The PHANTOM OF THE OPERA

AND OTHER GOTHIC TALES

The Phantom of the Opera

and Other Gothic Tales

BARNES & NOBLE
NEW YORK

BARNES & NOBLE

NEW YORK

This 2018 edition printed for Barnes & Noble Booksellers, Inc. by Sterling Publishing Co., Inc.

ISBN 978-1-4351-6713-1

Barnes & Noble Booksellers, Inc.
122 Fifth Avenue
New York, NY 10011

Manufactured in China

8 10 9

sterlingpublishing.com

Cover design by Raphael Geroni
Interior design by Sharon Jacobs
Endpaper art © Raphael Geroni

Contents

Introduction

"GOTHIC" IS A WORD THAT DESCRIBES BOTH A PARTICULAR literary era and a literary tradition that has persisted since that era into contemporary times. In the two-and-a-half centuries since Horace Walpole first subtitled his short novel *The Castle of Otranto* "A Gothic Story," the word *gothic*, as applied to works of literature, has become nearly synonymous with the tale of horror. In truth not all horror stories are gothic tales, but a mood of horror is prevalent in all gothic fiction.

The era of the gothic novel extends from the publication of *The Castle of Otranto* in 1764 to roughly 1820, at which point the literature was spent from exhaustive recyclings of its trademark tropes and set pieces and the effusions of hack writers who diluted what richness it had with cliché-ridden retreads of its better works. From the sea of gothic fiction published in the decades of the gothic era we can distill certain key elements that define the gothic. These elements are present in varying degrees in the stories collected in *The Phantom of the Opera and Other Gothic Tales*, most of which were published many years after the final flicker of the gothic era's flame.

Among these are a sense of antiquity and a past era when rationality and enlightenment had yet to triumph over superstition. Walpole sets the story told in his novel nearly seven centuries before his own time. In "Metzengerstein," Edgar Allan Poe paints a picture of a medieval Europe ruled by feudal lords. Both Vernon Lee's "Marsyas in Flanders" and Arthur Machen's "The Great God Pan" evoke a primitive pagan past, remnants of which have survived into the present.

Not every gothic tale is set in a castle, as Walpole's is, but the castle or similar work of architecture which proves a snare riddled with traps and menaces is perhaps the most iconic set piece in gothic literature. What is the Paris Opera House in Gaston Leroux's *The Phantom of the Opera*—haunted by a "ghost" and filled with secret passageways and subterranean chambers—but a glorified twentieth-century version of the gothic castle. Variations on the haunted castle can be found in other stories: the familial residences in

H. P. Lovecraft's "The Rats in the Walls" and M. P. Shiel's "The House of Sounds," the eerie churches in Mrs. J. H. Riddell's "The De Grabrooke Monument" and Robert W. Chambers' "In the Court of the Dragon," and the haunted convent in Ralph Adams Cram's "Sister Maddelena." Hanns Heinz Ewers' "The Spider" is set in a lowly apartment but the mesmerizing influence of the woman whom the narrator sees in the window across from his turns it into an environment as claustrophobic and inescapable as that of grander gothic structures.

The element that links all of the stories and that ties the classic gothic to its modern iteration is the suspension of the rational and the frequent incursion of the uncanny. This manifests sometimes in the form of supernatural entities who threaten everyday reality and its people—the vampires in John Polidori's *The Vampyre*, J. Sheridan Le Fanu's "Carmilla," and Aleksey Tolstoy's "The Family of a Vourdalak"; the poltergeist in M. Y. Halidom's "Execution"; the femme fatale whose touch is death in Nathaniel Hawthorne's "Rappaccini's Daughter"; the identity-exchanging being in Mary Shelley's "The Transformation"—but it can also present itself psychologically, as in the fantasies brought on by the tortured psyches of the characters in E. T. A. Hoffmann's "The Sandman" and Thomas Hardy's "The Withered Arm." Even when there is no overt supernatural element, as in Charles Brockden Brown's "Somnambulism: A Fragment" and Robert Louis Stevenson's "Olalla," the extraordinary circumstances that characters confront in these stories seem far removed from rational reality.

The degree to which the stories in *The Phantom of the Opera and Other Gothic Tales* take their cues from classic gothic literature has little bearing on how enjoyably they read. The twenty-five stories selected were written by some of the greatest writers of their time; some were written by writers now looked on as paragons of the gothic genre. Readers can decide for themselves which of these tales is more faithful to the gothic tradition in literature—or whether that even matters.

—Stefan Dziemianowicz

New York, 2018

The Vampyre

John Polidori

It happened that in the midst of the dissipations attendant upon a London winter, there appeared at the various parties of the leaders of the *ton* a nobleman, more remarkable for his singularities, than his rank. He gazed upon the mirth around him, as if he could not participate therein. Apparently, the light laughter of the fair only attracted his attention, that he might by a look quell it, and throw fear into those breasts where thoughtlessness reigned. Those who felt this sensation of awe, could not explain whence it arose: some attributed it to the dead grey eye, which, fixing upon the object's face, did not seem to penetrate, and at one glance to pierce through to the inward workings of the heart; but fell upon the cheek with a leaden ray that weighed upon the skin it could not pass. His peculiarities caused him to be invited to every house; all wished to see him, and those who had been accustomed to violent excitement, and now felt the weight of *ennui*, were pleased at having something in their presence capable of engaging their attention. In spite of the deadly hue of his face, which never gained a warmer tint, either from the blush of modesty, or from the strong emotion of passion, though its form and outline were beautiful, many of the female hunters after notoriety attempted to win his attentions, and gain, at least, some marks of what they might term affection: Lady Mercer, who had been the mockery of every monster shewn in drawing-rooms since her marriage, threw herself in his way, and did all but put on the dress of a mountebank, to attract his notice:—though in vain:—when she stood before him, though his eyes were apparently fixed upon hers, still it seemed as if they were unperceived;—even her unappalled impudence was baffled, and she left the field. But though the common adultress could not influence even the guidance of his eyes, it was not that the female sex was indifferent to him: yet such was the apparent caution with which he spoke to the virtuous wife and innocent daughter, that few knew he ever addressed himself to females. He had, however, the reputation of a winning tongue; and whether it was that it even overcame the dread of his singular character, or that they were moved by his apparent hatred of vice, he was as often among those females who form the boast of their sex from their domestic virtues, as among those who sully it by their vices.

About the same time, there came to London a young gentleman of the name of Aubrey: he was an orphan left with an only sister in the possession of great wealth, by parents who died while he was yet in childhood. Left also to himself by guardians, who thought it their duty merely to take care of his fortune, while they relinquished the more important charge of his mind to the care of mercenary subalterns, he cultivated more his imagination than his judgment. He had, hence, that high romantic feeling of honour and candour, which daily ruins so many milliners' apprentices. He believed all to sympathise with virtue, and thought that vice was thrown in by Providence merely for the picturesque effect of the scene, as we see in romances: he thought that the misery of a cottage merely consisted in the vesting of clothes, which were as warm, but which were better adapted to the painter's eye by their irregular folds and various coloured patches. He thought, in fine, that the dreams of poets were the realities of life. He was handsome, frank, and rich: for these reasons, upon his entering into the gay circles, many mothers surrounded him, striving which should describe with least truth their languishing or romping favourites: the daughters at the same time, by their brightening countenances when he approached, and by their sparkling eyes, when he opened his lips, soon led him into false notions of his talents and his merit. Attached as he was to the romance of his solitary hours, he was startled at finding, that, except in the tallow and wax candles that flickered, not from the presence of a ghost, but from want of snuffing, there was no foundation in real life for any of that congeries of pleasing pictures and descriptions contained in those volumes, from which he had formed his study. Finding, however, some compensation in his gratified vanity, he was about to relinquish his dreams, when the extraordinary being we have above described, crossed him in his career.

He watched him; and the very impossibility of forming an idea of the character of a man entirely absorbed in himself, who gave few other signs of his observation of external objects, than the tacit assent to their existence, implied by the avoidance of their contact: allowing his imagination to picture every thing that flattered its propensity to extravagant ideas, he soon formed this object into the hero of a romance, and determined to observe the offspring of his fancy, rather than the person before him. He became acquainted with him, paid him attentions, and so far advanced upon his notice, that his presence was always recognised. He gradually learnt that Lord Ruthven's affairs were embarrassed, and soon found, from the notes of preparation in —— Street, that he was about to travel. Desirous of gaining some information respecting this singular character, who, till now, had only whetted his curiosity, he hinted to his guardians, that it was time for him to perform the tour, which for many generations has been thought necessary to enable the young to take some rapid steps in the career of vice towards putting themselves upon an equality with the aged, and not allowing them to appear as if fallen from the skies, whenever scandalous intrigues are mentioned as the subjects of pleasantry or of praise, according to the degree of skill shewn in carrying them on. They consented: and Aubrey immediately mentioning his intentions to Lord Ruthven, was surprised to receive from him a proposal to join him. Flattered by such a mark of esteem from him, who, apparently, had nothing in common with other men, he gladly accepted it, and in a few days they had passed the circling waters.

Hitherto, Aubrey had had no opportunity of studying Lord Ruthven's character, and now he found, that, though many more of his actions were exposed to his view, the results offered different conclusions from the apparent motives to his conduct. His companion was profuse in his liberality;—the idle, the vagabond, and the beggar, received from his hand more than enough to relieve their immediate wants. But Aubrey could not avoid remarking, that it was not upon the virtuous, reduced to indigence by the misfortunes attendant even upon virtue, that he bestowed his alms;—these were sent from the door with hardly suppressed sneers; but when the profligate came to ask something, not to relieve his wants, but to allow him to wallow in his lust, or to sink him still deeper in his iniquity, he was sent away with rich charity. This was, however, attributed by him to the greater importunity of the vicious, which generally prevails over the retiring bashfulness of the virtuous indigent. There was one circumstance about the charity of his Lordship, which was still more impressed upon his mind: all those upon whom it was bestowed, inevitably found that there was a curse upon it, for they were all either led to the scaffold, or sunk to the lowest and the most abject misery. At Brussels and other towns through which they passed, Aubrey was surprized at the apparent eagerness with which his companion sought for the centres of all fashionable vice; there he entered into all the spirit of the faro table: he betted, and always gambled with success, except where the known sharper was his antagonist, and then he lost even more than he gained; but it was always with the same unchanging face, with which he generally watched the society around: it was not, however, so when he encountered the rash youthful novice, or the luckless father of a numerous family; then his very wish seemed fortune's law—this apparent abstractedness of mind was laid aside, and his eyes sparkled with more fire than that of the cat whilst dallying with the half-dead mouse. In every town, he left the formerly affluent youth, torn from the circle he adorned, cursing, in the solitude of a dungeon, the fate that had drawn him within the reach of this fiend; whilst many a father sat frantic, amidst the speaking looks of mute hungry children, without a single farthing of his late immense wealth, wherewith to buy even sufficient to satisfy their present craving. Yet he took no money from the gambling table; but immediately lost, to the ruiner of many, the last gilder he had just snatched from the convulsive grasp of the innocent: this might but be the result of a certain degree of knowledge, which was not, however, capable of combating the cunning of the more experienced. Aubrey often wished to represent this to his friend, and beg him to resign that charity and pleasure which proved the ruin of all, and did not tend to his own profit;—but he delayed it—for each day he hoped his friend would give him some opportunity of speaking frankly and openly to him; however, this never occurred. Lord Ruthven in his carriage, and amidst the various wild and rich scenes of nature, was always the same: his eye spoke less than his lip; and though Aubrey was near the object of his curiosity, he obtained no greater gratification from it than the constant excitement of vainly wishing to break that mystery, which to his exalted imagination began to assume the appearance of something supernatural.

They soon arrived at Rome, and Aubrey for a time lost sight of his companion; he left him in daily attendance upon the morning circle of an Italian countess, whilst he went in search of the memorials of another almost deserted city. Whilst he was thus engaged, letters arrived from England, which he opened with eager impatience; the first was from his sister, breathing nothing but affection; the others were from his guardians, the latter astonished him; if it had before entered into his imagination that there was an evil power resident in his companion, these seemed to give him almost sufficient reason for the belief. His guardians insisted upon his immediately leaving his friend, and urged, that his character was dreadfully vicious, for that the possession of irresistible powers of seduction, rendered his licentious habits more dangerous to society. It had been discovered, that his contempt for the adultress had not originated in hatred of her character; but that he had required, to enhance his gratification, that his victim, the partner of his guilt, should be hurled from the pinnacle of unsullied virtue, down to the lowest abyss of infamy and degradation: in fine, that all those females whom he had sought, apparently on account of their virtue, had, since his departure, thrown even the mask aside, and had not scrupled to expose the whole deformity of their vices to the public gaze.

Aubrey determined upon leaving one, whose character had not yet shown a single bright point on which to rest the eye. He resolved to invent some plausible pretext for abandoning him altogether, purposing, in the mean while, to watch him more closely, and to let no slight circumstances pass by unnoticed. He entered into the same circle, and soon perceived, that his Lordship was endeavouring to work upon the inexperience of the daughter of the lady whose house he chiefly frequented. In Italy, it is seldom that an unmarried female is met with in society; he was therefore obliged to carry on his plans in secret; but Aubrey's eye followed him in all his windings, and soon discovered that an assignation had been appointed, which would most likely end in the ruin of an innocent, though thoughtless girl. Losing no time, he entered the apartment of Lord Ruthven, and abruptly asked him his intentions with respect to the lady, informing him at the same time that he was aware of his being about to meet her that very night. Lord Ruthven answered, that his intentions were such as he supposed all would have upon such an occasion; and upon being pressed whether he intended to marry her, merely laughed. Aubrey retired; and, immediately writing a note, to say, that from that moment he must decline accompanying his Lordship in the remainder of their proposed tour, he ordered his servant to seek other apartments, and calling upon the mother of the lady, informed her of all he knew, not only with regard to her daughter, but also concerning the character of his Lordship. The assignation was prevented. Lord Ruthven next day merely sent his servant to notify his complete assent to a separation; but did not hint any suspicion of his plans having been foiled by Aubrey's interposition.

Having left Rome, Aubrey directed his steps towards Greece, and crossing the Peninsula, soon found himself at Athens. He then fixed his residence in the house of a Greek; and soon occupied himself in tracing the faded records of ancient glory upon monuments that apparently, ashamed of chronicling the deeds of freemen only before slaves, had hidden themselves beneath the sheltering soil or many coloured lichen. Under the same roof as himself, existed a being, so beautiful and delicate, that she might have formed the model for a painter, wishing to portray on canvas the promised hope of the faithful in Mahomet's paradise, save that her eyes spoke too much mind for any one to think she could belong to those who had no souls. As she danced upon the plain, or tripped along the mountain's side, one would have thought the gazelle a poor type of her beauties; for who would have exchanged her eye, apparently the eye of animated nature, for that sleepy luxurious look of the animal suited but to the taste of an epicure. The light step of Ianthe often accompanied Aubrey in his search after antiquities, and often would the unconscious girl, engaged in the pursuit of a Kashmere butterfly, show the whole beauty of her form, floating as it were upon the wind, to the eager gaze of him, who forgot the letters he had just decyphered upon an almost effaced tablet, in the contemplation of her sylph-like figure. Often would her tresses falling, as she flitted around, exhibit in the sun's ray such delicately brilliant and swiftly fading hues, its might well excuse the forgetfulness of the antiquary, who let escape from his mind the very object he had before thought of vital importance to the proper interpretation of a passage in Pausanias. But why attempt to describe charms which all feel, but none can appreciate?—It was innocence, youth, and beauty, unaffected by crowded drawing-rooms and stifling balls. Whilst he drew those remains of which lie wished to preserve a memorial for his future hours, she would stand by, and watch the magic effects of his pencil, in tracing the scenes of her native place; she would then describe to him the circling dance upon the open plain, would paint, to him in all the glowing colours of youthful memory, the marriage pomp she remembered viewing in her infancy; and then, turning to subjects that had evidently made a greater impression upon her mind, would tell him all the supernatural tales of her nurse. Her earnestness and apparent belief of what she narrated, excited the interest even of Aubrey; and often as she told him the tale of the living Vampyre, who had passed years amidst his friends, and dearest ties, forced every year, by feeding upon the life of a lovely female to prolong his existence for the ensuing months, his blood would run cold, whilst he attempted to laugh her out of such idle and horrible fantasies; but Ianthe cited to him the names of old men, who had at last detected one living among themselves, after several of their near relatives and children had been found marked with the stamp of the fiend's appetite; and when she found him so incredulous, she begged of him to believe her, for it had been, remarked, that those who had dared to question their existence, always had some proof given, which obliged them, with grief and heartbreaking, to confess it was true. She detailed to him the traditional appearance of these monsters, and his horror was increased, by hearing a pretty accurate description of Lord Ruthven; he, however, still persisted in persuading her, that there could be no truth in her fears, though at the same time he wondered at the many coincidences which had all tended to excite a belief in the supernatural power of Lord Ruthven.

Aubrey began to attach himself more and more to Ianthe; her innocence, so contrasted with all the affected virtues of the women among whom he had sought for his vision of romance, won his heart; and while he ridiculed the idea of a young man of English habits, marrying an uneducated Greek girl, still he found himself more and more attached to the almost fairy form before him. He would tear himself at times from her, and, forming a plan for some antiquarian research, he would depart, determined not to return until his object was attained; but he always found it impossible to fix his attention upon the ruins around him, whilst in his mind he retained an image that seemed alone the rightful possessor of his thoughts. Ianthe was unconscious of his love, and was ever the same frank infantile being he had first known. She always seemed to part from him with reluctance; but it was because she had no longer any one with whom she could visit her favourite haunts, whilst her guardian was occupied in sketching or uncovering some fragment which had yet escaped the destructive hand of time. She had appealed to her parents on the subject of Vampyres, and they both, with several present, affirmed their existence, pale with horror at the very name. Soon after, Aubrey determined to proceed upon one of his excursions, which was to detain him for a few hours; when they heard the name of the place, they all at once begged of him not to return at night, as he must necessarily pass through a wood, where no Greek would ever remain, after the day had closed, upon any consideration. They described it as the resort of the Vampyres in their nocturnal orgies, and denounced the most heavy evils as impending upon him who dared to cross their path. Aubrey made light of their representations, and tried to laugh them out of the idea; but when he saw them shudder at his daring thus to mock a superior, infernal power, the very name of which apparently made their blood freeze, he was silent.

Next morning Aubrey set off upon his excursion unattended; he was surprised to observe the melancholy face of his host, and was concerned to find that his words, mocking the belief of those horrible fiends, had inspired them with such terror. When he was about to depart, Ianthe came to the side of his horse, and earnestly begged of him to return, ere night allowed the power of these beings to be put in action;—he promised. He was, however, so occupied in his research, that lie did not perceive that day-light would soon end, and that in the horizon there was one of those specks which, in the warmer climates, so rapidly gather into a tremendous mass, and pour all their rage upon the devoted country.—He at last, however, mounted his horse, determined to make up by speed for his delay: but it was too late. Twilight, in these southern climates, is almost unknown; immediately the sun sets, night begins: and ere he had advanced far, the power of the storm was above—its echoing thunders had scarcely an interval of rest—its thick heavy rain forced its way through the canopying foliage, whilst the blue forked lightning seemed to fall and radiate at his very feet. Suddenly his horse took fright, and he was carried with dreadful rapidity through the entangled forest. The animal at last, through fatigue, stopped, and he found, by the glare of lightning, that he was in the neighbourhood of a hovel that hardly lifted itself up from the masses of dead leaves and brushwood which surrounded it. Dismounting, he approached, hoping to find some one to guide him to the town, or at least trusting to obtain shelter from the pelting of the storm. As he approached, the thunders, for a moment silent, allowed him to hear the dreadful shrieks of a woman mingling with the stifled, exultant mockery of a laugh, continued in one almost unbroken sound;—he was startled: but, roused by the thunder which again rolled over his head, he, with a sudden effort, forced open the door of the hut. He found himself in utter darkness: the sound, however, guided him. He was apparently unperceived; for, though he called, still the sounds continued, and no notice was taken of him. He found himself in contact with some one, whom he immediately seized; when a voice cried, "Again baffled!" to which a loud laugh succeeded; and he felt himself grappled by one whose strength seemed superhuman: determined to sell his life as dearly as he could, he struggled; but it was in vain: he was lifted from his feet and hurled with enormous force against the ground:—his enemy threw himself upon him, and kneeling upon his breast, had placed his hands upon his throat—when the glare of many torches penetrating through the hole that gave light in the day, disturbed him;—he instantly rose, and, leaving his prey, rushed through the door, and in a moment the crashing of the brandies, as he broke through the wood, was no longer heard. The storm was now still; and Aubrey, incapable of moving, was soon heard by those without. They entered; the light of their torches fell upon the mud walls, and the thatch loaded on every individual straw with heavy flakes of soot. At the desire of Aubrey they searched for her who had attracted him by her cries; he was again left in darkness; but what was his horror, when the light of the torches once more burst upon him, to perceive the airy form of his fair conductress brought in a lifeless corpse. He shut his eyes, hoping that it was but a vision arising from his disturbed imagination; but he again saw the same form, when he unclosed them, stretched by his side. There was no colour upon her cheek, not even upon her lip; yet there was a stillness about her face that seemed almost as attaching as the life that once dwelt there:—upon her neck and breast was blood, and upon her throat were the marks of teeth having opened the vein:—to this the men pointed, crying, simultaneously struck with horror, "A Vampyre! a Vampyre!" A litter was quickly formed, and Aubrey was laid by the side of her who had lately been to him the object of so many bright and fairy visions, now fallen with the flower of life that had died within her. He knew not what his thoughts were—his mind was benumbed and seemed to shun reflection, and take refuge in vacancy—he held almost unconsciously in his hand a naked dagger of a particular construction, which had been found in the hut. They were soon met by different parties who had been engaged in the search of her whom a mother had missed. Their lamentable cries, as they approached the city, forewarned the parents of some dreadful catastrophe.—To describe their grief would be impossible; but when they ascertained the cause of their child's death, they looked at Aubrey, and pointed to the corpse. They were inconsolable; both died broken-hearted.

Aubrey being put to bed was seized with a most violent fever, and was often delirious; in these intervals he would call upon Lord Ruthven and upon Ianthe—by some unaccountable combination he seemed to beg of his former companion to spare the being he loved. At other times he would imprecate maledictions upon his head, and curse him as her destroyer. Lord Ruthven chanced at this time to arrive at Athens, and, from whatever motive, upon hearing of the state of Aubrey, immediately placed himself in the same house, and became his constant attendant. When the latter recovered from his delirium, he was horrified and startled at the sight of him whose image he had now combined with that of a Vampyre; but Lord Ruthven, by his kind words, implying almost repentance for the fault that had caused their separation, and still more by the attention, anxiety, and care which he showed, soon reconciled him to his presence. His lordship seemed quite changed; he no longer appeared that apathetic being who had so astonished Aubrey; but as soon as his convalescence began to be rapid, he again gradually retired into the same state of mind, and Aubrey perceived no difference from the former man, except that at times he was surprised to meet his gaze fixed intently upon him, with a smile of malicious exultation playing upon his lips: he knew not why, but this smile haunted him. During the last stage of the invalid's recovery, Lord Ruthven was apparently engaged in watching the tideless waves raised by the cooling breeze, or in marking the progress of those orbs, circling, like our world, the moveless sun;—indeed, he appeared to wish to avoid the eyes of all.

Aubrey's mind, by this shock, was much weakened, and that elasticity of spirit which had once so distinguished him now seemed to have fled for ever. He was now as much a lover of solitude and silence as Lord Ruthven; but much as he wished for solitude, his mind could not find it in the neighbourhood of Athens; if he sought it amidst the ruins he had formerly frequented, Ianthe's form stood by his side—if he sought it in the woods, her light step would appear wandering amidst the underwood, in quest of the modest violet; then suddenly turning round, would show, to his wild imagination, her pale face and wounded throat, with a meek smile upon her lips. He determined to fly scenes, every feature of which created such bitter associations in his mind. He proposed to Lord Ruthven, to whom he held himself bound by the tender care he had taken of him during his illness, that they should visit those parts of Greece neither had yet seen. They travelled in every direction, and sought every spot to which a recollection could be attached: but though they thus hastened from place to place, yet they seemed not to heed what they gazed upon. They heard much of robbers, but they gradually began to slight these reports, which they imagined were only the invention of individuals, whose interest it was to excite the generosity of those whom they defended from pretended dangers. In consequence of thus neglecting the advice of the inhabitants, on one occasion they travelled with only a few guards, more to serve as guides than as a defence. Upon entering, however, a narrow defile, at the bottom of which was the bed of a torrent, with large masses of rock brought down from the neighbouring precipices, they had reason to repent their negligence; for scarcely were the whole of the party engaged in the narrow pass, when they were startled by the whistling of bullets close to their heads, and by the echoed report of several guns. In an instant their guards had left them, and, placing themselves behind rocks, had begun to fire in the direction whence the report came. Lord Ruthven and Aubrey, imitating their example, retired for a moment behind the sheltering turn of the defile: but ashamed of being thus detained by a foe, who with insulting shouts bade them advance, and being exposed to unresisting slaughter, if any of the robbers should climb above and take them in the rear, they determined at once to rush forward in search of the enemy. Hardly had they lost the shelter of the rock, when Lord Ruthven received a shot in the shoulder, which brought him to the ground. Aubrey hastened to his assistance; and, no longer heeding the contest or his own peril, was soon surprised by seeing the robbers' faces around him—his guards having, upon Lord Ruthven's being wounded, immediately thrown up their arms and surrendered.

By promises of great reward, Aubrey soon induced them to convey his wounded friend to a neighbouring cabin; and having agreed upon a ransom, he was no more disturbed by their presence—they being content merely to guard the entrance till their comrade should return with the promised sum, for which he had an order. Lord Ruthven's strength rapidly decreased; in two days mortification ensued, and death seemed advancing with hasty steps. His conduct and appearance had not changed; he seemed as unconscious of pain as he had been of the objects about him: but towards the close of the last evening, his mind became apparently uneasy, and his eye often fixed upon Aubrey, who was induced to offer his assistance with more than usual earnestness—"Assist me! you may save me—you may do more than that—I mean not my life, I heed the death of my existence as little as that of the passing day; but you may save my honour, your friend's honour."—"How? tell me how? I would do any thing," replied Aubrey.—"I need but little—my life ebbs apace—I cannot explain the whole—but if you would conceal all you know of me, my honour were free from stain in the world's mouth—and if my death were unknown for some time in England—I—I—but life."—"It shall not be known."—"Swear!" cried the dying man, raising himself with exultant violence, "Swear by all your soul reveres, by all your nature fears, swear that, for a year and a day you will not impart your knowledge of my crimes or death to any living being in any way, whatever may happen, or whatever you may see."—His eyes seemed bursting from their sockets: "I swear!" said Aubrey; he sunk laughing upon his pillow, and breathed no more.

Aubrey retired to rest, but did not sleep; the many circumstances attending his acquaintance with this man rose upon his mind, and he knew not why; when he remembered his oath a cold shivering came over him, as if from the presentiment of something horrible awaiting him. Rising early in the morning, he was about to enter the hovel in which he had left the corpse, when a robber met him, and informed him that it was no longer there, having been conveyed by himself and comrades, upon his retiring, to the pinnacle of a neighbouring mount, according to a promise they had given his lordship, that it should be exposed to the first cold ray of the moon that rose after his death. Aubrey astonished, and taking several of the men, determined to go and bury it upon the spot where it lay. But, when he had mounted to the summit he found no trace of either the corpse or the clothes, though the robbers swore they pointed out the identical rock on which they had laid the body. For a time his mind was bewildered in conjectures, but he at last returned, convinced that they had buried the corpse for the sake of the clothes.

Weary of a country in which he had met with such terrible misfortunes, and in which all apparently conspired to heighten that superstitious melancholy that had seized upon his mind, he resolved to leave it, and soon arrived at Smyrna. While waiting for a vessel to convey him to Otranto, or to Naples, he occupied himself in arranging those effects be had with him belonging to Lord Ruthven. Amongst other things there was a case containing several weapons of offence, more or less adapted to ensure the death of the victim. There were several daggers and ataghans. Whilst turning them over, and examining their curious forms, what was his surprise at finding a sheath apparently ornamented in the same style as the dagger discovered in the fatal hut—he shuddered—hastening to gain further proof, he found the weapon, and his horror may be imagined when he discovered that it fitted, though peculiarly shaped, the sheath he held in his hand. His eyes seemed to need no further certainty—they seemed gazing to be bound to the dagger; yet still he wished to disbelieve; but the particular form, the same varying tints upon the haft and sheath were alike in splendour on both, and left no room for doubt; there were also drops of blood on each.

He left Smyrna, and on his way home, at Rome, his first inquiries were concerning the lady he had attempted to snatch from Lord Ruthven's seductive arts.

Her parents were in distress, their fortune ruined, and she had not been heard of since the departure of his lordship. Aubrey's mind became almost broken under so many repeated horrors; he was afraid that this lady had fallen a victim to the destroyer of Ianthe. He became morose and silent; and his only occupation consisted in urging the speed of the postilions, as if he were going to save the life of some one he held dear. He arrived at Calais; a breeze, which seemed obedient to his will, soon wafted him to the English shores; and he hastened to the mansion of his fathers, and there, for a moment, appeared to lose, in the embraces and caresses of his sister, all memory of the past. If she before, by her infantine caresses, had gained his affection, now that the woman began to appear, she was still more attaching as a companion.

Miss Aubrey had not that winning grace which gains the gaze and applause of the drawing-room assemblies. There was none of that light brilliancy which only exists in the heated atmosphere of a crowded apartment. Her blue eye was never lit up by the levity of the mind beneath. There was a melancholy charm about it which did not seem to arise from misfortune, but from some feeling within, that appeared to indicate a soul conscious of a brighter realm. Her step was not that light footing, which strays where'er a butterfly or a colour may attract—it was sedate and pensive. When alone, her face was never brightened by the smile of joy; but when her brother breathed to her his affection, and would in her presence forget those griefs she knew destroyed his rest, who would have exchanged her smile for that of the voluptuary? It seemed as if those eyes,—that face were then playing in the light of their own native sphere. She was yet only eighteen, and had not been presented to the world, it having been thought by her guardians more fit that her presentation should be delayed until her brother's return from the continent, when he might be her protector. It was now, therefore, resolved that the next drawing-room, which was fast approaching, should be the epoch of her entry into the "busy scene." Aubrey would rather have remained in the mansion of his fathers, and fed upon the melancholy which overpowered him. He could not fed interest about the frivolities of fashionable strangers, when his mind had been so torn by the events he had witnessed; but he determined to sacrifice his own comfort to the protection of his sister. They soon arrived in town, and prepared for the next day, which had been announced as a drawing-room.

The crowd was excessive—a drawing-room had not been held for a long time, and all who were anxious to bask in the smile of royalty, hastened thither. Aubrey was there with his sister. While he was standing in a corner by himself, heedless of all around him, engaged in the remembrance that the first time he had seen Lord Ruthven was in that very place—he felt himself suddenly seized by the arm, and a voice he recognized too well, sounded in his ear—"Remember your oath."

He had hardly courage to turn, fearful of seeing a spectre that would blast him, when he perceived, at a little distance, the same figure which had attracted his notice on this spot upon his first entry into society. He gazed till his limbs almost refusing to bear their weight, he was obliged to take the arm of a friend, and forcing a passage through the crowd, he threw himself into his carriage, and was driven home. He paced the room with hurried steps, and fixed his hands upon his head, as if he were afraid his thoughts were bursting from his brain. Lord Ruthven again before him—circumstances started up in dreadful array—the dagger—his oath.—He roused himself, he could not believe it possible—the dead rise again!—He thought his imagination had conjured up the image, his mind was resting upon. It was impossible that it could be real—he determined, therefore, to go again into society; for though he attempted to ask concerning Lord Ruthven, the name hung upon his lips, and he could not succeed in gaining information. He went a few nights after with his sister to the assembly of a near relation. Leaving her under the protection of a matron, he retired into a recess, and there gave himself up to his own devouring thoughts. Perceiving, at last, that many were leaving, he roused himself, and entering another room, found his sister surrounded by several, apparently in earnest conversation; he attempted to pass and get near her, when one, whom he requested to move, turned round, and revealed to him those features he most abhorred. He sprang forward, seized his sister's arm, and, with hurried step, forced her towards the street: at the door he found himself impeded by the crowd of servants who were waiting for their lords; and while he was engaged in passing them, he again heard that voice whisper close to him—"Remember your oath!"—He did not dare to turn, but, hurrying his sister, soon reached home.

Aubrey became almost distracted. If before his mind had been absorbed by one subject, how much more completely was it engrossed, now that the certainty of the monster's living again pressed upon his thoughts. His sister's attentions were now unheeded, and it was in vain that she entreated him to explain to her what had caused his abrupt conduct. He only uttered a few words, and those terrified her. The more he thought, the more he was bewildered. His oath startled him;—was he then to allow this monster to roam, bearing ruin upon his breath, amidst all he held dear, and not avert its progress? His very sister might have been touched by him. But even if he were to break his oath, and disclose his suspicions, who would believe him? He thought of employing his own hand to free the world from such a wretch; but death, he remembered, had been already mocked. For days he remained in this state; shut up in his room, he saw no one, and ate only when his sister came, who, with eyes streaming with tears, besought him, for her sake, to support nature. At last, no longer capable of bearing stillness and solitude, he left his house, roamed from street to street, anxious to fly that image which haunted him. His dress became neglected, and he wandered, as often exposed to the noon-day sun as to the midnight damps. He was no longer to be recognized; at first he returned with the evening to the house; but at last he laid him down to rest wherever fatigue overtook him. His sister, anxious for his safety, employed people to follow him; but they were soon distanced by him who fled from a pursuer swifter than any—from thought. His conduct, however, suddenly changed. Struck with the idea that he left by his absence the whole of his friends, with a fiend amongst them, of whose presence they were unconscious, he determined to enter again into society, and watch him closely, anxious to forewarn, in spite of his oath, all whom Lord Ruthven approached with intimacy. But when he entered into a room, his haggard and suspicious looks were so striking, his inward shudderings so visible, that his sister was at last obliged to beg of him to abstain from seeking, for her sake, a society which affected him so strongly. When, however, remonstrance proved unavailing, the guardians thought proper to interpose, and, fearing that his mind was becoming alienated, they thought it high time to resume again that trust which had been before imposed upon them by Aubrey's parents.

Desirous of saving him from the injuries and sufferings he had daily encountered in his wanderings, and of preventing him from exposing to the general eye those marks of what they considered folly, they engaged a physician to reside in the house, and take constant care of him. He hardly appeared to notice it, so completely was his mind absorbed by one terrible subject. His incoherence became at last so great, that he was confined to his chamber. There he would often lie for days, incapable of being roused. He had become emaciated, his eyes had attained a glassy lustre;—the only sign of affection and recollection remaining displayed itself upon the entry of his sister; then he would sometimes start, and, seizing her hands, with looks that severely afflicted her, he would desire her not to touch him. "Oh, do not touch him—if your love for me is aught, do not go near him!" When, however, she inquired to whom he referred, his only answer was, "True! true!" and again he sank into a state, whence not even she could rouse him. This lasted many months: gradually, however, as the year was passing, his incoherences became less frequent, and his mind threw off a portion of its gloom, whilst his guardians observed, that several times in the day he would count upon his fingers a definite number, and then smile.

The time had nearly elapsed, when, upon the last day of the year, one of his guardians entering his room, began to converse with his physician upon the melancholy circumstance of Aubrey's being in so awful a situation, when his sister was going next day to be married. Instantly Aubrey's attention was attracted; he asked anxiously to whom. Glad of this mark of returning intellect, of which they feared he had been deprived, they mentioned the name of the Earl of Marsden. Thinking this was a young Earl whom he had met with in society, Aubrey seemed pleased, and astonished them still more by his expressing his intention to be present at the nuptials, and desiring to see his sister. They answered not, but in a few minutes his sister was with him. He was apparently again capable of being affected by the influence of her lovely smile; for he pressed her to his breast, and kissed her cheek, wet with tears, flowing at the thought of her brother's being once more alive to the feelings of affection. He began to speak with all his wonted warmth, and to congratulate her upon her marriage with a person so distinguished for rank and every accomplishment; when he suddenly perceived a locket upon her breast; opening it, what was his surprise at beholding the features of the monster who had so long influenced his life. He seized the portrait in a paroxysm of rage, and trampled it under foot. Upon her asking him why he thus destroyed the resemblance of her future husband, he looked as if he did not understand her—then seizing her hands, and gazing on her with a frantic expression of countenance, he bade her swear that she would never wed this monster, for he— But he could not advance—it seemed as if that voice again bade him remember his oath—he turned suddenly round, thinking Lord Ruthven was near him but saw no one. In the meantime the guardians and physician, who had heard the whole, and thought this was but a return of his disorder, entered, and forcing him from Miss Aubrey, desired her to leave him. He fell upon his knees to them, he implored, he begged of them to delay but for one day. They, attributing this to the insanity they imagined had taken possession of his mind, endeavoured to pacify him, and retired.

Lord Ruthven had called the morning after the drawing-room, and had been refused with every one else. When he heard of Aubrey's ill health, he readily understood himself to be the cause of it; but when he learned that he was deemed insane, his exultation and pleasure could hardly be concealed from those among whom he had gained this information. He hastened to the house of his former companion, and, by constant attendance, and the pretence of great affection for the brother and interest in his fate, he gradually won the ear of Miss Aubrey. Who could resist his power? His tongue had dangers and toils to recount—could speak of himself as of an individual having no sympathy with any being on the crowded earth, save with her to whom he addressed himself;—could tell how, since he knew her, his existence, had begun to seem worthy of preservation, if it were merely that he might listen to her soothing accents;—in fine, he knew so well how to use the serpent's art, or such was the will of fate, that he gained her affections. The title of the elder branch falling at length to him, he obtained an important embassy, which served as an excuse for hastening the marriage, (in spite of her brother's deranged state), which was to take place the very day before his departure for the continent.

Aubrey, when he was left by the physician and his guardians, attempted to bribe the servants, but in vain. He asked for pen and paper; it was given him; be wrote a letter to his sister, conjuring her, as she valued her own happiness, her own honour, and the honour of those now in the grave, who once held her in their arms as their hope and the hope of their house, to delay but for a few hours that marriage, on which he denounced the most heavy curses. The servants promised they would deliver it; but giving it to the physician, he thought it better not to harass any more the mind of Miss Aubrey by, what he considered, the ravings of a maniac. Night passed on without rest to the busy inmates of the house; and Aubrey heard, with a horror that may more easily be conceived than described, the notes of busy preparation. Morning came, and the sound of carriages broke upon his ear. Aubrey grew almost frantic. The curiosity of the servants at last overcame their vigilance, they gradually stole away, leaving him in the custody of an helpless old woman. He seized the opportunity, with one bound was out of the room, and in a moment found himself in the apartment where all were nearly assembled. Lord Ruthven was the first to perceive him: he immediately approached, and, taking his arm by force, hurried him from the room, speechless with rage. When on the staircase, Lord Ruthven whispered in his ear—"Remember your oath, and know, if not my bride to day, your sister is dishonoured. Women are frail!" So saying, he pushed him towards his attendants, who, roused by the old woman, had come in search of him. Aubrey could no longer support himself; his rage not finding vent, had broken a blood-vessel, and he was conveyed to bed. This was not mentioned to his sister, who was not present when he entered, as the physician was afraid of agitating her. The marriage was solemnized, and the bride and bridegroom left London.

Aubrey's weakness increased; the effusion of blood produced symptoms of the near approach of death. He desired his sister's guardians might be called, and when the midnight hour had struck, he related composedly what the reader has perused—he died immediately after.

The guardians hastened to protect Miss Aubrey; but when they arrived, it was too late. Lord Ruthven had disappeared, and Aubrey's sister had glutted the thirst of a VAMPYRE!

The Transformation

Mary Shelley

Forthwith this frame of mine was wrench'd
   With a woful agony,
Which forced me to begin my tale,
   And then it set me free.

Since then, at an uncertain hour,
   That agony returns;
And till my ghastly tale is told
   This heart within me burns.
—COLERIDGE'S ANCIENT MARINER

I HAVE HEARD IT SAID, THAT, WHEN ANY STRANGE, SUPERNATURAL, AND necromantic adventure has occurred to a human being, that being, however desirous he may be to conceal the same, feels at certain periods torn up as it were by an intellectual earthquake, and is forced to bare the inner depths of his spirit to another. I am a witness of the truth of this. I have dearly sworn to myself never to reveal to human ears the horrors to which I once, in excess of fiendly pride, delivered myself over. The holy man who heard my confession, and reconciled me to the Church, is dead. None knows that once—

Why should it not be thus? Why tell a tale of impious tempting of Providence, and soul-subduing humiliation? Why? answer me, ye who are wise in the secrets of human nature! I only know that so it is; and in spite of strong resolve,—of a pride that too much masters me—of shame, and even of fear, so to render myself odious to my species,—I must speak.

Genoa! my birthplace—proud city! looking upon the blue Mediterranean—dost thou remember me in my boyhood, when thy cliffs and promontories, thy bright sky and gay vineyards, were my world? Happy time! when to the young heart the narrow-bounded universe, which leaves, by its very limitation, free scope to the imagination, enchains our physical energies, and, sole period in our lives, innocence and enjoyment are united. Yet, who can look back to childhood, and not remember its sorrows and its harrowing fears? I was born with the most imperious, haughty, tameless spirit. I quailed before my father only; and he, generous and noble, but capricious and tyrannical, at once fostered and checked the wild impetuosity of my character, making obedience necessary, but inspiring no respect for the motives which guided his commands. To be a man, free, independent; or, in better words, insolent and domineering, was the hope and prayer of my rebel heart.

My father had one friend, a wealthy Genoese noble, who in a political tumult was suddenly sentenced to banishment, and his property confiscated. The Marchese Torella went into exile alone. Like my father, he was a widower: he had one child, the almost infant Juliet, who was left under my father's guardianship. I should certainly have been unkind to the lovely girl, but that I was forced by my position to become her protector. A variety of childish incidents all tended to one point,—to make Juliet see in me a rock of defence; I in her, one who must perish through the soft sensibility of her nature too rudely visited, but for my guardian care. We grew up together. The opening rose in May was not more sweet than this dear girl. An irradiation of beauty was spread over her face. Her form, her step, her voice—my heart weeps even now, to think of all of relying, gentle, loving, and pure, that she enshrined. When I was eleven and Juliet eight years of age, a cousin of mine, much older than either—he seemed to us a man—took great notice of my playmate; he called her his bride, and asked her to marry him. She refused, and he insisted, drawing her unwillingly towards him. With the countenance and emotions of a maniac I threw myself on him I strove to draw his sword I clung to his neck with the ferocious resolve to strangle him: he was obliged to call for assistance to disengage himself from me. On that night I led Juliet to the chapel of our house: I made her touch the sacred relics—I harrowed her child's heart, and profaned her child's lips with an oath, that she would be mine, and mine only.

Well, those days passed away. Torella returned in a few years, and became wealthier and more prosperous than ever. When I was seventeen, my father died; he had been magnificent to prodigality; Torella rejoiced that my minority would afford an opportunity for repairing my fortunes. Juliet and I had been affianced beside my father's deathbed—Torella was to be a second parent to me.

I desired to see the world, and I was indulged. I went to Florence, to Rome, to Naples; thence I passed to Toulon, and at length reached what had long been the bourne of my wishes, Paris. There was wild work in Paris then. The poor king, Charles the Sixth, now sane, now mad, now a monarch, now an abject slave, was the very mockery of humanity. The queen, the dauphin, the Duke of Burgundy, alternately friends and foes,—now meeting in prodigal feasts, now shedding blood in rivalry,—were blind to the miserable state of their country, and the dangers that impended over it, and gave themselves wholly up to dissolute enjoyment or savage strife. My character still followed me. I was arrogant and self-willed; I loved display, and above all, I threw off all control. My young friends were eager to foster passions which furnished them with pleasures. I was deemed handsome—I was master of every knightly accomplishment. I was disconnected with any political party. I grew a favourite with all: my presumption and arrogance was pardoned in one so young: I became a spoiled child. Who could control me? not the letters and advice of Torella—only strong necessity visiting me in the abhorred shape of an empty purse. But there were means to refill this void. Acre after acre, estate after estate, I sold. My dress, my jewels, my horses and their caparisons, were almost unrivalled in gorgeous Paris, while the lands of my inheritance passed into possession of others.

The Duke of Orleans was waylaid and murdered by the Duke of Burgundy. Fear and terror possessed all Paris. The dauphin and the queen shut themselves up; every pleasure was suspended. I grew weary of this state of things, and my heart yearned for my boyhood's haunts. I was nearly a beggar, yet still I would go there, claim my bride, and rebuild my fortunes. A few happy ventures as a merchant would make me rich again. Nevertheless, I would not return in humble guise. My last act was to dispose of my remaining estate near Albaro for half its worth, for ready money. Then I despatched all kinds of artificers, arras, furniture of regal splendour, to fit up the last relic of my inheritance, my palace in Genoa. I lingered a little longer yet, ashamed at the part of the prodigal returned, which I feared I should play. I sent my horses. One matchless Spanish jennet I despatched to my promised bride: its capirisona flamed with jewels and cloth of gold. In every part I caused to be entwined the initials of Juliet and her Guido. My present found favour in hers and in her father's eyes.

Still to return a proclaimed spendthrift, the mark of impertinent wonder, perhaps of scorn, and to encounter singly the reproaches or taunts of my fellow-citizens, was no alluring prospect. As a shield between me and censure, I invited some few of the most reckless of my comrades to accompany me: thus I went armed against the world, hiding a rankling feeling, half fear and half penitence, by bravado.

I arrived in Genoa. I trod the pavement of my ancestral palace. My proud step was no interpreter of my heart, for I deeply felt that, though surrounded by every luxury, I was a beggar. The first step I took in claiming Juliet must widely declare me such. I read contempt or pity in the looks of all. I fancied that rich and poor, young and old, all regarded me with derision. Torella came not near me. No wonder that my second father should expect a son's deference from me in waiting first on him. But, galled and stung by a sense of my follies and demerit, I strove to throw the blame on others. We kept nightly orgies in Palazzo Carega. To sleepless, riotous nights followed listless, supine mornings. At the Ave Maria we showed our dainty persons in the streets, scoffing at the sober citizens, casting insolent glances on the shrinking women. Juliet was not among them—no, no; if she had been there, shame would have driven me away, if love had not brought me to her feet.

I grew tired of this. Suddenly I paid the Marchese a visit. He was at his villa, one among the many which deck the suburb of San Pietro d'Arena. It was the month of May, the blossoms of the fruit-trees were fading among thick, green foliage; the vines were shooting forth; the ground strewed with the fallen olive blooms; the firefly was in the myrtle hedge; heaven and earth wore a mantle of surpassing beauty. Torella welcomed me kindly, though seriously; and even his shade of displeasure soon wore away. Some resemblance to my father—some look and tone of youthful ingenuousness, softened the good old man's heart. He sent for his daughter—he presented me to her as her betrothed. The chamber became hallowed by a holy light as she entered. Hers was that cherub look, those large, soft eyes, full dimpled cheeks, and mouth of infantine sweetness, that expresses the rare union of happiness and love. Admiration first possessed me; she is mine! was the second proud emotion, and my lips curled with haughty triumph. I had not been the *enfant gâté* of the beauties of France not to have learnt the art of pleasing the soft heart of woman. If towards men I was overbearing, the deference I paid to them was the more in contrast. I commenced my courtship by the display of a thousand gallantries to Juliet, who, vowed to me from infancy, had never admitted the devotion of others; and who, though accustomed to expressions of admiration, was uninitiated in the language of lovers.

For a few days all went well. Torella never alluded to my extravagance; he treated me as a favourite son. But the time came, as we discussed the preliminaries to my union with his daughter, when this fair face of things should be overcast. A contract had been drawn up in my father's lifetime. I had rendered this, in fact, void by having squandered the whole of the wealth which was to have been shared by Juliet and myself. Torella, in consequence, chose to consider this bond as cancelled, and proposed another, in which, though the wealth lie bestowed was immeasurably increased, there were so many restrictions as to the mode of spending it, that I, who saw independence only in free career being given to my own imperious will, taunted him as taking advantage of my situation, and refused utterly to subscribe to his conditions. The old man mildly strove to recall me to reason. Roused pride became the tyrant of my thought: I listened with indignation—I repelled him with disdain.

"Juliet, thou art mine! Did we not interchange vows in our innocent childhood? Are we not one in the sight of God? and shall thy cold-hearted, cold-blooded father divide us? Be generous, my love, be just; take not away a gift, last treasure of thy Guido retract not thy vows let us defy the world, and, setting at nought the calculations of age, find in our mutual affection a refuge from every ill."

Fiend I must have been with such sophistry to endeavour to poison that sanctuary of holy thought and tender love. Juliet shrank from me affrighted. Her father was the best and kindest of men, and she strove to show me how, in obeying him, every good would follow. He would receive my tardy submission with warm affection, and generous pardon would follow my repentance;—profitless words for a young and gentle daughter to use to a man accustomed to make his will law, and to feel in his own heart a despot so terrible and stern that he could yield obedience to nought save his own imperious desires! My resentment grew with resistance; my wild companions were ready to add fuel to the flame. We laid a plan to carry off Juliet. At first it appeared to be crowned with success. Midway, on our return, we were overtaken by the agonized father and his attendants. A conflict ensued. Before the city guard came to decide the victory in favour of our antagonists, two of Torella's servitors were dangerously wounded.

This portion of my history weighs most heavily with me. Changed man as I am, I abhor myself in the recollection. May none who hear this tale ever have felt as I. A horse driven to fury by a rider armed with barbed spurs was not more a slave than I to the violent tyranny of my temper. A fiend possessed my soul, irritating it to madness. I felt the voice of conscience within me; but if I yielded to it for a brief interval, it was only to be a moment after torn, as by a whirlwind, away—borne along on the stream of desperate rage—the plaything of the storms engendered by pride. I was imprisoned, and, at the instance of Torella, set free. Again I returned to carry off both him and his child to France, which hapless country, then preyed on by free booters and gangs of lawless soldiery, offered a grateful refuge to a criminal like me. Our plots were discovered. I was sentenced to banishment; and, as my debts were already enormous, my remaining property was put in the hands of commissioners for their payment. Torella again offered his mediation, requiring only my promise not to renew my abortive attempts on himself and his daughter. I spurned his offers, and fancied that I triumphed when I was thrust out from Genoa, a solitary and penniless exile. My companions were gone: they had been dismissed the city some weeks before, and were already in France. I was alone—friendless, with neither sword at my side, nor ducat in my purse.

I wandered along the sea-shore, a whirlwind of passion possessing and tearing my soul. It was as if a live coal had been set burning in my breast. At first I meditated on what *I should do*. I would join a band of freebooters. Revenge!—the word seemed balm to me; I hugged it, caressed it, till, like a serpent, it stung me. Then again I would abjure and despise Genoa, that little corner of the world. I would return to Paris, where so many of my friends swarmed; where my services would be eagerly accepted; where I would carve out fortune with my sword, and make my paltry birthplace and the false Torella rue the day when they drove me, a new Coriolanus, from her walls. I would return to Paris—thus on foot—a beggar—and present myself in my poverty to those I had formerly entertained sumptuously? There was gall in the mere thought of it.

The reality of things began to dawn upon my mind, bringing despair in its train. For several months I had been a prisoner: the evils of my dungeon had whipped my soul to madness, but they had subdued my corporeal frame. I was weak and wan. Torella had used a thousand artifices to administer to my comfort; I had detected and scorned them all, and I reaped the harvest of my obduracy. What was to be done? Should I crouch before my foe, and sue for forgiveness?—Die rather ten thousand deaths!—Never should they obtain that victory! Hate—I swore eternal hate! Hate from whom?—to whom?—From a wandering outcast—to a mighty noble! I and my feelings were nothing to them: already had they forgotten one so unworthy. And Juliet!—her angel face and sylph-like form gleamed among the clouds of my despair with vain beauty; for I had lost her—the glory and flower of the world! Another will call her his!—that smile of paradise will bless another!

Even now my heart fails within me when I recur to this rout of grim-visaged ideas. Now subdued almost to tears, now raving in my agony, still I wandered along the rocky shore, which grew at each step wilder and more desolate. Hanging rocks and hoar precipices overlooked the tideless ocean; black caverns yawned; and for ever, among the seaworn recesses, murmured and dashed the unfruitful waters. Now my way was almost barred by an abrupt promontory, now rendered nearly impracticable by fragments fallen from the cliff. Evening was at hand, when, seaward, arose, as if on the waving of a wizard's wand, a murky web of clouds, blotting the late azure sky, and darkening and disturbing the till now placid deep.

The clouds had strange, fantastic shapes, and they changed and mingled and seemed to be driven about by a mighty spell. The waves raised their white crests; the thunder first muttered, then roared from across the waste of waters, which took a deep purple dye, necked with foam. The spot where I stood looked, on one side, to the wide spread ocean; on the other, it was barred by a rugged promontory. Round this cape suddenly came, driven by the wind, a vessel. In vain the mariners tried to force a path for her to the open sea the gale drove her on the rocks. It will perish!—all on board will perish! Would I were among them! And to my young heart the, idea of death came for the first time blended with that of joy. It was an awful sight to behold that vessel struggling with her fate. Hardly could I discern the sailors, but I heard them. It was soon all over! A rock, just covered by the tossing waves, and so unperceived, lay in wait for its prey. A crash of thunder broke over my head at the moment that, with a frightful shock, the vessel dashed upon her unseen enemy. In a brief space of time she went to pieces. There I stood in safety; arid there were my fellow-creatures battling, how hopelessly, with annihilation. Methought I saw them struggling—too truly did I hear their shrieks, conquering the barking surges in their shrill agony. The dark breakers threw hither and thither the fragments of the wreck: soon it disappeared. I had been fascinated to gaze till the end: at last I sank on my knees—I covered my face with my hands. I again looked up; something was floating on the billows towards the shore. It neared and neared. Was that a human form? It grew more and more distinct; and at last a mighty wave, lifting the whole freight, lodged it upon a rock. A human being bestriding a sea-chest! a human being! Yet was it one? Surely never such had existed before—a misshapen dwarf, with squinting eyes, distorted features, and body deformed, till it became a horror to behold. My blood, lately warming towards a fellow-being so snatched from a watery tomb, froze in my heart. The dwarf got off his chest; he tossed his straight, struggling hair from his odious visage.

"By St. Beelzebub!" he exclaimed, "I have been well bested." He looked round and saw me. "Oh, by the fiend! here is another ally of the mighty One. To what saint did you offer prayers, friend—if not to mine? Yet I remember you not on board."

I shrank from the monster and his blasphemy. Again he questioned me, and I muttered some inaudible reply. He continued:—

"Your voice is drowned by this dissonant roar. What a noise the big ocean makes! Schoolboys bursting from their prison are not louder than these waves set free to play. They disturb me. I will no more of their ill-timed brawling. Silence, hoary One!—Winds, avaunt!—to your homes!—Clouds, fly to the antipodes, and leave our heaven clear!"

As he spoke, he stretched out his two long, lank arms, that looked like spider's claws, and seemed to embrace with them the expanse before him. Was it a miracle? The clouds became broken and fled; the azure sky first peeped out, and then was spread a calm field of blue above us; the stormy gale was exchanged to the softly breathing west; the sea grew calm; the waves dwindled to riplets.

"I like obedience even in these stupid elements," said the dwarf. "How much more in the tameless mind of man! It was a well-got-up storm, you must allow—and all of my own making."

It was tempting Providence to interchange talk with this magician. But *Power*, in all its shapes, is respected by man. Awe, curiosity, a clinging fascination, drew me towards him.

"Come, don t be frightened, friend," said the wretch: "I am good humoured when pleased; and something does please me in your well-proportioned body and handsome face, though you look a little woe-begone. You have suffered a land—I, a sea wreck. Perhaps I can allay the tempest of your futures as I did my own. Shall we be friends?"—And he held out his hand; I could not touch it. "Well, then, companions that will do as well. And now, while I rest after the buffeting I underwent just now, tell me why, young and gallant as you seem, you wander thus alone and downcast on this wild sea-shore."

The voice of the wretch was screeching and horrid, and his contortions as he spoke were frightful to behold. Yet he did gain a kind of influence over me, which I could not master, and I told him my tale. When it was ended, he laughed long and loud: the rocks echoed back the sound: hell seemed yelling around me.

"Oh, thou cousin of Lucifer!" said he; "so thou too hast fallen through thy pride; and, though bright as the son of Morning, thou art ready to give up thy good looks, thy bride, and thy well-being, rather than submit thee to the tyranny of good. I honour thy choice, by my soul!—So thou hast fled, and yield the day; and mean to starve on these rocks, and to let the birds peck out thy dead eyes, while thy enemy and thy betrothed rejoice in thy ruin. Thy pride is strangely akin to humility, methinks."

As he spoke, a thousand fanged thoughts stung me to the heart.

"What would you that I should do?" I cried.

"I!—Oh, nothing, but lie down and say your prayers before you die. But, were I you, I know the deed that should be done."

I drew near him. His supernatural powers made him an oracle in my eyes; yet a strange unearthly thrill quivered through my frame as I said, "Speak!—teach me—what act do you advise?"

"Revenge thyself, man!—humble thy enemies!—set thy foot on the old man's neck, and possess thyself of his daughter!"

"To the cast and west I turn," cried I, "and see no means! Had I gold, much could I achieve; but, poor and single, I am powerless."

The dwarf had been seated on his chest as he listened to my story. Now he got off; he touched a spring; it flew open! What a mine of wealth—of blazing jewels, beaming gold, and pale silver was displayed therein. A mad desire to possess this treasure was born within me.

"Doubtless," I said, "one so powerful as you could do all things."

"Nay," said the monster humbly, "I am less omnipotent than I seem. Some things I possess which you may covet; but I would give them all for a small share, or even for a loan of what is yours."

"My possessions are at your service," I replied bitterly—"my poverty, my exile, my disgrace I make a free gift of them all."

"Good! I thank you. Add one other thing to your gift, and my treasure is yours."

"As nothing is my sole inheritance, what besides nothing would you have?"

"Your comely face and well-made limbs."

I shivered. Would this all-powerful monster murder me? I had no dagger. I forgot to pray—but I grew pale.

"I ask for a loan, not a gift," said the frightful thing: "lend me your body for three days—you shall have mine to cage your soul the while, and, in payment, my chest. What say you to the bargain?—Three short days."

We are told that it is dangerous to hold unlawful talk; and well do I prove the same. Tamely written down, it may see in incredible that I should lend any ear to this proposition; but, in spite of his unnatural ugliness, there was something fascinating in a being whose voice could govern earth, air, and sea. I felt a keen desire to comply; for with that chest I could command the world. My only hesitation resulted from a fear that he would not be true to his bargain. Then, I thought, I shall soon die here on these lonely sands, and the limbs he covets will be mine no more:—it is worth the chance. And, besides, I knew that, by all the rules of art-magic, there were formula and oaths which none of its practisers dared break. I hesitated to reply; and he went on, now displaying his wealth, now speaking of the petty price he demanded, till it seemed madness to refuse. Thus is it;—place our bark in the current of the stream, and down, over fall and cataract it is hurried; give up our conduct to the wild torrent of passion, and we are away, we know not whither.

He swore many an oath, and I adjured him by many a sacred name; till I saw this wonder of power, this ruler of the elements, shiver like an autumn leaf before my words; and as if the spirit spake unwillingly and per force within him, at last, he, with broken voice, revealed the spell whereby he might be obliged, did he wish to play me false, to render up the unlawful spoil. Our warm life-blood must mingle to make and to mar the charm.

Enough of this unholy theme. I was persuaded—the thing was done. The morrow dawned upon me as I lay upon the shingles, and I knew not my own shadow as it fell from me. I felt myself changed to a shape of horror, and cursed my easy faith and blind credulity. The chest was there—there the gold and precious stones for which I had sold the frame of flesh which nature had given me. The sight a little stilled my emotions: three days would soon be gone.

They did pass. The dwarf had supplied me with a plenteous store of food. At first I could hardly walk, so strange and out of joint were all my limbs; and my voice—it was that of the fiend. But I kept silent, and turned my face to the sun, that I might not see my shadow, and I counted the hours, and ruminated on my future conduct. To bring Torella to my feet—to possess my Juliet in spite of him—all this my wealth could easily achieve. During dark night I slept, and dreamt of the accomplishment of my desires. Two suns had set—the third dawned. I was agitated, fearful. Oh expectation, what a frightful thing art thou, when kindled more by fear than hope! How dost thou twist thyself round the heart, torturing its pulsations! How dost thou dart unknown pangs all through our feeble mechanism, now seeming to shiver us like broken glass, to nothingness—now giving us a fresh strength, which can *do* nothing, and so torments us by a sensation, such as the strong man must feel who cannot break his fetters, though they bend in his grasp. Slowly paced the bright, bright orb up the eastern sky; long it lingered in the zenith, and still more slowly wandered down the west: it touched the horizon's verge—it was lost! Its glories were on the summits of the cliff—they grew dun and grey. The evening star shone bright. He will soon be here.

He came not!—By the living heavens, he came not!—and night dragged out its weary length, and, in its decaying age, "day began to grizzle its dark hair"; and the sun rose again on the most miserable wretch that ever upbraided its light. Three days thus I passed. The jewels and the gold—oh, how I abhorred them!

Well, well—I will not blacken these pages with demoniac ravings. All too terrible were the thoughts, the raging tumult of ideas that filled my soul. At the end of that time I slept; I had not before since the third sunset; and I dreamt that I was at Juliet's feet, and she smiled, and then she shrieked—for she saw my transformation—and again she smiled, for still her beautiful lover knelt before her. But it was not I—it was he, the fiend, arrayed in my limbs, speaking with my voice, winning her with my looks of love. I strove to warn her, but my tongue refused its office; I strove to tear him from her, but I was rooted to the ground I awoke with the agony. There were the solitary hoar precipices—there the plashing sea, the quiet strand, and the blue sky over all. What did it mean? was my dream but a mirror of the truth? was he wooing and winning my betrothed? I would on the instant back to Genoa—but I was banished. I laughed—the dwarf's yell burst from my lips—*I* banished! Oh no! they had not exiled the foul limbs I wore; I might with these enter, without fear of incurring the threatened penalty of death, my own, my native city.

I began to walk towards Genoa. I was somewhat accustomed to my distorted limbs; none were ever so ill-adapted for a straightforward movement; it was with infinite difficulty that I proceeded. Then, too, I desired to avoid all the hamlets strewed here and there on the sea-beach, for I was unwilling to make a display of my hideousness. I was not quite sure that, if seen, the mere boys would not stone me to death as I passed, for a monster; some ungentle salutations I did receive from the few peasants or fishermen I chanced to meet. But it was dark night before I approached Genoa. The weather was so balmy and sweet that it struck me that the Marchese and his daughter would very probably have quitted the city for their country retreat. It was from Villa Torella that I had attempted to carry off Juliet; I had spent many an hour reconnoitering the spot, and knew each inch of ground in its vicinity. It was beautifully situated, embosomed in trees, on the margin of a stream. As I drew near, it became evident that my conjecture was right; nay, moreover, that the hours were being then devoted to feasting and merriment. For the house was lighted up; strains of soft and gay music were wafted towards me by the breeze. My heart sank within me. Such was the generous kindness of Torella's heart that I felt sure that he would not have indulged in public manifestations of rejoicing just after my unfortunate banishment, but for a cause I dared not dwell upon.

The country people were all alive and flocking about; it became necessary that I should conceal myself; and yet I longed to address some one, or to hear others discourse, or in any way to gain intelligence of what was really going on. At length, entering the walks that were in immediate vicinity to the mansion, I found one dark enough to veil my excessive frightfulness; and yet others as well as I were loitering in its shade. I soon gathered all I wanted to know—all that first made my very heart die with horror, and then boil with indignation. To-morrow Juliet was to be given to the penitent, reformed, beloved Guido—to-morrow my bride was to pledge her vows to a fiend from hell! And I did this!—my accursed pride—my demoniac violence and wicked self-idolatry had caused this act. For if I had acted as the wretch who had stolen my form had acted—if, with a mien at once yielding and dignified, I had presented myself to Torella, saying, I have done wrong, forgive me; I am unworthy of your angel-child, but permit me to claim her hereafter, when my altered conduct shall manifest that I abjure my vices, and endeavour to become in some sort worthy of her. I go to serve against the infidels; and when my zeal for religion and my true penitence for the past shall appear to you to cancel my crimes, permit me again to call myself your son. Thus had he spoken; and the penitent was welcomed even as the prodigal son of Scripture: the fatted calf was killed for him; and lie, still pursuing the same path, displayed such open-hearted regret for his follies, so humble a concession of all his rights, and so ardent a resolve to reacquire them by a life of contrition and virtue, that he quickly conquered the kind old man; and full pardon, and the gift of his lovely child, followed in swift succession.

Oh, had an angel from Paradise whispered to me to act thus! But now, what would be the innocent Juliet's fate? Would God permit the foul union—or, some prodigy destroying it, link the dishonoured name of Carega with the worst of crimes? To-morrow at dawn they were to be married: there was but one way to prevent this—to meet mine enemy, and to enforce the ratification of our agreement. I felt that this could only be done by a mortal struggle. I had no sword—if indeed my distorted arms could wield a soldier's weapon but I had a dagger, and in that lay my hope. There was no time for pondering or balancing nicely the question: I might die in the attempt; but besides the burning jealousy and despair of my own heart, honour, mere humanity, demanded that I should fall rather than not destroy the machinations of the fiend.

The guests departed—the lights began to disappear; it was evident that the inhabitants of the villa were seeking repose. I hid myself among the trees—the garden grow desert the gates were closed I wandered round and came under a window—ah! well did I know the same!—a soft twilight glimmered in the room—the curtains were half withdrawn. It was the temple of innocence and beauty. Its magnificence was tempered, as it were, by the slight disarrangements occasioned by its being dwelt in, and all the objects scattered around displayed the taste of her who hallowed it by her presence. I saw her enter with a quick light step—I saw her approach the window—she drew back the curtain yet further, and looked out into the night. Its breezy freshness played among her ringlets, and wafted them from the transparent marble of her brow. She clasped her hands, she raised her eyes to heaven. I heard her voice. Guido! she softly murmured—mine own Guido! and then, as if overcome by the fulness of her own heart, she sank on her knees;—her upraised eyes—her graceful attitude—the beaming thankfulness that lighted up her face—oh, these are tame words! Heart of mine, thou imagest ever, though thou canst not portray, the celestial beauty of that child of light and love.

I heard a step—a quick firm step along the shady avenue. Soon I saw a cavalier, richly dressed, young and, methought, graceful to look on, advance. I hid myself yet closer. The youth approached; he paused beneath the window. She arose, and again looking out she saw him, and said—I cannot, no, at this distant time I cannot record her terms of soft silver tenderness; to me they were spoken, but they were replied to by him.

"I will not go," he cried: "here where you have been, where your memory glides like some heaven-visiting ghost, I will pass the long hours till we meet, never, my Juliet, again, day or night, to part. But do thou, my love, retire; the cold morn and fitful breeze will make thy cheek pale, and fill with languor thy love-lighted eyes. Ah, sweetest! could I press one kiss upon them, I could, methinks, repose.

And then he approached still nearer, and methought he was about to clamber into her chamber. I had hesitated, not to terrify her; now I was no longer master of myself. I rushed forward—I threw myself on him—I tore him away—I cried, "O loathsome and foul-shaped wretch!"

I need not repeat epithets, all tending, as it appeared, to rail at a person I at present feel some partiality for. A shriek rose from Juliet's lips. I neither heard nor saw—I *felt* only mine enemy, whose throat I grasped, and my dagger's hilt; he struggled, but could not escape. At length hoarsely he breathed these words: "Do!—strike home! destroy this body—you will still live: may your life be long and merry!"

The descending dagger was arrested at the word, and he, feeling my hold relax, extricated himself and drew his sword, while the uproar in the house, and flying of torches from one room to the other, showed that soon we should be separated. In the midst of my frenzy there was much calculation:—fall I might, and so that he did not survive, I cared not for the death-blow I might deal against myself. While still, therefore, he thought I paused, and while I saw the villainous resolve to take advantage of my hesitation, in the sudden thrust he made at me, I threw myself on his sword, and at the same moment plunged my dagger, with a true, desperate aim, in his side. We fell together, rolling over each other, and the tide of blood that flowed from the gaping wound of each mingled on the grass. More I know not—I fainted.

Again I return to life: weak almost to death, I found myself stretched upon a bed—Juliet was kneeling beside it. Strange! my first broken request was for a mirror. I was so wan and ghastly, that my poor girl hesitated, as she told me afterwards; but, by the mass! I thought myself a right proper youth when I saw the dear reflection of my own well-known features. I confess it is a weakness, but I avow it, I do entertain a considerable affection for the countenance and limbs I behold, whenever I look at a glass; and have more mirrors in my house, and consult them oftener, than any beauty in Genoa. Before you too much condemn me, permit me to say that no one better knows than I the value of his own body; no one, probably, except myself, ever having had it stolen from him.

Incoherently I at first talked of the dwarf and his crimes, and reproached Juliet for her too easy admission of his love. She thought me raving, as well she might; and yet it was some time before I could prevail on myself to admit that the Guido whose penitence had won her back for me was myself; and while I cursed bitterly the monstrous dwarf, and blest the well-directed blow that had deprived him of life, I suddenly checked myself when I heard her say, Amen! knowing that him whom she reviled was my very self. A little reflection taught me silence a little practice enabled me to speak of that frightful night without any very excessive blunder. The wound I had given myself was no mockery of one—it was long before I recovered—and as the benevolent and generous Torella sat beside me, talking such wisdom as might win friends to repentance, and mine own dear Juliet hovered near me, administering to my wants, and cheering me by her smiles, the work of my bodily cure and mental reform went on together. I have never, indeed, wholly recovered my strength—my cheek is paler since—my person a little bent. Juliet sometimes ventures to allude bitterly to the malice that caused this change, but I kiss her on the moment, and tell her all is for the best. I am a fonder and more faithful husband, and true is this—but for that wound, never had I called her mine.

I did not revisit the sea-shore, nor seek for the fiend's treasure; yet, while I ponder on the past, I often think, and my confessor was not backward in favouring the idea, that it might be a good rather than an evil spirit, sent by my guardian angel, to show me the folly and misery of pride. So well at least did I learn this lesson, roughly taught as I was, that I am known now by all my friends and fellow-citizens by the name of Guido il Cortese.

The Sandman

E. T. A. Hoffmann

NATHANIEL TO LOTHAIRE

CERTAINLY YOU MUST ALL BE UNEASY THAT I HAVE NOT WRITTEN for so long—so very long. My mother, I am sure, is angry, and Clara will believe that I am passing my time in dissipation, entirely forgetful of the fair angel-image that is so deeply imprinted in my heart and mind. Such, however, is not the case. Daily and hourly I think of you all, and in my sweet dreams the kindly form of my lovely Clara passes before me, and smiles upon me with her bright eyes as she was wont when I appeared among you. Alas, how could I write to you in the distracted mood which has hitherto disturbed my every thought! Something horrible has crossed my path of life. Dark forebodings of a cruel, threatening, fate spread themselves over me like dark clouds, which no friendly sunbeam can penetrate. Now will I tell you what has befallen me. I must do so, that I plainly see—but if I only think of it, it will laugh out of me like mad. Ah, my dear Lothaire, how shall I begin it? How shall I make you in any way sensible that that which occurred to me a few days ago could really have such a fatal effect on my life? If you were here you could see for yourself, but now you will certainly take me for a crazy ghost-seer. In a word, the horrible thing which happened to me, and the painful impression of which I in vain endeavour to escape, is nothing more than this; that some days ago, namely on the 30th of October, at twelve o'clock at noon, a barometer-dealer came into my room and offered me his wares. I bought nothing, and threatened to throw him down stairs, upon which he took himself off of his own accord.

You suspect that only relations of the most peculiar kind, and exerting the greatest influence over my life can give any import to this occurrence, nay, that the person of that unlucky dealer must have a hostile effect upon me. So it is, indeed. I collect myself with all my might, that patiently and quietly I may tell you so much of my early youth as will bring all plainly and clearly in bright images before your active mind. As I am about to begin I fancy that I hear you laughing and Clara saying: "Childish stories indeed!" Laugh at me I beseech you, laugh with all your heart. But, heavens, my hair stands on end, and it seems as if I am asking you to laugh at me, in mad despair, as Franz Moor asked Daniel. But to my story.

Excepting at dinner time I and my brothers and sisters saw my father very little during the day. He was, perhaps, busily engaged at his ordinary occupation. After supper, which, according to the old custom was served up at seven o'clock, we all went with my mother into my father's work-room, and seated ourselves at the round table. My father smoked tobacco and drank a large glass of beer. Often he told us a number of wonderful stories, and grew so warm over them that his pipe continually went out. I had to light it again, with burning paper, which I thought great sport. Often, too, he would give us picture-books, and sit in his arm-chair silent and thoughtful, puffing out such thick clouds of smoke that we all seemed to be swimming in the clouds. On such evenings as these my mother was very melancholy, and immediately the clock struck nine, she would say: "Now children, to bed—to bed! The Sandman is coming, I can see." And certainly on all these occasions I heard something with a heavy, slow step go bouncing up the stairs. That I thought must be the Sandman. Once that dull noise and footstep were particularly fearful, and I asked my mother, while she took us away: "Eh, mamma, who is this naughty Sandman, who always drives us away from papa? What does he look like?" "There is no Sandman, dear child," replied my mother. "When I say the Sandman comes, I only mean that you are sleepy and cannot keep your eyes open,—just as if sand had been sprinkled into them." This answer of my mother's did not satisfy me—nay, in my childish mind the thought soon matured itself that she only denied the existence of the Sandman to hinder us from being terrified at him. Certainly I always heard him coming up the stairs. Full of curiosity to hear more of this Sandman, and his particular connection with children, I at last asked the old woman who tended my youngest sister what sort of man he was. "Eh, Natty," said she, "do you not know that yet? He is a wicked man, who comes to children when they will not go to bed, and throws a handful of sand into their eyes, so that they start out bleeding from their heads. These eyes he puts in a bag and carries them to the half-moon to feed his own children, who sit in the nest up yonder, and have crooked beaks like owls with which they may pick up the eyes of the naughty human children."

A most frightful image of the cruel Sandman was horribly depicted in my mind, and when in the evening I heard the noise on the stairs, I trembled with agony and alarm. My mother could get nothing out of me, but the cry of "The Sandman, the Sandman!" which was stuttered forth through my tears. I then ran into the bed-room, where the frightful apparition of the Sandman terrified me during the whole night. I had already grown old enough to perceive that the nurse's tale about the Sandman and the nest of children in the half-moon could not be quite true, but, nevertheless, this Sandman remained a fearful spectre, and I was seized with the utmost horror, when I heard him not only come up the stairs, but violently force open my father's room-door and enter. Sometimes he staid away for a long period, but oftener his visits were in close succession. This lasted for years, and I could not accustom myself to the terrible goblin; the image of the dreadful Sandman did not become more faint. His intercourse with my father began more and more to occupy my fancy. An unconquerable fear prevented me from asking my father about it, but if I—I myself could penetrate the mystery, and behold the wondrous Sandman—that was the wish which grew upon me with years. The Sandman had brought me into the path of the marvellous and wonderful, which so readily finds a domicile in the mind of a child. Nothing was to me more delightful than to read or hear horrible stories of goblins, witches, pigmies, &c.; but above them all stood the Sandman, whom, in the oddest and most frightful shapes, I was always drawing with chalk or charcoal on the tables, cupboards, and walls. When I was ten years old, my mother removed me from the children's room into a little chamber, situated in a corridor near my father's room. Still, as before, we were obliged speedily to take our departure as soon as, on the stroke of nine, the unknown was heard in the house. I could hear in my little chamber how he entered my father's room, and then it soon appeared to me that a thin vapor of a singular odor diffused itself about the house. Stronger and stronger with my curiosity grew my resolution to form in some manner the Sandman's acquaintance. Often I sneaked from my room to the corridor, when my mother had passed, but never could I discover any thing, for the Sandman had always gone in at the door when I reached the place where I might have seen him. At last, urged by an irresistible impulse, I resolved to hide myself in my father's room and await the appearance of the Sandman.

By the silence of my father, and the melancholy of my mother, I perceived one evening that the Sandman was coming. I, therefore, feigned great weariness, left the room before nine o'clock, and hid myself in a corner close to the door. The house-door creaked, and the heavy, slow, groaning step went through the passage and towards the stairs. My mother passed me with the rest of the children. Softly—very softly, I opened the door of my father's room. He sat as usually, stiff and silent, with his back turned to the door. He did not perceive me, and I swiftly darted into the room and behind the curtain, drawn before an open press, which stood close to the door, and in which my father's clothes were hanging. The steps sounded nearer and nearer—there was a strange coughing and scraping and murmuring without. My heart trembled with anxiety and expectation. A sharp step close—very close to the door,—a smart stroke on the latch, and the door was open with a rattling noise. Screwing up my courage with all my might, I cautiously peeped out. The Sandman was standing before my father in the middle of the room, the light of the candles shone full upon his face. The Sandman, the fearful Sandman, was the old advocate Coppelius, who had often dined with us.

But the most hideous form could not have inspired me with deeper horror than this very Coppelius. Imagine a large broad-shouldered man, with a head disproportionately big, a face the colour of yellow ochre, a pair of gray bushy eyebrows, from beneath which a pair of green cat's eyes sparkled with the most penetrating lustre, and with a large nose curved over his upper lip. His wry mouth was often twisted into a malicious laugh, when a couple of dark red spots appeared upon his cheeks, and a strange hissing sound was heard through his compressed teeth. Coppelius always appeared in an ashen-gray coat, cut in old-fashioned style, with waistcoat and breeches of the same colour, while his stockings were black, and his shoes adorned with buckles set with precious stones. The little peruke scarcely reached further than the crown of his head, the curls stood high above his large red ears, and a broad hair-bag projected stiffly from his neck, so that the silver buckle which fastened his folded cravat might be plainly seen. The whole figure was hideous and repulsive, but most disgusting to us children were his coarse brown hairy fists; indeed, we did not like to eat what he had touched with them. This he had remarked, and it was his delight, under some pretext or other, to touch a piece of cake, or some nice fruit, that our kind mother might privately have put in our plate, in order that we, with tears in our eyes, might, from disgust and abhorrence, no longer be able to enjoy the treat intended for us. He acted in the same manner on holidays, when my father gave us a little glass of sweet wine. Then would he swiftly draw his fist over it, or perhaps he would even raise the glass to his blue lips, and laugh most devilishly, when we could only express our indignation by soft sobs. He always called us the little beasts, we dared not utter a sound when he was present, and we heartily cursed the ugly, unkind man, who deliberately marred our slightest pleasures. My mother seemed to hate the repulsive Coppelius as much as we did, since as soon as he showed himself her liveliness, her free and cheerful mind was changed into a gloomy solemnity. My father conducted himself towards him, as though he was a superior being, whose bad manners were to be tolerated, and who was to be kept in good humour at any rate. He need only give the slightest hint, and the favourite dishes were cooked, and the choicest wines served.

When I now saw this Coppelius, the frightful and terrific thought took possession of my soul, that indeed no one but he could be the Sandman. But the Sandman was no longer that bugbear of a nurse's tale, who provided the owl's nest in the half-moon with children's eyes,—no, he was a hideous spectral monster, who, wherever he appeared, brought with him grief, want, and destruction—temporal and eternal.

I was rivetted to the spot as if enchanted. At the risk of being discovered, and as I plainly foresaw, of being severely punished, I remained with my head peeping through the curtain. My father received Coppelius with solemnity. "Now to our work!" cried the latter with a harsh, grating voice, as he flung off his coat. My father silently and gloomily drew off his night-gown, and both attired themselves in long black frocks. Whence they took these, I did not see. My father opened the door of what I had always thought to be a cupboard, but I now saw that it was no cupboard, but rather a black hollow, in which there was a little hearth. Coppelius entered, and a blue flame began to crackle up on the hearth. All sorts of strange utensils lay around. Heavens!—As my old father now stooped down to the fire, he looked quite another man. A frightful convulsive pain seemed to have distorted his mild reverend features into a hideous repulsive diabolical countenance. He looked like Coppelius: the latter was brandishing red hot tongs, and with them taking shining masses busily out of the thick smoke, which he afterwards hammered. It seemed to me, as if I saw human faces around without any eyes—but with deep holes instead. "Eyes here, eyes!" said Coppelius in a dull roaring voice. Overcome by the wildest terror, I shrieked out, and fell from my hiding place upon the floor. Coppelius seized me, and showing his teeth, bleated out, "Ah—little wretch,—little wretch!"—then dragging me up, he flung me on the hearth, where the fire began to singe my hair. "Now we have eyes enough—a pretty pair of child's eyes." Thus whispered Coppelius and taking out of the flame some red-hot grains with his fists, he was about to sprinkle them in my eyes. My father upon this raised his hands in supplication, and cried: "Master, master, leave my Nathaniel his eyes!" Coppelius uttered a yelling laugh, and said: "Well let the lad have his eyes and cry his share in the world, but we will examine the mechanism of his hands and feet." And then he seized me so forcibly that my joints cracked, and screwed off my hands and feet, and then put them on again, one here and the other there. "Every thing is not right here!—As good as it was—the old one has understood it!" So did Coppelius say, in a hissing, lisping tone, but all around me became black and dark, a sudden cramp darted through my bones and nerves—and I lost all feeling. A gentle warm breath passed over my face; I woke as out of a sleep of death. My mother had been stooping over me. "Is the Sandman yet there?" I stammered. "No, no, my dear child, he has gone away long ago,—he will not hurt you!"—So said my mother, and she kissed and embraced her recovered darling.

Why should I weary you, my dear Lothaire! Why should I be so diffuse with details, when I have so much more to tell. Suffice it to say, that I had been discovered while watching, and ill-used by Coppelius. Agony and terror had brought on delirium and fever, of which I lay sick for several weeks. "Is the Sandman still there?" That was my first sensible word and the sign of my amendment—my recovery. I can now only tell you, the most frightful moment in my juvenile years. Then you will be convinced that it is no fault of my eyes, that all to me seems colourless, but that a dark fatality has actually suspended over my life a gloomy veil of clouds, which I shall perhaps only tear away in death.

Coppelius was no more to be seen; it was said he had left the town.

About a year might have elapsed, when, according to the old custom, we sat at the round table. My father was very cheerful, and told much that was entertaining, about his travels in his youth; when, as the clock struck nine, we heard the house-door creak on the hinges, and slow steps, heavy as iron, groaned through the passage and up the stairs. "That is Coppelius," said my mother, turning pale. "Yes!—that is Coppelius!" repeated my father, with a faint broken voice. The tears started from my mother's eyes. "But father—father!" she cried, "must it be so?" "He comes to me for the last time, I promise you," was the answer. "Only go now—go with the children—go—go to bed. Good night!"

I felt as if I were pressed into cold, heavy stone,—my breath was stopped. My mother caught me by the arm as I stood immoveable. "Come, come, Nathaniel!" I allowed myself to be led, and entered my chamber! "Be quiet—be quiet—go to bed—go to sleep!" cried my mother after me; but tormented by restlessness, and an inward anguish perfectly indescribable, I could not close my eyes. The hateful, abominable Coppelius stood before me with fiery eyes, and laughed at me maliciously. It was in vain that I endeavoured to get rid of his image. About midnight there was a frightful noise, like the firing of a gun. The whole house resounded. There was a rattling and a rustling by my door, and the house-door was closed with a violent sound. "That is Coppelius!" I cried, and I sprang out of bed in terror. There was then a shriek as if of acute inconsolable grief. I darted into my father's room; the door was open, a suffocating smoke rolled towards me, and the servant girl cried: "Ah, my master, my master!" On the floor of the smoking hearth lay my father dead, with his face burned and blackened, and hideously distorted,—my sisters were shrieking and moaning around him,—and my mother had fainted. "Coppelius!—cursed Satan, thou hast slain my father!" I cried, and lost my senses. When, two days afterwards, my father was laid in his coffin, his features were again as mild and gentle as they had been in his life. My soul was comforted by the thought that his compact with the devilish Coppelius could not have plunged him into eternal perdition.

The explosion had awakened the neighbours, the occurrence had become the common talk, and had reached the ears of the magistracy, who wished to make Coppelius answerable. He had, however, vanished from the spot, without leaving a trace.

If I tell you, my dear friend, that the barometer-dealer was the accursed Coppelius himself, you will not blame me for regarding a phenomenon so unpropitious as boding some heavy calamity. He was dressed differently, but the figure and features of Coppelius are too deeply imprinted in my mind, for an error in this respect to be possible. Besides, Coppelius has not even altered his name. As I hear he gives himself out as a Piedmontese optician, and calls himself Giuseppe Coppola.

I am determined to cope with him, and to avenge my father's death, be the issue what it may.

Tell my mother nothing of the hideous monster's appearance. Remember me to my dear sweet Clara, to whom I will write in a calmer mood.—Farewell.

CLARA TO NATHANIEL

It is true that you have not written to me for a long time, but nevertheless I believe that I am still in your mind and thoughts. For assuredly you were thinking of me most intently, when designing to send your last letter to my brother Lothaire, you directed it to me, instead of him. I joyfully opened the letter, and did not perceive my error till I came to the words: "Ah, my dear Lothaire." Now, by rights I should have read no farther, but should have handed over the letter to my brother. Although you have often in your childish teasing mood, charged me with having such a quiet, womanish, steady disposition, that like the lady, even if the house were about to fall in, I should smooth down a wrong fold in the window curtain before I ran away, I can hardly tell you how your letter shocked me. I could scarcely breathe,—my eyes became dizzy. Ah, my dear Nathaniel, how could such a horrible event have crossed your life? To be parted from you, never to see you again,—the thought darted through my breast like a burning dagger. I read and read. Your description of the repulsive Coppelius is terrific. For the first time I learned, how your good old father died a shocking violent death. My brother Lothaire, to whom I gave up the letter as his property, sought to calm me, but in vain. The fatal barometer-maker, Giuseppe Coppola, followed me at every step, and I am almost ashamed to confess that he disturbed my healthy and generally peaceful sleep with all sorts of horrible visions. Yet soon,—even the next day, I was quite changed again. Do not be offended, dearest one, if Lothaire tells you, that in spite of your strange misgiving, that Coppelius will in some manner injure you, I am in the same cheerful unembarrassed frame of mind as ever.

I will honestly confess to you that, according to my opinion, all the terrible things of which you speak, merely occurred in your own mind, and that the actual external world had little to do with them. Old Coppelius may have been repulsive enough, but his hatred of children was what really caused the abhorrence of your children towards him.

In your childish mind the frightful sandman in the nurse's tale was naturally associated with old Coppelius, who, even if you had not believed in the sandman, would still have been a spectral monster, especially dangerous to children. The awful nightly occupation with your father, was no more than this, that both secretly made alchemical experiments, and with these your mother was constantly dissatisfied, since besides a great deal of money being uselessly wasted, your father's mind being filled with a fallacious desire after higher wisdom was alienated from his family—as they say, is always the case with such experimentalists. Your father no doubt, by some act of carelessness, occasioned his own death, of which Coppelius was completely guiltless. Would you believe it, that I yesterday asked our neighbour, the clever apothecary, whether such a sudden and fatal explosion was possible in such chemical experiments? "Certainly," he replied, and in his way told me at great length and very circumstantially how such an event might take place, uttering a number of strange-sounding names, which I am unable to recollect. Now, I know you will be angry with your Clara; you will say that her cold disposition is impenetrable to every ray of the mysterious, which often embraces man with invisible arms, that she only sees the variegated surface of the world, and has the delight of a silly child, at some gold-glittering fruit, which contains within it a deadly poison.

Ah! my dear Nathaniel! Do you not then believe that even in free, cheerful, careless minds, here may dwell the suspicion of some dread power, which endeavours to destroy us in our own selves? Forgive me, if I, a silly girl, presume in any manner to indicate, what I really think of such an internal struggle; I shall not find out the right words after all, and you will laugh at me, not because my thoughts are foolish, but because I set about so clumsily to express them.

If there is a dark power, which with such enmity and treachery lays a thread within us, by which it holds us fast, and draws us along a path of peril and destruction, which we should not otherwise have trod; if, I say, there is such a power, it must form itself within us, or from ourselves; indeed, become identical with ourselves, for it is only in this condition that we can believe in it, and grant it the room which it requires, to accomplish its secret work. Now, if we have a mind, which is sufficiently firm, sufficiently strengthened by cheerful life, always to recognise this strange hostile operation as such, and calmly to follow the path which belongs to our inclination and calling, then will the dark power fail in its attempt to gain a power, that shall be a reflection of ourselves. Lothaire adds that it is certain, that the dark physical power, if of our own accord, we have yielded ourselves up to it, often draws within us some strange form, which the external world has thrown in our way, so that we ourselves kindle the spirit, which, as we in our strange delusion believe, speaks to us in that form. It is the phantom of our own selves, the close relationship with which, and its deep operation on our mind casts us into hell, or transports us into heaven. You see, dear Nathaniel, that I and my brother Lothaire have freely given our opinion on the subject of dark powers, which subject, now I find I have not been able to write down the chief part without trouble, appears to me somewhat deep. Lothaire's last words I do not quite comprehend. I can only suspect what he means, and yet I feel as if it were all very true. I beg of you, get the ugly advocate, Coppelius, and the barometer-seller, Giuseppe Coppola, quite out of your head. Be convinced that these strange fears have no power over you, and that it is only a belief in their hostile influence that can make them hostile in reality. If the great excitement of your mind did not speak from every line of your letter, if your situation did not give me the deepest pain, I could joke about the Sandman-Advocate, and the barometer-seller, Coppelius. Be cheerful, I have determined to appear before you as your guardian-spirit, and if the ugly Coppelius takes it in his head to annoy you in your dreams, to scare him away with loud peals of laughter. I am not a bit afraid of him nor of his disgusting hands; he shall neither spoil my sweetmeats as an advocate, nor my eyes as a sandman. Ever yours, my dear Nathaniel.

NATHANIEL TO LOTHAIRE

I AM VERY SORRY THAT IN CONSEQUENCE OF THE ERROR OCCASIONED by my wandering state of mind, Clara broke open the letter intended for you, and read it. She has written me a very profound philosophical epistle, in which she proves, at great length, that Coppelius and Coppola only exist in my own mind, and are phantoms of myself, which will be dissipated directly I recognise them as such. Indeed, one could not believe that the mind which often peers out of those bright, smiling, childish eyes, like a sweet charming dream, could define with such intelligence, in such a professor-like manner. She appeals to you—you, it seems have been talking about me. I suppose you read her logical lectures, that she may learn to divide and sift every thing acutely. Pray leave it off. Besides it is quite certain that the barometer-dealer, Guiseppe Coppola, is not the advocate Coppelius. I attend the lectures of the professor of physics, who has lately arrived. His name is the same as that of the famous natural philosopher, Spalanzani, and he is of Italian origin. He has known Coppola for years, and moreover it is clear from his accent that he is really a Piedmontese. Coppelius was a German, but I think no honest one. Calmed I am not, and though you and Clara may consider me a gloomy visionary, I cannot get rid of the impression, which the accursed face of Coppelius makes upon me. I am glad that Coppola has left the town, as Spalanzani says. This professor is a strange fellow—a little round man, with high cheek bones, sharp nose, pouting lips, and little piercing eyes. Yet you will get a better notion of him than by this description, if you look at the portrait of Cagliostro, designed by Chodowiecki, in one of the Berlin annuals, Spalanzani looks like that exactly. I lately went up stairs, and perceived that the curtain, which was generally drawn completely over a glass door, left a little opening on one side. I know not what curiosity impelled me to look through, a tall and very slender lady most symmetrically formed, and most splendidly attired, sat in the room by a little table on which she had laid her arms, her hands being folded together. She sat opposite to the door, so that I could completely see her angelic countenance. She did not appear to see me, and indeed there was something fixed about her eyes as if, I might almost say, she had no power of sight. It seemed to me that she was sleeping with her eyes open. I felt very uncomfortable, and therefore I slunk away into the auditorium, which was close at hand. Afterwards I learned that the form I had seen was that of Spalanzani's daughter Olympia, whom he kept confined in a very strange and improper manner, so that no one could approach her. After all, there may be something the matter with her; she is silly perhaps, or something of the kind. But why should I write you all this? I could have conveyed it better and more circumstantially by word of mouth. Know that I shall see you in a fortnight. I must again behold my dear; sweet, angelic Clara. The ill-humour will then be dispersed, which, I must confess, has endeavoured to get the mastery over me, since that fatal, sensible letter. Therefore I do not write to her to-day. A thousand greetings, & c.

Nothing more strange and chimerical can be imagined than that which occurred to my poor friend, the young student Nathaniel, and which I, gracious reader, have undertaken to tell you. Have you, kind reader, ever known a something that has completely filled your heart, thoughts, and senses, so as to exclude every thing else? There was in you a fermentation and a boiling, and your blood inflamed to the hottest glow bounded through your veins, and gave a higher colour to your cheeks. Your glance was so strange, as if you wished to perceive, in empty space, forms which to no other eyes are visible, and your speech flowed away into dark sighs. Then your friends asked you: "What is it, revered one?" "What is the matter, dear one?" And now you wished to express the internal picture with all its glowing tints, with all its light and shade, and laboured hard to find words only to begin. You thought that in the very first word you ought to crowd together all the wonderful, noble, horrible, comical, frightful, that had happened, so that it might strike all the hearers at once like an electric shock. But every word, every thing that is in the form of speech, appeared to you colourless, cold and dead. You hunt and hunt, and stutter and stammer, and the sober questions of your friends dart like icy breezes upon your internal fire until it is ready to go out; whereas if, like a bold painter, you had first with a few daring strokes drawn an outline of the internal picture, you might with small trouble have laid on the colours brighter and brighter, and the living throng of various forms would have carried your friends along with it, and they, like you, would have seen themselves in the picture that had proceeded from your mind. Now I must confess to you, kind reader, that no one has really asked me for the history of the young Nathaniel, but you know well enough that I belong to the queer race of authors, who, if they have any thing in their mind, such as I have just described, feel as if every one who comes near them, and indeed perhaps the whole world besides, is asking them: "What is it then—tell it, my dear friend?" Thus was I forcibly compelled to tell you of the momentous life of Nathaniel. The singularity and marvellousness of the story filled my entire soul, but for that very reason and because, my reader, I had to make you equally inclined to endure oddity, which is no small matter, I tormented myself to begin the history of Nathaniel in a manner as inspiring, original and striking as possible. "Once upon a time," the beautiful beginning of every tale, was too tame. "In the little provincial town of S—— lived"—was somewhat better, as it at least prepared for the climax. Or should I dart at once *medias in res*, with "Go to the devil, cried the student Nathaniel with rage and horror in his wild looks, when the barometer-seller, Guiseppe Coppola?"—I had indeed already written this down, when I fancied that in the wild looks of the student Nathaniel, I could detect something ludicrous, whereas the story is not comical at all. No form of language suggested itself to my mind, which even in the slightest degree seemed to reflect the colouring of the internal picture. I resolved that I would not begin it at all. So take, gentle reader, the three letters, which friend Lothaire was good enough to give me, as the sketch of the picture which I shall endeavour to colour more and more as I proceed in my narrative. Perhaps, like a good portrait-painter, I may succeed in catching many a form in such a manner, that you will find it is a likeness without having the original, and feel as if you had often seen the person with your own corporeal eyes. Perchance, dear reader, you will then believe that nothing is stranger and madder than actual life, and that this is all that the poet can conceive, as it were in the dull reflection of a dimly polished mirror.

In order that that which it is necessary in the first place to know, may be made clearer, we must add to these letters the circumstance, that shortly after the death of Nathaniel's father, Clara and Lothaire, the children of a distant relative, who had likewise died, and left them orphans, were taken by Nathaniel's mother to her own home. Clara and Nathaniel formed a strong attachment for each other, and no one in the world having any objection to make, they were betrothed, when Nathaniel left the place to pursue his studies in G——. He is, according to the date of his last letter, hearing the lectures of the celebrated professor of physics, Spalanzani.

Now I could proceed in my story with confidence, but at this moment Clara's image stands so plainly before me, that I cannot look another way, as indeed was always the case when she gazed at me, with one of her lively smiles. Clara could not by any means be reckoned beautiful; that was the opinion of all who are competent judges of beauty, by their calling. Nevertheless, the architects praised the exact symmetry of her frame, and the painters considered her neck, shoulders, and bosom almost too chastely formed, but then they all fell in love with her wondrous Magdalen-hair, and above every thing prated about *battonisch* colouring. One of them, a most fantastical fellow, singularly compared Clara's eyes to a lake by Ruysdael, in which the pure azure of a cloudless sky, the wood and flowery field, the whole cheerful life of the rich landscape are reflected. Poets and composers went still further. "What is a lake—what is a mirror!" said they, "can we look upon the girl without wondrous, heavenly songs and tunes flashing towards us from her glances, and penetrating our inmost soul, so that all there is awakened and stirred. If even then we sing nothing that is really sensible, there is not much in us, and that we can feelingly read in the delicate smile which plays on Clara's lips, when we presume to tinkle something before her, which is to pass for a song, although it is only a confused jumble of tones." So it was. Clara had the vivid fancy of a cheerful, unembarrassed child, a deep, tender, feminine disposition, an acute, clever understanding. The misty dreams had but a bad chance with her, since, though she did not talk,—as indeed talking would have been altogether repugnant to her tacit nature, her bright glance and her firm ironical smile would say to them: "Good friends, how can you imagine that I shall take your fleeting shadowy images for real forms with life and motion?" On this account Clara was censured by many as cold, unfeeling and prosaic; while others, who conceived life in its clear depth, greatly loved the feeling, acute, childlike girl, but none so much as Nathaniel, whose perception in art and science was clear and strong. Clara was attached to her lover with all her soul, and when he parted from her, the first cloud passed over her life. With what transport did she rush into his arms when, as he had promised in his last letter to Lothaire, he had actually returned to his native town and entered his mother's room. Nathaniel's expectations were completely fulfilled; for directly he saw Clara he thought neither of the Advocate Coppelius, nor of her "sensible" letter. All gloomy forebodings had gone.

However, Nathaniel was quite right, when he wrote to his friend Lothaire that the form of the repulsive barometer-seller, Coppola, had had a most hostile effect on his life. All felt, even in the first days, that Nathaniel had undergone a thorough change in his whole temperament. He sank into a gloomy reverie, and conducted himself in a strange manner, that had never been known in him before. Every thing, his whole life, had become to him a dream and a foreboding, and he was always saying that every man, although he might think himself free, only served for the cruel sport of dark powers. These he said it was vain to resist, and man must patiently resign himself to his fate. He went even so far as to say, that it is foolish to think that we do any thing in art and science according to our own self-acting will, for the inspiration which alone enables us to produce any thing, does not proceed from within ourselves, but is the effect of a higher principle without.

To the clear-headed Clara this mysticism was in the highest degree repugnant, but contradiction appeared to be useless. Only when Nathaniel proved that Coppelius was the evil principle, which had seized him at the moment when he was listening behind the curtain, and that this repugnant principle would in some horrible manner disturb the happiness of their life, Clara grew very serious, and said: "Yes, Nathaniel, you are right. Coppelius is an evil, hostile principle; he can produce terrible effects, like a diabolical power that has come invisibly into life; but only then, when you will not banish him from your mind and thoughts. So long as you believe in him he really exists, and exerts his influence; only your belief is his power."

Nathaniel, quite indignant that Clara established the demon's existence only in his own mind, would then come out with all the mystical doctrine of devils and fearful powers. But Clara would break off peevishly, by introducing some indifferent matter, to the no small annoyance of Nathaniel. He thought that such deep secrets were closed to cold, unsusceptible minds, without being clearly aware that he reckoned Clara among these subordinate natures, and therefore he constantly endeavoured to initiate her into the mysteries. In the morning, when Clara was getting breakfast ready, he stood by her, and read out of all sorts of mystical books, till she cried: "But, dear Nathaniel, suppose I blame you as the evil principle, that has a hostile effect upon my coffee? For if to please you, I leave every thing standing still, and look in your eyes, while you read, my coffee will run into the fire, and none of you will get any breakfast."

Nathaniel closed the book at once, and hurried indignantly to his chamber. Once he had a remarkable *forte* for graceful, lively tales, which he wrote down, and to which Clara listened with the greatest delight; now, his creations were gloomy, incomprehensible, formless, so that although Clara, out of compassion, did not say so, he plainly felt how little she was interested. Nothing was more insupportable to Clara than tediousness; in her looks and in her words a mental drowsiness, not to be conquered, was expressed. Nathaniel's productions were, indeed, very tedious. His indignation at Clara's cold, prosaic disposition, constantly increased, and Clara could not overcome her dislike of Nathaniel's dark, gloomy, tedious mysticism, so that they became more and more estranged from each other in mind, without perceiving it. The form of the ugly Coppelius, as Nathaniel himself was forced to confess, grew more dim in his fancy, and it often cost him trouble to colour with sufficient liveliness in his pictures, when he appeared as a ghastly bugbear of fate. At last it struck him that he would make the gloomy foreboding, that Coppelius would destroy his happiness in love, the subject of a poem. He represented himself and Clara as united by true love; but occasionally it seemed as though a black hand darted into their life, and tore away some newly springing joy. At last, while they were standing at the altar, the hideous Coppelius appeared, and touched Clara's lively eyes. They flashed into Nathaniel's heart, like bleeding sparks, scorching and burning, when Coppelius caught him, and flung him into a flaming, fiery circle, which flew round with the swiftness of the stream, and carried him along with it, amid its roaring. The roar is like that of the hurricane, when it fiercely lashes the foaming waves, which, like black giants with white heads, rise up for the furious combat. But through the wild tumult he hears Clara's voice: "Can you not, then, see me? Coppelius has deceived you. Those, indeed, were not my eyes, which so burned in your breast—they were glowing drops of your own heart's blood. I have my eyes still—only look at them!" Nathaniel reflects: "That is Clara, and I am hers for ever!" Then it seems to him as though thought forcibly entered the fiery circle, which stands still, while the noise dully ceases in the dark abyss. Nathaniel looks into Clara's eyes, but it is only death that, with Clara's eyes, kindly looks on him.

While Nathaniel composed this poem he was very calm and collected; he polished and improved every line, and having subjected himself to the fetters of metre, he did not rest till all was correct and melodious. When at last he had finished and read the poem aloud to himself, a wild horror seized him, and he cried out: "Whose horrible voice is that?" Soon, however, the whole appeared to him a very successful work, and he felt that it must inflame Clara's cold temperament, although he did not clearly consider for what Clara was to be excited, nor what purpose it would answer to torment her with the frightful images which threatened a horrible destiny, destructive to their love. Both of them—that is to say Nathaniel and Clara—were sitting in their mother's little garden, Clara very cheerful, because Nathaniel, during the three days in which he had been writing his poem, had not teased her with his dreams and his forebodings. Even Nathaniel spoke livelily and joyfully about pleasant matters, as he used to do formerly, so that Clara said: "Now for the first time I have you again! Do you not see that we have driven away the ugly Coppelius?" Then it first struck Nathaniel that he had in his pocket the poem, which he had intended to read. He at once drew the sheets out and began, while Clara, expecting something tedious as usual, resigned herself and began quietly to knit. But as the dark cloud rose ever blacker and blacker, she let the stocking fall and looked full into his face. He was carried along unceasingly by his poem, an internal fire deeply reddened his cheeks, tears flowed from his eyes. At last when he had concluded, he groaned in a state of utter exhaustion, and catching Clara's hand, sighed forth, as if melted into the most inconsolable grief: "Oh Clara!—Clara!" Clara pressed him gently to her bosom, and said softly, but very solemnly and sincerely: "Nathaniel, dearest Nathaniel, do throw that mad, senseless, insane stuff into the fire!" Upon this Nathaniel sprang up enraged, and thrusting Clara from him, cried: "Thou inanimate, accursed automaton!" He ran off; Clara, deeply offended, shed bitter tears, and sobbed aloud: "Ah, he has never loved me, for he does not understand me." Lothaire entered the arbour; Clara was obliged to tell him all that had occurred. He loved his sister with all his soul, and every word of her complaint fell like a spark of fire into his heart, so that the indignation which he had long harboured against the visionary Nathaniel, now broke out into the wildest rage. He ran to Nathaniel and reproached him for his senseless conduct towards his beloved sister in hard words, which the infuriated Nathaniel retorted in the same style. The appellation of "fantastical, mad fool," was answered by that of "miserable common-place fellow." A duel was inevitable. They agreed on the following morning, according to the academical custom of the place, to fight with sharp rapiers behind the garden. Silently and gloomily they slunk about. Clara had overheard the violent dispute, and seeing the fencing-master bring the rapiers at dawn, guessed what was to occur. Having reached the place of combat, Lothaire and Nathaniel had in gloomy silence flung off their coats, and with the fierce desire of fighting in their flaming eyes, were about to fall upon one another, when Clara rushed through the garden door. Sobbing, she cried aloud, "Ye wild cruel men! Strike me down before you attack each other, for how shall I live longer in the world if my lover murders my brother, or my brother murders my lover." Lothaire lowered his weapon, and looked in silence on the ground; but in Nathaniel's heart, amid the most poignant sorrow, revived all the love for the beautiful Clara, which he had felt in the best days of his happy youth. The weapon fell from his hand, he threw himself at Clara's feet. "Can you ever forgive me, my only—my beloved Clara? Can you forgive me, my dear brother, Lothaire?"

Lothaire was touched by the deep contrition of his friend; all three embraced in reconciliation amid a thousand tears, and vowed eternal love and fidelity.

Nathaniel felt as though a heavy burden, which pressed him to the ground, had been rolled away, as though by resisting the dark power, which held him fast, he had saved his whole being, which had been threatened with annihilation. Three happy days he passed with his dear friends, and then went to G——, where he intended to stay a year, and then to return to his native town for ever.

All that referred to Coppelius was kept a secret from the mother, for it was well known that she could not think of him without terror, as she, as well as Nathaniel, accused him of causing her husband's death.

How surprised was Nathaniel, when proceeding to his lodging, he saw that the whole house was burned down, and that only the bare walls stood up amid the ashes. However, notwithstanding the fire had broken out in the laboratory of the apothecary who lived on the ground-floor, and had therefore consumed the house from bottom to top, some bold active friends had succeeded in entering Nathaniel's room in the upper story, in time to save the books, manuscripts, and instruments. They carried all safe and sound into another house, where they took a room, which Nathaniel entered at once. He did not think it at all remarkable that he lodged opposite to Professor Spalanzani; neither did it appear singular when he perceived that his window looked straight into the room where Olympia often sat alone, so that he could plainly recognise her figure, although the features of her face were indistinct and confused. At last it struck him, that Olympia often remained for hours in this attitude, in which he had once seen her through the glass-door, sitting at a little table without any occupation, and that she plainly enough looked over at him with an unvarying glance. He was forced to confess that he had never seen a more lovely form, but with Clara in his heart, the stiff Olympia was perfectly indifferent to him. Occasionally, to be sure, he gave a transient look over his compendium, at the beautiful statue, but that was all. He was just writing to Clara, when he heard a light tap at the door; it paused at his words, and the repulsive face of Coppola peeped in. Nathaniel's heart trembled within him, but remembering what Spalanzani had told him about the countryman, Coppola, and also the sacred promises he had made to Clara with respect to the Sandman Coppelius, he felt ashamed of his childish fear, and collecting himself with all his might, said as softly and civilly as possible: "I do not want a barometer, my good friend; pray, go." Upon this, Coppola advanced a good way into the room, and said in a hoarse voice, while his wide mouth distorted itself into a hideous laugh, and his little eyes under their long gray lashes sparkled forth piercingly: "Eh, eh—no barometer—no barometer? I have besides pretty eyes—pretty eyes!"—"Madman!" cried Nathaniel with horror, "how can you have eyes?—Eyes?" But Coppola had already put his barometer aside, and plunged his hand into his wide coat-pocket, whence he drew lunettes and spectacles, which he placed upon the table "There—there—spectacles on the nose, those are my eyes—pretty eyes!" And so saying he drew out more and more spectacles so, that the whole table began to glisten and sparkle in the most extraordinary manner. A thousand eyes glanced, and quivered convulsively, and stared at Nathaniel; yet he could not look away from the table, and Coppola kept still laying down more and more spectacles, while flaming glances were intermingled more and more wildly, and shot their blood-red rays into Nathaniel's breast. Overcome with horror, he shrieked out: "Hold, hold, frightful man!" He seized fast by the arm Coppola, who was searching his pockets to bring out still more spectacles, although the whole table was already covered.

Coppola had greatly extricated himself with a hoarse repulsive laugh, and with the words: "Ah, nothing for you—but here are pretty glasses"; he had collected all the spectacles, put them up, and from the breast-pocket of his coat had drawn forth a number of telescopes large and small. As soon as the spectacles were removed Nathaniel felt quite easy, and thinking of Clara, perceived that the hideous phantom was but the creature of his own mind, and that Coppola was an honest optician, and could by no means be the accursed double of Coppelius. Moreover, in all the glasses which Coppola now placed on the table, there was nothing remarkable, or at least nothing so ghost-like as the spectacles, and to make matters right Nathaniel resolved to buy something of Coppola. He took up a little and very neatly worked pocket-telescope, and looked through the window to try it. Never in his life had he met a glass which brought the objects so sharply, plainly, and clearly before his eyes. Involuntarily he looked into Spalanzani's room; Olympia was sitting as usual before the little table, with her arms laid upon it, and her hands folded. For the first time could he see the wondrous beauty in the form of her face;—only the eyes seemed to him singularly stiff and dead. Nevertheless, as he looked more sharply through the glass, it seemed to him as if moist morn-beams were rising in the eyes of Olympia. It was as if the power of seeing was kindled for the first time; the glances flashed with constantly increasing liveliness. As if spell-bound, Nathaniel reclined against the window, meditating on the charming Olympia. A hemming and scraping aroused him as if from a dream. Coppola was standing behind him: "*Tre zecchini*—three ducats!" Nathaniel, who had quite forgotten the optician, quickly paid him what he asked. "Is it not so? A pretty glass—a pretty glass?" asked Coppola, in his hoarse, repulsive voice, and with his malicious smile. "Yes—yes," replied Nathaniel, peevishly; "good bye, friend." Coppola left the room, not without casting many strange glances at Nathaniel. He heard him laugh loudly on the stairs. "Ah," thought Nathaniel, "he is laughing at me because no doubt, I have paid him too much for this little glass." While he softly uttered these words, it seemed as if a deep deadly sigh was sounding fearfully through the room, and his breath was stopped by inward anguish. He perceived, however, that it was himself that had sighed. "Clara," he said to himself, "is right in taking me for a senseless dreamer, but it is pure madness—nay, more than madness, that the stupid thought, that I have paid Coppola too much for the glass, pains me even so strangely. I cannot see the cause." He now sat down to finish his letter to Clara; but a glance through the window convinced him that Olympia was still sitting there, and he instantly sprang out, as if impelled by an irresistible power, seized Coppola's glass, and could not tear himself from the seductive view of Olympia, till his friend and brother Sigismund, called him to go to Professor Spalanzani's lecture. The curtain was drawn close before the fatal room, and he could neither perceive Olympia now nor during the two following days, although he scarcely ever left the window, and constantly looked through Coppola's glass. On the third day the windows were completely covered. Quite in despair, and impelled by a burning wish, he ran out of the town-gate. Olympia's form floated before him in the air, stepped forth from the bushes, and peeped at him with large beaming eyes from the clear brook. Clara's image had completely vanished from his mind; he thought of nothing but Olympia, and complained aloud and in a murmuring tone: "Ah, thou noble, sublime star of my love, hast thou only risen upon me, to vanish immediately, and leave me in dark hopeless night?"

When he was retiring to his lodging, he perceived that there was a great bustle in Spalanzani's house. The doors were wide open, all sorts of utensils were being carried in, the windows of the first floor were being taken out, maid servants were going about sweeping and dusting with great hair-brooms, and carpenters and upholsterers were knocking and hammering within. Nathaniel remained standing in the street in a state of perfect wonder, when Sigismund came up to him, laughing, and said: "Now, what do you say to our old Spalanzani?" Nathaniel assured him that he could say nothing because he knew nothing about the professor, but on the contrary perceived with astonishment the mad proceedings in a house otherwise so quiet and gloomy. He then learnt from Sigismund that Spalanzani intended to give a grand festival on the following day,—a concert and ball—and that half the university was invited. It was generally reported that Spalanzani, who had so long kept his daughter most painfully from every human eye, would now let her appear for the first time.

Nathaniel found a card of invitation, and with heart beating highly went at the appointed hour to the professor's, where the coaches were already rolling, and the lights were shining in the decorated saloons. The company was numerous and brilliant. Olympia appeared dressed with great richness and taste. Her beautifully turned face, her figure called for admiration. The somewhat strange bend of her back inwards, the wasp-like thinness of her waist, seemed to be produced by too tight lacing. In her step and deportment there was something measured and stiff, which struck many as unpleasant, but it was ascribed to the constraint produced by the company. The concert began, Olympia played the piano with great dexterity, and executed a bravura, with a voice, like the sound of a glass bell, clear, and almost cutting. Nathaniel was quite enraptured; he stood in the hindermost row, and could not perfectly recognise Olympia's features in the dazzling light.

He, therefore, quite unperceived, took out Coppola's glass, and looked towards the fair Olympia. Ah! then he saw, with what a longing glance she looked towards him, how every tone first resolved itself plainly in the glance of love, which penetrated, in its glowing career, his inmost soul. The artistical *roulades* seemed to Nathaniel the exultation of a mind illuminated with love, and when, at last, after the cadence, the long trill sounded shrilly through the saloon, he felt as if grasped by glowing arms; he could no longer restrain himself, but with mingled pain and rapture shouted out, "Olympia!" All looked at him, and many laughed. The organist of the cathedral made a more gloomy face than usual, and simply said: "Well, well." The concert had finished, the ball began. "To dance with her—with her!" That was the aim of all Nathaniel's wishes, of all his efforts; but how to gain courage to ask her, the queen of the festival? Nevertheless—he himself did not know how it happened—no sooner had the dancing begun, than he was standing close to Olympia, who had not yet been asked to dance, and, scarcely able to stammer out a few words, had seized her hand. The hand of Olympia was as cold as ice; he felt a horrible deadly frost thrilling through him. He looked into her eye—that was beaming full of love and desire, and at the same time it seemed as though the pulse began to beat, and the stream of life to glow in the cold hand. And in the soul of Nathaniel the joy of love rose still higher; he clasped the beautiful Olympia, and with her flew through the dance. He thought that his dancing was usually correct as to time, but the peculiar rhythmical steadiness with which Olympia moved, and which often put him completely out, soon showed him, that his time was very defective. However, he would dance with no other lady, and would have liked to murder any one who approached Olympia for the purpose of asking her. But this only happened twice, and to his astonishment Olympia remained seated after every dance, when he lost no time in making her rise again. Had he been able to see any other object besides the fair Olympia, all sorts of unfortunate quarrels would have been inevitable, for the half-soft, scarcely suppressed laughter, which arose among the young people in every corner, was manifestly directed to Olympia, whom they pursued with very curious glances—one could not tell why. Heated by the dance, and by the wine, of which he had freely partaken, Nathaniel had laid aside all his ordinary reserve. He sat by Olympia, with her hand in his, and, highly inflamed and inspired, told his passion, in words which no one understood—neither himself nor Olympia. Yet, perhaps, *she* did; for she looked immoveably in his face, and sighed several times, "Ah, ah!" Upon this, Nathaniel said, "Oh, thou splendid, heavenly lady! Thou ray from the promised land of love—thou deep soul, in which all my being is reflected!" with much more stuff of the like kind; but

Olympia merely went on sighing, "Ah—ah!" Professor Spalanzani occasionally passed the happy pair, and smiled on them, with a look of singular satisfaction. To Nathaniel, although he felt in quite another region, it seemed all at once as though Professor Spalanzani was growing considerably darker; he looked around, and, to his no small horror, perceived that the two last candles in the empty saloon had burned down to their sockets, and were just going out. Music and dancing had ceased long ago. "Separation—separation!" he cried, wildly, and in despair; he kissed Olympia's hand, he bent towards her mouth, when his glowing lips were met by lips cold as ice! Just as when he touched Olympia's cold hand, he felt himself overcome by horror; the legend of the dead bride darted suddenly through his mind, but Olympia pressed him fast, and her lips seemed to recover to life at his kiss. Professor Spalanzani strode through the empty hall, his steps caused a hollow echo, and his figure, round which a flickering shadow played, had a fearful, spectral appearance. "Dost thou love me, dost thou love me, Olympia? Only this word!—Dost thou love me?" So whispered Nathaniel; but Olympia, as she rose, only sighed, "Ah—ah!" "Yes, my gracious, my beautiful star of love," said Nathaniel, "thou hast risen upon me, and thou wilt shine, ever illuminating my inmost soul." "Ah—ah!" replied Olympia, going. Nathaniel followed her; they both stood before the professor.

"You have had a very animated conversation with my daughter," said he, smiling; "so, dear Herr Nathaniel, if you have any taste for talking with a silly girl, your visits shall be welcome."

Nathaniel departed, with a whole heaven beaming in his bosom. The next day Spalanzani's festival was the subject of conversation. Notwithstanding the professor had done every thing to appear splendid, the wags had all sorts of incongruities and oddities to talk about, and were particularly hard upon the dumb, stiff Olympia, to whom, in spite of her beautiful exterior, they ascribed absolute stupidity, and were pleased to find therein the cause why Spalanzani kept her so long concealed. Nathaniel did not hear this without increased rage; but, nevertheless, he held his peace, for, thought he, "Is it worth while to convince these fellows that it is their own stupidity that prevents them from recognising Olympia's deep, noble mind?"

One day Sigismund said to him: "Be kind enough, brother, to tell me how it was possible for a sensible fellow like you to fall in love with that wax face, that wooden doll up there?"

Nathaniel was about to fly out in a passion, but he quickly recollected himself, and retorted: "Tell me, Sigismund, how it is that Olympia's heavenly charms could escape your glance, which generally perceives every thing so clearly—your active senses? But, for that very reason, Heaven be thanked, I have not you for my rival; otherwise, one of us must have fallen a bleeding corpse!"

Sigismund plainly perceived his friend's condition, so he skilfully gave the conversation a turn, and added, after observing that in love-affairs there was no disputing about the object: "Nevertheless it is strange, that many of us think much the same about Olympia. To us—pray do not take it ill, brother,—she appears singularly stiff and soulless. Her shape is symmetrical—so is her face—that is true! She might pass for beautiful, if her glance were not so utterly without a ray of life—without the power of seeing. Her pace is strangely measured, every movement seems to depend on some wound-up clockwork. Her playing—her singing has the unpleasantly correct and spiritless measure of a singing machine, and the same may be said of her dancing. To us, this Olympia has been quite unpleasant; we wished to have nothing to do with her; it seems as if she acts like a living being, and yet has some strange peculiarity of her own." Nathaniel did not completely yield to the bitter feeling, which was coming over him at these words of Sigismund; he mastered his indignation, and merely said, with great earnestness, "Well may Olympia appear awful to you, cold prosaic man. Only to the poetical mind does the similarly organised develop itself. To me alone was her glance of love revealed, beaming through mind and thought; only in the love of Olympia do I find myself again. It may not suit you, that she does not indulge in idle chit-chat like other shallow minds. She utters few words, it is true, but these few words appear as genuine hieroglyphics of the inner world, full of love and deep knowledge of the spiritual life in contemplation of the eternal *yonder*. But you have no sense for all this, and my words are wasted on you." "God preserve you, brother," said Sigismund very mildly, almost sorrowfully; "but it seems to me, that you are in an evil way. You may depend upon me, if all—no, no, I will not say any thing further." All of a sudden it seemed to Nathaniel as if the cold prosaic Sigismund meant very well towards him, and, therefore, he shook the proffered hand very heartily.

Nathaniel had totally forgotten, that there was in the world a Clara, whom he had once loved;—his mother—Lothaire—all had vanished from his memory; he lived only for Olympia, with whom he sat for hours every day, uttering strange fantastical stuff about his love, about the sympathy that glowed to life, about the affinity of souls, to all of which Olympia listened with great devotion. From the very bottom of his desk, he drew out all that he had ever written. Poems, fantasies, visions, romances, tales—this stock was daily increased with all sorts of extravagant sonnets, stanzas, and *canzone*, and he read all to Olympia for hours in succession without fatigue. Never had he known such an admirable listener. She neither embroidered nor knitted, she never looked out of window, she fed no favourite bird, she played neither with lap-dog nor pet cat, she did not twist a slip of paper nor any thing else in her hand, she was not obliged to suppress a yawn by a gentle forced cough. In short, she sat for hours, looking straight into her lover's eyes, without stirring, and her glance became more and more lively and animated. Only when Nathaniel rose at last, and kissed her hand and also her lips, she said "Ah, ah!" adding "good night, dearest!" "Oh deep, noble mind!" cried Nathaniel in his own room, "by thee, by thee, dear one, am I fully comprehended." He trembled with inward transport, when he considered the wonderful accordance that was revealed more and more every day in his own mind, and that of Olympia, for it seemed to him as if Olympia had spoken concerning him and his poetical talent out of the depths of his own mind;—as if the voice had actually sounded from within himself. That must indeed have been the case, for Olympia never uttered any words whatever beyond those which have been already mentioned. Even when Nathaniel, in clear and sober moments, as for instance, when he had just woke in the morning, remembered Olympia's utter passivity, and her paucity and scarcity of words, he said: "Words, words! The glance of her heavenly eye speaks more than any language here below. Can a child of heaven adapt herself to the narrow circle which a miserable earthly necessity has drawn?" Professor Spalanzani appeared highly delighted at the intimacy of his daughter with Nathaniel. To the latter he gave the most unequivocal signs of approbation, and when Nathaniel ventured at last to hint at an union with Olympia, he smiled with his white face, and thought "he would leave his daughter a free choice in the matter." Encouraged by these words, and with burning passion in his heart, Nathaniel resolved to implore Olympia on the very next day, that she would say directly, in plain words, that which her kind glance had told him long ago; namely, that she loved him. He sought the ring which his mother had given him at parting, that he might give it to Olympia as a symbol of his devotion, of his life which budded forth and bloomed with her alone. Clara's letters and Lothaire's came into his hands during the search; but he flung them aside indifferently, found the ring, put it up and hastened over to Olympia. Already on the steps, in the hall he heard a strange noise, which seemed to proceed from Spalanzani's room. There was a stamping, a clattering, a pushing, a hurling against the door, intermingled with curses and imprecations. "Let go, let go, rascal!—scoundrel! Body and soul ventured in it? Ha, ha, ha! that I never will consent to—I, I made the eyes, I the clockwork—stupid blockhead with your clockwork—accursed dog of a bungling watch-maker—off with you—Satan—stop, pipe-maker—infernal beast—hold—begone let go!"

These words were uttered by the voices of Spalanzani, and the hideous Coppelius, who was thus raging and clamoring. Nathaniel rushed in, overcome by the most inexpressible anguish. The professor held a female figure fast by the shoulders, the Italian Coppola grasped it by the feet, and thus they were tugging and pulling, this way and that, contending for the possession of it, with the utmost fury. Nathaniel started back with horror, when in the figure he recognised Olympia. Boiling with the wildest indignation, he was about to rescue his beloved from these infuriated men, but at that moment, Coppola, turning himself with the force of a giant, wrenched the figure from the professor's hand, and then with the figure itself gave him a tremendous blow, which made him reel and fall backwards over the table, where vials, retorts, bottles, and glass cylinders were standing. All these were dashed to a thousand shivers. Now Coppola flung the figure across his shoulders, and, with frightful, yelling laughter, dashed down the stairs, so that the feet of the figure, which dangled in the ugliest manner, rattled with a wooden sound on every step. Nathaniel stood paralysed; he had seen but too plainly that Olympia's waxen, deadly pale countenance had no eyes, but black holes instead—she was, indeed, a lifeless doll. Spalanzani was writhing on the floor; the pieces of glass had cut his head, heart, and arms, and the blood was spurting up, as from so many fountains. But he soon collected all his strength. "After him—after him—why do you pause? Coppelius, Coppelius, has robbed me of my best automaton—a work of twenty years—body and soul set upon it—the clock-work—the speech—the walk, mine; the eyes stolen from you. The infernal rascal—after him; fetch Olympia—there you have the eyes!"

And now Nathaniel saw how a pair of eyes, which lay upon the ground, were staring at him; these Spalanzani caught up, with the unwounded hand, and flung against his heart. At this, madness seized him with its burning claws, and clutched into his soul, tearing to pieces all his thoughts and senses. "Ho—ho—ho—a circle of fire! of fire!—turn thyself round, circle! merrily, merrily, ho, thou wooden doll—turn thyself, pretty doll!" With these words he flew at the professor and pressed in his throat. He would have strangled him, had not the noise attracted many people, who rushed in, forced open Nathaniel's grasp, and thus saved the professor, whose wounds were bound immediately. Sigismund, strong as he was, was not able to master the mad Nathaniel, who with frightful voice kept crying out: "Turn thyself, wooden doll!" and struck around him with clenched fists. At last the combined force of many succeeded in overcoming him, in flinging him to the ground, and binding him. His words were merged into a hideous roar, like that of a brute, and raging in this insane condition he was taken to the mad-house.

Before, gentle reader, I proceed to tell thee what more befell the unfortunate Nathaniel, I can tell thee, in case thou takest an interest in the skilfull optician and automaton-maker, Spalanzani, that he was completely healed of his wounds. He was, however, obliged to leave the university, because Nathaniel's story had created a sensation, and it was universally deemed an unpardonable imposition to smuggle wooden dolls instead of living persons into respectable tea-parties—for such Olympia had visited with success. The lawyers called it a most subtle deception, and the more culpable, inasmuch as he had planned it so artfully against the public, that not a single soul—a few cunning students excepted—had detected it, although all now wished to play the acute, and referred to various facts, which appeared to them suspicious. Nothing very clever was revealed in this way. For instance, could it strike any one as so very suspicious, that Olympia, according to the expression of an elegant tea-ite, had, contrary to all usage, sneezed oftener than she had yawned? "The *former*," remarked this elegant person, "was the self-winding-up of the concealed clockwork, which had, moreover, creaked audibly"—and so on. The professor of poetry and eloquence took a pinch of snuff, clapped first the lid of his box, cleared his throat, and said, solemnly, "Ladies and gentlemen, do you not perceive how the whole affair lies? It is all an allegory—a continued metaphor—you understand me—*Sapienti sat.*" But many were not satisfied with this; the story of the automaton had struck deep root into their souls, and, in fact, an abominable mistrust against human figures in general, began to creep in. Many lovers, to be quite convinced that they were not enamoured of wooden dolls, would request their mistress to sing and dance a little out of time, to embroider and knit, and play with their lap-dogs, while listening to reading, &c.; and, above all, not to listen merely, but also sometimes to talk, in such a manner as presupposed actual thought and feeling. With many did the bond of love become firmer, and more chaining, while others, on the contrary, slipped gently out of the noose. "One cannot really answer for this," said some. At tea-parties, yawning prevailed to an incredible extent, and there was no sneezing at all, that all suspicion might be avoided. Spalanzani, as already stated, was obliged to decamp, to escape the criminal prosecution for fraudulently introducing an automaton into human society. Coppola had vanished also.

Nathaniel awakened as from a heavy, frightful dream; he opened his eyes, and felt an indescribable sensation of pleasure streaming through him, with soft heavenly warmth. He was in bed in his own room, in his father's house, Clara was stooping over him, and Lothaire and his mother were standing near. "At last, at last, oh beloved Nathaniel, hast thou recovered from thy serious illness—

now thou art again mine!" So spoke Clara, from the very depth of her soul, and clasped Nathaniel in her arms. But with mingled sorrow and delight did the brightly glowing tears fall from his eyes, and he deeply groaned forth: "My own—my own Clara!" Sigismund, who had faithfully remained with his friend in the hour of trouble, now entered. Nathaniel stretched out his hand to him. "And thou, faithful brother, hast not deserted me?" Every trace of Nathaniel's madness had vanished, and he soon gained strength amid the care of his mother, his beloved, and his friends. Good fortune also had visited the house, for an old penurious uncle, of whom nothing had been expected, had died, and had left the mother, besides considerable property, an estate in a pleasant spot near the town. Thither Nathaniel, with his Clara, whom he now thought of marrying, his mother, and Lothaire, desired to go. Nathaniel had now grown milder and more docile than he had ever been, and he now understood, for the first time, the heavenly purity and the greatness of Clara's mind. No one, by the slightest hint, reminded him of the past. Only, when Sigismund took leave of him, Nathaniel said: "Heavens, brother, I was in an evil way, but a good angel led me betimes to the path of light! Ah, that was Clara!" Sigismund did not let him carry the discourse further for fear that deeply wounding recollections might burst forth bright and flaming. It was about this time that the four happy persons thought of going to the estate. They were crossing, at noon, the streets of the city, where they had made several purchases, and the high steeple of the town-house already cast its gigantic shadow over the market-place. "Oh," said Clara, "let us ascend it once more, and look at the distant mountains!" No sooner said than done. Nathaniel and Clara both ascended the steps, the mother returned home with the servant, and Lothaire, not inclined to clamber up so many steps, chose to remain below. The two lovers stood arm in arm in the highest gallery of the tower, and looked down upon the misty forests, behind which the blue mountains were rising like a gigantic city.

"Look there at that curious little gray bush, which actually seems as if it were striding towards us," said Clara. Nathaniel mechanically put his hand into his breast pocket—he found Coppola's telescope, and he looked on one side. Clara was before the glass. There was a convulsive movement in his pulse and veins,—pale as death, he stared at Clara, but soon streams of fire flashed and glared from his rolling eyes, and he roared frightfully, like a hunted beast. Then he sprang high into the air, and, in the intervals of a horrible laughter, shrieked out, in a piercing tone, "Wooden doll—turn thyself!" Seizing Clara with immense force he wished to hurl her down, but with the energy of a desperate death-struggle she clutched the railings. Lothaire heard the raging of the madman—he heard Clara's shriek of agony—fearful forebodings darted through his mind, he ran up, the door of the second flight was fastened, and the shrieks of Clara became louder and louder. Frantic with rage and anxiety, he dashed against the door, which, at last, burst open. Clara's voice became fainter and fainter. "Help—help—save me!"—with these words the voice seemed to die in the air. "She is gone—murdered by the madman!" cried Lothaire. The door of the gallery was also closed, but despair gave him a giant's strength, and he burst it from the hinges. Heavens—Clara, grasped by the mad Nathaniel, was hanging in the air over the gallery,—only with one hand she still held one of the iron railings. Quick as lightning Lothaire caught his sister, drew her in, and, at the same moment, struck the madman in the face with his clenched fist, so that he reeled and let go his prey.

Lothaire ran down with his fainting sister in his arms. She was saved. Nathaniel went raging about the gallery and bounded high in the air, crying, "Fire circle turn thyself—turn thyself!" The people collected at the sound of the wild shriek, and among them, prominent by his gigantic stature, was the advocate Coppelius, who had just come to the town, and was proceeding straight to the market-place. Some wished to ascend and secure the madman, but Coppelius laughed, saying, "Ha, ha,—only wait—he will soon come down of his own accord," and looked up like the rest. Nathaniel suddenly stood still as if petrified; he stooped down, perceived Coppelius, and yelling out, "Ah, pretty eyes—pretty eyes!"—he sprang over the railing.

When Nathaniel lay on the stone pavement, with his head shattered, Coppelius had disappeared in the crowd.

Many years afterwards it is said that Clara was seen in a remote spot, sitting hand in hand with a kind-looking man before the door of a country house, while two lively boys played before her. From this it may be inferred that she at last found that quiet domestic happiness which suited her serene and cheerful mind, and which the morbid Nathaniel would never have given her. J.O.

Somnambulism
A Fragment

Charles Brockden Brown

[The following fragment will require no other preface or commentary than an extract from the *Vienna Gazette* of June 14, 1784. "At Great Glogau, in Silesia, the attention of physicians, and of the people, has been excited by the case of a young man, whose behaviour indicates perfect health in all respects but one. He has a habit of rising in his sleep, and performing a great many actions with as much order and exactness as when awake. This habit for a long time showed itself in freaks and achievements merely innocent, or, at least, only troublesome and inconvenient, till about six weeks ago. At that period a shocking event took place about three leagues from the town, and in the neighbourhood where the youth's family resides. A young lady, travelling with her father by night, was shot dead upon the road, by some person unknown. The officers of justice took a good deal of pains to trace the author of the crime, and at length, by carefully comparing circumstances, a suspicion was fixed upon this youth. After an accurate scrutiny, by the tribunal of the circle, he has been declared author of the murder: but what renders the case truly extraordinary is, that there are good reasons for believing that the deed was perpetrated by the youth while asleep, and was entirely unknown to himself. The young woman was the object of his affection, and the journey in which she had engaged had given him the utmost anxiety for her safety."]

OUR GUESTS WERE PREPARING TO RETIRE FOR THE NIGHT, WHEN somebody knocked loudly at the gate. The person was immediately admitted, and presented a letter to Mr. Davis. This letter was from a friend, in which he informed our guest of certain concerns of great importance, on which the letter-writer was extremely anxious to have a personal conference with his friend; but knowing that he intended to set out from four days previous to his writing, he was hindered from setting out by the apprehension of missing him upon the way. Meanwhile, he had deemed it best to send a special message to quicken his motions, should he be able to find him.

The importance of this interview was such, that Mr. Davis declared his intention of setting out immediately. No solicitations could induce him to delay a moment. His daughter, convinced of the urgency of his motives, readily consented to brave the perils and discomforts of a nocturnal journey.

This event had not been anticipated by me: The shock that it produced in me was, to my own apprehension, a subject of surprise. I could not help perceiving that it was greater than the occasion would justify. The pleasures of this intercourse were, in a moment, to be ravished from me. I was to part from my new friend, and when we should again meet it was impossible to foresee. It was then that I recollected her expressions, that assured me that her choice was fixed upon another. If I saw her again, it would probably be as a wife. The claims of friendship, as well as those of love, would then be swallowed up by a superior and hateful obligation. But, though betrothed, she was not wedded. That was yet to come; but why should it be considered as inevitable: Our dispositions and views must change with circumstances. Who was he that Constantia Davis had chosen: Was he born to outstrip all competitors in ardour and fidelity? We cannot fail of choosing that which appears to us most worthy of choice. He had hitherto been unrivalled; but was not this day destined to introduce to her one, to whose merits every competitor must yield? He that would resign this prize, without an arduous struggle, would, indeed, be of all wretches the most pusillanimous and feeble.

Why, said I, do I cavil at her present choice? I will maintain that it does honour to her discernment. She would not be that accomplished being which she seems, if she had acted otherwise. It would be sacrilege to question the rectitude of her conduct. The object of her choice was worthy. The engagement of her heart in his favour was unavoidable, because her experience had not hitherto produced one deserving to be placed in competition with him. As soon as his superior is found, his claims will be annihilated. Has not this propitious accident supplied the defects of her former observation? But soft! is she not betrothed? If she be, what have I to dread? The engagement is accompanied with certain conditions. Whether they be openly expressed or not, they necessarily limit it. Her vows are binding on condition that the present situation continues, and that another does not arise, previously to marriage, by whose claims those of the present lover will be justly superseded.

But how shall I contend with this unknown admirer? She is going whither it will not be possible for me to follow her. An interview of a few hours is not sufficient to accomplish the important purpose that I meditate; but even this is now at an end. I shall speedily be forgotten by her. I have done nothing that entitles me to a place in her remembrance. While my rival will be left at liberty to prosecute his suit, I shall be abandoned to solitude, and have no other employment than to ruminate on the bliss that has eluded my grasp. If scope were allowed to my exertions, I might hope that they would ultimately be crowned with success; but, as it is, I am manacled and powerless. The good would easily be reached, if my hands were at freedom: now that they are fettered, the attainment is impossible.

But is it true that such is my forlorn condition? What is it that irrecoverably binds me to this spot? There are seasons of respite from my present occupations, in which I commonly indulge myself in journeys. This lady's habitation is not at an immeasurable distance from mine. It may be easily comprised within the sphere of my excursions. Shall I want a motive or excuse for paying her a visit? Her father has claimed to be better acquainted with my uncle. The lady has intimated, that the sight of me, at any future period, will give her pleasure. This will furnish ample apology for visiting their house. But why should I delay my visit? Why not immediately attend them on their way? If not on their whole journey, at least for a part of it? A journey in darkness is not unaccompanied with peril. Whatever be the caution or knowledge of their guide, they cannot be supposed to surpass mine, who have trodden this part of the way so often, that my chamber floor is scarcely more familiar to me. Besides, there is danger, from which, I am persuaded, my attendance would be a sufficient, an indispensable safeguard.

I am unable to explain why I conceived this journey to be attended with uncommon danger. My mind was, at first, occupied with the remoter consequences of this untimely departure, but my thoughts gradually returned to the contemplation of its immediate effects. There were twenty miles to a ferry, by which the travellers designed to cross the river, and at which they expected to arrive at sun-rise the next morning. I have said that the intermediate way was plain and direct. Their guide professed to be thoroughly acquainted with it.—From what quarter, then, could danger be expected to arise? It was easy to enumerate and magnify possibilities; that a tree, or ridge, or stone unobserved might overturn the carriage; that their horse might fail, or be urged, by some accident, to flight, were far from being impossible. Still they were such as justified caution. My vigilance would, at least, contribute to their security. But I could not for a moment divest myself of the belief, that my aid was indispensable. As I pondered on this image my emotions arose to terror.

All men are, at times, influenced by inexplicable sentiments. Ideas haunt them in spite of all their efforts to discard them. Prepossessions are entertained, for which their reason is unable to discover any adequate cause. The strength of a belief, when it is destitute of any rational foundation, seems, of itself, to furnish a new ground for credulity. We first admit a powerful persuasion, and then, from reflecting on the insufficiency of the ground on which it is built, instead of being prompted to dismiss it, we become more forcibly attached to it.

I had received little of the education of design. I owed the formation of my character chiefly to accident. I shall not pretend to determine in what degree I was credulous or superstitious. A belief, for which I could not rationally account, I was sufficiently prone to consider as the work of some invisible agent; as an intimation from the great source of existence and knowledge. My imagination was vivid. My passions, when I allowed them sway, were incontrollable. My conduct, as my feelings, was characterised by precipitation and headlong energy.

On this occasion I was eloquent in my remonstrances. I could not suppress my opinion, that unseen danger lurked in their way. When called upon to state the reasons of my apprehensions, I could only enumerate possibilities of which they were already apprised, but which they regarded in their true light. I made bold enquiries into the importance of the motives that should induce them to expose themselves to the least hazard. They could not urge their horse beyond his real strength. They would be compelled to suspend their journey for some time the next day. A few hours were all that they could hope to save by their utmost expedition. Were a few hours of such infinite moment?

In these representations I was sensible that I had over-leaped the bounds of rigid decorum. It was not my place to weigh his motives and inducements. My age and situation, in this family, rendered silence and submission my peculiar province. I had hitherto confined myself within bounds of scrupulous propriety, but now I had suddenly lost sight of all regards but those which related to the safety of the travellers.

Mr. Davis regarded my vehemence with suspicion. He eyed me with more attention than I had hitherto received from him. The impression which this unexpected interference made upon him, I was, at the time, too much absorbed in other considerations to notice. It was afterwards plain that he suspected my zeal to originate in a passion for his daughter, which it was by no means proper for him to encourage. If this idea occurred to him, his humanity would not suffer it to generate indignation or resentment in his bosom. On the contrary, he treated my arguments with mildness, and assured me that I had over-rated the inconveniences and perils of the journey. Some regard was to be paid to his daughter's ease and health. He did not believe them to be materially endangered. They should make suitable provision of cloaks and caps against the inclemency of the air. Had not the occasion been extremely urgent, and of that urgency he alone could be the proper judge, he should certainly not consent to endure even these trivial inconveniences. "But you seem," continued he, "chiefly anxious for my daughter's sake. There is, without doubt, a large portion of gallantry in your fears. It is natural and venial in a young man to take infinite pains for the service of the ladies; but, my dear, what say you? I will refer this important question to your decision. Shall we go, or wait till the morning?"

"Go, by all means," replied she. "I confess the fears that have been expressed appear to be groundless. I am bound to our young friend for the concern he takes in our welfare, but certainly his imagination misleads him. I am not so much a girl as to be scared merely because it is dark."

I might have foreseen this decision; but what could I say? My fears and my repugnance were strong as ever. The evil that was menaced was terrible. By remaining where they were till the next day they would escape it. Was no other method sufficient for their preservation? My attendance would effectually obviate the danger.

This scheme possessed irresistible attractions. I was thankful to the danger for suggesting it. In the fervour of my conceptions. I was willing to run to the world's end to show my devotion to the lady. I could sustain, with alacrity, the fatigue of many nights of travelling and watchfulness. I should unspeakably prefer them to warmth and ease, if I could thereby extort from this lady a single phrase of gratitude or approbation.

I proposed to them to bear them company, at least till the morning light. They would not listen to it. Half my purpose was indeed answered by the glistening eyes and affectionate looks of Miss Davis, but the remainder I was pertinaciously bent on likewise accomplishing. If Mr. Davis had not suspected my motives, he would probably have been less indisposed to compliance. As it was, however, his objections were insuperable. They earnestly insisted on my relinquishing my design. My uncle, also, not seeing any thing that justified extraordinary precautions, added his injunctions. I was conscious of my inability to show any sufficient grounds for my fears. As long as their representations rung in my ears, I allowed myself to be ashamed of my weakness, and conjured up a temporary persuasion that my attendance was, indeed, superfluous, and that I should show most wisdom in suffering them to depart alone.

But this persuasion was transient. They had no sooner placed themselves in their carriage, and exchanged the parting adieus, but my apprehensions returned upon me as forcibly as ever. No doubt part of my despondency flowed from the idea of separation, which, however auspicious it might prove to the lady, portended unspeakable discomforts to me. But this was not all. I was breathless with fear of some unknown and terrible disaster that awaited them. A hundred times I resolved to disregard their remonstrances, and hover near them till the morning. This might be done without exciting their displeasure. It was easy to keep aloof and be unseen by them. I should doubtless have pursued this method if my fears had assumed any definite and consistent form; if, in reality, I had been able distinctly to tell what it was that I feared. My guardianship would be of no use against the obvious sources of danger in the ruggedness and obscurity of the way. For that end I must have tendered them my services, which I knew would be refused, and, if pertinaciously obtruded on them, might justly excite displeasure. I was not insensible, too, of the obedience that was due to my uncle. My absence would be remarked. Some anger and much disquietude would have been the consequences with respect to him. And after all, what was this groundless and ridiculous persuasion that governed me? Had I profited nothing by experience of the effects of similar follies? Was I never to attend to the lessons of sobriety and truth? How ignominious to be thus the slave of a fortuitous and inexplicable impulse! To be the victim of terrors more chimerical than those which haunt the dreams of idiots and children. *They* can describe clearly, and attribute a real existence to the object of their terrors. Not so can I.

Influenced by these considerations, I shut the gate at which I had been standing, and turned towards the house. After a few steps I paused, turned, and listened to the distant sounds of the carriage. My courage was again on the point of yielding, and new efforts were requisite before I could resume my first resolutions. I spent a drooping and melancholy evening. My imagination continually hovered over our departed guests. I recalled every circumstance of the road. I reflected by what means they were to pass that bridge, or extricate themselves from this slough. I imagined the possibility of their guide's forgetting the position of a certain oak that grew in the road. It was an ancient tree, whose boughs extended, on all sides, to an extraordinary distance. They seemed disposed by nature in that way in which they would produce the most ample circumference of shade. I could not recollect any other obstruction from which much was to be feared. This indeed was several miles distant, and its appearance was too remarkable not to have excited attention.

The family retired to sleep. My mind had been too powerfully excited to permit me to imitate their example. The incidents of the last two days passed over my fancy like a vision. The revolution was almost incredible which my mind had undergone, in consequence of these incidents. It was so abrupt and entire that my soul seemed to have passed into a new form. I pondered on every incident till the surrounding scenes disappeared, and I forgot my real situation. I mused upon the image of Miss Davis till my whole soul was dissolved in tenderness, and my eyes overflowed with tears. There insensibly arose a sort of persuasion that destiny had irreversibly decreed that I should never see her more.

While engaged in this melancholy occupation, of which I cannot say how long it lasted, sleep overtook me as I sat. Scarcely a minute had elapsed during this period without conceiving the design, more or less strenuously, of sallying forth, with a view to overtake and guard the travellers; but this design was embarrassed with invincible objections, and was alternately formed and laid aside. At length, as I have said, I sunk into profound slumber, if that slumber can be termed profound, in which my fancy was incessantly employed in calling up the forms, into new combinations, which had constituted my waking reveries.—The images were fleeting and transient, but the events of the morrow recalled them to my remembrance with sufficient distinctness. The terrors which I had so deeply and unaccountably imbibed could not fail of retaining some portion of their influence, in spite of sleep.

In my dreams, the design which I could not bring myself to execute while awake I embraced without hesitation. I was summoned, methought, to defend this lady from the attacks of an assassin. My ideas were full of confusion and inaccuracy. All that I can recollect is, that my efforts had been unsuccessful to avert the stroke of the murderer. This, however, was not accomplished without drawing on his head a bloody retribution. I imagined myself engaged, for a long time, in pursuit of the guilty, and, at last, to have detected him in an artful disguise. I did not employ the usual preliminaries which honour prescribes, but, stimulated by rage, attacked him with a pistol, and terminated his career by a mortal wound.

I should not have described these phantoms had there not been a remarkable coincidence between them and the real events of that night. In the morning, my uncle, whose custom it was to rise first in the family, found me quietly reposing in the chair in which I had fallen asleep. His summons roused and startled me. This posture was so unusual that I did not readily recover my recollection, and perceive in what circumstances I was placed.

I shook off the dreams of the night. Sleep had refreshed and invigorated my frame, as well as tranquillized my thoughts. I still mused on yesterday's adventures, but my reveries were more cheerful and benign. My fears and bodements were dispersed with the dark, and I went into the fields, not merely to perform the duties of the day, but to ruminate on plans for the future.

My golden visions, however, were soon converted into visions of despair. A messenger arrived before noon, intreating my presence, and that of my uncle, at the house of Dr. Inglefield, a gentleman who resided at the distance of three miles from our house. The messenger explained the intention of this request. It appeared that the terrors of the preceding evening had some mysterious connection with truth. By some deplorable accident, Miss Davis had been shot on the road, and was still lingering in dreadful agonies at the house of this physician. I was in a field near the road when the messenger approached the house. On observing me, he called me. His tale was meagre and imperfect, but the substance of it was easy to gather. I stood for a moment motionless and aghast. As soon as I recovered my thoughts I set off full speed, and made not a moment's pause till I reached the house of Inglefield.

The circumstances of this mournful event, as I was able to collect them at different times, from the witnesses, were these. After they had parted from us, they proceeded on their way for some time without molestation. The clouds disappearing, the star-light enabled them with less difficulty to discern their path. They met not a human being till they came within less than three miles of the oak which I have before described. Here Miss Davis looked forward with some curiosity and said to her father, "Do you not see some one in the road before us? I saw him this moment move across from the fence on the right hand and stand still in the middle of the road."

"I see nothing, I must confess," said the father: "but that is no subject of wonder; your young eyes will of course see farther than my old ones."

"I see him clearly at this moment," rejoined the lady. "If he remain a short time where he is, of seems to be, we shall be able to ascertain his properties. Our horse's head will determine whether his substance be impassive or not."

The carriage slowly advancing, and the form remaining in the same spot, Mr. Davis at length perceived it, but was not allowed a clearer examination, for the person, having, as it seemed, ascertained the nature of the cavalcade, shot across the road, and disappeared. The behaviour of this unknown person furnished the travellers with a topic of abundant speculation.

Few possessed a firmer mind than Miss Davis; but whether she was assailed, on this occasion, with a mysterious foreboding of her destiny; whether the eloquence of my fears had not, in spite of resolution, infected her; or whether she imagined evils that my incautious temper might draw upon me, and which might originate in our late interview, certain it was that her spirits were visibly depressed. This accident made no sensible alteration in her. She was still disconsolate and incommunicative.

All the efforts of her father were insufficient to inspire her with cheerfulness. He repeatedly questioned her as to the cause of this unwonted despondency. Her answer was, that her spirits were indeed depressed, but she believed that the circumstance was casual. She knew of nothing that could justify despondency. But such is humanity. Cheerfulness and dejection will take their turns in the best regulated bosoms, and come and go when they will, and not at the command of reason. This observation was succeeded by a pause. At length Mr. Davis said, "A thought has just occurred to me. The person whom we just now saw is young Althorpe."

Miss Davis was startled: "Why, my dear father, should you think so? It is too dark to judge, at this distance, by resemblance of figure. Ardent and rash as he appears to be, I should scarcely suspect him on this occasion. With all the fiery qualities of youth, unchastised by experience, untamed by adversity, he is capable no doubt of extravagant adventures, but what could induce him to act in this manner?"

"You know the fears that he expressed concerning the issue of this night's journey. We know not what foundation he might have had for these fears. He told us of no danger that ought to deter us, but it is hard to conceive that he should have been thus vehement without cause. We know not what motives might have induced him to conceal from us the sources of his terror. And since he could not obtain our consent to his attending us, he has taken these means, perhaps, of effecting his purpose. The darkness might easily conceal him from our observation. He might have passed us without our noticing him, or he might have made a circuit in the woods we have just passed, and come out before us."

"That I own," replied the daughter, "is not improbable. If it be true, I shall be sorry for his own sake, but if there be any danger from which his attendance can secure us, I shall be well pleased for all our sakes. He will reflect with some satisfaction, perhaps, that he has done or intended us a service. It would be cruel to deny him a satisfaction so innocent."

"Pray, my dear, what think you of this young man? Does his ardour to serve us flow from a right source?"

"It flows, I have no doubt, from a double source. He has a kind heart, and delights to oblige others: but this is not all. He is likewise in love, and imagines that he cannot do too much for the object of his passion."

"Indeed!" exclaimed Mr. Davis, in some surprise. "You speak very positively. That is no more than I suspected; but how came you to know it with so much certainty?"

"The information came to me in the directest manner. He told me so himself."

"So ho! why, the impertinent young rogue!"

"Nay, my dear father, his behaviour did not merit that epithet. He is rash and inconsiderate. That is the utmost amount of his guilt. A short absence will show him the true state of his feelings. It was unavoidable, in one of his character, to fall in love with the first woman whose appearance was in any degree specious. But attachments like these will be extinguished as easily as they are formed. I do not fear for him on this account."

"Have you reason to fear for him on any account?"

"Yes. The period of youth will soon pass away. Overweening and fickle, he will go on committing one mistake after another, incapable of repairing his errors, or of profiting by the daily lessons of experience. His genius will be merely an implement of mischief. His greater capacity will be evinced merely by the greater portion of unhappiness that, by means of it, will accrue to others or rebound upon himself."

"I see, my dear, that your spirits are low. Nothing else, surely, could suggest such melancholy presages. For my part, I question not, but he will one day be a fine fellow and a happy one. I like him exceedingly. I shall take pains to be acquainted with his future adventures, and do him all the good that I can."

"That intention," said his daughter, "is worthy of the goodness of your heart. He is no less an object of regard to me than to you. I trust I shall want neither the power nor inclination to contribute to his welfare. At present, however, his welfare will be best promoted by forgetting me. Hereafter, I shall solicit a renewal of intercourse."

"Speak lower," said the father. "If I mistake not, there is the same person again." He pointed to the field that skirted the road on the left hand. The young lady's better eyes enabled her to detect his mistake. It was the trunk of a cherry-tree that he had observed.

They proceeded in silence. Contrary to custom, the lady was buried in musing. Her father, whose temper and inclinations were moulded by those of his child, insensibly subsided into the same state.

The re-appearance of the same figure that had already excited their attention diverted them anew from their contemplations. "As I live," exclaimed Mr. Davis, "that thing, whatever it be, haunts us. I do not like it. This is strange conduct for young Althorpe to adopt. Instead of being our protector, the danger, against which he so pathetically warned us, may be, in some inscrutable way, connected with this personage. It is best to be upon our guard."

"Nay, my father," said the lady, "be not disturbed. What danger can be dreaded by two persons from one? This thing, I dare say, means us no harm. What is at present inexplicable might be obvious enough if we were better acquainted with this neighbourhood. It is not worth a thought. You see it is now gone." Mr. Davis looked again, but it was no longer discernible.

They were now approaching a wood. Mr. Davis called to the guide to stop. His daughter enquired the reason of this command. She found it arose from his uncertainty as to the propriety of proceeding.

"I know not how it is," said he, "but I begin to be affected with the fears of young Althorpe. I am half resolved not to enter this wood.—That light yonder informs that a house is near. It may not be unadvisable to stop. I cannot think of delaying our journey till morning; but, by stopping a few minutes, we may possibly collect some useful information. Perhaps it will be expedient and practicable to procure the attendance of another person. I am not well pleased with myself for declining our young friend's offer."

To this proposal Miss Davis objected the inconveniences that calling at a farmer's house, at this time of night, when all were retired to rest, would probably occasion. "Besides," continued she, "the light which you saw is gone: a sufficient proof that it was nothing but a meteor."

At this moment they heard a noise, at a small distance behind them, as of shutting a gate. They called. Speedily an answer was returned in a tone of mildness. The person approached the chaise, and enquired who they were, whence they came, whither they were going, and, lastly, what they wanted.

Mr. Davis explained to this inquisitive person, in a few words, the nature of their situation, mentioned the appearance on the road, and questioned him, in his turn, as to what inconveniences were to be feared from prosecuting his journey. Satisfactory answers were returned to these enquiries.

"As to what you seed in the road," continued he, "I reckon it was nothing but a sheep or a cow. I am not more scary than some folks, but I never goes out a nights without I sees some *sich* thing as that, that I takes for a man or woman, and am scared a little oftentimes, but not much. I'm sure after to find that it's not nothing but a cow, or hog, or tree, or something. If it wasn't some sich thing you seed, I reckon it was *Nick Handyside*."

"Nick Handyside! who was he?"

"It was a fellow that went about the country a' nights. A shocking fool to be sure, that loved to plague and frighten people. Yes. Yes. It couldn't be nobody, he reckoned, but Nick. Nick was a droll thing. He wondered they'd never heard of Nick. He reckoned they were strangers in these here parts."

"Very true, my friend. But who is Nick: Is he a reptile to be shunned, or trampled on?"

"Why I don't know how as that. Nick is an odd soul to be sure; but he don't do nobody no harm, as ever I heard, except by scaring them. He is easily skeart though, for that matter, himself. He loves to frighten folks, but he's shocking apt to be frightened himself. I reckon you took Nick for a ghost. That's a shocking good story, I declare. Yet it's happened hundreds and hundreds of times, I guess, and more."

When this circumstance was mentioned, my uncle, as well as myself, was astonished at our own negligence. While enumerating, on the preceding evening, the obstacles and inconveniences which the travellers were likely to encounter, we entirely and unaccountably overlooked one circumstance, from which inquietude might reasonably have been expected. Near the spot where they now were, lived a Mr. Handyside, whose only son was an idiot. He also merited the name of monster, if a projecting breast, a mis-shapen head, features horrid and distorted, and a voice that resembled nothing that was ever before heard, could entitle him to that appellation. This being, besides the natural deformity of his frame, wore looks and practised gesticulations that were, in an inconceivable degree, uncouth and hideous. He was mischievous, but his freaks were subjects of little apprehension to those who were accustomed to them, though they were frequently occasions of alarm to strangers. He particularly delighted in imposing on the ignorance of strangers and the timidity of women. He was a perpetual rover. Entirely bereft of reason, his sole employment consisted in sleeping, and eating, and roaming. He would frequently escape at night, and a thousand anecdotes could have been detailed respecting the tricks which Nick Handyside had played upon way-farers.

Other considerations, however, had, in this instance, so much engrossed our minds, that Nick Handyside had never been once thought of or mentioned. This was the more remarkable, as there had very lately happened an adventure, in which this person had acted a principal part. He had wandered from home, and got bewildered in a desolate tract, known by the name of Norwood. It was a region, rude, sterile, and lonely, bestrewn with rocks, and embarrassed with bushes.

He had remained for some days in this wilderness. Unable to extricate himself, and, at length, tormented with hunger, he manifested his distress by the most doleful shrieks. These were uttered with most vehemence, and heard at greatest distance, by night. At first, those who heard them were panic-struck; but, at length, they furnished a clue by which those who were in search of him were guided to the spot. Notwithstanding the recentness and singularity of this adventure, and the probability that our guests would suffer molestation from this cause, so strangely forgetful had we been, that no caution on this head had been given. This caution, indeed, as the event testified, would have been superfluous, and yet I cannot enough wonder that in hunting for some reason, by which I might justify my fears to them or to myself, I had totally overlooked this mischief-loving idiot.

After listening to an ample description of Nick, being warned to proceed with particular caution in a part of the road that was near at hand being assured that they had nothing to dread from human interference, they resumed their journey with new confidence.

Their attention was frequently excited by rustling leaves or stumbling footsteps, and the figure which they doubted not to belong to Nick Handyside, occasionally hovered in their sight. This appearance no longer inspired them with apprehension. They had been assured that a stern voice was sufficient to repulse him, when most importunate. This antic being treated all others as children. He took pleasure in the effects which the sight of his own deformity produced, and betokened his satisfaction by a laugh, which might have served as a model to the poet who has depicted the ghastly risibilities of Death. On this occasion, however, the monster behaved with unusual moderation. He never came near enough for his peculiarities to be distinguished by star-light. There was nothing fantastic in his motions, nor any thing surprising, but the celerity of his transitions. They were unaccompanied by those howls, which reminded you at one time of a troop of hungry wolves, and had, at another, something in them inexpressibly wild and melancholy. This monster possessed a certain species of dexterity. His talents, differently applied, would have excited rational admiration. He was fleet as a deer. He was patient, to an incredible degree, of watchfulness, and cold, and hunger. He had improved the flexibility of his voice, till his cries, always loud and rueful, were capable of being diversified without end. Instances had been known, in which the stoutest heart was appalled by them; and some, particularly in the case of women, in which they had been productive of consequences truly deplorable.

When the travellers had arrived at that part of the wood where, as they had been informed, it was needful to be particularly cautious, Mr. Davis, for their greater security, proposed to his daughter to alight. The exercise of walking, he thought, after so much time spent in a close carriage, would be salutary and pleasant. The young lady readily embraced the proposal. They forthwith alighted, and walked at a small distance before the chaise, which was now conducted by the servant. From this moment the spectre, which, till now, had been occasionally visible, entirely disappeared. This incident naturally led the conversation to this topic. So singular a specimen of the forms which human nature is found to assume could not fail of suggesting a variety of remarks.

They pictured to themselves many combinations of circumstances in which Handyside might be the agent, and in which the most momentous effects might flow from his agency, without its being possible for others to conjecture the true nature of the agent. The propensities of this being might contribute to realize, on an American road, many of those imaginary tokens and perils which abound in the wildest romance. He would be an admirable machine, in a plan whose purpose was to generate or foster, in a given subject, the frenzy of quixotism.—No theatre was better adapted than Norwood to such an exhibition. This part of the country had long been deserted by beasts of prey. Bears might still, perhaps, be found during a very rigorous season, but wolves which, when the country was a desert, were extremely numerous, had now, in consequence of increasing population, withdrawn to more savage haunts. Yet the voice of Handyside, varied with the force and skill of which he was known to be capable, would fill these shades with outcries as ferocious as those which are to be heard in Siamese or Abyssinian forests. The tale of his recent elopement had been told by the man with whom they had just parted, in a rustic but picturesque style.

"But why," said the lady, "did not our kind host inform us of this circumstance? He must surely have been well acquainted with the existence and habits of this Handyside. He must have perceived to how many groundless alarms our ignorance, in this respect, was likely to expose us. It is strange that he did not afford us the slightest intimation of it."

Mr. Davis was no less surprised at this omission. He was at a loss to conceive how this should be forgotten in the midst of those minute directions, in which every cause had been laboriously recollected from which he might incur danger or suffer obstruction. This person, being no longer an object of terror, began to be regarded with a very lively curiosity. They even wished for his appearance and near approach, that they might carry away with them more definite conceptions of his figure. The lady declared she should be highly pleased by hearing his outcries, and consoled herself with the belief, that he would not allow them to pass the limits which he had prescribed to his wanderings, without greeting them with a strain or two. This wish had scarcely been uttered, when it was completely gratified.

The lady involuntarily started, and caught hold of her father's arm. Mr. Davis himself was disconcerted. A scream, dismally loud, and piercingly shrill, was uttered by one at less than twenty paces from them.

The monster had shown some skill in the choice of a spot suitable to his design. Neighbouring precipices, and a thick umbrage of oaks, on either side, contributed to prolong and to heighten his terrible notes. They were rendered more awful by the profound stillness that preceded and followed them. They were able speedily to quiet the trepidations which this hideous outcry, in spite of preparation and foresight, had produced, but they had not foreseen one of its unhappy consequences.

In a moment Mr. Davis was alarmed by the rapid sound of footsteps behind him. His presence of mind, on this occasion, probably saved himself and his daughter from instant destruction. He leaped out of the path, and, by a sudden exertion, at the same moment, threw the lady to some distance from the tract. The horse that drew the chaise rushed by them with the celerity of lightning. Affrighted at the sounds which had been uttered at a still less distance from the horse than from Mr. Davis, possibly with a malicious design to produce this very effect, he jerked the bridle from the hands that held it, and rushed forward with headlong speed. The man, before he could provide for his own safety, was beaten to the earth. He was considerably bruised by the fall, but presently recovered his feet, and went in pursuit of the horse.

This accident happened at about a hundred yards from the *oak*, against which so many cautions had been given. It was not possible, at any time, without considerable caution, to avoid it. It was not to be wondered at, therefore, that, in a few seconds, the carriage was shocked against the trunk, overturned, and dashed into a thousand fragments. The noise of the crash sufficiently informed them of this event. Had the horse been inclined to stop, a repetition, for the space of some minutes, of the same savage and terrible shrieks would have added tenfold to his consternation and to the speed of his flight. After this dismal strain had ended, Mr. Davis raised his daughter from the ground. She had suffered no material injury. As soon as they recovered from the confusion into which this accident had thrown them, they began to consult upon the measures proper to be taken upon this emergency. They were left alone. The servant had gone in pursuit of the flying horse. Whether he would be able to retake him was extremely dubious. Meanwhile they were surrounded by darkness. What was the distance of the next house could not be known. At that hour of the night they could not hope to be directed, by the far-seen taper, to any hospitable roof. The only alternative, therefore, was to remain where they were, uncertain of the fate of their companion, or to go forward with the utmost expedition.

They could not hesitate to embrace the latter. In a few minutes they arrived at the oak. The chaise appeared to have been dashed against a knotty projecture of the trunk, which was large enough for a person to be conveniently seated on it. Here they again paused.—Miss Davis desired to remain here a few minutes to recruit her exhausted strength. She proposed to her father to leave her here, and go forward in quest of the horse and the servant. He might return as speedily as he thought proper. She did not fear to be alone. The voice was still. Having accomplished his malicious purposes, the spectre had probably taken his final leave of them. At all events, if the report of the rustic was true, she had no personal injury to fear from him.

Through some deplorable infatuation, as he afterwards deemed it, Mr. Davis complied with her intreaties, and went in search of the missing. He had engaged in a most unpromising undertaking. The man and horse were by this time at a considerable distance. The former would, no doubt, shortly return. Whether his pursuit succeeded or miscarried, he would surely see the propriety of hastening his return with what tidings he could obtain, and to ascertain his master's situation. Add to this, the impropriety of leaving a woman, single and unarmed, to the machinations of this demoniac. He had scarcely parted with her when these reflections occurred to him. His resolution was changed. He turned back with the intention of immediately seeking her. At the same moment, he saw the flash and heard the discharge of a pistol. The light proceeded from the foot of the oak. His imagination was filled with horrible forebodings. He ran with all his speed to the spot. He called aloud upon the name of his daughter, but, alas! she was unable to answer him. He found her stretched at the foot of the tree, senseless, and weltering in her blood. He lifted her in his arms, and seated her against the trunk. He found himself stained with blood, flowing from a wound, which either the darkness of the night, or the confusion of his thoughts, hindered him from tracing. Overwhelmed with a catastrophe so dreadful and unexpected, he was divested of all presence of mind. The author of his calamity had vanished. No human being was at hand to succour him in his uttermost distress. He beat his head against the ground, tore away his venerable locks, and rent the air with his cries.

Fortunately there was a dwelling at no great distance from this scene. The discharge of a pistol produces a sound too loud not to be heard far and wide, in this lonely region. This house belonged to a physician. He was a man noted for his humanity and sympathy. He was roused, as well as most of his family, by a sound so uncommon. He rose instantly, and calling up his people, proceeded with lights to the road. The lamentations of Mr. Davis directed them to the place. To the physician the scene was inexplicable. Who was the author of this distress; by whom the pistol was discharged; whether through some untoward chance or with design, he was as yet uninformed, nor could he gain any information from the incoherent despair of Mr. Davis.

Every measure that humanity and professional skill could suggest were employed on this occasion. The dying lady was removed to the house. The ball had lodged in her brain, and to extract it was impossible. Why should I dwell on the remaining incidents of this tale? She languished till the next morning, and then expired.

The Castle of Otranto
A Gothic Story

Horace Walpole

PREFACE TO THE FIRST EDITION

THE FOLLOWING WORK WAS FOUND IN THE LIBRARY OF AN ANCIENT Catholic family in the north of England. It was printed at Naples, in the black letter, in the year 1529. How much sooner it was written does not appear. The principal incidents are such as were believed in the darkest ages of Christianity; but the language and conduct have nothing that savours of barbarism. The style is the purest Italian. If the story was written near the time when it is supposed to have happened, it must have been between 1095, the era of the first Crusade, and 1243, the date of the last, or not long afterwards. There is no other circumstance in the work that can lead us to guess at the period in which the scene is laid: the names of the actors are evidently fictitious, and probably disguised on purpose: yet the Spanish names of the domestics seem to indicate that this work was not composed until the establishment of the Arragonian Kings in Naples had made Spanish appellations familiar in that country. The beauty of the diction, and the zeal of the author (moderated, however, by singular judgment), concur to make me think that the date of the composition was little antecedent to that of the impression. Letters were then in their most flourishing state in Italy, and contributed to dispel the empire of superstition, at that time so forcibly attacked by the reformers. It is not unlikely that an artful priest might endeavour to turn their own arms on the innovators, and might avail himself of his abilities as an author to confirm the populace in their ancient errors and superstitions. If this was his view, he has certainly acted with signal address. Such a work as the following would enslave a hundred vulgar minds beyond half the books of controversy that have been written from the days of Luther to the present hour.

This solution of the author's motives is, however, offered as a mere conjecture. Whatever his views were, or whatever effects the execution of them might have, his work can only be laid before the public at present as a matter of entertainment. Even as such, some apology for it is necessary. Miracles, visions, necromancy, dreams, and other preternatural events, are exploded now even from romances. That was not the case when our author wrote; much less when the story itself is supposed to have happened. Belief in every kind of prodigy was so established in those dark ages, that an author would not be faithful to the manners of the times, who should omit all mention of them. He is not bound to believe them himself, but he must represent his actors as believing them.

If this *air* of the *miraculous* is excused, the reader will find nothing else unworthy of his perusal. Allow the possibility of the facts, and all the actors comport themselves as persons would do in their situation. There is no bombast, no similes, flowers, digressions, or unnecessary descriptions. Everything tends directly to the catastrophe. Never is the reader's attention relaxed. The rules of the drama are almost observed throughout the conduct of the piece. The characters are well drawn, and still better maintained. Terror, the author's principal engine, prevents the story from ever languishing; and it is so often contrasted by pity, that the mind is kept up in a constant vicissitude of interesting passions.

Some persons may perhaps think the characters of the domestics too little serious for the general cast of the story; but besides their opposition to the principal personages, the art of the author is very observable in his conduct of the subalterns. They discover many passages essential to the story, which could not be well brought to light but by their *naïveté* and simplicity. In particular, the womanish terror and foibles of Bianca, in the last chapter, conduce essentially towards advancing the catastrophe.

It is natural for a translator to be prejudiced in favour of his adopted work. More impartial readers may not be so much struck with the beauties of this piece as I was. Yet I am not blind to my author's defects. I could wish he had grounded his plan on a more useful moral than this: that *the sins of fathers are visited on their children to the third and fourth generation*. I doubt whether, in his time, any more than at present, ambition curbed its appetite of dominion from the dread of so remote a punishment. And yet this moral is weakened by that less direct insinuation, that even such anathemas may be diverted by devotion to St. Nicholas. Here the interest of the monk plainly gets the better of the judgment of the author. However, with all its faults, I have no doubt but the English reader will be pleased with a sight of this performance. The piety that reigns throughout, the lessons of virtue that are inculcated, and the rigid purity of the sentiments, exempt this work from the censure to which romances are but too liable. Should it meet with the success I hope for, I may be encouraged to reprint the original Italian, though it will tend to depreciate my own labour. Our language falls far short of the charms of the Italian, both for variety and harmony. The latter is peculiarly excellent for simple narrative. It is difficult in English *to relate* without falling too low or rising too high; a fault obviously occasioned by the little care taken to speak pure language in common conversation. Every Italian or Frenchman, of any rank, piques himself on speaking his own tongue correctly and with choice. I cannot flatter myself with having done justice to my author in this respect: his style is as elegant as his conduct of the passions is masterly. It is a pity that he did not apply his talents to what they were evidently proper for—the theatre.

I will detain the reader no longer, but to make one short remark. Though the machinery is invention, and the names of the actors imaginary, I cannot but believe that the groundwork of the story is founded on truth. The scene is undoubtedly laid in some real castle. The author seems frequently, without design, to describe particular parts. *The chamber*, says he, *on the right hand*; *the door on the left hand*; *the distance from the chapel to Conrad's apartment*. These and other passages are strong presumptions that the author had some certain building in his eye. Curious persons, who have leisure to employ in such researches, may possibly discover in the Italian writers the foundation on which our author has built. If a catastrophe, at all resembling that which he describes, is believed to have given rise to this work, it will contribute to interest the reader, and will make the "Castle of Otranto" a still more moving story.

I

MANFRED, PRINCE OF OTRANTO, HAD ONE SON AND ONE DAUGHTER: the latter, a most beautiful virgin, aged eighteen, was called Matilda. Conrad, the son, was three years younger; a homely youth, sickly, and of no promising disposition; yet he was the darling of his father, who never showed any symptoms of affection to Matilda. Manfred had contracted a marriage for his son with the marquis of Vicenza's daughter, Isabella: and she had already been delivered by her guardians into the hands of Manfred, that he might celebrate the wedding as soon as Conrad's infirm state of health would permit. Manfred's impatience for this ceremonial was remarked by his family and neighbours. The former, indeed, apprehending the severity of their prince's disposition, did not dare to utter their surmises on this precipitation. Hippolita, his wife, an amiable lady, did sometimes venture to represent the danger of marrying their only son so early, considering his great youth, and greater infirmities; but she never received any other answer than reflections on her own sterility, who had given him but one heir. His tenants and subjects were less cautious in their discourses. They attributed this hasty wedding to the prince's dread of seeing accomplished an ancient prophecy, which was said to have pronounced that the castle and lordship of Otranto *should pass from the present family, whenever the real owner should be grown too large to inhabit it*. It was difficult to make any sense of this prophecy; and still less easy to conceive what it had to do with the marriage in question. Yet these mysteries, or contradictions, did not make the populace adhere the less to their opinion.

Young Conrad's birth-day was fixed for his espousals. The company was assembled in the chapel of the Castle, and everything ready for beginning the divine office, when Conrad himself was missing. Manfred, impatient of the least delay, and who had not observed his son retire, despatched one of his attendants to summon the young prince. The servant, who had not stayed long enough to have crossed the court to Conrad's apartment, came running back breathless, in a frantic manner, his eyes staring, and foaming at the mouth. He said nothing, but pointed to the court. The company were struck with terror and amazement. The princess Hippolita, without knowing what was the matter, but anxious for her son, swooned away. Manfred, less apprehensive than enraged at the procrastination of the nuptials, and at the folly of his domestic, asked imperiously what was the matter? The fellow made no answer, but continued pointing towards the court-yard; and at last, after repeated questions put to him, cried out, "Oh! the helmet! the helmet!" In the mean time, some of the company had run into the court, from whence was heard a confused noise of shrieks, horror, and surprise. Manfred, who began to be alarmed at not seeing his son, went himself to get information of what occasioned this strange confusion. Matilda remained endeavouring to assist her mother; and Isabella staid for the same purpose, and to avoid showing any impatience for the bridegroom, for whom, in truth, she had conceived little affection.

The first thing that struck Manfred's eyes was a group of his servants endeavouring to raise something that appeared to him a mountain of sable plumes. He gazed without believing his sight. "What are ye doing?" cried Manfred, wrathfully; "where is my son?" A volley of voices replied, "Oh! my lord! the prince! the prince! the helmet! the helmet!" Shocked with these lamentable sounds, and dreading he knew not what, he advanced hastily;—but what a sight for a father's eyes!—he beheld his child dashed to pieces, and almost buried under an enormous helmet, an hundred times more large than any casque ever made for human being, and shaded with a proportionable quantity of black feathers.

The horror of the spectacle, the ignorance of all around how this misfortune had happened, and above all, the tremendous phenomenon before him, took away the prince's speech. Yet his silence lasted longer than even grief could occasion. He fixed his eyes on what he wished in vain to believe a vision; and seemed less attentive to his loss, than buried in meditation on the stupendous object that had occasioned it. He touched, he examined the fatal casque; nor could even the bleeding mangled remains of the young prince divert the eyes of Manfred from the portent before him. All who had known his partial fondness for young Conrad, were as much surprised at their prince's insensibility, as thunderstruck themselves at the miracle of the helmet. They conveyed the disfigured corpse into the hall, without receiving the least direction from Manfred. As little was he attentive to the ladies who remained in the chapel. On the contrary, without mentioning the unhappy princesses, his wife and daughter, the first sounds that dropped from Manfred's lips were, "Take care of the lady Isabella!"

The domestics, without observing the singularity of this direction, were guided by their affection to their mistress, to consider it as peculiarly addressed to her situation, and flew to her assistance. They conveyed her to her chamber more dead than alive, and indifferent to all the strange circumstances she heard, except the death of her son. Matilda, who doted on her mother, smothered her own grief and amazement, and thought of nothing but assisting and comforting her afflicted parent. Isabella, who had been treated by Hippolita like a daughter, and who returned that tenderness with equal duty and affection, was scarce less assiduous about the princess; at the same time endeavouring to partake and lessen the weight of sorrow which she saw Matilda strove to suppress, for whom she had conceived the warmest sympathy of friendship. Yet her own situation could not help finding its place in her thoughts. She felt no concern for the death of young Conrad, except commiseration; and she was not sorry to be delivered from a marriage which had promised her little felicity, either from her destined bridegroom, or from the severe temper of Manfred, who, though he had distinguished her by great indulgence, had imprinted her mind with terror, from his causeless rigour to such amiable princesses as Hippolita and Matilda.

While the ladies were conveying the wretched mother to her bed, Manfred remained in the court, gazing on the ominous casque, and regardless of the crowd which the strangeness of the event had now assembled around him. The few words he articulated, tended solely to inquiries, whether any man knew from whence it could have come. Nobody could give him the least information. However, as it seemed to be the sole object of his curiosity, it soon became so to the rest of the spectators, whose conjectures were as absurd and improbable, as the catastrophe itself was unprecedented. In the midst of their senseless guesses, a young peasant, whom rumour had drawn thither from a neighbouring village, observed that the miraculous helmet was exactly like that on the figure in black marble of Alfonso the Good, one of their former princes, in the church of St. Nicholas. "Villain! What sayest thou?" cried Manfred, starting from his trance in a tempest of rage, and seizing the young man by the collar; "how darest thou utter such treason? Thy life shall pay for it." The spectators, who as little comprehended the cause of the prince's fury as all the rest they had seen, were at a loss to unravel this new circumstance. The young peasant himself was still more astonished, not conceiving how he had offended the prince. Yet recollecting himself, with a mixture of grace and humility, he disengaged himself from Manfred's grip, and then with an obeisance, which discovered more jealousy of innocence than dismay, he asked, with respect, of what he was guilty? Manfred, more enraged at the vigour, however decently exerted, with which the young man had shaken off his hold, than appeased by his submission, ordered his attendants to seize him, and, if he had not been withheld by his friends whom he had invited to the nuptials, would have poignarded the peasant in their arms.

During this altercation, some of the vulgar spectators had run to the great church, which stood near the castle, and came back open-mouthed, declaring that the helmet was missing from Alfonso's statue. Manfred, at this news, grew perfectly frantic; and, as if he sought a subject on which to vent the tempest within him, he rushed again on the young peasant, crying, "Villain! Monster! Sorcerer! 'tis thou hast done this! 'tis thou hast slain my son!" The mob, who wanted some object within the scope of their capacities, on whom they might discharge their bewildered reasoning, caught the words from the mouth of their lord, and re-echoed, "Ay, ay! 'tis he, 'tis he! he has stolen the helmet from good Alfonso's tomb, and dashed out the brains of our young prince with it"—never reflecting how enormous the disproportion was between the marble helmet that had been in the church, and that of steel before their eyes; nor how impossible it was for a youth seemingly not twenty, to wield a piece of armour of so prodigious a weight.

The folly of these ejaculations brought Manfred to himself: yet whether provoked at the peasant having observed the resemblance between the two helmets, and thereby led to the farther discovery of the absence of that in the church, or wishing to bury any such rumour under so impertinent a supposition, he gravely pronounced that the young man was certainly a necromancer, and that till the Church could take cognizance of the affair, he would have the magician, whom they had thus detected, kept prisoner under the helmet itself, which he ordered his attendants to raise, and place the young man under it; declaring he should be kept there without food, with which his own infernal art might furnish him.

It was in vain for the youth to represent against this preposterous sentence: in vain did Manfred's friends endeavour to divert him from this savage and ill-grounded resolution. The generality were charmed with their lord's decision, which, to their apprehensions, carried great appearance of justice, as the magician was to be punished by the very instrument with which he had offended: nor were they struck with the least compunction at the probability of the youth being starved, for they firmly believed that, by his diabolic skill, he could easily supply himself with nutriment.

Manfred thus saw his commands even cheerfully obeyed; and appointing a guard with strict orders to prevent any food being conveyed to the prisoner, he dismissed his friends and attendants, and retired to his own chamber, after locking the gates of the castle, in which he suffered none but his domestics to remain.

In the mean time the care and zeal of the young ladies had brought the Princess Hippolita to herself, who amidst the transports of her own sorrow frequently demanded news of her lord, would have dismissed her attendants to watch over him, and at last enjoined Matilda to leave her, and visit and comfort her father. Matilda, who wanted no affectionate duty to Manfred, though she trembled at his austerity, obeyed the orders of Hippolita, whom she tenderly recommended to Isabella; and inquiring of the domestics for her father, was informed that he was retired to his chamber, and had commanded that nobody should have admittance to him. Concluding that he was immersed in sorrow for the death of her brother, and fearing to renew his tears by the sight of his sole remaining child, she hesitated whether she should break in upon his affliction; yet solicitude for him, backed by the commands of her mother, encouraged her to venture disobeying the orders he had given; a fault she had never been guilty of before. The gentle timidity of her nature made her pause for some minutes at his door. She heard him traverse his chamber backwards and forwards with disordered steps; a mood which increased her apprehensions. She was, however, just going to beg admittance, when Manfred suddenly opened the door; and as it was now twilight, concurring with the disorder of his mind, he did not distinguish the person, but asked angrily, who it was? Matilda replied, trembling, "My dearest father, it is I, your daughter." Manfred, stepping back hastily, cried, "Begone! I do not want a daughter!" and, flinging back abruptly, clapped the door against the terrified Matilda.

She was too well acquainted with her father's impetuosity to venture a second intrusion. When she had a little recovered the shock of so bitter a reception, she wiped away her tears to prevent the additional stab that the knowledge of it would give to Hippolita, who questioned her in the most anxious terms on the health of Manfred, and how he bore his loss. Matilda assured her he was well, and supported his misfortune with manly fortitude. "But will he not let me see him?" said Hippolita mournfully; "will he not permit me to blend my tears with his, and shed a mother's sorrows in the bosom of her lord? Or do you deceive me, Matilda? I know how Manfred doted on his son:—is not the stroke too heavy for him? has he not sunk under it?—You do not answer me—alas! I dread the worst! Raise me, my maidens; I will—I will see my lord. Bear me to him instantly. He is dearer to me even than my children." Matilda made signs to Isabella to prevent Hippolita's rising; and both those lovely young women were using their gentle violence to stop and calm the princess, when a servant, on the part of Manfred, arrived and told Isabella that his lord demanded to speak with her.

"With me!" cried Isabella. "Go," said Hippolita, relieved by a message from her lord; "Manfred cannot support the sight of his own family. He thinks you less disordered than we are, and dreads the shock of my grief. Console him, dear Isabella, and tell him I will smother my own anguish rather than add to his."

As it was now evening the servant who conducted Isabella bore a torch before her. When they came to Manfred, who was walking impatiently about the gallery, he started, and said hastily, "Take away that light, and begone." Then shutting the door impetuously, he flung himself upon a bench against the wall, and bade Isabella sit by him. She obeyed trembling. "I sent for you, lady,"—said he; and then stopped under great appearance of confusion. "My lord!"—"Yes, I sent for you on a matter of great moment," resumed he;—"dry your tears, young lady—you have lost your bridegroom. Yes, cruel fate! and I have lost the hopes of my race;—but Conrad was not worthy of your beauty."—"How! my lord?" said Isabella; "sure you do not suspect me of not feeling the concern I ought? my duty and affection would have always—" "Think no more of him," interrupted Manfred; "he was a sickly, puny child, and Heaven has, perhaps, taken him away, that I might not trust the honours of my house on so frail a foundation. The line of Manfred calls for numerous supports.

My foolish fondness for that boy blinded the eyes of my prudence.—But it is better as it is. I hope, in a few years, to have reason to rejoice at the death of Conrad."

Words cannot paint the astonishment of Isabella. At first she apprehended that grief had disordered Manfred's understanding. Her next thought suggested that this strange discourse was designed to ensnare her: she feared that Manfred had perceived her indifference for his son; and in consequence of that idea she replied, "Good my lord, do not doubt my tenderness; my heart would have accompanied my hand. Conrad would have engrossed all my care; and wherever fate shall dispose of me, I shall always cherish his memory, and regard your Highness and the virtuous Hippolita as my parents."—"Curse on Hippolita!" cried Manfred; "Forget her from this moment, as I do. In short, lady, you have missed a husband undeserving of your charms: they shall now be better disposed of. Instead of a sickly boy, you shall have a husband in the prime of his age, who will know how to value your beauties, and who may expect a numerous offspring."—"Alas! my lord," said Isabella, "my mind is too sadly engrossed by the recent catastrophe in your family to think of another marriage. If ever my father returns, and it shall be his pleasure, I shall obey, as I did when I consented to give my hand to your son: but, until his return, permit me to remain under your hospitable roof, and employ the melancholy hours in assuaging yours, Hippolita's, and the fair Matilda's affliction."

"I desired you once before," said Manfred, angrily, "not to name that woman. From this hour she must be a stranger to you, as she must be to me:—In short, Isabella, since I cannot give you my son, I offer you myself."—"Heavens!" cried Isabella, waking from her delusion, "what do I hear? You, my lord! you! my father-in-law! the father of Conrad! the husband of the virtuous and tender Hippolita!"—"I tell you," said Manfred, imperiously, "Hippolita is no longer my wife; I divorce her from this hour. Too long has she cursed me by her unfruitfulness. My fate depends on having sons,—and this night I trust will give a new date to my hopes." At those words he seized the cold hand of Isabella, who was half dead with fright and horror. She shrieked and started from him. Manfred rose to pursue her; when the moon, which was now up, and gleamed in at the opposite casement, presented to his sight the plumes of the fatal helmet, which rose to the height of the windows, waving backwards and forwards in a tempestuous manner, and accompanied with a hollow and rustling sound. Isabella, who gathered courage from her situation, and who dreaded nothing so much as Manfred's pursuit of his declaration, cried, "Look, my lord! see, Heaven itself declares against your impious intentions!"—"Heaven nor Hell shall impede my designs," said Manfred, advancing again to seize the princess. At that instant the portrait of his grandfather, which hung over the bench where they had been sitting, uttered a deep sigh, and heaved its breast. Isabella, whose back was turned to the picture, saw not the motion, nor knew whence the sound came, but started, and said, "Hark, my lord! what sound was that?" and at the same time, made towards the door. Manfred, distracted between the flight of Isabella, who had now reached the stairs, and yet unable to keep his eyes from the picture, which began to move, had, however, advanced some steps after her, still looking backwards on the portrait, when he saw it quit its panel, and descend on the floor with a grave and melancholy air. "Do I dream?" cried Manfred, returning, "or are the devils themselves in league against me? Speak, infernal spectre! or, if thou art my grandsire, why dost thou, too, conspire against thy wretched descendant, who too dearly pays for—" Ere he could finish the sentence, the vision sighed again, and made a sign to Manfred to follow him. "Lead on!" cried Manfred; "I will follow thee to the gulf of perdition!" The spectre marched sedately, but dejected, to the end of the gallery, and turned into a chamber on the right hand. Manfred accompanied him at a little distance, full of anxiety and horror, but resolved. As he would have entered the chamber, the door was clapped to with violence by an invisible hand. The prince, collecting courage from this delay, would have forcibly burst open the door with his foot, but found that it resisted his utmost efforts. "Since hell will not satisfy my curiosity," said Manfred, "I will use the human means in my power for preserving my race; Isabella shall not escape me."

The lady, whose resolution had given way to terror the moment she had quitted Manfred, continued her flight to the bottom of the principal staircase. There she stopped, not knowing whither to direct her steps, nor how to escape from the impetuosity of the prince. The gates of the castle, she knew, were locked, and guards placed in the court. Should she, as her heart prompted her, go and prepare Hippolita for the cruel destiny that awaited her, she did not doubt but Manfred would seek her there, and that his violence would incite him to double the injury he meditated, without leaving room for them to avoid the impetuosity of his passions. Delay might give him time to reflect on the horrid measures he had conceived, or produce some circumstance in her favour, if she could, for that night, at least, avoid his odious purpose. Yet, where conceal herself? how avoid the pursuit he would infallibly make throughout the castle? As these thoughts passed rapidly through her mind, she recollected a subterraneous passage which led from the vaults of the castle to the church of St. Nicholas. Could she reach the altar before she was overtaken, she knew even Manfred's violence would not dare to profane the sacredness of the place; and she determined, if no other means of deliverance offered, to shut herself up for ever among the holy virgins, whose convent was contiguous to the cathedral. In this resolution, she seized a lamp that burned at the foot of the staircase, and hurried towards the secret passage.

The lower part of the castle was hollowed into several intricate cloisters; and it was not easy for one under so much anxiety to find the door that opened into the cavern. An awful silence reigned throughout those subterraneous regions, except now and then some blasts of wind that shook the doors she had passed, and which, grating on the rusty hinges, were re-echoed through that long labyrinth of darkness. Every murmur struck her with new terror;—yet more she dreaded to hear the wrathful voice of Manfred urging his domestics to pursue her. She trod as softly as impatience would give her leave,—yet frequently stopped and listened to hear if she was followed. In one of those moments she thought she heard a sigh. She shuddered, and recoiled a few paces. In a moment she thought she heard the step of some person. Her blood curdled; she concluded it was Manfred. Every suggestion that horror could inspire rushed into her mind. She condemned her rash flight, which had thus exposed her to his rage in a place where her cries were not likely to draw anybody to her assistance.—Yet the sound seemed not to come from behind;—if Manfred knew where she was, he must have followed her. She was still in one of the cloisters, and the steps she had heard were too distinct to proceed from the way she had come. Cheered with this reflection, and hoping to find a friend in whoever was not the prince, she was going to advance, when a door that stood ajar, at some distance to the left, was opened gently: but ere her lamp, which she held up, could discover who opened it, the person retreated precipitately on seeing the light.

Isabella, whom every incident was sufficient to dismay, hesitated whether she should proceed. Her dread of Manfred soon outweighed every other terror. The very circumstance of the person avoiding her, gave her a sort of courage. It could only be, she thought, some domestic belonging to the castle. Her gentleness had never raised her an enemy; and conscious innocence made her hope that, unless sent by the prince's order to seek her, his servants would rather assist than prevent her flight. Fortifying herself with these reflections, and believing, by what she could observe, that she was near the mouth of the subterraneous cavern, she approached the door that had been opened; but a sudden gust of wind that met her at the door extinguished her lamp, and left her in total darkness.

Words cannot paint the horror of the princess's situation. Alone in so dismal a place, her mind imprinted with all the terrible events of the day, hopeless of escaping, expecting every moment the arrival of Manfred, and far from tranquil on knowing she was within reach of somebody, she knew not whom, who for some cause seemed concealed thereabouts; all these thoughts crowded on her distracted mind, and she was ready to sink under her apprehensions. She addressed herself to every saint in heaven, and inwardly implored their assistance. For a considerable time she remained in an agony of despair. At last, as softly as was possible, she felt for the door, and having found it, entered trembling into the vault from whence she had heard the sigh and steps. It gave her a kind of momentary joy to perceive an imperfect ray of clouded moonshine gleam from the roof of the vault, which seemed to be fallen in, and from whence hung a fragment of earth or building, she could not distinguish which, that appeared to have been crushed inwards. She advanced eagerly towards this chasm, when she discerned a human form standing close against the wall.

She shrieked, believing it the ghost of her betrothed Conrad. The figure, advancing, said, in a submissive voice, "Be not alarmed, lady; I will not injure you." Isabella, a little encouraged by the words and tone of voice of the stranger, and recollecting that this must be the person who had opened the door, recovered her spirits enough to reply, "Sir, whoever you are, take pity on a wretched princess, standing on the brink of destruction: assist me to escape from this fatal castle, or in a few moments I may be made miserable for ever."—"Alas!" said the stranger, "what can I do to assist you? I will die in your defence; but I am unacquainted with the castle, and want—" "Oh!" said Isabella, hastily interrupting him, "help me but to find a trap-door that must be hereabout, and it is the greatest service you can do me, for I have not a minute to lose." Saying these words, she felt about on the pavement, and directed the stranger to search likewise for a smooth piece of brass enclosed in one of the stones. "That," said she, "is the lock, which opens with a spring, of which I know the secret. If we can find that, I may escape—if not, alas! courteous stranger, I fear I shall have involved you in my misfortunes: Manfred will suspect you for the accomplice of my flight, and you will fall a victim to his resentment."—"I value not my life," said the stranger; "and it will be some comfort to lose it in trying to deliver you from his tyranny."—"Generous youth!" said Isabella, "how shall I ever requite—?" As she uttered those words, a ray of moonshine, streaming through a cranny of the ruin above, shone directly on the lock they sought.—"Oh! transport!" said Isabella, "here is the trap-door!" and, taking out the key, she touched the spring, which, starting aside, discovered an iron ring. "Lift up the door," said the princess. The stranger obeyed, and beneath appeared some stone steps descending into a vault totally dark. "We must go down here," said Isabella: "follow me; dark and dismal as it is, we cannot miss our way; it leads directly to the church of St. Nicholas.—But, perhaps," added the princess, modestly, "you have no reason to leave the castle, nor have I farther occasion for your service; in a few minutes I shall be safe from Manfred's rage—only let me know to whom I am so much obliged."—"I will never quit you," said the stranger, eagerly, "until I have placed you in safety—nor think me, princess, more generous than I am; though you are my principal care—" The stranger was interrupted by a sudden noise of voices that seemed approaching, and they soon distinguished these words: "Talk not to me of necromancers; I tell you she must be in the castle; I will find her in spite of enchantment."—"Oh, heavens!" cried Isabella, "it is the voice of Manfred! make haste, or we are ruined! and shut the trap-door after you." Saying this, she descended the steps precipitately; and as the stranger hastened to follow her, he let the door slip out of his hands: it fell, and the spring closed over it. He tried in vain to open it, not having observed Isabella's method of touching the spring; nor had he many moments to make an essay. The noise of the falling door had been heard by Manfred, who, directed by the sound, hastened thither, attended by his servants with torches. "It must be Isabella," cried Manfred, before he entered the vault. "She is escaping by the subterraneous passage, but she cannot have got far."—What was the astonishment of the prince when, instead of Isabella, the light of the torches discovered to him the young peasant, whom he thought confined under the fatal-helmet! "Traitor!" said Manfred; "how camest thou here? I thought thee in durance above in the court."—"I am no traitor," replied the young man boldly, "nor am I answerable for your thoughts."—"Presumptuous villain!" cried Manfred, "dost thou provoke my wrath? tell me, how hast thou escaped from above? Thou hast corrupted thy guards, and their lives shall answer it."—"My poverty," said the peasant calmly, "will disculpate them: though the ministers of a tyrant's wrath, to thee they are faithful, and but too willing to execute the orders which you unjustly imposed upon them."—"Art thou so hardy as to dare my vengeance?" said the prince; "but tortures shall force the truth from thee. Tell me; I will know thy accomplices."—"There was my accomplice!" said the youth, smiling, and pointing to the roof. Manfred ordered the torches to be held up, and perceived that one of the cheeks of the enchanted casque had forced its way through the pavement of the court, as his servants had let it fall over the peasant, and had broken through into the vault, leaving a gap, through which the peasant had pressed himself some minutes before he was found by Isabella. "Was that the way by which thou didst descend?" said Manfred.—"It was," said the youth. "But what noise was that," said Manfred, "which I heard as I entered the cloister?" "A door clapped,"—said the peasant: "I heard it as well as you."—"What door?" said Manfred hastily.—"I am not acquainted with your castle," said the peasant; "this is the first time I ever entered it, and this vault the only part of it within which

I ever was."—"But I tell thee," said Manfred, (wishing to find out if the youth had discovered the trap-door), "it was this way I heard the noise. My servants heard it too."—"My lord," interrupted one of them officiously, "to be sure it was the trap-door, and he was going to make his escape."—"Peace, blockhead," said the prince, angrily; "if he was going to escape, how should he come on this side? I will know from his own mouth what noise it was I heard. Tell me truly; thy life depends on thy veracity."—"My veracity is dearer to me than my life," said the peasant; "nor would I purchase the one by forfeiting the other." "Indeed, young philosopher!" said Manfred, contemptuously; "tell me, then, what was the noise I heard?"—"Ask me what I can answer," said he, "and put me to death instantly if I tell you a lie." Manfred, growing impatient at the steady valour and indifference of the youth, cried, "Well, then, thou man of truth, answer! Was it the fall of the trap-door that I heard?"—"It was," said the youth.—"It was!" said the prince; "and how didst thou come to know there was a trap-door here?"—"I saw the plate of brass by a gleam of moonshine," replied he. "But what told thee it was a lock?" said Manfred;—"How didst thou discover the secret of opening it?"—"Providence, that delivered me from the helmet, was able to direct me to the spring of a lock," said he. "Providence should have gone a little farther, and have placed thee out of the reach of my resentment," said Manfred. "When Providence had taught thee to open the lock, it abandoned thee for a fool, who did not know how to make use of its favours. Why didst thou not pursue the path pointed out for thy escape? Why didst thou shut the trap-door before thou hadst descended the steps?"—"I might ask you, my lord," said the peasant, "how I, totally unacquainted with your castle, was to know that those steps led to any outlet? but I scorn to evade your questions. Wherever those steps lead to, perhaps I should have explored the way—I could not be in a worse situation than I was. But the truth is, I let the trap-door fall: your immediate arrival followed. I had given the alarm—what imported it to me whether I was seized a minute sooner or a minute later?"—"Thou art a resolute villain for thy years," said Manfred; "yet on reflection I suspect thou dost but trifle with me: thou hast not yet told me how thou didst open the lock."—"That I will show you, my lord," said the peasant; and, taking up a fragment of stone that had fallen from above, he laid himself on the trap-door, and began to beat on the piece of brass that covered it, meaning to gain time for the escape of the princess. This presence of mind, joined to the frankness of the youth, staggered Manfred. He even felt a disposition towards pardoning one who had been guilty of no crime. Manfred was not one of those savage tyrants who wanton in cruelty unprovoked. The circumstances of his fortune had given an asperity to his temper, which was naturally humane; and his virtues were always ready to operate, when his passions did not obscure his reason.

While the prince was in this suspense, a confused noise of voices echoed through the distant vaults. As the sound approached, he distinguished the clamours of some of his domestics, whom he had dispersed through the castle in search of Isabella, calling out, "Where is my lord? where is the prince?"—"Here I am," said Manfred, as they came nearer; "have you found the princess?" The first that arrived, replied, "Oh! my lord! I am glad we have found you—" "Found me!" said Manfred; "have you found the princess?"—"We thought we had, my lord," said the fellow, looking terrified, "but—" "But, what?" cried the prince; "has she escaped?" —"Jaquez and I, my lord—" "Yes, I and Diego," interrupted the second, who came up in still greater consternation.—"Speak one of you at a time," said Manfred; "I ask you, where is the princess?"—"We do not know," said they, both together; "but we are frightened out of our wits—" "So I think, blockheads," said Manfred; "what is it has scared you thus?"—"Oh! my lord," said Jaquez, "Diego has seen such a sight! your Highness would not believe our eyes—" "What new absurdity is this?" cried Manfred; "give me a direct answer, or, by Heaven—" "Why, my lord, if it please your Highness to hear me," said the poor fellow, "Diego and I—" "Yes, I and Jaquez—" cried his comrade—"Did not I forbid you to speak both at a time?" said the prince: "you, Jaquez, answer; for the other fool seems more distracted than thou art; what is the matter?"—"My gracious lord," said Jaquez, "if it please your highness to hear me; Diego and I, according to your highness's orders, went to search for the young lady; but being comprehensive that we might meet the ghost of my young lord, your highness's son, God rest his soul, as he has not received Christian burial."—"Sot!" cried Manfred in a rage; "is it only a ghost, then, that thou hast seen?"—"Oh! worse! worse! my lord," cried Diego: "I had rather have seen ten whole ghosts—" "Grant me patience!" said Manfred; "these blockheads distract me!—Out of my sight, Diego! and thou, Jaquez, tell me in one word, art thou sober? art thou raving? Thou wast wont to have some sense: has the other sot frightened himself and thee too? Speak; what is it he fancies he has seen?"—"Why, my lord," replied Jaquez, trembling, "I was going to tell your Highness, that since the calamitous misfortune of my young lord, God rest his precious soul! not one of us your Highness's faithful servants—indeed we are, my lord, though poor men; I say, not one of us has dared to set a foot about the castle, but two together: so Diego and I, thinking that my young lady might be in the great gallery, went up there to look for her, and tell her your Highness wanted something to impart to her—" "O blundering fools!" cried Manfred; "and in the meantime, she has made her escape, because you were afraid of goblins!—Why, thou knave! she left me in the gallery; I came from thence myself."—"For all that, she may be there still for aught I know," said Jaquez; "but the devil shall have me before I seek her there again—poor Diego! I do not believe he will ever recover it."—"Recover what?" said Manfred; "am I never to learn what it is has terrified these rascals?—But I lose my time; follow me, slave; I will see if she is in the gallery—" "For Heaven's sake, my dear good lord," cried Jaquez, "do not go to the gallery. Satan himself I believe is in the chamber next to the gallery—" Manfred, who hitherto had treated the terror of his servants as an idle panic, was struck at this new circumstance. He recollected the apparition of the portrait, and the sudden closing of the door at the end of the gallery. His voice faltered, and he asked with disorder, "What is in the great chamber?"—"My lord," said Jaquez, "when Diego and I came into the gallery, he went first, for he said he had more courage than I. So when we came into the gallery we found nobody. We looked under every bench and stool; and still we found nobody—" "Were all the pictures in their places?" said Manfred. "Yes, my lord," answered Jaquez; "but we did not think of looking behind them."—"Well, well!" said Manfred; "proceed." "When we came to the door of the great chamber," continued Jaquez, "we found it shut—" "And could not you open it?" said Manfred. "Oh! yes, my lord; would to Heaven we had not!" replied he. "Nay, it was not I neither; it was Diego: he was grown fool-hardy, and would go on, though I advised him not—if ever I open a door that is shut again—" "Trifle not," said Manfred, shuddering, "but tell me what you saw in the great chamber on opening the door."—"I! my lord!" said Jaquez; "I was behind Diego; but I heard the noise—" "Jaquez," said Manfred, in a solemn tone of voice; "tell me, I adjure thee by the souls of my ancestors, what was it thou sawest? what was it thou heardest?"—"It was Diego saw it, my lord, it was not I," replied Jaquez; "I only heard the noise. Diego had no sooner opened the door, than he cried out, and ran back—I ran back too, and said, Is it the ghost? the ghost! No, no, said Diego, and his hair stood on end—it is a giant, I believe; he is all clad in armour, for I saw his foot and part of his leg, and they are as large as the helmet below in the court. As he said these words, my lord, we heard a violent motion and the rattling of armour, as if the giant was rising, for Diego has told me since that he believes the giant was lying down, for the foot and leg were stretched at length on the floor. Before we could get to the end of the gallery, we heard the door of the great chamber clap behind us, but we did not dare turn back to see if the giant was following us;—yet, now I think on it, we must have heard him if he had pursued us—but for Heaven's sake, good my lord, send for the chaplain, and have the castle exorcised, for, for certain, it is enchanted."—"Ay, pray do, my lord," cried all the servants at once, "or we must leave your Highness's service."—"Peace! dotards," said Manfred, "and follow me; I will know what all this means."—"We! my lord?" cried they with one voice, "we would not go up to the gallery for your Highness's revenue." The young peasant, who had stood silent, now spoke. "Will your Highness," said he, "permit me to try this adventure? My life is of consequence to nobody; I fear no bad angel, and have offended no good one."—"Your behaviour is above your seeming," said Manfred, viewing him with surprise and admiration; "hereafter I will reward your bravery—but now," continued he with a sigh, "I am so circumstanced, that I dare trust no eyes but my own. However, I give you leave to accompany me."

Manfred, when he first followed Isabella from the gallery, had gone directly to the apartment of his wife, concluding the princess had retired thither. Hippolita, who knew his step, rose with anxious fondness to meet her lord, whom she had not seen since the death of their son. She would have flown in a transport mixed of joy and grief to his bosom, but he pushed her rudely off, and said, "Where is Isabella?"—"Isabella! my lord?" said the astonished Hippolita. "Yes, Isabella," cried Manfred imperiously; "I want Isabella."—"My lord," replied Matilda, who perceived how much his behaviour had shocked her mother, "she has not been with us since your Highness summoned her to your apartment."—"Tell me where she is," said the prince; "I do not want to know where she has been."—"My good lord," says Hippolita, "your daughter tells you the truth: Isabella left us by your command, and has not returned since;—but, my good lord, compose yourself: retire to your rest: this dismal day has disordered you. Isabella shall wait your orders in the morning."—"What, then, you know where she is!" cried Manfred: "tell me directly, for I will not lose an instant—and you, woman," speaking to his wife, "order your chaplain to attend me forthwith."—"Isabella," said Hippolita, calmly, "is retired, I suppose, to her chamber: she is not accustomed to watch at this late hour. Gracious my lord," continued she, "let me know what has disturbed you. Has Isabella offended you?"—"Trouble me not with questions," said Manfred, "but tell me where she is."—"Matilda shall call her," said the princess. "Sit down, my lord, and resume your wonted fortitude."—"What, art thou jealous of Isabella?" replied he, "that you wish to be present at our interview?"—"Good heavens! my lord," said Hippolita, "what is it your highness means?"—"Thou wilt know ere many minutes are passed"; said the cruel prince. "Send your chaplain to me, and wait my pleasure here." At these words he flung out of the room in search of Isabella; leaving the amazed ladies thunderstruck with his words and frantic deportment, and lost in vain conjectures on what he was meditating.

Manfred was now returning from the vault, attended by the peasant and a few of his servants whom he had obliged to accompany him. He ascended the staircase without stopping till he arrived at the gallery, at the door of which he met Hippolita and her chaplain. When Diego had been dismissed by Manfred, he had gone directly to the princess's apartment with the alarm of what he had seen. That excellent lady, who no more than Manfred doubted of the reality of the vision, yet affected to treat it as a delirium of the servant. Willing, however, to save her lord from any additional shock, and prepared by a series of griefs not to tremble at any accession to it, she determined to make herself the first sacrifice, if fate had marked the present hour for their destruction. Dismissing the reluctant Matilda to her rest, who in vain sued for leave to accompany her mother, and attended only by her chaplain, Hippolita had visited the gallery and great chamber; and now with more serenity of soul than she had felt for many hours, she met her lord, and assured him that the vision of the gigantic leg and foot was all a fable; and no doubt an impression made by fear, and the dark and dismal hour of the night, on the minds of his servants. She and the chaplain had examined the chamber, and found everything in the usual order.

Manfred, though persuaded, like his wife, that the vision had been no work of fancy, recovered a little from the tempest of mind into which so many strange events had thrown him. Ashamed, too, of his inhuman treatment of a princess who returned every injury with new marks of tenderness and duty, he felt returning love forcing itself into his eyes—but not less ashamed of feeling remorse towards one against whom he was inwardly meditating a yet more bitter outrage, he curbed the yearnings of his heart, and did not dare to lean even towards pity. The next transition of his soul was to exquisite villainy. Presuming on the unshaken submission of Hippolita, he flattered himself that she would not only acquiesce with patience to a divorce, but would obey, if it was his pleasure, in endeavouring to persuade Isabella to give him her hand;—but, ere he could indulge his horrid hope, he reflected that Isabella was not to be found. Coming to himself, he gave orders that every avenue to the castle should be strictly guarded, and charged his domestics on pain of their lives to suffer nobody to pass out. The young peasant, to whom he spoke favourably, he ordered to remain in a small chamber on the stairs, in which there was a pallet-bed, and the key of which he took away himself, telling the youth he would talk with him in the morning. Then dismissing his attendants, and bestowing a sullen kind of half-nod on Hippolita, he retired to his own chamber.

II

Matilda, who, by Hippolita's order, had retired to her apartment, was ill disposed to take any rest. The shocking fate of her brother had deeply affected her. She was surprised at not seeing Isabella: but the strange words which had fallen from her father, and his obscure menace to the princess his wife, accompanied by the most furious behaviour, had filled her gentle mind with terror and alarm. She waited anxiously for the return of Bianca, a young damsel that attended her, whom she had sent to learn what was become of Isabella. Bianca soon appeared, and informed her mistress of what she had gathered from the servants, that Isabella was nowhere to be found. She related the adventure of the young peasant, who had been discovered in the vault, though with many simple additions from the incoherent accounts of the domestics; and she dwelt principally on the gigantic leg and foot which had been seen in the gallery chamber. This last circumstance had terrified Bianca so much, that she was rejoiced when Matilda told her that she would not go to rest, but would watch till the princess should rise.

The young princess wearied herself in conjectures on the flight of Isabella, and on the threats of Manfred to her mother. "But what business could he have so urgent with the chaplain?" said Matilda: "Does he intend to have my brother's body interred privately in the chapel?"—"Oh! madam!" said Bianca, "now I guess. As you are become his heiress, he is impatient to have you married: he has always been raving for more sons; I warrant he is now impatient for grandsons. As sure as I live, Madam, I shall see you a bride at last.—Good madam, you won't cast off your faithful Bianca: you won't put Donna Rosara over me, now you are a great princess."—"My poor Bianca," said Matilda, "how fast your thoughts amble! I a great princess! What hast thou seen in Manfred's behaviour since my brother's death that bespeaks any increase of tenderness to me? No, Bianca; his heart was ever a stranger to me;—but he is my father, and I must not complain. Nay, if Heaven shuts my father's heart against me, it overpays my little merit in the tenderness of my mother—O that dear mother!—Yes, Bianca, 'tis there I feel the rugged temper of Manfred. I can support his harshness to me with patience; but it wounds my soul when I am witness to his causeless severity towards her."—"Oh, madam," said Bianca, "all men use their wives so, when they are weary of them."—"And yet you congratulated me but now," said Matilda, "when you fancied my father intended to dispose of me!"—"I would have you a great lady," replied Bianca, "come what will. I do not wish to see you moped in a convent, as you would be if you had your will, and if my lady, your mother, who knows that a bad husband is better than no husband at all, did not hinder you.—Bless me! what noise is that? St. Nicholas forgive me! I was but in jest."—"It is the wind," said Matilda, "whistling through the battlements in the tower above: you have heard it a thousand times."—"Nay," said Bianca, "there was no harm neither in what I said: it is no sin to talk of matrimony—and so, madam, as I was saying, if my Lord Manfred should offer you a handsome young prince for a bridegroom, you would drop him a curtsey, and tell him you would rather take the veil?"—"Thank Heaven! I am in no such danger," said Matilda: "you know how many proposals for me he has rejected."—"And you thank him, like a dutiful daughter, do you, madam? But come, madam; suppose, to-morrow morning, he was to send for you to the great council-chamber, and there you should find at his elbow a lovely young prince, with large black eyes, a smooth white forehead, and manly curling locks like jet; in short, madam, a young hero resembling the picture of the good Alfonso in the gallery, which you sit and gaze at for hours together—?" "Do not speak lightly of that picture," interrupted Matilda sighing; "I know the adoration with which I look at that picture is uncommon—but I am not in love with a coloured panel. The character of that virtuous prince, the veneration with which my mother has inspired me for his memory, the orisons which, I know not why, she has enjoined me to pour forth at his tomb, all have concurred to persuade me that somehow or other my destiny is linked with something relating to him."—"Lord! madam, how should that be?" said Bianca; "I have always heard that your family was in no way related to his: and I am sure I cannot conceive why my lady, the princess, sends you in a cold morning or a damp evening to pray at his tomb: he is no saint by the almanac. If you must pray, why does she not bid you address yourself to our great St. Nicholas? I am sure he is the saint I pray to for a husband."—"Perhaps my mind would be less affected," said Matilda, "if my mother would explain her reasons to me: but it is the mystery she observes that inspires me with this—I know not what to call it. As she never acts from caprice, I am sure there is some fatal secret at bottom—nay, I know there is: in her agony of grief for my brother's death she dropped some words that intimated as much."—"Oh! dear Madam," cried Bianca, "what were they?"—"No," said Matilda, "if a parent lets fall a word, and wishes it recalled, it is not for a child to utter it."—"What! was she sorry for what she had said?" asked Bianca. "I am sure, madam, you may trust me."—"With my own little secrets when I have any, I may," said Matilda; "but never with my mother's: a child ought to have no ears or eyes but as a parent directs."—"Well! to be sure, madam, you were born to be a saint," said Bianca, "and there is no resisting one's vocation: you will end in a convent at last. But there is my

Lady Isabella would not be so reserved to me: she will let me talk to her of young men: and when a handsome cavalier has come to the castle, she has owned to me that she wished your brother Conrad resembled him."—"Bianca," said the princess, "I do not allow you to mention my friend disrespectfully. Isabella is of a cheerful disposition, but her soul is pure as virtue itself. She knows your idle babbling humour, and perhaps has now and then encouraged it, to divert melancholy, and enliven the solitude in which my father keeps us."—"Blessed Mary!" said Bianca, starting, "there it is again! Dear madam, do you hear nothing? this castle is certainly haunted!"—"Peace!" said Matilda, "and listen! I did think I heard a voice—but it must be fancy: your terrors, I suppose, have infected me."—"Indeed! indeed, madam," said Bianca, half-weeping with agony, "I am sure I heard a voice."—"Does anybody lie in the chamber beneath?" said the princess. "Nobody has dared to lie there," answered Bianca, "since the great astrologer, that was your brother's tutor, drowned himself. For certain, Madam, his ghost and the young prince's are now met in the chamber below—for Heaven's sake let us fly to your mother's apartment."—"I charge you not to stir," said Matilda. "If they are spirits in pain, we may ease their sufferings by questioning them. They can mean no hurt to us, for we have not injured them—and if they should, shall we be more safe in one chamber than in another? Reach me my beads; we will say a prayer, and then speak to them."—"Oh! dear lady, I would not speak to a ghost for the world!" cried Bianca. As she said those words they heard the casement of the little chamber below Matilda's open. They listened attentively, and, in a few minutes, thought they heard a person sing, but could not distinguish the words. "This can be no evil spirit," said the princess, in a low voice; "it is undoubtedly one of the family—open the window, and we shall know the voice."—"I dare not, indeed, madam," said Bianca. "Thou art a very fool," said Matilda, opening the window gently herself. The noise the princess made was, however, heard by the person beneath, who stopped; and they concluded had heard the casement open. "Is anybody below?" said the princess; "if there is, speak."—"Yes," said an unknown voice. "Who is it?" said Matilda. "A stranger," replied the voice. "What stranger?" said she; "and how didst thou come there at this unusual hour, when all the gates of the castle are locked?"—"I am not here willingly," answered the voice. "But pardon me, lady, if I have disturbed your rest; I knew not that I was overheard. Sleep had forsaken me; I left a restless couch, and came to waste the irksome hours with gazing on the fair approach of morning, impatient to be dismissed from this castle."—"Thy words and accents," said Matilda, "are of melancholy cast; if thou art unhappy, I pity thee. If poverty afflicts thee, let me know it; I will mention thee to the princess, whose beneficent soul ever melts for the distressed, and she will relieve thee."—"I am indeed unhappy," said the stranger; "and I know not what wealth is. But I do not complain of the lot which Heaven has cast for me:—I am young and healthy, and am not ashamed of owing my support to myself: yet think me not proud, or that I disdain your generous offers. I will remember you in my orisons, and will pray for blessings on your gracious self and your noble mistress. If I sigh, lady, it is for others, not for myself."—"Now I have it, Madam," said Bianca, whispering to the princess; "this is certainly the young peasant; and, by my conscience, he is in love—Well! this is a charming adventure!—do, madam, let us sift him. He does not know you, but takes you for one of my lady Hippolita's women."—"Art thou not ashamed, Bianca?" said the princess. "What right have we to pry into the secrets of this young man's heart? He seems virtuous and frank, and tells us he is unhappy. Are those circumstances that authorise us to make a property of him? How are we entitled to his confidence?"—"Lord, madam! how little you know of love!" replied Bianca: "why, lovers have no pleasure equal to talking of their mistress."—"And would you have *me* become a peasant's confidante?" said the princess. "Well, then, let me talk to him," said Bianca: "though I have the honour of being your highness's maid of honour, I was not always so great. Besides, if love levels ranks, it raises them too; I have a respect for any young man in love."—"Peace, simpleton!" said the princess. "Though he said he was unhappy, it does not follow that he must be in love. Think of all that has happened to-day, and tell me if there are no misfortunes but what love causes.—Stranger," resumed the princess, "if thy misfortunes have not been occasioned by thy own fault, and are within the compass of the Princess Hippolita's power to redress, I will take upon me to answer that she will be thy protectress. When thou art dismissed from this castle, repair to holy father Jerome, at the convent adjoining to the church of St. Nicholas, and make thy story known to him, as far as thou thinkest meet. He will not fail to inform the princess, who is the mother of all that want her assistance. Farewell; it is not seemly for me to hold farther converse with a man at this unwonted hour."—"May the saints guard thee, gracious lady!" replied the peasant: "but oh! if a poor and worthless stranger might presume to beg a minute's audience farther; am I so happy? the casement is not shut; might I venture to ask—" "Speak quickly," said Matilda: "the morning dawns apace: should the labourers come into the fields and perceive us—What wouldst thou ask?"—"I know not how, I know not if I dare," said the young stranger, faltering; "yet the humanity with which you have spoken to me emboldens—Lady! dare I trust you?"—"Heavens!" said Matilda, "what dost thou mean? With what wouldst thou trust me? Speak boldly, if thy secret is fit to be entrusted to a virtuous breast."—"I would ask," said the peasant, recollecting himself, "whether what I have heard from the domestics is true, that the princess is missing from the castle?"—"What imports it to thee to know?" replied Matilda. "Thy first words bespoke a prudent and becoming gravity. Dost thou come hither to pry into the secrets of Manfred? Adieu. I have been mistaken in thee." Saying these words she shut the casement hastily, without giving the young man time to reply. "I had acted more wisely," said the princess to Bianca, with some sharpness, "if I had let thee converse with this peasant; his inquisitiveness seems of a piece with thy own."—"It is not fit for me to argue with your highness," replied Bianca: "but perhaps the questions I should have put to him would have been more to the purpose than those you have been pleased to ask him."—"Oh! no doubt," said Matilda: "you are a very discreet personage! May I know what *you* would have asked him?"—"A bystander often sees more of the game than those that play," answered Bianca. "Does your highness think, madam, that this question about my lady Isabella was the result of mere curiosity? No, no, madam, there is more in it than you great folks are aware of. Lopez told me that all the servants believe this young fellow contrived my lady Isabella's escape; now, pray, Madam, observe you and I both know that my lady Isabella never much fancied the prince your brother. Well! he is killed just in a critical minute—I accuse nobody. A helmet falls from the moon—so, my lord, your father says; but Lopez and all the servants say that this young spark is a magician, and stole it from Alfonso's tomb."—"Have done with this rhapsody of impertinence," said Matilda. "Nay, madam, as you please," cried Bianca: "yet it is very particular though, that my lady Isabella should be missing the very same day, and that this young sorcerer should be found at the mouth of the trap-door. I accuse nobody; but if my young lord came honestly by his death—" "Dare not on thy duty," said Matilda, "to breathe a suspicion on the purity of my dear Isabella's fame."—"Purity, or not purity," said Bianca, "gone she is—a stranger is found that nobody knows; you question him yourself; he tells you he is in love, or unhappy, it is the same thing—nay, he owned he was unhappy about others; and is anybody unhappy about another, unless they are in love with them? and at the very next word, he asks innocently, poor soul! if my lady Isabella is missing—" "To be sure," said Matilda, "thy observations are not totally without foundation—Isabella's flight amazes me. The curiosity of the stranger is very particular; yet Isabella never concealed a thought from me."—"So she told you," said Bianca, "to fish out your secrets; but who knows, madam, but this stranger may be some prince in disguise? Do, Madam, let me open the window, and ask him a few questions."—"No," replied Matilda, "I will ask him myself, if he knows aught of Isabella; he is not worthy I should converse farther with him." She was going to open the casement, when they heard the bell ring at the postern-gate of the castle, which is on the right hand of the tower, where Matilda lay. This prevented the princess from renewing the conversation with the stranger.

After continuing silent for some time, "I am persuaded," said she to Bianca, "that whatever be the cause of Isabella's flight it had no unworthy motive. If this stranger was accessory to it, she must be satisfied with his fidelity and worth. I observed, did not you, Bianca? that his words were tinctured with an uncommon infusion of piety. It was no ruffian's speech; his phrases were becoming a man of gentle birth." —"I told you, Madam," said Bianca, "that I was sure he was some prince in disguise."—"Yet," said Matilda, "if he was privy to her escape, how will you account for his not accompanying her in her flight? why expose himself unnecessarily and rashly to my father's resentment?"—"As for that, madam," replied she, "if he could get from under the helmet, he will find ways of eluding your father's anger. I do not doubt but he has some talisman or other about him."—"You resolve everything into magic," said Matilda; "but a man who has any intercourse with infernal spirits, does not dare to make use of those tremendous and holy words which he uttered. Didst thou not observe with what fervour he vowed to remember *me* to heaven in his prayers? Yes; Isabella was undoubtedly convinced of his piety."—"Commend me to the piety of a young fellow and a damsel that consult to elope!" said Bianca. "No, no, madam, my lady Isabella is of another guess mould than you take her for. She used indeed to sigh and lift up her eyes in your company, because she knows you are a saint; but when your back was turned—" "You wrong her," said Matilda; "Isabella is no hypocrite; she has a due sense of devotion, but never affected a call she has not. On the contrary, she always combated my inclination for the cloister; and though I own the mystery she has made to me of her flight confounds me; though it seems inconsistent with the friendship between us; I cannot forget the disinterested warmth with which she always opposed my taking the veil. She wished to see me married, though my dower would have been a loss to her and my brother's children. For her sake I will believe well of this young peasant." "Then you do think there is some liking between them?" said Bianca.—While she was speaking, a servant came hastily into the chamber and told the princess that the lady Isabella was found. "Where?" said Matilda. "She has taken sanctuary in St. Nicholas's church," replied the servant; "Father Jerome has brought the news himself; he is below with his highness."—"Where is my mother?" said Matilda. "She is in her own chamber, Madam, and has asked for you."

Manfred had risen at the first dawn of light, and gone to Hippolita's apartment, to inquire if she knew aught of Isabella. While he was questioning her, word was brought that Jerome demanded to speak with him. Manfred, little suspecting the cause of the friar's arrival, and knowing he was employed by Hippolita in her charities, ordered him to be admitted, intending to leave them together, while he pursued his search after Isabella. "Is your business with me or the princess?" said Manfred. "With both," replied the holy man. "The lady Isabella—" "What of her?" interrupted Manfred, eagerly—"Is at St. Nicholas's altar," replied Jerome. "That is no business of Hippolita," said Manfred with confusion: "let us retire to my chamber, Father, and inform me how she came thither."—"No, my lord," replied the good man, with an air of firmness and authority, that daunted even the resolute Manfred, who could not help revering the saint-like virtues of Jerome: "my commission is to both, and with your highness's good-liking, in the presence of both I shall deliver it; but first, my lord, I must interrogate the princess, whether she is acquainted with the cause of the lady Isabella's retirement from your castle."—"No, on my soul," said Hippolita: "does Isabella charge me with being privy to it?"—"Father," interrupted Manfred, "I pay due reverence to your holy profession: but I am sovereign here, and will allow no meddling priest to interfere in the affairs of my domestic. If you have aught to say attend me to my chamber; I do not use to let my wife be acquainted with the secret affairs of my state; they are not within a woman's province."—"My lord," said the holy man, "I am no intruder into the secrets of families. My office is to promote peace, to heal divisions, to preach repentance, and teach mankind to curb their headstrong passions. I forgive your highness's uncharitable apostrophe; I know my duty, and am the minister of a mightier prince than Manfred. Hearken to him who speaks through my organs." Manfred trembled with rage and shame. Hippolita's countenance declared her astonishment and impatience to know where this would end. Her silence more strongly spoke her observance of Manfred.

"The lady Isabella," resumed Jerome, "commends herself to both your highnesses; she thanks both for the kindness with which she has been treated in your castle: she deplores the loss of your son, and her own misfortune in not becoming the daughter of such wise and noble princes, whom she shall always respect as parents; she prays for uninterrupted union and felicity between you": (Manfred's colour changed): "but as it is no longer possible for her to be allied to you, she entreats your consent to remain in sanctuary, till she can learn news of her father, or, by the certainty of his death, be at liberty, with the approbation of her guardians, to dispose of herself in suitable marriage."—"I shall give no such consent," said the prince, "but insist on her return to the castle without delay: I am answerable for her person to her guardians, and will not brook her being in any hands but my own."—"Your Highness will recollect whether that can any longer be proper," replied the friar. "I want no monitor," said Manfred, colouring: "Isabella's conduct leaves room for strange suspicions—and that young villain, who was at least the accomplice of her flight, if not the cause of it—" "The cause!" interrupted Jerome; "was a *young* man the cause?"—"This is not to be borne!" cried Manfred. "Am I to be bearded in my own palace by an insolent monk? Thou art privy, I guess, to their amours."—"I would pray to heaven to clear up your uncharitable surmises," said Jerome, "if your highness were not satisfied in your conscience how unjustly you accuse me. I do pray to heaven to pardon that uncharitableness: and I implore your Highness to leave the princess at peace in that holy place, where she is not liable to be disturbed by such vain and worldly fantasies as discourses of love from any man."—"Cant not to me," said Manfred, "but return and bring the princess to her duty."—"It is my duty to prevent her return hither," said Jerome. "She is where orphans and virgins are safest from the snares and wiles of this world; and nothing but a parent's authority shall take her thence."—"I am her parent," cried Manfred, "and demand her."—"She wished to have you for her parent," said the friar; "but Heaven that forbade that connection has for ever dissolved all ties betwixt you: and I announce to your highness—" "Stop! audacious man," said Manfred, "and dread my displeasure."—"Holy father," said Hippolita, "it is your office to be no respecter of persons: you must speak as your duty prescribes: but it is my duty to hear nothing that it pleases not my lord I should hear. Attend the prince to his chamber. I will retire to my oratory, and pray to the blessed virgin to inspire you with her holy counsels, and to restore the heart of my gracious lord to its wonted peace and gentleness."—"Excellent woman!" said the friar. "My lord, I attend your pleasure."

Manfred, accompanied by the friar, passed to his own apartment, where shutting the door, "I perceive, father," said he, "that Isabella has acquainted you with my purpose. Now hear my resolve, and obey. Reasons of state, most urgent reasons, my own and the safety of my people, demand that I should have a son. It is in vain to expect an heir from Hippolita. I have made choice of Isabella. You must bring her back; and you must do more. I know the influence you have with Hippolita: her conscience is in your hands. She is, I allow, a faultless woman: her soul is set on heaven, and scorns the little grandeur of this world: you can withdraw her from it entirely. Persuade her to consent to the dissolution of our marriage, and to retire into a monastery—she shall endow one if she will; and she shall have the means of being as liberal to your order as she or you can wish. Thus you will divert the calamities that are hanging over our heads, and have the merit of saying the principality of Otranto from destruction. You are a prudent man, and though the warmth of my temper betrayed me into some unbecoming expressions, I honour your virtue, and wish to be indebted to you for the repose of my life and the preservation of my family."

"The will of heaven be done!" said the friar. "I am but its worthless instrument. It makes use of my tongue to tell thee, prince, of thy unwarrantable designs. The injuries of the virtuous Hippolita have mounted to the throne of pity. By me thou art reprimanded for thy adulterous intention of repudiating her: by me thou art warned not to pursue the incestuous design on thy contracted daughter. Heaven that delivered her from thy fury, when the judgments so recently fallen on thy house ought to have inspired thee with other thoughts, will continue to watch over her. Even I, a poor and despised friar, am able to protect her from thy violence —I, sinner as I am, and uncharitably reviled by your highness as an accomplice of I know not what amours, scorn the allurements with which it has pleased thee to tempt mine honesty. I love my order; I honour devout souls; I respect the piety of thy princess—but I will not betray the confidence she reposes in me, nor serve even the cause of religion by foul and sinful compliances—but forsooth! the welfare of the state depends on your highness having a son! Heaven mocks the short-sighted views of man. But yester-morn, whose house was so great, so flourishing as Manfred's?—where is young Conrad now?—My lord, I respect your tears—but I mean not to check them—let them flow, prince! They will weigh more with heaven toward the welfare of thy subjects, than a marriage, which, founded on lust or policy, could never prosper. The sceptre, which passed from the race of Alfonso to thine, cannot be preserved by a match which the church will never allow. If it is the will of the most high that Manfred's name must perish, resign yourself, my lord, to its decrees; and thus deserve a crown that can never pass away. Come, my lord; I like this sorrow—let us return to the princess: she is not apprised of your cruel intentions; nor did I mean more than to alarm you. You saw with what gentle patience, with what efforts of love, she heard, she rejected hearing, the extent of your guilt. I know she longs to fold you in her arms, and assure you of her unalterable affection."—"Father," said the prince, "you mistake my compunction: true, I honour Hippolita's virtues; I think her a saint; and wish it were for my soul's health to tie faster the knot that has united us—but alas! Father, you know not the bitterest of my pangs! it is some time that I have had scruples on the legality of our union: Hippolita is related to me in the fourth degree—

it is true, we had a dispensation: but I have been informed that she had also been contracted to another. This it is that sits heavy at my heart: to this state of unlawful wedlock I impute the visitation that has fallen on me in the death of Conrad!—ease my conscience of this burden: dissolve our marriage, and accomplish the work of godliness—which your divine exhortations have commenced in my soul."

How cutting was the anguish which the good man felt, when he perceived this turn in the wily prince! He trembled for Hippolita, whose ruin he saw was determined; and he feared if Manfred had no hope of recovering Isabella, that his impatience for a son would direct him to some other object, who might not be equally proof against the temptation of Manfred's rank. For some time the holy man remained absorbed in thought. At length, conceiving some hopes from delay, he thought the wisest conduct would be to prevent the prince from despairing of recovering Isabella. Her the friar knew he could dispose, from her affection to Hippolita, and from the aversion she had expressed to him for Manfred's addresses, to second his views, till the censures of the church could be fulminated against a divorce. With this intention, as if struck with the prince's scruples, he at length said, "My lord, I have been pondering on what your highness has said; and if in truth it is delicacy of conscience that is the real motive of your repugnance to your virtuous lady, far be it from me to endeavour to harden your heart. The church is an indulgent mother: unfold your griefs to her: she alone can administer comfort to your soul, either by satisfying your conscience, or upon examination of your scruples, by setting you at liberty, and indulging you in the lawful means of continuing your lineage. In the latter case, if the lady Isabella can be brought to consent—" Manfred, who concluded that he had either over-reached the good man, or that his first warmth had been but a tribute paid to appearance, was overjoyed at this sudden turn, and repeated the most magnificent promises, if he should succeed by the friar's mediation. The well-meaning priest suffered him to deceive himself, fully determined to traverse his views, instead of seconding them.

"Since we now understand one another," resumed the prince, "I expect, father, that you satisfy me in one point. Who is the youth that I found in the vault? He must have been privy to Isabella's flight: tell me truly, is he her lover? or is he an agent for another's passion? I have often suspected Isabella's indifference to my son: a thousand circumstances crowd on my mind that confirm that suspicion. She herself was so conscious of it, that while I discoursed her in the gallery, she outran my suspicions, and endeavoured to justify herself from coolness to Conrad." The friar, who knew nothing of the youth, but what he had learnt occasionally from the princess, ignorant what was become of him, and not sufficiently reflecting on the impetuosity of Manfred's temper, conceived that it might not be amiss to sow the seeds of jealousy in his mind: they might be turned to some use hereafter, either by prejudicing the prince against Isabella, if he persisted in that union or by diverting his attention to a wrong scent, and employing his thoughts on a visionary intrigue, prevent his engaging in any new pursuit. With this unhappy policy, he answered in a manner to confirm Manfred in the belief of some connection between Isabella and the youth. The prince, whose passions wanted little fuel to throw them into a blaze, fell into a rage at the idea of what the friar suggested. "I will fathom to the bottom of this intrigue," cried he; and quitting Jerome abruptly, with a command to remain there till his return, he hastened to the great hall of the castle, and ordered the peasant to be brought before him.

"Thou hardened young impostor!" said the prince, as soon as he saw the youth; "what becomes of thy boasted veracity now? it was providence, was it, and the light of the moon, that discovered the lock of the trap-door to thee? Tell me, audacious boy, who thou art, and how long thou hast been acquainted with the princess—and take care to answer with less equivocation than thou didst last night, or tortures shall wring the truth from thee."

The young man, perceiving that his share in the flight of the princess was discovered, and concluding that anything he should say could no longer be of any service or detriment to her, replied, "I am no impostor, my lord, nor have I deserved opprobrious language. I answered to every question your highness put to me last night with the same veracity that I shall speak now: and that will not be from fear of your tortures, but because my soul abhors a falsehood. Please to repeat your questions, my lord; I am ready to give you all the satisfaction in my power."—"You know my questions," replied the prince, "and only want time to prepare an evasion. Speak directly; who art thou? and how long hast thou been known to the princess?"—"I am a labourer at the next village," said the peasant; "my name is Theodore. The princess found me in the vault last night: before that hour I never was in her presence."—"I may believe as much or as little as I please of this," said Manfred; "but I will hear thy own story before I examine into the truth of it. Tell me, what reason did the princess give thee for making her escape? thy life depends on thy answer."—"She told me," replied Theodore, "that she was on the brink of destruction, and that if she could not escape from the castle, she was in danger in a few moments of being made miserable for ever."—"And on this slight foundation, on a silly girl's report," said Manfred, "thou didst hazard my displeasure?"—"I fear no man's displeasure," said Theodore, "when a woman in distress puts herself under my protection." During this examination, Matilda was going to the apartment of Hippolita. At the upper end of the hall, where Manfred sat, was a boarded gallery with latticed windows, through which Matilda and Bianca were to pass. Hearing her father's voice, and seeing the servants assembled round him, she stopped to learn the occasion. The prisoner soon drew her attention: the steady and composed manner in which he answered, and the gallantry of his last reply, which were the first words she heard distinctly, interested her in his flavour. His person was noble, handsome, and commanding, even in that situation: but his countenance soon engrossed her whole care. "Heavens! Bianca," said the princess softly, "do I dream? or is not that youth the exact resemblance of Alfonso's picture in the gallery?" She could say no more, for her father's voice grew louder at every word. "This bravado," said he, "surpasses all thy former insolence. Thou shalt experience the wrath with which thou darest to trifle. Seize him," continued Manfred, "and bind him—the first news the princess hears of her champion shall be, that he has lost his head for her sake."—"The injustice of which thou art guilty towards me," said Theodore, "convinces me that I have done a good deed in delivering the princess from thy tyranny. May she be happy, whatever becomes of me!"—"This is a lover!" cried Manfred in a rage: "a peasant within sight of death is not animated by such sentiments. Tell me, tell me, rash boy, who thou art, or the rack shall force thy secret from thee."—"Thou hast threatened me with death already," said the youth, "for the truth I have told thee: if that is all the encouragement I am to expect for sincerity, I am not tempted to indulge thy vain curiosity farther."—"Then thou wilt not speak?" said Manfred. "I will not," replied he. "Bear him away into the courtyard," said Manfred; "I will see his head this instant severed from his body." Matilda fainted at hearing those words. Bianca shrieked, and cried, "Help! help! the princess is dead!" Manfred started at this ejaculation, and demanded what was the matter. The young peasant, who heard it too, was struck with horror, and asked eagerly the same question; but Manfred ordered him to be hurried into the court, and kept there for execution, till he had informed himself of the cause of Bianca's shrieks. When he learned the meaning, he treated it as a womanish panic, and ordering Matilda to be carried to her apartment, he rushed into the court, and calling for one of his guards, bade Theodore kneel down, and prepare to receive the fatal blow.

The undaunted youth received the bitter sentence with a resignation that touched every heart but Manfred's. He wished earnestly to know the meaning of the words he had heard relating to the princess; but fearing to exasperate the tyrant more against her, he desisted. The only boon he deigned to ask was, that he might be permitted to have a confessor, and make his peace with heaven. Manfred, who hoped by the confessor's means to come at the youth's history, readily granted his request; and being convinced that father Jerome was now in his interest, he ordered him to be called and shrive the prisoner. The holy man, who had little foreseen the catastrophe that his imprudence occasioned, fell on his knees to the prince, and adjured him in the most solemn manner not to shed innocent blood. He accused himself in the bitterest terms for his indiscretion, endeavoured to disculpate the youth, and left no method untried to soften the tyrant's rage. Manfred, more incensed than appeased by Jerome's intercession, whose retraction now made him suspect he had been imposed upon by both, commanded the friar to do his duty, telling him he would not allow the prisoner many minutes for confession. "Nor do I ask many, my lord," said the unhappy young man. "My sins, thank heaven, have not been numerous; nor exceed what might be expected at my years. Dry your tears, good father, and let us despatch. This is a bad world; nor have I had cause to leave it with regret."—"Oh wretched youth!" said Jerome; "how canst thou bear the sight of me with patience? I am thy murderer! it is I have brought this dismal hour upon thee!"—"I forgive thee from my soul," said the youth, "as I hope heaven will pardon me. Hear my confession, father; and give me thy blessing."—"How can I prepare thee for thy passage as I ought?" said Jerome. "Thou canst not be saved without pardoning thy foes—and canst thou forgive that impious man there?"—"I can," said Theodore: "I do."—"And does not this touch thee, cruel prince?" said the friar. "I sent for thee to confess him," said Manfred, sternly; "not to plead for him. Thou didst first incense me against him—his blood be upon thy head!"—"It will! it will!" said the good man, in an agony of sorrow. "Thou and I must never hope to go where this blessed youth is going!"—"Despatch!" said Manfred; "I am no more to be moved by the whining of priests than by the shrieks of women."—"What!" said the youth; "is it possible that my fate could have occasioned what I heard! Is the princess then again in thy power?"—"Thou dost but remember me of my wrath," said Manfred. "Prepare thee, for this moment is thy last." The youth, who felt his indignation rise, and who was touched with the sorrow which he saw he had infused into all the spectators, as well as into the friar, suppressed his emotions, and putting off his doublet, and unbuttoning, his collar, knelt down to his prayers. As he stooped, his shirt slipped down below his shoulder, and discovered the mark of a bloody arrow. "Gracious heaven!" cried the holy man, starting; "what do I see? It is my child! my Theodore!"

The passions that ensued must be conceived; they cannot be painted. The tears of the assistants were suspended by wonder, rather than stopped by joy. They seemed to inquire in the eyes of their lord what they ought to feel. Surprise, doubt, tenderness, respect, succeeded each other in the countenance of the youth. He received with modest submission the effusion of the old man's tears and embraces. Yet afraid of giving a loose to hope, and suspecting from what had passed the inflexibility of Manfred's temper, he cast a glance towards the prince, as if to say, canst thou be unmoved at such a scene as this?

Manfred's heart was capable of being touched. He forgot his anger in his astonishment; yet his pride forbade his owning himself affected. He even doubted whether this discovery was not a contrivance of the friar to save the youth. "What may this mean?" said he. "How can he be thy son? Is it consistent with thy profession or reputed sanctity to avow a peasant's offspring for the fruit of thy irregular amours!"—"Oh, God!" said the holy man, "dost thou question his being mine? Could I feel the anguish I do if I were not his father? Spare him! good prince! spare him! and revile me as thou pleasest."—"Spare him! spare him!" cried the attendants; "for this good man's sake!"—"Peace!" said Manfred, sternly. "I must know more ere I am disposed to pardon. A saint's bastard may be no saint himself."—"Injurious lord!" said Theodore, "add not insult to cruelty. If I am this venerable man's son, though no Prince, as thou art, know the blood that flows in my veins—" "Yes," said the friar, interrupting him, "his blood is noble; nor is he that abject thing, my lord, you speak him. He is my lawful son, and Sicily can boast of few houses more ancient than that of Falconara. But alas! my lord, what is blood! what is nobility! We are all reptiles, miserable, sinful creatures. It is piety alone that can distinguish us from the dust whence we sprung, and whither we must return."—"Truce to your sermon," said Manfred; "you forget you are no longer Friar Jerome, but the Count of Falconara. Let me know your history; you will have time to moralise hereafter, if you should not happen to obtain the grace of that sturdy criminal there."—"Mother of God!" said the friar, "is it possible my lord can refuse a father the life of his only, his long-lost, child! Trample me, my lord, scorn, afflict me, accept my life for his, but spare my son!"—"Thou canst feel, then," said Manfred, "what it is to lose an only son! A little hour ago thou didst preach up resignation to me: *my* house, if fate so pleased, must perish—but the Count of Falconara—" "Alas! my lord," said Jerome, "I confess I have offended; but aggravate not an old man's sufferings! I boast not of my family, nor think of such vanities—it is nature, that pleads for this boy; it is the memory of the dear woman that bore him. Is she, Theodore, is she dead?"—"Her soul has long been with the blessed," said Theodore. "Oh! how?" cried Jerome, "tell me—no—she is happy! Thou art all my care now!—Most dread lord! will you—will you grant me my poor boy's life?"—"Return to thy convent," answered Manfred; "conduct the princess hither; obey me in what else thou knowest; and I promise thee the life of thy son."—"Oh! my lord," said Jerome, "is my honesty the price I must pay for this dear youth's safety?"—"For me!" cried Theodore. "Let me die a thousand deaths, rather than stain thy conscience. What is it the tyrant would exact of thee? Is the princess still safe from his power? Protect her, thou venerable old man; and let all the weight of his wrath fall on me." Jerome endeavoured to check the impetuosity of the youth; and ere Manfred could reply, the trampling of horses was heard, and a brazen trumpet, which hung without the gate of the castle, was suddenly sounded. At the same instant the sable plumes on the enchanted helmet, which still remained at the other end of the court, were tempestuously agitated, and nodded thrice, as if bowed by some invisible wearer.

III

MANFRED'S HEART MISGAVE HIM WHEN HE BEHELD THE PLUMAGE ON the miraculous casque shaken in concert with the sounding of the brazen trumpet. "Father!" said he to Jerome, whom he now ceased to treat as Count of Falconara, "what mean these portents? If I have offended—" the plumes were shaken with greater violence than before. "Unhappy prince that I am," cried Manfred; "holy father! will you not assist me with your prayers?"—"My lord," replied Jerome, "heaven is no doubt displeased with your mockery of its servants. Submit yourself to the church; and cease to persecute her ministers. Dismiss this innocent youth; and learn to respect the holy character I wear. Heaven will not be trifled with: you see—" the trumpet sounded again. "I acknowledge I have been too hasty," said Manfred. "Father, do you go to the wicket, and demand who is at the gate."—"Do you grant me the life of Theodore?" replied the friar. "I do," said Manfred; "but inquire who is without."

Jerome, falling on the neck of his son, discharged a flood of tears, that spoke the fulness of his soul. "You promised to go to the gate," said Manfred. "I thought," replied the friar, "your highness would excuse my thanking you first in this tribute of my heart."—"Go, dearest sir," said Theodore, "obey the prince. I do not deserve that you should delay his satisfaction for me."

Jerome, inquiring who was without, was answered, "A herald." "From whom?" said he. "From the knight of the gigantic sabre," said the herald; "and I must speak with the usurper of Otranto." Jerome returned to the prince, and did not fail to repeat the message in the very words it had been uttered.

The first sounds struck Manfred with terror; but when he heard himself styled usurper, his rage rekindled, and all his courage revived. "Usurper!—insolent villain!" cried he, "who dares to question my title? Retire, father; this is no business for monks: I will meet this presumptuous man myself. Go to your convent and prepare the princess's return. Your son shall be a hostage for your fidelity: his life depends on your obedience."—"Good heaven! my lord," cried Jerome, "your highness did but this instant freely pardon my child—have you so soon forgot the interposition of heaven?"—"Heaven," replied Manfred, "does not send heralds to question the title of a lawful prince. I doubt whether it even notifies its will through friars—but that is your affair, not mine. At present you know my pleasure; and it is not a saucy herald that shall save your son, if you do not return with the princess."

It was in vain for the holy man to reply. Manfred commanded him to be conducted to the postern-gate, and shut out from the castle. And he ordered some of his attendants to carry Theodore to the top of the black tower, and guard him strictly; scarce permitting the father and son to exchange a hasty embrace at parting. He then withdrew to the hall, and seating himself in princely state, ordered the herald to be admitted to his presence.

"Well! thou insolent!" said the prince, "what wouldst thou with me?" —"I come," replied he, "to thee, Manfred, usurper of the principality of Otranto, from the renowned and invincible knight, the knight of the gigantic sabre: in the name of his lord, Frederic, Marquis of Vicenza, he demands the lady Isabella, daughter of that prince, whom thou hast basely and traitorously got into thy power, by bribing her false guardians during his absence; and he requires thee to resign the principality of Otranto, which thou hast usurped from the said Lord Frederic, the nearest of blood to the last rightful Lord, Alfonso the Good. If thou dost not instantly comply with these just demands, he defies thee to single combat to the last extremity." And so saying the herald cast down his warder.

"And where is this braggart who sends thee?" said Manfred. "At the distance of a league," said the herald: "he comes to make good his lord's claim against thee, as he is a true knight, and thou an usurper and ravisher."

Injurious as this challenge was, Manfred reflected that it was not his interest to provoke the Marquis. He knew how well founded the claim of Frederic was; nor was this the first time he had heard of it. Frederic's ancestors had assumed the style of princes of Otranto, from the death of Alfonso the Good without issue; but Manfred, his father, and grandfather, had been too powerful for the house of Vicenza to dispossess them. Frederic, a martial and amorous young prince, had married a beautiful young lady, of whom he was enamoured, and who had died in childbed of Isabella. Her death affected him so much that he had taken the cross and gone to the Holy Land, where he was wounded in an engagement against the infidels, made prisoner, and reported to be dead. When the news reached Manfred's ears, he bribed the guardians of the Lady Isabella to deliver her up to him as a bride for his son Conrad, by which alliance he had proposed to unite the claims of the two houses. This motive, on Conrad's death, had co-operated to make him so suddenly resolve on espousing her himself; and the same reflection determined him now to endeavour at obtaining the consent of Frederic to this marriage. A like policy inspired him with the thought of inviting Frederic's champion into the castle, lest he should be informed of Isabella's flight, which he strictly enjoined his domestics not to disclose to any of the knight's retinue.

"Herald," said Manfred, as soon as he had digested these reflections, "return to thy master, and tell him, ere we liquidate our differences by the sword, Manfred would hold some converse with him. Bid him welcome to my castle, where by my faith, as I am a true knight, he shall have courteous reception, and full security for himself and followers. If we cannot adjust our quarrel by amicable means, I swear he shall depart in safety, and shall have full satisfaction according to the laws of arms: So help me God and His Holy Trinity!" The herald made three obeisances and retired.

During this interview Jerome's mind was agitated by a thousand contrary passions. He trembled for the life of his son, and his first thought was to persuade Isabella to return to the castle. Yet he was scarce less alarmed at the thought of her union with Manfred. He dreaded Hippolita's unbounded submission to the will of her lord; and though he did not doubt but he could alarm her piety not to consent to a divorce, if he could get access to her; yet should Manfred discover that the obstruction came from him, it might be equally fatal to Theodore. He was impatient to know whence came the herald, who with so little management had questioned the title of Manfred: yet he did not dare absent himself from the convent, lest Isabella should leave it, and her flight be imputed to him. He returned disconsolately to the monastery, uncertain on what conduct to resolve. A monk, who met him in the porch and observed his melancholy air, said, "Alas! brother, is it then true that we have lost our excellent princess Hippolita?" The holy man started, and cried, "What meanest thou, brother? I come this instant from the castle, and left her in perfect health."—"Martelli," replied the other friar, "passed by the convent but a quarter of an hour ago on his way from the castle, and reported that her highness was dead. All our brethren are gone to the chapel to pray for her happy transit to a better life, and willed me to wait thy arrival. They know thy holy attachment to that good lady, and are anxious for the affliction it will cause in thee—indeed we have all reason to weep; she was a mother to our house. But this life is but a pilgrimage; we must not murmur—we shall all follow her! May our end be like hers!"—"Good brother, thou dreamest," said Jerome. "I tell thee I come from the castle, and left the princess well. Where is the Lady Isabella?"—"Poor gentlewoman!" replied the friar; "I told her the sad news, and offered her spiritual comfort. I reminded her of the transitory condition of mortality, and advised her to take the veil: I quoted the example of the holy Princess Sanchia of Arragon."—"Thy zeal was laudable," said Jerome, impatiently; "but at present it was unnecessary: Hippolita is well—at least I trust in the Lord she is; I heard nothing to the contrary—yet, methinks, the prince's earnestness— Well, brother, but where is the Lady Isabella?"—"I know not," said the friar; "she wept much, and said she would retire to her chamber." Jerome left his comrade abruptly, and hastened to the princess, but she was not in her chamber. He inquired of the domestics of the convent, but could learn no news of her. He searched in vain throughout the monastery and the church, and despatched messengers round the neighbourhood, to get intelligence if she had been seen; but to no purpose. Nothing could equal the good man's perplexity. He judged that Isabella, suspecting Manfred of having precipitated his wife's death, had taken the alarm, and withdrawn herself to some more secret place of concealment. This new flight would probably carry the prince's fury to the height. The report of Hippolita's death, though it seemed almost incredible, increased his consternation; and though Isabella's escape bespoke her aversion of Manfred for a husband, Jerome could feel no comfort from it, while it endangered the life of his son. He determined to return to the castle, and made several of his brethren accompany him to attest his innocence to Manfred, and, if necessary, join their intercession with his for Theodore.

The prince, in the meantime, had passed into the court, and ordered the gates of the castle to be flung open for the reception of the stranger knight and his train. In a few minutes the cavalcade arrived. First came two harbingers with wands. Next a herald, followed by two pages and two trumpets. Then a hundred foot-guards. These were attended by as many horse. After them fifty footmen, clothed in scarlet and black, the colours of the knight. Then a led horse. Two heralds on each side of a gentleman on horseback bearing a banner with the arms of Vicenza and Otranto quarterly—a circumstance that much offended Manfred—but he stifled his resentment. Two more pages. The knight's confessor telling his beads. Fifty more footmen clad as before. Two knights habited in complete armour, their beavers down, comrades to the principal knight. The squires of the two knights, carrying their shields and devices. The knight's own squire. A hundred gentlemen bearing an enormous sword, and seeming to faint under the weight of it. The knight himself on a chestnut steed, in complete armour, his lance in the rest, his face entirely concealed by his vizor, which was surmounted by a large plume of scarlet and black feathers. Fifty foot-guards with drums and trumpets closed the procession, which wheeled off to the right and left to make room for the principal knight.

As soon as he approached the gate he stopped; and the herald advancing, read again the words of the challenge. Manfred's eyes were fixed on the gigantic sword, and he scarce seemed to attend to the cartel: but his attention was soon diverted by a tempest of wind that rose behind him. He turned and beheld the plumes of the enchanted helmet agitated in the same extraordinary manner as before. It required intrepidity like Manfred's not to sink under a concurrence of circumstances that seemed to announce his fate. Yet scorning in the presence of strangers to betray the courage he had always manifested, he said boldly, "Sir Knight, whoever thou art, I bid thee welcome. If thou art of mortal mould, thy valour shall meet its equal: and if thou art a true knight, thou wilt scorn to employ sorcery to carry thy point. Be these omens from heaven or hell, Manfred trusts to the righteousness of his cause and to the aid of St. Nicholas, who has ever protected his house. Alight, Sir Knight, and repose thyself. To-morrow thou shalt have a fair field, and heaven befriend the juster side!"

The knight made no reply, but dismounting, was conducted by Manfred to the great hall of the castle. As they traversed the court, the knight stopped to gaze on the miraculous casque; and kneeling down, seemed to pray inwardly for some minutes. Rising, he made a sign to the prince to lead on. As soon as they entered the hall, Manfred proposed to the stranger to disarm, but the knight shook his head in token of refusal. "Sir Knight," said Manfred, "this is not courteous, but by my good faith I will not cross thee, nor shalt thou have cause to complain of the prince of Otranto. No treachery is designed on my part; I hope none is intended on thine; here take my gage" (giving him his ring): "your friends and you shall enjoy the laws of hospitality. Rest here until refreshments are brought. I will but give orders for the accommodation of your train, and return to you." The three knights bowed as accepting his courtesy. Manfred directed the stranger's retinue to be conducted to an adjacent hospital, founded by the princess Hippolita for the reception of pilgrims. As they made the circuit of the court to return towards the gate, the gigantic sword burst from the supporters, and falling to the ground opposite to the helmet, remained immovable. Manfred, almost hardened to preternatural appearances, surmounted the shock of this new prodigy; and returning to the hall, where by this time the feast was ready, he invited his silent guests to take their places. Manfred, however ill his heart was at ease, endeavoured to inspire the company with mirth. He put several questions to them, but was answered only by signs. They raised their vizors but sufficiently to feed themselves, and that sparingly. "Sirs," said the prince, "ye are the first guests I ever treated within these walls who scorned to hold any intercourse with me: nor has it oft been customary, I ween, for princes to hazard their state and dignity against strangers and mutes. You say you come in the name of Frederic of Vicenza; I have ever heard that he was a gallant and courteous knight; nor would he, I am bold to say, think it beneath him to mix in social converse with a prince that is his equal, and not unknown by deeds in arms. Still ye are silent—well! be it as it may—by the laws of hospitality and chivalry ye are masters under this roof: ye shall do your pleasure. But come, give me a goblet of wine; ye will not refuse to pledge me to the healths of your fair mistresses." The principal knight sighed and crossed himself, and was rising from the board—"Sir Knight," said Manfred, "what I said was but in sport: I shall constrain you in nothing: use your good liking. Since mirth is not your mood, let us be sad. Business may hit your fancies better. Let us withdraw, and hear if what I have to unfold may be better relished than the vain efforts I have made for your pastime."

Manfred then conducting the three knights into an inner chamber, shut the door, and inviting them to be seated, began thus, addressing himself to the chief personage:—

"You come, Sir Knight, as I understand, in the name of the Marquis of Vicenza, to re-demand the Lady Isabella, his daughter, who has been contracted in the face of Holy Church to my son, by the consent of her legal guardians; and to require me to resign my dominions to your lord, who gives himself for the nearest of blood to Prince Alfonso, whose soul God rest! I shall speak to the latter article of your demands first. You must know, your lord knows, that I enjoy the principality of Otranto from my father, Don Manuel, as he received it from his father, Don Ricardo. Alfonso, their predecessor, dying childless in the holy land, bequeathed his estates to my grandfather, Don Ricardo, in consideration of his faithful services." The stranger shook his head—"Sir Knight," said Manfred, warmly, "Ricardo was a valiant and upright man; he was a pious man; witness his munificent foundation of the adjoining church and two convents. He was peculiarly patronised by St. Nicholas—my grandfather was incapable— I say, sir, Don Ricardo was incapable— excuse me, your interruption has disordered me. I venerate the memory of my grandfather. Well, Sirs, he held this estate; he held it by his good sword and by the favour of St. Nicholas—so did my father; and so, sirs, will I, come what come will. But

Frederic, your lord, is nearest in blood. I have consented to put my title to the issue of the sword. Does that imply a vicious title? I might have asked, where is Frederic, your lord? Report speaks him dead in captivity. You say, your actions say, he lives—I question it not—I might, sirs, I might—but I do not. Other princes would bid Frederic take his inheritance by force, if he can: they would not stake their dignity on a single combat: they would not submit it to the decision of unknown mutes!—pardon me, gentlemen, I am too warm: but suppose yourselves in my situation: as ye are stout knights, would it not move your choler to have your own and the honour of your ancestors called in question?—But to the point. Ye require me to deliver up the lady Isabella. Sirs, I must ask if ye are authorised to receive her?" The knight nodded. "Receive her," continued Manfred; "well, you are authorised to receive her, but, gentle knight, may I ask if you have full powers?" The knight nodded. " 'Tis well," said Manfred; "then hear what I have to offer. Ye see, gentlemen, before you, the most unhappy of men! (he began to weep) afford me your compassion; I am entitled to it, indeed I am. Know, I have lost my only hope, my joy, the support of my house—Conrad died yester morning."—The knights discovered signs of surprise. "Yes, sirs, fate has disposed of my son. Isabella is at liberty."—"Do you then restore her?" cried the chief knight, breaking silence. "Afford me your patience," said Manfred. "I rejoice to find, by this testimony of your goodwill, that this matter may be adjusted without blood. It is no interest of mine dictates what little I have farther to say. Ye behold in me a man disgusted with the world: the loss of my son has weaned me from earthly cares. Power and greatness have no longer any charms in my eyes. I wished to transmit the sceptre I had received from my ancestors with honour to my son—but that is over! Life itself is so indifferent to me, that I accepted your defiance with joy. A good knight cannot go to the grave with more satisfaction than when falling in his vocation: whatever is the will of heaven, I submit; for alas! Sirs, I am a man of many sorrows. Manfred is no object of envy, but no doubt you are acquainted with my story." The knight made signs of ignorance, and seemed curious to have Manfred proceed. "Is it possible, sirs," continued the prince, "that my story should be a secret to you? Have you heard nothing relating to me and the princess Hippolita?"—They shook their heads. "No! Thus, then, sirs, it is. You think me ambitious: ambition, alas! is composed of more rugged materials. If I were ambitious, I should not for so many years have been a prey to all the hell of conscientious scruples. But I weary your patience: I will be brief. Know, then, that I have long been troubled in mind on my union with the princess Hippolita. Oh! sirs, if ye were acquainted with that excellent woman! if ye knew that I adore her like a mistress, and cherish her as a friend—but man was not born for perfect happiness!

She shares my scruples, and with her consent I have brought this matter before the church, for we are related within the forbidden degrees. I expect every hour the definitive sentence that must separate us for ever—I am sure you feel for me—I see you do—pardon these tears!" The knights gazed on each other, wondering where this would end. Manfred continued. "The death of my son betiding while my soul was under this anxiety, I thought of nothing but resigning my dominions, and retiring for ever from the sight of mankind. My only difficulty was to fix on a successor, who would be tender of my people, and to dispose of the Lady Isabella, who is dear to me as my own blood. I was willing to restore the line of Alfonso, even in his most distant kindred. And though, pardon me, I am satisfied it was his will that Ricardo's lineage should take place of his own relations; yet where was I to search for those relations? I knew of none but Frederic, your lord; he was a captive to the infidels, or dead; and were he living, and at home, would he quit the flourishing State of Vicenza for the inconsiderable principality of Otranto? If he would not, could I bear the thought of seeing a hard, unfeeling, Viceroy set over my poor faithful people? for, sirs, I love my people, and thank heaven am beloved by them.—But ye will ask whither tends this long discourse? Briefly, then, thus, sirs. Heaven in your arrival seems to point out a remedy for these difficulties and my misfortunes. The Lady Isabella is at liberty; I shall soon be so—I would submit to anything for the good of my people. Were it not the best, the only way to extinguish the feuds between our families, if I was to take the Lady Isabella to wife? You start. But though Hippolita's virtues will ever be dear to me, a prince must not consider himself; he is born for his people." A servant at that instant entering the chamber apprised Manfred that Jerome and several of his brethren demanded immediate access to him.

The prince, provoked at this interruption, and fearing that the friar would discover to the strangers that Isabella had taken sanctuary, was going to forbid Jerome's entrance. But recollecting that he was certainly arrived to notify the princess's return, Manfred began to excuse himself to the knights for leaving them for a few moments, but was prevented by the arrival of the friars. Manfred angrily reprimanded them for their intrusion, and would have forced them back from the chamber; but Jerome was too much agitated to be repulsed. He declared aloud the flight of Isabella, with protestations of his own innocence. Manfred, distracted at the news, and not less at its coming to the knowledge of the strangers, uttered nothing but incoherent sentences, now upbraiding the friar, now apologising to the knights, earnest to know what was become of Isabella, yet equally afraid of their knowing; impatient to pursue her, yet dreading to have them join in the pursuit. He offered to despatch messengers in quest of her, but the chief knight, no longer keeping silence, reproached Manfred in bitter terms for his dark and ambiguous dealing, and demanded the cause of Isabella's first absence from the castle. Manfred, casting a stern look at Jerome, implying a command of silence, pretended that on Conrad's death he had placed her in sanctuary until he could determine how to dispose of her. Jerome, who trembled for his son's life, did not dare contradict this falsehood, but one of his brethren, not under the same anxiety, declared frankly that she had fled to their church in the preceding night. The prince in vain endeavoured to stop this discovery, which overwhelmed him with shame and confusion. The principal stranger, amazed at the contradictions he heard, and more than half persuaded that Manfred had secreted the princess, notwithstanding the concern he expressed at her flight, rushing to the door, said, "Thou traitor-prince! Isabella shall be found." Manfred endeavoured to hold him, but the other knights assisting their comrade, he broke from the prince, and hastened into the court, demanding his attendants. Manfred, finding it vain to divert him from the pursuit, offered to accompany him and summoning his attendants, and taking Jerome and some of the friars to guide them, they issued from the castle; Manfred privately giving orders to have the knight's company secured, while to the knight he affected to despatch a messenger to require their assistance.

The company had no sooner quitted the castle than Matilda, who felt herself deeply interested for the young peasant, since she had seen him condemned to death in the hall, and whose thoughts had been taken up with concerting measures to save him, was informed by some of the female attendants that Manfred had despatched all his men various ways in pursuit of Isabella. He had in his hurry given this order in general terms, not meaning to extend it to the guard he had set upon Theodore, but forgetting it. The domestics, officious to obey so peremptory a prince, and urged by their own curiosity and love of novelty to join in any precipitate chase, had to a man left the castle. Matilda disengaged herself from her women, stole up to the black tower, and unbolting the door, presented herself to the astonished Theodore. "Young man," said she, "though filial duty and womanly modesty condemn the step I am taking, yet holy charity, surmounting all other ties, justifies this act. Fly; the doors of thy prison are open: my father and his domestics are absent; but they may soon return. Be gone in safety; and may the angels of heaven direct thy course!" —"Thou art surely one of those angels!" said the enraptured Theodore: "none but a blessed saint could speak, could act—could look—like thee!—May I not know the name of my divine protectress? Methought thou namedst thy father. Is it possible? Can Manfred's blood feel holy pity?—Lovely lady, thou answerest not—but how art thou here thyself? Why dost thou neglect thy own safety, and waste a thought on a wretch like Theodore? Let us fly together: the life thou bestowest shall be dedicated to thy defence."—"Alas! thou mistakest," said Matilda, sighing: "I am Manfred's daughter, but no dangers await me."—"Amazement!" said Theodore; "but last night I blessed myself for yielding thee the service thy gracious compassion so charitably returns me now."—"Still thou art in an error," said the princess; "but this is no time for explanation. Fly, virtuous youth, while it is in my power to save thee: should my father return, thou and I both should indeed have cause to tremble." —"How!" said Theodore; "thinkest thou, charming maid, that I will accept of life at the hazard of aught calamitous to thee? Better I endured a thousand deaths." —"I run no risk," said Matilda, "but by thy delay. Depart; it cannot be known that I have assisted thy flight."—"Swear by the saints above," said Theodore, "that thou canst not be suspected; else here I vow to await whatever can befall me." —"Oh! thou art too generous," said Matilda; "but rest assured that no suspicion can alight on me."—"Give me thy beauteous hand in token that thou dost not deceive me," said Theodore; "and let me bathe it with the warm tears of gratitude—" —"Forbear!" said the princess; "this must not be."—"Alas!" said Theodore, "I have never known but calamity until this hour—perhaps shall never know other fortune again: suffer the chaste raptures of holy gratitude: 'tis my soul would print its effusions on thy hand."—"Forbear, and begone," said Matilda. "How would Isabella approve of seeing thee at my feet?"—"Who is Isabella?" said the young man with surprise. "Ah, me! I fear," said the princess, "I am serving a deceitful one;—hast thou forgot thy curiosity this morning?"—"Thy looks, thy actions, all thy beauteous self seem an emanation of divinity," said Theodore; "but thy words are dark and mysterious;—speak, lady; speak to thy servant's comprehension." —"Thou understandest but too well!" said Matilda; "but once more I command thee to be gone: thy blood, which I may preserve, will be on my head, if I waste the time in vain discourse."—"I go, lady," said Theodore, "because it is thy will, and because I would not bring the grey hairs of my father with sorrow to the grave. Say but, adored lady, that I have thy gentle pity."—"Stay," said Matilda; "I will conduct thee to the subterraneous vault by which Isabella escaped; it will lead thee to the church of St. Nicholas, where thou mayst take sanctuary."—"What!" said Theodore, "was it another, and not thy lovely self that I assisted to find the subterraneous passage?"—"It was," said Matilda; "but ask no more; I tremble to see thee still abide here; fly to the sanctuary."—"To sanctuary," said Theodore; "no, princess; sanctuaries are for helpless damsels, or for criminals. Theodore's soul is free from guilt, nor will wear the appearance of it. Give me a sword, lady, and thy father shall learn that Theodore scorns an ignominious flight."—"Rash youth!" said Matilda; "thou wouldst not dare to lift thy presumptuous arm against the prince of Otranto?"—"Not against thy father; indeed, I dare not," said Theodore. "Excuse me, lady; I had forgotten. But could I gaze on thee, and remember thou art sprung from the tyrant Manfred?—But he is thy father, and from this moment my injuries are buried in oblivion." A deep and hollow groan, which seemed to come from above, startled the princess and Theodore. "Good Heaven, we are overheard!" said the princess. They listened; but perceiving no further noise, they both concluded it the effect of pent-up vapours. And the princess, preceding Theodore softly, carried him to her father's armoury, where, equipping him with a complete suit, he was conducted by Matilda to the postern-gate. "Avoid the town," said the princess, "and all the western side of the castle: 'tis there the search must be making by Manfred and the strangers: but hie thee to the opposite quarter. Yonder behind that forest to the east is a chain of rocks, hollowed into a labyrinth of caverns that reach to the sea-coast. There thou mayst lie concealed, till thou canst make signs to some vessel to put on shore, and take thee off. Go! heaven be thy guide!—and sometimes in thy prayers remember—Matilda!" Theodore flung himself at her feet, and seizing her lily hand, which with struggles she suffered him to kiss, he vowed on the earliest opportunity to get himself knighted, and fervently entreated her permission to swear himself eternally her knight. Ere the princess could reply, a clap of thunder was suddenly heard that shook the battlements. Theodore, regardless of the tempest, would have urged his suit: but the princess, dismayed, retreated hastily into the castle, and commanded the youth to be gone with an air that would not be disobeyed. He sighed, and retired, but with eyes fixed on the gate, until Matilda, closing it, put an end to an interview, in which the hearts of both had drunk so deeply of a passion, which both now tasted for the first time.

Theodore went pensively to the convent, to acquaint his father with his deliverance. There he learned the absence of Jerome, and the pursuit that was making after the Lady Isabella, with some particulars of whose story he now first became acquainted. The generous gallantry of his nature prompted him to wish to assist her; but the monks could lend him no lights to guess at the route she had taken. He was not tempted to wander far in search of her, for the idea of Matilda had imprinted itself so strongly on his heart, that he could not bear to absent himself at much distance from her abode. The tenderness Jerome had expressed for him concurred to confirm this reluctance; and he even persuaded himself that filial affection was the chief cause of his hovering between the castle and monastery. Until Jerome should return at night, Theodore at length determined to repair to the forest that Matilda had pointed out to him. Arriving there, he sought the gloomiest shades, as best suited to the pleasing melancholy that reigned in his mind. In this mood he roved insensibly to the caves which had formerly served as a retreat to hermits, and were now reported round the country to be haunted by evil spirits. He recollected to have heard this tradition; and being of a brave and adventurous disposition, he willingly indulged his curiosity in exploring the secret recesses of this labyrinth. He had not penetrated far before he thought he heard the steps of some person who seemed to retreat before him. Theodore, though firmly grounded in all our holy faith enjoins to be believed, had no apprehension that good men were abandoned without cause to the malice of the powers of darkness. He thought the place more likely to be infested by robbers than by those infernal agents who are reported to molest and bewilder travellers. He had long burned with impatience to approve his valour:—drawing his sabre, he marched sedately onwards, still directing his steps as the imperfect rustling sound before him led the way. The armour he wore was a like indication to the person who avoided him. Theodore, now convinced that he was not mistaken, redoubled his pace, and evidently gained on the person that fled, whose haste increasing, Theodore came up just as a woman fell breathless before him. He hasted to raise her, but her terror was so great that he apprehended she would faint in his arms. He used every gentle word to dispel her alarms, and assured her that far from injuring, he would defend her at the peril of his life. The lady recovering her spirits from his courteous demeanour, and gazing on her protector, said, "Sure, I have heard that voice before!"—"Not to my knowledge," replied Theodore; "unless, as I conjecture, thou art the Lady Isabella."—"Merciful Heaven!" cried she. "Thou art not sent in quest of me, art thou?" And saying those words, she threw herself at his feet, and besought him not to deliver her up to Manfred.—"To Manfred!" cried Theodore—"no, lady; I have once already delivered thee from his tyranny, and it shall fare hard with me now, but I will place thee out of the reach of his daring."—"Is it possible," said she, "that thou shouldst be the generous unknown whom I met last night in the vault of the castle? Sure thou art not a mortal, but my guardian angel. On my knees, let me thank—" "Hold! gentle princess," said Theodore, "nor demean thyself before a poor and friendless young man. If heaven has selected me for thy deliverer, it will accomplish its work, and strengthen my arm in thy cause:—but come, lady, we are too near the mouth of the cavern; let us seek its inmost recesses. I can have no tranquillity till I have placed thee beyond the reach of danger."—"Alas! what mean you, sir?" said she. "Though all your actions are noble, though your sentiments speak the purity of your soul, is it fitting that I should accompany you alone into these perplexed retreats? Should we be found together, what would a censorious world think of my conduct?"—"I respect your virtuous delicacy," said Theodore; "nor do you harbour a suspicion that wounds my honour. I meant to conduct you into the most private cavity of these rocks, and then at the hazard of my life to guard their entrance against every living thing. Besides, lady," continued he, drawing a deep sigh, "beauteous and all perfect as your form is, and though my wishes are not guiltless of aspiring, know, my soul is dedicated to another; and although—" A sudden noise prevented Theodore from proceeding. They soon distinguished these sounds, "Isabella! what, ho! Isabella!" The trembling princess relapsed into her former agony of fear. Theodore endeavoured to encourage her, but in vain. He assured her he would die rather than suffer her to return under Manfred's power; and begging her to remain concealed, he went forth to prevent the person in search of her from approaching.

At the mouth of the cavern he found an armed knight, discoursing with a peasant, who assured him he had seen a lady enter the passes of the rock. The knight was preparing to seek her, when Theodore, placing himself in his way, with his sword drawn, sternly forbad him at his peril to advance.—"And who art thou, who darest to cross my way?" said the knight, haughtily.—"One who does not dare more than he will perform," said Theodore. "I seek the Lady Isabella," said the knight, "and understand she has taken refuge among these rocks. Impede me not, or thou wilt repent having provoked my resentment."—"Thy purpose is as odious as thy resentment is contemptible," said Theodore. "Return whence thou camest, or we shall soon know whose resentment is most terrible." The stranger, who was the principal knight that had arrived from the Marquis of Vicenza, had galloped from Manfred as he was busied in getting information of the princess, and giving various orders to prevent her falling into the power of the three knights. Their chief had suspected Manfred of being privy to the princess's absconding, and this insult from a man, who he concluded was stationed by that prince to secrete her, confirming his suspicions, he made no reply, but discharging a blow with his sabre at Theodore, would soon have removed all obstruction, if Theodore, who took him for one of Manfred's captains, and who had no sooner given the provocation than prepared to support it, had not received the stroke on his shield. The valour that had so long been smothered in his breast broke forth at once; he rushed impetuously on the knight, whose pride and wrath were not less powerful incentives to hardy deeds. The combat was furious, but not long. Theodore wounded the knight in three several places, and at last disarmed him as he fainted by the loss of blood. The peasant, who had fled on the first onset, had given the alarm to some of Manfred's domestics, who, by his orders, were dispersed through the forest in pursuit of

Isabella. They came up as the knight fell, whom they soon discovered to be the noble stranger. Theodore, notwithstanding his hatred to Manfred, could not behold the victory he had gained without emotions of pity and generosity. But he was more touched when he learned the quality of his adversary, and was informed that he was no retainer, but an enemy, of Manfred. He assisted the servants of the latter in disarming the knight, and in endeavouring to stanch the blood that flowed from his wounds. The knight recovering his speech, said, in a faint and faltering voice, "Generous foe, we have both been in an error. I took thee for an instrument of the tyrant; I perceive thou hast made the like mistake—it is too late for excuses—I faint—if Isabella is at hand—call her—I have important secrets to—" "He is dying!" said one of the attendants; "has nobody a crucifix about them? Andrea, do thou pray over him."—"Fetch some water," said Theodore, "and pour it down his throat, while I hasten to the princess." Saying this, he flew to Isabella, and in few words told her modestly that he had been so unfortunate by mistake as to wound a gentleman from her father's court, who wished, ere he died, to impart something of consequence to her. The princess, who had been transported at hearing the voice of Theodore, as he called to her to come forth, was astonished at what she heard. Suffering herself to be conducted by Theodore, the new proof of whose valour recalled her dispersed spirits, she came where the bleeding knight lay speechless on the ground;—but her fears returned when she beheld the domestics of Manfred. She would again have fled if Theodore had not made her observe that they were unarmed, and had not threatened them with instant death if they should dare to seize the princess. The stranger, opening his eyes, and beholding a woman, said—"Art thou, pray tell me truly, art thou Isabella of Vicenza?"—"I am," said she: "good Heaven restore thee!"—"Then thou—then thou"—said the knight, struggling for utterance—"seest—thy father; give me one—" "Oh! amazement! horror! what do I hear! what do I see!" cried Isabella. "My father! You my father! How came you here, Sir? For Heaven's sake, speak!—oh! run for help, or he will expire!"—" 'Tis most true," said the wounded knight, exerting all his force; "I am Frederic, thy father;—yes, I came to deliver thee.—It will not be—give me a parting kiss, and take—" "Sir," said Theodore, "do not exhaust yourself; suffer us to convey you to the castle."—"To the castle!" said Isabella. "Is there no help nearer than the castle? Would you expose my father to the tyrant? If he goes thither, I dare not accompany him; and yet, can I leave him!"—"My child," said Frederic, "it matters not for me whither I am carried. A few minutes will place me beyond danger; but while I have eyes to dote on thee, forsake me not, dear Isabella! This brave knight, I know not who he is, will protect thy innocence.—Sir, you will not abandon my child, will you?" Theodore, shedding tears over his victim, and vowing to guard the princess at the expense of his life, persuaded Frederic to suffer himself to be conducted to the castle. They placed him on a horse belonging to one of the domestics, after binding up his wounds as well as they were able. Theodore marched by his side; and the afflicted Isabella, who could not bear to quit him, followed mournfully behind.

IV

The sorrowful troop no sooner arrived at the castle, than they were met by Hippolita and Matilda, whom Isabella had sent one of the domestics before to advertise of their approach. The ladies causing Frederic to be conveyed into the nearest chamber, retired, while the surgeons examined his wounds. Matilda blushed at seeing Theodore and Isabella together; but endeavoured to conceal it by embracing the latter, and condoling with her on her father's mischance. The surgeons soon came to acquaint Hippolita that none of the marquis's wounds were dangerous; and that he was desirous of seeing his daughter and the princesses. Theodore, under pretence of expressing his joy at being freed from his apprehensions of the combat being fatal to Frederic, could not resist the impulse of following Matilda. Her eyes were so often cast down on meeting his, that Isabella, who regarded Theodore as attentively as he gazed on Matilda, soon divined who the object was that he had told her in the cave engaged his affections. While this mute scene passed, Hippolita demanded of Frederic the cause of his having taken that mysterious course for reclaiming his daughter; and threw in various apologies to excuse her lord for the match contracted between their children. Frederic, however incensed against Manfred, was not insensible to the courtesy and benevolence of Hippolita: but he was still more struck with the lovely form of Matilda. Wishing to detain them by his bedside, he informed Hippolita of his story. He told her that, while prisoner to the infidels, he had dreamed that his daughter, of whom he had learned no news since his captivity, was detained in a castle, where she was in danger of the most dreadful misfortunes: and that if he obtained his liberty, and repaired to a wood near Joppa, he would learn more. Alarmed at this dream, and incapable of obeying the direction given by it, his chains became more grievous than ever. But while his thoughts were occupied on the means of obtaining his liberty, he received the agreeable news that the confederate princes who were warring in Palestine had paid his ransom. He instantly set out for the wood that had been marked in his dream. For three days he and his attendants had wandered in the forest without seeing a human form: but on the evening of the third they came to a cell, in which they found a venerable hermit in the agonies of death. Applying rich cordials, they brought the fainting man to his speech. "My sons," said he, "I am bounden to your charity—but it is in vain—I am going to my eternal rest—yet I die with the satisfaction of performing the will of heaven. When first I repaired to this solitude, after seeing my country become a prey to unbelievers—it is alas! above fifty years since I was witness to that dreadful scene! St. Nicholas appeared to me, and revealed a secret, which he bade me never disclose to mortal man, but on my death-bed. This is that tremendous hour, and ye are no doubt the chosen warriors to whom I was ordered to reveal my trust. As soon as ye have done the last offices to this wretched corse, dig under the seventh tree on the left hand of this poor cave, and your pains will—Oh! good Heaven receive my soul!" With those words the devout man breathed his last. "By break of day," continued Frederic, "when we had committed the holy relics to earth, we dug according to direction;—but what was our astonishment when about the depth of six feet we discovered an enormous sabre,—the very weapon yonder in the court. On the blade, which was then partly out of the scabbard, though since closed by our efforts in removing it, were written the following lines—no; excuse me, madam," added the marquis, turning to Hippolita; "if I forbear to repeat them: I respect your sex and rank, and would not be guilty of offending your ear with sounds injurious to aught that is dear to you."—He paused. Hippolita trembled. She did not doubt but Frederic was destined by Heaven to accomplish the fate that seemed to threaten her house. Looking with anxious fondness at Matilda, a silent tear stole down her cheek: but recollecting herself, she said, "Proceed, my lord; Heaven does nothing in vain: mortals must receive its divine behests with lowliness and submission. It is our part to deprecate its wrath, or bow to its decrees. Repeat the sentence, my lord; we listen resigned." Frederic was grieved that he had proceeded so far. The dignity and patient firmness of Hippolita penetrated him with respect, and the tender silent affection with which the princess and her daughter regarded each other, melted him almost to tears. Yet apprehensive that his forbearance to obey would be more alarming, he repeated in a faltering and low voice the following lines:—

"Where 'er a casque that suits this sword is found,
With perils is thy daughter compass'd round;
Alfonso's blood alone can save the maid,
And quiet a long restless prince's shade."

"What is there in these lines," said Theodore impatiently, "that affects these princesses? Why were they to be shocked by a mysterious delicacy, that has so little foundation?"—"Your words are rude, young man," said the marquis; "and though fortune has favoured you once—" "My honoured lord," said Isabella, who resented Theodore's warmth, which she perceived was dictated by his sentiments for Matilda, "discompose not yourself for the glosing of a peasant's son: he forgets the reverence he owes you; but he is not accustomed—" Hippolita, concerned at the heat that had arisen, checked Theodore for his boldness, but with an air acknowledging his zeal; and changing the conversation, demanded of Frederic where he had left her lord? As the marquis was going to reply, they heard a noise without, and rising to inquire the cause, Manfred, Jerome, and part of the troop, who had met an imperfect rumour of what had happened, entered the chamber. Manfred advanced hastily towards Frederic's bed to condole with him on his misfortune, and to learn the circumstances of the combat, when starting in an agony of terror and amazement, he cried, "Ha! what art thou? thou dreadful spectre! is my hour come?"—"My dearest, gracious lord," cried Hippolita, clasping him in her arms, "what is it you see! Why do you fix your eye-balls thus?"—"What!" cried Manfred breathless; "dost thou see nothing, Hippolita? Is this ghastly phantom sent to me alone;—to me, who did not—" "For mercy's sweetest self, my lord," said Hippolita, "resume your soul, command your reason:—there is none here, but us, your friends."—"What, is not that Alfonso?" cried Manfred. "Dost thou not see him? can it be my brain's delirium?"—"This! my lord," said Hippolita; "this is Theodore, the youth who has been so unfortunate."—"Theodore!" said Manfred mournfully, and striking his forehead; "Theodore or a phantom, he has unhinged the soul of Manfred.—But how comes he here? and how comes he in armour?"—"I believe he went in search of Isabella," said Hippolita. "Of Isabella!" said Manfred, relapsing into rage; "yes, yes, that is not doubtful: but how did he escape from durance in which I left him? Was it Isabella, or this hypocritical old friar, that procured his enlargement?"—"And would a parent be criminal, my lord," said Theodore, "if he meditated the deliverance of his child?" Jerome, amazed to hear himself in a manner accused by his son, and without foundation, knew not what to think. He could not comprehend how Theodore had escaped, how he came to be armed, and to encounter Frederic. Still he would not venture to ask any questions that might tend to inflame Manfred's wrath against his son. Jerome's silence convinced Manfred that he had contrived Theodore's release. "And is it thus, thou ungrateful old man," said the prince, addressing himself to the friar, "that thou repayest mine and Hippolita's bounties? And not content with traversing my heart's nearest wishes, thou armest thy bastard, and bringest him into my own castle to insult me!"—"My lord," said Theodore, "you wrong my father: neither he nor I are capable of harbouring a thought against your peace. Is it insolence thus to surrender myself to your Highness's pleasure?" added he, laying his sword respectfully at Manfred's feet. "Behold my bosom; strike, my lord, if you suspect that a disloyal thought is lodged there. There is not a sentiment engraven on my heart that does not venerate you and yours." The grace and fervour with which Theodore uttered these words interested every person present in his favour. Even Manfred was touched—yet still possessed with his resemblance to Alfonso, his admiration was dashed with secret horror. "Rise," said he; "thy life is not my present purpose. But tell me thy history, and how thou camest connected with this old traitor here."—"My lord," said Jerome eagerly—"Peace! impostor!" said Manfred; "I will not have him prompted."—"My lord," said Theodore, "I want no assistance; my story is very brief. I was carried at five years of age to Algiers with my mother, who had been taken by corsairs from the coast of Sicily. She died of grief in less than a twelvemonth." The tears gushed from Jerome's eyes, on whose countenance a thousand anxious passions stood expressed. "Before she died," continued Theodore, "she bound a writing about my arm under my garments, which told me I was the son of the Count Falconara."—"It is most true," said Jerome; "I am that wretched father."—"Again I enjoin thee silence," said Manfred: "proceed."—"I remained in slavery," said Theodore, "until within these two years, when attending on my master in his cruises, I was delivered by a Christian vessel, which overpowered the pirate; and discovering myself to the captain, he generously put me on shore in Sicily;—but alas! instead of finding a father, I learned that his estate, which was situated on the coast, had, during his absence, been laid waste by the rover, who had carried my mother and me into captivity: that his castle had been burnt to the ground, and that my father on his return had sold what remained, and was retired into religion in the kingdom of Naples, but where—no man could inform me. Destitute and friendless, hopeless almost of attaining the transport of a parent's embrace, I took the first opportunity of setting sail for Naples, from whence, within these six days, I wandered into this province, still supporting myself by the labour of my hands; nor until yestermorn did I believe that Heaven had reserved any lot for me but peace of mind and contented poverty. This, my lord, is Theodore's story. I am blessed beyond my hope in finding a father; I am unfortunate beyond my desert in having incurred your highness's displeasure." He ceased. A murmur of approbation gently arose from the audience. "This is not all," said Frederic; "I am bound in honour to add what he suppresses. Though he is modest, I must be generous;—he is one of the bravest youths on Christian ground. He is warm too; and from the short knowledge

I have of him, I will pledge myself for his veracity: if what he reports of himself were not true, he would not utter it—and for me, youth, I honour a frankness which becomes thy birth; but now, and thou didst offend me: yet the noble blood which flows in thy veins, may well be allowed to boil out, when it has so recently traced itself to its source. Come, my lord, (turning to Manfred,) if I can pardon him, surely you may; it is not the youth's fault, if you took him for a spectre." This bitter taunt galled the soul of Manfred. "If beings from another world," replied he haughtily, "have power to impress my mind with awe, it is more than living man can do; nor could a stripling's arm—" "My lord," interrupted Hippolita, "your guest has occasion for repose: shall we not leave him to his rest?" Saying this, and taking Manfred by the hand, she took leave of Frederic, and led the company forth. The prince, not sorry to quit a conversation which recalled to mind the discovery he had made of his most secret sensations, suffered himself to be conducted to his own apartment, after permitting Theodore, though under engagement to return to the castle on the morrow (a condition the young man gladly accepted), to retire with his father to the convent. Matilda and Isabella were too much occupied with their own reflections, and too little content with each other, to wish for farther converse that night. They separated each to her chamber, with more expressions of ceremony and fewer of affection than had passed between them since their childhood.

If they parted with small cordiality, they did but meet with greater impatience, as soon as the sun was risen. Their minds were in a situation that excluded sleep, and each recollected a thousand questions which she wished she had put to the other overnight. Matilda reflected that Isabella had been twice delivered by Theodore in very critical situations, which she could not believe accidental. His eyes, it was true, had been fixed on her in Frederic's chamber; but that might have been to disguise his passion for Isabella from the fathers of both. It were better to clear this up. She wished to know the truth, lest she should wrong her friend by entertaining a passion for Isabella's lover. Thus jealousy prompted, and at the same time borrowed an excuse from friendship to justify its curiosity.

Isabella, not less restless, had better foundation for her suspicions. Both Theodore's tongue and eyes had told her his heart was engaged—it was true—yet, perhaps, Matilda might not correspond to his passion:—she had ever appeared insensible to love: all her thoughts were set on Heaven. "Why did I dissuade her?" said Isabella to herself; "I am punished for my generosity—but when did they meet? where?—it cannot be; I have deceived myself—perhaps last night was the first time they ever beheld each other—it must be some other object that has prepossessed his affections—if it is, I am not so unhappy as I thought; if it is not my friend Matilda—how! can I stoop to wish for the affection of a man, who rudely and unnecessarily acquainted me with his indifference? and that at the very moment in which common courtesy demanded at least expressions of civility. I will go to my dear Matilda, who will confirm me in this becoming pride;—man is false—I will advise with her on taking the veil: she will rejoice to find me in this disposition; and I will acquaint her that I no longer oppose her inclination for the cloister." In this frame of mind, and determined to open her heart entirely to Matilda, she went to that princess's chamber, whom she found already dressed, and leaning pensively on her arm. This attitude, so correspondent to what she felt herself, revived Isabella's suspicions, and destroyed the confidence she had purposed to place in her friend. They blushed at meeting, and were too much novices to disguise their sensations with address. After some unmeaning questions and replies, Matilda demanded of Isabella the cause of her flight? The latter, who had almost forgotten Manfred's passion, so entirely was she occupied by her own, concluding that Matilda referred to her last escape from the convent, which had occasioned the events of the preceding evening, replied, "Martelli brought word to the convent that your mother was dead—" "Oh!" said Matilda, interrupting her, "Bianca has explained that mistake to me: on seeing me faint, she cried out, 'The princess is dead!' and Martelli, who had come for the usual dole to the castle—" "And what made you faint?" said Isabella, indifferent to the rest. Matilda blushed and stammered—"My father—he was sitting in judgment on a criminal—" "What criminal?" said Isabella eagerly.—"A young man," said Matilda—"I believe—I think it was that young man that—" "What, Theodore?" said Isabella. "Yes," answered she; "I never saw him before; I do not know how he had offended my father, but as he has been of service to you, I am glad my lord has pardoned him—" "Served me!" replied Isabella; "do you term it serving me, to wound my father, and almost occasion his death? Though it is but since yesterday that I am blessed with knowing a parent, I hope Matilda does not think I am such a stranger to filial tenderness as not to resent the boldness of that audacious youth, and that it is impossible for me ever to feel any affection for one who dared to lift his arm against the author of my being. No, Matilda, my heart abhors him; and if you still retain the friendship for me that you have vowed from your infancy, you will detest a man who has been on the point of making me miserable for ever." Matilda held down her head and replied: "I hope my dearest Isabella does not doubt her Matilda's friendship: I never beheld that youth until yesterday; he is almost a stranger to me: but as the surgeons have pronounced your father out of danger, you ought not to harbour uncharitable resentment against one, who I am persuaded did not know the marquis was related to you."—"You plead his cause very pathetically," said Isabella, "considering he is so much a stranger to you! I am mistaken, or he returns your charity."—"What mean you?" said Matilda.—"Nothing," said Isabella, repenting that she had given Matilda a hint of Theodore's inclination for her. Then changing the discourse, she asked Matilda what occasioned Manfred to take Theodore for a spectre? "Bless me," said Matilda, "did not you observe his extreme resemblance to the portrait of Alfonso in the gallery? I took notice of it to Bianca even before I saw him in armour; but with the helmet on, he is the very image of that picture."—"I do not much observe pictures," said Isabella: "much less have I examined this young man so attentively as you seem to have done—ah? Matilda, your heart is in danger—but let me warn you as a friend—he has owned to me that he is in love; it cannot be with you, for yesterday was the first time you ever met—was it not?"—"Certainly," replied Matilda; "but why does my dearest Isabella conclude from anything I have said, that"—she paused—then continuing: "he saw you first, and I am far from having the vanity to think that my little portion of charms could engage a heart devoted to you:—may you be happy, Isabella, whatever is the fate of Matilda!"—"My lovely friend," said Isabella, whose heart was too honest to resist a kind expression, "it is you that Theodore admires; I saw it; I am persuaded of it; nor shall a thought of my own happiness suffer me to interfere with yours." This frankness drew tears from the gentle Matilda; and jealousy that for a moment had raised a coolness between these amiable maidens soon gave way to the natural sincerity and candour of their souls. Each confessed to the other the impression that Theodore had made on her; and this confidence was followed by a struggle of generosity, each insisting on yielding her claim to her friend. At length the dignity of Isabella's virtue reminding her of the preference which Theodore had almost declared for her rival, made her determine to conquer her passion, and cede the beloved object to her friend.

During this contest of amity, Hippolita entered her daughter's chamber. "Madam," said she to Isabella, "you have so much tenderness for Matilda, and interest yourself so kindly in whatever affects our wretched house, that I can have no secrets with my child which are not proper for you to hear." The princesses were all attention and anxiety. "Know then, madam," continued Hippolita, "and you my dearest Matilda, that being convinced by all the events of these two last ominous days, that heaven purposes the sceptre of Otranto should pass from Manfred's hands into those of the Marquis Frederic, I have been perhaps inspired with the thought of averting our total destruction by the union of our rival houses. With this view I have been proposing to Manfred, my lord, to tender this dear, dear child to Frederic, your father—" "Me to Lord Frederic!" cried Matilda:—"good heavens! my gracious mother—and have you named it to my father?"—"I have," said Hippolita; "he listened benignly to my proposal, and is gone to break it to the marquis."—"Ah! wretched princess!" cried Isabella; "what hast thou done! what ruin has thy inadvertent goodness been preparing for thyself, for me, and for Matilda!"—"Ruin from me to you and to my child!" said Hippolita "what can this mean?"—"Alas!" said Isabella, "the purity of your own heart prevents your seeing the depravity of others. Manfred, your lord, that impious man—" "Hold," said Hippolita; "you must not in my presence, young lady, mention Manfred with disrespect: he is my lord and husband, and—" "Will not long be so," said Isabella, "if his wicked purposes can be carried into execution."—"This language amazes me," said Hippolita. "Your feeling, Isabella, is warm; but until this hour I never knew it betray you into intemperance. What deed of Manfred authorises you to treat him as a murderer, an assassin?"—"Thou virtuous, and too-credulous princess!" replied Isabella; "it is not thy life he aims at—it is to separate himself from thee! to divorce thee! to—" "To divorce me!"— "To divorce my mother!" cried Hippolita and Matilda at once.—"Yes," said Isabella; "and to complete his crime, he meditates—I cannot speak it!"—"What can surpass what thou hast already uttered?" said Matilda. Hippolita was silent. Grief choked her speech; and the recollection of Manfred's late ambiguous discourses confirmed what she heard. "Excellent, dear lady! madam! mother!" cried Isabella, flinging herself at Hippolita's feet in a transport of passion; "trust me, believe me, I will die a thousand deaths sooner than consent to injure you, than yield to so odious—oh!—" "This is too much!" cried Hippolita. "What crimes does one crime suggest! Rise, dear Isabella; I do not doubt your virtue. Oh! Matilda, this stroke is too heavy for thee! weep not, my child; and not a murmur, I charge thee. Remember, he is thy father still!"—"But you are my mother too," said Matilda fervently; "and you are virtuous, you are guiltless!—Oh! must not I, must not I complain?"—"You must not," said Hippolita:—"come, all will yet be well. Manfred, in the agony for the loss of thy brother, knew not what he said; perhaps Isabella misunderstood him; his heart is good—and, my child, thou knowest not all! There is a destiny hangs over us; the hand of Providence is stretched out. Oh! could I but save thee from the wreck!—yes," continued she in a firmer tone, "perhaps the sacrifice of myself may atone for all; I will go and offer myself to this divorce—it boots not what becomes of me. I will withdraw into the neighbouring monastery, and waste the remainder of life in prayers and tears for my child and—the prince!"—"Thou art as much too good for this world," said Isabella, "as Manfred is execrable; but think not, lady, that thy weakness shall determine for me. I swear, hear me all ye angels—" "Stop, I adjure thee," cried Hippolita: "remember thou dost not depend on thyself; thou hast a father—" "My father is too pious, too noble," interrupted Isabella, "to command an impious deed. But should he command it; can a father enjoin a cursed act? I was contracted to the son, can I wed the father? —No, madam, no; force should not drag me to Manfred's hated bed. I loathe him, I abhor him: divine and human laws forbid—and my friend, my dearest Matilda! would I wound her tender soul by injuring her adored mother? my own mother —I never have known another."—"Oh! she is the mother of both!" cried Matilda: "can we, can we, Isabella, adore her too much?"—"My lovely children," said the touched Hippolita, "your tenderness overpowers me—but I must not give way to it. It is not ours to make election for ourselves: Heaven, our fathers, and our husbands must decide for us. Have patience until you hear what Manfred and Frederic have determined. If the marquis accepts Matilda's hand, I know she will readily obey. Heaven may interpose and prevent the rest. What means my child?" continued she, seeing Matilda fall at her feet with a flood of speechless tears. —"But no; answer me not, my daughter: I must not hear a word against the pleasure of thy father."—"Oh! doubt not my obedience, my dreadful obedience to him and to you!" said Matilda: "but can I, most respected of women, can I experience all this tenderness, this world of goodness, and conceal a thought from the best of mothers?"—"What art thou going to utter?" said Isabella trembling. "Recollect thyself, Matilda."—"No, Isabella," said the princess, "I should not deserve this incomparable parent, if the inmost recesses of my soul harboured a thought without her permission—nay, I have offended her; I have suffered a passion to enter my heart without her avowal;—but here I disclaim it; here I vow to heaven and her—" "My child! my child!" said Hippolita, "what words are these! what new calamities has Fate in store for us! Thou, a passion? Thou, in this hour of destruction—" "Oh! I see all my guilt!" said Matilda. "I abhor myself, if I cost my mother a pang. She is the dearest thing I have on earth—Oh! I will never, never behold him more!"—"Isabella," said Hippolita, "thou art conscious to this unhappy secret, whatever it is—Speak!"—"What!" cried Matilda, "have I so forfeited my mother's love, that she will not permit me even to speak my own guilt?—oh! wretched, wretched Matilda!"—"Thou art too cruel," said Isabella to Hippolita: "canst thou behold this anguish of a virtuous mind, and not commiserate it?"—"Not pity my child!" said Hippolita, catching Matilda in her arms; "oh! I know she is good, she is all virtue, all tenderness, and duty. I do forgive thee, my excellent, my only hope!" The princesses then revealed to Hippolita their mutual inclination for Theodore, and the purpose of Isabella to resign him to Matilda. Hippolita blamed their imprudence, and showed them the improbability that either father would consent to bestow his heiress on so poor a man, though nobly born. Some comfort it gave her to find their passion of so recent a date, and that Theodore had had but little cause to suspect it in either. She strictly enjoined them to avoid all correspondence with him. This Matilda fervently promised: but Isabella, who flattered herself that she meant no more than to promote his union with her friend, could not determine to avoid him; and made no reply. "I will go to the convent," said Hippolita, "and order new masses to be said for a deliverance from these calamities."

"Oh! my mother," said Matilda, "you mean to quit us: you mean to take sanctuary, and to give my father an opportunity of pursuing his fatal intention. Alas! on my knees I supplicate you to forbear; will you leave me a prey to Frederic?—I will follow you to the convent."—"Be at peace, my child," said Hippolita: "I will return instantly. I will never abandon thee, until I know it is the will of heaven, and for thy benefit."—"Do not deceive me," said Matilda. "I will not marry Frederic until thou commandest it. Alas! what will become of me?"—"Why that exclamation?" said Hippolita. "I have promised thee to return."—"Ah! my mother," replied Matilda, "stay and save me from myself. A frown from thee can do more than all my father's severity. I have given away my heart, and you alone can make me recall it."—"No more," said Hippolita; "thou must not relapse, Matilda."—"I can quit Theodore," said she, "but must I wed another? let me attend thee to the altar, and shut myself from the world for ever."—"Thy fate depends on thy father," said Hippolita; "I have ill-bestowed my tenderness, if it has taught thee to revere aught beyond him. Adieu! my child: I go to pray for thee."

Hippolita's real purpose was to demand of Jerome, whether in conscience she might not consent to the divorce. She had oft urged Manfred to resign the principality, which the delicacy of her conscience rendered an hourly burthen to her. These scruples concurred to make the separation from her husband appear less dreadful to her than it would have seemed in any other situation.

Jerome, at quitting the castle overnight, had questioned Theodore severely why he had accused him to Manfred of being privy to his escape. Theodore owned it had been with design to prevent Manfred's suspicion from alighting on Matilda; and added, the holiness of Jerome's life and character secured him from the tyrant's wrath. Jerome was heartily grieved to discover his son's inclination for that princess; and leaving him to his rest, promised in the morning to acquaint him with important reasons for conquering his passion. Theodore, like Isabella, was too recently acquainted with parental authority to submit to its decisions against the impulse of his heart. He had little curiosity to learn the friar's reasons, and less disposition to obey them. The lovely Matilda had made stronger impressions on him than filial affection. All night he pleased himself with visions of love; and it was not till late after the morning-office, that he recollected the friar's commands to attend him at Alfonso's tomb.

"Young man," said Jerome, when he saw him, "this tardiness does not please me. Have a father's commands already so little weight?" Theodore made awkward excuses, and attributed his delay to having overslept himself. "And on whom were thy dreams employed?" said the friar sternly. His son blushed. "Come, come," resumed the friar, "inconsiderate youth, this must not be; eradicate this guilty passion from thy breast."—"Guilty passion!" cried Theodore: "Can guilt dwell with innocent beauty and virtuous modesty?"—"It is sinful," replied the friar, "to cherish those whom heaven has doomed to destruction. A tyrant's race must be swept from the earth to the third and fourth generation."—"Will heaven visit the innocent for the crimes of the guilty?" said Theodore. "The fair Matilda has virtues enough—" "To undo thee," interrupted Jerome. "Hast thou so soon forgotten that twice the savage Manfred has pronounced thy sentence?"—"Nor have I forgotten, sir," said Theodore, "that the charity of his daughter delivered me from his power. I can forget injuries, but never benefits."—"The injuries thou hast received from Manfred's race," said the friar, "are beyond what thou canst conceive. Reply not, but view this holy image! Beneath this marble monument rest the ashes of the good Alfonso; a prince adorned with every virtue: the father of his people! the delight of mankind! Kneel, headstrong boy, and list, while a father unfolds a tale of horror that will expel every sentiment from thy soul, but sensations of sacred vengeance.—Alfonso! much injured prince! let thy unsatisfied shade sit awful on the troubled air, while these trembling lips—Ha! who comes there?"—"The most wretched of women!" said Hippolita, entering the choir. "Good father, art thou at leisure?—But why this kneeling youth? what means the horror imprinted on each countenance?—why at this venerable tomb?—Alas! hast thou seen aught?"—"We were pouring forth our orisons to heaven," replied the friar, with some confusion, "to put an end to the woes of this deplorable province. Join with us, lady! thy spotless soul may obtain an exemption from the judgments which the portents of these days but too speakingly denounce against thy house."—"I pray fervently to heaven to divert them," said the pious princess. "Thou knowest it has been the occupation of my life to wrest a blessing for my lord and my harmless children. —One alas! is taken from me! would heaven but hear me for my poor Matilda! Father! intercede for her!"—"Every heart will bless her," cried Theodore with rapture. "Be dumb, rash youth!" said Jerome. "And thou, fond princess, contend not with the powers above!—The Lord giveth, and the Lord taketh away: bless his holy name, and submit to his decrees."—"I do most devoutly," said Hippolita; "but will he not spare my only comfort? must Matilda perish too?—ah! father, I came—but dismiss thy son. No ear but thine must hear what I have to utter." —"May Heaven grant thy every wish, most excellent princess!" said Theodore retiring. Jerome frowned.

Hippolita then acquainted the friar with the proposal she had suggested to Manfred, his approbation of it, and the tender of Matilda that he was gone to make to Frederic. Jerome could not conceal his dislike of the notion, which he covered under pretence of the improbability that Frederic, the nearest of blood to Alfonso, and who was come to claim his succession, would yield to an alliance with the usurper of his right. But nothing could equal the perplexity of the friar, when Hippolita confessed her readiness not to oppose the separation, and demanded his opinion on the legality of her acquiescence. The friar caught eagerly at her request of his advice, and without explaining his aversion to the proposed marriage of Manfred and Isabella, he painted to Hippolita in the most alarming colours the sinfulness of her consent, denounced judgments against her if she complied, and enjoined her in the severest terms to treat any such proposition with every mark of indignation and refusal.

Manfred, in the mean time, had broken his purpose to Frederic, and proposed the double marriage. That weak prince, who had been struck with the charms of Matilda, listened but too eagerly to the offer. He forgot his enmity to Manfred, whom he saw but little hope of dispossessing by force; and flattering himself that no issue might succeed from the union of his daughter with the tyrant, he looked upon his own succession to the principality as facilitated by wedding Matilda. He made faint opposition to the proposal; affecting, for form only, not to acquiesce unless Hippolita should consent to the divorce. Manfred took that upon himself. Transported with his success, and impatient to see himself in a situation to expect sons, he hastened to his wife's apartment, determined to extort her compliance. He learned with indignation that she was absent at the convent. His guilt suggested to him that she had probably been informed by Isabella of his purpose. He doubted whether her retirement to the convent did not import an intention of remaining there, until she could raise obstacles to their divorce; and the suspicions he had already entertained of Jerome, made him apprehend that the friar would not only traverse his views, but might have inspired Hippolita with the resolution of talking sanctuary. Impatient to unravel this clue, and to defeat its success, Manfred hastened to the convent, and arrived there as the friar was earnestly exhorting the princess never to yield to the divorce.

"Madam," said Manfred, "what business drew you hither? why did you not await my return from the marquis?"—"I came to implore a blessing on your councils," replied Hippolita. "My councils do not need a friar's intervention," said Manfred; "and of all men living is that hoary traitor the only one whom you delight to confer with?"—"Profane prince!" said Jerome; "is it at the altar that thou choosest to insult the servants of the altar?—But, Manfred, thy impious schemes are known. Heaven and this virtuous lady know them—nay, frown not, prince. The church despises thy menaces. Her thunders will be heard above thy wrath. Dare to proceed in thy cursed purpose of a divorce, until her sentence be known, and here I lance her anathema at thy head."—"Audacious rebel!" said Manfred, endeavouring to conceal the awe with which the friar's words inspired him. "Dost thou presume to threaten thy lawful prince?"—"Thou art no lawful prince," said Jerome; "thou art no prince,—go, discuss thy claim with Frederic; and when that is done—" "It is done," replied Manfred; "Frederic accepts Matilda's hand, and is content to waive his claim, unless I have no male issue." As he spoke those words three drops of blood fell from the nose of Alfonso's statue. Manfred turned pale, and the princess sank on her knees. "Behold!" said the friar; "mark this miraculous indication that the blood of Alfonso will never mix with that of Manfred!"—"My gracious lord," said Hippolita, "let us submit ourselves to Heaven. Think not thy ever obedient wife rebels against thy authority. I have no will but that of my lord and the Church. To that revered tribunal let us appeal. It does not depend on us to burst the bonds that unite us. If the Church shall approve the dissolution of our marriage, be it so. —I have but few years, and those of sorrow, to pass. Where can they be worn away so well as at the foot of this altar, in prayers for thine and Matilda's safety?" —"But thou shalt not remain here until then," said Manfred. "Repair with me to the castle, and there I will advise on the proper measures for a divorce;—but this meddling friar comes not thither; my hospitable roof shall never more harbour a traitor;—and for thy reverence's offspring," continued he, "I banish him from my dominions. He, I ween, is no sacred personage, nor under the protection of the Church. Whoever weds Isabella, it shall not be Father Falconara's started-up son."—"They start up," said the friar, "who are suddenly beheld in the seat of lawful princes; but they wither away like the grass, and their place knows them no more." Manfred, casting a look of scorn at the friar, led Hippolita forth; but at the door of the church whispered one of his attendants to remain concealed about the convent, and bring him instant notice, if any one from the castle should repair thither.

V

EVERY REFLECTION WHICH MANFRED MADE ON THE FRIAR'S BEHAVIOUR, conspired to persuade him that Jerome was privy to an amour between Isabella and Theodore. But Jerome's new presumption, so dissonant from his former meekness, suggested still deeper apprehensions. The prince even suspected that the friar depended on some secret support from Frederic, whose arrival, coinciding with the novel appearance of Theodore, seemed to bespeak a correspondence. Still more was he troubled with the resemblance of Theodore to Alfonso's portrait. The latter he knew had unquestionably died without issue. Frederic had consented to bestow Isabella on him. These contradictions agitated his mind with numberless pangs. He saw but two methods of extricating himself from his difficulties. The one was to resign his dominions to the marquis.—Pride, ambition, and his reliance on ancient prophecies, which had pointed out a possibility of his preserving them to his posterity, combated that thought. The other was to press his marriage with Isabella. After long ruminating on these anxious thoughts, as he marched silently with Hippolita to the castle, he at last discoursed with that princess on the subject of his disquiet, and used every insinuating and plausible argument to extract her consent to, even her promise of promoting the divorce. Hippolita needed little persuasions to bend her to his pleasure. She endeavoured to win him over to the measure of resigning his dominions; but finding her exhortations fruitless, she assured him, that as far as her conscience would allow, she would raise no opposition to a separation, though without better founded scruples than what he yet alleged, she would not engage to be active in demanding it.

This compliance, though inadequate, was sufficient to raise Manfred's hopes. He trusted that his power and wealth would easily advance his suit at the court of Rome, whither he resolved to engage Frederic to take a journey on purpose. That prince had discovered so much passion for Matilda, that Manfred hoped to obtain all he wished by holding out or withdrawing his daughter's charms, according as the marquis should appear more or less disposed to co-operate in his views. Even the absence of Frederic would be a material point gained, until he could take further measures for his security.

Dismissing Hippolita to her apartment, he repaired to that of the marquis; but crossing the great hall through which he was to pass he met Bianca. The damsel he knew was in the confidence of both the young ladies. It immediately occurred to him to sift her on the subject of Isabella and Theodore. Calling her aside into the recess of the oriel window of the hall, and soothing her with many fair words and promises, he demanded of her whether she knew aught of the state of Isabella's affections. "I! my lord! no my lord—yes my lord—poor lady! she is wonderfully alarmed about her father's wounds; but I tell her he will do well; don't your highness think so?"—"I do not ask you," replied Manfred, "what she thinks about her father; but you are in her secrets. Come, be a good girl and tell me; is there any young man—? ha!—you understand me"—"Lord bless me! understand your highness? no, not I. I told her a few vulnerary herbs and repose—" "I am not talking," replied the prince, impatiently, "about her father; I know he will do well—" "Bless me, I rejoice to hear your highness say so; for though I thought it not right to let my young lady despond, methought his greatness had a wan look, and a something—I remember when young Ferdinand was wounded by the Venetian—" "Thou answerest from the point," interrupted Manfred; "but here, take this jewel, perhaps that may fix thy attention—nay, no reverences; my favour shall not stop here—come, tell me truly; how stands Isabella's heart?"—"Well! your highness has such a way!" said Bianca—"to be sure—but can your highness keep a secret? if it should ever come out of your lips—" "It shall not, it shall not," cried Manfred. "Nay, but swear, your highness—by my halidame, if it should ever be known that I said it—why, truth is truth, I do not think my Lady Isabella ever much affectioned my young lord your son—yet he was a sweet youth as one should see; I am sure, if I had been a princess—but bless me! I must attend my Lady Matilda; she will marvel what is become of me."—"Stay," cried Manfred; "thou hast not satisfied my question. Hast thou ever carried any message, any letter—" "I! good gracious!" cried Bianca; "I carry a letter? I would not to be a queen. I hope your highness thinks, though I am poor, I am honest. Did your highness never hear what Count Marsigli offered me, when he came a wooing to my Lady Matilda?"—"I have not leisure," said Manfred, "to listen to thy tale. I do not question thy honesty. But it is thy duty to conceal nothing from me. How long has Isabella been acquainted with Theodore?"—"Nay, there is nothing can escape your highness!" said Bianca; "not that I know any thing of the matter—Theodore, to be sure, is a proper young man, and, as my Lady Matilda says, the very image of good Alfonso. Has not your highness remarked it?" "Yes, yes,—No—thou torturest me," said Manfred: "where did they meet? when?"—"Who! my Lady Matilda?" said Bianca. "No, no, not Matilda: Isabella; when did Isabella first become acquainted with this Theodore!"—"Virgin Mary!" said Bianca, "how should I know?"—"Thou dost know," said Manfred; "and I must know; I will—" "Lord! your highness is not jealous of young Theodore!" said Bianca. "Jealous! no, no. Why should I be jealous? perhaps I mean to unite them—If I were sure Isabella would have no repugnance—" "Repugnance!

no, I'll warrant her," said Bianca; "he is as comely a youth as ever trod on Christian ground. We are all in love with him; there is not a soul in the castle but would be rejoiced to have him for our prince:—I mean, when it shall please Heaven to call your highness to itself."—"Indeed!" said Manfred, "has it gone so far! oh! this cursed friar!—but I must not lose time—go, Bianca, attend Isabella; but I charge thee, not a word of what has passed. Find out how she is affected towards Theodore; bring me good news, and that ring has a companion. Wait at the foot of the winding staircase: I am going to visit the marquis, and will talk further with thee at my return."

Manfred, after some general conversation, desired Frederic to dismiss the two knights, his companions, having to talk with him on urgent affairs. As soon as they were alone, he began in artful guise to sound the marquis on the subject of Matilda; and finding him disposed to his wish, he let drop hints on the difficulties that would attend the celebration of their marriage, unless—At that instant Bianca burst into the room with a wildness in her look and gestures that spoke the utmost terror. "Oh! my lord, my lord!" cried she; "we are all undone! it is come again! it is come again!"—"What is come again?" cried Manfred amazed. "Oh! the hand! the giant! the hand!—support me! I am terrified out of my senses," cried Bianca. "I will not sleep in the castle to-night. Where shall I go? my things may come after me tomorrow—would I had been content to wed Francesco! this comes of ambition!" —"What has terrified thee thus, young woman?" said the marquis. "Thou art safe here; be not alarmed."—"Oh! your greatness is wonderfully good," said Bianca, "but I dare not—no, pray let me go—I had rather leave everything behind me, than stay another hour under this roof."—"Go to, thou hast lost thy senses," said Manfred. "Interrupt us not; we were communing on important matters:—My lord, this wench is subject to fits—Come with me, Bianca."—"Oh! the saints! No," said Bianca, "for certain it comes to warn your highness; why should it appear to me else? I say my prayers morning and evening.—Oh! if your highness had believed Diego! 'Tis the same hand that he saw the foot to in the gallery-chamber—Father Jerome has often told us the prophecy would be out one of these days—'Bianca,' said he, 'mark my words—'" "Thou ravest," said Manfred, in a rage; "be gone, and keep these fooleries to frighten thy companions."—"What! my lord," cried Bianca, "do you think I have seen nothing? go to the foot of the great stairs yourself—as I live I saw it."—"Saw what? tell us, fair maid, what thou hast seen," said Frederic. "Can your highness listen," said Manfred, "to the delirium of a silly wench, who has heard stories of apparitions until she believes them?"—"This is more than fancy," said the marquis; "her terror is too natural and too strongly impressed to be the work of imagination. Tell us, fair maiden, what it is has moved thee thus?"—"Yes, my lord, thank your greatness," said Bianca; "I believe I look very pale; I shall be better when I have recovered myself—I was going to my Lady Isabella's chamber, by his highness's order—" "We do not want the circumstances," interrupted Manfred, "since his highness will have it so, proceed; but be brief."—"Lord! your highness thwarts one so!" replied Bianca; "I fear my hair—I am sure I never in my life—well! as I was telling your greatness, I was going by his highness's order to my Lady Isabella's chamber; she lies in the watchet-coloured chamber, on the right hand, one pair of stairs: so when I came to the great stairs—I was looking on his Highness's present here—" "Grant me patience!" said Manfred, "will this wench never come to the point? what imports it to the marquis, that I gave thee a bauble for thy faithful attendance on my daughter?—We want to know what thou sawest." —"I was going to tell your highness," said Bianca, "if you would permit me.—So as I was rubbing the ring—I am sure I had not gone up three steps, but I heard the rattling of armour; for all the world such a clatter as Diego says he heard when the giant turned him about in the gallery-chamber."—"What giant is this, my lord?" said the marquis; "is your castle haunted by giants and goblins?"—"Lord! what, has not your greatness heard the story of the giant in the gallery-chamber?" cried Bianca. "I marvel his highness has not told you; mayhap you do not know there is a prophecy—" "This trifling is intolerable," interrupted Manfred. "Let us dismiss this silly wench, my lord! we have more important affairs to discuss." "By your favour," said Frederic, "these are no trifles:—the enormous sabre I was directed to in the wood, yon casque, its fellow;—are these visions of this poor maiden's brain?"—"So Jaquez thinks, may it please your greatness," said Bianca. "He says this moon will not be out without our seeing some strange revolution. For my part, I should not be surprised if it was to happen to-morrow; for, as I was saying, when I heard the clattering of armour, I was all in a cold sweat. I looked up, and, if your greatness will believe me, I saw upon the uppermost banister of the great stairs a hand in armour as big as big—I thought I should have swooned;—I never stopped until I came hither.—Would I were well out of this castle. My lady Matilda told me but yester-morning that her highness Hippolita knows something—" "Thou art an insolent!" cried Manfred. "Lord marquis, it much misgives me that this scene is concerted to affront me. Are my own domestics suborned to spread tales injurious to my honour? Pursue your claim by manly daring; or let us bury our feuds, as was proposed, by the intermarriage of our children. But trust me, it ill becomes a prince of your bearing to practise on mercenary wenches."—"I scorn your imputation," said Frederic: "until this hour I never set eyes on this damsel: I have given her no jewel: my lord, my lord, your conscience, your guilt accuses you, and would throw the suspicion on me—but keep your daughter, and think no more of Isabella. The judgments already fallen on your house forbid me matching into it."

Manfred, alarmed at the resolute tone in which Frederic delivered these words, endeavoured to pacify him. Dismissing Bianca, he made such submissions to the marquis, and threw in such artful encomiums on Matilda, that Frederic was once more staggered. However, as his passion was of so recent a date, it could not at once surmount the scruples he had conceived. He had gathered enough from Bianca's discourse to persuade him that heaven declared itself against Manfred. The proposed marriages too removed his claim to a distance; and the principality of Otranto was a stronger temptation than the contingent reversion of it with Matilda. Still he would not absolutely recede from his engagements; but purposing to gain time, he demanded of Manfred if it was true in fact that Hippolita consented to the divorce. The prince, transported to find no other obstacle, and depending on his influence over his wife, assured the marquis it was so, and that he might satisfy himself of the truth from her own mouth.

As they were thus discoursing, word was brought that the banquet was prepared. Manfred conducted Frederic to the great hall, where they were received by Hippolita and the young princesses. Manfred placed the marquis next to Matilda, and seated himself between his wife and Isabella. Hippolita comported herself with an easy gravity; but the young ladies were silent and melancholy. Manfred, who was determined to pursue his point with the marquis in the remainder of the evening, pushed on the feast until it waxed late; affecting unrestrained gaiety, and plying Frederic with repeated goblets of wine. The latter, more upon his guard than Manfred wished, declined his frequent challenges, on pretence of his late loss of blood; while the prince, to raise his own disordered spirits, and to counterfeit unconcern, indulged himself in plentiful draughts, though not to the intoxication of his senses.

The evening being far advanced, the banquet concluded. Manfred would have withdrawn with Frederic; but the latter pleading weakness and want of repose, retired to his chamber, gallantly telling the prince that his daughter should amuse his highness until himself could attend him. Manfred accepted the party, and to the no small grief of Isabella, accompanied her to her apartment. Matilda waited on her mother to enjoy the freshness of the evening on the ramparts of the castle.

Soon as the company were dispersed their several ways, Frederic, quitting his chamber, inquired if Hippolita was alone, and was told by one of her attendants, who had not noticed her going forth, that at that hour she generally withdrew to her oratory, where he probably would find her. The marquis, during the repast, had beheld Matilda with increase of passion. He now wished to find Hippolita in the disposition her lord had promised. The portents that had alarmed him were forgotten in his desires. Stealing softly and unobserved to the apartment of Hippolita, he entered it with a resolution to encourage her acquiescence to the divorce, having perceived that Manfred was resolved to make the possession of Isabella an unalterable condition, before he would grant Matilda to his wishes.

The marquis was not surprised at the silence that reigned in the princess's apartment. Concluding her, as he had been advertised, in her oratory, he passed on. The door was ajar; the evening gloomy and overcast. Pushing open the door gently, he saw a person kneeling before the altar. As he approached nearer, it seemed not a woman, but one in a long woollen weed, whose back was towards him. The person seemed absorbed in prayer. The marquis was about to return, when the figure, rising, stood some moments fixed in meditation, without regarding him. The marquis, expecting the holy person to come forth, and meaning to excuse his uncivil interruption, said, "Reverend father, I sought the lady Hippolita."—"Hippolita!" replied a hollow voice; "camest thou to this castle to seek Hippolita?" and then the figure, turning slowly round, discovered to Frederic the fleshless jaws and empty sockets of a skeleton, wrapt in a hermit's cowl. "Angels of grace protect me!" cried Frederic, recoiling. "Deserve their protection!" said the spectre. Frederic, falling on his knees, adjured the phantom to take pity on him. "Dost thou not remember me?" said the apparition. "Remember the wood of Joppa!"—"Art thou that holy hermit?" cried Frederic, trembling. "Can I do aught for thy eternal peace?"—"Wast thou delivered from bondage," said the spectre, "to pursue carnal delights? Hast thou forgotten the buried sabre, and the behest of heaven engraven on it?"—"I have not, I have not," said Frederic; "but say, blest spirit, what is thy errand to me? what remains to be done?"—"To forget Matilda!" said the apparition; and vanished.

Frederic's blood froze in his veins. For some minutes he remained motionless. Then falling prostrate on his face before the altar, he besought the intercession of every saint for pardon. A flood of tears succeeded to this transport; and the image of the beauteous Matilda rushing in spite of him on his thoughts, he lay on the ground in a conflict of penitence and passion. Ere he could recover from this agony of his spirits, the princess Hippolita with a taper in her hand entered the oratory alone. Seeing a man without motion on the floor, she gave a shriek, concluding him dead. Her fright brought Frederic to himself. Rising suddenly, his face bedewed with tears, he would have rushed from her presence; but Hippolita stopping him, conjured him in the most plaintive accents to explain the cause of his disorder, and by what strange chance she had found him there in that posture. "Ah, virtuous princess!" said the marquis, penetrated with grief,—and stopped. "For the love of heaven, my lord," said Hippolita, "disclose the cause of this transport! What mean these doleful sounds, this alarming exclamation on my name? What woes has heaven still in store for the wretched Hippolita?—Yet silent?—By every pitying angel, I adjure thee, noble prince," continued she, falling at his feet, "to disclose the purport of what lies at thy heart.—I see thou feelest for me; thou feelest the sharp pangs that thou inflictest—speak, for pity!—does aught thou knowest concern my child?"—"I cannot speak," cried Frederic, bursting from her—"oh, Matilda!"

Quitting the princess thus abruptly, he hastened to his own apartment. At the door of it he was accosted by Manfred, who flushed by wine and love had come to seek him, and to propose to waste some hours of the night in music and revelling. Frederic, offended at an invitation so dissonant from the mood of his soul, pushed him rudely aside, and entering his chamber, flung the door intemperately against Manfred, and bolted it inwards. The haughty prince, enraged at this unaccountable behaviour, withdrew in a frame of mind capable of the most fatal excesses. As he crossed the court, he was met by the domestic whom he had planted at the convent as a spy on Jerome and Theodore. This man, almost breathless with the haste he had made, informed his lord that Theodore, and some lady from the castle were, at that instant, in private conference at the tomb of Alfonso in St. Nicholas's church. He had dogged Theodore thither, but the gloominess of the night had prevented his discovering who the woman was.

Manfred, whose spirits were inflamed, and whom Isabella had driven from her on his urging his passion with too little reserve, did not doubt but the inquietude she had expressed had been occasioned by her impatience to meet Theodore. Provoked by this conjecture, and enraged at her father, he hastened secretly to the great church. Gliding softly between the aisles, and guided by an imperfect gleam of moonshine that shone faintly through the illuminated windows, he stole towards the tomb of Alfonso, to which he was directed by indistinct whispers of the persons he sought. The first sounds he could distinguish were—"Does it, alas! depend on me? Manfred will never permit our union—" "No, this shall prevent it!" cried the tyrant, drawing his dagger, and plunging it over her shoulder into the bosom of the person that spoke—"Ah, me, I am slain!" cried Matilda, sinking: "good Heaven, receive my soul!"—"Savage, inhuman monster, what hast thou done!" cried Theodore, rushing on him, and wrenching his dagger from him. "Stop, stop thy impious hand!" cried Matilda; "it is my father!" Manfred, waking as from a trance, beat his breast, twisted his hands in his locks, and endeavoured to recover his dagger from Theodore to despatch himself. Theodore, scarce less distracted, and only mastering the transports of his grief to assist Matilda, had now by his cries drawn some of the monks to his aid. While part of them endeavoured, in concert with the afflicted Theodore, to stop the blood of the dying princess, the rest prevented Manfred from laying violent hands on himself.

Matilda, resigning herself patiently to her fate, acknowledged with looks of grateful love the zeal of Theodore. Yet oft as her faintness would permit her speech its way, she begged the assistants to comfort her father. Jerome, by this time, had learnt the fatal news, and reached the church. His looks seemed to reproach Theodore, but turning to Manfred, he said, "Now, tyrant! behold the completion of woe fulfilled on thy impious and devoted head! The blood of Alfonso cried to heaven for vengeance; and heaven has permitted its altar to be polluted by assassination, that thou mightest shed thy own blood at the foot of that prince's sepulchre!"—"Cruel man!" cried Matilda, "to aggravate the woes of a parent; may heaven bless my father, and forgive him as I do! My lord, my gracious sire, dost thou forgive thy child? Indeed, I came not hither to meet Theodore. I found him praying at this tomb, whither my mother sent me to intercede for thee, for her—dearest father, bless your child, and say you forgive her."—"Forgive thee!—Murderous monster!" cried Manfred, "can assassins forgive? I took thee for Isabella; but heaven directed my bloody hand to the heart of my child. —Oh, Matilda!—I cannot utter it—canst thou forgive the blindness of my rage?"—"I can, I do; and may heaven confirm it!" said Matilda:—"but while I have life to ask it—oh! my mother! what will she feel?—will you comfort her, my lord? Will you not put her away? Indeed she loves you! Oh, I am faint! bear me to the castle. Can I live to have her close my eyes?"

Theodore and the monks besought her earnestly to suffer herself to be borne into the convent; but her instances were so pressing to be carried to the castle, that placing her on a litter, they conveyed her thither as she requested. Theodore, supporting her head with his arm, and hanging over her in an agony of despairing love, still endeavoured to inspire her with hopes of life. Jerome, on the other side, comforted her with discourses of heaven, and holding a crucifix before her, which she bathed with innocent tears, prepared her for her passage to immortality. Manfred, plunged in the deepest affliction, followed the litter in despair.

Ere they reached the castle, Hippolita, informed of the dreadful catastrophe, had flown to meet her murdered child; but when she saw the afflicted procession, the mightiness of her grief deprived her of her senses, and she fell lifeless to the earth in a swoon. Isabella and Frederic, who attended her, were overwhelmed in almost equal sorrow. Matilda alone seemed insensible to her own situation: every thought was lost in tenderness for her mother. Ordering the litter to stop, as soon as Hippolita was brought to herself, she asked for her father. He approached, unable to speak. Matilda, seizing his hand and her mother's, locked them in her own, and then clasped them to her heart. Manfred could not support this act of pathetic piety. He dashed himself on the ground, and cursed the day he was born. Isabella, apprehensive that these struggles of passion were more than Matilda could support, took upon herself to order Manfred to be borne to his apartment, while she caused Matilda to be conveyed to the nearest chamber. Hippolita, scarce more alive than her daughter, was regardless of everything but her; but when the tender Isabella's care would have likewise removed her, while the surgeons examined Matilda's wound, she cried, "Remove me! Never, never! I lived but in her, and will expire with her." Matilda raised her eyes at her mother's voice, but closed them again without speaking. Her sinking pulse and the damp coldness of her hand soon dispelled all hopes of recovery. Theodore followed the surgeons into the outer chamber, and heard them pronounce the fatal sentence with a transport equal to phrensy.—"Since she cannot live mine," cried he, "at least she shall be mine in death! Father! Jerome! will you not join our hands?" cried he to the friar, who, with the marquis, had accompanied the surgeons. "What means thy distracted rashness?" said Jerome: "is this an hour for marriage?"—"It is, it is," cried Theodore: "alas! there is no other!"—"Young man, thou art too unadvised," said Frederic. "Dost thou think we are to listen to thy fond transports in this hour of fate? What pretensions hast thou to the princess?"—"Those of a prince," said Theodore; "of the sovereign of Otranto. This reverend man, my father, has informed me who I am."—"Thou ravest," said the marquis. "There is no prince of Otranto but myself, now Manfred, by murder, by sacrilegious murder, has forfeited all pretensions."—"My lord," said Jerome, assuming an air of command, "he tells you true. It was not my purpose the secret should have been divulged so soon, but fate presses onward to its work. What his hot-headed passion has revealed, my tongue confirms. Know, prince, that when Alfonso set sail for the holy land—" "Is this a season for explanations?" cried Theodore. "Father, come and unite me to the princess; she shall be mine! In every other thing I will dutifully obey you. My life! my adored Matilda!" continued Theodore, rushing back into the inner chamber, "will you not be mine? Will you not bless your—" Isabella made signs to him to be silent, apprehending the princess was near her end. "What, is she dead?" cried Theodore; "is it possible!" The violence of his exclamations brought

Matilda to herself. Lifting up her eyes, she looked round for her mother. "Life of my soul, I am here!" cried Hippolita; "think not I will quit thee!"—"Oh! you are too good," said Matilda. "But weep not for me, my mother! I am going where sorrow never dwells—Isabella, thou hast loved me; wouldst thou not supply my fondness to this dear, dear woman?—Indeed I am faint!"—"Oh! my child! my child!" said Hippolita in a flood of tears, "can I not withhold thee a moment?"—"It will not be," said Matilda; "commend me to Heaven.—Where is my father? forgive him, dearest mother, forgive him my death; it was an error. Oh! I had forgotten—dearest mother, I vowed never to see Theodore more;—perhaps that has drawn down this calamity—but it was not intentional—can you pardon me?"—"Oh! wound not my agonising soul!" said Hippolita; "thou never couldst offend me—Alas! she faints! help! help!"—"I would say something more," said Matilda, struggling, "but it cannot be—Isabella—Theodore—for my sake—Oh!—" she expired. Isabella and her women tore Hippolita from the corse; but Theodore threatened destruction to all who attempted to remove him from it. He printed a thousand kisses on her clay-cold hands, and uttered every expression that despairing love could dictate.

Isabella, in the meantime, was accompanying the afflicted Hippolita to her apartment; but, in the middle of the court, they were met by Manfred, who, distracted with his own thoughts, and anxious once more to behold his daughter, was advancing to the chamber where she lay. As the moon was now at its height, he read in the countenances of this unhappy company the event he dreaded. "What! is she dead?" cried he in wild confusion. A clap of thunder at that instant shook the castle to its foundations; the earth rocked, and the clank of more than mortal armour was heard behind. Frederic and Jerome thought the last day was at hand. The latter, forcing Theodore along with them, rushed into the court. The moment Theodore appeared, the walls of the castle behind Manfred were thrown down with a mighty force, and the form of Alfonso, dilated to an immense magnitude, appeared in the centre of the ruins. "Behold in Theodore the true heir of Alfonso!" said the vision: And having pronounced those words, accompanied by a clap of thunder, it ascended solemnly towards heaven, where the clouds parting asunder, the form of St. Nicholas was seen, and receiving Alfonso's shade, they were soon wrapt from mortal eyes in a blaze of glory.

The beholders fell prostrate on their faces, acknowledging the divine will. The first that broke silence was Hippolita. "My lord," said she to the desponding Manfred, "behold the vanity of human greatness!—Conrad is gone! Matilda is no more! In Theodore we view the true prince of Otranto. By what miracle he is so I know not;—suffice it to us, our doom is pronounced! shall we not, can we but dedicate the few deplorable hours we have to live, in deprecating the further wrath of heaven? heaven ejects us;—whither can we fly, but to yon holy cells that yet offer us a retreat."—"Thou guiltless but unhappy woman! unhappy by my crimes!" replied Manfred, "my heart at last is open to thy devout admonitions. Oh! could—but it cannot be—ye are lost in wonder—let me at last do justice on myself! To heap shame on my own head is all the satisfaction I have left to offer to offended Heaven. My story has drawn down these judgments: Let my confession atone—but, ah! what can atone for usurpation and a murdered child?—a child murdered in a consecrated place? List, sirs, and may this bloody record be a warning to future tyrants!"

"Alfonso, ye all know, died in the holy land:—ye would interrupt me; ye would say he came not fairly to his end;—it is most true.—Why else this bitter cup which Manfred must drink to the dregs. Ricardo, my grandfather, was his chamberlain.—I would draw a veil over my ancestor's crimes—but it is in vain! Alfonso died by poison. A fictitious will declared Ricardo his heir. His crimes pursued him,—yet he lost no Conrad, no Matilda! I pay the price of usurpation for all! A storm overtook him. Haunted by his guilt he vowed to St. Nicholas to found a church and two convents, if he lived to reach Otranto. The sacrifice was accepted: the saint appeared to him in a dream, and promised that Ricardo's posterity should reign in Otranto until the rightful owner should be grown too large to inhabit the castle, and as long as issue male from Ricardo's loins should remain to enjoy it —Alas! alas! nor male nor female, except myself, remains of all his wretched race!—I have done;—the woes of these three days speak the rest. How this young man can be Alfonso's heir I know not;—yet I do not doubt it. His are these dominions: I resign them—yet I knew not Alfonso had an heir—I question not the will of Heaven.—Poverty and prayer must fill up the woeful space, until Manfred shall be summoned to Ricardo."

"What remains is my part to declare," said Jerome. "When Alfonso set sail for the holy land he was driven by a storm to the coast of Sicily. The other vessel, which bore Ricardo and his train, as your lordship must have heard, was separated from him."—"It is most true," said Manfred; "and the title you give me is more than an outcast can claim: well! be it so—proceed." Jerome blushed, and continued. "For three months Lord Alfonso was wind-bound in Sicily. There he became enamoured of a fair virgin named Victoria. He was too pious to tempt her to forbidden pleasures. They were married. Yet deeming this amour incongruous with the holy vow of arms by which he was bound, he determined to conceal their nuptials until his return from the crusade, when he purposed to seek and acknowledge her for his lawful wife. He left her pregnant. During his absence she was delivered of a daughter. But scarce had she felt a mother's pangs ere she heard the fatal rumour of her lord's death, and the succession of Ricardo. What could a friendless, helpless woman do? Would her testimony avail? —Yet, my lord, I have an authentic writing—" "It needs not," said Manfred; "the horrors of these days, the vision we have but now seen, all corroborate thy evidence beyond a thousand parchments. Matilda's death and my expulsion—" "Be composed, my lord," said Hippolita; "this holy man did not mean to recall your griefs." Jerome proceeded.

"I shall not dwell on what is needless. The daughter of which Victoria was delivered, was at her maturity bestowed in marriage on me. Victoria died; and the secret remained locked in my breast. Theodore's narrative has told the rest."

The friar ceased. The disconsolate company retired to the remaining part of the castle. In the morning Manfred signed his abdication of the principality, with the approbation of Hippolita, and each took on them the habit of religion in the neighbouring convents. Frederic offered his daughter to the new prince, which Hippolita's tenderness for Isabella concurred to promote: but Theodore's grief was too fresh to admit the thought of another love; and it was not until after frequent discourses with Isabella of his dear Matilda, that he was persuaded he could know no happiness but in the society of one with whom he could for ever indulge the melancholy that had taken possession of his soul.

Metzengerstein

Edgar Allan Poe

Pestis eram vivus—moriens tua mors ero.
—Martin Luther

HORROR AND FATALITY HAVE BEEN STALKING ABROAD IN ALL AGES. Why then give a date to this story I have to tell? Let it suffice to say, that at the period of which I speak, there existed, in the interior of Hungary, a settled although hidden belief in the doctrines of the Metempsychosis. Of the doctrines themselves—that is, of their falsity, or of their probability—I say nothing. I assert, however, that much of our incredulity (as La Bruyere says of all our unhappiness) "*vient de ne pouvoir être seuls*." *

But there are some points in the Hungarian superstition which were fast verging to absurdity. They—the Hungarians—differed very essentially from their Eastern authorities. For example, "*The soul*," said the former—I give the words of an acute and intelligent Parisian—"*ne demeure qu'un seul fois dans un corps sensible: au reste—un cheval, un chien, un homme meme, n'est que la ressemblance peu tangible de ces animaux*."

The families of Berlifitzing and Metzengerstein had been at variance for centuries. Never before were two houses so illustrious, mutually embittered by hostility so deadly. The origin of this enmity seems to be found in the words of an ancient prophecy—"A lofty name shall have a fearful fall when, as the rider over his horse, the mortality of Metzengerstein shall triumph over the immortality of Berlifitzing."

* Mercier, in "*L'an deux mille quarte cents quarante*," seriously maintains the doctrines of the Metempsychosis, and J. D'Israeli says that "no system is so simple and so little repugnant to the understanding." Colonel Ethan Allen, the "Green Mountain Boy," is also said to have been a serious metempsychosist.

To be sure the words themselves had little or no meaning. But more trivial causes have given rise—and that no long while ago—to consequences equally eventful. Besides, the estates, which were contiguous, had long exercised a rival influence in the affairs of a busy government. Moreover, near neighbors are seldom friends; and the inhabitants of the Castle Berlifitzing might look, from their lofty buttresses, into the very windows of the Palace Metzengerstein. Least of all had the more than feudal magnificence, thus discovered, a tendency to allay the irritable feelings of the less ancient and less wealthy Berlifitzings. What wonder, then, that the words, however silly, of that prediction, should have succeeded in setting and keeping at variance two families already predisposed to quarrel by every instigation of hereditary jealousy? The prophecy seemed to imply—if it implied anything—a final triumph on the part of the already more powerful house; and was of course remembered with the more bitter animosity by the weaker and less influential.

Wilhelm, Count Berlifitzing, although loftily descended, was, at the epoch of this narrative, an infirm and doting old man, remarkable for nothing but an inordinate and inveterate personal antipathy to the family of his rival, and so passionate a love of horses, and of hunting, that neither bodily infirmity, great age, nor mental incapacity, prevented his daily participation in the dangers of the chase.

Frederick, Baron Metzengerstein, was, on the other hand, not yet of age. His father, the Minister G——, died young. His mother, the Lady Mary, followed him quickly. Frederick was, at that time, in his eighteenth year. In a city, eighteen years are no long period; but in a wilderness—in so magnificent a wilderness as that old principality, the pendulum vibrates with a deeper meaning.

From some peculiar circumstances attending the administration of his father, the young Baron, at the decease of the former, entered immediately upon his vast possessions. Such estates were seldom held before by a nobleman of Hungary. His castles were without number. The chief in point of splendor and extent was the "Palace Metzengerstein." The boundary line of his dominions was never clearly defined; but his principal park embraced a circuit of fifty miles.

Upon the succession of a proprietor so young, with a character so well known, to a fortune so unparalleled, little speculation was afloat in regard to his probable course of conduct. And, indeed, for the space of three days, the behavior of the heir out-heroded Herod, and fairly surpassed the expectations of his most enthusiastic admirers. Shameful debaucheries—flagrant treacheries—unheard-of atrocities—gave his trembling vassals quickly to understand that no servile submission on their part—no punctilios of conscience on his own—were thenceforward to prove any security against the remorseless fangs of a petty Caligula. On the night of the fourth day, the stables of the Castle Berlifitzing were discovered to be on fire; and the unanimous opinion of the neighborhood added the crime of the incendiary to the already hideous list of the Baron's misdemeanors and enormities.

But during the tumult occasioned by this occurrence, the young nobleman himself, sat apparently buried in meditation, in a vast and desolate upper apartment of the family palace of Metzengerstein. The rich although faded tapestry hangings which swung gloomily upon the walls, represented the shadowy and majestic forms of a thousand illustrious ancestors. *Here*, rich-ermined priests, and pontifical dignitaries, familiarly seated with the autocrat and the sovereign, put a veto on the wishes of a temporal king, or restrained with the fiat of papal supremacy the rebellious sceptre of the Arch-enemy. *There*, the dark, tall statures of the Princes Metzengerstein—their muscular war-coursers plunging over the carcasses of fallen foes—startled the steadiest nerves with their vigorous expression; and *here*, again, the voluptuous and swan-like figures of the dames of days gone by, floated away in the mazes of an unreal dance to the strains of imaginary melody.

But as the Baron listened, or affected to listen, to the gradually increasing uproar in the stables of Berlifitzing—or perhaps pondered upon some more novel, some more decided act of audacity—his eyes were turned unwittingly to the figure of an enormous, and unnaturally colored horse, represented in the tapestry as belonging to a Saracen ancestor of the family of his rival. The horse itself, in the fore-ground of the design, stood motionless and statue-like—while, farther back, its discomfited rider perished by the dagger of a Metzengerstein.

On Frederick's lip arose a fiendish expression, as he became aware of the direction which his glance had, without his consciousness, assumed. Yet he did not remove it. On the contrary, he could by no means account for the overwhelming anxiety which appeared falling like a pall upon his senses. It was with difficulty that he reconciled his dreamy and incoherent feelings with the certainty of being awake. The longer he gazed, the more absorbing became the spell—the more impossible did it appear that he could ever withdraw his glance from the fascination of that tapestry. But the tumult without becoming suddenly more violent, with a compulsory exertion he diverted his attention to the glare of ruddy light thrown full by the flaming stables upon the windows of the apartment.

The action, however, was but momentary; his gaze returned mechanically to the wall. To his extreme horror and astonishment, the head of the gigantic steed had, in the meantime, altered its position. The neck of the animal, before arched, as if in compassion, over the prostrate body of its lord, was now extended, at full length, in the direction of the Baron. The eyes, before invisible, now wore an energetic and human expression, while they gleamed with a fiery and unusual red; and the distended lips of the apparently enraged horse left in full view his sepulchral and disgusting teeth.

Stupified with terror, the young nobleman tottered to the door. As he threw it open, a flash of red light, streaming far into the chamber, flung his shadow with a clear outline against the quivering tapestry; and he shuddered to perceive that shadow—as he staggered awhile upon the threshold—assuming the exact position, and precisely filling up the contour, of the relentless and triumphant murderer of the Saracen Berlifitzing.

To lighten the depression of his spirits, the Baron hurried into the open air. At the principal gate of the palace he encountered three equerries. With much difficulty, and at the imminent peril of their lives, they were restraining the convulsive plunges of a gigantic and fiery-colored horse.

"Whose horse? Where did you get him?" demanded the youth, in a querulous and husky tone, as he became instantly aware that the mysterious steed in the tapestried chamber was the very counterpart of the furious animal before his eyes.

"He is your own property, sire," replied one of the equerries, "at least he is claimed by no other owner. We caught him flying, all smoking and foaming with rage, from the burning stables of the Castle Berlifitzing. Supposing him to have belonged to the old Count's stud of foreign horses, we led him back as an estray. But the grooms there disclaim any title to the creature; which is strange, since he bears evident marks of having made a narrow escape from the flames."

"The letters W. V. B. are also branded very distinctly on his forehead," interrupted a second equerry; "I supposed them, of course, to be the initials of Wilhelm Von Berlifitzing—but all at the castle are positive in denying any knowledge of the horse."

"Extremely singular!" said the young Baron, with a musing air, and apparently unconscious of the meaning of his words. "He is, as you say, a remarkable horse—a prodigious horse! although, as you very justly observe, of a suspicious and untractable character; let him be mine, however," he added, after a pause, "perhaps a rider like Frederick of Metzengerstein, may tame even the devil from the stables of Berlifitzing."

"You are mistaken, my lord; the horse, as I think we mentioned, is *not* from the stables of the Count. If such had been the case, we know our duty better than to bring him into the presence of a noble of your family."

"True!" observed the Baron, drily; and at that instant a page of the bedchamber came from the palace with a heightened color, and a precipitate step. He whispered into his master's ear an account of the sudden disappearance of a small portion of the tapestry, in an apartment which he designated; entering, at the same time, into particulars of a minute and circumstantial character; but from the low tone of voice in which these latter were communicated, nothing escaped to gratify the excited curiosity of the equerries.

The young Frederick, during the conference, seemed agitated by a variety of emotions. He soon, however, recovered his composure, and an expression of determined malignancy settled upon his countenance, as he gave peremptory orders that the apartment in question should be immediately locked up, and the key placed in his own possession.

"Have you heard of the unhappy death of the old hunter Berlifitzing?" said one of his vassals to the Baron, as, after the departure of the page, the huge steed which that nobleman had adopted as his own, plunged and curveted, with redoubled fury, down the long avenue which extended from the palace to the stables of Metzengerstein.

"No!" said the Baron, turning abruptly toward the speaker, "dead! say you?"

"It is indeed true, my lord; and, to the noble of your name, will be, I imagine, no unwelcome intelligence."

A rapid smile shot over the countenance of the listener. "How died he?"

"In his rash exertions to rescue a favorite portion of his hunting stud, he has himself perished miserably in the flames."

"I—n—d—e—e—d—!" ejaculated the Baron, as if slowly and deliberately impressed with the truth of some exciting idea.

"Indeed," repeated the vassal.

"Shocking!" said the youth, calmly, and turned quietly into the palace.

From this date a marked alteration took place in the outward demeanor of the dissolute young Baron Frederick Von Metzengerstein. Indeed, his behaviour disappointed every expectation, and proved little in accordance with the views of many a manœuvring mamma; while his habits and manner, still less than formerly, offered anything congenial with those of the neighboring aristocracy. He was never to be seen beyond the limits of his own domain, and, in this wide and social world, was utterly companionless—unless, indeed, that unnatural, impetuous, and fiery-colored horse, which he henceforward continually bestrode, had any mysterious right to the title of his friend.

Numerous invitations on the part of the neighborhood for a long time, however, periodically came in. "Will the Baron honor our festivals with his presence?" "Will the Baron join us in a hunting of the boar?"—"Metzengerstein does not hunt"; "Metzengerstein will not attend," were the haughty and laconic answers.

These repeated insults were not to be endured by an imperious nobility. Such invitations became less cordial—less frequent—in time they ceased altogether. The widow of the unfortunate Count Berlifitzing was even heard to express a hope "that the Baron might be at home when he did not wish to be at home, since he disdained the company of his equals; and ride when he did not wish to ride, since he preferred the society of a horse." This to be sure was a very silly explosion of hereditary pique; and merely proved how singularly unmeaning our sayings are apt to become, when we desire to be unusually energetic.

The charitable, nevertheless, attributed the alteration in the conduct of the young nobleman to the natural sorrow of a son for the untimely loss of his parents;—forgetting, however, his atrocious and reckless behavior during the short period immediately succeeding that bereavement. Some there were, indeed, who suggested a too haughty idea of self-consequence and dignity. Others again (among them may be mentioned the family physician) did not hesitate in speaking of morbid melancholy, and hereditary ill-health; while dark hints, of a more equivocal nature, were current among the multitude.

Indeed, the Baron's perverse attachment to his lately-acquired charger—an attachment which seemed to attain new strength from every fresh example of the animal's ferocious and demon-like propensities—at length became, in the eyes of all reasonable men, a hideous and unnatural fervor. In the glare of noon—at the dead hour of night—in sickness or in health—in calm or in tempest—the young Metzengerstein seemed riveted to the saddle of that colossal horse, whose intractable audacities so well accorded with his own spirit.

There were circumstances, moreover, which, coupled with late events, gave an unearthly and portentous character to the mania of the rider, and to the capabilities of the steed. The space passed over in a single leap had been accurately measured, and was found to exceed by an astounding difference, the wildest expectations of the most imaginative. The Baron, besides, had no particular *name* for the animal, although all the rest in his collection were distinguished by characteristic appellations. His stable, too, was appointed at a distance from the rest; and with regard to grooming and other necessary offices, none but the owner in person had ventured to officiate, or even to enter the enclosure of that particular stall.

It was also to be observed, that although the three grooms, who had caught the steed as he fled from the conflagration at Berlifitzing, had succeeded in arresting his course, by means of a chain-bridle and noose—yet no one of the three could with any certainty affirm that he had, during that dangerous struggle, or at any period thereafter, actually placed his hand upon the body of the beast. Instances of peculiar intelligence in the demeanor of a noble and high-spirited horse are not to be supposed capable of exciting unreasonable attention, but there were certain circumstances which intruded themselves per force upon the most skeptical and phlegmatic; and it is said there were times when the animal caused the gaping crowd who stood around to recoil in horror from the deep and impressive meaning of his terrible stamp—times when the young Metzengerstein turned pale and shrunk away from the rapid and searching expression of his earnest and human-looking eye.

Among all the retinue of the Baron, however, none were found to doubt the ardor of that extraordinary affection which existed on the part of the young nobleman for the fiery qualities of his horse; at least, none but an insignificant and misshapen little page, whose deformities were in every body's way, and whose opinions were of the least possible importance. He (if his ideas are worth mentioning at all,) had the effrontery to assert that his master never vaulted into the saddle without an unaccountable and almost imperceptible shudder; and that, upon his return from every long-continued and habitual ride, an expression of triumphant malignity distorted every muscle in his countenance.

One tempestuous night, Metzengerstein, awaking from a heavy slumber, descended like a maniac from his chamber, and, mounting in hot haste, bounded away into the mazes of the forest. An occurrence so common attracted no particular attention, but his return was looked for with intense anxiety on the part of his domestics, when, after some hours' absence, the stupendous and magnificent battlements of the Palace Metzengerstein, were discovered crackling and rocking to their very foundation, under the influence of a dense and livid mass of ungovernable fire.

As the flames, when first seen, had already made so terrible a progress that all efforts to save any portion of the building were evidently futile, the astonished neighborhood stood idly around in silent, if not apathetic wonder. But a new and fearful object soon riveted the attention of the multitude, and proved how much more intense is the excitement wrought in the feelings of a crowd by the contemplation of human agony, than that brought about by the most appalling spectacles of inanimate matter.

Up the long avenue of aged oaks which led from the forest to the main entrance of the Palace Metzengerstein, a steed, bearing an unbonneted and disordered rider, was seen leaping with an impetuosity which outstripped the very Demon of the Tempest.

The career of the horseman was indisputably, on his own part, uncontrollable. The agony of his countenance, the convulsive struggle of his frame, gave evidence of superhuman exertion: but no sound, save a solitary shriek, escaped from his lacerated lips, which were bitten through and through in the intensity of terror. One instant, and the clattering of hoofs resounded sharply and shrilly above the roaring of the flames and the shrieking of the winds—another, and, clearing at a single plunge the gate-way and the moat, the steed bounded far up the tottering staircases of the palace, and, with its rider, disappeared amid the whirlwind of chaotic fire.

The fury of the tempest immediately died away, and a dead calm sullenly succeeded. A white flame still enveloped the building like a shroud, and, streaming far away into the quiet atmosphere, shot forth a glare of preternatural light; while a cloud of smoke settled heavily over the battlements in the distinct colossal figure of—*a horse*.

Rappaccini's Daughter

Nathaniel Hawthorne

A YOUNG MAN, NAMED GIOVANNI GUASCONTI, CAME, VERY LONG ago, from the more southern region of Italy, to pursue his studies at the University of Padua. Giovanni, who had but a scanty supply of gold ducats in his pocket, took lodgings in a high and gloomy chamber of an old edifice, which looked not unworthy to have been the palace of a Paduan noble, and which, in fact, exhibited over its entrance the armorial bearings of a family long since extinct. The young stranger, who was not unstudied in the great poem of his country, recollected that one of the ancestors of this family, and perhaps an occupant of this very mansion, had been pictured by Dante as a partaker of the immortal agonies of his Inferno. These reminiscences and associations, together with the tendency to heart-break natural to a young man for the first time out of his native sphere, caused Giovanni to sigh heavily as he looked around the desolate and ill-furnished apartment.

"Holy Virgin, signor!" cried old dame Lisabetta, who, won by the youth's remarkable beauty of person, was kindly endeavoring to give the chamber a habitable air, "what a sigh was that to come out of a young man's heart! Do you find this old mansion gloomy? For the love of heaven, then, put your head out of the window, and you will see as bright sunshine as you have left in Naples."

Guasconti mechanically did as the old woman advised, but could not quite agree with her that the Lombard sunshine was as cheerful as that of southern Italy. Such as it was, however, it fell upon a garden beneath the window and expended its fostering influences on a variety of plants, which seemed to have been cultivated with exceeding care.

"Does this garden belong to the house?" asked Giovanni.

"Heaven forbid, signor!—unless it were fruitful of better pot herbs than any that grow there now," answered old Lisabetta. "No: that garden is cultivated by the own hands of Signor Giacomo Rappaccini, the famous doctor, who, I warrant him, has been heard of as far as Naples. It is said that he distils these plants into medicines that are as potent as a charm. Oftentimes you may see the signor doctor at work, and perchance the signora, his daughter, too, gathering the strange flowers that grow in the garden."

The old woman had now done what she could for the aspect of the chamber, and, commending the young man to the protection of the saints, took her departure.

Giovanni still found no better occupation than to look down into the garden beneath his window. From its appearance, he judged it to be one of those botanic gardens, which were of earlier date in Padua than elsewhere in Italy, or in the world. Or, not improbably, it might once have been the pleasure-place of an opulent family; for there was the ruin of a marble fountain in the centre, sculptured with rare art, but so wofully shattered that it was impossible to trace the original design from the chaos of remaining fragments. The water, however, continued to gush and sparkle into the sunbeams as cheerfully as ever. A little gurgling sound ascended to the young man's window, and made him feel as if the fountain were an immortal spirit that sung its song unceasingly, and without heeding the vicissitudes around it; while one century imbodied it in marble, and another scattered the perishable garniture on the soil. All about the pool into which the water subsided grew various plants, that seemed to require a plentiful supply of moisture for the nourishment of gigantic leaves, and, in some instances, flowers gorgeously magnificent. There was one shrub in particular, set in a marble vase in the midst of the pool, that bore a profusion of purple blossoms, each of which had the lustre and richness of a gem; and the whole together made a show so resplendent that it seemed enough to illuminate the garden, even had there been no sunshine. Every portion of the soil was peopled with plants and herbs, which, if less beautiful, still bore tokens of assiduous care, as if all had their individual virtues, known to the scientific mind that fostered them. Some were placed in urns, rich with old carving, and others in common garden pots; some crept serpent-like along the ground or climbed on high, using whatever means of ascent was offered them. One plant had wreathed itself round a statue of Vertumnus, which was thus quite veiled and shrouded in a drapery of hanging foliage, so happily arranged that it might have served a sculptor for a study.

While Giovanni stood at the window he heard a rustling behind a screen of leaves, and became aware that a person was at work in the garden. His figure soon emerged into view, and showed itself to be that of no common laborer, but a tall, emaciated, sallow, and sickly-looking man, dressed in a scholar's garb of black. He was beyond the middle term of life, with grey hair, a thin grey beard, and a face singularly marked with intellect and cultivation, but which could never, even in his more youthful days, have expressed much warmth of heart.

Nothing could exceed the intentness with which this scientific gardener examined every shrub which grew in his path; it seemed as if he was looking into their inmost nature, making observations in regard to their creative essence, and discovering why one leaf grew in this shape and another in that, and wherefore such and such flowers differed among themselves in hue and perfume. Nevertheless, in spite of this deep intelligence on his part, there was no approach to intimacy between himself and these vegetable existences. On the contrary, he avoided their actual touch or the direct inhaling of their odors, with a caution that impressed Giovanni most disagreeably; for the man's demeanor was that of one walking among malignant influences, such as savage beasts, or deadly snakes, or evil spirits, which, should he allow them one moment of license, would wreak upon him some terrible fatality. It was strangely frightful to the young man's imagination to see this air of insecurity in a person cultivating a garden, that most simple and innocent of human toils, and which had been alike the joy and labor of the unfallen parents of the race. Was this garden, then, the Eden of the present world?—and this man, with such a perception of harm in what his own hands caused to grow, was he the Adam?

The distrustful gardener, while plucking away the dead leaves or pruning the too luxuriant growth of the shrubs, defended his hands with a pair of thick gloves. Nor were these his only armor. When, in his walk through the garden, he came to the magnificent plant that hung its purple gems beside the marble fountain, he placed a kind of mask over his mouth and nostrils, as if all this beauty did but conceal a deadlier malice. But, finding his task still too dangerous, he drew back, removed the mask, and called loudly, but in the infirm voice of a person affected with inward disease:

"Beatrice! Beatrice!"

"Here am I, my father. What would you?" cried a rich and youthful voice from the window of the opposite house; a voice as rich as a tropical sunset, and which made Giovanni, though he knew not why, think of deep hues of purple or crimson and of perfumes heavily delectable—"Are you in the garden?"

"Yes, Beatrice," answered the gardener, "and I need your help."

Soon there emerged from under a sculptured portal the figure of a young girl, arrayed with as much richness of taste as the most splendid of the flowers, beautiful as the day, and with a bloom so deep and vivid that one shade more would have been too much. She looked redundant with life, health, and energy;

all of which attributes were bound down and compressed, as it were and girdled tensely, in their luxuriance, by her virgin zone. Yet Giovanni's fancy must have grown morbid while he looked down into the garden; for the impression which the fair stranger made upon him was as if here were another flower, the human sister of those vegetable ones, as beautiful as they—more beautiful than the richest of them—but still to be touched only with a glove, nor to be approached without a mask. As Beatrice came down the garden path, it was observable that she handled and inhaled the odor of several of the plants which her father had most sedulously avoided.

"Here, Beatrice," said the latter,—"see how many needful offices require to be done to our chief treasure. Yet, shattered as I am, my life might pay the penalty of approaching it so closely as circumstances demand. Henceforth, I fear, this plant must be consigned to your sole charge."

"And gladly will I undertake it," cried again the rich tones of the young lady, as she bent towards the magnificent plant and opened her arms as if to embrace it. "Yes, my sister, my splendour, it shall be Beatrice's task to nurse and serve thee; and thou shalt reward her with thy kisses and perfumed breath, which to her is as the breath of life!"

Then, with all the tenderness in her manner that was so strikingly expressed in her words, she busied herself with such attentions as the plant seemed to require; and Giovanni, at his lofty window, rubbed his eyes and almost doubted whether it were a girl tending her favorite flower, or one sister performing the duties of affection to another. The scene soon terminated. Whether Dr. Rappaccini had finished his labors in the garden, or that his watchful eye had caught the stranger's face, he now took his daughter's arm and retired. Night was already closing in; oppressive exhalations seemed to proceed from the plants and steal upward past the open window; and Giovanni, closing the lattice, went to his couch and dreamed of a rich flower and beautiful girl. Flower and maiden were different, and yet the same, and fraught with some strange peril in either shape.

But there is an influence in the light of morning that tends to rectify whatever errors of fancy, or even of judgment, we may have incurred during the sun's decline, or among the shadows of the night, or in the less wholesome glow of moonshine. Giovanni's first movement, on starting from sleep, was to throw open the window and gaze down into the garden which his dreams had made so fertile of mysteries. He was surprised and a little ashamed to find how real and matter-of-fact an affair it proved to be, in the first rays of the sun which gilded the dew-drops that hung upon leaf and blossom, and, while giving a brighter beauty to each rare flower, brought everything within the limits of ordinary experience. The young man rejoiced that, in the heart of the barren city, he had the privilege of overlooking this spot of lovely and luxuriant vegetation. It would serve, he said to himself, as a symbolic language to keep him in communion with nature. Neither the sickly and thought-worn Dr. Giacomo Rappaccini, it is true, nor his brilliant daughter, were now visible; so that Giovanni could not determine how much of the singularity which he attributed to both, was due to their own qualities and how much to his wonder-working fancy. But he was inclined to take a most rational view of the whole matter.

In the course of the day he paid his respects to Signor Pietro Baglioni, professor of medicine in the university, a physician of eminent repute to whom Giovanni had brought a letter of introduction. The professor was an elderly personage, apparently of genial nature, and habits that might almost be called jovial; he kept the young man to dinner, and made himself very agreeable by the freedom and liveliness of his conversation, especially when warmed by a flask or two of Tuscan wine. Giovanni, conceiving that men of science, inhabitants of the same city, must needs be on familiar terms with one another, took an opportunity to mention the name of Dr. Rappaccini. But the professor did not respond with so much cordiality as he had anticipated.

"Ill would it become a teacher of the divine art of medicine," said Professor Pietro Baglioni, in answer to a question of Giovanni, "to withhold due and well-considered praise of a physician so eminently skilled as Rappaccini. But, on the other hand, I should answer it but scantily to my conscience were I to permit a worthy youth like yourself, Signor Giovanni, the son of an ancient friend, to imbibe erroneous ideas respecting a man who might hereafter chance to hold your life and death in his hands. The truth is, our worshipful Dr. Rappaccini has as much science as any member of the faculty—with perhaps one single exception—in Padua, or all Italy. But there are certain grave objections to his professional character."

"And what are they?" asked the young man.

"Has my friend Giovanni any disease of body or heart, that he is so inquisitive about physicians?" said the Professor, with a smile. "But as for Rappaccini, it is said of him—and I, who know the man well, can answer for its truth—that he cares infinitely more for science than for mankind. His patients are interesting to him only as subjects for some new experiment. He would sacrifice human life, his own among the rest, or whatever else was dearest to him, for the sake of adding so much as a grain of mustard seed to the great heap of his accumulated knowledge."

"Methinks he is an awful man, indeed," remarked Guasconti, mentally recalling the cold and purely intellectual aspect of Rappaccini. "And yet, worshipful Professor, is it not a noble spirit? Are there many men capable of so spiritual a love of science?"

"God forbid," answered the Professor, somewhat testily—"at least, unless they take sounder views of the healing art than those adopted by Rappaccini. It is his theory that all medicinal virtues are comprised within those substances which we term vegetable poisons. These he cultivates with his own hands, and is said even to have produced new varieties of poison, more horribly deleterious than Nature, without the assistance of this learned person, would ever have plagued the world with. That the Signor Doctor does less mischief than might be expected with such dangerous substances is undeniable. Now and then, it must be owned, he has effected—or seemed to effect—a marvellous cure. But, to tell you my private mind, Signor Giovanni, he should receive little credit for such instances of success,—they being probably the work of chance—but should be held strictly accountable for his failures, which may justly be considered his own work."

The youth might have taken Baglioni's opinions with many grains of allowance had he known that there was a professional warfare of long continuance between him and Doctor Rappaccini, in which the latter was generally thought to have gained the advantage. If the reader be inclined to judge for himself, we refer him to certain black-letter tracts on both sides, preserved in the medical department of the University of Padua.

"I know not, most learned Professor," returned Giovanni, after musing on what had been said of Rappaccini's exclusive zeal for science—"I know not how dearly this physician may love his art; but surely there is one object more dear to him. He has a daughter."

"Aha!" cried the Professor with a laugh. "So now our friend Giovanni's secret is out. You have heard of this daughter, whom all the young men in Padua are wild about, though not half a dozen have ever had the good hap to see her face. I know little of the Signora Beatrice save that Rappaccini is said to have instructed her deeply in his science, and that, young and beautiful as fame reports her, she is already qualified to fill a professor's chair. Perchance her father destines her for mine! Other absurd rumors there be, not worth talking about or listening to. So now, Signor Giovanni, drink off your glass of Lachryma."

Guasconti returned to his lodgings somewhat heated with the wine he had quaffed, and which caused his brain to swim with strange fantasies in reference to Dr. Rappaccini and the beautiful Beatrice. On his way, happening to pass by a florist's, he bought a fresh bouquet of flowers.

Ascending to his chamber, he seated himself near the window, but within the shadow thrown by the depth of the wall, so that he could look down into the garden with little risk of being discovered. All beneath his eye was a solitude. The strange plants were basking in the sunshine, and now and then nodding gently to one another, as if in acknowledgment of sympathy and kindred. In the midst, by the shattered fountain, grew the magnificent shrub, with its purple gems clustering all over it; they glowed in the air, and gleamed back again out of the depths of the pool, which thus seemed to overflow with colored radiance from the rich reflection that was steeped in it. At first, as we have said, the garden was a solitude. Soon, however,—as Giovanni had half hoped, half feared, would be the case,—a figure appeared beneath the antique sculptured portal, and came down between the rows of plants, inhaling their various perfumes as if she were one of those beings of old classic fable that lived upon sweet odors. On again beholding Beatrice, the young man was even startled to perceive how much her beauty exceeded his recollection of it; so brilliant, so vivid, was its character, that she glowed amid the sunlight, and, as Giovanni whispered to himself, positively illuminated the more shadowy intervals of the garden path. Her face being now more revealed than on the former occasion, he was struck by its expression of simplicity and sweetness; qualities that had not entered into his idea of her character, and which made him ask anew what manner of mortal she might be. Nor did he fail again to observe, or imagine, an analogy between the beautiful girl and the gorgeous shrub that hung its gemlike flowers over the fountain; a resemblance which Beatrice seemed to have indulged a fantastic humor in heightening, both by the arrangement of her dress and the selection of its hues.

Approaching the shrub, she threw open her arms, as with a passionate ardor, and drew its branches into an intimate embrace; so intimate that her features were hidden in its leafy bosom, and her glistening ringlets all intermingled with the flowers.

"Give me thy breath, my sister," exclaimed Beatrice; "for I am faint with common air! And give me this flower of thine, which I separate with gentlest fingers from the stem, and place it close beside my heart."

With these words the beautiful daughter of Rappaccini plucked one of the richest blossoms of the shrub, and was about to fasten it in her bosom. But now, unless Giovanni's draughts of wine had bewildered his senses, a singular incident occurred. A small orange-colored reptile, of the lizard or chameleon species, chanced to be creeping along the path, just at the feet of Beatrice. It appeared to Giovanni—but, at the distance from which he gazed, he could scarcely have seen anything so minute—it appeared to him, however, that a drop or two of moisture from the broken stem of the flower descended upon the lizard's head. For an instant the reptile contorted itself violently, and then lay motionless in the sunshine. Beatrice observed this remarkable phenomenon, and crossed herself, sadly, but without surprise; nor did she therefore hesitate to arrange the fatal flower in her bosom. There it blushed, and almost glimmered with the dazzling effect of a precious stone, adding to her dress and aspect the one appropriate charm which nothing else in the world could have supplied. But Giovanni, out of the shadow of his window, bent forward and shrank back, and murmured and trembled.

"Am I awake? Have I my senses?" said he to himself. "What is this being?—beautiful, shall I call her?—or inexpressibly terrible?"

Beatrice now strayed carelessly through the garden, approaching closer beneath Giovanni's window, so that he was compelled to thrust his head quite out of its concealment, in order to gratify the intense and painful curiosity which she excited. At this moment there came a beautiful insect over the garden wall; it had perhaps wandered through the city, and found no flowers or verdure among those antique haunts of men, until the heavy perfumes of Dr. Rappaccini's shrubs had lured it from afar. Without alighting on the flowers, this winged brightness seemed to be attracted by Beatrice, and lingered in the air and fluttered about her head. Now, here it could not be but that Giovanni Guasconti's eyes deceived him. Be that as it might, he fancied that, while Beatrice was gazing at the insect with childish delight, it grew faint and fell at her feet!—its bright wings shivered! it was dead!—from no cause that he could discern, unless it were the atmosphere of her breath. Again Beatrice crossed herself and sighed heavily as she bent over the dead insect.

An impulsive movement of Giovanni drew her eyes to the window. There she beheld the beautiful head of the young man—rather a Grecian than an Italian head, with fair, regular features, and a glistening of gold among his ringlets—gazing down upon her like a being that hovered in mid-air. Scarcely knowing what he did, Giovanni threw down the bouquet which he had hitherto held in his hand.

"Signora," said he, "there are pure and healthful flowers. Wear them for the sake of Giovanni Guasconti."

"Thanks, signor," replied Beatrice, with her rich voice, that came forth as it were like a gush of music; and with a mirthful expression half childish and half woman-like. "I accept your gift, and would fain recompense it with this precious purple flower; but if I toss it into the air, it will not reach you. So Signor Guasconti must even content himself with my thanks."

She lifted the bouquet from the ground, and then, as if inwardly ashamed at having stepped aside from her maidenly reserve to respond to a stranger's greeting, passed swiftly homeward through the garden. But few as the moments were, it seemed to Giovanni, when she was on the point of vanishing beneath the sculptured portal, that his beautiful bouquet was already beginning to wither in her grasp. It was an idle thought; there could be no possibility of distinguishing a faded flower from a fresh one at so great a distance.

For many days after this incident the young man avoided the window that looked into Dr. Rappaccini's garden, as if something ugly and monstrous would have blasted his eye-sight, had he been betrayed into a glance. He felt conscious of having put himself, to a certain extent, within the influence of an unintelligible power by the communication which he had opened with Beatrice. The wisest course would have been, if his heart were in any real danger, to quit his lodgings and Padua itself, at once; the next wiser, to have accustomed himself, as far as possible, to the familiar and day-light view of Beatrice; thus bringing her rigidly and systematically within the limits of ordinary experience. Least of all, while avoiding her sight, ought Giovanni to have remained so near this extraordinary being that the proximity and possibility even of intercourse should give a kind of substance and reality to the wild vagaries which his imagination ran riot continually in producing. Guasconti had not a deep heart—or, at all events, its depths were not sounded now—but he had a quick fancy, and an ardent southern temperament, which rose every instant to a higher fever-pitch. Whether or no Beatrice possessed those terrible attributes—that fatal breath—the affinity with those so beautiful and deadly flowers—which were indicated by what Giovanni had witnessed, she had at least instilled a fierce and subtle poison into his system. It was not love, although her rich beauty was a madness to him; nor horror, even while he fancied her spirit to be imbued with the same baneful essence that seemed to pervade her physical frame; but a wild offspring of both love and horror that had each parent in it, and burned like one and shivered like the other. Giovanni knew not what to dread; still less did he know what to hope; yet hope and dread kept a continual warfare in his breast, alternately vanquishing one another and starting up afresh to renew the contest. Blessed are all simple emotions, be they dark or bright! It is the lurid intermixture of the two that produces the illuminating blaze of the infernal regions.

Sometimes he endeavored to assuage the fever of his spirit by a rapid walk through the streets of Padua or beyond its gates; his footsteps kept time with the throbbings of his brain, so that the walk was apt to accelerate itself to a race. One day he found himself arrested; his arm was seized by a portly personage, who had turned back on recognizing the young man and expended much breath in overtaking him.

"Signor Giovanni!—stay, my young friend!" cried he. "Have you forgotten me? That might well be the case if I were as much altered as yourself."

It was Baglioni, whom Giovanni had avoided ever since their first meeting, from a doubt that the professor's sagacity would look too deeply into his secrets. Endeavoring to recover himself, he stared forth wildly from his inner world into the outer one and spoke like a man in a dream.

"Yes; I am Giovanni Guasconti. You are Professor Pietro Baglioni. Now let me pass!"

"Not yet—not yet, Signor Giovanni Guasconti," said the Professor, smiling, but at the same time scrutinizing the youth with an earnest glance—"What; did I grow up side by side with your father, and shall his son pass me like a stranger in these old streets of Padua? Stand still, Signor Giovanni; for we must have a word or two before we part."

"Speedily, then, most worshipful Professor, speedily!" said Giovanni, with feverish impatience. "Does not your worship see that I am in haste?"

Now, while he was speaking, there came a man in black along the street, stooping and moving feebly, like a person in inferior health. His face was all overspread with a most sickly and sallow hue, but yet so pervaded with an expression of piercing and active intellect, that an observer might easily have overlooked the merely physical attributes and have seen only this wonderful energy. As he passed, this person exchanged a cold and distant salutation with Baglioni, but fixed his eyes upon Giovanni with an intentness that seemed to bring out whatever was within him worthy of notice. Nevertheless, there was a peculiar quietness in the look, as if taking merely a speculative, not a human, interest in the young man.

"It is Dr. Rappaccini!" whispered the Professor when the stranger had passed.—"Has he ever seen your face before?"

"Not that I know," answered Giovanni, starting at the name.

"He *has* seen you! he must have seen you!" said Baglioni, hastily. "For some purpose or other, this man of science is making a study of you. I know that look of his! It is the same that coldly illuminates his face as he bends over a bird, a mouse, or a butterfly, which, in pursuance of some experiment, he has killed by the perfume of a flower; a look as deep as nature itself, but without nature's warmth of love. Signor Giovanni, I will stake my life upon it, you are the subject of one of Rappaccini's experiments!"

"Will you make a fool of me?" cried Giovanni, passionately. "*That*, Signor Professor, were an untoward experiment."

"Patience! patience!" replied the imperturbable Professor. "I tell thee, my poor

Giovanni, that Rappaccini has a scientific interest in thee. Thou hast fallen into fearful hands! And the Signora Beatrice? What part does she act in this mystery?"

But Guasconti, finding Baglioni's pertinacity intolerable, here broke away, and was gone before the Professor could again seize his arm. He looked after the young man intently and shook his head.

"This must not be," said Baglioni to himself. "The youth is the son of my old friend, and shall not come to any harm from which the arcana of medical science can preserve him. Besides, it is too insufferable an impertinence in Rappaccini, thus to snatch the lad out of my own hands, as I may say, and make use of him for his infernal experiments. This daughter of his! It shall be looked to. Perchance, most learned Rappaccini, I may foil you where you little dream of it!"

Meanwhile Giovanni had pursued a circuitous route, and at length found himself at the door of his lodgings. As he crossed the threshold he was met by old Lisabetta, who smirked and smiled, and was evidently desirous to attract his attention; vainly, however, as the ebullition of his feelings had momentarily subsided into a cold and dull vacuity. He turned his eyes full upon the withered face that was puckering itself into a smile, but seemed to behold it not. The old dame, therefore, laid her grasp upon his cloak.

"Signor!—Signor!" whispered she, still with a smile over the whole breadth of her visage, so that it looked not unlike a grotesque carving in wood, darkened by centuries.—"Listen, signor! There is a private entrance into the garden!"

"What do you say?" exclaimed Giovanni, turning quickly about, as if an inanimate thing should start into feverish life. "A private entrance into Dr. Rappaccini's garden?"

"Hush! hush!—not so loud!" whispered Lisabetta, putting her hand over his mouth. "Yes; into the worshipful Doctor's garden, where you may see all his fine shrubbery. Many a young man in Padua would give gold to be admitted among those flowers."

Giovanni put a piece of gold into her hand.

"Show me the way," said he.

A surmise, probably excited by his conversation with Baglioni, crossed his mind, that this interposition of old Lisabetta might perchance be connected with the intrigue, whatever were its nature, in which the Professor seemed to suppose that Dr. Rappaccini was involving him. But such a suspicion, though it disturbed Giovanni, was inadequate to restrain him. The instant that he was aware of the possibility of approaching Beatrice, it seemed an absolute necessity of his existence to do so. It mattered not whether she were angel or demon; he was irrevocably within her sphere, and must obey the law that whirled him onward, in ever-lessening circles, towards a result which he did not attempt to foreshadow. And yet, strange to say, there came across him a sudden doubt whether this intense interest on his part were not delusory—whether it were really of so deep and positive a nature as to justify him in now thrusting himself into an incalculable position—whether it were not merely the fantasy of a young man's brain, only slightly or not at all connected with his heart!

He paused—hesitated—turned half about—but again went on. His withered guide led him along several obscure passages, and finally undid a door, through which, as it was opened, there came the sight and sound of rustling leaves, with the broken sunshine glimmering among them. Giovanni stepped forth, and forcing himself through the entanglement of a shrub that wreathed its tendrils over the hidden entrance, stood beneath his own window, in the open area of Dr. Rappaccini's garden.

How often is it the case, that, when impossibilities have come to pass and dreams have condensed their misty substance into tangible realities, we find ourselves calm, and even coldly self-possessed, amid circumstances which it would have been a delirium of joy or agony to anticipate! Fate delights to thwart us thus. Passion will choose his own time to rush upon the scene, and lingers sluggishly behind when an appropriate adjustment of events would seem to summon his appearance. So was it now with Giovanni. Day after day, his pulses had throbbed with feverish blood at the improbable idea of an interview with Beatrice, and of standing with her, face to face, in this very garden, basking in the oriental sunshine of her beauty, and snatching from her full gaze the mystery which he deemed the riddle of his own existence. But now there was a singular and untimely equanimity within his breast. He threw a glance around the garden to discover if Beatrice or her father were present, and, perceiving that he was alone, began a critical observation of the plants.

The aspect of one and all of them dissatisfied him; their gorgeousness seemed fierce, passionate, and even unnatural. There was hardly an individual shrub which a wanderer, straying by himself through a forest, would not have been startled to find growing wild, as if an unearthly face had glared at him out of the thicket. Several also would have shocked a delicate instinct by an appearance of artificialness indicating that there had been such commixture, and, as it were, adultery, of various vegetable species, that the production was no longer of God's making, but the monstrous offspring of man's depraved fancy, glowing with only an evil mockery of beauty. They were probably the result of experiment, which in one or two cases had succeeded in mingling plants individually lovely into a compound possessing the questionable and ominous character that distinguished the whole growth of the garden. In fine, Giovanni recognized but two or three plants in the collection, and those of a kind that he well knew to be poisonous. While busy with these contemplations, he heard the rustling of a silken garment, and turning, beheld Beatrice emerging from beneath the sculptured portal.

Giovanni had not considered with himself what should be his deportment; whether he should apologize for his intrusion into the garden, or assume that he was there with the privity, at least, if not by the desire, of Doctor Rappaccini or his daughter. But Beatrice's manner placed him at his ease, though leaving him still in doubt by what agency he had gained admittance. She came lightly along the path and met him near the broken fountain. There was surprise in her face, but brightened by a simple and kind expression of pleasure.

"You are a connoisseur in flowers, Signor," said Beatrice, with a smile, alluding to the bouquet which he had flung her from the window. "It is no marvel, therefore, if the sight of my father's rare collection has tempted you to take a nearer view. If he were here, he could tell you many strange and interesting facts as to the nature and habits of these shrubs; for he has spent a life-time in such studies, and this garden is his world."

"And yourself, lady"—observed Giovanni—"if fame says true,—you likewise are deeply skilled in the virtues indicated by these rich blossoms and these spicy perfumes. Would you deign to be my instructress, I should prove an apter scholar than if taught by Signor Rappaccini himself."

"Are there such idle rumors?" asked Beatrice, with the music of a pleasant laugh. "Do people say that I am skilled in my father's science of plants? What a jest is there! No; though I have grown up among these flowers, I know no more of them than their hues and perfume; and sometimes methinks I would fain rid myself of even that small knowledge. There are many flowers here, and those not the least brilliant, that shock and offend me when they meet my eye. But pray, Signor, do not believe these stories about my science. Believe nothing of me save what you see with your own eyes."

"And must I believe all that I have seen with my own eyes?" asked Giovanni pointedly, while the recollection of former scenes made him shrink. "No, Signora; you demand too little of me. Bid me believe nothing save what comes from your own lips."

It would appear that Beatrice understood him. There came a deep flush to her cheek; but she looked full into Giovanni's eyes, and responded to his gaze of uneasy suspicion with a queenlike haughtiness.

"I do so bid you, Signor!" she replied. "Forget whatever you may have fancied in regard to me. If true to the outward senses, still it may be false in its essence. But the words of Beatrice Rappaccini's lips are true from the depths of the heart outward. Those you may believe!"

A fervor glowed in her whole aspect and beamed upon Giovanni's consciousness like the light of truth itself. But while she spoke there was a fragrance in the atmosphere around her, rich and delightful, though evanescent, yet which the young man, from an indefinable reluctance, scarcely dared to draw into his lungs. It might be the odor of the flowers. Could it be Beatrice's breath which thus embalmed her words with a strange richness, as if by steeping them in her heart? A faintness passed like a shadow over Giovanni and flitted away; he seemed to gaze through the beautiful girl's eyes into her transparent soul, and felt no more doubt or fear.

The tinge of passion that had colored Beatrice's manner vanished; she became gay, and appeared to derive a pure delight from her communion with the youth not unlike what the maiden of a lonely island might have felt conversing with a voyager from the civilized world. Evidently her experience of life had been confined within the limits of that garden. She talked now about matters as simple as the daylight or summer clouds, and now asked questions in reference to the city, or Giovanni's distant home, his friends, his mother, and his sisters; questions indicating such seclusion, and such lack of familiarity with modes and forms, that Giovanni responded as if to an infant. Her spirit gushed out before him like a fresh rill that was just catching its first glimpse of the sunlight and wondering at the reflections of earth and sky which were flung into its bosom. There came thoughts, too, from a deep source, and fantasies of a gem-like brilliancy, as if diamonds and rubies sparkled upward among the bubbles of the fountain. Ever and anon, there gleamed across the young man's mind a sense of wonder that he should be walking side by side with the being who had so wrought upon his imagination, whom he had idealized in such hues of terror—in whom he had positively witnessed such manifestations of dreadful attributes—that he should be conversing with Beatrice like a brother, and should find her so human and so maiden-like. But such reflections were only momentary; the effect of her character was too real not to make itself familiar at once.

In this free intercourse, they had strayed through the garden, and now, after many turns among its avenues, were come to the shattered fountain, beside which grew the magnificent shrub, with its treasury of glowing blossoms. A fragrance was diffused from it, which Giovanni recognized as identical with that which he had attributed to Beatrice's breath, but incomparably more powerful. As her eyes fell upon it, Giovanni beheld her press her hand to her bosom as if her heart were throbbing suddenly and painfully.

"For the first time in my life," murmured she, addressing the shrub, "I had forgotten thee!"

"I remember, Signora," said Giovanni, "that you once promised to reward me with one of these living gems for the bouquet which I had the happy boldness to fling to your feet. Permit me now to pluck it as a memorial of this interview."

He made a step towards the shrub with extended hand; but Beatrice darted forward, uttering a shriek that went through his heart like a dagger. She caught his hand and drew it back with the whole force of her slender figure. Giovanni felt her touch thrilling through his fibres.

"Touch it not!" exclaimed she, in a voice of agony. "Not for thy life! It is fatal!"

Then, hiding her face, she fled from him and vanished beneath the sculptured portal. As Giovanni followed her with his eyes, he beheld the emaciated figure and pale intelligence of Dr. Rappaccini, who had been watching the scene, he knew not how long, within the shadow of the entrance.

No sooner was Guasconti alone in his chamber than the image of Beatrice came back to his passionate musings, invested with all the witchery that had been gathering around it ever since his first glimpse of her, and now likewise imbued with a tender warmth of girlish womanhood. She was human: her nature was endowed with all gentle and feminine qualities; she was worthiest to be worshipped; she was capable, surely, on her part, of the height and heroism of love. Those tokens which he had hitherto considered as proofs of a frightful peculiarity in her physical and moral system were now either forgotten, or, by the subtle sophistry of passion transmitted into a golden crown of enchantment, rendering Beatrice the more admirable by so much as she was the more unique. Whatever had looked ugly was now beautiful; or, if incapable of such a change, it stole away and hid itself among those shapeless half-ideas, which throng the dim region beyond the daylight of our perfect consciousness. Thus did he spend the night, nor fell asleep, until the dawn had begun to awake the slumbering flowers in Dr. Rappaccini's garden, whither Giovanni's dreams doubtless led him. Up rose the sun in his due season, and, flinging his beams upon the young man's eyelids, awoke him to a sense of pain. When thoroughly aroused, he became sensible of a burning and tingling agony in his hand—in his right hand—the very hand which Beatrice had grasped in her own when he was on the point of plucking one of the gem-like flowers. On the back of that hand there was now a purple print like that of four small fingers, and the likeness of a slender thumb upon his wrist.

Oh, how stubbornly does love—or even that cunning semblance of love which flourishes in the imagination, but strikes no depth of root into the heart—how stubbornly does it hold its faith, until the moment comes when it is doomed to vanish into thin mist! Giovanni wrapt a handkerchief about his hand, and wondered what evil thing had stung him, and soon forgot his pain in a reverie of Beatrice.

After the first interview, a second was in the inevitable course of what we call fate. A third; a fourth; and a meeting with Beatrice in the garden was no longer an incident in Giovanni's daily life, but the whole space in which he might be said to live; for the anticipation and memory of that ecstatic hour made up the remainder. Nor was it otherwise with the daughter of Rappaccini. She watched for the youth's appearance, and flew to his side with confidence as unreserved as if they had been playmates from early infancy—as if they were such playmates still. If, by any unwonted chance, he failed to come at the appointed moment, she stood beneath the window and sent up the rich sweetness of her tones to float around him in his chamber and echo and reverberate throughout his heart—"Giovanni! Giovanni! Why tarriest thou? Come down!"—And down he hastened into that Eden of poisonous flowers.

But, with all this intimate familiarity, there was still a reserve in Beatrice's demeanor, so rigidly and invariably sustained that the idea of infringing it scarcely occurred to his imagination. By all appreciable signs, they loved; they had looked love with eyes that conveyed the holy secret from the depths of one soul into the depths of the other, as if it were too sacred to be whispered by the way; they had even spoken love in those gushes of passion when their spirits darted forth in articulated breath like tongues of long-hidden flame; and yet there had been no seal of lips, no clasp of hands, nor any slightest caress such as love claims and hallows. He had never touched one of the gleaming ringlets of her hair; her garment—so marked was the physical barrier between them—had never been waved against him by a breeze. On the few occasions when Giovanni had seemed tempted to overstep the limit, Beatrice grew so sad, so stern, and withal wore such a look of desolate separation, shuddering at itself, that not a spoken word was requisite to repel him. At such times he was startled at the horrible suspicions that rose, monster-like, out of the caverns of his heart, and stared him in the face; his love grew thin and faint as the morning-mist, his doubts alone had substance. But, when Beatrice's face brightened again after the momentary shadow, she was transformed at once from the mysterious, questionable being whom he had watched with so much awe and horror; she was now the beautiful and unsophisticated girl whom he felt that his spirit knew with a certainty beyond all other knowledge.

A considerable time had now passed since Giovanni's last meeting with Baglioni. One morning, however, he was disagreeably surprised by a visit from the Professor, whom he had scarcely thought of for whole weeks, and would willingly have forgotten still longer. Given up, as he had long been, to a pervading excitement, he could tolerate no companions, except upon condition of their perfect sympathy with his present state of feeling. Such sympathy was not to be expected from Professor Baglioni.

The visitor chatted carelessly, for a few moments, about the gossip of the city and the University, and then took up another topic.

"I have been reading an old classic author lately," said he, "and met with a story that strangely interested me. Possibly you may remember it. It is of an Indian prince, who sent a beautiful woman as a present to Alexander the Great. She was as lovely as the dawn and gorgeous as the sunset; but what especially distinguished her was a certain rich perfume in her breath—richer than a garden of Persian roses. Alexander, as was natural to a youthful conqueror, fell in love at first sight with this magnificent stranger. But a certain sage physician, happening to be present, discovered a terrible secret in regard to her."

"And what was that?" asked Giovanni, turning his eyes downward to avoid those of the Professor.

"That this lovely woman," continued Baglioni, with emphasis, "had been nourished with poisons from her birth upward, until her whole nature was so imbued with them that she herself had become the deadliest poison in existence. Poison was her element of life. With that rich perfume of her breath she blasted the very air. Her love would have been poison—her embrace death. Is not this a marvellous tale?"

"A childish fable," answered Giovanni, nervously starting from his chair. "I marvel how your worship finds time to read such nonsense, among your graver studies."

"By the bye," said the Professor, looking uneasily about him, "what singular fragrance is this in your apartment? Is it the perfume of your gloves? It is faint, but delicious, and yet, after all, by no means agreeable. Were I to breathe it long, methinks it would make me ill. It is like the breath of a flower—but I see no flowers in the chamber."

"Nor are there any," replied Giovanni, who had turned pale as the Professor spoke; "nor, I think, is there any fragrance except in your worship's imagination. Odors, being a sort of element combined of the sensual and the spiritual, are apt to deceive us in this manner. The recollection of a perfume—the bare idea of it—may easily be mistaken for a present reality."

"Aye; but my sober imagination does not often play such tricks," said Baglioni; "and, were I to fancy any kind of odor, it would be that of some vile apothecary drug, wherewith my fingers are likely enough to be imbued. Our worshipful friend Rappaccini, as I have heard, tinctures his medicaments with odors richer than those of Araby. Doubtless, likewise, the fair and learned Signora Beatrice would minister to her patients with draughts as sweet as a maiden's breath. But wo to him that sips them!"

Giovanni's face evinced many contending emotions. The tone in which the Professor alluded to the pure and lovely daughter of Rappaccini was a torture to his soul; and yet, the intimation of a view of her character opposite to his own, gave instantaneous distinctness to a thousand dim suspicions, which now grinned at him like so many demons. But he strove hard to quell them and to respond to Baglioni with a true lover's perfect faith.

"Signor Professor," said he, "you were my father's friend—perchance, too, it is your purpose to act a friendly part towards his son. I would fain feel nothing towards you save respect and deference; but I pray you to observe, Signor, that there is one subject on which we must not speak. You know not the Signora Beatrice. You cannot, therefore, estimate the wrong—the blasphemy, I may even say—that is offered to her character by a light or injurious word."

"Giovanni!—my poor Giovanni!" answered the Professor, with a calm expression of pity, "I know this wretched girl far better than yourself. You shall hear the truth in respect to the poisoner Rappaccini and his poisonous daughter. Yes; poisonous as she is beautiful! Listen; for, even should you do violence to my grey hairs, it shall not silence me. That old fable of the Indian woman has become a truth by the deep and deadly science of Rappaccini and in the person of the lovely Beatrice!"

Giovanni groaned and hid his face.

"Her father," continued Baglioni, "was not restrained by natural affection from offering up his child, in this horrible manner, as the victim of his insane zeal for science. For—let us do him justice—he is as true a man of science as ever distilled his own heart in an alembic. What, then, will be your fate? Beyond a doubt you are selected as the material of some new experiment. Perhaps the result is to be death—perhaps a fate more awful still! Rappaccini, with what he calls the interest of science before his eyes, will hesitate at nothing."

"It is a dream!" muttered Giovanni to himself, "surely it is a dream!"

"But," resumed the professor, "be of good cheer, son of my friend! It is not yet too late for the rescue. Possibly, we may even succeed in bringing back this miserable child within the limits of ordinary nature, from which her father's madness has estranged her. Behold this little silver vase! It was wrought by the hands of the renowned Benvenuto Cellini, and is well worthy to be a love-gift to the fairest dame in Italy. But its contents are invaluable. One little sip of this antidote would have rendered the most virulent poisons of the Borgias innocuous. Doubt not that it will be as efficacious against those of Rappaccini. Bestow the vase, and the precious liquid within it, on your Beatrice, and hopefully await the result."

Baglioni laid a small, exquisitely wrought silver vial on the table and withdrew, leaving what he had said to produce its effect upon the young man's mind.

"We will thwart Rappaccini yet!" thought he, chuckling to himself, as he descended the stairs. "But, let us confess the truth of him, he is a wonderful man!—a wonderful man indeed! A vile empiric, however, in his practice, and therefore not to be tolerated by those who respect the good old rules of the medical profession!"

Throughout Giovanni's whole acquaintance with Beatrice, he had occasionally, as we have said, been haunted by dark surmises as to her character. Yet, so thoroughly had she made herself felt by him as a simple, natural, most affectionate, and guileless creature, that the image now held up by Professor Baglioni, looked as strange and incredible as if it were not in accordance with his own original conception. True, there were ugly recollections connected with his first glimpses of the beautiful girl; he could not quite forget the bouquet that withered in her grasp, and the insect that perished amid the sunny air, by no ostensible agency save the fragrance of her breath. These incidents, however, dissolving in the pure light of her character, had no longer the efficacy of facts, but were acknowledged as mistaken fantasies, by whatever testimony of the senses they might appear to be substantiated. There is something truer and more real, than what we can see with the eyes and touch with the finger. On such better evidence, had Giovanni founded his confidence in Beatrice, though rather by the necessary force of her high attributes than by any deep and generous faith on his part. But, now, his spirit was incapable of sustaining itself at the height to which the early enthusiasm of passion had exalted it; he fell down, grovelling among earthly doubts, and defiled therewith the pure whiteness of Beatrice's image. Not that he gave her up; he did but distrust. He resolved to institute some decisive test that should satisfy him, once for all, whether there were those dreadful peculiarities in her physical nature, which could not be supposed to exist without some corresponding monstrosity of soul. His eyes, gazing down afar, might have deceived him as to the lizard, the insect, and the flowers. But if he could witness, at the distance of a few paces, the sudden blight of one fresh and healthful flower in Beatrice's hand, there would be room for no further question. With this idea he hastened to the florist's, and purchased a bouquet that was still gemmed with the morning dew-drops.

It was now the customary hour of his daily interview with Beatrice. Before descending into the garden, Giovanni failed not to look at his figure in the mirror; a vanity to be expected in a beautiful young man, yet, as displaying itself at that troubled and feverish moment, the token of a certain shallowness of feeling and insincerity of character. He did gaze, however, and said to himself that his features had never before possessed so rich a grace, nor his eyes such vivacity, nor his cheeks so warm a hue of superabundant life.

"At least," thought he, "her poison has not yet insinuated itself into my system. I am no flower to perish in her grasp!"

With that thought he turned his eyes on the bouquet, which he had never once laid aside from his hand. A thrill of indefinable horror shot through his frame, on perceiving that those dewy flowers were already beginning to droop; they wore the aspect of things that had been fresh and lovely, yesterday. Giovanni grew white as marble, and stood motionless before the mirror, staring at his own reflection there as at the likeness of something frightful. He remembered Baglioni's remark about the fragrance that seemed to pervade the chamber. It must have been the poison in his breath! Then he shuddered—shuddered at himself! Recovering from his stupor, he began to watch with curious eye a spider that was busily at work, hanging its web from the antique cornice of the apartment, crossing and re-crossing the artful system of interwoven lines, as vigorous and active a spider as ever dangled from an old ceiling. Giovanni bent towards the insect, and emitted a deep, long breath. The spider suddenly ceased its toil; the web vibrated with a tremor originating in the body of the small artizan. Again Giovanni sent forth a breath, deeper, longer, and imbued with a venomous feeling out of his heart: he knew not whether he were wicked or only desperate. The spider made a convulsive gripe with his limbs, and hung dead across the window.

"Accursed! Accursed!" muttered Giovanni, addressing himself. "Hast thou grown so poisonous that this deadly insect perishes by thy breath?"

At that moment a rich, sweet voice came floating up from the garden:—

"Giovanni! Giovanni! It is past the hour! Why tarriest thou? Come down!"

"Yes," muttered Giovanni again. "She is the only being whom my breath may not slay! Would that it might!"

He rushed down, and in an instant was standing before the bright and loving eyes of Beatrice. A moment ago his wrath and despair had been so fierce that he could have desired nothing so much as to wither her by a glance. But, with her actual presence, there came influences which had too real an existence to be at once shaken off; recollections of the delicate and benign power of her feminine nature, which had so often enveloped him in a religious calm; recollections of many a holy and passionate outgush of her heart, when the pure fountain had been unsealed from its depths, and made visible in its transparency to his mental eye; recollections which, had Giovanni known how to estimate them, would have assured him that all this ugly mystery was but an earthly illusion, and that, whatever mist of evil might seem to have gathered over her, the real Beatrice was a heavenly angel. Incapable as he was of such high faith, still her presence had not utterly lost its magic. Giovanni's rage was quelled into an aspect of sullen insensibility. Beatrice, with a quick spiritual sense, immediately felt that there was a gulf of blackness between them which neither he nor she could pass. They walked on together, sad and silent, and came thus to the marble fountain and to its pool of water on the ground, in the midst of which grew the shrub that bore gem-like blossoms. Giovanni was affrighted at the eager enjoyment—the appetite, as it were—with which he found himself inhaling the fragrance of the flowers.

"Beatrice," asked he, abruptly, "whence came this shrub!"

"My father created it," answered she, with simplicity.

"Created it! created it!" repeated Giovanni. "What mean you, Beatrice?"

"He is a man fearfully acquainted with the secrets of Nature," replied Beatrice; "and, at the hour when I first drew breath, this plant sprang from the soil, the offspring of his science, of his intellect, while I was but his earthly child. Approach it not!" continued she, observing with terror that Giovanni was drawing nearer to the shrub. "It has qualities that you little dream of. But I, dearest Giovanni,—I grew up and blossomed with the plant and was nourished with its breath. It was my sister, and I loved it with a human affection; for—alas! hast thou not suspected it? there was an awful doom."

Here Giovanni frowned so darkly upon her that Beatrice paused and trembled. But her faith in his tenderness reassured her, and made her blush that she had doubted for an instant.

"There was an awful doom," she continued,—"the effect of my father's fatal love of science—which estranged me from all society of my kind. Until Heaven sent thee, dearest Giovanni, oh, how lonely was thy poor Beatrice!"

"Was it a hard doom?" asked Giovanni, fixing his eyes upon her.

"Only of late have I known how hard it was," answered she tenderly. "Oh, yes; but my heart was torpid, and therefore quiet."

Giovanni's rage broke forth from his sullen gloom like a lightning-flash out of a dark cloud.

"Accursed one!" cried he, with venomous scorn and anger. "And, finding thy solitude wearisome, thou hast severed me likewise from all the warmth of life and enticed me into thy region of unspeakable horror!"

"Giovanni!" exclaimed Beatrice, turning her large bright eyes upon his face. The force of his words had not found its way into her mind; she was merely thunder-struck.

"Yes, poisonous thing!" repeated Giovanni, beside himself with passion. "Thou hast done it! Thou hast blasted me! Thou hast filled my veins with poison! Thou hast made me as hateful, as ugly, as loathsome and deadly a creature as thyself,—a world's wonder of hideous monstrosity! Now—if our breath be happily as fatal to ourselves as to all others—let us join our lips in one kiss of unutterable hatred, and so die!"

"What has befallen me?" murmured Beatrice, with a low moan out of her heart. "Holy Virgin pity me, a poor heart-broken child!"

"Thou! Dost thou pray?" cried Giovanni, still with the same fiendish scorn. "Thy very prayers, as they come from thy lips, taint the atmosphere with death. Yes, yes; let us pray! Let us to church, and dip our fingers in the holy water at the portal! They that come after us will perish as by a pestilence. Let us sign crosses in the air! It will be scattering curses abroad in the likeness of holy symbols!"

"Giovanni," said Beatrice, calmly, for her grief was beyond passion, "why dost thou join thyself with me thus in those terrible words? I, it is true, am the horrible thing thou namest me. But thou!—what hast thou to do, save with one other shudder at my hideous misery, to go forth out of the garden and mingle with thy race, and forget there ever crawled on earth such a monster as poor Beatrice?"

"Dost thou pretend ignorance?" asked Giovanni, scowling upon her. "Behold! This power have I gained from the pure daughter of Rappaccini!"

There was a swarm of summer-insects flitting through the air in search of the food promised by the flower-odors of the fatal garden. They circled round Giovanni's head, and were evidently attracted towards him by the same influence which had drawn them for an instant within the sphere of several of the shrubs. He sent forth a breath among them, and smiled bitterly at Beatrice as at least a score of the insects fell dead upon the ground.

"I see it! I see it!" shrieked Beatrice. "It is my father's fatal science! No, no, Giovanni; it was not I! Never, never! I dreamed only to love thee, and be with thee a little time, and so to let thee pass away, leaving but thine image in mine heart. For, Giovanni—believe it—though my body be nourished with poison, my spirit is God's creature, and craves love as its daily food. But my father!—he has united us in this fearful sympathy. Yes; spurn me!—tread upon me!—kill me! Oh, what is death, after such words as thine? But it was not I. Not for a world of bliss would I have done it!"

Giovanni's passion had exhausted itself in its outburst from his lips. There now came across him a sense, mournful, and not without tenderness, of the intimate and peculiar relationship between Beatrice and himself. They stood, as it were, in an utter solitude, which would be made none the less solitary by the densest throng of human life. Ought not, then, the desert of humanity around them to press this insulated pair closer together? If they should be cruel to one another, who was there to be kind to them? Besides, thought Giovanni, might there not still be a hope of his returning within the limits of ordinary nature, and leading Beatrice—the redeemed Beatrice—by the hand? O, weak, and selfish, and unworthy spirit, that could dream of an earthly union and earthly happiness as possible, after such deep love had been so bitterly wronged as was Beatrice's love by Giovanni's blighting words! No, no; there could be no such hope. She must pass heavily, with that broken heart, across the borders of Time—she must bathe her hurts in some fount of paradise, and forget her grief in the light of immortality—and *there* be well!

But Giovanni did not know it.

"Dear Beatrice," said he, approaching her, while she shrank away as always at his approach, but now with a different impulse—"dearest Beatrice, our fate is not yet so desperate. Behold! There is a medicine, potent, as a wise physician has assured me, and almost divine in its efficacy. It is composed of ingredients the most opposite to those by which thy awful father has brought this calamity upon thee and me. It is distilled of blessed herbs. Shall we not quaff it together, and thus be purified from evil?"

"Give it me!" said Beatrice, extending her hand to receive the little silver vial which Giovanni took from his bosom. She added, with a peculiar emphasis, "I will drink—but do thou await the result."

She put Baglioni's antidote to her lips; and, at the same moment, the figure of Rappaccini emerged from the portal and came slowly towards the marble fountain. As he drew near, the pale man of science seemed to gaze with a triumphant expression at the beautiful youth and maiden, as might an artist who should spend his life in achieving a picture or a group of statuary and finally be satisfied with his success. He paused—his bent form grew erect with conscious power; he spread out his hands over them in the attitude of a father imploring a blessing upon his children. But those were the same hands that had thrown poison into the stream of their lives. Giovanni trembled. Beatrice shuddered nervously, and pressed her hand upon her heart.

"My daughter," said Rappaccini, "thou art no longer lonely in the world! Pluck one of those precious gems from thy sister shrub and bid thy bridegroom wear it in his bosom. It will not harm him now. My science and the sympathy between thee and him have so wrought within his system that he now stands apart from common men, as thou dost, daughter of my pride and triumph, from ordinary women. Pass on, then, through the world, most dear to one another and dreadful to all besides!"

"My father," said Beatrice, feebly—and still as she spoke she kept her hand upon her heart—"wherefore didst thou inflict this miserable doom upon thy child?"

"Miserable!" exclaimed Rappaccini. "What mean you, foolish girl? Dost thou deem it misery to be endowed with marvellous gifts against which no power nor strength could avail an enemy? Misery, to be able to quell the mightiest with a breath? Misery, to be as terrible as thou art beautiful? Wouldst thou, then, have preferred the condition of a weak woman, exposed to all evil and capable of none?"

"I would fain have been loved, not feared," murmured Beatrice, sinking down upon the ground. "But now it matters not. I am going, father, where the evil which thou hast striven to mingle with my being will pass away like a dream-like the fragrance of these poisonous flowers, which will no longer taint my breath among the flowers of Eden. Farewell, Giovanni! Thy words of hatred are like lead within my heart—but they, too, will fall away as I ascend. Oh, was there not, from the first, more poison in thy nature than in mine?"

To Beatrice—so radically had her earthly part been wrought upon by Rappaccini's skill—as poison had been life, so the powerful antidote was death; and thus the poor victim of man's ingenuity and of thwarted nature, and of the fatality that attends all such efforts of perverted wisdom, perished there, at the feet of her father and Giovanni. Just at that moment Professor Pietro Baglioni looked forth from the window, and called loudly, in a tone of triumph mixed with horror, to the thunder-stricken man of science:—

"Rappaccini! Rappaccini! And is *this* the upshot of your experiment!"

Carmilla

J. Sheridan Le Fanu

I

AN EARLY FRIGHT

In Styria, we, though by no means magnificent people, inhabit a castle, or schloss. A small income, in that part of the world, goes a great way. Eight or nine hundred a year does wonders. Scantily enough ours would have answered among wealthy people at home. My father is English, and I bear an English name, although I never saw England. But here, in this lonely and primitive place, where everything is so marvelously cheap, I really don't see how ever so much more money would at all materially add to our comforts, or even luxuries.

My father was in the Austrian service, and retired upon a pension and his patrimony, and purchased this feudal residence, and the small estate on which it stands, a bargain.

Nothing can be more picturesque or solitary. It stands on a slight eminence in a forest. The road, very old and narrow, passes in front of its drawbridge, never raised in my time, and its moat, stocked with perch, and sailed over by many swans, and floating on its surface white fleets of water-lilies.

Over all this the schloss shows its many-windowed front; its towers, and its Gothic chapel.

The forest opens in an irregular and very picturesque glade before its gate, and at the right a steep Gothic bridge carries the road over a stream that winds in deep shadow through the wood.

I have said that this is a very lonely place. Judge whether I say truth. Looking from the hall door toward the road, the forest in which our castle stands extends fifteen miles to the right, and twelve to the left. The nearest inhabited village is about seven of your English miles to the left. The nearest inhabited schloss of any historic associations, is that of old General Spielsdorf, nearly twenty miles away to the right.

I have said "the nearest *inhabited* village," because there is, only three miles westward, that is to say in the direction of General Spielsdorf's schloss, a ruined village, with its quaint little church, now roofless, in the aisle of which are the moldering tombs of the proud family of Karnstein, now extinct, who once owned the equally-desolate château which, in the thick of the forest, overlooks the silent ruins of the town.

Respecting the cause of the desertion of this striking and melancholy spot, there is a legend which I shall relate to you another time.

I must tell you now, how very small is the party who constitute the inhabitants of our castle. I don't include servants, or those dependents who occupy rooms in the buildings attached to the schloss. Listen, and wonder! My father, who is the kindest man on earth, but growing old; and I, at the date of my story, only nineteen. Eight years have passed since then. I and my father constituted the family at the schloss. My mother, a Styrian lady, died in my infancy, but I had a good-natured governess, who had been with me from, I might almost say, my infancy. I could not remember the time when her fat, benignant face was not a familiar picture in my memory. This was Madame Perrodon, a native of Berne, whose care and good nature in part supplied to me the loss of my mother, whom I do not even remember, so early I lost her. She made a third at our little dinner party. There was a fourth, Mademoiselle De Lafontaine, a lady such as you term, I believe, a "finishing governess." She spoke French and German, Madame Perrodon French and broken English, to which my father and I added English, which, partly to prevent its becoming a lost language among us, and partly from patriotic motives, we spoke every day. The consequence was a Babel, at which strangers used to laugh, and which I shall make no attempt to reproduce in this narrative. And there were two or three young lady friends besides, pretty nearly of my own age, who were occasional visitors, for longer or shorter terms; and these visits I sometimes returned.

These were our regular social resources; but of course there were chance visits from "neighbours" of only five or six leagues' distance. My life was, notwithstanding, rather a solitary one, I can assure you.

My gouvernantes had just so much control over me as you might conjecture such sage persons would have in the case of a rather spoiled girl, whose only parent allowed her pretty nearly her own way in everything.

The first occurrence in my existence, which produced a terrible impression upon my mind, which, in fact, never has been effaced, was one of the very earliest incidents of my life which I can recollect. Some people will think it so trifling that it should not be recorded here. You will see, however, by-and-by, why I mention it. The nursery, as it was called, though I had it all to myself, was a large room in the upper story of the castle, with a steep oak roof. I can't have been more than six years old, when one night I awoke, and looking around the room from my bed, failed to see the nursery-maid. Neither was my nurse there; and I thought myself alone. I was not frightened, for I was one of those happy children who are studiously kept in ignorance of ghost stories, of fairy tales, and of all such lore as makes us cover up our heads when the door creaks suddenly, or the flicker of an expiring candle makes the shadow of a bed-post dance upon the wall, nearer to our faces. I was vexed and insulted at finding myself, as I conceived, neglected, and I began to whimper, preparatory to a hearty bout of roaring; when to my surprise, I saw a solemn, but very pretty face looking at me from the side of the bed. It was that of a young lady who was kneeling, with her hands under the coverlet. I looked at her with a kind of pleased wonder, and ceased whimpering. She caressed me with her hands, and lay down beside me on the bed, and drew me toward her, smiling; I felt immediately delightfully soothed, and fell asleep again. I was wakened by a sensation as if two needles ran into my breast very deep at the same moment, and I cried loudly. The lady started back, with her eyes fixed on me, and then slipped down upon the floor, and, as I thought, hid herself under the bed.

I was now for the first time frightened, and I yelled with all my might and main. Nurse, nursery-maid, housekeeper, all came running in, and hearing my story, they made light of it, soothing me all they could meanwhile. But, child as I was, I could perceive that their faces were pale with an unwonted look of anxiety, and I saw them look under the bed, and about the room, and peep under tables and pluck open cupboards; and the housekeeper whispered to the nurse: "Lay your hand along that hollow in the bed; some one did lie there, so sure as you did not; the place is still warm."

I remember the nursery-maid petting me, and all three examining my chest, where I told them I felt the puncture, and pronouncing that there was no sign visible that any such thing had happened to me.

The housekeeper and the two other servants who were in charge of the nursery, remained sitting up all night; and from that time a servant always sat up in the nursery until I was about fourteen.

I was very nervous for a long time after this. A doctor was called in, he was pallid and elderly. How well I remember his long saturnine face, slightly pitted with small-pox, and his chestnut wig. For a good while, every second day, he came and gave me medicine, which of course I hated.

The morning after I saw this apparition I was in a state of terror, and could not bear to be left alone, daylight though it was, for a moment.

I remember my father coming up and standing at the bedside, and talking cheerfully, and asking the nurse a number of questions, and laughing very heartily at one of the answers; and patting me on the shoulder, and kissing me, and telling me not to be frightened, that it was nothing but a dream and could not hurt me.

But I was not comforted, for I knew the visit of the strange woman was *not* a dream; and I was *awfully* frightened.

I was a little consoled by the nursery-maid's assuring me that it was she who had come and looked at me, and lain down beside me in the bed, and that I must have been half-dreaming not to have known her face. But this, though supported by the nurse, did not quite satisfy me.

I remembered, in the course of that day, a venerable old man, in a black cassock, coming into the room with the nurse and housekeeper, and talking a little to them, and very kindly to me; his face was very sweet and gentle, and he told me they were going to pray, and joined my hands together, and desired me to say, softly, while they were praying, "Lord hear all good prayers for us, for Jesus' sake." I think these were the very words, for I often repeated them to myself, and my nurse used for years to make me say them in my prayers.

I remembered so well the thoughtful sweet face of that white-haired old man, in his black cassock, as he stood in that rude, lofty, brown room, with the clumsy furniture of a fashion three hundred years old, about him, and the scanty light entering its shadowy atmosphere through the small lattice. He kneeled, and the three women with him, and he prayed aloud with an earnest quavering voice for, what appeared to me, a long time. I forget all my life preceding that event, and for some time after it is all obscure also; but the scenes I have just described stand out vivid as the isolated pictures of the phantasmagoria surrounded by darkness.

II

A GUEST

I AM NOW GOING TO TELL YOU SOMETHING SO STRANGE THAT IT WILL require all your faith in my veracity to believe my story. It is not only true, nevertheless, but truth of which I have been an eye-witness.

It was a sweet summer evening, and my father asked me, as he sometimes did, to take a little ramble with him along that beautiful forest vista which I have mentioned as lying in front of the schloss.

"General Spielsdorf cannot come to us so soon as I had hoped," said my father, as we pursued our walk.

He was to have paid us a visit of some weeks, and we had expected his arrival next day. He was to have brought with him a young lady, his niece and ward, Mademoiselle Rheinfeldt, whom I had never seen, but whom I had heard described as a very charming girl, and in whose society I had promised myself many happy days. I was more disappointed than a young lady living in a town, or a bustling neighbourhood can possibly imagine. This visit, and the new acquaintance it promised, had furnished my day dream for many weeks.

"And how soon does he come?" I asked.

"Not till autumn. Not for two months, I dare say," he answered. "And I am very glad now, dear, that you never knew Mademoiselle Rheinfeldt."

"And why?" I asked, both mortified and curious.

"Because the poor young lady is dead," he replied. "I quite forgot I had not told you, but you were not in the room when I received the General's letter this evening."

I was very much shocked. General Spielsdorf had mentioned in his first letter, six or seven weeks before, that she was not so well as he would wish her, but there was nothing to suggest the remotest suspicion of danger.

"Here is the General's letter," he said, handing it to me. "I am afraid he is in great affliction; the letter appears to me to have been written very nearly in distraction."

We sat down on a rude bench, under a group of magnificent lime trees. The sun was setting with all its melancholy splendor behind the sylvan horizon, and the stream that flows beside our home, and passes under the steep old bridge I have mentioned, wound through many a group of noble trees, almost at our feet, reflecting in its current the fading crimson of the sky. General Spielsdorf's letter was so extraordinary, so vehement, and in some places so self-contradictory, that I read it twice over—the second time aloud to my father—and was still unable to account for it, except by supposing that grief had unsettled his mind.

It said, "I have lost my darling daughter, for as such I loved her. During the last days of dear Bertha's illness I was not able to write to you. Before then I had no idea of her danger. I have lost her, and now learn *all*, too late. She died in the peace of innocence, and in the glorious hope of a blessed futurity. The fiend who betrayed our infatuated hospitality has done it all. I thought I was receiving into my house innocence, gaiety, a charming companion for my lost Bertha. Heavens! what a fool have I been! I thank God my child died without a suspicion of the cause of her sufferings. She is gone without so much as conjecturing the nature of her illness, and the accursed passion of the agent of all this misery. I devote my remaining days to tracking and extinguishing a monster. I am told I may hope to accomplish my righteous and merciful purpose. At present there is scarcely a gleam of light to guide me. I curse my conceited incredulity, my despicable affectation of superiority, my blindness, my obstinacy—all—too late. I cannot write or talk collectedly now. I am distracted. So soon as I shall have a little recovered, I mean to devote myself for a time to inquiry, which may possibly lead me as far as Vienna. Some time in the autumn, two months hence, or earlier if I live, I will see you —that is, if you permit me; I will then tell you all that I scarce dare put upon paper now. Farewell. Pray for me, dear friend."

In these terms ended this strange letter. Though I had never seen Bertha Rheinfeldt my eyes filled with tears at the sudden intelligence; I was startled, as well as profoundly disappointed.

The sun had now set, and it was twilight by the time I had returned the General's letter to my father.

I was a soft clear evening, and we loitered, speculating upon the possible meanings of the violent and incoherent sentences which I had just been reading. We had nearly a mile to walk before reaching the road that passes the schloss in front, and by that time the moon was shining brilliantly. At the drawbridge we met Madame Perrodon and Mademoiselle De Lafontaine, who had come out, without their bonnets, to enjoy the exquisite moonlight.

We heard their voices gabbling in animated dialogue as we approached. We joined them at the drawbridge, and turned about to admire with them the beautiful scene.

The glade through which we had just walked lay before us. At our left the narrow road wound away under clumps of lordly trees, and was lost to sight amid the thickening forest. At the right the same road crosses the steep and picturesque bridge, near which stands a ruined tower which once guarded that pass; and beyond the bridge an abrupt eminence rises, covered with trees, and showing in the shadows some grey ivy-clustered rocks.

Over the sward and low grounds a thin film of mist was stealing, like smoke, marking the distances with a transparent veil; and here and there we could see the river faintly flashing in the moonlight.

No softer, sweeter scene could be imagined. The news I had just heard made it melancholy; but nothing could disturb its character of profound serenity, and the enchanted glory and vagueness of the prospect.

My father, who enjoyed the picturesque, and I, stood looking in silence over the expanse beneath us. The two good governesses, standing a little way behind us, discoursed upon the scene, and were eloquent upon the moon.

Madame Perrodon was fat, middle-aged, and romantic, and talked and sighed poetically. Mademoiselle De Lafontaine—in right of her father, who was a German, assumed to be psychological, metaphysical, and something of a mystic—now declared that when the moon shone with a light so intense it was well known that it indicated a special spiritual activity. The effect of the full moon in such a state of brilliancy was manifold. It acted on dreams, it acted on lunacy, it acted on nervous people; it had marvelous physical influences connected with life. Mademoiselle related that her cousin, who was mate of a merchant ship, having taken a nap on deck on such a night lying on his back, with his face full in the light on the moon, had wakened, after a dream of an old woman clawing him by the cheek, with his features horribly drawn to one side; and his countenance had never quite recovered its equilibrium.

"The moon, this night," she said, "is full of odylic and magnetic influence—and see, when you look behind you at the front of the schloss how all its windows flash and twinkle with that silvery splendor, as if unseen hands had lighted up the rooms to receive fairy guests."

There are indolent states of the spirits in which, indisposed to talk ourselves, the talk of others is pleasant to our listless ears; and I gazed on, pleased with the tinkle of the ladies' conversation.

"I have got into one of my moping moods to-night," said my father, after a silence, and quoting Shakespeare, whom, by way of keeping up our English, he used to read aloud, he said:—

"In truth I know not why I am so sad:
It wearies me; you say it wearies you;
But how I got it—came by it.

"I forgot the rest. But I feel as if some great misfortune were hanging over us. I suppose the poor General's afflicted letter has had something to do with it."

At this moment the unwonted sound of carriage wheels and many hoofs upon the road, arrested our attention.

They seemed to be approaching from the high ground overlooking the bridge, and very soon the equipage emerged from that point. Two horsemen first crossed the bridge, then came a carriage drawn by four horses, and two men rode behind.

It seemed to be the traveling carriage of a person of rank; and we were all immediately absorbed in watching that very unusual spectacle. It became, in a few moments, greatly more interesting, for just as the carriage had passed the summit of the steep bridge, one of the leaders, taking fright, communicated his panic to the rest, and after a plunge or two, the whole team broke into a wild gallop together, and dashing between the horsemen who rode in front, came thundering along the road toward us with the speed of a hurricane.

The excitement of the scene was made more painful by the clear, long-drawn screams of a female voice from the carriage window.

We all advanced in curiosity and horror; my father in silence, the rest with various ejaculations of terror.

Our suspense did not last long. Just before you reach the castle drawbridge, on the route they were coming, there stands by the roadside a magnificent lime tree, on the other stands an ancient stone cross, at sight of which the horses, now going at a pace that was perfectly frightful, swerved so as to bring the wheel over the projecting roots of the tree.

I knew what was coming. I covered my eyes, unable to see it out, and turned my head away; at the same moment I heard a cry from my lady-friends, who had gone on a little.

Curiosity opened my eyes, and I saw a scene of utter confusion. Two of the horses were on the ground, the carriage lay upon its side with two wheels in the air; the men were busy removing the traces, and a lady, with a commanding air and figure had got out, and stood with clasped hands, raising the handkerchief that was in them every now and then to her eyes. Through the carriage door was now lifted a young lady, who appeared to be lifeless. My dear old father was already beside the elder lady, with his hat in his hand, evidently tendering his aid and the resources of his schloss. The lady did not appear to hear him, or to have eyes for anything but the slender girl who was being placed against the slope of the bank.

I approached; the young lady was apparently stunned, but she was certainly not dead. My father, who piqued himself on being something of a physician, had just had his fingers on her wrist and assured the lady, who declared herself her mother, that her pulse, though faint and irregular, was undoubtedly still distinguishable. The lady clasped her hands and looked upward, as if in a momentary transport of gratitude; but immediately she broke out again in that theatrical way which is, I believe, natural to some people.

She was what is called a fine-looking woman for her time of life, and must have been handsome; she was tall, but not thin, and dressed in black velvet, and looked rather pale, but with a proud and commanding countenance, though now agitated strangely.

"Was ever being so born to calamity?" I heard her say, with clasped hands, as I came up. "Here am I, on a journey of life and death, in prosecuting which to lose an hour is possibly to lose all. My child will not have recovered sufficiently to resume her route for who can say how long. I must leave her; I cannot, dare not, delay. How far on, sir, can you tell, is the nearest village? I must leave her there; and shall not see my darling, or even hear of her till my return, three months hence."

I plucked my father by the coat, and whispered earnestly in his ear: "Oh! papa, pray ask her to let her stay with us—it would be so delightful. Do, pray."

"If Madame will entrust her child to the care of my daughter, and of her good gouvernante, Madame Perrodon, and permit her to remain as our guest, under my charge, until her return, it will confer a distinction and an obligation upon us, and we shall treat her with all the care and devotion which so sacred a trust deserves."

"I cannot do that, sir, it would be to task your kindness and chivalry too cruelly," said the lady, distractedly.

"It would, on the contrary, be to confer on us a very great kindness at the moment when we most need it. My daughter has just been disappointed by a cruel misfortune, in a visit from which she had long anticipated a great deal of happiness. If you confide this young lady to our care it will be her best consolation. The nearest village on your route is distant, and affords no such inn as you could think of placing your daughter at; you cannot allow her to continue her journey for any considerable distance without danger. If, as you say, you cannot suspend your journey, you must part with her to-night, and nowhere could you do so with more honest assurances of care and tenderness than here."

There was something in this lady's air and appearance so distinguished, and even imposing, and in her manner so engaging, as to impress one, quite apart from the dignity of her equipage, with a conviction that she was a person of consequence.

By this time the carriage was replaced in its upright position, and the horses, quite tractable, in the traces again.

The lady threw on her daughter a glance which I fancied was not quite so affectionate as one might have anticipated from the beginning of the scene; then she beckoned slightly to my father, and withdrew two or three steps with him out of hearing; and talked to him with a fixed and stern countenance, not at all like that with which she had hitherto spoken.

I was filled with wonder that my father did not seem to perceive the change, and also unspeakably curious to learn what it could be that she was speaking, almost in his ear, with so much earnestness and rapidity.

Two or three minutes at most I think she remained thus employed, then she turned, and a few steps brought her to where her daughter lay, supported by Madame Perrodon. She kneeled beside her for a moment and whispered, as Madame supposed, a little benediction in her ear; then hastily kissing her she stepped into her carriage, the door was closed, the footmen in stately liveries jumped up behind, the outriders spurred on, the postilions cracked their whips, the horses plunged and broke suddenly into a furious canter that threatened soon again to become a gallop, and the carriage whirled away, followed at the same rapid pace by the two horsemen in the rear.

III

WE COMPARE NOTES

WE FOLLOWED THE *CORTÈGE* WITH OUR EYES UNTIL IT WAS SWIFTLY lost to sight in the misty wood; and the very sound of the hoofs and the wheels died away in the silent night air.

Nothing remained to assure us that the adventure had not been an illusion of a moment but the young lady, who just at that moment opened her eyes. I could not see, for her face was turned from me, but she raised her head, evidently looking about her, and I heard a very sweet voice ask complainingly. "Where is mamma?"

Our good Madame Perrodon answered tenderly, and added some comfortable assurances.

I then heard her ask:

"Where am I? What is this place?" and after that she said, "I don't see the carriage; and Matska, where is she?"

Madame answered all her questions in so far as she understood them; and gradually the young lady remembered how the misadventure came about, and was glad to hear that no one in, or in attendance on, the carriage was hurt; and on learning that her mamma had left her here, till her return in about three months, she wept.

I was going to add my consolations to those of Madame Perrodon when Mademoiselle de Lafontaine placed her hand upon my arm, saying:

"Don't approach, one at a time is as much as she can at present converse with; a very little excitement would possibly overpower her now."

As soon as she is comfortably in bed, I thought, I will run up to her room and see her.

My father in the meantime had sent a servant on horseback for the physician, who lived about two leagues away; and a bedroom was being prepared for the young lady's reception.

The stranger now rose, and leaning on Madame's arm, walked slowly over the drawbridge and into the castle gate.

In the hall, servants waited to receive her, and she was conducted forthwith to her room.

The room we usually sat in as our drawing-room is long, having four windows, that looked over the moat and drawbridge, upon the forest scene I have just described.

It is furnished in old carved oak, with large carved cabinets, and the chairs are cushioned with crimson Utrecht velvet. The walls are covered with tapestry, and surrounded with great gold frames, the figures being as large as life, in ancient and very curious costume, and the subjects represented are hunting, hawking, and generally festive. It is not too stately to be extremely comfortable; and here we had our tea, for with his usual patriotic leanings he insisted that the national beverage should make its appearance regularly with our coffee and chocolate.

We sat here this night, and with candles lighted, were talking over the adventure of the evening.

Madame Perrodon and Mademoiselle De Lafontaine were both of our party. The young stranger had hardly lain down in her bed when she sank into a deep sleep; and those ladies had left her in the care of a servant.

"How do you like our guest?" I asked, as soon as Madame entered. "Tell me all about her?"

"I like her extremely," answered Madame, "she is, I almost think, the prettiest creature I ever saw: about your age, and so gentle and nice."

"She is absolutely beautiful," threw in Mademoiselle, who had peeped for a moment into the stranger's room.

"And such a sweet voice!" added Madame Perrodon.

"Did you remark a woman in the carriage, after it was set up again, who did not get out," inquired Mademoiselle, "but only looked from the window?"

"No, we had not seen her."

Then she described a hideous black woman, with a sort of colored turban on her head, and who was gazing all the time from the carriage window, nodding and grinning derisively toward the ladies, with gleaming eyes and large white eyeballs, and her teeth set as if in fury.

"Did you remark what an ill-looking pack of men the servants were?" asked Madame.

"Yes," said my father, who had just come in, "ugly, hang-dog looking fellows, as ever I beheld in my life. I hope they mayn't rob the poor lady in the forest. They are clever rogues, however; they got everything to rights in a minute."

"I dare say they are worn out with too long traveling," said Madame. "Besides looking wicked, their faces were so strangely lean, and dark, and sullen. I am very curious, I own; but I dare say the young lady will tell us all about it to-morrow, if she is sufficiently recovered."

"I don't think she will," said my father, with a mysterious smile, and a little nod of his head, as if she knew more about it than he cared to tell us.

This made us all the more inquisitive as to what had passed between him and the lady in the black velvet, in the brief but earnest interview that had immediately preceded her departure.

We were scarcely alone, when I entreated him to tell me. He did not need much pressing.

"There is no particularly reason why I should not tell you. She expressed a reluctance to trouble us with the care of her daughter, saying she was in delicate health, and nervous, but not subject to any kind of seizure—she volunteered that—nor to any illusion; being, in fact, perfectly sane."

"How very odd to say all that!" I interpolated. "It was so unnecessary."

"At all events it *was* said," he laughed, "and as you wish to know all that passed, which was indeed very little, I tell you. She then said, 'I am making a long journey of *vital* importance'—she emphasized the word—'rapid and secret; I shall return for my child in three months; in the meantime, she will be silent as to who we are, whence we come, and whither we are traveling.' That is all she said. She spoke very pure French. When she said the word 'secret,' she paused for a few seconds, looking sternly, her eyes fixed on mine. I fancy she makes a great point of that. You saw how quickly she was gone. I hope I have not done a very foolish thing, in taking charge of the young lady."

For my part, I was delighted. I was longing to see and talk to her; and only waiting till the doctor should give me leave. You, who live in towns, can have no idea how great an event the introduction of a new friend is, in such a solitude as surrounded us.

The doctor did not arrive till nearly one o'clock; but I could no more have gone to my bed and slept, then I could have overtaken, on foot, the carriage in which the princess in black velvet had driven away.

When the physician came down into the drawing-room, it was to report very favorably upon his patient. She was now sitting up, her pulse quite regular, apparently perfectly well. She had sustained no injury, and the little shock to her nerves had passed away quite harmlessly. There could be no harm certainly in my seeing her, if we both wished it; and, with this permission, I sent, forthwith, to know whether she would allow me to visit her for a few minutes in her room.

The servant returned immediately to say that she desired nothing more.

You may be sure I was not long in availing myself of this permission.

Our visitor lay in one of the handsomest rooms in the schloss. It was, perhaps, a little stately. There was a sombre piece of tapestry opposite the foot of the bed, representing Cleopatra with the asps to her bosom; and other solemn classic scenes were displayed, a little faded, upon the other walls. But there was gold carving, and rich and varied color enough in the other decorations of the room, to more than redeem the gloom of the old tapestry.

There were candles at the bed side. She was sitting up; her slender pretty figure enveloped in the soft silk dressing-gown, embroidered with flowers, and lined with thick quilted silk, which her mother had thrown over her feet as she lay upon the ground.

What was it that, as I reached the bed side and had just begun my little greeting, struck me dumb in a moment, and made me recoil a step or two from before her? I will tell you.

I saw the very face which had visited me in my childhood at night, which remained so fixed in my memory, and on which I had for so many years so often ruminated with horror, when no one suspected of what I was thinking.

It was pretty, even beautiful; and when I first beheld it, wore the same melancholy expression.

But this almost instantly lighted into a strange fixed smile of recognition.

There was a silence of fully a minute, and then at length *she* spoke; *I* could not.

"How wonderful!" she exclaimed. "Twelve years ago, I saw your face in a dream, and it has haunted me ever since."

"Wonderful indeed!" I repeated, overcoming with an effort the horror that had for a time suspended my utterness. "Twelve years ago, in vision or reality, *I* certainly saw you. I could not forget your face. It has remained before my eyes ever since."

Her smile had softened. Whatever I had fancied strange in it, was gone, and it and her dimpling cheeks were now delightfully pretty and intelligent.

I felt reassured, and continued more in the vein which hospitality indicated, to bid her welcome, and to tell her how much pleasure her accidental arrival had given us all, and especially what a happiness it was to me.

I took her hand as I spoke. I was a little shy, as lonely people are, but the situation made me eloquent, and even bold. She pressed my hand, she laid hers upon it, and her eyes glowed, as, looking hastily into mine, she smiled again, and blushed.

She answered my welcome very prettily. I sat down beside her, still wondering, and she said:

"I must tell you my vision about you; it is so very strange that you and I should have had, each of the other so vivid a dream, that each should have seen, I you and you me, looking as we do now, when of course we both were mere children. I was a child, about six years old, and I awoke from a confused and troubled dream, and found myself in a room, unlike my nursery, wainscoted clumsily in some dark wood, and with cupboards and bedsteads, and chairs, and benches placed about it. The beds were, I thought, all empty, and the room itself without anyone but myself in it; and I, after looking about me for some time, and admiring especially an iron candlestick with two branches, which I should certainly know again, crept under one of the beds to reach the window; but as I got from under the bed, I heard someone crying; and looking up, while I was still upon my knees, I saw *you*—most assuredly you—as I see you now; a beautiful young lady, with golden hair and large blue eyes, and lips—your lips—you, as you are here. Your looks won me; I climbed on the bed and put my arms about you, and I think we both fell asleep. I was aroused by a scream; you were sitting up screaming. I was frightened, and slipped down upon the ground and, it seemed to me, lost consciousness for a moment; and when I came to myself, I was again in my nursery at home. Your face I have never forgotten since. I could not be misled by mere resemblance. You *are* the lady whom I then saw."

It was now my turn to relate my corresponding vision, which I did, to the undisguised wonder of my new acquaintance.

"I don't know which should be most afraid of the other," she said, again smiling. "If you were less pretty I think I should be very much afraid of you, but being as you are, and you and I both so young, I feel only that I have made your acquaintance twelve years ago, and have already a right to your intimacy; at all events it does seem as if we were destined, from our earliest childhood, to be friends. I wonder whether you feel as strangely drawn toward me as I do to you; I have never had a friend—shall I find one now?" She sighed, and her fine dark eyes gazed passionately on me.

Now the truth is, I felt rather unaccountably toward the beautiful stranger. I did feel, as she said, "drawn toward her," but there was also something of repulsion. In this ambiguous feeling, however, the sense of the attraction immensely prevailed. She interested and won me; she was so beautiful and so indescribably engaging.

I perceived now something of languor and exhaustion stealing over her, and hastened to bid her good night.

"The doctor thinks," I added, "that you ought to have a maid to sit up with you to-night; one of ours is waiting, and you will find her a very useful and quiet creature."

"How kind of you, but I could not sleep. I never could with an attendant in the room. I shan't require any assistance—and, shall I confess my weakness, I am haunted with a terror of robbers. Our house was robbed once, and two servants murdered, so I always lock my door. It has become a habit—and you look so kind I know you will forgive me. I see there is a key in the lock."

She held me close in her pretty arms for a moment and whispered in my ear, "Good night, darling, it is very hard to part with you, but good night; to-morrow, but not early, I shall see you again."

She sank back on the pillow with a sigh, and her fine eyes followed me with a fond and melancholy gaze, and she murmured again "Good-night, dear friend."

Young people like, and even love, on impulse. I was flattered by the evident, though as yet undeserved, fondness she showed me. I liked the confidence with which she at once received me. She was determined that we should be very near friends.

Next day came and we met again. I was delighted with my companion; that is to say, in many respects.

Her looks lost nothing in daylight—she was certainly the most beautiful creature I had ever seen, and the unpleasant remembrance of the face presented in my early dream, had lost the effect of the first unexpected recognition.

She confessed that she had experienced a similar shock on seeing me, and precisely the same faint antipathy that had mingled with my admiration of her. We now laughed together over our momentary horrors.

IV

HER HABITS—A SAUNTER

I told you that I was charmed with her in most particulars.

There were some that did not please me so well.

She was above the middle height of women. I shall begin by describing her. She was slender, and wonderfully graceful. Except that her movements were languid—*very* languid—indeed, there was nothing in her appearance to indicate an invalid. Her complexion was rich and brilliant; her features were small and beautifully formed; her eyes large, dark, and lustrous; her hair was quite wonderful, I never saw hair so magnificently thick and long when it was down about her shoulders; I have often placed my hands under it, and laughed with wonder at its weight. It was exquisitely fine and soft, and in color a rich very dark brown, with something of gold. I loved to let it down, tumbling with its own weight, as, in her room, she lay back in her chair talking in her sweet low voice, I used to fold and braid it, and spread it out and play with it. Heavens! If I had but known all!

I said there were particulars which did not please me. I have told you that her confidence won me the first night I saw her; but I found that she exercised with respect to herself, her mother, her history, everything in fact connected with her life, plans, and people, an ever wakeful reserve. I dare say I was unreasonable, perhaps I was wrong; I dare say I ought to have respected the solemn injunction laid upon my father by the stately lady in black velvet. But curiosity is a restless and unscrupulous passion, and no one girl can endure, with patience, that hers should be baffled by another. What harm could it do anyone to tell me what I so ardently desired to know? Had she no trust in my good sense or honor? Why would she not believe me when I assured her, so solemnly, that I would not divulge one syllable of what she told me to any mortal breathing.

There was a coldness, it seemed to me, beyond her years, in her smiling melancholy persistent refusal to afford me the last ray of light.

I cannot say we quarreled upon this point, for she would not quarrel upon any. It was, of course, very unfair of me to press her, very ill-bred, but I really could not help it; and I might just as well have let it alone.

What she did tell me amounted, in my unconscionable estimation—to nothing.

It was all summed up in three very vague disclosures:

First.—Her name was Carmilla.

Second.—Her family was very ancient and noble.

Third.—Her home lay in the direction of the west.

She would not tell me the name of her family, nor their armorial bearings, nor the name of their estate, nor even that of the country they lived in.

You are not to suppose that I worried her incessantly on these subjects. I watched opportunity, and rather insinuated than urged my inquiries. Once or twice, indeed, I did attack her more directly. But no matter what my tactics, utter failure was invariably the result. Reproaches and caresses were all lost upon her. But I must add this, that her evasion was conducted with so pretty a melancholy and deprecation, with so many, and even passionate declarations of her liking for me, and trust in my honor, and with so many promises that I should at last know all, that I could not find it in my heart long to be offended with her.

She used to place her pretty arms about my neck, draw me to her, and laying her cheek to mine, murmur with her lips near my ear, "Dearest, your little heart is wounded; think me not cruel because I obey the irresistible law of my strength and weakness; if your dear heart is wounded, my wild heart bleeds with yours. In the rapture of my enormous humiliation I live in your warm life, and you shall die—die, sweetly die—into mine. I cannot help it; as I draw near to you, you, in your turn, will draw near to others, and learn the rapture of that cruelty, which yet is love; so, for a while, seek to know no more of me and mine, but trust me with all your loving spirit."

And when she had spoken such a rhapsody, she would press me more closely in her trembling embrace, and her lips in soft kisses gently glow upon my cheek.

Her agitations and her language were unintelligible to me.

From these foolish embraces, which were not of very frequent occurrence, I must allow, I used to wish to extricate myself; but my energies seemed to fail me. Her murmured words sounded like a lullaby in my ear, and soothed my resistance into a trance, from which I only seemed to recover myself when she withdrew her arms.

In these mysterious moods I did not like her. I experienced a strange tumultuous excitement that was pleasurable, ever and anon, mingled with a vague sense of fear and disgust. I had no distinct thought about her while such scenes lasted, but I was conscious of a love growing into adoration, and also of abhorrence. This I know is paradox, but I can make no other attempt to explain the feeling.

I now write, after an interval of more than ten years, with a trembling hand, with a confused and horrible recollection of certain occurrences and situations, in the ordeal through which I was unconsciously passing; though with a vivid and very sharp remembrance of the main current of my story. But, I suspect, in all lives there are certain emotional scenes, those in which our passions have been most wildly and terribly roused, that are of all others the most vaguely and dimly remembered.

Sometimes after an hour of apathy, my strange and beautiful companion would take my hand and hold it with a fond pressure, renewed again and again; blushing softly, gazing in my face with languid and burning eyes, and breathing so fast that her dress rose and fell with the tumultuous respiration. It was like the ardor of a lover; it embarrassed me; it was hateful and yet overpowering; and with gloating eyes she drew me to her, and her hot lips traveled among my cheek in kisses; and she would whisper, almost in sobs, "You are mine, you *shall* be mine, you and I are one for ever." Then she threw herself back in her chair, with her small hands over her eyes, leaving me trembling.

"Are we related," I used to ask; "what can you mean by all this? I remind you perhaps of some one whom you love; but you must not, I hate it; I don't know you—I don't know myself when you look so and talk so."

She used to sigh at my vehemence, then turn away and drop my hand.

Respecting these very extraordinary manifestations I strove in vain to form any satisfactory theory—I could not refer them to affectation or trick. It was unmistakably the momentary breaking out of suppressed instinct and emotion. Was she, notwithstanding her mother's volunteered denial, subject to brief visitations of insanity; or was there here a disguise and a romance? I had read in old story books of such things. What if a boyish lover had found his way into the house, and sought to prosecute his suit in masquerade, with the assistance of a clever old adventuress. But there were many things against this hypothesis, highly interesting as it was to my vanity.

I could boast of no little attentions such as masculine gallantry delights to offer. Between these passionate moments there were long intervals of common-place, of gaiety, of brooding melancholy, during which, except that I detected her eyes so full of melancholy fire, following me, at times I might have been as nothing to her. Except in these brief periods of mysterious excitement her ways were girlish; and there was always a languor about her, quite incompatible with a masculine system in a state of health.

In some respects her habits were odd. Perhaps not so singular in the opinion of a town lady like you, as they appeared to us rustic people. She used to come down very late, generally not till one o'clock, she would then take a cup of chocolate, but eat nothing; we then went out for a walk, which was a mere saunter, and she seemed, almost immediately, exhausted, and either returned to the schloss or sat on one of the benches that were placed, here and there, among the trees. This was a bodily languor in which her mind did not sympathise. She was always an animated talker, and very intelligent.

She sometimes alluded for a moment to her own home, or mentioned an adventure or situation, or an early recollection, which indicated a people of strange manners, and described customs of which we knew nothing. I gathered from these chance hints that her native country was much more remote than I had at first fancied.

As we sat thus one afternoon under the trees a funeral passed us by. It was that of a pretty young girl, whom I had often seen, the daughter of one of the rangers of the forest. The poor man was walking behind the coffin of his darling; she was his only child, and he looked quite heartbroken. Peasants walking two-and-two came behind, they were singing a funeral hymn.

I rose to mark my respect as they passed, and joined in the hymn they were very sweetly singing.

My companion shook me a little roughly, and I turned surprised.

She said brusquely. "Don't you perceive how discordant that is?"

"I think it very sweet, on the contrary," I answered, vexed at the interruption, and very uncomfortable, lest the people who composed the little procession should observe and resent what was passing.

I resumed, therefore, instantly, and was again interrupted. "You pierce my ears," said Carmilla, almost angrily, and stopping her ears with her tiny fingers, "Besides, how can you tell that your religion and mine are the same; your forms wound me, and I hate funerals. What a fuss! Why *you* must die—*everyone* must die; and all are happier when they do. Come home."

"My father has gone on with the clergyman to the churchyard. I thought you knew she was to be buried to-day."

"*She?* I don't trouble my head about peasants. I don't know who she is," answered Carmilla, with a flash from her fine eyes.

"She is the poor girl who fancied she saw a ghost a fortnight ago, and has been dying ever since, till yesterday, when she expired."

"Tell me nothing about ghosts. I shan't sleep to-night if you do."

"I hope there is no plague or fever coming; all this looks very like it," I continued. "The swine-herd's young wife died only a week ago, and she thought something seized her by the throat as she lay in her bed, and nearly strangled her. Papa says such horrible fancies do accompany some forms of fever. She was quite well the day before. She sank afterward, and died before a week."

"Well, *her* funeral is over, I hope, and *her* hymn sung; and our ears shan't be tortured with that discord and jargon. It has made me nervous. Sit down here, beside me; sit close; hold my hand; press it hard—hard—harder."

We had moved a little back, and had come to another seat.

She sat down. Her face underwent a change that alarmed and even terrified me for a moment. It darkened, and became horribly livid; her teeth and hands were clenched, and she frowned and compressed her lips, while she stared down upon the ground at her feet, and trembled all over with a continued shudder as irrepressible as ague. All her energies seemed strained to suppress a fit, with which she was then breathlessly tugging; and at length a low convulsive cry of suffering broke from her, and gradually the hysteria subsided. "There! That comes of strangling people with hymns!" she said at last. "Hold me, hold me still. It is passing away."

And so gradually it did; and perhaps to dissipate the somber impression which the spectacle had left upon me, she became unusually animated and chatty; and so we got home.

This was the first time I had seen her exhibit any definable symptoms of that delicacy of health which her mother had spoken of. It was the first time, also, I had seen her exhibit anything like temper.

Both passed away like a summer cloud; and never but once afterward did I witness on her part a momentary sign of anger. I will tell you how it happened.

She and I were looking out of one of the long drawing-room windows, when there entered the courtyard, over the drawbridge, a figure of a wanderer whom I knew very well. He used to visit the schloss generally twice a year.

It was the figure of a hunchback, with the sharp lean features that generally accompany deformity. He wore a pointed black beard, and he was smiling from ear to ear, showing his white fangs. He was dressed in buff, black, and scarlet, and crossed with more straps and belts than I could count, from which hung all manner of things. Behind, he carried a magic-lantern, and two boxes, which I well knew, in one of which was a salamander, and in the other a mandrake. These monsters used to make my father laugh. They were compounded of parts of monkeys, parrots, squirrels, fish, and hedgehogs, dried and stitched together with great neatness and startling effect. He had a fiddle, a box of conjuring apparatus, a pair of foils and masks attached to his belt, several other mysterious cases dangling about him, and a black staff with copper ferrules in his hand. His companion was a rough spare dog, that followed at his heels, but stopped short, suspiciously at the drawbridge, and in a little while began to howl dismally.

In the meantime, the mountebank, standing in the midst of the court-yard, raised his grotesque hat, and made us a very ceremonious bow, paying his compliments very volubly in execrable French, and German not much better. Then, disengaging his fiddle, he began to scrape a lively air, to which he sang with merry discord, dancing with ludicrous airs and activity, that made me laugh, in spite of the dog's howling.

Then he advanced to the window with many smiles and salutations, and his hat in his left hand, his fiddle under his arm, and with a fluency that never took breath, he gabbled a long advertisement of all his accomplishments, and the resources of the various arts which he placed at our service, and the curiosities and entertainments which it was in his power, at our bidding, to display.

"Will your ladyships be pleased to buy an amulet against the oupire, which is going like the wolf, I hear, through these woods," he said, dropping his hat on the pavement. "They are dying of it right and left, and here is a charm that never fails; only pinned to the pillow, and you may laugh in his face."

These charms consisted of oblong slips of vellum, with cabalistic ciphers and diagrams upon them.

Carmilla instantly purchased one, and so did I.

He was looking up, and we were smiling down upon him, amused; at least, I can answer for myself. His piercing black eye, as he looked up in our faces, seemed to detect something that fixed for a moment his curiosity.

In an instant he unrolled a leather case, full of all manner of odd little steel instruments.

"See here, my lady," he said, displaying it, and addressing me, "I profess, among other things less useful, the art of dentistry. Plague take the dog!" he interpolated. "Silence, beast! He howls so that your ladyships can scarcely hear a word. Your noble friend, the young lady at your right, has the sharpest tooth—long, thin, pointed, like an awl, like a needle; ha, ha! With my sharp and long sight, as I look up, I have seen it distinctly; now if it happens to hurt the young lady, and I think it must, here am I, here are my file, my punch, my nippers; I will make it round and blunt, if her ladyship pleases; no longer the tooth of a fish, but of a beautiful young lady as she is. Hey? Is the young lady displeased? Have I been too bold? Have I offended her?"

The young lady, indeed, looked very angry as she drew back from the window.

"How does that mountebank insult us so? Where is your father? I shall demand redress from him. My father would have had the wretch tied up to the pump, and flogged with a cart-whip, and burnt to the bones with the castle brand!"

She retired from the window a step or two, and sat down, and had hardly lost sight of the offender, when her wrath subsided as suddenly as it had risen, and she gradually recovered her usual tone, and seemed to forget the little hunchback and his follies.

My father was out of spirits that evening. On coming in he told us that there had been another case very similar to the two fatal ones which had lately occurred. The sister of a young peasant on his estate, only a mile away, was very ill, had been, as she described it, attacked very nearly in the same way, and was now slowly but steadily sinking.

"All this," said my father, "is strictly referable to natural causes. These poor people infect one another with their superstitions, and so repeat in imagination the images of terror that have infested their neighbors."

"But that very circumstance frightens one horribly," said Carmilla.

"How so?" inquired my father.

"I am so afraid of fancying I see such things; I think it would be as bad as reality."

"We are in God's hands; nothing can happen without his permission, and all will end well for those who love him. He is our faithful creator; He had made us all, and will take care of us."

"Creator! *Nature!*" said the young lady in answer to my gentle father. "And this disease that invades the country is natural. Nature. All things proceed from Nature—don't they? All things in the heaven, in the earth, and under the earth, act and live as Nature ordains? I think so."

"The doctor said he would come here to-day," said my father, after a silence. "I want to know what he thinks about it, and what he thinks we had better do."

"Doctors never did me any good," said Carmilla.

"Then you have been ill?" I asked.

"More ill than ever you were," she answered.

"Long ago?"

"Yes, a long time. I suffered from this very illness; but I forget all my pain and weakness, and they were not so bad as are suffered in other diseases."

"You were very young then?"

"I dare say; let us talk no more of it. You would not wound a friend?" She looked languidly in my eyes, and passed her arm round my waist lovingly, and led me out of the room. My father was busy over some papers near the window.

"Why does your papa like to frighten us?" said the pretty girl, with a sigh and a little shudder.

"He doesn't, dear Carmilla, it is the very furthest thing from his mind."

"Are you afraid, dearest?"

"I should be very much if I fancied there was any real danger of my being attacked as those poor people were."

"You are afraid to die?"

"Yes, every one is."

"But to die as lovers may—to die together, so that they may live together. Girls are caterpillars while they live in the world, to be finally butterflies when the summer comes; but in the meantime there are grubs and larvae, don't you see—each with their peculiar propensities, necessities and structure. So says Monsieur Buffon, in his big book, in the next room."

Later in the day the doctor came, and was closeted with papa from some time. He was a skillful man, of sixty and upward, he wore powder, and shaved his pale face as smooth as a pumpkin. He and papa emerged from the room together, and I heard papa laugh, and say as they came out:

"Well, I do wonder at a wise man like you. What do you say to hippogriffs and dragons?"

The doctor was smiling, and made answer, shaking his head—

"Nevertheless, life and death are mysterious states, and we know little of the resources of either."

And so they walked on, and I heard no more. I did not then know what the doctor had been broaching, but I think I guess it now.

V

A WONDERFUL LIKENESS

THIS EVENING THERE ARRIVED FROM GRATZ THE GRAVE, DARK-FACED son of the picture-cleaner, with a horse and cart laden with two large packing cases, having many pictures in each. It was a journey of ten leagues, and whenever a messenger arrived at the schloss from our little capital of Gratz, we used to crowd about him in the hall, to hear the news.

This arrival created in our secluded quarters quite a sensation. The cases remained in the hall, and the messenger was taken charge of by the servants till he had eaten his supper. Then with assistants, and armed with hammer, ripping-chisel, and turnscrew, he met us in the hall, where we had assembled to witness the unpacking of the cases.

Carmilla sat looking listlessly on, while one after the other the old pictures, nearly all portraits, which had undergone the process of renovation, were brought to light. My mother was of an old Hungarian family, and most of these pictures, which were about to be restored to their places, had come to us through her.

My father had a list in his hand, from which he read, as the artist rummaged out the corresponding numbers. I don't know that the pictures were very good, but they were, undoubtedly, very old, and some of them very curious also. They had, for the most part, the merit of being now seen by me, I may say, for the first time; for the smoke and dust of time had all but obliterated them.

"There is a picture that I have not seen yet," said my father. "In one corner, at the top of it, is the name, as well as I could read, 'Marcia Karnstein,' and the date '1698'; and I am curious to see how it has turned out."

I remembered it; it was a small picture, about a foot and a half high, and nearly square, without a frame; but it was so blackened by age that I could not make it out.

The artist now produced it, with evident pride. It was quite beautiful; it was startling; it seemed to live. It was the effigy of Carmilla!

"Carmilla, dear, here is an absolute miracle. Here you are, living, smiling, ready to speak, in this picture. Isn't it beautiful, papa? And see, even the little mole on her throat."

My father laughed, and said, "Certainly it is a wonderful likeness," but he looked away, and to my surprise seemed but little struck by it, and went on talking to the picture-cleaner, who was also something of an artist, and discoursed with intelligence about the portraits or other works, which his art had just brought into light and color, while *I* was more and more lost in wonder the more I looked at the picture.

"Will you let me hang this picture in my room, papa?" I asked.

"Certainly, dear," said he, smiling, "I'm very glad you think it so like. It must be prettier even than I thought it, if it is."

The young lady did not acknowledge this pretty speech, did not seem to hear it. She was leaning back in her seat, her fine eyes under their long lashes gazing on me in contemplation, and she smiled in a kind of rapture.

"And now you can read quite plainly the name that is written in the corner. It is not Marcia; it looks as if it was done in gold. The name is Mircalla, Countess Karnstein, and this is a little coronet over it, and underneath A.D. 1698. I am descended from the Karnsteins; that is, mamma was."

"Ah!" said the lady, languidly, "so am I, I think, a very long descent, very ancient. Are they any Karnsteins living now?"

"None who bear the name, I believe. The family were ruined, I believe, in some civil wars, long ago, but the ruins of the castle are only about three miles away."

"How interesting!" she said, languidly. "But see what beautiful moonlight!" She glanced through the hall-door, which stood a little open. "Suppose you take a little ramble round the court, and look down at the road and river."

"It is so like the night you came to us," I said.

She sighed, smiling.

She rose, and each with her arm about the other's waist, we walked out upon the pavement.

In silence, slowly we walked down to the drawbridge, where the beautiful landscape opened before us.

"And so you were thinking of the night I came here?" she almost whispered. "Are you glad I came?"

"Delighted, dear Carmilla," I answered.

"And you asked for the picture you think like me, to hang in your room," she murmured with a sigh, as she drew her arm closer about my waist, and let her pretty head sink upon my shoulder.

"How romantic you are, Carmilla," I said. "Whenever you tell me your story, it will be made up chiefly of some one great romance."

She kissed me silently.

"I am sure, Carmilla, you have been in love; that there is, at this moment, an affair of the heart going on."

"I have been in love with no one, and never shall," she whispered, "unless it should be with you."

How beautiful she looked in the moonlight!

Shy and strange was the look with which she quickly hid her face in my neck and hair, with tumultuous sighs, that seemed almost to sob, and pressed in mine a hand that trembled.

Her soft cheek was glowing against mine. "Darling, darling," she murmured, "I live in you; and you would die for me, I love you so."

I started from her.

She was gazing on me with eyes from which all fire, all meaning had flown, and a face colorless and apathetic.

"Is there a chill in the air, dear?" she said drowsily. "I almost shiver; have I been dreaming? Let us come in. Come; come; come in."

"You look ill, Carmilla; a little faint. You certainly must take some wine," I said.

"Yes, I will, I'm better now. I shall be quite well in a few minutes. Yes, do give me a little wine," answered Carmilla, as we approached the door. "Let us look again for a moment; it is the last time, perhaps, I shall see the moonlight with you."

"How do you feel now, Carmilla? Are you really better?" I asked.

I was beginning to take alarm, lest she should have been stricken with the strange epidemic that they said had invaded the country about us.

"Papa would be grieved beyond measure," I added, "if he thought you were ever so little ill, without immediately letting us know. We have a very skillful doctor near this, the physician who was with papa to-day."

"I'm sure he is. I know how kind you all are; but, dear child, I am quite well again. There is nothing ever wrong with me, but a little weakness. People say I am languid; I am incapable of exertion; I can scarcely walk as far as a child of three years old; and every now and then the little strength I have falters, and I become as you have just seen me. But after all I am very easily set up again; in a moment I am perfectly myself. See how I have recovered."

So, indeed, she had; and she and I talked a great deal, and very animated she was; and the remainder of that evening passed without any recurrence of what I called her infatuations. I mean her crazy talk and looks, which embarrassed, and even frightened me.

But there occurred that night an event which gave my thoughts quite a new turn, and seemed to startle even Carmilla's languid nature into momentary energy.

VI

A VERY STRANGE AGONY

When we got into the drawing-room, and had sat down to our coffee and chocolate, although Carmilla did not take any, she seemed quite herself again, and Madame, and Mademoiselle De Lafontaine, joined us, and made a little card party, in the course of which papa came in for what he called his "dish of tea."

When the game was over he sat down beside Carmilla on the sofa, and asked her, a little anxiously, whether she had heard from her mother since her arrival.

She answered "No."

He then asked whether she knew where a letter would reach her at present.

"I cannot tell," she answered ambiguously, "but I have been thinking of leaving you; you have been already too hospitable and too kind to me. I have given you an infinity of trouble, and I should wish to take a carriage to-morrow, and post in pursuit of her; I know where I shall ultimately find her, although I dare not yet tell you."

"But you must not dream of any such thing," exclaimed my father, to my great relief. "We can't afford to lose you so, and I won't consent to your leaving us, except under the care of your mother, who was so good as to consent to your remaining with us till she should herself return. I should be quite happy if I knew that you heard from her; but this evening the accounts of the progress of the mysterious disease that has invaded our neighborhood, grow even more alarming; and my beautiful guest, I do feel the responsibility, unaided by advice from your mother, very much. But I shall do my best; and one thing is certain, that you must not think of leaving us without her distinct direction to that effect. We should suffer too much in parting from you to consent to it easily."

"Thank you, sir, a thousand times for your hospitality," she answered, smiling bashfully. "You have all been too kind to me; I have seldom been so happy in all my life before, as in your beautiful château, under your care, and in the society of your dear daughter."

So he gallantly, in his old-fashioned way, kissed her hand, smiling and pleased at her little speech.

I accompanied Carmilla as usual to her room, and sat and chatted with her while she was preparing for bed.

"Do you think," I said at length, "that you will ever confide fully in me?"

She turned round smiling, but made no answer, only continued to smile on me.

"You won't answer that?" I said. "You can't answer pleasantly; I ought not to have asked you."

"You were quite right to ask me that, or anything. You do not know how dear you are to me, or you could not think any confidence too great to look for. But I am under vows, no nun half so awfully, and I dare not tell my story yet, even to you. The time is very near when you shall know everything. You will think me cruel, very selfish, but love is always selfish; the more ardent the more selfish. How jealous I am you cannot know. You must come with me, loving me, to death; or else hate me and still come with me, and *hating* me through death and after. There is no such word as indifference in my apathetic nature."

"Now, Carmilla, you are going to talk your wild nonsense again," I said hastily.

"Not I, silly little fool as I am, and full of whims and fancies; for your sake I'll talk like a sage. Were you ever at a ball?"

"No; how you do run on. What is it like? How charming it must be."

"I almost forget, it is years ago."

I laughed.

"You are not so old. Your first ball can hardly be forgotten yet."

"I remember everything about it—with an effort. I see it all, as divers see what is going on above them, through a medium, dense, rippling, but transparent. There occurred that night what has confused the picture, and made its colours faint. I was all but assassinated in my bed, wounded *here*," she touched her breast, "and never was the same since."

"Were you near dying?"

"Yes, very—a cruel love—strange love, that would have taken my life. Love will have its sacrifices. No sacrifice without blood. Let us go to sleep now; I feel so lazy. How can I get up just now and lock my door?"

She was lying with her tiny hands buried in her rich wavy hair, under her cheek, her little head upon the pillow, and her glittering eyes followed me wherever I moved, and a kind of shy smile that I could not decipher.

I bid her good-night, and crept from the room with an uncomfortable sensation.

I often wondered whether our pretty guest ever said her prayers. *I* certainly had never seen her upon her knees. In the morning she never came down until long after our family prayers were over, and at night she never left the drawing-room to attend our brief evening prayers in the hall.

If it had not been that it had casually come out in one of our careless talks that she had been baptised, I should have doubted her being a Christian. Religion was a subject on which I had never heard her speak a word. If had known the world better, this particular neglect or antipathy would not have so much surprised me.

The precautions of nervous people are infectious, and persons of a like temperament are pretty sure, after a time, to imitate them. I had adopted Carmilla's habit of locking her bedroom door, having taken into my head all her whimsical alarms about midnight invaders and prowling assassins. I had also adopted her precaution of making a brief search through her room, to satisfy herself that no lurking assassin or robber was "ensconced."

These wise measures taken, I got into my bed and fell asleep. A light was burning in my room. This was an old habit, of very early date, and which nothing could have tempted me to dispense with.

Thus fortified I might take my rest in peace. But dreams come through stone walls, light up dark rooms, or darken light ones, and their persons make their exits and their entrances as they please, and laugh at locksmiths.

I had a dream that night that was the beginning of a very strange agony.

I cannot call it a nightmare, for I was quite conscious of being asleep. But I was equally conscious of being in my room, and lying in bed, precisely as I actually was. I saw, or fancied I saw, the room and its furniture just as I had seen it last, except that it was very dark, and I saw something moving round the foot of the bed, which at first I could not accurately distinguish. But I soon saw that it was a sooty-black animal that resembled a monstrous cat. It appeared to me about four or five feet long, for it measured fully the length of the hearthrug as it passed over it; and it continued to-ing and fro-ing with the lithe, sinister restlessness of a beast in a cage. I could not cry out, although as you may suppose, I was terrified. Its pace was growing faster, and the room rapidly darker and darker, and at length so dark that I could no longer see anything of it but its eyes. I felt it spring lightly on the bed. The two broad eyes approached my face, and suddenly I felt a stinging pain as if two large needles darted, an inch or two apart, deep into my breast. I waked with a scream. The room was lighted by the candle that burnt there all through the night, and I saw a female figure standing at the foot of the bed, a little at the right side. It was in a dark loose dress, and its hair was down and covered its shoulders. A block of stone could not have been more still. There was not the slightest stir of respiration. As I stared at it, the figure appeared to have changed its place, and was now nearer the door; then, close to it, the door opened, and it passed out.

I was now relieved, and able to breathe and move. My first thought was that Carmilla had been playing me a trick, and that I had forgotten to secure my door. I hastened to it, and found it locked as usual on the inside. I was afraid to open it—I was horrified. I sprang into my bed and covered my head up in the bed-clothes, and lay there more dead than alive till morning.

VII

DESCENDING

IT WOULD BE VAIN MY ATTEMPTING TO TELL YOU THE HORROR WITH which, even now, I recall the occurrence of that night. It was no such transitory terror as a dream leaves behind it. It seemed to deepen by time, and communicated itself to the room and the very furniture that had encompassed the apparition.

I could not bear next day to be alone for a moment. I should have told papa, but for two opposite reasons. At one time I thought he would laugh at my story, and I could not bear its being treated as a jest; and at another, I thought he might fancy that I had been attacked by the mysterious complaint which had invaded our neighborhood. I had myself no misgivings of the kind, and as he had been rather an invalid for some time, I was afraid of alarming him.

I was comfortable enough with my good-natured companions, Madame Perrodon, and the vivacious Mademoiselle De Lafontaine. They both perceived that I was out of spirits and nervous, and at length I told them what lay so heavy at my heart.

Mademoiselle laughed, but I fancied that Madame Perrodon looked anxious.

"By-the-by," said Mademoiselle, laughing, "the long lime tree walk, behind Carmilla's bedroom window, is haunted!"

"Nonsense," exclaimed Madame, who probably thought the theme rather inopportune, "and who tells the story, my dear?"

"Martin says that he came up twice, when the old yard-gate was being repaired, before sunrise, and twice saw the same female figure walking down the lime tree avenue."

"So he well might, as long as there are cows to milk in the river fields," said Madame.

"I daresay; but Martin chooses to be frightened, and never did I see fool *more* frightened."

"You must not say a word about it to Carmilla, because she can see down that walk from her room window," I interposed, "and she is, if possible, a greater coward than I."

Carmilla came down rather later than usual that day.

"I was so frightened last night," she said, so soon as were together, "and I am sure I should have seen something dreadful if it had not been for that charm I bought from the poor little hunchback whom I called such hard names. I had a dream of something black coming round my bed, and I awoke in a perfect horror, and I really thought, for some seconds, I saw a dark figure near the chimney-piece, but I felt under my pillow for my charm, and the moment any fingers touched it, the figure disappeared, and I felt quite certain, only that I had it by me, that something frightful would have made its appearance, and, perhaps, throttled me, as it did those poor people we heard of."

"Well, listen to me," I began, and recounted my adventure, at the recital of which she appeared horrified.

"And had you the charm near you?" she asked, earnestly.

"No, I had dropped it into a china vase in the drawing-room, but I shall certainly take it with me to-night, as you have so much faith in it."

At this distance of time I cannot tell you, or even understand, how I overcame my horror so effectually as to lie alone in my room that night. I remember distinctly that I pinned the charm to my pillow. I fell asleep almost immediately, and slept even more soundly than usual all night.

Next night I passed as well. My sleep was delightfully deep and dreamless. But I wakened with a sense of lassitude and melancholy, which, however, did not exceed a degree that was almost luxurious.

"Well, I told you so," said Carmilla, when I described my quiet sleep, "I had such delightful sleep myself last night; I pinned the charm to the breast of my nightdress. It was too far away the night before. I am quite sure it was all fancy, except the dreams. I used to think that evil spirits made dreams, but our doctor told me it is no such thing. Only a fever passing by, or some other malady, as they often do, he said, knocks at the door, and not being able to get in, passes on, with that alarm."

"And what do you think the charm is?" said I.

"It has been fumigated or immersed in some drug, and is an antidote against the malaria," she answered.

"Then it acts only on the body?"

"Certainly; you don't suppose that evil spirits are frightened by bits of ribbon, or the perfumes of a druggist's shop? No, these complaints, wandering in the air, begin by trying the nerves, and so infect the brain, but before they can seize upon you, the antidote repels them. That I am sure is what the charm has done for us. It is nothing magical, it is simply natural."

I should have been happier if I could have quite agreed with Carmilla, but I did my best, and the impression was a little losing its force.

For some nights I slept profoundly; but still every morning I felt the same lassitude, and a languor weighed upon me all day. I felt myself a changed girl. A strange melancholy was stealing over me, a melancholy that I would not have interrupted. Dim thoughts of death began to open, and an idea that I was slowly sinking took gentle, and, somehow, not unwelcome, possession of me. If it was sad, the tone of mind which this induced was also sweet. Whatever it might be, my soul acquiesced in it.

I would not admit that I was ill, I would not consent to tell my papa, or to have the doctor sent for.

Carmilla became more devoted to me than ever, and her strange paroxysms of languid adoration more frequent. She used to gloat on me with increasing ardor the more my strength and spirits waned. This always shocked me like a momentary glare of insanity.

Without knowing it, I was now in a pretty advanced stage of the strangest illness under which mortal ever suffered. There was an unaccountable fascination in its earlier symptoms that more than reconciled me to the incapacitating effect of that stage of the malady. This fascination increased for a time, until it reached a certain point, when gradually a sense of the horrible mingled itself with it, deepening, as you shall hear, until it discoloured and perverted the whole state of my life.

The first change I experienced was rather agreeable. It was very near the turning point from which began the descent of Avernus.

Certain vague and strange sensations visited me in my sleep. The prevailing one was of that pleasant, peculiar cold thrill which we feel in bathing, when we move against the current of a river. This was soon accompanied by dreams that seemed interminable, and were so vague that I could never recollect their scenery and persons, or any one connected portion of their action. But they left an awful impression, and a sense of exhaustion, as if I had passed through a long period of great mental exertion and danger. After all these dreams there remained on waking a remembrance of having been in a place very nearly dark, and of having spoken to people whom I could not see; and especially of one clear voice, of a female's, very deep, that spoke as if at a distance, slowly, and producing always the same sensation of indescribable solemnity and fear. Sometimes there came a sensation as if a hand was drawn softly along my cheek and neck. Sometimes it was as if warm lips kissed me, and longer and more lovingly as they reached my throat, but there the caress fixed itself. My heart beat faster, my breathing rose and fell rapidly and full drawn; a sobbing, that rose into a sense of strangulation, supervened, and turned into a dreadful convulsion, in which my senses left me and I became unconscious.

It was now three weeks since the commencement of this unaccountable state. My sufferings had, during the last week, told upon my appearance. I had grown pale, my eyes were dilated and darkened underneath, and the languor which I had long felt began to display itself in my countenance.

My father asked me often whether I was ill; but, with an obstinacy which now seems to me unaccountable, I persisted in assuring him that I was quite well.

In a sense this was true. I had no pain. I could complain of no bodily derangement. My complaint seemed to be one of the imagination, or the nerves, and, horrible as my sufferings were, I kept them, with a morbid reserve, very nearly to myself.

It could not be that terrible complaint which the peasants called the oupire, for I had now been suffering for three weeks, and they were seldom ill for much more than three days, when death put an end to their miseries.

Carmilla complained of dreams and feverish sensations, but by no means of so alarming a kind as mine. I say that mine were extremely alarming. Had I been capable of comprehending my condition, I would have invoked aid and advice on my knees. The narcotic of an unsuspected influence was acting upon me, and my perceptions were benumbed.

I am going to tell you now of a dream that led immediately to an odd discovery.

One night, instead of the voice I was accustomed to hear in the dark, I heard one, sweet and tender, and at the same time terrible, which said, "Your mother warns you to beware of the assassin." At the same time a light unexpectedly sprang up, and I saw Carmilla, standing, near the foot of my bed, in her white nightdress, bathed, from her chin to her feet, in one great stain of blood.

I wakened with a shriek, possessed with the one idea that Carmilla was being murdered. I remember springing from my bed, and my next recollection is that of standing on the lobby, crying for help.

Madame and Mademoiselle came scurrying out of their rooms in alarm; a lamp burned always on the lobby, and seeing me, they soon learned the cause of my terror.

I insisted on our knocking at Carmilla's door. Our knocking was unanswered. It soon became a pounding and an uproar. We shrieked her name, but all was vain.

We all grew frightened, for the door was locked. We hurried back, in panic, to my room. There we rang the bell long and furiously. If my father's room had been at that side of the house we would have called him up at once to our aid. But, alas! he was quite out of hearing, and to reach him involved an excursion for which we none of us had courage.

Servants, however, soon came running up the stairs; I had got on my dressing-gown and slippers meanwhile, and my companions were already similarly furnished. Recognizing the voices of the servants on the lobby, we sallied out together; and having renewed, as fruitlessly, our summons at Carmilla's door, I ordered the men to force the lock. They did so, and we stood, holding our lights aloft, in the doorway, and so stared into the room.

We called her by name; but there was still no reply. We looked around the room. Everything was undisturbed. It was exactly in the state in which I had left it on bidding her good night. But Carmilla was gone.

VIII

SEARCH

AT SIGHT OF THE ROOM, PERFECTLY UNDISTURBED EXCEPT FOR OUR violent entrance, we began to cool a little, and soon recovered our senses sufficiently to dismiss the men. It had struck Mademoiselle that possibly Carmilla had been wakened by the uproar at her door, and in her first panic had jumped from her bed, and hid herself in a press, or behind a curtain, from which she could not, of course, emerge until the majordomo and his myrmidons had withdrawn. We now recommenced our search, and began to call her by name again.

It was all to no purpose. Our perplexity and agitation increased. We examined the windows, but they were secured. I implored of Carmilla, if she had concealed herself, to play this cruel trick no longer—to come out, and to end our anxieties. It was all useless. I was by this time convinced that she was not in the room, nor in the dressing-room, the door of which was still locked on this side. She could not have passed it. I was utterly puzzled. Had Carmilla discovered one of those secret passages which the old housekeeper said were known to exist in the schloss, although the tradition of their exact situation had been lost? A little time would, no doubt, explain all—utterly perplexed as, for the present, we were.

It was past four o'clock, and I preferred passing the remaining hour of darkness in Madame's room. Daylight brought no solution of the difficulty.

The whole household, with my father at its head, was in a state of agitation next morning. Every part of the château was searched. The grounds were explored. Not a trace of the missing lady could be discovered. The stream was about to be dragged; my father was in distraction; what a tale to have to tell the poor girl's mother on her return. I, too, was almost beside myself, though my grief was quite of a different kind.

The morning was passed in alarm and excitement. It was now one o'clock, and still no tidings. I ran up to Carmilla's room, and found her standing at her dressing-table. I was astounded. I could not believe my eyes. She beckoned me to her with her pretty finger, in silence. Her face expressed extreme fear.

I ran to her in an ecstasy of joy; I kissed and embraced her again and again. I ran to the bell and rang it vehemently, to bring others to the spot, who might at once relieve my father's anxiety.

"Dear Carmilla, what has become of you all this time? We have been in agonies of anxiety about you," I exclaimed. "Where have you been? How did you come back?"

"Last night has been a night of wonders," she said.

"For mercy's sake, explain all you can."

"It was past two last night," she said, "when I went to sleep as usual in my bed, with my doors locked, that of the dressing-room, and that opening upon the gallery. My sleep was uninterrupted, and, so far as I know, dreamless; but I woke just now on the sofa in the dressing-room there, and I found the door between the rooms open, and the other door forced. How could all this have happened without my being wakened? It must have been accompanied with a great deal of noise, and I am particularly easily wakened; and how could I have been carried out of my bed without my sleep having been interrupted, I whom the slightest stir startles?"

By this time, Madame, Mademoiselle, my father, and a number of the servants were in the room. Carmilla was, of course, overwhelmed with inquiries, congratulations, and welcomes. She had but one story to tell, and seemed the least able of all the party to suggest any way of accounting for what had happened.

My father took a turn up and down the room, thinking. I saw Carmilla's eye follow him for a moment with a sly, dark glance.

When my father had sent the servants away, Mademoiselle having gone in search of a little bottle of valerian and sal-volatile, and there being no one now in the room with Carmilla, except my father, Madame, and myself, he came to her thoughtfully, took her hand very kindly, led her to the sofa, and sat down beside her.

"Will you forgive me, my dear, if I risk a conjecture, and ask a question?"

"Who can have a better right?" she said. "Ask what you please, and I will tell you everything. But my story is simply one of bewilderment and darkness. I know absolutely nothing. Put any question you please. But you know, of course, the limitations mamma has placed me under."

"Perfectly, my dear child. I need not approach the topics on which she desires our silence. Now, the marvel of last night consists in your having been removed from your bed and your room, without being wakened, and this removal having occurred apparently while the windows were still secured, and the two doors locked upon the inside. I will tell you my theory, and first ask you a question."

Carmilla was leaning on her hand dejectedly; Madame and I were listening breathlessly.

"Now, my question is this. Have you ever been suspected of walking in your sleep?"

"Never, since I was very young indeed."

"But you did walk in your sleep when you were young?"

"Yes; I know I did. I have been told so often by my old nurse."

My father smiled and nodded.

"Well, what has happened is this. You got up in your sleep, unlocked the door, not leaving the key, as usual, in the lock, but taking it out and locking it on the outside; you again took the key out, and carried it away with you to some one of the five-and-twenty rooms on this floor, or perhaps upstairs or downstairs. There are so many rooms and closets, so much heavy furniture, and such accumulations of lumber, that it would require a week to search this old house thoroughly. Do you see, now, what I mean?"

"I do, but not all," she answered.

"And how, papa, do you account for her finding herself on the sofa in the dressing-room, which we had searched so carefully?"

"She came there after you had searched it, still in her sleep, and at last awoke spontaneously, and was as much surprised to find herself where she was as any one else. I wish all mysteries were as easily and innocently explained as yours, Carmilla," he said, laughing. "And so we may congratulate ourselves on the certainty that the most natural explanation of the occurrence is one that involves no drugging, no tampering with locks, no burglars, or poisoners, or witches—nothing that need alarm Carmilla, or anyone else, for our safety."

Carmilla was looking charmingly. Nothing could be more beautiful than her tints. Her beauty was, I think, enhanced by that graceful languor that was peculiar to her. I think my father was silently contrasting her looks with mine, for he said:—

"I wish my poor Laura was looking more like herself"; and he sighed.

So our alarms were happily ended, and Carmilla restored to her friends.

IX

THE DOCTOR

AS CARMILLA WOULD NOT HEAR OF AN ATTENDANT SLEEPING IN HER ROOM, my father arranged that a servant should sleep outside her door, so that she could not attempt to make another such excursion without being arrested at her own door.

That night passed quietly; and next morning early, the doctor, whom my father had sent for without telling me a word about it, arrived to see me.

Madame accompanied me to the library; and there the grave little doctor, with white hair and spectacles, whom I mentioned before, was waiting to receive me.

I told him my story, and as I proceeded he grew graver and graver.

We were standing, he and I, in the recess of one of the windows, facing one another. When my statement was over, he leaned with his shoulders against the wall, and with his eyes fixed on me earnestly, with an interest in which was a dash of horror.

After a minute's reflection, he asked Madame if he could see my father.

He was sent for accordingly, and as he entered, smiling, he said:

"I dare say, doctor, you are going to tell me that I am an old fool for having brought you here; I hope I am."

But his smile faded into shadow as the doctor, with a very grave face, beckoned him to him.

He and the doctor talked for some time in the same recess where I had just conferred with the physician. It seemed an earnest and argumentative conversation. The room is very large, and I and Madame stood together, burning with curiosity, at the farther end. Not a word could we hear, however, for they spoke in a very low tone, and the deep recess of the window quiet concealed the doctor from view, and very nearly my father, whose foot, arm, and shoulder only could we see; and the voices were, I suppose, all the less audible for the sort of closet which the thick wall and window formed.

After a time my father's face looked into the room; it was pale, thoughtful, and, I fancied, agitated.

"Laura, dear, come here for a moment. Madame, we shan't trouble you, the doctor says, at present."

Accordingly I approached, for the first time a little alarmed; for, although I felt very weak, I did not feel ill; and strength, one always fancies, is a thing that may be picked up when we please.

My father held out his hand to me, as I drew near, but he was looking at the doctor, and he said:

"It certainly *is* very odd; I don't understand it quite. Laura, come here, dear; now attend to Doctor Spielsberg, and recollect yourself."

"You mentioned a sensation like that of two needles piercing the skin, somewhere about your neck, on the night when you experienced your first horrible dream. Is there still any soreness?"

"None at all," I answered.

"Can you indicate with your finger about the point at which you think this occurred?"

"Very little below my throat—*here,*" I answered.

I wore a morning dress, which covered the place I pointed to.

"Now you can satisfy yourself," said the doctor. "You won't mind your papa's lowering your dress a very little. It is necessary, to detect a symptom of the complaint under which you have been suffering."

I acquiesced. It was only an inch or two below the edge of my collar.

"God bless me!—so it is," exclaimed my father, growing pale.

"You see it now with your own eyes," said the doctor, with a gloomy triumph.

"What is it?" I exclaimed, beginning to be frightened.

"Nothing, my dear young lady, but a small blue spot, about the size of the tip of your little finger; and now," he continued, turning to papa, "the question is what is best to be done?"

"Is there any danger?" I urged, in great trepidation.

"I trust not, my dear," answered the doctor. "I don't see why you should not recover. I don't see why you should not begin *immediately* to get better. That is the point at which the sense of strangulation begins?"

"Yes," I answered.

"And—recollect as well as you can—the same point was a kind of center of that thrill which you described just now, like the current of a cold stream running against you?"

"It may have been; I think it was."

"Ay, you see?" he added, turning to my father. "Shall I say a word to Madame?"

"Certainly," said my father.

He called Madame to him, and said:

"I find my young friend here far from well. It won't be of any great consequence, I hope; but it will be necessary that some steps be taken, which I will explain by-and-by; but in the meantime, Madame, you will be so good as not to let Miss Laura be alone for one moment. That is the only direction I need give for the present. It is indispensable."

"We may rely upon your kindness, Madame, I know," added my father.

Madame satisfied him eagerly.

"And you, dear Laura, I know you will observe the doctor's direction."

"I shall have to ask your opinion upon another patient, whose symptoms slightly resemble those of my daughter, that have just been detailed to you—very much milder in degree, but I believe quite of the same sort. She is a young lady—our guest; but as you say you will be passing this way again this evening, you can't do better than take your supper here, and you can then see her. She does not come down till the afternoon."

"I thank you," said the doctor. "I shall be with you, then, at about seven this evening."

And then they repeated their directions to me and to Madame, and with this parting charge my father left us, and walked out with the doctor; and I saw them pacing together up and down between the road and the moat, on the grassy platform in front of the castle, evidently absorbed in earnest conversation.

The doctor did not return. I saw him mount his horse there, take his leave, and ride away eastward through the forest.

Nearly at the same time I saw the man arrive from Dranfield with the letters, and dismount and hand the bag to my father.

In the meantime, Madame and I were both busy, lost in conjecture as to the reasons of the singular and earnest direction which the doctor and my father had concurred in imposing. Madame, as she afterward told me, was afraid the doctor apprehended a sudden seizure, and that, without prompt assistance, I might either lose my life in a fit, or at least be seriously hurt.

The interpretation did not strike me; and I fancied, perhaps luckily for my nerves, that the arrangement was prescribed simply to secure a companion, who would prevent my taking too much exercise, or eating unripe fruit, or doing any of the fifty foolish things to which young people are supposed to be prone.

About half-an-hour after my father came in—he had a letter in his hand—and said:

"This letter had been delayed; it is from General Spielsdorf. He might have been here yesterday, he may not come till to-morrow or he may be here to-day."

He put the open letter into my hand; but he did not look pleased, as he used when a guest, especially one so much loved as the General, was coming. On the contrary, he looked as if he wished him at the bottom of the Red Sea. There was plainly something on his mind which he did not choose to divulge.

"Papa, darling, will you tell me this?" said I, suddenly laying my hand on his arm, and looking, I am sure, imploringly in his face.

"Perhaps," he answered, smoothing my hair caressingly over my eyes.

"Does the doctor think me very ill?"

"No, dear; he thinks, if right steps are taken, you will be quite well again, at least, on the high road to a complete recovery, in a day or two," he answered, a little drily. "I wish our good friend, the General, had chosen any other time; that is, I wish you had been perfectly well to receive him."

"But do tell me, papa," I insisted, "*what* does he think is the matter with me?"

"Nothing; you must not plague me with questions," he answered, with more irritation than I ever remember him to have displayed before; and seeing that I looked wounded, I suppose, he kissed me, and added, "You shall know all about it in a day or two; that is, all that I know. In the meantime you are not to trouble your head about it."

He turned and left the room, but came back before I had done wondering and puzzling over the oddity of all this; it was merely to say that he was going to Karnstein, and had ordered the carriage to be ready at twelve, and that I and Madame should accompany him; he was going to see the priest who lived near those picturesque grounds, upon business, and as Carmilla had never seen them, she could follow, when she came down, with Mademoiselle, who would bring materials for what you call a picnic, which might be laid for us in the ruined castle.

At twelve o'clock, accordingly, I was ready, and not long after, my father, Madame and I set out upon our projected drive.

Passing the drawbridge we turn to the right, and follow the road over the steep Gothic bridge, westward, to reach the deserted village and ruined castle of Karnstein.

No sylvan drive can be fancied prettier. The ground breaks into gentle hills and hollows, all clothed with beautiful wood, totally destitute of the comparative formality which artificial planting and early culture and pruning impart.

The irregularities of the ground often lead the road out of its course, and cause it to wind beautifully round the sides of broken hollows and the steeper sides of the hills, among varieties of ground almost inexhaustible.

Turning one of these points, we suddenly encountered our old friend, the General, riding toward us, attended by a mounted servant. His portmanteaus were following in a hired wagon, such as we term a cart.

The General dismounted as we pulled up, and, after the usual greetings, was easily persuaded to accept the vacant seat in the carriage and send his horse on with his servant to the schloss.

X

BEREAVED

IT WAS ABOUT TEN MONTHS SINCE WE HAD LAST SEEN HIM; BUT THAT time had sufficed to make an alteration of years in his appearance. He had grown thinner; something of gloom and anxiety had taken the place of that cordial serenity which used to characterize his features. His dark blue eyes, always penetrating, now gleamed with a sterner light from under his shaggy gray eyebrows. It was not such a change as grief alone usually induces, and angrier passions seemed to have had their share in bringing it about.

We had not long resumed our drive, when the General began to talk, with his usual soldierly directness, of the bereavement, as he termed it, which he had sustained in the death of his beloved niece and ward; and he then broke out in a tone of intense bitterness and fury, inveighing against the "hellish arts" to which she had fallen a victim, and expressing, with more exasperation than piety, his wonder that Heaven should tolerate so monstrous an indulgence of the lusts and malignity of hell

My father, who saw at once that something very extraordinary had befallen, asked him, if not too painful to him, to detail the circumstances which he thought justified the strong terms in which he expressed himself.

"I should tell you all with pleasure," said the General, "but you would not believe me."

"Why should I not?" he asked.

"Because," he answered testily, "you believe in nothing but what consists with your own prejudices and illusions. I remember when I was like you, but I have learned better."

"Try me," said my father; "I am not such a dogmatist as you suppose. Besides which, I very well know that you generally require proof for what you believe, and am, therefore, very strongly predisposed to respect your conclusions."

"You are right in supposing that I have not been led lightly into a belief in the marvelous—for what I have experienced *is* marvelous—and I have been forced by extraordinary evidence to credit that which ran counter, diametrically, to all my theories. I have been made the dupe of a preternatural conspiracy."

Notwithstanding his professions of confidence in the General's penetration, I saw my father, at this point, glance at the General, with, as I thought, a marked suspicion of his sanity.

The General did not see it, luckily. He was looking gloomily and curiously into the glades and vistas of the woods that were opening before us.

"You are going to the Ruins of Karnstein?" he said. "Yes, it is a lucky coincidence; do you know I was going to ask you to bring me there to inspect them. I have a special object in exploring. There is a ruined chapel, ain't there, with a great many tombs of that extinct family?"

"So there are—highly interesting," said my father. "I hope you are thinking of claiming the title and estates?"

My father said this gaily, but the General did not recollect the laugh, or even the smile, which courtesy exacts for a friend's joke; on the contrary, he looked grave and even fierce, ruminating on a matter that stirred his anger and horror.

"Something very different," he said, gruffly. "I mean to unearth some of those fine people. I hope, by God's blessing, to accomplish a pious sacrilege here, which will relieve our earth of certain monsters, and enable honest people to sleep in their beds without being assailed by murderers. I have strange things to tell you, my dear friend, such as I myself would have scouted as incredible a few months since."

My father looked at him again, but this time not with a glance of suspicion—with an eye, rather, of keen intelligence and alarm.

"The house of Karnstein," he said, "has been long extinct: a hundred years at least. My dear wife was maternally descended from the Karnsteins. But the name and title have long ceased to exist. The castle is a ruin; the very village is deserted; it is fifty years since the smoke of a chimney was seen there; not a roof left."

"Quite true. I have heard a great deal about that since I last saw you; a great deal that will astonish you. But I had better relate everything in the order in which it occurred," said the General. "You saw my dear ward—my child, I may call her. No creature could have been more beautiful, and only three months ago none more blooming."

"Yes, poor thing! when I saw her last she certainly was quite lovely," said my father. "I was grieved and shocked more than I can tell you, my dear friend; I knew what a blow it was to you."

He took the General's hand, and they exchanged a kind pressure. Tears gathered in the old soldier's eyes. He did not seek to conceal them. He said:

"We have been very old friends; I knew you would feel for me, childless as I am. She had become an object of very near interest to me, and repaid my care by an affection that cheered my home and made my life happy. That is all gone. The years that remain to me on earth may not be very long; but by God's mercy I hope to accomplish a service to mankind before I die, and to subserve the vengeance of Heaven upon the friends who have murdered my poor child in the spring of her hopes and beauty!"

"You said, just now, that you intended relating everything as it occurred," said my father. "Pray do; I assure you that it is not mere curiosity that prompts me."

By this time we had reached the point at which the Drunstall road, by which the General had come, diverges from the road which we were traveling to Karnstein.

"How far is it to the ruins?" inquired the General, looking anxiously forward.

"About half a league," answered my father. "Pray let us hear the story you were so good as to promise."

XI

THE STORY

"WITH ALL MY HEART," SAID THE GENERAL, WITH AN EFFORT; AND AFTER a short pause in which to arrange his subject, he commenced one of the strangest narratives I ever heard.

"My dear child was looking forward with great pleasure to the visit you had been so good as to arrange for her to your charming daughter." Here he made me a gallant but melancholy bow. "In the meantime we had an invitation to my old friend the Count Carlsfeld, whose schools is about six leagues to the other side of Karnstein. It was to attend the series of fêtes which, you remember, were given by him in honor of his illustrious visitor, the Grand Duke Charles."

"Yes; and very splendid, I believe, they were," said my father.

"Princely! But then his hospitalities are quite regal. He has Aladdin's lamp. The night from which my sorrow dates was devoted to a magnificent masquerade. The grounds were thrown open, the trees hung with colored lamps. There was such a display of fireworks as Paris itself had never witnessed. And such music—music, you know, is my weakness—such ravishing music! The finest instrumental band, perhaps, in the world, and the finest singers who could be collected from all the great operas in Europe. As you wandered through these fantastically illuminated grounds, the moon-lighted château throwing a rosy light from its long rows of windows, you would suddenly hear these ravishing voices stealing from the silence of some grove, or rising from boats upon the lake. I felt myself, as I looked and listened, carried back into the romance and poetry of my early youth.

"When the fireworks were ended, and the ball beginning, we returned tothe noble suite of rooms that were thrown open to the dancers. A masked bail, you know, is a beautiful sight; but so brilliant a spectacle of the kind I never saw before.

"It was a very aristocratic assembly. I was myself almost the only 'nobody' present.

"My dear child was looking quite beautiful. She wore no mask. Her excitement and delight added an unspeakable charm to her features, always lovely. I remarked a young lady, dressed magnificently, but wearing a mask, who appeared to me to be observing my ward with extraordinary interest. I had seen her, earlier in the evening, in the great hall, and again, for a few minutes, walking near us, on the terrace under the castle windows, similarly employed. A lady, also masked, richly and gravely dressed, and with a stately air, like a person of rank, accompanied her as a chaperon. Had the young lady not worn a mask, I could, of course, have been much more certain upon the question whether she was really watching my poor darling. I am now well assured that she was.

"We were now in one of the *salons*. My poor dear child had been dancing, and was resting a little in one of the chairs near the door; I was standing near. The two ladies I have mentioned had approached and the younger took the chair next my ward; while her companion stood beside me, and for a little time addressed herself, in a low tone, to her charge.

"Availing herself of the privilege of her mask, she turned to me, and in the tone of an old friend, and calling me by my name, opened a conversation with me, which piqued my curiosity a good deal. She referred to many scenes where she had met me—at Court, and at distinguished houses. She alluded to little incidents which I had long ceased to think of, but which, I found, had only lain in abeyance in my memory, for they instantly started into life at her touch.

"I became more and more curious to ascertain who she was, every moment. She parried my attempts to discover very adroitly and pleasantly. The knowledge she showed of many passages in my life seemed to me all but unaccountable; and she appeared to take a not unnatural pleasure in foiling my curiosity, and in seeing me flounder in my eager perplexity, from one conjecture to another.

"In the meantime the young lady, whom her mother called by the odd name of Millarca, when she once or twice addressed her, had, with the same ease and grace, got into conversation with my ward.

"She introduced herself by saying that her mother was a very old acquaintance of mine. She spoke of the agreeable audacity which a mask rendered practicable; she talked like a friend; she admired her dress, and insinuated very prettily her admiration of her beauty. She amused her with laughing criticisms upon the people who crowded the ballroom, and laughed at my poor child's fun. She was very witty and lively when she pleased, and after a time they had grown very good friends, and the young stranger lowered her mask, displaying a remarkably beautiful face. I had never seen it before, neither had my dear child. But though it was new to us, the features were so engaging, as well as lovely, that it was impossible not to feel the attraction powerfully. My poor girl did so. I never saw anyone more taken with another at first sight, unless, indeed, it was the stranger herself, who seemed quite to have lost her heart to her.

"In the meantime, availing myself of the license of a masquerade, I put not a few questions to the elder lady.

" 'You have puzzled me utterly,' I said, laughing. 'Is that not enough? Won't you, now, consent to stand on equal terms, and do me the kindness to remove your mask?'

"'Can any request be more unreasonable?' she replied. 'Ask a lady to yield an advantage! Beside, how do you know you should recognize me? Years make changes.'

"'As you see,' I said, with a bow, and, I suppose, a rather melancholy little laugh.

"'As philosophers tell us,' she said; 'and how do you know that a sight of my face would help you?'

"'I should take chance for that,' I answered. 'It is vain trying to make yourself out an old woman; your figure betrays you.'

"'Years, nevertheless, have passed since I saw you, rather since you saw me, for that is what I am considering. Millarca, there, is my daughter; I cannot then be young, even in the opinion of people whom time has taught to be indulgent, and I may not like to be compared with what you remember me. You have no mask to remove. You can offer me nothing in exchange.'

"'My petition is to your pity, to remove it.'

"'And mine to yours, to let it stay where it is,' she replied.

"'Well, then, at least you will tell me whether you are French or German; you speak both languages so perfectly.'

"'I don't think I shall tell you that, General; you intend a surprise, and are meditating the particular point of attack.'

"'At all events, you won't deny this,' I said, 'that being honored by your permission to converse, I ought to know how to address you. Shall I say Madame la Comtesse?'

"She laughed, and she would, no doubt, have met me with another evasion—if, indeed, I can treat any occurrence in an interview every circumstance of which was pre-arranged, as I now believe, with the profoundest cunning, as liable to be modified by accident.

"'As to that,' she began; but she was interrupted, almost as she opened her lips, by a gentleman, dressed in black, who looked particularly elegant and distinguished, with this drawback, that his face was the most deadly pale I ever saw, except in death. He was in no masquerade—in the plain evening dress of a gentleman; and he said, without a smile, but with a courtly unusually low bow:—

"'Will Madame la Comtesse permit me to say a very few words which may interest her?'

"The lady turned quickly to him, and touched her lip in token of silence; she then said to me, 'Keep my place for me, General; I shall return when I have said a few words.'

"And with this injunction, playfully given, she walked a little aside with the gentleman in black, and talked for some minutes, apparently very earnestly. They then walked away slowly together in the crowd, and I lost them for some minutes.

"I spent the interval in cudgeling my brains for a conjecture as to the identity of the lady who seemed to remember me so kindly, and I was thinking of turning about and joining in the conversation between my pretty ward and the Countess' daughter, and trying whether, by the time she returned, I might not have a surprise in store for her, by having her name, title, château, and estates at my fingers' ends. But at this moment she returned, accompanied by the pale man in black, who said:

"'I shall return and inform Madame la Comtesse when her carriage is at the door.'

"He withdrew with a bow."

XII

A PETITION

"'THEN WE ARE TO LOSE MADAME LA COMTESSE, BUT I HOPE ONLY FOR A few hours,' I said, with a low bow.

"'It may be that only, or it may be a few weeks. It was very unlucky his speaking to me just now as he did. Do you now know me?'

"I assured her I did not.

"'You shall know me,' she said, 'but not at present. We are older and better friends than, perhaps, you suspect. I cannot yet declare myself. I shall in there weeks pass your beautiful schools, about which I have been making inquiries. I shall then look in upon you for an hour or two, and renew a friendship which I never think of without a thousand pleasant recollections. This moment a piece of news has reached me like a thunderbolt. I must set out now and travel by a devious route, nearly a hundred miles, with all the dispatch I can possibly make. My perplexities multiply. I am only deterred by the compulsory reserve I practice as to my name from making a very singular request of you. My poor child has not quite recovered her strength. Her horse fell with her, at a hunt which she had ridden out to witness, her nerves have not yet recovered the shock, and our physician says that she must on no account exert herself for some time to come. We came here, in consequence, by very easy stages—hardly six leagues a day. I must now travel day and night, on a mission of life and death—a mission the critical and momentous nature of which I shall be able to explain to you when we meet, as I hope we shall, in a few weeks, without the necessity of any concealment.'

"She went on to make her petition, and it was in the tone of a person from whom such a request amounted to conferring, rather than seeking a favor. This was only in manner, and, as it seemed, quite unconsciously. Than the terms in which it was expressed, nothing could be more deprecatory. It was simply that I would consent to take charge of her daughter during her absence.

"This was, all things considered, a strange, not to say, an audacious request. She in some sort disarmed me, by stating and admitting everything that could be urged against it, and throwing herself entirely upon my chivalry. At the same moment, by a fatality that seems to have predetermined all that happened, my poor child came to my side, and, in an undertone, besought me to invite her new friend, Millarca, to pay us a visit. She had just been sounding her, and thought, if her mamma would allow her, she would like it extremely.

"At another time I should have told her to wait a little, until, at least, we knew who they were. But I had not a moment to think in. The two ladies assailed me together, and I must confess the refined and beautiful face of the young lady, about which there was something extremely engaging, as well as the elegance and fire of high birth, determined me; and, quite overpowered, I submitted, and undertook, too easily, the care of the young lady, whom her mother called Millarca.

"The Countess beckoned to her daughter, who listened with grave attention while she told her, in general terms, how suddenly and peremptorily she had been summoned, and also of the arrangement she had made for her under my care, adding that I was one of her earliest and most valued friends.

"I made, of course, such speeches as the case seemed to call for, and found myself, on reflection, in a position which I did not half like.

"The gentleman in black returned, and very ceremoniously conducted the lady from the room.

"The demeanour of this gentleman was such as to impress me with the conviction that the Countess was a lady of very much more importance than her modest title alone might have led me to assume.

"Her last charge to me was that no attempt was to be made to learn more about her than I might have already guessed, until her return. Our distinguished host, whose guest she was, knew her reasons.

"'But here,' she said, 'neither I nor my daughter could safely remain for more than a day. I removed my mask imprudently for a moment, about an hour ago, and, too late, I fancied you saw me. So I resolved to seek an opportunity of talking a little to you. Had I found that you *had* seen me, I should have thrown myself on your high sense of honour to keep my secret for some weeks. As it is, I am satisfied that you did not see me; but if you now *suspect,* or, on reflection, *should* suspect, who I am, I commit myself, in like manner, entirely to your honor. My daughter will observe the same secrecy, and I will know that you will, from time to time remind her, lest she should thoughtlessly disclose it.'

"She whispered a few words to her daughter, kissed her hurriedly twice, and went away, accompanied by the pale gentleman in black, and disappeared in the crowd.

"'In the next room,' said Millarca, 'there is a window that looks upon the hall door. I should like to see the last of mamma, and to kiss my hand to her.'

"We assented, of course, and accompanied her to the window. We looked out, and saw a handsome old-fashioned carriage, with a troop of couriers and footmen. We saw the slim figure of the pale gentleman in black, as he held a thick velvet cloak, and placed it about her shoulders and threw the hood over her head. She nodded to him, and just touched his hand with hers. He bowed low repeatedly as the door closed, and the carriage began to move.

"'She is gone,' said Millarca, with a sigh.

"'She is gone,' I repeated to myself, for the first time—in the hurried moments that had elapsed since my consent—reflecting upon the folly of my act.

"'She did not look up,' said the young lady, plaintively.

"'The Countess had taken off her mask, perhaps, and did not care to show her face,' I said; 'and she could not know that you were in the window.'

"She sighed, and looked in my face. She was so beautiful that I relented. I was sorry I had for a moment repented of my hospitality, and I determined to make her amends for the unavowed churlishness of my reception.

"The young lady, replacing her mask, joined my ward in persuading me to return to the grounds, where the concert was soon to be renewed. We did so, and walked up and down the terrace that lies under the castle windows. Millarca became very intimate with us, and amused us with lively descriptions and stories of most of the great people whom we saw upon the terrace. I liked her more and more every minute. Her gossip, without being ill-natured, was extremely diverting to me, who had been so long out of the great world. I thought what life she would give to our sometimes lonely evenings at home.

"This ball was not over until the morning sun had almost reached the horizon. It pleased the Grand Duke to dance till then, so loyal people could not go away, or think of bed.

"We had just got through a crowded saloon, when my ward asked me what had become of Millarca. I thought she had been by her side, and she fancied she was by mine. The fact was, we had lost her.

"All my efforts to find her were vain. I feared that she had mistaken, in the confusion of a momentary separation from us, other people for her new friends, and had, possibly, pursued and lost them in the extensive grounds which were thrown open to us.

"Now, in its full force, I recognized a new folly in my having undertaken the charge of a young lady without so much as knowing her name; and fettered as I was by promises, of the reasons for imposing which I knew nothing, I could not even point my inquiries by saying that the missing young lady was the daughter of the Countess who had taken her departure a few hours before.

"Morning broke. It was clear daylight before I gave up my search. It was not till near two o'clock next day that we heard anything of my missing charge.

"At about that time a servant knocked at my niece's door, to say that he had been earnestly requested by a young lady, who appeared to be in great distress, to make out where she could find the General Baron Spielsdorf and the young lady his daughter, in whose charge she had been left by her mother.

"There could be no doubt, notwithstanding the slight inaccuracy, that our young friend had turned up; and so she had. Would to heaven we had lost her!

"She told my poor child a story to account for her having failed to recover us for so long. Very late, she said, she had got to the housekeeper's bedroom in despair of finding us, and had then fallen into a deep sleep which, long as it was, had hardly sufficed to recruit her strength after the fatigues of the ball.

"That day Millarca came home with us. I was only too happy, after all, to have secured so charming a companion for my dear girl."

XIII

THE WOOD-MAN

"THERE SOON, HOWEVER, APPEARED SOME DRAWBACKS. IN THE FIRST place, Millarca complained of extreme languor—the weakness that remained after her late illness—and she never emerged from her room till the afternoon was pretty far advanced. In the next place, it was accidentally discovered, although she always locked her door on the inside, and near disturbed the key from its place till she admitted the maid to assist at her toilet, that she was undoubtedly sometimes absent from her room in the very early morning, and at various times later in the day, before she wished it to be understood that she was stirring. She was repeatedly seen from the windows of the schloss, in the first faint gray of the morning, walking through the trees, in an easterly direction, and looking like a person in a trance. This convinced me that she walked in her sleep. But this hypothesis did not solve the puzzle. How did she pass out from her room, leaving the door locked on the inside? How did she escape from the house without unbarring door or window?

"In the midst of my perplexities, an anxiety of a far more urgent kind presented itself.

"My dear child began to lose her looks and health and that in a manner so mysterious, and even horrible, that I became thoroughly frightened.

"She was at first visited by appalling dreams; then, as she fancied, by a specter, sometimes resembling Millarca, sometimes in the shape of a beast, indistinctly seen, walking round the foot of her bed, from side to side. Lastly came sensations. One, not unpleasant, but very peculiar, she said, resembled the flow of an icy stream against her breast. At a later time, she felt something like a pair of large needles pierce her, a little below the throat, with a very sharp pain. A few nights after, followed a gradual and convulsive sense of strangulation; then came unconsciousness."

I could hear distinctly every word the kind old General was saying, because by this time we were driving upon the short grass that spreads on either side of the road as you approach the roofless village which had not shown the smoke of a chimney for more than half a century.

You may guess how strangely I felt as I heard my own symptoms so exactly described in those which had been experienced by the poor girl who, but for the catastrophe which followed, would have been at that moment a visitor at my father's château. You may suppose, also, how I felt as I heard him detail habits and mysterious peculiarities which were, in fact, those of our beautiful guest, Carmilla!

A vista opened in the forest; we were of a sudden under the chimneys and gables of the ruined village, and the towers and battlements of the dismantled castle, round which gigantic trees are grouped, overhung us from a slight eminence.

In a frightened dream I got down from the carriage, and in silence, for we had each abundant matter for thinking; we soon mounted the ascent, and were among the spacious chambers, winding stairs, and dark corridors of the castle.

"And this was once the palatial residence of the Karnsteins!" said the old General at length, as from a great window he looked out across the village, and saw the wide, undulating expanse of forest. "It was a bad family, and here its bloodstained annals were written," he continued. "It is hard that they should, after death, continue to plague the human race with their atrocious lusts. That is the chapel of the Karnsteins, down there."

He pointed down to the grey walls of the Gothic building, partly visible through the foliage, a little way down the steep. "And I hear the axe of a woodman," he added, "busy among the trees that surround it; he possibly may give us the information of which I am in search, and point out the grave of Mircalla, Countess of Karnstein. These rustics preserve the local traditions of great families, whose stories die out among the rich and titled as soon as the families themselves become extinct."

"We have a portrait, at home, of Mircalla, the Countess Karnstein; should you like to see it?" asked my father.

"Time enough, dear friend," replied the General. "I believe that I have seen the original; and one motive which has led me to you earlier than I at first intended, was to explore the chapel which we are now approaching."

"What! see the Countess Mircalla," exclaimed my father; "why, she has been dead more than a century!"

"Not so dead as you fancy, I am told," answered the General.

"I confess, General, you puzzle me utterly," replied my father, looking at him, I fancied, for a moment with a return of the suspicion I detected before. But although there was anger and detestation, at times, in the old General's manner, there was nothing flighty.

"There remains to me," he said, as we passed under the heavy arch of the Gothic church—for its dimensions would have justified its being so styled—"but one object which can interest me during the few years that remain to me on earth, and that is to wreak on her the vengeance which, I thank God, may still be accomplished by a mortal arm."

"What vengeance can you mean?" asked my father, in increasing amazement.

"I mean, to decapitate the monster," he answered, with a fierce flush, and a stamp that echoed mournfully through the hollow ruin, and his clenched hand was at the same moment raised, as if it grasped the handle of an axe, while he shook it ferociously in the air.

"What?" exclaimed my father, more than ever bewildered.

"To strike her head off."

"Cut her head off!"

"Aye, with a hatchet, with a spade, or with anything that can cleave through her murderous throat. You shall hear," he answered, trembling with rage. And hurrying forward he said:

"That beam will answer for a seat; your dear child is fatigued; let her be seated, and I will, in a few sentences, close my dreadful story."

The squared block of wood, which lay on the grass-grown pavement of the chapel, formed a bench on which I was very glad to seat myself, and in the meantime the General called to the woodman, who had been removing some boughs which leaned upon the old walls; and, axe in hand, the hardy old fellow stood before us.

He could not tell us anything of these monuments; but there was an old man, he said, a ranger of this forest, at present sojourning in the house of the priest, about two miles away, who could point out every monument of the old Karnstein family; and, for a trifle, he undertook to bring him back with him, if we would lend him one of our horses, in little more than half-an-hour.

"Have you been long employed about this forest?" asked my father of the old man.

"I have been a woodman here," he answered in his *patois*, "under the forester, all my days; so has my father before me, and so on, as many generations as I can count up. I could show you the very house in the village here, in which my ancestors lived."

"How came the village to be deserted?" asked the General.

"It was troubled by *revenants*, sir; several were tracked to their graves, there detected by the usual tests, and extinguished in the usual way, by decapitation, by the stake, and by burning; but not until many of the villagers were killed.

"But after all these proceedings according to law," he continued—"so many graves opened, and so many vampires deprived of their horrible animation—the village was not relieved. But a Moravian nobleman, who happened to be traveling this way, heard how matters were, and being skilled—as many people are in his country—in such affairs, he offered to deliver the village from its tormentor. He did so thus: There being a bright moon that night, he ascended, shortly after sunset, the towers of the chapel here, from whence he could distinctly see the churchward beneath him; you can see it from that window. From this point he watched until he saw the vampire come out of his grave, and place near it the linen clothes in which he had been folded, and then glide away toward the village to plague its inhabitants.

"The stranger, having seen all this, came down from the steeple, took the linen wrappings of the vampire, and carried them up to the top of the tower, which he again mounted. When the vampire returned from his prowlings and missed his clothes, he cried furiously to the Moravian, whom he saw at the summit of the tower, and who, in reply, beckoned him to ascend and take them. Whereupon the vampire, accepting his invitation, began to climb the steeple, and so soon as he had reached the battlements, the Moravian, with a stroke of his sword, clove his skull in twain, hurling him down to the churchyard, whither, descending by the winding stairs, the stranger followed and cut his head off, and the next day delivered it and the body to the villagers, who duly impaled and burnt them.

"This Moravian nobleman had authority from the then head of the family to remove the tomb of Mircalla, Countess Karnstein, which he did effectually, so that in a little while its site was quite forgotten."

"Can you point out where it stood?" asked the General, eagerly.

The forester shook his head, and smiled.

"Not a soul living could tell you that now," he said; "besides, they say her body was removed; but no one is sure of that either."

Having thus spoken, as time pressed, he dropped his axe and departed, leaving us to hear the remainder of the General's strange story.

XIV

THE MEETING

"MY BELOVED CHILD," HE RESUMED, "WAS NOW GROWING RAPIDLY worse. The physician who attended her had failed to produce the slightest impression upon her disease, for such I then supposed it to be. He saw my alarm, and suggested a consultation. I called in an abler physician, from Gratz. Several days elapsed before he arrived. He was a good and pious, as well as a learned man. Having seen my poor ward together, they withdrew to my library to confer and discuss. I, from the adjoining room, where I awaited their summons, heard these two gentlemen's voices raised in something sharper than a strictly philosophical discussion. I knocked at the door and entered. I found the old physician from Gratz maintaining his theory. His rival was combating it with undisguised ridicule, accompanied with bursts of laughter. This unseemly manifestation subsided and the altercation ended on my entrance.

"'Sir,' said my first physician, 'my learned brother seems to think that you want a conjuror, and not a doctor.'

"'Pardon me,' said the old physician from Gratz, looking displeased, 'I shall state my own view of the case in my own way another time. I grieve, Monsieur le Général, that by my skill and science I can be of no use. Before I go I shall do myself the honour to suggest something to you.'

"He seemed thoughtful, and sat down at a table and began to write. Profoundly disappointed, I made my bow, and as I turned to go, the other doctor pointed over his shoulder to his companion who was writing, and then, with a shrug, significantly touched his forehead.

"This consultation, then, left me precisely where I was. I walked out into the grounds, all but distracted. The doctor from Gratz, in ten or fifteen minutes, overtook me. He apologized for having followed me, but said that he could not conscientiously take his leave without a few words more. He told me that he could not be mistaken; no natural disease exhibited the same symptoms; and that death was already very near. There remained, however, a day, or possibly two, of life. If the fatal seizure were at once arrested, with great care and skill her strength might possibly return. But all hung now upon the confines of the irrevocable. One more assault might extinguish the last spark of vitality which is, every moment, ready to die.

"'And what is the nature of the seizure you speak of?' I entreated.

"'I have stated all fully in this note, which I place in your hands upon the distinct condition that you send for the nearest clergyman, and open my letter in his presence, and on no account read it till he is with you; you would despise it else, and it is a matter of life and death. Should the priest fail you, then, indeed, you may read it.'

"He asked me, before taking his leave finally, whether I would wish to see a man curiously learned upon the very subject, which, after I had read his letter, would probably interest me above all others, and he urged me earnestly to invite him to visit him there; and so took his leave.

"The ecclesiastic was absent, and I read the letter by myself. At another time, or in another case, it might have excited my ridicule. But into what quackeries will not people rush for a last chance, where all accustomed means have failed, and the life of a beloved object is at stake?

"Nothing, you will say could be more absurd than the learned man's letter. It was monstrous enough to have consigned him to a madhouse. He said that the patient was suffering from the visits of a vampire! The punctures which she described as having occurred near the throat, were, he insisted, the insertion of those two long, thin, and sharp teeth which, it is well known, are peculiar to vampires; and there could be no doubt, he added, as to the well-defined presence of the small livid mark which all concurred in describing as that induced by the demon's lips, and every symptom described by the sufferer was in exact conformity with those recorded in every case of a similar visitation.

"Being myself wholly skeptical as to the existence of any such portent as the vampire, the supernatural theory of the good doctor furnished, in my opinion, but another instance of learning and intelligence oddly associated with some one hallucination. I was so miserable, however, that, rather than try nothing, I acted upon the instructions of the letter.

"I concealed myself in the dark dressing-room, that opened upon the poor patient's room, in which a candle was burning, and watched there till she was fast asleep. I stood at the door, peeking through the small crevice, my sword laid on the table beside me, as my directions prescribed, until, a little after one, I saw a large black object, very ill-defined, crawl, as it seemed to me, over the foot of the bed, and swiftly spread itself up to the poor girl's throat, where it swelled, in a moment, into a great, palpitating mass.

"For a few moments I had stood petrified. I now sprang forward, with my sword in my hand. The black creature suddenly contracted toward the foot of the bed, glided over it, and, standing on the floor about a yard below the foot of the bed, with a glare of skulking ferocity and horror fixed on me, I saw Millarca. Speculating I know not what, I struck at her instantly with my sword; but I saw her standing near the door, unscathed. Horrified, I pursued, and struck again. She was gone; and my sword flew to shivers against the door.

"I can't describe to you all that passed on that horrible night. The whole house was up and stirring. The spectre Millarca was gone. But her victim was sinking fast, and before the morning dawned, she died."

The old General was agitated. We did not speak to him. My father walked to some little distance, and began reading the inscriptions on the tombstones: and thus occupied, he strolled into the door of a side chapel to prosecute his researches. The General leaned against the wall, dried his eyes, and sighed heavily. I was relieved on hearing the voices of Carmilla and Madame, who were at that moment approaching. The voices died away.

In this solitude, having just listened to so strange a story, connected, as it was, with the great and titled dead, whose monuments were moldering among the dust and ivy round us, and every incident of which bore so awfully upon my own mysterious case—in this haunted spot, darkened by the towering foliage that rose on every side dense and high above its noiseless walls—a horror began to steal over me, and my heart sank as I thought that my friends were, after all, not about to enter and disturb this triste and ominous scene.

The old General's eyes were fixed on the ground, as he leaned with his hand upon the basement of a shattered monument.

Under a narrow, arched doorway, surmounted by one of those demoniacal grotesques in which the cynical and ghastly fancy of old Gothic carving delights, I saw very gladly the beautiful face and figure of Carmilla enter the shadowy chapel.

I was just about to rise and speak, and nodded smiling, in answer to her peculiarly engaging smile; when with a cry, the old man by my side caught up the woodman's hatchet, and started forward. On seeing him a brutalized change came over her features. It was an instantaneous and horrible transformation, as she made a crouching step backward. Before I could utter a scream, he struck at her with all his force, but she dived under his blow, and unscratched, caught him in her tiny grasp by the wrist. He struggled for a moment to release his arm, but his hand opened, the axe fell to the ground, and the girl was gone.

He staggered against the wall. His gray hair stood upon his head, and a moisture shone over his face, as if he were at the point of death.

The frightful scene had passed in a moment. The first thing I recollect after, is Madame standing before me, and impatiently repeating again and again, and question, "Where is Mademoiselle Carmilla?"

I answered at length. "I don't know—I can't tell—she went there," and I pointed to the door through which Madame had just entered; "only a minute or two since."

"But I have been standing there, in the passage, ever since Mademoiselle Carmilla entered; and she did not return."

She then began to call "Carmilla," through every door and passage and from the windows, but no answer came.

"She called herself Carmilla?" asked the General, still agitated.

"Carmilla, yes," I answered.

"Aye," he said; "that is Millarca. That is the same person who long ago was called Mircalla, Countess Karnstein. Depart from this accursed ground, my poor child, as quickly as you can. Drive to the clergyman's house, and stay there till we come. Begone! May you never behold Carmilla more; you will not find her here."

XV

ORDEAL AND EXECUTION

AS HE SPOKE ONE OF THE STRANGEST LOOKING MEN I EVER BEHELD entered the chapel at the door through which Carmilla had made her entrance and her exit. He was tall, narrow-chested, stooping, with high shoulders, and dressed in black. His face was brown and dried in with deep furrows; he wore an oddly-shaped hat with a broad leaf. His hair, long and grizzled, hung on his shoulders. He wore a pair of gold spectacles, and walked slowly, with an odd shambling gait, with his face sometimes turned up to the sky, and sometimes bowed down toward the ground, seemed to wear a perpetual smile; his long thin arms were swinging, and his lank hands, in old black gloves ever so much too wide for them, waving and gesticulating in utter abstraction.

"The very man!" exclaimed the General, advancing with manifest delight. "My dear Baron, how happy I am to see you, I had no hope of meeting you so soon." He signed to my father, who had by this time returned, and leading the fantastic old gentleman, whom he called the Baron to meet him. He introduced him formally, and they at once entered into earnest conversation. The stranger took a roll of paper from his pocket, and spread it on the worn surface of a tomb that stood by. He had a pencil case in his fingers, with which he traced imaginary lines from point to point on the paper, which from their often glancing from it, together, at certain points of the building, I concluded to be a plan of the chapel. He accompanied, what I may term, his lecture, with occasional readings from a dirty little book, whose yellow leaves were closely written over.

They sauntered together down the side aisle, opposite to the spot where I was standing, conversing as they went; then they began measuring distances by paces, and finally they all stood together, facing a piece of the side-wall, which they began to examine with great minuteness; pulling off the ivy that clung over it, and rapping the plaster with the ends of their sticks, scraping here, and knocking there. At length they ascertained the existence of a broad marble tablet, with letters carved in relief upon it.

With the assistance of the woodman, who soon returned, a monumental inscription, and carved escutcheon, were disclosed. They proved to be those of the long lost monument of Mircalla, Countess Karnstein.

The old General, though not I fear given to the praying mood, raised his hands and eyes to heaven, in mute thanksgiving for some moments.

"To-morrow," I heard him say; "the commissioner will be here, and the Inquisition will be held according to law."

Then turning to the old man with the gold spectacles, whom I have described, he shook him warmly by both hands and said:

"Baron, how can I thank you? How can we all thank you? You will have delivered this region from a plague that has scourged its inhabitants for more than a century. The horrible enemy, thank God, is at last tracked."

My father led the stranger aside, and the General followed. I knew that he had led them out of hearing, that he might relate my case, and I saw them glance often quickly at me, as the discussion proceeded.

My father came to me, kissed me again and again, and leading me from the chapel, said:

"It is time to return, but before we go home, we must add to our party the good priest, who lives but a little way from this; and persuade him to accompany us to the schloss."

In this quest we were successful: and I was glad, being unspeakably fatigued when we reached home. But my satisfaction was changed to dismay, on discovering that there were no tidings of Carmilla. Of the scene that had occurred in the ruined chapel, no explanation was offered to me, and it was clear that it was a secret which my father for the present determined to keep from me.

The sinister absence of Carmilla made the remembrance of the scene more horrible to me. The arrangements for the night were singular. Two servants, and Madame, were to sit up in my room that night; and the ecclesiastic with my father kept watch in the adjoining dressing-room.

The priest had performed certain solemn rites that night, the purport of which I did not understand any more than I comprehended the reason of this extraordinary precaution taken for my safety during sleep.

I saw all clearly a few days later.

The disappearance of Carmilla was followed by the discontinuance of my nightly sufferings.

You have heard, no doubt, of the appalling superstition that prevails in Upper and Lower Styria, in Moravia, Silesia, in Turkish Serbia, in Poland, even in Russia; the superstition, so we must call it, of the vampire.

If human testimony, taken with every care and solemnity, judicially, before commissions innumerable, each consisting of many members, all chosen for integrity and intelligence, and constituting reports more voluminous perhaps than exist upon any one other class of cases, is worth anything, it is difficult to deny, or even to doubt the existence of such a phenomenon as the vampire.

For my part I have heard no theory by which to explain what I myself have witnessed and experienced, other than that supplied by the ancient and well-attested belief of the country.

The next day the formal proceedings took place in the Chapel of Karnstein. The grave of the Countess Mircalla was opened; and the General and my father recognized each his perfidious and beautiful guest, in the face now disclosed to view. The features, though a hundred and fifty years had passed since her funeral, were tinted with the warmth of life. Her eyes were open; no cadaverous smell exhaled from the coffin. The two medical men, one officially present, the other on the part of the promoter of the inquiry, attested the marvelous fact that there was a faint but appreciable respiration, and a corresponding action of the heart. The limbs were perfectly flexible, the flesh elastic; and the leaden coffin floated with blood, in which to a depth of seven inches, the body lay immersed. Here then, were all the admitted signs and proofs of vampirism. The body, therefore, in accordance with the ancient practice, was raised, and a sharp stake driven through the heart of the vampire, who uttered a piercing shriek at the moment, in all respects such as might escape from a living person in the last agony. Then the head was struck off, and a torrent of blood flowed from the severed neck. The body and head was next placed on a pile of wood, and reduced to ashes, which were thrown upon the river and borne away, and that territory has never since been plagued by the visits of a vampire.

My father has a copy of the report of the Imperial Commission, with the signatures of all who were present at these proceedings, attached in verification of the statement. It is from this official paper that I have summarized my account of this last shocking scene.

XVI

CONCLUSION

I WRITE ALL THIS YOU SUPPOSE WITH COMPOSURE. BUT FAR FROM IT; I cannot think of it without agitation. Nothing but your earnest desire so repeatedly expressed, could have induced me to sit down to a task that has unstrung my nerves for months to come, and reinduced a shadow of the unspeakable horror which years after my deliverance continued to make my days and nights dreadful, and solitude insupportably terrific.

Let me add a word or two about that quaint Baron Vordenburg, to whose curious lore we were indebted for the discovery of the Countess Mircalla's grave.

He had taken up his abode in Gratz, where, living upon a mere pittance, which was all that remained of him of the once princely estates of his family, in Upper Styria, he devoted himself to the minute and laborious investigation of the marvelously authenticated tradition of Vampirism. He had at his fingers' ends all the great and little works upon the subject. "Magia Posthuma," "Phlegon de Mirabilibus," "Augustinus de curâ pro Mortuis," "Philosophicæ et Christianæ Cogitationes de Vampiris," by John Christofer Herenberg; and a thousand others, among which I remember only a few of those which he lent to my father. He had a voluminous digest of all the judicial cases, from which he had extracted a system of principles that appear to govern—some always, and others occasionally only—the condition of the vampire. I may mention, in passing, that the deadly pallor attributed to that sort of *revenants*, is a mere melodramatic fiction. They present, in the grave, and when they show themselves in human society, the appearance of healthy life. When disclosed to light in their coffins, they exhibit all the symptoms that are enumerated as those which proved the vampire-life of the long-dead Countess Karnstein.

How they escape from their graves and return to them for certain hours every day without displacing the clay or leaving any trace of disturbance in the state of the coffin or the cerements, has always been admitted to be utterly inexplicable. The amphibious existence of the vampire is sustained by daily renewed slumber in the grave. Its horrible lust for living blood supplies the vigor of its waking existence. The vampire is prone to be fascinated with an engrossing vehemence, resembling the passion of love, by particular persons. In pursuit of these it will exercise inexhaustible patience and stratagem, for access to a particular object may be obstructed in a hundred ways. It will never desist until it has satiated its passion, and drained the very life of its coveted victim. But it will, in these cases, husband and protract its murderous enjoyment with the refinement of an epicure, and heighten it by the gradual approaches of an artful courtship. In these cases it seems to yearn for something like sympathy and consent. In ordinary ones it goes direct to its object, overpowers with violence, and strangles and exhausts often at a single feast.

The vampire is, apparently, subject, in certain situations, to special conditions. In the particular instance of which I have given you a relation, Mircalla seemed to be limited to a name which, if not her real one, should at least reproduce, without the omission or addition of a single letter, those, as we say, anagrammatically, which compose it. *Carmilla* did this; so did *Millarca*.

My father related to the Baron Vordenburg, who remained with us for two or three weeks after the expulsion of Carmilla, the story about the Moravian nobleman and the vampire at Karnstein churchyard, and then he asked the Baron how he had discovered the exact position of the long-concealed tomb of the Countess Mircalla? The Baron's grotesque features puckered up into a mysterious smile; he looked down, still smiling on his worn spectacle-case and fumbled with it. Then, looking up, he said:

"I have many journals, and other papers, written by that remarkable man; the most curious among them is one treating of the visit of which you speak, to Karnstein. The tradition, of course, discolors and distorts a little. He might have been termed a Moravian nobleman, for he had changed his abode to that territory, and was, beside, a noble. But he was, in truth, a native of Upper Styria. It is enough to say that in very early youth he had been a passionate and favored lover of the beautiful Mircalla, Countess Karnstein. Her early death plunged him into inconsolable grief. It is the nature of vampires to increase and multiply, but according to an ascertained and ghostly law.

"Assume, at starting, a territory perfectly free from that pest. How does it begin, and how does it multiply itself? I will tell you. A person, more or less wicked, puts an end to himself. A suicide, under certain circumstances, becomes a vampire. That specter visits living people in their slumbers; *they* die, and almost invariably, in the grave develop into vampires. This happened in the case of the beautiful Mircalla, who was haunted by one of those demons. My ancestor, Vordenburg, whose title I still bear, soon discovered this, and in the course of the studies to which he devoted himself, learned a great deal more.

"Among other things, he concluded that suspicion of vampirism would probably fall, sooner or later, upon the dead Countess, who in life had been his idol. He conceived a horror, be she what she might, of her remains being profaned by the outrage of a posthumous execution. He has left a curious paper to prove that the vampire, on its expulsion from its amphibious existence, is projected into a far more horrible life; and he resolved to save his once beloved Mircalla from this.

"He adopted the strategem of a journey here, a pretended removal of her remains, and a real obliteration of her monument. When age had stolen upon him, and from the vale of years, he looked back on the scenes he was leaving, he considered, in a different spirit, what he had done, and a horror took possession of him. He made the tracings and notes which have guided me to the very spot, and drew up a confession of the deception that he had practiced. If he had intended any further action in this matter, death prevented him; and the hand of a remote descendant has, too late for many, directed the pursuit to the lair of the beast."

We talked a little more, and among other things he said was this:

"One sign of the vampire is the power of the hand. The slender hand of Mircalla closed like a vice of steel on the General's wrist when he raised the hatchet to strike. But its power is not confined to its grasp; it leaves a numbness in the limb it seizes, which is slowly, if ever, recovered from."

The following Spring my father took me on a tour through Italy. We remained away for more than a year. It was long before the terror of recent events subsided; and to this hour the image of Carmilla returns to memory with ambiguous alterations—sometimes the playful, languid, beautiful girl; sometimes the writhing fiend I saw in the ruined church; and often from a reverie I have started, fancying I heard the light step of Carmilla at the drawing-room door.

Olalla

Robert Louis Stevenson

"Now," said the Doctor, "my part is done, and, I may say, with some vanity, well done. It remains only to get you out of this cold and poisonous city, and to give you two months of a pure air and an easy conscience. The last is your affair. To the first I think I can help you. It falls indeed rather oddly; it was but the other day the Padre came in from the country; and as he and I are old friends, although of contrary professions, he applied to me in a matter of distress among some of his parishioners. This was a family—but you are ignorant of Spain, and even the names of our grandees are hardly known to you; suffice it, then, that they were once great people, and are now fallen to the brink of destitution. Nothing now belongs to them but the residencia, and certain leagues of desert mountain, in the greater part of which not even a goat could support life. But the house is a fine old place, and stands at a great height among the hills, and most salubriously; and I had no sooner heard my friend's tale than I remembered you. I told him I had a wounded officer, wounded in the good cause, who was now able to make a change; and I proposed that his friends should take you for a lodger. Instantly the Padre's face grew dark, as I had maliciously foreseen it would. It was out of the question, he said. Then let them starve, said I, for I have no sympathy with tatterdemalion pride. Thereupon we separated, not very content with one another; but yesterday, to my wonder, the Padre returned and made a submission: the difficulty, he said, he had found upon inquiry to be less than he had feared; or, in other words, these proud people had put their pride in their pocket. I closed with the offer; and, subject to your approval, I have taken rooms for you in the residencia. The air of these mountains will renew your blood; and the quiet in which you will there live is worth all the medicines in the world."

"Doctor," said I, "you have been throughout my good angel, and your advice is a command. But tell me, if you please, something of the family with which I am to reside."

"I am coming to that," replied my friend; "and, indeed, there is a difficulty in the way. These beggars are, as I have said, of very high descent, and swollen with the most baseless vanity; they have lived for some generations in a growing isolation, drawing away, on either hand, from the rich who had now become too high for them, and from the poor, whom they still regarded as too low; and even to-day, when poverty forces them to unfasten their door to a guest, they cannot do so without a most ungracious stipulation. You are to remain, they say, a stranger; they will give you attendance, but they refuse from the first the idea of the smallest intimacy."

I will not deny that I was piqued, and perhaps the feeling strengthened my desire to go, for I was confident that I could break down that barrier if I desired. "There is nothing offensive in such a stipulation," said I; "and I even sympathise with the feeling that inspired it."

"It is true they have never seen you," returned the doctor politely; "and if they knew you were the handsomest and the most pleasant man that ever came from England (where I am told that handsome men are common, but pleasant ones not so much so), they would doubtless make you welcome with a better grace. But since you take the thing so well, it matters not. To me, indeed, it seems discourteous. But you will find yourself the gainer. The family will not much tempt you. A mother, a son, and a daughter; an old woman said to be half-witted, a country lout, and a country girl, who stands very high with her confessor, and is, therefore," chuckled the physician, "most likely plain; there is not much in that to attract the fancy of a dashing officer."

"And yet you say they are high-born," I objected.

"Well, as to that, I should distinguish," returned the doctor. "The mother is; not so the children. The mother was the last representative of a princely stock, degenerate both in parts and fortune. Her father was not only poor, he was mad: and the girl ran wild about the residencia till his death. Then, much of the fortune having died with him, and the family being quite extinct, the girl ran wilder than ever, until at last she married, Heaven knows whom, a muleteer some say, others a smuggler; while there are some who uphold there was no marriage at all, and that Felipe and Olalla are bastards. The union, such as it was, was tragically dissolved some years ago; but they live in such seclusion, and the country at that time was in so much disorder, that the precise manner of the man's end is known only to the priest—if even to him."

"I begin to think I shall have strange experiences," said I.

"I would not romance, if I were you," replied the doctor; "you will find, I fear, a very grovelling and commonplace reality. Felipe, for instance, I have seen. And what am I to say? He is very rustic, very cunning, very loutish, and, I should say, an innocent; the others are probably to match. No, no, señor commandante, you must seek congenial society among the great sights of our mountains; and in these at least, if you are at all a lover of the works of nature, I promise you will not be disappointed."

The next day Felipe came for me in a rough country cart, drawn by a mule; and a little before the stroke of noon, after I had said farewell to the doctor, the innkeeper, and different good souls who had befriended me during my sickness, we set forth out of the city by the eastern gate, and began to ascend into the Sierra. I had been so long a prisoner, since I was left behind for dying after the loss of the convoy, that the mere smell of the earth set me smiling. The country through which we went was wild and rocky, partially covered with rough woods, now of the cork-tree, and now of the great Spanish chestnut, and frequently intersected by the beds of mountain torrents. The sun shone, the wind rustled joyously; and we had advanced some miles, and the city had already shrunk into an inconsiderable knoll upon the plain behind us, before my attention began to be diverted to the companion of my drive. To the eye, he seemed but a diminutive, loutish, well-made country lad, such as the doctor had described, mighty quick and active, but devoid of any culture; and this first impression was with most observers final. What began to strike me was his familiar, chattering talk; so strangely inconsistent with the terms on which I was to be received; and partly from his imperfect enunciation, partly from the sprightly incoherence of the matter, so very difficult to follow clearly without an effort of the mind. It is true I had before talked with persons of a similar mental constitution; persons who seemed to live (as he did) by the senses, taken and possessed by the visual object of the moment and unable to discharge their minds of that impression. His seemed to me (as I sat, distantly giving ear) a kind of conversation proper to drivers, who pass much of their time in a great vacancy of the intellect and threading the sights of a familiar country. But this was not the case of Felipe; by his own account, he was a home-keeper; "I wish I was there now," he said; and then, spying a tree by the wayside, he broke off to tell me that he had once seen a crow among its branches.

"A crow?" I repeated, struck by the ineptitude of the remark, and thinking I had heard imperfectly.

But by this time he was already filled with a new idea; hearkening with a rapt intentness, his head on one side, his face puckered; and he struck me rudely, to make me hold my peace. Then he smiled and shook his head.

"What did you hear?" I asked.

"Oh, it is all right," he said; and began encouraging his mule with cries that echoed unhumanly up the mountain walls.

I looked at him more closely. He was superlatively well-built, light, and lithe and strong; he was well-featured; his yellow eyes were very large, though, perhaps, not very expressive; take him altogether, he was a pleasant-looking lad, and I had no fault to find with him, beyond that he was of a dusky hue, and inclined to hairyness; two characteristics that I disliked. It was his mind that puzzled, and yet attracted me. The doctor's phrase—an innocent—came back to me; and I was wondering if that were, after all, the true description, when the road began to go down into the narrow and naked chasm of a torrent. The waters thundered tumultuously in the bottom; and the ravine was filled full of the sound, the thin spray, and the claps of wind, that accompanied their descent. The scene was certainly impressive; but the road was in that part very securely walled in; the mule went steadily forward; and I was astonished to perceive the paleness of terror in the face of my companion. The voice of that wild river was inconstant, now sinking lower as if in weariness, now doubling its hoarse tones; momentary freshets seemed to swell its volume, sweeping down the gorge, raving and booming against the barrier walls; and I observed it was at each of these accessions to the clamour that my driver more particularly winced and blanched. Some thoughts of Scottish superstition and the river Kelpie passed across my mind; I wondered if perchance the like were prevalent in that part of Spain; and turning to Felipe, sought to draw him out.

"What is the matter?" I asked.

"O, I am afraid," he replied.

"Of what are you afraid?" I returned. "This seems one of the safest places on this very dangerous road."

"It makes a noise," he said, with a simplicity of awe that set my doubts at rest.

The lad was but a child in intellect; his mind was like his body, active and swift, but stunted in development; and I began from that time forth to regard him with a measure of pity, and to listen at first with indulgence, and at last even with pleasure, to his disjointed babble.

By about four in the afternoon we had crossed the summit of the mountain line, said farewell to the western sunshine, and began to go down upon the other side, skirting the edge of many ravines and moving through the shadow of dusky woods. There rose upon all sides the voice of falling water, not condensed and formidable as in the gorge of the river, but scattered and sounding gaily and musically from glen to glen. Here, too, the spirits of my driver mended, and he began to sing aloud in a falsetto voice, and with a singular bluntness of musical perception, never true either to melody or key, but wandering at will, and yet somehow with an effect that was natural and pleasing, like that of the song of birds. As the dusk increased, I fell more and more under the spell of this artless warbling, listening and waiting for some articulate air, and still disappointed; and when at last I asked him what it was he sang—"O," cried he, "I am just singing!" Above all, I was taken with a trick he had of unweariedly repeating the same note at little intervals; it was not so monotonous as you would think, or, at least, not disagreeable; and it seemed to breathe a wonderful contentment with what is, such as we love to fancy in the attitude of trees, or the quiescence of a pool.

Night had fallen dark before we came out upon a plateau, and drew up a little after, before a certain lump of superior blackness which I could only conjecture to be the residencia. Here my guide, getting down from the cart, hooted and whistled for a long time in vain; until at last an old peasant man came towards us from somewhere in the surrounding dark, carrying a candle in his hand. By the light of this I was able to perceive a great arched doorway of a Moorish character: it was closed by iron-studded gates, in one of the leaves of which Felipe opened a wicket. The peasant carried off the cart to some out-building; but my guide and I passed through the wicket, which was closed again behind us; and, by the glimmer of the candle, passed through a court, up a stone stair, along a section of an open gallery, and up more stairs again, until we came at last to the door of a great and somewhat bare apartment. This room, which I understood was to be mine, was pierced by three windows, lined with some lustrous wood disposed in panels, and carpeted with the skins of many savage animals. A bright fire burned in the chimney, and shed abroad a changeful flicker; close up to the blaze there was drawn a table, laid for supper; and in the far end a bed stood ready. I was pleased by these preparations, and said so to Felipe; and he, with the same simplicity of disposition that I had already remarked in him, warmly re-echoed my praises. "A fine room," he said; "a very fine room. And fire, too; fire is good; it melts out the pleasure in your bones. And the bed," he continued, carrying over the candle in that direction—"see what fine sheets—how soft, how smooth, smooth"; and he passed his hand again and again over their texture, and then laid down his head and rubbed his cheeks among them with a grossness of content that somehow offended me. I took the candle from his hand (for I feared he would set the bed on fire) and walked back to the supper-table, where, perceiving a measure of wine, I poured out a cup and called to him to come and drink of it. He started to his feet at once and ran to me with a strong expression of hope; but when he saw the wine he visibly shuddered.

"Oh, no," he said, "not that; that is for you. I hate it."

"Very well, Señor," said I; "then I will drink to your good health, and to the prosperity of your house and family. Speaking of which," I added, after I had drunk, "shall I not have the pleasure of laying my salutations in person at the feet of the Señora, your mother?"

But at these words all the childishness passed out of his face, and was succeeded by a look of indescribable cunning and secrecy. He backed away from me at the same time, as though I were an animal about to leap or some dangerous fellow with a weapon, and when he had got near the door, glowered at me sullenly with contracted pupils. "No," he said at last, and the next moment was gone noiselessly out of the room; and I heard his footing die away downstairs as light as rainfall, and silence closed over the house.

After I had supped I drew up the table nearer to the bed and began to prepare for rest; but in the new position of the light, I was struck by a picture on the wall. It represented a woman, still young. To judge by her costume and the mellow unity which reigned over the canvas, she had long been dead; to judge by the vivacity of the attitude, the eyes and the features, I might have been beholding in a mirror the image of life. Her figure was very slim and strong, and of a just proportion; red tresses lay like a crown over her brow; her eyes, of a very golden brown, held mine with a look; and her face, which was perfectly shaped, was yet marred by a cruel, sullen, and sensual expression. Something in both face and figure, something exquisitely intangible, like the echo of an echo, suggested the features and bearing of my guide; and I stood a while unpleasantly attracted and wondering at the oddity of the resemblance. The common, carnal stock of that race, which had been originally designed for such high dames as the one now looking on me from the canvas, had fallen to baser uses, wearing country clothes, sitting on the shaft and holding the reins of a mule cart, to bring home a lodger. Perhaps an actual link subsisted; perhaps some scruple of the delicate flesh that was once clothed upon with the satin and brocade of the dead lady, now winced at the rude contact of Felipe's frieze.

The first light of the morning shone full upon the portrait, and, as I lay awake, my eyes continued to dwell upon it with growing complacency; its beauty crept about my heart insidiously, silencing my scruples one after another; and while I knew that to love such a woman were to sign and seal one's own sentence of degeneration, I still knew that, if she were alive, I should love her. Day after day the double knowledge of her wickedness and of my weakness grew clearer. She came to be the heroine of many day-dreams, in which her eyes led on to, and sufficiently rewarded, crimes. She cast a dark shadow on my fancy, and when I was out in the free air of heaven, taking vigorous exercise and healthily renewing the current of my blood, it was often a glad thought to me that my enchantress was safe in the grave, her wand of beauty broken, her lips closed in silence, her philtre spilt. And yet I had a half-lingering terror that she might not be dead after all, but re-arisen in the body of some descendant.

Felipe served my meals in my own apartment; and his resemblance to the portrait haunted me. At times it was not; at times, upon some change of attitude or flash of expression, it would leap out upon me like a ghost. It was above all in his ill tempers that the likeness triumphed. He certainly liked me; he was proud of my notice, which he sought to engage by many simple and childlike devices; he loved to sit close before my fire, talking his broken talk or singing his odd, endless, wordless, songs, and sometimes drawing his hand over my clothes with an affectionate manner of caressing that never failed to cause in me an embarrassment of which I was ashamed. But for all that, he was capable of flashes of causeless anger and fits of sturdy sullenness. At a word of reproof, I have seen him upset the dish of which I was about to eat, and this not surreptitiously, but with defiance; and similarly at a hint of inquisition. I was not unnaturally curious, being in a strange place and surrounded by strange people; but at the shadow of a question he shrank back, lowering and dangerous. Then it was that, for a fraction of a second, this rough lad might have been the brother of the lady in the frame. But these humours were swift to pass; and the resemblance died along with them.

In these first days I saw nothing of any one but Felipe, unless the portrait is to be counted; and since the lad was plainly of weak mind, and had moments of passion, it may be wondered that I bore his dangerous neighbourhood with equanimity. As a matter of fact, it was for some time irksome; but it happened before long that I obtained over him so complete a mastery as set my disquietude at rest.

It fell in this way. He was by nature slothful, and much of a vagabond, and yet he kept by the house, and not only waited upon my wants, but laboured every day in the garden or small farm to the south of the residencia. Here he would be joined by the peasant whom I had seen on the night of my arrival, and who dwelt at the far end of the enclosure, about half a mile away, in a rude out-house; but it was plain to me that of these two, it was Felipe who did most; and though I would sometimes see him throw down his spade and go to sleep among the very plants he had been digging, his constancy and energy were admirable in themselves, and still more so since I was well assured they were foreign to his disposition, and the fruit of an ungrateful effort. But while I admired, I wondered what had called forth in a lad so shuttle-witted this enduring sense of duty. How was it sustained? I asked myself, and to what length did it prevail over his instincts? The priest was possibly his inspirer; but the priest came one day to the residencia. I saw him both come and go after an interval of close upon an hour, from a knoll where I was sketching, and all that time Felipe continued to labour undisturbed in the garden.

At last, in a very unworthy spirit, I determined to debauch the lad from his good resolutions, and, waylaying him at the gate, easily persuaded him to join me in a ramble. It was a fine day, and the woods to which I led him were green and pleasant and sweet-smelling and alive with the hum of insects. Here he discovered himself in a fresh character, mounting up to heights of gaiety that abashed me, and displaying an energy and grace of movement that delighted the eye. He leaped, he ran round me in mere glee; he would stop, and look and listen, and seem to drink in the world like a cordial; and then he would suddenly spring into a tree with one bound, and hang and gambol there like one at home. Little as he said to me, and that of not much import, I have rarely enjoyed more stirring company; the sight of his delight was a continual feast; the speed and accuracy of his movements pleased me to the heart; and I might have been so thoughtlessly unkind as to make a habit of these walks, had not chance prepared a very rude conclusion to my pleasure. By some swiftness or dexterity the lad captured a squirrel in a tree-top. He was then some way ahead of me, but I saw him drop to the ground and crouch there, crying aloud for pleasure like a child. The sound stirred my sympathies, it was so fresh and innocent; but as I bettered my pace to draw near, the cry of the squirrel knocked upon my heart. I have heard and seen much of the cruelty of lads, and above all, of peasants; but what I now beheld struck me into a passion of anger. I thrust the fellow aside, plucked the poor brute out of his hands, and with swift mercy killed it. Then I turned upon the torturer, spoke to him long out of the heat of my indignation, calling him names at which he seemed to wither; and at length, pointing towards the residencia, bade him begone and leave me, for I chose to walk with men, not with vermin. He fell upon his knees, and, the words coming to him with more clearness than usual, poured out a stream of the most touching supplications, begging me in mercy to forgive him, to forget what he had done, to look to the future. "Oh, I try so hard," he said. "Oh, commandante, bear with Felipe this once; he will never be a brute again!" Thereupon, much more affected than I cared to show, I suffered myself to be persuaded, and at last shook hands with him and made it up. But the squirrel, by way of penance, I made him bury; speaking of the poor thing's beauty, telling him what pains it had suffered, and how base a thing was the abuse of strength. "See, Felipe," said I, "you are strong indeed; but in my hands you are as helpless as that poor thing of the trees. Give me your hand in mine. You cannot remove it. Now suppose that I were cruel like you, and took a pleasure in pain. I only tighten my hold, and see how you suffer." He screamed aloud, his face stricken ashy and dotted with needle points of sweat; and when I set him free, he fell to the earth and nursed his hand and moaned over it like a baby. But he took the lesson in good part; and whether from that, or from what I had said to him, or the higher notion he now had of my bodily strength, his original affection was changed into a dog-like, adoring fidelity.

Meanwhile I gained rapidly in health. The residencia stood on the crown of a stony plateau; on every side the mountains hemmed it about; only from the roof, where was a bartizan, there might be seen, between two peaks, a small segment of plain blue, with extreme distance. The air in these altitudes moved freely and largely; great clouds congregated there, and were broken up by the wind and left in tatters on the hilltops; a hoarse and yet faint rumbling of torrents rose from all round; and one could there study all the ruder and more ancient characters of nature in something of their pristine force. I delighted from the first in the vigorous scenery and changeful weather; nor less in the antique and dilapidated mansion where I dwelt. This was a large oblong, flanked at two opposite corners by bastion-like projections, one of which commanded the door, while both were loopholed for musketry. The lower story was, besides, naked of windows, so that the building, if garrisoned, could not be carried without artillery. It enclosed an open court planted with pomegranate trees. From this a broad flight of marble stairs ascended to an open gallery, running all round and resting, towards the court, on slender pillars. Thence again, several enclosed stairs led to the upper stories of the house, which were thus broken up into distinct divisions. The windows, both within and without, were closely shuttered; some of the stonework in the upper parts had fallen; the roof, in one place, had been wrecked in one of the flurries of wind which were common in these mountains; and the whole house, in the strong, beating sunlight, and standing out above a grove of stunted cork-trees, thickly laden and discoloured with dust, looked like the sleeping palace of the legend. The court, in particular, seemed the very home of slumber. A hoarse cooing of doves haunted about the eaves; the winds were excluded, but when they blew outside, the mountain dust fell here as thick as rain, and veiled the red bloom of the pomegranates; shuttered windows and the closed doors of numerous cellars, and the vacant arches of the gallery, enclosed it; and all day long the sun made broken profiles on the four sides, and paraded the shadow of the pillars on the gallery floor. At the ground level there was, however, a certain pillared recess, which bore the marks of human habitation.

Though it was open in front upon the court, it was yet provided with a chimney, where a wood fire would be always prettily blazing; and the tile floor was littered with the skins of animals.

It was in this place that I first saw my hostess. She had drawn one of the skins forward and sat in the sun, leaning against a pillar. It was her dress that struck me first of all, for it was rich and brightly coloured, and shone out in that dusty courtyard with something of the same relief as the flowers of the pomegranates. At a second look it was her beauty of person that took hold of me. As she sat back—watching me, I thought, though with invisible eyes—and wearing at the same time an expression of almost imbecile good-humour and contentment, she showed a perfectness of feature and a quiet nobility of attitude that were beyond a statue's. I took off my hat to her in passing, and her face puckered with suspicion as swiftly and lightly as a pool ruffles in the breeze; but she paid no heed to my courtesy. I went forth on my customary walk a trifle daunted, her idol-like impassivity haunting me; and when I returned, although she was still in much the same posture, I was half surprised to see that she had moved as far as the next pillar, following the sunshine. This time, however, she addressed me with some trivial salutation, civilly enough conceived, and uttered in the same deep-chested, and yet indistinct and lisping tones, that had already baffled the utmost niceness of my hearing from her son. I answered rather at a venture; for not only did I fail to take her meaning with precision, but the sudden disclosure of her eyes disturbed me. They were unusually large, the iris golden like Felipe's, but the pupil at that moment so distended that they seemed almost black; and what affected me was not so much their size as (what was perhaps its consequence) the singular insignificance of their regard. A look more blankly stupid I have never met. My eyes dropped before it even as I spoke, and I went on my way upstairs to my own room, at once baffled and embarrassed. Yet when I came there and saw the face of the portrait, I was again reminded of the miracle of family descent. My hostess was, indeed, both older and fuller in person; her eyes were of a different colour; her face, besides, was not only free from the ill-significance that offended and attracted me in the painting; it was devoid of either good or bad—a moral blank expressing literally naught. And yet there was a likeness, not so much speaking as immanent, not so much in any particular feature as upon the whole. It should seem, I thought, as if when the master set his signature to that grave canvas, he had not only caught the image of one smiling and false-eyed woman, but stamped the essential quality of a race.

From that day forth, whether I came or went, I was sure to find the Señora seated in the sun against a pillar, or stretched on a rug before the fire; only at times she would shift her station to the top round of the stone staircase, where she lay with the same nonchalance right across my path. In all these days, I never knew her to display the least spark of energy beyond what she expended in brushing and re-brushing her copious copper-coloured hair, or in lisping out, in the rich and broken hoarseness of her voice, her customary idle salutations to myself. These, I think, were her two chief pleasures, beyond that of mere quiescence. She seemed always proud of her remarks, as though they had been witticisms: and, indeed, though they were empty enough, like the conversation of many respectable persons, and turned on a very narrow range of subjects, they were never meaningless or incoherent; nay, they had a certain beauty of their own, breathing, as they did, of her entire contentment. Now she would speak of the warmth, in which (like her son) she greatly delighted; now of the flowers of the pomegranate trees, and now of the white doves and long-winged swallows that fanned the air of the court. The birds excited her. As they raked the eaves in their swift flight, or skimmed sidelong past her with a rush of wind, she would sometimes stir, and sit a little up, and seem to awaken from her doze of satisfaction. But for the rest of her days she lay luxuriously folded on herself and sunk in sloth and pleasure. Her invincible content at first annoyed me, but I came gradually to find repose in the spectacle, until at last it grew to be my habit to sit down beside her four times in the day, both coming and going, and to talk with her sleepily, I scarce knew of what. I had come to like her dull, almost animal neighbourhood; her beauty and her stupidity soothed and amused me. I began to find a kind of transcendental good sense in her remarks, and her unfathomable good nature moved me to admiration and envy. The liking was returned; she enjoyed my presence half-unconsciously, as a man in deep meditation may enjoy the babbling of a brook. I can scarce say she brightened when I came, for satisfaction was written on her face eternally, as on some foolish statue's; but I was made conscious of her pleasure by some more intimate communication than the sight. And one day, as I sat within reach of her on the marble step, she suddenly shot forth one of her hands and patted mine. The thing was done, and she was back in her accustomed attitude, before my mind had received intelligence of the caress; and when I turned to look her in the face I could perceive no answerable sentiment. It was plain she attached no moment to the act, and I blamed myself for my own more uneasy consciousness.

The sight and (if I may so call it) the acquaintance of the mother confirmed the view I had already taken of the son. The family blood had been impoverished, perhaps by long in-breeding, which I knew to be a common error among the proud and the exclusive. No decline, indeed, was to be traced in the body, which had been handed down unimpaired in shapeliness and strength; and the faces of to-day were struck as sharply from the mint as the face of two centuries ago that smiled upon me from the portrait. But the intelligence (that more precious heirloom) was degenerate; the treasure of ancestral memory ran low; and it had required the potent, plebeian crossing of a muleteer or mountain contrabandista to raise what approached hebetude in the mother into the active oddity of the son. Yet of the two, it was the mother I preferred. Of Felipe, vengeful and placable, full of starts and shyings, inconstant as a hare, I could even conceive as a creature possibly noxious. Of the mother I had no thoughts but those of kindness. And indeed, as spectators are apt ignorantly to take sides, I grew something of a partisan in the enmity which I perceived to smoulder between them. True, it seemed mostly on the mother's part. She would sometimes draw in her breath as he came near, and the pupils of her vacant eyes would contract as if with horror or fear. Her emotions, such as they were, were much upon the surface and readily shared; and this latent repulsion occupied my mind, and kept me wondering on what grounds it rested, and whether the son was certainly in fault.

I had been about ten days in the residencia, when there sprang up a high and harsh wind, carrying clouds of dust. It came out of malarious lowlands, and over several snowy sierras. The nerves of those on whom it blew were strung and jangled; their eyes smarted with the dust; their legs ached under the burthen of their body; and the touch of one hand upon another grew to be odious. The wind, besides, came down the gullies of the hills and stormed about the house with a great, hollow buzzing and whistling that was wearisome to the ear and dismally depressing to the mind. It did not so much blow in gusts as with the steady sweep of a waterfall, so that there was no remission of discomfort while it blew. But higher up on the mountain it was probably of a more variable strength, with accesses of fury; for there came down at times a far-off wailing, infinitely grievous to hear; and at times, on one of the high shelves or terraces, there would start up, and then disperse, a tower of dust, like the smoke of an explosion.

I no sooner awoke in bed than I was conscious of the nervous tension and depression of the weather, and the effect grew stronger as the day proceeded. It was in vain that I resisted; in vain that I set forth upon my customary morning's walk; the irrational, unchanging fury of the storm had soon beat down my strength and wrecked my temper; and I returned to the residencia, glowing with dry heat, and foul and gritty with dust. The court had a forlorn appearance; now and then a glimmer of sun fled over it; now and then the wind swooped down upon the pomegranates, and scattered the blossoms, and set the window shutter clapping on the wall. In the recess the Señora was pacing to and fro with a flushed countenance and bright eyes; I thought, too, she was speaking to herself, like one in anger. But when I addressed her with my customary salutation, she only replied by a sharp gesture and continued her walk. The weather had distempered even this impassive creature; and as I went on upstairs I was the less ashamed of my own discomposure.

All day the wind continued; and I sat in my room and made a feint of reading, or walked up and down, and listened to the riot overhead. Night fell, and I had not so much as a candle. I began to long for some society, and stole down to the court. It was now plunged in the blue of the first darkness; but the recess was redly lighted by the fire. The wood had been piled high, and was crowned by a shock of flames, which the draught of the chimney brandished to and fro. In this strong and shaken brightness the Señora continued pacing from wall to wall with disconnected gestures, clasping her hands, stretching forth her arms, throwing back her head as in appeal to heaven. In these disordered movements the beauty and grace of the woman showed more clearly; but there was a light in her eye that struck on me unpleasantly; and when I had looked on a while in silence, and seemingly unobserved, I turned tail as I had come, and groped my way back again to my own chamber.

By the time Felipe brought my supper and lights, my nerve was utterly gone; and, had the lad been such as I was used to seeing him, I should have kept him (even by force, had that been necessary) to take off the edge from my distasteful solitude. But on Felipe, also, the wind had exercised its influence. He had been feverish all day; now that the night had come he was fallen into a low and tremulous humour that reacted on my own. The sight of his scared face, his starts and pallors and sudden hearkenings, unstrung me; and when he dropped and broke a dish, I fairly leaped out of my seat.

"I think we are all mad to-day," said I, affecting to laugh.

"It is the black wind," he replied dolefully. "You feel as if you must do something, and you don't know what it is."

I noted the aptness of the description; but, indeed, Felipe had sometimes a strange felicity in rendering into words the sensations of the body. "And your mother, too," said I; "she seems to feel this weather much. Do you not fear she may be unwell?"

He stared at me a little, and then said, "No," almost defiantly; and the next moment, carrying his hand to his brow, cried out lamentably on the wind and the noise that made his head go round like a millwheel. "Who can be well?" he cried; and, indeed, I could only echo his question, for I was disturbed enough myself.

I went to bed early, wearied with day-long restlessness; but the poisonous nature of the wind, and its ungodly and unintermittent uproar, would not suffer me to sleep. I lay there and tossed, my nerves and senses on the stretch. At times I would doze, dream horribly, and wake again; and these snatches of oblivion confused me as to time. But it must have been late on in the night, when I was suddenly startled by an outbreak of pitiable and hateful cries. I leaped from my bed, supposing I had dreamed; but the cries still continued to fill the house, cries of pain, I thought, but certainly of rage also, and so savage and discordant that they shocked the heart. It was no illusion; some living thing, some lunatic or some wild animal was being foully tortured. The thought of Felipe and the squirrel flashed into my mind, and I ran to the door; but it had been locked from the outside, and I might shake it as I pleased, I was a fast prisoner. Still the cries continued. Now they would dwindle down into a moaning that seemed to be articulate, and at these times I made sure they must be human; and again they would break forth and fill the house with ravings worthy of hell. I stood at the door and gave ear to them, till at last they died away. Long after that, I still lingered and still continued to hear them mingle in fancy with the storming of the wind; and when at last I crept to my bed, it was with a deadly sickness and a blackness of horror on my heart.

It was little wonder if I slept no more. Why had I been locked in? What had passed? Who was the author of these indescribable and shocking cries? A human being? It was inconceivable. A beast? The cries were scarce quite bestial; and what animal, short of a lion or a tiger, could thus shake the solid walls of the residencia? And while I was thus turning over the elements of the mystery, it came into my mind that I had not yet set eyes upon the daughter of the house. What was more probable than that the daughter of the Señora, and the sister of Felipe, should be herself insane? Or, what more likely than that these ignorant and half-witted people should seek to manage an afflicted kinswoman by violence? Here was a solution; and yet when I called to mind the cries (which I never did without a shuddering chill) it seemed altogether insufficient: not even cruelty could wring such cries from madness. But of one thing I was sure: I could not live in a house where such a thing was half conceivable, and not probe the matter home and, if necessary, interfere.

The next day came, the wind had blown itself out, and there was nothing to remind me of the business of the night. Felipe came to my bedside with obvious cheerfulness; as I passed through the court the Señora was sunning herself with her accustomed immobility; and when I issued from the gateway I found the whole face of nature austerely smiling, the heavens of a cold blue, and sown with great cloud islands, and the mountain-sides mapped forth into provinces of light and shadow. A short walk restored me to myself, and renewed within me the resolve to plumb this mystery; and when, from the vantage of my knoll, I had seen Felipe pass forth to his labours in the garden, I returned at once to the residencia to put my design in practice. The Señora appeared plunged in slumber; I stood a while and marked her, but she did not stir; even if my design were indiscreet, I had little to fear from such a guardian; and turning away, I mounted to the gallery and began my exploration of the house.

All morning I went from one door to another, and entered spacious and faded chambers, some rudely shuttered, some receiving their full charge of daylight, all empty and unhomely. It was a rich house, on which Time had breathed its tarnish and dust had scattered disillusion. The spider swung there; the bloated tarantula scampered on the cornices; ants had their crowded highways on the floor of halls of audience; the big and foul fly, that lives on carrion and is often the messenger of death, had set up his nest in the rotten woodwork, and buzzed heavily about the rooms. Here and there a stool or two, a couch, a bed, or a great carved chair remained behind, like islets on the bare floors, to testify of man's bygone habitation; and everywhere the walls were set with the portraits of the dead. I could judge, by these decaying effigies, in the house of what a great and what a handsome race I was then wandering. Many of the men wore orders on their breasts and had the port of noble offices; the women were all richly attired; the canvases most of them by famous hands. But it was not so much these evidences of greatness that took hold upon my mind, even contrasted, as they were, with the present depopulation and decay of that great house. It was rather the parable of family life that I read in this succession of fair faces and shapely bodies. Never before had I so realised the miracle of the continued race, the creation and re-creation, the weaving and changing and handing down of fleshly elements. That a child should be born of its mother, that it should grow and clothe itself (we know not how) with humanity, and put on inherited looks, and turn its head with the manner of one ascendant, and offer its hand with the gesture of another, are wonders dulled for us by repetition. But in the singular unity of look, in the common features and common bearing, of all these painted generations on the walls of the residencia, the miracle started out and looked me in the face. And an ancient mirror falling opportunely in my way, I stood and read my own features a long while, tracing out on either hand the filaments of descent and the bonds that knit me with my family.

At last, in the course of these investigations, I opened the door of a chamber that bore the marks of habitation. It was of large proportions and faced to the north, where the mountains were most wildly figured. The embers of a fire smouldered and smoked upon the hearth, to which a chair had been drawn close. And yet the aspect of the chamber was ascetic to the degree of sternness; the chair was uncushioned; the floor and walls were naked; and beyond the books which lay here and there in some confusion, there was no instrument of either work or pleasure. The sight of books in the house of such a family exceedingly amazed me; and I began with a great hurry, and in momentary fear of interruption, to go from one to another and hastily inspect their character. They were of all sorts, devotional, historical, and scientific, but mostly of a great age and in the Latin tongue. Some I could see to bear the marks of constant study; others had been torn across and tossed aside as if in petulance or disapproval. Lastly, as I cruised about that empty chamber, I espied some papers written upon with pencil on a table near the window. An unthinking curiosity led me to take one up. It bore a copy of verses, very roughly metred in the original Spanish, and which I may render somewhat thus—

Pleasure approached with pain and shame,
Grief with a wreath of lilies came.
Pleasure showed the lovely sun;
Jesu dear, how sweet it shone!
Grief with her worn hand pointed on,
  Jesu dear, to thee!

Shame and confusion at once fell on me; and, laying down the paper, I beat an immediate retreat from the apartment. Neither Felipe nor his mother could have read the books nor written these rough but feeling verses. It was plain I had stumbled with sacrilegious feet into the room of the daughter of the house. God knows, my own heart most sharply punished me for my indiscretion. The thought that I had thus secretly pushed my way into the confidence of a girl so strangely situated, and the fear that she might somehow come to hear of it, oppressed me like guilt. I blamed myself besides for my suspicions of the night before; wondered that I should ever have attributed those shocking cries to one of whom I now conceived as of a saint, spectral of mien, wasted with maceration, bound up in the practices of a mechanical devotion, and dwelling in a great isolation of soul with her incongruous relatives; and as I leaned on the balustrade of the gallery and looked down into the bright close of pomegranates and at the gaily dressed and somnolent woman, who just then stretched herself and delicately licked her lips as in the very sensuality of sloth, my mind swiftly compared the scene with the cold chamber looking northward on the mountains, where the daughter dwelt.

That same afternoon, as I sat upon my knoll, I saw the Padre enter the gates of the residencia. The revelation of the daughter's character had struck home to my fancy, and almost blotted out the horrors of the night before; but at sight of this worthy man the memory revived. I descended, then, from the knoll, and making a circuit among the woods, posted myself by the wayside to await his passage. As soon as he appeared I stepped forth and introduced myself as the lodger of the residencia. He had a very strong, honest countenance, on which it was easy to read the mingled emotions with which he regarded me, as a foreigner, a heretic, and yet one who had been wounded for the good cause. Of the family at the residencia he spoke with reserve, and yet with respect. I mentioned that I had not yet seen the daughter, whereupon he remarked that that was as it should be, and looked at me a little askance. Lastly, I plucked up courage to refer to the cries that had disturbed me in the night. He heard me out in silence, and then stopped and partly turned about, as though to mark beyond doubt that he was dismissing me.

"Do you take tobacco-powder?" said he, offering his snuff-box; and then, when I had refused, "I am an old man," he added, "and I may be allowed to remind you that you are a guest."

"I have, then, your authority," I returned, firmly enough, although I flushed at the implied reproof, "to let things take their course, and not to interfere?"

He said "yes," and with a somewhat uneasy salute turned and left me where I was. But he had done two things: he had set my conscience at rest, and he had awakened my delicacy. I made a great effort, once more dismissed the recollections of the night, and fell once more to brooding on my saintly poetess. At the same time, I could not quite forget that I had been locked in, and that night when Felipe brought me my supper I attacked him warily on both points of interest.

"I never see your sister," said I casually.

"Oh, no," said he; "she is a good, good girl," and his mind instantly veered to something else.

"Your sister is pious, I suppose," I asked in the next pause.

"Oh," he cried, joining his hands with extreme fervour, "a saint; it is she that keeps me up."

"You are very fortunate," said I, "for the most of us, I am afraid, and myself among the number, are better at going down."

"Señor," said Felipe earnestly, "I would not say that. You should not tempt your angel. If one goes down, where is he to stop?"

"Why, Felipe," said I, "I had no guess you were a preacher, and I may say a good one; but I suppose that is your sister's doing?"

He nodded at me with round eyes.

"Well, then," I continued, "she has doubtless reproved you for your sin of cruelty?"

"Twelve times!" he cried; for this was the phrase by which the odd creature expressed the sense of frequency. "And I told her you had done so—I remembered that," he added proudly—"and she was pleased."

"Then, Felipe," said I, "what were those cries that I heard last night? for surely they were cries of some creature in suffering."

"The wind," returned Felipe, looking in the fire.

I took his hand in mine, at which, thinking it to be a caress, he smiled with a brightness of pleasure that came near disarming my resolve. But I trod the weakness down. "The wind," I repeated; "and yet I think it was this hand," holding it up, "that had first locked me in." The lad shook visibly, but answered never a word. "Well," said I, "I am a stranger and a guest. It is not my part either to meddle or to judge in your affairs; in these you shall take your sister's counsel, which I cannot doubt to be excellent. But in so far as concerns my own I will be no man's prisoner, and I demand that key." Half an hour later my door was suddenly thrown open, and the key tossed ringing on the floor.

A day or two after I came in from a walk a little before the point of noon. The Senõra was lying lapped in slumber on the threshold of the recess; the pigeons dozed below the eaves like snowdrifts; the house was under a deep spell of noontide quiet; and only a wandering and gentle wind from the mountain stole round the galleries, rustled among the pomegranates, and pleasantly stirred the shadows. Something in the stillness moved me to imitation, and I went very lightly across the court and up the marble staircase. My foot was on the topmost round, when a door opened, and I found myself face to face with Olalla. Surprise transfixed me; her loveliness struck to my heart; she glowed in the deep shadow of the gallery, a gem of colour; her eyes took hold upon mine and clung there, and bound us together like the joining of hands; and the moments we thus stood face to face, drinking each other in, were sacramental and the wedding of souls. I know not how long it was before I awoke out of a deep trance, and, hastily bowing, passed on into the upper stair. She did not move, but followed me with her great, thirsting eyes; and as I passed out of sight it seemed to me as if she paled and faded.

In my own room, I opened the window and looked out, and could not think what change had come upon that austere field of mountains that it should thus sing and shine under the lofty heaven. I had seen her—Olalla! And the stone crags answered, Olalla! and the dumb, unfathomable azure answered, Olalla! The pale saint of my dreams had vanished for ever; and in her place I beheld this maiden on whom God had lavished the richest colours and the most exuberant energies of life, whom he had made active as a deer, slender as a reed, and in whose great eyes he had lighted the torches of the soul. The thrill of her young life, strung like a wild animal's, had entered into me; the force of soul that had looked out from her eyes and conquered mine, mantled about my heart and sprang to my lips in singing. She passed through my veins: she was one with me.

I will not say that this enthusiasm declined; rather my soul held out in its ecstasy as in a strong castle, and was there besieged by cold and sorrowful considerations. I could not doubt but that I loved her at first sight, and already with a quivering ardour that was strange to my experience. What then was to follow? She was the child of an afflicted house, the Señora's daughter, the sister of Felipe; she bore it even in her beauty. She had the lightness and swiftness of the one, swift as an arrow, light as dew; like the other, she shone on the pale background of the world with the brilliancy of flowers. I could not call by the name of brother that half-witted lad, nor by the name of mother that immovable and lovely thing of flesh, whose silly eyes and perpetual simper now recurred to my mind like something hateful. And if I could not marry, what then? She was helplessly unprotected; her eyes, in that single and long glance, which had been all our intercourse, had confessed a weakness equal to my own; but in my heart I knew her for the student of the cold northern chamber, and the writer of the sorrowful lines; and this was a knowledge to disarm a brute. To flee was more than I could find courage for; but I registered a vow of unsleeping circumspection.

As I turned from the window, my eyes alighted on the portrait. It had fallen dead, like a candle after sunrise; it followed me with eyes of paint. I knew it to be like, and marvelled at the tenacity of type in that declining race; but the likeness was swallowed up in difference. I remembered how it had seemed to me a thing unapproachable in the life, a creature rather of the painter's craft than of the modesty of nature, and I marvelled at the thought, and exulted in the image of Olalla. Beauty I had seen before, and not been charmed, and I had been often drawn to women, who were not beautiful except to me; but in Olalla all that I desired and had not dared to imagine was united.

I did not see her the next day, and my heart ached and my eyes longed for her, as men long for morning. But the day after, when I returned, about my usual hour, she was once more on the gallery, and our looks once more met and embraced.

I would have spoken, I would have drawn near to her; but strongly as she plucked at my heart, drawing me like a magnet, something yet more imperious withheld me; and I could only bow and pass by; and she, leaving my salutation unanswered, only followed me with her noble eyes.

I had now her image by rote, and as I conned the traits in memory it seemed as if I read her very heart. She was dressed with something of her mother's coquetry and love of positive colour. Her robe, which I knew she must have made with her own hands, clung about her with a cunning grace. After the fashion of that country, besides, her bodice stood open in the middle, in a long slit, and here, in spite of the poverty of the house, a gold coin, hanging by a ribbon, lay on her brown bosom. These were proofs, had any been needed, of her inborn delight in life and her own loveliness. On the other hand, in her eyes that hung upon mine, I could read depth beyond depth of passion and sadness, lights of poetry and hope, blacknesses of despair, and thoughts that were above the earth. It was a lovely body, but the inmate, the soul, was more than worthy of that lodging. Should I leave this incomparable flower to wither unseen on these rough mountains? Should I despise the great gift offered me in the eloquent silence of her eyes? Here was a soul immured; should I not burst its prison? All side considerations fell off from me; were she the child of Herod I swore I should make her mine; and that very evening I set myself, with a mingled sense of treachery and disgrace, to captivate the brother. Perhaps I read him with more favourable eyes, perhaps the thought of his sister always summoned up the better qualities of that imperfect soul; but he had never seemed to me so amiable, and his very likeness to Olalla, while it annoyed, yet softened me.

A third day passed in vain—an empty desert of hours. I would not lose a chance, and loitered all afternoon in the court, where (to give myself a countenance) I spoke more than usual with the Señora. God knows it was with a most tender and sincere interest that I now studied her; and even as for Felipe, so now for the mother, I was conscious of a growing warmth of toleration. And yet I wondered. Even while I spoke with her, she would doze off into a little sleep, and presently awake again without embarrassment; and this composure staggered me. And again, as I marked her make infinitesimal changes in her posture, savouring and lingering on the bodily pleasure of the movement, I was driven to wonder at this depth of passive sensuality. She lived in her body; and her consciousness was all sunk into and disseminated through her members, where it luxuriously dwelt. Lastly, I could not grow accustomed to her eyes. Each time she turned on me those great beautiful and meaningless orbs, wide open to the day, but closed against human inquiry—

each time I had occasion to observe the lively changes of her pupils which expanded and contracted in a breath—I know not what it was came over me, I can find no name for the mingled feeling of disappointment, annoyance, and distaste that jarred along my nerves. I tried her on a variety of subjects, equally in vain; and at last led the talk to her daughter. But even there she proved indifferent; said she was pretty, which (as with children) was her highest word of commendation, but was plainly incapable of any higher thought; and when I remarked that Olalla seemed silent, merely yawned in my face and replied that speech was of no great use when you had nothing to say. "People speak much, very much," she added, looking at me with expanded pupils; and then again yawned, and again showed me a mouth that was as dainty as a toy. This time I took the hint, and, leaving her to her repose, went up into my own chamber to sit by the open window, looking on the hills and not beholding them, sunk in lustrous and deep dreams, and hearkening in fancy to the note of a voice that I had never heard.

I awoke on the fifth morning with a brightness of anticipation that seemed to challenge fate. I was sure of myself, light of heart and foot, and resolved to put my love incontinently to the touch of knowledge. It should lie no longer under the bonds of silence, a dumb thing, living by the eye only, like the love of beasts; but should now put on the spirit, and enter upon the joys of the complete human intimacy. I thought of it with wild hopes, like a voyager to El Dorado; into that unknown and lovely country of her soul, I no longer trembled to adventure. Yet when I did indeed encounter her, the same force of passion descended on me and at once submerged my mind; speech seemed to drop away from me like a childish habit; and I but drew near to her as the giddy man draws near to the margin of a gulf. She drew back from me a little as I came; but her eyes did not waver from mine, and these lured me forward. At last, when I was already within reach of her, I stopped. Words were denied me; if I advanced I could but clasp her to my heart in silence; and all that was sane in me, all that was still unconquered, revolted against the thought of such an accost. So we stood for a second, all our life in our eyes, exchanging salvos of attraction and yet each resisting; and then, with a great effort of the will, and conscious at the same time of a sudden bitterness of disappointment, I turned and went away in the same silence.

What power lay upon me that I could not speak? And she, why was she also silent? Why did she draw away before me dumbly, with fascinated eyes? Was this love? or was it a mere brute attraction, mindless and inevitable, like that of the magnet for the steel? We had never spoken, we were wholly strangers; and yet an influence, strong as the grasp of a giant, swept us silently together. On my side, it filled me with impatience; and yet I was sure that she was worthy; I had seen her books, read her verses, and thus, in a sense, divined the soul of my mistress. But on her side, it struck me almost cold. Of me, she knew nothing but my bodily favour; she was drawn to me as stones fall to the earth; the laws that rule the earth conducted her, unconsenting, to my arms; and I drew back at the thought of such a bridal, and began to be jealous for myself. It was not thus that I desired to be loved. And then I began to fall into a great pity for the girl herself. I thought how sharp must be her mortification, that she, the student, the recluse, Felipe's saintly monitress, should have thus confessed an overweening weakness for a man with whom she had never exchanged a word. And at the coming of pity, all other thoughts were swallowed up; and I longed only to find and console and reassure her; to tell her how wholly her love was returned on my side, and how her choice, even if blindly made, was not unworthy.

The next day it was glorious weather; depth upon depth of blue over-canopied the mountains; the sun shone wide; and the wind in the trees and the many fallen torrents in the mountains filled the air with delicate and haunting music. Yet I was prostrated with sadness. My heart wept for the sight of Olalla, as a child weeps for its mother. I sat down on a boulder on the verge of the low cliffs that bound the plateau to the north. Thence I looked down into the wooded valley of a stream, where no foot came. In the mood I was in, it was even touching to behold the place untenanted; it lacked Olalla; and I thought of the delight and glory of a life passed wholly with her in that strong air, and among these rugged and lovely surroundings, at first with a whimpering sentiment, and then again with such a fiery joy that I seemed to grow in strength and stature, like a Samson.

And then suddenly I was aware of Olalla drawing near. She appeared out of a grove of cork-trees, and came straight towards me; and I stood up and waited. She seemed in her walking a creature of such life and fire and lightness as amazed me; yet she came quietly and slowly. Her energy was in the slowness; but for inimitable strength, I felt she would have run, she would have flown to me. Still, as she approached, she kept her eyes lowered to the ground; and when she had drawn quite near, it was without one glance that she addressed me. At the first note of her voice I started. It was for this I had been waiting; this was the last test of my love. And lo, her enunciation was precise and clear, not lisping and incomplete like that of her family; and the voice, though deeper than usual with women, was still both youthful and womanly. She spoke in a rich chord; golden contralto strains mingled with hoarseness, as the red threads were mingled with the brown among her tresses. It was not only a voice that spoke to my heart directly; but it spoke to me of her. And yet her words immediately plunged me back upon despair.

"You will go away," she said, "to-day."

Her example broke the bonds of my speech; I felt as lightened of a weight, or as if a spell had been dissolved. I know not in what words I answered; but, standing before her on the cliffs, I poured out the whole ardour of my love, telling her that I lived upon the thought of her, slept only to dream of her loveliness, and would gladly forswear my country, my language, and my friends, to live for ever by her side. And then, strongly commanding myself, I changed the note; I reassured, I comforted her; I told her I had divined in her a pious and heroic spirit, with which I was worthy to sympathise, and which I longed to share and lighten. "Nature," I told her, "was the voice of God, which men disobey at peril; and if we were thus dumbly drawn together, ay, even as by a miracle of love, it must imply a divine fitness in our souls; we must be made," I said—"made for one another. We should be mad rebels," I cried out—"mad rebels against God, not to obey this instinct."

She shook her head. "You will go to-day," she repeated, and then with a gesture, and in a sudden, sharp note—"no, not to-day," she cried, "to-morrow!"

But at this sign of relenting, power came in upon me in a tide. I stretched out my arms and called upon her name; and she leaped to me and clung to me. The hills rocked about us, the earth quailed; a shock as of a blow went through me and left me blind and dizzy. And the next moment she had thrust me back, broken rudely from my arms, and fled with the speed of a deer among the cork-trees.

I stood and shouted to the mountains; I turned and went back towards the residencia, walking upon air. She sent me away, and yet I had but to call upon her name and she came to me. These were but the weaknesses of girls, from which even she, the strangest of her sex, was not exempted. Go? Not I, Olalla—Oh, not I, Olalla, my Olalla! A bird sang near by; and in that season birds were rare. It bade me be of good cheer. And once more the whole countenance of nature, from the ponderous and stable mountains down to the lightest leaf and the smallest darting fly in the shadow of the groves, began to stir before me and to put on the lineaments of life and wear a face of awful joy. The sunshine struck upon the hills, strong as a hammer on the anvil, and the hills shook; the earth, under that vigorous insolation, yielded up heady scents; the woods smouldered in the blaze. I felt the thrill of travail and delight run through the earth. Something elemental, something rude, violent, and savage, in the love that sang in my heart, was like a key to nature's secrets; and the very stones that rattled under my feet appeared alive and friendly. Olalla! Her touch had quickened, and renewed, and strung me up to the old pitch of concert with the rugged earth, to a swelling of the soul that men learn to forget in their polite assemblies. Love burned in me like rage; tenderness waxed fierce;

I hated, I adored, I pitied, I revered her with ecstasy. She seemed the link that bound me in with dead things on the one hand, and with our pure and pitying God upon the other: a thing brutal and divine, and akin at once to the innocence and to the unbridled forces of the earth.

My head thus reeling, I came into the courtyard of the residencia, and the sight of the mother struck me like a revelation. She sat there, all sloth and contentment, blinking under the strong sunshine, branded with a passive enjoyment, a creature set quite apart, before whom my ardour fell away like a thing ashamed. I stopped a moment, and, commanding such shaken tones as I was able, said a word or two. She looked at me with her unfathomable kindness; her voice in reply sounded vaguely out of the realm of peace in which she slumbered, and there fell on my mind, for the first time, a sense of respect for one so uniformly innocent and happy, and I passed on in a kind of wonder at myself that I should be so much disquieted.

On my table there lay a piece of the same yellow paper I had seen in the north room; it was written on with pencil in the same hand, Olalla's hand, and I picked it up with a sudden sinking of alarm, and read, "If you have any kindness for Olalla, if you have any chivalry for a creature sorely wrought, go from here to-day; in pity, in honour, for the sake of Him who died, I supplicate that you shall go." I looked at this a while in mere stupidity, then I began to awaken to a weariness and horror of life; the sunshine darkened outside on the bare hills, and I began to shake like a man in terror. The vacancy thus suddenly opened in my life unmanned me like a physical void. It was not my heart, it was not my happiness, it was life itself that was involved. I could not lose her. I said so, and stood repeating it. And then, like one in a dream, I moved to the window, put forth my hand to open the casement, and thrust it through the pane. The blood spurted from my wrist; and with an instantaneous quietude and command of myself, I pressed my thumb on the little leaping fountain, and reflected what to do. In that empty room there was nothing to my purpose; I felt, besides, that I required assistance. There shot into my mind a hope that Olalla herself might be my helper, and I turned and went downstairs, still keeping my thumb upon the wound.

There was no sign of either Olalla or Felipe, and I addressed myself to the recess, whither the Señora had now drawn quite back and sat dozing close before the fire, for no degree of heat appeared too much for her.

"Pardon me," said I, "if I disturb you, but I must apply to you for help."

She looked up sleepily and asked me what it was, and with the very words I thought she drew in her breath with a widening of the nostrils and seemed to come suddenly and fully alive.

"I have cut myself," I said, "and rather badly. See!" And I held out my two hands, from which the blood was oozing and dripping.

Her great eyes opened wide, the pupils shrank into points; a veil seemed to fall from her face, and leave it sharply expressive and yet inscrutable. And as I still stood, marvelling a little at her disturbance, she came swiftly up to me, and stooped and caught me by the hand; and the next moment my hand was at her mouth, and she had bitten me to the bone. The pang of the bite, the sudden spurting of blood, and the monstrous horror of the act, flashed through me all in one, and I beat her back; and she sprang at me again and again, with bestial cries, cries that I recognised, such cries as had awakened me on the night of the high wind. Her strength was like that of madness; mine was rapidly ebbing with the loss of blood; my mind besides was whirling with the abhorrent strangeness of the onslaught, and I was already forced against the wall, when Olalla ran betwixt us, and Felipe, following at a bound, pinned down his mother on the floor.

A trance-like weakness fell upon me; I saw, heard, and felt, but I was incapable of movement. I heard the struggle roll to and fro upon the floor, the yells of the catamount ringing up to heaven as she strove to reach me. I felt Olalla clasp me in her arms, her hair falling on my face, and, with the strength of a man, raise and half drag, half carry me upstairs into my own room, where she cast me down upon the bed. Then I saw her hasten to the door and lock it, and stand an instant listening to the savage cries that shook the residencia. And then, swift and light as a thought, she was again beside me, binding up my hand, laying it in her bosom, moaning and mourning over it, with dove-like sounds. They were not words that came to her, they were sounds more beautiful than speech, infinitely touching, infinitely tender; and yet as I lay there, a thought stung to my heart, a thought wounded me like a sword, a thought, like a worm in a flower, profaned the holiness of my love. Yes, they were beautiful sounds, and they were inspired by human tenderness; but was their beauty human?

All day I lay there. For a long time the cries of that nameless female thing, as she struggled with her half-witted whelp, resounded through the house, and pierced me with despairing sorrow and disgust. They were the death-cry of my love; my love was murdered; it was not only dead, but an offence to me; and yet, think as I pleased, feel as I must, it still swelled within me like a storm of sweetness, and my heart melted at her looks and touch. This horror that had sprung out, this doubt upon Olalla, this savage and bestial strain that ran not only through the whole behaviour of her family, but found a place in the very foundations and story of our love—though it appalled, though it shocked and sickened me, was yet not of power to break the knot of my infatuation.

When the cries had ceased, there came a scraping at the door, by which I knew Felipe was without; and Olalla went and spoke to him—I know not what. With that exception, she stayed close beside me, now kneeling by my bed and fervently praying, now sitting with her eyes upon mine. So then, for these six hours I drank in her beauty, and silently perused the story in her face. I saw the golden coin hover on her breaths; I saw her eyes darken and brighten, and still speak no language but that of an unfathomable kindness; I saw the faultless face, and, through the robe, the lines of the faultless body. Night came at last, and in the growing darkness of the chamber the sight of her slowly melted; but even then the touch of her smooth hand lingered in mine and talked with me. To lie thus in deadly weakness and drink in the traits of the beloved, is to reawake to love from whatever shock of disillusion. I reasoned with myself; and I shut my eyes on horrors, and again I was very bold to accept the worst. What mattered it, if that imperious sentiment survived; if her eyes still beckoned and attached me; if now, even as before, every fibre of my dull body yearned and turned to her? Late on in the night some strength revived in me, and I spoke:—

"Olalla," I said, "nothing matters; I ask nothing; I am content; I love you."

She knelt down a while and prayed, and I devoutly respected her devotions. The moon had begun to shine in upon one side of each of the three windows, and make a misty clearness in the room, by which I saw her indistinctly. When she rearose she made the sign of the cross.

"It is for me to speak," she said, "and for you to listen. I know; you can but guess. I prayed, how I prayed for you to leave this place. I begged it of you, and I know you would have granted me even this; or if not, oh let me think so!"

"I love you," I said.

"And yet you have lived in the world," she said; after a pause, "you are a man and wise; and I am but a child. Forgive me, if I seem to teach, who am as ignorant as the trees of the mountain; but those who learn much do but skim the face of knowledge; they seize the laws, they conceive the dignity of the design—the horror of the living fact fades from their memory. It is we who sit at home with evil who remember, I think, and are warned and pity. Go, rather, go now, and keep me in mind. So I shall have a life in the cherished places of your memory; a life as much my own as that which I lead in this body."

"I love you," I said once more; and reaching out my weak hand, took hers, and carried it to my lips, and kissed it. Nor did she resist, but winced a little; and I could see her look upon me with a frown that was not unkindly, only sad and baffled. And then it seemed she made a call upon her resolution; plucked my hand towards her, herself at the same time leaning somewhat forward, and laid it on the beating of her heart. "There," she cried, "you feel the very footfall of my life. It only moves for you; it is yours. But is it even mine? It is mine indeed to offer you, as I might take the coin from my neck, as I might break a live branch from a tree, and give it you. And yet not mine! I dwell, or I think I dwell (if I exist at all), somewhere apart, an impotent prisoner, and carried about and deafened by a mob that I disown. This capsule, such as throbs against the sides of animals, knows you at a touch for its master; ay, it loves you! But my soul, does my soul? I think not; I know not, fearing to ask. Yet when you spoke to me, your words were of the soul; it is of the soul that you ask—it is only from the soul that you would take me."

"Olalla," I said, "the soul and the body are one, and mostly so in love. What the body chooses, the soul loves; where the body clings, the soul cleaves; body for body, soul to soul, they come together at God's signal; and the lower part (if we can call aught low) is only the footstool and foundation of the highest."

"Have you," she said, "seen the portraits in the house of my fathers? Have you looked at my mother or at Felipe? Have your eyes never rested on that picture that hangs by your bed? She who sat for it died ages ago; and she did evil in her life. But, look again: there is my hand to the least line, there are my eyes and my hair. What is mine, then, and what am I? If not a curve in this poor body of mine (which you love, and for the sake of which you dotingly dream that you love me), not a gesture that I can frame, not a tone of my voice, not any look from my eyes, no, not even now when I speak to him I love, but has belonged to others? Others, ages dead, have wooed other men with my eyes; other men have heard the pleading of the same voice that now sounds in your ears. The hands of the dead are in my bosom; they move me, they pluck me, they guide me; I am a puppet at their command; and I but reinform features and attributes that have long been laid aside from evil in the quiet of the grave. Is it me you love, friend? or the race that made me? The girl who does not know and cannot answer for the least portion of herself? or the stream of which she is a transitory eddy, the tree of which she is the passing fruit? The race exists; it is old, it is ever young, it carries its eternal destiny in its bosom; upon it, like waves upon the sea, individual succeeds to individual, mocked with a semblance of self-control, but they are nothing. We speak of the soul, but the soul is in the race."

"You fret against the common law," I said. "You rebel against the voice of God, which he has made so winning to convince, so imperious to command. Hear it, and how it speaks between us! Your hand clings to mine, your heart leaps at my touch, the unknown elements of which we are compounded awake and run together at a look; the clay of the earth remembers its independent life and yearns to join us; we are drawn together as the stars are turned about in space, or as the tides ebb and flow; by things older and greater than we ourselves."

"Alas!" she said, "what can I say to you? My fathers, eight hundred years ago, ruled all this province: they were wise, great, cunning, and cruel; they were a picked race of the Spanish; their flags led in war; the king called them his cousin; the people, when the rope was slung for them or when they returned and found their hovels smoking, blasphemed their name. Presently a change began. Man has risen; if he has sprung from the brutes, he can descend again to the same level. The breath of weariness blew on their humanity and the cords relaxed; they began to go down; their minds fell on sleep, their passions awoke in gusts, heady and senseless like the wind in the gutters of the mountains; beauty was still handed down, but no longer the guiding wit nor the human heart; the seed passed on, it was wrapped in flesh, the flesh covered the bones, but they were the bones and the flesh of brutes, and their mind was as the mind of flies. I speak to you as I dare; but you have seen for yourself how the wheel has gone backward with my doomed race. I stand, as it were, upon a little rising ground in this desperate descent, and see both before and behind, both what we have lost and to what we are condemned to go farther downward. And shall I—I that dwell apart in the house of the dead, my body, loathing its ways—shall I repeat the spell? Shall I bind another spirit, reluctant as my own, into this bewitched and tempest-broken tenement that I now suffer in? Shall I hand down this cursed vessel of humanity, charge it with fresh life as with fresh poison, and dash it, like a fire, in the faces of posterity? But my vow has been given; the race shall cease from off the earth. At this hour my brother is making ready; his foot will soon be on the stair; and you will go with him and pass out of my sight for ever. Think of me sometimes as one to whom the lesson of life was very harshly told, but who heard it with courage; as one who loved you indeed, but who hated herself so deeply that her love was hateful to her; as one who sent you away and yet would have longed to keep you for ever: who had no dearer hope than to forget you, and no greater fear than to be forgotten."

She had drawn towards the door as she spoke, her rich voice sounding softer and farther away; and with the last word she was gone, and I lay alone in the moonlit chamber. What I might have done had not I lain bound by my extreme weakness, I know not; but as it was, there fell upon me a great and blank despair. It was not long before there shone in at the door the ruddy glimmer of a lantern, and Felipe, coming, charged me without a word upon his shoulders, and carried me down to the great gate, where the cart was waiting. In the moonlight the hills stood out sharply, as if they were of cardboard; on the glimmering surface of the plateau, and from among the low trees which swung together and sparkled in the wind, the great black cube of the residencia stood out bulkily, its mass only broken by three dimly lighted windows in the northern front above the gate. They were Olalla's windows, and as the cart jolted onwards I kept my eyes fixed upon them till, where the road dipped into a valley, they were lost to my view for ever. Felipe walked in silence beside the shafts, but from time to time he would check the mule and seem to look back upon me; and at length drew quite near and laid his hand upon my head. There was such kindness in the touch, and such a simplicity, as of the brutes, that tears broke from me like the bursting of an artery.

"Felipe," I said, "take me where they will ask no questions."

He said never a word, but he turned his mule about, end for end, retraced some part of the way we had gone, and, striking into another path, led me to the mountain village, which was, as we say in Scotland, the kirkton of that thinly peopled district. Some broken memories dwell in my mind of the day breaking over the plain, of the cart stopping, of arms that helped me down, of a bare room into which I was carried, and of a swoon that fell upon me like sleep.

The next day and the days following, the old priest was often at my side with his snuff-box and prayer book, and after a while, when I began to pick up strength, he told me that I was now on a fair way to recovery, and must as soon as possible hurry my departure; whereupon, without naming any reason, he took snuff and looked at me sideways. I did not affect ignorance; I knew he must have seen Olalla. "Sir," said I, "you know that I do not ask in wantonness. What of that family?"

He said they were very unfortunate; that it seemed a declining race, and that they were very poor and had been much neglected.

"But she has not," I said. "Thanks, doubtless, to yourself, she is instructed and wise beyond the use of women."

"Yes," he said, "the Señorita is well-informed. But the family has been neglected."

"The mother?" I queried.

"Yes, the mother too," said the Padre, taking snuff. "But Felipe is a well-intentioned lad."

"The mother is odd?" I asked.

"Very odd," replied the priest.

"I think, sir, we beat about the bush," said I. "You must know more of my affairs than you allow. You must know my curiosity to be justified on many grounds. Will you not be frank with me?"

"My son," said the old gentleman, "I will be very frank with you on matters within my competence; on those of which I know nothing it does not require much discretion to be silent. I will not fence with you, I take your meaning perfectly; and what can I say, but that we are all in God's hands, and that His ways are not our ways? I have even advised with my superiors in the Church, but they, too, were dumb. It is a great mystery."

"Is she mad?" I asked.

"I will answer you according to my belief. She is not," returned the Padre, "or she was not. When she was young—God help me, I fear I neglected that wild lamb—she was surely sane; and yet, although it did not run to such heights, the same strain was already notable; it had been so before her in her father, ay, and before him, and this inclined me, perhaps, to think too lightly of it. But these things go on growing, not only in the individual but in the race."

"When she was young," I began, and my voice failed me for a moment, and it was only with a great effort that I was able to add, "was she like Olalla?"

"Now God forbid!" exclaimed the Padre. "God forbid that any man should think so slightingly of my favourite penitent. No, no; the Señorita (but for her beauty, which I wish most honestly she had less of) has not a hair's resemblance to what her mother was at the same age. I could not bear to have you think so; though, heaven knows, it were, perhaps, better that you should."

At this I raised myself in bed, and opened my heart to the old man; telling him of our love and of her decision; owning my own horrors, my own passing fancies, but telling him that these were at an end; and with something more than a purely formal submission, appealing to his judgment.

He heard me very patiently and without surprise; and when I had done he sat for some time silent. Then he began: "The church," and instantly broke off again to apologise. "I had forgotten, my child, that you were not a Christian," said he. "And indeed, upon a point so highly unusual, even the church can scarce be said to have decided. But would you have my opinion? The Señorita is, in a matter of this kind, the best judge; I would accept her judgment."

On the back of that he went away, nor was he thence-forward so assiduous in his visits; indeed, even when I began to get about again, he plainly feared and deprecated my society, not as in distaste, but much as a man might be disposed to flee from the riddling sphinx. The villagers, too, avoided me; they were unwilling to be my guides upon the mountain. I thought they looked at me askance, and I made sure that the more superstitious crossed themselves on my approach. At first I set this down to my heretical opinions; but it began at length to dawn upon me that if I was thus redoubted it was because I had stayed at the residencia. All men despise the savage notions of such peasantry; and yet I was conscious of a chill shadow that seemed to fall and dwell upon my love. It did not conquer, but I may not deny that it restrained, my ardour.

Some miles westward of the village there was a gap in the sierra, from which the eye plunged direct upon the residencia; and thither it became my daily habit to repair. A wood crowned the summit; and just where the pathway issued from its fringes, it was overhung by a considerable shelf of rock, and that, in its turn, was surmounted by a crucifix of the size of life and more than usually painful in design. This was my perch; thence, day after day, I looked down upon the plateau, and the great old house, and could see Felipe, no bigger than a fly, going to and fro about the garden. Sometimes mists would draw across the view, and be broken up again by mountain winds; sometimes the plain slumbered below me in unbroken sunshine; it would sometimes be all blotted out by rain. This distant post, these interrupted sights of the place where my life had been so strangely changed, suited the indecision of my humour. I passed whole days there, debating with myself the various elements of our position, now leaning to the suggestions of love, now giving an ear to prudence, and in the end halting irresolute between the two.

One day, as I was sitting on my rock, there came by that way a somewhat gaunt peasant wrapped in a mantle. He was a stranger, and plainly did not know me even by repute; for, instead of keeping the other side, he drew near and sat down beside me, and we had soon fallen in talk. Among other things, he told me he had been a muleteer, and in former years had much frequented these mountains; later on, he had followed the army with his mules, had realised a competence, and was now living retired with his family.

"Do you know that house?" I inquired at last, pointing to the residencia, for I readily wearied of any talk that kept me from the thought of Olalla.

He looked at me darkly and crossed himself.

"Too well," he said, "it was there that one of my comrades sold himself to Satan; the Virgin shield us from temptations! He has paid the price; he is now burning in the reddest place in Hell!"

A fear came upon me; I could answer nothing; and presently the man resumed, as if to himself: "Yes," he said, "O yes, I know it. I have passed its doors. There was snow upon the pass, the wind was driving it; sure enough there was death that night upon the mountains, but there was worse beside the hearth. I took him by the arm, Señor, and dragged him to the gate; I conjured him, by all he loved and respected, to go forth with me; I went on my knees before him in the snow; and I could see he was moved by my entreaty. And just then she came out on the gallery, and called him by his name; and he turned, and there was she, standing with a lamp in her hand and smiling on him to come back. I cried out aloud to God, and threw my arms about him, but he put me by, and left me alone. He had made his choice; God help us. I would pray for him, but to what end? there are sins that not even the Pope can loose."

"And your friend," I asked, "what became of him?"

"Nay, God knows," said the muleteer. "If all be true that we hear, his end was like his sin, a thing to raise the hair."

"Do you mean that he was killed?" I asked.

"Sure enough, he was killed," returned the man. "But how? Ah, how? But these are things that it is sin to speak of."

"The people of that house . . ." I began.

But he interrupted me with a savage outburst. "The people?" he cried. "What people? There are neither men nor women in that house of Satan's! What? have you lived here so long, and never heard?" And here he put his mouth to my ear and whispered, as if even the fowls of the mountain might have overheard and been stricken with horror.

What he told me was not true, nor was it even original; being, indeed, but a new edition, vamped up again by village ignorance and superstition, of stories nearly as ancient as the race of man. It was rather the application that appalled me. In the old days, he said, the church would have burned out that nest of basilisks; but the arm of the church was now shortened; his friend Miguel had been unpunished by the hands of men, and left to the more awful judgment of an offended God. This was wrong; but it should be so no more. The Padre was sunk in age; he was even bewitched himself; but the eyes of his flock were now awake to their own danger; and some day—ay, and before long—the smoke of that house should go up to heaven.

He left me filled with horror and fear. Which way to turn I knew not; whether first to warn the Padre, or to carry my ill-news direct to the threatened inhabitants of the residencia. Fate was to decide for me; for, while I was still hesitating, I beheld the veiled figure of a woman drawing near to me up the pathway. No veil could deceive my penetration; by every line and every movement I recognised Olalla; and keeping hidden behind a corner of the rock, I suffered her to gain the summit. Then I came forward. She knew me and paused, but did not speak; I, too, remained silent; and we continued for some time to gaze upon each other with a passionate sadness.

"I thought you had gone," she said at length. "It is all that you can do for me—to go. It is all I ever asked of you. And you still stay. But do you know, that every day heaps up the peril of death, not only on your head, but on ours? A report has gone about the mountain; it is thought you love me, and the people will not suffer it."

I saw she was already informed of her danger, and I rejoiced at it. "Olalla," I said, "I am ready to go this day, this very hour, but not alone."

She stepped aside and knelt down before the crucifix to pray, and I stood by and looked now at her and now at the object of her adoration, now at the living figure of the penitent, and now at the ghastly, daubed countenance, the painted wounds, and the projected ribs of the image. The silence was only broken by the wailing of some large birds that circled sidelong, as if in surprise or alarm, about the summit of the hills. Presently Olalla rose again, turned towards me, raised her veil, and, still leaning with one hand on the shaft of the crucifix, looked upon me with a pale and sorrowful countenance.

"I have laid my hand upon the cross," she said. "The Padre says you are no Christian; but look up for a moment with my eyes, and behold the face of the Man of Sorrows. We are all such as He was—the inheritors of sin; we must all bear and expiate a past which was not ours; there is in all of us—ay, even in me—a sparkle of the divine. Like Him, we must endure for a little while, until morning returns, bringing peace. Suffer me to pass on upon my way alone; it is thus that I shall be least lonely, counting for my friend Him who is the friend of all the distressed; it is thus that I shall be the most happy, having taken my farewell of earthly happiness, and willingly accepted sorrow for my portion."

I looked at the face of the crucifix, and, though I was no friend to images, and despised that imitative and grimacing art of which it was a rude example, some sense of what the thing implied was carried home to my intelligence. The face looked down upon me with a painful and deadly contraction; but the rays of a glory encircled it, and reminded me that the sacrifice was voluntary. It stood there, crowning the rock, as it still stands on so many highway sides, vainly preaching to passers-by, an emblem of sad and noble truths; that pleasure is not an end, but an accident; that pain is the choice of the magnanimous; that it is best to suffer all things and do well. I turned and went down the mountain in silence; and when I looked back for the last time before the wood closed about my path, I saw Olalla still leaning on the crucifix.

The Withered Arm

Thomas Hardy

I

A LORN MILKMAID

IT WAS AN EIGHTY-COW DAIRY, AND THE TROOP OF MILKERS, REGULAR and supernumerary, were all at work; for, though the time of year was as yet but early April, the feed lay entirely in water-meadows, and the cows were "in full pail." The hour was about six in the evening, and three-fourths of the large, red, rectangular animals having been finished off, there was opportunity for a little conversation.

"He do bring home his bride to-morrow, I hear. They've come as far as Anglebury to-day."

The voice seemed to proceed from the belly of the cow called Cherry, but the speaker was a milking-woman, whose face was buried in the flank of that motionless beast.

"Hav' anybody seen her?" said another.

There was a negative response from the first. "Though they say she's a rosy-cheeked, tisty-tosty little body enough," she added; and as the milkmaid spoke she turned her face so that she could glance past her cow's tail to the other side of the barton, where a thin, fading woman of thirty milked somewhat apart from the rest.

"Years younger than he, they say," continued the second, with also a glance of reflectiveness in the same direction.

"How old do you call him, then?"

"Thirty or so."

"More like forty," broke in an old milkman near, in a long white pinafore or "wropper," and with the brim of his hat tied down, so that he looked like a woman. "'A was born before our Great Weir was builded, and I hadn't man's wages when I laved water there."

The discussion waxed so warm that the purr of the milk-streams became jerky, till a voice from another cow's belly cried with authority, "Now then, what the Turk do it matter to us about Farmer Lodge's age, or Farmer Lodge's new mis'ess? I shall have to pay him nine pound a year for the rent of every one of these milchers, whatever his age or hers. Get on with your work, or 'twill be dark afore we have done. The evening is pinking in a'ready." This speaker was the dairyman himself; by whom the milkmaids and men were employed.

Nothing more was said publicly about Farmer Lodge's wedding, but the first woman murmured under her cow to her next neighbour, "'Tis hard for *she*," signifying the thin worn milkmaid aforesaid.

"O no," said the second. "He ha'n't spoke to Rhoda Brook for years."

When the milking was done they washed their pails and hung them on a many-forked stand made of the peeled limb of an oak-tree, set upright in the earth, and resembling a colossal antlered horn. The majority then dispersed in various directions homeward. The thin woman who had not spoken was joined by a boy of twelve or thereabout, and the twain went away up the field also.

Their course lay apart from that of the others, to a lonely spot high above the water-meads, and not far from the border of Egdon Heath, whose dark countenance was visible in the distance as they drew nigh to their home.

"They've just been saying down in barton that your father brings his young wife home from Anglebury to-morrow," the woman observed. "I shall want to send you for a few things to market, and you'll be pretty sure to meet 'em."

"Yes, mother," said the boy. "Is father married then?"

"Yes. . . . You can give her a look, and tell me what's she's like, if you do see her."

"Yes, mother."

"If she's dark or fair, and if she's tall—as tall as I. And if she seems like a woman who has ever worked for a living, or one that has been always well off, and has never done anything, and shows marks of the lady on her, as I expect she do."

"Yes."

They crept up the hill in the twilight, and entered the cottage. It was built of mud-walls, the surface of which had been washed by many rains into channels and depressions that left none of the original flat face visible; while here and there in the thatch above a rafter showed like a bone protruding through the skin.

She was kneeling down in the chimney-corner, before two pieces of turf laid together with the heather inwards, blowing at the red-hot ashes with her breath till the turves flamed. The radiance lit her pale cheek, and made her dark eyes, that had once been handsome, seem handsome anew. "Yes," she resumed, "see if she is dark or fair, and if you can, notice if her hands be white; if not, see if they look as though she had ever done housework, or are milker's hands like mine."

The boy again promised, inattentively this time, his mother not observing that he was cutting a notch with his pocket-knife in the beech-backed chair.

II

THE YOUNG WIFE

The road from Anglebury to Holmstoke is in general level; but there is one place where a sharp ascent breaks its monotony. Farmers homeward-bound from the former market-town, who trot all the rest of the way, walk their horses up this short incline.

The next evening, while the sun was yet bright, a handsome new gig, with a lemon-coloured body and red wheels, was spinning westward along the level highway at the heels of a powerful mare. The driver was a yeoman in the prime of life, cleanly shaven like an actor, his face being toned to that bluish-vermilion hue which so often graces a thriving farmer's features when returning home after successful dealings in the town. Beside him sat a woman, many years his junior—almost, indeed, a girl. Her face too was fresh in colour, but it was of a totally different quality—soft and evanescent, like the light under a heap of rose-petals.

Few people travelled this way, for it was not a main road; and the long white riband of gravel that stretched before them was empty, save of one small scarce-moving speck, which presently resolved itself into the figure of boy, who was creeping on at a snail's pace, and continually looking behind him—the heavy bundle he carried being some excuse for, if not the reason of, his dilatoriness. When the bouncing gig-party slowed at the bottom of the incline above mentioned, the pedestrian was only a few yards in front. Supporting the large bundle by putting one hand on his hip, he turned and looked straight at the farmer's wife as though he would read her through and through, pacing along abreast of the horse.

The low sun was full in her face, rendering every feature, shade, and contour distinct, from the curve of her little nostril to the colour of her eyes. The farmer, though he seemed annoyed at the boy's persistent presence, did not order him to get out of the way; and thus the lad preceded them, his hard gaze never leaving her, till they reached the top of the ascent, when the farmer trotted on with relief in his lineaments—having taken no outward notice of the boy whatever.

"How that poor lad stared at me!" said the young wife.

"Yes, dear; I saw that he did."

"He is one of the village, I suppose?"

"One of the neighbourhood. I think he lives with his mother a mile or two off."

"He knows who we are, no doubt?"

"O yes. You must expect to be stared at just at first, my pretty Gertrude."

"I do,—though I think the poor boy may have looked at us in the hope we might relieve him of his heavy load, rather than from curiosity."

"O no," said her husband off-handedly. "These country lads will carry a hundredweight once they get it on their backs; besides his pack had more size than weight in it. Now, then, another mile and I shall be able to show you our house in the distance—if it is not too dark before we get there." The wheels spun round, and particles flew from their periphery as before, till a white house of ample dimensions revealed itself, with farm-buildings and ricks at the back.

Meanwhile the boy had quickened his pace, and turning up a by-lane some mile and half short of the white farmstead, ascended towards the leaner pastures, and so on to the cottage of his mother.

She had reached home after her day's milking at the outlying dairy, and was washing cabbage at the doorway in the declining light. "Hold up the net a moment," she said, without preface, as the boy came up.

He flung down his bundle, held the edge of the cabbage-net, and as she filled its meshes with the dripping leaves she went on, "Well, did you see her?"

"Yes; quite plain."

"Is she ladylike?"

"Yes; and more. A lady complete."

"Is she young?"

"Well, she's growed up, and her ways be quite a woman's."

"Of course. What colour is her hair and face?"

"Her hair is lightish, and her face as comely as a live doll's."

"Her eyes, then, are not dark like mine?"

"No—of a bluish turn, and her mouth is very nice and red; and when she smiles, her teeth show white."

"Is she tall?" said the woman sharply.

"I couldn't see. She was sitting down."

"Then do you go to Holmstoke church to-morrow morning: she's sure to be there. Go early and notice her walking in, and come home and tell me if she's taller than I."

"Very well, mother. But why don't you go and see for yourself?"

"*I* go to see her! I wouldn't look up at her if she were to pass my window this instant. She was with Mr. Lodge, of course. What did he say or do?"

"Just the same as usual."

"Took no notice of you?"

"None."

Next day the mother put a clean shirt on the boy, and started him off for Holmstoke church. He reached the ancient little pile when the door was just being opened, and he was the first to enter. Taking his seat by the font, he watched all the parishioners file in. The well-to-do Farmer Lodge came nearly last; and his young wife, who accompanied him, walked up the aisle with the shyness natural to a modest woman who had appeared thus for the first time. As all other eyes were fixed upon her, the youth's stare was not noticed now.

When he reached home his mother said, "Well?" before he had entered the room.

"She is not tall. She is rather short," he replied.

"Ah!" said his mother, with satisfaction.

"But she's very pretty—very. In fact, she's lovely." The youthful freshness of the yeoman's wife had evidently made an impression even on the somewhat hard nature of the boy.

"That's all I want to hear," said his mother quickly. "Now, spread the table-cloth. The hare you caught is very tender; but mind that nobody catches you.—You've never told me what sort of hands she had."

"I have never seen 'em. She never took off her gloves."

"What did she wear this morning?"

"A white bonnet and a silver-coloured gownd. It whewed and whistled so loud when it rubbed against the pews that the lady coloured up more than ever for very shame at the noise, and pulled it in to keep it from touching; but when she pushed into her seat, it whewed more than ever. Mr. Lodge, he seemed pleased, and his waistcoat stuck out, and his great golden seals hung like a lord's; but she seemed to wish her noisy gownd anywhere but on her."

"Not she! However, that will do now."

These descriptions of the newly-married couple were continued from time to time by the boy at his mother's request, after any chance encounter he had had with them. But Rhoda Brook, though she might easily have seen young Mrs. Lodge for herself by walking a couple of miles, would never attempt an excursion towards the quarter where the farmhouse lay. Neither did she, at the daily milking in the dairyman's yard on Lodge's outlying second farm, ever speak on the subject of the recent marriage. The dairyman, who rented the cows of Lodge, and knew perfectly the tall milkmaid's history, with manly kindliness always kept the gossip in the cow-barton from annoying Rhoda. But the atmosphere thereabout was full of the subject during the first days of Mrs. Lodge's arrival; and from her boy's description and the casual words of the other milkers, Rhoda Brook could raise a mental image of the unconscious Mrs. Lodge that was realistic as a photograph.

III

A VISION

ONE NIGHT, TWO OR THREE WEEKS AFTER THE BRIDAL RETURN, when the boy was gone to bed, Rhoda sat a long time over the turf ashes that she had raked out in front of her to extinguish them. She contemplated so intently the new wife, as presented to her in her mind's eye over the embers, that she forgot the lapse of time. At last, wearied with her day's work, she too retired.

But the figure which had occupied her so much during this and the previous days was not to be banished at night. For the first time Gertrude Lodge visited the supplanted woman in her dreams. Rhoda Brook dreamed—since her assertion that she really saw, before falling asleep, was not to be believed—that the young wife, in the pale silk dress and white bonnet, but with features shockingly distorted, and wrinkled as by age, was sitting upon her chest as she lay. The pressure of Mrs. Lodge's person grew heavier; the blue eyes peered cruelly into her face; and then the figure thrust forward its left hand mockingly, so as to make the wedding-ring it wore glitter in Rhoda's eyes. Maddened mentally, and nearly suffocated by pressure, the sleeper struggled; the incubus, still regarding her, withdrew to the foot of the bed, only, however, to come forward by degrees, resume her seat, and flash her left hand as before.

Gasping for breath, Rhoda, in a last desperate effort, swung out her right hand, seized the confronting spectre by its obtrusive left arm, and whirled it backward to the floor, starting up herself as she did so with a low cry.

"O, merciful heaven!" she cried, sitting on the edge of the bed in a cold sweat; "that was not a dream—she was here!"

She could feel her antagonist's arm within her grasp even now—the very flesh and bone of it, as it seemed. She looked on the floor whither she had whirled the spectre, but there was nothing to be seen.

Rhoda Brook slept no more that night, and when she went milking at the next dawn they noticed how pale and haggard she looked. The milk that she drew quivered into the pail; her hand had not calmed even yet, and still retained the feel of the arm. She came home to breakfast as wearily as if it had been suppertime.

"What was that noise in your chimmer, mother, last night?" said her son. "You fell off the bed, surely?"

"Did you hear anything fall? At what time?"

"Just when the clock struck two."

She could not explain, and when the meal was done went silently about her household work, the boy assisting her, for he hated going afield on the farms, and she indulged his reluctance. Between eleven and twelve the garden-gate clicked, and she lifted her eyes to the window. At the bottom of the garden, within the gate, stood the woman of her vision. Rhoda seemed transfixed.

"Ah, she said she would come!" exclaimed the boy, also observing her.

"Said so—when? How does she know us?"

"I have seen and spoken to her. I talked to her yesterday."

"I told you," said the mother, flushing indignantly, "never to speak to anybody in that house, or go near the place."

"I did not speak to her till she spoke to me. And I did not go near the place. I met her in the road."

"What did you tell her?"

"Nothing. She said, 'Are you the poor boy who had to bring the heavy load from market?' And she looked at my boots, and said they would not keep my feet dry if it came on wet, because they were so cracked. I told her I lived with my mother, and we had enough to do to keep ourselves, and that's how it was; and she said then, 'I'll come and bring you some better boots, and see your mother.' She gives away things to other folks in the meads besides us."

Mrs. Lodge was by this time close to the door—not in her silk, as Rhoda had seen her in the bed-chamber, but in a morning hat, and gown of common light material, which became her better than silk. On her arm she carried a basket.

The impression remaining from the night's experience was still strong. Brook had almost expected to see the wrinkles, the scorn, and the cruelty on her visitor's face.

She would have escaped an interview, had escape been possible. There was, however, no backdoor to the cottage, and in an instant the boy had lifted the latch to Mrs. Lodge's gentle knock.

"I see I have come to the right house," said she, glancing at the lad, and smiling. "But I was not sure till you opened the door."

The figure and action were those of the phantom; but her voice was so indescribably sweet, her glance so winning, her smile so tender, so unlike that of Rhoda's midnight visitant, that the latter could hardly believe the evidence of her senses. She was truly glad that she had not hidden away in sheer aversion, as she had been inclined to do. In her basket Mrs. Lodge brought the pair of boots that she had promised to the boy, and other useful articles.

At these proofs of a kindly feeling towards her and hers Rhoda's heart reproached her bitterly. This innocent young thing should have her blessing and not her curse. When she left them a light seemed gone from the dwelling. Two days later she came again to know if the boots fitted; and less than a fortnight after that paid Rhoda another call. On this occasion the boy was absent.

"I walk a good deal," said Mrs. Lodge, "and your house is the nearest outside our own parish. I hope you are well. You don't look quite well."

Rhoda said she was well enough; and, indeed, though the paler of the two, there was more of the strength that endures in her well-defined features and large frame, than in the soft-cheeked young woman before her. The conversation became quite confidential as regarded their powers and weaknesses; and when Mrs. Lodge was leaving, Rhoda said, "I hope you will find this air agree with you, ma'am, and not suffer from the damp of the water-meads."

The younger one replied that there was not much doubt of it, her general health being usually good. "Though, now you remind me," she added, "I have one little ailment which puzzles me. It is nothing serious, but I cannot make it out."

She uncovered her left hand and arm; and their outline confronted Rhoda's gaze as the exact original of the limb she had beheld and seized in her dream. Upon the pink round surface of the arm were faint marks of an unhealthy colour, as if produced by a rough grasp. Rhoda's eyes became riveted on the discolorations; she fancied that she discerned in them the shape of her own four fingers.

"How did it happen?" she said mechanically.

"I cannot tell," replied Mrs. Lodge, shaking her head. "One night when I was sound asleep, dreaming I was away in some strange place, a pain suddenly shot into my arm there, and was so keen as to awaken me. I must have struck it in the daytime, I suppose, though I don't remember doing so." She added, laughing,

"I tell my dear husband that it looks just as if he had flown into a rage and struck me there. O, I daresay it will soon disappear."

"Ha, ha! Yes. . . . On what night did it come?"

Mrs. Lodge considered, and said it would be a fortnight ago on the morrow. "When I awoke I could not remember where I was," she added, "till the clock striking two reminded me."

She had named the night and the hour of Rhoda's spectral encounter, and Brook felt like a guilty thing. The artless disclosure startled her; she did not reason on the freaks of coincidence; and all the scenery of that ghastly night returned with double vividness to her mind.

"O, can it be," she said to herself, when her visitor had departed, "that I exercise a malignant power over people against my own will?" She knew that she had been slily called a witch since her fall; but never having understood why that particular stigma had been attached to her, it had passed disregarded. Could this be the explanation, and had such things as this ever happened before?

IV

A SUGGESTION

THE SUMMER DREW ON, AND RHODA BROOK ALMOST DREADED TO MEET Mrs. Lodge again, notwithstanding that her feeling for the young wife amounted well-nigh to affection. Something in her own individuality seemed to convict Rhoda of crime. Yet a fatality sometimes would direct the steps of the latter to the outskirts of Holmstoke whenever she left her house for any other purpose than her daily work; and hence it happened that their next encounter was out of doors. Rhoda could not avoid the subject which had so mystified her, and after the first few words she stammered, "I hope your—arm is well again, ma'am?" She had perceived with consternation that Gertrude Lodge carried her left arm stiffly.

"No; it is not quite well. Indeed it is no better at all; it is rather worse. It pains me dreadfully sometimes."

"Perhaps you had better go to a doctor, ma'am."

She replied that she had already seen a doctor. Her husband had insisted upon her going to one. But the surgeon had not seemed to understand the afflicted limb at all; he had told her to bathe it in hot water, and she had bathed it, but the treatment had done no good.

"Will you let me see it?" said the milkwoman.

Mrs. Lodge pushed up her sleeve and disclosed the place, which was a few inches above the wrist. As soon as Rhoda Brook saw it, she could hardly preserve her composure. There was nothing of the nature of a wound, but the arm at that point had a shrivelled look, and the outline of the four fingers appeared more distinct than at the former time. Moreover, she fancied that they were imprinted in precisely the relative position of her clutch upon the arm in the trance; the first finger towards Gertrude's wrist, and the fourth towards her elbow.

What the impress resembled seemed to have struck Gertrude herself since their last meeting. "It looks almost like finger-marks," she said; adding with a faint laugh, "my husband says it is as if some witch, or the devil himself, had taken hold of me there, and blasted the flesh."

Rhoda shivered. "That's fancy," she said hurriedly. "I wouldn't mind it, if I were you."

"I shouldn't so much mind it," said the younger, with hesitation, "if—if I hadn't a notion that it makes my husband—dislike me—no, love me less. Men think so much of personal appearance."

"Some do—he for one."

"Yes; and he was very proud of mine, at first."

"Keep your arm covered from his sight."

"Ah—he knows the disfigurement is there!" She tried to hide the tears that filled her eyes.

"Well, ma'am, I earnestly hope it will go away soon."

And so the milkwoman's mind was chained anew to the subject by a horrid sort of spell as she returned home. The sense of having been guilty of an act of malignity increased, affect as she might to ridicule her superstition. In her secret heart Rhoda did not altogether object to a slight diminution of her successor's beauty, by whatever means it had come about; but she did not wish to inflict upon her physical pain. For though this pretty young woman had rendered impossible any reparation which Lodge might have made Rhoda for his past conduct, everything like resentment at the unconscious usurpation had quite passed away from the elder's mind.

If the sweet and kindly Gertrude Lodge only knew of the scene in the bed-chamber, what would she think? Not to inform her of it seemed treachery in the presence of her friendliness; but tell she could not of her own accord—neither could she devise a remedy.

She mused upon the matter the greater part of the night; and the next day, after the morning milking, set out to obtain another glimpse of Gertrude Lodge if she could, being held to her by a gruesome fascination. By watching the house from a distance the milkmaid was presently able to discern the farmer's wife in a ride she was taking alone—probably to join her husband in some distant field. Mrs. Lodge perceived her, and cantered in her direction.

"Good morning, Rhoda!" Gertrude said, when she had come up. "I was going to call."

Rhoda noticed that Mrs. Lodge held the reins with some difficulty.

"I hope—the bad arm," said Rhoda.

"They tell me there is possibly one way by which I might be able to find out the cause, and so perhaps the cure, of it," replied the other anxiously. "It is by going to some clever man over in Egdon Heath. They did not know if he was still alive—and I cannot remember his name at this moment; but they said that you knew more of his movements than anybody else hereabout, and could tell me if he were still to be consulted. Dear me—what was his name? But you know."

"Not Conjuror Trendle?" said her thin companion, turning pale.

"Trendle—yes. Is he alive?"

"I believe so," said Rhoda, with reluctance.

"Why do you call him conjuror?"

"Well—they say—they used to say he was a—he had powers other folks have not."

"O, how could my people be so superstitious as to recommend a man of that sort! I thought they meant some medical man. I shall think no more of him."

Rhoda looked relieved, and Mrs. Lodge rode on. The milkwoman had inwardly seen, from the moment she heard of her having been mentioned as a reference for this man, that there must exist a sarcastic feeling among the work-folk that a sorceress would know the whereabouts of the exorcist. They suspected her, then. A short time ago this would have given no concern to a woman of her common-sense. But she had a haunting reason to be superstitious now; and she had been seized with sudden dread that this Conjuror Trendle might name her as the malignant influence which was blasting the fair person of Gertrude, and so lead her friend to hate her for ever, and to treat her as some fiend in human shape.

But all was not over. Two days after, a shadow intruded into the window-pattern thrown on Rhoda Brook's floor by the afternoon sun. The woman opened the door at once, almost breathlessly.

"Are you alone?" said Gertrude. She seemed to be no less harassed and anxious than Brook herself.

"Yes," said Rhoda.

"The place on my arm seems worse, and troubles me!" the young farmer's wife went on. "It is so mysterious! I do hope it will not be an incurable wound. I have again been thinking of what they said about Conjuror Trendle. I don't really believe in such men, but I should not mind just visiting him, from curiosity—though on no account must my husband know. Is it far to where he lives?"

"Yes—five miles," said Rhoda backwardly. "In the heart of Egdon."

"Well, I should have to walk. Could not you go with me to show me the way—say to-morrow afternoon?"

"O, not I—that is," the milkwoman murmured, with a start of dismay. Again the dread seized her that something to do with her fierce act in the dream might be revealed, and her character in the eyes of the most useful friend she had ever had be ruined irretrievably.

Mrs. Lodge urged, and Rhoda finally assented, though with much misgiving. Sad as the journey would be to her, she could not conscientiously stand in the way of a possible remedy for her patron's strange affliction. It was agreed that, to escape suspicion of their mystic intent, they should meet at the edge of the heath at the corner of a plantation which was visible from the spot where they now stood.

V

CONJUROR TRENDLE

BY THE NEXT AFTERNOON RHODA WOULD HAVE DONE ANYTHING TO escape this inquiry. But she had promised to go. Moreover, there was a horrid fascination at times in becoming instrumental in throwing such possible light on her own character as would reveal her to be something greater in the occult world than she had ever herself suspected.

She started just before the time of day mentioned between them, and half-an-hour's brisk walking brought her to the south-eastern extension of the Egdon tract of country, where the fir plantation was. A slight figure, cloaked and veiled, was already there. Rhoda recognized, almost with a shudder, that Mrs. Lodge bore her left arm in a sling.

They hardly spoke to each other, and immediately set out on their climb into the interior of this solemn country, which stood high above the rich alluvial soil they had left half-an-hour before. It was a long walk; thick clouds made the atmosphere dark, though it was as yet only early afternoon; and the wind howled dismally over the hills of the heath—not improbably the same heath which had witnessed the agony of the Wessex King Ina, presented to after-ages as Lear. Gertrude Lodge talked most, Rhoda replying with monosyllabic preoccupation. She had a strange dislike to walking on the side of her companion where hung the afflicted arm, moving round to the other when inadvertently near it. Much heather had been brushed by their feet when they descended upon a cart-track, beside which stood the house of the man they sought.

He did not profess his remedial practices openly, or care anything about their continuance, his direct interests being those of a dealer in furze, turf, "sharp sand," and other local products. Indeed, he affected not to believe largely in his own powers, and when warts that had been shown him for cure miraculously disappeared—which it must be owned they infallibly did—he would say lightly, "O, I only drink a glass of grog upon 'em—perhaps it's all chance," and immediately turn the subject.

He was at home when they arrived, having in fact seen them descending into his valley. He was a gray-bearded man, with a reddish face, and he looked singularly at Rhoda the first moment he beheld her. Mrs. Lodge told him her errand; and then with words of self-disparagement he examined her arm.

"Medicine can't cure it," he said promptly. "'Tis the work of an enemy."

Rhoda shrank into herself, and drew back.

"An enemy? What enemy?" asked Mrs. Lodge.

He shook his head. "That's best known to yourself," he said. "If you like, I can show the person to you, though I shall not myself know who it is. I can do no more; and don't wish to do that."

She pressed him; on which he told Rhoda to wait outside where she stood, and took Mrs. Lodge into the room. It opened immediately from the door; and, as the latter remained ajar, Rhoda Brook could see the proceedings without taking part in them. He brought a tumbler from the dresser, nearly filled it with water, and fetching an egg, prepared it in some private way; after which he broke it on the edge of the glass, so that the white went in and the yolk remained. As it was getting gloomy, he took the glass and its contents to the window, and told Gertrude to watch them closely. They leant over the table together, and the milkwoman could see the opaline hue of the egg-fluid changing form as it sank in the water, but she was not near enough to define the shape that it assumed.

"Do you catch the likeness of any face or figure as you look?" demanded the conjuror of the young woman.

She murmured a reply, in tones so low as to be inaudible to Rhoda, and continued to gaze intently into the glass. Rhoda turned, and walked a few steps away.

When Mrs. Lodge came out, and her face was met by the light, it appeared exceedingly pale—as pale as Rhoda's—against the sad dun shades of the upland's garniture. Trendle shut the door behind her, and they at once started homeward together. But Rhoda perceived that her companion had quite changed.

"Did he charge much?" she asked tentatively.

"O no—nothing. He would not take a farthing," said Gertrude.

"And what did you see?" inquired Rhoda.

"Nothing I—care to speak of." The constraint in her manner was remarkable; her face was so rigid as to wear an oldened aspect, faintly suggestive of the face in Rhoda's bed-chamber.

"Was it you who first proposed coming here?" Mrs. Lodge suddenly inquired, after a long pause. "How very odd, if you did!"

"No. But I am not sorry we have come, all things considered," she replied. For the first time a sense of triumph possessed her, and she did not altogether deplore that the young thing at her side should learn that their lives had been antagonized by other influences than their own.

The subject was no more alluded to during the long and dreary walk home. But in some way or other a story was whispered about the many-dairied lowland that winter that Mrs. Lodge's gradual loss of the use of her left arm was owing to her being "overlooked" by Rhoda Brook. The latter kept her own counsel about the incubus, but her face grew sadder and thinner; and in the spring she and her boy disappeared from the neighbourhood of Holmstoke.

VI

A SECOND ATTEMPT

HALF-A-DOZEN YEARS PASSED AWAY, AND MR. AND MRS. LODGE'S married experience sank into prosiness, and worse. The farmer was usually gloomy and silent: the woman whom he had wooed for her grace and beauty was contorted and disfigured in the left limb; moreover, she had brought him no child, which rendered it likely that he would be the last of a family who had occupied that valley for some two hundred years. He thought of Rhoda Brook and her son; and feared this might be a judgment from heaven upon him.

The once blithe-hearted and enlightened Gertrude was changing into an irritable, superstitious woman, whose whole time was given to experimenting upon her ailment with every quack remedy she came across. She was honestly attached to her husband, and was ever secretly hoping against hope to win back his heart again by regaining some at least of her personal beauty. Hence it arose that her closet was lined with bottles, packets, and ointment-pots of every description—nay, bunches of mystic herbs, charms, and books of necromancy, which in her schoolgirl time she would have ridiculed as folly.

"Damned if you won't poison yourself with these apothecary messes and witch mixtures some time or other," said her husband, when his eye chanced to fall upon the multitudinous array.

She did not reply, but turned her sad, soft glance upon him in such heart-swollen reproach that he looked sorry for his words, and added, "I only meant it for your good, you know, Gertrude."

"I'll clear out the whole lot, and destroy them," said she huskily, "and try such remedies no more!"

"You want somebody to cheer you," he observed. "I once thought of adopting a boy; but he is too old now. And he is gone away I don't know where."

She guessed to whom he alluded; for Rhoda Brook's story had in the course of years become known to her; though not a word had ever passed between her husband and herself on the subject. Neither had she ever spoken to him of her visit to Conjuror Trendle, and of what was revealed to her, or she thought was revealed to her, by that solitary heath-man.

She was now five-and-twenty; but she seemed older. "Six years of marriage, and only a few months of love," she sometimes whispered to herself. And then she thought of the apparent cause, and said, with a tragic glance at her withering limb, "If I could only again be as I was when he first saw me!"

She obediently destroyed her nostrums and charms; but there remained a hankering wish to try something else—some other sort of cure altogether. She had never revisited Trendle since she had been conducted to the house of the solitary by Rhoda against her will; but it now suddenly occurred to Gertrude that she would, in a last desperate effort at deliverance from this seeming curse, again seek out the man, if he yet lived. He was entitled to a certain credence, for the indistinct form he had raised in the glass had undoubtedly resembled the only woman in the world who—as she now knew, though not then—could have a reason for bearing her ill-will. The visit should be paid.

This time she went alone, though she nearly got lost on the heath, and roamed a considerable distance out of her way. Trendle's house was reached at last, however: he was not indoors, and instead of waiting at the cottage, she went to where his bent figure was pointed out to her at work a long way off. Trendle remembered her, and laying down the handful of furze-roots which he was gathering and throwing into a heap, he offered to accompany her in her homeward direction, as the distance was considerable and the days were short. So they walked together, his head bowed nearly to the earth, and his form of a colour with it.

"You can send away warts and other excrescences I know," she said; "why can't you send away this?" And the arm was uncovered.

"You think too much of my powers!" said Trendle; "and I am old and weak now, too. No, no; it is too much for me to attempt in my own person. What have ye tried?"

She named to him some of the hundred medicaments and counterspells which she had adopted from time to time. He shook his head.

"Some were good enough," he said approvingly; "but not many of them for such as this. This is of the nature of a blight, not of the nature of a wound; and if you ever do throw it off; it will be all at once."

"If I only could!"

"There is only one chance of doing it known to me. It has never failed in kindred afflictions,—that I can declare. But it is hard to carry out, and especially for a woman."

"Tell me!" said she.

"You must touch with the limb the neck of a man who's been hanged."

She started a little at the image he had raised.

"Before he's cold—just after he's cut down," continued the conjuror impassively.

"How can that do good?"

"It will turn the blood and change the constitution. But, as I say, to do it is hard. You must get into jail, and wait for him when he's brought off the gallows. Lots have done it, though perhaps not such pretty women as you. I used to send dozens for skin complaints. But that was in former times. The last I sent was in '13—near twenty years ago."

He had no more to tell her; and, when he had put her into a straight track homeward, turned and left her, refusing all money as at first.

VII

A RIDE

The communication sank deep into Gertrude's mind. her nature was rather a timid one; and probably of all remedies that the white wizard could have suggested there was not one which would have filled her with so much aversion as this, not to speak of the immense obstacles in the way of its adoption.

Casterbridge, the county-town, was a dozen or fifteen miles off; and though in those days, when men were executed for horse-stealing, arson, and burglary, an assize seldom passed without a hanging, it was not likely that she could get access to the body of the criminal unaided. And the fear of her husband's anger made her reluctant to breathe a word of Trendle's suggestion to him or to anybody about him.

She did nothing for months, and patiently bore her disfigurement as before. But her woman's nature, craving for renewed love, through the medium of renewed beauty (she was but twenty-five), was ever stimulating her to try what, at any rate, could hardly do her any harm. "What came by a spell will go by a spell surely," she would say. Whenever her imagination pictured the act she shrank in terror from the possibility of it: then the words of the conjuror, "It will turn your blood," were seen to be capable of a scientific no less than a ghastly interpretation; the mastering desire returned, and urged her on again.

There was at this time but one county paper, and that her husband only occasionally borrowed. But old-fashioned days had old-fashioned means, and news was extensively conveyed by word of mouth from market to market, or from fair to fair, so that, whenever such an event as an execution was about to take place, few within a radius of twenty miles were ignorant of the coming sight; and, so far as Holmstoke was concerned, some enthusiasts had been known to walk all the way to Casterbridge and back in one day, solely to witness the spectacle. The next assizes were in March; and when Gertrude Lodge heard that they had been held, she inquired stealthily at the inn as to the result, as soon as she could find opportunity.

She was, however, too late. The time at which the sentences were to be carried out had arrived, and to make the journey and obtain admission at such short notice required at least her husband's assistance. She dared not tell him, for she had found by delicate experiment that these smouldering village beliefs made him furious if mentioned, partly because he half entertained them himself. It was therefore necessary to wait for another opportunity.

Her determination received a fillip from learning that two epileptic children had attended from this very village of Holmstoke many years before with beneficial results, though the experiment had been strongly condemned by the neighbouring clergy. April, May, June, passed; and it is no overstatement to say that by the end of the last-named month Gertrude well-nigh longed for the death of a fellow-creature. Instead of her formal prayers each night, her unconscious prayer was, "O Lord, hang some guilty or innocent person soon!"

This time she made earlier inquiries, and was altogether more systematic in her proceedings. Moreover, the season was summer, between the haymaking and the harvest, and in the leisure thus afforded him her husband had been holiday-taking away from home.

The assizes were in July, and she went to the inn as before. There was to be one execution—only one—for arson.

Her greatest problem was not how to get to Casterbridge, but what means she should adopt for obtaining admission to the jail. Though access for such purposes had formerly never been denied, the custom had fallen into desuetude; and in contemplating her possible difficulties, she was again almost driven to fall back upon her husband. But, on sounding him about the assizes, he was so uncommunicative, so more than usually cold, that she did not proceed, and decided that whatever she did she would do alone.

Fortune, obdurate hitherto, showed her unexpected favour. On the Thursday before the Saturday fixed for the execution, Lodge remarked to her that he was going away from home for another day or two on business at a fair, and that he was sorry he could not take her with him.

She exhibited on this occasion so much readiness to stay at home that he looked at her in surprise. Time had been when she would have shown deep disappointment at the loss of such a jaunt. However, he lapsed into his usual taciturnity, and on the day named left Holmstoke.

It was now her turn. She at first had thought of driving, but on reflection held that driving would not do, since it would necessitate her keeping to the turnpike-road, and so increase by tenfold the risk of her ghastly errand being found out. She decided to ride, and avoid the beaten track, notwithstanding that in her husband's stables there was no animal just at present which by any stretch of imagination could be considered a lady's mount, in spite of his promise before marriage to always keep a mare for her. He had, however, many cart-horses, fine ones of their kind; and among the rest was a serviceable creature, an equine Amazon, with a back as broad as a sofa, on which Gertrude had occasionally taken an airing when unwell. This horse she chose.

On Friday afternoon one of the men brought it round. She was dressed, and before going down looked at her shrivelled arm. "Ah!" she said to it, "if it had not been for you this terrible ordeal would have been saved me!"

When strapping up the bundle in which she carried a few articles of clothing, she took occasion to say to the servant, "I take these in case I should not get back to-night from the person I am going to visit. Don't be alarmed if I am not in by ten, and close up the house as usual. I shall be at home to-morrow for certain." She meant then to privately tell her husband: the deed accomplished was not like the deed projected. He would almost certainly forgive her.

And then the pretty palpitating Gertrude Lodge went from her husband's homestead; but though her goal was Casterbridge she did not take the direct route thither through Stickleford. Her cunning course at first was in precisely the opposite direction. As soon as she was out of sight, however, she turned to the left, by a road which led into Egdon, and on entering the heath wheeled round, and set out in the true course, due westerly. A more private way down the county could not be imagined; and as to direction, she had merely to keep her horse's head to a point a little to the right of the sun. She knew that she would light upon a furze-cutter or cottager of some sort from time to time, from whom she might correct her bearing.

Though the date was comparatively recent, Egdon was much less fragmentary in character than now. The attempts—successful and otherwise—at cultivation on the lower slopes, which intrude and break up the original heath into small detached heaths, had not been carried far; Enclosure Acts had not taken effect, and the banks and fences which now exclude the cattle of those villagers who formerly enjoyed rights of commonage thereon, and the carts of those who had turbary privileges which kept them in firing all the year round, were not erected. Gertrude, therefore, rode along with no other obstacles than the prickly furze bushes, the mats of heather, the white water-courses, and the natural steeps and declivities of the ground.

Her horse was sure, if heavy-footed and slow, and though a draught animal, was easy-paced; had it been otherwise, she was not a woman who could have ventured to ride over such a bit of country with a half-dead arm. It was therefore nearly eight o'clock when she drew rein to breathe the mare on the last outlying high point of heath-land towards Casterbridge, previous to leaving Egdon for the cultivated valleys.

She halted before a pool called Rushy-pond, flanked by the ends of two hedges; a railing ran through the centre of the pond, dividing it in half. Over the railing she saw the low green country; over the green trees the roofs of the town; over the roofs a white flat façade, denoting the entrance to the county jail. On the roof of this front specks were moving about; they seemed to be workmen erecting something. Her flesh crept. She descended slowly, and was soon amid corn-fields and pastures. In another half-hour, when it was almost dusk, Gertrude reached the White Hart, the first inn of the town on that side.

Little surprise was excited by her arrival; farmers' wives rode on horseback then more than they do now; though, for that matter, Mrs. Lodge was not imagined to be a wife at all; the innkeeper supposed her some harum-skarum young woman who had come to attend "hang-fair" next day. Neither her husband nor herself ever dealt in Casterbridge market, so that she was unknown. While dismounting she beheld a crowd of boys standing at the door of a harness-maker's shop just above the inn, looking inside it with deep interest.

"What is going on there?" she asked of the ostler.

"Making the rope for to-morrow."

She throbbed responsively, and contracted her arm.

"'Tis sold by the inch afterwards," the man continued. "I could get you a bit, miss, for nothing, if you'd like?"

She hastily repudiated any such wish, all the more from a curious creeping feeling that the condemned wretch's destiny was becoming interwoven with her own; and having engaged a room for the night, sat down to think.

Up to this time she had formed but the vaguest notions about her means of obtaining access to the prison. The words of the cunning-man returned to her mind. He had implied that she should use her beauty, impaired though it was, as a pass-key. In her inexperience she knew little about jail functionaries; she had heard of a high-sheriff and an under-sheriff; but dimly only. She knew, however, that there must be a hangman, and to the hangman she determined to apply.

VIII

A WATER-SIDE HERMIT

AT THIS DATE, AND FOR SEVERAL YEARS AFTER, THERE WAS A HANGMAN to almost every jail. Gertrude found, on inquiry, that the Casterbridge official dwelt in a lonely cottage by a deep slow river flowing under the cliff on which the prison buildings were situate—the stream being the self-same one, though she did not know it, which watered the Stickleford and Holmstoke meads lower down in its course.

Having changed her dress, and before she had eaten or drunk—for she could not take her ease till she had ascertained some particulars—Gertrude pursued her way by a path along the water-side to the cottage indicated. Passing thus the outskirts of the jail, she discerned on the level roof over the gateway three rectangular lines against the sky, where the specks had been moving in her distant view; she recognized what the erection was, and passed quickly on. Another hundred yards brought her to the executioner's house, which a boy pointed out. It stood close to the same stream, and was hard by a weir, the waters of which emitted a steady roar.

While she stood hesitating the door opened, and an old man came forth shading a candle with one hand. Locking the door on the outside, he turned to a flight of wooden steps fixed against the end of the cottage, and began to ascend them, this being evidently the staircase to his bedroom. Gertrude hastened forward, but by the time she reached the foot of the ladder he was at the top. She called to him loudly enough to be heard above the roar of the weir; he looked down and said, "What d'ye want here?"

"To speak to you a minute."

The candle-light, such as it was, fell upon her imploring, pale, upturned face, and Davies (as the hangman was called) backed down the ladder. "I was just going to bed," he said; "'Early to bed and early to rise,' but I don't mind stopping a minute for such a one as you. Come into house." He reopened the door, and preceded her to the room within.

The implements of his daily work, which was that of a jobbing gardener, stood in a corner, and seeing probably that she looked rural, he said, "If you want me to undertake country work I can't come, for I never leave Casterbridge for gentle nor simple—not I. My real calling is officer of justice," he added formally.

"Yes, yes! That's it. To-morrow!"

"Ah! I thought so. Well, what's the matter about that? 'Tis no use to come here about the knot—folks do come continually, but I tell 'em one knot is as merciful as another if ye keep it under the ear. Is the unfortunate man a relation; or, I should say, perhaps" (looking at her dress) "a person who's been in your employ?"

"No. What time is the execution?"

"The same as usual—twelve o'clock, or as soon after as the London mail-coach gets in. We always wait for that, in case of a reprieve."

"O—a reprieve—I hope not!" she said involuntarily.

"Well,—hee, hee!—as a matter of business, so do I! But still, if ever a young fellow deserved to be let off, this one does; only just turned eighteen, and only present by chance when the rick was fired. Howsomever, there's not much risk of it, as they are obliged to make an example of him, there having been so much destruction of property that way lately."

"I mean," she explained, "that I want to touch him for a charm, a cure of an affliction, by the advice of a man who has proved the virtue of the remedy."

"O yes, miss! Now I understand. I've had such people come in past years. But it didn't strike me that you looked of a sort to require blood-turning. What's the complaint? The wrong kind for this, I'll be bound."

"My arm." She reluctantly showed the withered skin.

"Ah—'tis all a-scram!" said the hangman, examining it.

"Yes," said she.

"Well," he continued, with interest, "that *is* the class o' subject, I'm bound to admit! I like the look of the place; it is truly as suitable for the cure as any I ever saw. 'Twas a knowing-man that sent 'ee, whoever he was."

"You can contrive for me all that's necessary?" she said breathlessly.

"You should really have gone to the governor of the jail, and your doctor with 'ee, and given your name and address—that's how it used to be done, if I recollect. Still, perhaps, I can manage it for a trifling fee."

"O, thank you! I would rather do it this way, as I should like it kept private."

"Lover not to know, eh?"

"No—husband."

"Aha! Very well. I'll get ee' a touch of the corpse."

"Where is it now?" she said, shuddering.

"It?—*he*, you mean; he's living yet. Just inside that little small winder up there in the glum." He signified the jail on the cliff above.

She thought of her husband and her friends. "Yes, of course," she said; "and how am I to proceed?"

He took her to the door. "Now, do you be waiting at the little wicket in the wall, that you'll find up there in the lane, not later than one o'clock. I will open it from the inside, as I shan't come home to dinner till he's cut down. Good-night. Be punctual; and if you don't want anybody to know 'ee, wear a veil. Ah—once I had such a daughter as you!"

She went away, and climbed the path above, to assure herself that she would be able to find the wicket next day. Its outline was soon visible to her—a narrow opening in the outer wall of the prison precincts. The steep was so great that, having reached the wicket, she stopped a moment to breathe; and, looking back upon the water-side cot, saw the hangman again ascending his outdoor staircase.

He entered the loft or chamber to which it led, and in a few minutes extinguished his light.

The town clock struck ten, and she returned to the White Hart as she had come.

IX

A RENCOUNTER

IT WAS ONE O'CLOCK ON SATURDAY. GERTRUDE LODGE, HAVING BEEN admitted to the jail as above described, was sitting in a waiting-room within the second gate, which stood under a classic archway of ashlar, then comparatively modern, and bearing the inscription, "covnty jail: 1793." This had been the façade she saw from the heath the day before. Near at hand was a passage to the roof on which the gallows stood.

The town was thronged, and the market suspended; but Gertrude had seen scarcely a soul. Having kept her room till the hour of the appointment, she had proceeded to the spot by a way which avoided the open space below the cliff where the spectators had gathered; but she could, even now, hear the multitudinous babble of their voices, out of which rose at intervals the hoarse croak of a single voice uttering the words, "Last dying speech and confession!" There had been no reprieve, and the execution was over; but the crowd still waited to see the body taken down.

Soon the persistent girl heard a trampling overhead, then a hand beckoned to her, and, following directions, she went out and crossed the inner paved court beyond the gatehouse, her knees trembling so that she could scarcely walk. One of her arms was out of its sleeve, and only covered by her shawl.

On the spot at which she had now arrived were two trestles, and before she could think of their purpose she heard heavy feet descending stairs somewhere at her back. Turn her head she would not, or could not, and, rigid in this position, she was conscious of a rough coffin passing her shoulder, borne by four men. It was open, and in it lay the body of a young man, wearing the smockfrock of a rustic, and fustian breeches. The corpse had been thrown into the coffin so hastily that the skirt of the smockfrock was hanging over. The burden was temporarily deposited on the trestles.

By this time the young woman's state was such that a gray mist seemed to float before her eyes, on account of which, and the veil she wore, she could scarcely discern anything: it was as though she had nearly died, but was held up by a sort of galvanism.

"Now!" said a voice close at hand, and she was just conscious that the word had been addressed to her.

By a last strenuous effort she advanced, at the same time hearing persons approaching behind her. She bared her poor curst arm; and Davies, uncovering the face of the corpse, took Gertrude's hand, and held it so that her arm lay across the dead man's neck, upon a line the colour of an unripe blackberry, which surrounded it.

Gertrude shrieked: "the turn o' the blood," predicted by the conjuror, had taken place. But at that moment a second shriek rent the air of the enclosure: it was not Gertrude's, and its effect upon her was to make her start round.

Immediately behind her stood Rhoda Brook, her face drawn, and her eyes red with weeping. Behind Rhoda stood Gertrude's own husband; his countenance lined, his eyes dim, but without a tear.

"D——n you! what are you doing here?" he said hoarsely.

"Hussy—to come between us and our child now!" cried Rhoda. "This is the meaning of what Satan showed me in the vision! You are like her at last!" And clutching the bare arm of the younger woman, she pulled her unresistingly back against the wall. Immediately Brook had loosened her hold the fragile young Gertrude slid down against the feet of her husband. When he lifted her up she was unconscious.

The mere sight of the twain had been enough to suggest to her that the dead young man was Rhoda's son. At that time the relatives of an executed convict had the privilege of claiming the body for burial, if they chose to do so; and it was for this purpose that Lodge was awaiting the inquest with Rhoda. He had been summoned by her as soon as the young man was taken in the crime, and at different times since; and he had attended in court during the trial. This was the "holiday" he had been indulging in of late. The two wretched parents had wished to avoid exposure; and hence had come themselves for the body, a waggon and sheet for its conveyance and covering being in waiting outside.

Gertrude's case was so serious that it was deemed advisable to call to her the surgeon who was at hand. She was taken out of the jail into the town; but she never reached home alive. Her delicate vitality, sapped perhaps by the paralyzed arm, collapsed under the double shock that followed the severe strain, physical and mental, to which she had subjected herself during the previous twenty-four hours. Her blood had been "turned" indeed—too far. Her death took place in the town three days after.

Her husband was never seen in Casterbridge again; once only in the old market-place at Anglebury, which he had so much frequented, and very seldom in public anywhere. Burdened at first with moodiness and remorse, he eventually changed for the better, and appeared as a chastened and thoughtful man. Soon after attending the funeral of his poor young wife he took steps towards giving up the farms in Holmstoke and the adjoining parish, and, having sold every head of his stock, he went away to Port-Bredy, at the other end of the county, living there in solitary lodgings till his death two years later of a painless decline. It was then found that he had bequeathed the whole of his not inconsiderable property to a reformatory for boys, subject to the payment of a small annuity to Rhoda Brook, if she could be found to claim it.

For some time she could not be found; but eventually she reappeared in her old parish,—absolutely refusing, however, to have anything to do with the provision made for her. Her monotonous milking at the dairy was resumed, and followed for many long years, till her form became bent, and her once abundant dark hair white and worn away at the forehead—perhaps by long pressure against the cows. Here, sometimes, those who knew her experiences would stand and observe her, and wonder what sombre thoughts were beating inside that impassive, wrinkled brow, to the rhythm of the alternating milk-streams.

The Abbot's Ghost, or, Maurice Treherne's Temptation

A Christmas Story

Louisa May Alcott

I

DRAMATIS PERSONAE

"How goes it, Frank? down first, as usual."

"The early bird gets the worm, Major."

"Deuced ungallant speech, considering that the lovely Octavia is the worm," and with a significant laugh the major assumed an Englishman's favorite attitude before the fire.

His companion shot a quick glance at him, and an expression of anxiety passed over his face as he replied, with a well-feigned air of indifference:

"You are altogether too sharp, major; I must be on my guard while you are in the house. Any new arrivals? I thought I heard a carriage drive up not long ago."

"It was General Snowdon and his charming wife. Maurice Treherne came while we were out, and I've not seen him yet, poor fellow!"

"Aye, you may well say that; his is a hard case, if what I heard is true. I'm not booked up in the matter, and I should be, lest I make some blunder here, so tell me how things stand, Major. We've a good half hour before dinner. Sir Jasper is never punctual."

"Yes, you've a right to know, if you are going to try your fortune with Octavia."

The major marched through the three drawing-rooms to see that no inquisitive servant was eavesdropping, and, finding all deserted, he resumed his place, while young Annon lounged on a couch as he listened with intense interest to the major's story.

"You know it was supposed that old Sir Jasper, being a bachelor, would leave his fortune to his two nephews. But he was an oddity, and as the title *must* go to young Jasper by right, the old man said Maurice should have the money. He was poor, young Jasper rich, and it seemed but just, though *Madame Mère* was very angry when she learned how the will was made."

"But Maurice didn't get the fortune, how was that?"

"There was some mystery there which I shall discover in time. All went smoothly till that unlucky yachting trip, when the cousins were wrecked. Maurice saved Jasper's life, and almost lost his own in so doing. I fancy he wishes he had, rather than remain the poor cripple he is. Exposure, exertion, and neglect afterward brought on paralysis of the lower limbs, and there he is, a fine, talented, spirited fellow tied to that cursed chair like a decrepit old man."

"How does he bear it?" asked Annon, as the major shook his gray head, with a traitorous huskiness in his last words.

"Like a philosopher or a hero. He is too proud to show his despair at such a sudden end to all his hopes, too generous to complain, for Jasper is desperately cut up about it, and too brave to be daunted by a misfortune which would drive many a man mad."

"Is it true that Sir Jasper, knowing all this, made a new will and left every cent to his namesake?"

"Yes, and there lies the mystery. Not only did he leave it away from poor Maurice, but so tied it up that Jasper cannot transfer it, and at his death it goes to Octavia."

"The old man must have been demented. What in heaven's name did he mean by leaving Maurice helpless and penniless after all his devotion to Jasper? Had he done anything to offend the old party?"

"No one knows; Maurice hasn't the least idea of the cause of this sudden whim, and the old man would give no reason for it. He died soon after, and the instant Jasper came to the title and estate he brought his cousin home, and treats him like a brother. Jasper is a noble fellow, with all his faults, and this act of justice increases my respect for him," said the major, heartily.

"What will Maurice do, now that he can't enter the army as he intended?" asked Annon, who now sat erect, so full of interest was he.

"Marry Octavia, and come to his own, I hope."

"An excellent little arrangement, but Miss Treherne may object," said Annon, rising with sudden kindling of the eye.

"I think not, if no one interferes. Pity, with women, is akin to love, and she pities her cousin in the tenderest fashion. No sister could be more devoted, and as Maurice is a handsome, talented fellow, one can easily foresee the end, if, as I said before, no one interferes to disappoint the poor lad again."

"You espouse his cause, I see, and tell me this that I may stand aside. Thanks for the warning, major; but as Maurice Treherne is a man of unusual power in many ways, I think we are equally matched, in spite of his misfortune. Nay, if anything, he has the advantage of me, for Miss Treherne pities him, and that is a strong ally for my rival. I'll be as generous as I can, but I'll *not* stand aside and relinquish the woman I love without a trial first."

With an air of determination Annon faced the major, whose keen eyes had read the truth which he had but newly confessed to himself. Major Royston smiled as he listened, and said briefly, as steps approached, "Do your best. Maurice will win."

"We shall see," returned Annon between his teeth.

Here their host entered, and the subject of course was dropped. But the major's words rankled in the young man's mind, and would have been doubly bitter had he known that their confidential conversation had been overheard. On either side of the great fireplace was a door leading to a suite of rooms which had been old Sir Jasper's. These apartments had been given to Maurice Treherne, and he had just returned from London, whither he had been to consult a certain famous physician. Entering quietly, he had taken possession of his rooms, and having rested and dressed for dinner, rolled himself into the library, to which led the curtained door on the right. Sitting idly in his light, wheeled chair, ready to enter when his cousin appeared, he had heard the chat of Annon and the major. As he listened, over his usually impassive face passed varying expressions of anger, pain, bitterness, and defiance, and when the young man uttered his almost fierce "We shall see," Treherne smiled a scornful smile and clenched his pale hand with a gesture which proved that a year of suffering had not conquered the man's spirit, though it had crippled his strong body.

A singular face was Maurice Treherne's; well-cut and somewhat haughty features; a fine brow under the dark locks that carelessly streaked it; and remarkably piercing eyes. Slight in figure and wasted by pain, he still retained the grace as native to him as the stern fortitude which enabled him to hide the deep despair of an ambitious nature from every eye, and bear his affliction with a cheerful philosophy more pathetic than the most entire abandonment to grief. Carefully dressed, and with no hint at invalidism but the chair, he bore himself as easily and calmly as if the doom of lifelong helplessness did not hang over him. A single motion of the hand sent him rolling noiselessly to the curtained door, but as he did so, a voice exclaimed behind him:

"Wait for me, cousin." And as he turned, a young girl approached, smiling a glad welcome as she took his hand, adding in a tone of soft reproach, "Home again, and not let me know it, till I heard the good news by accident."

"Was it good news, Octavia?" and Maurice looked up at the frank face with a new expression in those penetrating eyes of his. His cousin's open glance never changed as she stroked the hair off his forehead with the caress one often gives a child, and answered eagerly:

"The best to me; the house is dull when you are away, for Jasper always becomes absorbed in horses and hounds, and leaves mamma and me to mope by ourselves. But tell me, Maurice, what they said to you, since you would not write."

"A little hope, with time and patience. Help me to wait, dear, help me to wait."

His tone was infinitely sad, and as he spoke, he leaned his cheek against the kind hand he held, as if to find support and comfort there. The girl's face brightened beautifully, though her eyes filled, for to her alone did he betray his pain, and in her alone did he seek consolation.

"I will, I will with heart and hand! Thank heaven for the hope, and trust me it shall be fulfilled. You look very tired, Maurice. Why go in to dinner with all those people? Let me make you cozy here," she added, anxiously.

"Thanks, I'd rather go in, it does me good; and if I stay away, Jasper feels that he must stay with me. I dressed in haste, am I right, little nurse?"

She gave him a comprehensive glance, daintily settled his cravat, brushed back a truant lock, and, with a maternal air that was charming, said:

"My boy is always elegant, and I'm proud of him. Now we'll go in." But with her hand on the curtain she paused, saying quickly, as a voice reached her, "Who is that?"

"Frank Annon, didn't you know he was coming?" Maurice eyed her keenly.

"No, Jasper never told me. Why did he ask him?"

"To please you."

"Me! when he knows I detest the man. No matter, I've got on the color he hates, so he won't annoy me, and Mrs. Snowdon can amuse herself with him. The general has come, you know?"

Treherne smiled, well pleased, for no sign of maiden shame or pleasure did the girl's face betray, and as he watched her while she peeped, he thought with satisfaction.

"Annon is right, *I* have the advantage, and I'll keep it at all costs."

"Here is mamma, we must go in," said Octavia, as a stately old lady made her appearance in the drawing-room.

The cousins entered together and Annon watched them covertly, while seemingly intent on paying his respects to "Madame Mère," as his hostess was called by her family.

"Handsomer than ever," he muttered, as his eye rested on the blooming girl, looking more like a rose than ever in the peach-colored silk which he had once condemned because a rival admired it. She turned to reply to the major, and Annon glanced at Treherne with an irrepressible frown, for sickness had not marred the charm of that peculiar face, so colorless and thin that it seemed cut in marble; but the keen eyes shone with a wonderful brilliancy, and the whole countenance was alive with a power of intellect and will which made the observer involuntarily exclaim:

"That man must suffer a daily martyrdom, so crippled and confined; if it last long he will go mad or die."

"General and Mrs. Snowdon," announced the servant, and a sudden pause ensued as everyone looked up to greet the new-comers.

A feeble, white-haired old man entered, leaning on the arm of an indescribably beautiful woman. Not thirty yet, tall and nobly moulded, with straight black brows over magnificent eyes; rippling dark hair gathered up in a great knot, and ornamented with a single band of gold. A sweeping dress of wine-colored velvet, set off with a dazzling neck and arms decorated like her stately head with ornaments of Roman gold. At the first glance she seemed a cold, haughty creature, born to dazzle but not to win. A deeper scrutiny detected lines of suffering in that lovely face, and behind the veil of reserve, which pride forced her to wear, appeared the anguish of a strong-willed woman burdened by a heavy cross. No one would dare express pity or offer sympathy, for her whole air repelled it, and in her gloomy eyes sat scorn of herself mingled with defiance of the scorn of others. A strange, almost tragical-looking woman, in spite of beauty, grace and the cold sweetness of her manner. A faint smile parted her lips as she greeted those about her, and as her husband seated himself beside Lady Treherne, she lifted her head with a long breath, and a singular expression of relief, as if a burden was removed, and for the time being she was free. Sir Jasper was at her side, and as she listened, her eye glanced from face to face.

"Who is with you now?" she asked, in a low, mellow voice that was full of music.

"My sister and my cousin are yonder. You may remember Tavie as a child, she is little more now. Maurice is an invalid, but the finest fellow breathing."

"I understand," and Mrs. Snowdon's eyes softened with a sudden glance of pity for one cousin and admiration for the other, for she knew the facts.

"Major Royston, my father's friend, and Frank Annon, my own. Do you know him?" asked Sir Jasper.

"No."

"Then allow me to make him happy by presenting him, may I?"

"Not now, I'd rather see your cousin."

"Thanks, you are very kind. I'll bring him over."

"Stay, let me go to him," began the lady, with more feeling in face and voice than one would believe her capable of showing.

"Pardon, it will offend him; he will not be pitied, or relinquish any of the duties or privileges of a gentleman which he can possibly perform. He is proud, we can understand the feeling, so let us humor the poor fellow."

Mrs. Snowdon bowed silently, and Sir Jasper called out in his hearty, blunt way, as if nothing was amiss with his cousin:

"Maurice, I've an honor for you. Come and receive it."

Divining what it was, Treherne noiselessly crossed the room, and with no sign of self-consciousness or embarrassment, was presented to the handsome woman. Thinking his presence might be a restraint, Sir Jasper went away. The instant his back was turned, a change came over both: an almost grim expression replaced the suavity of Treherne's face, and Mrs. Snowdon's smile faded suddenly, while a deep flush rose to her brow, as her eyes questioned his beseechingly.

"How dared you come?" he asked below his breath.

"The general insisted."

"And you could not change his purpose; poor woman!"

"You will not be pitied, neither will I," and her eyes flashed; then the fire was quenched in tears, and her voice lost all its pride in a pleading tone.

"Forgive me, I longed to see you since your illness, and so I 'dared' to come."

"You shall be gratified; look, quite helpless, crippled for life, perhaps."

The chair was turned from the groups about the fire, and as he spoke, with a bitter laugh Treherne threw back the skin which covered his knees, and showed her the useless limbs once so strong and fleet. She shrank and paled, put out her hand to arrest him, and cried in an indignant whisper:

"No, no, not that! You know I never meant such cruel curiosity, such useless pain to both—"

"Be still, some one is coming," he returned, inaudibly; adding aloud, as he adjusted the skin and smoothed the rich fur as if speaking of it:

"Yes, it is a very fine one, Jasper gave it to me; he spoils me, like a dear, generous-hearted fellow as he is. Ah, Octavia, what can I do for you?"

"Nothing, thank you. I want to recall myself to Mrs. Snowdon's memory, if she will let me."

"No need of that; I never forget happy faces and pretty pictures. Two years ago I saw you at your first ball, and longed to be a girl again."

As she spoke, Mrs. Snowdon pressed the hand shyly offered, and smiled at the spirited face before her, though the shadow in her own eyes deepened as she met the bright glance of the girl.

"How kind you were that night! I remember you let me chatter away about my family, my cousin, and my foolish little affairs with the sweetest patience, and made me very happy by your interest. I was homesick, and aunt could never bear to hear of those things. It was before your marriage, and all the kinder, for you were the queen of the night, yet had a word for poor little me."

Mrs. Snowdon was pale to the lips, and Maurice impatiently tapped the arm of his chair, while the girl innocently chatted on:

"I am sorry the general is such an invalid; yet I dare say you find great happiness in taking care of him. It is so pleasant to be of use to those we love." And as she spoke, Octavia leaned over her cousin to hand him the glove he had dropped. The affectionate smile that accompanied the act made the color deepen again in Mrs. Snowdon's cheek, and lit a spark in her softened eyes. Her lips curled and her voice was sweetly sarcastic as she answered:

"Yes, it is charming to devote one's life to these dear invalids, and find one's reward in their gratitude. Youth, beauty, health and happiness are small sacrifices if one wins a little comfort for the poor sufferers."

The girl felt the sarcasm under the soft words and drew back with a troubled face.

Maurice smiled, and glanced from one to the other, saying significantly:

"Well for me that my little nurse loves her labor, and finds no sacrifice in it. I am fortunate in my choice."

"I trust it may prove so—" Mrs. Snowdon got no further, for at that moment dinner was announced, and Sir Jasper took her away. Annon approached with him and offered his arm to Miss Treherne, but with an air of surprise, and a little gesture of refusal, she said coldly:

"My cousin always takes me in to dinner. Be good enough to escort the major." And with her hand on the arm of the chair, she walked away with a mischievous glitter in her eyes.

Annon frowned and fell back, saying sharply:

"Come, Major, what are you doing there?"

"Making discoveries."

II

BY-PLAY

A right splendid old dowager was Lady Treherne, in her black velvet and point lace, as she sat erect and stately on a couch by the drawing-room fire, a couch which no one dare occupy in her absence, or share uninvited. The gentlemen were still over their wine, and the three ladies were alone. My lady never dozed in public, Mrs. Snowdon never gossiped, and Octavia never troubled herself to entertain any guests but those of her own age, so long pauses fell, and conversation languished, till Mrs. Snowdon roamed away into the library. As she disappeared, Lady Treherne beckoned to her daughter, who was idly making chords at the grand piano. Seating herself on the ottoman at her mother's feet, the girl took the still handsome hand in her own and amused herself with examining the old-fashioned jewels that covered it, a pretext for occupying her telltale eyes, as she suspected what was coming.

"My dear, I'm not pleased with you, and I tell you so at once, that you may amend your fault," began Madame Mère in a tender tone, for though a haughty, imperious woman, she idolized her children.

"What have I done, mamma?" asked the girl.

"Say rather, what have you left undone. You have been very rude to Mr. Annon; it must not occur again; not only because he is a guest, but because he is your—brother's friend."

My lady hesitated over the word "lover," and changed it, for to her Octavia still seemed a child, and though anxious for the alliance, she forbore to speak openly, lest the girl should turn willful, as she inherited her mother's high spirit.

"I'm sorry, mamma. But how can I help it, when he teases me so that I detest him?" said Octavia, petulantly.

"How tease, my love?"

"Why, he follows me about like a dog, puts on a sentimental look when I appear; blushes, and beams, and bows at everything I say, if I am polite; frowns and sighs if I'm not; and glowers tragically at every man I speak to, even poor Maurice.

Oh, mamma, what foolish creatures men are!" And the girl laughed blithely, as she looked up for the first time into her mother's face.

My lady smiled, as she stroked the bright head at her knee, but asked quickly:

"Why say '*even poor Maurice*,' as if it were impossible for anyone to be jealous of him?"

"But isn't it, mamma? I thought strong, well men regarded him as one set apart and done with, since his sad misfortune."

"Not entirely; while women pity and pet the poor fellow, his comrades will be jealous, absurd as it is."

"No one pets him but me, and I have a right to do it, for he is my cousin," said the girl, feeling a touch of jealousy herself.

"Rose and Blanche Talbot outdo you, my dear, and there is no cousinship to excuse them."

"Then let Frank Annon be jealous of them, and leave me in peace. They promised to come to-day; I'm afraid something has happened to prevent them." And Octavia gladly seized upon the new subject. But my lady was not to be eluded.

"They said they could not come till after dinner. They will soon arrive. Before they do so, I must say a few words, Tavia, and I beg you to give heed to them. I desire you to be courteous and amiable to Mr. Annon, and before strangers to be less attentive and affectionate to Maurice. You mean it kindly, but it looks ill, and causes disagreeable remarks."

"Who blames me for being devoted to my cousin? Can I ever do enough to repay him for his devotion? Mamma, you forget he saved your son's life."

Indignant tears filled the girl's eyes, and she spoke passionately, forgetting that Mrs. Snowdon was within ear-shot of her raised voice. With a frown my lady laid her hand on her daughter's lips, saying coldly:

"I do not forget, and I religiously discharge my every obligation by every care and comfort it is in my power to bestow. You are young, romantic, and tender-hearted. You think you must give your time and health, must sacrifice your future happiness to this duty. You are wrong, and unless you learn wisdom in season, you will find that you have done harm, not good."

"God forbid! How can I do that? Tell me, and I will be wise in time."

Turning the earnest face up to her own, Lady Treherne whispered anxiously:

"Has Maurice ever looked or hinted anything of love during this year he has been with us, and you his constant companion?"

"Never, mamma; he is too honorable and too unhappy to speak or think of that. I am his little nurse, sister, and friend, no more, nor ever shall be. Do not suspect us, or put such fears into my mind, else all our comfort will be spoiled."

Flushed and eager was the girl, but her clear eyes betrayed no tender confusion as she spoke, and all her thought seemed to be to clear her cousin from the charge of loving her too well. Lady Treherne looked relieved, paused a moment, then said, seriously but gently,

"This is well, but, child, I charge you tell me at once, if ever he forgets himself, for this thing cannot be. Once I hoped it might, now it is impossible; remember that he continue a friend and cousin, nothing more. I warn you in time, but if you neglect the warning, Maurice must go. No more of this; recollect my wish regarding Mr. Annon, and let your cousin amuse himself without you in public."

"Mamma, do you wish me to like Frank Annon?"

The abrupt question rather disturbed my lady, but knowing her daughter's frank, impetuous nature, she felt somewhat relieved by this candor, and answered decidedly:

"I do; he is your equal in all respects; he loves you, Jasper desires it, I approve, and you, being heart-whole, can have no just objection to the alliance."

"Has he spoken to you?"

"No, to your brother."

"You wish this much, mamma?"

"Very much, my child."

"I will try to please you, then." And stifling a sigh, the girl kissed her mother with unwonted meekness in tone and manner.

"Now I am well pleased. Be happy, my love. No one will urge or distress you. Let matters take their course, and if this hope of ours can be fulfilled, I shall be relieved of the chief care of my life."

A sound of girlish voices here broke on their ears, and springing up, Octavia hurried to meet her friends, exclaiming joyfully:

"They have come! they have come!"

Two smiling, blooming girls met her at the door, and, being at an enthusiastic age, they gushed in girlish fashion for several minutes, making a pretty group as they stood in each other's arms, all talking at once, with frequent kisses and little bursts of laughter, as vents for their emotion. Madame Mère welcomed them and then went to join Mrs. Snowdon, leaving the trio to gossip unrestrained.

"My dearest creature, I thought we never should get here, for papa had a tiresome dinner-party, and we were obliged to stay, you know," cried Rose, the lively sister, shaking out the pretty dress and glancing at herself in the mirror as she fluttered about the room like a butterfly.

"We were dying to come, and so charmed when you asked us, for we haven't seen you this age, darling," added Blanche, the pensive one, smoothing her blond curls after a fresh embrace.

"I'm sorry the Ulsters couldn't come to keep Christmas with us, for we have no gentlemen but Jasper, Frank Annon, and the major. Sad, isn't it?" said Octavia, with a look of despair, which caused a fresh peal of laughter.

"One apiece, my dear, it might be worse." And Rose privately decided to appropriate Sir Jasper.

"Where is your cousin?" asked Blanche, with a sigh of sentimental interest.

"He is here, of course. I forget him, but he is not on the flirting list, you know. We must amuse him, and not expect him to amuse us, though really, all the capital suggestions and plans for merry-making always come from him."

"He is better, I hope?" asked both sisters with real sympathy, making their young faces womanly and sweet.

"Yes, and has hopes of entire recovery. At least, they tell him so, though Dr. Ashley said there was no chance of it."

"Dear, dear, how sad! Shall we see him, Tavia?"

"Certainly; he is able to be with us now in the evening, and enjoys society as much as ever. But please take no notice of his infirmity, and make no inquiries beyond the usual 'How do you do.' He is sensitive, and hates to be considered an invalid more than ever."

"How charming it must be to take care of him, he is so accomplished and delightful. I quite envy you," said Blanche pensively.

"Sir Jasper told us that the General and Mrs. Snowdon were coming. I hope they will, for I've a most intense curiosity to see her—" began Rose.

"Hush, she is here with mamma! Why curious? What is the mystery? For you look as if there was one," questioned Octavia under her breath.

The three charming heads bent toward one another as Rose replied in a whisper, "If I knew, I shouldn't be inquisitive. There was a rumor that she married the old general in a fit of pique, and now repents. I asked mamma once, but she said such matters were not for young girls to hear, and not a word more would she say. *N'importe*, I have wits of my own, and I can satisfy myself. The gentlemen are coming! Am I all right, dear?" And the three glanced at one another with a swift scrutiny that nothing could escape, then grouped themselves prettily, and waited, with a little flutter of expectation in each young heart.

In came the gentlemen, and instantly a new atmosphere seemed to pervade the drawing-room, for with the first words uttered, several romances began. Sir Jasper was taken possession of by Rose, Blanche intended to devote herself to Maurice Treherne, but Annon intercepted her, and Octavia was spared any effort at politeness by this unexpected move on the part of her lover.

"He is angry, and wishes to pique me by devoting himself to Blanche. I wish he would, with all my heart, and leave me in peace. Poor Maurice, he expects me, and I long to go to him, but must obey mamma." And Octavia went to join the group formed by my lady, Mrs. Snowdon, the general, and the major.

The two young couples flirted in different parts of the room, and Treherne sat alone, watching them all with eyes that pierced below the surface, reading the hidden wishes, hopes, and fears that ruled them. A singular expression sat on his face as he turned from Octavia's clear countenance to Mrs. Snowdon's gloomy one. He leaned his head upon his hand and fell into deep thought, for he was passing through one of those fateful moments which come to us all, and which may make or mar a life. Such moments come when least looked for: an unexpected meeting, a peculiar mood, some trivial circumstance, or careless word produces it, and often it is gone before we realize its presence, leaving after-effects to show us what we have gained or lost. Treherne was conscious that the present hour, and the acts that filled it, possessed unusual interest, and would exert an unusual influence on his life. Before him was the good and evil genius of his nature in the guise of those two women. Edith Snowdon had already tried her power, and accident only had saved him. Octavia, all unconscious as she was, never failed to rouse and stimulate the noblest attributes of mind and heart. A year spent in her society had done much for him, and he loved her with a strange mingling of passion, reverence, and gratitude. He knew why Edith Snowdon came, he felt that the old fascination had not lost its charm, and though fear was unknown to him, he was ill pleased at the sight of the beautiful, dangerous woman. On the other hand, he saw that Lady Treherne desired her daughter to shun him and smile on Annon; he acknowledged that he had no right to win the young creature, crippled and poor as he was, and a pang of jealous pain wrung his heart as he watched her.

Then a sense of power came to him, for helpless, poor, and seemingly an object of pity, he yet felt that he held the honor, peace and happiness of nearly every person present in his hands. It was a strong temptation to this man, so full of repressed passion and power, so set apart and shut out from the more stirring duties and pleasures of life. A few words from his lips, and the pity all felt for him would be turned to fear, respect and admiration. Why not utter them, and enjoy all that was possible? He owed the Trehernes nothing; why suffer injustice, dependence, and the compassion that wounds a proud man deepest? Wealth, love, pleasure might be his with a breath. Why not secure them now?

His pale face flushed, his eye kindled, and his thin hand lay clenched like a vise as these thoughts passed rapidly through his mind. A look, a word at that moment would sway him; he felt it, and leaned forward, waiting in secret suspense for the glance, the speech which should decide him for good or ill. Who shall say what subtle instinct caused Octavia to turn and smile at him with a wistful, friendly look that warmed his heart? He met it with an answering glance, which thrilled her strangely, for love, gratitude, and some mysterious intelligence met and mingled in the brilliant yet soft expression which swiftly shone and faded in her face. What it was she could not tell; she only felt that it filled her with an indescribable emotion never experienced before. In an instant it all passed, Lady Treherne spoke to her, and Blanche Talbot addressed Maurice, wondering, as she did so, if the enchanting smile he wore was meant for her.

"Mr. Annon having mercifully set me free, I came to try to cheer your solitude; but you look as if solitude made you happier than society does the rest of us," she said without her usual affectation, for his manner impressed her.

"You are very kind and very welcome. I do find pleasures to beguile my loneliness, which gayer people would not enjoy, and it is well that I can, else I should turn morose and tyrannical, and doom some unfortunate to entertain me all day long," he answered with a gentle curtesy which was his chief attraction to womankind.

"Pray tell me some of your devices. I'm often alone in spirit, if not so in the flesh, for Rose, though a dear girl, is not congenial, and I find no kindred soul."

A humorous glimmer came to Treherne's eyes, as the sentimental damsel beamed a soft sigh and drooped her long lashes effectively. Ignoring the topic of "kindred souls," he answered, coldly:

"My favorite amusement is studying the people around me. It may be rude, but tied to my corner, I cannot help watching the figures around me, and discovering their little plots and plans. I'm getting very expert, and really surprise myself sometimes by the depth of my researches."

"I can believe it; your eyes look as if they possessed that gift. Pray don't study *me*." And the girl shrank away with an air of genuine alarm.

Treherne smiled involuntarily, for he had read the secret of that shallow heart long ago, and was too generous to use the knowledge, however flattering it might be to him. In a reassuring tone he said, turning away the keen eyes she feared, "I give you my word I never will, charming as it might be to study the white pages of a maidenly heart. I find plenty of others to read, so rest tranquil, Miss Blanche."

"Who interests you most just now?" asked the girl, coloring with pleasure at his words. "Mrs. Snowdon looks like one who has a romance to be read, if you have the skill."

"I have read it. My lady is my study just now. I thought I knew her well, but of late she puzzles me. Human minds are more full of mysteries than any written book and more changeable than the cloud-shapes in the air."

"A fine old lady, but I fear her so intensely I should never dare to try to read her, as you say." Blanche looked toward the object of discussion as she spoke, and added, "Poor Tavia, how forlorn she seems. Let me ask her to join us, may I?"

"With all my heart," was the quick reply.

Blanche glided away but did not return, for my lady kept her as well as her daughter.

"That test satisfies me; well, I submit for a time, but I think I can conquer my aunt yet." And with a patient sigh Treherne turned to observe Mrs. Snowdon.

She now stood by the fire talking with Sir Jasper, a handsome, reckless, generous-hearted young gentleman, who very plainly showed his great admiration for the lady. When he came, she suddenly woke up from her listless mood and became as brilliantly gay as she had been unmistakably melancholy before. As she chatted, she absently pushed to and fro a small antique urn of bronze on the chimney-piece, and in doing so she more than once gave Treherne a quick, significant glance, which he answered at last by a somewhat haughty nod. Then, as if satisfied, she ceased toying with the ornament and became absorbed in Sir Jasper's gallant badinage.

The instant her son approached Mrs. Snowdon, Madame Mère grew anxious, and leaving Octavia to her friends and lover, she watched Jasper. But her surveillance availed little, for she could neither see nor hear anything amiss, yet could not rid herself of the feeling that some mutual understanding existed between them. When the party broke up for the night, she lingered till all were gone but her son and nephew.

"Well, madame-ma-mère, what troubles you?" asked Sir Jasper, as she looked anxiously into his face before bestowing her good-night kiss.

"I cannot tell, yet I feel ill at ease. Remember, my son, that you are the pride of my heart, and any sin or shame of yours would kill me. Good-night, Maurice." And with a stately bow she swept away.

Lounging with both elbows on the low chimney-piece, Sir Jasper smiled at his mother's fears, and said to his cousin, the instant they were alone:

"She is worried about E. S. Odd, isn't it, what instinctive antipathies women take to one another?"

"Why did you ask E. S. here?" demanded Treherne.

"My dear fellow, how could I help it? My mother wanted the general, my father's friend, and of course his wife must be asked also. I couldn't tell my mother that the lady had been a most arrant coquette, to put it mildly, and had married the old man in a pet, because my cousin and I declined to be ruined by her."

"You *could* have told her what mischief she makes wherever she goes, and for Octavia's sake have deferred the general's visit for a time. I warn you, Jasper, harm will come of it."

"To whom, you or me?"

"To both, perhaps, certainly to you. She was disappointed once when she lost us both by wavering between your title and my supposed fortune. She is miserable with the old man, and her only hope is in his death, for he is very feeble. You are free, and doubly attractive now, so beware, or she will entangle you before you know it."

"Thanks, Mentor, I've no fear, and shall merely amuse myself for a week—they stay no longer." And with a careless laugh, Sir Jasper strolled away.

"Much mischief may be done in a week, and this is the beginning of it," muttered Treherne, as he raised himself to look under the bronze vase for the note. It was gone!

III

WHO WAS IT?

WHO HAD TAKEN IT? THIS QUESTION TORMENTED TREHERNE ALL THAT sleepless night. He suspected three persons, for only these had approached the fire after the note was hidden. He had kept his eye on it, he thought, till the stir of breaking up. In that moment it must have been removed by the major, Frank Annon, or my lady; Sir Jasper was out of the question, for he never touched an ornament in the drawing-room since he had awkwardly demolished a whole *étagère* of costly trifles, to his mother's and sister's great grief. The major evidently suspected something, Annon was jealous, and my lady would be glad of a pretext to remove her daughter from his reach. Trusting to his skill in reading faces, he waited impatiently for morning, resolving to say nothing to anyone but Mrs. Snowdon, and from her merely to inquire what the note contained.

Treherne usually was invisible till lunch, often till dinner; therefore, fearing to excite suspicion by unwonted activity, he did not appear till noon. The mail-bag had just been opened, and everyone was busy over their letters, but all looked up to exchange a word with the newcomer, and Octavia impulsively turned to meet him, then checked herself and hid her suddenly crimsoned face behind a newspaper. Treherne's eye took in everything, and saw at once in the unusually late arrival of the mail a pretext for discovering the pilferer of the note.

"All have letters but me, yet, I expected one last night. Major, have you got it among yours?" And as he spoke, Treherne fixed his penetrating eyes full on the person he addressed.

With no sign of consciousness, no trace of confusion, the major carefully turned over his pile, and replied in the most natural manner:

"Not a trace of it; I wish there was, for nothing annoys me more than any delay or mistake about my letters."

"He knows nothing of it," thought Treherne, and turned to Annon, who was deep in a long epistle from some intimate friend, with a talent for imparting news, to judge from the reader's interest.

"Annon, I appeal to you, for I *must* discover who has robbed me of my letter."

"I have but one, read it, if you will, and satisfy yourself," was the brief reply.

"No, thank you. I merely asked in joke; it is doubtless among my lady's. Jasper's letters and mine often get mixed, and my lady takes care of his for him. I think you must have it, aunt."

Lady Treherne looked up impatiently.

"My dear Maurice, what a coil about a letter! We none of us have it, so do not punish us for the sins of your correspondent or the carelessness of the post."

"She was not the thief, for she is always intensely polite when she intends to thwart me," thought Treherne, and, apologizing for his rudeness in disturbing them, he rolled himself to his nook in a sunny window and became apparently absorbed in a new magazine.

Mrs. Snowdon was opening the general's letters for him, and, having finished her little task, she roamed away into the library, as if in search of a book. Presently returning with one, she approached Treherne, and, putting it into his hand, said, in her musically distinct voice:

"Be so kind as to find for me the passage you spoke of last night. I am curious to see it."

Instantly comprehending her stratagem, he opened it with apparent carelessness, secured the tiny note laid among the leaves, and, selecting a passage at hazard, returned her book and resumed his own. Behind the cover of it he unfolded and read these words:

> I understand, but do not be anxious; the line I left was merely this—"I must see you alone, tell me when and where." No one can make much of it, and I will discover the thief before dinner. Do nothing, but watch to whom I speak first on entering, when we meet in the evening, and beware of that person.

Quietly transferring the note to the fire with the wrapper of the magazine, he dismissed the matter from his mind and left Mrs. Snowdon to play detective as she pleased, while he busied himself about his own affairs.

It was a clear, bright December day, and when the young people separated to prepare for a ride, while the general and the major sunned themselves on the terrace, Lady Treherne said to her nephew:

"I am going for an airing in the pony carriage; will you be my escort, Maurice?"

"With pleasure," replied the young man, well knowing what was in store for him.

My lady was unusually taciturn and grave, yet seemed anxious to say something which she found difficult to utter. Treherne saw this, and ended an awkward pause by dashing boldly into the subject which occupied both.

"I think you want to say something to me about Tavie, aunt; am I right?"

"Yes."

"Then let me spare you the pain of beginning, and prove my sincerity by openly stating the truth, as far as I am concerned. I love her very dearly, but I am not mad enough to dream of telling her so. I know that it is impossible, and I relinquish my hopes. Trust me. I will keep silent and see her marry Annon without a word of complaint, if you will it. I see by her altered manner that you have spoken to her, and that my little friend and nurse is to be mine no longer. Perhaps you are wise, but if you do this on my account, it is in vain—the mischief is done, and while I live I shall love my cousin. If you do it to spare her, I am dumb, and will go away rather than cause her a care or pain."

"Do you really mean this, Maurice?" And Lady Treherne looked at him with a changed and softened face.

Turning upon her, Treherne showed her a countenance full of suffering and sincerity, of resignation and resolve, as he said earnestly:

"I do mean it; prove me in any way you please. I am not a bad fellow, aunt, and I desire to be better. Since my misfortune I've had time to test many things, myself among others, and in spite of many faults, I do cherish the wish to keep my soul honest and true, even though my body be a wreck. It is easy to say these things, but in spite of temptation, I think I can stand firm, if you trust me."

"My dear boy, I do trust you, and thank you gratefully for this frankness. I never forget that I owe Jasper's life to you, and never expect to repay that debt. Remember this when I seem cold or unkind, and remember also that I say now, had you been spared this affliction, I would gladly have given you my girl. But—"

"But, aunt, hear one thing," broke in Treherne; "they tell me that any sudden and violent shock of surprise, joy or sorrow may do for me what they hope time will achieve. I said nothing of this, for it is but a chance; yet, while there is any hope, need I utterly renounce Octavia?"

"It is hard to refuse, and, yet, I cannot think it wise to build upon a chance so slight. Once let her have you, and both are made unhappy, if the hope fail. No, Maurice, it is better to be generous, and leave her free to make her own happiness elsewhere. Annon loves her, she is heart-whole, and will soon learn to love him, if you are silent. My poor boy, it seems cruel, but I must say it."

"Shall I go away, aunt?" was all his answer, very firmly uttered, though his lips were white.

"Not yet, only leave them to themselves, and hide your trouble if you can. Yet, if you prefer, you shall go to town, and Benson shall see that you are comfortable. Your health will be a reason, and I will come, or write often, if you are homesick. It shall depend on you, for I want to be just and kind in this hard case. You shall decide."

"Then I will stay. I can hide my love; and to see them together will soon cease to wound me, if Octavia is happy."

"So let it rest then, for a time. You shall miss your companion as little as possible, for I will try to fill her place. Forgive me, Maurice, and pity a mother's solicitude, for these two are the last of many children, and I am a widow now."

Lady Treherne's voice faltered, and if any selfish hope or plan lingered in her nephew's mind, that appeal banished it and touched his better nature. Pressing her hand he said gently:

"Dear aunt, do not lament over me. I am one set apart for afflictions, yet I will not be conquered by them. Let us forget my youth and be friendly counselors together for the good of the two whom we both love. I must say a word about Jasper, and you will not press me to explain more than I can without breaking my promise."

"Thank you, thank you! It is regarding that woman, I know. Tell me all you can; I will not be importunate, but I disliked her the instant I saw her, beautiful and charming as she seems."

"When my cousin and I were in Paris, just before my illness, we met her. She was with her father then, a gay old man, who led a life of pleasure, and was no fit guardian for a lovely daughter. She knew our story and, having fascinated both, paused to decide which she would accept: Jasper, for his title, or me, for my fortune. This was before my uncle changed his will, and I believed myself his heir; but, before she made her choice, something (don't ask me what, if you please) occurred to send us from Paris. On our return voyage we were wrecked, and then came my illness, disinheritance and helplessness. Edith Dubarry heard the story, but rumor reported it falsely, and she believed both of us had lost the fortune. Her father died penniless, and in a moment of despair she married the general, whose wealth surrounds her with the luxury she loves, and whose failing health will soon restore her liberty—"

"And then, Maurice?" interrupted my lady.

"She hopes to win Jasper, I think."

"Never! We must prevent that at all costs. I had rather see him dead before me, than the husband of such a woman. Why is she permitted to visit homes like mine? I should have been told this sooner," exclaimed my lady angrily.

"I should have told you had I known it, and I reproved Jasper for his neglect. Do not be needlessly troubled, aunt, there is no blemish on Mrs. Snowdon's name, and, as the wife of a brave and honorable man, she is received without question; for beauty, grace or tact like hers can make their way anywhere. She stays but a week, and I will devote myself to her; this will save Jasper, and, if necessary, convince Tavie of my indifference—" Then he paused to stifle a sigh.

"But yourself, have you no fears for your own peace, Maurice? You must not sacrifice happiness or honor, for me or mine."

"I am safe; I love my cousin, and that is my shield. Whatever happens remember that I tried to serve you, and sincerely endeavored to forget myself."

"God bless you, my son! Let me call you so, and feel that, though I deny you my daughter, I give you heartily a mother's care and affection."

Lady Treherne was as generous as she was proud, and her nephew had conquered her by confidence and submission. He acted no part, yet, even in relinquishing all, he cherished a hope that he might yet win the heart he coveted. Silently they parted, but from that hour a new and closer bond existed between the two, and exerted an unsuspected influence over the whole household.

Maurice waited with some impatience for Mrs. Snowdon's entrance, not only because of his curiosity to see if she had discovered the thief, but because of the part he had taken upon himself to play. He was equal to it, and felt a certain pleasure in it for a three-fold reason. It would serve his aunt and cousin, would divert his mind from its own cares, and, perhaps by making Octavia jealous, waken love; for, though he had chosen the right, he was but a man, and moreover a lover.

Mrs. Snowdon was late, she always was, for her toilet was elaborate, and she liked to enjoy its effects upon others. The moment she entered, Treherne's eye was on her, and to his intense surprise and annoyance she addressed Octavia, saying blandly:

"My dear Miss Treherne, I've been admiring your peacocks. Pray let me see you feed them to-morrow. Miss Talbot says it is a charming sight."

"If you are on the terrace just after lunch, you will find them there, and may feed them yourself, if you like," was the cool, civil reply.

"She looks like a peacock herself in that splendid green and gold dress, doesn't she?" whispered Rose to Sir Jasper, with a wicked laugh.

"Faith, so she does. I wish Tavie's birds had voices like Mrs. Snowdon's; their squalling annoys me intensely."

"I rather like it, for it is honest, and no malice or mischief is hidden behind it. I always distrust those smooth, sweet voices; they are insincere. I like a full, clear tone; sharp, if you please, but decided and true."

"Well said, Octavia. I agree with you, and your own is a perfect sample of the kind you describe." And Treherne smiled as he rolled by to join Mrs. Snowdon, who evidently waited for him, while Octavia turned to her brother to defend her pets.

"Are you sure? How did you discover?" said Maurice, affecting to admire the lady's bouquet, as he paused beside her.

"I suspected it the moment I saw her this morning. She is no actress; and dislike, distrust and contempt were visible in her face when we met. Till you so cleverly told me my note was lost, I fancied she was disturbed about her brother—or you."

A sudden pause and a keen glance followed the last softly-uttered word, but Treherne met it with an inscrutable smile and a quiet:

"Well, what next?"

"The moment I learned that you did not get the note I was sure she had it, and, knowing that she must have seen me put it there, in spite of her apparent innocence, I quietly asked her for it. This surprised her, this robbed the affair of any mystery, and I finished her perplexity by sending it to the major the moment she returned it to me, as if it had been intended for him. She begged pardon, said her brother was thoughtless, and she watched over him lest he should get into mischief; professed to think I meant the line for him, and behaved like a charming simpleton, as she is."

"Quite a tumult about nothing. Poor little Tavie! You doubtlessly frightened her so that we may safely correspond hereafter."

"You may give me an answer now, and here."

"Very well, meet me on the terrace to-morrow morning; the peacocks will make the meeting natural enough. I usually loiter away an hour or two there, in the sunny part of the day."

"But the girl?"

"I'll send her away."

"You speak as if it would be an easy thing to do."

"It will, both easy and pleasant."

"Now you are mysterious or uncomplimentary. You either care nothing for a *tête-à-tête* with her, or you will gladly send her out of my way. Which is it?"

"You shall decide. Can I have this?"

She looked at him as he touched a rose with a warning glance, for the flower was both an emblem of love and of silence. Did he mean to hint that he recalled the past, or to warn her that someone was near? She leaned from the shadow of the curtain where she sat, and caught a glimpse of a shadow gliding away.

"Who was it?" she asked, below her breath.

"A Rose," he answered, laughing. Then, as if the danger was over, he said, "How will you account to the major for the message you sent him?"

"Easily, by fabricating some interesting perplexity in which I want sage counsel. He will be flattered, and by seeming to take him into my confidence, I can hoodwink the excellent man to my heart's content, for he annoys me by his odd way of mounting guard over me at all times. Now take me in to dinner, and be your former delightful self."

"That is impossible," he said, yet proved that it was not.

IV

FEEDING THE PEACOCKS

It was indeed a charming sight, the twelve stately birds perched on the broad stone balustrade, or prancing slowly along the terrace, with the sun gleaming on their green and golden necks and the glories of their gorgeous plumes, widespread, or sweeping like rich trains behind them. In pretty contrast to the splendid creatures was their young mistress, in her simple morning dress and fur-trimmed hood and mantle, as she stood feeding the tame pets from her hand, calling their fanciful names, laughing at their pranks, and heartily enjoying the winter sunshine, the fresh wind, and the girlish pastime. As Treherne slowly approached, he watched her with lover's eyes, and found her very sweet and blithe, and dearer in his sight than ever. She had shunned him carefully all the day before, had parted at night with a hasty handshake, and had not come as usual to bid him good-morning in the library. He had taken no notice of the change as yet, but now, remembering his promise to his aunt, he resolved to let the girl know that he fully understood the relation which henceforth was to exist between them.

"Good-morning, cousin. Shall I drive you away, if I take a turn or two here?" he said, in a cheerful tone, but with a half-reproachful glance.

She looked at him an instant, then went to him with extended hand and cheeks rosier than before, while her frank eyes filled, and her voice had a traitorous tremor in it, as she said, impetuously:

"I *will* be myself for a moment, in spite of everything. Maurice, don't think me unkind, don't reproach me, or ask my leave to come where I am. There is a reason for the change you see in me; it's not caprice, it is obedience."

"My dear girl, I know it; I meant to speak of it, and show you that I understand. Annon is a good fellow, as worthy of you as any man can be, and I wish you all the happiness you deserve."

"Do you?" and her eyes searched his face keenly.

"Yes; do you doubt it?" and so well did he conceal his love, that neither face, voice nor manner betrayed a hint of it.

Her eyes fell, a cloud passed over her clear countenance, and she withdrew her hand, as if to caress the hungry bird that gently pecked at the basket she held. As if to change the conversation, she said playfully:

"Poor Argus, you have lost your fine feathers, and so all desert you, except kind little Juno, who never forgets her friends. There, take it all, and share between you."

Treherne smiled, and said quickly:

"I am a human Argus, and you have been a kind little Juno to me since I lost my plumes. Continue to be so, and you will find me a very faithful friend."

"I will." And as she answered, her old smile came back and her eyes met his again.

"Thanks! Now we shall get on happily. I don't ask or expect the old life—that is impossible. I knew that when lovers came, the friend would fall into the background; and I am content to be second, where I have so long been first. Do not think you neglect me; be happy with your lover, dear, and when you have no pleasanter amusement, come and see old Maurice."

She turned her head away, that he might not see the angry color in her cheeks, the trouble in her eyes, and when she spoke, it was to say petulantly:

"I wish Jasper and mamma would leave me in peace. I hate lovers and want none. If Frank teases, I'll go into a convent and so be rid of him."

Maurice laughed, and turned her face towards himself, saying, in his persuasive voice:

"Give him a trial first, to please your mother. It can do no harm and may amuse you. Frank is already lost, and, as you are heart-whole, why not see what you can do for him? I shall have a new study, then, and not miss you so much."

"You are very kind; I'll do my best. I wish Mrs. Snowdon would come, if she is coming; I've an engagement at two, and Frank will look tragical if I'm not ready. He is teaching me billiards, and I really like the game, though I never thought I should."

"That looks well. I hope you'll learn a double lesson, and Annon find a docile pupil in both."

"You are very pale this morning; are you in pain, Maurice?" suddenly asked Octavia, dropping the tone of assumed ease and gayety under which she had tried to hide her trouble.

"Yes, but it will soon pass. Mrs. Snowdon is coming. I saw her at the hall door a moment ago. I will show her the peacocks, if you want to go. She won't mind the change, I dare say, as you don't like her, and I do."

"No, I am sure of that. It was an arrangement, perhaps? I understand. I will not play Mademoiselle De Trop."

Sudden fire shone in the girl's eyes, sudden contempt curled her lip, and a glance full of meaning went from her cousin to the door, where Mrs. Snowdon appeared, waiting for her maid to bring her some additional wrappings.

"You allude to the note you stole. How came you to play that prank, Tavie?" asked Treherne tranquilly.

"I saw her put it under the urn. I thought it was for Jasper, and I took it," she said boldly.

"Why for Jasper?"

"I remembered his speaking of meeting her long ago, and describing her beauty enthusiastically—and so did you."

"You have a good memory."

"I have for everything concerning those I love. I observed her manner of meeting my brother, his devotion to her, and, when they stood laughing together before the fire, I felt sure that she wished to charm him again."

"Again? Then she did charm him once?" asked Treherne, anxious to know how much Jasper had told his sister.

"He always denied it, and declared that you were the favorite."

"Then why not think the note for me?" he asked.

"I do now," was the sharp answer.

"But she told you it was for the major, and sent it."

"She deceived me; I am not surprised. I am glad Jasper is safe, and I wish you a pleasant *tête-à-tête*."

Bowing with unwonted dignity, Octavia set down her basket, and walked away in one direction as Mrs. Snowdon approached in another.

"I have done it now," sighed Treherne, turning from the girlish figure to watch the stately creature who came sweeping toward him with noiseless grace.

Brilliancy and splendor became Mrs. Snowdon; she enjoyed luxury, and her beauty made many things becoming which in a plainer woman would have been out of taste, and absurd. She had wrapped herself in a genuine Eastern burnous of scarlet, blue and gold; the hood drawn over her head framed her fine face in rich hues, and the great gilt tassels shone against her rippling black hair. She wore it with grace, and the barbaric splendor of the garment became her well. The fresh air touched her cheeks with a delicate color; her usually gloomy eyes were brilliant now, and the smile that parted her lips was full of happiness.

"Welcome, Cleopatra!" cried Treherne, with difficulty repressing a laugh, as the peacocks screamed and fled before the rustling amplitude of her drapery.

"I might reply by calling you Thaddeus of Warsaw, for you look very romantic and Polish with your pale, pensive face, and your splendid furs," she answered, as she paused beside him with admiration very visibly expressed in her eyes.

Treherne disliked the look, and rather abruptly said, as he offered her the basket of bread:

"I have disposed of my cousin, and offered to do the honors of the peacocks. Here they are—will you feed them?"

"No, thank you—I care nothing for the fowls, as you know; I came to speak to you," she said impatiently.

"I am at your service."

"I wish to ask you a question or two—is it permitted?"

"What man ever refused Mrs. Snowdon a request?"

"Nay, no compliments; from you they are only satirical evasions. I was deceived when abroad, and rashly married that old man. Tell me truly how things stand."

"Jasper has all. I have nothing."

"I am glad of it."

"Many thanks for the hearty speech. You at least speak sincerely," he said bitterly.

"I do, Maurice—I do; let me prove it."

Treherne's chair was close beside the balustrade. Mrs. Snowdon leaned on the carved railing, with her back to the house and her face screened by a tall urn. Looking steadily at him, she said rapidly and low:

"You thought I wavered between you and Jasper, when we parted two years ago. I did; but it was not between title and fortune that I hesitated. It was between duty and love. My father, a fond, foolish old man, had set his heart on seeing me a lady. I was his all; my beauty was his delight, and no untitled man was deemed worthy of me. I loved him tenderly. You may doubt this, knowing how selfish, reckless, and vain I am, but I have a heart, and with better training had been a better woman. No matter, it is too late now. Next my father, I loved you. Nay, hear me—I *will* clear myself in your eyes. I mean no wrong to the general. He is kind, indulgent, generous; I respect him—I am grateful, and while he lives, I shall be true to him."

"Then be silent now. Do not recall the past, Edith; let it sleep, for both our sakes," began Treherne; but she checked him imperiously.

"It shall, when I am done. I loved you, Maurice; for, of all the gay, idle, pleasure-seeking men I saw about me, you were the only one who seemed to have a thought beyond the folly of the hour. Under the seeming frivolity of your life lay something noble, heroic and true. I felt that you had a purpose, that your present mood was but transitory—a young man's holiday, before the real work of his life began. This attracted, this won me; for even in the brief regard you then gave me, there was an earnestness no other man had shown. I wanted your respect; I longed to earn your love, to share your life, and prove that even in my neglected nature slept the power of canceling a frivolous past by a noble future. O Maurice, had you lingered one week more, I never should have been the miserable thing I am!"

There her voice faltered and failed, for all the bitterness of lost love, peace and happiness sounded in the pathetic passion of that exclamation. She did not weep, for tears seldom dimmed those tragical eyes of hers; but she wrung her hands in mute despair, and looked down into the frost-blighted gardens below, as if she saw there a true symbol of her own ruined life. Treherne uttered not a word, but set his teeth with an almost fierce glance toward the distant figure of Sir Jasper, who was riding gaily away, like one unburdened by a memory or a care. Hurriedly Mrs. Snowdon went on:

"My father begged and commanded me to choose your cousin. I could not break his heart, and asked for time, hoping to soften him. While I waited, that mysterious affair hurried you from Paris, and then came the wreck, the illness, and the rumor that old Sir Jasper had disinherited both nephews. They told me you were dying, and I became a passive instrument in my father's hands. I promised to recall and accept your cousin, but the old man died before it was done, and then I cared not what became of me. General Snowdon was my father's friend; he pitied me; he saw my desolate, destitute state, my despair and helplessness. He comforted, sustained and saved me. I was grateful; and when he offered me his heart and home, I accepted them. He knew I had no love to give; but as a friend, a daughter, I would gladly serve him, and make his declining years as happy as I could. It was all over, when I heard that you were alive, afflicted and poor. I longed to come and live for you. My new bonds became heavy fetters then, my wealth oppressed me, and I was doubly wretched—for I dared not tell my trouble, and it nearly drove me mad. I have seen you now; I know that you are happy; I read your cousin's love and see a peaceful life in store for you. This must content me, and I must learn to bear it as I can."

She paused, breathless and pale, and walked rapidly along the terrace, as if to hide or control the agitation that possessed her. Treherne still sat silent, but his heart leaped within him, as he thought:

"She sees that Octavia loves me! A woman's eye is quick to detect love in another, and she asserts what I begin to hope. My cousin's manner just now, her dislike of Annon, her new shyness with me; it may be true, and if it is—Heaven help me—what am I saying! I must not hope, nor wish, nor dream; I must renounce and forget."

He leaned his head upon his hand, and sat so still Mrs. Snowdon rejoined him, pale, but calm and self-possessed. As she drew near, she marked his attitude, the bitter sadness of his face, and hope sprang up within her. Perhaps she was mistaken; perhaps he did not love his cousin; perhaps he still remembered the past, and still regretted the loss of the heart she had just laid bare before him. Her husband was failing, and might die any day. And then, free, rich, beautiful and young, what might she not become to Treherne, helpless, poor and ambitious. With all her faults, she was generous, and this picture charmed her fancy, warmed her heart, and comforted her pain.

"Maurice," she said softly, pausing again beside him, "if I mistake you and your hopes, it is because I dare ask nothing for myself; but if ever a time shall come when I have liberty to give or help, ask of me *anything*, and it is gladly yours."

He understood her, pitied her, and, seeing that she found consolation in a distant hope, he let her enjoy it while she might. Gravely, yet gratefully, he spoke, and pressed the hand extended to him with an impulsive gesture.

"Generous as ever, Edith, and impetuously frank. Thank you for your sincerity, your kindness, and the affection you once gave me. I say 'once,' for now duty, truth and honor bar us from each other. My life must be solitary, yet I shall find work to do, and learn to be content. You owe all devotion to the good old man who loves you, and will not fail him, I am sure. Leave the future and the past, but let us make the present what it may be—a time to forgive and forget, to take heart and begin anew. Christmas is a fitting time for such resolves, and the birth of friendship such as ours may be."

Something in his tone and manner struck her, and, eyeing him with soft wonder, she exclaimed:

"How changed you are!"

"Need you tell me that?" And he glanced at his helpless limbs with a bitter yet pathetic look of patience.

"No, no—not so! I mean in mind, not body. Once you were gay and careless, eager and fiery, like Jasper; now you are grave and quiet, or cheerful, and so very kind. Yet, in spite of illness and loss, you seem twice the man you were, and something wins respect, as well as admiration—and love."

Her dark eyes filled as the last word left her lips, and the beauty of a touched heart shone in her face. Maurice looked up quickly, asking with sudden earnestness:

"Do you see it? Then it is true. Yes, I *am* changed, thank God! and she has done it."

"Who?" demanded his companion, jealously.

"Octavia. Unconsciously, yet surely, she has done much for me, and this year of seeming loss and misery has been the happiest, most profitable of my life. I have often heard that afflictions were the best teachers, and I believe it now."

Mrs. Snowdon shook her head sadly.

"Not always; they are tormentors to some. But don't preach, Maurice. I am still a sinner, though you incline to sainthood, and I have one question more to ask. What was it that took you and Jasper so suddenly away from Paris?"

"That I can never tell you."

"I shall discover it for myself, then."

"It is impossible."

"Nothing is impossible to a determined woman."

"You can neither wring, surprise nor bribe this secret from the two persons who hold it. I beg of you to let it rest," said Treherne earnestly.

"I have a clew, and I shall follow it; for I am convinced that something is wrong, and you are—"

"Dear Mrs. Snowdon, are you so charmed with the birds that you forget your fellow-beings, or so charmed with one fellow-being that you forget the birds?"

As the sudden question startled both, Rose Talbot came along the terrace, with hands full of holly and a face full of merry mischief, adding as she vanished:

"I shall tell Tavie that feeding the peacocks is such congenial amusement for lovers, she and Mr. Annon had better try it."

"Saucy gipsey!" muttered Treherne.

But Mrs. Snowdon said, with a smile of double meaning:

"Many a true word is spoken in jest."

V

UNDER THE MISTLETOE

Unusually gay and charming the three young friends looked, dressed alike in fleecy white, with holly wreaths in their hair, as they slowly descended the wide oaken stairway arm in arm. A footman was lighting the hall lamps, for the winter dusk gathered early, and the girls were merrily chatting about the evening's festivity when suddenly a loud, long shriek echoed through the hall. A heavy glass shade fell from the man's hand with a crash, and the young ladies clung to one another aghast, for mortal terror was in the cry, and a dead silence followed it.

"What was it, John?" demanded Octavia, very pale, but steady in a moment.

"I'll go and see, miss." And the man hurried away.

"Where did the dreadful scream come from?" asked Rose, collecting her wits as rapidly as possible.

"Above us somewhere. Oh, let us go down among people; I am frightened to death," whispered Blanche, trembling and faint.

Hurrying into the parlor, they found only Annon and the major, both looking startled, and both staring out of the windows.

"Did you hear it? What could it be? Don't go and leave us!" cried the girls in a breath, as they rushed in.

The gentlemen had heard, couldn't explain the cry, and were quite ready to protect the pretty creatures who clustered about them like frightened fawns. John speedily appeared, looking rather wild, and as eager to tell his tale as they to listen.

"It's Patty, one of the maids, miss, in a fit. She went up to the north gallery to see that the fires was right, for it takes a power of wood to warm the gallery even enough for dancing, as you know, miss. Well, it was dark, for the fires was low and her candle went out as she whisked open the door, being flurried, as the maids always is when they go in there. Halfway down the gallery she says she heard a rustling, and stopped. She's the pluckiest of 'em all, and she called out, 'I see you!' thinking it was some of us trying to fright her. Nothing answered, and she went on a bit, when suddenly the fire flared up one flash, and there right before her was the ghost."

"Don't be foolish, John. Tell us what it was," said Octavia sharply, though her face whitened and her heart sank as the last word passed the man's lips.

"It was a tall, black figger, miss, with a dead-white face and a black hood. She see it plain, and turned to go away, but she hadn't gone a dozen steps when there it was again before her, the same tall, dark thing with the dead-white face looking out from the black hood. It lifted its arm as if to hold her, but she gave a spring and dreadful screech, and ran to Mrs. Benson's room, where she dropped in a fit."

"How absurd to be frightened by the shadows of the figures in armor that stand along the gallery!" said Rose, boldly enough, though she would have declined entering the gallery without a light.

"Nay, I don't wonder, it's a ghostly place at night. How is the poor thing?" asked Blanche, still hanging on the major's arm in her best attitude.

"If mamma knows nothing of it, tell Mrs. Benson to keep it from her, please. She is not well, and such things annoy her very much," said Octavia, adding as the man turned away, "Did anyone look in the gallery after Patty told her tale?"

"No, miss. I'll go and do it myself; I'm not afraid of man, ghost, or devil, saving your presence, ladies," replied John.

"Where is Sir Jasper?" suddenly asked the major.

"Here I am. What a deuce of a noise some one has been making. It disturbed a capital dream. Why, Tavie, what is it?" And Sir Jasper came out of the library with a sleepy face and tumbled hair.

They told him the story, whereat he laughed heartily, and said the maids were a foolish set to be scared by a shadow. While he still laughed and joked, Mrs. Snowdon entered, looking alarmed, and anxious to know the cause of the confusion.

"How interesting! I never knew you kept a ghost. Tell me all about it, Sir Jasper, and soothe our nerves by satisfying our curiosity," she said in her half-persuasive, half-commanding way, as she seated herself on Lady Treherne's sacred sofa.

"There's not much to tell, except that this place used to be an abbey, in fact as well as in name. An ancestor founded it, and for years the monks led a jolly life here, as one may see, for the cellar is twice as large as the chapel, and much better preserved. But another ancestor, a gay and gallant baron, took a fancy to the site for his castle, and, in spite of prayers, anathemas, and excommunication, he turned the poor fellows out, pulled down the abbey, and built this fine old place. Abbot Boniface, as he left his abbey, uttered a heavy curse on all who should live here, and vowed to haunt us till the last Treherne vanished from the face of the earth. With this amiable threat the old party left Baron Roland to his doom, and died as soon as he could in order to begin his cheerful mission."

"Did he haunt the place?" asked Blanche eagerly.

"Yes, most faithfully from that time to this. Some say many of the monks still glide about the older parts of the abbey, for Roland spared the chapel and the north gallery which joined it to the modern building. Poor fellows, they are welcome, and once a year they shall have a chance to warm their ghostly selves by the great fires always kindled at Christmas in the gallery."

"Mrs. Benson once told me that when the ghost walked, it was a sure sign of a coming death in the family. Is that true?" asked Rose, whose curiosity was excited by the expression of Octavia's face, and a certain uneasiness in Sir Jasper's manner in spite of his merry mood.

"There is a stupid superstition of that sort in the family, but no one except the servants believes it, of course. In times of illness some silly maid or croaking old woman can easily fancy they see a phantom, and, if death comes, they are sure of the ghostly warning. Benson saw it before my father died, and old Roger, the night my uncle was seized with apoplexy. Patty will never be made to believe that this warning does not forebode the death of Maurice or myself, for the gallant spirit leaves the ladies of our house to depart in peace. How does it strike you, cousin?"

Turning as he spoke, Sir Jasper glanced at Treherne, who had entered while he spoke.

"I am quite skeptical and indifferent to the whole affair, but I agree with Octavia that it is best to say nothing to my aunt if she is ignorant of the matter. Her rooms are a long way off, and perhaps she did not hear the confusion."

"You seem to hear everything; you were not with us when I said that." And Octavia looked up with an air of surprise.

Smiling significantly, Treherne answered:

"I hear, see and understand many things that escape others. Jasper, allow me to advise you to smooth the hair which your sleep has disarranged. Mrs. Snowdon, permit me. This rich velvet catches the least speck." And with his handkerchief he delicately brushed away several streaks of white dust which clung to the lady's skirt.

Sir Jasper turned hastily on his heel and went to remake his toilet; Mrs. Snowdon bit her lip, but thanked Treherne sweetly and begged him to fasten her glove. As he did so, she said softly:

"Be more careful next time. Octavia has keen eyes, and the major may prove inconvenient."

"I have no fear that *you* will," he whispered back, with a malicious glance.

Here the entrance of my lady put an end to the ghostly episode, for it was evident that she knew nothing of it. Octavia slipped away to question John, and learn that no sign of a phantom was to be seen. Treherne devoted himself to Mrs. Snowdon, and the major entertained my lady, while Sir Jasper and the girls chatted apart.

It was Christmas-eve, and a dance in the great gallery was the yearly festival at the abbey. All had been eager for it, but the maid's story seemed to have lessened their enthusiasm, though no one would own it. This annoyed Sir Jasper, and he exerted himself to clear the atmosphere by affecting gaiety he did not feel. The moment the gentlemen came in after dinner he whispered to his mother, who rose, asked the general for his arm, and led the way to the north gallery, whence the sound of music now proceeded. The rest followed in a merry procession, even Treherne, for two footmen carried him up the great stairway, chair and all.

Nothing could look less ghostly now than the haunted gallery. Fires roared up a wide chimney at either end, long rows of figures clad in armor stood on each side, one mailed hand grasping a lance, the other bearing a lighted candle, a device of Sir Jasper's. Narrow windows pierced in the thick walls let in gleams of wintry moonlight; ivy, holly and evergreen glistened in the ruddy glow of mingled firelight and candle shine. From the arched stone roof hung tattered banners, and in the midst depended a great bunch of mistletoe. Red-cushioned seats stood in recessed window nooks, and from behind a high-covered screen of oak sounded the blithe air of Sir Roger de Coverly.

With the utmost gravity and stateliness my lady and the general led off the dance, for, according to the good old fashion, the men and maids in their best array joined the gentlefolk and danced with their betters in a high state of pride and bashfulness. Sir Jasper twirled the old housekeeper till her head spun around and around and her decorous skirts rustled stormily; Mrs. Snowdon captivated the gray-haired butler by her condescension, and John was made a proud man by the hand of his young mistress. The major came out strong among the pretty maids, and Rose danced the footmen out of breath long before the music paused.

The merriment increased from that moment, and when the general surprised my lady by gallantly saluting her as she unconsciously stood under the mistletoe, the applause was immense. Everyone followed the old gentleman's example as fast as opportunities occurred, and the young ladies soon had as fine a color as the housemaids. More dancing, games, songs and all manner of festival devices filled the evening, yet under cover of the gaiety more than one little scene was enacted that night, and in an hour of seeming frivolity the current of several lives was changed.

By a skillful manœuvre Annon led Octavia to an isolated recess, as if to rest after a brisk game, and, taking advantage of the auspicious hour, pleaded his suit. She heard him patiently and, when he paused, said slowly, yet decidedly, and with no sign of maiden hesitation:

"Thanks for the honor you do me, but I cannot accept it, for I do not love you. I think I never can."

"Have you tried?" he asked eagerly.

"Yes, indeed I have. I like you as a friend, but no more. I know mamma desires it, that Jasper hopes for it, and I try to please them, but love will not be forced, so what can I do?" And she smiled in spite of herself at her own blunt simplicity.

"No, but it can be cherished, strengthened, and in time won, with patience and devotion. Let me try, Octavia; it is but fair, unless you have already learned from another the lesson I hope to teach. Is it so?"

"No, I think not. I do not understand myself as yet, I am so young, and this so sudden. Give me time, Frank."

She blushed and fluttered now, looked half angry, half beseeching, and altogether lovely.

"How much time shall I give? It cannot take long to read a heart like yours, dear." And fancying her emotion a propitious omen, he assumed the lover in good earnest.

"Give me time till the New Year. I will answer then, and, meantime, leave me free to study both myself and you. We have known each other long, I own, but, still, this changes everything, and makes you seem another person. Be patient, Frank, and I will try to make my duty a pleasure."

"I will. God bless you for the kind hope, Octavia. It has been mine for years, and if I lose it, it will go hardly with me."

Later in the evening General Snowdon stood examining the antique screen. In many places carved oak was pierced quite through, so that voices were audible from behind it. The musicians had gone down to supper, the young folk were quietly busy at the other end of the hall, and as the old gentleman admired the quaint carving, the sound of his own name caught his ear. The housekeeper and butler still remained, though the other servants had gone, and sitting cosily behind the screen chatted in low tones believing themselves secure.

"It *was* Mrs. Snowdon, Adam, as I'm a living woman, though I wouldn't say it to anyone but you. She and Sir Jasper were here wrapped in cloaks, and up to mischief, I'll be bound. She is a beauty, but I don't envy her, and there'll be trouble in the house if she stays long."

"But how do you know, Mrs. Benson, she was here? Where's your proof, mum?" asked the pompous butler.

"Look at this, and then look at the outlandish trimming of the lady's dress. You men are so dull about such matters you'd never observe these little points. Well, I was here first after Patty, and my light shone on this jet ornament lying near where she saw the spirit. No one has any such tasty trifles but Mrs. Snowdon, and these are all over her gown. If that ain't proof, what is?"

"Well, admitting it, I then say what on earth should she and Master be up here for, at such a time?" asked the slow-witted butler.

"Adam, we are old servants of the family, and to you I'll say what tortures shouldn't draw from to another. Master has been wild, as you know, and it's my belief that he loved this lady abroad. There was a talk of some mystery, or misdeed, or misfortune, more than a year ago, and she was in it. I'm loath to say it, butI think master loves her still, and she him. The general is an old man, she is but young, and so spirited and winsome she can't in reason care for him as for a fine, gallant gentleman like Sir Jasper. There's trouble brewing, Adam, mark my words. There's trouble brewing for the Trehernes."

So low had the voices fallen that the listener could not have caught the words had not his ear been strained to the utmost. He did hear all, and his wasted face flashed with the wrath of a young man, then grew pale and stern as he turned to watch his wife. She stood apart from the others talking to Sir Jasper, who looked unusually handsome and debonair as he fanned her with a devoted air.

"Perhaps it is true," thought the old man, bitterly. They are well matched, were lovers once, no doubt, and long to be so again. Poor Edith, I was very blind. And with his gray head bowed upon his breast the general stole away, carrying an arrow in his brave old heart.

"Blanche, come here and rest, you will be ill to-morrow; and I promised mamma to take care of you." With which elder-sisterly command Rose led the girl to an immense old chair, which held them both. "Now listen to me and follow my advice, for I am wise in my generation, though not yet gray. They are all busy, so leave them alone, and let me show you what is to be done."

Rose spoke softly, but with great resolution, and nodded her pretty head so energetically that the holly-berries came rolling over her white shoulders.

"We are not as rich as we might be, and must establish ourselves as soon and as well as possible. I intend to be Lady Treherne. You can be the Honorable Mrs. Annon, if you give your mind to it."

"My dear child, are you mad?" whispered Blanche.

"Far from it, but you will be if you waste your time on Maurice. He is poor, and a cripple, though very charming, I admit. He loves Tavie, and she will marry him, I am sure. She can't endure Frank, but tries to because my lady commands it. Nothing will come of it, so try your fascinations and comfort the poor man; sympathy now will foster love hereafter."

"Don't talk so here, Rose, someone will hear us," began her sister, but the other broke in briskly:

"No fear, a crowd is the best place for secrets. Now remember what I say, and make your game while the ball is rolling. Other people are careful not to put their plans into words, but I'm no hypocrite, and say plainly what I mean. Bear my sage counsel in mind and act wisely. Now come and begin."

Treherne was sitting alone by one of the great fires, regarding the gay scene with serious air. For him there was neither dancing nor games; he could only roam about catching glimpses of forbidden pleasures, impossible delights and youthful hopes forever lost to him. Sad but not morose was his face, and to Octavia it was a mute reproach which she could not long resist. Coming up as if to warm herself, she spoke to him in her usually frank and friendly way, and felt her heart beat fast when she saw how swift a change her cordial manner wrought in him.

"How pretty your holly is! Do you remember how we used to go and gather it for festivals like this, when we were happy children?" he asked, looking up at her with eyes full of tender admiration.

"Yes, I remember. Everyone wears it to-night as a badge, but you have none. Let me get you a bit, I like to have you one of us in all things."

She leaned forward to break a green sprig from the branch over the chimney-piece; the strong draft drew in her fleecy skirt, and in an instant she was enveloped in flames.

"Maurice, save me, help me!" cried a voice of fear and agony, and before anyone could reach her, before he himself knew how the deed was done, Treherne had thrown himself from his chair, wrapt the tiger skin tightly about her, and knelt there clasping her in his arms heedless of fire, pain or the incoherent expressions of love that broke from his lips.

VI

MIRACLES

GREAT WAS THE CONFUSION AND ALARM WHICH REIGNED FOR MANY minutes, but when the panic subsided two miracles appeared. Octavia was entirely uninjured, and Treherne was standing on his feet, a thing which for months he had not done without crutches. In the excitement of the moment, no one observed the wonder; all were crowding about the girl, who, pale and breathless but now self-possessed, was the first to exclaim, pointing to her cousin, who had drawn himself up, with the help of his chair, and leaned there smiling, with a face full of intense delight.

"Look at Maurice! Oh, Jasper, help him or he'll fall!"

Sir Jasper sprung to his side and put a strong arm about him, while a chorus of wonder, sympathy and congratulations rose about them.

"Why, lad, what does it mean? Have you been deceiving us all this time?" cried Jasper, as Treherne leaned on him, looking exhausted but truly happy.

"It means that I am not to be a cripple all my life; that they did not deceive me when they said a sudden shock might electrify me with a more potent magnetism than any they could apply. It *has*, and if I am cured I owe it all to you, Octavia."

He stretched his hands to her with a gesture of such passionate gratitude that the girl covered her face to hide its traitorous tenderness, and my lady went to him, saying brokenly, as she embraced him with maternal warmth:

"God bless you for this act, Maurice, and reward you with a perfect cure. To you I owe the lives of both my children; how can I thank you as I ought?"

"I dare not tell you yet," he whispered eagerly, then added, "I am growing faint, aunt, get me away before I make a scene."

This hint recalled my lady to her usual state of dignified self-possession. Bidding Jasper and the major help Treherne to his room without delay, she begged Rose to comfort her sister, who was sobbing hysterically, and as they all obeyed her, she led her daughter away to her own apartment, for the festivities of the evening were at an end. At the same time Mrs. Snowdon and Annon bade my lady good-night, as if they also were about to retire, but as they reached the door of the gallery Mrs. Snowdon paused and beckoned Annon back. They were alone now, and, standing before the fire which had so nearly made that Christmas Eve a tragical one, she turned to him with a face full of interest and sympathy as she said, nodding toward the blackened shreds of Octavia's dress, and the scorched tiger skin which still lay at their feet:

"That was both a fortunate and an unfortunate little affair, but I fear Maurice's gain will be your loss. Pardon my frankness for Octavia's sake; she is a fine creature, and I long to see her given to one worthy of her. I am a woman to read faces quickly; I know that your suit does not prosper as you would have it, and I desire to help you—may I?"

"Indeed you may, and command any service of me in return. But to what do I owe this unexpected friendliness?" cried Annon, both grateful and surprised.

"To my regard for the young lady, my wish to save her from an unworthy man."

"Do you mean Treherne?" asked Annon, more and more amazed.

"I do. Octavia must not marry a gambler!"

"My dear lady, you labor under some mistake; Treherne is by no means a gambler. I owe him no good-will, but I cannot hear him slandered."

"You are generous, but I am not mistaken. Can you, on your honor, assure me that Maurice never played?"

Mrs. Snowdon's keen eyes were on him, and he looked embarrassed for a moment, but answered with some hesitation:

"Why, no, I cannot say that, but I can assure you that he is not an habitual gambler. All young men of his rank play more or less, especially abroad. It is merely an amusement with most, and among men is not considered dishonorable or dangerous. Ladies think differently, I believe, at least in England."

At the word "abroad," Mrs. Snowdon's face brightened, and she suddenly dropped her eyes, as if afraid of betraying some secret purpose.

"Indeed we do, and well we may, many of us having suffered from this pernicious habit. I have had special cause to dread and condemn it, and the fear that Octavia should in time suffer what I have suffered as a girl urges me to interfere where otherwise I should be dumb. Mr. Annon, there was a rumor that Maurice was forced to quit Paris, owing to some dishonorable practices at the gaming-table. Is this true?"

"Nay, don't ask me; upon my soul I cannot tell you. I only know that something was amiss, but what I never learned. Various tales were whispered at the clubs, and Sir Jasper indignantly denied them all. The bravery with which Maurice saved his cousin, and the sad affliction which fell upon him, silenced the gossip, and it was soon forgotten."

Mrs. Snowdon remained silent for a moment, with brows knit in deep thought, while Annon uneasily watched her. Suddenly she glanced over her shoulder, drew nearer, and whispered cautiously:

"Did the rumors of which you speak charge him with—" and the last word was breathed into Annon's ear almost inaudibily.

He started, as if some new light broke on him, and stared at the speaker with a troubled face for an instant, saying hastily:

"No, but now you remind me that when an affair of that sort was discussed the other day Treherne looked very odd, and rolled himself away, as if it didn't interest him. I can't believe it, and yet it may be something of the kind. That would account for old Sir Jasper's whim, and Treherne's steady denial of any knowledge of the cause. How in heaven's name did you learn this?"

"My woman's wit suggested it, and my woman's will shall confirm or destroy the suspicion. My lady and Octavia evidently know nothing, but they shall if there is any danger of the girl's being won by him."

"You would not tell her!" exclaimed Annon.

"I will, unless you do it," was the firm answer.

"Never! To betray a friend, even to gain the woman I love, is a thing I cannot do; my honor forbids it."

Mrs. Snowdon smiled scornfully.

"Men's code of honor is a strong one, and we poor women suffer from it. Leave this to me; do your best, and if all other means fail, you may be glad to try my device to prevent Maurice from marrying his cousin. Gratitude and pity are strong allies, and if he recovers, his strong will will move heaven and earth to gain her. Good-night." And leaving her last words to rankle in Annon's mind, Mrs. Snowdon departed to endure sleepless hours full of tormenting memories, new-born hopes, and alternations of determination and despair.

Treherne's prospect of recovery filled the whole house with delight, for his patient courage and unfailing cheerfulness had endeared him to all. It was no transient amendment, for day by day he steadily gained strength and power, passing rapidly from chair to crutches, from crutches to a cane and a friend's arm, which was always ready for him. Pain returned with returning vitality, but he bore it with a fortitude that touched all who witnessed it. At times motion was torture, yet motion was necessary lest the torpidity should return, and Treherne took his daily exercise with unfailing perseverance, saying with a smile, though great drops stood upon his forehead:

"I have something dearer even than health to win. Hold me up, Jasper, and let me stagger on, in spite of everything, till my twelve turns are made."

He remembered Lady Treherne's words, "If you were well, I'd gladly give my girl to you." This inspired him with strength, endurance, and a happiness which could not be concealed. It overflowed in looks, words and acts; it infected everyone, and made these holidays the blithest the old abbey had seen for many a day.

Annon devoted himself to Octavia, and in spite of her command to be left in peace till the New Year, she was very kind—so kind that hope flamed up in his heart, though he saw that something like compassion often shone on him from her frank eyes, and her compliance had no touch of the tender docility which lovers long to see. She still avoided Treherne, but so skillfully that few observed the change but Annon and himself. In public Sir Jasper appeared to worship at the sprightly Rose's shrine, and she fancied her game was prospering well. But had any one peeped behind the scenes it would have been discovered that during the half hour before dinner, when everyone was in their dressing rooms and the general taking his nap, a pair of ghostly black figures flitted about the haunted gallery, where no servant ventured without orders. The major fancied himself the only one who had made this discovery, for Mrs. Snowdon affected Treherne's society in public, and was assiduous in serving and amusing the "dear convalescent," as she called him. But the general did not sleep; he too watched and waited, longing yet dreading to speak, and hoping that this was but a harmless freak of Edith's, for her caprices were many, and till now he had indulged them freely. This hesitation disgusted the major, who, being a bachelor, knew little of women's ways, and less of their powers of persuasion. The day before New Year he took a sudden resolution, and demanded a private interview with the general.

"I have come on an unpleasant errand, sir," he abruptly began, as the old man received him with an expression which rather daunted the major. "My friendship for Lady Treherne, and my guardianship of her children, makes me jealous of the honor of the family. I fear it is in danger, sir; pardon me for saying it, but your wife is the cause."

"May I trouble you to explain, Major Royston," was all the general's reply, as his old face grew stern and haughty.

"I will, sir, briefly. I happen to know from Jasper that there were love passages between Miss Dubarry and himself a year or more ago in Paris. A whim parted them, and she married. So far no reproach rests upon either, but since she came here it has been evident to others as well as myself that Jasper's affection has revived, and that Mrs. Snowdon does not reject and reprove it as she should. They often meet, and from Jasper's manner I am convinced that mischief is afloat. He is ardent, headstrong and utterly regardless of the world's opinion in some cases. I have watched them, and what I tell you is true."

"Prove it."

"I will. They meet in the north gallery, wrapt in dark cloaks, and play ghost if anyone comes. I concealed myself behind the screen last evening at dusk, and satisfied myself that my suspicions were correct. I heard little of their conversation, but that little was enough."

"Repeat it, if you please."

"Sir Jasper seemed pleading for some promise which she reluctantly gave, saying, 'While you live I will be true to my word with everyone but him. He will suspect, and it will be useless to keep it from him.' 'He will shoot me for this if he knows I am the traitor,' expostulated Jasper. 'He shall not know that; I can hoodwink him easily, and serve my purpose also.' 'You are mysterious, but I leave all to you and wait for my reward. When shall I have it, Edith?' She laughed, and answered so low I could not hear, for they left the gallery as they spoke. Forgive me, general, for the pain I inflict. You are the only person to whom I have spoken, and you are the only person who can properly and promptly prevent this affair from bringing open shame and scandal on an honorable house. To you I leave it, and will do my part with this infatuated young man if you will withdraw the temptation which will ruin him."

"I will, thank you, major; trust to me, and by tomorrow I will prove that I can act as becomes me."

The grief and misery in the general's face touched the major; he silently wrung his hand and went away, thanking heaven more fervently than ever that no cursed coquette of a woman had it in her power to break his heart.

While this scene was going on above, another was taking place in the library. Treherne sat there alone, thinking happy thoughts evidently, for his eyes shone and his lips smiled as he mused, while watching the splendors of a winter sunset. A soft rustle and the faint scent of violets warned him of Mrs. Snowdon's approach, and a sudden foreboding told him that danger was near. The instant he saw her face his fear was confirmed, for exultation, resolve and love met and mingled in the expression it wore. Leaning in the window recess, where the red light shone full on her lovely face and queenly figure, she said, softly yet with a ruthless accent below the softness:

"Dreaming dreams, Maurice, which will never come to pass, unless I will it. I know your secret, and I shall use it to prevent the fulfillment of the foolish hope you cherish."

"Who told you?" he demanded, with an almost fierce flash of the eye and an angry flush.

"I discovered it, as I warned you I should. My memory is good, I recall the gossip of long ago, I observe the faces, words and acts of those whom I suspect, and unconscious hints from them give me the truth."

"I doubt it"; and Treherne smiled securely.

She stooped and whispered one short sentence into his ear. Whatever it was it caused him to start up with a pale, panic-stricken face, and eye her as if she had pronounced his doom.

"Do you doubt it now?" she asked coldly.

"He told you! Even your skill and craft could not discover it alone," he muttered.

"Nay, I told you nothing was impossible to a determined woman. I needed no help, for I knew more than you think."

He sank down again in a despairing attitude and hid his face, saying mournfully, "I might have known you would hunt me down and dash my hopes when they were surest. How will you use this unhappy secret?"

"I will tell Octavia, and make her duty less hard. It will be kind to both of you, for even with her this memory would mar your happiness; and it saves her from the shame and grief of discovering, when too late, that she has given herself to a—"

"Stop!" he cried, in a tone that made her start and pale, as he rose out of his chair white with a stern indignation which awed her for a moment. "You shall not utter that word—you know but half the truth, and if you wrong me or trouble the girl I will turn traitor also, and tell the general the game you are playing with my cousin. You feign to love me as you feigned before, but his title is the bait now as then, and you fancy that by threatening to mar my hopes you will secure my silence, and gain your end."

"Wrong, quite wrong. Jasper is nothing to me; I use *him* as a tool, not you. If I threaten, it is to keep you from Octavia, who cannot forgive the past and love you for yourself, as I have done all these miserable months. You say I know but half the truth. Tell me the whole and I will spare you."

If ever a man was tempted to betray a trust it was Treherne then. A word, and Octavia might be his; silence, and she might be lost; for this woman was in earnest, and possessed the power to ruin his good name forever. The truth leaped to his lips and would have passed them, had not his eye fallen on the portrait of Jasper's father. This man had loved and sheltered the orphan all his life, had made of him a son, and, dying, urged him to guard and serve and save the rebellious youth he left, when most needing a father's care.

"I promised, and I will keep my promise at all costs," sighed Treherne, and with a gesture full of pathetic patience he waved the fair tempter from him, saying steadily, "I will never tell you, though you rob me of that which is dearer than my life. Go and work your will, but remember that when you might have won the deepest gratitude of the man you profess to love, you chose instead to earn his hatred and contempt."

Waiting for no word of hers, he took refuge in his room, and Edith Snowdon sank down upon the couch, struggling with contending emotions of love and jealousy, remorse and despair. How long she sat there she could not tell; an approaching step recalled her to herself, and looking up she saw Octavia. As the girl approached down the long vista of the drawing-rooms, her youth and beauty, innocence and candor touched that fairer and more gifted woman with an envy she had never known before. Something in the girl's face struck her instantly: a look of peace and purity, a sweet serenity more winning than loveliness, more impressive than dignity or grace. With a smile on her lips, yet a half-sad, half-tender light in her eyes, and a cluster of pale winter roses in her hand, she came on till she stood before her rival and, offering the flowers, said, in words as simple as sincere:

"Dear Mrs. Snowdon, I cannot let the last sun of the old year set on any misdeeds of mine for which I may atone. I have disliked, distrusted, and misjudged you, and now I come to you in all humility to say forgive me."

With the girlish abandon of her impulsive nature Octavia knelt down before the woman who was plotting to destroy her happiness, laid the roses like a little peace-offering on her lap, and with eloquently pleading eyes waited for pardon. For a moment Mrs. Snowdon watched her, fancying it a well-acted ruse to disarm a dangerous rival; but in that sweet face there was no art; one glance showed her that. The words smote her to the heart and won her in spite of pride or passion, as she suddenly took the girl into her arms, weeping repentant tears. Neither spoke, but in the silence each felt the barrier which had stood between them vanishing, and each learned to know the other better in that moment than in a year of common life. Octavia rejoiced that the instinct which had prompted her to make this appeal had not misled her, but assured her that behind the veil of coldness, pride and levity which this woman wore there was a heart aching for sympathy and help and love. Mrs. Snowdon felt her worser self slip from her, leaving all that was true and noble to make her worthy of the test applied. Art she could meet with equal art, but nature conquered her. For spite of her misspent life and faulty character, the germ of virtue, which lives in the worst, was there, only waiting for the fostering sun and dew of love to strengthen it, even though the harvest be a late one.

"Forgive you!" she cried, brokenly. "It is I who should ask forgiveness of you—I who should atone, confess and repent. Pardon *me*, pity me, love me, for I am more wretched than you know."

"Dear, I do with heart and soul. Believe it, and let me be your friend" was the soft answer.

"God knows I need one!" sighed the poor woman, still holding fast the only creature who had wholly won her. "Child, I am not good, but not so bad that I dare not look in your innocent face and call you friend. I never had one of my own sex. I never knew my mother; and no one ever saw in me the possibility of goodness, truth and justice but you. Trust and love and help me, Octavia, and I will reward you with a better life, if I can do no more."

"I will, and the new year shall be happier than the old."

"God bless you for that prophecy; may I be worthy of it."

Then as a bell warned them away, the rivals kissed each other tenderly, and parted friends. As Mrs. Snowdon entered her room, she saw her husband sitting with his gray head in his hands, and heard him murmur despairingly to himself:

"My life makes her miserable. But for the sin of it I'd die to free her."

"No, live for me, and teach me to be happy in your love."

The clear voice startled him, but not so much as the beautiful changed face of the wife who laid the gray head on her bosom, saying tenderly:

"My kind and patient husband, you have been deceived. From me you shall know all the truth, and when you have forgiven my faulty past, you shall see how happy I will try to make your future."

VII

A GHOSTLY REVEL

"BLESS ME, HOW DULL WE ARE TO-NIGHT!" EXCLAIMED ROSE, AS THE younger portion of the party wandered listlessly about the drawing-rooms that evening, while my lady and the major played an absorbing game of piquet, and the general dozed peacefully at last.

"It is because Maurice is not here; he always keeps us going, for he is a fellow of infinite resources," replied Sir Jasper, suppressing a yawn.

"Have him out then," said Annon.

"He won't come. The poor lad is blue tonight, in spite of his improvement. Something is amiss, and there is no getting a word from him."

"Sad memories afflict him, perhaps," sighed Blanche.

"Don't be absurd, dear, sad memories are all nonsense; melancholy is always indigestion, and nothing is so sure a cure as fun," said Rose briskly. "I'm going to send in a polite invitation begging him to come and amuse us. He'll accept, I haven't a doubt."

The message was sent, but to Rose's chagrin a polite refusal was returned.

"He *shall* come. Sir Jasper, do you and Mr. Annon go as a deputation from us, and return without him at your peril" was her command.

They went, and while waiting their re-appearance the sisters spoke of what all had observed.

"How lovely Mrs. Snowdon looks to-night. I always thought she owed half her charms to her skill in dress, but she never looked so beautiful as in that plain black silk, with those roses in her hair," said Rose.

"What has she done to herself?" replied Blanche. "I see a change, but can't account for it. She and Tavie have made some beautifying discovery, for both look altogether uplifted and angelic all of a sudden."

"Here come the gentlemen, and, as I'm a Talbot, they haven't got him!" cried Rose as the deputation appeared, looking very crestfallen. "Don't come near me," she added, irefully, "you are disloyal cowards, and I doom you to exile till I want you. *I* am infinite in resources as well as this recreant man, and come he shall. Mrs. Snowdon, would you mind asking Mr. Treherne to suggest something to wile away the rest of this evening? we are in despair, and can think of nothing, and you are all-powerful with him."

"I must decline, since he refuses you," was the decided answer, as Mrs. Snowdon moved away.

"Tavie, dear, do go; we *must* have him; he always obeys you, and you would be such a public benefactor, you know."

Without a word Octavia wrote a line and sent it by a servant. Several minutes passed, and the gentlemen began to lay wagers on the success of her trial. "He will not come for me, you may be sure," said Octavia. As the words passed her lips he appeared.

A general laugh greeted him, but, taking no notice of the jests at his expense, he turned to Octavia, saying quietly, "What can I do for you, cousin?"

His colorless face and weary eyes reproached her for disturbing him, but it was too late for regret, and she answered hastily:

"We are in want of some new and amusing occupation to wile away the evening. Can you suggest something appropriate?"

"Why not sit round the hall fire and tell stories, while we wait to see the old year out, as we used to do long ago?" he asked, after a moment's thought.

"I told you so! There it is, just what we want." And Sir Jasper looked triumphant.

"It's capital—let us begin at once. It is after ten now, so we shall not have long to wait," cried Rose, and, taking Sir Jasper's arm, she led the way to the hall.

A great fire always burned there, and in winter time thick carpets and curtains covered the stone floor and draped the tall windows. Plants blossomed in the warm atmosphere, and chairs and lounges stood about invitingly. The party was soon seated, and Treherne was desired to begin.

"We must have ghost-stories, and in order to be properly thrilling and effective, the lights must be put out," said Rose, who sat next him, and spoke first, as usual.

This was soon done, and only a ruddy circle of firelight was left to oppose the rapt gloom that filled the hall, where shadows now seemed to lurk in every corner.

"Don't be very dreadful, or I shall faint away," pleaded Blanche, drawing nearer to Annon, for she had taken her sister's advice, and laid close siege to that gentleman's heart.

"I think your nerves will bear my little tale," replied Treherne. "When I was in India, four years ago, I had a very dear friend in my regiment—a Scotchman; I'm half Scotch myself, you know, and clannish, of course. Gordon was sent up the country on a scouting expedition, and never returned. His men reported that he left them one evening to take a survey, and his horse came home bloody and riderless. We searched, but could not find a trace of him, and I was desperate to discover and avenge his murder. About a month after his disappearance, as I sat in my tent one fearfully hot day, suddenly the canvas door flap was raised and there stood Gordon. I saw him as plainly as I see you, Jasper, and should have sprung to meet him, but something held me back. He was deathly pale, dripping with water, and in his bonny blue eyes was a wild, woeful look that made my blood run cold. I stared dumbly, for it was awful to see my friend so changed and so unearthly. Stretching his arm to me he took my hand, saying solemnly, 'Come!' The touch was like ice; an ominous thrill ran through me; I started up to obey, and he was gone."

"A horrid dream, of course. Is that all?" asked Rose.

With his eyes on the fire and his left hand half extended, Treherne went on as if he had not heard her.

"I thought it was a fancy, and soon recovered myself, for no one had seen or heard anything of Gordon, and my native servant lay just outside my tent. A strange sensation remained in the hand the phantom touched. It was cold, damp and white. I found it vain to try to forget this apparition; it took strong hold of me; I told Yermid, my man, and he bade me consider it a sign that I was to seek my friend. That night I dreamed I was riding up the country in hot haste; what led me I know not, but I pressed on and on, longing to reach the end. A half-dried river crossed my path, and, riding down the steep bank to ford it, I saw Gordon's body lying in the shallow water looking exactly as the vision looked. I woke in a strange mood, told the story to my commanding officer, and, as nothing was doing just then, easily got leave of absence for a week. Taking Yermid, I set out on my sad quest. I thought it folly, but I could not resist the impulse that drew me on. For seven days I searched, and the strangest part of the story is that all that time I went on exactly as in the dream, seeing what I saw then, and led by the touch of a cold hand on mine. On the seventh day I reached the river, and found my friend's body."

"How horrible!—is it really true?" cried Mrs. Snowdon.

"As true as I am a living man. Nor is that all: this left hand of mine never has been warm since that time. See and feel for yourselves."

He opened both hands, and all satisfied themselves that the left was smaller, paler and colder than the right.

"Pray someone tell another story to put this out of my mind; it makes me nervous," said Blanche.

"I'll tell one, and you may laugh to quiet your nerves. I want to have mine done with, so that I can enjoy the rest with a free mind." With these words Rose began her tale in the good old fashion.

"Once upon a time, when we were paying a visit to my blessed grandmamma, I saw a ghost in this wise: The dear old lady was ill with a cold and kept her room, leaving us to mope, for it was very dull in the great lonely house. Blanche and

I were both homesick, but didn't like to leave till she was better, so we ransacked the library and solaced ourselves with all manner of queer books. One day I found grandmamma very low and nervous, and evidently with something on her mind. She would say nothing, but the next day was worse, and I insisted on knowing the cause, for the trouble was evidently mental. Charging me to keep it from Blanche, who was, and is, a sad coward, she told me that a spirit had appeared to her two successive nights. 'If it comes a third time, I shall prepare to die,' said the foolish old lady. 'No, you won't, for I'll come and stay with you and lay your ghost,' I said. With some difficulty I made her yield, and after Blanche was asleep I slipped away to grandmamma, with a book and candle for a long watch, as the spirit didn't appear till after midnight. She usually slept with her door unlocked, in case of fire or fright, and her maid was close by. That night I locked the door, telling her that spirits could come through the oak if they chose, and I preferred to have a fair trial. Well, I read and chatted and dozed till dawn and nothing appeared, so I laughed at the whole affair, and the old lady pretended to be convinced that it was all a fancy. Next night I slept in my own room, and in the morning was told that not only grandmamma but Janet had seen the spirit. All in white, with streaming hair, a pale face, and a red streak at the throat. It came and parted the bed-curtains, looking in a moment, and then vanished. Janet had slept with grandmamma and kept a lamp burning on the chimney, so both saw it. I was puzzled, but not frightened; I never am, and I insisted on trying again. The door was left unlocked, as on the previous night, and I lay with Grandmamma, a light burning as before. About two she clutched me as I was dropping off. I looked, and there, peeping in between the dark curtains, was a pale face with long hair all about it, and a red streak at the throat. It was very dim, the light being low, but I saw it, and after one breathless minute sprang up, caught my foot, fell down with a crash, and by the time I was around the bed, not a vestige of the thing appeared. I was angry, and vowed I'd succeed at all hazards, though I'll confess I was just a bit daunted. Next time Janet and I sat up in easy chairs, with bright lights burning, and both wide awake with the strongest coffee we could make. As the hour drew near we got nervous, and when the white shape came gliding in Janet hid her face. I didn't, and after one look was on the point of laughing, for the spirit was Blanche walking in her sleep. She wore a coral necklace in those days, and never took it off, and her long hair half hid her face, which had the unnatural, uncanny look somnambulists always wear. I had the sense to keep still and tell Janet what to do, so the poor child went back unwaked, and grandmamma's spirit never walked again for I took care of that."

"Why did you haunt the old lady?" asked Annon, as the laughter ceased.

"I don't know, unless it was that I wanted to ask leave to go home, and was afraid to do it awake, so tried when asleep. I shall not tell any story, as I was the heroine of this, but will give my turn to you, Mr. Annon," said Blanche, with a soft glance, which was quite thrown away, for the gentleman's eyes were fixed on Octavia, who sat on a low ottoman at Mrs. Snowdon's feet in the full glow of the fire-light.

"I've had very small experience in ghosts, and can only recall a little fright I once had when a boy at college. I'd been out to a party, got home tired, couldn't find my matches, and retired in the dark. Toward morning I woke, and glancing up to see if the dim light was dawn or moonshine I was horrified to see a coffin standing at the bed's foot. I rubbed my eyes to be sure I was awake, and looked with all my might. There it was, a long black coffin, and I saw the white plate in the dusk, for the moon was setting and my curtain was not drawn. 'It's some trick of the fellows,' I thought; 'I'll not betray myself, but keep cool.' Easy to say but hard to do, for it suddenly flashed into my mind that I might be in the wrong room. I glanced about, but there were the familiar objects as usual, as far as the indistinct light allowed me to see, and I made sure by feeling on the wall at the bed's head for my watchcase. It was there, and mine beyond a doubt, being peculiar in shape and fabric. Had I been to a college wine party I could have accounted for the vision, but a quiet evening in a grave professor's well-conducted family could produce no ill effects. 'It's an optical illusion, or a prank of my mates; I'll sleep and forget it,' I said, and for a time endeavored to do so, but curiosity overcame my resolve, and soon I peeped again. Judge of my horror when I saw the sharp white outline of a dead face, which seemed to be peeping up from the coffin. It gave me a terrible shock for I was but a lad and had been ill. I hid my face and quaked like a nervous girl, still thinking it some joke and too proud to betray fear lest I should be laughed at. How long I lay there I don't know, but when I looked again the face was farther out and the whole figure seemed rising slowly. The moon was nearly down, I had no lamp, and to be left in the dark with that awesome thing was more than I could bear. Joke or earnest, I must end the panic, and bolting out of my room I roused my neighbor. He told me I was mad or drunk, but lit a lamp and returned with me, to find my horror only a heap of clothes thrown on the table in such a way that, as the moon's pale light shot it, it struck upon my black student's gown, with a white card lying on it, and produced the effect of a coffin and plate. The face was a crumpled handkerchief, and what seemed hair a brown muffler. As the moon sank, these outlines changed and, incredible as it may seem, grew like a face. My friend not having had the fright enjoyed the joke, and 'coffins' was my sobriquet for a long while."

"You get worse and worse. Sir Jasper, do vary the horrors by a touch of fun, or I shall run away," said Blanche, glancing over her shoulder nervously.

"I'll do my best, and tell a story my uncle used to relate of his young days. I forget the name of the place, but it was some little country town famous among anglers. My uncle often went to fish, and always regretted that a deserted house near the trout stream was not occupied, for the inn was inconveniently distant. Speaking of this one evening as he lounged in the landlady's parlor, he asked why no one took it and let the rooms to strangers in the fishing season. 'For fear of the ghostissess, your honor,' replied the woman, and proceeded to tell, him that three distinct spirits haunted the house. In the garret was heard the hum of a wheel and the tap of high-heeled shoes, as the ghostly spinner went to and fro. In a chamber sounded the sharpening of a knife, followed by groans and the drip of blood. The cellar was made awful by a skeleton sitting on a half-buried box and chuckling fiendishly. It seems a miser lived there once, and was believed to have starved his daughter in the garret, keeping her at work till she died. The second spirit was that of the girl's rejected lover, who cut his throat in the chamber, and the third of the miser who was found dead on the money chest he was too feeble to conceal. My uncle laughed at all this, and offered to lay the ghosts if anyone would take the house.

"This offer got abroad, and a crusty old fellow accepted it, hoping to turn a penny. He had a pretty girl, whose love had been thwarted by the old man, and whose lover was going to sea in despair. My uncle knew this and pitied the young people. He had made acquaintance with a wandering artist, and the two agreed to conquer the prejudices against the house by taking rooms there. They did so, and after satisfying themselves regarding the noises, consulted a wise old woman as to the best means of laying the ghosts. She told them if any young girl would pass a night in each haunted room, praying piously the while, that all would be well. Peggy was asked if she would do it, and being a stout-hearted lass she consented, for a round sum, to try it. The first night was in the garret, and Peggy, in spite of the prophecies of the village gossips, came out alive, though listeners at the door heard the weird humming and tapping all night long. The next night all went well, and from that time no more sharpening, groaning, or dripping was heard. The third time she bade her friends good-bye and, wrapped in her red cloak, with a lamp and prayer book, went down into the cellar. Alas for pretty Peggy! When day came she was gone, and with her the miser's empty box, though his bones remained to prove how well she had done her work.

"The town was in an uproar, and the old man furious. Some said the devil had flown away with her, others that the bones were hers, and all agreed that henceforth another ghost would haunt the house. My uncle and the artist did their best to comfort the father, who sorely reproached himself for thwarting the girl's love, and declared that if Jack would find her he should have her. But Jack had sailed, and the old man 'was left lamenting.' The house was freed from its unearthly visitors, however, for no ghost appeared; and when my uncle left, old Martin found money and letter informing him that Peggy had spent her first two nights preparing for flight, and on the third had gone away to marry and sail with Jack. The noises had been produced by the artist, who was a ventriloquist, the skeleton had been smuggled from the surgeons, and the whole thing was a conspiracy to help Peggy and accommodate the fishermen."

"It is evident that roguery is hereditary," laughed Rose as the narrator paused.

"I strongly suspect that Sir Jasper the second was the true hero of that story," added Mrs. Snowdon.

"Think what you like, I've done my part, and leave the stage for you, madam."

"I will come last. It is your turn, dear." As Mrs. Snowdon softly uttered the last word, and Octavia leaned upon her knee with an affectionate glance, Treherne leaned forward to catch a glimpse of the two changed faces, and looked as if bewildered when both smiled at him, as they sat hand in hand while the girl told her story.

"Long ago a famous actress suddenly dropped dead at the close of a splendidly played tragedy. She was carried home, and preparations were made to bury her. The play had been gotten up with great care and expense, and a fine actor was the hero. The public demanded a repetition, and an inferior person was engaged to take the dead lady's part. A day's delay had been necessary, but when the night came the house was crowded. They waited both before and behind the curtain for the debut of the new actress, with much curiosity. She stood waiting for her cue, but as it was given, to the amazement of all, the great tragedienne glided upon the stage. Pale as marble, and with a strange fire in her eyes, strange pathos in her voice, strange power in her acting, she went through her part, and at the close vanished as mysteriously as she came. Great was the excitement that night, and intense the astonishment and horror next day when it was whispered abroad that the dead woman never had revived, but had lain in her coffin before the eyes of watchers all the evening, when hundreds fancied they were applauding her at the theater. The mystery never was cleared up, and Paris was divided by two opinions: one that some person marvelously like Madame Z. had personated her for the sake of a sensation; the other that the ghost of the dead actress, unable to free itself from the old duties so full of fascination to an ambitious and successful woman, had played for the last time the part which had made her famous."

"Where did you find that, Tavie? It's very French, and not bad if you invented it," said Sir Jasper.

"I read it in an old book, where it was much better told. Now, Edith, there is just time for your tale."

As the word "Edith" passed her lips, again Treherne started and eyed them both, and again they smiled, as Mrs. Snowdon caressed the smooth cheek leaning on her knee, and looking full at him began the last recital.

"You have been recounting the pranks of imaginary ghosts; let me show you the workings of some real spirits, evil and good, that haunt every heart and home, making its misery or joy. At Christmastime, in a country house, a party of friends met to keep the holidays, and very happily they might have done so had not one person marred the peace of several. Love, jealousy, deceit and nobleness were the spirits that played their freaks with these people. The person of whom I speak was more haunted than the rest, and much tormented, being willful, proud and jealous. Heaven help her, she had had no one to exorcise these ghosts for her, and they goaded her to do much harm. Among these friends there were more than one pair of lovers, and much tangling of plots and plans, for hearts are wayward and mysterious things, and cannot love as duty bids or prudence counsels. This woman held the key to all the secrets of the house, and, having a purpose to gain, she used her power selfishly, for a time. To satisfy a doubt, she feigned a fancy for a gentleman who once did her the honor of admiring her, and, to the great scandal of certain sage persons, permitted him to show his regard for her, knowing that it was but a transient amusement on his part as well as upon hers. In the hands of this woman lay a secret which could make or mar the happiness of the best and dearest of the party. The evil spirits which haunted her urged her to mar their peace and gratify a sinful hope. On the other side, honor, justice, and generosity prompted her to make them happy, and while she wavered there came to her a sweet enchantress who, with a word, banished the tormenting ghosts forever, and gave the haunted woman a talisman to keep her free henceforth."

There the earnest voice faltered, and with a sudden impulse Mrs. Snowdon bent her head and kissed the fair forehead which had bent lower and lower as she went on. Each listener understood the truth, lightly veiled in that hasty fable, and each found in it a different meaning. Sir Jasper frowned and bit his lips, Annon glanced anxiously from face to face, Octavia hid hers, and Treherne's flashed with sudden intelligence, while Rose laughed low to herself, enjoying the scene. Blanche, who was getting sleepy, said, with a stifled gape, "That is a very nice, moral little story, but I wish there had been some real ghosts in it."

"There was. Will you come and see them?"

As she put the question, Mrs. Snowdon rose abruptly, wishing to end the seance, and beckoning them to follow glided up the great stairway. All obeyed, wondering what whim possessed her, and quite ready for any jest in store for them.

VIII

JASPER

SHE LED THEM TO THE NORTH GALLERY AND, PAUSING AT THE DOOR, said merrily:

"The ghost—or ghosts rather, for there were two—which frightened Patty were Sir Jasper and myself, meeting to discuss certain important matters which concerned Mr. Treherne. If you want to see spirits we will play phantom for you, and convince you of our power."

"Good, let us go and have a ghostly dance, as a proper finale of our revel," answered Rose as they flocked into the long hall.

At that moment the great clock struck twelve, and all paused to bid the old year adieu. Sir Jasper was the first to speak, for, angry with Mrs. Snowdon, yet thankful to her for making a jest to others of what had been earnest to him, he desired to hide his chagrin under a gay manner; and taking Rose around the waist was about to waltz away as she proposed, saying cheerily:

"Come one and all, and dance the new year in,"

when a cry from Octavia arrested him, and turning he saw her stand, pale and trembling, pointing to the far end of the hall.

Eight narrow Gothic windows pierced either wall of the north gallery. A full moon sent her silvery light strongly in upon the eastern side, making broad bars of brightness across the floor. No fires burned there now, and wherever the moonlight did not fall deep shadows lay. As Octavia cried out, all looked, and all distinctly saw a tall, dark figure moving noiselessly across the second bar of light far down the hall.

"Is it some jest of yours?" asked Sir Jasper of Mrs. Snowdon, as the form vanished in the shadow.

"No, upon my honor, I know nothing of it! I only meant to relieve Octavia's superstitious fears by showing her our pranks," was the whispered reply as Mrs. Snowdon's cheek paled, and she drew nearer to Jasper.

"Who is there?" called Treherne in a commanding tone.

No answer, but a faint, cold breath of air seemed to sigh along the arched roof and die away as the dark figure crossed the third streak of moonlight. A strange awe fell upon them all, and no one spoke, but stood watching for the appearance of the shape. Nearer and nearer it came, with soundless steps, and as it reached the sixth window its outlines were distinctly visible. A tall, wasted figure, all in black, with a rosary hanging from the girdle, and a dark beard half concealing the face.

"The Abbot's ghost, and very well got up," said Annon, trying to laugh but failing decidedly, for again the cold breath swept over them, causing a general shudder.

"Hush!" whispered Treherne, drawing Octavia to his side with a protecting gesture.

Once more the phantom appeared and disappeared, and as they waited for it to cross the last bar of light that lay between it and them, Mrs. Snowdon stepped forward to the edge of the shadow in which they stood, as if to confront the apparition alone. Out of the darkness it came, and in the full radiance of the light it paused. Mrs. Snowdon, being nearest, saw the face first, and uttering a faint cry dropped down upon the stone floor, covering up her eyes. Nothing human ever wore a look like that of the ghastly, hollow-eyed, pale-lipped countenance below the hood. All saw it and held their breath as it slowly raised a shadowy arm and pointed a shriveled finger at Sir Jasper.

"Speak, whatever you are, or I'll quickly prove whether you are man or spirit!" cried Jasper fiercely, stepping forward as if to grasp the extended arm that seemed to menace him alone.

An icy gust swept through the hall, and the phantom slowly receded into the shadow. Jasper sprang after it, but nothing crossed the second stream of light, and nothing remained in the shade. Like one possessed by a sudden fancy he rushed down the gallery to find all fast and empty, and to return looking very strangely. Blanche had fainted away and Annon was bearing her out of the hall. Rose was clinging to Mrs. Snowdon, and Octavia leaned against her cousin, saying in a fervent whisper:

"Thank God it did not point at you!"

"Am I then dearer than your brother?" he whispered back.

There was no audible reply, but one little hand involuntarily pressed his, though the other was outstretched toward Jasper, who came up white and startled but firm and quiet. Affecting to make light of it, he said, forcing a smile as he raised Mrs. Snowdon:

"It is some stupid joke of the servants. Let us think no more of it. Come, Edith, this is not like your usual self."

"It was nothing human, Jasper; you know it as well as I. O, why did I bring you here to meet the warning phantom that haunts your house!"

"Nay, if my time is near the spirit would have found me out wherever I might be. I have no faith in that absurd superstition—I laugh at and defy it. Come down and drink my health in wine from the Abbot's own cellar."

But no one had heart for further gaiety, and, finding Lady Treherne already alarmed by Annon, they were forced to tell her all, and find their own bewilderment deepened by her unalterable belief in the evil omen.

At her command the house was searched, the servants cross-questioned, and every effort made to discover the identity of the apparition. All in vain; the house was as usual, and not a man or maid but turned pale at the idea of entering the gallery at midnight. At my lady's request, all promised to say no more upon the mystery, and separated at last to such sleep as they could enjoy.

Very grave were the faces gathered about the breakfast table next morning, and very anxious the glances cast on Sir Jasper as he came in, late as usual, looking uncommonly blithe and well. Nothing serious ever made a deep impression on his mercurial nature. Treherne had more the air of a doomed man, being very pale and worn, in spite of an occasional gleam of happiness as he looked at Octavia. He haunted Jasper like a shadow all the morning, much to that young gentleman's annoyance, for both his mother and sister hung about him with faces of ill-dissembled anxiety. By afternoon his patience gave out, and he openly rebelled against the tender guard kept over him. Ringing for his horse he said decidedly:

"I'm bored to death with the solemnity which pervades the house today, so I'm off for a brisk gallop, before I lose my temper and spirits altogether."

"Come with me in the pony carriage, Jasper. I've not had a drive with you for a long while, and should enjoy it so much," said my lady, detaining him.

"Mrs. Snowdon looks as if she needed air to revive her roses, and the pony carriage is just the thing for her, so I will cheerfully resign my seat to her," he answered laughing, as he forced himself from his mother's hand.

"Take the girls in the clarence, we all want a breath of air, and you are the best whip we know. Be gallant and say yes, dear."

"No, thank you, Tavie, that wont do. Rose and Blanche are both asleep, and you are dying to go and do likewise, after your vigils last night. As a man and a brother I beg you'll do so, and let me ride as I like."

"Suppose you ask Annon to join you—" began Treherne with well-assumed indifference; but Sir Jasper frowned and turned sharply on him, saying, half-petulantly, half-jocosely:

"Upon my life I should think I was a boy or a baby, by the manner in which you mount guard over me to-day. If you think I'm going to live in daily fear of some mishap, you are all much mistaken. Ghost or no ghost, I shall make merry while I can; a short life and a jolly one has always been my motto, you know, so fare you well till dinner time."

They watched him gallop down the avenue, and then went their different ways, still burdened with a nameless foreboding. Octavia strolled into the conservatory, thinking to refresh herself with the balmy silence which pervaded the place, but Annon soon joined her, full of a lover's hopes and fears.

"Miss Treherne, I have ventured to come for my answer. Is my New Year to be a blissful or a sad one?" he asked eagerly.

"Forgive me if I give you an unwelcome reply, but I must be true, and so regretfully refuse the honor you do me," she said sorrowfully.

"May I ask why?"

"Because I do not love you."

"And you do love your cousin," he cried angrily, pausing to watch her half-averted face.

She turned it fully toward him and answered, with her native sincerity, "Yes, I do, with all my heart, and now my mother will not thwart me, for Maurice has saved my life, and I am free to devote it all to him."

"Happy man, I wish I had been a cripple!" sighed Annon. Then with a manful effort to be just and generous, he added heartily, "Say no more, he deserves you; I want no sacrifice to duty; I yield, and go away, praying heaven to bless you now and always."

He kissed her hand and left her to seek my lady and make his adieus, for no persuasion could keep him. Leaving a note for Sir Jasper, he hurried away, to the great relief of Treherne and the deep regret of Blanche, who, however, lived in hopes of another trial later in the season.

"Here comes Jasper, mamma, safe and well," cried Octavia an hour or two later, as she joined her mother on the terrace, where my lady had been pacing restlessly to and fro nearly ever since her son rode away.

With a smile of intense relief she waved her handkerchief as he came clattering up the drive, and seeing her he answered with hat and hand. He usually dismounted at the great-hall door, but a sudden whim made him ride along the wall that lay below the terrace, for he was a fine horseman, and Mrs. Snowdon was looking from her window. As he approached, the peacocks fled screaming, and one flew up just before the horse's eyes as his master was in the act of dismounting. The spirited creature was startled, sprang partway up the low, broad steps of the terrace, and, being sharply checked, slipped, fell, and man and horse rolled down together.

Never did those who heard it forget the cry that left Lady Treherne's lips as she saw the fall. It brought out both guests and servants, to find Octavia recklessly struggling with the frightened horse, and my lady down upon the stones with her son's bleeding head in her arms.

They bore in the senseless, shattered body, and for hours tried everything that skill and sciences could devise to save the young man's life. But every effort was in vain, and as the sun set Sir Jasper lay dying. Conscious at last, and able to speak, he looked about him with a troubled glance, and seemed struggling with some desire that overmastered pain and held death at bay.

"I want Maurice," he feebly said, at length.

"Dear lad, I'm here," answered his cousin's voice from a seat in the shadow of the half-drawn curtains.

"Always near when I need you. Many a scrape have you helped me out of, but this is beyond your power," and a faint smile passed over Jasper's lips as the past flitted before his mind. But the smile died, and a groan of pain escaped him as he cried, suddenly, "Quick! Let me tell it before it is too late! Maurice never will, but bear the shame all his life that my dead name may be untarnished. Bring Edith; she must hear the truth."

She was soon there, and, lying in his mother's arms, one hand in his cousin's, and one on his sister's bent head, Jasper rapidly told the secret which had burdened him for a year.

"I did it; I forged my uncle's name when I had lost so heavily at play that I dared not tell my mother, or squander more of my own fortune. I deceived Maurice, and let him think the cheque a genuine one; I made him present it and get the money, and when all went well I fancied I was safe. But my uncle discovered it secretly, said nothing, and, believing Maurice the forger, disinherited him. I never knew this till the old man died, and then it was too late. I confessed to Maurice, and he forgave me. He said, 'I am helpless now, shut out from the world, with nothing to lose or gain, and soon to be forgotten by those who once knew me, so let the suspicion of shame, if any such there be, still cling to me, and do you go your way, rich, happy, honorable and untouched by any shadow on your fame.' Mother, I let him do it, unconscious as he was that many knew the secret sin and fancied him the doer of it."

"Hush, Jasper, let it pass. I can bear it; I promised your dear father to be your staunch friend through life, and I have only kept my word."

"God knows you have, but now my life ends, and I cannot die till you are cleared. Edith, I told you half the truth, and you would have used it against him had not some angel sent this girl to touch your heart. You have done your part to atone for the past, now let me do mine. Mother, Tavie loves him, he has risked life and honor for me. Repay him generously and give him this."

With feeble touch Sir Jasper tried to lay his sister's hand in Treherne's as he spoke; Mrs. Snowdon helped him, and as my lady bowed her head in silent acquiescence, a joyful smile shone on the dying man's face.

"One more confession, and then I am ready," he said, looking up into the face of the woman whom he had loved with all the power of a shallow nature. "It was a jest to you, Edith, but it was bitter earnest to me, for I loved you, sinful as it was. Ask your husband to forgive me, and tell him it was better I should die than live to mar a good man's peace. Kiss me once, and make him happy for my sake."

She touched his cold lips with remorseful tenderness, and in the same breath registered a vow to obey that dying prayer.

"Tavie dear, Maurice, my brother, God bless you both. Good-by, Mother. He will be a better son than I have been to you." Then, the reckless spirit of the man surviving to the last, Sir Jasper laughed faintly, as he seemed to beckon some invisible shape, and died saying gaily, "Now, Father Abbot, lead on, I'll follow you."

A year later three weddings were celebrated on the same day and in the same church. Maurice Treherne, a well man, led up his cousin. Frank Annon rewarded Blanche's patient siege by an unconditional surrender, and, to the infinite amusement of Mrs. Grundy, Major Royston publicly confessed himself outgeneraled by merry Rose. The triple wedding feast was celebrated at Treherne Abbey, and no uncanny visitor marred its festivities, for never again was the north gallery haunted by the ghostly Abbot.

Marsyas in Flanders

Vernon Lee

I

"You are right. This is not the original crucifix at all. Another one has been put instead. *Il y a eu substitution,*" and the little old Antiquary of Dunes nodded mysteriously, fixing his ghostseer's eyes upon mine.

He said it in a scarce audible whisper. For it happened to be the vigil of the Feast of the Crucifix, and the once famous church was full of semi-clerical persons decorating it for the morrow, and of old ladies in strange caps, clattering about with pails and brooms. The Antiquary had brought me there the very moment of my arrival, lest the crowd of faithful should prevent his showing me everything next morning.

The famous crucifix was exhibited behind rows and rows of unlit candles and surrounded by strings of paper flowers and coloured muslin and garlands of sweet resinous maritime pine; and two lighted chandeliers illumined it.

"There has been an exchange," he repeated, looking round that no one might hear him. "*Il y a eu substitution.*"

For I had remarked, as anyone would have done, at the first glance, that the crucifix had every appearance of French work of the thirteenth century, boldly realistic, whereas the crucifix of the legend, which was a work of St. Luke, which had hung for centuries in the Holy Sepulchre at Jerusalem and been miraculously cast ashore at Dunes in 1195, would surely have been a more or less Byzantine image, like its miraculous companion of Lucca.

"But why should there have been a substitution?" I inquired innocently.

"Hush, hush," answered the Antiquary, frowning, "not here—later, later—"

He took me all over the church, once so famous for pilgrimages; but from which, even like the sea which has left it in a salt marsh beneath the cliffs, the tide of devotion has receded for centuries. It is a very dignified little church, of charmingly restrained and shapely Gothic, built of a delicate pale stone, which the sea damp has picked out, in bases and capitals and carved foliation, with stains of a lovely bright green. The Antiquary showed me where the transept and belfry had been left unfinished when the miracles had diminished in the fourteenth century. And he took me up to the curious warder's chamber, a large room up some steps in the triforium; with a fireplace and stone seats for the men who guarded the precious crucifix day and night. There had even been beehives in the window, he told me, and he remembered seeing them still as a child.

"Was it usual, here in Flanders, to have a guardroom in churches containing important relics?" I asked, for I could not remember having seen anything similar before.

"By no means," he answered, looking round to make sure we were alone, "but it was necessary here. You have never heard in what the chief miracles of this church consisted?"

"No," I whispered back, gradually infected by his mysteriousness, "unless you allude to the legend that the figure of the Saviour broke all the crosses until the right one was cast up by the sea?"

He shook his head but did not answer, and descended the steep stairs into the nave, while I lingered a moment looking down into it from the warder's chamber. I have never had so curious an impression of a church. The chandeliers on either side of the crucifix swirled slowly round, making great pools of light which were broken by the shadows of the clustered columns, and among the pews of the nave moved the flicker of the sacristan's lamp. The place was full of the scent of resinous pine branches, evoking dunes and mountainsides; and from the busy groups below rose a subdued chatter of women's voices, and a splash of water and clatter of pattens. It vaguely suggested preparations for a witches' sabbath.

"What sort of miracles did they have in this church?" I asked, when we had passed into the dusky square, "and what did you mean about their having exchanged the crucifix—about a *substitution?*"

It seemed quite dark outside. The church rose black, a vague lopsided mass of buttresses and high-pitched roofs, against the watery, moonlit sky; the big trees of the churchyard behind wavering about in the seawind; and the windows shone yellow, like flaming portals, in the darkness.

"Please remark the bold effect of the gargoyles," said the Antiquary pointing upwards.

They jutted out, vague wild beasts, from the roof-line; and, what was positively frightening, you saw the moonlight, yellow and blue through the open jaws of some of them. A gust swept through the trees, making the weathercock clatter and groan.

"Why, those gargoyle wolves seem positively to howl," I exclaimed.

The old Antiquary chuckled. "Aha," he answered, "did I not tell you that this church has witnessed things like no other church in Christendom? And it still remembers them! There—have you ever known such a wild, savage church before?"

And as he spoke there suddenly mingled with the sough of the wind and the groans of the weather-vane, a shrill quavering sound as of pipers inside.

"The organist trying his vox humana for tomorrow," remarked the Antiquary.

II

NEXT DAY I BOUGHT ONE OF THE PRINTED HISTORIES OF THE MIRACULOUS crucifix which they were hawking all round the church; and next day also, my friend the Antiquary was good enough to tell me all that he knew of the matter. Between my two informants, the following may be said to be the true story.

In the autumn of 1195, after a night of frightful storm, a boat was found cast upon the shore of Dunes, which was at that time a fishing village at the mouth of the Nys, and exactly opposite a terrible sunken reef.

The boat was broken and upset; and close to it, on the sand and bent grass, lay a stone figure of the crucified Saviour, without its cross and, as seems probable, also without its arms, which had been made of separate blocks. A variety of persons immediately came forward to claim it; the little church of Dunes, on whose glebe it was found; the Barons of Cröy, who had the right of jetsam on that coast, and also the great Abbey of St. Loup of Arras, as possessing the spiritual overlordship of the place. But a holy man who lived close by in the cliffs, had a vision which settled the dispute. St. Luke in person appeared and told him that he was the original maker of the figure; that it had been one of three which had hung round the Holy Sepulchre of Jerusalem; that three knights, a Norman, a Tuscan, and a man of Arras, had with the permission of Heaven stolen them from the Infidels and placed them on unmanned boats, that one of the images had been cast upon the Norman coast near Salenelles; that the second had run aground not far from the city of Lucca, in Italy, and that this third was the one which had been embarked by the knight from Artois. As regarded its final resting place, the hermit, on the authority of St. Luke, recommended that the statue should be left to decide the matter itself. Accordingly the crucified figure was solemnly cast back into the sea. The very next day it was found once more in the same spot, among the sand and bent grass at the mouth of the Nys. It was therefore deposited in the little church of Dunes; and very soon indeed the flocks of pious persons who brought it offerings from all parts made it necessary and possible to rebuild the church thus sanctified by its presence.

The Holy Effigy of Dunes—Sacra Dunarum Effigies as it was called—did not work the ordinary sort of miracles. But its fame spread far and wide by the unexampled wonders which became the constant accompaniment of its existence. The Effigy, as above mentioned, had been discovered without the cross to which it had evidently been fastened, nor had any researches or any subsequent storms brought the missing blocks to light, despite the many prayers which were offered for the purpose. After some time therefore, and a deal of discussion, it was decided that a new cross should be provided for the effigy to hang upon. And certain skilful stonemasons of Arras were called to Dunes for this purpose. But behold! the very day after the cross had been solemnly erected in the church, an unheard of and terrifying fact was discovered. The Effigy, which had been hanging perfectly straight the previous evening, had shifted its position, and was bent violently to the right, as if in an effort to break loose.

This was attested not merely by hundreds of laymen, but by the priests of the place, who notified the fact in a document, existing in the episcopal archives of Arras until 1790, to the Abbot of St. Loup their spiritual overlord.

This was the beginning of a series of mysterious occurrences which spread the fame of the marvellous crucifix all over Christendom. The Effigy did not remain in the position into which it had miraculously worked itself: it was found, at intervals of time, shifted in some other manner upon its cross, and always as if it had gone through violent contortions. And one day, about ten years after it had been cast up by the sea, the priests of the church and the burghers of Dunes discovered the Effigy hanging in its original outstretched, symmetrical attitude, but O wonder! with the cross, broken in three pieces, lying on the steps of its chapel.

Certain persons, who lived in the end of the town nearest the church, reported to have been roused in the middle of the night by what they had taken for a violent clap of thunder, but which was doubtless the crash of the Cross falling down, or perhaps, who knows? the noise with which the terrible Effigy had broken loose and spurned the alien cross from it. For that was the secret: the Effigy, made by a saint and come to Dunes by miracle, had evidently found some trace of unholiness in the stone to which it had been fastened. Such was the ready explanation afforded by the Prior of the church, in answer to an angry summons of the Abbot of St. Loup, who expressed his disapproval of such unusual miracles. Indeed, it was discovered that the piece of marble had not been cleaned from sinful human touch with the necessary rites before the figure was fastened on; a most grave, though excusable oversight. So a new cross was ordered, although it was noticed that much time was lost about it; and the consecration took place only some years later.

Meanwhile the Prior had built the warder's chamber, with the fireplace and recess, and obtained permission from the Pope himself that a clerk in orders should watch day and night, on the score that so wonderful a relic might be stolen. For the relic had by this time entirely cut out all similar crucifixes, and the village of Dunes, through the concourse of pilgrims, had rapidly grown into a town, the property of the now fabulously wealthy Priory of the Holy Cross.

The Abbots of St. Loup, however, looked upon the matter with an unfavourable eye. Although nominally remaining their vassals, the Priors of Dunes had contrived to obtain gradually from the Pope privileges which rendered them virtually independent, and in particular, immunities which sent to the treasury of St. Loup only a small proportion of the tribute money brought by the pilgrims. Abbot Walterius in particular, showed himself actively hostile. He accused the Prior of Dunes of having employed his warders to trump up stories of strange movements and sounds on the part of the still crossless Effigy, and of suggesting, to the ignorant, changes in its attitude which were more credulously believed in now that there was no longer the straight line of the cross by which to verify. So finally the new cross was made, and consecrated, and on Holy Cross Day of the year, the Effigy was fastened to it in the presence of an immense concourse of clergy and laity. The Effigy, it was now supposed, would be satisfied, and no unusual occurrences would increase or perhaps fatally compromise its reputation for sanctity.

These expectations were violently dispelled. In November, 1293, after a year of strange rumours concerning the Effigy, the figure was again discovered to have moved, and continued moving, or rather (judging from the position on the cross) writhing; and on Christmas Eve of the same year, the cross was a second time thrown down and dashed in pieces. The priest on duty was, at the same time, found, it was thought, dead, in his warder's chamber. Another cross was made and this time privately consecrated and put in place, and a hole in the roof made a pretext to close the church for a while, and to perform the rites of purification necessary after its pollution by workmen. Indeed, it was remarked that on this occasion the Prior of Dunes took as much trouble to diminish and if possible to hide away the miracles, as his predecessor had done his best to blazon the preceding ones abroad. The priest who had been on duty on the eventful Christmas Eve disappeared mysteriously, and it was thought by many persons that he had gone mad and was confined in the Prior's prison, for fear of the revelations he might make. For by this time, and not without some encouragement from the Abbots at Arras, extraordinary stories had begun to circulate about the goings-on in the church of Dunes. This church, be it remembered, stood a little above the town, isolated and surrounded by big trees. It was surrounded by the precincts of the Priory and, save on the water side, by high walls. Nevertheless, persons there were who affirmed that, the wind having been in that direction, they had heard strange noises come from the church of nights. During storms, particularly, sounds had been heard which were variously described as howls, groans, and the music of rustic dancing. A master mariner affirmed that one Halloween, as his boat approached the mouth of the Nys, he had seen the church of Dunes brilliantly lit up, its immense windows flaming. But he was suspected of being drunk and of having exaggerated the effect of the small light shining from the warder's chamber. The interest of the townsfolk of Dunes coincided with that of the Priory, since they prospered greatly by the pilgrimages, so these tales were promptly hushed up. Yet they undoubtedly reached the ear of the Abbot of St. Loup. And at last there came an event which brought them all back to the surface.

For, on the Vigil of All Saints, 1299, the church was struck by lightning. The new warder was found dead in the middle of the nave, the cross broken in two; and oh, horror! the Effigy was missing. The indescribable fear which overcame everyone was merely increased by the discovery of the Effigy lying behind the high altar, in an attitude of frightful convulsion, and, it was whispered, blackened by lightning.

This was the end of the strange doings at Dunes.

An ecclesiastical council was held at Arras, and the church shut once more for nearly a year. It was opened this time and re-consecrated by the Abbot of St. Loup, whom the Prior-of Holy Cross served humbly at mass. A new chapel had been built, and in it the miraculous crucifix was displayed, dressed in more splendid brocade and gems than usual, and its head nearly hidden by one of the most gorgeous crowns ever seen before; a gift, it was said, of the Duke of Burgundy.

All this new splendour, and the presence of the great Abbot himself was presently explained to the faithful, when the Prior came forward to announce that a last and greatest miracle had now taken place. The original cross, on which the figure had hung in the Church of the Holy Sepulchre, and for which the Effigy had spurned all others made by less holy hands, had been cast on the shore of Dunes, on the very spot where, a hundred years before, the figure of the Saviour had been discovered in the sands. "This," said the Prior, "was the explanation of the terrible occurrences which had filled all hearts with anguish. The Holy Effigy was now satisfied, it would rest in peace and its miraculous powers would be engaged only in granting the prayers of the faithful."

One-half of the forecast came true: from that day forward the Effigy never shifted its position, but from that day forward also, no considerable miracle was ever registered; the devotion of Dunes diminished, other relics threw the Sacred Effigy into the shade; and the pilgrimages dwindling to mere local gatherings, the church was never brought to completion.

What had happened? No one ever knew, guessed, or perhaps even asked. But, when in 1790 the Archiepiscopal palace of Arras was sacked, a certain notary of the neighbourhood bought a large portion of the archives at the price of waste paper, either from historical curiosity, or expecting to obtain thereby facts which might gratify his aversion to the clergy. These documents lay unexamined for many years, till my friend the Antiquary bought them. Among them taken helter skelter from the Archbishop's palace, were sundry papers referring to the suppressed Abbey of St. Loup of Arras, and among these latter, a series of notes concerning the affairs of the church of Dunes; they were, so far as their fragmentary nature explained, the minutes of an inquest made in 1309, and contained the deposition of sundry witnesses. To understand their meaning it is necessary to remember that this was the time when witch trials had begun, and when the proceedings against the Templars had set the fashion of inquests which could help the finances of the country while furthering the interests of religion.

What appears to have happened is that after the catastrophe of the Vigil of All Saints, October, 1299, the Prior, Urbain de Luc, found himself suddenly threatened with a charge of sacrilege and witchcraft, of obtaining miracles of the Effigy by devilish means, and of converting his church into a chapel of the Evil One.

Instead of appealing to high ecclesiastical tribunals, as the privileges obtained from the Holy See would have warranted, Prior Urbain guessed that this charge came originally from the wrathful Abbot of St. Loup, and, dropping all his pretensions in order to save himself, he threw himself upon the mercy of the Abbot whom he had hitherto flouted. The Abbot appears to have been satisfied by his submission, and the matter to have dropped after a few legal preliminaries, of which the notes found among the archiepiscopal archives of Arras represented a portion.

Some of these notes my friend the Antiquary kindly allowed me to translate from the Latin, and I give them here, leaving the reader to make what he can of them.

> Item. The Abbot expresses himself satisfied that His Reverence the Prior has had no personal knowledge of or dealings with the Evil One (Diabolus). Nevertheless, the gravity of the charge requires . . . — here the page is torn.
>
> Hugues Jacquot, Simon le Couvreur, Pierre Denis, burghers of Dunes, being interrogated, witness:
>
> That the noises from the Church of the Holy Cross always happened on nights of bad storms, and foreboded shipwrecks on the coast; and were very various, such as terrible rattling, groans, howls as of wolves, and occasional flute playing. A certain Jehan, who has twice been branded and flogged for lighting fires on the coast and otherwise causing ships to wreck at the mouth of the Nys, being promised immunity, after two or three slight pulls on the rack, witnesses as follows: That the band of wreckers to which he belongs always knew when a dangerous storm was brewing, on account of the noises which issued from the church of Dunes. Witness has often climbed the walls and prowled round in the churchyard, waiting to hear such noises. He was not unfamiliar with the howlings and roarings mentioned by the previous witnesses. He has heard tell by a countryman who passed in the night that the howling was such that the countryman thought himself pursued by a pack of wolves, although it is well known that no wolf has been seen in these parts for thirty years. But the witness himself is of the opinion that the most singular of all the noises, and the one which always accompanied or foretold the worst storms, was a noise of flutes and pipes (quod vulgo dicuntur flustes et musettes) so sweet that the King of France could not have sweeter at his Court. Being interrogated whether he had ever seen anything? the witness answers: "That he has seen the church brightly lit up from the sands; but on approaching found all dark, save the light from the warder's chamber. That once, by moonlight, the piping and fluting and howling being uncommonly loud, he thought he had seen wolves, and a human figure on the roof, but that he ran away from fear, and cannot be sure."

Item. His Lordship the Abbot desires the Right Reverend Prior to answer truly, placing his hand on the Gospels, whether or not he had himself heard such noises.

The Right Reverend Prior denies ever having heard anything similar. But, being threatened with further proceedings (the rack?) acknowledges that he had frequently been told of these noises by the Warder on duty.

Query: Whether the Right Reverend Prior was ever told anything else by the Warder?

Answer: Yes; but under the seal of confession. The last Warder, moreover, the one killed by lightning, had been a reprobate priest, having committed the greatest crimes and obliged to take asylum, whom the Prior had kept there on account of the difficulty of finding a man sufficiently courageous for the office.

Query: Whether the Prior has ever questioned previous Warders?

Answer: That the Warders were bound to reveal only in confession whatever they had heard, that the Prior's predecessors had kept the seal of confession inviolate, and that though unworthy, the Prior himself desired to do alike.

Query: What had become of the Warder who had been found in a swoon after the occurrences of Hallow Even?

Answer: That the Prior does not know. The Warder was crazy. The Prior believes he was secluded for that reason.

A disagreeable surprise had been, apparently, arranged for Prior Urbain de Luc. For the next entry states that:

Item. By order of His Magnificence the Lord Abbot, certain servants of the Lord Abbot aforesaid introduce Robert Baudouin priest, once Warder in the Church of the Holy Cross, who has been kept ten years in prison by His Reverence the Prior, as being of unsound mind. Witness manifests great terror on finding himself in the presence of their Lordships, and particularly of His Reverence the Prior. And refuses to speak, hiding his face in his hands and uttering shrieks. Being comforted with kind words by those present, nay even most graciously by My Lord the Abbot himself, *etiam* threatened with the rack if he continue obdurate, this witness deposes as follows, not without much lamentation, shrieking and senseless jabber after the manner of mad men.

Query: Can he remember what happened on the Vigil of All Saints, in the church of Dunes, before he swooned on the floor of the church?

Answer: He cannot. It would be sin to speak of such things before great spiritual Lords. Moreover he is but an ignorant man, and also mad. Moreover his hunger is great.

Being given white bread from the Lord Abbot's own table, witness is again cross-questioned.

Query: What can he remember of the events of the Vigil of All Saints?

Answer: Thinks he was not always mad. Thinks he has not always been in prison. Thinks he once went in a boat on sea, etc.

Query: Does witness think he has ever been in the church of Dunes?

Answer: Cannot remember. But is sure that he was not always in prison.

Query: Has witness ever heard anything like that? (My Lord the Abbot having secretly ordered that a certain fool in his service, an excellent musician, should suddenly play the pipes behind the Arras.)

At which sound witness began to tremble and sob and fall on his knees, and catch hold of the robe even of My Lord the Abbot, hiding his head therein.

Query: Wherefore does he feel such terror, being in the fatherly presence of so clement a prince as the Lord Abbot?

Answer: That witness cannot stand that piping any longer. That it freezes his blood. That he has told the Prior many times that he will not remain any longer in the warder's chamber. That he is afraid for his life. That he dare not make the sign of the Cross nor say his prayers for fear of the Great Wild Man. That the Great Wild Man took the Cross and broke it in two and played at quoits with it in the nave. That all the wolves trooped down from the roof howling, and danced on their hind legs while the Great Wild man played the pipes on the high altar. That witness had surrounded himself with a hedge of little crosses, made of broken rye straw, to keep off the Great Wild Man from the warder's chamber. Ah—ah—ah! He is piping again! The wolves are howling! He is raising the tempest.

Item. That no further information can be extracted from witness who falls on the floor like one possessed and has to be removed from the presence of His Lordship the Abbot and His Reverence the Prior.

III

HERE THE MINUTES OF THE INQUEST BREAK OFF. DID THOSE GREAT spiritual dignitaries ever get to learn more about the terrible doings in the church of Dunes? Did they ever guess at their cause?

"For there was a cause," said the Antiquary, folding his spectacles after reading me these notes, "or more strictly the cause still exists. And you will understand, though those learned priests of six centuries ago could not."

And rising, he fetched a key from a shelf and preceded me into the yard of his house, situated on the Nys, a mile below Dunes.

Between the low steadings one saw the salt marsh, lilac with sea lavender, the Island of Birds, a great sandbank at the mouth of the Nys, where every kind of sea fowl gathers; and beyond, the angry whitecrested sea under an angry orange afterglow. On the other side, inland, and appearing above the farm roofs, stood the church of Dunes, its pointed belfry and jagged outlines of gables and buttresses and gargoyles and wind-warped pines black against the easterly sky of ominous livid red.

"I told you," said the Antiquary, stopping with the key in the lock of a big outhouse, "that there had been a *substitution*; that the crucifix at present at Dunes is not the one miraculously cast up by the storm of 1195. I believe the present one may be identified as a life-size statue, for which a receipt exists in the archives of Arras, furnished to the Abbot of St. Loup by Estienne Le Mas and Guillaume Pernel, stonemasons, in the year 1299, that is to say the year of the inquest and of the cessation of all supernatural occurrences at Dunes. As to the original effigy, you shall see it and understand everything."

The Antiquary opened the door of a sloping, vaulted passage, lit a lantern and led the way. It was evidently the cellar of some mediaeval building, and a scent of wine, of damp wood, and of fir branches from innumerable stacked up faggots, filled the darkness among thickset columns.

"Here," said the Antiquary, raising his lantern, "he was buried beneath this vault and they had run an iron stake through his middle, like a vampire, to prevent his rising."

The Effigy was erect against the dark wall, surrounded by brushwood. It was more than life-size, nude, the arms broken off at the shoulders, the head, with stubbly beard and clotted hair, drawn up with an effort, the face contracted with agony; the muscles dragged as of one hanging crucified, the feet bound together with a rope. The figure was familiar to me in various galleries. I came forward to examine the ear: it was leaf-shaped.

"Ah, you have understood the whole mystery," said the Antiquary.

"I have understood," I answered, not knowing how far his thought really went, "that this supposed statue of Christ is an antique satyr, a Marsyas awaiting his punishment."

The Antiquary nodded. "Exactly," he said drily, "that is the whole explanation. Only I think the Abbot and the Prior were not so wrong to drive the iron stake through him when they removed him from the church."

The Dead Smile

F. Marion Crawford

I

Sir Hugh Ockram smiled as he sat by the open window of his study, in the late August afternoon; and just then a curiously yellow cloud obscured the low sun, and the clear summer light turned lurid, as if it had been suddenly poisoned and polluted by the foul vapours of a plague. Sir Hugh's face seemed, at best, to be made of fine parchment drawn skin-tight over a wooden mask, in which two eyes were sunk out of sight, and peered from far within through crevices under the slanting, wrinkled lids, alive and watchful like two toads in their holes, side by side and exactly alike. But as the light changed, then a little yellow glare flashed in each. Nurse Macdonald said once that when Sir Hugh smiled he saw the faces of two women in hell—two dead women he had betrayed. (Nurse Macdonald was a hundred years old.) And the smile widened, stretching the pale lips across the discoloured teeth in an expression of profound self-satisfaction, blended with the most unforgiving hatred and contempt for the human doll. The hideous disease of which he was dying had touched his brain. His son stood beside him, tall, white and delicate as an angel in a primitive picture; and though there was deep distress in his violet eyes as he looked at his father's face, he felt the shadow of that sickening smile stealing across his own lips and parting them and drawing them against his will. And it was like a bad dream, for he tried not to smile and smiled the more. Beside him, strangely like him in her wan, angelic beauty, with the same shadowy golden hair, the same sad violet eyes, the same luminously pale face, Evelyn Warburton rested one hand upon his arm. And as she looked into her uncle's eyes, and could not turn her own away, she knew that the deathly smile was hovering on her own red lips, drawing them tightly across her little teeth, while two bright tears ran down her cheeks to her mouth, and dropped from the upper to the lower lip while she smiled—and the smile was like the shadow of death and the seal of damnation upon her pure, young face.

"Of course," said Sir Hugh very slowly, and still looking out at the trees, "if you have made up your mind to be married, I cannot hinder you, and I don't suppose you attach the smallest importance to my consent—"

"Father!" exclaimed Gabriel reproachfully.

"No; I do not deceive myself," continued the old man, smiling terribly. "You will marry when I am dead, though there is a very good reason why you had better not—why you had better not," he repeated very emphatically, and he slowly turned his toad eyes upon the lovers.

"What reason?" asked Evelyn in a frightened voice.

"Never mind the reason, my dear. You will marry just as if it did not exist." There was a long pause. "Two gone," he said, his voice lowering strangely, "and two more will be four—all together—for ever and ever, burning, burning, burning bright."

At the last words his head sank slowly back, and the little glare of the toad eyes disappeared under the swollen lids; and the lurid cloud passed from the westering sun, so that the earth was green again and the light pure. Sir Hugh had fallen asleep, as he often did in his last illness, even while speaking.

Gabriel Ockram drew Evelyn away, and from the study they went out into the dim hall, softly closing the door behind them, and each audibly drew breath, as though some sudden danger had been passed. They laid their hands each in the other's, and their strangely-like eyes met in a long look, in which love and perfect understanding were darkened by the secret terror of an unknown thing. Their pale faces reflected each other's fear.

"It is his secret," said Evelyn at last. "He will never tell us what it is."

"If he dies with it," answered Gabriel, "let it be on his own head!"

"On his head!" echoed the dim hall. It was a strange echo, and some were frightened by it, for they said that if it were a real echo it should repeat everything and not give back a phrase here and there, now speaking, now silent. But Nurse Macdonald said that the great hall would never echo a prayer when an Ockram was to die, though it would give back curses ten for one.

"On his head!" it repeated quite softly, and Evelyn started and looked round.

"It is only the echo," said Gabriel, leading her away.

They went out into the late afternoon light, and sat upon a stone seat behind the chapel, which was built across the end of the east wing. It was very still, not a breath stirred, and there was no sound near them. Only far off in the park a songbird was whistling the high prelude to the evening chorus.

"It is very lonely here," said Evelyn, taking Gabriel's hand nervously, and speaking as if she dreaded to disturb the silence. "If it were dark, I should be afraid."

"Of what? Of me?" Gabriel's sad eyes turned to her.

"Oh no! How could I be afraid of you? But of the old Ockrams—they say they are just under our feet here in the north vault outside the chapel, all in their shrouds, with no coffins, as they used to bury them."

"As they always will—as they will bury my father, and me. They say an Ockram will not lie in a coffin."

"But it cannot be true—these are fairy tales—ghost stories!" Evelyn nestled nearer to her companion, grasping his hand more tightly, and the sun began to go down.

"Of course. But there is the story of old Sir Vernon, who was beheaded for treason under James II. The family brought his body back from the scaffold in an iron coffin with heavy locks, and they put it in the north vault. But ever afterwards, whenever the vault was opened to bury another of the family, they found the coffin wide open, and the body standing upright against the wall, and the head rolled away in a corner, smiling at it."

"As Uncle Hugh smiles?" Evelyn shivered.

"Yes, I suppose so," answered Gabriel, thoughtfully. "Of course I never saw it, and the vault has not been opened for thirty years—none of us have died since then."

"And if—if Uncle Hugh dies—shall you—" Evelyn stopped, and her beautiful thin face was quite white.

"Yes. I shall see him laid there too—with his secret, whatever it is." Gabriel sighed and pressed the girl's little hand.

"I do not like to think of it," she said unsteadily. "O Gabriel, what can the secret be? He said we had better not marry—not that he forbade it—but he said it so strangely, and he smiled—ugh!" Her small white teeth chattered with fear, and she looked over her shoulder while drawing still closer to Gabriel. "And, somehow, I felt it in my own face—"

"So did I," answered Gabriel in a low, nervous voice. "Nurse Macdonald—" He stopped abruptly.

"What? What did she say?"

"Oh—nothing. She has told me things—they would frighten you, dear. Come, it is growing chilly." He rose, but Evelyn held his hand in both of hers, still sitting and looking up into his face.

"But we shall be married, just the same—Gabriel! Say that we shall!"

"Of course, darling—of course. But while my father is so very ill, it is impossible—"

"O Gabriel, Gabriel, dear! I wish we were married now!" cried Evelyn in sudden distress. "I know that something will prevent it and keep us apart."

"Nothing shall!"

"Nothing?"

"Nothing human," said Gabriel Ockram, as she drew him down to her.

And their faces, that were so strangely alike, met and touched—and Gabriel knew that the kiss had a marvellous savour of evil, but on Evelyn's lips it was like the cool breath of a sweet and mortal fear. And neither of them understood, for they were innocent and young. Yet she drew him to her by her lightest touch, as a sensitive plant shivers and waves its thin leaves, and bends and closes softly upon what it wants; and he let himself be drawn to her willingly, as he would if her touch had been deadly and poisonous; for she strangely loved that half voluptuous breath of fear, and he passionately desired the nameless evil something that lurked in her maiden lips.

"It is as if we loved in a strange dream," she said.

"I fear the waking," he murmured.

"We shall not wake, dear—when the dream is over it will have already turned into death, so softly that we shall not know it. But until then—"

She paused, and her eyes sought his, and their faces slowly came nearer. It was as if they had thoughts in their red lips that foresaw and foreknew the deep kiss of each other.

"Until then—" she said again, very low, and her mouth was nearer to his.

"Dream—till then," murmured his breath.

II

Nurse Macdonald was a hundred years old. She used to sleep sitting all bent together in a great old leathern arm-chair with wings, her feet in a bag footstool lined with sheepskin, and many warm blankets wrapped about her, even in summer. Beside her a little lamp always burned at night by an old silver cup, in which there was something to drink.

Her face was very wrinkled, but the wrinkles were so small and fine and near together that they made shadows instead of lines. Two thin locks of hair, that was turning from white to a smoky yellow again, were drawn over her temples from under her starched white cap. Every now and then she woke, and her eyelids were drawn up in tiny folds like little pink silk curtains, and her queer blue eyes looked straight before her through doors and walls and worlds to a far place beyond. Then she slept again, and her hands lay one upon the other on the edge of the blanket; the thumbs had grown longer than the fingers with age, and the joints shone in the low lamplight like polished crab-apples.

It was nearly one o'clock in the night, and the summer breeze was blowing the ivy branch against the panes of the window with a hushing caress. In the small room beyond, with the door ajar, the girl-maid who took care of Nurse Macdonald was fast asleep. All was very quiet. The old woman breathed regularly, and her indrawn lips trembled each time as the breath went out, and her eyes were shut.

But outside the closed window there was a face, and violet eyes were looking steadily at the ancient sleeper, for it was like the face of Evelyn Warburton, though there were eighty feet from the sill of the window to the foot of the tower. Yet the cheeks were thinner than Evelyn's, and as white as a gleam, and the eyes stared, and the lips were not red with life; they were dead, and painted with new blood.

Slowly Nurse Macdonald's wrinkled eyelids folded themselves back, and she looked straight at the face at the window while one might count ten.

"Is it time?" she asked in her little old, faraway voice.

While she looked the face at the window changed, for the eyes opened wider and wider till the white glared all round the bright violet, and the bloody lips opened over gleaming teeth, and stretched and widened and stretched again, and the shadowy golden hair rose and streamed against the window in the night breeze. And in answer to Nurse Macdonald's question came the sound that freezes the living flesh.

That low-moaning voice that rises suddenly, like the scream of storm, from a moan to a wail, from a wail to a howl, from a howl to the fear-shriek of the tortured dead—he who has heard knows, and he can bear witness that the cry of the banshee is an evil cry to hear alone in the deep night. When it was over and the face was gone, Nurse Macdonald shook a little in her great chair, and still she looked at the black square of the window, but there was nothing more there, nothing but the night, and the whispering ivy branch. She turned her head to the door that was ajar, and there stood the girl in her white gown, her teeth chattering with fright.

"It is time, child," said Nurse Macdonald. "I must go to him, for it is the end."

She rose slowly, leaning her withered hands upon the arms of the chair, and the girl brought her a woollen gown and a great mantle, and her crutch-stick, and made her ready. But very often the girl looked at the window and was unjointed with fear, and often Nurse Macdonald shook her head and said words which the maid could not understand.

"It was like the face of Miss Evelyn," said the girl at last, trembling.

But the ancient woman looked up sharply and angrily, and her queer blue eyes glared. She held herself by the arm of the great chair with her left hand, and lifted up her crutch-stick to strike the maid with all her might. But she did not.

"You are a good girl," she said, "but you are a fool. Pray for wit, child, pray for wit—or else find service in another house than Ockram Hall. Bring the lamp and help me under my left arm."

The crutch-stick clacked on the wooden floor, and the low heels of the woman's slippers clappered after her in slow triplets, as Nurse Macdonald got toward the door. And down the stairs each step she took was a labour in itself, and by the clacking noise the waking servants knew that she was coming, very long before they saw her.

No one was sleeping now, and there were lights, and whisperings, and pale faces in the corridors near Sir Hugh's bedroom, and now some one went in, and now some one came out, but every one made way for Nurse Macdonald, who had nursed Sir Hugh's father more than eighty years ago.

The light was soft and clear in the room. There stood Gabriel Ockram by his father's bedside, and there knelt Evelyn Warburton, her hair lying like a golden shadow down her shoulders, and her hands clasped nervously together. And opposite Gabriel, a nurse was trying to make Sir Hugh drink. But he would not, and though his lips were parted, his teeth were set. He was very, very thin and yellow now, and his eyes caught the light sideways and were as yellow coals.

"Do not torment him," said Nurse Macdonald to the woman who held the cup. "Let me speak to him, for his hour is come."

"Let her speak to him," said Gabriel in a dull voice.

So the ancient woman leaned to the pillow and laid the feather-weight of her withered hand, that was like a brown moth, upon Sir Hugh's yellow fingers, and she spoke to him earnestly, while only Gabriel and Evelyn were left in the room to hear.

"Hugh Ockram," she said, "this is the end of your life; and as I saw you born, and saw your father born before you, I am come to see you die. Hugh Ockram, will you tell me the truth?"

The dying man recognised the little faraway voice he had known all his life, and he very slowly turned his yellow face to Nurse Macdonald; but he said nothing. Then she spoke again.

"Hugh Ockram, you will never see the daylight again. Will you tell the truth?"

His toad-like eyes were not yet dull. They fastened themselves on her face.

"What do you want of me?" he asked, and each word struck hollow upon the last. "I have no secrets. I have lived a good life."

Nurse Macdonald laughed—a tiny, cracked laugh, that made her old head bob and tremble a little, as if her neck were on a steel spring. But Sir Hugh's eyes grew red, and his pale lips began to twist.

"Let me die in peace," he said slowly.

But Nurse Macdonald shook her head, and her brown, moth-like hand left his and fluttered to his forehead.

"By the mother that bore you and died of grief for the sins you did, tell me the truth!"

Sir Hugh's lips tightened on his discoloured teeth.

"Not on earth," he answered slowly.

"By the wife who bore your son and died heartbroken, tell me the truth!"

"Neither to you in life, nor to her in eternal death."

His lips writhed, as if the words were coals between them, and a great drop of sweat rolled across the parchment of his forehead. Gabriel Ockram bit his hand as he watched his father die. But Nurse Macdonald spoke a third time.

"By the woman whom you betrayed, and who waits for you this night, Hugh Ockram, tell me the truth!"

"It is too late. Let me die in peace."

The writhing lips began to smile across the set yellow teeth, and the toad eyes glowed like evil jewels in his head.

"There is time," said the ancient woman. "Tell me the name of Evelyn Warburton's father. Then I will let you die in peace."

Evelyn started back, kneeling as she was, and stared at Nurse Macdonald, and then at her uncle.

"The name of Evelyn's father?" he repeated slowly, while the awful smile spread upon his dying face.

The light was growing strangely dim in the great room. As Evelyn looked, Nurse Macdonald's crooked shadow on the wall grew gigantic. Sir Hugh's breath came thick, rattling in his throat, as death crept in like a snake and choked it back. Evelyn prayed aloud, high and clear.

Then something rapped at the window, and she felt her hair rise upon her head in a cool breeze, as she looked around in spite of herself. And when she saw her own white face looking in at the window, and her own eyes staring at her through the glass, wide and fearful, and her own hair streaming against the pane, and her own lips dashed with blood, she rose slowly from the floor and stood rigid for one moment, till she screamed once and fell straight back into Gabriel's arms. But the shriek that answered hers was the fear-shriek of the tormented corpse, out of which the soul cannot pass for shame of deadly sins, though the devils fight in it with corruption, each for their due share.

Sir Hugh Ockram sat upright in his deathbed, and saw and cried aloud:

"Evelyn!" His harsh voice broke and rattled in his chest as he sank down. But still Nurse Macdonald tortured him, for there was a little life left in him still.

"You have seen the mother as she waits for you, Hugh Ockram. Who was this girl Evelyn's father? What was his name?"

For the last time the dreadful smile came upon the twisted lips, very slowly, very surely now, and the toad eyes glared red, and the parchment face glowed a little in the flickering light. For the last time words came.

"They know it in hell."

Then the glowing eyes went out quickly, the yellow face turned waxen pale, and a great shiver ran through the thin body as Hugh Ockram died.

But in death he still smiled, for he knew his secret and kept it still, on the other side, and he would take it with him, to lie with him for ever in the north vault of the chapel where the Ockrams lie uncoffined in their shrouds—all but one. Though he was dead, he smiled, for he had kept his treasure of evil truth to the end, and there was none left to tell the name he had spoken, but there was all the evil he had not undone left to bear fruit.

As they watched—Nurse Macdonald and Gabriel, who held Evelyn still unconscious in his arms while he looked at the father—they felt the dead smile crawling along their own lips—the ancient crone and the youth with the angel's face. Then they shivered a little, and both looked at Evelyn as she lay with her head on his shoulder, and, though she was very beautiful, the same sickening smile was twisting her young mouth too, and it was like the foreshadowing of a great evil which they could not understand.

But by and by they carried Evelyn out, and she opened her eyes and the smile was gone. From far away in the great house the sound of weeping and crooning came up the stairs and echoed along the dismal corridors, for the women had begun to mourn the dead master, after the Irish fashion, and the hall had echoes of its own all that night, like the far-off wail of the banshee among forest trees.

When the time was come they took Sir Hugh in his winding-sheet on a trestle bier, and bore him to the chapel and through the iron door and down the long descent to the north vault, with tapers, to lay him by his father. And two men went in first to prepare the place, and came back staggering like drunken men, and white, leaving their lights behind them.

But Gabriel Ockram was not afraid, for he knew. And he went in alone and saw that the body of Sir Vernon Ockram was leaning upright against the stone wall, and that its head lay on the ground near by with the face turned up, and the dried leathern lips smiled horribly at the dried-up corpse, while the iron coffin, lined with black velvet, stood open on the floor.

Then Gabriel took the thing in his hands, for it was very light, being quite dried by the air of the vault, and those who peeped in from the door saw him lay it in the coffin again, and it rustled a little, like a bundle of reeds, and sounded hollow as it touched the sides and the bottom. He also placed the head upon the shoulders and shut down the lid, which fell to with a rusty spring that snapped.

After that they laid Sir Hugh beside his father, with the trestle bier on which they had brought him, and they went back to the chapel.

But when they saw one another's faces, master and men, they were all smiling with the dead smile of the corpse they had left in the vault, so that they could not bear to look at one another until it had faded away.

III

GABRIEL OCKRAM BECAME SIR GABRIEL, INHERITING THE BARONETCY with the half-ruined fortune left by his father, and still Evelyn Warburton lived at Ockram Hall, in the south room that had been hers ever since she could remember anything. She could not go away, for there were no relatives to whom she could have gone, and, besides, there seemed to be no reason why she should not stay. The world would never trouble itself to care what the Ockrams did on their Irish estates, and it was long since the Ockrams had asked anything of the world.

So Sir Gabriel took his father's place at the dark old table in the dining-room, and Evelyn sat opposite to him, until such time as their mourning should be over, and they might be married at last. And meanwhile their lives went on as before, since Sir Hugh had been a hopeless invalid during the last year of his life, and they had seen him but once a day for a little while, spending most of their time together in a strangely perfect companionship.

But though the late summer saddened into autumn, and autumn darkened into winter, and storm followed storm, and rain poured on rain through the short days and the long nights, yet Ockram Hall seemed less gloomy since Sir Hugh had been laid in the north vault beside his father. And at Christmastide Evelyn decked the great hall with holly and green boughs, and huge fires blazed on every hearth. Then the tenants were all bidden to a New Year's dinner, and they ate and drank well, while Sir Gabriel sat at the head of the table. Evelyn came in when the port wine was brought, and the most respected of the tenants made a speech to propose her health.

It was long, he said, since there had been a Lady Ockram. Sir Gabriel shaded his eyes with his hand and looked down at the table, but a faint colour came into Evelyn's transparent cheeks. But, said the grey-haired farmer, it was longer still since there had been a Lady Ockram so fair as the next was to be, and he gave the health of Evelyn Warburton.

Then the tenants all stood up and shouted for her, and Sir Gabriel stood up likewise, beside Evelyn. And when the men gave the last and loudest cheer of all there was a voice not theirs, above them all, higher, fiercer, louder—a scream not earthly, shrieking for the bride of Ockram Hall. And the holly and the green boughs over the great chimney-piece shook and slowly waved as if a cool breeze were blowing over them. But the men turned very pale, and many of them set down their glasses, but others let them fall upon the floor for fear. And looking into one another's faces, they were all smiling strangely, a dead smile, like dead Sir Hugh's. One cried out words in Irish, and the fear of death was suddenly upon them all, so that they fled in panic, falling over one another like wild beasts in the burning forest, when the thick smoke runs along before the flame; and the tables were over-set, and drinking glasses and bottles were broken in heaps, and the dark red wine crawled like blood upon the polished floor.

Sir Gabriel and Evelyn stood alone at the head of the table before the wreck of the feast, not daring to turn to see each other, for each knew that the other smiled. But his right arm held her and his left hand clasped her right as they stared before them; and but for the shadows of her hair one might not have told their two faces apart. They listened long, but the cry came not again, and the dead smile faded from their lips, while each remembered that Sir Hugh Ockram lay in the north vault, smiling in his winding-sheet, in the dark, because he had died with his secret.

So ended the tenants' New Year's dinner. But from that time on Sir Gabriel grew more and more silent, and his face grew even paler and thinner than before. Often, without warning and without words, he would rise from his seat, as if something moved him against his will, and he would go out into the rain or the sunshine to the north side of the chapel, and sit on the stone bench, staring at the ground as if he could see through it, and through the vault below, and through the white winding-sheet in the dark, to the dead smile that would not die.

Always when he went out in that way Evelyn came out presently and sat beside him. Once, too, as in summer, their beautiful faces came suddenly near, and their lids drooped, and their red lips were almost joined together. But as their eyes met, they grew wide and wild, so that the white showed in a ring all round the deep violet, and their teeth chattered, and their hands were like hands of corpses, each in the other's, for the terror of what was under their feet, and of what they knew but could not see.

Once, also, Evelyn found Sir Gabriel in the chapel alone, standing before the iron door that led down to the place of death, and in his hand there was the key to the door; but he had not put it into the lock. Evelyn drew him away, shivering, for she had also been driven in waking dreams to see that terrible thing again, and to find out whether it had changed since it had lain there.

"I'm going mad," said Sir Gabriel, covering his eyes with his hand as he went with her. "I see it in my sleep, I see it when I am awake—it draws me to it, day and night—and unless I see it I shall die!"

"I know," answered Evelyn, "I know. It is as if threads were spun from it, like a spider's, drawing us down to it." She was silent for a moment, and then she started violently and grasped his arm with a man's strength, and almost screamed the words she spoke. "But we must not go there!" she cried. "We must not go!"

Sir Gabriel's eyes were half shut, and he was not moved by the agony of her face.

"I shall die, unless I see it again," he said, in a quiet voice not like his own. And all that day and that evening he scarcely spoke, thinking of it, always thinking, while Evelyn Warburton quivered from head to foot with a terror she had never known.

She went alone, on a grey winter's morning, to Nurse Macdonald's room in the tower, and sat down beside the great leathern easy-chair, laying her thin white hand upon the withered fingers.

"Nurse," she said, "what was it that Uncle Hugh should have told you, that night before he died? It must have been an awful secret—and yet, though you asked him, I feel somehow that you know it, and that you know why he used to smile so dreadfully."

The old woman's head moved slowly from side to side.

"I only guess—I shall never know," she answered slowly in her cracked little voice.

"But what do you guess? Who am I? Why did you ask who my father was? You know I am Colonel Warburton's daughter, and my mother was Lady Ockram's sister, so that Gabriel and I are cousins. My father was killed in Afghanistan. What secret can there be?"

"I do not know. I can only guess."

"Guess what?" asked Evelyn imploringly, and pressing the soft withered hands, as she leaned forward. But Nurse Macdonald's wrinkled lids dropped suddenly over her queer blue eyes, and her lips shook a little with her breath, as if she were asleep.

Evelyn waited. By the fire the Irish maid was knitting fast, and the needles clicked like three or four clocks ticking against each other. And the real clock on the wall solemnly ticked alone, checking off the seconds of the woman who was a hundred years old, and had not many days left. Outside the ivy branch beat the window in the wintry blast, as it had beaten against the glass a hundred years ago.

Then as Evelyn sat there she felt again the waking of a horrible desire—the sickening wish to go down, down to the thing in the north vault, and to open the winding-sheet, and see whether it had changed; and she held Nurse Macdonald's hands as if to keep herself in her place and fight against the appalling attraction of the evil dead.

But the old cat that kept Nurse Macdonald's feet warm, lying always on the bag footstool, got up and stretched itself, and looked up into Evelyn's eyes, while its back arched, and its tail thickened and bristled, and its ugly pink lips drew back in a devilish grin, showing its sharp teeth. Evelyn stared at it, half fascinated by its ugliness. Then the creature suddenly put out one paw with all its claws spread, and spat at the girl, and all at once the grinning cat was like the smiling corpse far down below, so that Evelyn shivered down to her small feet, and covered her face with her free hand, lest Nurse Macdonald should wake and see the dead smile there, for she could feel it.

The old woman had already opened her eyes again, and she touched her cat with the end of her crutch-stick, whereupon its back went down and its tail shrunk, and it sidled back to its place on the bag footstool. But its yellow eyes looked up sideways at Evelyn, between the slits of its lids.

"What is it that you guess, nurse?" asked the young girl again.

"A bad thing—a wicked thing. But I dare not tell you, lest it might not be true, and the very thought should blast your life. For if I guess right, he meant that you should not know, and that you two should marry, and pay for his old sin with your souls."

"He used to tell us that we ought not to marry—"

"Yes—he told you that, perhaps—but it was as if a man put poisoned meat before a starving beast, and said 'do not eat,' but never raised his hand to take the meat away. And if he told you that you should not marry, it was because he hoped you would; for of all men living or dead, Hugh Ockram was the falsest man that ever told a cowardly lie, and the cruelest that ever hurt a weak woman, and the worst that ever loved a sin."

"But Gabriel and I love each other," said Evelyn very sadly.

Nurse Macdonald's old eyes looked far away, at sights seen long ago, and that rose in the grey winter air amid the mists of an ancient youth.

"If you love, you can die together," she said, very slowly. "Why should you live, if it is true? I am a hundred years old. What has life given me? The beginning is fire; the end is a heap of ashes; and between the end and the beginning lies all the pain of the world. Let me sleep, since I cannot die."

Then the old woman's eyes closed again, and her head sank a little lower upon her breast.

So Evelyn went away and left her asleep, with the cat asleep on the bag footstool; and the young girl tried to forget Nurse Macdonald's words, but she could not, for she heard them over and over again in the wind, and behind her on the stairs. And as she grew sick with fear of the frightful unknown evil to which her soul was bound, she felt a bodily something pressing her, and pushing her, and forcing her on, and from the other side she felt the threads that drew her mysteriously: and when she shut her eyes, she saw in the chapel behind the altar, the low iron door through which she must pass to go to the thing.

And as she lay awake at night, she drew the sheet over her face, lest she should see shadows on the wall beckoning to her; and the sound of her own warm breath made whisperings in her ears, while she held the mattress with her hands, to keep from getting up and going to the chapel. It would have been easier if there had not been a way thither through the library, by a door which was never locked. It would be fearfully easy to take her candle and go softly through the sleeping house. And the key of the vault lay under the altar behind a stone that turned. She knew the little secret. She could go alone and see.

But when she thought of it, she felt her hair rise on her head, and first she shivered so that the bed shook, and then the horror went through her in a cold thrill that was agony again, like myriads of icy needles boring into her nerves.

IV

The old clock in Nurse Macdonald's tower struck midnight. From her room she could hear the creaking chains and weights in their box in the corner of the staircase, and overhead the jarring of the rusty lever that lifted the hammer. She had heard it all her life. It struck eleven strokes clearly, and then came the twelfth, with a dull half stroke, as though the hammer were too weary to go on, and had fallen asleep against the bell.

The old cat got up from the bag footstool and stretched itself, and Nurse Macdonald opened her ancient eyes and looked slowly round the room by the dim light of the night lamp. She touched the cat with her crutch-stick, and it lay down upon her feet. She drank a few drops from her cup and went to sleep again.

But downstairs Sir Gabriel sat straight up as the clock struck, for he had dreamed a fearful dream of horror, and his heart stood still, till he awoke at its stopping, and it beat again furiously with his breath, like a wild thing set free. No Ockram had ever known fear waking, but sometimes it came to Sir Gabriel in his sleep.

He pressed his hands to his temples as he sat up in bed, and his hands were icy cold, but his head was hot. The dream faded far, and in its place there came the master thought that racked his life; with the thought also came the sick twisting of his lips in the dark that would have been a smile. Far off, Evelyn Warburton dreamed that the dead smile was on her mouth, and awoke, starting with a little moan, her face in her hands, shivering.

But Sir Gabriel struck a light and got up and began to walk up and down his great room. It was midnight, and he had barely slept an hour, and in the north of Ireland the winter nights are long.

"I shall go mad," he said to himself, holding his forehead. He knew that it was true. For weeks and months the possession of the thing had grown upon him like a disease, till he could think of nothing without thinking first of that. And now all at once it outgrew his strength, and he knew that he must be its instrument or lose his mind—that he must do the deed he hated and feared, if he could fear anything, or that something would snap in his brain and divide him from life while he was yet alive. He took the candlestick in his hand, the old-fashioned heavy candlestick that had always been used by the head of the house. He did not think of dressing, but went as he was, in his silk night clothes and his slippers, and he opened the door. Everything was very still in the great old house. He shut the door behind him and walked noiselessly on the carpet through the long corridor. A cool breeze blew over his shoulder and blew the flame of his candle straight out from him. Instinctively he stopped and looked round, but all was still, and the upright flame burned steadily. He walked on, and instantly a strong draught was behind him, almost extinguishing the light. It seemed to blow him on his way, ceasing whenever he turned, coming again when he went on—invisible, icy.

Down the great staircase to the echoing hall he went, seeing nothing but the flaring flame of the candle standing away from him over the guttering wax, while the cold wind blew over his shoulder and through his hair. On he passed through the open door into the library, dark with old books and carved bookcases; on through the door in the shelves, with painted shelves on it, and the imitated backs of books, so that one needed to know where to find it—and it shut itself after him with a soft click. He entered the low-arched passage, and though the door was shut behind him and fitted tightly in its frame, still the cold breeze blew the flame forward as he walked. And he was not afraid; but his face was very pale, and his eyes were wide and bright, looking before him, seeing already in the dark air the picture of the thing beyond. But in the chapel he stood still, his hand on the little turning stone tablet in the back of the stone altar. On the tablet were engraved words: "*Clavis sepulchri Clarissimorum Dominorum De Ockram*"—("the key to the vault of the most illustrious lords of Ockram"). Sir Gabriel paused and listened. He fancied that he heard a sound far off in the great house where all had been so still, but it did not come again. Yet he waited at the last, and looked at the low iron door. Beyond it, down the long descent, lay his father uncoffined, six months dead, corrupt, terrible in his clinging shroud. The strangely preserving air of the vault could not yet have done its work completely. But on the thing's ghastly features, with their half-dried, open eyes, there would still be the frightful smile with which the man had died—the smile that haunted—

As the thought crossed Sir Gabriel's mind, he felt his lips writhing, and he struck his own mouth in wrath with the back of his hand so fiercely that a drop of blood ran down his chin, and another, and more, falling back in the gloom upon the chapel pavement. But still his bruised lips twisted themselves. He turned the tablet by the simple secret. It needed no safer fastening, for had each Ockram been coffined in pure gold, and had the door been open wide, there was not a man in

Tyrone brave enough to go down to that place, saving Gabriel Ockram himself, with his angel's face and his thin, white hands, and his sad unflinching eyes. He took the great old key and set it into the lock of the iron door; and the heavy, rattling noise echoed down the descent beyond like footsteps, as if a watcher had stood behind the iron and were running away within, with heavy dead feet. And though he was standing still, the cool wind was from behind him, and blew the flame of the candle against the iron panel. He turned the key.

Sir Gabriel saw that his candle was short. There were new ones on the altar, with long candlesticks, and he lit one, and left his own burning on the floor. As he set it down on the pavement his lip began to bleed again, and another drop fell upon the stones.

He drew the iron door open and pushed it back against the chapel wall, so that it should not shut of itself, while he was within; and the horrible draught of the sepulchre came up out of the depths in his face, foul and dark. He went in, but though the fetid air met him, yet the flame of the tall candle was blown straight from him against the wind while he walked down the easy incline with steady steps, his loose slippers slapping the pavement as he trod.

He shaded the candle with his hand, and his fingers seemed to be made of wax and blood as the light shone through them. And in spite of him the unearthly draught forced the flame forward, till it was blue over the black wick, and it seemed as if it must go out. But he went straight on, with shining eyes.

The downward passage was wide, and he could not always see the walls by the struggling light, but he knew when he was in the place of death by the larger, drearier echo of his steps in the greater space, and by the sensation of a distant blank wall. He stood still, almost enclosing the flame of the candle in the hollow of his hand. He could see a little, for his eyes were growing used to the gloom. Shadowy forms were outlined in the dimness, where the biers of the Ockrams stood crowded together, side by side, each with its straight, shrouded corpse, strangely preserved by the dry air, like the empty shell that the locust sheds in summer. And a few steps before him he saw clearly the dark shape of headless Sir Vernon's iron coffin, and he knew that nearest to it lay the thing he sought.

He was as brave as any of those dead men had been, and they were his fathers, and he knew that sooner or later he should lie there himself, beside Sir Hugh, slowly drying to a parchment shell. But he was still alive, and he closed his eyes a moment, and three great drops stood on his forehead.

Then he looked again, and by the whiteness of the winding-sheet he knew his father's corpse, for all the others were brown with age; and, moreover, the flame of the candle was blown toward it. He made four steps till he reached it, and suddenly the light burned straight and high, shedding a dazzling yellow glare upon the fine linen that was all white, save over the face, and where the joined hands were laid on the breast. And at those places ugly stains had spread, darkened with outlines of the features and of the tight-clasped fingers. There was a frightful stench of drying death.

As Sir Gabriel looked down, something stirred behind him, softly at first, then more noisily, and something fell to the stone floor with a dull thud and rolled up to his feet; he started back and saw a withered head lying almost face upward on the pavement, grinning at him. He felt the cold sweat standing on his face, and his heart beat painfully.

For the first time in all his life that evil thing which men call fear was getting hold of him, checking his heart-strings as a cruel driver checks a quivering horse, clawing at his backbone with icy hands, lifting his hair with freezing breath, climbing up and gathering in his midriff with leaden weight.

Yet presently he bit his lip and bent down, holding the candle in one hand, to lift the shroud back from the head of the corpse with the other. Slowly he lifted it. Then it clove to the half-dried skin of the face, and his hand shook as if some one had struck him on the elbow, but half in fear and half in anger at himself, he pulled it, so that it came away with a little ripping sound. He caught his breath as he held it, not yet throwing it back, and not yet looking. The horror was working in him, and he felt that old Vernon Ockram was standing up in his iron coffin, headless, yet watching him with the stump of his severed neck.

While he held his breath he felt the dead smile twisting his lips. In sudden wrath at his own misery, he tossed the death-stained linen backward, and looked at last. He ground his teeth lest he should shriek aloud.

There it was, the thing that haunted him, that haunted Evelyn Warburton, that was like a blight on all that came near him.

The dead face was blotched with dark stains, and the thin, grey hair was matted about the discoloured forehead. The sunken lids were half open, and the candle light gleamed on something foul where the toad eyes had lived.

But yet the dead thing smiled, as it had smiled in life; the ghastly lips were parted and drawn wide and tight upon the wolfish teeth, cursing still, and still defying hell to do its worst—defying, cursing, and always and for ever smiling alone in the dark.

Sir Gabriel opened the winding-sheet where the hands were, and the blackened, withered fingers were closed upon something stained and mottled. Shivering from head to foot, but fighting like a man in agony for his life, he tried to take the package from the dead man's hold. But as he pulled at it the claw-like fingers seemed to close more tightly, and when he pulled harder the shrunken hands and arms rose from the corpse with a horrible look of life following his motion—then as he wrenched the sealed packet loose at last, the hands fell back into their place still folded.

He set down the candle on the edge of the bier to break the seals from the stout paper. And, kneeling on one knee, to get a better light, he read what was within, written long ago in Sir Hugh's queer hand.

He was no longer afraid.

He read how Sir Hugh had written it all down that it might perchance be a witness of evil and of his hatred; how he had loved Evelyn Warburton, his wife's sister; and how his wife had died of a broken heart with his curse upon her, and how Warburton and he had fought side by side in Afghanistan, and Warburton had fallen; but Ockram had brought his comrade's wife back a full year later, and little Evelyn, her child, had been born in Ockram Hall. And next, how he had wearied of the mother, and she had died like her sister with his curse on her. And then, how Evelyn had been brought up as his niece, and how he had trusted that his son Gabriel and his daughter, innocent and unknowing, might love and marry, and the souls of the women he had betrayed might suffer another anguish before eternity was out. And, last of all, he hoped that some day, when nothing could be undone, the two might find his writing and live on, not daring to tell the truth for their children's sake and the world's word, man and wife.

This he read, kneeling beside the corpse in the north vault, by the light of the altar candle; and when he had read it all, he thanked God aloud that he had found the secret in time. But when he rose to his feet and looked down at the dead face it was changed, and the smile was gone from it for ever, and the jaw had fallen a little, and the tired, dead lips were relaxed. And then there was a breath behind him and close to him, not cold like that which had blown the flame of the candle as he came, but warm and human. He turned suddenly.

There she stood, all in white, with her shadowy golden hair—for she had risen from her bed and had followed him noiselessly, and had found him reading, and had herself read over his shoulder. He started violently when he saw her, for his nerves were unstrung—and then he cried out her name in the still place of death:

"Evelyn!"

"My brother!" she answered softly and tenderly, putting out both hands to meet his.

The De Grabrooke Monument

Mrs. J. H. RIDDELL

I

YOU WANT TO KNOW WHY I DO NOT CARE TO LOOK AT PICTURES of our great cathedrals, why, indeed, the very name of cathedral fills me with a shivering terror. Well, I will tell you, though it is a story I do not much like to repeat.

Far away from London, hundreds of miles away, there is an old, old town, a town grey and worn with age, where the many gabled houses have high-peaked, red-tiled roofs, where the streets are narrow and the lanes tortuous, where the five arched bridge spanning a sluggish river is covered with lichens and tender cushions of emerald moss, a marvellous piece of colour when the sun shines warm and bright upon it.

I was born there, not quite in the town, but on its outskirts, in a pleasant house, that had its gardens sloping down to the river, and was well-shaded from the high road which it faced, by a high holly hedge and a line of interlacing lime trees planted inside. It was a lovely house, a rambling, old-fashioned mansion, that had once belonged to some great family—quaint, and homely, and picturesque—all covered over with roses and jasmine and honeysuckle, and clematis—the common white with the small star-like flowers which smells so sweet in the fine autumnal weather.

Out on the other side of the town—inland as we called it, to distinguish our district from that which lay away from the windings of the river—there resided a sister of my father's, a sister so much older, that while we were children we always fancied she must have been his mother. When quite a girl, she married the then agent of the De Grabrooke estates. A great match it was considered at the time, for Mr. Herington had a nice little property of his own, and was high in favour with Sir Roland de Grabrooke, who was at that time the reigning baronet.

Sir Roland died, and other baronets succeeded, but Mr. Herington still remained agent; and when, at length, he too died, my aunt was permitted to remain on at the cottage, not far from the northern entrance to Grabrooke, which is the admiration of every stranger who sees it, and is certainly the most beautiful house of its size, I ever beheld.

My aunt was elderly and childless, and as there were—I will not say too many of us at home—but a very sufficient number—few days passed without one or other of her nieces finding time to walk across Oldstone and out along the main London road to Grabrooke.

Sometimes—often, indeed, it chanced that when we stayed later, or the weather grew inclement, or my aunt had an unexpected visitor, we remained with her for the night—indeed, it had grown to be an understood thing if we did not return home before twilight, no one was to feel uneasy at our absence.

"Aunt Hilda had kept us," and we would return with a budget of news, and a hamper full of good things, driven sedately through Oldstone by Thomas, aunt's staid old servant, in her little phaeton, drawn by a fat, lazy pony, we could all of us remember so long as we could remember anything.

We had no mother, or perhaps so easy an arrangement might not have satisfied the home anxieties and proprieties. My father might well be excused if, when he came back at night, tired and fagged, one face, more or less, was scarcely noticed amongst the number at hand to greet him; and for the rest, every one in Oldstone knew every one else, and an adventure, whether agreeable or disagreeable, was the last thing likely to occur to any person living within the shadow of that cathedral town.

Unless, indeed, the cathedral itself fell down some day, and buried us all in its ruins. That calamity had been freely prophecied for years past, by great architects, who were at the trouble of travelling all the way from London, to tell the clerical and municipal authorities of Oldstone, that the building in which every inhabitant of Oldstone felt a pride was most insecure, and that it would cost a large sum of money to render it ordinarily safe.

For a short time after one of these visits, the more timid of the population eschewed the narrow paths which ran through the churchyard, and were wont to look about them nervously from their accustomed seats on Sundays; but ere long, finding that nothing happened—that the old building showed no more signs of tumbling about our ears than had been the case for years previously, they took courage again, and began to talk of the impertinence of persons who talked as if those who reared such a pile did not understand their business.

Great architects repair in these days to Oldstone, but merely in order to pay homage to the greater genius of one of their guild, who has restored the cathedral, and rendered it perfectly unrecognisable by any one who remember the building in its olden state.

Cleaned it has been, inside and out. The marks left by Time's fingers are obliterated. It has been scraped; it has been swept and garnished. The dear old monuments look as spick and span, as bright and clean as if only just turned out of the stonemason's yard. Not an inscription now on any wall is difficult to decipher. He who runs may read all about the good folks who departed this life a few hundred years ago, all about their pedigree, their deeds of valour, the names of their wives, the number of their children. The brasses are rubbed up as bright as door-plates; the pavement looks as if it had just been hearth-stoned. The old glass in the windows stares in sullen amazement at the new; the organ loft has been swept away bodily, and you can see the whole building at a glance.

Not a scrap of mystery left about the place now. The secrets of every nook and corner have been laid bare by the hand of innovation; fancy has not a place left wherein to weave a web. The most nervous person might pace the nuns' gallery without fear, and the way to the leads is as safe as the pavements in the Close. I can remember when the traditions of the cathedral were things not to be lightly spoken of—rather they were legends it was considered most seemly only to hint of in the firelight, or to whisper concerning when the autumn evenings were growing chill and drear.

In the watches of the night I have awakened and thought of the cathedral standing solitary and mighty in the darkness, its massive towers rising to Heaven, its stones worn with the tread of men and women, whose very names were forgotten, its history interwoven with the history of the country, till I have grown so frightened with the pictures fancy drew, that I dare not even turn my head upon my pillow.

But in the daytime we—Alick and I—could be brave enough. Not even the sexton, who had no doubt once been young and active, though our memories were not long enough to recall him as otherwise than tottering and feeble, was not so well acquainted with all the ins and outs of the cathedral as we.

No dean of Oldstone, I am satisfied, ever knew half so much about the building as my brother and myself.

We had climbed the worn and slippery steps scores—ay, hundreds of times; we had crept along the nun's gallery, unimpeded by rubbish, unappalled by danger; we had gone like cats over the leads, and looked down upon the houses in the Close, and taken bird's-eye views of the quaint old town and surrounding country; we had burrowed into the vaults, and on one occasion Alick penetrated so far into one of the subterranean passages, that in the firm belief he had died of suffocation, I was about to rush away and alarm the town, when he re-appeared, his clothes very much torn, and his face and hands begrimed with dirt, but otherwise none the worse for his adventure.

Oh! Alick, my brother, you can never return to tell me whether in that far-away land, where you were laid to rest, your thoughts turned with tender longing to dreamy Oldstone, with its softly flowing river and its grand cathedral, where hand clasped in hand we used, evening after evening, to stand in the dark nave, and listen while the organist practised, and rolled out harmonies that never seemed to us quite the same when we heard them in the daylight and amongst the congregation.

But I must hurry on, or I shall never have space to tell you my story.

I was quite grown up, nearly twenty years old, and Alick had got his regimentals and was home with us for a few weeks before going to India, when one afternoon I went across to Grabrooke to visit Aunt Hilda. She wanted me to remain the night; she was in the mood for a long talk, and she had heaps to tell me, she said, about Sir Edwin De Grabrooke, who was having the Court done up, inside and out, before he brought home his bride.

"They say she is not a willing bride," went on my aunt, settling herself more comfortably in her easy-chair. "Poor little thing, she was attached, you know, to young Sir Clement, and I think it is a sin and a shame for this marriage to be forced upon her."

"But perhaps she may be fond of Sir Edwin," I remarked, "if only out of gratitude for his kindness to his nephew."

Aunt Hilda was an elderly lady and privileged; moreover, she had always energetic ways of expressing herself. Consequently I was not so much surprised as might be supposed when, in answer to my innocent observation, she said—

"Fiddle-de-dee!"

"But, aunt," I persisted, "he was very kind to Sir Clement. I have heard papa say no father could have been more devoted. Who else would have nursed him in that dreadful fever?"

"I would," interrupted Mrs. Herington. "I offered to do it. I went up to the Court myself for the purpose, and saw that doctor who is such a non-such in

Sir Edwin's opinion, and told him I—Hilda Herington—was not afraid of fever or of death, if either met me in the way of my duty, and that I would gladly nurse the youth, whose mother I had known and loved, and whom I had held in my arms when he was not a day old."

"It was like you, aunt," I said.

"It was not like me, child," she answered; "I was never a person to thrust myself forward, where no one wanted me, to offer help, except where I knew it would be appreciated. I could not tell then what made me do it, but I am sure now that it was the certainty I, and no one else, could save him urged me on. Well, he is gone, poor lad—and now Sir Edwin is to marry pretty Lily in his stead."

"Aunt," I said, "I must be going. I would not stay a night away from home while Alick is with us for any consideration. There will be plenty of nights and days too, when I can stop with you, after he is gone—gone!"

And then I broke down. I burst into such a passion of tears, that my aunt, who, despite her brusque manner, was one of the kindest creatures that ever breathed, kissed and soothed and cooed over me; and then, putting on my shawl, and tying my bonnet-strings with her fair, withered hands, bade me run away home, and make haste, or I should find darkness surprising me.

It was getting late to be out—late, that is, for the autumn time of year; and I hurried along as my aunt had advised, lest evening should close in ere I reached Oldstone.

But fast as I walked, my thoughts travelled faster. They kept flitting hither and thither: now back to the De Grabrookes who were dead and gone, now forward to the future Lady De Grabrooke, whom I had known when we were children, and she, a tiny, golden-haired, blue-eyed mite, was called Clement's little wife.

It all came back as though not a day had passed since Sir Clement—he was Sir Clement from six years old—said to Lily, standing in my father's garden—

"Make haste and grow, Lily. They won't let me marry you unless you are as tall as Miss Atterton."

Miss Atterton was the Dean's daughter, and five feet ten exact measurement; but the lad loved to tease golden hair and blue eyes.

And now Sir Clement was dead, and his uncle meant to marry Lily. In secret I had always admired Sir Edwin myself.

His dark, set face—his cold, proud bearing—his curt address—his look of grave, settled determination—were far more attractive to my girlish fancy than Sir Clement's sunny face and boyish manner and cheery voice had ever been.

"Ah! how he must have loved his nephew," I considered, "to nurse him in that dreadful fever, and never to smile since his death."

Except Aunt Hilda, every one in Oldstone I think shared my opinion of Sir Edwin; and I had never before heard Mrs. Herington cast, even by implication, a doubt on the perfect amiability of Sir Edwin's character. Since his nephew's death he had been studiously kind to every one for whom Sir Clement entertained a preference; and it was entirely of his goodness that my aunt remained on at the Cottage, for which reason it seemed strange she should object to his marrying Lilian, or any other person he fancied.

But then Mrs. Herington always was a little odd, and no good purpose could be served by thinking about her likes and dislikes; besides, it was growing dusk, and if I did not hurry along still faster, I should find the cathedral closed, and have to make a long detour in consequence.

How it may be at Oldstone since the restoration I cannot tell, but in those days we used the cathedral as a short cut—just as one might a field-path—in at the north door, out at the south, or *vice versâ*, if it suited our convenience. St. Paul's before the fire was not a more common thoroughfare than Oldstone Cathedral when Alick and I were young.

Panting and out of breath, I reached the north door as twilight was settling down over the town, and shrouding everything in the cathedral in gloom and mystery; but I had not time then to do more than glance around while I sped along the chancel and across the nave. There was not a creature apparently in the building but myself, and my footsteps rang out through the stillness the while I hurried over the stones, beneath which lay prelates and warriors, lords and ladies, and humbler persons, whose inscriptions were worn away, whose very names were forgotten, save by the Almighty.

I reached the south door: I could have found my way to it blindfold, but there was some light in the nave, which found its way down from the long line of windows near the roof. Yes, there was the door, closed. I put my hand out and lifted the ponderous latch; *the door was locked*. Never before—never—had I known Jardin, the sexton, lock the south door before fastening the north. He lived in one of the streets leading to the river—one of the streets close to the Green—and it had hitherto been his invariable practice to secure the north door, and then hobble slowly across to the south—all on his way home.

But now it was locked, true enough; and if I could not reach the north door before Jardin made it fast, I should be in a pretty fix. You may be quite sure I did not waste any time knocking at the south door. I took up my dress, and ran as for my life back to the other entrance.

Just as I got to the screen dividing the chancel from the nave, I heard the door banged violently.

"Stop, stop, stop!" I cried—I shouted—but only the lonely echoes answered me. The north door was fast when I reached it, and though I hammered on the oak till my fingers were sore, and kicked upon the lower panels till the dead might almost have heard,—Jardin made no sign.

"What shall I do?—oh! what shall I do?" I thought, standing there on the cold stones, with that iron-studded door between me and human companionship; and then, my dears, I did just what it has often fallen to my lot to do since—I bore it.

I submitted; when once I felt assured Jardin was really gone I beat the door no longer—I cried aloud no more.

"I shall have to stop here all night," I thought. "Aunt Hilda will think I am at home, and at home they will think I am with Aunt Hilda."

That was the position. There was not the slightest chance of any one coming to look for me; and if I shrieked myself hoarse, I knew my cries would never be heard.

Was I afraid? you ask.

Well, yes. Though I knew every inch of the cathedral as thoroughly as I knew our own house—though I could not be considered a coward. I was afraid—cruelly, mortally afraid.

Hitherto I had thought little enough about the dead lying all around and within the cathedral, filling the vaults below—mouldering away to dust beneath the stones of the nave.

In the insolence of our youth, Alick and I had often mocked at the gruesome effigies upon the tombs, and laughed over the Old World inscriptions; but, my word! when I came to be left alone among them in darkness I seemed to feel, my mood was the reverse of merry.

Oh! for the sound of a human voice, the touch of a living hand, the glimmer even of a taper! And then came a new horror to me—or rather an old horror in a new shape—some day I should be in just such a place—not for a night merely, but for all the days and nights till the Resurrection morn. I should be one of the silent army by which I was then encompassed—one of the forgotten dead—one of the lonely, lonely folks, sleeping as quietly in the darkness as in the sunlight.

If I had never felt before—and probably I never really had—the need of religion, the necessity for belief, I felt it then; words to which I paid little attention when read by the old dean, came back to my ears with quite a new meaning, and

I fell on my knees and prayed as throughout the twenty years of my life I had never prayed before.

When I raised my head and looked around me into the darkness, I knew that half my fear had departed. I was not alone—no, I felt that, though no human friend or relative was near, though no created being was at hand, I knew I was not left solitary; though there was no hand I could touch, no voice I could hear, no face I could see, I comprehended vaguely it might be—for the faith like the religion of youth is mostly vague—yet certainly—that no harm could come to me, that I was as safe all alone in the cathedral as I had ever been in my earthly father's house.

The hours went by—surely hours never seemed so long. I heard the quarters strike, the half hours, the hours. I thought of what they were doing home—thought of at my aunt sitting in her pretty drawing-room, of all the people in Oldstone, not one of whom guessed any person was locked up alone in the great cathedral; and then my thoughts always drifted back to the dead by whom I was surrounded, and of whom I knew quite well I should never think carelessly and lightly again.

I tried to go to sleep—but I could not. I counted hundreds and thousands. I strove to recall all the heads of last Sunday's sermons, and recollect forgotten verses of the Psalms—but it was useless. The very darkness seemed to be awake. In broad daylight I had never felt my eyes so wide open as they were during the time I sat in Oldstone Cathedral whiling the weary hours away.

At length there came a light stealing into the building; faint and feeble at first, it grew stronger by degrees, till at length every object stood out clear and cold in the beams of the risen moon. The stalls, the bishop's throne, the pulpit, the organ put up so high, the tombs of abbots and barons; all these things were as visible now to my outward eyes, as they had been to my mental vision during the vigil I had kept.

There was the great De Grabrooke monument, a pile against the wall—of cumbrous marble and rude sculpture—a huge tasteless monument which quite blocked up one window, and, yet large as it was, had not sufficed the love or ostentation of the family, for in a memorial chapel hard by, quite discernible from the seat it occupied, another tomb had been erected.

At the base of the larger monument, knelt a baronet, his wife and children; on the top of the tomb lay another baronet, his head resting on a stone pillow, a bible in his left hand crossed over his breast, a sword in his right stretched out stiff beside him.

As for Sir Clement, a memorial window was to be erected ere long in remembrance of his short life, but as yet the cathedral contained no record of him save the plate on his coffin-lid hidden away from sight in the deep vault beneath the chapel.

If the cathedral had been lonely and terrible in the darkness, it was ten times more lonely in the moonlight creeping down the walls and stealing along the aisles, penetrating into mysterious corners, and chasing lingering shadows round the tombs.

The silvery beams seemed to flit here and there and everywhere, now shining on the pipes of the organ, now glimmering through the stained glass of the great east window, now throwing white patches on the steps leading to the communion table, and now throwing themselves as if weary across the recumbent effigy of some forgotten prelate.

Up and down the aisles, dodging in and out amongst the arches and behind the pillars, darting with quick haste into the aide chapels, peeping into the stalls, wandering like careless visitors hither and thither! Never since that night have I beheld the moonbeams without thinking of Oldstone Cathedral, and the shadows and the light playing at a weird game of hide and seek in the gloomy cloisters and the grand lonely nave.

There was a fascination I could not resist about the light and the scene, though both terrified me; and so I sat in a familiar corner, and looked and looked till my eyes ached, till my eyelids closed with very weariness.

Higher and higher rose the moon; slowly she sailed from east to west till she left the chancel in comparative darkness; but of all this I saw nothing, knew nothing. At length I was fast asleep—slumbering as deeply and soundly as though I had been lying in my white-curtained bed at home instead of being all alone in Oldstone Cathedral surrounded by the great and mighty dead.

II

HOW LONG I SLEPT I CANNOT TELL, BUT, WHEN WITH A START AND A SHIVER I awoke, it was to find myself numbed and dazed in a darkness I could just discern, in a building which seemed to my scattered senses full of every known and unknown horror.

Yet I did not cry out—I knew that my lips uttered no sound—I made no frantic efforts to escape as one so often tries to do in dreams, as one sometimes actually does in the first moments of returning consciousness.

The terror of it instead of unchaining my voice laid an icy hand upon my mouth and kept me still and silent.

And then I was cold—never before or since have I been so cold. Not after a night's vigil by a sick bed, not at daybreak upon the sea, never have I felt such an intensity of cold as I did awakening to find myself solitary in that lonely pile.

"Will morning never come?" I thought; and then half reproachfully contrasted my condition with that of the dear ones at home, feeling first angry at the idea of their comfortable safety, and then quite subdued when I considered the alarm and anxiety they would experience if they knew I was not at Aunt Hilda's.

Many a soldier lying wounded on a battle-field, many a sailor clinging to the shrouds of a doomed vessel, must, I think, have experienced the same transitions of feeling as those through which I passed that night.

Often I have wondered whether Alick—but there that tragedy was mercifully hidden in the future on the night when chilled to my very bones I sat in the darkness and prayed for the morning to dawn.

No, it was not fancy; I shut my eyes and opened them again; I lifted my hand and rubbed them stealthily, so stealthily that not even a mouse would have been disturbed by my movements.

I was wide awake, and it was not fancy! My senses were playing no tricks with me—my imagination was not cheating me with any optical delusion! I turned away my head, and then turned and looked again.

In the Grabrooke chapel there was a faint flickering light, which as I gazed, grew stronger.

At first a mere glimmer, it spread and spread, till I could see the great monument and the quaint old tomb.

It was not fire—I knew that well enough from the beginning, though I could not tell you how I knew it.

Just for a moment the idea crossed my mind that thieves might have been concealed in the chapel, pillagers of the dead about to commence their unholy work, and under this impression, I crouched down in my seat, and concealed myself behind the high oaken partition.

"They will kill me if they find me here," I considered; and I sank down in the stall a trembling icicle amongst the stools and hassocks, on the matting.

I am particular in telling you all these details that you may understand I made no mistake as to what I beheld afterwards.

The light increased; slowly but steadily the body of flame grew and grew, till I could see the vaulted roof, the beautiful aisles, the carving on the top of the columns, the tattered banners pendant from the walls. And then there came a sound as of many muffled footsteps and by degrees soft at first and as if at some distance, swelling in volume as it approached nearer, music, sad, stately, solemn, floated through the building—a requiem for the dead.

You will wonder that I kept my senses; but with the opening note of the mysterious music fear seemed to flee away, and sadness to take its place.

My eyes filled with tears; my heart thrilled with an exquisite melancholy. I covered my face with my hands and sobbed in silence as I had often done before at a soldier's funeral only with a subtler sense of sadness.

For this music was grander and more mournful than the "Dead March in Saul"; it was more touching than Mozart's "Requiem"; more heart-breaking than anything I had ever heard.

And it was produced from no instrument fashioned by man; above my head the mellow organ was dumb and silent, yet the air was full of the divine harmony so awfully majestic, and yet so replete with woe.

No longer in dread of wicked men, but with a shivering fear upon me of what I might behold I slowly lifted my head, and kneeling on the ground raised my eyes till they were on a level with the top of the pew.

What a sight met my gaze! The Grabrooke chapel was ablaze with lights; hundreds of tapers illumined the monument, the kneeling figures, and the time-stained tomb.

In the aisle stood a goodly company of the dead and gone—priest and warrior, abbot and crusader, sainted nun and courtly beauty. The mouth of the vault yawned wide and black, and gathered round and about it were the De Grabrookes of generations past; De Grabrookes who had died abroad, who had been drowned and buried in the great deep, who had been slain in battle, beheaded on Tower Hill, burned at the stake, turned their faces to the wall in their own familiar rooms and gathered up their feet in their beds ere passing into the broad eternity. Here they were all, habited once more in their earthly robes of flesh, waiting, I could see, for one who tarried in the coming.

The chiefest among them carried torches; and, as I gazed, they formed into procession, and advanced to a small door beside the monument, which had in former days given private access to the De Grabrooke chapel. Many a mourner must in the times departed have come in by that door to pray, but I had never seen it opened, not even when Sir Clement was borne to his last resting-place. The hinges were stiff, the bolts red with rust, no key would have turned in the massive lock. The armour in the hall at Grabrooke Court did not seem less necessary to the family now than that heavy door which once swung wide so easily, and yet it was towards this door the ghostly company pressed forward—the while the music rose and fell died away almost to a whisper, and then wailed out in louder notes of woe.

There was one I had known among the De Grabrookes missing—young Sir Clement. With a terrified curiosity my eyes looked for him, searched for him without success.

They waited—but I could see they were growing impatient. Though there was no speech nor voice amongst them, I knew they were all swayed by a common purpose—that they had gathered together to confront some one who ought to have been there ere now.

"He is coming!"

I heard the words distinctly—as distinctly as I heard the sobbing wail of the mysterious music, and yet none of the De Grabrookes uttered them; rather the sound seemed to come from a far away part of the cathedral.

"He is coming!" and there was a stir of expectation, a thrill of human emotion amongst the dead men and the dead women.

"Buried at night," was almost whispered in my ear. Turning suddenly, I tried to see who spoke, but there was no one near me.

At that moment there came a blast of keen, cold air through the cathedral; the torches nickered and the names waved with the force of the wind which rushed in through the open door of the De Grabrooke chapel.

That door stood wide; through it I could see the graves in the Cathedral yard, the railings round the tombs, the trees in the green, the canons' houses on the other side the road.

Quick, quick, up the flagged path leading to the door so long disused, came a man hurrying fast; his footsteps rung out on the stones. Looking neither to right nor to left, he strode to meet awful company.

It was he they had expected—he they were waiting for; and he was coming, he was at hand.

They all pressed forward as he entered—a terrible band—all men, women, and children. He had sped thither in hot haste, of that there could be no question; his dress was careless, his looks wild, his hair in disorder, and as he took off his hat when he passed through the door, I could see his face looked ghastly as of one in the throes of some mortal agony or terror.

From his brow he wiped the moisture which gathered there, and would have passed on towards the vault, but that the De Grabrooke dead gathered together and prevented him.

He looked at them each individually, and then around.

It was Sir Edwin De Grabrooke!

I thought I must have shrieked aloud. The light of the tapers fell full upon him as he stood there repulsed. The dead did not look more corpse like than he; the countenances of the dead were not more terrible in their rigid sternness, than his in its desperate defiance.

Once again he made a movement as if to pass on towards the open vault, and again the silent dead barred his passage.

Then in a moment they drew back forming on each side in line, and leaving a path wide enough for him to have pushed on had he chosen to do so.

But he did not so choose, rather he stood rooted to the spot, gazing at a figure which issued from the vault and came slowly towards him.

Sir Clement—robed not in any garments he had worn in life, but with his grave clothes draped about him; Sir Clement—with a look of sorrowful reproach in his young eyes; Sir Clement for whom all the other dead made way—falling aside and behind till he and his kinsman stood face to face.

Great as was my fear, my curiosity was greater. I slipped from my place and crossed the aisle and crept along, keeping well in the shade till I could hide myself behind what we called the King's Tomb, as there was a tradition that some Danish monarch lay mouldering there.

Scarcely venturing to draw my breath—though not one of the ghostly throng had a thought to spare for me—I peeped from between an angel's wings and beheld the uncle and the nephew standing still, the one confronting the other in a silence more appalling than the wildest tumult.

Slowly the dead youth bared his heart, and drawing it open a ghastly spectacle disclosed a sharp long weapon, fine as a needle, fatal as the cruellest sword, which penetrated it through and through.

The grave had given up its secrets; only a morsel of steel; only a human life; only one who had stood between sent in a moment to his long account; and now, all the dead De Grabrookes had risen to drive out the traitor from amongst them.

There was a sound as of a rising storm, as of a gathering tempest, and while one wild blast swept round the cathedral, they thrust him out into the night, and with skeleton hands closed and bolted the door behind.

Then there came utter darkness.

III

For weeks I hovered on the borderland. Now the doctors told the dear ones who moved about my bed that it must be death; then a slight change for the better gave them hope, and they said it was possible I might live.

I had been found in the early morning by the organist of the cathedral, lying insensible on the cold pavement beside the King's Tomb. From the cathedral I was carried into the Deanery close at hand, and then, the doctors having pronounced that life was not extinct, my father insisted on taking me home, where Aunt Hilda came to help in the weary nursing which followed.

Of all these details I remembered not one. My memory was a complete blank from the time the De Grabrooke chapel door was shut till I came back, after weeks of mortal sickness, to the knowledge that I was still alive, that the weak, wan, helpless creature who lay back on the pillows, was the shadow of the robust, light-hearted girl who had walked into Oldstone Cathedral strong and well to be carried out of it fourteen hours later a mere wreck of her former self.

When I could speak connectedly I did not tell of what I had seen during the course of that awful night. In all the years which have come and gone since then I have never told the story right through until to-night. During my illness I had raved of terrible things, reproducing doubtless the horrors my eyes had witnessed, but those around me attributed all I said to delirium.

"The terror of finding herself shut up in the cathedral was too much for her," declared my relatives, and Oldstone echoed this opinion.

"I am quite sure, Patty, you were not well when you left me that night," said Aunt Hilda, who never ceased searching about for natural causes to account for my illness. I did not contradict her. I knew she desired to believe there was nothing at the bottom of the wild ravings she had listened to, and so I held my peace. Only once, when a visitor remarked in my presence that Lily's wedding was to be in the spring, I spoke out suddenly, and declared, "Oh! she must not marry Sir Edwin; she must not."

Then my aunt signed to her friend to be silent, and turning to me entreated that I would keep myself quite quiet.

"You will begin to wander again, Patty, if you excite yourself," she added.

This was how they managed, and they treated me one and all so judiciously, I declare at length the memory of that night came to be merely as the memory of some bad dream. Before the crocuses and the snowdrops peeped through the bare earth, I learned to regard the visions I had seen as a part of my delirium, as one of the many terrible pageants at which I had assisted, while my flesh and my spirit fought out their battle as to whether they were then to part company or remain together for years to come.

All this time Alick, for whose sake I had hurried home from Aunt Hilda's snug little bower, was still in England. At the eleventh hour some alteration had taken place in the minds of those who rule at the Horse Guards, and orders were sent countermanding the departure of his regiment when it was almost on the eve of embarkation.

Thus it came to pass he was able to spend Christmas with us, and when May came—May with all its sweet airs and lovely blossoms—he was at Oldstone once again, this time paying really his last visit, for he sailed two months afterwards, and—but that has nothing to do with this story.

It was May, then, and Alick and I were wandering after breakfast up and down the walk beside the river, he laughing and merry, I more quiet than had been my wont before that long exhausting illness, but serenely happy in his companionship, and rejoicing, as who does not rejoice in the sights and sounds of spring.

It was a perfect morning, the blue heaven was reflected in the water gliding past us, the scent of the hawthorn came wafted from the bushes growing on the opposite bank of the river. Our own garden was a mass of flowers, and I who, had been almost dead, was alive again, able to walk amid all this beauty, and thank God for the comparative strength and health He had restored to me.

"What an exquisite day," I said, as we stood looking at the sunshine lying across fields where cattle were lazily grazing.

"Yes. Lily could not have had a more delicious morning for her wedding, could she?"

"Lily!" I repeated, "What do you mean, Alick?"

He laughed and coloured.

"By the by, I ought not to have mentioned the matter. We were all bound over to silence, but I quite forgot Aunt Hilda's injunction. She thought you had better hear nothing about the marriage till it was over and done with."

"Because of what I said when I was delirious, I suppose?" I remarked, thoughtfully. "Certainly I had the strangest notions."

"Do not think of them," he entreated. "We cannot have you laid up again, Patty."

We took a few turns in silence, then I said, "Alick, I would give the world to have just one peep at Lily as a bride."

He shook his head. "You are not strong enough yet, little woman, to go sight-seeing."

"But I am strong," I persisted, "as strong as I ever shall be again; and it will do me harm to cross my fancy; I feel it will, Alick. You know the doctors said I was to have everything I asked for."

Alick laughed outright, mine was such barefaced casuistry, but again negative my proposition.

"You must not think of it, dear," he said in his kind, loving way. "I am quite sure you have had enough of the cathedral to last you for the remainder of your natural life."

Still I persisted—insisted rather. I could give fifty reasons for my desire where he could only give one against it, and so at length I gained my point, all the more readily, perhaps, because he was at heart as eager as I to see the show.

"We will not try though to get in amongst the crowd," he bargained. "All Oldstone is certain to be there, and you are not fit to be hustled about or stared at by the good people in the town. We will just go round the cloisters, and steal through our own particular little door, and get up into the nun's gallery, and we shall see everything there, and nobody be a bit the wiser."

Entering at the most remote gate, and creeping our way in and out amongst the tombs and headstones, we reached the cloisters, which were quite deserted, and surreptitiously made our way high up to a point where, without being seen, we could obtain a view of the whole of the proceedings.

The cathedral was full—full to over-flowing. Every available seat was occupied. People in the aisles were craning their heads over the shoulders of those in front of them. Only one passage, and that the principal one, was kept clear for the bridal party. We could not have obtained standing-room had we tried our chance amongst the crowd.

The sun was shining in through the windows, stained and unstained. It was the brightest of all bright sights to look down from our eyrie—and see the ladies' dresses—and the lovely flowers—and the rich colours cast by the old glass. Everything seemed so bright, so gay that for the time I quite forgot myself—forgot I had ever spent a night alone in the cathedral—and that I had there either dreamed strange dreams, or beheld terrible visions.

"Why, I believe coming has done you good," said my brother in a low voice, surveying me with wondering eyes. "You look quite bright and cheerful, Patty."

For answer I only squeezed his fingers, and then began to pick out our most intimate friends from amidst the spectators.

"Do you see Miss Atterton, Alick?" I whispered; "she has got a new bonnet; and see, there is aunt, and Mrs. James Herington, and Nina Lovelace, is not she pretty! And look, Alick—"

"Hist!" he interposed. "Here they come."

Yes, there they came. In a minute more they were ranged before the altar, and the dean began the service.

I could not take my eyes off Lily, she was as white as her floral namesake, and there was a look in her face I had never before seen in any living face, and that I trust I may never see again.

In a moment all the brightness and sunshine seemed to fade away, leaving nothing save a dull darkness before my eyes. The goodly company, the many coloured dresses, the delicate flowers vanished, and in their places there came desolation and silence, save for the voice of the dean beginning "Dearly beloved."

"Alick, I am afraid I am going to be ill—I feel very faint!" I gasped.

"For mercy's sake, Patty, keep up for a little, we can't get away without making some noise, and one might almost hear a pin drop below. Have you not some smelling-salts with you?"

I had, and with a great effort kept myself up, figuratively, as he desired. I leaned my head against the rough wall behind me, and tried to steady the objects in the cathedral which would keep slipping, slipping from my sight.

At intervals I could see distinctly Sir Edwin's dark face, and Lily's so ghastly, ghastly white, the evil countenance of the doctor who had attended Sir Clement in his last illness, and then they would all blend with the figures kneeling before the De Grabrooke monument, with the stiff effigy on the De Grabrooke tomb.

"Into which holy estate," proceeded the dean, "these two persons present come now to be joined. Therefore, if any man can show any just cause why they may not lawfully be joined together, let him now speak, or else hereafter for ever hold his peace."

"*I can. He is a murderer!*"

The words rang out through the ancient edifice clear as a bell, and echoed along the roof of the cathedral, as if the sentence were taken up and repeated by fifty voices. In a moment all was confusion, every one seemed to be moving, hundreds of people appeared to be pressing forward to one spot, a thousand colours danced before my eyes, a hum as of a multitude of people talking sounded in my ears; then I felt myself hurried along, dragged down this dark steep broken steps, and so breathless out into the open air.

"*I* did not speak, Alick!" I cried. "*I* said nothing!"

His face and clothes were covered with dust and dirt, he was panting as if he had run a race, drops of perspiration were on his forehead, but he did not answer a word.

He took me in his arms, and keeping well out of sight till we were clear of the Close, struck into a narrow passage between two blank walls.

Then he put me to the ground and catching my hand, said—

"Run, Patty! whether you are able or not, you must run now."

I do not know how I did it. I cannot imagine how my limbs so weak and feeble carried me along, but at last we were safe—quite safe on the bank of our own tranquil river, and we had not met a creature by the way.

How long we sat there I do not know—not very long, I daresay, though it seemed hours to me.

As well as he could Alick brushed the cobwebs and dirt from his clothes, and washed his hands and face in the river, then with very pale cheeks he turned to me and said—

"Patty, we will get home now; we can go through the garden, and you must lie down in your own room. I will return to the town and see what has happened; but remember one thing, to no human being, not to father or aunt, or any one else, must you confess we were in the cathedral this day: you understand me, dear?"

His tone was very tender and pitiful, though his words were so urgent.

For answer I held out my hands and began to cry.

"*I* did not speak, Alick. I assure you I did not say a word."

"Never mind that, dear," he answered, kissing me still with the same sorrowful tenderness; "only keep your own counsel and I will keep it too."

I had another illness. Whatever my ravings revealed, or my family suspected, was kept so close a secret that not a creature in Oldstone guessed Alick and I had been in the nun's gallery when the dean's exhortation met with so fearful a response.

Before I could leave my room Alick had to say good-by in reality.

It was one evening at twilight he came to part with me, and we sat for a while hand clasped in hand in total silence, our hearts too full for speech.

At last he said—

"Patty, before I go to India there is something I want to tell you. No one else will, perhaps, and you may hear it suddenly."

"About—about—I understand," I exclaimed feebly.

"Yes, about that morning. Even father does not know for certain that we were there."

"I am glad of it," I said.

"The marriage did not go on," he proceeded after a pause.

"Not then?" I asked.

"Not ever," he answered; "it will never take place now."

I raised myself on my elbow and tried to see his face, for his tone implied more even than his words, but it was too dark for me to distinguish his features.

"Sir Edwin had a fit!" he went on speaking, slowly and cautiously.

"Yes?" I said, interrogatively.

"And somehow—we cannot tell how such things grow—there got about a belief that Sir Clement did not die of fever—that he came to his end unfairly. Do you feel faint, Patty?"

"No, go on. I would rather hear it from you."

"Well, at last there was such a fuss made that an order came for the body to be exhumed."

"You need not go on," I said. "I know—I know—I know. It was not delirium then, Alick, it was truth?"

"It was truth," he answered.

"And Sir Edwin?" I asked, half afraid to inquire, and yet feeling that I must put the question.

"Sir Edwin destroyed himself; that is what most of all I wanted to tell you."

"And was he buried in the De Grabrooke vault?"

Alick hesitated a minute, but then replied—

"No, he was buried in another place at midnight. Now, Patty, you know everything."

That is the story, my dears, and we will talk no more about it.

The Family of a Vourdalak

Aleksey Tolstoy

GATHERED IN VIENNA IN THE YEAR 1815 WAS THE CREAM OF EUROPE'S intellectuals, the elite of the international diplomatic set and all the towering social figures of the day. The congress was coming to an end. Royalist émigrés were preparing to return to their restored chateaux, and Russian fighters to their forsaken homes, while a number of discontented Poles were scheming to bring to Cracow their dreams of liberty and freedom, dubiously promised them by Prince Metternich, Prince Gartenberg and Count Nesselrode.

The scene resembled the aftermath of an animated social ball. For, in those late hours, after the fanfare and revelry had subsided, there remained a small core of people, still possessing a taste for amusement and the delightful company of the Austrian ladies, who were delaying their departures. This congenial circle, of which I was a member, gathered twice weekly in the manor of the Dowager Princess Schwartzenberg, several miles from the city on the outskirts of the tiny village of Gitzing. The aristocratic bearing of the mistress of the manor, her gracious amiability and her astute intellect held for her guests a magnetic attraction. On these blissful occasions, the mornings were devoted to promenades, and the afternoons to lunching in the manor or its environs. Evenings we spent luxuriating by the hearth, chatting—but never about politics, which was strictly forbidden. We surely had our fill of that. Sometimes we related tales, either the superstitions and legends of our mother countries or our own experiences.

One evening, after a round of story-telling which left everyone in that strained condition relieved only by the enveloping semidarkness, the Marquis d'Urfé, an elderly émigré who was loved for his youthful gaiety and penetrating wit, interrupted the ensuing silence.

"Your tales, gentlemen, are unusual, of course, but each, it seems to me, lacks the critical ingredient of personal involvement. I don't know whether any of you has actually witnessed the supernatural phenomenon of which you speak or if you can back it up with your word of honor."

Since not one of us could comply, the old man continued, decorously straightening his jabot.

"As for myself, gentlemen, I know of only one case similar to yours, but so strange, horrible and, what is most essential, authentic is it that even the most incredulous man will be left horror-stricken. I unfortunately was both witness and actor, and though I rarely like to recall the experience, I will do so if our charming ladies will only grant me their permission."

General consent followed immediately. A few apprehensive faces glanced toward the moonlit square on the parquet marble of the hall where we assembled. Slowly our small circle drew closer together, silently awaiting the tale. The marquis took out his gold snuffbox, drew a pinch, languorously inhaled and thus began.

"First of all, mesdames, I wish to ask your forgiveness if during my story I allude to affairs of the heart more often than is agreeable for a man of my age. But, as you will see, they are essential for the clarity of my story. And since it is excusable in old age to forget oneself, I hope none of you will mind if I imagine myself a young man again. It was in 1769 that I fell hopelessly in love with the exquisite Duchess de Gramont. This passion, which at the time I considered deep indeed, left me no peace either day or night, and the duchess, like most beautiful women, prolonged my anguish. In a moment of extreme agitation, I requested and received a diplomatic mission to the Gospodar of Moldavia, where negotiations were being held with Versailles on matters of great importance to France. Before my departure, I visited the duchess. She greeted me less mockingly than ever before; in fact, with genuine concern.

"D'Urfé, you are acting like a madman. But I know you, and I know you will never change your mind. And so, I beg you for only one thing. Please accept this small cross as a token of my friendship. Wear it until you return. It's a family relic which we value highly."

"With gallantry perhaps misplaced that moment, I kissed not the family relic but the delicate hand and fastened the cross around my neck. I have never removed it since.

"I shan't tire you, mesdames, with the details of my trip, with my observations about the Hungarians and the Serbs—those poor but brave and honest people who, in spite of Turkish enslavement, had forsaken neither their dignity nor their former independence. It's enough to tell you that having learned Polish during my extended stay in Warsaw, I also managed to acquire some Serbian. Thus I was able to make myself understood when I finally came upon a particular village, the name of which does not matter. Upon arriving at my quarters, I found my hosts in a state of profound confusion. This seemed especially strange since it was Sunday, the day Serbs abandon themselves to such amusements as dancing, sharpshooting, wrestling and the like. Ascribing their mood to some recent misfortune I was about to depart when an imposing young man approached and took my hand.

"'Enter. Enter, foreigner,' he urged. 'Don't be upset by our sadness. You will understand when I explain its origin.'

"He told me that his elderly father, Gorcha, a restless and wild-tempered man, arose one morning and took a long Turkish rifle from the wall.

"'Children,' said he to his two sons, George and Peter, 'I'm going up in the mountains to join the brave ones who are chasing the scoundrel, Ali Beg.'

"Such was called the Turkish bandit who continued to harass the neighborhood.

"'Wait ten days for me, and if by then I do not return, have a priest say a funeral Mass, for it will mean that I have been killed. But,' added old Gorcha sternly, 'if, and may God save you, I should return after those ten days, then, for your own sakes, do not permit me to enter the house. I order you to pierce me with a stake made of ash, regardless of what I will say or do. Because then I will no longer be myself, but rather a cursed vourdalak come to suck your blood.'

"I must digress, mesdames, to explain that the vourdalaks, or vampires, are, according to local opinion in Slavic nations, dead bodies that rise from graves in order to suck blood from the living. Although their habits are similar to vampires in other countries, vourdalaks prefer to suck the blood of close relatives and friends, who die and become vampires also. In Estonia and Herzegovina entire villages may be composed of vourdalaks. Indeed, the Abbot Augustine Colline, in his curious book on ghosts, indicates terrible examples of this phenomenon. Moreover, commissioners appointed by German emperors to investigate cases of vampirism have printed evidence of vourdalaks, who, being pierced through the heart with ash stakes, were buried in the village squares. Testimony offered by those officials who had been present at the piercings assure us they heard the corpses moaning as the stakes struck their hearts. I might add that all such testimony was delivered under oath and backed by signatures and authoritative seals.

"Keeping this in mind, it should be easy, Mesdames, for you to comprehend the effect of Gorcha's words upon his sons. Both threw themselves at his feet, pleading that he let them go to the mountains in his place. Gorcha didn't even reply. He simply turned his back on them and set forth, whistling an old ballad.

"The day I arrived in this village was the day appointed by Gorcha for his return, so it is not difficult for me to appreciate his family's alarm. Also, this was a fine family. George, the elder of the two sons, married and with two children, seemed to be the serious and firm one. His brother, Peter, a handsome eighteen-year-old youth, had a gentle manner. He was obviously a favorite of his younger sister, Zdenka, a true Slavic beauty. I was immediately struck by her resemblance to the Duchesse de Gramont, particularly with respect to one characteristic, a delicate line on her forehead. To this day, I have never seen it on anyone other than those two. This fault line, which did not seem appealing at first, became irresistible once you had noticed it a few times.

"Perhaps too impressionable then, or maybe this characteristic resemblance combined with Zdenka's charming naïveté was, in fact, irresistible. Having spoken to her briefly, I felt an affection that was destined to become even more tender.

"I remember we were all sitting at the table that was set with farmer's cheese and a jug of milk. Zdenka was weaving; her sister-in-law was preparing supper for the children who were playing in the sand at her feet. Peter was lightheartedly whistling as he cleaned his *jitagan*, a long Turkish dagger. George, who was leaning his elbows on the table with his chin in his hands, could not take his eyes off the main road. He sat there brooding.

"I, also confused by the melancholy atmosphere, stared at the evening clouds and at the monastery rising above the pines of a nearby forest. This monastery, as I later discovered, had been famous at one time for its miraculous icon of the Holy Virgin which, according to legend, was brought by the angels and hung on the branches of an oak tree. During the preceding century, the invading Turks had slaughtered the monks and destroyed this cloister. Now there remained only the walls and a shrine where a mysterious hermit served Mass. He also guided travelers through the ruins and sheltered pilgrim who, journeying from shrine to shrine, preferred to stop at Our Lady under the Oak. Of course, I learned all of this later, since that evening my thoughts were hardly on the archeology of Serbia. As often happens when one gives free rein to thought, I became engrossed with the memory of earlier days with the enchanting period of my childhood and with friends whom I left for this remote and uncivilized country. And I was dreaming about the Duchesse de Gramont, and—but what is the use of hiding my sinful thoughts?—I mused, Mesdames, about several other contemporaries of your grandmothers', whose beauty, in spite of my will, reminded me, each in turn, of the charming duchess. Thus obsessed, I was soon oblivious to my hosts and their anxiety.

"Suddenly, George broke the silence to ask his wife about the exact time the old man had left.

"'At eight o'clock,' she replied. 'I remember hearing the monastery bell strike then.'

"'Well, now it must be no later than half past seven,' he said, becoming pensive and gazing again at the long road leading into the forest.

"I failed to mention, mesdames, that when the Serbs suspect someone of vampirism, they avoid referring to him directly. Otherwise they would call him forth from his grave. Consequently, George alluded to his father as the 'old man.'"

"Several minutes of silence lasted until one of the boys pulled Zdenka by the apron, asking 'Auntie, when is Grandfather coming home?'

"George responded to this question with a violent slap. The child began to cry, whereupon his younger brother asked, surprised and frightened, 'Why do you forbid us, Father, to speak of Grandfather?' Another slap silenced him instantly. Then both began to howl as the rest of the family made a sign of the cross. At that very moment the monastery clock struck the first chime of eight and a human figure emerged from the forest.

"'It's he, thank God!' exclaimed Zdenka, Peter and their sister-in-law all at once.

"'God protect us,' George cried. 'And how are we to tell if the ten days appointed by him have passed or not?'

"Everyone gazed at him in horror. Meanwhile, the human figure was approaching closer, closer, closer. A tall old man with a gray mustache and a pale stern face dragged himself with the aid of a stick. The closer he drew, the gloomier George became. Finally, the newcomer stopped and circled his family with a look that seemed oblivious, so glazed and distant were his eyes.

"'Well,' he said in a timbreless voice, 'why does no one meet me? What does this silence mean? Don't you see I'm wounded?'

"Then we all noticed that the old man's left side was drenched with blood.

"'Hold your father up,' I motioned to George. 'And you, Zdenka, give him something to strengthen him; otherwise, he will collapse.'

"'Father,' said George approaching Gorcha, 'show me your wound. I know about wounds and I'll bandage it for you.' But as soon as the son attempted to take off his coat, the old man pushed him away viciously, clasping his side with both hands.

"'Let go, clumsy one. You are hurting me.'

"'That means you're wounded in the heart!' George exclaimed, his face blanching. 'Take off your coat! Take it off, do you hear! It's crucial, do you hear me!'

"The old man rose to his full height. 'Watch out!' he warned, in that same flat voice. 'If you touch me, I shall curse you.'

"Peter placed himself between George and his father. 'Let him be. You must see he's suffering.'

"'Don't go against his will,' his wife advised. 'You know he'll never tolerate such a thing.'

"At that moment we saw the herd heading toward the house in a cloud of dust. It was not certain whether the dog escorting them did not recognize her old master or if something else influenced her, for as soon as she spied Gorcha, she halted. Her fur bristled. She growled, shivering in her tracks as if she were seeing something extraordinary.

"'What's the matter with the dog?' the old man asked, his frown deepening. 'Have I become a stranger to my own family? Did the ten days in the mountains change me so much that my dog does not recognize me?'

"'Do you hear?' George nudged his wife.

"'What, George?'

"'He said himself that ten days have passed.'

"'Oh, no! And he did not come at the appointed hour?'

"'Yes, yes. It's clear what has to be done.'

"'The accursed dog is still howling. Shoot her!' Gorcha commanded. 'Do you hear me?'

"George didn't move. But Peter, with tears in his eyes, arose, lifted his father's rifle and shot the dog, which whimpered, rolling in the dust. 'This one was my favorite,' he said huskily. 'I don't know why my father had to have her killed.'

"'Because that's all she was worth,' Gorcha snapped. 'But it has grown cool. I want to be under the roof.'

"While all this took place, Zdenka prepared a drink of vodka with pears, honey and raisins for the old man, which he pushed away with disgust. He displayed the same loathing for the lamb and rice that George placed before him. Then he went to sit in a corner, muttering unintelligibly.

"The pine logs were flaming in the fireplace, their flicker illuminating the old man's gaunt and pallid face. Were it not for the fire's glow, he could have been taken for a dead man. Zdenka sat down beside him.

"'Father, you do not eat or rest. But do tell us about your adventures in the mountain.'

"By saying this, the girl knew she was striking the most sensitive cord in the old man's heart. He loved to recount his battles and exploits against the Turks.

A faint smile crossed his livid lips, though his eyes remained unexpressive. He responded by stroking his daughter's lovely blond hair.

"'Zdenka,' he said, 'I will tell you what I saw in the mountain, but not now, not today. I am tired after all. I can tell you one thing. Ali Beg is dead. He perished by your father's stroke. If anyone doubts it, here is the proof!' He pulled open the bag which was slung across his shoulder, removing a bloody head, not much less cadaverous than his own. We all turned away with a shudder. Gorcha, handing it to Peter, said, 'Hang it over the door of our house so that all who pass may know that Ali Beg is dead, that the roads are free of villains—unless one counts the Yanychars of the Sultan!'

"Peter obeyed, though with obvious aversion. 'Now everything's clear to me,' he reflected. 'The poor dog was growling because she smelled dead flesh.'

"'Yes, she smelled dead flesh . . .' George mumbled, after having returned unobtrusively with something in his hand which he rested in a nearby corner. It looked like a sharply pointed pole.

"'George,' whispered his wife, 'you don't mean you intend to . . .'

"'Brother,' murmured Zdenka, 'what do you have in mind? No, no, no. You're not going to do this! It's inconceivable!'

"'Let me be,' warned George. 'I know what I'm doing and it won't be anything rash.'

"Meanwhile, night had fallen and the family wandered off to sleep in that part of the house which was separated from my own room by a thin partition. I must confess that everything I had observed affected me strangely. I snuffed out the candle. The moon shone through my window, casting bluish reflections on the floor—similar to those, Mesdames, you see before your very eyes. I felt sleepy, but, needless to say, I could not fall asleep. Attributing it to the moonlight, I searched for something to drape across the window. But I could find nothing. I was startled by voices coming from the other side of the partition and strained to hear what they were saying.

"'Lie down, wife,' George said soothingly. 'You, Peter, and you, Zdenka, don't worry about anything. I'll stand watch.'

"'No, George,' answered his wife. 'It's I who should not be sleeping. You worked all last night; you're exhausted. Besides, I have to attend our elder son who's been ill since yesterday. Don't worry. Lie down. I'll watch for you.'

"'Brother,' Zdenka said in her caressing voice, 'it seems that nobody has to watch for anything. See how peacefully Father sleeps.'

"'Not my wife, nor you, nor anyone seems to have much sense,' George replied in a voice that left no room for contradiction. 'Now I've told you to go to sleep. I'll be the guard!'

"Complete silence followed. Soon, my eyelids grew heavy, and I too fell asleep. The slow creaking of my door awakened me. The old man, Gorcha, was entering. I could feel his presence through the pitch darkness. He seemed to be observing me through his vacant eyes. He lifted one foot after another, stealthily, until he was by my side. Consumed with terror, I nevertheless managed to remain still. The old man bent over me, his livid face so close to mine that I could feel his corpselike breath. Then, exerting superhuman effort, I discovered myself sitting up in bed, perspiring profusely. No one was in the room. But through the window I detected Gorcha, his face pressed against the pane, his uncanny eyes riveted upon me. I didn't have the strength to cry out, only enough composure to remain in bed and pretend I saw nothing. The old man was evidently reassuring himself that I was asleep, for, having stared at me thus, he slowly moved away from the window. George was snoring so loudly that the walls rattled. Then I heard Gorcha's voice in the next room. The sick child coughed.

"'You're not asleep my little boy,' Gorcha asked.

"'No, Grandfather, and I'd like very much to talk to you.'

"'Ah, you want to talk with me. And what will it be about?'

"'I'd like you to tell me how you fought the Turks because I want to fight them.'

"'I thought you would, my dear child. Tomorrow, I will give you the small dagger I've been saving.'

"'Oh, Grandfather, please give it to me now.'

"'Well, my little one, why didn't you talk to me earlier today?'

"'Because . . . because Father wouldn't let me.'

"'Your father is very cautious. But you want the dagger very much' . . .

"'Yes, I want it very much. Only not here because Father might wake up.'

"'Where then?'

"'Well, let's go outside quietly, Grandfather, so no one can hear us.'

"Gorcha seemed to laugh as the boy got out of bed. I didn't believe in vampires. But my nerves had been so shattered by my nightmare that I got up and slammed my fist against the partition lest I reproach myself later. No one woke, though my blow sounded loud enough to waken the seven sleepers in the Arabian fairy tale. Determined to save the child, I hurled myself against the door, but it was locked from the outside. To intensify my frustration, the old man was already passing the window with the child in his arms.

"'Get up! Get up!' I screamed with all my might, shaking the partition vehemently. Only then did George awaken.

"'Hurry,' I cried. 'He's carrying your child away.' With one swift kick, George broke down the door and darted toward the forest. With some trouble I wakened Peter, then his sister-in-law and Zdenka. Huddled in front of the house, we saw George a few minutes later returning with the boy in his arms. The child had already fainted when George stumbled upon him on the main highway. We revived him, though he appeared no sicker than before. To our anxious interrogation, he explained that Grandfather had done him no harm, that they had strolled together, quietly chatting; that once they were in the fresh air, he had fainted, though he couldn't remember how or why.

"Gorcha was nowhere to be found, so the remainder of the night was spent in hushed consultation.

"The next morning I learned that ice was floating in the river, preventing anyone from crossing to the mainland for several days. Even if it were possible for me too leave, however, I could not have done so. The more I saw Zdenka, the more I craved her. And, Mesdames, I am not, mind you, one of those who believe in sudden, uncontrollable passion, the kind exalted in novels. Yet I do believe that love can develop sometimes more quickly than is usual. In Zdenka's remarkable beauty I encountered the Duchesse de Gramont, the duchess transformed by pastoral garb and melodious foreign speech. The characteristic line both had on their foreheads was the *coup de grâce*. Yet perhaps it was really the incredible situation in which I had become an actor that ignited my intense passion.

"During the day I overheard Zdenka speaking with her younger brother. 'What do you think about Father, Peter?' she asked. 'I can't believe you suspect him.'

"'I dare not suspect him, especially since the boy assured us father didn't harm him. As for his sudden disappearance, well, you know he had done this before, and never explained his activities and departures.'

"'I know,' Zdenka agreed. 'But you know that George is—'

"'Yes, I know. I know. It's useless talking to him. I'm afraid we'll have to hide the stake. He won't be able to get another one. There are no ash trees on this side of the mountain.'

"'Yes, let's hide it. But don't tell the children, for they'll surely tell George.'

"'We must be cautious,' Peter urged, and they separated.

"Night came, and still not a trace of the old man, Gorcha. Like the previous night, I was in bed, distracted by the moonbeams that illuminated my room. Sleep was beginning to distort my thoughts when I instinctively felt the presence of the old man. Opening my eyes, I saw his deathlike face pressed against the pane.

This time I tried to get up, but my limbs were paralyzed. I heard the old man go around the house and knock on George's window. The child tossed and moaned in his sleep. For a while, silence prevailed. Then there was a knock at the child's window. He moaned again and woke up.

"'Is that you, Grandfather?'

"'It's me,' he answered solemnly. 'I brought you the little dagger.'

"'I don't dare come out. Father has forbidden it.'

"'But you don't have to. Just open the window and kiss me.'

"As the window was being opened, I summoned all of my nerve, jumped off the bed, and began knocking on the partition. George was immediately up. I heard him cursing and his wife screaming. A minute later the entire household clustered around the fainted child. As before, Gorcha vanished. We revived the child, though he was weak and could barely breathe. The poor little thing didn't understand why he had fainted. His mother and Zdenka ascribed it to the child's fear of being caught in a forbidden conversation with his grandfather. I said nothing. When the boy grew quiet everyone but George went to sleep. At dawn I heard him awakened with his wife. They were whispering. Zdenka joined them. The women were crying.

"The child died. I shall not elaborate on the family's despair, except to mention that, peculiarly enough, nobody attributed his death to Gorcha. At least not publicly.

"George remained reticent, his gloomy expression menacing. For two days the old man did not reappear. The third night, on the day of the little one's burial, I sensed that somebody was roaming through the house murmuring the name of the child who was still alive. It even seemed to me, momentarily, that Gorcha glanced into my window. I couldn't be sure, since the moon was obscured by the clouds. Nevertheless I reported this to George. He questioned the child, who acknowledged that he had heard his grandfather calling him and had seen him at the window outside his room. George commanded his son to awaken him the next time the old man appeared.

"These events curiously intensified my tenderness for Zdenka. I existed in constant agitation. During the day it was impossible to speak with her alone. At night, I was tormented by the prospect of my imminent departure.

"Zdenka's room was separated from mine by a hall which led on one side to the street, on the other to the yard. On my way for a walk before sleeping, I passed through the hall and noticed her door slightly ajar. In spite of myself I stood behind it, listening. The familiar rustle of her dress made my heart pound. She was singing a song about a Serbian knight saying farewell to his girl:

"'Oh, my young poplar,' the old king said, 'I am off to the wars and you will forget me.
The trees that grow at the foot of the mountain are slender and easily bent, but your young body is even more slender and easily bent.
Bittersweet berries are red. They are effortlessly blown by the wind.
But your lips are redder than the berries. And I am like the old oak without leaves; my beard whiter than the Danube's foam.
You will forget me, little heart, and I will perish from longing, for the enemy will not dare to kill the old king.'
Then the beautiful girl answered, 'I swear to remain faithful to you, never to forget you. If I break my oath then return after death to suck my heart's blood.'
To which the old king replied, 'Amen.'
He went off to war and the beautiful girl forgot him."

"Here Zdenka stopped as if afraid to finish the song. I could not contain myself. Her soft eloquence was an echo of the Duchesse de Gramont. Disregarding the consequences, I flung open the door. My intrusion made her blush, for she had just removed her outer garment and was wearing only a gold-embroidered red silk blouse and a richly colored petticoat. The outline of her supple limbs was visible and her abundant blond hair unbraided. In this state of half-undress, she looked more ravishing than ever.

"'Zdenka, my life, please do not fear me,' I implored. 'Everybody is asleep. Only the crickets in the grass and the dragonfly in the air can hear what I'm going to tell you.'

"'Go away, go away, my dearest. If my brother sees us, I am lost.'

"'Zdenka, I will not leave you until you promise to love me as the lovely maiden in your song promised to love the king. Zdenka, I soon will have to depart. Who knows whether we will ever see each other again. I love you more than my own soul, more than my salvation. My life and my blood are yours. Won't you give me but an hour?'

"'Too much can happen in an hour,' Zdenka said softly, leaving her hand in mine. 'You don't know my brother. I have a premonition that he will see us.'

"'Don't worry, Zdenka, my darling Zdenka. Your brother is exhausted by these sleepless nights. He is lulled by the wind rustling through the trees.

His slumber is deep. Our night is long, and I beg you for only one hour, whereas farewell may last forever.'

"'No, no. Not forever!'

"'Perhaps, Zdenka. Yet I see only you, hear only you. I am no longer master over my own fate. It's as if I were compelled by a superior power. Forgive me!' and like a madman I pressed her to my heart.

"'You're not a friend to me, no, no, no,' she gasped, breaking away from my arms and hiding in a corner.

"I don't recall what I replied to her at that moment, for my sudden boldness alarmed me though not because I was inhibited in the past, but because, in spite of my passion, I deeply respected Zdenka's purity. Thus, my gallant manner, so successful with the beautiful maidens of the time, shamed me. I realized that the young girl, in all her simplicity, had not fathomed the intent of my artful words, though, Mesdames, judging from your smiles, I can see it is readily apparent to you. I stood before her, bewildered, when unexpectedly she pointed toward the window, shivering. There was Gorcha peering at us. A heavy arm grabbed my shoulder. I turned around. It was George.

"'What are you doing here?' he scowled.

"Embarrassed by this turn of events, I directed his attention toward his father, who was still standing at the window but who vanished once George saw him.

"'I heard the old man came to warn your sister,' I explained. George stared as if to penetrate my innermost thoughts. Taking my arm, he walked me to my room and left without a word.

"The next day the family was gathered in front of the house at a table set with dairy foods.

"'Where is the boy?' asked George.

"'In the yard,' his wife answered. 'He's playing his favorite game, imagining that he's fighting against the Turks.'

"No sooner had she said this than to our great surprise we detected the hulking form of old Gorcha lumbering toward us from the forest, in a manner reminiscent of his initial arrival.

"'You are most welcome, Father,' said his daughter-in-law in a low tone.

"'We are happy to see you, Father,' chorused Zdenka and Peter.

"'Father,' George said, 'we were expecting you. Will you say grace?'

"The old man turned away, frowning.

"'Say grace this very minute,' urged George, 'and make the sign of the cross. Or, I swear by St. George . . .'

"Zdenka and her sister-in-law begged the old man to say grace.

"'No,' insisted Gorcha. 'He doesn't dare give me orders. If he tries to force me, I will curse him.'

"George darted into the house, returning in a fury. 'Where is the stake?' he cried. 'Where did you put the stake?'

"Zdenka and Peter glanced at each other furtively.

"'You corpse!' George shouted at his father. 'What have you done with my elder son? Give me my son, you dead man!'

"Speaking this way, he turned more and more pale as rage burned in his eyes. The old man stood motionless, an evil sneer on his lips.

"'Where in heaven's name is the stake? Where is that stake?' George continued. 'Let misery befall those who have hidden it, all the misery possible in one lifetime.'

"Then the most terrible thing occurred. Riding toward us on an enormous stake was the younger son, his blood-curdling laughter resounding in our ears. As he neared us, he screeched the Serbian battle cry.

"George flushed, grabbing the stake away from the child. The youngster threw himself on his father, who let forth a howl, then darted away in the direction of the forest with a speed that seemed supernatural. George chased him across the field and also faded out of sight. The sun already set when George, pale as death, his hair on end, came back. As he sat by the fire, his teeth seemed to be chattering. Nobody dared question him. As bedtime approached, he regained his self-control and, calling me to his side, spoke in a casual manner.

"'My dear guest, I just saw that the river is cleared of ice. Nothing detains you any longer. No need to say good-bye to my family,' he added, glancing at Zdenka. 'She wishes you well and hopes you remember us kindly. At dawn, you will find your horse saddled and a guide to direct you out of the village. Farewell, and forgive your hosts for the difficult times you spent with them.'

"George seemed almost friendly as he accompanied me to my room and shook my hand for the last time. Then he shuddered and his teeth chattered as if from the cold.

"Once alone, I thought of the despaired I had suffered over former love affairs, the tenderness, jealousy and rage. Yet never until that moment, not even during encounters with the Duchesse de Gramont, had I experienced such despondence. I changed into my traveling clothes before the sun had risen, hoping to see Zdenka before my departure. But George was already awaiting me in the hall.

"I spurred my horse on, promising myself that I would stop at the village when returning from Yassa. Although this was a long time off, the prospect relieved my sadness. I was already contemplating a pleasurable return, and my imagination was working out the sweet details, when my horse bolted, almost hurling me from my saddle. She stopped, stretched out her forelegs and snorted as if in danger. I looked about in every direction until I noticed a wolf about a hundred steps ahead of us, digging in the ground. Seeing us, it raced away. I rode over and found a freshly dug hole, with a stake sticking out a few inches above the ground. Yet I couldn't be sure of this, since I rode by swiftly."

At this point the marquis stopped talking and took a pinch of snuff.

"Is that all?" the ladies asked.

"Oh, no, not at all," assured d'Urfé. "It's very painful for me to recall what I am about to relate. Gladly would I forfeit worldly pleasures to free my mind forever of these memories.

"It took me about a year to conclude my affairs in Yassa, much longer than anticipated. How can I tell you what I experienced through that stretch of time? It's the sad truth that stable emotions do not exist in this world. The success of my negotiations regarding the revolting politics which have recently cause so much trouble brought me strong praise from Versailles. But my tormenting memories of Zdenka were intensified. Even the ladies, particularly the wife of the Seigneur of Modlavia—a beauty who spoke out language to perfection and who singled me out from all the other young foreigners in Yassa—could not relieve my pain. Yet, reared according to French gallantry and ruled by Gallic bloods in my veins, I, of course, could not refuse this lady's flattering approaches. Moreover, considering that I was the French representative at the court of her husband, I regarded it my singular duty to satisfy the desires of the seigneur's noble wife. As you can see, Mesdames, I always put the interest of my country above all else.

"Upon my return home, I journeyed by the same road I had taken to Yassa. By then I had forgotten Zdenka and her family and was reminded of them while riding through a field where I heard a bell ring eight times. Its ring was familiar. My guide informed me that it came from a nearby shrine, the Monastery of Our Lady under the Oak. With this, I headed for the guest house, which was swarming with pilgrims. A monk assured me I could find lodging practically anywhere, that, due to 'damned Gorcha,' there were many empty houses.

"'Do you mean,' I gasped, 'that the old man is still alive?'

"'No. Apparently, he is lying quietly in the earth with a stake through his heart. He sucked the blood of his grandson, the younger child of George. One night, the little boy knocked at the house begging to be admitted, crying that he was cold. His foolish mother, though she herself had buried him that very day, was unable to summon the courage to send her son back to the grave. No sooner had she let him in than he threw himself upon her, sucking her life's blood. After she was buried, she in turn came for the blood of her husband and her brother-in-law. They all shared the same fate.'

"'And Zdenka. What happened to her?' I asked, trembling.

"'Well, as for her, the poor thing went mad from sorrow. It's really better we don't speak of her.'

"The monk's comments were puzzling, but I had no heart to pursue them further.

"'Still,' he continued 'vampirism is contagious. Many families in the village suffer from it. If you accept my advice, you'll remain in the monastery for the night. Out there, whether the vourdalaks get you or not, you'll undergo such terror that your hair will turn snow white before I ring for early Mass. Of course, I'm only a poor monk, yet the generosity of the travelers enables me to care for their needs. I can offer you such excellent farmer's cheese and currants that your mouth will water at the sight of them. There are a few bottles of Tokay wine which are as fine as those served at the table of His Holiness.'

"I seemed to be speaking with an innkeeper rather than a monk, and his purpose in relating these horror stories appeared bent upon coercing me into imitating the generosity of other travelers who provided the holy man with the means of gratifying their needs. Aside from this, the word 'terror' never fails to affect me like a trumpet affects a warhorse. How ashamed I would have been had I not proceeded to investigate the rumors.

"My shivering guide begged permission, which I granted, to remain at the monastery. I thus arrived alone at the deserted village. No lights were on; no songs sung. Though the eerie silence, I passed those familiar houses until I reached George's. Whether I was influenced by a romantic whim or simply by youthful boldness, I resolved to spend the night, though no one answered my knock at the gates. Pushing, I managed to get them open. I tied my saddled horse to the shed and crept up to the house. Not a single door was locked, yet the house seemed abandoned. Zdenka's room appeared to have been forsaken that very day. Several dresses lay across the bed. A few pieces of jewelry, gifts from me, were scattered on the bureau. A small enamel cross, which I had purchased in Budapest, sparkled in the moonlight.

"My heart pounded at a dreadful speed. Regardless of my waning love, I sighed, wrapped myself in my cape, stretched out on the bed and slept. I can't recall the precise details, but I do remember envisioning Zdenka as a charming, ingenuous, devoted creature shamed by my fickleness. How, I agonized, could I have forgotten the sweet maiden who had loved me so very much? The vision of her became intertwined with my memories of the Duchesse de Gramont, and, in those two silhouettes, I saw one and the same person. Kneeling at Zdenka's feet, I prayed for her forgiveness. My entire being, my very soul, became infused with both sadness and happiness. Thus, I continued to dream until gently wakened by wheat stalks waving in the wind. I heard the distant chirping of birds, the rushing of a waterfall and the brushing of leaves, when it seemed that all those sounds could actually have emanated from the rustling of a lady's dress. With this notion, I opened my eyes and beheld Zdenka by my bedside. So bright was the moon that I could distinguish every feature, each more enchanting than I remembered. She was dressed in the garb she had worn on the eve of our farewell: her silk peasant blouse embroidered in gold and dirndl skirt gathered tightly around her slim waist.

"'Zdenka,' I cried, rising quickly from the bed. 'Is it you?'

"'Yes, it is me,' she responded in a small, pathetic voice. 'Yes, it is your forgotten Zdenka. Why didn't you return sooner? Now everything is ended and you must leave at once. A moment's delay and you are lost. Farewell, my friend. Farewell forever.'

"'Zdenka, Zdenka, you have been through so much sorrow. Please speak with me at least. It will relieve your anxiety.'

"'My friend, do not believe all you hear about us. But do go. Go quickly, or else you will die without reprieve.'

"'But Zdenka, what is there to fear? Is it possible you will not grant me an hour?' She shuddered and for a second seemed almost imperceptibly transformed.

"'All right. An hour—just one. Is it not the same request you made the night you overheard me singing about the old king? So be it again. I'll permit you this hour . . . But no, no,' she screamed, as if coming to her senses. 'Go. Run. Run far away. I'm telling you to hurry while you still have the chance.'

"A wild frenzy distorted her features. I could understand what forced her to speak this way. I only knew how lovely she was and decided to remain in spite of her wishes. Finally, complying with my request, she sat beside me and confessed that she had loved me at first sight. As she spoke, the change in her became gradually more and more distinct. Her eyes glinted boldly. Her movements challenged me provocatively. Indeed, she was emerging as someone quite unmaidenly, even wicked, completely different from the reserved young virgin of my memories.

"Is it possible, I asked myself, that Zdenka was never the chaste girl she appeared to be six months ago? Is it possible that being afraid of her brother, she had assumed a convenient disguise? Had I been tricked by a modest façade? But then, I countered, why did she urge me to leave? Was this simply a coy move? I imagined for a moment that I saw the former Zdenka . . . But no, she was still transfigured . . . If Zdenka is not the Diana I thought she was, could she not be compared to another goddess at least as charming? Anyway, I prefer the fate of Adonis to that of Acteon. If this classical reference seems out of place, Mesdames, please remember that I am relating events of 1769. At that time, mythology was à la mode, and I made the pretense of being avant-garde. Since then, times have changed, for the revolution has eclipsed both paganism and Christianity. The new religion, reason, is erected in their place. I never favored this cult, reason, especially in the company of women. As my story was transpiring, I was particularly unwilling to worship this deity. Quite naturally, I abandoned myself to Zdenka, responding pleasurably to her irresistible advances. Some time passed in sweet forgetfulness. Zdenka amused me by trying on one piece of jewelry after another, until it occurred to me to place the enamel cross around her swanlike neck. Anticipating my intention, Zdenka withdrew with a shudder.

"'Enough of his foolishness, my love,' she smiled, regaining her composure. 'Let us leave all these trinkets and discuss you and your intentions.'

"In spite of my feelings, Zdenka's odd behavior forced me to study her more closely. Unlike the past, she did not have the gold medals and relics which Serbians commonly wear from childhood to death. I questioned her about this.

"'I lost them,' she answered, impatient to change the subject.

"A sense of foreboding came over me. I decided to leave, but Zdenka stood in my way.

"'What's the meaning of this?' she scowled. 'You begged me for an hour of my time, and now you're leaving so abruptly.'

"'Zdenka, you were right in convincing me to leave. I just heard a noise. I'm afraid we will be discovered together,' I said, attempting to conciliate her.

"'Don't worry, my friend. Everyone around us is asleep. Only the cricket in the grass and the dragonfly in the air can hear what we say.'

"'No, no, Zdenka, this won't do. I must go.'

"'Please wait,' she implored. 'I love you more than my own soul, more than my salvation. You once told me that your life and blood were mine.'

"'But your brother! I have the feeling he is about to arrive.'

"'Be still, my heart. My brother is asleep, too, lulled by the wind that is rustling in the trees. His sleep is deep and the night is long. I am requesting but a moment longer.'

"As she said this, Zdenka looked so beautiful that the anxiety that had gripped me vanished with my desire to remain by her side. A strange mixture of fright and rapture filled me. Slowly, as my will weakened, Zdenka became increasingly tender. I resolved to give in to her while I maintained my guard. But alas! I was only half sensible, as usual. Noticing my reserve, she offered me a few drafts of wine to warm myself, saying that she had purchased it from the good monk. My compliance elicited a smile, and the wine surely produced its intended effect. After the second glass, my reservations over the little cross and holy medals were completely erased from my consciousness. Zdenka, in her informal attire, her blond hair unbraided, her bracelets gleaming in the moonlight, was hopelessly enticing. I could not restrain myself and impulsively embraced her.

Then, Mesdames, then one of those inexplicable signs appeared. I have never been able to explain it to myself. In fact, at that time I was inclined not to believe in it at all. Nevertheless, when I pressed Zdenka's body to my own, one of the points of the cross, which the Duchesse de Gramont had given me, stuck into my chest. That momentary pain served as a bolt from heaven. Glancing at Zdenka, I saw that her features, though beautiful, were imprinted with death, that her eyes were glazed and that her smile was convulsed with the agony of a condemned prisoner. Simultaneously, I sense in the room a putrid odor like some half-opened tomb. The loathsome truth stunned me. Only too late did I recall the monk's warning. What a desperate situation I was in! Everything depended upon boldness and cunning. No wanting her to notice my doubt, I turned away. My gaze passed for a second across the window where Gorcha was leaning on a bloody stake, peering at me with the eyes of a hyena. In the other window stood George, looking exactly like his father. They were both following my movements closely. Undoubtedly they would descend upon me at my slightest effort to escape. So I pretended not to have seen them but continued, with all my will, to caress Zdenka as if nothing unusual were happening. My mind raced through plans of escape. The wailing of women and children floated from the yard, piercing the silence like the howling of wild cats.

"It is time to escape, I said to myself, and the sooner the better. Turning to Zdenka, I spoke loudly enough for her ghastly relatives to hear. 'I am tired my dearest, and must lie down for a while. Yet, first, my horse should be fed. I beg you not to leave. Wait for me,' I said, kissing her cold mouth. Outside, my horse was covered with foam, trying vainly to gallop out of the shed. Her neighing made me wary lest she give me away. But the vourdalaks who overheard my conversation with Zdenka did not move. Certain that the gates were ajar, I jumped onto the saddle and spurred my horse on. Having passed swiftly through the gates, I barely noticed the crowd gathered round the house, gaping through the windows. My sudden departure must have startled them. Yet for those first few moments I only concentrated on the rhythmic clatter of my horse's hoofs as they resounded in the unearthly silence.

"On the verge of congratulating myself on a safe escape, I was interrupted by a noise that resembled a hurricane. Voices moaned, howled and argued with one another. Silence. Then a resounding beat as if a corps of infantrymen were in hot pursuit, I spurred on until my horse spurted blood and my veins almost burst from the fire within. A voice was calling me.

"'Wait, wait, my dear. I love you more than my soul, more than my salvation. Wait, wait. Your blood is mine.'

"A cold breath touched my ears as Zdenka leaped upon my horse from behind.

"'My heart, my soul,' she whispered to me. 'I see only you. I want only you. I have no power over myself. I obey a superior force. Forgive me, my dear one, forgive me.' Placing her arms around me, she bit my neck and tried to throw me from my horse.

"A terrible struggle ensued between us. Mustering all my energy, I managed to grab Zdenka with one arm around her waist, the other hand on her braids. Lifting myself in the stirrups, I hurled her to the ground. My strength drained, I became delirious. Gruesome images menaced me. First George, then Peter, was running along the road's edge trying to veer me off course. Neither one succeeded. I was rejoicing over this victory when, turning back, I saw old man Gorcha leaning on his stake, making incredible leaps with it as the Tyroleans do when they jump over crevices. But even he remained behind. His daughter-in-law, who was dragging the two children, threw one of them to him. He caught it on the sharp point, then, operating the stake like a slingshot, hurled the child at me. I avoided the blow, but the child, like a fierce bulldog, set his teeth in the neck of my horse. With some effort, I tore him away. Gorcha discharged the other one at me, but he was crushed under my horse's hoofs. I don't know what happened next. When I regained consciousness, it was already daylight, and I was sprawled at the end of the road, my horse dying nearby.

"And so, Mesdames, ended the love affair which, it would seem, should have numbed all my subsequent desires to search for others among your grandmothers. Those who still survive will testify that I did become far more sensible.

"The events I have related to you this evening are strange indeed. To this very day I shiver at the thought that I might have fallen into the power of my enemies. I might have become a vampire in turn. But Providence did not permit this, and I, mesdames, am not thirsty for your blood. And, though an old man, I am prepared to defend you till the last drop of blood courses from my veins."

The Spider

Hanns Heinz Ewers

And a will therein lieth, which dieth not. Who knoweth the mysteries of a will with its vigor?

—GLANVILLE

WHEN RICHARD BRACQUERNONT, MEDICAL STUDENT, MADE UP his mind to take Room 7 in the Hotel Stevens, a small place at Rue Alfred Stevens 6, three persons on three successive Fridays had hanged themselves to its window-cross.

Of these the first was a Swiss traveling salesman. They found his body by Saturday evening. The doctor maintained it must have been between five and six o'clock Friday afternoon that death befell. The corpse hung to a great hook fixed in the transom sill. The window was closed. The dead man had used the curtain cord for a rope. Since it was a low window, the man's knees almost rested on the floor. Thus, the suicide must have exercised strong will-power to accomplish his design. It was further evidenced that he was married, had four children, enjoyed a very steady and remunerative position and had proved himself of cheerful, evenly sanguine character. They found not a scrap of writing that bore upon the suicide, much less a will. Also he had never given any of his friends the slightest intimation.

Not far otherwise did it chance the second time. Carl Krause, featured at the nearby *Cirque Médrano* as quick change bicycle specialty man, had engaged Room 7 two days later. When he did not appear for that Friday night's performance the manager dispatched a stagehand to the hotel. The room was not locked; so the fellow entering found the actor hanging from the window rail. The suicide appeared no less inexplicable. The popular artist drew a handsome salary; and, being a young man of twenty-five, knew how to enjoy life.

Here again, no papers, no verbal insinuations. The only living relative was his old mother, toward whose support he had been in the habit of sending two hundred marks the first of every month.

Madam Dubonnet, the proprietress of this cheap little hotel, counted for her patronage almost entirely on the neighboring Montmartre-Varietés. For her this second inscrutable case of death in the same room had very unpleasant results. By now, several of her guests had left, and other regular patrons had not put in an appearance. She turned to the police commissioner of the Ninth Precinct, who, as a personal friend, promised to do everything for her that lay in his power. Hence, he not only busied himself with especial zeal in the investigations toward some possible motive for the suicide of the two lodgers, but he also placed an officer at her disposal, who moved into the mysterious room. For this, the guardsman, Charles-Marie Chaumié, had volunteered his services. This sergeant, an old "Marsouin" and marine-infantrist of eleven years service, had stood guard in Tonkiri and Annam so many a night alone at his post, had greeted with a rousing shot so many a surreptitious visit of cat-footed, yellow river pirates, that he indeed seemed capable of engaging the ghostly visitants, about which there was such great talk in Rue Alfred Stevens. Thus he moved into the room by Sunday evening, and composed himself for peaceful slumber, but not before he had handsomely praised the food and drink of the worthy Madam Dubonnet.

Every morning and evening Chaumié paid the police precinct a short visit, in order to make a report. For the first days these amounted to the declaration that he had noticed not the slightest thing. Wednesday evening, however, he stated his finding a clue. When urged to say more, he begged to remain silent for the time, for he was by no means sure that his discovery had any real connection with the death of the unfortunates, and he quite dreaded to make a fool of himself and be laughed at. Thursday his appearance was less confident and more grave; yet, again, he had nothing to report. Friday morning he showed more excitement. He remarked, half laughing, half serious, that this window, at all events, had a peculiar fascination.

Nevertheless, he insisted that this stood in no relation whatsoever to the suicides, and that if he said more he would surely be made fun of. In the evening of this day he did not report again to the station-house, but was discovered, caught on the hook of the window-cross, dead.

Here again the circumstances matched in the minutest particular those of the other cases. The legs spraddled on the floor, the curtain cord used as a rope, the window closed, the door unlocked, and death in the sixth hour of the afternoon. The dead man's mouth gaped wide open. The livid tongue curled out—

This third death in Room 7 brought about the departure that very day of all guests, with the exception of a German high school teacher in No. 16, who used the chance to reduce rent by a third. It was a feeble consolation for Madam Dubonnet when Mary Garden, star of the Opéra Comique, rode by in her Renault, and bargained for the red curtain cord at two hundred francs—first of all because that brought luck, and then because it appeared in the dailies.

If this affair had happened in the summer, say in July or August, then Madam Dubonnet might well have secured three times that amount for the cord. The papers would not have failed to fill their columns, even for weeks, with this stuff. But here, in the middle of the season, with elections, Morocco, Persia, bank-crash in New York, and not less than three political affairs, really they scarcely knew where to find room for it. Consequently, the topic of Rue Alfred Stevens became perceptibly less bruited than it really deserved; and, further, the reports, direct and short, rehearsed but the police records and kept themselves free from exaggeration.

This evidence was all that the medical student, Richard Bracquemont, knew of the matter. He was aware of one other little circumstance. It appeared so extraneous that neither the commissioner nor any other of the witnesses mentioned it to the reporters. Only later, after the adventure of the medical student, did anybody recall that, when the policeman cut down the body of Sergeant Charles-Marie Chaumié from the window-cross, there crept out of the open mouth of the corpse a great black spider. The porter flipped it away with his finger, crying, "The devil! Another damned bug!"

In the course of those later investigations that had to do with Bracquemont, he declared that, when the body of the Swiss traveling salesman was carried out, a very similar spider had been seen by him running over the shoulder.

Of this Bracquemont knew nothing.

He moved into the room on a Sunday, a good fortnight after the last suicide. What he there experienced was daily recorded with great fidelity in a notebook.

DIARY OF RICHARD BRACQUEMONT, MEDICAL STUDENT

Monday, February 28

Moved in here yesterday evening. Unpacked both suitcases and put things to rights; then went to bed. I slept well. It just struck nine o'clock when a knocking woke me. It was the housekeeper, who herself brought me breakfast. She is very anxious about me; that's proven by the eggs, ham and excellent coffee. I washed, dressed, then looked on as the porter tidied the room, the while smoking my pipe.

Well, then, here I am! I know perfectly well that the affair is risky, but I also realize that there's a fortune in it for me if I succeed in getting at the bottom of it. And if Paris long ago was reckoned at a holy mass—(one couldn't get it so cheaply today)—why, then, I can put up my bit of a life for such a prize. Here is a chance—all right—I'll attempt it.

Besides, a lot of people were clever enough to get into my game—not less than twenty-seven persons. Some through the police, some directly through the proprietress, wanted to secure the room; among them three ladies. There was plenty of competition; all of them apparently just as hard up as myself.

But I "got the job." How? Well, it seems I was the only one who could offer the wise police an idea! A fine idea! Of course it was a bluff.

Since those reports are prepared for the eyes of the police, it amuses me to tell the gentlemen, right at the beginning, that I have led them by the nose. Suppose the commissioner is sensible. He'll say: "Hm! just for this reason Bracquemont appears to be the right man!"

But it's all the same to me what he says later on; for the present here I sit. And I regard it as a good omen that I have started my activities by hoodwinking the gentlemen so thoroughly.

I first looked up Madam Dubonnet, who directed me to the station-house. I loafed around there every day for a whole week. It was always "Your application will be considered," which amounted to the request that I come again. Most of my rivals had cleared out; probably had more urgent business than to drowse in the musty old guard-room. The commissioner was showing signs of anger at my obstinacy. Finally, he gave me to understand that I needn't apply any more. To me, as to the others, he was extremely grateful, but he simply couldn't use the promising suggestions of outsiders. Unless I had some sort of a worked-out plan—

So I told him that's the very thing I had. And really I could not have gotten beyond the first word. Nevertheless, I stipulated, I would declare my plan if he would give his word of honor to carry it out himself, for it was really dangerous, and might well come to the same end as the efforts of the unfortunate policeman. He very cordially answered that he had not a moment to spare for anything like that. But I saw that I was gaining ground when he inquired whether I could not give him at least a hint—

And that I did. I gave him a piece of blooming nonsense that had come into my head a second before. I am in the dark where this sudden notion came from. I told him that of all the hours of the week there was one marked by a singular and mysterious power. That was the hour in which the Christ vanished from His grave and descended into hell—the sixth hour in the evening of the next to the last day of the Jewish week. And he, perchance, recalled it was this hour Friday between 5 and 6 o'clock in which all three suicides occurred. I might not tell him more at that time except to refer him to the Revelations of St. John.

The commissioner put on a visage of comprehension, was again cordial and made an evening appointment with me. I walked into his office on the dot. I saw the New Testament spread out before him on the table. In the meantime I had looked up the same reference as himself. Had hunted through the Revelations and found them absolutely unintelligible. Perhaps the commissioner was a brighter man than I. At all events, he informed me very courteously, that in spite of my vague suggestions he believed that he understood my train of thought. He added his readiness to follow out my wishes and to further them in every way possible.

In fact, I must credit him with having been very helpful to me. He made arrangements with the housekeeper whereby I was to be boarded free during my stay tat the hotel. He also loaned me a splendid revolver and a police whistle. The policemen on duty were ordered to go through Rue Alfred Stevens as often as possible and to rush to my assistance at the least sign of trouble. But his chief kindness was to have brought into my room a portable telephone, through which I have direct connection with police headquarters. Since this is scarcely four minutes away, I can obtain quickest help in any emergency. Thus fortified, I can't very well see what should make me afraid.

Tuesday, March 1

Nothing has occurred, neither yesterday nor today. Madam Dubonnet brought a new curtain cord from another room—surely she has enough of them empty! She does not miss any opportunity to visit me, and brings something along every time. I asked to hear again each detail of what had happened, but have gained nothing new. Concerning the death motives she has her own opinions. The trouble with the artist she believes was an unhappy love affair. When he was with her last year, a young lady called upon him frequently, but this year she had not shown herself. What had touched the Swiss gentleman to desperate impulse, she simply did not understand—one couldn't know everything! But the sergeant, the sergeant, undoubtedly committed suicide just to spite her. I must confess that these explanations of Madam Dubonnet sounded a bit thin. But I tolerate her prattling—anyhow, it serves to break the monotony.

Thursday, March 3

Still absolutely nothing. The commissioner rings me up several times a day. Although I told him that all goes well, he is clearly not reassured. I lugged out my medicine books and now I study. My self-imposed durance is not without one good purpose.

Friday, March 4, 2 P.M.

Dandy lunch today! To crown all, the landlady brought me half a bottle of champagne. It was a regular hangman's feast. She regards me as already three-quarters dead. Before going out she implored me, with tears in her eyes, to come away with her. She indeed dreaded that I too would hang myself—"just to spite her."

I have scrutinized the new cord. Must I go to work and choke myself with it? Hm, I haven't the least desire. Then, too, the rope hangs rough and stiff and forms a clumsy loop. Surely, a fellow would need a strong bent in order to emulate the example of the others. Here I sit at the table, with the telephone to my left and to my right the revolver. Fear I have none, but I'm very curious.

6 P.M.

Nothing has occurred. I as about to write—"unfortunately." The ominous hour came and sped, and was like all the rest. Of course, I will not deny that several times I had a certain impulse to be at the window. Oh, yes; but for other reasons. Between 5 and 6 the commissioner must have run me up at least ten times. He was just as impatient as I myself. But Madam Dubonnet is delighted; for a whole week somebody has lived in No. 7 without hanging himself. Preposterous!

Monday, March 7

I am now convinced that I shall find out nothing, and I incline to the belief that the suicides were mere coincidences. I requested the commissioner to have further investigations into all three cases, as I am convinced that they will eventually be cleared up. As for me, I am going to stay on as long as I can. 'Tis true that I will not master Paris here, but this is high living, all right, and I'm getting fat on it. Then, too, I'm studying faithfully and my progress is noticeable. Besides this, I have a new purpose to hold me here.

Wednesday, March 9

So now I'm advanced a step further. Clarimonde—Ah, yes; I have related nothing yet of Clarimonde. She is my purpose for remaining here. And it is she, too, in whose behest, gladly would I have gone in that impending hour to the window—but most certainly not to hang myself. Clarimonde—must I call her merely that?—I have no knowledge of her real name. But Clarimonde, I feel, it must be. And I'd bet that's the very way she'd call herself if one were to ask her. Right at the very start I noticed Clarimonde. She lives on the opposite side of this close street and her window directly faces mine. She sits there behind the curtains. I may as well confess that she espied me sooner than I noticed her, and surely betrayed an interest in me. No wonder! Thanks to the tongue of Madam Dubonnet, the whole neighborhood knows the fact and the reason for my being here.

I have truly a very impassive nature and my connections with women have always been rather cold. When a fellow leaves Verdun and goes to Paris to study, taking scarcely enough money along to be well fed three days out of the week, he has something else to think about than love. So, you see, I have little experience, and probably I play the silly ass in this case. After all, it suits me just as it goes. At first I had a desire to bring her nearer. I thought to myself that since I am here on the watch and, do what I may, have nothing to find out, why, then, I might as well gaze at the creature opposite. How the deuce can anybody sit still the live long day over nothing but books?

I have determined that Clarimonde is apparently solitary in her tiny quarters. She has three windows, but she always sits at the window opposite my own—sits there and spins—spins from a small old-fashioned wheel. I once saw a spinning wheel like hers at my grandmother's, but the old lady had never used this heirloom of some great-aunt. It was a surprise to me that anybody still used one. Moreover, the spinning wheel of Clarimonde is a wee, precious contrivance—white, as if of ivory. Surely those must be subtle threads of her spinning! Through the long day she sits there behind the curtains and pauselessly weaves, ceasing only at twilight. In these dark days it soon becomes dusk over this narrow street. At five o'clock we have the very beauty of sunset. I have never seen light in her room.

Her appearance—Oh, I'm not quite sure. Her black tresses are sleek and close, and she has a certain pallor. Her nose is aquiline and delicate and the nostrils quiver. Her lips are blanched and I feel as if the little teeth were pointed like the teeth of carnivora. The eyelids give great shadows, but when they open her large dark eyes are luminous. Yet I have intimations of all this rather than direct knowledge. It is difficult to perceive anything exactly behind those hangings.

One thing further: She always wears a snug black garment—great lilac tufts distinguish it—and she is forever wearing long black gloves—no doubt to preserve her hands from toil. Now and then, as I regard the antic black fingers plying away, in and out, plucking and leading the filaments, it actually reminds me of the spasmodic twitching of insect tentacles.

Our mutual bearing? Well, it is rather superficial, and yet it occurs to me that it may be much deeper. It began, you see, in her looking over to my window and I to hers. She gazes at me and I at her. Evidently she must have been pleased with me, for one day when she gazed over she smiled. I did the same, of course. So things continued for several days. We smiled more and more often to one another. Next I resolved to greet her, but ever experienced some intangible restraint. At last I took that step—this very afternoon. And Clarimonde greeted me. Quite delicately, you may be sure, but I am convinced that she inclined her head.

Thursday, March 10

Yesterday I wearied myself with books. I can't exactly say that I studied a good deal. I have been building air-castles and dreaming of Clarimonde. Slept restlessly until far into the morning.

When I stepped to the window there Clarimonde sat. I saluted and she nodded again. She smiled and peered long at me.

I meant to study, but could not concentrate. I placed myself at the window and stared at her. Still another thing I noticed, how she placed her hands in her lap. I tugged at the curtains and almost at the same instant—she did likewise. We both smiled and looked upon each other. I believe we certainly sat there an hour.

Then she continued spinning.

Saturday, March 12

These days run along thus: I eat and drink and sit down at the desk; I then light my pipe and pore over a book, but I do not read a single syllable. I am trying right along, but I feel that it is entirely fruitless. Then I go to the window and wave a greeting. Clarimonde shows thanks. We smile and look fixedly at each other, hours at a time—

About six o'clock yesterday afternoon I was a bit restless. Twilight stole over us very early, and I caught some foreboding. I sat and waited. I received an indomitable impulse toward the window—of course, not to hang myself, but just to look at Clarimonde. I leaped up and stopped behind the curtain. Never had I seen her so distinctly, in spite of its being now quite dark. She was spinning, but her eyes, her eyes were fastened upon me. I experienced a strange pervading comfort, and the least touch of misgiving.

The telephone bell!

I could have killed the doddering commissioner, who with his gruff questions rasped me out of my dreams.

This morning he paid me a visit, together with Madam Dubonnet. She is pretty well pleased with what I am doing, and is quite content with my two weeks' occupancy of Room 7. But the commissioner's one idea is to get results. I have hinted that I am on the track of a most singular discovery. The ass believed every word of it. So my bunk is safe for weeks more—and that's my one desire. Not because of Madam Dubonnet's cakes and wine—Good Lord! how soon food becomes wearisome when one has his fill!—No, only because of the window that she hates and fears and which I am so fond of; this window which lets me see Clarimonde.

When I light my lamp she vanishes. I have peered my eyes out to know whether she goes elsewhere. But never have I seen her set foot on the street. I have a big, snug easy chair and a green shade on the lamp, whose light pours warmly over me. The commissioner brought me a large package of tobacco, the best I've ever smoked—and yet with all this I can't work. I read over two, three pages, and at the end I know that I haven't grasped any of it. Only my eye catches up letters, my brain resists every new impression. Odd! As though it carried a sign: "No admittance"—as though it now entertained no other thought but—Clarimonde.

At last I stick the books away, snuggle back into my cushions and dream.

Sunday, March 13

This morning I witnessed a little spectacle. I paced up and down the corridor while the porter put my room in order. Before the small courtyard window hangs a web wherein a crossbacked spider sways. Madam Dubonnet will not have it brushed away; spiders bring luck, and she has had quite enough misfortune in her house. Then I noticed how another and much smaller spider, a male, was running guardedly about the web. Up a frail gray filament it drew cautiously toward the middle, but at the slightest movement of the female it swung back, made for another strand and again struggled to draw near. At least, the taut pudgy female seemed to tolerate his advances; she stirred no more. Gently, at first, then more assuredly, did the male tug at a gossamer, till the whole weavement fluttered, but his adored one stayed quiescent. Nearer and nearer, quickly, but with unceasing precaution he ascended. The female took it composedly, and was gently and yieldingly indulgent to his passionate embracings. Immovably, then, they two hung together upon the ample web.

Next I regarded how the male spider gradually released one leg from another; it was as if he would gently withdraw and leave the consort alone in her voluptuous musings. Suddenly he pulled away and scampered affrightedly out of the net. But in the same instant a wild life stirred in the female. Madly, she hunted him down. The spindling male let fall on a thread; at once the beloved matched his art. Both dropped to the windowsill. With a summoning of his supremest energy, the hunted one tried to escape. Too late! Relentlessly even then the consort gripped him and hauled him again up into the very middle of the net. And this place, which had just served as bed for lustful cravings, showed now another picture. In vain the lover writhed, ever stretching out the weakening legs, striving to avoid this wild embracement. Never more would the beloved release him. In a few minutes she had spun him motionless. Now she was plunging her sharp pincers into his belly, and sucking in full gulps his new white blood—

I regarded also how she finally freed the wretched, unrecognizable mass of legs, skin and fiber, and contemptuously cast it from the web.

So this is the way these creatures love! Well, I'm glad that I am no spider-youthling.

Monday, March 14

Haven't a glance more for my books. I spend the live long day at the window. And when it is dark, even then I remain sitting. She is no longer there, but I shut my eyes and still see her—

So! This diary has certainly become different from my anticipations of it. It runs on about Madam Dubonnet and the commissioner and spiders and Clarimonde, but not a syllable about the discoveries that I wanted to make. But what should I care?

Tuesday, March 15

We have hit upon a rare game, Clarimonde and I, and this we play the whole day long. From her I receive an immediate response to my greetings. Thereupon I drum with my finger against the pane, which she no sooner notices than she begins to do the same. I wave my hand to her and she waves hack. I move my lips, as if I were speaking to her, and she mutely answers me. Then I push back the hair from my temples, and at once her hand, too, is on her forehead. A regular child's play, and the two of us laugh over it. This is, of course, she doesn't laugh—it is merely a smile, gentle, indulgent I believe I must smile very similarly.

But now, all this is not quite so stupid as it might seem. It is no mere imitation. We would both very soon tire of that. Something of thought transference must surely be in it; because Clarimonde follows my motions in the merest fraction of a second. With scarcely time to notice them, she already responds. Many a time I get the notion that all is simultaneous with us. To put into action an entirely unexpected whim gives me a delicate thrill, and mine the astonishment at her immediate answer. I have often endeavored to confound her. I twist a rapid succession of varied contortions. Once more the same, and yet again—I end with a third repetition of these antics, but change the sequence, or throw in something new, or leave something out. It is quite extraordinary that Clarimonde never makes a slip, although I change so quickly that she can scarcely have time to observe every little variance.

And so I trifle the hours away! But it never seems to me that I am merely killing time. On the contrary, I think I never have pursued anything more necessary.

Wednesday, March 16

How strange it is that I have never entertained the idea of placing my relations with Clarimonde upon a more reasonable basis than these childish diversions! Last night I thought the matter over. There is nothing simpler than to take hat and coat and go down two flights of stairs, five steps across the street, then up two flights. On the door is a little plate with the name "Clarimonde"—Clarimonde—What? I do not know, but surely "Clarimonde" is there engraven. I knock, and then—

So far I can anticipate every least detail; every slightest motion I would make I see before me. But I cannot picture what might follow. The door opens, that is clear. I stop there in front of it and stare within, into a blackness that reveals nothing, absolutely nothing. She does not appear. Nothing appears. Really, there is nothing there—only black, impenetrable gloom. Often I imagine that there is not or could not be a different Clarimonde than the one I see yonder at the window, the one that plays with me. I cannot conceive of this woman wearing a hat, or wearing clothes, or anything other than the black habit with the startling lavender rosettes. I cannot even portray her without the gloves! See her on the street, or perhaps in a restaurant, eating, drinking, conversing?—I must laugh. It seems so impossible. Sometimes I ask myself whether I love her. I cannot answer that strictly, since I have never yet been in love. If this feeling that I entertain toward Clarimonde is really love, then, at all events, it is very, very different from what I have seen among my comrades or read of in novels.

It is becoming more and more difficult to comprehend the states of my mind. It is growing exceedingly difficult to think of anything that does not center in Clarimonde, or rather, in our game. For undoubtedly it is this game which excites me, and nothing else. And that's the very thing I least understand.

Clarimonde—yes, I feel myself being drawn toward her, but there steals in a furtive sense that I am in dread. Dread? No, not that! But a sort of timidity—an intangible fear—of something or other that I cannot know. And it is just this fear, holding something compelling, strangely passionate, which wards me off from her and yet lures me closer. It seems as if I were coursing about her in a great circle, oft times coming nearer, then swinging further away, venturing toward another point and the shrinking back until at the last I know I must eventually go to her.

Clarimonde sits at the window and spins—long, thin everlastingly fine threads. From them she prepares a fabric whose nature I do not know; and it is incomprehensible to me how she can ply this intrication without perplexing and severing those flimsy threads. There form wondrous devices in her nice handiwork, feverous fervid creatures and fascinating grotesques.

But come, now—what's this I am writing? In sober truth it is utterly impossible for me to see what she is really spinning; the web is imperceptible, and yet it impresses me that her work is exactly as I see it—when I close my eyes. Exactly so: A great net and many inwoven animal-fablings, and pattern-monsters, and awful, hideous grotesques.

Thursday, March 17

I am in a remarkable state of excitement. No longer do I speak to anybody, not even a "good morning" to Madam Dubonnet or to the porter—Scarcely allow myself time to eat. I want to be at the window and play with her. It is an enthralling game, really, without doubt, and I have the apprehension that something must come of it.

Friday, March 18

Yes, yes, something must befall today, I keep telling myself—(Quite loudly I soliloquize in order to hear my voice)—that I am here for that single reason. The worst of it is, I am afraid. And this fear that something terrible might visit me just as it has my predecessors in this room fuses curiously with the other dread—that of Clarimonde. I find them quite inseparable. I am afraid. I would like to scream.

6 P.M.

Just a few words with my hat and coat on—

At the stroke of five I felt my strength at its ebb. But now I believe that it must have some connection with this sixth hour of the next to the last day of the week. I no longer find the deception I perpetrated against the commissioner at all amusing. Seated within my wide armchair I struggle to remain firm. But always I am hauled, almost torn to the window. I must play with Clarimonde! And then again that hideous horror of the window. I saw them hanged there—the Swiss traveling salesman—bulky, fat-necked, stubble-faced—the slender artist—and the squat, powerful sergeant. All three I saw there, first one by one and then together—all three on the same hook; all with gaping mouths and thick tongues, far-lolling. And then I saw myself hanged in the midst of them.

Oh, what fear! I felt that I had as much fear of the window-cross and the devilish hook up there as I have of Clarimonde. She must forgive my thinking so; but in my contemptible dread I repeatedly pictured her presence fitfully flitting among the three hanged men, whose legs sprawled to the floor. It is true I never for a moment received a longing to strangle myself. I had not even fear of doing so. No, my terror was only of the window itself and of Clarimonde, of something alarming, inconceivable, which was now in event. I had the gripping, unshakable desire to get up and rush to the window. And I was driven to do it—

Then the telephone rang out. I took the receiver, and before I could distinguish a word, I had myself yelled into it: "Come at once; Come!" It seemed as if the piercing cry of my voice had instantly chased all of the shadows right into the cracks of the floor. At once I was calm. I brushed the drops from my brow and drank a glass of water. Then I cast about to find what I could say to the commissioner when he arrived. At last I returned to the window, nodding and smiling.

And Clarimonde nodded and smiled. Five minutes later the commissioner was on the scene. I informed him that now I had gotten down to the very bottom of the matter. Today he might spare me further questioning, but I would shortly make him remarkable disclosures. The funny part of it was that while I was brazenly lying to him the conviction was deepening upon me that I was telling the truth, and of that, at this very minute, I am quite as certain—despite my better knowledge.

He remarked my somewhat peculiar manner, especially when I attempted to excuse and make as commonplace as possible my anguished cry over the telephone—but still could not appreciate a vital cause. He then observed very graciously that I need take no consideration for him. He would ever be at my service: that was his duty. Better to come a dozen times in vain than that he should once fail in a crisis. Then he invited me to go out for the evening. That would tranquillize me. It was not well for me to remain so entirely alone. I accepted—although with a twinge. I do not care to part from this room.

Saturday, March 19

We went to the Gaité Rochechouart into the Cigale and into Lune Rousse. The commissioner was right. It did me good to get away from here and to breathe other air. At first I had quite an unpleasant feeling, just as if I were doing something wrong, as if I were a deserter, who turns his back upon the colors. That feeling vanished. We had many drinks, laughed and chatted. When I went up to the window this morning I thought I could detect a reproach in Clarimonde's glance. But perhaps that was only imagination, for how could she possibly know that I went out last evening? Anyway, that only lasted a minute—then she smiled again.

The whole day we played.

Sunday, twentieth of March

Today I can but write again: "The whole day we have played."

March 21st, Monday

The whole day we have been playing.

Tuesday, March 22

Yes, and we were at it today as well. Nothing, absolutely nothing else. Now and then I ask myself: Well, to what end, and why? Or—

What do I really want; where will this take me? But I cannot reply to my own questions. For it is settled that I want nothing. Just that! And whatever may be the outcome of this—that is what I'm longing for.

We have been talking together these last few days; but, of course, without a spoken word. Many times our lips have moved. More often we have simply looked at each other. But even then we have well understood.

I was not in error. Clarimonde did reproach me for running away last Friday. I replied by begging her pardon, and declaring that now I could see how stupid and hateful of me it had been. She forgave me, and I vowed that I would never more stir from the window. And we kissed one another, pressing our lips against the pane.

Wednesday, March 23

I know now that I love her. It must be so. I am pervaded with her to the very last fiber. Maybe the love of other people is different. But is there then a head, an ear, even a hand, which truly resembles one of a thousand million? All are at variance! No love is ever like another. And strangely remarkable is my love, I am sure. But is it, therefore, less beautiful?

I were contented in my love, but for this dominance of fear. Often it sleeps and I forget about it; but only for a few minutes, when it wakes again and grips me firmly. It appears to me like a poor little mouse struggling against a huge, splendid snake, whose mighty coils seek to crush it. Just wait, you silly little fear, you will soon be devoured by this great love.

Thursday, March 24

Then there was a knocking. The porter had fetched my boots. I took them. Just as I was going back to the window my glance fell on the paper with the directions for my flourishes. And then I saw that I had not carried out a single one of these movements. I staggered and almost fell. I clutched the arms of the chair and let myself drop. I could not believe my eyes. I scanned the paper over, but there it was. I had just gone through a series of gestures at the window—and not one of them my own!

I had a feeling come over me again that a door was opening wide—her door. There I stood and gaped within. Nothing, nothing. Only this vacant darkness. And I realized if I could leave right now I were saved. And I really felt that I had the power to go, and yet did not. That was because I had the decided conviction, I was holding the secret fast in my hands. Paris, *Paris* to be conquered. For a single moment the call of Paris prevailed over Clarimonde.

Oh, I scarcely ever think of that any more. I am swayed only by love; and with it this silent, passionate fear.

But at that moment it brought me strength. Once more I conned my first set of gestures, and made sure of each distinct motion. Then I returned to the window, paid strict attention to what I was doing, yet could not stir a muscle according to my own plan. Then I proposed to rub my nose with the index finger, but found myself kissing the window pane. It was in my mind to drum upon the window frame, but I ran my fingers through my hair. Thus it was final; Clarimonde was not bound to repeat my promptings, but it was I who copied her imperative signals. And so rapidly, so lightning fast did it happen that I could still imagine the motive as proceeding directly from me.

I, then, I the proud one at influencing her thoughts, it is I, who so completely am influenced. Yet—this direction is so gentle, so imperceptible, that there is nothing could be more gracious.

Yes; I have made still other experiments besides. Thrust my hands into my pockets, resolved not to move them, and at the same time staring over at her. And I perceived how she was lifting her hand and smiling, and how her pointing finger was gently threatening. I did not move. My right hand itched to be out of the pocket, but I tortured my fingers into the cloth. Finally, after some minutes, the fingers had to relax, the hand drew out of the pocket, and the arm moved upwards. I threatened her with my finger and smiled. It appeared as if I were not doing it at all, but rather some stranger whom I was watching. No—no—that was not it. I, it was really I, and a stranger was watching me.

This same stranger who so desired to make a great discovery. But I was not this man—what matters a fool discovery to me. Here I am to do the will of Clarimonde, whom I love in precious dread.

Friday, March 25

I have severed the telephone wire. I haven't the slightest wish to be disturbed by a nonsensical commissioner just when the peculiar hour approaches—

—God in Heaven! Why am I writing this now? Not a word of it is true. It's just as if some one were moving my pen. But I will—will—will write down the truth. It is costing me a frightful effort, but I will do it, if only once more—what—what I will.

I cut the telephone wire—

Because I had to! There it stands at last! Because I had to do it, had to. We stood at the window this morning and played. Our sport has changed since yesterday. She makes a motion which I resist as long as I can, until at the last, I must give in, and do her will without volition. And I cannot declare the wonderful pleasure it is—this investment, this surrender to her will. We were playing, when suddenly she stood up and went back into the room. It was so dark that I could not perceive her any longer. She seemed swallowed in the black. But she returned soon, bearing in her hands a portable telephone, exactly like mine. Smiling, she put it down on the windowsill, took a knife, cut the cord through and carried the phone back.

For a good quarter hour I fought it off. My terror was greater than ever before; and all the more acute this terror because of the long delay. At length I got my telephone, snipped its wire and put it back on the table.

So it's done.

I am sitting at my table. I have had a cup of tea. Just now the porter took out the dishes. I questioned him about the time, for my watch is slow: Five-fifteen o'clock, five-fifteen o'clock.

I know, if I raise my head now, Clarimonde is going to do something. She's going to do something or other that I must repeat.

Well, I am looking up. She stands there and smiles. Oh, if I could only turn my eyes away! Now she is moving toward the curtain. She loosens the rope—just like that of my window, it is red—she is making a loop. She hangs the rope up on the hook of the window-cross.

She sits down and smiles. No, I've passed beyond anxiety, It is a terrible, smothering revulsion. Yet nothing in the world would make me want to feel differently. It is so unspeakable a force, and yet so sweetly insinuating with its inevitable cruelty.

I burn to leap up and obey, but I wait, struggle, resist. I feel her becoming stronger and stronger every minute . . .

So I am sitting here again. I sprang up quickly and did what she wanted: Took the rope, made the loop, and hung it on the hook—

And now I am determined not to look up again. I know what she will do if I look at her once more—Now in the sixth hour of the next to the last day of the week. See her again and I must do what she wants. I must then—

I will not look at her.

There I was laughing aloud. No, I didn't laugh, but something within me. I know at what; at this: "I will not—"

I will not, and yet I know for sure that I must—Must do it—and then—the rest.

I wait only to linger out the torment still longer. These breathless agonies which are the keenest ravishment.

I write fast, fast, in order to sit here still longer, to drag out these aching seconds while the lusts of my love mount and mount—

Still more, longer still—again the dread, again!—I know I will look at her—will stand up—will hang myself. Not of that am I afraid. Oh, no! That is enticing, that is precious.

But something, something else creeps in—that which is to come! I don't know what's going to happen—but it is surely inevitable . . . The bliss of my torment is so outrageously strong that I feel, oh I feel, that something atrocious must follow.

Only keep from thinking!

Write something, write something, never mind what. But fast, don't think—my name—Richard Bracquemont, Richard Bracquemont, Richard—Oh, I can't go any further—Richard Bracquemont, Richard Bracquemont, now—now—I must look at her—Richard Bracquemont—I must. No, still more—Richard Bracque—

The commissioner on the Ninth Precinct, who, upon repeated efforts to establish communication by telephone, had received no answer, reached Hotel Stevens at five minutes past six. He found the corpse of the student Richard Bracquemont in Room 7, hanging at the window-cross in exactly the same posture as the three other suicides.

One thing was different: The face was twisted in hideous fright,—the eyes, wide open, bulged from their sockets—from the strong, powerfully locked teeth the lips stretched tightly back.

And between the teeth stuck, fanged and mashed, a great black spider, with strange violet mottlings.

On the table lay the diary of the medical student. The commissioner read it and rushed straight to the house opposite. He ascertained that the second-story had been empty and unoccupied for months.

Execution

M. Y. Halidom

A RESPECTABLE ANCESTOR OF MINE, FAR BACK IN THE MIDDLE AGES, went to study at a German university. I cannot call to mind the name of it, but that is of no consequence. I think he studied medicine, but I will not be sure even of that. I know that he belonged to a "chor," or company of students who pride themselves on their liberty, who have their own laws and customs, who fight duels with rival chors, and who settle disputes among themselves by outvieing each other in the drinking of beer, who revel in street brawls and other such respectable amusements, playing practical jokes upon the peaceful citizens; in fact, making night hideous.

I know not whether my ancestor was any better or any worse than his fellow students, but he seems to have entered with pleasure into all their amusements, and never to have held himself aloof when any mischief was going on. He was consequently looked up to rather than otherwise by his companions.

It was the custom then, and still is among Germans, especially among German students, to travel long distances on foot, going together often in large numbers and putting up at night, if they could, at some inn; if not, in some cottage, stables, or loft, with nothing but straw to sleep upon.

But German students are not pampered mortals, and can put up with very homely accommodation. If after a fatiguing day's march a student can find at his quarters sufficient beer, black bread, sausage, raw ham, or a little strong cheese, he is perfectly satisfied. Should he be so fortunate as to light upon a dish of "sauer kraut," he would fancy himself in the seventh heaven.

The German is hardy, yet studious, highly sensitive, and keenly susceptible to the beauties of nature. Though somewhat penurious, he is fond of good fellowship, and is a staunch friend.

The foot tour in Germany is a thing common to all classes, from the nobility down to the "handwerks-bursch," or journeying mechanic, which latter class is often unmercifully persecuted by the university student. From time immemorial there seems to have been a feeling of animosity between the two classes, as nearer home we find existing between the "town and gown."

The German student of the middle ages, as in our times, was fond of swagger, delighted in wearing high boots, enormous spurs, an exaggerated sword, a preposterous hat, was provoked to a duel on the slightest occasion, boasted of the number of "schoppen" or "seidel" of beer that he could stow away beneath his doublet, and ran up long bills without a thought of how they were to be paid.

In those days every student had his guitar or other musical instrument wherewith to serenade his "Liebchen" or lady-love, for that latter article was indispensable to the life of a student, and though much grossness and barbarity has been attributed to him, he is, nevertheless, at times capable of being elevated by a pure and refined passion, for he has much poetry in his nature, and is both sentimental and romantic in the extreme.

In all ages students have meddled much in politics, and princes have been known to tremble before their audacity and resolution.

But enough of this digression, gentlemen. My present tale demands only that you should call up in your minds the German student on his foot tour in the long vacation, with his keen relish of the beautiful, his lusty and well-trained frame, that laughs at fatigue, his love of good-fellowship, his tender thoughts of home with the image of his lady-love.

> Which pined although it spoke not, and grew keen,
> Entering with every step it took through many a scene.
>
> —BYRON*

I must now return to my ancestor, who at the time this story commences was on one of these pedestrian rambles, accompanied by some twenty of his fellow-students, all stout, hearty youths who could eat, drink, and fight with any in the university, and flirt, too, I've no doubt, when occasion tempted them.

* The reader is begged to excuse the anachronism. Byron did not write these lines until several years later.

These attributes, you will say, are not strictly necessary to the student preparing for honours, yet, nevertheless, somehow German students manage to find time for other amusements besides dry study. They *can* play, but when they *do* study, they study hard.

My ancestor at the time I speak of was a young man of about twenty, and had already been two years at the university. We may presume, therefore, that he spoke German tolerably well, if not well.

I believe it was in the Harz mountains, the Thüringer Wald, and about those parts that he was travelling on foot with his friends.

They rose at daybreak and walked hard, with their knapsacks on their backs, singing or conversing as they went, reposing at noon in some shady spot to avoid the heat of the day. When the sun began to abate a little they would resume their journey till night overshadowed them, when they would encamp, as hungry as hunters, in some rude quarters, where they would make merry together over a simple but plentiful supper, and talk over the fatigues of the day.

They had been following this sort of life for some time, when one evening as they were hastening towards their quarters in groups of twos, threes, and fours, my ancestor asked of his friend, "What is the name of the township where we are to sleep to-night, Hans?"

"——dorf," answered his friend; "but we shall have to hasten in order to reach it before nightfall. Look, how the mist is rising!"

"Ah! so it is," replied my relative, whose name was Frederick, but who was never called otherwise than "Fritz" by his companions.

Our Fritz had remained behind to enjoy the last dying glow of a gorgeous sunset, and was wrapt in meditation, while his friend Hans hurried on.

"Now then, Fritz!" cried one, Max, "don't lag behind so; or are your English legs not strong enough for our German mountains?"

Our Englishman was stung at this taunt, implying, as it did a disparagement of himself and countrymen, however undeserved it was, for the Germans knew that he could outwalk the best of them when he chose. Yet it had the effect of making him hasten his steps a little.

The dusky hue of night fast overshadowed our students, and the mist now rose at their feet in thick clouds, so that it was with the utmost difficulty that they could find their way.

My ancestor was still a long distance behind the rest, but he was gaining fast on them, when in the darkness, he stumbled over a clump of rock and sprained his ankle. All hope of catching up his companions was now gone. The most he could do was to hobble on slowly with the help of his staff, now losing his way, now finding it, whenever the moon peeped out to light up his path, then losing it again when the moon hid itself behind a cloud, till he began to despair of ever finding anything in the shape of a roof to shelter him from the night air during sleep, and he more than half made up his mind to encamp on the spot, but just then he felt a large drop of rain on his face, then another, and another.

It had been a broiling hot day, and the air was still sultry. Presently a flash of vivid forked lightning danced before his eyes, followed by a clap of thunder so terrific that it bid fair to burst the drum of his ear.

The storm was now overhead; the flashes grew more frequent and more vivid, and the thunder growled more fiercely than ever. In a few minutes the rain poured down in torrents, and the English student was drenched to the skin.

"Here is a nice situation for a man on a pleasure trip!" muttered my ancestor to himself. "Lost, in the dead of night, in the midst of a thunderstorm, in an open plain without shelter, drenched like a drowned rat, as hungry as a wolf, and hardly able to crawl, from a sprained ankle!"

His reflections were anything but of a pleasing sort, as you may imagine, yet he hobbled on as best he could, endeavouring to comfort himself with the vague hope of finding some sort of shelter for the night as soon as the storm should pass off.

After dragging on his limbs with exemplary patience for another half-mile, it being then about midnight, he perceived a light from a cottage window not very far distant. His courage began to revive, and with halting gait he made for the door of the cottage.

He knocked loudly, but no one answered. Thinking that he had not been heard for the rumbling of the thunder, he knocked again and again. Still no one came to the door.

"I mean to lodge here for the night," said the Englishman to himself, "if I have to break the door open to effect an entrance." And he kept up a furious knocking for about three-quarters-of-an-hour. At length he heard a harsh, grating voice within break out in a string of choice Teutonic oaths, and the word "schweinhund" (pig-dog) pronounced once or twice.

Footsteps were then heard descending the stairs, and the next moment a quaint-looking personage appeared at the door in dressing-gown and slippers, with night-cap on head and candle in hand, and demanded in a surly tone what the "teufel" he wanted at that hour of night.

My ancestor apologised with much courtesy for having roused up so worthy an individual at such an unearthly hour, but pleaded that he was a poor benighted traveller, hungry and soaked to the skin.

"Then you should have moved further on," was the curt reply.

"But whither?" asked my relative.

"To the township. This house is not a 'wirthshaus.'"

"How far distant is it?"

"A mile."

By this he meant a German mile—equal to four English miles.

"A mile!" exclaimed the Englishman. "I could not walk a mile to save my life. I've sprained my ankle and can't move a step further. I'm sorry to put you to such inconvenience, my good fellow, but I really must put up here."

"But there is no accommodation," growled the inmate.

"No matter. I dare say you have a little straw; if not, the bare ground will do."

The inmate sulkily suffered the traveller to enter, and showing him into a parlour on the ground-floor, was about to leave him to himself.

"Stop a bit, my good host," said the student. "I must beg to remind you that I am as hungry as a wolf, and as cold as an icicle. If you could find me something in your larder to keep soul and body together, and light me a nice little fire to dry my clothes, you will make me your friend for life."

"Food! Fire! at this time of night!" exclaimed the host, with a look that seemed to say, "Is the man mad?"

"My dear friend," said the Englishman, putting his hand in his pocket and passing a reichsgulden into the hand of his host, "I do not want you to do anything for me gratis. Make me as comfortable as you can for that—on my departure I'll give you more."

"Oh, mein Herr!" said our host, softening at the touch of the bright metal, "that alters the case entirely. You shall have everything you want. I am sorry I haven't another bed, but you can have some straw, and a fire to dry your clothes. I'll go and see directly what there is in the house by way of refreshment, for you must be hungry indeed!"

Our host left the apartment, and returned shortly with some firewood and a heap of straw.

To light a fire and arrange the straw for the traveller in a corner of the room was the work of a moment. He then hurried off to get supper ready, and returned soon afterwards with a dish of sausage, some black bread, some strong cheese and a bottle of "schnaps."

"Our fare is homely, you see, sir," said the host, apologetically; "but it is all we have in the house. We are poor people, and not accustomed to entertain travellers."

"Never mind that, mine host," said the student, "as long as there is plenty of it, we'll excuse the quality."

So saying, he began to strip himself and to hang his clothes before the fire. Then taking from his knapsack a clean shirt and another pair of hose, he donned his slippers and drew his chair close to the table.

The host, after trimming a lamp and lighting it, placed it in the centre of the table, and was just about to return to his bed, when the student called out with his mouth full of sausage, "What! mine host, will you not honour me with your company whilst I discuss my supper? Company helps digestion, you know, and I'm sure you wouldn't like to have my undigested supper on your conscience."

The host returned with a grunt, saying that he couldn't stop long, as he had to rise early on the morrow.

"Oh, so have I, good mine host," said my ancestor, "so we are equal. Come, sit down here, and let me see you toss off a glass or two of this most excellent schnaps. It will keep out the cold and give you pleasant dreams, besides adding a still richer tint to that glorious nose of yours."

"Humph!" replied the host, little pleased at this personal allusion; but he drew a chair to the table and made an effort at being sociable.

My ancestor until now had hardly had time to give more than a cursory glance at the features of his host, but finding himself now at table opposite him, he took a minute survey of his countenance in all its details.

The exterior of our host was striking, to say the least. He was a man of about five-and-forty, of middle height, broad rather than tall. His neck and chest might have served as a model for the Farnese Hercules. His hair and beard, which were matted and unkempt, were of a flaming red, and he was just beginning to turn bald. His brow was low, knotted, and streaked with red. His eyebrows, which were of the same tint as his hair, were enormous, and overhung a pair of small, deep-set brown eyes that moved furtively from right to left with the rapidity of lightning, giving to his countenance a remarkably sinister expression.

His complexion was florid, and the nose, which was large and bottle-shaped, was of so bright a red that it made the eyes water to look upon it, and spoke little for its owner's temperance. His ears, large and red, stood out at the sides of his head like those of an animal, and their orifices were carefully protected by fierce tufts of red hair. The back part of his head was excessively developed, and the jaw was large and massive. His arms were very muscular, and hairy as an ape's, with strongly-defined purple veins, and his hands, the fingers of which were short and stunted, were the colour of raw meat. The legs were somewhat short for the body, and slightly bowed.

My ancestor, as he scanned the grim features of his host, could not help imagining himself a prince in a fairy-tale who had been lured by the evil genius of the storm into the castle of some ogre, who would sooner or later devour him unless rescued by the good fairies. The ogre was not a communicative person. He had not opened his mouth once since he had taken his seat at the table, save to toss down a glass of schnaps.

At length the Englishman, curious to know something of the life and habits of this mysterious individual, was the first to break silence.

"You live in a very isolated spot, mine host," said he.

"Ja," was the laconic reply.

"Have you no nearer neighbours than those of the township?" demanded his guest.

"Nein," grunted the ogre.

"And do you enjoy this solitary existence?" pursued the traveller.

"Ja!" was the inevitable monosyllabic response.

"I shall not get much out of him," said my ancestor to himself, and again there was silence for the space of five minutes.

As if searching for some topic wherewith to renew the conversation, the student cast his eyes round the apartment, taking in at a glance the minutest article of furniture or other commodity that the room contained.

It was a homely, undecorated apartment, built after the fashion of the period, and differed little from most other apartments of the sort. If it was remarkable for anything, it was for its extreme simplicity, not to say nakedness, but there was one object hanging on the wall that at once attracted the traveller's eye. It was a two-handed sword of peculiar shape, and appeared bright and sharp as if ready for use.

"Aha!" exclaimed the Englishman, fixing his eye on the object, "you have been a soldier, I see."

"Not I," said the host.

"No? Ah! I see that your sword is not of the same form as those used in battle. It is probably antique—an heirloom, perhaps."

The man answered with a nod of the head.

"I thought so," said the stranger; "and yet it seems bright and well cared for. It has evidently been sharpened lately. Do you always keep it well sharpened?"

"On great occasions, yes," was the reply, and our host gave a peculiar wink, accompanying it with a significant gesture with both hands, in imitation of wielding the two-handed instrument over his head, then slapping his own neck he uttered a low whistle and a sort of chuckle thus: "Wh—ew!—click!" being his mode of expressing the action of cutting off a head.

"Ho! ho!" exclaimed the Englishman, "is that in your line?"

The ogre answered by a savage laugh.

At this moment the crying of a child was heard overhead, together with the harsher tones of its mother scolding it.

"Then you do not live perfectly solitary, as I thought," said the student; "you have also wife and children?"

"One boy only," replied the man.

"Ah! An only son—a great pet, I'll warrant," said his guest, finishing his last morsel of supper.

"What age may he be?"

"Ten years old—fine boy—just like me—bringing him up like his father," said the strange individual.

"If he turns out like his father, he'll be a beauty," thought my ancestor. Then he asked aloud of his host:

"And what profession may that be that you wish to apprentice him to?"

"Like his father," was the curt reply; but it was followed by the same sort of expressive gesture that I have just described.

"What!" exclaimed the student, "to cut off people's heads?"

"Yes," replied the ruffian; "I am a Scharfrichter."

"A what?" inquired my ancestor, who though he could make himself generally understood in German, had never yet come across the word "Scharfrichter" in his vocabulary.

"A Scharfrichter," repeated the man, raising his voice. "Don't you know what that means? Why, one who cuts off heads."

"An executioner!" muttered the foreigner, half-aloud. "Have I been constrained to crave the hospitality of an executioner?"

These words were inaudible to his host, but the ruffian evidently observed a change in his guest's countenance when he informed him of the nature of his profession, for he hastened to reply.

"One sees at once that you are a foreigner, and unused to the customs of this country. You shudder at meeting an executioner, and sicken at the thought of cutting off a head. No matter, it is always so at first. In fact, the pleasure derived from seeing executions is an acquired taste; but I'll show you some sport to-morrow. There is to be some rare fun down at the township at daybreak," and the wretch gave another wink and a chuckle. "I'll show you how to cut off a head. One blow—click!—cuts like cheese."

"Horrible being!" muttered my ancestor to himself in his native tongue. "Is it possible that anything human can actually revel in such brutality?" and he shuddered in spite of himself. Then he said aloud to his host—

"What was it that first gave you a taste for so horrible a profession?"

"Hm! I hardly know. I had a natural genius for it, I suppose. My father was a butcher, and I was brought up from infancy to see cattle slaughtered. At a very early age I took to slaughtering the animals myself. I seemed to take a liking to it from the very beginning. I happened to have an uncle at that time who was a Scharfrichter, and my greatest delight was to see him cut off the heads of the criminals. I began to long to do the same.

"I was a very young man when this uncle died, and as he had no male issue to take his place, and no one else seemed to come forward, I thought I would offer my services, and they were accepted. I have been headsman of the town these thirty years, and when I die my son will step into my shoes."

"But if he doesn't take to it?"

"He *must* take to it—he'll *have* to take to it."

"Why, are there not many other noble professions just as inviting as that of chopping off the heads of one's fellow-mortals?"

"Not for the son of a headsman. I see you are ignorant of the laws of this country. Here in Germany the son of a headsman is bound by law to adopt the profession of his father, and should the executioner have a daughter instead of a son, in that case, the man who marries his daughter is bound to be headsman. Then the Scharfrichter is obliged to build his house a mile away from other men, for he is a being hated and shunned by everyone."

"This then is the reason of your solitude?"

"It is; and so far is this superstitious fear of contamination carried in this country, that your citizen considers himself defiled if by chance he has eaten out of the same plate that a headsman has once used. Accordingly all vendors of crockery have orders to knock a chip out of every earthen vessel that they sell to the headsman."

"Dear me!" exclaimed my ancestor, "what a peculiar custom! I never heard that before. I certainly did remark that your crockery was in a most dilapidated state, but I didn't consider the remark worth making, although more than once in the course of the evening I felt inclined to ask you how on earth you contrived to knock out chips of such a peculiar shape by mere accident."

"Ah!" sighed the headsman, "what between the crockery-seller and—"

Here he put his finger to his lip and looked round the room suspiciously.

"What is the matter?" asked the student.

"Hush!" said the headsman, "it isn't always safe to talk of mischievous people—they are apt to appear. You know the saying, 'Talk of the devil.'"

"Well," said my ancestor, "but what has that to do with your broken crockery?"

"Hush!" answered his host, looking round him half-timidly; then whispered, "I have a certain mischievous lodger that does my crockery more harm than either the crockery-seller or my boy upstairs when he's fractious."

"Ah!" exclaimed the traveller in surprise, "you have a lodger in your house?"

"Ay!—a lodger who never pays his rent, and who drives me to my wit's end by shying my crockery at my head. Look here, what a cut he gave my wrist once in one of his pranks. I shall bear this mark to my grave." So saying, he bared his wrist and displayed a deep, livid wound, long since healed, but which left behind a scar which nothing could efface.

"An ugly cut, to be sure," remarked the Englishman. "But why on earth do you not get rid of so playful a lodger?"

"Get rid of him! I only wish the devil I could. He comes here uninvited and— But let us not talk of him, or he may pay us another of his pleasant visits, when you will be able to make his acquaintance. He never stands upon ceremony, but comes just whenever he likes. He may be in the room now, for what I know. I shall be off to bed."

My ancestor gazed round the room, vainly endeavouring to discover in some hidden nook the object of his host's terror, when, marvellous to relate! a dish on the top shelf was pitched, as if by some invisible hand, from its post, and shattered into pieces against the opposite wall, nearly hitting him on the head as it passed.

The traveller stared first at the shelf, then at his host, and turned pale.

"Good Heavens!" he cried. "What was that?"

"What was it? Ay! You may well ask what it is," answered his host, peevishly. "What in the devil's name should it be but that pest of a 'Poltergeist' again. I told you you would make his acquaintance ere long."

"A what?—a '*Poltergeist*'?"

"Ay, Poltergeist—a malignant spirit, whose chief delight seems to be to strike terror into the house of a poor honest headsman, and smash all his crockery that he has to pay for out of his hard-earned wages."

"Holy Virgin!" ejaculated my ancestor, crossing himself (for he was a good Catholic). "A malignant spirit! Saints protect us!"

But the words were hardly out of his mouth when crash! went another plate upon the floor, just grazing his host's auburn head as it passed.

"Oh! come now, my fine fellow," said our host, in a tone of mild remonstrance; a little of that goes a long way."

Then turning to his guest, he remarked:

"I wonder why he honours me especially with his visits, and not other people. I shouldn't wonder if he is someone that I have had the honour of decapitating, and he comes to pay me an occasional visit in order to impress upon me that he hasn't forgotten the little service I did him."

A large pointed knife that lay peacefully on the table was then suddenly and powerfully thrown from the traveller's side, and remained with the point sticking in the panel of the door opposite.

"Ho! ho," cried the headsman; "this is getting warm work. Now, my good friend, do let me entreat you to be more moderate in your manifestations, and if you are quiet, to-morrow I will send you a companion."

This promise, so far from quieting our spiritual guest, seemed to infuriate him more than ever, for the bottle of schnaps, more than half full, was now raised in the air and dashed to pieces on the table, the candle being overturned at the same time, and falling flame downwards on to the spirit spilled on the table, it ignited, and in a moment everything was in a blaze.

"Fire! Fire!" cried the headsman, in a voice that roused up his wife and child, who came tumbling downstairs in no time, to learn what was the matter.

There is no knowing what mischief might not have taken place had not my ancestor, with great presence of mind, snatched up his damp clothes from before the fire, and succeeded in extinguishing the flame.

"What *is* the matter, Franz?" exclaimed our host's better half, appearing at the door just as matters were being set to rights again.

"Oh, nothing," said her fond spouse, "only that d——d Poltergeist again, who seems bent upon burning us all in our beds before he has done with us."

"Hush!" said his wife, "don't swear, or he may do as you say in real earnest. Come to bed now, or tomorrow you won't be able to get up in time. Remember—"

"Ah, true; I must have my night's rest, as it would not do for my hand to tremble to-morrow when I mount the scaffold. *Gute nacht, mein Herr.*"

And our worthy host followed his partner out of the room, leaving my ancestor to his reflections.

"Well," soliloquised my relative, "of all the strange adventures that ever occurred to me, this beats all. Oh! there is not the slightest doubt that what I have just witnessed is the work of the infernal powers—some diabolical agency.

"When I see a knife jump up from the table by itself without anyone near and deliberately fix itself in the panel of the door before my very eyes; when I see a bottle of spirit overturned and broken in pieces, and then a candle after that knocked over as if on purpose to ignite the spirit, and withal no way of accounting for such a phenomenon; moreover, when I see plates and dishes hurled from one end of the room to the other, and apparently aimed at people's heads, and yet the perpetrator of such pranks has the power of making himself invisible to the naked eye, then, I say, this is not through human agency, but something superhuman, and as it is not exactly an angelic mode of proceeding, it must be the reverse."

My ancestor shuddered, and crossed himself. The manifestations, however, had ceased for the night, and in five minutes our weary traveller was fast asleep.

His dreams that night were not of the pleasantest. He imagined that he mounted the scaffold with a crowd of eager eyes gazing at him, amongst whom were his friends and travelling companions. His host, the Scharfrichter, stood brandishing his terrible two-handed sword, and in another moment his head would have been off, but at the critical time the dream changed, and he was being pelted with crockery in the midst of a cemetery at night by innumerable sheeted "poltergeister."

These and such-like visions were flitting before his brain, when a loud thump at the door brought him back to earth again. There was the Scharfrichter before him, not in dressing gown and slippers, as on the previous evening, but attired in doublet and hose of a blood red, a black *barello* with scarlet cock's feather.

"Now then, mein Herr," said the headsman, taking down his fearful instrument from the wall, "time's up."

My ancestor, only just awake, rubbed his eyes and imagined that he was really and truly called away to execution, and that his last hour had come.

The executioner, seeing that he hesitated, added: "If you want to witness the cunning of my hand, now's your time."

My relation gave a sigh of relief when he began to recollect that his own head was quite safe, and that he was only called to witness the execution of another man.

"But I can't go; I have sprained my ankle," pleaded the Englishman.

"Oh, I don't intend to walk myself," replied the executioner. "I have my horse and cart ready, and can give you a lift."

"Oh, if that's the case," said the student, "I shall be glad to go, as I wish to meet my friends in the township."

"Come on, then," and the headsman assisted the Englishman into the cart.

As they were about starting, a little red-haired ruffian of about ten, stout and well-built, and bearing a striking likeness to our host, appeared on the threshold.

"Papa, you'll bring me home a football, won't you?" said the youth.

"Ay, my boy, that will I, a good sized one," answered his father.

"That's your son?" asked the student of his host.

"Ah, a fine little fellow. Here, my little man," said he to the child, and slipping a small coin into his little fat fist, he patted him on the cheek and stepped into the cart.

"Ah, he's a fine boy," said our host with a paternal pride, as he whipped on his horse. "There is nothing of the milksop about him. *He's* not afraid of the devil himself."

"You do well to be proud of him. I'll warrant you buy him many a pretty toy," observed the Englishman. "Buy him toys!" exclaimed the headsman, laughing. "As long as I bring him home a football now and then, he is quite content." And he laughed again.

"Well, that is a toy, isn't it?" said the student, not as yet comprehending the headsman's meaning.

"Yes, a toy that costs me nothing, and gives him no end of amusement. You should see how he kicks the heads about that I bring him home. It's quite a pleasure to see the youngster enjoy himself in his innocent way."

"You do not mean to say," said the Englishman, in horror, "that the football you promised him is to be *a human head*!"

"Aye, to be sure," replied the Scharfrichter, "What else should it be? What kicks he'll give it to be sure! Ha! ha! ha! that's the way to bring up boys; makes them hardy. He's not afraid of a little blood. Talk of his not taking a liking to my business! Why he's always saying to me, 'Papa, when I am big enough to wield your sword, you'll let me cut off heads, won't you?'

"'Yes, my boy, that you shall,' say I, for I like to give him encouragement. That's what I call bringing up boys well. I wouldn't give a fig for one of your milksops that scream or faint at the sight of blood, not I."

"Humph," muttered my ancestor, and he remained silent for some minutes, absorbed in meditation.

The headsman whipped on his horse in silence; at length he said to his guest: "Here we are at last. Look at yon crowd waiting to receive us."

My relative lifted his head, and sure enough there was the mound of earth erected for the criminal already surrounded by soldiers, close to which thronged the crowd. All the inhabitants of ——dorf were astir, and in the crowd our Englishman now recognised his fellow students. A cry of "*Der Henker! der henker!*"* arose on all sides. Room was at once made for the headsman and his companion, and Fritz's fellow students, seeing their friend arrive in a Henker's cart, pushed their way through the crowd to ask him all sorts of questions.

Fritz descended with difficulty after paying his host for his board and lodging, and joined his companions. In a few minutes more the criminal's cart arrived with the "*armer sünder*" or poor sinner, accompanied by two priests. Loud execrations broke from the mob, amidst which the wretched being descended from the cart and mounted the scaffold. A dead silence reigned around. One of the priests whispered something earnestly in the ear of the condemned, who was as pale as death, and he took his seat on the chair prepared for him, while an expression of savage delight appeared on the countenance of the headsman.

He felt all eyes were upon him. The terrible two-handed weapon was raised aloft, and brandished over the Henker's head. One blow and the head of the unhappy wretch was severed from his body. Loud cheering rent the air as the Scharfrichter, holding the head of the criminal by the hair, presented it to the public gaze. But at this moment a most unexpected and revolting scene ensued.

Several persons from among the crowd rushed forward toward the scaffold with mugs, which they filled at the fresh fountain of blood spurting up from the severed neck of the criminal and drank off at a draught.

My ancestor sickened at so disgusting a spectacle, and demanded the reason of some bystander. He was informed that those persons believed human blood fresh from the neck of a beheaded criminal to be an infallible remedy for epileptic fits. The superstition exists to this day. Violent exercise after the draught, he was informed, was considered necessary, in order to effect a cure.

The crowd began to disperse, and my ancestor, leaning on the arm of a friend, also retired from the scene, disgusted with himself at having been present at such a spectacle. Before leaving the spot he had time to notice his host of the previous night start off in his cart towards home with the promised football.

Our English student was laid up for some little time with his sprained ankle, and some of his companions remained behind to keep him company, while others moved onward.

The ankle being cured, my relative continued his foot tour with his friends, and afterwards returned to the university, where he studied hard till the time came

* Another name for the headsman or hangman.

round for an examination, which he passed, and shortly afterwards returned to England.

We hear nothing more of my ancestor until ten or twelve years afterwards, when we again find him in Germany, whither he had been suddenly called to visit some relative, then in a dying state.

He arrived just in time to close his relative's eyes, after which he saw him quietly interred in his last home.

This sad office over, he was thinking of returning to England, when, in turning over the articles of his travelling trunk, he suddenly came across a German book belonging to a college friend of his, one Ludwig Engstein, that had been lent him when at the university, and which he had forgotten to return before leaving college. His friend used to live, he remembered, in Weimar, and not being far distant, he resolved to visit that town and to find out his friend's house.

Many changes take place in twelve years, and my ancestor only half expected to meet his fellow-student again. He might have changed his residence—he might be dead. Who could tell what might not have happened to him after so long a lapse of time?

Nevertheless, the Englishman, finding himself on German soil once more, resolved to enquire after the friend of his youth, and should he succeed in discovering him, to put him in possession of his book again, and chat with him over their student's days.

Accordingly, he set off for the town of Weimar, and having arrived there, proceeded with the said book under his arm to the house of his friend. He had been once on a visit of a fortnight at his friend's house when a student, and had known his mother and sisters intimately, therefore he had no difficulty in finding the house again.

The town of Weimar had changed but little during these ten or twelve years, and once more he found himself on the old familiar door-step.

"*Ist der Herr Advocat Engstein zu Hause?*" he demanded of an old woman who answered the door.

"*Ja mein Herr*," replied the crone. "What name shall I give?"

"Oh, never mind announcing me," said the Englishman; "I'll announce myself."

So saying, he pushed past the old woman, and knocked at his friend's study.

"*Herein!*" called out a voice from within, which my ancestor had no difficulty in recognising as his friend's, and the Englishman entered.

Ludwig Engstein was seated at a table strewed with papers and documents, and was busily writing. He was still young looking, but his friend Fritz noticed that his face had assumed a more thoughtful expression than when at the university. He was now a lawyer in good practice, and the moment his friend entered he was so busy that he did not even raise his head.

"I am sorry to disturb you, Herr Advocat," said Fritz, suddenly, "but I've come to return a book you lent me some time back."

And placing the book on the table, he marched straight out of the room, shutting the door after him. He then peeped through the key-hole and listened awhile to note the effect of his abrupt departure on his friend.

The young lawyer's ear caught his friend's English accent, and at once lifted his head, though not in time to catch a glimpse of his retreating figure.

I have said that Engstein recognised Fritz's accent as English, but little did he suspect that it was his old college friend who had called upon him and left so suddenly.

He looked surprised, took up the book upon the table to look at the title, and muttered to himself, "Who can it have been? I do not recollect now who it was I lent it to, but it must have been a long while ago."

He was about to ring the bell, and rose for that purpose when he noticed a face peeping at him through the opening of the door, which was now ajar.

"Who's that? Come in!" cried the lawyer.

"You are busy, Herr advocat—another time.

"*Ich empfähle mich Ihnen*," said my relative, closing the door slowly after him.

But this time Ludwig had a better view of the Englishman's face.

"*Potztausend*!" exclaimed the lawyer; "I shall know that face. *Ach! lieber freund Fritz*. Can it be really you? *Nein was für ein angenehme Ueberaschung*!" he cried, rushing forward and throwing the door wide open while he kissed his friend forcibly on both cheeks.

"Sit down here and tell me to what for a fortuitous and never-to-be-expected train of circumstances I am indebted for this friendly and to me most agreeable and blissful-past-days-recalling visit."

Fritz then went on to relate the circumstances of his relative's death, and how he had been called from home to attend him in his last moments.

"I am sorry for the death of your relation," said Ludwig, "but I cannot sufficiently express my extreme joy at seeing my old friend Fritz again after so many years! Ha! ha! ha!" he laughed, partly from delight at meeting his friend, and partly at his friend's mode of introducing himself.

"What for an eccentric and of you and your strange countryman-characteristic way of saluting your old friend after so long!"

And the German again laughed again heartily.

"And what for a busy and for-ever-with-documents-and-papers-occupied-German business man, not even to notice his swiftly entering, and though long departed from German soil, speedily-vanishing and almost-forgotten English friend!" retorted Fritz, mimicking the high-flown, wordy phraseology of the German.

"No, on my honour, Fritz," replied his friend; "not forgotten, I assure you. Do you know that I had a dream of you only last night. It never struck me till now. It is strange that I should have dreamed of you just the night before your unexpected and to me most grateful arrival. How strange it is that our dreams often prognosticate coming events! It is as if the mind, partly freed from its material covering during sleep, received the power of peering with greater accuracy into that to-us-in-our-waking-state-obscure-and-unfathomable future which—"

"Precisely; I understand you," answered my relative, cutting short his friend's philosophic remark; "but let us talk a little over old times; that is if you are at leisure."

"Yes, to be sure," answered the lawyer; "what I am doing now has no need of hurry. Oh, by the way, Fritz, talking of old times, do you remember the night you spent at the house of old Franz Wenzel the Scharfrichter?"

"If I remember? Shall I ever forget it? ask, rather," answered my ancestor.

"It seems to me only yesterday that I witnessed that execution; and then that Poltergeist—it seems as if I had witnessed his pranks only last night. I can remember the minutest incident that happened on that unhallowed evening."

"Well," resumed the lawyer, "poor old Franz is no more."

"What—dead, eh?"

"Ay, murdered. Horrible to relate, his body was discovered minus the head, which has been carried off or hidden somewhere, for it hasn't been found yet, but his son recognised the body by the clothes, besides Franz has never returned home since, so it must be he. There appears to be a mystery about it, however. The murderer has not as yet been discovered, neither can people guess at what prompted the murderer to take the life of a man who was never over-burdened with money. Then the head being cut off without care being taken to bury the body, and all, too, within a few steps of the Henker's own house. What could have been the murderer's object in carrying off the head?"

"A mere act of spite, I suppose," replied the Englishman.

"Well, it may be so," replied his friend, "for it seems that his life had been often threatened by the friends or relations of those he had beheaded. It may be as you say, out of spite. The murderer may, by way of wreaking his vengeance have cut off the head of the man who had put some friend or relation to death as a trophy, but why just at this moment? Why not before, as there has been no execution in the town lately? I believe there has been none since that execution we two witnessed together. If the avenger had made up his mind to avenge his friend, why did he not do so at once, instead of waiting these twelve years?"

"It may be some other private quarrel," replied Fritz. "Are you mixed up in it?"

"Yes, I shall be at the trial."

"It happened recently it would seem."

"Only two days ago."

"Then the body is still fresh—of course it has been exposed and examined?"

"Yes, but it was recognised at once by the family. I dare say it is buried by this time. I am going there to-morrow. If you have time, my friend, I should be most glad of your company."

"Well, I don't mind giving you a day or so, as I am taking a holiday."

"Agreed, then; we start to-morrow."

The two friends then discoursed until dinner-time, when Ludwig invited Fritz to share his meal.

The Englishman accepted the offer, and they chatted and laughed the time away till the evening.

Ludwig lived quite alone. His sisters had married, his mother was dead. Ludwig was still a batchelor, and so was my ancestor at this time.

"You have not yet put your neck under the yoke it appears," said my relative to his friend, in allusion to the conjugal tie.

"Not I," replied his friend. "At least, not yet."

"I understand," said Fritz; "not married, but *verlobt*."

"No, nor that either."

"No? *Verliebt*, then, perhaps."

"No, neither '*verlobt*' nor '*verliebt*.'"

"What!" exclaimed the Englishman, "not even that! Nevertheless, if I remember rightly, the student Ludwig Engstein was not once averse to the fair sex."

"Oh, recall not the follies of the past, my friend, or I may retaliate," answered the German.

"True, true," said the Englishman. "We all have our weaknesses, and youth is the season in which they mostly flourish, but now we have both grown into sober-minded *Philister*,* and are more wary."

* Philister or Philistine.

"Yes, yes," rejoined his friend; "we are not to be caught now by a pair of blue eyes, flaxen tresses, and a jimp waist, however well these charms may be set off with the allurements of dress. When men get to our advanced age, they want '*geist*,' and look out for a good housewife who can cook them a dish of '*sauer kraut*' or a '*pfankuchen*' when '*das moos*'* is wanting, which is another very useful accessory we desire to have thrown in."

Here he made a significant gesture with his finger and thumb, intended to express the counting of money.

"I hope, my friend, you have not become so worldly as to look upon marriage in the light of bettering yourself," said my relative.

"*Ach! lieber freund*," replied Ludwig. "It is all very well for you rich milords who have '*löwen*'† to talk in that style, but we '*armer teufeln*' are bound to take even that into consideration."

"This is what the world makes of noble fellows when it has once got them in its grasp!" sighed my ancestor to himself, and he hastened to change the conversation.

They then discoursed on various other topics, sitting up to a late hour of night, until wearied with incessant talking, each retired to rest.

Early the next morning both were dressed and ready to start on their journey. They reached ——dorf towards evening, and having fixed their quarters at the very same inn they had put up at on their memorable tour, they beguiled the time until the morrow by discoursing with the townspeople about the mysterious murder.

The body, it seems, was not yet underground, but was to be buried the next day. They accordingly both resolved to examine it.

"The head has not been found yet?" asked Ludwig after supper of the landlord of the inn, who had come in for a gossip.

"No sir, not yet," replied their host. "Ah, there are some strange rumours in the town about that same murder."

"Indeed!" cried Fritz; "what do the people say?"

"Some say one thing, and some another, but all seem to agree that there is something supernatural about the murder of the Henker."

"Something supernatural! Why—what reason have they to jump at that conclusion?"

* Das moss—The moss. Slang word among German students for money.

† Löwen—also money.

"Well, sir, I don't know if you have ever heard of the Henker's Poltergeist, but it is a fact well known to all in the township."

"Yes, yes—even we know it. In fact—but never mind, proceed."

"Well, gentlemen, this Poltergeist—this evil spirit—that no doubt was permitted to haunt the headsman for his sins—for a headsman must of necessity be a cruel, hard-hearted, unnatural villain to choose such a profession."

"Well, well—this evil spirit."

"Well then the Scharfrichter, at least, so people say, had sold his soul to this demon, and when the time came round for him to give up his soul according to the bargain, he refused, and the demon wrested it from him by force by cutting off his head and carrying it away with him."

"Oh, but why this strange supposition? Why put down a thing to supernatural agency before sufficient time has elapsed to investigate the matter properly? A person is murdered, and the body discovered without the head, and because the head cannot be found at once, you say that the devil has run off with it. My dear sir, the thing's absurd."

"Well, we must wait and see what evidence will turn up," said the host.

"Yes, but if everybody merely *waits* for evidence to turn up instead of actively searching for it, the matter will come to a standstill," said the Englishman. "I myself am interested in the murder, as I knew the Scharfrichter twelve years ago, when I was a student."

"Ah, in that case, sir—of course you would. By-the-by, there is another murder now talked about besides the Henker's. They seem to be getting in fashion."

"What! another body?"

"Well, sir, the body isn't exactly found yet, but there is a certain Count, well-known to be rich, who was taking a foot tour through the country alone. His family expected him home on a certain day, and as he hasn't turned up yet, they suspect that he has been robbed and murdered."

"That may be merely a suspicion. How long has he been missing?"

"Three days, they say."

"Three days! Why, a man doesn't bind himself to a day or two when out on a foot tour. He may remain another three days, or a week longer, and then return unhurt."

"Well, sir, it may be as you say, but as the Count was known by his relations to be a very punctual man, and never to fail in his appointments, you see, it is natural they should feel uneasy."

"True, especially as three days ago was about the time of the other murder, and they may get it into their heads that the two murders occurred in the same night. Was he a married man?"

"No, sir; quite young, they say."

"Humph! When did you say the body of the Henker would be buried—tomorrow?"

"About ten, I think, sir."

"Ah! then I must be there early, as I want to examine the corpse myself."

"Oh, decidedly, sir. I will bring you to the place to-morrow in good time."

Our friends now felt inclined for their night's rest, so their host showed them into a room with two beds, and wishing them a good night, left them to undress, and before many minutes had passed both were sound asleep.

The following morning early our two friends, in the company of their host, started from the inn to visit the corpse of the murdered executioner. As they entered the hall where the body lay exposed, Fritz instantly recognised the clothes; if not the identical vestments worn by the defunct twelve years ago, at least, of the same colour and material, being, as I have said before, a doublet and hose of crimson, a colour that he seems to have been partial to.

"Yes," said Fritz; "these are the Henker's clothes, I've no doubt."

Then, after examining the form laid out before him, he was observed to start slightly, and he added in a whisper to his friend: "Ludwig, this is not the body of Franz Wenzel—I'll take my oath of that."

"How! Not Franz Wenzel! Who else should it be, then?"

"That I am not prepared to say, but it is not the body of the Henker; that is certain. Remember that I passed a night at Wenzel's house; during that time I took note of the features and figure of the Scharfrichter, and though twelve years have passed since I saw him, I can swear—"

"But how! His own family have recognized him. What further proof would you have?"

Then addressing the landlord, Ludwig said: "Is it true, landlord, that his own family have recognised the body?"

"Yes, sir; at least, the son did. I don't know whether his wife did or not, as she has been laid up for ever so long with paralysis, poor soul. It may be she has never been informed of the murder. One does not like to frighten invalids, you know."

"Well, well—enough if the corpse has been recognised by the son."

"Yes, sir, he recognised it. It is true, he was a little the worse for liquor when they brought him before the corpse of his father; but when is he otherwise, for the matter of that? As sad a young dog as ever lived that same—inherits all the vices of his father. Nevertheless, who is there in the township that does not recognise the Henker's red legs?"

"You see, therefore, my friend," said Ludwig, turning to his companion, "that you are mistaken. Everybody recognises him."

"I see nothing of the sort," replied the Englishman, doggedly; "and I am still prepared to swear that the corpse before us is not that of Franz Wenzel."

"My dear Fritz," said Engstein, "you are obstinate. What reason can you possibly have for saying so?"

"Observe the hands of the corpse," said Fritz, in a low tone. "Do they look like the hands of an executioner? They are long and delicate. Those of Franz Wenzel were hard, rough, and hairy, with square stunted fingers; besides, the headsman wore no ring. This hand, though no ring is visible, has a depression on the forefinger, as if the owner were in the constant habit of wearing one."

"Ha! say you so?" exclaimed his friend, and a strange expression came over his face.

"Then," pursued Fritz, "observe the clothes. Do they look as if they were made for the body? Franz Wenzel had enormously developed calves, and his hose fitted tightly. Do these hose fit tightly? Look at these limbs, that, compared with the Henker's, are but those of a boy."

"Humph! I believe you are right, Fritz, after all," said Engstein; "but it never would have struck me if you had not pointed it out, as it is so long ago since I set eyes upon him, and then only for a moment. You took a more complete survey of him, and your evidence may prove useful. We will look into the matter together. It is strange, however, that no one should have been struck in the same manner as yourself."

"Well, I don't know," responded Fritz. "The people in these small villages are not always of the brightest. Then the headsman's house being so far away from the town, few people have the opportunity of taking a minute survey of him. The people here content themselves with recognising the clothes. Franz's wife is laid up with paralysis, and has not seen the body, while his son only recognised it when in a drunken state. Do you call that sufficient evidence to prove that the corpse before us is that of the executioner? Would you like another proof that this is no more Franz Wenzel than I am?"

"Well," said Ludwig.

"I remember a scar upon the right wrist that he showed me the night I put up at his house," said the Englishman; "and which he told me had been inflicted on him by a piece of broken plate hurled at him by his Poltergeist. I remember that he said he should carry that mark with him to the grave. If this is the corpse of Franz Wenzel we shall not fail to discover the mark."

So saying, he bared the right arm of the corpse and examined it carefully. No such mark was to be found. The arm was free from scar or brand, and was delicate in form, almost like that of a maiden's. Moreover, there was a scanty covering of dark hair upon it, while the hair on the arms of the executioner, if you remember rightly, was red and profuse. Even Engstein remarked this, and was now convinced beyond a doubt that the murdered man was not Franz Wenzel.

"Is any search being made now for the head of the corpse?" demanded Engstein of his host, who had withdrawn some paces from the two friends, and consequently had not heard the doubt that had been suddenly cast upon the public opinion.

"No active search, I believe, sir," was the reply.

"We will make the search ourselves, my friend," whispered Engstein to Fritz; then added to his host, "My friend and I will take a stroll together. It is uncertain when we shall return to the inn, but get something savoury for us against we come back," and he waved his hand towards his host, who doffed his cap and walked towards his inn, while our two friends set off together in the direction of the Henker's house, which they reached in about an hour.

"Yes," said Fritz, "this is the place. I remember it well. What did our host tell us? That the murder took place only a few paces from the headsman's door. Let us look well round the spot. How solitary it is! Just the place where a murder would be committed. What do you say to yon hollow flanked with brushwood, Ludwig? Is it not a likely place for a murderer to await his victim?"

"You are right, Fritz, let us make a strict search, but if the head has been carried far distant—"

"Let us, nevertheless, search well here first," said my ancestor, and the two friends set to work at once, lifting up every bush and bramble, following every track, until finally they came upon some blood stains.

An old dried well they discovered not far from this spot. Common sense would have suggested this as a likely place for the concealment of the missing head, and there is no doubt that the same idea struck the inhabitants of ——dorf, for there was evident traces of a great number of feet in the sand round about it; besides which there was a chip recently made in the brickwork, which appeared caused by the letting down of a rope or chain.

This seemed evidence enough for our two friends that the well had already been searched, and without effect. Further search in that direction appeared to them to be useless, especially as no bloodstains were to be found near.

They then proceeded to examine more closely than ever the bushes around, stamping on the ground to ascertain if a hole had recently been made, but the ground was firm, and there was nothing to attract suspicion save a few bloodstains, which, instead of leading up to the well as one would have imagined, led up to the foot of an old chestnut-tree, and there seemed to end.

On examining the bark of the tree attentively they observed blood also on the trunk, but this might have been occasioned by the splashing of the blood from the neck after the decapitation of the head. There was no hollow visible in the tree where suspicion would lead one to suppose that the head could be concealed; nevertheless, when men make up their minds to make a rigid search, they often pry into the most unlikely and impossible places, so our friends determined to ascend the tree to ascertain if by any chance the head could have lodged between its leafy branches.

Previous to mounting, Ludwig, who, together with his friend, had provided himself with a long branch wherewith to beat down the bushes, struck the chestnut-tree a blow on the trunk with the branch he carried, when a hollow sound proceeded from the tree, and instantly a large owl fluttered out from the foliage before their faces with its beak and plumage stained with blood. Blinded with the sunlight, it hovered distractedly hither and thither for a time, and then vanished with a screech.

"Did you notice the beak and feathers of the bird, Ludwig?" asked Fritz.

"I did," said Ludwig, "and what is more, I am convinced that the whole of this seemingly robust chestnut-tree is hollow, and I have not a doubt that the murderer, aware of the fact, has hidden the head of his victim at the bottom, and that this fell bird has been gorging itself and its young upon it ever since."

"That is just my opinion," said Fritz. "Let us climb the tree and look within."

My ancestor was the first to mount, and having arrived at the point where the trunk divides itself into branches, he discovered a large hole thickly covered over with leaves. Sitting upon the edge, with his legs dangling within the hollow trunk, he proceeded to strike a light, and having ignited a taper, he commenced carefully to descend into the hollow of the tree. In his descent, however, his foot slipped, his taper extinguished itself, and he came down rather suddenly upon his feet. He soon became aware from a feeble smothered shriek that he was treading upon a nest of young owlets.

He began to dread lest he might encounter some venomous reptile in this unexplored region, but taking courage he struck another light and searched about. He had not looked long when he discovered what appeared to be a human scalp. He grasped it firmly by the hair, and by the light of his taper soon knew it to be in reality the head of a man, one half of which had been already eaten away to the bone.

"Eureka!" exclaimed Fritz, "I have it."

His friend uttered an exclamation of delight, while my relative clambered up again, and the two friends examined the disgusting treasure under the fair light of day.

"You see the hair is black," said Fritz. "I hope you are satisfied now that this is not the head of the Scharfrichter."

"There is no doubt about that now, I think," said Ludwig. "And do you know, Fritz, now that I scan these features, they seem familiar to me as my own in the looking-glass. Himmel! Can it be possible!"

"What?" demanded my ancestor, anxiously.

"Why, I'll swear that this is no other than my old friend and fellow-student, the Count of Waffenburg!" exclaimed Engstein.

"What! Graf von Waffenberg! Is it really so? I knew him well. Let me examine the features," said Fritz.

"Yes, it is he beyond a doubt," said Ludwig. "We had a quarrel once, and I wounded him in the cheek. Here is the wound I myself inflicted; but afterwards we became staunch friends."

"True," said Fritz. "I remember the duel well, being present myself on the occasion. What a curious coincidence! It is certainly he, and no other. The more I look at the features the more satisfied I am. Let us hasten with this proof of the identity of the murdered man to the township and spread abroad the news of the murder of the count. His relations will then come to claim his body."

The two friends then made a covering of chestnut leaves for the head, and tying it up in a handkerchief, retraced their steps towards the township, discoursing on the cunning of the murderer, who appeared to them to be no other than the Scharfrichter himself.

"For when a body is found minus the head," argued Ludwig, "and dressed in the clothes of another man, and that other man is nowhere to be found, it follows as a matter of course that the man missing must be the murderer."

"Yes," said the Englishman, "unless the murdered man had previously stolen the clothes of another, and then afterwards been murdered by some unknown assassin."

"But when the deceased has been proved beyond a doubt to be the Graf von Waffenburg, a man whose name is above so ridiculous a suspicion," said Engstein.

"Oh, of course the blackest suspicion attaches itself to Wenzel," said Fritz; "yet, in the case of a mysterious murder, evidence, occasionally of so startling and unexpected a nature, turns up as to completely alter the state of the case.

"The headsman is missing, and a corpse has been found dressed in his clothes. We presume, therefore, that *he* is the murderer, but if after a time the Henker's corpse should also be found—"

"Oh, in that case," said Ludwig, "the aspect of the whole affair would be changed. Well, we must wait for further evidence. To-morrow the case will begin in court, and my services will be required. I doubt not before long that sufficient light will be thrown on the subject to enable us to discover the true murderer."

Thus our two friends chatted by the way, till in due time they arrived at the township, and having deposited the head of the murdered man at the town hall, where the body had been exposed, they spread abroad the result of their expedition, and clearly proved to the somewhat obtuse inhabitants their error.

On the following morning, then, the trial began. The court was crowded to suffocation. Evidence of a very extraordinary nature had turned up, so it was said, and Ludwig Engstein, attired in his professional robes, was preparing to conduct the case.

My ancestor was amongst the crowd, and had placed himself as near as he possibly could to his friend.

"Call in Gottlieb Kräger," cried the examiner.

A hoary peasant entered the witness-box, and the examination proceeded in this wise:

"You are a farmer from the village of ——, are you not?"

"I am."

"Just inform us, if you please, what you were doing on the night of the murder."

"I was returning home after selling some cattle at the ——dorf market, and it was about midnight when I passed close to the Henker's cottage. I heard cries and groans as of someone being murdered not far off. I stopped and listened for a moment, then set off on tiptoe to the spot whence the sounds proceeded. It was very dark, and the groans at length ceased.

"I placed myself behind some brushwood to watch who should issue from the copse, when a friar passed me."

"Stay, are you quite sure the friar came from the very spot from whence you heard the groans?"

"Well, as to swearing to it, I don't know, but I heard the sound as of brushwood being trampled under foot, and the next instant the friar passed close to me. He did not appear to observe me, but moved onward in the direction of the village of Ahlden."

"Did you follow him or take any further notice of him?"

"To say the truth, I was too frightened to move, but I kept my eye on him as far as I could see him."

"But you tell me it was very dark."

"Just at that moment the moon had burst from behind the clouds, and enabled me to see distinctly."

"Well, did you observe anything peculiar in the manner or gait of the friar?"

"Yes; after he had passed me some ten paces he halted, as if he were counting money, after which he threw away something that glittered in the moonlight and then walked on. I followed stealthily behind to discover what it was that he had thrown away, when I picked up this."

The witness held up a long silk purse knitted with silver beads.

"Give it to me—so—can you recollect anything else about this friar? Could you manage to catch a glimpse of his face?"

"No, I could not exactly distinguish the features, but—"

"But what?"

"I observed a peculiar patch in his amice over the left shoulder."

"Should you be able to swear to the amice?"

"Aye, that I should, among a thousand."

"Is this the amice of the friar you saw issue from the copse?" asked Ludwig, holding up a patched amice such as is worn by the Capuchin friars.

"The very same, I'll swear to it."

"Take care, you are on your oath."

"Well, if it is not the same, it is one made after the same fashion, patch and all complete. I'll swear to the shape of the patch, for I observed the garment well."

"Enough; you may retire. Call in Hans Schultz."

A dapper little man with oiled hair and closely-shaven face entered the court, and having taken his post at the witness-box, gave his evidence as follows:—

"I am by profession a barber. The morning after the murder I was shaving an elderly gentleman in my shop. I suggested that a little hair dye would improve his personal appearance, and offered him a bottle. He refused to buy it, so I placed it on a table behind me, and continued to shave him. Whilst I was recommending the hair dye to my customer I noticed a Capuchin friar pass several times in front of my shop. He appeared to be listening to our conversation.

"Shortly afterwards he entered the shop and begged for alms for the convent. I gave him a creuzer, and after he had chatted a little he left the shop. I could not see his face well, as he kept it covered with his hood, but I remember that he had a red beard. He had hardly left my shop when on looking on the table behind me I found the bottle of hair dye gone. No one else but the friar and my customer had entered the shop since I laid the bottle down upon the table, yet I could not suspect my customer of having stolen the bottle, and I was much at a loss to conceive what a Capuchin friar should want with hair dye.

"I concluded, therefore, that I must have been mistaken, and must have laid the bottle down somewhere else without thinking, so I thought no more of it.

"On the same day I was called to cut the hair of a gentleman at the other end of the village, when I passed a friar who appeared to be the same as he who not long ago had entered my shop. I looked at him in the face, but he had a black beard. I could have sworn it was the same, for his amice was patched in a peculiar manner on the shoulder, as was that of the first friar."

"Is this the amice that the friar wore?" asked Engstein, holding up the patched garment.

"It is like it. I could all but swear to it."

"Did you address him when you met him, as you thought, a second time?"

"I was about to do so, but he pulled out his beads, and began counting them. Not liking to disturb him in his devotions, I passed on, thinking that after all I might have been deceived."

"That is sufficient, you may go,"

The little barber left the court, and another witness was called for.

"Your name?"

"Max Offenbrunnen."

"Profession?"

"I am host of the Bear Inn in the village of M——."

"Can you tell us anything that happened at your inn within this last week?"

"Yes; three days after the murder a Capuchin friar stopped at my inn and called for a tankard of beer. He kept his hood down all the time, so that I could not see his face, but I remember that he had a black beard, and I also noticed that he had a patch in his amice over one shoulder of rather an unusual form."

The patched garment was held up again in court, and recognised also by the third witness, after which he proceeded as follows:—

"He called for more beer, and I began to enter into conversation with him and asked him where he came from. He told me from a Capuchin convent at W——, about a mile off. Just at that moment another friar, an old friend of mine, passed my inn, who belonged to the aforementioned convent.

"'Then you know each other,'" said I to my friend the second friar, and I sought to bring them together, but my friend, after eyeing the former from head to foot, denied all knowledge of him. The first friar then somewhat confusedly stammered an excuse, saying that he had spoken without thinking, but that he had intended to say St. Mary's, another Capuchin convent, six miles further off. Then my friend the second friar said that he knew all the friars at St. Mary's, but still denied that he knew this one.

"The former began to mumble that he had only lately arrived, and began to turn the conversation. My friend whispered to me that he didn't believe he was a friar at all, but someone in disguise. After my friend had left, the former friar called for more beer (I never saw a friar drink so much beer as this one), and being curious to discover who the man was I tried to draw him out. At first he answered cautiously, but after drinking deeper he became less cautious and more confidential, but his utterance was now thick and unintelligible. He drew his chair closer to mine, and seemed about to let me into some secret, when some other customers of mine at the next table began to talk about the murder.

"I noticed that the would-be friar started, and instead of continuing his conversation with me, got up suddenly and muttered some excuse for taking his departure. He paid me hurriedly by lying down a Reichsgulden, saying that whatever change there might be I might keep for myself. He had hardly left my house when certain of the guard who had been on the track of the murderer stopped to question him, and finding he could give no satisfactory account of himself, took him into custody."

Other witnesses were then examined in their turn, among which were certain members of the family of the murdered count, and a certain Fraulein von Berlichingen, his affianced bride, all of whom recognised the body to be that of the missing Graf von Waffenburg. The silken purse with silver beads picked up by the first witness was also recognised by Fraulein von Berlichingen as having been knitted by herself and presented by her to her lover.

The remains of the murdered count were decently interred. The melancholy event caused no small commotion in the neighbourhood. The funeral was followed by a large crowd of relatives and intimate friends, among which were our two heroes Fritz and Ludwig. The grief of Fraulein von Berlichingen was too great to allow her to appear at the funeral. She was inconsolable, and shortly afterwards entered a convent.

But to return to the trial.

The prisoner was now conducted into court. He was a man somewhat passed middle-age, though his frame was square built and powerful, and his hair, beard, and eyebrows were of a deep black, yet an observer might have noticed that whenever a ray of sunlight entered the court and shone full in the face of the prisoner that his hair and beard turned to a glowing purple, demonstrating beyond a doubt the presence of dye. Those who chanced to be stationed near the prisoner declared afterwards that the hairs of his head towards the roots were of a bright red, and many were they who recognised, in spite of this disguise, the person of Franz Wenzel, the executioner.

The prisoner, however, when examined, gave his name as Adolf Schmidt, and denied stoutly that he was Franz Wenzel, or to having ever had dealings with such a person.

He denied having stolen a bottle of hair-dye for the purpose of disguising himself, and maintained that he was an honest citizen who had donned a holy garb for penitence, which had been imposed upon him by his father confessor.

The prisoner was then asked if such were the case, why he had tried to deceive the host of the Bear Inn and the Capuchin friar when they asked him whence he came. To this the prisoner replied that he loved not to gratify the idle curiosity of others respecting his private affairs. Ludwig Engstein then asked the prisoner how he came in possession of the friar's amice, for which he responded that it had been lent him some time ago by his father confessor, who had obtained it from some Capuchin friar of his acquaintance.

When asked for particulars concerning his father confessor, he replied vaguely and confusedly, and when begged to be more explicit, he refused, saying he had private reasons for not divulging the affairs of his friends.

Other witnesses were then called for, who stated that they had been robbed of money and various sorts of ware more than once within the last three years, about half a (German) mile from the house of the Scharfrichter by a man who wore a mask, and who corresponded in height and width of person to the prisoner. Among these latter was a Jew pedlar, who three years ago had been robbed of a large sum and various articles of clothing, among which he declared was the identical friar's amice held up in court, and which he perfectly remembered to have patched himself.

This and such like evidence naturally went very much against the prisoner; neither will it be wondered at that his disguise was easily seen through, and his person recognised as that of Franz Wenzel, the executioner. He was consequently found guilty of wilful murder and finally condemned to be beheaded. The day of the execution was fixed, and the prisoner conducted to the condemned cell.

We have mentioned before in an early part of this story that the profession of the headsman was hereditary, that the law forced the son of an executioner to follow in the steps of his father.

The unhappy wretch then, according to this law, was doomed to lose his life at the hands of his own son. Much speculation, however, among the inhabitants of ——dorf had arisen as to whether the law would actually enforce so rigorous a decree, and whether the son of the Scharfrichter would rebel against it if it did, or bow submissively to so harsh and unfeeling an order.

Some there were who thought that an exception ought to be made in this case, and a new Henker selected, as it was hard for the son to suffer for the crimes of the father; but even if the law were disposed to be lenient, who was the new aspirant to be? Who would like to come forward to offer his services?

The office of the Scharfrichter was in such bad odour that it would be difficult to find a man in the whole village who could be persuaded to undertake the task, even by the offer of a large reward.

However, after much speculation and gossip, the inhabitants came to the conclusion that everything might be done with money, and that someone would be certainly found to accept the bribe.

Others began to spread throughout the village that the man had already been found, and ventured to point out such or such a citizen as the new practitioner. Meanwhile the law had remained passive and had not troubled itself to make an exception in the case, and the burgomaster who had the superintendence of such affairs was far too phlegmatic and indifferent even to give the matter a thought.

He knew that an execution had to take place, that someone would be paid for amputating the head of the criminal, but whether it was to be one man's duty or another's was all the same to him.

The headsman's trade was hereditary, and he (the burgomaster) had never heard of any such innovation as that of selecting a new headsman during the lifetime of the rightful heir; therefore, as a matter of course, the young scharfrichter was to decapitate his own father, and there was an end of the matter.

What to him were the feelings of the son at being forced to obey so unnatural a dictate? He was paid for it like anyone else, and very good pay he got, too.

What to him was the additional anguish of the criminal at being executed by his own son? He knew well enough that his son would step into his shoes when he himself should be deprived of office, and if he didn't like to lose his head at the hands of his own son, he ought to have reflected before he committed the murder.

Now, the burgomaster had a confidential servant, one Heinrich Göbel, a man of heartless and revengeful nature, who cherished an ill-will against the prisoner's son for having dared to supplant him in the affections of a certain blue-eyed damsel, the daughter of a tavern-keeper in the village.

The father of the lady in question was not over pleased with the attentions of either of these individuals towards his Lieschen, one of the aspirants for his daughter's hand being a drunkard, the son of an executioner, who besides the stigma inevitably attached to his character for life, would be obliged to maintain his daughter by the scanty proceeds of his loathsome profession.

The other, a man of notoriously bad character, and dependent upon the wages he received from his master for a living. Of the two, the maid herself decidedly favoured Leo Wenzel, the young headsman, and seeing this, Heinrich Göbel inwardly resolved to take vengeance on his rival upon the first opportunity.

Whilst plotting vengeance thus in his heart, Göbel sought his master and shaped his conversation in this wise:

"Herr Burgermeister, this will be a somewhat difficult business, this execution."

"How so?" inquired his master.

"Why, according to law," answered his servant, "young Leo will have to take the life of his own father."

"Well, what of that?" said the burgomaster.

"They say he is a young man of spirit, and he might refuse to take his father's life."

"Refuse! would he? The law will force him."

"But if he is obstinate and persists? He is a young man of spirit."

"Ugh! I hate these young men of spirit, they are always making trouble and subverting order. Well, if he makes a disturbance, he will be imprisoned, that's all."

"Yes, yes, of course; but for all that, if he positively refuses to lift his arm against his father, the law cannot force him to do it."

"Well, not exactly, but—but what has put it into your head that he *will* refuse? He will be rewarded for his services."

"But if he could not be tempted by a reward, if by chance he should refuse at the last moment to act the part of executioner towards his own father, and no one should be found to accept the post—why, in that case, if *my* services should be accepted, I should be most glad to officiate."

"What, *you* Heinrich! *you* turn scharfrichter! Ha! ha!—this is something quite new. I was not aware that that was anything in your line."

"Well, sir, knowing your dislike to a disturbance among the populace (a thing very likely to occur if the headsman should not be found at his post)—rather than such an old vagabond as Franz Wenzel should get off in the confusion, why, I'll undertake the job myself."

"You would? Ha! ha!—but stay, if there *should* be a disturbance (which Heaven forfend, as any excitement sadly upsets my digestion), I am not so sure that I should like my servant to take upon himself the office of scharfrichter, for the odium of the populace that he would naturally incur would reflect likewise upon his master, and—"

"Well sir, if you fear that, I should then advise another line of conduct."

"Indeed! What may that be?"

"To keep young Leo in ignorance that it is his father that he is called upon to execute. Listen to me! The Scharfrichter's house is a mile distant; our villagers have a superstitious dread of the spot, and are not likely yet to have communicated with the young man, and I know that he hasn't been in the township since he was last called to swear to the identity of the murdered man, then commonly believed to be his father. You will recollect that he identified the corpse as that of his father. In his lonely dwelling, he can have heard nothing of the trial, and is consequently still under the impression that it is his father that has been murdered.

"Now, if you will leave the matter to me I will contrive that he shall not be undeceived until too late."

"Yes; but how?"

"First of all I will go there myself with the news that the murderer of his father has been arrested, that the day has been fixed for his execution, and that he will have the pleasure of trying his hand for the first time in his life on his father's murderer. Everything will go straight, provided he has as yet heard nothing from other tongues."

"But if he has?"

"Then our plan is frustrated; but I go to ascertain that, and if he has not, the greatest care must be taken that no one communicates with him from this town, to which end you should give orders for the gates of the town to be closed for some days, under the excuse that you have been robbed of certain valuables, and have taken this precaution to catch the thief. It would be as well, perhaps, to hurry on the execution as quickly as possible."

"Well, but there is one point I don't understand. Supposing all to go on smoothly, as you seem so confident that it will, won't the young man recognise his father when led up to the scaffold in the 'poor sinner's' cart, and afterwards takes his seat on the chair placed for him?"

"There is our great difficulty, but let us hope for the best. The prisoner, as you know, took the precaution to dye his red head black in order to escape recognition. This will aid our project. The 'poor sinner's' garb that he will don the morning of the execution will also help the disguise. Young Leo is but a superficial observer, and before he has well taken note of the criminal his head will be off."

"You are very hopeful as to the success of your scheme, but if the father, in his last moments, makes himself known to his son—should rush into his arms to embrace him and say: 'My son, do you not know me? I am your father—you will not have the heart to execute your own father, the author of your existence.'"

"We must prevent this. Let a handkerchief be tied round his jaw that he cannot open his mouth to speak. This, after all, will be nothing more than is usually done to catch hold of the head in order to exhibit it to the public after decapitation, the only difference being that it is generally tied on after the criminal has taken his seat on the scaffold, while in this case it will be done before. Another bandage should be bound round his eyes at the same time, which is also customary; thus a great portion of the prisoner's face will be hidden. His arms will be pinioned firmly to his sides, so as to render all attempt at the removal of the bandage impossible, and everything will pass off quietly."

"Well, well, you're a queer dog. See that it *does* pass off quietly, that's all, and don't bother me any more about it. Mind, I leave the matter entirely in your hands."

"Never fear, sir, I am off at once to the house of the Scharfrichter; trust everything to me. Stay, you had better issue an order for the gates of the town to be closed at once. You can give me a pass before I start, or they will shut me out with the rest."

"True; just wait one moment. Here—the pen and ink—so now be off as fast as you can."

Off started the servant of the burgomaster with the order to the gatekeeper to close the gates, and the pass which was to admit none but himself, and after the gatekeeper had received the necessary instructions, Heinrich passed rapidly through the gates and directed his steps towards the house of the Scharfrichter. He chuckled to himself as he contemplated the success of his scheme.

"What would the death of his father at my hands be to him to the discovery of having taken his father's life himself! That will be revenge indeed! Now to the fulfilment of my scheme there is no obstacle."

He had proceeded about an English mile on his way when, suddenly lifting his eyes, he descried in the distance the figure of an aged man, who appeared to be going the same road as himself. He hastened his steps, and soon overtook the veteran, whom he now recognised as one of his fellow citizens, a certain Gustav Meyer, and known to be one of the greatest gossips in the neighbourhood.

"Good-day, Gustav," said Göbel, with forced good humour. "Where are you off to on those venerable pins of yours?"

"Ach! lieber, freund Göbel!" exclaimed the loquacious old man; "how are you? I have not seen you for an age. You have grown proud since you have been in the burgomaster's service, and forget that it was I who got you the situation, for you never come to see me now, though we used to be such cronies, you know. But you young folks never think it worth while to give us old fogies a call to see how we are. Why, I might be dead and buried for all you would know about it, and even if you did hear of it, I suppose it would be all the same to you, eh?

"Well, well, 'ingratitude is the reward of the world,' as the proverb says, and we old fogies with one foot in the grave and the other about to follow must make up our minds to be put on the shelf. We all have our turn; I have had mine, you are having yours, but old age comes at last, and then there is an end of us all, even to the best of us. Even I have been young, friend Göbel. Ha! ha! You'd hardly think so to look at me now with these silvery locks and tottering limbs. I say you'd hardly think so now, would you, eh? Now, how many years should you think I could count, friend Göbel, tell me?"

"I haven't the slightest idea," said Göbel, impatiently.

"I am hard upon ninety years old, and all tell me that I carry my years well. I may say I haven't had a day's illness in all my life. I have nearly all my teeth yet, and—"

"I have no doubt all you say is very true, my friend," interrupted Göbel; "but you have hardly answered my question satisfactorily yet. I asked you where you were going?"

"Friend Göbel," said the old man, "now I'll just tell you what I propose doing this morning, just by way of stretching my old limbs, seeing that I have not had a walk for an age. It does old folks good to go out for a stroll every now and then in the country. Too much staying at home over the fire isn't good, even for the likes of me."

"Well, well," broke in Göbel, beginning to lose all patience. "I asked you where you were going."

"Did you? Ah yes, I had nearly forgot. We old folks are apt to lose our memories at times, you know, my friend, so you young folks ought to have compassion on us, and recollect that we were once like you, and that you will one day become like us, therefore—"

"This is insufferable," burst out Göbel, whose forbearance was quite at an end. "I ask you a plain question, and I expect a plain answer. I repeat the question—Where are you going?"

"Hoity, toity! friend Göbel," cried the old man, in great surprise. "What! so impatient with your old friend Gustav! Don't you remember how often I have taken you upon my knee and danced you? We used to be great friends then. Don't you recollect? But I suppose you have forgotten all that now, eh?—since you have become a man. Let me see, how long ago must that be? Full thirty years ago, if it's a day, I'll warrant."

"Will you, or will you not, give me a plain answer to a plain question. Tell me where you are going?" cried Göbel, now quite furious, and shaking the old man violently by both shoulders.

"Softly, softly! friend Göbel," cried the veteran, much alarmed. "Save my life. Prithee, save my life, and I will tell you where I am going, if you will have patience."

"Well, tell me at once, and let us have no more chattering," said Göbel, leaving go his hold.

"Well, in the first place, then," began old Gustav, recovering himself—"in the first place—but stay, upon second thoughts, I'll just leave you to guess where I am going. Now, where do you think?"

"Dotard, have a care!" cried Göbel, threateningly, "and trifle with me no longer. Tell me where you are going, or—"

"Well, well, friend Göbel, I'll tell you; don't be afraid, don't let two such old friends as we are quarrel for a trifle,—I'll tell you where I am going, although I must say that I think you seem to take an uncommon interest in the doings of an old man like me, who, though he be an old friend—"

"Take care now!"

"Well, well, my friend, wait one moment; I'll tell you. I told you before that I would tell you, and I will be as good as my word, if you will have one moment's patience—for patience, friend Göbel, patience, I say, is a virtue that we ought all to cultivate, and which we all of us more or less are sadly wanting in. But to proceed; though, after all, my friend, what hurry can you possibly have to learn so simple a fact? It appears to me that the world has grown wondrously impatient since my time; that is, if everybody is like you, but as I said before—"

"Tell me! tell me!" screamed Göbel, seizing his venerable friend a second time by the shoulders.

"Well, then, my friend," said Gustav, drawing out his words at a most provoking length, "if I *must* tell you, and you are quite sure that you have sufficient patience to listen to me, learn that I am going to pay a visit at the house of the Scharfrichter, to have a quiet little gossip. You know I am fond of a nice little gossip. Well, I am just going to have a little chat with that poor young man Leo Wenzel. What do you think? He doesn't know yet that his father is the real murderer, for he lives so far off and no one ever goes near the house to tell him the news, and he is still under the delusion that his father has been murdered and that the assassin has not yet been caught. Poor young man, I shall have to break the news very gently to him, for he will feel it deeply. He must know the truth sooner or later, so I have taken upon myself to be the first to communicate the unwelcome news.

"According to the law he will be obliged to take the life of his own father. It will be a dreadful blow him, poor boy, and I am sure I don't know how he will be induced to act executioner in the present instance. I know not if the law in this case will make an exception and choose someone else in his place; it will be very hard upon him if the law really should insist on being carried out to the very letter. Let us hope that mercy will be shown to the son, but in any case it is a very dreadful affair, so I thought I would just go to comfort him a little, to see how he takes the matter, and give him courage, in case—"

"I thought as much!" muttered Göbel to himself; then aloud to his friend, "So that is where you are going is it? Ah, then I will save you the trouble. Being a matter of no importance, you need not be in a hurry. Listen to me; my master has lost certain valuables, and has given orders for the gates of the town to be closed until he has discovered the thief, and has strictly commanded me to arrest any person I might find leaving the town, until his valuables shall have been recovered. I should be sorry to suspect you, but as the law respects the person of no man, it is my painful duty to take you back to the town. Let us have no more cackling or resistance, but come at once.—"

"But my dear friend Göbel!" pleaded the veteran, "you surely can't suspect—you will not for one moment imagine—nay, if you have any doubt of my honesty search me. I can assure it will be useless, I am innocent."

"If you are innocent, you will be proved so in due time, meanwhile I have orders—"

"But friend Göbel, I assure you again and again upon my oath that I have taken nothing. There—look—search me all over, if you will, and let me go in peace. Is not my character enough? Am I not well known in——dorf? Have I ever been known to touch my neighbour's goods? Pray satisfy yourself that I have taken nothing, and let me go. Why trouble yourself to bring back a man to the town to be searched whom you know to be innocent? Besides, it will upset my plan. I wouldn't miss my little gossip with young Leo for all the world just at this moment. Just consider, my friend—"

"Cease your cackling and come along with me!" shouted Göbel, seizing him by the collar and dragging him forcibly back towards the town.

"But—but—" stammered the astonished and terrified old man.

"But me no buts, but do my bidding instantly, Sir Driveller, or it will be the worse for you."

So saying, he dragged his old friend home again at a hurried pace, regardless of his tottering limbs and of his prayers and entreaties.

It was just mid day, and the sun shone hot, when Göbel returned to the township, perspiring at every pore, and deposited his charge, more dead than alive, within the walls of ——dorf. He then retraced his steps under the broiling sun, cursing and swearing as he went at his plan having been so nearly frustrated by the cackling gossip of an old dotard.

"*Potz—Himmel, Donnerwetter, Schock, Schwerer, Noth, noch mal*!" he muttered to himself. "A pretty obstacle in my path! *Tausend Teufel*! I had a mind to dash his brains out on the spot, the old idiot, for his drivelling."

With these and such like elaborately strung together oaths the servant of the burgomaster beguiled the time, until at length he arrived at the door of the Scharfrichter's house, where he discovered young Leo at work in his garden. The young executioner looked up at the sound of stranger footsteps, and though he would rather the visitor had been anyone else than his rival, yet upon the whole he was not displeased to see a human face after so long. His manner even warmed towards his visitor when he saw him advance with a smile on his face and an extended hand.

"Leo," began Heinrich Göbel with feigned friendship, "we have long been enemies, but everything has an end. I have now come to offer you my hand in friendship, for henceforth we are no longer rivals, but friends. Lieschen, think of her no more. Her father positively refuses to give her to either of us, so she has at length plighted her troth to another man."

"What! Lieschen? Impossible!" cried Leo, mopping his forehead.

"Ay, my friend, it is too true; nay, pray calm yourself. I, too, loved her as you did, but since the matter has turned out thus, I have made up my mind to console myself by paying my addresses to another as soon as possible."

"You never *could* have loved her as I loved her," gasped out Leo, as he staggered for support against the garden wall.

"Well, well, my friend, I knew you would feel the blow, but calm yourself and dismiss these gloomy thoughts. I have better news than that in store for you."

"What care I for news now that *she* has deserted me?" groaned Leo distractedly.

"Come, come now, let me comfort you a little," said Göbel. "What do you think? *The murderer of your father has been discovered*!"

"What do I hear? Caught? Safe?"

"Ay, the murder has been proved, and the murderer condemned to die by the sword. The execution has been fixed for the day after to-morrow. It will take place at daybreak as usual, and you will have the satisfaction of taking vengeance on your father's murderer with your own hands. You will wield your father's sword for the first time in your life before an admiring crowd. Think of that."

"Vengeance at last!" cried the young headsman, with flushed face and distorted features. "Vengeance at last! Thank God! thank God!"

"Bravo, old friend!" cried Göbel, slapping his heartily detested rival on the shoulder in the friendliest manner possible. "I knew you would take heart at this piece of news. Come, let us sit down together and console ourselves."

Leo, then entering the house, took from a cupboard a large bottle of schnaps and two glasses. The two companions, seating themselves, began to drink deeply and to chat incessantly, the subject of the discourse being the particulars of the murder according to the version of Göbel. We need hardly say that the whole was a fabrication of Heinrich's own brain. At length the servant of the burgomaster rose to take his departure, and having enjoined his rival to be of good cheer, bent his steps again towards the township, chuckling by the way at his own devices. Arrived at the gates of the town, he showed his pass, and was permitted to enter without let or hindrance. Hurrying through the streets until he reached the burgomaster's house, he presented himself before that worthy, whom he found seated at a table before a plate of sausage, and in the act of draining to the dregs an enormous tankard of beer.

"Well, what news?" asked his master.

"Oh! the very best; he took the bait greedily. It was quite a pleasure to see how he enjoyed the news. No one had been before me, so I had him all to myself. The matter will now go off as smoothly as could be desired; but, by the saints! I had a narrow escape of failure."

"Indeed! How was that?"

"When I was nearly half way to the Scharfrichter's house, who should I see just ahead of me but that cursed old gossip, Gustav Meyer. I stopped him and asked him where he was going. *Potzausend*! what a chatterbox! I thought I should not get an answer out of him before nightfall, and when I did, where do you think he was going? Why, straight to the house of the Henker to have a quiet chat with young Leo upon the subject of the murder, and reveal to him all that I had taken such pains to keep secret. He seemed delighted at the idea of being the first to deliver the news."

The burgomaster laughed heartily.

"Well, what did you do?" said he, at length.

"What did I do! I told him his presence was particularly wanted at the township, and seizing him by the collar, dragged him all the way back again, regardless of his cackling. I informed him that you had lost some valuables, and had given me orders to arrest anyone leaving the town on suspicion. He was indignant at the charge. Protested, declared his innocence, and spoke of the high character he had always borne in the town, etc., etc. He seemed in despair at being deprived of his little gossip with the Henker's son, and begged and entreated me to let him have it out quietly; but, deaf to all his chattering, I dragged him home again in spite of himself, and lodged him safely within the gates of the town. *Donner und Blitzen*! but it was enough to raise the bile of a saint to listen to the wanderings of that antique driveller, to say nothing of having one's plan so nearly frustrated; by such a worm as that too!"

Here and again the burgomaster burst into a loud laugh, in which Göbel, in spite of himself, joined.

"Ah," said he, at length recovering himself, "there is one thing yet to be done. I must go to the jailor of the prison with private orders from you to prevent the prisoner having an interview with his son, should he ask for one. This accomplished, there will be no more difficulty."

"Ah, yes," said the burgomaster, "it would be as well. But what an interest you seem to take in this case, Heinrich! One would imagine that you had a private grudge against the prisoner."

"I like to see things well done," was the reply, and the servant shortly after left the presence of his master.

A great sensation was caused in ——dorf when it was given out that the execution had been hurried on a week, and much speculation arose as to what could have been the burgomaster's motive. Half the town already knew by the tongue of old Gustav of his having been arrested by the servant of the burgomaster on suspicion of having robbed his master of certain valuables just at the very time when he (Gustav) was contemplating the pleasure he would have in being the first to communicate the melancholy tidings of the murder to the young headsman. They therefore concluded that Leo must still be in ignorance of the real state of the case. The other half of ——dorf, however, never gave a thought as to whether he knew it or not; enough for them that someone was going to be beheaded and that they should have a spectacle to vary the monotony of their humdrum lives.

At length the fatal day arrived. The gates of the town were thrown open (for the servant of the burgomaster gave out that the thief had been discovered and the valuables regained), and now all ——dorf was in an uproar, while crowds of peasants from all the surrounding villages flocked to witness the bloody spectacle.

The scaffold, or the mound of earth which was to serve as such, had been erected half way between the township and the house of the executioner, and was already surrounded by a file of soldiers, around which thronged the mob so closely that they were every now and then repulsed by the military. From the sea of human heads that inundated the place of execution resounded a hum of voices, in which salutations, sallies, bad language, coarse jokes, and coarser laughter, together with murmurs and imprecations, and an occasional scream from the women when the crowd pressed too closely, were confusedly mingled, and resembled at a little distance the bleating of an immense flock of sheep. Classes of all sorts were jostled together, from the lowest grade of handwerksbursch to the university student. There were pretty peasant girls in their holiday costumes, and sturdy peasants from all parts of the country. There were Jew hawkers, sharpers, pickpockets, ruffianly bullies, cripples, and mendicants. There were mothers with young children in their arms, which latter contributed their feeble cries to the general buzz.

All had turned out to feast their eyes upon the death of a fellow mortal. Nor was this an ordinary execution like that described in an earlier part of this story. No; this was an exceptional case—something out of the common way, a sublimer spectacle.

In this case the condemned was no obscure handwerksbursch, of whose career the multitude knew nothing, and cared as little about. The criminal was no less a man than Franz Wenzel, the far-famed Scharfrichter, who had amputated the heads of "poor sinners" for the last thirty or forty years, and was now doomed to lose his own.

The interest in the case was considerably heightened when it was known that the veteran executioner was to be operated upon by the hands of his own son. Then the facts of the murder were so strange, so unnatural. Fancy the cunning of that hardened old sinner, the ex-headsman, who, according to his own confession, made in prison the day before the execution, had waylaid, robbed, and murdered the innocent Count of Waffenburg, a scion of one of the most wealthy and respected noble families for miles round, disguised as a Capuchin friar, and in order to conceal the identity of the murdered man, had dissevered the head of the corpse, which he had endeavoured to hide for ever from the eye of man by throwing it into the trunk of a hollow chestnut tree. Then having stripped the corpse of its clothes, and afterwards having stripped himself of his outer garments, he dressed up the corpse of his victim in his own well known crimson-coloured doublet and hose, thereby conveying the idea to the public mind that the corpse found was his own, after which, returning to his house close by, having again donned the friar's habit, he deposited the sword usually set apart for the beheading of criminals, and in this case used for amputating the head of the murdered count, and wiping it well, he lighted a fire on his hearth where he burned one by one the habiliments of his victim. He then left his house a second time, still disguised as a friar and laden with his ill-gotten treasure, passed once more the scene of the murder and wandered all night in the direction of ——. How strange the evidence, too, that convicted him, the theft of the bottle of hair dye, the remarkable patch on his amice. Every particular of the murder had an indescribable interest in the minds of the populace of ——dorf and its surrounding villages. No wonder the adjacent townships vomited forth their scum of the curious, idle, and depraved! This was a sight not to be missed on any account, and would furnish them with gossip for the next six months at least. At length, when the long streaky rose-tipped clouds announced the approach of the fatal hour, the crowd burst out simultaneously into a cry of "He comes! he comes! the Henker comes!"

The crowd made room for a young man in a cart, who, having thrown the reins on the horse's neck, passed through the file of soldiers and mounted the hillock of earth, armed with the two-handed weapon that he was about to use for the first time in his life.

"Look!" said one of the crowd; "it *is* young Leo, after all. I thought they had found a substitute."

"What a hardhearted young ruffian to consent to take the life of his father with his own hands!" said another.

"And he doesn't seem to feel it a bit," said a third; "why, he is actually smiling."

"Some folks say that he does not know who it is that he is going to behead," said a fourth.

"Not know that the criminal is his father?" exclaimed the former speaker. "Nonsense, I don't believe it."

The young headsman was attired in a buff leather jerkin slashed with red and hose of a dark green. He appeared about two-and-twenty, and was as yet beardless. He was considerably taller than his father, but his frame, though powerfully built, was devoid of that excessive and almost preternatural muscular development that characterised that of the old executioner. His hair was of a reddish brown, his complexion florid, his eyes light blue, and his features, though somewhat coarse, had something in them not altogether disagreeable. He leaned firmly on his sword and gazed around calmly on the crowd, when suddenly the human sea became violently agitated and began to groan and hiss in its fury.

The cause of this tumult became speedily known.

It was the arrival of the "poor sinner," who was drawn in a cart between two priests and habited according to the custom of the condemned on such occasions. Loud hooting and execrations burst forth on all sides from the crowd as it made way for the condemned cart.

"But that is not Franz Wenzel," said one to his neighbour. "The old Henker had red hair; this man's hair is black."

"Fool, don't you know how that is?" said his neighbour. "Haven't you heard yet how he dyed his hair black in order not to be recognised?"

"No, did he though?" said the former. "But look! why is his head tied up so with two handkerchiefs? I can't see anything of his face."

"H'm, I don't know; some innovation I suppose. The handkerchief always used to be tied on when on the scaffold in my time," answered his friend. The criminal had now alighted from the cart, and, followed by the two priests, ascended the place of execution, where he took his seat on the chair placed for him. The assistant executioner, whose face was most successfully disguised with a black mask, pushed his way through the crowd and mounted the platform.

"Who is *he*?" was a question asked by everyone of everybody; "and why is he masked while Leo, who bears the sword, is unmasked?"

"Who knows? Perhaps he is the new headsman that they all talked about, and young Leo will not really behead his own father; but we shall see."

The crowd had grown more curious than ever. Every one stood on the tiptoe of expectation with his eyes and mouth wide open. An intense silence reigned around, during which the man in the mask bound the criminal firmly to his seat with a strong cord, then seizing the handkerchief that was tied round the head of the condemned, he gave the signal for the blow. The two priests who had hitherto been whispering consolation in the ear of the criminal now retreated a few paces to the rear, while young Leo advanced, flushed and triumphant, his whole countenance distorted with an expression of malice and revenge. Before brandishing his sword to give the final blow he lowered his head close to the ear of the victim and hissed out in accents sufficiently audible to be overheard by that part of the crowd that had assembled nearest to the scaffold: "Wretch! thine hour has come at last. Learn now the vengeance of a wronged son. Thou shalt see if I am the son of my father or no, and whether it is for nothing that I have been bred a Scharfrichter. Prepare now, for thou art soon to learn how I have profited by my lessons—whether I am an apt pupil. My sword is sharpened well on purpose for thee, and when thou feelest the cold steel close to thy neck, then, then, to h——l with thee, and bear throughout eternity the curses of a ruined son!"

During this speech of the young headsman the criminal was observed to tremble convulsively, as if struggling to speak, but the assistant executioner grasped the handkerchief still tighter round his head and repeated the signals impatiently.

"Did you hear?" said one of the foremost in the crowd. "Did you hear how he cursed his father? He actually reproached him in his last moments for having brought him up a Scharfrichter! Oh! the unfeeling young villain! What a heart he must have."

"Ah! neighbour," answered another, "these executioners are not like other mortals; they do not know what it is to feel. They are brought up to kill their fellow creatures as butchers are to kill cattle, and they think nothing of it. Bless you, there is nothing these men would not do for money."

"'Tis strange, too," said another close by. "I always thought young Leo loved his father. I never thought so bad of him as to think that he would curse him in his dying moments, wretch though he may have been."

"Take my word for it, neighbour," said a sturdy inhabitant of ——dorf, "that young Leo does not know yet that it is his father."

At this moment everyone suddenly broke short his discourse, and the crowd again was silent for a moment. The two-handed weapon was raised high in the air, glittered for a moment in the rays of the rising sun, then descended with the rapidity of lightning, while the head of the murderer having slipped out of the handkerchief with the force of the blow, fell with a crash on the platform.

A loud cheer is raised by the crowd, and young Leo having thrown away his sword and pushed aside the assistant executioner, has seized the head of the criminal and torn off the bandage from his eyes. He holds it high in the air by its purple locks and gloats with fiendish satisfaction on its writhing features. The muscles of the face are fearfully convulsed, as if the spirit had not as yet quite departed, but still lingered about the corpse, being loath to leave its tenement. The eyes roll hideously and appear to gaze reproachfully upon the face of the young executioner. Suddenly a change comes over the features of the young man. His countenance, the moment before so flushed with triumph and revenge, now assumes a ghastly pallor; a cold sweat breaks out on his forehead, his matted locks stand on end. His eyes start from his head, his jaw drops low. Then, with a preternatural shriek, he drops the head, which rolls down the hillock of earth among the crowd, staggers and falls heavily upon the platform, gasping out "*Oh, Gott! mein Vater*!"

No words can describe the sensation created among the crowd at this horrible scene. Questions and explanations ensued, and a rush was made towards the scaffold. Assistance was at length procured, and the son of the late executioner was lifted from the ground and driven toward his own house in the cart that he had set out in that morning, to execute his fearful mission. A doctor was sent for, who declared that he was in an apoplectic fit. In time, however, he recovered, and the doctor left someone with him to attend to him and keep him quiet. Nevertheless, when he came to reflect upon what had happened that morning, in spite of all restraint, he rushed wildly into the chamber where his poor paralytic mother lay on her death-bed, and losing all caution and reflection in his emotion, he related in a wild and excited manner the dreadful events of the day. The result may be anticipated. The poor woman, long given up by the doctors, sank under the startling news, and expired almost instantaneously.

Young Leo, who, with the exception of his drunkenness had really nothing very bad in him, now gave way to the most excessive grief, for he loved his mother tenderly. He felt himself now guilty of the murder of both his parents, and refused all consolation. What had he now to live for, thought he. His father he had murdered with his own hands and sent with curses to the tomb; his mother, so dear to him he had hurried to the grave through his insane want of self-restraint. His ladylove, false (as he thought), for secretly they had plighted their troth together. What was life to him now but a burden? He loathed it. These gloomy thoughts clouded his mind with a profound melancholy, a deep incurable despair. On the following morning Leo Wenzel, the young executioner, fell upon his own sword, yet moist with the blood of his father, by him so unconsciously shed on the day before.

With the death of Leo Wenzel the family became extinct, and the profession of the Scharfrichter went begging. But who was the assistant executioner? Nobody could find out. He had disappeared as mysteriously as he had made his appearance. Some said it was one, and some another, while the most settled belief was that it could be none other than the arch-fiend himself who had come to carry off the Henker's soul. In the confusion that followed the swoon of young Leo he had vanished, and no one had seen whither. No human being could have passed through a crowd without being seen by someone, therefore it must have been the arch enemy of mankind. Thus reasoned the people of ——dorf.

And Lieschen, what became of her? Poor girl! the news of her lover's suicide, for she had truly loved the youthful headsman, had completely overwhelmed her. She fell into a decline and outlived her lover but one year.

The servant of the burgomaster was mistaken in believing that after Leo's death the course would be now clear for him. His heartless scheme had come to light (for it was difficult to keep anything long a secret in ——dorf), and he found the door of Lieschen's house closed upon him for ever.

He soon knew himself hated by all the town, and tradition goes on to relate that some years afterwards, when he was in the service of another master, his employer having missed certain articles of plate and called in the police to search his coffers, they found not only the missing articles, but also a black mask and a suit of sad coloured clothes, recognised as having been worn by the assistant on the day of Wenzel's execution.

Finding his reputation lost in ——dorf, he deemed it advisable to retire to another village, where he afterwards married. The last we hear of him is that he ultimately accepted the office of Scharfrichter, and took up his abode in the house of Franz Wenzel, where he reared up a long line of executioners, which was only broken many years later by the profession of the Henker ceasing to be obligatory.

But what of our two friends Fritz and Ludwig? We had nigh forgotten them. That they were both of them present at the execution is undoubted from certain passages in their correspondence after my ancestor had left Germany for ever. The day after Wenzel's execution was the last time they met on earth. They each of them passed the remainder of their days in their own respective countries though they corresponded frequently. The most recently dated letter from Ludwig Engstein bears with it the news of his marriage, and in a postscript he mentions having been just informed that since the execution of Franz Wenzel the tricks of the Poltergeist had ceased for ever.

The Great God Pan

Arthur Machen

THE EXPERIMENT

"I AM GLAD YOU CAME, CLARKE; VERY GLAD INDEED. I WAS NOT SURE you could spare the time."

"I was able to make arrangements for a few days; things are not very lively just now. But have you no misgivings, Raymond? Is it absolutely safe?"

The two men were slowly pacing the terrace in front of Dr. Raymond's house. The sun still hung above the western mountain-line, but it shone with a dull red glow that cast no shadows, and all the air was quiet; a sweet breath came from the great wood on the hillside above, and with it, at intervals, the soft murmuring call of the wild doves. Below, in the long lovely valley, the river wound in and out between the lonely hills and, as the sun hovered and vanished into the west, a faint mist, pure white, began to rise from the banks. Dr. Raymond turned sharply to his friend.

"Safe? Of course it is. In itself the operation is a perfectly simple one; any surgeon could do it."

"And there is no danger at any other stage?"

"None; absolutely no physical danger whatever, I give you my word. You were always timid, Clarke, always, but you know my history. I have devoted myself to transcendental medicine for the last twenty years. I have heard myself called quack, and charlatan, and impostor, but all the while I knew I was on the right path. Five years ago I reached the goal, and since then every day has been a preparation for what we shall do to-night."

"I should like to believe it is all true." Clarke knit his brows and looked doubtfully at Dr. Raymond. "Are you perfectly sure, Raymond, that your theory is not a phantasmagoria, a splendid vision, certainly, but a mere vision after all?"

Dr. Raymond stopped in his walk and turned sharply. He was a middle-aged man, gaunt and thin, of a pale yellow complexion, but as he answered Clarke and faced him, there was a flush on his cheek.

"Look about you, Clarke, you see the mountain, and hill following after hill, as wave on wave, you see the woods and orchards, the field of ripe corn, and the meadows reaching to the reed-beds by the river. You see me standing here beside you, and hear my voice; but I tell you that all these things, yes, from that star that has just shone out in the sky to the solid ground beneath our feet, I say that all these are but dreams and shadows: the shadows that hide the real world from our eyes. There *is* a real world, but it is beyond this glamour and this vision, beyond these 'chases in Arras, dreams in a career,' beyond them all as beyond a veil. I do not know whether any human being has ever lifted that veil; but I do know, Clarke, that you and I shall see it lifted this very night from before another's eyes. You may think all this strange nonsense; it may be strange, but it is true, and the ancients knew what lifting the veil means. They called it seeing the God Pan."

Clarke shivered; the white mist gathering over the river was chilly.

"It is wonderful indeed," he said. "We are standing on the brink of a strange world, Raymond, if what you say is true. I suppose the knife is absolutely necessary!"

"Yes; a slight lesion in the gray matter, that is all; a trifling rearrangement of certain cells, a microscopical alteration that would escape the attention of ninety-nine brain specialists out of a hundred. I don't want to bother you with 'shop,' Clarke; I might give you a mass of technical detail which would sound very imposing, and would leave you as enlightened as you are now. But I suppose you have read, casually, in out-of-the-way corners of your paper, that immense strides have been made recently in the physiology of the brain. I saw a paragraph the other day about Digby's theory and Browne Faber's discoveries. Theories and discoveries! Where they are standing now, I stood fifteen years ago, and I need not tell you that I have not been standing still for the last fifteen years. It will be enough if I say that five years ago I made the discovery to which I alluded when I said that then I reached the goal. After years of labor, after years of toiling and groping in the dark, after days and nights of disappointment and sometimes of despair, in which I used now and then to tremble and grow cold with the thought that perhaps there were others seeking for what I sought, at last, after so long, a pang of sudden joy thrilled my soul, and I knew the long journey was at an end. By what seemed then and still seems a chance, the suggestion of a moment's idle thought followed up upon familiar lines and paths that I had tracked a hundred times already, the great truth burst upon me, and I saw, mapped out in lines of light, a whole world, a sphere unknown; continents and islands, and great oceans in which no ship has sailed (to my belief) since a Man first lifted up his eyes and beheld the sun, and the stars of heaven, and the quiet earth beneath. You will think all this high-flown language, Clarke, but it is hard to be literal. And yet, I do not know whether what I am hinting at cannot be set forth in plain and homely terms. For instance, this world of ours is pretty well girded now with the telegraph wires and cables; thought, with something less than the speed of thought, flashes from sunrise to sunset, from north to south, across the floods and the desert places. Suppose that an electrician of to-day were suddenly to perceive that he and his friends have merely been playing with pebbles and mistaking them for the foundations of the world; suppose that such a man saw uttermost space lie open before the current, and words of men flash forth to the sun and beyond the sun into the systems beyond, and the voices of articulate-speaking-men echo in the waste void that bounds our thought. As analogies go, that is a pretty good analogy of what I have done; you can understand now a little of what I felt as I stood here one evening; it was a summer evening, and the valley looked much as it does now; I stood here, and saw before me the unutterable, the unthinkable gulf that yawns profound between two worlds, the world of matter and the world of spirit; I saw the great empty deep stretch dim before me, and in that instant a bridge of light leapt from the earth to the unknown shore, and the abyss was spanned. You may look in Browne Faber's book, if you like, and you will find that to the present day men of science are unable to account for the presence, or to specify the functions of a certain group of nerve-cells in the brain. That group is, as it were, land to let, a mere waste place for fanciful theories. I am not in the position of Browne Faber and the specialists, I am perfectly instructed as to the possible functions of those nerve-centres in the scheme of things. With a touch I can bring them into play; with a touch, I say, I can set free the current; with a touch I can complete the communication between this world of sense and we shall be able to finish the sentence later on. Yes, the knife is necessary; but think what that knife will effect. It will level utterly the solid wall of sense, and, probably for the first time since man was made, a spirit will gaze on a spirit world. Clarke, Mary will see the god Pan!"

"But you remember what you wrote to me? I thought it would be requisite that she—"

He whispered the rest into the doctor's ear.

"Not at all, not at all. That is nonsense, I assure you. Indeed, it is better as it is, I am quite certain of that."

"Consider the matter well, Raymond. It's a great responsibility. Something might go wrong; you would be a miserable man for the rest of your days."

"No, I think not, even if the worst happened. As you know, I rescued Mary from the gutter, and from almost certain starvation, when she was a child; I think her life is mine, to use as I see fit. Come, it is getting late, we had better go in."

Dr. Raymond led the way into the house, through the hall, and down a long dark passage. He took a key from his pocket and opened a heavy door, and motioned Clarke into his laboratory. It had once been a billiard room, and was lighted by a glass dome in the centre of the ceiling, whence there still shone a sad gray light on the figure of the doctor as he lit a lamp with a heavy shade, and placed it on a table in the middle of the room.

Clarke looked about him. Scarcely a foot of wall remained bare; there were shelves all around laden with bottles and phials of all shapes and colors, and at one end stood a little Chippendale book-case. Raymond pointed to this.

"You see that parchment Oswald Crollius? He was one of the first to show me the way, though I don't think he ever found it himself. That is a strange saying of his: 'In every grain of wheat there lies hidden the soul of a star!'"

There was not much of furniture in the laboratory. The table in the centre, a stone slab with a drain in one corner, the two armchairs on which Raymond and Clarke were sitting; that was all, except an odd-looking chair at the furthest end of the room. Clarke looked at it and raised his eyebrows.

"Yes, that is the chair," said Raymond. "We may as well place it in position." He got up and wheeled the chair to the light, and began raising and lowering it, letting down the seat, setting the back at various angles, and adjusting the foot-rest. It looked comfortable enough, and Clarke passed his hand over the soft green velvet, as the doctor manipulated the levers.

"Now, Clarke, make yourself quite comfortable. I have a couple of hours' work before me; I was obliged to leave certain matters to the last."

Raymond went to the stone slab, and Clarke watched him drearily as he bent over a row of phials and lit the flame under the crucible. The doctor had a small hand-lamp, shaded as the larger one, on a ledge above his apparatus, and Clarke who sat in the shadows looked down the great dreary room, wondering at the bizarre effects of brilliant light and undefined darkness contrasting with one another. Soon he became conscious of an odd odor, at first the merest suggestion of odor, in the room; and as it grew more decided he felt surprised that he was not reminded of the chemist's shop or the surgery. Clarke found himself idly endeavoring to analyze the sensation, and, half conscious, he began to think of a day, fifteen years ago, that he had spent in roaming through the woods and meadows near his old home. It was a burning day at the beginning of August, the heat had dimmed the outlines of all things and all distances with a faint mist, and people who observed the thermometer spoke of an abnormal register, of a temperature that was almost tropical. Strangely that wonderful hot day of 185— rose up in Clarke's imagination; the sense of dazzling all-pervading sunlight seemed to blot out the shadows and the lights of the laboratory, and he felt again the heated air beating in gusts about his face, saw the shimmer rising from the turf, and heard the myriad murmur of the summer.

"I hope the smell doesn't annoy you, Clarke; there's nothing unwholesome about it. It may make you a bit sleepy, that's all."

Clarke heard the words quite distinctly, and knew that Raymond was speaking to him, but for the life of him he could not rouse himself from his lethargy. He could only think of the lonely walk he had taken fifteen years ago; it was his last look at the fields and woods he had known since he was a child, and now it all stood out in brilliant light, as a picture, before him. Above all there came to his nostrils the scent of summer, the smell of flowers mingled, and the odor of the woods, of cool shaded places, deep in the green depths, drawn forth by the sun's heat; and the scent of the good earth, lying as it were with arms stretched forth, and smiling lips, overpowered all. His fancies made him wander, as he had wandered long ago, from the fields into the wood, tracking a little path between the shining undergrowth of beech-trees; and the trickle of water dropping from the limestone rock sounded as a clear melody in the dream. Thoughts began to go astray and to mingle with other recollections; the beech-alley was transformed to a path beneath ilex-trees, and here and there a vine climbed from bough to bough, and sent up waving tendrils and drooped with purple grapes, and the sparse gray green leaves of a wild olive-tree stood out against the dark shadows of the ilex. Clarke, in the deep folds of dream, was conscious that the path from his father's house had led him into an undiscovered country, and he was wondering at the strangeness of it all, when suddenly, in place of the hum and murmur of the summer, an infinite silence seemed to fall on all things, and the wood was hushed, and for a moment of time he stood face to face there with a presence that was neither man nor beast, neither the living nor the dead, but all things mingled, the form of all things but devoid of all form, and in that moment, the sacrament of body and soul was dissolved, and a voice seemed to cry "let us go hence," and then the darkness of darkness beyond the stars, the darkness of everlasting.

When Clarke woke up with a start, he saw Raymond pouring a few drops of some oily fluid into a green phial, which he stoppered tightly.

"You have been dozing," he said, "the journey must have tired you out. It is done now. I am going to fetch Mary; I shall be back in ten minutes."

Clarke lay back in his chair and wondered. It seemed as if he had but passed from one dream into another. He half expected to see the walls of the laboratory melt and disappear, and to awake in London shuddering at his own sleeping fancies. But at last the door opened, and the doctor returned, and behind him came a girl of about seventeen, dressed all in white. She was so beautiful that Clarke did not wonder at what the doctor had written to him. She was blushing now over face and neck and arms, but Raymond seemed unmoved.

"Mary," he said, "the time has come. You are quite free. Are you willing to trust yourself to me entirely?"

"Yes, dear."

"You hear that, Clarke? You are my witness. Here is the chair, Mary. It is quite easy. Just sit in it and lean back! Are you ready?"

"Yes, dear, quite ready. Give me a kiss before you begin."

The doctor stooped and kissed her mouth, kindly enough. "Now shut your eyes," he said. The girl closed her eyelids, as if she were tired, and longed for sleep, and Raymond held the green phial to her nostrils. Her face grew white, whiter than her dress; she struggled faintly, and then with the feeling of submission strong within her, crossed her arms upon her breast as a little child about to say her prayers. The bright light of the lamp beat full upon her, and Clarke watched changes fleeting over that face as the changes of the hills when the summer clouds float across the sun. And then she lay all white and still, and the doctor turned up one of her eyelids. She was quite unconscious. Raymond pressed hard on one of the levers, and the chair instantly sank back. Clarke saw him cutting away a circle, like a tonsure, from her hair, and the lamp was moved nearer. Raymond took a small glittering instrument from a little case, and Clarke turned away shuddering. When he looked again the doctor was binding up the wound he had made.

"She will awake in five minutes." Raymond was still perfectly cool. "There is nothing further to be done; we can only wait."

The minutes passed slowly; they could hear a slow, heavy ticking. There was an old clock in the passage. Clarke felt sick and faint; his knees shook beneath him, he could hardly stand.

Suddenly, as they watched, they heard a long-drawn sigh, and suddenly did the color that had vanished return to the girl's cheeks, and suddenly her eyes opened. Clarke quailed before them. They shone with an awful light, looking far away, and a great wonder fell upon her face, and her hand stretched out as if to touch what was invisible; but in an instant the wonder faded, and gave place to the most awful terror. The muscles of her face were hideously convulsed, she shook from head to foot; the soul seemed struggling and shuddering within the house of flesh. It was a horrible sight, and Clarke rushed forward, as she fell shrieking to the floor.

Three days later Raymond took Clarke to Mary's bedside. She was lying wide awake, rolling her head from side to side, and grinning vacantly.

"Yes," said the doctor, still quite cool, "it is a great pity; she is a hopeless idiot. However it could not be helped; and after all, she has seen the Great God Pan."

MR. CLARKE'S MEMOIRS

MR. CLARKE, THE GENTLEMAN CHOSEN BY DR. RAYMOND TO WITNESS the strange experiment of the god Pan, was a person in whose character caution and curiosity were oddly mingled; in his sober moments he thought of the unusual and the eccentric with undisguised aversion, and yet, deep in his heart there was a wide-eyed inquisitiveness with respect to all the more recondite and esoteric elements in the nature of men. The latter tendency had prevailed when he accepted Raymond's invitation, for though his considered judgment had always repudiated the doctor's theories, as the wildest nonsense, yet he secretly hugged a belief in fantasy, and would have rejoiced to see that belief confirmed. The horrors that he witnessed in the dreary laboratory were to a certain extent salutary; he was conscious of being involved in an affair not altogether reputable, and for many years afterwards he clung bravely to the commonplace, and rejected all occasions of occult investigation. Indeed, on some homoeopathic principle, he for some time attended the séances of distinguished mediums, hoping that the clumsy tricks of these gentlemen would make him altogether disgusted with mysticism of every kind; but the remedy, though caustic, was not efficacious. Clarke knew that he still pined for the unseen, and little by little, the old passion began to reassert itself, as the face of Mary, shuddering and convulsed with an unknowable terror, faded slowly from his memory. Occupied all day in pursuits both serious and lucrative, the temptation to relax in the evening was too great, especially in the winter months when the fire cast a warm glow over his snug bachelor apartment, and a bottle of some choice claret stood ready by his elbow. His dinner digested, he would make a brief pretence of reading the evening paper, but the mere catalogue of news soon palled upon him, and Clarke would find himself casting glances of warm desire in the direction of an old Japanese bureau, which stood at a pleasant distance from the hearth. Like a boy before a jam-closet, for a few minutes he would hover indecisive, but lust always prevailed, and Clarke ended by drawing up his chair, lighting a candle, and sitting down before the bureau. Its pigeon-holes and drawers teemed with documents on the most morbid subjects, and in the well reposed a large manuscript volume, in which he had painfully entered the gems of his collection. Clarke had a fine contempt for published literature; the most ghostly story ceased to interest him if it happened to be printed; his sole pleasure was in the reading, compiling, arranging and re-arranging what he called his "Memoirs to prove the Existence of the Devil," and engaged in this pursuit the evening seemed to fly and the night appeared too short.

On one particular evening, an ugly December night, black with fog, and raw with frost, Clarke hurried over his dinner, and scarcely deigned to observe his customary ritual of taking up the paper, and laying it down again. He paced two or three times up and down the room, and opened the bureau, stood still a moment, and sat down. He leant back, absorbed in one of those dreams to which he was subject, and at length drew out his book, and opened it at the last entry. There were three or four pages densely covered with Clarke's round, set penmanship, and at the beginning he had written in a somewhat larger hand:

> Singular Narrative told me by my Friend, Dr. Phillips. He assures me that all the Facts related therein are strictly and wholly True, but refuses to give either the Surnames of the Persons Concerned, or the Place where these Extraordinary Events occurred.

Mr. Clarke began to read over the account for the tenth time, glancing now and then at the pencil notes he had made when it was told him by his friend. It was one of his humors to pride himself on a certain literary ability; he thought well of his style, and took pains in arranging the circumstances in dramatic order. He read the following story:

The persons concerned in this statement are Helen V., who, if she is still alive, must now be a woman of twenty-three, Rachel M., since deceased, who was a year younger than the above, and Trevor W., an imbecile, aged eighteen. These persons were, at the period of the story, inhabitants of a village on the borders of Wales, a place of some importance in the time of the Roman occupation, but now a scattered hamlet, of not more than five hundred souls. It is situated on rising ground, about six miles from the sea, and is sheltered by a large and picturesque forest.

Some eleven years ago, Helen V. came to the village under rather peculiar circumstances. It is understood that she, being an orphan, was adopted in her infancy by a distant relative, who brought her up in his own house till she was twelve years old. Thinking, however, that it would be better for the child to have playmates of her own age, he advertised in several local papers for a good home in a comfortable farm-house for a girl of twelve, and this advertisement was answered by Mr. R., a well-to-do farmer in the above-mentioned village. His references proving satisfactory, the gentleman sent his adopted daughter to Mr. R., with a letter, in which he stipulated that the girl should have a room to herself, and stated that her guardians need be at no trouble in the matter of education, as she was already sufficiently educated for the position in life which she would occupy. In fact, Mr. R. was given to understand that the girl was to be allowed to find her own occupations, and to spend her time almost as she liked. Mr. R. duly met her at the nearest station, a town some seven miles away from his house, and seems to have remarked nothing extraordinary about the child, except that she was reticent as to her former life and her adopted father. She was, however, of a very different type from the inhabitants of the village; her skin was a pale, clear olive, and her features were strongly marked, and of a somewhat foreign character. She appears to have settled down easily enough into farm-house life, and became a favorite with the children, who, sometimes, went with her on her rambles in the forest, for this was her amusement. Mr. R. states that he has known her go out by herself directly after their early breakfast, and not return till after dusk, and that, feeling uneasy at a young girl being out alone for so many hours, he communicated with her adopted father, who replied in a brief note that Helen must do as she chose. In the winter, when the forest paths are impassable, she spent most of her time in her bedroom, where she slept alone, according to the instructions of her relative. It was on one of these expeditions to the forest that the first of the singular incidents with which this girl is connected occurred, the date being about a year after her arrival at the village. The preceding winter had been remarkably severe, the snow drifting to a great depth, and the frost continuing for an unexampled period; and the summer following was as noteworthy for its extreme heat. On one of the very hottest days in this summer, Helen V. left the farmhouse for one of her long rambles in the forest, taking with her, as usual, some bread and meat for lunch. She was seen by some men in the fields making for the old Roman Road, a green causeway which traverses the highest part of the wood, and they were astonished to observe that the girl had taken off her hat, though the heat of the sun was already almost tropical. As it happened, a laborer, Joseph W. by name, was working in the forest near the Roman Road, and at twelve o'clock his little son, Trevor, brought the man his dinner of bread and cheese. After the meal the boy, who was about seven years old at the time, left his father at work, and, as he says, went to look for flowers in the wood, and the man, who could hear him shouting with delight over his discoveries, felt no uneasiness. Suddenly however he was horrified at hearing the most dreadful screams, evidently the result of great terror, proceeding from the direction in which his son had gone, and he hastily threw down his tools and ran to see what had happened. Tracing his path by the sound, he met the little boy, who was running headlong, and was evidently terribly frightened; and on questioning him, the man at last elicited that after picking a posy of flowers he felt tired, and lay down on the grass and fell asleep. He was suddenly awakened, as he stated, by a peculiar noise, a sort of singing he called it, and on peeping through the branches he saw Helen V. playing on the grass with a "strange naked man," whom he seemed unable to describe further. He said he felt dreadfully frightened, and ran away, crying for his father. Joseph W. proceeded in the direction indicated by his son, and found Helen V. sitting on the grass, in the middle of a glade or open space left by charcoal-burners. He angrily charged her with frightening his little boy; but she entirely denied the accusation, and laughed at the child's story of a "strange man," to which he himself did not attach much credence. Joseph W. came to the conclusion that the boy had woke up with a sudden fright, as children sometimes do; but Trevor persisted in his story, and continued in such evident distress that at last his father took him home, hoping that his mother would be able to soothe him. For many weeks, however, the boy gave his parents much anxiety; he became nervous and strange in his manner, refusing to leave the cottage by himself, and constantly alarming the household by waking in the night with cries of "The man in the wood! Father! father!" In course of time, however, the impression seemed to have worn off, and about three months later he accompanied his father to the house of a gentleman in the neighborhood, for whom Joseph W. occasionally did work. The man was shown into the study, and the little boy was left sitting in the hall; and a few minutes later, while the gentleman was giving W. his instructions, they were both horrified by a piercing shriek and the sound of a fall, and, rushing out, they found the child lying senseless on the floor, his face contorted with terror. The doctor was immediately summoned; and, after some examination, he pronounced the child to be suffering from a kind of fit, apparently produced by a sudden shock. The boy was taken to one of the bedrooms, and after some time recovered consciousness, but only to pass into a condition described by the medical man as one of violent hysteria. The doctor exhibited a strong sedative, and in the course of two hours pronounced him fit to walk home; but in passing through the hall the paroxysms of fright returned, and with additional violence. The father perceived that the child was pointing at some object, and heard the old cry, "the man in the wood," and, looking in the direction indicated, saw a stone head, of grotesque appearance, which had been built into the wall above one of the doors. It seems that the owner of the house had recently made alterations in his premises, and on digging the foundations for some offices, the men had found a curious head, evidently of the Roman period, which had been placed in the hall in the manner described. The head is pronounced by the most experienced archaeologists of the district to be that of a faun or satyr.*

From whatever cause arising, this second shock seemed too severe for the boy Trevor, and at the present date he suffers from a weakness of intellect, which gives but little promise of amending. The matter caused a good deal of sensation at the time, and the girl Helen was closely questioned by Mr. R., but to no purpose, she steadfastly denying that she had frightened or in any way molested Trevor.

The second event with which this girl's name is connected took place about six years ago, and is of still more extraordinary character.

At the beginning of the summer of 188— Helen contracted a friendship of a peculiarly intimate character with Rachel M., the daughter of a prosperous farmer in the neighbourhood. This girl, who was a year younger than Helen, was considered by most people to be the prettier of the two, though Helen's features had to a great extent softened as she became older. The two girls, who were together on every available opportunity, presented a singular contrast; the one with her clear olive skin and almost Italian appearance, and the other of the proverbial red and white of our rural districts. It must be stated that the payments made to Mr. R. for the maintenance of Helen were known in the village for their excessive liberality, and the impression was general that she would one day inherit a large sum of money from her relative. The parents of Rachel were, therefore, not averse to their daughter's friendship with the girl, and even encouraged the intimacy, though they now bitterly regret having done so. Helen still retained her extraordinary fondness for the forest, and on several occasions Rachel accompanied her; the two friends setting out early in the morning, and remaining in the wood till dusk. Once or twice after these excursions Mrs. M. thought her daughter's manner rather peculiar; she seemed languid and dreamy, and as it has been expressed, "different from herself," but these peculiarities

* Dr. Phillips tells me that he has seen the head in question, and assures me that he has never received such a vivid presentment of intense evil.

seem to have been thought too trifling for remark. One evening, however, after Rachel had come home, her mother heard a noise which sounded like suppressed weeping in the girl's room; and on going in, found her lying, half-undressed, upon the bed, evidently in the greatest distress. As soon as she saw her mother, she exclaimed, "Ah, mother, mother, why did you let me go to the forest with Helen?" Mrs. M. was astonished at so strange a question, and proceeded to make inquiries. Rachel told her a wild story. She said—

Clarke closed the book with a snap, and turned his chair towards the fire. When his friend sat one evening in that very chair, and told his story, Clarke had interrupted him at a point a little subsequent to this, had cut short his words in a paroxysm of horror. "My God!" he had exclaimed, "think, think, what you are saying. It is too incredible, too monstrous; such things can never be in this quiet world, where men and women live and die and struggle and conquer, or maybe fail, and fall down under sorrow, and grieve, and suffer strange fortunes for many a year; but not this, Phillips, not such things as this. There must be some explanation, some way out of the terror. Why, man, if such a case were possible, our earth would be a nightmare."

But Phillips had told his story to the end, concluding:

"Her flight remains a mystery to this day; she vanished in broad sunlight; they saw her walking in a meadow, and a few moments later, she was not there."

Clarke tried to conceive the thing again as he sat by the fire, and again his mind shuddered and shrank back, appalled before the sight of such awful, unspeakable elements enthroned, as it were, and triumphant in human flesh. Before him stretched the long dim vista of the green causeway in the forest, as his friend had described it; he saw the swaying leaves and the quivering shadows on the grass, he saw the sunlight and the flowers, and far away, far in the long distance, the two figures moved towards him. One was Rachel; but the other?

Clarke had tried his best to disbelieve it all, but at the end of the account, as he had written it in his book, he had placed the inscription:

ET DIABOLUS INCARNATUS EST. ET HOMO FACTUS EST.

THE CITY OF RESURRECTIONS

"HERBERT! GOOD GOD! IS IT POSSIBLE?"

"Yes, my name's Herbert. I think I know your face too, but I don't remember your name. My memory is very queer."

"Don't you recollect Villiers of Wadham?"

"So it is, so it is. I beg your pardon, Villiers, I didn't think I was begging of an old college friend. Good-night."

"My dear fellow, this haste is unnecessary. My rooms are close by, but we won't go there just yet. Suppose we walk up Shaftesbury Avenue a little way? But how in Heaven's name have you come to this pass, Herbert?"

"It's a long story, Villiers, and a strange one too; but you can hear it if you like."

"Come on, then. Take my arm, you don't seem very strong."

The ill-assorted pair moved slowly up Rupert Street; the one in dirty, evil looking rags, and the other attired in the regulation uniform of a man about town, trim, glossy, and eminently well-to-do. Villiers had emerged from his restaurant after an excellent dinner of many courses, assisted by an ingratiating little flask of Chianti, and in that frame of mind which was with him almost chronic, had delayed a moment by the door, peering round in the dimly lighted street in search of those mysterious incidents and persons with which the streets of London teem in every quarter and at every hour. Villiers prided himself as a practiced explorer of such obscure mazes and byways of London life, and in this unprofitable pursuit he displayed an assiduity which was worthy of more serious employment. Thus he stood beside the lamp post surveying the passers-by with undisguised curiosity, and, with that gravity only known to the systematic diner, had just enunciated in his mind the formula: "London had been called the city of encounters; it is more than that, it is the city of Resurrections," when these reflections were suddenly interrupted by a piteous whine at his elbow, and a deplorable appeal for alms. He looked round in some irritation, and with a sudden shock found himself confronted with the embodied proof of his somewhat stilted fancies. There, close beside him, his face altered and disfigured by poverty and disgrace, his body barely covered by greasy ill-fitting rags, stood his old friend Charles Herbert, who had matriculated on the same day as himself, and with whom he had been merry and wise for twelve revolving terms. Different occupations and varying interests had interrupted the friendship, and it was six years since Villiers had seen Herbert; and now he looked upon this wreck of a man with grief and dismay, mingled with a certain inquisitiveness as to what dreary chain of circumstance had dragged him down to such a doleful pass.

Villiers felt together with compassion all the relish of the amateur in mysteries, and congratulated himself on his leisurely speculations outside the restaurant.

They walked on in silence for some time, and more than one passer-by stared in astonishment at the unaccustomed spectacle of a well-dressed man with an unmistakable beggar hanging on to his arm, and, observing this, Villiers led the way to an obscure street in Soho. Here he repeated his question.

"How on earth has it happened, Herbert? I always understood you would succeed to an excellent position in Dorsetshire. Did your father disinherit you? Surely not!"

"No, Villiers; I came into all the property at my poor father's death; he died a year after I left Oxford. He was a very good father to me, and I mourned his death sincerely enough. But you know what young men are; a few months later I came up to town and went a good deal into society. Of course I had excellent introductions, and I managed to enjoy myself very much in a harmless sort of way. I played a little, certainly, but never for heavy stakes, and the few bets I made on races brought me in money—only a few pounds, you know, but enough to pay for cigars and such petty pleasures. It was in my second season that the tide turned. Of course you have heard of my marriage?"

"No, I never heard anything about it."

"Yes, I married, Villiers. I met a girl, a girl of the most wonderful and most strange beauty, at the house of some people whom I knew. I cannot tell you her age; I never knew it, but, so far as I can guess, I should think she must have been about nineteen when I made her acquaintance. My friends had come to know her at Florence; she told them she was an orphan, the child of an English father, and an Italian mother, and she charmed them as she charmed me. The first time I saw her was at an evening party; I was standing by the door talking to a friend, when suddenly, above the hum and babble of conversation, a voice which seemed to thrill to my heart. She was singing an Italian song. I was introduced to her that evening, and in three months I married Helen. Villiers, that woman, if I can call her woman, corrupted my soul. The night of the wedding I found myself sitting in her bedroom in the hotel, listening to her talk. She was sitting up in bed, and I listened to her as she spoke in her beautiful voice, spoke of things which even now I would not dare whisper in blackest night, though I stood in the midst of a wilderness. You, Villiers, you may think you know life, and London, and what goes on, day and night, in this dreadful city; for all I can say you may have heard the talk of the vilest, but I tell you you can have no conception of what I know; no, not in your most fantastic, hideous dreams can you have imaged forth the faintest shadow of what I have heard and seen. Yes, seen. I have seen the incredible, such horrors that even I myself sometimes stop in the middle of the street, and ask whether it is possible for a man to behold such things and live. In a year, Villiers, I was a ruined man, in body and soul—in body and soul."

"But your property, Herbert? You had land in Dorset."

"I sold it all; the fields and woods, the dear old house—everything."

"And the money?"

"She took it all from me."

"And then left you?"

"Yes, she disappeared one night. I don't know where she went, but I am sure if I saw her again it would kill me. The rest of my story is of no interest; sordid misery, that is all. You may think, Villiers, that I have exaggerated and talked for effect, but I have not told you half. I could tell you certain things which would convince you, but you would never know a happy day again; you would pass the rest of your life, as I pass mine, a haunted man, a man who has seen hell."

Villiers took the unfortunate man to his rooms, and gave him a meal. Herbert could eat little, and scarcely touched the glass of wine set before him. He sat moody and silent by the fire, and seemed relieved when Villiers sent him away with a small present of money.

"By the way, Herbert," said Villiers, as they parted at the door, "what was your wife's name? You said Helen, I think? Helen what?"

"The name she passed under when I met her was Helen Vaughan, but what her real name was I can't say. I don't think she had a name. No, no, not in that sense. Only human beings have names, Villiers; I can't say any more. Good-bye; yes, I will not fail to call if I see any way in which you can help me. Good-night."

The man went out into the bitter night, and Villiers returned to his fireside. There was something about Herbert which shocked him inexpressibly; not his poor rags or the marks which poverty had set upon his face, but rather an indefinite terror which hung about him like a mist. He had acknowledged that he himself was not devoid of blame; the woman, he had avowed, had corrupted him body and soul, and Villiers felt that this man, once his friend, had been an actor in scenes evil beyond the power of words. His story needed no confirmation; he himself was the embodied proof of it.

Villiers mused curiously over the story he had heard, and wondered whether he had heard both the first and the last of it. "No," he thought, "certainly not the last, probably only the beginning. A case like this is like a nest of Chinese boxes;

you open one after another, and find a quainter workmanship in every box. Most likely poor Herbert is merely one of the outside boxes; there are stranger ones to follow."

Villiers could not take his mind away from Herbert and his story, which seemed to grow wilder as the night wore on. The fire began to burn low, and the chilly air of the morning crept into the room; Villiers got up with a glance over his shoulder, and shivering slightly went to bed.

A few days later he saw at his club a gentleman of his acquaintance, named Austin, who was famous for his intimate knowledge of London life, both in its tenebrous and luminous phases. Villiers, still full of his encounter in Soho and its consequences, thought Austin might possibly be able to shed some light on Herbert's history, and so after some casual talk he suddenly put the question:

"Do you happen to know anything of a man named Herbert—Charles Herbert?"

Austin turned round sharply and stared at Villiers with some astonishment.

"Charles Herbert? Weren't you in town three years ago? No; then you have not heard of the Paul Street case? It caused a good deal of sensation at the time."

"What was the case?"

"Well, a gentleman, a man of very good position, was found dead, stark dead, in the area of a certain house in Paul Street, off Tottenham Court Road. Of course the police did not make the discovery; if you happen to be sitting up all night and have a light in your window, the constable will ring the bell, but if you happen to be lying dead in somebody's area you will be left alone. In this instance as in many others the alarm was raised by some kind of vagabond; I don't mean a common tramp, or a public-house loafer, but a gentleman, whose business or pleasure or both made him a spectator of the London streets at five o'clock in the morning. This individual was, as he said, 'going home,' it did not appear whence or whither, and had occasion to pass through Paul Street between four and five A.M. Something or other caught his eye at Number 20; he said, absurdly enough, that the house had the most unpleasant physiognomy he had ever observed; but, at any rate, he glanced down the area, and was a good deal astonished to see a man lying on the stones, his limbs all huddled together, and his face turned up. Our gentleman thought this face looked peculiarly ghastly, and so set off at a run in search of the nearest policeman. The constable was at first inclined to treat the matter lightly, suspecting a mere drunken freak; however, he came, and after looking at the man's face, changed his tone quickly enough. The early bird who had picked up this fine worm, was sent off for a doctor, and the policeman rang and knocked at the door till a slatternly servant girl came down looking more than half asleep. The constable pointed out the contents of the area to the maid, who screamed loudly enough to wake up the street, but she knew nothing of the man; had never seen him at the house, and so forth. Meanwhile the original discoverer had come back with a medical man, and the next thing was to get into the area. The gate was open, so the whole quartet stumped down the steps. The doctor hardly needed a moment's examination; he said the poor fellow had been dead for several hours, and he was moved away to the police-station for the time being. It was then the case began to get interesting. The dead man had not been robbed, and in one of his pockets were papers identifying him as—well, as a man of good family and means, a favorite in society, and nobody's enemy, so far as could be known. I don't give his name, Villiers, because it has nothing to do with the story, and because it's no good raking up these affairs about the dead, when there are relations living. The next curious point was that the medical men couldn't agree as to how he met his death. There were some slight bruises on his shoulders, but they were so slight that it looked as if he had been pushed roughly out of the kitchen door, and not thrown over the railings from the street, or even dragged down the steps. But there were positively no other marks of violence about him, certainly none that would account for his death; and when they came to the autopsy there wasn't a trace of poison of any kind. Of course the police wanted to know all about the people at Number 20; and here again, so I have heard from private sources, one or two other very curious points came out. It appears that the occupants of the house were a Mr. and Mrs. Charles Herbert; he was said to be a landed proprietor, though it struck most people that Paul Street was not exactly the place to look for county gentry. As for Mrs. Herbert nobody seemed to know who or what she was, and, between ourselves, I fancy the divers after her history found themselves in rather strange waters. Of course they both denied knowing anything about the deceased, and in default of any evidence against them they were discharged. But some very odd things came out about them. Though it was between five and six in the morning when the dead man was removed, a large crowd had collected, and several of the neighbors ran to see what was going on. They were pretty free with their comments, by all accounts, and from these it appeared that Number 20 was in very bad odor in Paul Street. The detectives tried to trace down these rumors to some solid foundation of fact, but could not get hold of anything. People shook their heads and raised their eyebrows and thought the Herberts rather 'queer,' 'would rather not be seen going into their house,' and so on, but there was nothing tangible. The authorities were morally certain that the man met his death in some way or another in the house and was thrown out by the kitchen door, but they couldn't prove it, and the absence of any indications of violence or poisoning left them helpless. An odd case, wasn't it? But curiously enough, there's something more that I haven't told you. I happened to know one of the doctors who was consulted as to the cause of death, and some time after the inquest, I met him, and asked him about it. 'Do you really mean to tell me,' I said, 'that you were baffled by the case, that you actually don't know what the man died of?' 'Pardon me,' he replied, 'I know perfectly well what caused death. Blank died of fright, of sheer, awful terror; I never saw features so hideously contorted in the entire course of my practice, and I have seen the faces of a whole host of dead.' The doctor was usually a cool customer enough, and a certain vehemence in his manner struck me, but I couldn't get anything more out of him. I suppose the Treasury didn't see their way to prosecuting the Herberts for frightening a man to death; at any rate, nothing was done, and the case dropped out of men's minds. Do you happen to know anything of Herbert?"

"Well," replied Villiers, "he was an old college friend of mine."

"You don't say so? Have you ever seen his wife?"

"No, I haven't. I have lost sight of Herbert for many years."

"It's queer, isn't it, parting with a man at the college gate or at Paddington, seeing nothing of him for years, and then finding him pop up his head in such an odd place. But I should like to have seen Mrs. Herbert; people said extraordinary things about her."

"What sort of things?"

"Well, I hardly know how to tell you. Every one who saw her at the police court said she was at once the most beautiful woman and the most repulsive they had ever set eyes on. I have spoken to a man who saw her, and I assure you he positively shuddered as he tried to describe the woman, but he couldn't tell why. She seems to have been a sort of enigma; and I expect if that one dead man could have told tales, he would have told some uncommonly queer ones. And there you are again in another puzzle; what could a respectable country gentleman like Mr. Blank (we'll call him that if you don't mind) want in such a very queer house as Number 20? It's altogether a very odd case, isn't it?"

"It is indeed, Austin, an extraordinary case. I didn't think, when I asked you about my old friend, I should strike on such strange metal. Well, I must be off; good-day."

Villiers went away, thinking of his own conceit of the Chinese boxes; here was quaint workmanship indeed.

THE DISCOVERY IN PAUL STREET

A FEW MONTHS AFTER VILLIERS'S MEETING WITH HERBERT, MR. CLARKE was sitting, as usual, by his after-dinner hearth, resolutely guarding his fancies from wandering in the direction of the bureau. For more than a week he had succeeded in keeping away from the "Memoirs," and he cherished hopes of a complete self-reformation; but in spite of his endeavors he could not hush the wonder and the strange curiosity that that last case he had written down had excited within him. He had put the case, or rather the outline of it, conjecturally to a scientific friend, who shook his head, and thought Clarke getting queer, and on this particular evening Clarke was making an effort to rationalize the story, when a sudden knock at his door roused him from his meditations.

"Mr. Villiers to see you, sir."

"Dear me, Villiers, it is very kind of you to look me up; I have not seen you for many months; I should think nearly a year. Come in, come in. And how are you, Villiers? Want any advice about investments?"

"No, thanks, I fancy everything I have in that way is pretty safe. No, Clarke, I have really come to consult you about a rather curious matter that has been brought under my notice of late. I am afraid you will think it all rather absurd when I tell my tale, I sometimes think so myself, and that's just why I made up my mind to come to you, as I know you're a practical man."

Mr. Villiers was ignorant of the "Memoirs to prove the Existence of the Devil."

"Well, Villiers, I shall be happy to give you my advice to the best of my ability. What is the nature of the case?"

"It's an extraordinary thing altogether. You know my ways; I always keep my eyes open in the streets, and in my time I have chanced upon some queer customers, and queer cases, too, but this, I think, beats all I was coming out of a restaurant one nasty winter night, about three months ago; I had had a capital dinner and a good bottle of Chianti, and I stood for a moment on the pavement, thinking what a mystery there is about London streets and the companies that pass along them. A bottle of red wine encourages these fancies, Clarke, and I daresay I should have thought a page of small type, but I was cut short by a beggar who had come behind me, and was making the usual appeals. Of course I looked round, and this beggar turned out to be what was left of an old friend of mine, a man named Herbert. I asked him how he had come to such a wretched pass, and he told me. We walked up and down one of those long, dark Soho streets, and there I listened to his story. He said he had married a beautiful girl, some years younger than himself, and, as he put it, she had corrupted him body and soul. He wouldn't go into details; he said he dared not, that what he had seen and heard haunted him by night and day, and when I looked in his face I knew he was speaking the truth. There was something about the man that made me shiver, I don't know why, but it was there. I gave him a little money and sent him away, and I assure you that when he was gone I gasped for breath. His presence seemed to chill one's blood."

"Isn't all this just a little fanciful, Villiers? I suppose the poor fellow had made an imprudent marriage, and, in plain English, gone to the bad."

"Well, listen to this." Villiers told Clarke the story he had heard from Austin.

"You see," he concluded, "there can be but little doubt that this Mr. Blank, whoever he was, died of sheer terror he saw something so awful, so terrible, that it cut short his life. And what he saw, he most certainly saw in that house, which, somehow or other, had got a bad name in the neighborhood. I had the curiosity to go and look at the place for myself. It's a saddening kind of street; the houses are old enough to be mean and dreary, but not old enough to be quaint. As far as I could see most of them are let in lodgings, furnished and unfurnished, and almost every door has three bells to it. Here and there the ground floors have been made into shops of the commonest kind; it's a dismal street in every way. I found Number 20 was to let, and I went to the agent's and got the key. Of course I should have heard nothing of the Herberts in that quarter, but I asked the man, fair and square, how long they have left the house, and whether there had been other tenants in the meanwhile. He looked at me queerly for a minute, and told me the Herberts had left immediately after the unpleasantness, as he called it, and since then the house had been empty."

Mr. Villiers paused for a moment.

"I have always been rather fond of going over empty houses; there's a sort of fascination about the desolate empty rooms, with the nails sticking in the walls, and the dust thick upon the window-sills. But I didn't enjoy going over Number 20 Paul Street. I had hardly put my foot inside the passage before I noticed a queer, heavy feeling about the air of the house. Of course all empty houses are stuffy, and so forth, but this was something quite different; I can't describe it to you, but it seemed to stop the breath. I went into the front room, and the back room, and the kitchens downstairs; they were all dirty and dusty enough, as you would expect, but there was something strange about them all. I couldn't define it to you, I only know I felt queer. It was one of the rooms on the first floor, though, that was the worst. It was a largish room, and once on a time the paper must have been cheerful enough, but when I saw it, paint, paper, and every tiling were most doleful. But the room was full of horror; I felt my teeth grinding as I put my hand on the door, and when I went in, I thought I should have fallen fainting to the floor. However I pulled myself together, and stood against the end wall, wondering what on earth there could be about the room to make my limbs tremble, and my heart beat as if I were at the hour of death. In one corner there was a pile of newspapers littered about on the floor, and I began looking at them; they were papers of three or four years ago, some of them half torn, and some crumpled as if they had been used for packing. I turned the whole pile over, and amongst them I found a curious drawing; I will show it you presently. But I couldn't stay in the room; I felt it was overpowering me. I was thankful to come out, safe and sound, into the open air. People stared at me as I walked along the street, and one man said I was drunk. I was staggering about from one side of the pavement to the other, and it was as much as I could do to take the key back to the agent and get home. I was in bed for a week, suffering from what my doctor called nervous shock and exhaustion. One of those days I was reading the evening paper, and happened to notice a paragraph headed, 'Starved to Death.' It was the usual style of thing, a model lodging-house in Marylebone, a door locked for several days, and a dead man in his chair when they broke in. 'The deceased,' said the paragraph, 'was known as Charles Herbert, and is believed to have been once a prosperous country gentleman. His name was familiar to the public three years ago in connection with the mysterious death in Paul Street, Tottenham Court Road, the deceased being the tenant of the house Number 20, in the area of which a gentleman of good position was found dead under circumstances not devoid of suspicion.' A tragic ending, wasn't it? But, after all, if what he told me were true, which I am sure it was, the man's life was all a tragedy, and a tragedy of a stranger sort than they put on the boards."

"And that is the story, is it?" said Clarke, musingly.

"Yes, that is the story."

"Well, really, Villiers, I scarcely know what to say about it. There are no doubt circumstances in the case which seem peculiar, the finding of the dead man in the area of the Herberts' house, for instance, and the extraordinary opinion of the physician as to the cause of death, but, after all, it is conceivable that the facts may be explained in a straightforward manner. As to your own sensations when you went to see the house, I would suggest that they were due to a vivid imagination; you must have been brooding, in a semi-conscious way, over what you had heard. I don't exactly see what more can be said or done in the matter; you evidently think there is a mystery of some kind, but Herbert is dead; where then do you propose to look?"

"I propose to look for the woman; the woman whom he married. *She* is the mystery."

The two men sat silent by the fireside; Clarke secretly congratulating himself on having successfully kept up the character of advocate of the commonplace, and Villiers wrapt in his gloomy fancies.

"I think I will have a cigarette," he said at last, and put his hand in his pocket to feel for the cigarette-case.

"Ah," he said, starting slightly, "I forgot I had something to show you. You remember my saying that I had found a rather curious sketch amongst the pile of old newspapers at the house in Paul Street; here it is."

Villiers drew out a small thin parcel from his pocket. It was covered with brown paper and secured with string, and the knots were troublesome. In spite of himself Clarke felt inquisitive; he bent forward on his chair as Villiers painfully undid the string, and unfolded the outer covering. Inside was a second wrapping of tissue, and Villiers took it off, and handed the small piece of paper to Clarke without a word.

There was dead silence in the room for five minutes or more; the two men sat so still, that they could hear the ticking of the tall old-fashioned clock that stood outside, in the hall, and in the mind of one of them, the slow monotony of sound woke up a far, far memory. He was looking intently at the small pen-and-ink sketch of a woman's head; it had evidently been drawn with great care, and by a true artist, for the woman's soul looked out of the eyes, and the lips were parted with a strange smile. Clarke gazed still at the face; it brought to his memory one summer evening long ago; he saw again the long lovely valley, the river winding between the hills, the meadows and the cornfields, the dull red sun, and the cold white mist rising from the water. He heard a voice speaking to him across the waves of many years, and saying, "Clarke, Mary will see the God Pan!" and then he was standing in the grim room beside the doctor, listening to the heavy ticking of the clock, waiting and watching, watching the figure lying on the green chair beneath the lamp light. Mary rose up, and he looked into her eyes, and his heart grew cold within him.

"Who is this woman?" he said at last. His voice was dry and hoarse.

"That is the woman whom Herbert married."

Clarke looked again at the sketch; it was not Mary after all. There certainly was Mary's face, but there was something else, something he had not seen on Mary's features when the white-clad girl entered the laboratory with the doctor, nor at her terrible awakening, nor when she lay, grinning, on the bed. Whatever it was, the glance that came from those eyes, the smile on the full lips, or the expression of the whole face, Clarke shuddered before it in his inmost soul, and thought, unconsciously, of Dr. Phillips's words, "the most vivid presentment of evil, I have ever seen." He turned the paper over, mechanically, in his hand, and glanced at the back.

"Good God! Clarke, what is the matter? You are as white as death."

Villiers had started wildly from his chair, as Clarke fell back with a groan, and let the paper drop from his hands.

"I don't feel very well, Villiers, I am subject to these attacks. Pour me out a little wine; thanks, that will do. I shall be better in a few minutes."

Villiers picked up the fallen sketch, and turned it over as Clarke had done.

"You saw that?" he said. "That's how I identified it as being a portrait of Herbert's wife, or I should say his widow. How do you feel now?"

"Better, thanks, it was only a passing faintness. I don't think I quite catch your meaning. What did you say enabled you to identify the picture?"

"This word—Helen—written on the back. Didn't I tell you her name was Helen? Yes; Helen Vaughan."

Clarke groaned; there could be no shadow of doubt.

"Now, don't you agree with me," said Villiers, "that in the story I have told you to-night, and in the part this woman plays in it, there are some very strange points?"

"Yes, Villiers," Clarke muttered, "it is a strange story indeed, a strange story indeed. You must give me time to think it over; I may be able to help you, or I may not. Must you be going now? Well, good-night, Villiers, good-night. Come and see me in the course of a week."

THE LETTER OF ADVICE

"DO YOU KNOW, AUSTIN," SAID VILLIERS, AS THE TWO FRIENDS WERE PACING sedately along Piccadilly one pleasant morning in May, "do you know I am convinced that what you told me about Paul Street and the Herberts is a mere episode in an extraordinary history. I may as well confess to you that when I asked you about Herbert a few months ago I had just seen him."

"You had seen him? Where?"

"He begged of me in the street one night. He was in the most pitiable plight, but I recognized the man, and I got him to tell me his history, or at least the outline of it. In brief, it amounted to this, he had been ruined by his wife."

"In what manner?"

"He would not tell me; he would only say that she had destroyed him body and soul. The man is dead now."

"And what has become of his wife?"

"Ah, that's what I should like to know, and I mean to find her sooner or later. I know a man named Clarke, a dry fellow, in fact a man of business, but shrewd enough. You understand my meaning; not shrewd in the mere business sense of the word, but a man who really knows something about men and life. Well I laid the case before him, and he was evidently impressed. He said it needed consideration, and asked me to come again in the course of a week. A few days later I received this extraordinary letter."

Austin took the envelope, drew out the letter, and read it curiously. It ran as follows:—

> MY DEAR VILLIERS,—I have thought over the matter on which you consulted me the other night, and my advice to you is this. Throw the portrait into the fire, blot out the story from your mind. Never give it another thought, Villiers, or you will be sorry. You will think, no doubt, that I am in possession of some secret information, and to a certain extent that is the case. But I only know a little; I am like a traveller who has peered over an abyss, and has drawn back in terror. What I know is strange enough and horrible enough, but beyond my knowledge there are depths and horrors more frightful still, more incredible than any tale told of winter nights about the fire. I have resolved, and nothing shall shake that resolve, to explore no whit farther, and if you value your happiness you will make the same determination. Come and see me by all means; but we will talk on more cheerful topics than this.

Austin folded the letter methodically, and returned it to Villiers.

"It is certainly an extraordinary letter," he said, "what does he mean by the portrait?"

"Ah, I forgot to tell you I have been to Paul Street and have made a discovery."

Villiers told his story, as he had told it to Clarke, and Austin listened in silence. He seemed puzzled.

"How very curious that you should experience such an unpleasant sensation in that room," he said at length. "I hardly gather that it was a mere matter of the imagination; a feeling of repulsion, in short."

"No, it was more physical than mental. It was as if I were inhaling at every breath some deadly fume, which seemed to penetrate to every nerve and bone and sinew of my body. I felt racked from head to foot, my eyes began to grow dim; it was like the entrance of death."

"Yes, yes, very strange, certainly. You see, your friend confesses that there is some very black story connected with this woman. Did you notice any particular emotion in him when you were telling your tale?"

"Yes, I did. He became very faint, but he assured me that it was a mere passing attack to which he was subject."

"Did you believe him?"

"I did at the time, but I don't now. He heard what I had to say with a good deal of indifference till I showed him the portrait. It was then he was seized with the attack of which I spoke. He looked ghastly, I assure you."

"Then he must have seen the woman before. But there might be another explanation; it might have been the name, and not the face, which was familiar to him. What do you think?"

"I couldn't say. To the best of my belief it was after turning the portrait in his hands that he nearly dropped from his chair. The name, you know, was written on the back."

"Quite so. After all, it is impossible to come to any resolution in a case like this. I hate melodrama, and nothing strikes me as more commonplace and tedious than the ordinary ghost story of commerce; but really, Villiers, it looks as if there were something very queer at the bottom of all this."

The two men had, without noticing it, turned up Ashley Street, leading northward from Piccadilly. It was a long street, and rather a gloomy one, but here and there a brighter taste had illuminated the dark houses with flowers, and gay curtains, and a cheerful paint on the doors. Villiers glanced up as Austin stopped speaking, and looked at one of these houses; geraniums, red and white, drooped from every sill, and daffodil-colored curtains were draped back from each window.

"It looks cheerful, doesn't it?" he said.

"Yes, and the inside is still more cheery. One of the pleasantest houses of the season, so I have heard. I haven't been there myself, but I have met several men who have, and they tell me it's uncommonly jovial."

"Whose house is it?"

"A Mrs. Beaumont's."

"And who is she?"

"I couldn't tell you. I have heard she comes from South America, but, after all, who she is is of little consequence. She is a very wealthy woman, there's no doubt of that, and some of the best people have taken her up. I hear she has some wonderful claret, really marvellous wine, which must have cost a fabulous sum. Lord Argentine was telling me about it; he was there last Sunday evening. He assures me he has never tasted such a wine, and Argentine, as you know, is an expert. By the way, that reminds me, she must be an oddish sort of woman, this Mrs. Beaumont. Argentine asked her how old the wine was, and what do you think she said? 'About a thousand years, I believe.' Lord Argentine thought she was chaffing him, you know, but when he laughed she said she was speaking quite seriously, and offered to show him the jar. Of course, he couldn't say anything more after that, but it seems rather antiquated for a beverage, doesn't it? Why, here we are at my rooms. Come in, won't you?"

"Thanks, I think I will. I haven't seen the curiosity shop for some time."

It was a room furnished richly, yet oddly, where every chair and bookcase and table, every rug and jar and ornament seemed to be a thing apart, preserving each its own individuality.

"Anything fresh lately?" said Villiers, after a while.

"No, I think not; you saw those queer jugs, didn't you? I thought so. I don't think I have come across anything for the last few weeks."

Austin glanced round the room from cupboard to cupboard, from shelf to shelf, in search of some new oddity. His eyes fell at last on an old chest, pleasantly and quaintly carved, which stood in a dark corner of the room.

"Ah," he said, "I was forgetting, I have got something to show you." Austin unlocked the chest, drew out a thick quarto volume, laid it on the table, and resumed the cigar he had put down.

"Did you know Arthur Meyrick, the painter, Villiers?"

"A little; I met him two or three times at the house of a friend of mine. What has become of him? I haven't heard his name mentioned for some time."

"He's dead."

"You don't say so! Quite young, wasn't he?"

"Yes, only thirty when he died."

"What did he die of?"

"I don't know. He was an intimate friend of mine, and a thoroughly good fellow. He used to come here and talk to me for hours, and he was one of the best talkers I have met. He could even talk about painting, and that's more than can be said of most painters. About eighteen months ago he was feeling rather overworked, and partly at my suggestion he went off on a sort of roving expedition, with no very definite end or aim about it. I believe New York was to be his first port, but I never heard from him. Three months ago I got this book, with a very civil letter from an English doctor practising at Buenos Ayres, stating that he had attended the late Mr. Meyrick during his illness, and that the deceased had expressed an earnest wish that the enclosed packet should be sent to me after his death. That was all."

"And haven't you written for further particulars?"

"I have been thinking of doing so. You would advise me to write to the doctor?"

"Certainly. And what about the book?"

"It was sealed up when I got it. I don't think the doctor had seen it."

"It is something very rare? Meyrick was a collector, perhaps?"

"No, I think not, hardly a collector. Now, what do you think of those Ainu jugs?"

"They are peculiar, but I like them. But aren't you going to show me poor Meyrick's legacy?"

"Yes, yes, to be sure. The fact is, it's rather a peculiar sort of thing, and I haven't shown it to any one. I wouldn't say anything about it, if I were you. There it is."

Villiers took the book, and opened it at haphazard. "It isn't a printed volume, then?" he said.

"No. It is a collection of drawings in black and white by my poor friend Meyrick."

Villiers turned to the first page, it was blank; the second bore a brief inscription, which he read:

> Silet per diem universus, nec sine horrore secretus est; lucet nocturnis ignibus, chorus Ægipanum undique personatur: audiuntur et cantus tibiarum, et tinnitus cymbalorum per oram maritimam.

On the third page was a design which made Villiers start and look up at Austin; he was gazing abstractedly out of the window. Villiers turned page after page, absorbed, in spite of himself, in the frightful Walpurgis Night of evil, strange monstrous evil, that the dead artist had set forth in hard black and white. The figures of Fauns and Satyrs and Ægipans danced before his eyes; the darkness of the thicket, the dance on the mountain-top, the scenes by lonely shores, in green vineyards, by rocks and desert places, passed before him; a world before which the human soul seemed to shrink back and shudder. Villiers whirled over the remaining pages, he had seen enough, but the picture on the last leaf caught his eye, as he almost closed the book.

"Austin!"

"Well, what is it?"

"Do you know who that is?"

It was a woman's face, alone on the white page.

"Know who it is? No, of course not."

"I do."

"Who is it?"

"It is Mrs. Herbert."

"Are you sure?"

"I am perfectly certain of it. Poor Meyrick! He is one more chapter in her history."

"But what do you think of the designs?"

"They are frightful. Lock the book up again, Austin. If I were you I would burn it; it must be a terrible companion, even though it be in a chest."

"Yes, they are singular drawings. But I wonder what connection there could be between Meyrick and Mrs. Herbert, or what link between her and these designs?"

"Ah, who can say? It is possible that the matter may end here, arid we shall never know, but in my own opinion this Helen Vaughan, or Mrs. Herbert, is only beginning. She will come back to London, Austin, depend upon it, she will come back, and we shall hear more about her then. I don't think it will be very pleasant news."

THE SUICIDES

LORD ARGENTINE WAS A GREAT FAVORITE IN LONDON SOCIETY. At twenty he had been a poor man, decked with the surname of an illustrious family, but forced to earn a livelihood as best he could, and the most speculative of money-lenders would not have entrusted him with fifty pounds on the chance of his ever changing his name for a title, and his poverty for a great fortune. His father had been near enough to the fountain of good things to secure one of the family livings, but the son, even if he had taken orders, would scarcely have obtained so much as this, and moreover felt no vocation for the ecclesiastical estate. Thus he fronted the world with no better armor than the bachelor's gown and the wits of a younger son's grandson, with which equipment he contrived in some way to make a very tolerable fight of it. At twenty-five Mr. Charles Aubernoun saw himself still a man of struggles and of warfare with the world, but out of the seven who stood between him and the high places of his family three only remained. These three, however, were "good lives," but yet not proof against the Zulu assegais and typhoid fever, and so one morning Aubernoun woke up and found himself Lord Argentine, a man of thirty who had faced the difficulties of existence, and had conquered. The situation amused him immensely, and he resolved that riches should be as pleasant to him as poverty had always been. Argentine, after some little consideration, came to the conclusion that dining, regarded as a fine art, was perhaps the most amusing pursuit open to fallen humanity, and thus his dinners became famous in London, and an invitation to his table a thing covetously desired. After ten years of lordship and dinners Argentine still declined to be jaded, still persisted in enjoying life, and by a kind of infection had become recognized as the cause of joy in others, in short as the best of company. His sudden and tragical death therefore caused a wide and deep sensation. People could scarce believe it, even though the newspaper was before their eyes, and the cry of "Mysterious Death of a Nobleman" came ringing up from the street. But there stood the brief paragraph: "Lord Argentine was found dead this morning by his valet under distressing circumstances. It is stated that there can be no doubt that his lordship committed suicide, though no motive can be assigned for the act. The deceased nobleman was widely known in society, and much liked for his genial manner and sumptuous hospitality. He is succeeded by etc. etc."

By slow degrees the details came to light, but the case still remained a mystery. The chief witness at the inquest was the dead nobleman's valet, who said that the night before his death Lord Argentine had dined with a lady of good position, whose name was suppressed in the newspaper reports. At about eleven o'clock Lord Argentine had returned, and informed his man that he should not require his services till the next morning. A little later the valet had occasion to cross the hall and was somewhat astonished to see his master quietly letting himself out at the front door. He had taken off his evening clothes, and was dressed in a Norfolk coat and knickerbockers, and wore a low brown hat. The valet had no reason to suppose that Lord Argentine had seen him, and though his master rarely kept late hours, thought little of the occurrence till the next morning when he knocked at the bedroom door at a quarter to nine as usual. He received no answer, and, after knocking two or three times, entered the room, and saw Lord Argentine's body leaning forward at an angle from the bottom of the bed. He found that his master had tied a cord securely to one of the short bedposts, and, after making a running noose and slipping it round his neck, the unfortunate man must have resolutely fallen forward, to die by slow strangulation. He was dressed in the light suit in which the valet had seen him go out, and the doctor who was summoned pronounced that life had been extinct for more than four hours. All papers, letters, and so forth, seemed in perfect order, and nothing was discovered which pointed in the most remote way to any scandal either great or small. Here the evidence ended; nothing more could be discovered. Several persons had been present at the dinner-party at which Lord Argentine had assisted, and to all these he seemed in his usual genial spirits. The valet, indeed, said he thought his master appeared a little excited when he came home, but he confessed that the alteration in his manner was very slight, hardly noticeable indeed. It seemed hopeless to seek for any clew, and the suggestion that Lord Argentine had been suddenly attacked by acute suicidal mania was generally accepted.

It was otherwise, however, when within three weeks three more gentlemen, one of them a nobleman, and the two others men of good position and ample means, perished miserably in almost precisely the same manner. Lord Swanleigh was found one morning in his dressing-room, hanging from a peg affixed to the wall, and Mr. Collier-Stuart and Mr. Herries had chosen to die as Lord Argentine. There was no explanation in either case; a few bald facts; a living man in the evening and a dead body with a black swollen face in the morning. The police had been forced to confess themselves powerless to arrest or to explain the sordid murders of Whitechapel; but before the horrible suicides of Piccadilly and Mayfair they were dumfoundered, for not even the mere ferocity which did duty as an explanation of the crimes of the East End could be of service in the West. Each of these men who had resolved to die a tortured shameful death was rich, prosperous, and to all appearance in love with the world, and not the acutest research could ferret out any shadow of a lurking motive in either case. There was a horror in the air, and men looked at one another's faces when they met, each wondering whether the other was to be the victim of a fifth nameless tragedy. Journalists sought in vain in their scrapbooks for materials whereof to concoct reminiscent articles; and the morning paper was unfolded in many a house with a feeling of awe; no man knew when or where the blow would next light.

A short while after the last of these terrible events, Austin came to see Mr. Villiers. He was curious to know whether Villiers had succeeded in discovering any fresh traces of Mrs. Herbert, either through Clarke or by other sources, and he asked the question soon after he had sat down.

"No," said Villiers, "I wrote to Clarke, but he remains obdurate, and I have tried other channels, but without any result. I can't find out what became of Helen Vaughan after she left Paul Street, but I think she must have gone abroad. But to tell the truth, Austin, I haven't paid very much attention to the matter for the last few weeks; I knew poor Herries intimately, and his terrible death has been a great shock to me, a great shock."

"I can well believe it," answered Austin, gravely, "you know Argentine was a friend of mine. If I remember rightly, we were speaking of him that day you came to my rooms."

"Yes, it was in connection with that house in Ashley Street, Mrs. Beaumont's house. You said something about Argentine's dining there."

"Quite so. Of course you know it was there Argentine dined the night before his death."

"No, I haven't heard that."

"Oh, yes, the name was kept out of the papers to spare Mrs. Beaumont. Argentine was a great favorite of hers, and it is said she was in a terrible state for some time after."

A curious look came over Villiers's face; he seemed undecided whether to speak or not. Austin began again.

"I never experienced such a feeling of horror as when I read the account of Argentine's death. I didn't understand it at the time, and I don't now. I knew him well, and it completely passes my understanding for what possible cause he or any of the others for the matter of that could have resolved in cold blood to die in such an awful manner. You know how men babble away each other's characters in London, you may be sure any buried scandal or hidden skeleton would have been brought to light in such a case as this; but nothing of the sort has taken place. As for the theory of mania, that is very well of course for the coroner's jury, but everybody knows that it's all nonsense. Suicidal mania is not smallpox."

Austin relapsed into gloomy silence. Villiers sat silent also, watching his friend. The expression of indecision still fleeted across his face; he seemed as if weighing his thoughts in the balance, and the considerations he was revolving left him still silent. Austin tried to shake off the remembrance of tragedies as hopeless and perplexed as the labyrinth of Dædalus, and began to talk in an indifferent voice of the more pleasant incidents and adventures of the season.

"That Mrs. Beaumont," he said, "of whom we were speaking, is a great success; she has taken London almost by storm. I met her the other night at Fulham's; she is really a remarkable woman."

"You have met Mrs. Beaumont?"

"Yes; she had quite a court around her. She would be called very handsome, I suppose, and yet there is something about her face which I didn't like. The features are exquisite, but the expression is strange; and all the time I was looking at her, and afterwards, when I was going home, I had a curious feeling that that very expression was in some way or other familiar to me."

"You must have seen her in the Row."

"No, I am sure I never set eyes on the woman before; it is that which makes it puzzling. And to the best of my belief I have never seen anybody like her; what I felt was a kind of dim far-off memory, vague but persistent. The only sensation I can compare it to is that odd feeling one sometimes has in a dream, when fantastic cities and wondrous lands and phantom personages appear familiar and accustomed."

Villiers nodded, and glanced aimlessly round the room, possibly in search of something on which to turn the conversation. His eyes fell on an old chest somewhat like that in which the artist's strange legacy lay hid beneath a Gothic scutcheon.

"Have you written to the doctor about poor Meyrick?" he asked.

"Yes; I wrote asking for full particulars as to his illness and death. I don't expect to have an answer for another three weeks or a month. I thought I might as well inquire whether Meyrick knew an Englishwoman named Herbert, and if so, whether the doctor could give me any information about her. But it's very possible that Meyrick fell in with her at New York, or Mexico, or San Francisco; I have no idea as to the extent or direction of his travels."

"Yes, and it's very possible that the woman may have more than one name."

"Exactly. I wish I had thought of asking you to lend me the portrait of her which you possess. I might have enclosed it in my letter to Dr. Mathews."

"So you might, that never occurred to me. We might even now do so. Hark! what are those boys calling?"

While the two men had been talking together a confused noise of shouting had been gradually growing louder. The noise rose from the eastward, and swelled down Piccadilly, drawing nearer and nearer, a very torrent of sound; surging tip streets usually quiet, and making every window a frame for a face, curious or excited. The cries and voices came echoing up the silent street where Villiers lived, growing more distinct as they advanced, and, as Villiers spoke, an answer rang up from the pavement:

"The West End Horrors: Another Awful Suicide; Full Details!"

Austin rushed down the stairs and bought a paper and read out the paragraph to Villiers, as the uproar in the street rose and fell. The window was open and the air seemed full of noise and terror.

"Another gentlemen has fallen a victim to the terrible epidemic of suicide which for the last month has prevailed in the West End. Mr. Sidney Crashaw of Stoke House, Fulham, and King's Pomeroy, Devon, was found, after a prolonged search, hanging from the branch of a tree in his garden at one o'clock to-day. The deceased gentleman dined last night at the Carlton Club, and seemed in his usual health and spirits. He left the Club at about ten o'clock, and was seen walking leisurely up St. James's Street a little later. Subsequent to this his movements cannot be traced. On the discovery of the body medical aid was at once summoned, but life had evidently been long extinct. So far as is known Mr. Crashaw had no trouble or anxiety of any kind. This painful suicide, it will be remembered, is the fifth of the kind in the last month. The authorities at Scotland Yard are unable to suggest any explanation of these terrible occurrences."

Austin put down the paper in mute horror.

"I shall leave London to-morrow," he said, "it is a city of nightmares. How awful this is, Villiers!"

Mr. Villiers was sitting by the window quietly looking out into the street. He had listened to the newspaper report attentively, and the hint of indecision was no longer on his face.

"Wait a moment, Austin," he replied, "I have made up my mind to mention a little matter that occurred last night. It is stated, I think, that Crashaw was last seen alive in St. James's Street, shortly after ten?"

"Yes, I think so. I will look again. Yes, you are quite right."

"Quite so. Well, I am in a position to contradict that statement at all events. Crashaw was seen after that; considerably later indeed."

"How do you know?"

"Because I happened to see Crashaw myself at about two o'clock this morning."

"You saw Crashaw? You, Villiers?"

"Yes, I saw him quite distinctly; indeed there were but a few feet between us."

"Where, in heaven's name, did you see him?"

"Not far from here. I saw him in Ashley Street. He was just leaving a house."

"Did you notice what house it was?"

"Yes, it was Mrs. Beaumont's."

"Villiers! Think what you are saying; there must be some mistake. How could Crashaw be in Mrs. Beaumont's house at two o' clock in the morning? Surely, surely, you must have been dreaming, Villiers, you were always rather fanciful."

"No, I was wide awake enough. Even if I had been dreaming as you say, what I saw would have roused me effectually."

"What you saw? What did you see? Was there anything strange about Crashaw? But I can't believe it; it is impossible."

"Well, if you like I will tell you what I saw, or if you please, what I think I saw, and you can judge for yourself."

"Very good, Villiers."

The noise and clamor of the street had died away, though now and then the sound of shouting still came from the distance, and the dull, leaden silence seemed like the quiet after an earthquake or a storm. Villiers turned from the window and began speaking.

"I was at a house near Regent's Park last night, and when I came away the fancy took me to walk home instead of taking a hansom. It was a clear pleasant night enough, and after a few minutes I had the streets pretty much to myself. It's a curious thing, Austin, to be alone in London at night, the gas lamps stretching away in perspective, and the dead silence, and then perhaps the rush and clatter of a hansom on the stones, and the fire starting up under the horse's hoofs. I walked along pretty briskly, for I was feeling a little tired of being out in the night, and as the clocks were striking two I turned down Ashley Street, which, you know, is on my way. It was quieter than ever there, and the lamps were fewer; altogether it looked as dark and gloomy as a forest in winter. I had done about half the length of the street when I heard a door closed very softly, and naturally I looked up to see who was abroad, like myself, at such an hour. As it happens, there is a street lamp close to the house in question, and I saw a man standing on the step. He had just shut the door, and his face was towards me, and I recognized Crashaw directly. I never knew him to speak to, but I had often seen him, and I am positive that I was not mistaken in my man. I looked into his face for a moment, and then, I will confess the truth, I set off at a good run, and kept it up till I was within my own door."

"Why?"

"Why? Because it made my blood run cold to see that man's face. I could never have supposed that such an infernal medley of passions could have glared out of any human eyes; I almost fainted as I looked. I knew I had looked into the eyes of a lost soul, Austin, the man's outward form remained, but all hell was within it. Furious lust, and hate that was like fire, and the loss of all hope, and horror that seemed to shriek aloud to the night, though his teeth were shut; and the utter blackness of despair. I am sure he did not see me; he saw nothing that you or I can see, but he saw what I hope we never shall. I do not know when he died; I suppose in an hour, or perhaps two, but when I passed down Ashley Street and heard the closing door, that man no longer belonged to this world; it was a devil's face that I looked upon."

There was an interval of silence in the room when Villiers ceased speaking. The light was failing, and all the tumult of an hour ago was quite hushed. Austin had bent his head at the close of the story, and his hand covered his eyes.

"What can it mean?" he said at length.

"Who knows, Austin, who knows? It's a black business, but I think we had better keep it to ourselves, for the present at any rate. I will see if I cannot learn anything about that house through private channels of information, and if I do light upon anything I will let you know."

THE ENCOUNTER IN SOHO

THREE WEEKS LATER AUSTIN RECEIVED A NOTE FROM VILLIERS, ASKING him to call either that afternoon or the next. He chose the nearer date and found Villiers sitting as usual by the window, apparently lost in meditation on the drowsy traffic of the street. There was a bamboo table by his side, a fantastic thing, enriched with gilding and queer painted scenes, and on it lay a little pile of papers, arranged and docketed as neatly as anything in Mr. Clarke's office.

"Well, Villiers, have you made any discoveries in the last three weeks?"

"I think so; I have here one or two memoranda which struck me as singular, and there is a statement to which I shall call your attention."

"And these documents relate to Mrs. Beaumont? it was really Crashaw whom you saw that night standing on the doorstep of the house in Ashley Street?"

"As to that matter, my belief remains unchanged, but neither my inquiries nor their results have any special relation to Crashaw. But my investigations have had a strange issue; I have found out who Mrs. Beaumont is!"

"Who she is? In what way do you mean?"

"I mean that you and I know her better under another name."

"What name is that?"

"Herbert."

"Herbert!" Austin repeated the word, dazed with astonishment.

"Yes, Mrs. Herbert of Paul Street, Helen Vaughan of earlier adventures unknown to me. You had reason to recognize the expression of her face; when you go home look at the face in Meyrick's book of horrors, and you will know the sources of your recollection."

"And you have proof of this?"

"Yes, the best of proof; I have seen Mrs. Beaumont, or shall we say Mrs. Herbert?"

"Where did you see her?"

"Hardly in a place where you would expect to see a lady who lives in Ashley Street, Piccadilly. I saw her entering a house in one of the meanest and most disreputable streets in Soho. In fact, I had made an appointment, though not with her, and she was precise, both to time and place."

"All this seems very wonderful, but I cannot call it incredible. You must remember, Villiers, that I have seen this woman, in the ordinary adventure of London society, talking and laughing, and sipping her chocolate in a commonplace drawing-room, with commonplace people. But you know what you are saying."

"I do; I have not allowed myself to be led by surmises or fancies. It was with no thought of finding Helen Vaughan that I searched for Mrs. Beaumont in the dark waters of the life of London, but such has been the issue."

"You must have been in strange places, Villiers."

"Yes, I have been in very strange places. It would have been useless, you know, to go to Ashley Street, and ask Mrs. Beaumont to kindly give me a short sketch of her previous history. No; assuming, as I had to assume, that her record was not of the cleanest, it would be pretty certain that at some previous time she must have moved in circles not quite so refined as her present ones. If you see mud on the top of a stream, you may be sure that it was once at the bottom. I went to the bottom. I have always been fond of diving into Queer Street for my amusement, and I found my knowledge of that locality and its inhabitants very useful. It is perhaps needless to say that my friends had never heard the name of Beaumont, and as I had never seen the lady, and was quite unable to describe her, I had to set to work in an indirect way. The people there know me, I have been able to do some of them a service now and again, so they made no difficulty about giving their information; they were aware I had no communication direct or indirect with Scotland Yard. I had to cast out a good many lines though, before I got what I wanted, and when I landed the fish I did not for a moment suppose it was my fish. But I listened to what I was told out of a constitutional liking for useless information, and I found myself in possession of a very curious story, though, as I imagined, not the story I was looking for. It was to this effect. Some five or six years ago, a woman named Raymond suddenly made her appearance in the neighborhood to which I am referring. She was described to me as being quite young, probably not more than seventeen or eighteen, very handsome, and looking as if she came from the country. I should be wrong in saying that she found her level in going to this particular quarter, or associating with these people, for, from what I was told, I should think the worst den in London far too good for her. The person from whom I got my information, as you may suppose, no great Puritan, shuddered and grew sick in telling me of the nameless infamies which were laid to her charge. After living there for a year, or perhaps a little more, she disappeared as suddenly as she came, and they saw nothing of her till about the time of the Paul Street case. At first she came to her old haunts only occasionally, then more frequently, and finally took up her abode there as before and remained for six or eight months. It's of no use my going into details as to the life that woman led; if you want particulars you can look at Meyrick's legacy. Those designs were not drawn from his imagination. She again disappeared, and the people of the place saw nothing of her till a few months ago. My informant told me that she had taken some rooms in a house which he pointed out, and these rooms she was in the habit of visiting two or three times a week, and always at ten in the morning. I was led to expect that one of these visits would be paid on a certain day about a week ago, and I accordingly managed to be on the lookout in company with my cicerone at a quarter to ten, and the hour and the lady came with equal punctuality. My friend and I were standing under an archway, a little way back from the street, but she saw us, and gave me a glance that I shall be long in forgetting. That look was quite enough for me; I knew Miss Raymond to be Mrs. Herbert; as for Mrs. Beaumont she had quite gone out of my head. She went into the house, and I watched it till four o'clock, when she came out, and then I followed her. It was a long chase, and I had to be very careful to keep a long way in the background, and yet not to lose sight of the woman. She took me down to the Strand, and then to Westminster, and then up St. James's Street, and along Piccadilly. I felt queerish when I saw her turn up Ashley Street; the thought that Mrs. Herbert was Mrs. Beaumont came into my mind, but it seemed too improbable to be true. I waited at the corner, keeping my eye on her all the time, and I took particular care to note the house at which she stopped. It was the house with the gay curtains, the house of flowers, the house out of which Crashaw came the night he hanged himself in his garden. I was just going away with my discovery, when I saw an empty carriage come round and draw up in front of the house, and I came to the conclusion that Mrs. Herbert was going out for a drive, and I was right. I took a hansom and followed the carriage into the Park. There, as it happened, I met a man I know, and we stood talking together a little distance from the carriage-way, to which I had my back. We had not been there for ten minutes when my friend took off his hat, and I glanced round and saw the lady I had been following all day. 'Who is that?' I said, and his answer was, 'Mrs. Beaumont; lives in Ashley Street.' Of course there could be no doubt after that. I don't know whether she saw me, but I don't think she did. I went home at once, and, on consideration, I thought that I had a sufficiently good case with which to go to Clarke."

"Why to Clarke?"

"Because I am sure that Clarke is in possession of facts about this woman, facts of which I know nothing."

"Well, what then?"

Mr. Villiers leaned back in his chair and looked reflectively at Austin for a moment before he answered.

"My idea was that Clarke and I should call on Mrs. Beaumont."

"You would never go into such a house as that? No, no, Villiers, you cannot do it. Besides, consider; what result . . ."

"I will tell you soon. But I was going to say that my information does not end here; it has been completed in an extraordinary manner.

"Look at this neat little packet of manuscript, it is paginated, you see, and I have indulged in the civil coquetry of a ribbon of red tape. It has almost a legal air, hasn't it? Run your eye over it, Austin. It is an account of the entertainment Mrs. Beaumont provided for her choicer guests. The man who wrote this escaped with his life, but I do not think he will live many years. The doctors tell him he must have sustained some severe shock to the nerves."

Austin took the manuscript, but never read it. Opening the neat pages at haphazard, his eye was caught by a word and a phrase that followed it; and, sick at heart, with white lips and a cold sweat pouring like water from his temples, he flung the paper down.

"Take it away, Villiers, never speak of this again. Are you made of stone, man? Why, the dread and horror of death itself, the thoughts of the man who stands in the keen morning air on the black platform, bound, the bell tolling in his ears, and waits for the harsh rattle of the bolt, are as nothing compared to this. I will not read it; I should never sleep again."

"Very good. I can fancy what you saw. Yes; it is horrible enough; but after all, it is an old story, an old mystery played in our day, and in dim London streets instead of amidst the vineyards and the olive gardens. We know what happened to those who chanced to meet the Great God Pan, and those who are wise know that all symbols are symbols of something, not of nothing. It was, indeed, an exquisite symbol beneath which men long ago veiled their knowledge of the most awful, most secret forces which lie at the heart of all things; forces before which the souls of men must wither and die and blacken, as their bodies blacken under the electric current. Such forces cannot be named, cannot be spoken, cannot be imagined except under a veil and a symbol, a symbol to the most of us appearing a quaint, poetic fancy, to some a foolish, silly tale. But you and I, at all events, have known something of the terror that may dwell in the secret place of life, manifested under human flesh; that which is without form taking to itself a form. Oh, Austin, how can it be? How is it that the very sunlight does not turn to blackness before this thing, the hard earth melt and boil beneath such a burden?"

Villiers was pacing up and down the room, and the beads of sweat stood out on his forehead. Austin sat silent for a while, but Villiers saw him make a sign upon his breast.

"I say again, Villiers, you will surely never enter such a house as that? You would never pass out alive."

"Yes, Austin, I shall go out alive—I, and Clarke with me."

"What do you mean? You cannot, you would not dare . . ."

"Wait a moment. The air was very pleasant and fresh this morning; there was a breeze blowing, even through this dull street, and I thought I would take a walk. Piccadilly stretched before me a clear, bright vista, and the sun flashed on the carriages and on the quivering leaves in the park. It was a joyous morning, and men and women looked at the sky and smiled as they went about their work or their pleasure, and the wind blew as blithely as upon the meadows and the scented gorse. But somehow or other I got out of the bustle and the gaiety, and found myself walking slowly along a quiet, dull street, where there seemed to be no sunshine and no air, and where the few foot-passengers loitered as they walked, and hung indecisively about corners and archways. I walked along, hardly knowing where I was going or what I did there, but feeling impelled, as one sometimes is, to explore still further, with a vague idea of reaching some unknown goal. Thus I forged up the street, noting the small traffic of the milk-shop, and wondering at the incongruous medley of penny pipes, black tobacco, sweets, newspapers, and comic songs, which here and there jostled one another in the short compass of a single window. I think it was a cold shudder that suddenly passed through me that first told me I had found what I wanted. I looked up from the pavement and stopped before a dusty shop, above which the lettering had faded, where the red bricks of two hundred years ago had grimed to black; where the windows had gathered to themselves the fog and the dirt of winters innumerable. I saw what I required; but I think it was five minutes before I had steadied myself and could walk in and ask for it, in a cool voice and with a calm face. I think there must even then have been a tremor in my words, for the old man, who came out from his back parlor and fumbled slowly amongst his goods, looked oddly at me as he tied the parcel. I paid what he asked, and stood leaning by the counter, with a strange reluctance to take up my goods and go. I asked about the business, and learnt that trade was bad and profits cut down sadly; but then the street was not what it was before traffic had been diverted, but that was done forty years ago, 'just before my father died,' he said. I got away at last, and walked along sharply; it was a dismal street indeed, and I was glad to return to the bustle and the noise. Would you like to see my purchase?"

Austin said nothing, but nodded his head slightly; he still looked white and sick. Villiers pulled out a drawer in the bamboo table, and showed Austin a long coil of cord, hard and new; and at one end was a running noose.

"It is the best hempen cord," said Villiers, "just as it used to be made for the old trade, the man told me. Not an inch of jute from end to end."

Austin set his teeth hard, and stared at Villiers, growing whiter as he looked.

"You would not do it," he murmured at last. "You would not have blood on your hands. My God!" he exclaimed, with sudden vehemence, "you cannot mean this, Villiers, that you will make yourself a hangman?"

"No. I shall offer a choice, and leave the thing alone with this cord in a locked room for fifteen minutes. If when we go in it is not done, I shall call the nearest policeman. That is all."

"I must go now. I cannot stay here any longer; I cannot bear this. Good-night."

"Good-night, Austin."

The door shut, but in a moment it was opened again, and Austin stood, white and ghastly, in the entrance.

"I was forgetting," he said, "that I too have something to tell. I have received a letter from Dr. Harding of Buenos Ayres. He says that he attended Meyrick for three weeks before his death."

"And does he say what carried him off in the prime of life? It was not fever?"

"No, it was not fever. According to the doctor, it was an utter collapse of the whole system, probably caused by some severe shock. But he states that the patient would tell him nothing, and that he was consequently at some disadvantage in treating the case."

"Is there anything more?"

"Yes. Dr. Harding ends his letter by saying: 'I think this is all the information I can give you about your poor friend. He had not been long in Buenos Ayres, and knew scarcely any one, with the exception of a person who did not bear the best of characters, and has since left—a Mrs. Vaughan.'"

THE FRAGMENTS

[AMONGST THE PAPERS OF THE WELL-KNOWN PHYSICIAN, DR. ROBERT MATHESON, of Ashley Street, Piccadilly, who died suddenly of apoplectic seizure, at the beginning of 1892, a leaf of manuscript paper was found, covered with pencil jottings. These notes were in Latin, much abbreviated, and had evidently been made in great haste. The ms. was only deciphered with great difficulty, and some words have up to the present time evaded all the efforts of the expert employed. The date, "xxv Jul. 1888," is written on the right-hand corner of the ms. The following is a translation of Dr. Matheson's manuscript.]

Whether science would benefit by these brief notes if they could be published, I do not know, but rather doubt. But certainly I shall never take the responsibility of publishing or divulging one word of what is here written, not only on account of my oath freely given to those two persons who were present, but also because the details are too loathsome. It is probable that upon mature consideration, and after weighing the good and evil, I shall one day destroy this paper, or at least leave it under seal to my friend D., trusting in his discretion, to use it or to burn it, as he may think fit.

As was befitting I did all that my knowledge suggested to make sure that I was suffering under no delusion. At first astounded, I could hardly think, but in a minute's time I was sure that my pulse was steady and regular and that I was in my real and true senses. I ran over the anatomy of the foot and arm and repeated the formulae of some of the carbon compounds, and then fixed my eyes quietly on what was before me.

Though horror and revolting nausea rose up within me, and an odor of corruption choked my breath, I remained firm. I was then privileged or accursed, I dare not say which, to see that which was on the bed, lying there black like ink, transformed before my eyes. The skin, and the flesh, and the muscles, and the bones, and the firm structure of the human body that I had thought to be unchangeable; and permanent as adamant began to melt and dissolve.

I knew that the body may be separated into its elements by external agencies, but I should have refused to believe what I saw. For here there was some internal force of which I knew nothing that caused dissolution and change.

Here too was all the work by which man has been made repeated before my eyes. I saw the form waver from sex to sex, dividing itself from itself, and then again reunited. Then I saw the body descend to the beasts whence it ascended, and that which was on the heights go down to the depths, even to the abyss of all being. The principle of life, which makes organism, always remained, while the outward form changed.

The light within the room had turned to blackness, not the darkness of night, in which objects are seen dimly, for I could see clearly and without difficulty. But it was the negation of light; objects were presented to my eyes, if I may say so, without any medium, in such a manner that if there had been a prism in the room, I should have seen no colors represented in it.

I watched, and at last I saw nothing but a substance as jelly. Then the ladder was ascended again . . . [Here the MS. is illegible] for one instant I saw a Form, shaped in dimness before me, which I will not further describe. But the symbol of this form may be seen in ancient sculptures, and in paintings which survived beneath the lava, too foul to be spoken of . . . as a horrible and unspeakable shape, neither man nor beast, was changed into human form, there came finally death.

I who saw all this, not without great horror and loathing of soul, here write my name declaring all that I have set on this paper to be true.

—ROBERT MATHESON, Med. Dr.

. . . Such, Raymond, is the story of what I know, and what I have seen. The burden of it was too heavy for me to bear alone, and yet I could tell it to none but you. Villiers, who was with me at the last knows nothing of that awful secret of the wood, of how what we both saw die, lay upon the smooth sweet turf amidst the summer flowers, half in sun and half in shadow, and holding the girl Rachel's hand, called and summoned those companions, and shaped in solid form, upon the earth we tread on, the horror which we can but hint at, which we can only name under a figure. I would not tell Villiers of this, nor of that resemblance, which struck me as with a blow upon my heart, when I saw the portrait, which filled the cup of terror at the end. What this can mean I dare not guess. I know that what I saw perish was not Mary, and yet in the last agony Mary's eyes looked into mine. Whether there be any one who can show the last link in this chain of awful mystery, I do not know, but if there be any one who can do this, you, Raymond, are the man. And if you know the secret, it rests with you to tell it or not, as you please.

I am writing this letter to you immediately on my getting back to town. I have been in the country for the last few days; perhaps you may be able to guess in what part. While the horror and wonder of London was at its height—for "Mrs. Beaumont," as I have told you, was well known in society—I wrote to my friend Dr. Phillips, giving some brief outline, or rather hint, of what had happened, and asking him to tell me the name of the village where the events he had related to me occurred. He gave me the name, as he said with the less hesitation, because Rachel's father and mother were dead, and the rest of the family had gone to a relative in the State of Washington six months before. The parents, he said, had undoubtedly died of grief and horror caused by the terrible death of their daughter, and by what had gone before that death. On the evening of the day on which I received Phillips's letter I was at Caermaen, and standing beneath the mouldering Roman walls, white with the winters of seventeen hundred years, I looked over the meadow where once had stood the older temple of the "God of the Deeps" and saw a house gleaming in the sunlight. It was the house where Helen had lived. I stayed at Caermaen for several days. The people of the place, I found, knew little and had guessed less. Those whom I spoke to on the matter seemed surprised that an antiquarian (as I professed myself to be) should trouble about a village tragedy, of which they gave a very commonplace version, and, as you may imagine, I told nothing of what I knew. Most of my time was spent in the great wood that rises just above the village and climbs the hillside, and goes down to the river in the valley; such another long lovely valley, Raymond, as that on which we looked one summer night, walking to and fro before your house. For many an hour I strayed through the maze of the forest, turning now to right and now to left, pacing slowly down long alleys of undergrowth, shadowy and chill, even under the mid-day sun, and halting beneath great oaks; lying on the short turf of a clearing where the faint sweet scent of wild roses came to me on the wind and mixed with the heavy perfume of the elder whose mingled odor is like the odor of the room of the dead, a vapor of incense and corruption. I stood by rough banks at the edges of the wood gazing at all the pomp and procession of the foxgloves towering amidst the bracken and shining red in the broad sunshine, and beyond them into deep thickets of close undergrowth where springs boil up from the rock and nourish the waterweeds, dank and evil. But in all my wanderings I avoided one part of the wood; it was not till yesterday that I climbed to the summit of the hill, and stood upon the ancient Roman road that threads the highest ridge of the wood. Here they had walked, Helen and

Rachel, along this quiet causeway upon the pavement of green turf, shut in on either side by high banks of red earth, and tall hedges of shining beech, and here I followed in their steps, looking out, now and again, through partings in the boughs, and seeing on one side the sweep of the wood stretching far to right and left, and sinking into the broad level, and beyond, the yellow sea, and the land over the sea. On the other side was the valley and the river, and hill following hill as wave on wave, and wood and meadow, and cornfield, and white houses gleaming, and a great wall of mountain, and far blue peaks in the north. And so at last, I came to the place. The track went up a gentle slope and widened out into an open space with a wall of thick undergrowth around it, and then, narrowing again, passed on into the distance and the faint blue mist of summer heat. And into this pleasant summer glade Rachel passed a girl and left it, who shall say what? I did not stay long there.

In a small town near Caermaen there is a museum, containing for the most part Roman remains which have been found in the neighborhood at various times. On the day after my arrival at Caermaen I walked over to the town in question, and took the opportunity of inspecting this museum. After I had seen most of the sculptured stones, the coffins, rings, coins, and fragments of tessellated pavement which the place contains, I was shown a small square pillar of white stone, which had been recently discovered in the wood of which I have been speaking, and, as I found on inquiry, in that open space where the Roman road broadens out. On one side of the pillar was an inscription, of which I took a note. Some of the letters have been defaced, but I do not think there can be any doubt as to those which I supply. The inscription is as follows:

DEVOMNODENT*i*
FLA*v*IVSSENILISPOSSV*it*
PROPTERNVP*tias*
*quas*VIDITSVBVMB*ra*

"To the great god Nodens (the god of the Great Deep or Abyss), Flavins Senilis has erected this pillar on account of the marriage which he saw beneath the shade."

The custodian of the museum informed me that local antiquaries were much puzzled, not by the inscription, or by any difficulty in translating it, but as to the circumstance or rite to which allusion is made.

. . . And now, my dear Clarke, as to what you tell me about Helen Vaughan, whom you say you saw die under circumstances of the utmost and almost incredible horror. I was interested in your account, but a good deal, nay, all of what you told me, I knew already. I can understand the strange likeness you remarked both in the portrait and in the actual face; you have seen Helen's mother. You remember that still summer night so many years ago, when I talked to you of the world beyond the shadows, and of the God Pan. You remember Mary. She was the mother of Helen Vaughan, who was born nine months after that night.

Mary never recovered her reason. She lay, as you saw her, all the while upon her bed, and a few days after the child was born, she died. I fancy that just at the last she knew me; I was standing by the bed, and the old look came into her eyes for a second, and then she shuddered and groaned and died. It was an ill work I did that night, when you were present; I broke open the door of the house of life, without knowing or caring what might pass forth or enter in. I recollect your telling me at the time, sharply enough, and rightly enough too, in one sense, that I had ruined the reason of a human being by a foolish experiment, based on an absurd theory. You did well to blame me, but my theory was not all absurdity. What I said Mary would see, she saw, but I forgot that no human eyes could look on such a vision with impunity. And I forgot, as I have just said, that when the house of life is thus thrown open, there may enter in that for which we have no name, and human flesh may become the veil of a horror one dare not express. I played with energies which I did not understand and you have seen the ending of it. Helen Vaughan did well to bind the cord about her neck and die, though the death was horrible. The blackened face, the hideous form upon the bed, changing and melting before your eyes from woman to man, from man to beast, and from beast to worse than beast, all the strange horror that you witnessed, surprises me but little. What you say the doctor whom you sent for saw and shuddered at I noticed long ago; I knew what I had done the moment the child was born, and when it was scarcely five years old I surprised it, not once or twice but several times with a playmate, you may guess of what kind. It was for me a constant, and incarnate horror, and after a few years I felt I could bear it no longer, and I sent Helen Vaughan away. You know now what frightened the boy in the wood. The rest of the strange story, and all else that you tell me, as discovered by your friend, I have contrived to learn from time to time, almost to the last chapter. And now Helen is with her companions. . . .

NOTE—*Helen Vaughan was born on August 5th, 1865, at the Red House, Breconshire, and died on July 25th, 1888, in her house in a street off Piccadilly, called Ashley Street in the story.*

The House of Sounds

M. P. Shiel

"E caddi come l'uom cui sonno piglia."
—Dante

A GOOD MANY YEARS AGO, WHEN A YOUNG MAN, A STUDENT IN PARIS, I knew the great Carot, and witnessed by his side several of those cases of mind-malady, in the analysis of which he was such a master. I remember one little maid of the Marais, who, until the age of nine, did not differ from her playmates; but one night, lying abed, she whispered into her mother's ear: "Mama, can you not hear the *sound of the world*?" It appears that her geography had just taught her that our globe reels with an enormous velocity, on an orbit about the sun; and that this *sound of the world* of hers was merely a murmur in the ear, heard in the silence of night, and attributed by her fancy to the song of this high motion. Within six months she was as mad as a March-hare.

I mentioned the incident to my friend, Haco Harfager, then occupying with me an old mansion in St.Germain, shut in by a wall and a jungle of shrubbery. He listened with singular interest, and during a good while sat wrapped in gloom.

Another case which I gave made a great impression upon my friend: A young man, a toy-maker of St. Antoine, suffering from consumption—but sober, industrious—returning one gloaming to his garret, happened to purchase one of those factious journals which circulate by lamplight over the Boulevards. This simple act was the beginning of his doom. He had never been a reader: knew little of the reel and turmoil of the world. But the next night he purchased another journal. Soon he acquired a knowledge of politics, the huge movements, the tumult of life. And this interest grew absorbing. Till late into the night, every night, he lay poring over the roar of action, the printed passion. He would awake sick, but brisk of spirit—and bought a morning paper. And the more his teeth gnashed, the less they ate. He grew negligent, irregular at work, turning on his bed through the day. Rags overtook him. As the grand grew upon his frail soul, so every lesser interest failed him. There came a day when he no more cared for his own life; and another day when he tore the hairs from his head.

As to this man, the great Carot said to me:

"Really, one does not know whether to chuckle or to weep over such a business. Observe, for one thing, how diversely men are made! There are minds precisely so sensitive as a thread of melted lead: *every* breath will fret and trouble them: and how about the hurricane? For such this scheme is clearly no fit habitation, but a Machine of Death, a baleful Immense. *Too* cruel to some is the rushing shriek of Being—they *cannot* stand the world. Let each look well to his own little shred of existence, I say, and leave the monstrous Automaton alone! Here, in this poor toy-maker you have a case of the ear: it is only the neurosis, Oxyecoia. Splendid was that Greek myth of 'the Harpies'—by *them* was this creature snatched away—or say, caught by a limb in the wheels of the universe, and so perished. It is quite a ravishing exit—translation in a chariot of flame. Only remember the first seized was *the pinna*—he bent *ear* to the howl of the world, and ended by himself howling. Between chaos and our shoes swings, I assure you, the thinnest film! I knew a man who had this aural peculiarity: that every sound brought him some knowledge of the matter causing the sound: a rod, for instance, of mixed copper and tin striking upon a rod of mixed copper and lead, conveyed to him not merely the proportion of each metal in each rod, but some knowledge of the essential meaning and spirit, as it were, of copper, of tin, of iron and of lead. Him also did the Harpies snatch aloft."

I have mentioned that I related some of these cases to my friend, Harfager: and I was astonished at the obvious pains which he gave himself to his interest, his gaping nostrils. . . .

From first days when we happened to attend the same seminary in Stockholm, an intimacy accompanied by ordinary signs of friendship. Harfager was the shyest, most isolated, of beings. Though our joint housekeeping (brought about by a chance meeting at a midnight *séance*) had now lasted some months, I knew nothing of his plans. Through the day we read together, he rapt back into the past, I engrossed with the present; late at night we reclined on sofas within the vast cave of an old hearthplace *Louis Onze*, and smoked over the dying flame in a silence. Occasionally a *soirée* or lecture might draw me from the house; except once, I never understood that Harfager left it. On that occasion I was hurrying through the Rue St. Honoré, where a rush of traffic rattles over the old pavers retained there, when I came upon him. In this tumult he stood in a listening attitude; and for a moment did not know me.

Even as a boy I had seen in my friend the genuine patrician—not that his personality gave an impression of loftiness or opulence: on the contrary. He did, however, suggest an incalculable *ancientness;* and I have I have known no nobleman who bore in his expression the assurance of the essential Prince, whose pale blossom is of yesterday, and will perish to-morrow, but whose root shoots through the ages. This much I knew of Harfager; also that on one or other of his islands north of Zetland lived his mother and an aunt; that he was somewhat deaf; but liable to a thousand torments or delights at certain sounds, the whine of a door, the note of a bird. . . .

He was somewhat under middle height; and inclined to portliness. His nose rose highly aquiline from that sort of brow called "the musical"—that is, with temples which incline *outward* to the cheek-bones, making breadth for the base of the brain; while the direction of the heavy-lidded eyes, and of the eyebrows, was a downward *droop* from the nose of their outer ends. He wore a thin chin-beard. But the feature of his face were the ears, which were nearly circular, very small and flat, without that outer curve called "the helix." I came to understand that this had long been a trait of his race. Over the whole wan face of my friend was engraved an air of woeful inability, utter gravity of sorrow: one said "Sardanapalus," frail last of the race of Nimrod.

After a year I found it necessary to mention to Harfager my intention of leaving Paris, as we reclined one night in our nooks within the fireplace. He replied to my tidings with a polite "Indeed!" and continued to gloat over the gate; but after an hour turned to me and observed: "Well, it seems to be a hard world."

Truisms uttered with just such a tone of discovery I occasionally heard from him; but his earnest gaze, his despondency, now astonished me.

"Apropos of what?" I asked.

"My friend, do not leave me!" He spread his arms.

I learned that he was the object of a devilish malice; that he was the prey of a hellish temptation. That a lure, a becking hand, a lurking lust, which it was the effort of his life to escape (and to which he was especially liable in solitude) perpetually enticed him; and that so it had been almost from the day when, at time age of five, he had been sent by his father from his desolate home in time ocean.

And whose was this malice?

He told me his mother's and aunt's.

And what was this temptation?

He said it was the temptation to go back—to hurry with the frenzy of hunger—back to that home.

I demanded with what motives, and in what way, the malice of his mother and aunt manifested itself. He answered that there was, he fancied, no definite motive, but only a fated malevolence, involuntary and fated; and that the respect in which it manifested itself was the prayers and commands with which they plagued him to go again to the hold of his ancestors.

All this I could in not understand, and said so. In what consisted this magnetism, and this peril, of his home? To this Harfager did not reply, but rising from his seat, disappeared behind the hearth-curtains, and left the apartment. When he returned, it was with a quarto tome bound in hide, which proved to be Hugh Gascoigne's "Chronicle of Norse Families" in English black-letter. The passage to which he pointed I read as follows:

> Nowe, of thise two brethors the older, Harold, being of seemely personage and prowess, did go a pilgrimage into Danemarke, wherein he repaired again home to Hjaltland (Zetland), and with him fetched the amiable Thronda for his wife, who was a daughter of the sank (blood) royal of Danemark. And his younger brother, Sweyn, that was sad and debonair, but far surpassed the other in cunning, received him with all good cheer.
>
> But eftsoons (soon after) fell Sweyn sick for all his love that he had of Thronda, his brother's wife. And while the worthy Harold ministered about the bed where Sweyne lay sick, lo, Sweyn fastened on him with a violent stroke with a sword, and with no longer tarring enclosed his hands in bonds, and cast him in the bottom of a deep hold. And because Harold would not deprive himself of the governance of Thronda his wife, Sweyn cut off both his ear[s], and put out one of his eyes, and after diverse such torments was ready to slay him. But on a day the valliant Harold, breaking his bonds, and embracing his adversary, did by the sleight of wrestling overthrow him, and escaped. Notwithstanding, he faltered when he came to the Somburgh Head not far from the Castle, and albeit that he was swift-foot, could no farther run, by reason that he was faint with the long plagues of his brother. And whilst he there lay in a swoon, did Sweyne come upon him, and whan he had striken him with a dart, cast him from Somburgh Head into the sea.

Not long hereafterward did the lady Thronda (though she knew not the manner of her lord's death, nor, verily, if he was dead or alive) receive Sweyn in to favour, and with great gaudying and blowing of beamous (trumpets) did become his wife. And right so they two went thence to sojourn in far parts.

Now, it befell that Sweyn was minded by a dream to have built a great mansion in Hjaltland for the home-coming of the lady Thronda; wherefore he called to him a cunning Master-workman, and sent him to England to gather men for the building of this lusty House, while he himself remained with his lady at Rome. Then came this architect to London, but passing thence to Hjaltland was drowned, he and his feers (mates), all and some.

And after two years, which was the time assigned, Sweyn Harfager sent a letter to Hjaltland to understand how his great House did: for he knew not the drowning of the Architect; and soon after he received answer that the House *did well*, and was building on the Isle of Rayba; but that was not the Ilse where Sweyn had appointed the building to be; and he was afeard, and near fell down ded for dread, because in the letter, he saw before him the manner of writing of his brother Harold. And he said in this form: "Surely Harold is alive, else be this a letter writ with ghost hand." And he was wo many days, seeing that this was a deadly stroke.

Thereafter, he took himself back to Hjaltland to know how the matter was, and there the old Castle on Somburg Head was break down to the earth. Then Sweyne was wode-wrorth, and cried: "Jhesu mercy, where is all the great house of my fathers gone? alas! this wicked day of destiny." An one of the people told him that a host of workmen from far parts had break it down. And he said: "Who hath bid them?" but that could none answer. Then he said again: "nis (is not) my brother Harold alive? for I have behold his writing"; and that, too, none could answer. So he went to Rayba, and saw there a great House stand, and when he looked on it, he said: "This, sooth, was y-built by my brother Harold, be he dead, or be he on-live." And there he dwelt, and his lady, and his son's sons until now: for that the House is ruthless and without pity; wherefore 'tis said that up on all who dwell there falleth a wicked madness and a lecherous anguish; and that by way of the ears do they drink the cup of the furie of the earless Harold, til the time of the House be ended.

After I had read the narrative half-aloud, I smiled, saying: "This, Harfager, is very tolerable romance on the part of the good Gascoigne, but has the look of indifferent history."

"It is, nevertheless, *history,*" he replied.

"You believe that?"

"The house still stands solidly on Rayba."

"But you believe that mediæval ghosts superintended the building of their family mansions?"

"Gascoigne nowhere says that; for to be 'stricken with a darte,' is not necessarily to die; nor, if he did say it, have I any knowledge on the subject."

"And what, Harfager, is the nature of that 'wicked madness,' that 'lecherous anguish,' of which Gascoigne speaks?"

"Do you ask me?"—he spread his arms—"what do I know? I know nothing! I was banished from the place at the age of five. Yet the cry of it still rings in my mind. And have I not *told* you of anguishes—even in myself—of inherited longing and loathing . . ."

Anyway, I *had* to go to Heidelberg just then; so I said I would compromise by making my absence short, and rejoin him in a few weeks for me. I took his moody silence to mean assent; and soon afterwards left him.

But I was detained; and when I got back to our old house found it empty. Harfager was gone.

It was only after twelve years that a letter was forwarded me—a rather wild letter, an awfully long one—in the writing of my friend. It was dated at Rayba. From the writing I understood that it had been dashed off *with furious haste,* so I was the more astonished at the very trivial nature of the contents. On the first half page he spoke of our old friendship, and asked if I would see his mother, who was dying; the rest of the epistle consisted of an analysis of his mother's family-tree, the apparent aim being to show that she was a genuine Harfager, and a distant cousin of his father. He then went on to comment on the great prolificness of his race, stating that since the fourteenth century, over *four millions* of its members had lived; three only of them, he believed, being now left. That settled, the letter ended.

Influenced by this, I travelled northward; reached Caithness; passed the stormy Orkneys; reached Lerwick; and from Unst, the most bleak and northerly of the Zetlands, contrived, by dint of bribes, to pit the weather-worthiness of a lug-sailed "sixern" (identical with the "lang-schips" of the Vikings) against a flowing sea and an ugly sky. The trip, I was told, was at such a season of some risk. It was the sombre December of those seas; and the weather, they said, although never cold, is seldom other than tempestuous. A mist now lay over the billows, enclosing our boat in a dome of doleful gloaming; and there was a ghostly something in the look of the silent sea and brooding sky which produced upon my nerves the mood of a journey out of nature, a cruise beyond the world. Occasionally, however, we ran past one of those solitary "skerries," or sea-stacks, whose craggy sea-walls, disintegrated by the struggles of the Gulf Stream with the North Sea, had a look of awful ruin and havoc. But I only noticed three of these: for before the dun day had well run half its course, sudden darkness was upon us; and with it one of those storms, of which the winter of this semi-Arctic sea is one succession. During the haggard glimpses of the following day the rain did not stop; but before darkness had quite fallen, my skipper (who talked continuously to a mate of seal-maidens, and water-horses, and *grüles*), paused to point me out a mound of gloomier grey on the weather-bow, which, he said, should be Rayba.

Rayba, he said, was the centre of quite a system of those *rösts* (dangerous eddies) and cross-currents, which the tidal wave hurls with complicated swirlings among all of the islands: but at Rayba they ran with more than usual angriness, owing to the row of sea-crags which garrisoned the land around: approach was therefore at all times difficult, and at night foolhardy. With a running sea, however, we came sufficiently close to see the mane of foam which railed round the coast-wall. Its shock, according to the captain, had often more than all the efficiency of artillery, tossing tons of rock to heights of six hundred feet upon the island.

When the sun next pried above the horizon, we had closely approached the coast; and it was then that for the first time the impression of some *spinning* motion of the island (due probably to the swirling movement of the water) was produced upon me. We affected a landing at a *voe*, or sea-arm, on the west coast; the east, though the point of my aim, was out of the question on account of the swell. Here I found two *skeoes* (or sheds), thatched with feal, five or six seamen, who gained a livelihood by trading for the groceries of the great house on the east; and, taking one of them for guide, I began the climb of the island.

Now, during the night in the boat, I had been aware of a booming in the ears for which even the roar of the sea round the coast seemed insufficient to account; and this now, as we went on, became sufficiently augmented—and with it, once more, the conviction within me of *spinning* motions. Rayba I found discovered to be a land of precipices of granite and flaggy gneiss; at about the centre, however, we came upon a tableland, sloping from west to east, and covered by lots of lochs, which sullenly flowed into one another. I could see no shore eastward to this chain of waters, and by dint of shouting to my leader, and bending ear to his shoutings, I came to know that there *was* no such shore—I say *shout,* for nothing less could have sounded through the steady bellowing as of ten thousand bisons that now resounded on every side. A certain trembling, too, of the earth became distinct. In vain, meantime, did the eye in its dreary survey seek a tree or shrub—for no kind of vegetation, save peat, could brave for a day the perennial tempest of this benighted island. Darkness, half an hour after noon, commenced to fall upon us: and it was soon afterwards that my guide, pointing down a defile near the eastern coast, hurriedly started back the way he had come. I bawled a question after him, as he went: but at this point the voice of mortals had ceased to be in the least audible.

Down this defile, with a sinking of the heart, and a most singular sickness of giddiness, I passed; and, on reaching its end, emerged upon a ledge of rock which shuddered to the immediate onsets of the sea—though all this part of the island was, besides, in the grip of an ague not due to the great guns of the sea. Hugging a crag of cliff for steadiness from the gusts, I gazed forth upon a scene not less eerily dismal than some drear district of the dreams of Dante. Three "skerries," flanked by stacks as fantastic and twisted as a witch's finger, and giving a home to hosts of osprey and scart, seal and walrus, lay at some fathoms distance; and from its rush among them, the sea in blanched, tumultuous, but inaudible wrath, like an army with banners, ranted toward the land. Letting go my crag, I staggered some distance to the left: and now all at once an amphitheatre opened before me, and there broke upon my view a panorama of such appalling majesty as had never entered my heart to fancy.

"An amphitheatre" I said: but it was rather the form of a Norman door that I saw. Fancy such a door, half a mile wide, flat on the ground, the rounded part farthest from the sea; and all round it let a wall of rock tower perpendicular forty yards: and now down this rounded door shape, and *over its whole extent,* let a roaring ocean roll its tonnage in hoary fury—and the stupor with which I looked, and then the shrinking, and then the instinct of flight, will find comprehension.

This was the disemboguement of the lochs of Rayba.

And within the curve of this Norman cataract, robed in the world of its smokes and far-excursive surfs, stood a fabric of brass.

The last beam of the day had now nearly passed; but I could still see through the mist which had bleakly nimbused it as in tears, that the building was low in proportion to the hugeness of its circumference; that it was roofed with a dome; and that about it ran two rows of Norman windows, the upper smaller than the lower.

Certain indications led me to infer that the house had been founded upon a bed of rock which lay, circular and detached, within the curve of the cataract; but this nowhere emerged above the flood: for the whole floor which I had before me dashed one reeking deep river to the beachless sea—passage to the mansion being made possible by a massive causeway-bridge, with arches, all bearded with sea-weed.

Descending from my ledge, I passed along it, now drenched in spray; and as I came nearer, could see that this house, too, was to half its height more thickly bearded than an old hull with barnacles and every variety of bright sea-weed; also—what was very surprising—that from many spots near the top of the brazen wall ponderous chains, dropping beards, reached out in rays: so that the fabric had the aspect of a many-anchored ark. But without pausing to look closely, I pushed forward, and rushing through the smooth waterfall which poured all round from the roof, by one of its many porches I entered the dwelling.

Darkness now was around me—and sound. I seemed to stand in the very centre of some yelling planet, the low resembling the sounding of many thousands of cannon, purchased by strange crashing and breaking uproars. And a madness descended on me; I was near to tears. "Here," I said, "is the place of weeping; not elsewhere is the vale of sighing." However, I passed forward through a succession of halls, and was wondering where to go next, when a hideous figure, with a lamp in his hand, stalked rapidly towards me. I shrank from him! It seemed the skeleton of a lank man wrapped in a winding-sheet till the light of one tiny eye, and a film of skin over a portion of the face reassured one. Of ears he showed no sign. His name, I afterwards learned, was Aith; and his appearance was explained by his pretence (true or false) that he had once suffered *burning*, almost to the cinder-stage, but had somehow recovered. With an expression of malice, and agitated gestures, he led the way to a chamber on the upper stage, where, having struck light to a taper, he made signs toward a spread table, and left me.

For a long time I sat in solitude, conscious of the shaking of the mansion, though every sense was swallowed up and confounded in the one impression of sound. Water, water, was the world—a nightmare on my breast, a tingling on my nerves, a sense of being infinitely drowned and buried in boundless deluges; and when the feeling of giddiness, too, increased, I sprang up and paced—but suddenly stopped, angry, I scarce knew why, with myself. I had, in fact, caught myself walking with a certain *hurry*, not usual with me, not natural to me. So I forced myself to stand and take note of the hall. It was large, and damp with mists, so that its tattered, but rich, furniture looked lost in it, its centre occupied by a tomb bearing the name of a

Harfager of the fourteenth century, and its walls old panels of oak. Having drearily seen these things, I waited on with an intolerable consciousness of solitude; but a little after midnight the tapestry parted, and Harfager with a rapid stalk walked in.

In twelve years my friend had grown old. He showed, it is true, a tendency to portliness: yet, to a knowing eye, he was in reality tabid, ill-nourished. And his neck stuck forward from his chest; and the lower part of his back had quite a forward bend of age; and his hair floated about his face and shoulders in a wildness of awful whiteness, while a white chin-beard hung to his chest. His dress was a robe of bauge, which, as he went, waved aflaunt from his bare and hairy shins, and he was shod in those soft slippers called *rivlins.*

To my astonishment, he spoke. When I passionately shouted that I could gather no fragment of sound from his moving mouth, he clapped both his palms to his ears, and then anew besieged mine: but again without result: and now, with an angry throw of the hand, he caught up his taper, and walked from the apartment.

There was something strikingly unnatural in his manner—something which reminded me of the skeleton, Aith: an excess of zeal, a fever, a rage, a *loudness,* an eagerness of gait, a great extravagance of gesture. His hand constantly dashed the whiffs of hair from his face which, though of the saffron of death, had red eyes—thick-lidded eyes, fixed in a downward and sideward gaze. When he came back to me, it was with a leaf a folio of ivory, and a piece of graphite, hanging from the cord tied round his garment; and he rapidly wrote a petition that, if not too tired, I would take part with him in the funeral of his mother.

I shouted assent.

Once more he clapped palms to his ears; then wrote: "Do not shout: no whisper in any part of the building is inaudible to me."

I remembered that, in early life, he had been slightly *deaf.*

We passed together through many apartments, he shading the taper with his hand—a necessary action, for, as I quickly discovered, in no nook of the quivering building was the air in a state of rest, but was forever commoved by a curious agitation, a faint windiness, like an echo of tempests, which communicated a universal nervousness to the curtains. Everywhere I met the same past grandeur, present raggedness and decay. In many of the rooms were tombs; one was a museum thronged with bronzes, but broken, grown with fungoids, dripping with moisture—it was as if the mansion, in ardour of travail, sweated; and a miasma of decomposition tainted all the air.

I followed Harfager through the maze of his way with some difficulty, for he went headlong—only once stopping, when with a face ungainly wild over the glare of the light, he tossed up his fingers, and gave out a single word: from the form of his lips I guessed the word "*Hark*!"

Presently we entered a very long chamber, in which, on chairs beside a bed, lay a coffin, flanked by a file of candles. The coffin was very deep, and had this singularity—that the foot-piece was absent, so that the soles of the corpse could be seen as we approached. I saw, too, three upright rods secured to a side of the coffin, each rod fitted at its top with a little silver bell of the sort called *morrice*, pendent from a flexible spring. At the head of the bed, Aith, with an air of irascibility, was stamping to and fro with a narrow area.

Harfager deposited the taper upon a stone table, and stood poring with a crazy intentness over the body. I, too, stood and looked at death so grim and rigorous as I think I never saw. The coffin looked angrily full of tangled grey locks, the lady being of great age, bony and hook-nosed; and her face shook with solemn constancy to the quivering of the building. I noticed that over the body had been set fixed three bridges, like the bridge of a violin; their sides fitting into groves in the coffin's sides, and their tops of a shape to fit the slope of the two coffin-lids when closed. One of these bridges passed over the knees of the dead lady; another bridged her stomach; the third her neck. In each of them was a hole, and across each of the three holes passed a string from the morrice-bell above it—the three holes being thus divided by the three tight strings into six semi-circles. Before I could guess the significance of all this, Harfager closed the folding coffin-lids, which had little holes for the passage of the three strings. He then turned the key in the lock, and uttered a word which I took to be, "come."

Aith now took hold of the handle at the coffin's head; and out of the dark part of the hall a lady in black walked forward. She was very tall, pallid, of imposing aspect; and from the curvature of the nose, and her circular ears, I guessed her the lady Swertha, aunt of Harfager. Her eyes were red—if with crying I could not tell.

Harfager and I taking each a handle near the coffin-foot, and the lady bearing before us one of the black candlesticks, the obsequies began. When we got to the doorway, I noticed in a corner there were two more coffins, engraved with the names of Harfager and his aunt. Thence we wound our way down a wide stairway winding to a lower floor; and descending thence still lower by narrow brass steps, came to a portal of metal, where the lady, depositing the candlestick, left us.

The chamber of death into which we now bore the body had for its outer wall the brazen outer wall of the whole house at a spot where this approached the cataract, and was no doubt profoundly drowned in the world of surge without: so that the earthquake there was urgent. On every side the place was piled with coffins, ranged high and wide upon shelves; and the huge rush and scampering which ensued on our entrance proved it was the paradise of troops of rats. As it was inconceivable that these could have eaten a way through sixteen brazen feet—for even the floor here was brazen—I assumed that some fruitful pair must have found in the house, on its building, an ark from the waters. Even this guess, though, seemed wild; and Harfager afterwards confided to me his suspicion that they had for some reason been *placed* there by the original builder.

We deposited our load upon a stone bench in the centre; whereupon Aith made haste to be away. Harfager then repeatedly walked from end to end of the place, scrutinising with many a stoop and peer and upward stretch the shelves and their props. Could he, I was led to wonder, have any doubts as to their soundness? Damp, in fact, and decay pervaded everything. A bit of which I touched crumbled to dust under my thumb.

He presently beckoned to me, and with yet one halt and "*Hark*!" from him, we passed through the house to my chamber; where, left alone, I paced long about, agitated with a strange anger; then tumbled to an agony of slumber.

In the far interior of the mansion even the bleared day of this land of bleakness never rose upon our gloom; but I was able to regulate my gettings-up by a clock which stood in my chamber; or I was called by Harfager, with whom in a short time, I renewed more than all our former friendship. That I should say *more* is curious: but so it *was*: and this was proved by the fact that we grew to take, and to excuse, freedoms of speech and manner which, as two persons of more than usual reserve, we had once never dreamed of permitting to ourselves in respect of each other. Down corridors that vanished either way in darkness and length of perspective remoteness we linked ourselves in perambulations of purposeless urgency. Once, for example, in our pacings of aimless haste down passages that vanished in shadow and length of perspective remoteness, he wrote that my step was very slow. I replied that it was just such a step as suited my then mood. He wrote: "You have developed an tendency to *fret*." I was very offended, and said: "Certainly there are more fingers than one in the world which that ring will fit!"

Another day he was no less than rude to me for seeking to reveal to him the secret of the unhuman keenness of his hearing—and of mine! For I, too, to my dismay, began, as time passed, to catch hints of shouted sounds. The cause might be found, I asserted, in a fervour of the auditory nerve, which, if the cataract were absent, the roar of the ocean, and the perpetual tempest about us, might be sufficient to bring about; his own ear interior, I said, must be inflamed to an exquisite pitch of fever; and I named the disease to him as the Paracusis Wilisü.

When he frowned dissent, I, quite undeterred, proceeded to relate the case (that had occurred within my own experience) of a very deaf lady who could hear the drop of a pin in a railway-train*; and now he made me the reply: "Of ignorant persons I am accustomed to consider the mere scientist the most ignorant!"

But I, for my part, regarded it as merely far-fetched that he should pretend to be in the dark as to the morbid state of his hearing! He himself, indeed, confessed to me his own, Aith's, and the lady Swertha's pronness to paroxysms of *vertigo.* I was startled; for I had myself shortly previously roused out of sleep by feelings of reeling and nausea, and an assurance that the room flew furiously round with me. The impression passed away, and I attributed it, perhaps hastily, to some disturbance in the nerve-endings of the "labyrinth," or inner ear. In Harfager, however, the conviction of whirling motions in the house, in the world, got to so horrible a degree of certainty, that its effects sometimes resembled those of lunacy or energumenal possession. Never, he said, was the sensation of giddiness altogether dead in him; seldom the sensation that he gazed with stretched-out arms over the brink of abysms which wooed his half-consenting foot. Once, as we walked, he was hurled, as by unearthly powers, to the ground; and there for an hour sprawled, bathed in sweat, with distraught bedazzlement and amaze in his stare, while watched the racing walls. He was constantly racked, moreover, with the consciousness of sounds so peculiar in their character, that I could account for them on no other supposition than that of a *tinnitùs* infinitely sick. Through the roar there sometimes visited him, he told me, the lullaby of some bird, from the burden of whose song he had the consciousness that she derived from a very remote country, was of the whiteness of foam, and crested with a comb of mauve. Or else he knew aware of accumulated human tones, distant yet articulate, busily contending in volubility, and in the end melting into a medley of musical movements. Or, anon, he was shocked by an infinite and imminent crashing, like the monstrous racket of the crackling of a cosmos of crockery round his ears. He told me, moreover, that he could frequently see, rather than hear, the parti-coloured wheels of a mazy sphere-music deep, deep, within the black dark of the cataract's roar. These impressions, which I protested *must* be merely entotic, had sometimes a pleasing effect upon him, and he would stand long to listen with a lifted hand to their seduction: others again inflamed him to a mad angry madness. I guessed that they were the cause of those "*Harks*!" that at intervals of about an hour did not fail to break from him. But in truth I was wrong: and it was with a thrill of dismay that I shortly came to know the truth.

* Such cases are known to many medical men. The concussion on the deaf nerve is the cause of the acquired sensitiveness; nor is there any limit to that sensitiveness when the tumult is immensely augmented.

For, as once we were once passing by an iron door on the lower floor, he stopped, and for some minutes stood, listening with a leer most keen and cunning. Presently the cry "*Hark*!" escaped him; and he then turned to me and wrote up the tablet: "Did you did not hear?" I heard nothing but the roar; and he howled into my ear in sounds now audible to me as an echo caught far off in dreams: "You shall see."

He took up the candlestick; produced from the pocket of his robe a key; unlocked the iron door; and we passed into a room very loftily domed in proportion to its area, and empty, save that a pair of steps lay against its wall, and that in the centre of its marble floor was a pool, like a Roman "impluvium," only round like the room—a pool evidently profound in depth, full of a thick and inky fluid. I was very perturbed by its present aspect, for as the candle burned upon its surface, I observed that this had been quite recently *disturbed*, in a style for which the shivering of the house could not account, since *ripples* of slime were now rounding out from its middle to its brink. When I glanced at Harfager for explanation; he gave me a signal to wait; and now for about an hour, with his hands behind his back, paced the chamber; but then paused, and we two stood together by the pool's margin, gazing into the water. Suddenly his clutch tightened on my arm, and I saw, with a touch of horror, a tiny ball, probably of lead, but daubed blood-red by some chemical, fall from the roof, and sink into the middle of the pool. It hissed on contact with the water a whiff of mist.

"In the name of all that is sinister," I whispered, "what thing is this?"

Again he made me a busy and confident signal to wait, moved the ladder-steps toward toward the pool, handed me the taper. When I had mounted, holding high the light, I saw hanging out of the fogs in dome a globe of old copper, lengthened into balloon-shape by a neck, at the end of which I could spy a tiny hole. Painted over the globe was barely visible in red print-letters:

HARFAGER-HOUS: 1388–188

I was down quicker than I went up!

"But the meaning?" I panted.

"Did you see the writing?"

"Yes. The meaning?"

He wrote: "By comparing Gascoigne with Thrunster, I find that the mansion was *built* around 1389."

"But the final figures?"

"After the last 8," he replied, "there is another figure not quite obliterated by a tarnish-spot."

"What figure?" I asked.

"It cannot be read, but may be surmised. The year 1888 is now all but passed. It can only be the figure 9."

"Oh, you are depraved in mind!" I cried, very irritated; "you assume—you *state*—in a manner which no mind trained to base its conclusions on facts can bear with patience."

"And you are irrational," he wrote. "You know, I suppose, the formula of Archimedes by which, the diameter of a globe being known, its volume also is know. Now, the diameter of the globe in the dome I know to be four and a half feet; and the diameter of the leaden balls about a third of an inch. Supposing, then, that 1389 was the year in which the globe was full of balls, you may readily calculate that not many fellows of the four million and odd which have since dropped at the rate of one an hour are now left within. The fall of balls *cannot* persist another year. The figure 9 is therefore forced upon us."

"But you assume, Harfager," I cried: "Oh, believe me, my friend, this is the very wantonness of wickedness! By what algebra of despair do you know that each ball represents one of your house, or that the last date was intended to correspond with the stoppage of the horologe. And, even if so, what is the significance of it? It can have no *significance*!"

"Do you want to madden me?" he shouted. Then furiously writing: "I swear that I know nothing of its significance! But is it not evident to you that the thing is a big hour-glass, intended to count the hours, not of a day, but of a cycle; and of a cycle of five hundred years?"

"But the whole contrivance," I passionately cried, "is a baleful phantasm of our brains! an evil impossibility! How is the fall of the balls regulated? Ah, my friend, you wander—your mind is debauched in this brawl of waters."

"I have not ascertained," he replied, "by what internal works, or clammy medium, or spiral coil, dependent probably for its action upon the vibration of the mansion, the balls are retarded in their fall: that was a matter well within the skill of the mediæval mechanic, the inventor of the clock; but this at least is clear, that one element of their retardation is the smallness of the aperture through which they have to pass; that this element, by known laws of stats, will cease to operate when no more than three balls remain; and that, consequently, the last three will fall at almost the same instant."

"In Heaven's name!" I exclaimed, careless now what folly I poured out, "but your mother is dead, Harfager! Do you deny that there remain but you and the lady Swertha?"

A glance of disdain was all the answer he then gave me as to this.

But he confessed to me a day later that the leaden drops were a constant sorrow to his ears; that from hour to hour his life was a keen waiting for their fall; that even from his brief sleeps he infallibly started awake at each descent; that in whatever reach of the mansion he chanced to be, they found him out with a crashing *loudness;* and that each drop tweaked him with a twinge of anguish within the ear. I was therefore shocked at his declaration that these droppings had now become to as the life of life to him; had acquired an entwining so close with the tone of his mind, that their ceasing might even mean for him the reeling of Reason: at which confession he sobbed, with his face buried, as he leant upon a column. When this paroxysm was past, I asked him if it was out of the question that he should once and for all cast off the fascination of the horologe, and escape with me from the place. He wrote in mysterious reply: "A *three-fold* cord is not easily broken." I started, asking—"How three-fold?" He wrote with a bitter smile: "To be in love with pain—to pine after aching—is not that a wicked madness?" I stood astonished that he had unconsciously quoted Gascoigne! "a wicked madness!" "a lecherous anguish!" "You have seen my aunt's face," he proceeded; "your eyes were dim if you did not see in it an impious calm, the glee of a blasphemous patience, a grin behind her daring smile." He then spoke of a prospect at the terror of which his whole soul trembled, yet which sometimes laughed in his heart in the form of a *hope.* It was the prospect of any considerable increase in the volume of sound about his ears. At *that,* he said, the brain must totter. On the night of my arrival the noise of my boots, and since then, my voice occasionally raised voice, had produced acute pain in him. To such an ear, I understood him to say, the luxury of torture involved in a large sound-increase around was an allurement from which no human virtue could turn: and when I said that I could not even conceive such an increase, much less the means by which it could be effected, he brought out from the archives of the mansion some annals kept by the heads of the family. From these it appeared that the tempests that ever lacerated the latitude of Rayba did not fail to give place, at intervals of some years, to one mammoth madness, one Samson among the merry men, and Sirius among the suns. At such periods the rains descended—and the floods came—even as in the first world-deluge; those *rösts,* or eddies, which ever encircled Rayba, spurning the bands of lateral space, burst aloft into a whirl of water-spouts, to dance about the little land, upon which, converging, some of them discharged their waters: and the locks which flowed to the cataract thus redoubled their volume, and crashed with redoubled roar. Harfager said that it was miraculous that for eighteen years no such great event had transacted itself at Rayba.

"And what," I asked, "in addition to the dropping balls, and the prospect of an increase of sound, is the third strand of that '*three-fold cord*' of which you have spoken?"

For answer he led me to a circular hall which, he said, he had ascertained to be the center of the circular mansion. It was a very large hall—so large as I think I never saw—so large that the amount of wall lighted at any one time by the candle seemed nearly flat: and nearly the whole of its area, from floor to roof, was occupied by a column of brass, the space between wall and cylinder being only such as to admit of a stretched-out arm.

"This column," Harfager wrote, "goes up to the dome and passes beyond it; it goes down to the lower floor, and passes through that; it goes down thence to the brazen flooring of the vaults, and *passes through that* into the bedrock. Under each floor it spreads out, helping to support the floor. What is the precise quality of the impression which I have made upon your mind by this description?"

"I do not know!" I answered, turning from him: "ask me none of your enigmas, Harfager: I feel a giddiness. . . ."

"But answer me," he said: "consider *the strangeness* of that brazen lowest floor, which I have discovered to be some six feet thick, and whose under-surface, I have reason to think, is somewhat *above* the bed-rock; remember that the fabric is at no point *fastened* to the column; think of the *chains* that ray out from the outer wall, apparently *anchoring* the house to the ground. Tell me, what impression have I *now* made?"

"And is it for *this* you wait?" I cried. "Yet there may have been no malevolent intention! You jump at conclusions! Any fixed building in such a land and spot as this would at any time be liable to be broken up by some sovereign tempest! What if it was the intention of the builder that in such a case the chains should break, and the building, by yielding, be saved?"

"You have no lack of charity at least," he replied; and we returned to the book we then read together.

He had not wholly lost the old habit of study, although he could no longer get himself to *sit* to read; so with a volume (often tossed down) he would stamp about within the region of the lamplight; or I, unconscious of my voice, might read to him. By a whim of his mood the few books which now lay within the limits of his patience had all for their motive something of the *picaresque*, or the foppishly speculative: Quevedo's "Tacaño"; or the system of Tycho Brahe; above all, George Hakewill's "Power and Providence of God." One day, however, as I read, he interrupted me with the sentence, *à propos* of nothing: "What I cannot understand is that you, a scientist, should believe that the physical life ceases with the ceasing of breathing"—

and from that moment the tone of our reading changed. For he led me to the crypts of the library in the lowest part of the building, and hour after hour, with a *furore* of triumph, overwhelmed me with books proving the length of life after "death." What, he asked, was my opinion of Baron Verulam's account of the dead man who was heard to utter words of prayer? or of the bounding bowels of the dead convict? On my expressing unbelief, he seemed surprised, and reminded me of the writhings of dead cobras, of the long beatings of a frog's heart after "death." "She is not dead," he quoted, "but *sleepeth*." The idea of Bacon and Paracelsus that the principle of life resides in the spirit or fluid was proof to him that such fluid could not, from its very nature, undergo any sudden annihilation, while the organs which it pervades remain. When I asked him what limit he, then, set to the persistence of "life" in the "dead," he answered that when decay had so far advanced that the nerves could no longer be called nerves, or when the brain had been disconnected at the neck from the body, as by rats gnawing, then the king of terrors was king verily. With an indiscretion strange to me before my residence at Rayba, I now blurted out the question whether all this could be referring to his mother? For a while he stood thoughtful, then wrote: "Even if I had I not reason to believe that my own and Swertha's life in some way hung upon the final cessation of hers, I should still have taken precautions to ascertain the march of the destroyer on her frame: as it is, I shall not lack even the exactest information." He then explained that the rats which ran riot in the place of death would in their time do their full work upon her; but would be unable to reach the region of the throat without first gnawing their way through the three strings stretched across the holes of the bridges within the coffin, and thus, one by one, liberating the three morrisco-bells to a tinkling.

The winter solstice had gone; another year began. I was sleeping in a deep sleep by night when Harfager came into my chamber, and shook me. His face was ghastly in the taper's glare. A change within a short time had taken place upon him. He was hardly the same. He was like some poor wight into whose surprised eyes in the night have pried into the eyes of Affright.

He said that he was aware of strainings and creakings, which gave him the feeling of being suspended in airy spaces by a thread which must break to his weight; and he begged me, for God's sake, to accompany him to the coffins. We passed together through the house, he craven, haggard, his gate now laggard, into the chamber of the dead, where he stole to and fro examining the shelves. Out of the footless coffin of the dowager trembling on its bench I saw a water-rat crawl; and as Harfager passed beneath one of the shortest of the shelves which bore one coffin, it suddenly dropped from a height with to dust at his feet. He screamed the cry of a frighted creature; tottered to my support; and I bore him back to the upper parts of the palace.

He sat, with his face buried, in a corner of a small chamber, doddering, overtaken, as it were, with the extremity of age, no longer marking with his "*Hark*!" the fall of the leaden drops. To my remonstrances he answered only with the moan, "so soon!" Whenever I looked for him, I found him there, his manhood now collapsed in an ague. I do not think that during this time he slept.

On the second night, as I was approaching him, he sprang suddenly upright with the outcry: "The first bell is tinkling!"

And he had screamed it when, from some long way off, a faint wail, which at its origin must have been a fierce shriek, reached my now feverish ears. Harfager, for his part, clapped his palms to his ears, and dashed from his place, I following in hot chase through the black breadth of the mansion: till we came to a chamber containing a candelabrum, and arrased in faded red. On the floor in swoon lay the lady Swertha, her dark-grey hair in disarray wrapping her like an angry sea; tufts of it scattered, torn from the roots; and on her throat prints of strangling fingers. We bore her to the bed in an alcove; and, having discovered some tincture in a cabinet, I administered it between her fixed teeth. In her rapt countenance I saw that death was not; and, as I found something appalling in her aspect, shortly afterwards left her to Harfager.

When I next saw him his manner had undergone a kind of change which I can only describe as gruesome. It resembled the officious self-importance seen in a person of weak intellect who spurs himself with the thought, "to business! the time is short!" while his walk sickened me with a hint of *ataxie locomotrice*. When I asked him as to his aunt, as to the meaning of the marks of violence on her body, bending ear to his deep and unctuous tone, I could hear: "An attempt has been made upon her the skeleton, Aith."

He seemed not share my astonishment at this thing! nor could give me any clear answer as to his reason for retaining such a servant, or as to the origin of Aith's service. Aith, he told me, had been admitted into the palace during the period of his own absence in youth, and he knew little of him beyond the fact that he was extraordinarily strong. *Whence* he had come, or how, no person except the lady Swertha was aware: and she, it seems, feared, or at least persistently flinched from admitting him into the mystery. He added that, as a matter of fact, the lady, from the day of his coming back to Rayba, had with some object imposed upon herself a dumbness on all subjects, which he had never once known her to break through, except by an occasional note.

With an ataxic strenuousness, with the airs of a drunken man constraining himself to ordered action, Harfager now set himself to the doing of a host of trivial things: he collected chronicles and arranged them in order of date; he docketed or ticketed packets of documents; he insisted upon my assistance in turning the faces of paintings to the wall. He was, however, now constantly stopped by bursts of vertigo, six times in a single hour being hurled to the ground, while blood frequently guttered from his ears. He complained to me in a tone of piteous wail of the wooing of a silver *piccolo* that continually seduced him. As he bent, sweating, over his momentous nothings, his hands fluttered like aspen. I noted the movements of his whimpering lips, the rheum of his sunken eyes: sudden dotage had come upon his youth.

On a day he threw it utterly off, and was young anew. He entered my room; roused me from my dreams; I observed the lunacy of bliss in his eyes, heard his hiss in my ear:

"Up! The *storm*!"

Ah! I had known it—in the nightmare of the night. I felt it in the air of the room. It had come. I saw it lurid by the lamplight on the hell of Harfager's face.

A glee burst at once into birth within me, as I sprang from my couch, glancing at the clock: it was eight—in the morning. Harfager, with the naked stalk of some maniac prophet, had already taken himself away; and I started out after him. A deepening was clearly felt in the quivering of the edifice; anon for a second it stopped still, as if, breathlessly, to listen; its air was troubled with a vague gustiness. Occasionally there came to me as it were the noising of some far-off lamentation and voice in Ramah, but whether this was in my ear or the screaming of the gale, I could not tell; or again I could hear one clear chord of an organ's vaunt. About noon I spied Harfager, lamp in hand, running along a corridor, with naked soles. As we met he looked at me, but hardly with recognition, and passed by; stopped, however, and ran back to howl into my ear the question: "Would you *see*?" He then beckoned before me, and I followed to a very small window in the outer wall, closed with a slab of brass. As he lifted a latch, the slab dashed inward with instant impetuosity and tossed him a long way, while the breath of the tempest, braying through the brazen tube with a brutal bravura, caught and pinned me upon a corner of a wall, and all down the corridor a long crashing racket of crowds of pictures and couches followed. I nevertheless managed to push my way on the belly to the opening. Hence the sea should have been visible; but my senses were met by nothing but a vision of tumbled tenebrousness, and a general impression of the letter O. The sun of Rayba had gone out. In a moment of opportunity our two forces got the shutter again.

"Come"—he had obtained fresh glimmer, and beckoned before me—"let us see how the dead fare in the great desolation": and we ran, but had hardly got to the middle of the stairway, when I was thrilled by the consciousness of some great shock, the bass of a dull thud, which nothing save the thumping to the floor of the whole lump of the coffins could have caused. I looked for Harfager, and for a moment only saw his heels skedaddling, panic-hounded, his ears stopped ears, his mouth round! Then, indeed, fear reached me—a tremor in the audacity of my heart, a thought that at any rate I must desert him in his extremity, and work out my own salvation. Yet it was with a hesitancy that I turned to search him for the last farewell—a hesitancy which I felt not to be unselfish, but selfish, and unhealthy. I rambled through the night, seeking light, and having happened upon a lamp, proceeded to hunt for Harfager. Several hours went by in this way, during which I could not doubt from the state of the air in the house that the violence about me was being wildly heightened. Sounds as of screams—unreal, like the shriekings of demons—now reached my ears. As the time of night came on, I began to detect in the greatly augmented baritone of the cataract a fresh character—a shrillness—the whistle of rapture—a malice—the menace of a rabies blind and deaf. It must have been at about the hour of six that I found Harfager. He sat in an obscure room, with his head bowed down, his hands on his knees, his face was covered with hair, and blood from the ears. The right sleeve of his robe had been rent away in some renewed attempt, I imagine, to manipulate a window, and the rather crushed arm hung lank from the shoulder. For some time I stood and eyed him mouthing his mumblings; but now that I had found him uttered nothing as to my departure. Presently he looked sharply up with the call "*Hark*!"—then with impatience, "Hark! Hark!"—then with a shout, "The second bell!" And *again*, in an immediate sequence upon his shout, there sounded a wail, vague yet real, through the house. Harfager at the instant dropped reeling with giddiness; but I, snatching up a lamp, dashed out, shivering, but eager. For some while the wild wailing went on (either actually, or by reflex action of my ear); and as I ran for the lady's apartment, I saw, opposite to it the open door of an armoury, into which I passed, caught up a battle-axe, and was not about to dart in to her aid, when Aith, with a blazing eye, shied out of her chamber. I cast up my axe, and, shouting, dashed forward to down him: but by some chance the lamp fell from me, and before I knew anything more, the axe sprang from my grasp, and I was cast far backward by some grim vigour. There was, however, enough light shining out of the chamber to show that the skeleton had darted into a door of the armoury, so I instantly slammed and locked the door near me by which I had procured the axe, and hurrying to the other, secured it, too. Aith was thus a prisoner. I entered the lady's chamber. She lay over the bed in the alcove, and to my bent ear grossly croaked the ruckle of death. A glance at the mangled throat convincing me that her last moments were come, I settled her on the bed, curtained her within the loosened festoons of the hangings of black, and turned from the cursedness of her aspect. On an *escritoire* near I noticed a note, intended apparently for Harfager: "I mean to defy, and fly; not from fear, but for the light of the defiance itself. *Can* you come?" Taking a flame from the candelabrum, I left her to her loneliness, and throes of her death.

I had passed some distance backward when I was startled by a queer sound—a crash—resembling the crash of a tamboureen; and as I could hear it pretty clearly, and from a distance, this meant some prodigious energy. In two minutes it again broke out, and thenceforth at regular intervals—with an effect of pain upon me; and the conviction grew gradually within me that Aith had unhung two of the old brass shields from their pegs, and holding them by their handles, and dash them viciously together, thus expressed the frenzy that had now overtaken him. When I found my way back to Harfager, very anguish now stamping in him about the chamber; he shook his head like a tormented horse, brushing and barring from his hearing each crash of the brass shields. "Ah, when—when—" he hoarsely groaned into my ear, "will that ruckle cease in her throat? I will myself, I tell you—*with my own hand*—oh God . . ." Since the morning his auditory fever (as indeed my own also) apeared to have increased in steady proportion with the roaring and screeching chaos round; and the death-struggle in the lady's throat bitterly filled for him the intervals of the grisly cymbaling of Aith. He presently sent twinkling fingers into the air, and with arms cast out, darted into the darkness.

And again I sought him, and long again in vain. As the hours passed, and the day deepened toward its baleful midnight, the cry of the now redoubled cataract, mixed with the mass and majesty of the now climactic tempest, took on too intentional a *shriek* to be longer tolerable to any reason. My own mind escaped my sway, and went its way; for here, in the hot-bed of fever, I was fevered. I wandered from chamber to chamber, precipitate, dizzy on the upbuoyance of a joy. "As a man upon whom sleep seizes," so had I fallen. Even yet, as I passed near the region of the armoury, the rapturous shields of Aith did not fail to smash faintly upon my ear. Harfager I did not see, for he, too, was doubtless roaming a hurtling Ahasuerus round the world of the house. However, at about midnight, observing light shining from a door on the lower stage, I entered and saw him there—the chamber of the dropping horologe. He sat hugging himself on the ladder-steps, gazing at the gloomy pool. The final lights of the riot of the day seemed dying in his eyes; and he gave me no glance as I ran in. His hands, his bare arm, were all washed with new-shed blood; but of this, too, he looked unconscious; his mouth was hanging open to his pantings. As I eyed him, he suddenly leapt high, smiting hands with the yell, "The last bell tinkling!" and ran out raving. He therefore did not see (though he may have understood by hearing) the thing which, with cowering awe, I now saw: for a ball slipped from the horologe with a hiss and mist of smoke into the pool; and while the clock once ticked another: and while the clock yet ticked, another! and the smoke of the first had not perfectly thinned, when the smoke of the third, mixing with it, floated toward the dome. Understanding that the sands of the mansion were run, I, too, throwing up my arms, rushed from the spot; but was suddenly stopped in my flight by the sense of some stupendous destiny emptying its vials upon the edifice; and was quickly made aware by a cracking racket like musketry, above, and the downpour of a world of waters, that some water-spout, in the waltz and whirl, had hurled its broken summit upon us, and burst through the dome. At that moment I beheld Harfager running toward me, his hands buried in his hair; and, as he raced past, I caught him, crying: "Harfager, save yourself! the very fountains, Harfager—by the grand God, man"—I hissed it into his inmost ear—"*the very fountains of the Great Deep* . . . !" He glared at me and went on his way while I, whisking myself into a room, closed the door. Here for some time with weak knees I waited, I waited; but the eagerness of my frenzy pressed me, and I again stepped out, to find the corridors everywhere thigh-deep with water; while rags of the storm, bragging through the whole in the dome, were now blustering about the house. My light was at once puffed out, but I was surprised by the presence of *another* light—most ghostly, gloomy, bluish—mild, yet wild—which now gloated everywhere through the house. I was staring in wonder at this when a gust of auguster passion galloped up the mansion; and, with it, I was made aware of the *snap* of something somewhere. There was a minute's infinite waiting—and then—quick—ever quicker—came the throb, snap, pop, in spacious succession, of the anchoring chains of the mansion before the hurried shoulder of the hurricane. And *again* a second of breathless stillness—and then—deliberately—its hour came—the house *moved*. My flesh worked like the flesh of worms which squirm. Slowly moved and stopped—then was a sweep—and a swirl—and a pause! then a swirl—and a sweep—and a pause!—then steady labour on the brazen axis, as the labourer tramps by the harrow; then a heightening of zest—then intensity—then the final liveliness of flight. And now once again, as, staggering and plunging I spun, the notion of escape for a moment came to me, but this time I shook an impious fist. "No, but God, no, no," I gasped, "I will no more go from here: there waltzing let me pass, in this carnival of the vortices, anarchy of the thunders!"—and I ran staggering. But memory gropes in a greying gloaming as to all that followed. I struggled up the stairway, now flowing a river, and for a good while ran plunging, full of wild rantings, about, amid the downfall of roofs now, save three rafters, having been snatched by the wind away, and in the blush of that bluish moonshine the tapestries were flapping and trailing wildly out after the flying place, like the streaming hair of some ranting fakir stung reeling by the tarantulas of distraction. At one point, where the largest of the porticoes protruded, the mansion began at every revolution to bump with grum shudderings against some obstruction: it bumped, and while the lips said one-two-three it three times bumped again. It was the mænadism of mass! Swift—still swifter—in ague of flurry it raced, every portico a sail to the gale, racking its great frame to fragments. I, running by the door of a room littered with the ruins of a fallen wall, saw through that livid moonlight Harfager sitting on a tomb—a drum by him, upon which, with a club in his bloody fist, he feebly but persistingly, beat. The speed of the leaning house had now attained the *sleeping* stage, that last pitch of the spinning-top; and now all at once. Harfager dashed away mat of hair which wrapped his face, sprang, stretched his arms, and began to spin—giddily—in the same direction as the mansion—nor less sleep-embathed—with lifted hair, with quivering cheeks . . . from such a sight I shied with retching; and, staggering, plunging, presently found myself on the lower floor opposite a porch, where an outer door chancing to crash before me, the breath of the tempest smote freshly upon me. On this impulse, partly of madness, more of sanity, spurred in my soul; and I spurted out of the doorway, to be whirled far out into the limbo without.

The river at once rushed me deep-drenched toward the sea—though even there, in the depth of the whirlpool, a shrill din like the splitting of a world, reached my ears. It had hardly passed when my body butted in its course upon one of the arches, cushioned with seaweed, of the not all-demolished causeway. Nor had I utterly lost consciousness. A clutch freed my head from the drench; and in the end I heaved myself to the level of the summit. Hence to the ledge of rock by which I had come, the bridge being intact, I rowed myself on my face under the thumps of wind, and under a rushing of rain, like a shimmering of silk, through the air. Noticing the same wild shining about me which had blushed through the broken dome into the mansion, I glanced backward—and the whole northern heaven, to the zenith, shone one ocean of variegated glories—the *aurora borealis,* which was being fairly blushed and flustered by the gail. At the augustness of which sight, I was touched to a gush of tears. And with them, the dream broke! the infatuation passed! a palm seemed to skin back from my brain the films and media of delusion; and on my knees I threw my hands to heaven in thankfulness for the marvel of my rescue from all the temptation, and the tribulation, and the breakage, of Rayba.

The Secret of the Growing Gold

Bram Stoker

When Margaret Delandre went to live at Brent's Rock the whole neighbourhood awoke to the pleasure of an entirely new scandal. Scandals in connection with either the Delandre family or the Brents of Brent's Rock, were not few; and if the secret history of the county had been written in full both names would have been found well represented. It is true that the status of each was so different that they might have belonged to different continents—or to different worlds for the matter of that—for hitherto their orbits had never crossed. The Brents were accorded by the whole section of the country a unique social dominance, and had ever held themselves as high above the yeoman class to which Margaret Delandre belonged, as a blue-blooded Spanish hidalgo out-tops his peasant tenantry.

The Delandres had an ancient record and were proud of it in their way as the Brents were of theirs. But the family had never risen above yeomanry; and although they had been once well-to-do in the good old times of foreign wars and protection, their fortunes had withered under the scorching of the free trade sun and the "piping times of peace." They had, as the elder members used to assert, "stuck to the land," with the result that they had taken root in it, body and soul. In fact, they, having chosen the life of vegetables, had flourished as vegetation does—blossomed and thrived in the good season and suffered in the bad. Their holding, Dander's Croft, seemed to have been worked out, and to be typical of the family which had inhabited it. The latter had declined generation after generation, sending out now and again some abortive shoot of unsatisfied energy in the shape of a soldier or sailor, who had worked his way to the minor grades of the services and had there stopped, cut short either from unheeding gallantry in action or from that destroying cause to men without breeding or youthful care—the recognition of a position above them which they feel unfitted to fill. So, little by little, the family dropped lower and lower, the men brooding and dissatisfied, and drinking themselves into the grave, the women drudging at home, or marrying beneath them—or worse. In process of time all disappeared, leaving only two in the Croft, Wykham Delandre and his sister Margaret. The man and woman seemed to have inherited in masculine and feminine form respectively the evil tendency of their race, sharing in common the principles, though manifesting them in different ways, of sullen passion, voluptuousness and recklessness.

The history of the Brents had been something similar, but showing the causes of decadence in their aristocratic and not their plebeian forms. They, too, had sent their shoots to the wars; but their positions had been different and they had often attained honour—for without flaw they were gallant, and brave deeds were done by them before the selfish dissipation which marked them had sapped their vigour.

The present head of the family—if family it could now be called when one remained of the direct line—was Geoffrey Brent. He was almost a type of worn-out race, manifesting in some ways its most brilliant qualities, and in others its utter degradation. He might be fairly compared with some of those antique Italian nobles whom the painters have preserved to us with their courage, their unscrupulousness, their refinement of lust and cruelty—the voluptuary actual with the fiend potential. He was certainly handsome, with that dark, aquiline, commanding beauty which women so generally recognise as dominant. With men he was distant and cold; but such a bearing never deters womankind. The inscrutable laws of sex have so arranged that even a timid woman is not afraid of a fierce and haughty man. And so it was that there was hardly a woman of any kind or degree, who lived within view of Brent's Rock, who did not cherish some form of secret admiration for the handsome wastrel. The category was a wide one, for Brent's Rock rose up steeply from the midst of a level region and for a circuit of a hundred miles it lay on the horizon, with its high old towers and steep roofs cutting the level edge of wood and hamlet, and far-scattered mansions.

So long as Geoffrey Brent confined his dissipations to London and Paris and Vienna—anywhere out of sight and sound of his home—opinion was silent. It is easy to listen to far off echoes unmoved, and we can treat them with disbelief, or scorn, or disdain, or whatever attitude of coldness may suit our purpose. But when the scandal came close home it was another matter; and the feelings of independence and integrity which is in people of every community which is not utterly spoiled, asserted itself and demanded that condemnation should be expressed. Still there was a certain reticence in all, and no more notice was taken of the existing facts than was absolutely necessary. Margaret Delandre bore herself so fearlessly and so openly—she accepted her position as the justified companion of Geoffrey Brent so naturally that people came to believe that she was secretly married to him, and therefore thought it wiser to hold their tongues lest time should justify her and also make her an active enemy.

The one person who, by his interference, could have settled all doubts was debarred by circumstances from interfering in the matter. Wykham Delandre had quarrelled with his sister—or perhaps it was that she had quarrelled with him—and they were on terms not merely of armed neutrality but of bitter hatred. The quarrel had been antecedent to Margaret going to Brent's Rock. She and Wykham had almost come to blows. There had certainly been threats on one side and on the other; and in the end Wykham, overcome with passion, had ordered his sister to leave his house. She had risen straightway, and, without waiting to pack up even her own personal belongings, had walked out of the house. On the threshold she had paused for a moment to hurl a bitter threat at Wykham that he would rue in shame and despair to the last hour of his life his act of that day. Some weeks had since passed; and it was understood in the neighbourhood that Margaret had gone to London, when she suddenly appeared driving out with Geoffrey Brent, and the entire neighbourhood knew before nightfall that she had taken up her abode at the Rock. It was no subject of surprise that Brent had come back unexpectedly, for such was his usual custom. Even his own servants never knew when to expect him, for there was a private door, of which he alone had the key, by which he sometimes entered without anyone in the house being aware of his coming. This was his usual method of appearing after a long absence.

Wykham Delandre was furious at the news. He vowed vengeance—and to keep his mind level with his passion drank deeper than ever. He tried several times to see his sister, but she contemptuously refused to meet him. He tried to have an interview with Brent and was refused by him also. Then he tried to stop him in the road, but without avail, for Geoffrey was not a man to be stopped against his will. Several actual encounters took place between the two men, and many more were threatened and avoided. At last Wykham Delandre settled down to a morose, vengeful acceptance of the situation.

Neither Margaret nor Geoffrey was of a pacific temperament, and it was not long before there began to be quarrels between them. One thing would lead to another, and wine flowed freely at Brent's Rock. Now and again the quarrels would assume a bitter aspect, and threats would be exchanged in uncompromising language that fairly awed the listening servants. But such quarrels generally ended where domestic altercations do, in reconciliation, and in a mutual respect for the fighting qualities proportionate to their manifestation. Fighting for its own sake is found by a certain class of persons, all the world over, to be a matter of absorbing interest, and there is no reason to believe that domestic conditions minimise its potency. Geoffrey and Margaret made occasional absences from Brent's Rock, and on each of these occasions Wykham Delandre also absented himself; but as he generally heard of the absence too late to be of any service, he returned home each time in a more bitter and discontented frame of mind than before.

At last there came a time when the absence from Brent's Rock became longer than before. Only a few days earlier there had been a quarrel, exceeding in bitterness anything which had gone before; but this, too, had been made up, and a trip on the Continent had been mentioned before the servants. After a few days Wykham Delandre also went away, and it was some weeks before he returned. It was noticed that he was full of some new importance—satisfaction, exaltation—they hardly knew how to call it. He went straightway to Brent's Rock, and demanded to see Geoffrey Brent, and on being told that he had not yet returned, said, with a grim decision which the servants noted:

"I shall come again. My news is solid—it can wait!" and turned away. Week after week went by, and month after month; and then there came a rumour, certified later on, that an accident had occurred in the Zermatt valley. Whilst crossing a dangerous pass the carriage containing an English lady and the driver had fallen over a precipice, the gentleman of the party, Mr. Geoffrey Brent, having been fortunately saved as he had been walking up the hill to ease the horses. He gave information, and search was made. The broken rail, the excoriated roadway, the marks where the horses had struggled on the decline before finally pitching over into the torrent—all told the sad tale. It was a wet season, and there had been much snow in the winter, so that the river was swollen beyond its usual volume, and the eddies of the stream were packed with ice. All search was made, and finally the wreck of the carriage and the body of one horse were found in an eddy of the river. Later on the body of the driver was found on the sandy, torrent-swept waste near Täsch; but the body of the lady, like that of the other horse, had quite disappeared, and was—what was left of it by that time—whirling amongst the eddies of the Rhone on its way down to the Lake of Geneva.

Wykham Delandre made all the enquiries possible, but could not find any trace of the missing woman. He found, however, in the books of the various hotels the name of "Mr. and Mrs. Geoffrey Brent." And he had a stone erected at Zermatt to his sister's memory, under her married name, and a tablet put up in the church at Bretten, the parish in which both Brent's Rock and Dander's Croft were situated.

There was a lapse of nearly a year, after the excitement of the matter had worn away, and the whole neighbourhood had gone on its accustomed way. Brent was still absent, and Delandre more drunken, more morose, and more revengeful than before.

Then there was a new excitement. Brent's Rock was being made ready for a new mistress. It was officially announced by Geoffrey himself in a letter to the Vicar, that he had been married some months before to an Italian lady, and that they were then on their way home. Then a small army of workmen invaded the house; and hammer and plane sounded, and a general air of size and paint pervaded the atmosphere. One wing of the old house, the south, was entirely re-done; and then the great body of the workmen departed, leaving only materials for the doing of the old hall when Geoffrey Brent should have returned, for he had directed that the decoration was only to be done under his own eyes. He had brought with him accurate drawings of a hall in the house of his bride's father, for he wished to reproduce for her the place to which she had been accustomed. As the moulding had all to be re-done, some scaffolding poles and boards were brought in and laid on one side of the great hall, and also a great wooden tank or box for mixing the lime, which was laid in bags beside it.

When the new mistress of Brent's Rock arrived the bells of the church rang out, and there was a general jubilation. She was a beautiful creature, full of the poetry and fire and passion of the South; and the few English words which she had learned were spoken in such a sweet and pretty broken way that she won the hearts of the people almost as much by the music of her voice as by the melting beauty of her dark eyes.

Geoffrey Brent seemed more happy than he had ever before appeared; but there was a dark, anxious look on his face that was new to those who knew him of old, and he started at times as though at some noise that was unheard by others.

And so months passed and the whisper grew that at last Brent's Rock was to have an heir. Geoffrey was very tender to his wife, and the new bond between them seemed to soften him. He took more interest in his tenants and their needs than he had ever done; and works of charity on his part as well as on his sweet young wife's were not lacking. He seemed to have set all his hopes on the child that was coming, and as he looked deeper into the future the dark shadow that had come over his face seemed to die gradually away.

All the time Wykham Delandre nursed his revenge. Deep in his heart had grown up a purpose of vengeance which only waited an opportunity to crystallise and take a definite shape. His vague idea was somehow centred in the wife of Brent, for he knew that he could strike him best through those he loved, and the coming time seemed to hold in its womb the opportunity for which he longed. One night he sat alone in the living-room of his house. It had once been a handsome room in its way, but time and neglect had done their work and it was now little better than a ruin, without dignity or picturesqueness of any kind. He had been drinking heavily for some time and was more than half stupefied. He thought he heard a noise as of someone at the door and looked up. Then he called half savagely to come in; but there was no response. With a muttered blasphemy he renewed his potations. Presently he forgot all around him, sank into a daze, but suddenly awoke to see standing before him someone or something like a battered, ghostly edition of his sister. For a few moments there came upon him a sort of fear. The woman before him, with distorted features and burning eyes seemed hardly human, and the only thing that seemed a reality of his sister, as she had been, was her wealth of golden hair, and this was now streaked with grey. She eyed her brother with a long, cold stare; and he, too, as he looked and began to realise the actuality of her presence, found the hatred of her which he had had, once again surging up in his heart. All the brooding passion of the past year seemed to find a voice at once as he asked her:

"Why are you here? You're dead and buried."

"I am here, Wykham Delandre, for no love of you, but because I hate another even more than I do you!" A great passion blazed in her eyes.

"Him?" he asked, in so fierce a whisper that even the woman was for an instant startled till she regained her calm.

"Yes, him!" she answered. "But make no mistake, my revenge is my own; and I merely use you to help me to it." Wykham asked suddenly:

"Did he marry you?"

The woman's distorted face broadened out in a ghastly attempt at a smile. It was a hideous mockery, for the broken features and seamed scars took strange shapes and strange colours, and queer lines of white showed out as the straining muscles pressed on the old cicatrices.

"So you would like to know! It would please your pride to feel that your sister was truly married! Well, you shall not know. That was my revenge on you, and I do not mean to change it by a hair's breadth. I have come here tonight simply to let you know that I am alive, so that if any violence be done me where I am going there may be a witness."

"Where are you going?" demanded her brother.

"That is my affair! and I have not the least intention of letting you know!" Wykham stood up, but the drink was on him and he reeled and fell. As he lay on the floor he announced his intention of following his sister; and with an outburst of splenetic humour told her that he would follow her through the darkness by the light of her hair, and of her beauty. At this she turned on him, and said that there were others beside him that would rue her hair and her beauty too. "As he will," she hissed; "for the hair remains though the beauty be gone. When he withdrew the lynch-pin and sent us over the precipice into the torrent, he had little thought of my beauty. Perhaps his beauty would be scarred like mine were he whirled, as I was, among the rocks of the Visp, and frozen on the ice pack in the drift of the river. But let him beware! His time is coming!" and with a fierce gesture she flung open the door and passed out into the night.

Later on that night, Mrs. Brent, who was but half-asleep, became suddenly awake and spoke to her husband:

"Geoffrey, was not that the click of a lock somewhere below our window?"

But Geoffrey—though she thought that he, too, had started at the noise—seemed sound asleep, and breathed heavily. Again Mrs. Brent dozed; but this time awoke to the fact that her husband had arisen and was partially dressed. He was deadly pale, and when the light of the lamp which he had in his hand fell on his face, she was frightened at the look in his eyes.

"What is it, Geoffrey? What dost thou?" she asked.

"Hush! little one," he answered, in a strange, hoarse voice. "Go to sleep. I am restless, and wish to finish some work I left undone."

"Bring it here, my husband," she said; "I am lonely and I fear when thou art away."

For reply he merely kissed her and went out, closing the door behind him. She lay awake for a while, and then nature asserted itself, and she slept.

Suddenly she started broad awake with the memory in her ears of a smothered cry from somewhere not far off. She jumped up and ran to the door and listened, but there was no sound. She grew alarmed for her husband, and called out: "Geoffrey! Geoffrey!"

After a few moments the door of the great hall opened, and Geoffrey appeared at it, but without his lamp.

"Hush!" he said, in a sort of whisper, and his voice was harsh and stern.

"Hush! Get to bed! I am working, and must not be disturbed. Go to sleep, and do not wake the house!"

With a chill in her heart—for the harshness of her husband's voice was new to her—she crept back to bed and lay there trembling, too frightened to cry, and listened to every sound. There was a long pause of silence, and then the sound of some iron implement striking muffled blows! Then there came a clang of a heavy stone falling, followed by a muffled curse. Then a dragging sound, and then more noise of stone on stone. She lay all the while in an agony of fear, and her heart beat dreadfully. She heard a curious sort of scraping sound; and then there was silence. Presently the door opened gently, and Geoffrey appeared. His wife pretended to be asleep; but through her eyelashes she saw him wash from his hands something white that looked like lime.

In the morning he made no allusion to the previous night, and she was afraid to ask any question.

From that day there seemed some shadow over Geoffrey Brent. He neither ate nor slept as he had been accustomed, and his former habit of turning suddenly as though someone were speaking from behind him revived. The old hall seemed to have some kind of fascination for him. He used to go there many times in the day, but grew impatient if anyone, even his wife, entered it. When the builder's foreman came to inquire about continuing his work Geoffrey was out driving; the man went into the hall, and when Geoffrey returned the servant told him of his arrival and where he was. With a frightful oath he pushed the servant aside and hurried up to the old hall. The workman met him almost at the door; and as Geoffrey burst into the room he ran against him. The man apologised:

"Beg pardon, sir, but I was just going out to make some enquiries. I directed twelve sacks of lime to be sent here, but I see there are only ten."

"Damn the ten sacks and the twelve too!" was the ungracious and incomprehensible rejoinder.

The workman looked surprised, and tried to turn the conversation.

"I see, sir, there is a little matter which our people must have done; but the governor will of course see it set right at his own cost."

"What do you mean?"

"That 'ere 'arth-stone, sir: Some idiot must have put a scaffold pole on it and cracked it right down the middle, and it's thick enough you'd think to stand hanythink." Geoffrey was silent for quite a minute, and then said in a constrained voice and with much gentler manner:

"Tell your people that I am not going on with the work in the hall at present. I want to leave it as it is for a while longer."

"All right sir. I'll send up a few of our chaps to take away these poles and lime bags and tidy the place up a bit."

"No! No!" said Geoffrey, "leave them where they are. I shall send and tell you when you are to get on with the work." So the foreman went away, and his comment to his master was:

"I'd send in the bill, sir, for the work already done. 'Pears to me that money's a little shaky in that quarter."

Once or twice Delandre tried to stop Brent on the road, and, at last, finding that he could not attain his object rode after the carriage, calling out:

"What has become of my sister, your wife?" Geoffrey lashed his horses into a gallop, and the other, seeing from his white face and from his wife's collapse almost into a faint that his object was attained, rode away with a scowl and a laugh.

That night when Geoffrey went into the hall he passed over to the great fireplace, and all at once started back with a smothered cry. Then with an effort he pulled himself together and went away, returning with a light. He bent down over the broken hearth-stone to see if the moonlight falling through the storied window had in any way deceived him. Then with a groan of anguish he sank to his knees.

There, sure enough, through the crack in the broken stone were protruding a multitude of threads of golden hair just tinged with grey!

He was disturbed by a noise at the door, and looking round, saw his wife standing in the doorway. In the desperation of the moment he took action to prevent discovery, and lighting a match at the lamp, stooped down and burned away the hair that rose through the broken stone. Then rising nonchalantly as he could, he pretended surprise at seeing his wife beside him.

For the next week he lived in an agony; for, whether by accident or design, he could not find himself alone in the hall for any length of time. At each visit the hair had grown afresh through the crack, and he had to watch it carefully lest his terrible secret should be discovered. He tried to find a receptacle for the body of the murdered woman outside the house, but someone always interrupted him; and once, when he was coming out of the private doorway, he was met by his wife, who began to question him about it, and manifested surprise that she should not have before noticed the key which he now reluctantly showed her. Geoffrey dearly and passionately loved his wife, so that any possibility of her discovering his dread secrets, or even of doubting him, filled him with anguish; and after a couple of days had passed, he could not help coming to the conclusion that, at least, she suspected something.

That very evening she came into the hall after her drive and found him there sitting moodily by the deserted fireplace. She spoke to him directly.

"Geoffrey, I have been spoken to by that fellow Delandre, and he says horrible things. He tells to me that a week ago his sister returned to his house, the wreck and ruin of her former self, with only her golden hair as of old, and announced some fell intention. He asked me where she is—and oh, Geoffrey, she is dead, she is dead! So how can she have returned? Oh! I am in dread, and I know not where to turn!"

For answer, Geoffrey burst into a torrent of blasphemy which made her shudder. He cursed Delandre and his sister and all their kind, and in especial he hurled curse after curse on her golden hair.

"Oh, hush! hush!" she said, and was then silent, for she feared her husband when she saw the evil effect of his humour. Geoffrey in the torrent of his anger stood up and moved away from the hearth; but suddenly stopped as he saw a new look of terror in his wife's eyes. He followed their glance, and then he too, shuddered—for there on the broken hearth-stone lay a golden streak as the point of the hair rose though the crack.

"Look, look!" she shrieked. "Is it some ghost of the dead! Come away—come away!" and seizing her husband by the wrist with the frenzy of madness, she pulled him from the room.

That night she was in a raging fever. The doctor of the district attended her at once, and special aid was telegraphed for to London. Geoffrey was in despair, and in his anguish at the danger of his young wife almost forgot his own crime and its consequences. In the evening the doctor had to leave to attend to others; but he left Geoffrey in charge of his wife. His last words were:

"Remember, you must humour her till I come in the morning, or till some other doctor has her case in hand. What you have to dread is another attack of emotion. See that she is kept warm. Nothing more can be done."

Late in the evening, when the rest of the household had retired, Geoffrey's wife got up from her bed and called to her husband.

"Come!" she said. "Come to the old hall! I know where the gold comes from! I want to see it grow!"

Geoffrey would fain have stopped her, but he feared for her life or reason on the one hand, and lest in a paroxysm she should shriek out her terrible suspicion, and seeing that it was useless to try to prevent her, wrapped a warm rug around her and went with her to the old hall. When they entered, she turned and shut the door and locked it.

"We want no strangers amongst us three tonight!" she whispered with a wan smile.

"We three! nay we are but two," said Geoffrey with a shudder; he feared to say more.

"Sit here," said his wife as she put out the light. "Sit here by the hearth and watch the gold growing. The silver moonlight is jealous! See, it steals along the floor towards the gold—our gold!" Geoffrey looked with growing horror, and saw that during the hours that had passed the golden hair had protruded further through the broken hearth-stone. He tried to hide it by placing his feet over the broken place; and his wife, drawing her chair beside him, leant over and laid her head on his shoulder.

"Now do not stir, dear," she said; "let us sit still and watch. We shall find the secret of the growing gold!" He passed his arm round her and sat silent; and as the moonlight stole along the floor she sank to sleep.

He feared to wake her; and so sat silent and miserable as the hours stole away.

Before his horror-struck eyes the golden-hair from the broken stone grew and grew; and as it increased, so his heart got colder and colder, till at last he had not power to stir, and sat with eyes full of terror watching his doom.

In the morning when the London doctor came, neither Geoffrey nor his wife could be found. Search was made in all the rooms, but without avail. As a last resource the great door of the old hall was broken open, and those who entered saw a grim and sorry sight.

There by the deserted hearth Geoffrey Brent and his young wife sat cold and white and dead. Her face was peaceful, and her eyes were closed in sleep; but his face was a sight that made all who saw it shudder, for there was on it a look of unutterable horror. The eyes were open and stared glassily at his feet, which were twined with tresses of golden hair, streaked with grey, which came through the broken hearth-stone.

In the Court of the Dragon

Robert W. Chambers

Oh, thou who burn'st in heart for those who burn
In Hell, whose fires thyself shall feed in turn;
How long be crying—"Mercy on them, God!"
Why, who art thou to teach and He to learn?

In the church of St. Barnabé Vespers were over; the clergy left the altar; the little choir-boys flocked across the chancel and settled in the stalls. A Suisse in rich uniform marched down the south aisle, sounding his staff at every fourth step on the stone pavement; behind him came that eloquent preacher and good man, Monseigneur C——.

My chair was near the chancel rail. I now turned toward the west end of the church. The other people between the altar and the pulpit turned too. There was a little scraping and rustling while the congregation seated itself again; the preacher mounted the pulpit stairs, and the organ voluntary ceased.

I had always found the organ-playing at St. Barnabé highly interesting. Learned and scientific it was, too much so for my small knowledge, but expressing a vivid if cold intelligence. Moreover, it possessed the French quality of taste: taste reigned supreme, self-controlled, dignified and reticent.

To-day, however, from the first chord I had felt a change for the worse, a sinister change. During vespers it had been chiefly the chancel organ which supported the beautiful choir, but now and again, quite wantonly as it seemed, from the west gallery where the great organ stands, a heavy hand had struck across the church at the serene peace of those clear voices. It was something more than harsh and dissonant, and it betrayed no lack of skill. As it recurred again and again, it set me thinking of what my architect's books say about the custom in early times to consecrate the choir as soon as it was built, and that the nave, being finished sometimes half a century later, often did not get any blessing at all: I wondered idly if that had been the case at St. Barnabé, and whether something not usually supposed to be at home in a Christian church might have entered undetected and taken possession of the west gallery. I had read of such things happening, too, but not in works on architecture.

Then I remembered that St. Barnabé was not much more than a hundred years old, and smiled at the incongruous association of mediaeval superstitions with that cheerful little piece of eighteenth century rococo.

But now vespers were over, and there should have followed a few quiet chords, fit to accompany meditation, while we waited for the sermon. Instead of that, the discord at the lower end of the church broke out with the departure of the clergy, as if now nothing could control it.

I belong to those children of an older and simpler generation who do not love to seek for psychological subtleties in art; and I have ever refused to find in music anything more than melody and harmony, but I felt that in the labyrinth of sounds now issuing from that instrument there was something being hunted. Up and down the pedals chased him, while the manuals blared approval. Poor devil! whoever he was, there seemed small hope of escape!

My nervous annoyance changed to anger. Who was doing this? How dare he play like that in the midst of divine service? I glanced at the people near me: not one appeared to be in the least disturbed. The placid brows of the kneeling nuns, still turned towards the altar, lost none of their devout abstraction under the pale shadow of their white head-dress. The fashionable lady beside me was looking expectantly at Monseigneur C——. For all her face betrayed, the organ might have been singing an Ave Maria.

But now, at last, the preacher had made the sign of the cross, and commanded silence. I turned to him gladly. Thus far I had not found the rest I had counted on when I entered St. Barnabé that afternoon.

I was worn out by three nights of physical suffering and mental trouble: the last had been the worst, and it was an exhausted body, and a mind benumbed and yet acutely sensitive, which I had brought to my favourite church for healing. For I had been reading *The King in Yellow*.

"The sun ariseth; they gather themselves together and lay them down in their dens." Monseigneur C—— delivered his text in a calm voice, glancing quietly over the congregation. My eyes turned, I knew not why, toward the lower end of the church. The organist was coming from behind his pipes, and passing along the gallery on his way out, I saw him disappear by a small door that leads to some stairs which descend directly to the street. He was a slender man, and his face was as white as his coat was black. "Good riddance!" I thought, "with your wicked music! I hope your assistant will play the closing voluntary."

With a feeling of relief, with a deep, calm feeling of relief, I turned back to the mild face in the pulpit and settled myself to listen. Here, at last, was the ease of mind I longed for.

"My children," said the preacher, "one truth the human soul finds hardest of all to learn; that it has nothing to fear. It can never be made to see that nothing can really harm it."

"Curious doctrine!" I thought, "for a Catholic priest. Let us see how he will reconcile that with the Fathers."

"Nothing can really harm the soul," he went on, in, his coolest, clearest tones, "because—"

But I never heard the rest; my eye left his face, I knew not for what reason, and sought the lower end of the church. The same man was coming out from behind the organ, and was passing along the gallery *the same way*. But there had not been time for him to return, and if he had returned, I must have seen him. I felt a faint chill, and my heart sank; and yet, his going and coming were no affair of mine. I looked at him: I could not look away from his black figure and his white face. When he was exactly opposite to me, he turned and sent across the church straight into my eyes, a look of hate, intense and deadly: I have never seen any other like it; would to God I might never see it again! Then he disappeared by the same door through which I had watched him depart less than sixty seconds before.

I sat and tried to collect my thoughts. My first sensation was like that of a very young child badly hurt, when it catches its breath before crying out.

To suddenly find myself the object of such hatred was exquisitely painful: and this man was an utter stranger. Why should he hate me so? Me, whom he had never seen before? For the moment all other sensation was merged in this one pang: even fear was subordinate to grief, and for that moment I never doubted; but in the next I began to reason, and a sense of the incongruous came to my aid.

As I have said, St. Barnabé is a modern church. It is small and well lighted; one sees all over it almost at a glance. The organ gallery gets a strong white light from a row of long windows in the clere-story, which have not even colored glass.

The pulpit being in the middle of the church, it followed that, when I was turned toward it, whatever moved at the west end could not fail to attract my eye. When the organist passed it was no wonder that I saw him: I had simply miscalculated the interval between his first and his second passing. He had come in that last time by the other side-door. As for the look which had so upset me, there had been no such thing, and I was a nervous fool.

I looked about. This was a likely place to harbour supernatural horrors! That clear-cut, reasonable face of Monseigneur C——, his collected manner and easy, graceful gestures, were they not just a little discouraging to the notion of a gruesome mystery? I glanced above his head, and almost laughed. That flyaway lady supporting one corner of the pulpit canopy, which looked like a fringed damask table-cloth in a high wind, at the first attempt of a basilisk to pose up there in the organ loft, she would point her gold trumpet at him, and puff him out of existence! I laughed to myself over this conceit, which, at the time, I thought very amusing, and sat and chaffed myself and everything else, from the old harpy outside the railing, who had made me pay ten centimes for my chair, before she would let me in (she was more like a basilisk, I told myself, than was my organist with the anæmic complexion): from that grim old dame, to, yes, alas! Monseigneur C—— himself. For all devoutness had fled. I had never yet done such a thing in my life, but now I felt a desire to mock.

As for the sermon, I could not hear a word of it for the jingle in my ears of

"The skirts of St. Paul has reached.
Having preached us those six Lent lectures,
More unctuous than ever he preached":

keeping time to the most fantastic and irreverent thoughts.

It was no use to sit there any longer: I must get out of doors and shake myself free from this hateful mood. I knew the rudeness I was committing, but still I rose and left the church.

A spring sun was shining on the rue St. Honoré, as I ran down the church steps. On one corner stood a barrow full of yellow jonquils, pale violets from the Riviera, dark Russian violets, and white Roman hyacinths in a golden cloud of mimosa. The street was full of Sunday pleasure-seekers. I swung my cane and laughed with the rest. Some one overtook and passed me. He never turned, but there was the same deadly malignity in his white profile that there had been in his eyes. I watched him as long as I could see him. His lithe back expressed the same menace; every step that carried him away from me seemed to bear him on some errand connected with my destruction.

I was creeping along, my feet almost refusing to move. There began to dawn in me a sense of responsibility for something long forgotten. It began to seem as if I deserved that which he threatened: it reached a long way back—a long, long way back. It had lain dormant all these years: it was there, though, and presently it would rise and confront me. But I would try to escape; and I stumbled as best I could into the rue de Rivoli, across the Place de la Concorde and on to the Quai. I looked with sick eyes upon the sun, shining through the white foam of the fountain, pouring over the backs of the dusky bronze river-gods, on the far-away Arc, a structure of amethyst mist, on the countless vistas of gray stems and bare branches faintly green. Then I saw him again coming down one of the chestnut alleys of the Cours la Reine.

I left the river side, plunged blindly across to the Champs Elysées and turned toward the Arc. The setting sun was sending its rays along the green sward of the Rond-point: in the full glow he sat on a bench, children and young mothers all about him. He was nothing but a Sunday lounger, like the others, like myself. I said the words almost aloud, and all the while I gazed on the malignant hatred of his face. But he was not looking at me. I crept past and dragged my leaden feet up the Avenue. I knew that every time I met him brought him nearer to the accomplishment of his purpose and my fate. And still I tried to save myself.

The last rays of sunset were pouring through the great Arc. I passed under it, and met him face to face. I had left him far down the Champs Elysées, and yet he came in with a stream of people who were returning from the Bois de Boulogne. He came so close that he brushed me. His slender frame felt like iron inside its loose black covering. He showed no signs of haste, nor of fatigue, nor of any human feeling. His whole being expressed one thing: the will, and the power to work me evil.

In anguish I watched him where he went down the broad crowded Avenue, that was all flashing with wheels and the trappings of horses and the helmets of the Garde Republicaine.

He was soon lost to sight; then I turned and fled. Into the Bois, and far out beyond it—I know not where I went, but after a long while as it seemed to me, night had fallen, and I found myself sitting at a table before a small café. I had wandered back into the Bois. It was hours now since I had seen him. Physical fatigue and mental suffering had left me no power to think or feel. I was tired, so tired! I longed to hide away in my own den. I resolved to go home. But that was a long way off.

I live in the Court of the Dragon, a narrow passage that leads from the rue de Rennes to the rue du Dragon.

It is an "impasse"; traversable only for foot passengers. Over the entrance on the rue de Rennes is a balcony, supported by an iron dragon. Within the court tall old houses rise on either side, and close the ends that give on the two streets. Huge gates, swung back during the day into the walls of the deep archways, close this court, after midnight, and one must enter then by ringing at certain small doors on the side. The sunken pavement collects unsavory pools. Steep stairways pitch down to doors that open on the court. The ground floors are occupied by shops of second-hand dealers, and by iron workers. All day long the place rings with the clink of hammers and the clang of metal bars.

Unsavory as it is below, there is cheerfulness, and comfort, and hard, honest work above.

Five flights up are the ateliers of architects and painters, and the hiding-places of middle-aged students like myself who want to live alone. When I first came here to live I was young, and not alone.

I had to walk a while before any conveyance appeared, but at last, when I had almost reached the Arc de Triomphe again, an empty cab came along and I took it.

From the Arc to the rue de Rennes is a drive of more than half an hour, especially when one is conveyed by a tired cab horse that has been at the mercy of Sunday fête makers.

There had been time before I passed under the Dragon's wings to meet my enemy over and over again, but I never saw him once, and now refuge was close at hand.

Before the wide gateway a small mob of children were playing. Our concierge and his wife walked among them, with their black poodle, keeping order; some couples were waltzing on the side-walk. I returned their greetings and hurried in.

All the inhabitants of the court had trooped out into the street. The place was quite deserted, lighted by a few lanterns hung high up, in which the gas burned dimly.

My apartment was at the top of a house, halfway down the court, reached by a staircase that descended almost into the street, with only a bit of passageway intervening. I set my foot on the threshold of the open door, the friendly old ruinous stairs rose before me, leading up to rest and shelter. Looking back over my right shoulder, I saw *him,* ten paces off. He must have entered the court with me.

He was coming straight on, neither slowly, nor swiftly, but straight on to me. And now he was looking at me. For the first time since our eyes encountered across the church they met now again, and I knew that the time had come.

Retreating backward, down the court, I faced him. I meant to escape by the entrance on the rue du Dragon. His eyes told me that I never should escape.

It seemed ages while we were going, I retreating, he advancing, down the court in perfect silence; but at last I felt the shadow of the archway, and the next step brought me within it. I had meant to turn here and spring through into the street. But the shadow was not that of an archway; it was that of a vault. The great doors on the rue du Dragon were closed. I felt this by the blackness which surrounded me, and at the same instant I read it in his face. How his face gleamed in the darkness, drawing swiftly nearer! The deep vaults, the huge closed doors, their cold iron clamps were all on his side. The thing which he had threatened had arrived: it gathered and bore down on me from the fathomless shadows; the point from which it would strike was his infernal eyes. Hopeless, I set my back against the barred doors and defied him.

There was a scraping of chairs on the stone floor, and a rustling as the congregation rose. I could hear the Suisse's staff in the south aisle, preceding Monseigneur C—— to the sacristy.

The kneeling nuns, roused from their devout abstraction, made their reverence and went away. The fashionable lady, my neighbor, rose also, with graceful reserve. As she departed her glance just flitted over my face in disapproval.

Half dead, or so it seemed to me, yet intensely alive to every trifle, I sat among the leisurely moving crowd, then rose too and went toward the door.

I had slept through the sermon. Had I slept through the sermon? I looked up and saw him passing along the gallery to his place. Only his side I saw; the thin bent arm in its black covering looked like one of those devilish, nameless instruments which lie in the disused torture-chambers of mediaeval castles.

But I had escaped him, though his eyes had said I should not. *Had* I escaped him? That which gave him the power over me came back out of oblivion, where I had hoped to keep it. For I knew him now. Death and the awful abode of lost souls, whither my weakness long ago had sent him—they had changed him for every other eye, but not for mine. I had recognized him almost from the first; I had never doubted what he was come to do; and now I knew while my body sat safe in the cheerful little church, he had been hunting my soul in the Court of the Dragon.

I crept to the door; the organ broke out overhead with a blare. A dazzling light filled the church, blotting the altar from my eyes. The people faded away, the arches, the vaulted roof vanished. I raised my seared eyes to the fathomless glare, and I saw the black stars hanging in the heavens: and the wet winds from the Lake of Hali chilled my face.

And now, far away, over leagues of tossing cloud-waves, I saw the moon dripping with spray; and beyond, the towers of Carcosa rose behind the moon.

Death and the awful abode of lost souls, whither my weakness long ago had sent him, had changed him for every other eye but mine. And now I heard *his voice*, rising, swelling, thundering through the flaring light, and as I fell, the radiance increasing, increasing, poured over me in waves of flame. Then I sank into the depths, and I heard the King in Yellow whispering to my soul: "It is a fearful thing to fall into the hands of the living God!"

Sister Maddelena

Ralph Adams Cram

ACROSS THE VALLEY OF THE ORETO FROM MONREALE, ON THE slopes of the mountains just above the little village of Parco, lies the old convent of Sta. Catarina. From the cloister terrace at Monreale you can see its pale walls and the slim campanile of its chapel rising from the crowded citron and mulberry orchards that flourish, rank and wild, no longer cared for by pious and loving hands. From the rough road that climbs the mountains to Assunto, the convent is invisible, a gnarled and ragged olive grove intervening, and a spur of cliffs as well, while from Palermo one sees only the speck of white, flashing in the sun, indistinguishable from the many similar gleams of desert monastery or pauper village.

Partly because of this seclusion, partly by reason of its extreme beauty, partly, it may be, because the present owners are more than charming and gracious in their pressing hospitality, Sta. Catarina seems to preserve an element of the poetic, almost magical; and as I drove with the Cavaliere Valguanera one evening in March out of Palermo, along the garden valley of the Oreto, then up the mountain side where the warm light of the spring sunset swept across from Monreale, lying golden and mellow on the luxuriant growth of figs, and olives, and orange-trees, and fantastic cacti, and so up to where the path of the convent swung off to the right round a dizzy point of cliff that reached out gaunt and gray from the olives below,—as I drove thus in the balmy air, and saw of a sudden a vision of creamy walls and orange roofs, draped in fantastic festoons of roses, with a single curving palm-tree stuck black and feathery against the gold sunset, it is hardly to be wondered at that I should slip into a mood of visionary enjoyment, looking for a time on the whole thing as the misty phantasm of a summer dream.

The Cavaliere had introduced himself to us,—Tom Rendel and me,—one morning soon after we reached Palermo, when, in the first bewilderment of architects in this paradise of art and color, we were working nobly at our sketches in that dream of delight, the Capella Palatina. He was himself an amateur archæologist, he told us, and passionately devoted to his island; so he felt impelled to speak to any one whom he saw appreciating the almost—and in a way fortunately—unknown beauties of Palermo. In a little time we were fully acquainted, and talking like the oldest friends. Of course he knew acquaintances of Rendel's,—some one always does: this time they were officers on the tubby U. S. S. *Quinebaug*, that, during the summer of 1888, was trying to uphold the maritime honor of the United States in European waters. Luckily for us, one of the officers was a kind of cousin of Rendel's, and came from Baltimore as well, so, as he had visited at the Cavaliere's place, we were soon invited to do the same. It was in this way that, with the luck that attends Rendel wherever he goes, we came to see something of domestic life in Italy, and that I found myself involved in another of those adventures for which I naturally sought so little.

I wonder if there is any other place in Sicily so faultless as Sta. Catarina? Taormina is a paradise, an epitome of all that is beautiful in Italy,—Venice excepted. Girgenti is a solemn epic, with its golden temples between the sea and hills. Cefalú is wild and strange, and Monreale a vision out of a fairy tale; but Sta. Catarina!—

Fancy a convent of creamy stone and rose-red brick perched on a ledge of rock midway between earth and heaven, the cliff falling almost sheer to the valley two hundred feet and more, the mountain rising behind straight towards the sky; all the rocks covered with cactus and dwarf fig-trees, the convent draped in smothering roses, and in front a terrace with a fountain in the midst; and then—nothing—between you and the sapphire sea, six miles away. Below stretches the Eden valley, the Concha d'Oro, gold-green fig orchards alternating with smoke-blue olives, the mountains rising on either hand and sinking undulously away towards the bay where, like a magic city of ivory and nacre, Palermo lies guarded by the twin mountains, Monte Pellegrino and Capo Zafferano, arid rocks like dull amethysts, rose in sunlight, violet in shadow: lions couchant, guarding the sleeping town.

Seen as we saw it for the first time that hot evening in March, with the golden lambent light pouring down through the valley, making it in verity a "shell of gold," sitting in Indian chairs on the terrace, with the perfume of roses and jasmines all around us, the valley of the Oreto, Palermo, Sta. Catarina, Monreale,—all were but parts of a dreamy vision, like the heavenly city of Sir Percivale, to attain which he passed across the golden bridge that burned after him as he vanished in the intolerable light of the Beatific Vision.

It was all so unreal, so phantasmal, that I was not surprised in the least when, late in the evening after the ladies had gone to their rooms, and the Cavaliere, Tom, and I were stretched out in chairs on the terrace, smoking lazily under the multitudinous stars, the Cavaliere said, "There is something I really must tell you both before you go to bed, so that you may be spared any unnecessary alarm."

"You are going to say that the place is haunted," said Rendel, feeling vaguely on the floor beside him for his glass of Amaro: "thank you; it is all it needs."

The Cavaliere smiled a little: "Yes, that is just it. Sta. Catarina is really haunted; and much as my reason revolts against the idea as superstitious and savoring of priestcraft, yet I must acknowledge I see no way of avoiding the admission. I do not presume to offer any explanations, I only state the fact; and the fact is that to-night one or other of you will, in all human—or unhuman—probability, receive a visit from Sister Maddelena. You need not be in the least afraid, the apparition is perfectly gentle and harmless; and, moreover, having seen it once, you will never see it again. No one sees the ghost, or whatever it is, but once, and that usually the first night he spends in the house. I myself saw the thing eight—nine years ago, when I first bought the place from the Marchese di Muxaro; all my people have seen it, nearly all my guests, so I think you may as well be prepared."

"Then tell us what to expect," I said; "what kind of a ghost is this nocturnal visitor?"

"It is simple enough. Some time to-night you will suddenly awake and see before you a Carmelite nun who will look fixedly at you, say distinctly and very sadly, 'I cannot sleep,' and then vanish. That is all, it is hardly worth speaking of, only some people are terribly frightened if they are visited unwarned by strange apparitions; so I tell you this that you may be prepared."

"This was a Carmelite convent, then?" I said.

"Yes; it was suppressed after the unification of Italy, and given to the House of Muxaro; but the family died out, and I bought it. There is a story about the ghostly nun, who was only a novice, and even that unwillingly, which gives an interest to an otherwise very commonplace and uninteresting ghost."

"I beg that you will tell it us," cried Rendel.

"There is a storm coming," I added, "See, the lightning is flashing already up among the mountains at the head of the valley; if the story is tragic, as it must be, now is just the time for it. You will tell it, will you not?"

The Cavaliere smiled that slow, cryptic smile of his that was so unfathomable.

"As you say, there is a shower coming, and as we have fierce tempests here, we might not sleep; so perhaps we may as well sit up a little longer, and I will tell you the story."

The air was utterly still, hot and oppressive; the rich, sick odor of the oranges just bursting into bloom came up from the valley in a gently rising tide. The sky, thick with stars, seemed mirrored in the rich foliage below, so numerous were the glow-worms under the still trees, and the fireflies that gleamed in the hot air. Lightning flashed fitfully from the darkening west; but as yet no thunder broke the heavy silence.

The Cavaliere lighted another cigar, and pulled a cushion under his head so that he could look down to the distant lights of the city. "This is the story," he said.

"Once upon a time, late in the last century, the Duca di Castiglione was attached to the court of Charles III, King of the Two Sicilies, down at Palermo. They tell me he was very ambitious, and, not content with marrying his son to one of the ladies of the House of Tuscany, had betrothed his only daughter, Rosalia, to Prince Antonio, a cousin of the king. His whole life was wrapped up in the fame of his family, and he quite forgot all domestic affection in his madness for dynastic glory. His son was a worthy scion, cold and proud; but Rosalia was, according to legend, utterly the reverse,—a passionate, beautiful girl, wilful and headstrong, and careless of her family and the world.

"The time had nearly come for her to marry Prince Antonio, a typical *roué* of the Spanish court, when, through the treachery of a servant, the Duke discovered that his daughter was in love with a young military officer whose name I don't remember, and that an elopement had been planned to take place the next night. The fury and dismay of the old autocrat passed belief; he saw in a flash the downfall of all his hopes of family aggrandizement through union with the royal house, and, knowing well the spirit of his daughter, despaired of ever bringing her to subjection. Nevertheless, he attacked her unmercifully, and, by bullying and threats, by imprisonment, and even bodily chastisement, he tried to break her spirit and bend her to his indomitable will. Through his power at court he had the lover sent away to the mainland, and for more than a year he held his daughter closely imprisoned in his palace on the Toledo,—that one, you may remember, on the right, just beyond the Via del Collegio dei Gesuiti, with the beautiful iron-work grilles at all the windows, and the painted frieze. But nothing could move her, nothing bend her stubborn will; and at last, furious at the girl he could not govern, Castiglione sent her to this convent, then one of the few houses of barefoot Carmelite nuns in Italy. He stipulated that she should take the name of Maddelena, that he should never hear of her again, and that she should be held an absolute prisoner in this conventual castle.

"Rosalia—or Sister Maddelena, as she was now—believed her lover dead, for her father had given her good proofs of this, and she believed him; nevertheless she refused to marry another, and seized upon the convent life as a blessed relief from the tyranny of her maniacal father.

"She lived here for four or five years; her name was forgotten at court and in her father's palace. Rosalia di Castiglione was dead, and only Sister Maddelena lived, a Carmelite nun, in her place.

"In 1798 Ferdinand IV found himself driven from his throne on the mainland, his kingdom divided, and he himself forced to flee to Sicily. With him came the lover of the dead Rosalia, now high in military honor. He on his part had thought Rosalia dead, and it was only by accident that he found that she still lived, a Carmelite nun. Then began the second act of the romance that until then had been only sadly commonplace, but now became dark and tragic. Michele—Michele Biscari,—that was his name; I remember now—haunted the region of the convent, striving to communicate with Sister Maddelena; and at last, from the cliffs over us, up there among the citrons—you will see by the next flash of lightning—he saw her in the great cloister, recognized her in her white habit, found her the same dark and splendid beauty of six years before, only made more beautiful by her white habit and her rigid life. By and by he found a day when she was alone, and tossed a ring to her as she stood in the midst of the cloister. She looked up, saw him, and from that moment lived only to love him in life as she had loved his memory in the death she had thought had overtaken him.

"With the utmost craft they arranged their plans together. They could not speak, for a word would have aroused the other inmates of the convent. They could make signs only when Sister Maddelena was alone. Michele could throw notes to her from the cliff,—a feat demanding a strong arm, as you will see, if you measure the distance with your eye,—and she could drop replies from the window over the cliff, which he picked up at the bottom. Finally he succeeded in casting into the cloister a coil of light rope. The girl fastened it to the bars of one of the windows, and—so great is the madness of love—Biscari actually climbed the rope from the valley to the window of the cell, a distance of almost two hundred feet, with but three little craggy resting-places in all that height. For nearly a month these nocturnal visits were undiscovered, and Michele had almost completed his arrangements for carrying the girl from Sta. Catarina and away to Spain, when unfortunately one of the sisters, suspecting some mystery, from the changed face of Sister Maddelena, began investigating, and at length discovered the rope neatly coiled up by the nun's window, and hidden under some clinging vines. She instantly told the Mother Superior; and together they watched from a window in the crypt of the chapel,—the only place, as you will see to-morrow, from which one could see the window of Sister Maddelena's cell. They saw the figure of Michele daringly ascending the slim rope; watched hour after hour, the Sister remaining while the Superior went to say the hours in the chapel, at each of which Sister Maddelena was present; and at last, at prime, just as the sun was rising, they saw the figure slip down the rope, watched the rope drawn up and concealed, and knew that Sister Maddelena was in their hands for vengeance and punishment,—a criminal.

"The next day, by the order of the Mother Superior, Sister Maddelena was imprisoned in one of the cells under the chapel, charged with her guilt, and commanded to make full and complete confession. But not a word would she say, although they offered her forgiveness if she would tell the name of her lover. At last the Superior told her that after this fashion would they act the coming night: she herself would be placed in the crypt, tied in front of the window, her mouth gagged; that the rope would be lowered, and the lover allowed to approach even to the sill of her window, and at that moment the rope would be cut, and before her eyes her lover would be dashed to death on the ragged cliffs. The plan was feasible, and Sister Maddelena knew that the Mother was perfectly capable of carrying it out. Her stubborn spirit was broken, and in the only way possible; she begged for mercy, for the sparing of her lover. The Mother Superior was deaf at first; at last she said, 'It is your life or his. I will spare him on condition that you sacrifice your own life.' Sister Maddelena accepted the terms joyfully, wrote a last farewell to Michele, fastened the note to the rope, and with her own hands cut the rope and saw it fall coiling down to the valley bed far below.

"Then she silently prepared for death; and at midnight, while her lover was wandering, mad with the horror of impotent fear, around the white walls of the convent, Sister Maddelena, for love of Michele, gave up her life. How, was never known. That she was indeed dead was only a suspicion, for when Biscari finally compelled the civil authorities to enter the convent, claiming that murder had been done there, they found no sign. Sister Maddelena had been sent to the parent house of the barefoot Carmelites at Avila in Spain, so the Superior stated, because of her incorrigible contumacy. The old Duke of Castiglione refused to stir hand or foot in the matter, and Michele, after fruitless attempts to prove that the Superior of Sta. Catarina had caused the death, was forced to leave Sicily. He sought in Spain for very long; but no sign of the girl was to be found, and at last he died, exhausted with suffering and sorrow.

"Even the name of Sister Maddelena was forgotten, and it was not until the convents were suppressed, and this house came into the hands of the Muxaros, that her story was remembered. It was then that the ghost began to appear; and, an explanation being necessary, the story, or legend, was obtained from one of the nuns who still lived after the suppression. I think the fact—for it is a fact—of the ghost rather goes to prove that Michele was right, and that poor Rosalia gave her life a sacrifice for love,—whether in accordance with the terms of the legend or not, I cannot say. One or the other of you will probably see her to-night. You might ask her for the facts. Well, that is all the story of Sister Maddelena, known in the world as Rosalia di Castiglione. Do you like it?"

"It is admirable," said Rendel, enthusiastically. "But I fancy I should rather look on it simply as a story, and not as a warning of what is going to happen. I don't much fancy real ghosts myself."

"But the poor Sister is quite harmless"; and Valguanera rose, stretching himself. "My servants say she wants a mass said over her, or something of that kind; but I haven't much love for such priestly hocus-pocus,—I beg your pardon" (turning to me), "I had forgotten that you were a Catholic: forgive my rudeness."

"My dear Cavaliere, I beg you not to apologize. I am sorry you cannot see things as I do; but don't for a moment think I am hypersensitive."

"I have an excuse,—perhaps you will say only an explanation; but I live where I see all the absurdities and corruptions of the Church."

"Perhaps you let the accidents blind you to the essentials; but do not let us quarrel to-night,—see, the storm is close on us. Shall we go in?"

The stars were blotted out through nearly all the sky; low, thunderous clouds, massed at the head of the valley, were sweeping over so close that they seemed to brush the black pines on the mountain above us. To the south and east the storm-clouds had shut down almost to the sea, leaving a space of black sky where the moon in its last quarter was rising just to the left of Monte Pellegrino,—a black silhouette against the pallid moonlight. The rosy lightning flashed almost incessantly, and through the fitful darkness came the sound of bells across the valley, the rushing torrent below, and the dull roar of the approaching rain, with a deep organ point of solemn thunder through it all.

We fled indoors from the coming tempest, and taking our candles, said "good-night," and sought each his respective room.

My own was in the southern part of the old convent, giving on the terrace we had just quitted, and about over the main doorway. The rushing storm, as it swept down the valley with the swelling torrent beneath, was very fascinating, and after wrapping myself in a dressing-gown I stood for some time by the deeply embrasured window, watching the blazing lightning and the beating rain whirled by fitful gusts of wind around the spurs of the mountains. Gradually the violence of the shower seemed to decrease, and I threw myself down on my bed in the hot air, wondering if I really was to experience the ghostly visit the Cavaliere so confidently predicted.

I had thought out the whole matter to my own satisfaction, and fancied I knew exactly what I should do, in case Sister Maddelena came to visit me. The story touched me: the thought of the poor faithful girl who sacrificed herself for her lover,—himself, very likely, quite unworthy,—and who now could never sleep for reason of her unquiet soul, sent out into the storm of eternity without spiritual aid or counsel. I could not sleep; for the still vivid lightning, the crowding thoughts of the dead nun, and the shivering anticipation of my possible visitation, made slumber quite out of the question. No suspicion of sleepiness had visited me, when, perhaps an hour after midnight, came a sudden vivid flash of lightning, and, as my dazzled eyes began to regain the power of sight, I saw her as plainly as in life,—a tall figure, shrouded in the white habit of the Carmelites, her head bent, her hands clasped before her. In another flash of lightning she slowly raised her head and looked at me long and earnestly. She was very beautiful, like the Virgin of Beltraffio in the National Gallery,—more beautiful than I had supposed possible, her deep, passionate eyes very tender and pitiful in their pleading, beseeching glance. I hardly think I was frightened, or even startled, but lay looking steadily at her as she stood in the beating lightning.

Then she breathed, rather than articulated, with a voice that almost brought tears, so infinitely sad and sorrowful was it, "I cannot sleep!" and the liquid eyes grew more pitiful and questioning as bright tears fell from them down the pale dark face.

The figure began to move slowly towards the door, its eyes fixed on mine with a look that was weary and almost agonized. I leaped from the bed and stood waiting. A look of utter gratitude swept over the face, and, turning, the figure passed through the doorway.

Out into the shadow of the corridor it moved, like a drift of pallid storm-cloud, and I followed, all natural and instinctive fear or nervousness quite blotted out by the part I felt I was to play in giving rest to a tortured soul. The corridors were velvet black; but the pale figure floated before me always, an unerring guide, now but a thin mist on the utter night, now white and clear in the bluish lightning through some window or doorway.

Down the stairway into the lower hall, across the refectory, where the great frescoed Crucifixion flared into sudden clearness under the fitful lightning, out into the silent cloister.

It was very dark. I stumbled along the heaving bricks, now guiding myself by a hand on the whitewashed wall, now by a touch on a column wet with the storm. From all the eaves the rain was dripping on to the pebbles at the foot of the arcade: a pigeon, startled from the capital where it was sleeping, beat its way into the cloister close. Still the white thing drifted before me to the farther side of the court, then along the cloister at right angles, and paused before one of the many doorways that led to the cells.

A sudden blaze of fierce lightning, the last now of the fleeting trail of storm, leaped around us, and in the vivid light I saw the white face turned again with the look of overwhelming desire, of beseeching pathos, that had choked my throat with an involuntary sob when first I saw Sister Maddelena. In the brief interval that ensued after the flash, and before the roaring thunder burst like the crash of battle over the trembling convent, I heard again the sorrowful words, "I cannot sleep," come from the impenetrable darkness. And when the lightning came again, the white figure was gone.

I wandered around the courtyard, searching in vain for Sister Maddelena, even until the moonlight broke through the torn and sweeping fringes of the storm. I tried the door where the white figure vanished: it was locked; but I had found what I sought, and, carefully noting its location, went back to my room, but not to sleep.

In the morning the Cavaliere asked Rendel and me which of us had seen the ghost, and I told him my story; then I asked him to grant me permission to sift the thing to the bottom; and he courteously gave the whole matter into my charge, promising that he would consent to anything.

I could hardly wait to finish breakfast; but no sooner was this done than, forgetting my morning pipe, I started with Rendel and the Cavaliere to investigate.

"I am sure there is nothing in that cell," said Valguanera, when we came in front of the door I had marked. "It is curious that you should have chosen the door of the very cell that tradition assigns to Sister Maddelena; but I have often examined that room myself, and I am sure that there is no chance for anything to be concealed. In fact, I had the floor taken up once, soon after I came here, knowing the room was that of the mysterious Sister, and thinking that there, if anywhere, the monastic crime would have taken place; still, we will go in, if you like."

He unlocked the door, and we entered, one of us, at all events, with a beating heart. The cell was very small, hardly eight feet square. There certainly seemed no opportunity for concealing a body in the tiny place; and although I sounded the floor and walls, all gave a solid, heavy answer,—the unmistakable sound of masonry.

For the innocence of the floor the Cavaliere answered. He had, he said, had it all removed, even to the curving surfaces of the vault below; yet somewhere in this room the body of the murdered girl was concealed,—of this I was certain. But where? There seemed no answer; and I was compelled to give up the search for the moment, somewhat to the amusement of Valguanera, who had watched curiously to see if I could solve the mystery.

But I could not forget the subject, and towards noon started on another tour of investigation. I procured the keys from the Cavaliere, and examined the cells adjoining; they were apparently the same, each with its window opposite the door, and nothing—Stay, were they the same? I hastened into the suspected cell; it was as I thought: this cell, being on the corner, could have had two windows, yet only one was visible, and that to the left, at right angles with the doorway. Was it imagination? As I sounded the wall opposite the door, where the other window should be, I fancied that the sound was a trifle less solid and dull. I was becoming excited. I dashed back to the cell on the right, and, forcing open the little window, thrust my head out.

It was found at last! In the smooth surface of the yellow wall was a rough space, following approximately the shape of the other cell windows, not plastered like the rest of the wall, but showing the shapes of bricks through its thick coatings of whitewash. I turned with a gasp of excitement and satisfaction: yes, the embrasure of the wall was deep enough; what a wall it was!—four feet at least, and the opening of the window reached to the floor, though the window itself was hardly three feet square. I felt absolutely certain that the secret was solved, and called the Cavaliere and Rendel, too excited to give them an explanation of my theories.

They must have thought me mad when I suddenly began scraping away at the solid wall in front of the door; but in a few minutes they understood what I was about, for under the coatings of paint and plaster appeared the original bricks; and as my architectural knowledge had led me rightly, the space I had cleared was directly over a vertical joint between firm, workmanlike masonry on one hand, and rough amateurish work on the other, bricks laid anyway, and without order or science.

Rendel seized a pick, and was about to assail the rude wall, when I stopped him.

"Let us be careful," I said; "who knows what we may find?" So we set to work digging out the mortar around a brick at about the level of our eyes.

How hard the mortar had become! But a brick yielded at last, and with trembling fingers I detached it. Darkness within, yet beyond question there was a cavity there, not a solid wall; and with infinite care we removed another brick. Still the hole was too small to admit enough light from the dimly illuminated cell. With a chisel we pried at the sides of a large block of masonry, perhaps eight bricks in size. It moved, and we softly slid it from its bed.

Valguanera, who was standing watching us as we lowered the bricks to the floor, gave a sudden cry, a cry like that of a frightened woman,—terrible, coming from him. Yet there was cause.

Framed by the ragged opening of the bricks, hardly seen in the dim light, was a face, an ivory image, more beautiful than any antique bust, but drawn and distorted by unspeakable agony: the lovely mouth half open, as though gasping for breath; the eyes cast upward; and below, slim chiselled hands crossed on the breast, but clutching the folds of the white Carmelite habit, torture and agony visible in every tense muscle, fighting against the determination of the rigid pose.

We stood there breathless, staring at the pitiful sight, fascinated, bewitched. So this was the secret. With fiendish ingenuity, the rigid ecclesiastics had blocked up the window, then forced the beautiful creature to stand in the alcove, while with remorseless hands and iron hearts they had shut her into a living tomb. I had read of such things in romance; but to find the verity here, before my eyes—

Steps came down the cloister, and with a simultaneous thought we sprang to the door and closed it behind us. The room was sacred; that awful sight was not for curious eyes. The gardener was coming to ask some trivial question of Valguanera. The Cavaliere cut him short. "Pietro, go down to Parco and ask Padre Stefano to come here at once." (I thanked him with a glance.) "Stay!" He turned to me: "Signore, it is already two o'clock and too late for mass, is it not?"

I nodded.

Valguanera thought a moment, then he said, "Bring two horses; the Signor Americano will go with you,—do you understand?" Then, turning to me, "You will go, will you not? I think you can explain matters to Padre Stefano better than I."

"Of course I will go, more than gladly." So it happened that after a hasty luncheon I wound down the mountain to Parco, found Padre Stefano, explained my errand to him, found him intensely eager and sympathetic, and by five o'clock had him back at the convent with all that was necessary for the resting of the soul of the dead girl.

In the warm twilight, with the last light of the sunset pouring into the little cell through the window where almost a century ago Rosalia had for the last time said farewell to her lover, we gathered together to speed her tortured soul on its journey, so long delayed. Nothing was omitted; all the needful offices of the Church were said by Padre Stefano, while the light in the window died away, and the flickering flames of the candles carried by two of the acolytes from San Francesco threw fitful flashes of pallid light into the dark recess where the white face had prayed to Heaven for a hundred years.

Finally, the Padre took the asperge from the hands of one of the acolytes, and with a sign of the cross in benediction while he chanted the *Asperges*, gently sprinkled the holy water on the upturned face. Instantly the whole vision crumbled to dust, the face was gone, and where once the candlelight had flickered on the perfect semblance of the girl dead so very long, it now fell only on the rough bricks which closed the window, bricks laid with frozen hearts by pitiless hands.

But our task was not done yet. It had been arranged that Padre Stefano should remain at the convent all night, and that as soon as midnight made it possible he should say the first mass for the repose of the girl's soul. We sat on the terrace talking over the strange events of the last crowded hours, and I noted with satisfaction that the Cavaliere no longer spoke of the Church with that hardness, which had hurt me so often. It is true that the Padre was with us nearly all the time; but not only was Valguanera courteous, he was almost sympathetic; and I wondered if it might not prove that more than one soul benefited by the untoward events of the day.

With the aid of the astonished and delighted servants, and no little help as well from Signora Valguanera, I fitted up the long cold Altar in the chapel, and by midnight we had the gloomy sanctuary beautiful with flowers and candles. It was a curiously solemn service, in the first hour of the new day, in the midst of blazing candles and the thick incense, the odor of the opening orange-blooms drifting up in the fresh morning air, and mingling with the incense smoke and the perfume of flowers within. Many prayers were said that night for the soul of the dead girl, and I think many afterwards; for after the benediction I remained for a little time in my place, and when I rose from my knees and went towards the chapel door, I saw a figure kneeling still, and, with a start, recognized the form of the Cavaliere. I smiled with quiet satisfaction and gratitude, and went away softly, content with the chain of events that now seemed finished.

The next day the alcove was again walled up, for the precious dust could not be gathered together for transportation to consecrated ground; so I went down to the little cemetery at Parco for a basket of earth, which we cast in over the ashes of Sister Maddelena.

By and by, when Rendel and I went away, with great regret, Valguanera came down to Palermo with us; and the last act that we performed in Sicily was assisting him to order a tablet of marble, whereon was carved this simple inscription:—

HERE LIES THE BODY OF

ROSALIA DI CASTIGLIONI,

CALLED

SISTER MADDELENA.

HER SOUL

IS WITH HIM WHO GAVE IT.

To this I added in thought:—

"Let him that is without sin among you cast the first stone."

The Ghost of Mohammed Din

Clark Ashton Smith

"I'll wager a hundred rupees that you won't stay there over-night," said Nicholson.

It was late in the afternoon, and we were seated on the veranda of my friend's bungalow in the Begum suburb at Hyderabad. Our conversation had turned to ghosts, on which subject I was, at the time, rather skeptical, and Nicholson, after relating a number of blood-curdling stories, had finished by remarking that a nearby house, which was said to be haunted, would give me an excellent chance to put the matter to the test.

"Done!" I answered, laughing.

"It's no joking matter," said my friend, seriously. "However, if you really wish to encounter the ghost, I can easily secure you the necessary permission. The house, a six-roomed bungalow, owned by one Yussuf Au Borah, is tenanted only by the spirit who appears to regard it as his exclusive property.

"Two years ago it was occupied by a Moslem merchant named Mohammed Din, and his family and servants. One morning they found the merchant dead—stabbed through the heart, and no trace of his murderer, whose identity still remains unrevealed.

"Mohammed Din's people left, and the place was let to a Parsee up from Bombay on business. He vacated the premises abruptly about midnight, and told a wild tale the next morning of having encountered a number of disembodied spirits, describing the chief one as Mohammed Din.

"Several other people took the place in turn, but their occupancy was generally of short duration. All told tales similar to the Parsee's. Gradually it acquired a bad reputation, and the finding of tenants became impossible."

"Have you ever seen the ghost yourself?" I asked.

"Yes; I spent a night, or rather part of one, there, for I went out of the window about one o'clock. My nerves were not strong enough to stand it any longer. I wouldn't enter the place again for almost any sum of money."

Nicholson's story only confirmed my intention of occupying the haunted house. Armed with a firm disbelief in the supernatural, and a still firmer intention to prove it all rot, I felt myself equal to all the ghosts, native and otherwise, in India. Of my ability to solve the mystery, if there were any, I was quite assured.

"My friend," said Nicholson to Yussuf Ali Borah an hour later, "wishes to spend a night in your haunted bungalow."

The person addressed, a fat little Moslem gentleman, looked at me curiously.

"The house is at your service, Sahib," he said, "I presume that Nicholson Sahib has told you the experiences of the previous tenants?"

I replied that he had. "If the whole thing is not a trumped-up story, there is doubtless some trickery afoot," said I, "and I warn you that the trickster will not come off unharmed. I have a loaded revolver, and shall not hesitate to use it if I meet any disembodied spirits."

Yussuf's only answer was to shrug his shoulders.

He gave us the keys, and we set out for the bungalow, which was only a few minutes' walk distant. Night had fallen when we reached it. Nicholson unlocked the door and we entered, and lighting a lamp I had brought with me, set out on a tour of inspection. The furniture consisted chiefly of two charpoys, three tabourets, an old divan quite innocent of cushions, a broken punkah, a three-legged chair and a dilapidated rug. Everything was covered with dust; the shutters rattled disconsolately, and all the doors creaked. The other rooms were meagrely furnished. I could hear rats running about in the dark.

There was a compound adjoining, filled with rank reed and a solitary pipal tree. Nicholson said that the ghost generally appeared in one of the rooms opening upon it, and this I selected as the one in which to spend the night. It was a fitting place for ghosts to haunt. The ceiling sagged listlessly, and the one charpoy which it contained had a wobbly look.

"Sleep well," said Nicholson. "You will find the atmosphere of this spirit-ridden place most conducive to slumber."

"Rats!" said I.

"Yes, there are plenty of rats here," he answered as he went out.

Placing the lamp on a tabouret, I lay down, with some misgivings as to its stability, on the charpoy. Happily, these proved unfounded, and laying my revolver close at hand, I took out a newspaper and began to read.

Several hours passed and nothing unusual happened. The ghost failed to materialize, and about eleven, with my fine skepticism greatly strengthened, and feeling a trifle ashamed concerning the hundred rupees which my friend would have to hand over the next morning, I lay down and tried to go to sleep. I had no doubt that my threat about the revolver to Yussuf Ali Borah had checked any plans for scaring me that might have been entertained.

Scarcely were my eyes closed when all the doors and windows, which had been creaking and rattling all evening, took on renewed activity. A light breeze had sprung up, and one shutter, which hung only by a single hinge, began to drum a tune on the wall. The rats scuttled about with redoubled energy, and a particularly industrious fellow gnawed something in the further corner for about an hour. It was manifestly impossible to sleep. I seemed to hear whisperings in the air, and once thought that I detected faint footsteps going and coming through the empty rooms. A vague feeling of eeriness crept upon me, and it required a very strong mental effort to convince myself that these sounds were entirely due to imagination.

Finally the breeze died down, the loose shutter ceased to bang, the rat stopped gnawing, and comparative quiet being restored, I fell asleep. Two hours later I woke, and taking out my watch, saw, though the lamp had begun to burn dimly, that the hands pointed to two o'clock. I was about to turn over, when again I heard the mysterious footsteps, this time quite audibly. They seemed to approach my room, but when I judged them to be in the next apartment, ceased abruptly. I waited five minutes in a dead silence, with my nerves on edge and my scalp tingling.

Then I became aware that there was something between me and the opposite wall. At first it was a dim shadow, but as I watched, it darkened into a body. A sort of phosphorescent light emanated from it, surrounding it with pale radiance.

The lamp flared up and went out, but the figure was still visible. It was that of a tall native dressed in flowing white robes and a blue turban. He wore a bushy beard and had eyes like burning coals of fire. His gaze was directed intently upon me, and I felt cold shivers running up and down my spine. I wanted to shriek, but my tongue seemed glued to the roof of my mouth. The figure stepped forward and I noticed that the robe was red at the breast as though with blood.

This, then, was the ghost of Mohammed Din. Nicholson's story was true, and for a moment my conviction that the supernatural was all nonsense went completely to pieces. Only momentarily, however, for I remembered that I had a revolver, and the thought gave me courage. Perhaps it was a trick after all, and anger arose in me, and a resolve not to let the trickster escape unscathed.

I raised the weapon with a quick movement and fired. The figure being not over five paces distant, it was impossible to miss, but when the smoke had cleared it had not changed its position.

It began to advance, making no sound, and in a few moments was beside the charpoy. With one remaining vestige of courage I raised my revolver and pulled the trigger three times in succession, but without visible effect. I hurled the weapon at the figure's head, and heard it crash against the opposite wall an instant later. The apparition, though visible, was without tangibility.

Now it began to disappear. Very slowly at first it faded, then more rapidly until I could make out only the bare outlines. Another instant and all was gone but the outline of one hand, which hung motionless in the air. I got up and made a step towards it, then stopped abruptly, for the outlines again began to fill in, the hand to darken and solidify. Now I noticed something I had not before seen—a heavy gold ring set with some green gem, probably an emerald, appeared to be on the middle finger.

The hand began to move slowly past me towards the door opening into the next apartment. Lighting the lamp, I followed, all fear being thrown aside and desiring to find the explanation of the phenomenon. I could hear faint footfalls beneath the hand, as though the owner, though invisible, were still present. I followed it through the adjoining apartment and into the next, where it again stopped and hung motionless. One finger was pointed toward the further corner, where stood a tabouret, or stand.

Impelled, I think, by some force other than my own volition, I went over and lifting the tabouret, found a small wooden box, covered with dust, beneath.

Turning about I saw that the hand had disappeared.

Taking the box with me, I returned to my room. The thing was made of very hard wood and in size was perhaps ten inches in length by eight in width and four in height. It was light, and the contents rustled when I shook it. I guessed them to be letters or papers, but having nothing to pry the box open with, I concluded to wait until morning before trying to.

Strange as it may seem I soon fell asleep. You would naturally think that a man would not feel inclined to slumber immediately after encountering a disembodied spirit. I can give no explanation of it.

The sun was streaming through the window when I awoke, and so cheerful and matter-of-fact was the broad daylight that I wondered if the events of the night were not all a dream. The presence of the box, however, convinced me that they were not.

Nicholson came in and appeared much surprised and a trifle discomfited to find me still in possession.

"Well," he inquired, "what happened? What did you see?"

I told him what had occurred and produced the box as proof.

An hour afterwards, Nicholson, with a short native sword and considerable profanity, was trying to pry the thing open. He finally succeeded. Within were a number of closely-written sheets of paper and some letters, most of which were addressed to Mohammed Din.

The papers were mostly in the form of memoranda and business accounts such as would be made by a merchant. They were written in execrable Urdu, hopelessly jumbled together, and though all were dated, it was no small task to sort them out. The letters were mostly regarding business affairs, but several, which were written in a very fair hand, were from a cousin of Mohammed Din's, one Ali Bagh, an Agra horse-trader. These, too, with one exception, were commonplace enough. Nicholson knitted his brows as he read it, and then handed it to me. The greater part, being of little interest, has escaped my memory, but I recollect that the last paragraph ran thus:

"I do not understand how you came by the knowledge, nor why you wish to use it to ruin me. It is all true. If you have any love for me, forbear."

"What does that mean?" asked Nicholson. "What secret did Mohammed Din possess that he could have used to ruin his cousin?"

We went through the memoranda carefully, and near the bottom found the following, dated April 21, 1881, according to our notation:

> To-day I found the letters which I have long been seeking. They are ample proof of what I have long known, but have hitherto been unable to substantiate, that Ali Bagh is a counterfeiter, the chief of a large band. I have but to turn them over to the police, and he will be dragged away to jail, there to serve a term of many years. It will be good revenge—part compensation, at least, for the injuries he has done me.

"That explains Ali Bagh's letter," said Nicholson. "Mohammed Din was boastful enough to write to him, telling him that he knew of his guilt and intended to prove it."

Next were several sheets in a different hand and signed "Mallek Khan." Mallek Khan, it seemed, was a friend of Ali Bagh's, and the sheets were in the form of a letter. But being without fold, it was quite evident they had not been posted.

The communication related to certain counterfeiting schemes, and the names of a number of men implicated appeared. This, plainly, was the proof alluded to by Mohammed Din, and which he had threatened his cousin to turn over to the police.

There was nothing else of interest save the following in Mohammed Din's hand, dated April 17th, 1881:

"To-morrow I shall give the papers to the authorities. I have delayed too long, and was very foolish to write to Ali Bagh.

"I passed a man in the street today who bore a resemblance to my cousin. . . . I could not be sure . . . But if he is here, then may Allah help me, for he will hesitate at nothing. . . ."

What followed was illegible.

"On the night of April 21st," said Nicholson, "Mohammed Din was killed by a person or persons unknown." He paused and then went on: "This Ali Bagh is a man with whom I have had some dealings in horses, and an especially vicious crook it was that he got three hundred rupees out of me for. He has a bad reputation as a horse-dealer, and the Agra police have long been patiently seeking evidence of his implication in several bold counterfeiting schemes. Mallek Khan, one of his accomplices, was arrested, tried and sentenced to fifteen years' imprisonment, but refused to turn State's evidence on Ali Bagh. The police are convinced that Ali Bagh was as much, if not more implicated, than Mallek Khan, but they can do nothing for lack of proof. The turning over of these papers, however, as poor Mohammed Din would have done had he lived, will lead to his arrest and conviction.

"It was Ali Bagh who killed Mohammed Din, I am morally convinced, his motive, of course, being to prevent the disclosure of his guilt. Your extraordinary experience last night and the murdered man's papers point to it. Yet we can prove nothing, and your tale would be laughed at in court."

Some blank sheets remained in the bottom of the box, and my friend tilted them out as he spoke. They fluttered to the veranda and something rolled out from amongst them and lay glittering in the sunshine. It was a heavy gold ring set with an emerald—the very same that I had seen upon the apparition's finger several hours before.

A week or so later, as the result of the papers that Nicholson sent to the Agra police, accompanied by an explanatory note, one Ali Bagh, horse-trader, found himself on trial, charged with counterfeiting. It was a very short trial, his character and reputation going badly against him, and it being proven that he was the leader of the gang of which Mallek Khan was thought to be a member, he was sentenced to a somewhat longer term in jail than his accomplice.

The Rats in the Walls

H. P. Lovecraft

On July 16, 1923, I moved into Exham Priory after the last workman had finished his labours. The restoration had been a stupendous task, for little had remained of the deserted pile but a shell-like ruin; yet because it had been the seat of my ancestors I let no expense deter me. The place had not been inhabited since the reign of James the First, when a tragedy of intensely hideous, though largely unexplained, nature had struck down the master, five of his children, and several servants; and driven forth under a cloud of suspicion and terror the third son, my lineal progenitor and the only survivor of the abhorred line. With this sole heir denounced as a murderer, the estate had reverted to the crown, nor had the accused man made any attempt to exculpate himself or regain his property. Shaken by some horror greater than that of conscience or the law, and expressing only a frantic wish to exclude the ancient edifice from his sight and memory, Walter de la Poer, eleventh Baron Exham, fled to Virginia and there founded the family which by the next century had become known as Delapore.

Exham Priory had remained untenanted, though later allotted to the estates of the Norrys family and much studied because of its peculiarly composite architecture; an architecture involving Gothic towers resting on a Saxon or Romanesque substructure, whose foundation in turn was of a still earlier order or blend of orders—Roman, and even Druidic or native Cymric, if legends speak truly. This foundation was a very singular thing, being merged on one side with the solid limestone of the precipice from whose brink the priory overlooked a desolate valley three miles west of the village of Anchester. Architects and antiquarians loved to examine this strange relic of forgotten centuries, but the country folk hated it. They had hated it hundreds of years before, when my ancestors lived there, and they hated it now, with the moss and mould of abandonment on it. I had not been a day in Anchester before I knew I came of an accursed house. And this week workmen have blown up Exham Priory, and are busy obliterating the traces of its foundations.

The bare statistics of my ancestry I had always known, together with the fact that my first American forbear had come to the colonies under a strange cloud. Of details, however, I had been kept wholly ignorant through the policy of reticence always maintained by the Delapores. Unlike our planter neighbours, we seldom boasted of crusading ancestors or other mediaeval and Renaissance heroes; nor was any kind of tradition handed down except what may have been recorded in the sealed envelope left before the Civil War by every squire to his eldest son for posthumous opening. The glories we cherished were those achieved since the migration; the glories of a proud and honourable, if somewhat reserved and unsocial Virginia line.

During the war our fortunes were extinguished and our whole existence changed by the burning of Carfax, our home on the banks of the James. My grandfather, advanced in years, had perished in that incendiary outrage, and with him the envelope that bound us all to the past. I can recall that fire today as I saw it then at the age of seven, with the Federal soldiers shouting, the women screaming, and the negroes howling and praying. My father was in the army, defending Richmond, and after many formalities my mother and I were passed through the lines to join him. When the war ended we all moved north, whence my mother had come; and I grew to manhood, middle age, and ultimate wealth as a stolid Yankee. Neither my father nor I ever knew what our hereditary envelope had contained, and as I merged into the greyness of Massachusetts business life I lost all interest in the mysteries which evidently lurked far back in my family tree. Had I suspected their nature, how gladly I would have left Exham Priory to its moss, bats, and cobwebs!

My father died in 1904, but without any message to leave me, or to my only child, Alfred, a motherless boy of ten. It was this boy who reversed the order of family information; for although I could give him only jesting conjectures about the past, he wrote me of some very interesting ancestral legends when the late war took him to England in 1917 as an aviation officer. Apparently the Delapores had a colourful and perhaps sinister history, for a friend of my son's, Capt. Edward Norrys of the Royal Flying Corps, dwelt near the family seat at Anchester and related some peasant superstitions which few novelists could equal for wildness and incredibility. Norrys himself, of course, did not take them seriously; but they amused my son and made good material for his letters to me. It was this legendry which definitely turned my attention to my transatlantic heritage, and made me resolve to purchase and restore the family seat which Norrys shewed to Alfred in its picturesque desertion, and offered to get for him at a surprisingly reasonable figure, since his own uncle was the present owner.

I bought Exham Priory in 1918, but was almost immediately distracted from my plans of restoration by the return of my son as a maimed invalid. During the two years that he lived I thought of nothing but his care, having even placed my business under the direction of partners. In 1921, as I found myself bereaved and aimless, a retired manufacturer no longer young, I resolved to divert my remaining years with my new possession. Visiting Anchester in December, I was entertained by Capt. Norrys, a plump, amiable young man who had thought much of my son, and secured his assistance in gathering plans and anecdotes to guide in the coming restoration. Exham Priory itself I saw without emotion, a jumble of tottering mediaeval ruins covered with lichens and honeycombed with rooks' nests, perched perilously upon a precipice, and denuded of floors or other interior features save the stone walls of the separate towers.

As I gradually recovered the image of the edifice as it had been when my ancestor left it over three centuries before, I began to hire workmen for the reconstruction. In every case I was forced to go outside the immediate locality, for the Anchester villagers had an almost unbelievable fear and hatred of the place. This sentiment was so great that it was sometimes communicated to the outside labourers, causing numerous desertions; whilst its scope appeared to include both the priory and its ancient family.

My son had told me that he was somewhat avoided during his visits because he was a de la Poer, and I now found myself subtly ostracised for a like reason until I convinced the peasants how little I knew of my heritage. Even then they sullenly disliked me, so that I had to collect most of the village traditions through the mediation of Norrys. What the people could not forgive, perhaps, was that I had come to restore a symbol so abhorrent to them; for, rationally or not, they viewed Exham Priory as nothing less than a haunt of fiends and werewolves.

Piecing together the tales which Norrys collected for me, and supplementing them with the accounts of several savants who had studied the ruins, I deduced that Exham Priory stood on the site of a prehistoric temple; a Druidical or ante-Druidical thing which must have been contemporary with Stonehenge. That indescribable rites had been celebrated there, few doubted; and there were unpleasant tales of the transference of these rites into the Cybele-worship which the Romans had introduced. Inscriptions still visible in the sub-cellar bore such unmistakable letters as "DIV . . . OPS . . . MAGNA. MAT . . ." sign of the Magna Mater whose dark worship was once vainly forbidden to Roman citizens. Anchester had been the camp of the third Augustan legion, as many remains attest, and it was said that the temple of Cybele was splendid and thronged with worshippers who performed nameless ceremonies at the bidding of a Phrygian priest. Tales added that the fall of the old religion did not end the orgies at the temple, but that the priests lived on in the new faith without real change. Likewise was it said that the rites did not vanish with the Roman power, and that certain among the Saxons added to what remained of the temple, and gave it the essential outline it subsequently preserved, making it the centre of a cult feared through half the heptarchy. About 1000 A.D. the place is mentioned in a chronicle as being a substantial stone priory housing a strange and powerful monastic order and surrounded by extensive gardens which needed no walls to exclude a frightened populace. It was never destroyed by the Danes, though after the Norman Conquest it must have declined tremendously; since there was no impediment when Henry the Third granted the site to my ancestor, Gilbert de la Poer, First Baron Exham, in 1261.

Of my family before this date there is no evil report, but something strange must have happened then. In one chronicle there is a reference to a de la Poer as "cursed of God" in 1307, whilst village legendry had nothing but evil and frantic fear to tell of the castle that went up on the foundations of the old temple and priory. The fireside tales were of the most grisly description, all the ghastlier because of their frightened reticence and cloudy evasiveness. They represented my ancestors as a race of hereditary daemons beside whom Gilles de Retz and the Marquis de Sade would seem the veriest tyros, and hinted whisperingly at their responsibility for the occasional disappearance of villagers through several generations.

The worst characters, apparently, were the barons and their direct heirs; at least, most was whispered about these. If of healthier inclinations, it was said, an heir would early and mysteriously die to make way for another more typical scion. There seemed to be an inner cult in the family, presided over by the head of the house, and sometimes closed except to a few members. Temperament rather than ancestry was evidently the basis of this cult, for it was entered by several who married into the family. Lady Margaret Trevor from Cornwall, wife of Godfrey, the second son of the fifth baron, became a favourite bane of children all over the countryside, and the daemon heroine of a particularly horrible old ballad not yet extinct near the Welsh border. Preserved in balladry, too, though not illustrating the same point, is the hideous tale of Lady Mary de la Poer, who shortly after her marriage to the Earl of Shrewsfield was killed by him and his mother, both of the slayers being absolved and blessed by the priest to whom they confessed what they dared not repeat to the world.

These myths and ballads, typical as they were of crude superstition, repelled me greatly. Their persistence, and their application to so long a line of my ancestors, were especially annoying; whilst the imputations of monstrous habits proved unpleasantly reminiscent of the one known scandal of my immediate forbears—the case of my cousin, young Randolph Delapore of Carfax, who went among the negroes and became a voodoo priest after he returned from the Mexican War.

I was much less disturbed by the vaguer tales of wails and howlings in the barren, windswept valley beneath the limestone cliff; of the graveyard stenches after the spring rains; of the floundering, squealing white thing on which Sir John Clave's horse had trod one night in a lonely field; and of the servant who had gone mad at what he saw in the priory in the full light of day. These things were hackneyed spectral lore, and I was at that time a pronounced sceptic. The accounts of vanished peasants were less to be dismissed, though not especially significant in view of mediaeval custom. Prying curiosity meant death, and more than one severed head had been publicly shewn on the bastions—now effaced—around Exham Priory.

A few of the tales were exceedingly picturesque, and made me wish I had learnt more of comparative mythology in my youth. There was, for instance, the belief that a legion of bat-winged devils kept Witches' Sabbath each night at the priory—a legion whose sustenance might explain the disproportionate abundance of coarse vegetables harvested in the vast gardens. And, most vivid of all, there was the dramatic epic of the rats—the scampering army of obscene vermin which had burst forth from the castle three months after the tragedy that doomed it to desertion—the lean, filthy, ravenous army which had swept all before it and devoured fowl, cats, dogs, hogs, sheep, and even two hapless human beings before its fury was spent. Around that unforgettable rodent army a whole separate cycle of myths revolves, for it scattered among the village homes and brought curses and horrors in its train.

Such was the lore that assailed me as I pushed to completion, with an elderly obstinacy, the work of restoring my ancestral home. It must not be imagined for a moment that these tales formed my principal psychological environment. On the other hand, I was constantly praised and encouraged by Capt. Norrys and the antiquarians who surrounded and aided me. When the task was done, over two years after its commencement, I viewed the great rooms, wainscotted walls, vaulted ceilings, mullioned windows, and broad staircases with a pride which fully compensated for the prodigious expense of the restoration. Every attribute of the Middle Ages was cunningly reproduced, and the new parts blended perfectly with the original walls and foundations. The seat of my fathers was complete, and I looked forward to redeeming at last the local fame of the line which ended in me. I would reside here permanently, and prove that a de la Poer (for I had adopted again the original spelling of the name) need not be a fiend. My comfort was perhaps augmented by the fact that, although Exham Priory was mediaevally fitted, its interior was in truth wholly new and free from old vermin and old ghosts alike.

As I have said, I moved in on July 16, 1923. My household consisted of seven servants and nine cats, of which latter species I am particularly fond. My eldest cat, "Nigger-Man," was seven years old and had come with me from my home in Bolton, Massachusetts; the others I had accumulated whilst living with Capt. Norrys' family during the restoration of the priory. For five days our routine proceeded with the utmost placidity, my time being spent mostly in the codification of old family data. I had now obtained some very circumstantial accounts of the final tragedy and flight of Walter de la Poer, which I conceived to be the probable contents of the hereditary paper lost in the fire at Carfax. It appeared that my ancestor was accused with much reason of having killed all the other members of his household, except four servant confederates, in their sleep, about two weeks after a shocking discovery which changed his whole demeanour, but which, except by implication, he disclosed to no one save perhaps the servants who assisted him and afterward fled beyond reach.

This deliberate slaughter, which included a father, three brothers, and two sisters, was largely condoned by the villagers, and so slackly treated by the law that its perpetrator escaped honoured, unharmed, and undisguised to Virginia; the general whispered sentiment being that he had purged the land of an immemorial curse. What discovery had prompted an act so terrible, I could scarcely even conjecture. Walter de la Poer must have known for years the sinister tales about his family, so that this material could have given him no fresh impulse. Had he, then, witnessed some appalling ancient rite, or stumbled upon some frightful and revealing symbol in the priory or its vicinity? He was reputed to have been a shy, gentle youth in England. In Virginia he seemed not so much hard or bitter as harassed and apprehensive. He was spoken of in the diary of another gentleman-adventurer, Francis Harley of Bellview, as a man of unexampled justice, honour, and delicacy.

On July 22 occurred the first incident which, though lightly dismissed at the time, takes on a preternatural significance in relation to later events. It was so simple as to be almost negligible, and could not possibly have been noticed under the circumstances; for it must be recalled that since I was in a building practically fresh and new except for the walls, and surrounded by a well-balanced staff of servitors, apprehension would have been absurd despite the locality. What I afterward remembered is merely this—that my old black cat, whose moods I know so well, was undoubtedly alert and anxious to an extent wholly out of keeping with his natural character. He roved from room to room, restless and disturbed, and sniffed constantly about the walls which formed part of the old Gothic structure. I realise how trite this sounds—like the inevitable dog in the ghost story, which always growls before his master sees the sheeted figure—yet I cannot consistently suppress it.

The following day a servant complained of restlessness among all the cats in the house. He came to me in my study, a lofty west room on the second story, with groined arches, black oak panelling, and a triple Gothic window overlooking the limestone cliff and desolate valley; and even as he spoke I saw the jetty form of Nigger-Man creeping along the west wall and scratching at the new panels which overlaid the ancient stone. I told the man that there must be some singular odour or emanation from the old stonework, imperceptible to human senses, but affecting the delicate organs of cats even through the new woodwork. This I truly believed, and when the fellow suggested the presence of mice or rats, I mentioned that there had been no rats there for three hundred years, and that even the field mice of the surrounding country could hardly be found in these high walls, where they had never been known to stray. That afternoon I called on Capt. Norrys, and he assured me that it would be quite incredible for field mice to infest the priory in such a sudden and unprecedented fashion.

That night, dispensing as usual with a valet, I retired in the west tower chamber which I had chosen as my own, reached from the study by a stone staircase and short gallery—the former partly ancient, the latter entirely restored. This room was circular, very high, and without wainscotting, being hung with arras which I had myself chosen in London. Seeing that Nigger-Man was with me, I shut the heavy Gothic door and retired by the light of the electric bulbs which so cleverly counterfeited candles, finally switching off the light and sinking on the carved and canopied four-poster, with the venerable cat in his accustomed place across my feet. I did not draw the curtains, but gazed out at the narrow north window which I faced. There was a suspicion of aurora in the sky, and the delicate traceries of the window were pleasantly silhouetted.

At some time I must have fallen quietly asleep, for I recall a distinct sense of leaving strange dreams, when the cat started violently from his placid position. I saw him in the faint auroral glow, head strained forward, fore feet on my ankles, and hind feet stretched behind. He was looking intensely at a point on the wall somewhat west of the window, a point which to my eye had nothing to mark it, but toward which all my attention was now directed. And as I watched, I knew that Nigger-Man was not vainly excited. Whether the arras actually moved I cannot say. I think it did, very slightly. But what I can swear to is that behind it I heard a low, distinct scurrying as of rats or mice. In a moment the cat had jumped bodily on the screening tapestry, bringing the affected section to the floor with his weight, and exposing a damp, ancient wall of stone; patched here and there by the restorers, and devoid of any trace of rodent prowlers. Nigger-Man raced up and down the floor by this part of the wall, clawing the fallen arras and seemingly trying at times to insert a paw between the wall and the oaken floor. He found nothing, and after a time returned wearily to his place across my feet. I had not moved, but I did not sleep again that night.

In the morning I questioned all the servants, and found that none of them had noticed anything unusual, save that the cook remembered the actions of a cat which had rested on her windowsill. This cat had howled at some unknown hour of the night, awaking the cook in time for her to see him dart purposefully out of the open door down the stairs. I drowsed away the noontime, and in the afternoon called again on Capt. Norrys, who became exceedingly interested in what I told him. The odd incidents—so slight yet so curious—appealed to his sense of the picturesque, and elicited from him a number of reminiscences of local ghostly lore. We were genuinely perplexed at the presence of rats, and Norrys lent me some traps and Paris green, which I had the servants place in strategic localities when I returned.

I retired early, being very sleepy, but was harassed by dreams of the most horrible sort. I seemed to be looking down from an immense height upon a twilit grotto, knee-deep with filth, where a white-bearded daemon swineherd drove about with his staff a flock of fungous, flabby beasts whose appearance filled me with unutterable loathing. Then, as the swineherd paused and nodded over his task, a mighty swarm of rats rained down on the stinking abyss and fell to devouring beasts and man alike.

From this terrific vision I was abruptly awaked by the motions of Nigger-Man, who had been sleeping as usual across my feet. This time I did not have to question the source of his snarls and hisses, and of the fear which made him sink his claws into my ankle, unconscious of their effect; for on every side of the chamber the walls were alive with nauseous sound—the verminous slithering of ravenous, gigantic rats. There was now no aurora to shew the state of the arras—the fallen section of which had been replaced—but I was not too frightened to switch on the light.

As the bulbs leapt into radiance I saw a hideous shaking all over the tapestry, causing the somewhat peculiar designs to execute a singular dance of death. This motion disappeared almost at once, and the sound with it. Springing out of bed,

I poked at the arras with the long handle of a warming-pan that rested near, and lifted one section to see what lay beneath. There was nothing but the patched stone wall, and even the cat had lost his tense realisation of abnormal presences. When I examined the circular trap that had been placed in the room, I found all of the openings sprung, though no trace remained of what had been caught and had escaped.

Further sleep was out of the question, so, lighting a candle, I opened the door and went out in the gallery toward the stairs to my study, Nigger-Man following at my heels. Before we had reached the stone steps, however, the cat darted ahead of me and vanished down the ancient flight. As I descended the stairs myself, I became suddenly aware of sounds in the great room below; sounds of a nature which could not be mistaken. The oak-panelled walls were alive with rats, scampering and milling, whilst Nigger-Man was racing about with the fury of a baffled hunter. Reaching the bottom, I switched on the light, which did not this time cause the noise to subside. The rats continued their riot, stampeding with such force and distinctness that I could finally assign to their motions a definite direction. These creatures, in numbers apparently inexhaustible, were engaged in one stupendous migration from inconceivable heights to some depth conceivably, or inconceivably, below.

I now heard steps in the corridor, and in another moment two servants pushed open the massive door. They were searching the house for some unknown source of disturbance which had thrown all the cats into a snarling panic and caused them to plunge precipitately down several flights of stairs and squat, yowling, before the closed door to the sub-cellar. I asked them if they had heard the rats, but they replied in the negative. And when I turned to call their attention to the sounds in the panels, I realised that the noise had ceased. With the two men, I went down to the door of the sub-cellar, but found the cats already dispersed. Later I resolved to explore the crypt below, but for the present I merely made a round of the traps. All were sprung, yet all were tenantless. Satisfying myself that no one had heard the rats save the felines and me, I sat in my study till morning; thinking profoundly, and recalling every scrap of legend I had unearthed concerning the building I inhabited.

I slept some in the forenoon, leaning back in the one comfortable library chair which my mediaeval plan of furnishing could not banish. Later I telephoned to Capt. Norrys, who came over and helped me explore the sub-cellar. Absolutely nothing untoward was found, although we could not repress a thrill at the knowledge that this vault was built by Roman hands. Every low arch and massive pillar was Roman—not the debased Romanesque of the bungling Saxons, but the severe and harmonious classicism of the age of the Caesars; indeed, the walls abounded with inscriptions familiar to the antiquarians who had repeatedly explored the place—things like "P.GETAE. PROP . . . TEMP . . . DONA . . ." and "L. PRAEC . . . VS . . . PONTIFI . . . ATYS . . ."

The reference to Atys made me shiver, for I had read Catullus and knew something of the hideous rites of the Eastern god, whose worship was so mixed with that of Cybele. Norrys and I, by the light of lanterns, tried to interpret the odd and nearly effaced designs on certain irregularly rectangular blocks of stone generally held to be altars, but could make nothing of them. We remembered that one pattern, a sort of rayed sun, was held by students to imply a non-Roman origin, suggesting that these altars had merely been adopted by the Roman priests from some older and perhaps aboriginal temple on the same site. On one of these blocks were some brown stains which made me wonder. The largest, in the centre of the room, had certain features on the upper surface which indicated its connexion with fire—probably burnt offerings.

Such were the sights in that crypt before whose door the cats had howled, and where Norrys and I now determined to pass the night. Couches were brought down by the servants, who were told not to mind any nocturnal actions of the cats, and Nigger-Man was admitted as much for help as for companionship. We decided to keep the great oak door—a modern replica with slits for ventilation—tightly closed; and, with this attended to, we retired with lanterns still burning to await whatever might occur.

The vault was very deep in the foundations of the priory, and undoubtedly far down on the face of the beetling limestone cliff overlooking the waste valley. That it had been the goal of the scuffling and unexplainable rats I could not doubt, though why, I could not tell. As we lay there expectantly, I found my vigil occasionally mixed with half-formed dreams from which the uneasy motions of the cat across my feet would rouse me. These dreams were not wholesome, but horribly like the one I had had the night before. I saw again the twilit grotto, and the swineherd with his unmentionable fungous beasts wallowing in filth, and as I looked at these things they seemed nearer and more distinct—so distinct that I could almost observe their features. Then I did observe the flabby features of one of them—and awaked with such a scream that Nigger-Man started up, whilst Capt. Norrys, who had not slept, laughed considerably. Norrys might have laughed more—or perhaps less—had he known what it was that made me scream. But I did not remember myself till later. Ultimate horror often paralyses memory in a merciful way.

Norrys waked me when the phenomena began. Out of the same frightful dream I was called by his gentle shaking and his urging to listen to the cats. Indeed, there was much to listen to, for beyond the closed door at the head of the stone steps was a veritable nightmare of feline yelling and clawing, whilst Nigger-Man, unmindful of his kindred outside, was running excitedly around the bare stone walls, in which I heard the same babel of scurrying rats that had troubled me the night before.

An acute terror now rose within me, for here were anomalies which nothing normal could well explain. These rats, if not the creatures of a madness which I shared with the cats alone, must be burrowing and sliding in Roman walls I had thought to be of solid limestone blocks . . . unless perhaps the action of water through more than seventeen centuries had eaten winding tunnels which rodent bodies had worn clear and ample. . . . But even so, the spectral horror was no less; for if these were living vermin why did not Norrys hear their disgusting commotion? Why did he urge me to watch Nigger-Man and listen to the cats outside, and why did he guess wildly and vaguely at what could have aroused them?

By the time I had managed to tell him, as rationally as I could, what I thought I was hearing, my ears gave me the last fading impression of the scurrying; which had retreated *still downward,* far underneath this deepest of sub-cellars till it seemed as if the whole cliff below were riddled with questing rats. Norrys was not as sceptical as I had anticipated, but instead seemed profoundly moved. He motioned to me to notice that the cats at the door had ceased their clamour, as if giving up the rats for lost; whilst Nigger-Man had a burst of renewed restlessness, and was clawing frantically around the bottom of the large stone altar in the centre of the room, which was nearer Norrys' couch than mine.

My fear of the unknown was at this point very great. Something astounding had occurred, and I saw that Capt. Norrys, a younger, stouter, and presumably more naturally materialistic man, was affected fully as much as myself—perhaps because of his lifelong and intimate familiarity with local legend. We could for the moment do nothing but watch the old black cat as he pawed with decreasing fervour at the base of the altar, occasionally looking up and mewing to me in that persuasive manner which he used when he wished me to perform some favour for him.

Norrys now took a lantern close to the altar and examined the place where Nigger-Man was pawing; silently kneeling and scraping away the lichens of centuries which joined the massive pre-Roman block to the tessellated floor. He did not find anything, and was about to abandon his effort when I noticed a trivial circumstance which made me shudder, even though it implied nothing more than I had already imagined. I told him of it, and we both looked at its almost imperceptible manifestation with the fixedness of fascinated discovery and acknowledgment. It was only this—that the flame of the lantern set down near the altar was slightly but certainly flickering from a draught of air which it had not before received, and which came indubitably from the crevice between floor and altar where Norrys was scraping away the lichens.

We spent the rest of the night in the brilliantly lighted study, nervously discussing what we should do next. The discovery that some vault deeper than the deepest known masonry of the Romans underlay this accursed pile—some vault unsuspected by the curious antiquarians of three centuries—would have been sufficient to excite us without any background of the sinister. As it was, the fascination became twofold; and we paused in doubt whether to abandon our search and quit the priory forever in superstitious caution, or to gratify our sense of adventure and brave whatever horrors might await us in the unknown depths. By morning we had compromised, and decided to go to London to gather a group of archaeologists and scientific men fit to cope with the mystery. It should be mentioned that before leaving the sub-cellar we had vainly tried to move the central altar which we now recognised as the gate to a new pit of nameless fear. What secret would open the gate, wiser men than we would have to find.

During many days in London Capt. Norrys and I presented our facts, conjectures, and legendary anecdotes to five eminent authorities, all men who could be trusted to respect any family disclosures which future explorations might develop. We found most of them little disposed to scoff, but instead intensely interested and sincerely sympathetic. It is hardly necessary to name them all, but I may say that they included Sir William Brinton, whose excavations in the Troad excited most of the world in their day. As we all took the train for Anchester I felt myself poised on the brink of frightful revelations, a sensation symbolised by the air of mourning among the many Americans at the unexpected death of the President on the other side of the world.

On the evening of August 7th we reached Exham Priory, where the servants assured me that nothing unusual had occurred. The cats, even old Nigger-Man, had been perfectly placid; and not a trap in the house had been sprung. We were to begin exploring on the following day, awaiting which I assigned well-appointed rooms to all my guests. I myself retired in my own tower chamber, with Nigger-Man across my feet. Sleep came quickly, but hideous dreams assailed me. There was a vision of a Roman feast like that of Trimalchio, with a horror in a covered platter. Then came that damnable, recurrent thing about the swineherd and his filthy drove in the twilit grotto. Yet when I awoke it was full daylight, with normal sounds in the house below. The rats, living or spectral, had not troubled me; and Nigger-Man was quietly asleep. On going down, I found that the same tranquillity had prevailed elsewhere; a condition which one of the assembled savants—a fellow named Thornton, devoted to the psychic—rather absurdly laid to the fact that I had now been shewn the thing which certain forces had wished to shew me.

All was now ready, and at 11 A.M. our entire group of seven men, bearing powerful electric searchlights and implements of excavation, went down to the sub-cellar and bolted the door behind us. Nigger-Man was with us, for the investigators found no occasion to despise his excitability, and were indeed anxious that he be present in case of obscure rodent manifestations. We noted the Roman inscriptions and unknown altar designs only briefly, for three of the savants had already seen them, and all knew their characteristics. Prime attention was paid to the momentous central altar, and within an hour Sir William Brinton had caused it to tilt backward, balanced by some unknown species of counterweight.

There now lay revealed such a horror as would have overwhelmed us had we not been prepared. Through a nearly square opening in the tiled floor, sprawling on a flight of stone steps so prodigiously worn that it was little more than an inclined plane at the centre, was a ghastly array of human or semi-human bones. Those which retained their collocation as skeletons shewed attitudes of panic fear, and over all were the marks of rodent gnawing. The skulls denoted nothing short of utter idiocy, cretinism, or primitive semi-apedom. Above the hellishly littered steps arched a descending passage seemingly chiselled from the solid rock, and conducting a current of air. This current was not a sudden and noxious rush as from a closed vault, but a cool breeze with something of freshness in it. We did not pause long, but shiveringly began to clear a passage down the steps. It was then that Sir William, examining the hewn walls, made the odd observation that the passage, according to the direction of the strokes, must have been chiselled *from beneath*.

I must be very deliberate now, and choose my words.

After ploughing down a few steps amidst the gnawed bones we saw that there was light ahead; not any mystic phosphorescence, but a filtered daylight which could not come except from unknown fissures in the cliff that overlooked the waste valley. That such fissures had escaped notice from outside was hardly remarkable, for not only is the valley wholly uninhabited, but the cliff is so high and beetling that only an aëronaut could study its face in detail. A few steps more, and our breaths were literally snatched from us by what we saw; so literally that Thornton, the psychic investigator, actually fainted in the arms of the dazed man who stood behind him. Norrys, his plump face utterly white and flabby, simply cried out inarticulately; whilst I think that what I did was to gasp or hiss, and cover my eyes. The man behind me—the only one of the party older than I—croaked the hackneyed "My God!"

in the most cracked voice I ever heard. Of seven cultivated men, only Sir William Brinton retained his composure; a thing more to his credit because he led the party and must have seen the sight first.

It was a twilit grotto of enormous height, stretching away farther than any eye could see; a subterraneous world of limitless mystery and horrible suggestion. There were buildings and other architectural remains—in one terrified glance I saw a weird pattern of tumuli, a savage circle of monoliths, a low-domed Roman ruin, a sprawling Saxon pile, and an early English edifice of wood—but all these were dwarfed by the ghoulish spectacle presented by the general surface of the ground. For yards about the steps extended an insane tangle of human bones, or bones at least as human as those on the steps. Like a foamy sea they stretched, some fallen apart, but others wholly or partly articulated as skeletons; these latter invariably in postures of daemoniac frenzy, either fighting off some menace or clutching other forms with cannibal intent.

When Dr. Trask, the anthropologist, stooped to classify the skulls, he found a degraded mixture which utterly baffled him. They were mostly lower than the Piltdown man in the scale of evolution, but in every case definitely human. Many were of higher grade, and a very few were the skulls of supremely and sensitively developed types. All the bones were gnawed, mostly by rats, but somewhat by others of the half-human drove. Mixed with them were many tiny bones of rats—fallen members of the lethal army which closed the ancient epic.

I wonder that any man among us lived and kept his sanity through that hideous day of discovery. Not Hoffmann or Huysmans could conceive a scene more wildly incredible, more frenetically repellent, or more Gothically grotesque than the twilit grotto through which we seven staggered; each stumbling on revelation after revelation, and trying to keep for the nonce from thinking of the events which must have taken place there three hundred years, or a thousand, or two thousand, or ten thousand years ago. It was the antechamber of hell, and poor Thornton fainted again when Trask told him that some of the skeleton things must have descended as quadrupeds through the last twenty or more generations.

Horror piled on horror as we began to interpret the architectural remains. The quadruped things—with their occasional recruits from the biped class—had been kept in stone pens, out of which they must have broken in their last delirium of hunger or rat-fear. There had been great herds of them, evidently fattened on the coarse vegetables whose remains could be found as a sort of poisonous ensilage at the bottom of huge stone bins older than Rome. I knew now why my ancestors had had such excessive gardens—would to heaven I could forget! The purpose of the herds I did not have to ask.

Sir William, standing with his searchlight in the Roman ruin, translated aloud the most shocking ritual I have ever known; and told of the diet of the antediluvian cult which the priests of Cybele found and mingled with their own. Norrys, used as he was to the trenches, could not walk straight when he came out of the English building. It was a butcher shop and kitchen—he had expected that—but it was too much to see familiar English implements in such a place, and to read familiar English *graffiti* there, some as recent as 1610. I could not go in that building—that building whose daemon activities were stopped only by the dagger of my ancestor Walter de la Poer.

What I did venture to enter was the low Saxon building, whose oaken door had fallen, and there I found a terrible row of ten stone cells with rusty bars. Three had tenants, all skeletons of high grade, and on the bony forefinger of one I found a seal ring with my own coat-of-arms. Sir William found a vault with far older cells below the Roman chapel, but these cells were empty. Below them was a low crypt with cases of formally arranged bones, some of them bearing terrible parallel inscriptions carved in Latin, Greek, and the tongue of Phrygia. Meanwhile, Dr. Trask had opened one of the prehistoric tumuli, and brought to light skulls which were slightly more human than a gorilla's, and which bore indescribable ideographic carvings. Through all this horror my cat stalked unperturbed. Once I saw him monstrously perched atop a mountain of bones, and wondered at the secrets that might lie behind his yellow eyes.

Having grasped to some slight degree the frightful revelations of this twilit area—an area so hideously foreshadowed by my recurrent dream—we turned to that apparently boundless depth of midnight cavern where no ray of light from the cliff could penetrate. We shall never know what sightless Stygian worlds yawn beyond the little distance we went, for it was decided that such secrets are not good for mankind. But there was plenty to engross us close at hand, for we had not gone far before the searchlights shewed that accursed infinity of pits in which the rats had feasted, and whose sudden lack of replenishment had driven the ravenous rodent army first to turn on the living herds of starving things, and then to burst forth from the priory in that historic orgy of devastation which the peasants will never forget.

God! those carrion black pits of sawed, picked bones and opened skulls! Those nightmare chasms choked with the pithecanthropoid, Celtic, Roman, and English bones of countless unhallowed centuries! Some of them were full, and none can say how deep they had once been. Others were still bottomless to our searchlights, and peopled by unnamable fancies. What, I thought, of the hapless rats that stumbled into such traps amidst the blackness of their quests in this grisly Tartarus?

Once my foot slipped near a horribly yawning brink, and I had a moment of ecstatic fear. I must have been musing a long time, for I could not see any of the party but the plump Capt. Norrys. Then there came a sound from that inky, boundless, farther distance that I thought I knew; and I saw my old black cat dart past me like a winged Egyptian god, straight into the illimitable gulf of the unknown. But I was not far behind, for there was no doubt after another second. It was the eldritch scurrying of those fiend-born rats, always questing for new horrors, and determined to lead me on even unto those grinning caverns of earth's centre where Nyarlathotep, the mad faceless god, howls blindly to the piping of two amorphous idiot flute-players.

My searchlight expired, but still I ran. I heard voices, and yowls, and echoes, but above all there gently rose that impious, insidious scurrying; gently rising, rising, as a stiff bloated corpse gently rises above an oily river that flows under endless onyx bridges to a black, putrid sea. Something bumped into me—something soft and plump. It must have been the rats; the viscous, gelatinous, ravenous army that feast on the dead and the living. . . . Why shouldn't rats eat a de la Poer as a de la Poer eats forbidden things? . . . The war ate my boy, damn them all . . . and the Yanks ate Carfax with flames and burnt Grandsire Delapore and the secret . . . No, no, I tell you, I am *not* that daemon swineherd in the twilit grotto! It was *not* Edward Norrys' fat face on that flabby, fungous thing! Who says I am a de la Poer? He lived, but my boy died! . . . Shall a Norrys hold the lands of a de la Poer? . . . It's voodoo, I tell you. . . that spotted snake. . . Curse you, Thornton, I'll teach you to faint at what my family do! . . . 'Sblood, thou stinkard, I'll learn ye how to gust . . . wolde ye swynke me thilke wys?. . . *Magna Mater! Magna Mater! . . . Atys . . . Dia ad aghaidh 's ad aodann . . . agus bas dunach ort! Dhonas 's dholas ort, agus leat-sa! . . . Ungl . . . ungl . . . rrrlh . . . chchch . . .*

That is what they say I said when they found me in the blackness after three hours; found me crouching in the blackness over the plump, half-eaten body of Capt. Norrys, with my own cat leaping and tearing at my throat. Now they have blown up Exham Priory, taken my Nigger-Man away from me, and shut me into this barred room at Hanwell with fearful whispers about my heredity and experiences. Thornton is in the next room, but they prevent me from talking to him. They are trying, too, to suppress most of the facts concerning the priory. When I speak of poor Norrys they accuse me of a hideous thing, but they must know that I did not do it. They must know it was the rats; the slithering, scurrying rats whose scampering will never let me sleep; the daemon rats that race behind the padding in this room and beckon me down to greater horrors than I have ever known; the rats they can never hear; the rats, the rats in the walls.

The Phantom of the Opera

Gaston Leroux

Prologue

IN WHICH THE AUTHOR OF THIS SINGULAR WORK INFORMS THE READER HOW HE ACQUIRED THE CERTAINTY THAT THE OPERA GHOST REALLY EXISTED

THE OPERA GHOST REALLY EXISTED. HE WAS NOT, AS WAS LONG believed, a creature of the imagination of the artists, the superstition of the managers, or a product of the absurd and impressionable brains of the young ladies of the ballet, their mothers, the box-keepers, the cloak-room attendants or the concierge. Yes, he existed in flesh and blood, although he assumed the complete appearance of a real phantom; that is to say, of a spectral shade.

When I began to ransack the archives of the National Academy of Music I was at once struck by the surprising coincidences between the phenomena ascribed to the "ghost" and the most extraordinary and fantastic tragedy that ever excited the Paris upper classes; and I soon conceived the idea that this tragedy might reasonably be explained by the phenomena in question. The events do not date more than thirty years back; and it would not be difficult to find at the present day, in the foyer of the ballet, old men of the highest respectability, men upon whose word one could absolutely rely, who would remember as though they happened yesterday the mysterious and dramatic conditions that attended the kidnapping of Christine Daaé, the disappearance of the Vicomte de Chagny and the death of his elder brother, Count Philippe, whose body was found on the bank of the lake that exists in the lower cellars of the Opera on the Rue-Scribe side. But none of those witnesses had until that day thought that there was any reason for connecting the more or less legendary figure of the Opera ghost with that terrible story.

The truth was slow to enter my mind, puzzled by an inquiry that at every moment was complicated by events which, at first sight, might be looked upon as superhuman; and more than once I was within an ace of abandoning a task in which I was exhausting myself in the hopeless pursuit of a vain image. At last, I received the proof that my presentiments had not deceived me, and I was rewarded for all my efforts on the day when I acquired the certainty that the Opera ghost was more than a mere shade.

On that day, I had spent long hours over *The Memoirs of a Manager*, the light and frivolous work of the too-skeptical Moncharmin, who, during his term at the Opera, understood nothing of the mysterious behavior of the ghost and who was making all the fun of it that he could at the very moment when he became the first victim of the curious financial operation that went on inside the "magic envelope."

I had just left the library in despair, when I met the delightful acting-manager of our National Academy, who stood chatting on a landing with a lively and well-groomed little old man, to whom he introduced me gaily. The acting-manager knew all about my investigations and how eagerly and unsuccessfully I had been trying to discover the whereabouts of the examining magistrate in the famous Chagny case, M. Faure. Nobody knew what had become of him, alive or dead; and here he was back from Canada, where he had spent fifteen years, and the first thing he had done, on his return to Paris, was to come to the secretarial offices at the Opera and ask for a free seat. The little old man was M. Faure himself.

We spent a good part of the evening together and he told me the whole Chagny case as he had understood it at the time. He was bound to conclude in favor of the madness of the viscount and the accidental death of the elder brother, for lack of evidence to the contrary; but he was nevertheless persuaded that a terrible tragedy had taken place between the two brothers in connection with Christine Daaé. He could not tell me what became of Christine or the viscount. When I mentioned the ghost, he only laughed. He, too, had been told of the curious manifestations that seemed to point to the existence of an abnormal being, residing in one of the most mysterious corners of the Opera, and he knew the story of the envelope; but he had never seen anything in it worthy of his attention as magistrate in charge of the Chagny case, and it was as much as he had done to listen to the evidence of a witness who appeared of his own accord and declared that he had often met the ghost. This witness was none other than the man whom all Paris called the "Persian" and who was well-known to every subscriber to the Opera. The magistrate took him for a visionary.

I was immensely interested by this story of the Persian. I wanted, if there were still time, to find this valuable and eccentric witness. My luck began to improve and I discovered him in his little flat in the Rue de Rivoli, where he had lived ever since and where he died five months after my visit. I was at first inclined to be suspicious; but when the Persian had told me, with child-like candor, all that he knew about the ghost and had handed me the proofs of the ghost's existence—including the strange correspondence of Christine Daaé—to do as I pleased with, I was no longer able to doubt. No, the ghost was not a myth!

I have, I know, been told that this correspondence may have been forged from first to last by a man whose imagination had certainly been fed on the most seductive tales; but fortunately I discovered some of Christine's writing outside the famous bundle of letters and, on a comparison between the two, all my doubts were removed. I also went into the past history of the Persian and found that he was an upright man, incapable of inventing a story that might have defeated the ends of justice.

This, moreover, was the opinion of the more serious people who, at one time or other, were mixed up in the Chagny case, who were friends of the Chagny family, to whom I showed all my documents and set forth all my inferences. In this connection, I should like to print a few lines which I received from General D———:

> Sir:
>
> I can not urge you too strongly to publish the results of your inquiry. I remember perfectly that, a few weeks before the disappearance of that great singer, Christine Daaé, and the tragedy which threw the whole of the Faubourg Saint-Germain into mourning, there was a great deal of talk, in the foyer of the ballet, on the subject of the "ghost"; and I believe that it only ceased to be discussed in consequence of the later affair that excited us all so greatly. But, if it be possible—as, after hearing you, I believe—to explain the tragedy through the ghost, then I beg you, sir, to talk to us about the ghost again. Mysterious though the ghost may at first appear, he will always be more easily explained than the dismal story in which malevolent people have tried to picture two brothers killing each other who had worshiped each other all their lives.
>
> Believe me, etc.

Lastly, with my bundle of papers in hand, I once more went over the ghost's vast domain, the huge building which he had made his kingdom. All that my eyes saw, all that my mind perceived, corroborated the Persian's documents precisely; and a wonderful discovery crowned my labors in a very definite fashion. It will be remembered that, later, when digging in the substructure of the Opera, before burying the phonographic records of the artist's voice, the workmen laid bare a corpse. Well, I was at once able to prove that this corpse was that of the Opera ghost. I made the acting-manager put this proof to the test with his own hand; and it is now a matter of supreme indifference to me if the papers pretend that the body was that of a victim of the Commune.

The wretches who were massacred, under the Commune, in the cellars of the Opera, were not buried on this side; I will tell where their skeletons can be found in a spot not very far from that immense crypt which was stocked during the siege with all sorts of provisions. I came upon this track just when I was looking for the remains of the Opera ghost, which I should never have discovered but for the unheard-of chance described above.

But we will return to the corpse and what ought to be done with it. For the present, I must conclude this very necessary introduction by thanking M. Mifroid (who was the commissary of police called in for the first investigations after the disappearance of Christine Daaé), M. Rémy, the late secretary, M. Mercier, the late acting-manager, M. Gabriel, the late chorus-master, and more particularly Mme. la Baronne de Castelot-Barbezac, who was once the "little Meg" of the story (and who is not ashamed of it), the most charming star of our admirable *corps de ballet*, the eldest daughter of the worthy Mme. Giry, now deceased, who had charge of the ghost's private box. All these were of the greatest assistance to me; and, thanks to them, I shall be able to reproduce those hours of sheer love and terror, in their smallest details, before the reader's eyes.

And I should be ungrateful indeed if I omitted, while standing on the threshold of this dreadful and veracious story, to thank the present management of the Opera, which has so kindly assisted me in all my inquiries, and M. Messager in particular, together with M. Gabion, the acting-manager, and that most amiable of men, the architect intrusted with the preservation of the building, who did not hesitate to lend me the works of Charles Gamier, although he was almost sure that I would never return them to him. Lastly, I must pay a public tribute to the generosity of my friend and former collaborator, M. J. Le Croze, who allowed me to dip into his splendid theatrical library and to borrow the rarest editions of books by which he set great store.

—Gaston Leroux

I

IS IT THE GHOST?

IT WAS THE EVENING ON WHICH MM. DEBIENNE AND POLIGNY, THE managers of the Opera, were giving a last gala performance to mark their retirement. Suddenly the dressing-room of La Sorelli, one of the principal dancers, was invaded by half-a-dozen young ladies of the ballet, who had come up from the stage after "dancing" *Polyeucte*. They rushed in amid great confusion, some giving vent to forced and unnatural laughter, others to cries of terror. Sorelli, who wished to be alone for a moment to "run through" the speech which she was to make to the resigning managers, looked around angrily at the mad and tumultuous crowd. It was little Jammes—the girl with the tip-tilted nose, the forget-me-not eyes, the rose-red cheeks and the lily-white neck and shoulders—who gave the explanation in a trembling voice:

"It's the ghost!" And she locked the door.

Sorelli's dressing-room was fitted up with official, commonplace elegance. A pier-glass, a sofa, a dressing-table and a cupboard or two provided the necessary furniture. On the walls hung a few engravings, relics of the mother, who had known the glories of the old Opera in the Rue le Peletier; portraits of Vestris, Gardel, Dupont, Bigottini. But the room seemed a palace to the brats of the *corps de ballet*, who were lodged in common dressing-rooms where they spent their time singing, quarreling, smacking the dressers and hair-dressers and buying one another glasses of *cassis*, beer, or even *rhum*, until the callboy's bell rang.

Sorelli was very superstitious. She shuddered when she heard little Jammes speak of the ghost, called her a "silly little fool" and then, as she was the first to believe in ghosts in general, and the Opera ghost in particular, at once asked for details:

"Have you seen him?"

"As plainly as I see you now!" said little Jammes, whose legs were giving way beneath her, and she dropped with a moan into a chair.

Thereupon little Giry—the girl with eyes black as sloes, hair black as ink, a swarthy complexion and a poor little skin stretched over poor little bones—little Giry added:

"If that's the ghost, he's very ugly!"

"Oh, yes!" cried the chorus of ballet-girls.

And they all began to talk together. The ghost had appeared to them in the shape of a gentleman in dress-clothes, who had suddenly stood before them in the passage, without their knowing where he came from. He seemed to have come straight through the wall.

"Pooh!" said one of them, who had more or less kept her head. "You see the ghost everywhere!"

And it was true. For several months, there had been nothing discussed at the Opera but this ghost in dress-clothes who stalked about the building, from top to bottom, like a shadow, who spoke to nobody, to whom nobody dared speak and who vanished as soon as he was seen, no one knowing how or where. As became a real ghost, he made no noise in walking. People began by laughing and making fun of this specter dressed like a man of fashion or an undertaker; but the ghost legend soon swelled to enormous proportions among the *corps de ballet*. All the girls pretended to have met this supernatural being more or less often. And those who laughed the loudest were not the most at ease. When he did not show himself, he betrayed his presence or his passing by accident, comic or serious, for which the general superstition held him responsible. Had any one met with a fall, or suffered a practical joke at the hands of one of the other girls, or lost a powder-puff, it was at once the fault of the ghost, of the Opera ghost.

After all, who had seen him? You meet so many men in dress-clothes at the Opera who are not ghosts. But this dress-suit had a peculiarity of its own. It covered a skeleton. At least, so the ballet-girls said. And, of course, it had a death's head.

Was all this serious? The truth is that the idea of the skeleton came from the description of the ghost given by Joseph Buquet, the chief scene-shifter, who had really seen the ghost. He had run up against the ghost on the little staircase, by the footlights, which leads to "the cellars." He had seen him for a second—for the ghost had fled—and to any one who cared to listen to him he said:

"He is extraordinarily thin and his dress-coat hangs on a skeleton frame. His eyes are so deep that you can hardly see the fixed pupils. You just see two big black holes, as in a dead man's skull. His skin, which is stretched across his bones like a drumhead, is not white, but a nasty yellow. His nose is so little worth talking about that you can't see it side-face; and *the absence* of that nose is a horrible thing *to look at*. All the hair he has is three or four long dark locks on his forehead and behind his ears."

This chief scene-shifter was a serious, sober, steady man, very slow at imagining things. His words were received with interest and amazement; and soon there were other people to say that they too had met a man in dress-clothes with a death's head on his shoulders. Sensible men who had wind of the story began by saying that Joseph Buquet had been the victim of a joke played by one of his assistants. And then, one after the other, there came a series of incidents so curious and so inexplicable that the very shrewdest people began to feel uneasy.

For instance, a fireman is a brave fellow! He fears nothing, least of all fire! Well, the fireman in question, who had gone to make a round of inspection in the cellars and who, it seems, had ventured a little farther than usual, suddenly reappeared on the stage, pale, scared, trembling, with his eyes starting out of his head, and practically fainted in the arms of the proud mother of little Jammes.* And why? Because he had seen coming toward him, *at the level of his head, but without a body attached to it, a head of fire*! And, as I said, a fireman is not afraid of fire.

The fireman's name was Pampin.

The *corps de ballet* was flung into consternation. At first sight, this fiery head in no way corresponded with Joseph Buquet's description of the ghost. But the young ladies soon persuaded themselves that the ghost had several heads, which he changed about as he pleased. And, of course, they at once imagined that they were in the greatest danger. Once a fireman did not hesitate to faint, leaders and front-row and back-row girls alike had plenty of excuses for the fright that made them quicken their pace when passing some dark corner or ill-lighted corridor. Sorelli herself, on the day after the adventure of the fireman, placed a horse-shoe on the table in front of the stage-door-keeper's box, which every one who entered the Opera otherwise than as a spectator must touch before setting foot on the first tread of the staircase. This horse-shoe was not invented by me—any more than any other part of this story, alas!—and may still be seen on the table in the passage outside the stage-door-keeper's box, when you enter the Opera through the court known as the Cour de l'Administration.

To return to the evening in question.

"It's the ghost!" little Jammes had cried.

An agonizing silence now reigned in the dressing-room. Nothing was heard but the hard breathing of the girls. At last, Jammes, flinging herself upon the farthest corner of the wall, with every mark of real terror on her face, whispered:

"Listen!"

Everybody seemed to hear a rustling outside the door. There was no sound of footsteps. It was like light silk sliding over the panel. Then it stopped.

Sorelli tried to show more pluck than the others. She went up to the door and, in a quavering voice, asked:

"Who's there?"

* I have the anecdote, which is quite authentic, from M. Pedro Gailhard himself, the late manager of the Opera.

But nobody answered. Then feeling all eyes upon her, watching her last movement, she made an effort to show courage, and said very loudly:

"Is there any one behind the door?"

"Oh, yes, yes! Of course there is!" cried that little dried plum of a Meg Giry, heroically holding Sorelli back by her gauze skirt. "Whatever you do, don't open the door! Oh, Lord, don't open the door!"

But Sorelli, armed with a dagger that never left her, turned the key and drew back the door, while the ballet-girls retreated to the inner dressing-room and Meg Giry sighed:

"Mother! Mother!"

Sorelli looked into the passage bravely. It was empty; a gas-flame, in its glass prison, cast a red and suspicious light into the surrounding darkness, without succeeding in dispelling it. And the dancer slammed the door again, with a deep sigh.

"No," she said, "there is no one there."

"Still, we saw him!" Jammes declared, returning with timid little steps to her place beside Sorelli. "He must be somewhere prowling about. I shan't go back to dress. We had better all go down to the foyer together, at once, for the 'speech,' and we will come up again together."

And the child reverently touched the little coral finger-ring which she wore as a charm against bad luck, while Sorelli, stealthily, with the tip of her pink right thumb-nail, made a St. Andrew's cross on the wooden ring which adorned the fourth finger of her left hand. She said to the little ballet-girls:

"Come, children, pull yourselves together! I dare say no one has ever seen the ghost."

"Yes, yes, we saw him—we saw him just now!" cried the girls. "He had his death's head and his dress-coat, just as when he appeared to Joseph Buquet!"

"And Gabriel saw him too!" said Jammes. "Only yesterday! Yesterday afternoon—in broad daylight—"

"Gabriel, the chorus-master?"

"Why, yes, didn't you know?"

"And he was wearing his dress-clothes, in broad daylight?"

"Who? Gabriel?"

"Why, no, the ghost!"

"Certainly! Gabriel told me so himself. That's what he knew him by. Gabriel was in the stage-manager's office. Suddenly the door opened and the Persian entered. You know the Persian has the evil eye—"

"Oh, yes!" answered the little ballet-girls in chorus, warding off ill-luck by pointing their forefinger and little finger at the absent Persian, while their second and third fingers were bent on the palm and held down by the thumb.

"And you know how superstitious Gabriel is," continued Jammes. "However, he is always polite. When he meets the Persian, he just puts his hand in his pocket and touches his keys. Well, the moment the Persian appeared in the doorway, Gabriel gave one jump from his chair to the lock of the cupboard, so as to touch iron! In doing so, he tore a whole skirt of his overcoat on a nail. Hurrying to get out of the room, he banged his forehead against a hat-peg and gave himself a huge bump; then, suddenly stepping back, he skinned his arm on the screen, near the piano; he tried to lean on the piano, but the lid fell on his hands and crushed his fingers; he rushed out of the office like a madman, slipped on the staircase and came down the whole of the first flight on his back. I was just passing with mother. We picked him up. He was covered with bruises and his face was all over blood. We were frightened out of our lives, but, all at once, he began to thank Providence that he had got off so cheaply. Then he told us what had frightened him. He had seen the ghost behind the Persian, *the ghost with the death's head*, just like Joseph Buquet's description!"

Jammes had told her story ever so quickly, as though the ghost were at her heels, and was quite out of breath at the finish. A silence followed, while Sorelli polished her nails in great excitement. It was broken by little Giry, who said:

"Joseph Buquet would do better to hold his tongue."

"Why should he hold his tongue?" asked somebody.

"That's mother's opinion," replied Meg, lowering her voice and looking all about her as though fearing lest other ears than those present might overhear.

"And why is it your mother's opinion?"

"Hush! Mother says the ghost doesn't like being talked about."

"And why does your mother say so?"

"Because—because—nothing—"

This reticence exasperated the curiosity of the young ladies, who crowded round little Giry, begging her to explain herself. They were there, side by side, leaning forward simultaneously in one movement of entreaty and fear, communicating their terror to one another, taking a keen pleasure in feeling their blood freeze in their veins.

"I swore not to tell!" gasped Meg.

But they left her no peace and promised to keep the secret, until Meg, burning to say all she knew, began, with her eyes fixed on the door:

"Well, it's because of the private box."

"What private box?"

"The ghost's box!"

"Has the ghost a box? Oh, do tell us, do tell us!"

"Not so loud!" said Meg. "It's Box Five, you know, the box on the grand tier, next to the stage-box, on the left."

"Oh, nonsense!"

"I tell you it is. Mother has charge of it. But you swear you won't say a word?"

"Of course, of course."

"Well, that's the ghost's box. No one has had it for over a month, except the ghost, and orders have been given at the box-office that it must never be sold."

"And does the ghost really come there?"

"Yes."

"Then somebody does come?"

"Why, no! The ghost comes, but there is nobody there."

The little ballet-girls exchanged glances. If the ghost came to the box, he must be seen, because he wore a dress-coat and a death's head. This was what they tried to make Meg understand, but she replied:

"That's just it! The ghost is not seen. And he has no dress-coat and no head! All that talk about his death's head and his head of fire is nonsense! There's nothing in it. You only hear him when he is in the box. Mother has never seen him, but she has heard him. Mother knows, because she gives him his program."

Sorelli interfered.

"Giry, child, you're getting at us!"

Thereupon little Giry began to cry.

"I ought to have held my tongue—if mother ever came to know! But I was quite right, Joseph Buquet had no business to talk of things that don't concern him—it will bring him bad luck—mother was saying so last night—"

There was a sound of hurried and heavy footsteps in the passage and a breathless voice cried:

"Cecile! Cecile! Are you there?"

"It's mother's voice," said Jammes. "What's the matter?"

She opened the door. A respectable lady, built on the lines of a Pomeranian grenadier, burst into the dressing-room and dropped groaning into a vacant arm-chair. Her eyes rolled madly in her brick-dust colored face.

"How awful!" she said. "How awful!"

"What? What?"

"Joseph Buquet—"

"What about him?"

"Joseph Buquet is dead!"

The room became filled with exclamations, with astonished outcries, with scared requests for explanations.

"Yes, he was found hanging in the third-floor cellar!"

"It's the ghost!" little Giry blurted, as though in spite of herself; but she at once corrected herself, with her hands pressed to her mouth: "No, no!—I didn't say it!—I didn't say it!—"

All around her, her panic-stricken companions repeated under their breaths:

"Yes—it must be the ghost!"

Sorelli was very pale.

"I shall never be able to recite my speech," she said.

Ma Jammes gave her opinion, while she emptied a glass of liqueur that happened to be standing on a table; the ghost must have something to do with it.

The truth is that no one ever knew how Joseph Buquet met his death. The verdict at the inquest was "natural suicide." In his *Memoirs of a Manager*, M. Moncharmin, one of the joint managers who succeeded MM. Debienne and Poligny, describes the incident as follows:

> A grievous accident spoiled the little party which MM. Debienne and Poligny gave to celebrate their retirement. I was in the manager's office, when Mercier, the acting-manager, suddenly came darting in. He seemed half mad and told me that the body of a scene-shifter had been found hanging in the third cellar under the stage, between a farm-house and a scene from the Roi de Lahore. I shouted:
>
> "Come and cut him down!"
>
> By the time I had rushed down the staircase and the Jacob's ladder, the man was no longer hanging from his rope!

So this is an event which M. Moncharmin thinks natural. A man hangs at the end of a rope; they go to cut him down; the rope has disappeared. Oh, M. Moncharmin found a very simple explanation! Listen to him:

> It was just after the ballet; and leaders and dancing-girls lost no time in taking their precautions against the evil eye.

There you are! Picture the *corps de ballet* scuttling down the Jacob's ladder and dividing the suicide's rope among themselves in less time than it takes to write! When, on the other hand, I think of the exact spot where the body was discovered—the third cellar underneath the stage—I imagine that somebody must have been interested in seeing that the rope disappeared after it had effected its purpose; and time will show if I am wrong.

The horrid news soon spread all over the Opera, where Joseph Buquet was very popular. The dressing-rooms emptied and the ballet-girls, crowding around Sorelli like timid sheep around their shepherdess, made for the foyer through the ill-lit passages and staircases, trotting as fast as their little pink legs could carry them.

II

THE NEW MARGARITA

ON THE FIRST LANDING, SORELLI RAN AGAINST THE COMTE DE CHAGNY, who was coming up-stairs. The count, who was generally so calm, seemed greatly excited.

"I was just going to you," he said, taking off his hat. "Oh, Sorelli, what an evening! And Christine Daaé: what a triumph!"

"Impossible!" said Meg Giry. "Six months ago, she used to sing like a *crock*! But do let us get by, my dear count," continues the brat, with a saucy curtsey. "We are going to inquire after a poor man who was found hanging by the neck."

Just then the acting-manager came fussing past and stopped when he heard this remark.

"What!" he exclaimed roughly. "Have you girls heard already? Well, please forget about it for tonight—and above all don't let M. Debienne and M. Poligny hear; it would upset them too much on their last day."

They all went on to the foyer of the ballet, which was already full of people. The Comte de Chagny was right; no gala performance ever equalled this one. All the great composers of the day had conducted their own works in turns. Faure and Krauss had sung; and, on that evening, Christine Daaé had revealed her true self, for the first time, to the astonished and enthusiastic audience. Gounod had conducted the *Funeral March of a Marionnette*; Reyer, his beautiful overture to *Siguar*; Saint Saëns, the *Danse Macabre* and a *Rêverie Orientale*; Massenet, an unpublished Hungarian march; Guiraud, his *Carnaval*; Delibes, the *Valse lente* from *Sylvia* and the *Pizzicati* from *Coppelia*. Mlle. Krauss had sung the bolero in the *Vespri Siciliani*; and Mlle. Denise Bloch the drinking song in *Lucrezia Borgia*.

But the real triumph was reserved for Christine Daaé, who had begun by singing a few passages from *Romeo and Juliet*. It was the first time that the young artist sang in this work of Gounod, which had not been transferred to the Opera and which was revived at the Opéra Comique after it had been produced at the old Theatre Lyrique by Mme. Carvalho. Those who heard her say that her voice, in these passages, was seraphic; but this was nothing to the superhuman notes that she gave forth in the prison scene and the final trio in *Faust*, which she sang in the place of La Carlotta, who was ill. No one had ever heard or seen anything like it.

Daaé revealed a new Margarita that night, a Margarita of a splendor, a radiance hitherto unsuspected. The whole house went mad, rising to its feet, shouting, cheering, clapping, while Christine sobbed and fainted in the arms of her fellow-singers and had to be carried to her dressing-room. A few subscribers, however, protested. Why had so great a treasure been kept from them all that time? Till then, Christine Daaé had played a good Siebel to Carlotta's rather too splendidly material Margarita. And it had needed Carlotta's incomprehensible and inexcusable absence from this gala night for the little Daaé, at a moment's warning, to show all that she could do in a part of the program reserved for the Spanish diva! Well, what the subscribers wanted to know was, why had Debienne and Poligny applied to Daaé, when Carlotta was taken ill? Did they know of her hidden genius? And, if they knew of it, why had they kept it hidden? And why had she kept it hidden? Oddly enough, she was not known to have a professor of singing at that moment. She had often said she meant to practise alone for the future. The whole thing was a mystery.

The Comte de Chagny, standing up in his box, listened to all this frenzy and took part in it by loudly applauding. Philippe Georges Marie Comte de Chagny was just forty-one years of age. He was a great aristocrat and a good-looking man, above middle height and with attractive features, in spite of his hard forehead and his rather cold eyes. He was exquisitely polite to the women and a little haughty to the men, who did not always forgive him for his successes in society. He had an excellent heart and an irreproachable conscience. On the death of old Count Philibert, he became the head of one of the oldest and most distinguished families in France, whose arms dated back to the fourteenth century. The Chagnys owned a great deal of property; and, when the old count, who was a widower, died, it was no easy task for Philippe to accept the management of so large an estate. His two sisters and his brother, Raoul, would not hear of a division and waived their claim to their shares, leaving themselves entirely in Philippe's hands, as though the right of primogeniture had never ceased to exist. When the two sisters married, on the same day, they received their portion from their brother, not as a thing rightfully belonging to them, but as a dowry for which they thanked him.

The Comtesse de Chagny, *née* de Moerogis de La Martyniere, had died in giving birth to Raoul, who was born twenty years after his elder brother. At the time of the old count's death, Raoul was twelve years of age. Philippe busied himself actively with the youngster's education. He was admirably assisted in this work first by his sisters and afterward by an old aunt, the widow of a naval officer, who lived at Brest and gave young Raoul a taste for the sea. The lad entered the *Borda* training-ship, finished his course with honors and quietly made his trip round the world. Thanks to powerful influence, he had just been appointed a member of the official expedition on board the *Requin*, which was to be sent to the Arctic Circle in search of the survivors of the D'Artoi's expedition, of whom nothing had been heard for three years. Meanwhile, he was enjoying a long furlough which would not be over for six months; and already the dowagers of the Faubourg Saint-Germain were pitying the handsome and apparently delicate stripling for the hard work in store for him.

The shyness of the sailor-lad—I was almost saying his innocence—was remarkable. He seemed to have but just left the women's apron-strings. As a matter of fact, petted as he was by his two sisters and his old aunt, he had retained from this purely feminine education manners that were almost candid and stamped with a charm that nothing had yet been able to sully. He was a little over twenty-one years of age and looked eighteen. He had a small, fair mustache, beautiful blue eyes and a complexion like a girl's.

Philippe spoiled Raoul. To begin with, he was very proud of him and pleased to foresee a glorious career for his junior in the navy in which one of their ancestors, the famous Chagny de La Roche, had held the rank of admiral. He took advantage of the young man's leave of absence to show him Paris, with all its luxurious and artistic delights. The count considered that, at Raoul's age, it is not good to be too good. Philippe himself had a character that was very well-balanced in work and pleasure alike; his demeanor was always faultless; and he was incapable of setting his brother a bad example. He took him with him wherever he went. He even introduced him to the foyer of the ballet. I know that the count was said to be "on terms" with Sorelli. But it could hardly be reckoned as a crime for this nobleman, a bachelor, with plenty of leisure, especially since his sisters were settled, to come and spend an hour or two after dinner in the company of a dancer, who, though not so very, very witty, had the finest eyes that ever were seen! And, besides, there are places where a true Parisian, when he has the rank of the Comte de Chagny, is bound to show himself; and at that time the foyer of the ballet at the Opera was one of those places.

Lastly, Philippe would perhaps not have taken his brother behind the scenes of the Opera if Raoul had not been the first to ask him, repeatedly renewing his request with a gentle obstinacy which the count remembered at a later date.

On that evening, Philippe, after applauding the Daaé, turned to Raoul and saw that he was quite pale.

"Don't you see," said Raoul, "that the woman's fainting?"

"You look like fainting yourself," said the count. "What's the matter?"

But Raoul had recovered himself and was standing up.

"Let's go and see," he said, "she never sang like that before."

The count gave his brother a curious smiling glance and seemed quite pleased. They were soon at the door leading from the house to the stage. Numbers of subscribers were slowly making their way through. Raoul tore his gloves without knowing what he was doing and Philippe had much too kind a heart to laugh at him for his impatience. But he now understood why Raoul was absent-minded when spoken to and why he always tried to turn every conversation to the subject of the Opera.

They reached the stage and pushed through the crowd of gentlemen, scene-shifters, supers and chorus-girls, Raoul leading the way, feeling that his heart no longer belonged to him, his face set with passion, while Count Philippe followed him with difficulty and continued to smile. At the back of the stage, Raoul had to stop before the inrush of the little troop of ballet-girls who blocked the passage which he was trying to enter. More than one chaffing phrase darted from little made-up lips, to which he did not reply; and at last he was able to pass, and dived into the semi-darkness of a corridor ringing with the name of "Daaé! Daaé!" The count was surprised to find that Raoul knew the way. He had never taken him to Christine's himself and came to the conclusion that Raoul must have gone there alone while the count stayed talking in the foyer with Sorelli, who often asked him to wait until it was her time to "go on" and sometimes handed him the little gaiters in which she ran down from her dressing-room to preserve the spotlessness of her satin dancing-shoes and her flesh-colored tights. Sorelli had an excuse; she had lost her mother.

Postponing his usual visit to Sorelli for a few minutes, the count followed his brother down the passage that led to Daaé's dressing-room and saw that it had never been so crammed as on that evening, when the whole house seemed excited by her success and also by her fainting fit. For the girl had not yet come to; and the doctor of the theater had just arrived at the moment when Raoul entered at his heels. Christine, therefore, received the first aid of the one, while opening her eyes in the arms of the other. The count and many more remained crowding in the doorway.

"Don't you think, Doctor, that those gentlemen had better clear the room?" asked Raoul coolly. "There's no breathing here."

"You're quite right," said the doctor.

And he sent every one away, except Raoul and the maid, who looked at Raoul with eyes of the most undisguised astonishment. She had never seen him before and yet dared not question him; and the doctor imagined that the young man was only acting as he did because he had the right to. The viscount, therefore, remained in the room watching Christine as she slowly returned to life, while even the joint managers, Debienne and Poligny, who had come to offer their sympathy and congratulations, found themselves thrust into the passage among the crowd of dandles. The Comte de Chagny, who was one of those standing outside, laughed:

"Oh, the rogue, the rogue!" And he added, under his breath: "Those youngsters with their school-girl airs! So he's a Chagny after all!"

He turned to go to Sorelli's dressing-room, but met her on the way, with her little troop of trembling ballet-girls, as we have seen.

Meanwhile, Christine Daaé uttered a deep sigh, which was answered by a groan. She turned her head, saw Raoul and started. She looked at the doctor, on whom she bestowed a smile, then at her maid, then at Raoul again.

"Monsieur," she said, in a voice not much above a whisper, "who are you?"

"Mademoiselle," replied the young man, kneeling on one knee and pressing a fervent kiss on the diva's hand, "*I am the little boy who went into the sea to rescue your scarf.*"

Christine again looked at the doctor and the maid; and all three began to laugh.

Raoul turned very red and stood up.

"Mademoiselle," he said, "since you are pleased not to recognize me, I should like to say something to you in private, something very important."

"When I am better, do you mind?" And her voice shook. "You have been very good."

"Yes, you must go," said the doctor, with his pleasantest smile. "Leave me to attend to mademoiselle."

"I am not ill now," said Christine suddenly, with strange and unexpected energy.

She rose and passed her hand over her eyelids.

"Thank you. Doctor. I should like to be alone. Please go away, all of you. Leave me. I feel very restless this evening."

The doctor tried to make a short protest, but, perceiving the girl's evident agitation, he thought the best remedy was not to thwart her. And he went away, saying to Raoul, outside:

"She is not herself to-night. She is usually so gentle."

Then he said good night and Raoul was left alone. The whole of this part of the theater was now deserted. The farewell ceremony was no doubt taking place in the foyer of the ballet. Raoul thought that Daaé might go to it and he waited in the silent solitude, even hiding in the favoring shadow of a doorway. He felt a terrible pain at his heart and it was of this that he wanted to speak to Daaé without delay.

Suddenly the dressing-room door opened and the maid came out by herself, carrying bundles. He stopped her and asked how her mistress was. The woman laughed and said that she was quite well, but that he must not disturb her, for she wished to be left alone. And she passed on. One idea alone filled Raoul's burning brain: of course, Daaé wished to be left alone *for him*! Had he not told her that he wanted to speak to her privately?

Hardly breathing, he went up to the dressing-room and, with his ear to the door to catch her reply, prepared to knock. But his hand dropped. He had heard *a man's voice* in the dressing-room, saying, in a curiously masterful tone:

"Christine, you must love me!"

And Christine's voice, infinitely sad and trembling, as though accompanied by tears, replied:

"How can you talk like that? *When I sing only for you*!"

Raoul leaned against the panel to ease his pain. His heart, which had seemed gone for ever, returned to his breast and was throbbing loudly. The whole passage echoed with its beating and Raoul's ears were deafened. Surely, if his heart continued to make such a noise, they would hear it inside, they would open the door and the young man would be turned away in disgrace. What a position for a Chagny! To be caught listening behind a door! He took his heart in his two hands to make it stop.

The man's voice spoke again:

"Are you very tired?"

"Oh, to-night I gave you my soul and I am dead!" Christine replied.

"Your soul is a beautiful thing, child," replied the grave man's voice, "and I thank you. No emperor ever received so fair a gift. *The angels wept tonight*."

Raoul heard nothing after that. Nevertheless, he did not go away, but, as though he feared lest he should be caught, he returned to his dark corner, determined to wait for the man to leave the room. At one and the same time, he had learned what love meant, and hatred. He knew that he loved. He wanted to know whom he hated. To his great astonishment, the door opened and Christine Daaé appeared, wrapped in furs, with her face hidden in a lace veil, alone. She closed the door behind her, but Raoul observed that she did not lock it. She passed him. He did not even follow her with his eyes, for his eyes were fixed on the door, which did not open again.

When the passage was once more deserted, he crossed it, opened the door of the dressing-room, went in and shut the door. He found himself in absolute darkness. The gas had been turned out.

"There is some one here!" said Raoul, with his back against the closed door, in a quivering voice. "What are you hiding for?"

All was darkness and silence. Raoul heard only the sound of his own breathing. He quite failed to see that the indiscretion of his conduct was exceeding all bounds.

"You shan't leave this until I let you!" he exclaimed. "If you don't answer, you are a coward! But I'll expose you!"

And he struck a match. The blaze lit up the room. There was no one in the room! Raoul, first turning the key in the door, lit the gas-jets. He went into the dressing-closet, opened the cupboards, hunted about, felt the walls with his moist hands. Nothing!

"Look here!" he said, aloud. "Am I going mad?"

He stood for ten minutes listening to the gas flaring in the silence of the empty room; lover though he was, he did not even think of stealing a ribbon that would have given him the perfume of the woman he loved. He went out, not knowing what he was doing nor where he was going. At a given moment in his wayward progress, an icy draft struck him in the face. He found himself at the bottom of a staircase, down which, behind him, a procession of workmen were carrying a sort of stretcher, covered with a white sheet.

"Which is the way out, please?" he asked or one of the men.

"Straight in front of you, the door is open. But let us pass."

Pointing to the stretcher, he asked mechanically:

"What's that?"

The workmen answered:

"'That' is Joseph Buquet, who was found in the third cellar, hanging between a farm-house and a scene from the *Roi de Lahore*."

He took off his hat, fell back to make room for the procession and went out.

III

THE MYSTERIOUS REASON

During this time, the farewell ceremony was taking place. I have already said that this magnificent function was being given on the occasion of the retirement of M. Debienne and M. Poligny, who had determined to "die game," as we say nowadays. They had been assisted in the realization of their ideal, though melancholy, program by all that counted in the social and artistic world of Paris. All these people met, after the performance, in the foyer of the ballet, where Sorelli waited for the arrival of the retiring managers with a glass of champagne in her hand and a little prepared speech at the tip of her tongue. Behind her, the members of the *corps de ballet*, young and old, discussed the events of the day in whispers or exchanged discreet signals with their friends, a noisy crowd of whom surrounded the supper-tables arranged along the slanting floor.

A few of the dancers had already changed into ordinary dress; but most of them wore their skirts of gossamer gauze; and all had thought it the right thing to put on a special face for the occasion: all, that is, except little Jammes, whose fifteen summers—happy age!—seemed already to have forgotten the ghost and the death of Joseph Buquet. She never ceased to laugh and chatter, to hop about and play practical jokes, until MM. Debienne and Poligny appeared on the steps of the foyer, when she was severely called to order by the impatient Sorelli.

Everybody remarked that the retiring managers looked cheerful, as is the Paris way. None will ever be a true Parisian who has not learned to wear a mask of gaiety over his sorrows and one of sadness, boredom or indifference over his inward joy. You know that one of your friends is in trouble; do not try to console him: he will tell you that he is already comforted; but, should he have met with good fortune, be careful how you congratulate him: he thinks it so natural that he is surprised that you should speak of it. In Paris, our lives are one masked ball; and the foyer of the ballet is the last place in which two men so "knowing" as M. Debienne and M. Poligny would have made the mistake of betraying their grief, however genuine it might be. And they were already smiling rather too broadly upon Sorelli, who had begun to recite her speech, when an exclamation from that little madcap of a Jammes broke the smile of the managers so brutally that the expression of distress and dismay that lay beneath it became apparent to all eyes:

"The Opera ghost!"

Jammes yelled these words in a tone of unspeakable terror; and her finger pointed, among the crowd of dandies, to a face so pallid, so lugubrious and so ugly, with two such deep black cavities under the straddling eyebrows, that the death's head in question immediately scored a huge success.

"The Opera ghost! The Opera ghost!"

Everybody laughed and pushed his neighbor and wanted to offer the Opera ghost a drink, but he was gone. He had slipped through the crowd; and the others vainly hunted for him, while two old gentlemen tried to calm little Jammes and while little Giry stood screaming like a peacock.

Sorelli was furious; she had not been able to finish her speech; the managers had kissed her, thanked her and run away as fast as the ghost himself. No one was surprised at this, for it was known that they were to go through the same ceremony on the floor above, in the foyer of the singers, and that finally they were themselves to receive their personal friends, for the last time. In the great lobby outside the managers' office, where a regular supper would be served.

Here they found the new managers, M. Armand Moncharmin and M. Firmin Richard, whom they hardly knew; nevertheless, they were lavish in protestations of friendship and received a thousand flattering compliments in reply, so that those of the guests who had feared that they had a rather tedious evening in store for them at once put on brighter faces. The supper was almost gay and a particularly clever speech of the representative of the government, mingling the glories of the past with the successes of the future, caused the greatest cordiality to prevail.

The retiring managers had already handed over to their successors the two tiny master-keys which opened all the doors—thousands of doors—of the Opera house. And those little keys, the object of general curiosity, were being passed from hand to hand, when the attention of some of the guests was diverted by their discovery, at the end of the table, of that strange, wan and fantastic face, with the hollow eyes, which had already appeared in the foyer of the ballet and been greeted by little Jammes' exclamation:

"The Opera ghost!"

There sat the ghost, as natural as could be, except that he neither ate nor drank. Those who began by looking at him with a smile ended by turning away their heads, for the sight of him at once provoked the most funereal thoughts. No one repeated the joke of the foyer, no one exclaimed:

"There's the Opera ghost!"

He himself did not speak a word and his very neighbors could not have stated at what precise moment he had sat down between them; but every one felt that if the dead did ever come and sit at the table of the living, they could not cut a more ghastly figure. The friends of Firmin Richard and Armand Moncharmin thought that this lean and skinny guest was an acquaintance of Debienne's or Poligny's, while Debienne's and Poligny's friends believed that the cadaverous individual belonged to Firmin Richard and Armand Moncharmin's party.

The result was that no request was made for an explanation; no unpleasant remark; no joke in bad taste, which might have offended this visitor from the tomb. A few of those present who knew the story of the ghost and the description of him given by the chief scene-shifter—they did not know of Joseph Buquet's death—thought, in their own minds, that the man at the end of the table might easily have passed for him; and yet, according to the story, the ghost had no nose and the person in question had. But M. Moncharmin declares, in his *Memoirs*, that the guest's nose was transparent: "long, thin and transparent" are his exact words. I, for my part, will add that this might very well apply to a false nose. M. Moncharmin may have taken for transparency what was only shininess. Everybody knows that orthopædic science provides beautiful false noses for those who have lost their noses naturally or as the result of an operation.

Did the ghost really take a seat at the managers' supper-table that night, uninvited? And can we be sure that the figure was that of the Opera ghost himself? Who would venture to assert as much? I mention the incident, not because I wish for a second to make the reader believe—or even to try to make him believe—that the ghost was capable of such a sublime piece of impudence; but because, after all, the thing is impossible.

M. Armand Moncharmin, in chapter eleven of his *Memoirs*, says:

> When I think of this first evening, I can not separate the secret confided to us by MM. Debienne and Poligny in their office from the presence at our supper of that ghostly person whom none of us knew.

What happened was this: MM. Debienne and Poligny, sitting at the center of the table, had not seen the man with the death's head. Suddenly he began to speak.

"The ballet-girls are right," he said. "The death of that poor Buquet is perhaps not so natural as people think."

Debienne and Poligny gave a start.

"Is Buquet dead?" they cried.

"Yes," replied the man, or the shadow of a man, quietly. "He was found, this evening, hanging in the third cellar, between a farm-house and a scene from the *Roi de Lahore*."

The two managers, or rather ex-managers, at once rose and stared strangely at the speaker. They were more excited than they need have been, that is to say, more excited than any one need be by the announcement of the suicide of a chief scene-shifter. They looked at each other. They had both turned whiter than the table-cloth. At last, Debienne made a sign to MM. Richard and Moncharmin; Poligny muttered a few words of excuse to the guests; and all four went into the managers' office. I leave M. Moncharmin to complete the story. In his *Memoirs*, he says:

> MM. Debienne and Poligny seemed to grow more and more excited, and they appeared to have something very difficult to tell us. First, they asked us if we knew the man, sitting at the end of the table, who had told them of the death of Joseph Buquet; and, when we answered in the negative, they looked still more concerned. They took the master-keys from our hands, stared at them for a moment and advised us to have new locks made, with the greatest secrecy, for the rooms, closets and presses that we might wish to have hermetically closed. They said this so funnily that we began to laugh and to ask if there were thieves at the Opera. They replied that there was something worse, which was the ghost. We began to laugh again, feeling sure that they were indulging in some joke that was intended to crown our little entertainment. Then, at their request, we became "serious," resolving to humor them and to enter into the spirit of the game. They told us that they never would have spoken to us of the ghost, if they had not received formal orders from the ghost himself to ask us to be pleasant to him and to grant any request that he might make. However, in their relief at leaving a domain where that tyrannical shade held sway, they had hesitated until the last moment to tell us this curious story, which our skeptical minds were certainly not prepared to entertain. But the announcement of the death of Joseph Buquet had served them as a brutal reminder that, whenever they had disregarded the ghost's wishes, some fantastic or disastrous event had brought them to a sense of their dependence.
>
> During these unexpected utterances made in a tone of the most secret and important confidence, I looked at Richard. Richard, in his student days, had acquired a great reputation for practical joking, and he seemed to relish the dish which was being served up to him in his turn. He did not miss a morsel of it, though the seasoning was a little

gruesome because of the death of Buquet. He nodded his head sadly, while the others spoke, and his features assumed the air of a man who bitterly regretted having taken over the Opera, now that he knew that there was a ghost mixed up in the business. I could think of nothing better than to give him a servile imitation of this attitude of despair. However, in spite of all our efforts, we could not, at the finish, help bursting out laughing in the faces of MM. Debienne and Poligny, who, seeing us pass straight from the gloomiest state of mind to one of the most insolent merriment, acted as though they thought that we had gone mad.

The joke became a little tedious; and Richard asked half-seriously and half in jest:

"But, after all, what does this ghost of yours want?"

M. Poligny went to his desk and returned with a copy of the memorandum-book. The memorandum book begins with the well-known words saying that "the management of the Opera shall give to the performance of the National Academy of Music the splendor that becomes the first lyric stage in France" and ends with Clause 98, which says that the privilege can be withdrawn If the manager infringes the conditions stipulated In the memorandum-book. This is followed by the conditions, which are four in number.

The copy produced by M. Poligny was written in black ink and exactly similar to that in our possession, except that, at the end, it contained a paragraph in red ink and in a queer, labored handwriting, as though it had been produced by dipping the heads of matches into the ink, the writing of a child that has never got beyond the down-strokes and has not learned to join its letters. This paragraph ran, word for word, as follows:

"5. Or if the manager, in any month, delay for more than a fortnight the payment of the allowance which he shall make to the Opera ghost, an allowance of twenty thousand francs a month, say two hundred and forty thousand francs a year."

M. Poligny pointed with a hesitating finger to this last clause, which we certainly did not expect.

"Is this all? Does he not want anything else?" asked Richard, with the greatest coolness.

"Yes, he does," replied Poligny.

"And he turned over the pages of the memorandum-book until he came to the clause specifying the days on which certain private boxes were to be reserved for the free use of the president of the republic, the ministers and so on. At the end of this clause, a line had been added, also in red ink:

"Box Five on the grand tier shall be placed at the disposal of the Opera ghost for every performance."

When we saw this, there was nothing else for us to do but to rise from our chairs, shake our two predecessors warmly by the hand and congratulate them on thinking of this charming little joke, which proved that the old French sense of humor was never likely to become extinct. Richard added that he now understood why MM. Debienne and Poligny were retiring from the management of the National Academy of Music. Business was impossible with so unreasonable a ghost.

"Certainly, two hundred and forty thousand francs are not be picked up for the asking," said M. Poligny, without moving a muscle of his face. "And have you considered what the loss over Box Five meant to us? We did not sell it once; and not only that, but we had to return the subscription: why, it's awful! We really can't work to keep ghosts! We prefer to go away!"

"Yes," echoed M. Debienne, "we prefer to go away. Let us go."

And he stood up. Richard said: "But, after all, it seems to me that you were much too kind to the ghost. If I had such a troublesome ghost as that, I should not hesitate to have him arrested—"

"But how? Where?" they cried, in chorus. "We have never seen him!"

"But when he comes to his box?"

"We have never seen him in his box."

"Then sell it."

"Sell the Opera ghost's box! Well, gentlemen, try it."

Thereupon we all four left the office. Richard and I had "never laughed so much in our lives."

IV

BOX FIVE

Armand Moncharmin wrote such voluminous *Memoirs* during the fairly long period of his co-management that we may well ask if he ever found time to attend to the affairs of the Opera otherwise than by telling what went on there. M. Moncharmin did not know a note of music, but he called the minister of education and fine arts by his Christian name, had dabbled a little in society journalism and enjoyed a considerable private income. Lastly, he was a charming fellow and showed that he was not lacking in intelligence, for, as soon as he made up his mind to be a sleeping partner in the Opera, he selected the best possible active manager and went straight to Firmin Richard.

Firmin Richard was a very distinguished composer, who had published a number of successful pieces of all kinds and who liked nearly every form of music and every sort of musician. Clearly, therefore, it was the duty of every sort of musician to like M. Firmin Richard. The only things to be said against him were that he was rather masterful in his ways and endowed with a very hasty temper.

The first few days which the partners spent at the Opera were given over to the delight of finding themselves the head of so magnificent an enterprise; and they had forgotten all about that curious, fantastic story of the ghost, when an incident occurred that proved to them that the joke—if joke it were—was not over. M. Firmin Richard reached his office that morning at eleven o'clock. His secretary, M. Rémy, showed him half a dozen letters which he had not opened because they were marked "private." One of the letters had at once attracted Richard's attention not only because the envelope was addressed in red ink, but because he seemed to have seen the writing before. He soon remembered that it was the red handwriting in which the memorandum-book had been so curiously completed. He recognized the clumsy childish hand. He opened the letter and read:

> Dear Mr. Manager:
>
> I am sorry to have to trouble you at a time when you must be so very busy, renewing important engagements, signing fresh ones and generally displaying your excellent taste. I know what you have done for Carlotta, Sorelli and little Jammes and for a few others whose admirable qualities of talent or genius you have suspected.

Of course, when I use these words, I do not mean to apply them to La Carlotta, who sings like a squirt and who ought never to have been allowed to leave the Ambassadeurs and the Café Jacquin; nor to La Sorelli, who owes her success mainly to the coachbuilders; nor to little Jammes, who dances like a calf in a field. And I am not speaking of Christine Daaé either, though her genius is certain, whereas your jealousy prevents her from creating any important part. When all is said, you are free to conduct your little business as you think best, are you not?

All the same, I should like to take advantage of the fact that you have not yet turned Christine Daaé out of doors by hearing her this evening in the part of Siebel, as that of Margarita has been forbidden her since her triumph of the other evening; and I will ask you not to dispose of my box to-day nor on the following days, for I can not end this letter without telling you how disagreeably surprised I have been once or twice, to hear, on arriving at the Opera, that my box had been sold, at the box-office, by your orders.

I did not protest, first, because I dislike scandal, and, second, because I thought that your predecessors, MM. Debienne and Poligny, who were always charming to me, had neglected, before leaving, to mention my little fads to you. I have now received a reply from those gentlemen to my letter asking for an explanation, and this reply proves that you know all about my *memorandum-book* and, consequently, that you are treating me with outrageous contempt. If you wish to live in peace, you must not begin by taking away my private box.

Believe me to be, dear Mr. Manager, without prejudice to these little observations.

Your Most Humble and Obedient Servant,

—OPERA GHOST

The letter was accompanied by a cutting from the agony-column of the *Revue Théâtrale*, which ran:

O. G.—There is no excuse for R. and M. We told them and left your memorandum-book in their hands. Kind regards.

M. Firmin Richard had hardly finished reading this letter when M. Armand Moncharmin entered, carrying one exactly similar. They looked at each other and burst out laughing.

"They are keeping up the joke," said M. Richard, "but I don't call it funny."

"What does it all mean?" asked M. Moncharmin. "Do they imagine that, because they have been managers of the Opera, we are going to let them have a box for an indefinite period?"

"I am not in the mood to let myself be laughed at long," said Firmin Richard.

"It's harmless enough," observed Armand Moncharmin. "What is it they really want? A box for to-night?"

M. Firmin Richard told his secretary to send Box Five on the grand tier to MM. Debienne and Poligny, if it was not sold. It was not. It was sent off to them. Debienne lived at the corner of the Rue Scribe and the Boulevard des Capucines; Poligny, in the Rue Auber. O. Ghost's two letters had been posted at the Boulevard des Capucines post-office, as Moncharmin remarked after examining the envelopes.

"You see!" said Richard.

They shrugged their shoulders and regretted that two men of that age should amuse themselves with such childish tricks.

"They might have been civil, for all that!" said Moncharmin. "Did you notice how they treat us with regard to Carlotta, Sorelli and Little Jammes?"

"Why, my dear fellow, these two are mad with jealousy! To think that they went to the expense of an advertisement in the *Revue Théâtrale*! Have they nothing better to do?"

"By the way," said Moncharmin, "they seem to be greatly interested in that little Christine Daaé!"

"You know as well as I do that she has the reputation of being quite good," said Richard.

"Reputations are easily obtained," replied Moncharmin. "Haven't I a reputation for knowing all about music? And I don't know one key from another."

"Don't be afraid: you never had that reputation," Richard declared.

Thereupon he ordered the artists to be shown in, who, for the last two hours, had been walking up and down outside the door behind which fame and fortune—or dismissal—awaited them.

The whole day was spent in discussing, negotiating, signing or cancelling contracts; and the two overworked managers went to bed early, without so much as casting a glance at Box Five to see whether M. Debienne and M. Poligny were enjoying the performance.

Next morning, the managers received a card of thanks from the ghost:

> DEAR MR. MANAGER:
>
> Thanks. Charming evening. Daaé exquisite. Choruses want waking up. Carlotta a splendid commonplace instrument. Will write you soon for the 240,000 francs, or 233,424 fr. 70 c, to be correct. MM. Debienne and Poligny have sent me the 6,575 fr. 30 c. representing the first ten days of my allowance for the current year; their privileges finished on the evening of the tenth inst. Kind regards,
>
> O. G.

On the other hand, there was a letter from MM. Debienne and Poligny:

> GENTLEMEN:
>
> We are much obliged for your kind thought of us, but you will easily understand that the prospect of again hearing *Faust*, pleasant though it is to ex-managers of the Opera, can not make us forget that we have no right to occupy Box Five on the grand tier, which is the exclusive property of him of whom we spoke to you when we went through the memorandum-book with you for the last time. See Clause 98, final paragraph.
>
> Accept, gentlemen, etc.

"Oh, those fellows are beginning to annoy me!" shouted Firmin Richard, snatching up the letter.

And that evening Box Five was sold.

The next morning, MM. Richard and Moncharmin, on reaching their office, found an inspector's report relating to an incident that had happened, the night before, in Box Five. I give the essential part of the report:

> I was obliged to call in a municipal guard twice, this evening, to clear Box Five on the grand tier, once at the beginning and once in the middle of the second act. The occupants, who arrived as the curtain rose on the second act, created a regular scandal by their laughter and their ridiculous observations. There were cries of "Hush!" all around them and the whole house was beginning to protest, when the box-keeper came to fetch me. I entered the box and said what I thought

> necessary. The people did not seem to me to be in their right mind; and they made stupid remarks. I said that, if the noise was repeated, I should be compelled to clear the box. The moment I left, I heard the laughing again, with fresh protests from the house. I returned with a municipal guard, who turned them out. They protested, still laughing, saying they would not go unless they had their money back. At last, they became quiet and I allowed them to enter the box again. The laughter at once recommenced; and, this time, I had them turned out definitely.

"Send for the inspector," said Richard to his secretary, who had already read the report and marked it with blue pencil.

M. Rémy, the secretary, had foreseen the order and called the inspector at once.

"Tell us what happened," said Richard bluntly.

The inspector began to splutter and referred to the report.

"Well, but what were those people laughing at?" asked Moncharmin.

"They must have been dining, sir, and seemed more inclined to lark about than to listen to good music. The moment they entered the box, they came out again and called the box-keeper, who asked them what they wanted. They said, 'Look in the box: there's no one there. Is there?' 'No,' said the woman. 'Well,' said they, 'when we went in, we heard a voice saying *that the box was taken*!'"

M. Moncharmin could not help smiling as he looked at M. Richard; but M. Richard did not smile. He himself had done too much in that way in his time not to recognize, in the inspector's story, all the marks of one of those practical jokes which begin by amusing and end by enraging the victims. The inspector, to curry favor with M. Moncharmin, who was smiling, thought it best to give a smile too. A most unfortunate smile! M. Richard glared at his subordinate who thenceforth made it his business to display a face of utter consternation.

"However, when the people arrived," roared Richard, "there was no one in the box, was there?"

"Not a soul, sir, not a soul! Nor in the box on the right, nor in the box on the left: not a soul, sir, I swear! The box-keeper told it me often enough, which proves that it was all a joke."

"Oh, you agree, do you?" said Richard. "You agree! It's a joke! And you think it funny, no doubt?"

"I think it in very bad taste, sir."

"And what did the box-keeper say?"

"Oh, she just said that it was the Opera ghost. That's all she said!"

And the inspector grinned. But he soon found that he had made a mistake in grinning, for the words had no sooner left his mouth than M. Richard, from gloomy, became furious.

"Send for the box-keeper!" he shouted. "Send for her! This minute! This minute! And bring her in to me here! And turn all those people out!"

The inspector tried to protest, but Richard closed his mouth with an angry order to hold his tongue. Then, when the wretched man's lips seemed shut for ever, the manager commanded him to open them once more.

"Who is this 'Opera ghost?'" he snarled.

But the inspector was by this time incapable of speaking a word. He managed to convey, by a despairing gesture, that he knew nothing about it, or rather that he did not wish to know.

"Have you ever seen him, have you seen the Opera ghost?"

The inspector, by means of a vigorous shake of the head, denied ever having seen the ghost in question.

"Very well!" said M. Richard coldly.

The inspector's eyes started out of his head, as though to ask why the manager had uttered that ominous "Very well!"

"Because I'm going to settle the account of any one who has not seen him!" explained the manager. "As he seems to be everywhere, I can't have people telling me that they see him nowhere. I like people to work for me when I employ them!"

Having said this, M. Richard paid no attention to the inspector and discussed various matters of business with his acting-manager, who had entered the room meanwhile. The inspector thought he could go and was gently—oh, so gently!—sidling toward the door, when M. Richard nailed the man to the floor with a thundering:

"Stay where you are!"

M. Rémy had sent for the box-keeper to the Rue de Provence, close to the Opera, where she was engaged as a porteress. She soon made her appearance.

"What's your name?"

"Mame Giry. You know me well enough, sir; I'm the mother of little Giry, little Meg, what!"

This was said in so rough and solemn a tone that, for a moment, M. Richard was impressed. He looked at Mame Giry, in her faded shawl, her worn shoes, her old taffeta dress and dingy bonnet. It was quite evident from the manager's attitude, that he either did not know or could not remember having met Mame

Giry, nor even little Giry, nor even "little Meg!" But Mame Giry's pride was so great that the celebrated box-keeper imagined that everybody knew her.

"Never heard of her!" the manager declared. "But that's no reason, Mame Giry, why I shouldn't ask you what happened last night to make you and the inspector call in a municipal guard . . ."

"I was just wanting to see you, sir, and talk to you about it, so that you mightn't have the same unpleasantness as M. Debienne and M. Poligny. They wouldn't listen to me either, at first."

"I'm not asking you about all that. I'm asking what happened last night."

Mame Giry turned purple with indignation. Never had she been spoken to like that. She rose as though to go, gathering up the folds of her skirt and waving the feathers of her dingy bonnet with dignity, but, changing her mind, she sat down again and said, in a haughty voice:

"I'll tell you what happened. The ghost was annoyed again!"

Thereupon, as M. Richard was on the point of bursting out, M. Moncharmin interfered and conducted the interrogatory, whence it appeared that Mame Giry thought it quite natural that a voice should be heard to say that a box was taken, when there was nobody in the box. She was unable to explain this phenomenon, which was not new to her, except by the intervention of the ghost. Nobody could see the ghost in his box, but everybody could hear him. She had often heard him; and they could believe her, for she always spoke the truth. They could ask M. Debienne and M. Poligny, and anybody who knew her; and also M. Isidore Saack, who had had a leg broken by the ghost!

"Indeed!" said Moncharmin, interrupting her. "Did the ghost break poor Isidore Saack's leg?"

Mame Giry opened her eyes with astonishment at such ignorance. However, she consented to enlighten those two poor innocents. The thing had happened in M. Debienne and M. Poligny's time, also in Box Five and also during a performance of *Faust*. Mame Giry coughed, cleared her throat—it sounded as though she were preparing to sing the whole of Gounod's score—and began:

"It was like this, sir. That night, M. Maniera and his lady, the jewelers in the Rue Mogador, were sitting in the front of the box, with their great friend, M. Isidore Saack, sitting behind Mme. Maniera. Mephistopheles was singing"—Mame Giry here burst into song herself—"'Catarina, while you play at sleeping,' and then M. Maniera heard a voice in his right ear (his wife was on his left) saying, 'Ha, ha! Julie's not playing at sleeping!' His wife happened to be called Julie. So, M. Maniera turns to the right to see who was talking to him like that. Nobody there! He rubs his ear and asks himself if he's dreaming. Then Mephistopheles went on with his serenade. . . .But, perhaps I'm boring you gentlemen?"

"No, no, go on."

"You are too good, gentlemen," with a smirk. "Well, then, Mephistopheles went on with his serenade"—Mame Giry, burst into song again—"'Saint, unclose thy portals holy and accord the bliss, to a mortal bending lowly, of a pardon-kiss.' And then M. Maniera again hears the voice in his right ear, saying, this time, 'Ha, ha! Julie wouldn't mind according a kiss to Isidore!' Then he turns round again, but, this time, to the left; and what do you think he sees? Isidore, who had taken his lady's hand and was covering it with kisses through the little round place in the glove—like this, gentlemen"—rapturously kissing the bit of palm left bare in the middle of her thread gloves. "Then they had a lively time between them! Bang! Bang! M. Maniera, who was big and strong, like you, M. Richard, gave two blows to M. Isidore Saack, who was small and weak like M. Moncharmin, saving his presence. There was a great uproar. People in the house shouted, 'That will do! Stop them! He'll kill him!' Then, at last, M. Isidore Saack managed to run away."

"Then the ghost had not broken his leg?" asked M. Moncharmin, a little vexed that his figure had made so little impression on Mame Giry.

"He did break it for him, sir," replied Mame Giry haughtily. "He broke it for him on the grand staircase, which he ran down too fast, sir, and it will be long before the poor gentleman will be able to go up it again!"

"Did the ghost tell you what he said in M. Maniera's right ear?" asked M. Moncharmin, with a gravity which he thought exceedingly humorous.

"No, sir, it was M. Maniera himself. So—"

"But you have spoken to the ghost, my good lady?"

"As I'm speaking to you now, my good sir!" Mame Giry replied.

"And, when the ghost speaks to you, what does he say?"

"Well, he tells me to bring him a footstool!"

This time, Richard burst out laughing, as did Moncharmin and Rémy, the secretary. Only the inspector, warned by experience, was careful not to laugh, while Mame Giry ventured to adopt an attitude that was positively threatening.

"Instead of laughing," she cried indignantly, "you'd do better to do as M. Poligny did, who found out for himself."

"Found out about what?" asked Moncharmin, who had never been so much amused in his life.

"About the ghost, of course! . . . Look here . . ."

She suddenly calmed herself, feeling that this was a solemn moment in her life:

"*Look here*," she repeated. "They were playing *La Juive*. M. Poligny thought he would watch the performance from the ghost's box. . . .Well, when Leopold cries, 'Let us fly!'—you know—and Eléazer stops them and says, 'Whither go ye?' . . . well, M. Poligny—I was watching him from the back of the next box, which was empty—M. Poligny got up and walked out quite stiffly, like a statue, and before I had time to ask him, 'Whither go ye?' like Eléazer, he was down the staircase, but without breaking his leg. . . ."

"Still, that doesn't let us know how the Opera ghost came to ask you for a footstool," insisted M. Moncharmin.

"Well, from that evening, no one tried to take the ghost's private box from him. The manager gave orders that he was to have it at each performance. And, whenever he came, he asked me for a footstool."

"Tut, tut! A ghost asking for a footstool! Then this ghost of yours is a woman?"

"No, the ghost is a man."

"How do you know?"

"He has a man's voice, oh, such a lovely man's voice! This is what happens: When he comes to the opera, it's usually in the middle of the first act. He gives three little taps on the door of Box Five. The first time I heard those three taps, when I knew there was no one in the box, you can think how puzzled I was! I opened the door, listened, looked; nobody! And then I heard a voice say, 'Mame Jules'—my poor husband's name was Jules—'a footstool, please.' Saving your presence, gentlemen, it made me feel all-overish like. But the voice went on, 'Don't be frightened, Mame Jules, I'm the Opera ghost!' And the voice was so soft and kind that I hardly felt frightened. *The voice was sitting in the corner chair, on the right, in the front row.*"

"Was there any one in the box on the right of Box Five?" asked Moncharmin.

"No; Box Seven, and Box Three, the one on the left, were both empty. The curtain had only just gone up."

"And what did you do?"

"Well, I brought the footstool. Of course, it wasn't for himself he wanted it, but for his lady! But I never heard her nor saw her."

"Eh? What? So now the ghost is married!" The eyes of the two managers traveled from Mame Giry to the inspector, who, standing behind the boxkeeper, was waving his arms to attract their attention. He tapped his forehead with a distressful forefinger, to convey his opinion that the widow Jules Giry was most certainly mad, a piece of pantomime which confirmed M. Richard in his determination to get rid of an inspector who kept a lunatic in his service. Meanwhile, the worthy lady went on about her ghost, now painting his generosity:

"At the end of the performance, he always gives me two francs, sometimes five, sometimes even ten, when he has been many days without coming. Only, since people have begun to annoy him again, he gives me nothing at all. . . ."

"Excuse me, my good woman," said Moncharmin, while Mame Giry tossed the feathers in her dingy hat at this persistent familiarity, "excuse me, how does the ghost manage to give you your two francs?"

"Why, he leaves them on the little shelf in the box, of course. I find them with the program, which I always give him. Some evenings, I find flowers in the box, a rose that must have dropped from his lady's bodice . . . for he brings a lady with him sometimes; one day, they left a fan behind them."

"Oh, the ghost left a fan, did he? And what did you do with it?"

"Well, I brought it back to the box next night."

Here the inspector's voice was raised.

"You've broken the rules; I shall have to fine you, Mame Giry."

"Hold your tongue, you fool!" muttered M. Firmin Richard.

"You brought back the fan. And then?"

"Well, then, they took it away with them, sir; it was not there at the end of the performance; and in its place they left me a box of English sweets, which I'm very fond of. That's one of the ghost's pretty thoughts."

"That will do, Mame Giry. You can go." When Mame Giry had bowed herself out, with the dignity that never deserted her, the manager told the inspector that they had decided to dispense with that old madwoman's services; and, when he had gone in his turn, they instructed the acting-manager to make up the inspector's accounts. Left alone, the managers told each other of the idea which they both had in mind, which was that they should look into that little matter of Box Five themselves.

V

THE ENCHANTED VIOLIN

CHRISTINE DAAÉ, OWING TO INTRIGUES TO WHICH I WILL RETURN later, did not immediately continue her triumph at the Opera. After the famous gala night, she sang once at the Duchess de Zurich's; but this was the last occasion on which she was heard in private. She refused, without plausible excuse, to appear at a charity concert to which she had promised her assistance. She acted throughout as though she were no longer the mistress of her own destiny and as though she feared a fresh triumph.

She knew that the Comte de Chagny, to please his brother, had done his best on her behalf with M. Richard; and she wrote to thank him and also to ask him to cease speaking in her favor. Her reason for this curious attitude was never known. Some pretended that it was due to overweening pride; others spoke of her heavenly modesty. But people on the stage are not so modest as all that; and I think that I shall not be far from the truth if I ascribe her action simply to fear. Yes, I believe that Christine Daaé was frightened by what had happened to her. I have a letter of Christine's (it forms part of the Persian's collection), relating to this period, which suggests a feeling of absolute dismay:

"I don't know myself when I sing," writes the poor child.

She showed herself nowhere; and the Vicomte de Chagny tried in vain to meet her. He wrote to her, asking to call upon her, but despaired of receiving a reply when, one morning, she sent him the following note:

> Monsieur:
>
> I have not forgotten the little boy who went into the sea to rescue my scarf. I feel that I must write to you to-day, when I am going to Perros, in fulfilment of a sacred duty. To-morrow is the anniversary of the death of my poor father, whom you knew and who was very fond of you. He is buried there, with his violin, in the graveyard of the little church, at the bottom of the slope where we used to play as children, beside the road where, when we were a little bigger, we said good-by for the last time.

The Vicomte de Chagny hurriedly consulted a railway guide, dressed as quickly as he could, wrote a few lines for his valet to take to his brother and jumped into a cab which brought him to the Gare Montparnasse just in time to miss the morning train. He spent a dismal day in town and did not recover his spirits until the evening, when he was seated in his compartment in the Brittany express. He read Christine's note over and over again, smelling its perfume, recalling the sweet pictures of his childhood, and spent the rest of that tedious night journey in feverish dreams that began and ended with Christine Daaé. Day was breaking when he alighted at Lannion. He hurried to the diligence for Perros-Guirec. He was the only passenger. He questioned the driver and learned that, on the evening of the previous day, a young lady who looked like a Parisian had gone to Perros and put up at the inn known as the Setting Sun.

The nearer he drew to her, the more fondly he remembered the story of the little Swedish singer. Most of the details are still unknown to the public.

There was once, in a little market-town not far from Upsala, a peasant who lived there with his family, digging the earth during the week and singing in the choir on Sundays. This peasant had a little daughter to whom he taught the musical alphabet before she knew how to read. Daaé's father was a great musician, perhaps without knowing it. Not a fiddler throughout the length and breadth of Scandinavia played as he did. His reputation was widespread and he was always invited to set the couples dancing at weddings and other festivals. His wife died when Christine was entering upon her sixth year. Then the father, who cared only for his daughter and his music, sold his patch of ground and went to Upsala in search of fame and fortune. He found nothing but poverty.

He returned to the country, wandering from fair to fair, strumming his Scandinavian melodies, while his child, who never left his side, listened to him in ecstasy or sang to his playing. One day, at Ljimby Fair, Professor Valérius heard them and took them to Gothenburg. He maintained that the father was the first violinist in the world and that the daughter had the making of a great artist. Her education and instruction were provided for. She made rapid progress and charmed everybody with her prettiness, her grace of manner and her genuine eagerness to please.

When Valérius and his wife went to settle in. France, they took Daaé and Christine with them. "Mamma" Valérius treated Christine as her daughter. As for Daaé, he began to pine away with homesickness. He never went out of doors in Paris, but lived in a sort of dream which he kept up with his violin. For hours at a time, he remained locked up in his bedroom with his daughter, fiddling and singing, very, very softly. Sometimes Mamma Valérius would come and listen behind the door, wipe away a tear and go down-stairs again on tiptoe, sighing for her Scandinavian skies.

Daaé seemed not to recover his strength until the summer, when the whole family went to stay at Perros-Guirec, in a far-away corner of Brittany, where the sea was of the same color as in his own country. Often he would play his saddest tunes on the beach and pretend that the sea stopped its roaring to listen to them. And then he induced Mamma Valérius to indulge a queer whim of his. At the time of the "pardons," or Breton pilgrimages, the village festival and dances, he went off with his fiddle, as in the old days, and was allowed to take his daughter with him for a week. They gave the smallest hamlets music to last them for a year and slept at night in a barn, refusing a bed at the inn, lying close together on the straw, as when they were so poor in Sweden. At the same time, they were very neatly dressed, made no collection, refused the halfpence offered them; and the people around could not understand the conduct of this rustic fiddler, who tramped the roads with that pretty child who sang like an angel from Heaven. They followed them from village to village.

One day, a little boy, who was out with his governess, made her take a longer walk than he intended, for he could not tear himself from the little girl whose pure, sweet voice seemed to bind him to her. They came to the shore of an inlet which is still called Trestraou, but which now, I believe, harbors a casino or something of the sort. At that time, there was nothing but sky and sea and a stretch of golden beach. Only, there was also a high wind, which blew Christine's scarf out to sea. Christine gave a cry and put out her arms, but the scarf was already far on the waves. Then she heard a voice say:

"It's all right, I'll go and fetch your scarf out of the sea."

And she saw a little boy running fast, in spite of the outcries and the indignant protests of a worthy lady in black. The little boy ran into the sea, dressed as he was, and brought her back her scarf. Boy and scarf were both soaked through. The lady in black made a great fuss, but Christine laughed merrily and kissed the little boy, who was none other than the Vicomte Raoul de Chagny, staying at Lannion with his aunt.

During the season, they saw each other and played together almost every day. At the aunt's request, seconded by Professor Valérius, Daaé consented to give the young viscount some violin lessons. In this way, Raoul learned to love the same airs that had charmed Christine's childhood. They also both had the same calm and dreamy little cast of mind. They delighted in stories, in old Breton legends; and their favorite sport was to go and ask for them at the cottage-doors, like beggars:

"Ma'am . . ." or, "Kind gentleman . . . have you a little story to tell us, please?"

And it seldom happened that they did not have one "given" them; for nearly every old Breton grandame has, at least once in her life, seen the "korrigans" dance by moonlight on the heather.

But their great treat was, in the twilight, in the great silence of the evening, after the sun had set in the sea, when Daaé came and sat down by them on the roadside and, in a low voice, as though fearing lest he should frighten the ghosts whom he evoked, told them the legends of the land of the North. And, the moment he stopped, the children would ask for more.

There was one story that began:

"A king sat in a little boat on one of those deep, still lakes that open like a bright eye in the midst of the Norwegian mountains . . ."

And another:

"Little Lotte thought of everything and nothing. Her hair was golden as the sun's rays and her soul as clear and blue as her eyes. She wheedled her mother, was kind to her doll, took great care of her frock and her little red shoes and her fiddle, but most of all loved, when she went to sleep, to hear the Angel of Music."

While the old man told this story, Raoul looked at Christine's blue eyes and golden hair; and Christine thought that Lotte was very lucky to hear the Angel of Music when she went to sleep. The Angel of Music played a part in all Daddy Daaé's tales; and he maintained that every great musician, every great artist received a visit from the Angel at least once in his life. Sometimes the Angel leans over their cradle, as happened to Lotte, and that is how there are little prodigies who play the fiddle at six better than men at fifty, which, you must admit, is very wonderful. Sometimes, the Angel comes much later, because the children are naughty and won't learn their lessons or practise their scales. And, sometimes, he does not come at all, because the children have a bad heart or a bad conscience.

No one ever sees the Angel; but he is heard by those who are meant to hear him. He often comes when they least expect him, when they are sad and disheartened. Then their ears suddenly perceive celestial harmonies, a divine voice, which they remember all their lives. Persons who are visited by the Angel quiver with a thrill unknown to the rest of mankind. And they can not touch an instrument, or open their mouths to sing, without producing sounds that put all other human sounds to shame. Then people who do not know that the Angel has visited those persons say that they have genius.

Little Christine asked her father if he had heard the Angel of Music. But Daddy Daaé shook his head sadly; and then his eyes lit up, as he said:

"You will hear him one day, my child! When I am in Heaven, I will send him to you!"

Daddy was beginning to cough at that time.

Three years later, Raoul and Christine met again at Perros. Professor Valérius was dead, but his widow remained in France with Daddy Daaé and his daughter, who continued to play the violin and sing, wrapping in their dream of harmony their kind patroness, who seemed henceforth to live on music alone. The young man, as he now was, had come to Perros on the chance of finding them and went straight to the house in which they used to stay. He first saw the old man; and then Christine entered, carrying the tea-tray. She flushed at the sight of Raoul, who went up to her and kissed her. She asked him a few questions, performed her duties as hostess prettily, took up the tray again and left the room. Then she ran into the garden and took refuge on a bench, a prey to feelings that stirred her young heart for the first time. Raoul followed her and they talked till the evening, very shyly. They were quite changed, cautious as two diplomatists, and told each other things that had nothing to do with their budding sentiments. When they took leave of each other by the roadside, Raoul, pressing a kiss on Christine's trembling hand, said:

"Mademoiselle, I shall never forget you!"

And he went away regretting his words, for he knew that Christine could not be the wife of the Vicomte de Chagny.

As for Christine, she tried not to think of him and devoted herself wholly to her art. She made wonderful progress and those who heard her prophesied that she would be the greatest singer in the world. Meanwhile, the father died; and, suddenly, she seemed to have lost, with him, her voice, her soul and her genius. She retained just, but only just, enough of this to enter the *conservatoire*, where she did not distinguish herself at all, attending the classes without enthusiasm and taking a prize only to please old Mamma Valérius, with whom she continued to live.

The first time that Raoul saw Christine at the Opera, he was charmed by the girl's beauty and by the sweet images of the past which it evoked, but was rather surprised at the negative side of her art. He returned to listen to her. He followed her in the wings. He waited for her behind a Jacob's ladder. He tried to attract her attention. More than once, he walked after her to the door of her box, but she did not see him. She seemed, for that matter, to see nobody. She was all indifference. Raoul suffered, for she was very beautiful and he was shy and dared not confess his love, even to himself. And then came the lightning-flash of the gala performance: the heavens torn asunder and an angel's voice heard upon earth for the delight of mankind and the utter capture of his heart.

And then . . . and then there was that man's voice behind the door—"You must love me!"—and no one in the room. . . .

Why did she laugh when he reminded her of the incident of the scarf? Why did she not recognize him? And why had she written to him? . . .

Perros was reached at last. Raoul walked Into the smoky sitting-room of the Setting Sun and at once saw Christine standing before him, smiling and showing no astonishment.

"So you have come," she said. "I felt that I should find you here, when I came back from mass. Some one told me so, at the church."

"Who?" asked Raoul, taking her little hand in his.

"Why, my poor father, who is dead."

There was a silence; and then Raoul asked:

"Did your father tell you that I love you, Christine, and that I can not live without you?"

Christine blushed to the eyes and turned away her head. In a trembling voice, she said:

"Me? You are dreaming, my friend!"

And she burst out laughing, to put herself in countenance.

"Don't laugh, Christine; I am quite serious," Raoul answered.

And she replied gravely: "I did not make you come to tell me such things as that."

"You 'made me come,' Christine; you knew that your letter would not leave me indignant and that I should hasten to Perros. How can you have thought that, if you did not think I loved you?"

"I thought you would remember our games here, as children, in which my father so often joined. I really don't know what I thought.... Perhaps I was wrong to write to you.... This anniversary and your sudden appearance in my room at the Opera, the other evening, reminded me of the time long past and made me write to you as the little girl that I then was...."

There was something in Christine's attitude that seemed to Raoul not natural. He did not feel any hostility in her; far from it: the distressed affection shining in her eyes told him that. But why was this affection distressed? That was what he wished to know and what was irritating him.

"When you saw me in your dressing-room, was that the first time you noticed me, Christine?"

She was incapable of lying.

"No," she said, "I had seen you several times in your brother's box. And also on the stage."

"I thought so!" said Raoul, compressing his lips. "But then why, when you saw me in your room, at your feet, reminding you that I had rescued your scarf from the sea, why did you answer as though you did not know me and also why did you laugh?"

The tone of these questions was so rough that Christine stared at Raoul without replying. The young man himself was aghast at the sudden quarrel which he had dared to raise at the very moment when he had resolved to speak words of gentleness, love and submission to Christine. A husband, a lover with all rights, would talk no differently to a wife, a mistress who had offended him. But he had gone too far and saw no other way out of the ridiculous position than to behave odiously.

"You don't answer!" he said angrily and unhappily. "Well, I will answer for you. It was because there was some one in the room who was in your way, Christine, some one that you did not wish to know that you could be interested in any one else!"

"If any one was in my way, my friend," Christine broke in coldly, "if any one was in my way, that evening, it was yourself, since I told you to leave the room!"

"Yes, so that you might remain with the other!"

"What are you saying, monsieur?" asked the girl excitedly. "And to what other do you refer?"

"To the man to whom you said, 'I sing only for you! . . . to-night I gave you my soul and I am dead!'"

Christine seized Raoul's arm and clutched it with a strength which no one would have suspected in so frail a creature.

"Then you were listening behind the door?"

"Yes, because I love you . . . And I heard everything. . . ."

"You heard what?"

And the young girl, becoming strangely calm, released Raoul's arm.

"He said to you, 'Christine, you must love me!'"

At these words, a deathly pallor spread over Christine's face, dark rings formed round her eyes, she staggered and seemed on the point of swooning. Raoul darted forward, with arms outstretched, but Christine had overcome her passing faintness and said, in a low voice:

"Go on! Go on! Tell me all you heard!"

At an utter loss to understand, Raoul answered: "I heard him reply, when you said you had given him your soul, 'Your soul is a beautiful thing, child, and I thank you. No emperor ever received so fair a gift. The angels wept to-night.'"

Christine carried her hand to her heart, a prey to indescribable emotion. Her eyes stared before her like a madwoman's. Raoul was terror-stricken. But suddenly Christine's eyes moistened and two great tears trickled, like two pearls, down her ivory cheeks.

"Christine!"

"Raoul!"

The young man tried to take her in his arms, but she escaped and fled in great disorder.

While Christine remained locked in her room, Raoul was at his wit's end what to do. He refused to breakfast. He was terribly concerned and bitterly grieved to see the hours, which he had hoped to find so sweet, slip past without the presence of the young Swedish girl. Why did she not come to roam with him through the country where they had so many memories in common? He heard that she had had a mass said, that morning, for the repose of her father's soul and spent a long time praying in the little church and on the fiddler's tomb. Then, as she seemed to have nothing more to do at Perros and, in fact, was doing nothing there, why did she not go back to Paris at once?

Raoul walked away, dejectedly, to the graveyard in which the church stood and was indeed alone among the tombs, reading the inscriptions; but, when he turned behind the apse, he was suddenly struck by the dazzling note of the flowers that straggled over the white ground. They were marvelous red roses that had blossomed in the morning, in the snow, giving a glimpse of life among the dead, for death was all around him. It also, like the flowers, issued from the ground, which had flung back a number of its corpses. Skeletons and skulls by the hundred were heaped against the wall of the church, held in position by a wire that left the whole gruesome stack visible. Dead men's bones, arranged in rows, like bricks, to form the first course upon which the walls of the sacristy had been built. The door of the sacristy opened in the middle of that bony structure, as is often seen in old Breton churches.

Raoul said a prayer for Daaé and then, painfully impressed by all those eternal smiles on the mouths of skulls, he climbed the slope and sat down on the edge of the heath overlooking the sea. The wind fell with the evening. Raoul was surrounded by icy darkness, but he did not feel the cold. It was here, he remembered, that he used to come with little Christine to see the Korrigans dance at the rising of the moon. He had never seen any, though his eyes were good, whereas Christine, who was a little shortsighted, pretended that she had seen many. He smiled at the thought and then suddenly gave a start. A voice behind him said:

"Do you think the Korrigans will come this evening?"

It was Christine. He tried to speak. She put her gloved hand on his mouth.

"Listen, Raoul. I have decided to tell you something, serious, very serious. . . . Do you remember the legend of the Angel of Music?"

"I do indeed," he said. "I believe it was here that your father first told it to us."

"And it was here that he said, 'When I am in Heaven, my child, I will send him to you.' Well, Raoul, my father is in Heaven, and I have been visited by the Angel of Music."

"I have no doubt of it," replied the young man gravely, for it seemed to him that his friend, in obedience to a pious thought, was connecting the memory of her father with the brilliancy of her last triumph.

Christine appeared astonished at the Vicomte de Chagny's coolness:

"How do you understand it?" she asked, bringing her pale face so close to his that he might have thought that Christine was going to give him a kiss; but she only wanted to read his eyes in spite of the dark.

"I understand," he said, "that no human being can sing as you sang the other evening without the intervention of some miracle. No professor on earth can teach you such accents as those. You have heard the Angel of Music, Christine."

"Yes," she said solemnly, "in my dressing-room. That is where he comes to give me my lessons daily."

"In your dressing-room?" he echoed stupidly.

"Yes, that is where I have heard him; and I have not been the only one to hear him."

"Who else heard him, Christine?"

"You, my friend."

"I? I heard the Angel of Music?"

"Yes, the other evening. It was he who was talking when you were listening behind the door. It was he who said, 'You must love me.' But I then thought that I was the only one to hear his voice. Imagine my astonishment when you told me, this morning, that you could hear him too."

Raoul burst out laughing. The first rays of the moon came and shrouded the two young people in their light. Christine turned on Raoul with a hostile air. Her eyes, usually so gentle, flashed fire.

"What are you laughing at? You think you heard a man's voice, I suppose?"

"Well! . . ." replied the young man, whose ideas began to grow confused in the face of Christine's determined attitude.

"It's you, Raoul, who say that? You, an old playfellow of my own! A friend of my father's! But you have changed since those days. What are you thinking of? I am an honest girl, M. le Vicomte de Chagny, and I don't lock myself up in my dressing-room with men's voices. If you had opened the door, you would have seen that there was nobody in the room!"

"That's true! I did open the door, when you were gone, and I found no one in the room."

"So you see! . . . Well?"

The viscount summoned up all his courage.

"Well, Christine, I think that somebody is making game of you."

She gave a cry and ran away. He ran after her, but, in a tone of fierce anger, she called out: "Leave me! Leave me!" And she disappeared.

Raoul returned to the inn feeling very weary, very low-spirited and very sad. He was told that Christine had gone to her bedroom saying that she would not be down to dinner. Raoul dined alone, in a very gloomy mood. Then he went to his room and tried to read, went to bed and tried to sleep. There was no sound in the next room.

The hours passed slowly. It was about half-past eleven when he distinctly heard some one moving, with a light, stealthy step, in the room next to his. Then Christine had not gone to bed! Without troubling for a reason, Raoul dressed, taking care not to make a sound, and waited. Waited for what? How could he tell? But his heart thumped in his chest when he heard Christine's door turn slowly on its hinges. Where could she be going, at this hour, when every one was fast asleep at Perros? Softly opening the door, he saw Christine's white form, in the moonlight, slipping along the passage. She went down the stairs and he leaned over the baluster above her.

Suddenly he heard two voices in rapid conversation. He caught one sentence: "Don't lose the key."

It was the landlady's voice. The door facing the sea was opened and locked again. Then all was still.

Raoul ran back to his room and threw back the window. Christine's white form stood on the deserted quay.

The first floor of the Setting Sun was at no great height and a tree growing against the wall held out its branches to Raoul's impatient arms and enabled him to climb down unknown to the landlady. Her amazement, therefore, was all the greater when, the next morning, the young man was brought back to her half frozen, more dead than alive, and when she learned that he had been found stretched at full length on the steps of the high altar of the little church. She ran at once to tell Christine, who hurried down and, with the help of the landlady, did her best to revive him. He soon opened his eyes and was not long in recovering when he saw his friend's charming face leaning over him.

A few weeks later, when the tragedy at the Opera compelled the Intervention of the public prosecutor, M. Mifroid, the commissary of police, examined the Vicomte de Chagny touching the events of the night at Perros. I quote the questions and answers as given in the official report pp. 150 *et seq*.:

> Q. "Did Mlle. Daaé not see you come down from your room by the curious road which you selected?"
>
> R. "No, monsieur, no, although, when walking behind her, I took no pains to deaden the sound of my footsteps. In fact, I was anxious that she should turn round and see me. I realized that I had no excuse for following her and that this way of spying on her was unworthy of me. But she seemed not to hear me and acted exactly as though I were not there. She quietly left the quay and then suddenly walked quickly up the road. The church-clock had struck a quarter to twelve and

I thought that this must have made her hurry, for she began almost to run and continued hastening until she came to the church."

Q. "Was the gate open?"

R. "Yes, monsieur, and this surprised me, but did not seem to surprise Mlle. Daaé."

Q. "Was there no one in the churchyard?"

R. "I did not see any one; and, if there had been, I must have seen him. The moon was shining on the snow and made the night quite light."

Q. "Was it possible for any one to hide behind the tombstones?"

R. "No, monsieur. They were quite small, poor tombstones, partly hidden under the snow, with their crosses just above the level of the ground. The only shadows were those of the crosses and ourselves. The church stood out quite brightly. I never saw so clear a night. It was very fine and very cold and one could see everything."

Q. "Are you at all superstitious?"

R. "No, monsieur, I am a practising Catholic."

Q. "In what condition of mind were you?"

R. "Very healthy and peaceful, I assure you. Mlle. Daaé's curious action in going out at that hour had worried me at first; but, as soon as I saw her go to the churchyard, I thought that she meant to fulfil some pious duty on her father's grave and I considered this so natural that I recovered all my calmness. I was only surprised that she had not heard me walking behind her, for my footsteps were quite audible on the hard snow. But she must have been taken up with her intentions and I resolved not to disturb her. She knelt down by her father's grave, made the sign of the cross and began to pray. At that moment, it struck midnight. At the last stroke, I saw Mlle. Daaé lift her eyes to the sky and stretch out her arms as though in ecstasy. I was wondering what the reason could be, when I myself raised my head and everything within me seemed drawn toward the invisible, which was *playing the most perfect music*! Christine and I knew that music; we had heard it as children. But it had never been executed with such divine art, even by M. Daaé. I remembered all that Christine had told me of the Angel of Music. The air was *The Resurrection of Lazarus*, which old M. Daaé used to play to us in his hours of melancholy and of faith. If Christine's Angel had existed, he could not have played better, that night, on the late musician's violin. When the music stopped, I seemed to hear a noise from the skulls in the heap of bones; it was as though they were chuckling and I could not help shuddering."

Q. "Did it not occur to you that the musician might be hiding behind that very heap of bones?"

R. "It was the one thought that did occur to me, monsieur, so much so that I omitted to follow Mlle. Daaé, when she stood up and walked slowly to the gate. She was so much absorbed just then that I am not surprised that she did not see me."

Q. "Then what happened that you were found in the morning lying half-dead on the steps of the high altar?"

R. "First a skull rolled to my feet . . . then another . . . then another . . . It was as if I were the mark of that ghastly game of bowls. And I had an idea that false step must have destroyed the balance of the structure behind which our musician was concealed. This surmise seemed to be confirmed when I saw a shadow suddenly glide along the sacristy wall. I ran up. The shadow had already pushed open the door and entered the church. But I was quicker than the shadow and caught hold of a corner of its cloak. At that moment, we were just in front of the high altar; and the moonbeams fell straight upon us through the stained-glass windows of the apse. As I did not let go of the cloak, the shadow turned round; and I saw a terrible death's head, which darted a look at me from a pair of scorching eyes. I felt as if I were face to face with Satan; and, in the presence of this unearthly apparition, my heart gave way, my courage failed me . . . and I remember nothing more until I recovered consciousness at the Setting Sun."

VI

A VISIT TO BOX FIVE

We left M. Firmin Richard and M. Armand Moncharmin at the moment when they were deciding "to look into that little matter of Box Five."

Leaving behind them the broad staircase which leads from the lobby outside the managers' offices to the stage and its dependencies, they crossed the stage, went out by the subscribers' door and entered the house through the first little passage on the left. Then they made their way through the front rows of stalls and looked at Box Five on the grand tier. They could not see it well, because it was half in darkness and because great covers were flung over the red velvet of the ledges of all the boxes.

They were almost alone in the huge, gloomy house; and a great silence surrounded them. It was the time when most of the stage-hands go out for a drink. The staff had left the boards for the moment, leaving a scene half set. A few rays of light, a wan, sinister light, that seemed to have been stolen from an expiring luminary, fell through some opening or other upon an old tower that raised its pasteboard battlements on the stage; everything, in this deceptive light, adopted a fantastic shape. In the orchestra stalls, the drugget covering them looked like an angry sea, whose glaucous waves had been suddenly rendered stationary by a secret order from the storm phantom, who, as everybody knows, is called Adamastor. MM. Moncharmin and Richard were the shipwrecked mariners amid this motionless turmoil of a calico sea. They made for the left boxes, plowing their way like sailors who leave their ship and try to struggle to the shore. The eight great polished columns stood up in the dusk like so many huge piles supporting the threatening, crumbling, big-bellied cliffs whose layers were represented by the circular, parallel, waving lines of the balconies of the grand, first and second tiers of boxes. At the top, right on top of the cliff, lost in M. Lenepveu's copper ceiling, figures grinned and grimaced, laughed and jeered at MM. Richard and Moncharmin's distress. And yet these figures were usually very serious. Their names were Isis, Amphitrite, Hebe, Pandora, Psyche, Thetis, Pomona, Daphne, Clytie, Galatea and Arethusa. Yes, Arethusa herself and Pandora, whom we all know by her box, looked down upon the two new managers of the Opera, who ended by clutching at some piece of wreckage and from there stared silently at Box Five on the grand tier.

I have said that they were distressed. At least, I presume so. M. Moncharmin, in any case, admits that he was impressed. To quote his own words, in his *Memoirs*:

> This moonshine about the Opera ghost in which, since we first took over the duties of MM. Poligny and Debienne, we had been so nicely steeped [Moncharmin's style is not always irreproachable] had no doubt ended by blinding my imaginative and also my visual faculties. It may be that the exceptional surroundings in which we found ourselves, in the midst of an incredible silence, impressed us to an unusual extent. It may be that we were the sport of a kind of hallucination brought about by the semidarkness of the theater and the partial gloom that filled Box Five. At any rate, I saw and Richard also saw a shape in the box. Richard said nothing, nor I either. But we spontaneously seized each other's hand. We stood like that for some minutes, without moving, with our eyes fixed on the same point; but the figure had disappeared. Then we went out and, in the lobby, communicated our impressions to each other and talked about "the shape." The misfortune was that my shape was not in the least like Richard's. I had seen a thing like a death's head resting on the ledge of the box, whereas Richard saw the shape of an old woman who looked like Mame Giry. We soon discovered that we had really been the victims of an illusion, whereupon, without further delay and laughing like madmen, we ran to Box Five on the grand tier, went inside and found no shape of any kind.

Box Five is just like all the other grand tier boxes. There is nothing to distinguish it from any of the others. M. Moncharmin and M. Richard, ostensibly highly amused and laughing at each other, moved the furniture of the box, lifted the cloths and the chairs and particularly examined the arm-chair in which "the man's voice" used to sit. But they saw that it was a respectable arm-chair, with no magic about it. Altogether, the box was the most ordinary box in the world, with its red hangings, its chairs, its carpet and its ledge covered in red velvet. After feeling the carpet in the most serious manner possible, and discovering nothing more here or anywhere else, they went down to the corresponding box on the pit tier below. In Box Five on the pit tier, which is, just inside the first exit from the stalls on the left, they found nothing worth mentioning either.

"Those people are all making fools of us!" Firmin Richard ended by exclaiming. "It will be *Faust* on Saturday: let us both see the performance from Box Five on the grand tier!"

VII

FAUST AND WHAT FOLLOWED

On the Saturday morning, on reaching their office, the joint managers found a letter from O. G. worded in these terms:

> My Dear Managers:
>
> So it is to be war between us?
>
> If you still care for peace, here is my ultimatum. It consists of the four following conditions:
>
> 1. You must give me back my private box; and I wish it to be at my free disposal from henceforward.
> 2. The part of Margarita shall be sung this evening by Christine Daaé. Never mind about Carlotta; she will be ill.
> 3. I absolutely insist upon the good and loyal services of Mme. Giry, my box-keeper, whom you will reinstate in her functions forthwith.
> 4. Let me know by a letter handed to Mme. Giry, who will see that it reaches me, that you accept, as your predecessors did, the conditions in my memorandum-book relating to my monthly allowance. I will inform you later how you are to pay it to me.
>
> If you refuse, you will give Faust to-night in a house with a curse upon it.
>
> Take my advice and be warned in time.
>
> O. G.

"Look here, I'm getting sick of him, sick of him!" shouted Richard, bringing his fists down on his office-table.

Just then, Mercier, the acting-manager, entered.

"Lachenel would like to see one of you gentlemen," he said. "He says that his business is urgent and he seems quite upset."

"Who's Lachenel?" asked Richard.

"He's your stud-groom."

"What do you mean? My stud-groom?"

"Yes, sir," explained Mercier, "there are several grooms at the Opera and M. Lachenel is at the head of them."

"And what does this groom do?"

"He has the chief management of the stable."

"What stable?"

"Why, yours, sir, the stable of the Opera."

"Is there a stable at the Opera? Upon my word, I didn't know. Where is it?"

"In the cellars, on the Rotunda side. It's a very important department; we have twelve horses."

"Twelve horses! And what for, in Heaven's name?"

"Why, we want trained horses for the processions In the *Juive*, the *Profeta* and so on; horses 'used to the boards.' It is the grooms' business to teach them. M. Lachenel is very clever at it. He used to manage Franconi's stables."

"Very well . . . but what does he want?"

"I don't know; I never saw him in such a state."

"He can come in."

M. Lachenel came in, carrying a riding-whip, with which he struck his right boot in an irritable manner.

"Good morning, M. Lachenel," said Richard, somewhat impressed. "To what do we owe the honor of your visit?"

"Mr. Manager, I have come to ask you to get rid of the whole stable."

"What, you want to get rid of our horses?"

"I'm not talking of the horses, but of the stablemen."

"How many stablemen have you, M. Lachenel?"

"Six."

"Six stablemen! That's at least two too many."

"These are 'places,'" Mercier interposed, "created and forced upon us by the under-secretary for fine arts. They are filled by protégées of the government and, if I may venture to . . ."

"I don't care a hang for the government!" roared Richard. "We don't need more than four stablemen for twelve horses."

"Eleven," said the head riding-master, correcting him.

"Twelve," repeated Richard.

"Eleven," repeated Lachenel.

"Oh, the acting-manager told me that you had twelve horses!"

"I did have twelve, but I have only eleven since César was stolen."

And M. Lachenel gave himself a great smack on the boot with his whip.

"Has César been stolen?" cried the acting-manager. "César, the white horse in the *Profeta*?"

"There are not two Césars," said the stud-groom dryly. "I was ten years at Franconi's and I have seen plenty of horses in my time. Well, there are not two Césars. And he's been stolen."

"How?"

"I don't know. Nobody knows. That's why I have come to ask you to sack the whole stable."

"What do your stablemen say?"

"All sorts of nonsense. Some of them accuse the supers. Others pretend that it's the acting-manager's doorkeeper . . ."

"My doorkeeper? I'll answer for him as I would for myself!" protested Mercier.

"But, after all, M. Lachenel," cried Richard, "you must have some idea."

"Yes, I have," M. Lachenel declared. "I have an idea and I'll tell you what it is. There's no doubt about it in my mind." He walked up to the two managers and whispered. "It's the ghost who did the trick!"

Richard gave a jump.

"What, you too! You too!"

"How do you mean, I too? Isn't it natural, after what I saw?"

"What did you see?"

"I saw, as clearly as I now see you, a black shadow riding a white horse that was as like César as two peas!"

"And did you run after them?"

"I did and I shouted, but they were too fast for me and disappeared in the darkness of the underground gallery."

M. Richard rose. "That will do, M. Lachenel. You can go . . . . We will lodge a complaint against *the ghost*."

"And sack my stable?"

"Oh, of course! Good morning."

M. Lachenel bowed and withdrew. Richard foamed at the mouth.

"Settle that idiot's account at once, please."

"He is a friend of the government representative's!" Mercier ventured to say.

"And he takes his vermouth at Tortoni's with Lagréné, Scholl and Pertuiset, the lion-hunter," added Moncharmin. "We shall have the whole press against us! He'll tell the story of the ghost; and everybody will be laughing at our expense! We may as well be dead as ridiculous!"

"All right, say no more about it."

At that moment the door opened. It must have been deserted by its usual Cerberus, for Mame Giry entered without ceremony, holding a letter in her hand, and said hurriedly:

"I beg your pardon, excuse me, gentlemen, but I had a letter this morning from the Opera ghost. He told me to come to you, that you had something to . . ."

She did not complete the sentence. She saw Firmin Richard's face; and it was a terrible sight. He seemed ready to burst. He said nothing, he could not speak. But suddenly he acted. First, his left arm seized upon the quaint person of Mame Giry and made her describe so unexpected a semicircle that she uttered a despairing cry. Next, his right foot imprinted its sole on the black taffeta of a skirt which certainly had never before undergone a similar outrage in a similar place. The thing happened so quickly that Mame Giry, when in the passage, was still quite bewildered and seemed not to understand. But, suddenly, she understood; and the Opera rang with her indignant yells, her violent protests and threats.

About the same time, Carlotta, who had a small house of her own in the Rue du Faubourg St.-Honoré, rang for her maid, who brought her letters to her bed. Among them was an anonymous missive, written in red ink, in a hesitating, clumsy hand, which ran:

> If you appear to-night, you must be prepared for a great misfortune at the moment when you open your mouth to sing . . . a misfortune worse than death.

The letter took away Carlotta's appetite for breakfast. She pushed back her chocolate, sat up in bed and thought hard. It was not the first letter of the kind which she had received, but she never had one couched in such threatening terms.

She thought herself, at that time, the victim of a thousand jealous attempts and went about saying that she had a secret enemy who had sworn to ruin her. She pretended that a wicked plot was being hatched against her, a cabal which would come to a head one of those days; but she added that she was not the woman to be intimidated.

The truth is that, if there was a cabal, it was led by Carlotta herself against poor Christine, who had no suspicion of it. Carlotta had never forgiven Christine for the triumph which she had achieved when taking her place at a moment's notice. When Carlotta heard of the astounding reception bestowed upon her understudy, she was at once cured of an incipient attack of bronchitis and a bad fit of sulking against the management and lost the slightest inclination to shirk her duties. From that time, she worked with all her might to "smother" her rival, enlisting the services of influential friends to persuade the managers not to give Christine an opportunity for a fresh triumph. Certain newspapers which had begun to extol the talent of Christine now interested themselves only in the fame of Carlotta. Lastly, in the theater itself, the celebrated, but heartless and soulless diva made the most scandalous remarks about Christine and tried to cause her endless minor unpleasantnesses.

When Carlotta had finished thinking over the threat contained in the strange letter, she got up.

"We shall see," she said, adding a few oaths in her native Spanish with a very determined air.

The first thing she saw, when looking out of her window, was a hearse. She was very superstitious; and the hearse and the letter convinced her that she was running the most serious dangers that evening. She collected all her supporters, told them that she was threatened at that evening's performance with a plot organized by Christine Daaé and declared that they must play a trick upon that chit by filling the house with her, Carlotta's, admirers. She had no lack of them, had she? She relied upon them to hold themselves prepared for any eventuality and to silence the adversaries, if, as she feared, they created a disturbance.

M. Richard's private secretary called to ask after the diva's health and returned with the assurance that she was perfectly well and that, "were she dying," she would sing the part of Margarita that evening. The secretary urged her, in his chief's name, to commit no imprudence, to stay at home all day and to be careful of drafts; and Carlotta could not help, after he had gone, comparing this unusual and unexpected advice with the threats contained in the letter.

It was five o'clock when the post brought a second anonymous letter in the same hand as the first. It was short and said simply:

> You have a bad cold. If you are wise, you will see that it is madness to try to sing to-night.

Carlotta sneered, shrugged her handsome shoulders and sang two or three notes to reassure herself.

Her friends were faithful to their promise. They were all at the Opera that night, but looked round in vain for the fierce conspirators whom they were instructed to suppress. The only unusual thing was the presence of M. Richard and M. Moncharmin in Box Five. Carlotta's friends thought that, perhaps, the managers had wind, on their side, of the proposed disturbance and that they had determined to be in the house, so as to stop it then and there; but this was unjustifiable supposition, as the reader knows. M. Richard and M. Moncharmin were thinking of nothing but their ghost.

"Vain! In vain do I call, through my vigil weary,
On creation and its Lord!
Never reply will break the silence dreary!
No sign! No single word!"

The famous baritone, Carolus Fonta, had hardly finished Doctor Faust's first appeal to the powers of darkness, when M. Firmin Richard, who was sitting in the ghost's own chair, the front chair on the right, leaned over to his partner and asked him chaffingly:

"Well, has the ghost whispered a word in your ear yet?"

"Wait, don't be in such a hurry," replied M. Armand Moncharmin, in the same gay tone. "The performance has only begun and you know that the ghost does not usually come until the middle of the first act."

The first act passed without incident, which did not surprise Carlotta's friends, because Margarita does not sing in this act. As for the managers, they looked at each other, when the curtain fell.

"That's one!" said Moncharmin.

"Yes, the ghost is late," said Firmin Richard.

"It's not a bad house," said Moncharmin, "for 'a house with a curse on it.'"

M. Richard smiled and pointed to a fat, rather vulgar woman, dressed in black, sitting in a stall in the middle of the auditorium with a man in a broadcloth frock-coat on either side of her.

"Who on earth are 'those?'" asked Moncharmin.

"'Those,' my dear fellow, are my concierge, her husband and her brother."

"Did you give them their tickets?"

"I did . . . My concierge had never been to the Opera—this is the first time—and, as she is now going to come every night, I wanted her to have a good seat, before spending her time showing other people to theirs."

Moncharmin asked what he meant and Richard answered that he had persuaded his concierge, in whom he had the greatest confidence, to come and take Mame Giry's place. Yes, he would like to see if, with that woman instead of the old lunatic, Box Five would continue to astonish the natives?

"By the way," said Moncharmin, "you know that Mother Giry is going to lodge a complaint against you."

"With whom? The ghost?"

The ghost! Moncharmin had almost forgotten him. However, that mysterious person did nothing to bring himself to the memory of the managers; and they were just saying so to each other for the second time, when the door of the box suddenly opened to admit the startled stage-manager.

"What's the matter?" they both asked, amazed at seeing him there at such a time.

"It seems there's a plot got up by Christine Daaé's friends against Carlotta. Carlotta's furious."

"What on earth . . . ?" said Richard, knitting his brows.

But the curtain rose on the kermess scene and Richard made a sign to the stage-manager to go away. When the two were alone again, Moncharmin leaned over to Richard:

"Then Daaé has friends?" he asked.

"Yes, she has."

"Whom?"

Richard glanced across at a box on the grand tier containing no one but two men.

"The Comte de Chagny?"

"Yes, he spoke to me in her favor with such warmth that, if I had not known him to be Sorelli's friend . . ."

"Really? Really?" said Moncharmin. "And who is that pale young man beside him?"

"That's his brother, the viscount."

"He ought to be in his bed. He looks ill."

The stage rang with gay song:

"Red or white liquor.
Coarse or fine!
What can it matter,
So we have wine?"

Students, citizens, soldiers, girls and matrons whirled light-heartedly before the inn with the figure of Bacchus for a sign. Siebel made her entrance. Christine

Daaé looked charming in her boy's clothes; and Carlotta's partisans expected to hear her greeted with an ovation which would have enlightened them as to the intentions of her friends. But nothing happened.

On the other hand, when Margarita crossed the stage and sang the only two lines allotted her in this second act:

> "No, my lord, not a lady am I, nor yet a beauty,
> And do not need an arm to help me on my way."

Carlotta was received with enthusiastic applause. It was so unexpected and so uncalled for that those who knew nothing about the rumors looked at one another and asked what was happening. And this act also was finished without incident.

Then everybody said: "Of course, it will be during the next act."

Some, who seemed to be better informed than the rest, declared that the "row" would begin with the ballad of the *King of Thule* and rushed to the subscribers' entrance to warn Carlotta. The managers left the box during the entr'acte to find out more about the cabal of which the stage-manager had spoken; but they soon returned to their seats, shrugging their shoulders and treating the whole affair as silly.

The first thing they saw, on entering the box, was a box of English sweets on the little shelf of the ledge. Who had put it there? They asked the boxkeepers, but none of them knew. Then they went back to the shelf and, next to the box of sweets, found an opera glass. They looked at each other. They had no inclination to laugh. All that Mme. Giry had told them returned to their memory ... and then... and then ... they seemed to feel a curious sort of draft around them.... They sat down in silence.

The scene represented Margarita's garden:

> "Gentle flow'rs in the dew,
> Be message from me ..."

As she sang these first two lines, with her bunch of roses and lilacs in her hand, Christine, raising her head, saw the Vicomte de Chagny in his box; and, from that moment, her voice seemed less sure, less crystal-clear than usual. Something seemed to deaden and dull her singing....

"What a queer girl she is!" said one of Carlotta's friends in the stalls, almost aloud. "The other day she was divine; and to-night she's simply bleating. She has no experience, no training."

"Gentle flow'rs, lie ye there
And tell her from me . . ."

The viscount put his head under his hands and wept. The count, behind him, viciously gnawed his mustache, shrugged his shoulders and frowned. For him, usually so cold and correct, to betray his inner feelings like that, by outward signs, the count must be very angry. He was. He had seen his brother return from a rapid and mysterious journey in an alarming state of health. The explanation that followed was unsatisfactory and the count asked Christine Daaé for an appointment. She had the audacity to reply that she could not see either him or his brother. . . .

"Would she but deign to hear me
And with one smile to cheer me. . . ."

"The little baggage!" growled the count.

And he wondered what she wanted. What she was hoping for. . . . She was a virtuous girl, she was said to have no friend, no protector of any sort. . . .That angel from the North must be very artful!

Raoul, behind the curtain of his hands that veiled his boyish tears, thought only of the letter which he received on his return to Paris, where Christine, fleeing from Perros like a thief in the night, had arrived before him:

MY DEAR LITTLE PLAYFELLOW:

You must have the courage not to see me again, not to speak of me again. If you love me just a little, do this for me, for me who will never forget you, my dear Raoul. My life depends upon it. Your life depends upon it.

YOUR LITTLE CHRISTINE

Thunders of applause. Carlotta made her entrance.

"I wish I could but know who was he
That addressed me,
If he was noble, or, at least, what his name is . . ."

When Margarita had finished singing the ballad of the *King of Thule*, she was loudly cheered and again when she came to the end of the jewel song:

"Ah, the joy of past compare
These jewels bright to wear! . . ."

Thenceforth, certain of herself, certain of her friends in the house, certain of her voice and her success, fearing nothing, Carlotta flung herself into her part without restraint of modesty. . . . She was no longer Margarita, she was Carmen. She was applauded all the more; and her debut with Faust seemed about to bring her a new success, when suddenly. . . a terrible thing happened.

Faust had knelt on one knee:

"Let me gaze on the form below me,
While from yonder ether blue
Look how the star of eve, bright and tender, lingers o'er me,
To love thy beauty too!"

And Margarita replied:

"Oh, how strange!
Like a spell does the evening bind me!
And a deep languid charm
I feel without alarm
With its melody enwind me
And all my heart subdue."

At that moment, at that identical moment, the terrible thing happened. . . . Carlotta croaked like a toad:

"Co-ack!"

There was consternation on Carlotta's face and consternation on the faces of all the audience. The two managers in their box could not suppress an exclamation of horror. Every one felt that the thing was not natural, that there was witchcraft behind it. That toad smelt of brimstone. Poor, wretched, despairing, crushed Carlotta!

The uproar in the house was indescribable. If the thing had happened to any one but Carlotta, she would have been hooted. But everybody knew how perfect an instrument her voice was; and there was no display of anger, but only of horror and dismay, the sort of dismay which men would have felt if they had witnessed the catastrophe that broke the arms of the Venus de Milo. . . . And even then they would have seen . . . and understood . . .

But here that toad was incomprehensible! So much so that, after some seconds spent in asking herself if she had really heard that note, that sound, that infernal noise issue from her throat, she tried to persuade herself that it was not so, that she was the victim of an illusion, an illusion of the ear, and not of an act of treachery on the part of her voice.

Meanwhile, in Box Five, Moncharmin and Richard had turned very pale. This extraordinary and inexplicable incident filled them with a dread which was the more mysterious inasmuch as for some little while, they had fallen within the direct influence of the ghost.

They had felt his breath. Moncharmin's hair stood on end. Richard wiped the perspiration from his forehead. Yes, the ghost was there, around them, behind them, beside them; they felt his presence without seeing him, they heard his breath, close, close, close to them! . . . They were sure that there were three people in the box. . . . They trembled. . . . They thought of running away. . . . They dared not. . . . They dared not make a movement or exchange a word that would have told the ghost that they knew that he was there! . . . What was going to happen?

This happened.

"Co-ack!"

Their joint exclamation of horror was heard all over the house. *They felt that they were smarting under the ghost's attacks.* Leaning over the ledge of their box, they stared at Carlotta as though they did not recognize her. That infernal girl must have given the signal for some catastrophe. Ah, they were waiting for the catastrophe! The ghost had told them it would come! The house had a curse upon it! The two managers gasped and panted under the weight of the catastrophe. Richard's stifled voice was heard calling to Carlotta:

"Well, go on!"

No, Carlotta did not go on. . . . Bravely, heroically, she started afresh on the fatal line at the end of which the toad had appeared.

An awful silence succeeded the uproar. Carlotta's voice alone once more filled the resounding house:

"I feel without alarm . . ."

The audience also felt, but not without alarm . . .

"I feel without alarm . . .
I feel without alarm—co-ack!

With its melody enwind me—co-ack!
And all my heart sub—co-ack!"

The toad also had started afresh!

The house broke into a wild tumult. The two managers collapsed in their chairs and dared not even turn round; they had not the strength; the ghost was chuckling behind their backs! And, at last, they distinctly heard his voice in their right ears, the impossible voice, the mouthless voice, saying:

"*She is singing to-night to bring the chandelier down!*"

With one accord, they raised their eyes to the ceiling and uttered a terrible cry. The chandelier, the immense mass of the chandelier was slipping down, coming toward them, at the call of that fiendish voice. Released from its hook, it plunged from the ceiling and came smashing into the middle of the stalls, amid a thousand shouts of terror. A wild rush for the doors followed.

The papers of the day state that there were numbers wounded and one killed. The chandelier had crashed down upon the head of the wretched woman who had come to the Opera for the first time in her life, the one whom M. Richard had appointed to succeed Mame Giry, the ghost's box-keeper, in her functions! She died on the spot and, the next morning, a newspaper appeared with this heading:

TWO HUNDRED KILOS ON THE HEAD OF A CONCIERGE

That was her sole epitaph!

VIII

THE MYSTERIOUS BROUGHAM

THAT TRAGIC EVENING WAS BAD FOR EVERYBODY. CARLOTTA FELL ILL. As for Christine Daaé, she disappeared after the performance. A fortnight elapsed during which she was seen neither at the Opera nor outside.

Raoul, of course, was the first to be astonished at the prima donna's absence. He wrote to her at Mme. Valérius' flat and received no reply. His grief increased and he ended by being seriously alarmed at never seeing her name on the program. *Faust* was played without her.

One afternoon he went to the managers' office to ask the reason of Christine's disappearance. He found them both looking extremely worried. Their own friends did not recognize them: they had lost all their gaiety and spirits. They were seen crossing the stage with hanging heads, care-worn brows, pale cheeks, as though pursued by some abominable thought or a prey to some persistent sport of fate.

The fall of the chandelier had involved them in no little responsibility; but it was difficult to make them speak about it. The inquest had ended in a verdict of accidental death, caused by the wear and tear of the chains by which the chandelier was hung from the ceiling; but it was the duty of both the old and the new managers to have discovered this wear and tear and to have remedied it in time. And I feel bound to say that MM. Richard and Moncharmin at this time appeared so changed, so absent-minded, so mysterious, so incomprehensible that many of the subscribers thought that some event even more horrible than the fall of the chandelier must have affected their state of mind.

In their daily intercourse, they showed themselves very impatient, except with Mme. Giry, who had been reinstated in her functions. And their reception of the Vicomte de Chagny, when he came to ask about Christine, was anything but cordial. They merely told him that she was taking a holiday. He asked how long the holiday was for, and they replied curtly that it was for an unlimited period, as Mlle. Daaé had requested leave of absence for reasons of health.

"Then she is ill!" he cried. "What is the matter with her?"

"We don't know."

"Didn't you send the doctor of the Opera to see her?"

"No, she did not ask for him; and, as we trust her, we took her word."

Raoul left the building a prey to the gloomiest thoughts. He resolved, come what might, to go and inquire of Mamma Valérius. He remembered the strong phrases in Christine's letter, forbidding him to make any attempt to see her. But what he had seen at Perros, what he had heard behind the dressing-room door, his conversation with Christine at the edge of the moor made him suspect some machination which, devilish though it might be, was none the less human. The girl's highly strung imagination, her affectionate and credulous mind, the primitive education which had surrounded her childhood with a circle of legends, the constant brooding over her dead father and, above all, the state of sublime ecstasy into which music threw her from the moment that this art was made manifest to her in certain exceptional conditions, as in the churchyard at Perros; all this seemed to him to constitute a moral ground only too favorable for the malevolent designs of some mysterious and unscrupulous person. Of whom was Christine Daaé the victim? This was the very reasonable question which Raoul put to himself as he hurried off to Mamma Valérius.

He trembled as he rang at a little flat in the Rue Notre-Dame-des-Victoires. The door was opened by the maid whom he had seen coming out of Christine's dressing-room one evening. He asked if he could speak to Mme. Valérius. He was told that she was ill in bed and was not receiving visitors.

"Take in my card, please," he said.

The maid soon returned and showed him into a small and scantily furnished drawing-room, in which portraits of Professor Valérius and old Daaé hung on opposite walls.

"Madame begs *monsieur le vicomte* to excuse her," said the servant. "She can only see him in her bedroom, because she can no longer stand on her poor legs."

Five minutes later, Raoul was ushered into an ill-lit room where he at once recognized the good, kind face of Christine's benefactress in the semi-darkness of an alcove. Mamma Valérius' hair was now quite white, but her eyes had grown no older; never, on the contrary, had their expression been so bright, so pure, so child-like.

"M. de Chagny!" she cried gaily, putting out both her hands to her visitor. "Ah, it's Heaven that sends you here! . . . We can talk of *her*."

This last sentence sounded very gloomily in the young man's ears. He at once asked:

"Madame . . . where is Christine?"

And the old lady replied calmly:

"She is with her good genius!"

"What good genius?" exclaimed poor Raoul.

"Why, the Angel of Music!"

The viscount dropped Into a chair. Really? Christine was with the Angel of Music? And there lay Mamma Valérius in bed, smiling to him and putting her finger to her lips, to warn him to be silent! And she added:

"You must not tell anybody!"

"You can rely on me," said Raoul.

He hardly knew what he was saying, for his ideas about Christine, already greatly confused, were becoming more and more entangled; and it seemed as if everything was beginning to turn around him, around the room, around that extraordinary good lady with the white hair and forget-me-not eyes.

"I know! I know I can!" she said, with a happy laugh. "But why don't you come near me, as you used to do when you were a little boy? Give me your hands, as when you brought me the story of little Lotte, which Daddy Daaé had told you. I am very fond of you, M. Raoul, you know. And so is Christine too!"

"She is fond of me!" sighed the young man. He found a difficulty in collecting his thoughts and bringing them to bear on Mamma Valérius' "good genius," on the Angel of Music of whom Christine had spoken to him so strangely, on the death's head which he had seen in a sort of nightmare on the high altar at Perros and also on the Opera ghost, whose fame had come to his ears one evening when he was standing behind the scenes, within hearing of a group of sceneshifters who were repeating the ghastly description which the hanged man, Joseph Buquet, had given of the ghost before his mysterious death.

He asked in a low voice: "What makes you think that Christine is fond of me, madame?"

"She used to speak of you every day."

"Really? . . . And what did she tell you?"

"She told me that you had made her a proposal!" And the good old lady began laughing wholeheartedly. Raoul sprang from his chair, flushing to the temples, suffering agonies.

"What's this? Where are you going? . . . Sit down again at once, will you? . . . Do you think I will let you go like that? . . . If you're angry with me for laughing, I beg your pardon . . . After all, what has happened isn't your fault . . . Didn't you know? . . . Did you think that Christine was free? . . ."

"Is Christine engaged to be married?" the wretched Raoul asked, in a choking voice.

"Why no! Why no! . . . You know as well as I do that Christine couldn't marry, even if she wanted to! . . ."

"But I don't know anything about it! . . . And why can't Christine marry?"

"Because of the Angel of Music, of course! . . ."

"I don't follow. . ."

"Yes, he forbids her to! . . ."

"He forbids her! . . . The Angel of Music forbids her to marry! . . ."

"Oh, he forbids her . . . without forbidding her. It's like this: he tells her that, if she got married, she would never hear him again. That's all! . . . And that he would go away for ever! . . . So, you understand, she can't let the Angel of Music go. It's quite natural."

"Yes, yes," echoed Raoul submissively, "it's quite natural."

"Besides, I thought Christine had told you all that, when she met you at Perros, where she went with her good genius."

"Oh, she went to Perros with her good genius, did she?"

"That is to say, he arranged to meet her down there, in Perros churchyard, at Daaé's grave. He promised to play her *The Resurrection of Lazarus* on her father's violin!"

Raoul de Chagny rose and, with a very authoritative air, pronounced these peremptory words:

"Madame, you will have the goodness to tell me where that genius lives."

The old lady did not seem surprised at this indiscreet command. She raised her eyes and said:

"In Heaven!"

Such simplicity baffled him. He did not know what to say in the presence of this candid and perfect faith in a genius who came down nightly from Heaven to haunt the dressing-rooms at the Opera.

He now realized the possible state of mind of a girl brought up between a superstitious fiddler and a visionary old lady and he shuddered when he thought of the consequences of it all.

"Is Christine still a good girl?" he asked suddenly, in spite of himself.

"I swear it, as I hope to be saved!" exclaimed the old woman, who, this time, seemed to be incensed. "And, if you doubt it, sir, I don't know what you are here for!"

Raoul tore at his gloves.

"How long has she known this 'genius?'"

"About three months. . . .Yes, it's quite three months since he began to give her lessons."

The viscount threw up his arms with a gesture of despair.

"The genius gives her lessons! . . . And where, pray?"

"Now that she has gone away with him, I can't say; but, up to a fortnight ago, it was in Christine's dressing-room. It would be impossible in this little flat. The whole house would hear them. Whereas, at the Opera, at eight o'clock in the morning, there is no one about, do you see!"

"Yes, I see! I see!" cried the viscount.

And he hurriedly took leave of Mme. Valérius, who asked herself if the young nobleman was not a little off his head.

He walked home to his brother's house in a pitiful state. He could have struck himself, banged his head against the walls! To think that he had believed in her innocence, in her purity! The Angel of Music! He knew him now! He saw him! It was beyond a doubt some unspeakable tenor, a good-looking jackanapes, who mouthed and simpered as he sang! He thought himself as absurd and as wretched as could be. Oh, what a miserable, little, insignificant, silly young man was M. le Vicomte de Chagny! thought Raoul furiously. And she, what a bold and damnable sly creature!

His brother was waiting for him and Raoul fell into his arms, like a child. The count consoled him, without asking for explanations; and Raoul would: certainly have long hesitated before telling him the story of the Angel of Music. His brother suggested taking him out to dinner. Overcome as he was with despair, Raoul would probably have refused any invitation that evening, if the count had not, as an inducement, told him that the lady of his thoughts had been seen, the night before, in company of the other sex in the Bois. At first, the viscount refused to believe; but he received such exact details that he ceased protesting. She had been seen, it appeared, driving in a brougham, with the window down. She seemed to be slowly taking in the icy night air. There was a glorious moon shining. She was recognized beyond a doubt. As for her companion, only his shadowy outline was distinguished leaning back in the dark. The carriage was going at a walking pace in a lonely drive behind the grand stand at Longchamp.

Raoul dressed in frantic haste, prepared to forget his distress by flinging himself, as people say, into "the vortex of pleasure." Alas, he was a very sorry guest and, leaving his brother early, found himself, by ten o'clock in the evening, in a cab, behind the Longchamp race-course.

It was bitterly cold. The road seemed deserted and very bright under the moonlight. He told the driver to wait for him patiently at the corner of a near turning and, hiding himself as well as he could, stood stamping his feet to keep warm. He had been indulging in this healthy exercise for half an hour or so, when a carriage turned the corner of the road and came quietly in his direction, at a walking pace.

As it approached, he saw that a woman was leaning her head from the window. And, suddenly, the moon shed a pale gleam over her features.

"Christine!"

The sacred name of his love had sprung from his heart and his lips. He could not keep it back . . . He would have given anything to withdraw it, for that name, proclaimed in the stillness of the night, had acted as though it were the preconcerted signal for a furious rush on the part of the whole turn-out, which dashed past him before he could put into execution his plan of leaping at the horses' heads. The carriage window had been closed and the girl's face had disappeared. And the brougham, behind which he was now running, was no more than a black spot on the white road.

He called out again: "Christine!"

No reply. And he stopped in the midst of the silence.

With a lack-luster eye, he stared down that cold, desolate road and into the pale, dead night. Nothing was colder than his heart, nothing half so dead: he had loved an angel and now he despised a woman!

Raoul, how that little fairy of the North has trifled with you! Was it really, was it really necessary to have so fresh and young a face, a forehead so shy and always ready to cover itself with the pink blush of modesty in order to pass in the lonely night, in a carriage and pair, accompanied by a mysterious lover? Surely there should be some limit to hypocrisy and lying! . . .

She had passed without answering his cry. . . . And he was thinking of dying; and he was twenty years old! . . .

His valet found him in the morning sitting on his bed. He had not undressed and the servant feared, at the sight of his face, that some disaster had occurred. Raoul snatched his letters from the man's hands. He had recognized Christine's paper and hand-writing. She said:

> Dear:
>
> Go to the masked ball at the Opera on the night after to-morrow. At twelve o'clock, be in the little room behind the chimney-place of the big crush-room. Stand near the door that leads to the Rotunda. Don't mention this appointment to any one on earth. Wear a white domino and be carefully masked. As you love me, do not let yourself be recognized.
>
> Christine

IX

AT THE MASKED BALL

The envelope was covered with mud and unstamped. It bore the words "To be handed to M. le Vicomte Raoul de Chagny," with the address in pencil. It must have been flung out in the hope that a passer-by would pick up the note and deliver it, which was what happened. The note had been picked up on the pavement of the Place de l'Opera.

Raoul read it over again with fevered eyes. No more was needed to revive his hope. The somber picture which he had for a moment imagined of a Christine forgetting her duty to herself made way for his original conception of an unfortunate, innocent child, the victim of imprudence and exaggerated sensibility.

To what extent, at this time, was she really a victim? Whose prisoner was she? Into what whirlpool had she been dragged? He asked himself these questions with a crude anguish; but even this pain seemed endurable beside the frenzy into which he was thrown at the thought of a lying and deceitful Christine. What had happened? What influence had she undergone? What monster had carried her off and by what means? . . .

By what means indeed but that of music? He knew Christine's story. After her father's death, she acquired a distaste of everything in life, including her art. She went through the *conservatoire* like a poor soulless singing-machine. And, suddenly, she awoke as though through the intervention of a god. The Angel of Music appeared upon the scene! She sang Margarita in *Faust* and triumphed! . . .

The Angel of Music! . . . For three months the Angel of Music had been giving Christine lessons. . . . Ah, he was a punctual singing-master! . . . And now he was taking her for drives in the Bois! . . .

Raoul's lingers clutched at his flesh, above his jealous heart. In his inexperience, he now asked himself with terror what game the girl was playing? Up to what point could an opera-singer make a fool of a good-natured young man, quite new to love? O misery! . . .

Thus did Raoul's thoughts fly from one extreme to the other. He no longer knew whether to pity Christine or to curse her; and he pitied and cursed her turn and turn about. At all events, he bought a white domino.

The hour of the appointment came at last. With his face in a mask trimmed with long, thick lace, looking like a pierrot in his white wrap, the viscount thought himself very ridiculous. Men of the world do not go to the Opera ball in fancy-dress! It was absurd. One thought, however, consoled the viscount: he would certainly never be recognized!

This ball was an exceptional affair, given some time before Shrovetide, in honor of the anniversary of the birth of a famous draftsman; and it was expected to be much gayer, noisier, more Bohemian than the ordinary masked ball. Numbers of artists had arranged to go, accompanied by a whole cohort of models and pupils, who, by midnight, began to create a tremendous din. Raoul climbed the grand staircase at five minutes to twelve, did not linger to look at the motley dresses displayed all the way up the marble steps, one of the richest settings in the world, allowed no facetious mask to draw him into a war of wits, replied to no jests and shook off the bold familiarity of a number of couples who had already become a trifle too gay. Crossing the big crush-room and escaping from a mad whirl of dancers in which he was caught for a moment, he at last entered the room mentioned in Christine's letter. He found it crammed; for this small space was the point where all those who were going to supper in the Rotunda crossed those who were returning from taking a glass of champagne. The fun, here, waxed fast and furious.

Raoul leaned against a door-post and waited. He did not wait long. A black domino passed and gave a quick squeeze to the tips of his fingers. He understood that it was she and followed her:

"Is that you, Christine?" he asked, between his teeth.

The black domino turned round promptly and raised her finger to her lips, no doubt to warn him not to mention her name again. Raoul continued to follow her in silence.

He was afraid of losing her, after meeting her again in such strange circumstances. His grudge against her was gone. He no longer doubted that she had "nothing to reproach herself with," however peculiar and inexplicable her conduct might seem. He was ready to make any display of clemency, forgiveness or cowardice. He was in love. And, no doubt, he would soon receive a very natural explanation of her curious absence.

The black domino turned back from time to time to see if the white domino was still following.

As Raoul once more passed through the great crush-room, this time in the wake of his guide, he could not help noticing a group crowding round a person whose disguise, eccentric air and gruesome appearance were causing a sensation. It was a man dressed all in scarlet, with a huge hat and feathers on the top of a wonderful death's head. From his shoulders hung an immense red-velvet cloak, which trailed along the floor like a king's train; and on this cloak was embroidered, in gold letters, which every one read and repeated aloud, "Don't touch me! I am Red Death stalking abroad!"

Then one, greatly daring, did try to touch him . . . but a skeleton hand shot out of a crimson sleeve and violently seized the rash one's wrist; and he, feeling the clutch of the knucklebones, the furious grasp of Death, uttered a cry of pain and terror. When Red Death released him at last, he ran away like a very madman, pursued by the jeers of the bystanders.

It was at this moment that Raoul passed in front of the funereal masquerader, who had just happened to turn in his direction. And he nearly exclaimed:

"The death's head of Perros-Guirec!"

He had recognized him! . . . He wanted to dart forward, forgetting Christine; but the black domino, who also seemed a prey to some strange excitement, caught him by the arm and dragged him from the crush-room, far from the mad crowd through which Red Death was stalking. . . .

The black domino kept on turning back and, apparently, on two occasions saw something that startled her, for she hurried her pace and Raoul's as though they were being pursued.

They went up two floors. Here, the stairs and corridors were almost deserted. The black domino opened the door of a private box and beckoned to the white domino to follow her. Then Christine, whom he recognized by the sound of her voice, closed the door behind them and warned him, in a whisper, to remain at the back of the box and on no account to show himself. Raoul took off his mask. Christine kept hers on. And, when Raoul was about to ask her to remove it, he was surprised to see her put her ear to the partition and listen eagerly for a sound outside. Then she opened the door ajar, looked out into the corridor and, in a low voice, said:

"He must have gone up higher." Suddenly she exclaimed: "He is coming down again!"

She tried to close the door, but Raoul prevented her; for he had seen, on the top step of the staircase that led to the floor above, *a red foot*, followed by another . . . and slowly, majestically, the whole scarlet dress of Red Death met his eyes. And he once more saw the death's head of Perros-Guirec.

"It's he!" he exclaimed. "This time, he shall not escape me! . . ."

But Christine had slammed the door at the moment when Raoul was on the point of rushing out. He tried to push her aside.

"Whom do you mean by 'he'?" she asked, in a changed voice. "Who shall not escape you?"

Raoul tried to overcome the girl's resistance by force, but she repelled him with a strength which he would not have suspected in her. He understood, or thought he understood, and at once lost his temper.

"Who?" he repeated angrily. "Why, he, the man who hides behind that hideous mask of death! The evil genius of the churchyard at Perros! . . . Red Death! . . . In a word, madam, your friend . . . your Angel of Music! . . . But I shall snatch off his mask, as I shall snatch off my own; and, this time, we shall look each other in the face, he and I, with no veil and no lies between us; and I shall know whom you love and who loves you!"

He burst into a mad laugh, while Christine gave a disconsolate moan behind her velvet mask. With a tragic gesture, she flung out her two arms, which fixed a barrier of white flesh against the door.

"In the name of our love, Raoul, you shall not pass! . . ."

He stopped. What had she said? . . . In the name of their love? . . . Never before had she confessed that she loved him. And yet she had had opportunities enough. . . . Pooh, her only object was to gain a few seconds! . . . She wished to give the Red Death time to escape . . . And, in accents of childish hatred, he said:

"You lie, madam, for you do not love me and you have never loved me! What a poor fellow I must be to let you mock and flout me as you have done! Why did you give me every reason for hope, at Perros . . . for honest hope, madam, for I am an honest man and I believed you to be an honest woman, when your only intention was to deceive me! Alas, you have deceived us all! You have taken a shameful advantage of the candid affection of your benefactress herself, who continues to believe in your sincerity while you go about the Opera ball with Red Death! . . . I despise you! . . ."

And he burst into tears. She allowed him to insult her. She thought of but one thing, to keep him from leaving the box.

"You will beg my pardon, one day, for all those ugly words, Raoul, and when you do I shall forgive you!"

He shook his head. "No, no, you have driven me mad! When I think that I had only one object in life: to give my name to an opera wench!"

"Raoul! . . . How can you?"

"I shall die of shame!"

"No, dear, live!" said Christine's grave and changed voice. "And . . . good-by. Good-by, Raoul . . ."

The boy stepped forward, staggering as he went. He risked one more sarcasm:

"Oh, you must let me come and applaud you from time to time!"

"I shall never sing again, Raoul! . . ."

"Really?" he replied, still more satirically. "So he is taking you off the stage: I congratulate you! . . . But we shall meet in the Bois, one of these evenings!"

"Not in the Bois nor anywhere, Raoul: you shall not see me again . . ."

"May one ask at least to what darkness you are returning? . . . For what hell are you leaving, mysterious lady . . . or for what paradise?"

"I came to tell you, dear, but I can't tell you now . . . you would not believe me! You have lost faith in me, Raoul; it is finished!"

She spoke in such a despairing voice that the lad began to feel remorse for his cruelty.

"But look here!" he cried. "Can't you tell me what all this means! . . . You are free, there is no one to interfere with you. . . . You go about Paris. . . . You put on a domino to come to the ball. . . . Why do you not go home? . . . What have you been doing this past fortnight?. . . What is this tale about the Angel of Music, which you have been telling Mamma Valérius? Some one may have taken you in, played upon your innocence. I was a witness of it myself, at Perros . . . but you know what to believe now! You seem to me quite sensible, Christine. You know what you are doing . . . . And meanwhile Mamma Valérius lies waiting for you at home and appealing to your 'good genius!' . . . Explain yourself, Christine, I beg of you! Any one might have been deceived as I was. What is this farce?"

Christine simply took off her mask and said: "Dear, it is a tragedy!"

Raoul now saw her face and could not restrain an exclamation of surprise and terror. The fresh complexion of former days was gone. A mortal pallor covered those features, which he had known so charming and so gentle, and sorrow had furrowed them with pitiless lines and traced dark and unspeakably sad shadows under her eyes.

"My dearest! My dearest!" he moaned, holding out his arms. "You promised to forgive me . . ."

"Perhaps! . . . Some day, perhaps!" she said, resuming her mask; and she went away, forbidding him, with a gesture, to follow her.

He tried to disobey her; but she turned round and repeated her gesture of farewell with such authority that he dared not move a step.

He watched her till she was out of sight. Then he also went down among the crowd, hardly knowing what he was doing, with throbbing temples and an aching heart; and, as he crossed the dancing-floor, he asked if anybody had seen Red Death. Yes, every one had seen Red Death; but Raoul could not find him; and, at two o'clock in the morning, he turned down the passage, behind the scenes, that led to Christine Daaé's dressing-room.

His footsteps took him to that room where he had first known suffering. He tapped at the door. There was no answer. He entered, as he had entered when he looked everywhere for "the man's voice." The room was empty. A gas-jet was burning, turned down low. He saw some writing-paper on a little desk. He thought of writing to Christine, but he heard steps in the passage. He had only time to hide in the inner room, which was separated from the dressing-room by a curtain.

Christine entered, took off her mask with a weary movement and flung it on the table. She sighed and let her pretty head fall into her two hands. What was she thinking of? Of Raoul? No, for Raoul heard her murmur: "Poor Erik!"

At first, he thought he must be mistaken. To begin with, he was persuaded that, if any one was to be pitied, it was he, Raoul. It would have been quite natural if she had said, "Poor Raoul," after what had happened between them. But, shaking her head, she repeated: "Poor Erik!"

What had this Erik to do with Christine's sighs and why was she pitying Erik when Raoul was so unhappy?

Christine began to write, deliberately, calmly and so placidly that Raoul, who was still trembling from the effects of the tragedy that separated them, was painfully impressed.

"What coolness!" he said to himself.

She wrote on, filling two, three, four sheets. Suddenly, she raised her head and hid the sheets in her bodice.... She seemed to be listening... Raoul also listened... Whence came that strange sound, that distant rhythm?... A faint singing seemed to issue from the walls... yes, it was as though the walls themselves were singing! ... The song became plainer... the words were now distinguishable... he heard a voice, a very beautiful, very soft, very captivating voice... but, for all its softness, it remained a male voice... The voice came nearer and nearer... it came through the wall... it approached... and now the voice was *in the room*, in front of Christine. Christine rose and addressed the voice, as though speaking to some one:

"Here I am, Erik," she said. "I am ready. But you are late."

Raoul, peeping from behind the curtain, could not believe his eyes, which showed him nothing. Christine's face lit up. A smile of happiness appeared upon her bloodless lips, a smile like that of sick people when they receive the first hope of recovery.

The voice without a body went on singing; and certainly Raoul had never in his life heard anything more absolutely and heroically sweet, more gloriously insidious, more delicate, more powerful, in short, more irresistibly triumphant. He listened to it in a fever and he now began to understand how Christine Daaé was able to appear one evening, before the stupefied audience, with accents of a beauty hitherto unknown, of a superhuman exaltation, while doubtless still under the influence of the mysterious and invisible master.

The voice was singing the Wedding-night Song from *Romeo and Juliet*. Raoul saw Christine stretch out her arms to the voice as she had done, in Perros churchyard, to the invisible violin playing *The Resurrection of Lazarus*. And nothing could describe the passion with which the voice sang:

"Fate links thee to me for ever and a day!"

The strains went through Raoul's heart. Struggling against the charm that seemed to deprive him of all his will and all his energy and of almost all his lucidity at the moment when he needed them most, he succeeded in drawing back the curtain that hid him and he walked to where Christine stood. She herself was moving to the back of the room, the whole wall of which was occupied by a great mirror that reflected her image, but not his, for he was just behind her and entirely covered by her.

"Fate links thee to me for ever and a day!"

Christine walked toward her image in the glass and the image came toward her. The two Christines—the real one and the reflection—ended by touching; and Raoul put out his arms to clasp the two in one embrace. But, by a sort of dazzling miracle that sent him staggering, Raoul was suddenly flung back, while an icy blast swept over his face; he saw, not two, but four, eight, twenty Christines spinning round him, laughing at him and fleeing so swiftly that he could not touch one of them. At last, everything stood still again; and he saw himself in the glass. But Christine had disappeared.

He rushed up to the glass. He struck at the walls. Nobody! And meanwhile the room still echoed with a distant passionate singing:

"Fate links thee to me for ever and a day!"

Which way, which way had Christine gone? . . . Which way would she return? . . .

Would she return? Alas, had she not declared to him that everything was finished? And was the voice not repeating:

"Fate links thee to me for ever and a day!"

To me? To whom?

Then, worn out, beaten, empty-brained, he sat down on the chair which Christine had just left. Like her, he let his head fall into his hands. When he raised it, the tears were streaming down his young cheeks, real, heavy tears like those which jealous children shed, tears that wept for a sorrow which was in no way fanciful, but which is common to all the lovers on earth and which he expressed aloud:

"Who is this Erik?" he said.

X

FORGET THE NAME OF THE MAN'S VOICE

THE DAY AFTER CHRISTINE HAD VANISHED BEFORE HIS EYES IN A SORT of dazzlement that still made him doubt the evidence of his senses, M. le Vicomte de Chagny called to inquire at Mamma Valérius'. He came upon a charming picture. Christine herself was seated by the bedside of the old lady, who was sitting up against the pillows, knitting. The pink and white had returned to the young girl's cheeks. The dark rings round her eyes had disappeared. Raoul no longer recognized the tragic face of the day before. If the veil of melancholy over those adorable features had not still appeared to the young man as the last trace of the weird drama in whose toils that mysterious child was struggling, he could have believed that Christine was not its heroine at all.

She rose, without showing any emotion, and offered him her hand. But Raoul's stupefaction was so great that he stood there dumfounded, without a gesture, without a word.

"Well, M. de Chagny," exclaimed Mamma Valérius, "don't you know our Christine? Her good genius has sent her back to us!"

"Mamma!" the girl broke in promptly, while a deep blush mantled to her eyes. "I thought, mamma, that there was to be no more question of that! . . . You know there is no such thing as the Angel of Music!"

"But, child, he gave you lessons for three months!"

"Mamma, I have promised to explain everything to you one of these days; and I hope to do so . . . but you have promised me, until that day, to be silent and to ask me no more questions whatever!"

"Provided that you promised never to leave me again! But have you promised that, Christine?"

"Mamma, all this can not interest M. de Chagny."

"On the contrary, mademoiselle," said the young man, in a voice which he tried to make firm and brave, but which still trembled, "anything that concerns you interests me to an extent which perhaps you will one day understand. I do not deny that my surprise equals my pleasure at finding you with your adopted mother and that, after what happened between us yesterday, after what you said and what I was able to guess, I hardly expected to see you here so soon. I should be the first to delight at your return, if you were not so bent on preserving a secrecy that may be fatal to you . . . and I have been your friend too long not to be alarmed, with Mme. Valérius, at a disastrous adventure which will remain dangerous so long as we have not unraveled its threads and of which you will certainly end by being the victim, Christine."

At these words. Mamma Valérius tossed about in her bed.

"What does this mean?" she cried. "Is Christine in danger?"

"Yes, madame," said Raoul courageously, notwithstanding the signs which Christine made to him.

"My God!" exclaimed the good, simple old woman, gasping for breath. "You must tell me everything, Christine! Why did you try to reassure me? And what danger is it, M. de Chagny?"

"An impostor is abusing her good faith."

"Is the Angel of Music an impostor?"

"She told you herself that there is no Angel of Music."

"But then what is it, in Heaven's name? You will be the death of me!"

"There is a terrible mystery around us, madame, around you, around Christine, a mystery much more to be feared than any number of ghosts or genii!"

Mamma Valérius turned a terrified face to Christine, who had already run to her adopted mother and was holding her in her arms.

"Don't believe him, mummy, don't believe him," she repeated.

"Then tell me that you will never leave me again," implored the widow.

Christine was silent and Raoul resumed.

"That is what you must promise, Christine. It is the only thing that can reassure your mother and me. We will undertake not to ask you a single question about the past, if you promise us to remain under our protection in future."

"That is an undertaking which I have not asked of you and a promise which I refuse to make you!" said the young girl haughtily. "I am mistress of my own actions, M. de Chagny: you have no right to control them, and I will beg you to desist henceforth. As to what I have done during the last fortnight, there is only one man in the world who has the right to demand an account of me: my husband! Well, I have no husband and I never mean to marry!"

She threw out her hands to emphasize her words and Raoul turned pale, not only because of the words which he had heard, but because he had caught sight of a plain gold ring on Christine's finger.

"You have no husband and yet you wear a wedding-ring."

He tried to seize her hand, but she swiftly drew it back.

"That's a present!" she said, blushing once more and vainly striving to hide her embarrassment.

"Christine! As you have no husband, that ring can only have been given by one who hopes to make you his wife! Why deceive us further? Why torture me still more? That ring is a promise; and that promise has been accepted!"

"That's what I said!" exclaimed the old lady.

"And what did she answer, madame?"

"What I chose," said Christine, driven to exasperation. "Don't you think, monsieur, that this cross-examination has lasted long enough? As far as I am concerned . . ."

Raoul was afraid to let her finish her speech. He interrupted her:

"I beg your pardon for speaking as I did, mademoiselle. You know the good intentions that make me meddle, just now, in matters which, you no doubt think, have nothing to do with me. But allow me to tell you what I have seen—and I have seen more than you suspect, Christine—or what I thought I saw, for, to tell you the truth, I have sometimes been inclined to doubt the evidence of my eyes."

"Well, what did you see, sir, or think you saw?"

"I saw your ecstasy *at the sound of the voice*, Christine: the voice that came from the wall or the next room to yours. . . yes, *your ecstasy*! And that is what makes me alarmed on your behalf. You are under a very dangerous spell. And yet it seems that you are aware of the imposture, because you say to-day *that there is no Angel of Music*! In that case, Christine, why did you follow him that time? Why did you stand up, with radiant features, as though you were really hearing angels? . . . Ah, it is a very dangerous voice, Christine, for I myself, when I heard it, was so much fascinated by it that you vanished before my eyes without my seeing which way you passed! Christine, Christine, in the name of Heaven, in the name of your father who is in Heaven now and who loved you so dearly and who loved me too, Christine, tell us, tell your benefactress and me, to whom does that voice belong? If you do, we will save you in spite of yourself. Come, Christine, the name of the man! The name of the man who had the audacity to put a ring on your finger!"

"M. de Chagny," the girl declared coldly, "you shall never know!"

Thereupon, seeing the hostility with which her ward had addressed the viscount, Mamma Valérius suddenly took Christine's part.

"And, if she does love that man, *monsieur le vicomte*, even then it is no business of yours!"

"Alas, madame," Raoul humbly replied, unable to restrain his tears, "alas, I believe that Christine really does love him! . . . But it is not only that which drives me to despair; for what I am not certain of, madame, is that the man whom Christine loves is worthy of her love!"

"It is for me to be the judge of that, monsieur!" said Christine, looking Raoul angrily in the face.

"When a man," continued Raoul, "adopts such romantic methods to entice a young girl's affections . . ."

"The man must be either a villain, or the girl a fool: is that it?"

"Christine!"

"Raoul, why do you condemn a man whom you have never seen, whom no one knows and about whom you yourself know nothing?"

"Yes, Christine. . . . Yes. . . . I at least know the name that you thought to keep from me for ever. . . . The name of your Angel of Music, mademoiselle, is Erik!"

Christine at once betrayed herself. She turned as white as a sheet and stammered:

"Who told you?"

"You yourself!"

"How do you mean?"

"By pitying him the other night, the night of the masked ball. When you went to your dressing-room, did you not say, 'Poor Erik?' Well, Christine, there was a poor Raoul who overheard you."

"This is the second time that you have listened behind the door, M. de Chagny!"

"I was not behind the door . . . I was in the dressing-room, in the inner room, mademoiselle."

"Oh, unhappy man!" moaned the girl, showing every sign of unspeakable terror. "Unhappy man! Do you want to be killed?"

"Perhaps."

Raoul uttered this "perhaps" with so much love and despair in his voice that Christine could not keep back a sob. She took his hands and looked at him with all the pure affection of which she was capable:

"Raoul," she said, "forget *the man's voice* and do not even remember its name... You must never try to fathom the mystery of *the man's voice*."

"Is the mystery so very terrible?"

"There is no more awful mystery on this earth. Swear to me that you will make no attempt to find out," she insisted. "Swear to me that you will never come to my dressing-room, unless I send for you."

"Then you promise to send for me sometimes, Christine?"

"I promise."

"When?"

"To-morrow."

"Then I swear to do as you ask."

He kissed her hands and went away, cursing Erik and resolving to be patient.

XI

ABOVE THE TRAP-DOORS

THE NEXT DAY, HE SAW HER AT THE OPERA. SHE WAS STILL WEARING the plain gold ring. She was gentle and kind to him. She talked to him of the plans which he was forming, of his future, of his career.

He told her that the date of the Polar expedition had been put forward and that he would leave France in three weeks, or a month at latest. She suggested, almost gaily, that he must look upon the voyage with delight, as a stage toward his coming fame. And when he replied that fame without love was no attraction in his eyes, she treated him as a child whose sorrows were only short-lived.

"How can you speak so lightly of such serious things?" he asked. "Perhaps we shall never see each other again! I may die during that expedition."

"Or I," she said simply.

She no longer smiled or jested. She seemed to be thinking of some new thing that had entered her mind for the first time. Her eyes were all aglow with it.

"What are you thinking of, Christine?"

"I am thinking that we shall not see each other again . . ."

"And does that make you so radiant?"

"And that, in a month, we shall have to say good-by for ever!"

"Unless, Christine, we pledge our faith and wait for each other for ever."

She put her hand on his mouth.

"Hush, Raoul! . . . You know there is no question of that . . . And we shall never be married: that is understood!"

She seemed suddenly almost unable to contain an overpowering gaiety. She clapped her hands with childish glee. Raoul stared at her in amazement.

"But . . . but," she continued, holding out her two hands to Raoul, or rather giving them to him, as though she had suddenly resolved to make him a present of them, "but if we can not be married, we can . . . we can be engaged! Nobody will know but ourselves, Raoul. There have been plenty of secret marriages: why not a secret engagement? . . . We are engaged, dear, for a month! In a month, you will go away, and I can be happy at the thought of that month all my life long!"

She was enchanted with her inspiration. Then she became serious again.

"This," she said, "*is a happiness that will harm no one.*"

Raoul jumped at the idea. He bowed to Christine and said:

"Mademoiselle, I have the honor to ask for your hand."

"Why, you have both of them already, my dear betrothed! . . . Oh, Raoul, how happy we shall be! . . . We must play at being engaged all day long."

It was the prettiest game in the world and they enjoyed it like the children that they were. Oh, the wonderful speeches they made to each other and the eternal vows they exchanged! They played at hearts as other children might play at ball; only, as it was really their two hearts that they flung to and fro, they had to be very, very handy to catch them, each time, without hurting them.

One day, about a week after the game began, Raoul's heart was badly hurt and he stopped playing and uttered these wild words:

"I shan't go to the North Pole!"

Christine, who, in her innocence, had not dreamed of such a possibility, suddenly discovered the danger of the game and reproached herself bitterly. She did not say a word in reply to Raoul's remark and went straight home.

This happened in the afternoon, in the singer's dressing-room, where they met every day and where they amused themselves by dining on three biscuits, two glasses of port and a bunch of violets. In the evening, she did not sing; and he did not receive his usual letter, though they had arranged to write to each other daily during that month. The next morning, he ran off to Mamma Valérius, who told him that Christine had gone away for two days. She had left at five o'clock the day before.

Raoul was distracted. He hated Mamma Valérius for giving him such news as that with such stupefying calmness. He tried to sound her, but the old lady obviously knew nothing.

Christine returned on the following day. She returned in triumph. She renewed her extraordinary success of the gala performance. Since the adventure of the "toad," Carlotta had not been able to appear on the stage. The terror of a fresh "co-ack" filled her heart and deprived her of all her power of singing; and the theater that had witnessed her incomprehensible disgrace had become odious to her. She contrived to cancel her contract. Daaé was offered the vacant place for the time. She received thunders of applause in the *Juive*.

The viscount, who, of course, was present, was the only one to suffer on hearing the thousand echoes of this fresh triumph; for Christine still wore her plain gold ring. A distant voice whispered in the young man's ear:

"She is wearing the ring again to-night; and you did not give it to her. She gave her soul again tonight and did not give it to you. . . . If she will not tell you what she has been doing the past two days . . . you must go and ask Erik!"

He ran behind the scenes and placed himself in her way. She saw him for her eyes were looking for him. She said:

"Quick! Quick! . . . Come!"

And she dragged him to her dressing-room.

Raoul at once threw himself on his knees before her. He swore to her that he would go and he entreated her never again to withhold a single hour of the ideal happiness which she had promised him. She let her tears flow. They kissed like a despairing brother and sister who have been smitten with a common loss and who meet to mourn a dead parent.

Suddenly, she snatched herself from the young man's soft and timid embrace, seemed to listen to something, and, with a quick gesture, pointed to the door. When he was on the threshold, she said, in so low a voice that the viscount guessed rather than heard her words:

"To-morrow, my dear betrothed! And be happy, Raoul: I sang for you to-night!"

He returned the next day. But those two days of absence had broken the charm of their delightful make-believe. They looked at each other, in the dressing-room, with their sad eyes, without exchanging a word. Raoul had to restrain himself not to cry out:

"I am jealous! I am jealous! I am jealous!"

But she heard him all the same. Then she said:

"Come for a walk, dear. The air will do you good."

Raoul thought that she would propose a stroll in the country, far from that building which he detested as a prison whose jailer he could feel walking within the walls . . . the jailer Erik. . . . But she took him to the stage and made him sit on the wooden curb of a well, in the doubtful peace and coolness of a first scene set for the evening's performance.

On another day, she wandered with him, hand in hand, along the deserted paths of a garden whose creepers had been cut out by a decorator's skilful hands. It was as though the real sky, the real flowers, the real earth were forbidden her for all time and she condemned to breathe no other air than that of the theater. An occasional fireman passed, watching over their melancholy idyll from afar. And she would drag him up above the clouds, in the magnificent disorder of the grid, where she loved to make him giddy by running in front of him along the frail bridges, among the thousands of ropes fastened to the pulleys, the windlasses, the rollers, in the midst of a regular forest of yards and masts. If he hesitated, she said, with an adorable pout of her lips:

"You, a sailor!"

And then they returned to *terra firma*, that is to say, to some passage that led them to the little girls' dancing-school, where brats between six and ten were practising their steps, in the hope of becoming great dancers one day, "covered with diamonds. . . ." Meanwhile, Christine gave them sweets instead.

She took him to the wardrobe and property-rooms, took him all over her empire, which was artificial, but immense, covering seventeen stories from the ground-floor to the roof and inhabited by an army of subjects. She moved among them like a popular queen, encouraging them in their labors, sitting down in the workshops, giving words of advice to the workmen whose hands hesitated to cut into the rich stuffs that were to clothe heroes. There were inhabitants of that country who practised every trade. There were cobblers, there were goldsmiths. All had learned to know her and to love her, for she always interested herself in all their troubles and all their little hobbies.

She knew unsuspected corners that were secretly occupied by little old couples. She knocked at their door and introduced Raoul to them as a Prince Charming who had asked for her hand; and the two of them, sitting on some worm-eaten "property," would listen to the legends of the Opera, even as, in their childhood, they had listened to the old Breton tales. Those old people remembered nothing outside the Opera. They had lived there for years without number. Past managements had forgotten them; palace revolutions had taken no notice of them; the history of France had run its course unknown to them; and nobody recollected their existence.

The precious days sped in this way; and Raoul and Christine, by affecting excessive interest in outside matters, strove awkwardly to hide from each other the one thought of their hearts. One fact was certain, that Christine, who until then had shown herself the stronger of the two, became suddenly inexpressibly nervous. When on their expeditions, she would start running without reason or else suddenly stop; and her hand, turning ice-cold in a moment, would hold the young man back. Sometimes her eyes seemed to pursue imaginary shadows. She cried, "This way," and "This way," and "This way," laughing a breathless laugh that often ended in tears. Then Raoul tried to speak, to question her, in spite of his promises. But, even before he had worded his question, she answered feverishly:

"Nothing . . . I swear it is nothing."

Once, when they were passing before an open trapdoor on the stage, Raoul stopped over the dark cavity.

"You have shown me over the upper part of your empire, Christine, but there are strange stories told of the lower part. Shall we go down?"

She caught him in her arms, as though she feared to see him disappear down the black hole, and, in a trembling voice, whispered:

"Never! . . . I will not have you go there! Besides, it's not mine . . . *everything that is underground belongs to him*!"

Raoul looked her in the eyes and said roughly:

"So he lives down there, does he?"

"I never said so. . . . Who told you a thing like that? Come away! I sometimes wonder if you are quite sane, Raoul. . . . You always take things in such an impossible way. . . . Come along! Come!"

And she literally dragged him away, for he was obstinate and wanted to remain by the trap-door; that hole attracted him.

Suddenly, the trap-door was closed and so quickly that they did not even see the hand that worked it; and they remained quite dazed.

"Perhaps he was there," Raoul said, at last.

She shrugged her shoulders, but did not seem easy.

"No, no, it was the 'trap-door-shutters.' They must do something, you know. . . . They open and shut the trap-doors without any particular reason. . . . It's like the 'door-shutters': they must spend their time somehow."

"But suppose it were *he*, Christine?"

"No, no! He has shut himself up, he is working."

"Oh, really! He's working, is he?"

"Yes, he can't open and shut the trap-doors and work at the same time." She shivered.

"What is he working at?"

"Oh, something terrible! . . . But it's all the better for us. . . . When he's working at that, he sees nothing; he does not eat, drink, or breathe for days and nights at a time . . . he becomes a living dead man and has no time to amuse himself with the trap-doors."

She shivered again. She was still holding him in her arms. Then she sighed and said, in her turn:

"Suppose it were *he*!"

"Are you afraid of him?"

"No, no, of course not," she said.

For all that, on the next day and the following days, Christine was careful to avoid the trap-doors. Her agitation only increased as the hours passed. At last, one afternoon, she arrived very late, with her face so desperately pale and her eyes so desperately red, that Raoul resolved to go to all lengths, including that which he foreshadowed when he blurted out that he would not go on the North Pole expedition unless she first told him the secret of the man's voice.

"Hush! Hush, in Heaven's name! Suppose *he* heard you, you unfortunate Raoul!"

And Christine's eyes stared wildly at everything around her.

"I will remove you from his power, Christine, I swear it. And you shall not think of him any more."

"Is it possible?"

She allowed herself this doubt, which was an encouragement, while dragging the young man up to the topmost floor of the theater, far, very far from the trap-doors.

"I shall hide you in some unknown corner of the world, where *he* can not come to look for you. You will be safe; and then I shall go away . . . as you have sworn never to marry."

Christine seized Raoul's hands and squeezed them with incredible rapture. But, suddenly becoming alarmed again, she turned away her head. "Higher!" was all she said. "Higher still!" And she dragged him up toward the summit. He had a difficulty in following her. They were soon under the very roof, in the maze of timber-work. They slipped through the buttresses, the rafters, the joists; they ran from beam to beam as they might have run from tree to tree in a forest.

And, despite the care which she took to look behind her at every moment, she failed to see a shadow which followed her like her own shadow, which stopped when she stopped, which started again when she did and which made no more noise than a well-conducted shadow should. As for Raoul, he saw nothing either; for, when he had Christine in front of him, nothing interested him that happened behind.

XII

APOLLO'S LYRE

IN THIS WAY, THEY REACHED THE ROOF. CHRISTINE TRIPPED OVER IT AS lightly as a swallow. Their eyes swept the empty space between the three domes and the triangular pediment. She breathed freely over Paris, the whole valley of which was seen at work below. She called Raoul to come quite close to her and they walked side by side along the zinc streets, in the leaden avenues; they looked at their twin shapes in the huge tanks, full of stagnant water, where, in the hot weather, the little boys of the ballet, a score or so, learn to swim and dive.

The shadow had followed behind them, clinging to their steps; and the two children little suspected its presence when they at last sat down, trustingly, under the mighty protection of Apollo, who, with a great bronze gesture, lifted his huge lyre to the heart of a crimson sky.

It was a gorgeous spring evening. Clouds, which had just received their gossamer robe of gold and purple from the setting sun, drifted slowly by; and Christine said to Raoul:

"Soon we shall go farther and faster than the clouds, to the end of the world, and then you will leave me, Raoul. But, if, when the moment comes for you to take me away, I refuse to go with you—well you must carry me off by force!"

"Are you afraid that you will change your mind, Christine?"

"I don't know," she said, shaking her head in an odd fashion. "He is a demon!" And she shivered and nestled in his arms with a moan. "I am afraid now of going back to live with him . . . in the ground!"

"What compels you to go back, Christine?"

"If I do not go back to him, terrible misfortunes may happen! . . . But I can't do it, I can't do it! . . . I know one ought to be sorry for people who live underground . . . .But he is too horrible! And yet the time is at hand; I have only a day left; and. If I do not go, he will come and fetch me with his voice. And he will drag me with him, underground, and go on his knees before me, with his death's head. And he will tell me that he loves me! And he will cry! Oh, those tears, Raoul, those tears in the two black eye-sockets of the death's head! I can not see those tears flow again!"

She wrung her hands in anguish, while Raoul pressed her to his heart.

"No, no, you shall never again hear him tell you that he loves you! You shall not see his tears! Let us fly, Christine, let us fly at once!"

And he tried to drag her away, then and there. But she stopped him.

"No, no," she said, shaking her head sadly. "Not now! . . . It would be too cruel . . . let him hear me sing to-morrow evening . . . and then we will go away. You must come and fetch me in my dressing-room at midnight exactly. He will then be waiting for me in the dining-room by the lake . . . we shall be free and you shall take me away. . . . You must promise me that, Raoul, even if I refuse; for I feel that, if I go back this time, I shall perhaps never return."

And she gave a sigh to which it seemed to her that another sigh, behind her, replied.

"Didn't you hear?"

Her teeth chattered.

"No," said Raoul, "I heard nothing."

"It is too terrible," she confessed, "to be always trembling like this! . . . And yet we run no danger here; we are at home, in the sky. In the open air. In the light. The sun is flaming; and night-birds can not bear to look at the sun. I have never seen *him* by daylight . . . It must be awful! . . . Oh, the first time I saw him! . . . I thought that he was going to die."

"Why?" asked Raoul, really frightened at the aspect which this strange confidence was taking.

"*Because I had seen him*!"

This time, Raoul and Christine turned round at the same time:

"There is some one in pain," said Raoul. "Perhaps some one has been hurt. Did you hear?"

"I can't say," Christine confessed. "Even when he is not there, my ears are full of his sighs. Still, if you heard . . ."

They stood up and looked around them. They were quite alone on the immense lead roof. They sat down again and Raoul said:

"Tell me how you saw him first."

"I had heard him for three months without seeing him. The first time I heard it, I thought, as you did, that that adorable voice was singing in another room. I went out and looked everywhere; but, as you know, Raoul, my dressing-room is very much by itself; and I could not find the voice outside my room, whereas it went on steadily inside. And it not only sang, but it spoke to me and answered my questions, like a real man's voice, with this difference, that it was as beautiful as the voice of an angel. I had never got the Angel of Music whom my poor father had promised to send me as soon as he was dead. I really think that Mamma Valérius was a little bit to blame. I told her about it; and she at once said, 'It must be the Angel; at any rate, you can do no harm by asking him.' I did so; and the man's voice replied that, yes, it was the Angel's voice, the voice which I was expecting and which my father had promised me. From that time onward, the voice and I became great friends. It asked leave to give me lessons every day. I agreed and never failed to keep the appointment which it gave me in my dressing-room. You have no idea, though you have heard the voice, of what those lessons were like."

"No, I have no idea," said Raoul. "What was your accompaniment?"

"We were accompanied by a music which I do not know: it was behind the wall and wonderfully accurate. The voice seemed to understand mine exactly, to know precisely where my father had left off teaching me. In a few weeks' time, I hardly knew myself when I sang. I was even frightened. I seemed to dread a sort of witchcraft behind it; but Mamma Valérius reassured me. She said that she knew I was much too simple a girl to give the devil a hold on me. . . . My progress, by the voice's own order, was kept a secret between the voice, Mamma Valérius and myself. It was a curious thing, but, outside the dressing-room, I sang with my ordinary, every-day voice and nobody noticed anything. I did all that the voice asked. It said, 'Wait and see: we shall astonish Paris!' And I waited and lived on in a sort of ecstatic dream. It was then that I saw you for the first time one evening, in the house. I was so glad that I never thought of concealing my delight when I reached my dressing-room. Unfortunately, the voice was there before me and soon noticed, by my air, that something had happened. It asked what was the matter and I saw no reason for keeping our story secret or concealing the place which you filled in my heart. Then the voice was silent. I called to it, but it did not reply; I begged and entreated, but in vain. I was terrified lest it had gone for good. I wish to Heaven it had, dear! . . . That night, I went home in a desperate condition. I told Mamma Valérius, who said, 'Why, of course, the voice is jealous!' And that, dear, first revealed to me that I loved you."

Christine stopped and laid her head on Raoul's shoulder. They sat like that for a moment, in silence, and they did not see, did not perceive the movement, at a few steps from them, of the creeping shadow of two great black wings, a shadow that came along the roof so near, so near them that it could have stifled them by closing over them.

"The next day," Christine continued, with a sigh, "I went back to my dressing-room in a very pensive frame of mind. The voice was there, spoke to me with great sadness and told me plainly that, if I must bestow my heart on earth, there was nothing for the voice to do but to go back to Heaven. And it said this with such an accent of *human* sorrow that I ought then and there to have suspected and begun to believe that I was the victim of my deluded senses. But my faith in the voice, with which the memory of my father was so closely intermingled, remained undisturbed. I feared nothing so much as that I might never hear it again; I had thought about my love for you and realized all the useless danger of it; and I did not even know if you remembered me. Whatever happened, your position in society forbade me to contemplate the possibility of ever marrying you; and I swore to the voice that you were no more than a brother to me nor ever would be and that my heart was incapable of any earthly love. And that, dear, was why I refused to recognize or see you when I met you on the stage or in the passages. Meanwhile, the hours during which the voice taught me were spent in a divine frenzy, until, at last, the voice said to me, 'You can now, Christine Daaé, give to men a little of the music of Heaven.' I don't know how it was that Carlotta did not come to the theater that night nor why I was called upon to sing in her stead; but I sang with a rapture I had never known before and I felt for a moment as if my soul were leaving my body!"

"Oh, Christine," said Raoul, "my heart quivered that night at every accent of your voice. I saw the tears stream down your cheeks and I wept with you. How could you sing, sing like that while crying?"

"I felt myself fainting," said Christine, "I closed my eyes. When I opened them, you were by my side. But the voice was there also, Raoul! I was afraid for your sake and again I would not recognize you and began to laugh when you reminded me that you had picked up my scarf in the sea! Alas, there is no deceiving the voice! . . . The voice recognized you and the voice was jealous! It said that, if I did not love you, I would not avoid you, but treat you like any other old friend. It made me scene upon scene. At last, I said to the voice, 'That will do! I am going to Perros to-morrow, to pray on my father's grave, and I shall ask M. Raoul de Chagny to go with me.' 'Do as you please,' replied the voice, 'but I shall be at Perros too, for I am wherever you are, Christine; and, if you are still worthy of me, if you have not lied to me, I will play you *The Resurrection of Lazarus,* on the stroke of midnight, on your father's tomb and on your father's violin.' That, dear, was how I came to write you the letter that brought you to Perros. How could I have been so beguiled? How was it, when I saw the personal, the selfish point of view of the voice, that I did not suspect some impostor? Alas, I was no longer mistress of myself: I had become his thing!"

"But, after all," cried Raoul, "you soon came to know the truth! Why did you not at once rid yourself of that abominable nightmare?"

"Know the truth, Raoul? Rid myself of that nightmare? But, my poor boy, I was not caught in the nightmare until the day when I learned the truth! . . . Pity me, Raoul, pity me! . . . You remember the terrible evening when Carlotta thought that she had been turned into a toad on the stage and when the house was suddenly plunged in darkness through the chandelier crashing to the floor? There were killed and wounded that night and the whole theater rang with terrified screams. My first thought was for you and the voice. I was at once easy, where you were concerned, for I had seen you in your brother's box and I knew that you were not in danger. But the voice had told me that it would be at the performance and I was really afraid for it, just as if it had been an ordinary person who was capable of dying. I thought to myself, 'The chandelier may have come down upon the voice.' I was then on the stage and was nearly running into the house, to look for the voice among the killed and wounded, when I thought that, if the voice was safe, it would be sure to be in my dressing-room and I rushed to my room. The voice was not there. I locked my door and, with tears in my eyes, besought it, if it were still alive, to manifest itself to me. The voice did not reply, but suddenly I heard a long, beautiful wail which I knew well. It is the plaint of Lazarus when, at the sound of the Redeemer's voice, he begins to open his eyes and see the light of day. It was the music which you and I, Raoul, heard at Perros. And then the voice began to sing the leading phrase, 'Come! And believe in me! Whoso believes in me shall live! Walk! Whoso hath believed in me shall never die! . . . ' I can not tell you the effect which that music had upon me. It seemed to command me, personally, to come, to stand up and come to it. It retreated and I followed. 'Come! And believe in me!' I believed in it, I came. . . . I came and—this was the extraordinary thing—my dressing-room, as I moved, seemed to lengthen out . . . to lengthen out. Evidently, it must have been an effect of mirrors for I had the mirror in front of me . . . And, suddenly, I was outside the room without knowing how!"

"What! Without knowing how? Christine, Christine, you must really stop dreaming!"

"I was not dreaming, dear, I was outside my room without knowing how. You, who saw me disappear from my room one evening, may be able to explain it; but I can not. I can only tell you that, suddenly, there was no mirror before me and no dressing-room. I was in a dark passage, I was frightened and I cried out. It was quite dark, but for a faint red glimmer at a distant corner of the wall. I cried out. My voice was the only sound, for the singing and the violin had stopped. And, suddenly, a hand was laid on mine . . . or rather a stone-cold, bony thing that seized my wrist and did not let go. I cried out again. An arm took me round the waist and supported me. I struggled for a little while and then gave up the attempt. I was dragged toward the little red light and then I saw that I was in the hands of a man wrapped in a large cloak and wearing a mask that hid his whole face. I made one last effort; my limbs stiffened, my mouth opened to scream, but a hand closed it, a hand which I felt on my lips, on my skin . . . a hand that smelt of death. Then I fainted away.

"When I opened my eyes, we were still surrounded by darkness. A lantern, standing on the ground, showed a bubbling well. The water splashing from the well disappeared, almost at once, under the floor on which I was lying, with my head on the knee of the man in the black cloak and the black mask. He was bathing my temples and his hands smelt of death. I tried to push them away and asked, 'Who are you? Where is the voice?' His only answer was a sigh. Suddenly, a hot breath passed over my face and I perceived a white shape, beside the man's black shape, in the darkness. The black shape lifted me on to the white shape, a glad neighing greeted my astounded ears and I murmured, 'César!' The animal quivered. Raoul, I was lying half back on a saddle and I had recognized the white horse out of the *Profeta*, which I had so often fed with sugar and sweets. I remembered that, one evening, there was a rumor in the theater that the horse had disappeared and that it had been stolen by the Opera ghost. I believed in the voice, but had never believed in the ghost. Now, however, I began to wonder, with a shiver, whether I was the ghost's prisoner. I called upon the voice to help me, for I should never have imagined that the voice and the ghost were one. You have heard about the Opera ghost, have you not, Raoul?"

"Yes, but tell me what happened when you were on the white horse of the *Profeta*?"

"I made no movement and let myself go. The black shape held me up, and I made no effort to escape. A curious feeling of peacefulness came over me and I thought that I must be under the influence of some cordial. I had the full command of my senses; and my eyes became used to the darkness, which was lit, here and there, by fitful gleams. I calculated that we were in a narrow circular gallery, probably running all round the Opera, which is immense, underground. I had once been down into those cellars, but had stopped at the third floor, though there were two lower still, large enough to hold a town. But the figures of which I caught sight had made me run away. There are demons down there, quite black, standing in front of boilers, and they wield shovels and pitchforks and poke up fires and stir up flames and, if you come too near them, they frighten you by suddenly opening the red mouths of their furnaces. . . . Well, while César was quietly carrying me on his back, I saw those black demons in the distance, looking quite small, in front of the red fires of their furnaces: they came into sight, disappeared and came into sight again, as we went on our winding way. At last, they disappeared altogether. The shape was still holding me up and César walked on, unled and sure-footed. I could not tell you, even approximately, how long this ride lasted; I only know that we seemed to turn and turn and often went down a spiral stair into the very heart of the earth. Even then, it may be that my head was turning, but I don't think so: no, my mind was quite clear. At last, César raised his nostrils, sniffed the air and quickened his pace a little. I felt a moistness in the air and César stopped. The darkness had lifted. A sort of bluey light surrounded us. We were on the edge of a lake, whose leaden waters stretched into the distance, into the darkness; but the blue light lit up the bank and I saw a little boat fastened to an iron ring on the wharf!"

"A boat!"

"Yes, but I knew that all that existed and that there was nothing supernatural about that underground lake and boat. But think of the exceptional conditions in which I arrived upon that shore! I don't know whether the effects of the cordial had worn off when the man's shape lifted me into the boat, but my terror began all over again. My gruesome escort must have noticed it, for he sent César back and I heard his hoofs trampling up a staircase while the man jumped into the boat, untied the rope that held it and seized the oars. He rowed with a quick, powerful stroke; and his eyes, under the mask, never left me. We slipped across the noiseless water in the bluey light which I told you of; then we were in the dark again and we touched shore. And I was once more taken up in the man's arms. I cried aloud. And then, suddenly, I was silent, dazed by the light.... Yes, a dazzling light in the midst of which I had been put down. I sprang to my feet. I was in the middle of a drawing-room that seemed to me to be decorated, adorned and furnished with nothing but flowers, flowers both magnificent and stupid, because of the silk ribbons that tied them to baskets, like those which they sell in the shops on the boulevards. They were much too civilized flowers, like those which I used to find in my dressing-room after a first night. And, in the midst of all these flowers, stood the black shape of the man in the mask, with arms crossed, and he said, 'Don't be afraid, Christine; you are in no danger.' *It was the voice*!

"My anger equaled my amazement. I rushed at the mask and tried to snatch it away, so as to see the face of the voice. The man said, 'You are in no danger, so long as you do not touch the mask.' And, taking me gently by the wrists, he forced me into a chair and then went down on his knees before me and said nothing more! His humility gave me back some of my courage; and the light restored me to the realities of life. However extraordinary the adventure might be, I was now surrounded by mortal, visible, tangible things. The furniture, the hangings, the candles, the vases and the very flowers in their baskets, of which I could almost have told whence they came and what they cost, were bound to confine my imagination to the limits of a drawing-room quite as commonplace as any that, at least, had the excuse of not being in the cellars of the Opera. I had, no doubt, to do with a terrible, eccentric person, who, in some mysterious fashion, had succeeded in taking up his abode there, under the Opera house, five stories below the level of the ground. And the voice, the voice which I had recognized under the mask, was on its knees before me, *was a man*! And I began to cry. . . . The man, still kneeling, must have understood the cause of my tears, for he said, 'It is true, Christine! . . . I am not an Angel, nor a genius, nor a ghost . . . I am Erik!' "

Christine's narrative was again interrupted. An echo behind them seemed to repeat the word after her.

"Erik!"

What echo? . . . They both turned round and saw that night had fallen. Raoul made a movement as though to rise, but Christine kept him beside her.

"Don't go," she said. "I want you to know everything *here*!"

"But why here, Christine? I am afraid of your catching cold."

"We have nothing to fear except the trap-doors, dear, and here we are miles away from the trap-doors . . . and I am not allowed to see you outside the theater. This is not the time to annoy him. We must not arouse his suspicion."

"Christine! Christine! Something tells me that we are wrong to wait till tomorrow evening and that we ought to fly at once."

"I tell you that, if he does not hear me sing tomorrow, it will cause him infinite pain."

"It is difficult not to cause him pain and yet to escape from him for good."

"You are right in that, Raoul, for certainly he will die of my flight." And she added in a dull voice, "But then it counts both ways . . . for we risk his killing us."

"Does he love you so much?"

"He would commit murder for me."

"But one can find out where he lives. One can go in search of him. Now that we know that Erik is not a ghost, one can speak to him and force him to answer!"

Christine shook her head.

"No, no! There is nothing to be done with Erik . . . except to run away!"

"Then why, when you were able to run away, did you go back to him?"

"Because I had to. And you will understand that when I tell you how I left him."

"Oh, I hate him!" cried Raoul. "And you, Christine, tell me, do you hate him too?"

"No," said Christine simply.

"No, of course not. . . . Why, you love him! Your fear, your terror, all of that is just love and love of the most exquisite kind, the kind which people do not admit even to themselves," said Raoul bitterly. "The kind that gives you a thrill, when you think of it. . . . Picture it: a man who lives in a palace underground!" And he gave a leer.

"Then you want me to go back there?" said the young girl cruelly. "Take care, Raoul; I have told you: I should never return!"

There was an appalling silence between the three of them: the two who spoke and the shadow that listened, behind them.

"Before answering that," said Raoul, at last, speaking very slowly, "I should like to know with what feeling he inspires you, since you do not hate him."

"With horror!" she said. "That is the terrible thing about it. He fills me with horror and I do not hate him. How can I hate him, Raoul? Think of Erik at my feet, in the house on the lake, underground. He accuses himself, he curses himself, he implores my forgiveness! . . . He confesses his cheat. He loves me! He lays at my feet an immense and tragic love. . . . He has carried me off for love! . . . He has imprisoned me with him, underground, for love! . . . But he respects me: he crawls, he moans, he weeps! . . . And, when I stood up, Raoul, and told him that I could only despise him if he did not, then and there, give me my liberty . . . he offered it . . . he offered to show me the mysterious road . . . Only . . . only he rose too . . . and I was made to remember that, though he was not an angel, nor a ghost, nor a genius, he remained the voice . . . for he sang. And I listened . . . and stayed! . . . That night, we did not exchange another word. He sang me to sleep.

"When I woke up, I was alone, lying on a sofa in a simply furnished little bedroom, with an ordinary mahogany bedstead, lit by a lamp standing on the marble top of an old Louis-Philippe chest of drawers. I soon discovered that I was a prisoner and that the only outlet from my room led to a very comfortable bathroom. On returning to the bedroom, I saw on the chest of drawers a note, in red ink, which said, 'My dear Christine, you need have no concern as to your fate. You have no better nor more respectful friend in the world than myself. You are alone, at present, in this home which is yours. I am going out shopping to fetch you all the things that you can need.' I felt sure that I had fallen into the hands of a madman. I ran round my little apartment, looking for a way of escape which I could not find. I upbraided myself for my absurd superstition, which had caused me to fall into the trap. I felt inclined to laugh and to cry at the same time.

"This was the state of mind in which Erik found me. After giving three taps on the wall, he walked in quietly through a door which I had not noticed and which he left open. He had his arms full of boxes and parcels and arranged them on the bed, in a leisurely fashion, while I overwhelmed him with abuse and called upon him to take off his mask, if it covered the face of an honest man. He replied serenely, 'You shall never see Erik's face.' And he reproached me with not having finished dressing at that time of day: he was good enough to tell me that it was two o'clock in the afternoon. He said he would give me half an hour and, while he spoke, wound up my watch and set it for me. After which, he asked me to come to the dining-room, where a nice lunch was waiting for us.

"I was very angry, slammed the door in his face and went to the bath-room.... When I came out again, feeling greatly refreshed, Erik said that he loved me, but that he would never tell me so except when I allowed him and that the rest of the time would be devoted to music. 'What do you mean by the rest of the time?' I asked. 'Five days,' he said, with decision. I asked him if I should then be free and he said, 'You will be free, Christine, for, when those five days are past, you will have learned not to see me; and then, from time to time, you will come to see your poor Erik!' He pointed to a chair opposite him, at a small table, and I sat down, feeling greatly perturbed. However, I ate a few prawns and the wing of a chicken and drank half a glass of tokay, which he had himself, he told me, brought from the Königsberg cellars. Erik did not eat or drink. I asked him what his nationality was and if that name of Erik did not point to his Scandinavian origin. He said that he had no name and no country and that he had taken the name of Erik by accident.

"After lunch, he rose and gave me the tips of his fingers, saying he would like to show me over his flat; but I snatched away my hand and gave a cry. What I had touched was cold and, at the same time, bony; and I remembered that his hands smelt of death. 'Oh, forgive me!' he moaned. And he opened a door before me. 'This is my bedroom, if you care to see it. It is rather curious.' His manners, his words, his attitude gave me confidence and I went in without hesitation. I felt as if I were entering the room of a dead person. The walls were all hung with black, but, instead of the white trimmings that usually set off that funereal upholstery, there was an enormous stave of music with the notes of the *Dies Iræa*, many times repeated. In the middle of the room was a canopy, from which hung curtains of red brocaded stuff, and, under the canopy, an open coffin. 'That is where I sleep,' said Erik. 'One has to get used to everything in life, even to eternity.' The sight upset me so much that I turned away my head.

"Then I saw the keyboard of an organ which filled one whole side of the walls. On the desk was a music-book covered with red notes. I asked leave to look at it and read, *Don Juan Triumphant*. 'Yes,' he said, 'I compose sometimes. I began that work twenty years ago. When I have finished, I shall take it away with me in that coffin and never wake up again.' 'You must work at it as seldom as you can,' I said. He replied, 'I sometimes work at it for fourteen days and nights together, during which I live on music only, and then I rest for years at a time.' 'Will you play me something out of your *Don Juan Triumphant*?' I asked, thinking to please him. 'You must never ask me that,' he said, in a gloomy voice. 'I will play you Mozart, if you like, which will only make you weep; but my *Don Juan*, Christine, burns; and yet he is not struck by fire from Heaven.' Thereupon we returned to the drawing-room. I noticed that there was no mirror in the whole apartment. I was going to remark upon this, but Erik had already sat down to the piano. He said, 'You see, Christine, there is some music that is so terrible that it consumes all those who approach it. Fortunately, you have not come to that music yet, for you would lose all your pretty coloring and nobody would know you when you returned to Paris. Let us sing something from the Opera, Christine Daaé.' He spoke these last words as though he were flinging an insult at me."

"What did you do?"

"I had no time to think about the meaning he put into his words. We at once began the duet in *Othello* and already the catastrophe was upon us. I sang *Desdemona* with a despair, a terror which I had never displayed before. As for him, his voice thundered forth his revengeful soul at every note. Love, jealousy, hatred, burst out around us in harrowing cries. Erik's black mask made me think of the natural mask of the Moor of Venice. He was Othello himself. Suddenly, I felt a need to see beneath the mask. I wanted to know the face of the voice, and, with a movement which I was utterly unable to control, swiftly my fingers tore away the mask. Oh, horror, horror, horror!"

Christine stopped, at the thought of the vision that had scared her, while the echoes of the night, which had repeated the name of Erik, now thrice moaned the cry:

"Horror! . . . Horror! . . . Horror!"

Raoul and Christine, clasping each other closely, raised their eyes to the stars that shone in a clear and peaceful sky. Raoul said:

"Strange, Christine, that this calm, soft night should be so full of plaintive sounds. One would think that it was sorrowing with us."

"When you know the secret, Raoul, your ears, like mine, will be full of lamentations."

She took Raoul's protecting hands in hers and, with a long shiver, continued:

"Yes, if I lived to be a hundred, I should always hear the superhuman cry of grief and rage which he uttered when the terrible sight appeared before my eyes.... Raoul, you have seen death's heads, when they have been dried and withered by the centuries, and, perhaps, if you were not the victim of a nightmare, you saw his death's head at Perros. And then you saw Red Death stalking about at the last masked ball. But all those death's heads were motionless and their dumb horror was not alive. But imagine, if you can, Red Death's mask suddenly coming to life in order to express, with the four black holes of its eyes, its nose, and its mouth, the extreme anger, the mighty fury of a demon; *and not a ray of light from the sockets*, for, as I learned later, you can not see his blazing eyes except in the dark.

"I fell back against the wall and he came up to me, grinding his teeth, and, as I fell upon my knees, he hissed mad, incoherent words and curses at me. Leaning over me, he cried, 'Look! You want to see! See! Feast your eyes, glut your soul on my cursed ugliness! Look at Erik's face! Now you know the face of the voice! You were not content to hear me, eh? You wanted to know what I looked like! Oh, you women are so inquisitive! Well, are you satisfied? I'm a very good-looking fellow, eh?... When a woman has seen me, as you have, she belongs to me. She loves me for ever. I am a kind of Don Juan, you know!' And, drawing himself up to his full height, with his hand on his hip, wagging the hideous thing that was his head on his shoulders, he roared, 'Look at me! *I am Don Juan triumphant*!' And, when I turned away my head and begged for mercy, he drew it to him, brutally, twisting his dead fingers into my hair."

"Enough! Enough!" cried Raoul. "I will kill him. In Heaven's name, Christine, tell me where the dining-room on the lake is! I must kill him!"

"Oh, be quiet, Raoul, if you want to know!"

"Yes, I want to know how and why you went back; I must know! ... But, in any case, I will kill him!"

"Oh, Raoul, listen, listen! ... He dragged me by my hair and then ... and then ... Oh, it is too horrible!"

"Well, what? Out with it!" exclaimed Raoul fiercely. "Out with it, quick!"

"Then he hissed at me. 'Ah, I frighten you, do I?... I dare say! ... Perhaps you think that I have another mask, eh, and that this ... this ... my head is a mask? Well,' he roared, 'tear it off as you did the other! Come! Come along! I insist! Your hands! Your hands! Give me your hands!' And he seized my hands and dug them into his awful face. He tore his flesh with my nails, tore his terrible dead flesh with my nails! ... 'Know,' he shouted, while his throat throbbed and panted like a furnace, 'know that I am built up of death from head to foot and that it is a corpse that loves you and adores you and will never, never leave you! . . . Look, I am not laughing now, I am crying, crying for you, Christine, who have torn off my mask and who therefore can never leave me again! . . . As long as you thought me handsome, you could have come back, I know you would have come back . . . but, now that you know my hideousness, you would run away for good. . . . So I shall keep you here! . . . Why did you want to see me? Oh, mad Christine, who wanted to see me! . . . When my own father never saw me and when my mother, so as not to see me, made me a present of my first mask!'

"He had let go of me at last and was dragging himself about on the floor, uttering terrible sobs. And then he crawled away like a snake, went into his room, closed the door and left me alone to my reflections. Presently I heard the sound of the organ; and then I began to understand Erik's contemptuous phrase when he spoke about Opera music. What I now heard was utterly different from what I had heard up to then. His *Don Juan Triumphant* (for I had not a doubt but that he had rushed to his masterpiece to forget the horror of the moment) seemed to me at first one long, awful, magnificent sob. But, little by little, it expressed every emotion, every suffering of which mankind is capable. It intoxicated me; and I opened the door that separated us. Erik rose, as I entered, *but dared not turn in my direction*. 'Erik,' I cried, 'show me your face without fear! I swear that you are the most unhappy and sublime of men; and, if ever again I shiver when I look at you, it will be because I am thinking of the splendor of your genius!' Then Erik turned round, for he believed me, and I also had faith in myself. He fell at my feet, with words of love . . . with words of love in his dead mouth and the music had ceased . . . He kissed the hem of my dress and did not see that I closed my eyes.

"What more can I tell you, dear? You now know the tragedy. It went on for a fortnight—a fortnight during which I lied to him. My lies were as hideous as the monster who inspired them; but they were the price of my liberty. I burned his mask; and I managed so well that, even when he was not singing, he tried to catch my eye, like a dog sitting by its master. He was my faithful slave and paid me endless little attentions. Gradually, I gave him such confidence that he ventured to take me walking on the banks of the lake and to row me in the boat on its leaden waters; toward the end of my captivity he let me out through the gates that closed the underground passages in the Rue Scribe. Here a carriage awaited us and took us to the Bois. The night when we met you was nearly fatal to me, for he is terribly jealous of you and I had to tell him that you were soon going away. . . . Then, at last, after a fortnight of that horrible captivity, during which I was filled with pity, enthusiasm, despair and horror by turns, he believed me when I said, '*I will come back*!'"

"And you went back, Christine," groaned Raoul.

"Yes, dear, and I must tell you that it was not his frightful threats when setting me free that helped me to keep my word, but the harrowing sob which he gave on the threshold of the tomb. . . . That sob attached me to the unfortunate man more than I myself suspected when saying good-by to him. Poor Erik! Poor Erik!"

"Christine," said Raoul, rising, "you tell me that you love me; but you had recovered your liberty hardly a few hours before you returned to Erik! Remember the masked ball!"

"Yes; and do you remember those hours which I passed with you, Raoul. . . to the great danger of both of us?"

"I doubted your love for me, during those hours."

"Do you doubt it still, Raoul? . . . Then know that each of my visits to Erik increased my horror of him; for each of those visits, instead of calming him, as I hoped, made him mad with love! . . . And I am so frightened, so frightened! . . ."

"You are frightened . . . but do you love me? If Erik were good-looking, would you love me, Christine?"

She rose in her turn, put her two trembling arms round the young man's neck and said:

"Oh, my betrothed of a day, if I did not love you, I would not give you my lips! Take them, for the first time and the last."

He kissed her lips; but the night that surrounded them was rent asunder, they fled as at the approach of a storm and their eyes, filled with dread of Erik, showed them, before they disappeared, high up above them, an immense night-bird that stared at them with its blazing eyes and seemed to cling to the string of Apollo's lyre.

XIII

A MASTER-STROKE OF THE TRAP-DOOR LOVER

RAOUL AND CHRISTINE RAN, EAGER TO ESCAPE FROM THE ROOF AND the blazing eyes that showed only in the dark; and they did not stop before they came to the eighth floor on the way down.

There was no performance at the Opera that night and the passages were empty. Suddenly, a queer-looking form stood before them and blocked the road:

"No, not this way!"

And the form pointed to another passage by which they were to reach the wings. Raoul wanted to stop and ask for an explanation. But the form, which wore a sort of long frock-coat and a pointed cap, said:

"Quick! Go away quickly!"

Christine was already dragging Raoul, compelling him to start running again.

"But who is he? Who is that man?" he asked.

Christine replied: "It's the Persian."

"What's he doing here?"

"Nobody knows. He is always in the Opera."

"You are making me run away, for the first time in my life. If we really saw Erik, what I ought to have done was to nail him to Apollo's lyre, just as we nail the owls to the walls of our Breton farms; and there would have been no more question of him."

"My dear Raoul, you would first have had to climb up to Apollo's lyre: that is no easy matter."

"The blazing eyes were there!"

"Oh, you are getting like me now, seeing him everywhere! What I took for blazing eyes was probably a couple of stars shining through the strings of the lyre."

And Christine went down another floor, with Raoul following her.

"As you have quite made up your mind to go, Christine, I assure you it would be better to go at once. Why wait for to-morrow? He may have heard us to-night."

"No, no, he is working, I tell you, at his *Don Juan Triumphant* and not thinking of us."

"You're so sure of that you keep on looking behind you!"

"Come to my dressing-room."

"Hadn't we better meet outside the Opera?"

"Never, till we go away for good! It would bring us bad luck, if I did not keep my word. I promised him to see you only here."

"It's a good thing for me that he allowed you even that. Do you know," said Raoul bitterly, "that it was very plucky of you to let us play at being engaged?"

"Why, my dear, he knows all about it! He said, 'I trust you, Christine. M. de Chagny is in love with you and is going abroad. Before he goes, I want him to be as happy as I am.' Are people so unhappy when they love?"

"Yes, Christine, when they love and are not sure of being loved."

They came to Christine's dressing-room.

"Why do you think that you are safer in this room than on the stage?" asked Raoul. "You heard him through the walls here, therefore he can certainly hear us."

"No. He gave me his word not to be behind the walls of my dressing-room again and I believe Erik's word. This room and my bedroom on the lake are for me, exclusively, and not to be approached by him."

"How can you have gone from this room into that dark passage, Christine? Suppose we try to repeat your movements; shall we?"

"It is dangerous, dear, for the glass might carry me off again; and, instead of running away, I should be obliged to go to the end of the secret passage to the lake and there call Erik."

"Would he hear you?"

"Erik will hear me wherever I call him. He told me so. He is a very curious genius. You must not think, Raoul, that he is simply a man who amuses himself by living underground. He does things that no other man could do; he knows things which nobody in the world knows."

"Take care, Christine, you are making a ghost of him again!"

"No, he is not a ghost; he is a man of Heaven and earth, that is all."

"A man of Heaven and earth . . . that is all! A nice way to speak of him! . . . And are you still resolved to run away from him?"

"Yes, to-morrow."

"To-morrow, you will have no resolve left!"

"Then, Raoul, you must run away with me in spite of myself; is that understood?"

"I shall be here at twelve to-morrow night; I shall keep my promise, whatever happens. You say that, after listening to the performance, he is to wait for you in the dining-room on the lake?"

"Yes."

"And how are you to reach him, if you don't know how to go out by the glass?"

"Why, by going straight to the edge of the lake."

Christine opened a box, took out an enormous key and showed it to Raoul.

"What's that?" he asked.

"The key of the gate to the underground passage in the Rue Scribe."

"I understand, Christine. It leads straight to the lake. Give it to me, Christine, will you?"

"Never!" she said. "That would be treacherous!"

Suddenly Christine changed color. A mortal pallor overspread her features.

"Oh heavens!" she cried. "Erik! Erik! Have pity on me!"

"Hold your tongue!" said Raoul. "You told me he could hear you!"

But the singer's attitude became more and more inexplicable. She wrung her fingers, repeating, with a distraught air:

"Oh, Heaven! Oh, Heaven!"

"But what is it? What is it?" Raoul implored.

"The ring . . . the gold ring he gave me."

"Oh, so Erik gave you that ring!"

"You know he did, Raoul! But what you don't know is that, when he gave it to me, he said, 'I give you back your liberty, Christine, on condition that this ring is always on your finger. As long as you keep it, you will be protected against all danger and Erik will remain your friend. But woe to you if you ever part with it, for Erik will have his revenge!' . . . My dear, my dear, the ring is gone! Woe to us both!"

They both looked for the ring, but could not find it. Christine refused to be pacified.

"It was while I gave you that kiss, up above, under Apollo's lyre," she said. "The ring must have slipped from my finger and dropped into the street! We can never find it. And what misfortunes are in store for us now! Oh, to run away!"

"Let us run away at once," Raoul insisted, once more.

She hesitated. He thought that she was going to say yes. . . . Then her bright pupils became dimmed and she said:

"No! To-morrow!"

And she left him hurriedly, still wringing and rubbing her fingers, as though she hoped to bring the ring back like that.

Raoul went home, greatly perturbed at all that he had heard.

"If I don't save her from the hands of that humbug," he said, aloud, as he went to bed, "she is lost. But I shall save her."

He put out his lamp and felt a need to insult Erik in the dark. Thrice over, he shouted:

"Humbug! . . . Humbug! . . . Humbug!"

But, suddenly, he raised himself on his elbow. A cold sweat poured from his temples. Two eyes, like blazing coals, had appeared at the foot of his bed. They stared at him fixedly, terribly, in the darkness of the night.

Raoul was no coward; and yet he trembled. He put out a groping, hesitating hand toward the table by his bedside. He found the matches and lit his candle. The eyes disappeared.

Still uneasy in his mind, he thought to himself:

"She told me that *his* eyes only showed in the dark. His eyes have disappeared in the light, but *he* may be there still."

And he rose, hunted about, went round the room. He looked under his bed, like a child. Then he thought himself absurd, got into bed again and blew out the candle. The eyes reappeared.

He sat up and stared back at them with all the courage he possessed. Then he cried:

"Is that you, Erik? Man, genius, or ghost, is it you?"

He reflected: "If it's he, he's on the balcony!"

Then he ran to the chest of drawers and groped for his revolver. He opened the balcony window, looked out, saw nothing and closed the window again. He went back to bed, shivering, for the night was cold, and put the revolver on the table within his reach.

The eyes were still there, at the foot of the bed. Were they between the bed and the window-pane or behind the pane, that is to say, on the balcony? That was what Raoul wanted to know. He also wanted to know if those eyes belonged to a human being.... He wanted to know everything.

Then, patiently, calmly, he seized his revolver and took aim. He aimed a little above the two eyes. Surely, if they were eyes and if above those two eyes there was a forehead and if Raoul was not too clumsy...

The shot made a terrible din amid the silence of the slumbering house. And, while footsteps came hurrying along the passages, Raoul sat up with outstretched arm, ready to fire again, if need be.

This time, the two eyes had disappeared.

Servants appeared, carrying lights; Count Philippe, terribly anxious:

"What is it?"

"I think I have been dreaming," replied the young man. "I fired at two stars that kept me from sleeping."

"You're raving! Are you ill? For God's sake, tell me, Raoul: what happened?"

And the count seized hold of the revolver.

"No, no, I'm not raving... Besides, we shall soon see..."

He got out of bed, put on a dressing-gown and slippers, took a light from the hands of a servant and, opening the window, stepped out on the balcony.

The count saw that the window had been pierced by a bullet at a man's height. Raoul was leaning over the balcony with his candle:

"Aha!" he said. "Blood!... Blood!... Here, there, more blood!... That's a good thing! A ghost who bleeds is less dangerous!" he grinned.

"Raoul! Raoul! Raoul!"

The count was shaking him as though he were trying to waken a sleep-walker.

"But, my dear brother, I'm not asleep!" Raoul protested impatiently. "You can see the blood for yourself. I thought I had been dreaming and firing at two stars. It was Erik's eyes . . . and here is his blood! . . . After all, perhaps I was wrong to shoot; and Christine is quite capable of never forgiving me. . . . All this would not have happened if I had drawn the curtains before going to bed."

"Raoul, have you suddenly gone mad? Wake up!"

"What, still? You would do better to help me find Erik . . . for, after all, a ghost who bleeds can always be found."

The count's valet said:

"That is so, sir; there is blood on the balcony."

The other man-servant brought a lamp, by the light of which they examined the balcony carefully. The marks of blood followed the rail till they reached a gutter-spout; then they went up the gutter-spout.

"My dear fellow," said Count Philippe, "you have fired at a cat."

"The misfortune is," said Raoul, with a grin, "that it's quite possible. With Erik, you never know. Is it Erik? Is it the cat? Is it the ghost? No, with Erik, you can't tell!"

Raoul went on making this strange sort of remarks which corresponded so intimately and logically with the preoccupation of his brain and which, at the same time, tended to persuade many people that his mind was unhinged. The count himself was seized with this idea; and, later, the examining magistrate, on receiving the report of the commissary of police, came to the same conclusion.

"Who is Erik?" asked the count, pressing his brother's hand.

"He is my rival. And, if he's not dead, it's a pity."

He dismissed the servants with a wave of the hand and the two Chagnys were left alone. But the men were not out of earshot before the count's valet heard Raoul say, distinctly and emphatically:

"I shall carry off Christine Daaé to-night."

This phrase was afterward repeated to M. Faure, the examining-magistrate. But no one ever knew exactly what passed between the two brothers at this interview. The servants declared that this was not their first quarrel. Their voices penetrated the wall; and it was always an actress called Christine Daaé that was in question.

At breakfast—the early morning breakfast, which the count took in his study—Philippe sent for his brother, Raoul arrived silent and gloomy. The scene was a very short one. Philippe handed his brother a copy of the *Epoque* and said:

"Read that!"

The viscount read:

> The latest news in the Faubourg is that there is a promise of marriage between Mlle. Christine Daaé, the opera-singer, and M. le Vicomte Raoul de Chagny. If the gossips are to be credited, Count Philippe has sworn that, for the first time on record, the Chagnys shall not keep their promise. But, as love is all-powerful, at the Opera as—and even more than—elsewhere, we wonder how Count Philippe intends to prevent the viscount, his brother, from leading the new Margarita to the altar. The two brothers are said to adore each other; but the count is curiously mistaken if he imagines that brotherly love will triumph over love pure and simple.

"You see, Raoul," said the count, "you are making us ridiculous! That little girl has turned your head with her ghost-stories."

The viscount had evidently repeated Christine's narrative to his brother, during the night. All that he now said was:

"Good-by, Philippe."

"Have you quite made up your mind? You are going to-night? With her?"

No reply.

"Surely you will not do anything so foolish? I *shall* know how to prevent you!"

"Good-by, Philippe," said the viscount again and left the room.

This scene was described to the examining-magistrate by the count himself, who did not see Raoul again until that evening, at the Opera, a few minutes before Christine's disappearance.

Raoul, in fact, devoted the whole day to his preparations for the flight. The horses, the carriage, the coachman, the provisions, the luggage, the money required for the journey, the road to be taken (he had resolved not to go by train, so as to throw the ghost off the scent): all this had to be settled and provided for; and it occupied him until nine o'clock at night.

At nine o'clock, a sort of traveling-barouche with the curtains of its windows close-down, took its place in the rank on the Rotunda side. It was drawn by two powerful horses driven by a coachman whose face was almost concealed in the long folds of a muffler. In front of this traveling-carriage were three broughams, belonging respectively to Carlotta, who had suddenly returned to Paris, to Sorelli and, at the head of the rank, to Comte Philippe de Chagny. No one left the barouche. The coachman remained on his box, and the three other coachmen remained on theirs.

A shadow in a long black cloak and a soft black felt hat passed along the pavement between the Rotunda and the carriages, examined the barouche carefully, went up to the horses and the coachman and then moved away without saying a word. The magistrate afterward believed that this shadow was that of the Vicomte Raoul de Chagny; but I do not agree, seeing that that evening, as every evening, the Vicomte de Chagny was wearing a tall hat, which hat, besides, was subsequently found. I am more inclined to think that the shadow was that of the ghost, who knew all about the whole affair, as the reader will soon perceive.

They were giving *Faust*, as it happened, before a splendid house. The Faubourg was magnificently represented; and the paragraph in that morning's *Epoque* had already produced its effect, for all eyes were turned to the box in which Count Philippe sat alone, apparently in a very indifferent and careless frame of mind. The feminine element in the brilliant audience seemed curiously puzzled; and the viscount's absence gave rise to any amount of whispering behind the fans. Christine Daaé met with a rather cold reception. That special audience could not forgive her for aiming so high.

The singer noticed this unfavorable attitude of a portion of the house and was confused by it.

The regular frequenters of the Opera, who pretended to know the truth about the viscount's love-story, exchanged significant smiles at certain passages in Margarita's part; and they made a show of turning and looking at Philippe de Chagny's box when Christine sang:

> "I wish I could but know who was he
> That addressed me,
> If he was noble, or, at least, what his name is."

The count sat with his chin on his hand and seemed to pay no attention to these manifestations. He kept his eyes fixed on the stage; but his thoughts appeared to be far away.

Christine lost her self-assurance more and more. She trembled. She felt on the verge of a breakdown. . . . Carolus Fonta wondered if she was ill, if she could keep the stage until the end of the Garden Act. In the front of the house, people remembered the catastrophe that had befallen Carlotta at the end of that act and the historic "co-ack" which had momentarily interrupted her career in Paris.

Just then, Carlotta made her entrance in a box facing the stage, a sensational entrance. Poor Christine raised her eyes upon this fresh subject of excitement. She recognized her rival. She thought she saw a sneer on her lips. That saved her. She forgot everything, in order to triumph once more.

From that moment the prima donna sang with all her heart and soul. She tried to surpass all that she had done till then; and she succeeded. In the last act when she began the invocation to the angels, she made all the members of the audience feel as though they too had wings.

In the center of the amphitheater a man stood up and remained standing, facing the singer. It was Raoul.

"Holy angel. In Heaven blessed . . ."

And Christine, her arms outstretched, her throat filled with music, the glory of her hair falling over her bare shoulders, uttered the divine cry:

"My spirit longs with thee to rest!"

It was at that moment that the stage was suddenly plunged in darkness. It happened so quickly that the spectators hardly had time to utter a sound of stupefaction, for the gas at once lit up the stage again. But Christine Daaé was no longer there!

What had become of her? What was that miracle? All exchanged glances without understanding, and the excitement at once reached its height. Nor was the tension any less great on the stage itself. Men rushed from the wings to the spot where Christine had been singing that very instant. The performance was interrupted amid the greatest disorder.

Where had Christine gone? What witchcraft had snatched her away before the eyes of thousands of enthusiastic onlookers and from the arms of Carolus Fonta himself? It was as though the angels had really carried her up "to rest."

Raoul, still standing up in the amphitheater, had uttered a cry. Count Philippe had sprung to his feet in his box. People looked at the stage, at the count, at Raoul, and wondered if this curious event was connected in any way with the paragraph in that morning's paper. But Raoul hurriedly left his seat, the count disappeared, from his box and, while the curtain was lowered, the subscribers rushed to the door that led behind the scenes. The rest of the audience waited amid an indescribable hubbub. Every one spoke at once. Every one tried to suggest an explanation of the extraordinary incident.

At last, the curtain rose slowly and Carolus Fonta stepped to the conductor's desk and, in a sad and serious voice, said:

"Ladies and gentlemen, an unprecedented event has taken place and thrown us into a state of the greatest alarm. Our sister-artist, Christine Daaé, has disappeared before our eyes and nobody can tell us how!"

XIV

THE SINGULAR ATTITUDE OF A SAFETY-PIN

BEHIND THE CURTAIN, THERE WAS AN INDESCRIBABLE CROWD. ARTISTS, scene-shifters, dancers, supers, choristers, subscribers were all asking questions, shouting and hustling one another.

"What became of her?"

"She's run away."

"With the Vicomte de Chagny, of course!"

"No, with the count!"

"Ah, here's Carlotta! Carlotta did the trick!"

"No, it was the ghost!"

And a few laughed, especially as a careful examination of the trap-doors and boards had put the idea of an accident out of the question.

Amid this noisy throng, three men stood talking in a low voice and with despairing gestures. They were Gabriel, the chorus-master; Mercier, the acting-manager; and Rémy, the secretary. They retired to a corner of the lobby by which the stage communicates with the wide passage leading to the foyer of the ballet. Here they stood and argued behind some enormous "properties."

"I knocked at the door," said Rémy. "They did not answer. Perhaps they are not in the office. In any case, it's impossible to find out, for they took the keys with them."

"They" were obviously the managers, who had given orders, during the last entr'acte, that they were not to be disturbed on any pretext whatever. They were not in to anybody.

"All the same," exclaimed Gabriel, "a singer isn't run away with, from the middle of the stage, every day!"

"Did you shout that to them?" asked Mercier, impatiently.

"I'll go back again," said Rémy, and disappeared at a run.

Thereupon the stage-manager arrived.

"Well, M. Mercier, are you coming? What are you two doing here? You're wanted, Mr. Acting-Manager."

"I refuse to know or to do anything before the commissary arrives," declared Mercier. "I have sent for Mifroid. We shall see when he comes!"

"And I tell you that you ought to go down to the organ at once."

"Not before the commissary comes."

"I've been down to the organ myself already."

"Ah! And what did you see?"

"Well, I saw nobody! Do you hear—nobody!"

"What do you want me to do down there for?"

"You're right!" said the stage-manager, frantically pushing his hands through his rebellious hair. "You're right! But there might be some one at the organ who could tell us how the stage came to be suddenly darkened. Now Mauclair is nowhere to be found. Do you understand that?"

Mauclair was the gas-man, who dispensed day and night at will on the stage of the Opera.

"Mauclair is not to be found!" repeated Mercier, taken aback. "Well, what about his assistants?"

"There's no Mauclair and no assistants! No one at the lights, I tell you! You can imagine," roared the stage-manager, "that that little girl must have been carried off by somebody else: she didn't run away by herself! It was a calculated stroke and we have to find out about it. . . . And what are the managers doing all this time? . . . I gave orders that no one was to go down to the lights and I posted a fireman in front of the gas-man's box beside the organ. Wasn't that right?"

"Yes, yes, quite right, quite right. And now let's wait for the commissary."

The stage-manager walked away, shrugging his .shoulders, fuming, muttering insults at those milksops who remained quietly squatting in a corner while the whole theater was topsy-turvy.

Gabriel and Mercier were not so quiet as all that. Only they had received an order that paralyzed them. The managers were not to be disturbed on any account. Rémy had violated that order and met with no success.

At that moment he returned from his new expedition, wearing a curiously startled air.

"Well, have you seen them?" asked Mercier.

"Moncharmin opened the door at last. His eyes were starting out of his head. I thought he meant to strike me. I could not get a word in; and what do you think he shouted at me? 'Have you a safety-pin?' 'No!' 'Well, then, clear out!' I tried to tell him that an unheard-of thing had happened on the stage, but he roared,

'A safety-pin! Give me a safety-pin at once!' A boy heard him—he was bellowing like a bull—ran up with a safety-pin and gave it to him; whereupon Moncharmin slammed the door in my face, and there you are!"

"And couldn't you have said, 'Christine Daaé.'"

"I should like to have seen you in my place. He was foaming at the mouth. He thought of nothing but his safety-pin. I believe, if they hadn't brought him one on the spot, he would have fallen down in a fit! . . . Oh, all this isn't natural; and our managers are going mad! . . . Besides, it can't go on like this! I'm not used to being treated in that fashion!"

Suddenly Gabriel whispered:

"It's another trick of O. G.'s."

Rémy gave a grin, Mercier a sigh and seemed about to speak . . . but, meeting Gabriel's eye, said nothing.

However, Mercier felt his responsibility increased as the minutes passed without the managers' appearing; and, at last, he could stand it no longer.

"Look here, I'll go and hunt them out myself!"

Gabriel, turning very gloomy and serious, stopped him.

"Be careful what you're doing, Mercier! If they're staying in their office, it's probably because they have to! O. G. has more than one trick in his bag!"

But Mercier shook his head.

"That's their lookout! I'm going! If people had listened to me, the police would have known everything long ago!"

And he went.

"What's everything?" asked Rémy. "What was there to tell the police? Why don't you answer, Gabriel? . . . Ah, so you know something! Well, you would do better to tell me, too, if you don't want me to shout out that you are all going mad! . . . Yes, that's what you are: mad!"

Gabriel put on a stupid look and pretended not to understand the private secretary's unseemly outburst.

"What 'something' am I supposed to know?" he said. "I don't know what you mean."

Rémy began to lose his temper.

"This evening, Richard and Moncharmin were behaving like lunatics, here, between the acts."

"I never noticed it," growled Gabriel, very much annoyed.

"Then you're the only one! . . . Do you think that I didn't see them? . . . And that M. Parabise, the manager of the Crédit Central, noticed nothing? . . .

And that M. de La Borderie, the ambassador, has no eyes to see with? Why, all the subscribers were pointing at our managers!"

"But what were our managers doing?" asked Gabriel, putting on his most innocent air.

"What were they doing? You know better than any one what they were doing! . . . You were there! . . . And you were watching them, you and Mercier! . . . And you were the only two who didn't laugh. . . ."

"I don't understand!"

Gabriel raised his arms and dropped them to his sides again, which gesture was meant to convey that the question did not interest him in the least. Rémy continued:

"What is the sense of this new mania of theirs? *Why won't they have any one come near them now?*"

"What? *Won't they have any one come near them?*"

"*And they won't let any one touch them!*"

"Really? Have you noticed *that they won't let any one touch them?* That is certainly odd!"

"Oh, so you admit it! And high time, too! And *then, they walk backward!*"

"*Backward!* You have seen our managers *walk backward?* Why, I thought that only crabs walked backward!"

"Don't laugh, Gabriel; don't laugh!"

"I'm not laughing," protested Gabriel, looking as solemn as a judge.

"Perhaps you can tell me this, Gabriel, as you're an intimate friend of the management: When I went up to M. Richard, outside the foyer, during the Garden interval, with my hand out before me, why did M. Moncharmin hurriedly whisper to me, 'Go away! Go away! Whatever you do, don't touch *M. le directeur!*' Am I supposed to have an infectious disease?"

"It's incredible!"

"And, a little later, when M. de La Borderie went up to M. Richard, didn't you see M. Moncharmin fling himself between them and hear him exclaim, '*M. l'ambassadeur*, I entreat you not to touch *M. le directeur*'?"

"It's terrible! . . . And what was Richard doing meanwhile?"

"What was he doing? Why, you saw him! He turned about, *bowed in front of him, though there was nobody in front of him*, and withdrew *backward*."

"*Backward?*"

"And Moncharmin, behind Richard, also turned about; that is, he described a semicircle behind Richard and also *walked backward!* . . . And they went like that to the staircase leading to the managers' office: *backward, backward, backward*! . . . Well, if they are not mad, will you explain what it means?"

"Perhaps they were practising a figure in the ballet," suggested Gabriel, without much conviction in his voice.

The secretary was furious at this wretched joke, made at so dramatic a moment. He knit his brows and contracted his lips. Then he put his mouth to Gabriel's ear:

"Don't be so sly, Gabriel. There are things going on for which you and Mercier are partly responsible."

"What do you mean?" asked Gabriel.

"Christine Daaé is not the only one who suddenly disappeared to-night."

"Oh, nonsense!"

"There's no nonsense about it. Perhaps you can tell me why, when Mother Giry came down to the foyer just now, Mercier took her by the hand and hurried her away with him?"

"Really?" said Gabriel, "I never saw it."

"You did see it, Gabriel, for you went with Mercier and Mother Giry to Mercier's office. Since then, you and Mercier have been seen, but no one has seen Mother Giry."

"Do you think we've eaten her?"

"No, but you've locked her up in the office; and any one passing the office can hear her yelling, 'Oh, the scoundrels! Oh, the scoundrels!'"

At this point of this singular conversation, Mercier arrived, all out of breath.

"There!" he said, in a gloomy voice. "It's worse than ever! . . . I shouted, 'It's a serious matter! Open the door! It's I, Mercier.' I heard footsteps. The door opened and Moncharmin appeared. He was very pale. He said, 'What do you want?' I answered, 'Some one has run away with Christine Daaé.' What do you think he said? 'And a good job, too!' And he shut the door, after putting this in my hand."

Mercier opened his hand; Rémy and Gabriel looked.

"The safety-pin!" cried Rémy.

"Strange! Strange!" muttered Gabriel, who could not help shivering.

Suddenly a voice made them all three turn round.

"I beg your pardon, gentlemen. Could you tell me where Christine Daaé is?"

In spite of the seriousness of the circumstances, the absurdity of the question would have made them roar with laughter, if they had not caught sight of a face so sorrow-stricken that they were at once seized with pity. It was the Vicomte Raoul de Chagny.

XV

CHRISTINE! CHRISTINE!

Raoul's first thought, after Christine Daaé's fantastic disappearance, was to accuse Erik. He no longer doubted the almost supernatural powers of the Angel of Music, in this domain of the Opera in which he had set up his empire. And Raoul rushed on the stage, in a mad fit of love and despair.

"Christine! Christine!" he moaned, calling to her as he felt that she must be calling to him from the depths of that dark pit to which the monster had carried her. "Christine! Christine!"

And he seemed to hear the girl's screams through the frail boards that separated him from her. He bent forward, he listened, . . . he wandered over the stage like a madman. Ah, to descend, to descend into that pit of darkness every entrance to which was closed to him, . . . for the stairs that led below the stage were forbidden to one and all that night!

"Christine! Christine! . . ."

People pushed him aside, laughing. They made fun of him. They thought the poor lover's brain was gone!

By what mad road, through what passages of mystery and darkness known to him alone had Erik dragged that pure-souled child to the awful haunt, with the Louis-Philippe room, opening out on the lake?

"Christine! Christine! . . . Why don't you answer? . . . Are you alive? . . ."

Hideous thoughts flashed through Raoul's congested brain. Of course, Erik must have discovered their secret, must have known that Christine had played him false. What a vengeance would be his!

And Raoul thought again of the yellow stars that had come, the night before, and roamed over his balcony. Why had he not put them out for good? There were some men's eyes that dilated in the darkness and shone like stars or like cats' eyes. Certainly Albinos, who seemed to have rabbits' eyes by day, had cats' eyes at night: everybody knew that! . . . Yes, yes, he had undoubtedly fired at Erik. Why had he not killed him? The monster had fled up the gutter-spout like a cat or a convict who—everybody knew that also—would scale the very skies, with the help of a gutter-spout. . . . No doubt Erik was at that time contemplating some decisive step against Raoul, but he had been wounded and had escaped to turn against poor Christine instead.

Such were the cruel thoughts that haunted Raoul as he ran to the singer's dressing-room.

"Christine! Christine!"

Bitter tears scorched the boy's eyelids as he saw scattered over the furniture the clothes which his beautiful bride was to have worn at the hour of their flight. Oh, why had she refused to leave earlier?

Why had she toyed with the threatening catastrophe? Why toyed with the monster's heart? Why, in a final access of pity, had she insisted on flinging, as a last sop to that demon's soul, her divine song:

"Holy angel, in Heaven blessed,
My spirit longs with thee to rest!"

Raoul, his throat filled with sobs, oaths and insults, fumbled awkwardly at the great mirror that had opened one night, before his eyes, to let Christine pass to the murky dwelling below. He pushed, pressed, groped about, but the glass apparently obeyed no one but Erik. . . . Perhaps actions were not enough with a glass of the kind? Perhaps he was expected to utter certain words? When he was a little boy, he had heard that there were things that obeyed the spoken word!

Suddenly, Raoul remembered something about a gate opening into the Rue Scribe, an underground passage running straight to the Rue Scribe from the lake . . . . Yes, Christine had told him about that . . . . And, when he found that the key was no longer in the box, he nevertheless ran to the Rue Scribe.

Outside, in the street, he passed his trembling hands over the huge stones, felt for outlets . . . met with iron bars . . . were those they? . . . Or these? . . . Or could it be that air-hole? . . . He plunged his useless eyes through the bars. . . . How dark it was in there! . . . He listened. . . . All was silence! . . . He went round the building . . . and came to bigger bars, immense gates! . . . It was the entrance to the Cour de l'Administratlon.

Raoul rushed into the doorkeeper's lodge.

"I beg your pardon, madame, could you tell me where to find a gate or door, made of bars, iron bars, opening into the Rue Scribe. . . and leading to the lake?. . . You know the lake! mean?. . . Yes, the underground lake . . . under the Opera."

"Yes, sir, I know there is a lake under the Opera, but I don't know which door leads to it. I have never been there!"

"And the Rue Scribe, madame, the Rue Scribe? Have you never been to the Rue Scribe?"

The woman laughed, screamed with laughter! Raoul darted away, roaring with anger, ran up-stairs, four stairs at a time, down-stairs, rushed through the whole of the business side of the opera-house, found himself once more in the light of the stage.

He stopped, with his heart thumping in his chest: suppose Christine Daaé had been found? He saw a group of men and asked:

"I beg your pardon, gentlemen. Could you tell me where Christine Daaé is?"

And somebody laughed.

At the same moment the stage buzzed with a new sound and, amid a crowd of men in evening-dress, all talking and gesticulating together, appeared a man who seemed very calm and displayed a pleasant face, all pink and chubby-cheeked, crowned with curly hair and lit up by a pair of wonderfully serene blue eyes.

Mercier, the acting-manager, called the Vicomte de Chagny's attention to him and said:

"This is the gentleman to whom you should put your question, monsieur. Let me introduce M. Mifroid, the commissary of police."

"Ah, M. le Vicomte de Chagny! Delighted to meet you, monsieur," said the commissary. "Would you mind coming with me? . . . And now where are the managers? . . . Where are the managers? . . ."

Mercier did not answer, and Rémy, the secretary, volunteered the information that the managers were locked up in their office and that they knew nothing as yet of what had happened.

"You don't mean to say so! Let us go up to the office!"

And M. Mifroid, followed by an ever-increasing crowd, turned toward the business side of the building. Mercier took advantage of the confusion to slip a key into Gabriel's hand:

"This is all going very badly," he whispered. "You had better let Mother Giry out."

And Gabriel moved away.

They soon came to the managers' door. Mercier stormed in vain: the door remained closed.

"Open in the name of the law!" commanded M. Mifroid, in a loud and rather anxious voice.

At last the door was opened. All rushed in to the office, on the commissary's heels.

Raoul was the last to enter. As he was about to follow the rest into the room, a hand was laid on his shoulder and he heard these words spoken in his ear:

"*Erik's secrets concern no one but himself*!"

He turned around, with a stifled exclamation. The hand that was laid on his shoulder was now placed on the lips of a person with an ebony skin, with eyes of jade and with an astrakhan cap on his head: the Persian!

The stranger kept up the gesture that recommended discretion and then, at the moment when the astonished viscount was about to ask the reason of his mysterious intervention, bowed and disappeared.

XVI

MME. GIRY'S ASTOUNDING REVELATIONS AS TO HER PERSONAL RELATIONS WITH THE OPERA GHOST

BEFORE FOLLOWING THE COMMISSARY INTO THE MANAGER'S OFFICE I must describe certain extraordinary occurrences that took place in that office which Rémy and Mercier had vainly tried to enter and into which MM. Richard and Moncharmin had locked themselves with an object which the reader does not yet know, but which it is my duty, as an historian, to reveal without further postponement.

I have had occasion to say that the managers' mood had undergone a disagreeable change for some time past and to convey the fact that this change was due not only to the fall of the chandelier on the famous night of the gala performance.

The reader must know that the ghost had calmly been paid his first twenty thousand francs. Oh, there had been walling and gnashing of teeth, indeed! And yet the thing had happened as simply as could be.

One morning, the managers found on their table an envelope addressed to "Monsieur O. G. (private)" and accompanied by a note from O. G. himself:

> The time has come to carry out the clause in the memorandum-book. Please put twenty notes of a thousand francs each into this envelope, seal it with your own seal and hand it to Mme. Giry, who will do what is necessary.

The managers did not hesitate; without wasting time in asking how these confounded communications came to be delivered in an office which they were careful to keep locked, they seized this opportunity of laying hands on the mysterious blackmailer. And, after telling the whole story, under the promise of secrecy, to Gabriel and Mercier, they put the twenty thousand francs into the envelope and without asking for explanations, handed it to Mme. Giry, who had been reinstated in her functions. The box-keeper displayed no astonishment. I need hardly say that she was well watched. She went straight to the ghost's box and placed the precious envelope on the little shelf attached to the ledge. The two managers, as well as Gabriel and Mercier, were hidden in such a way that they did not lose sight of the envelope for a second during the performance and even afterward, for, as the envelope had not moved, those who watched it did not move either; and Mme. Giry went away while the managers, Gabriel and Mercier were still there. At last, they became tired of waiting and opened the envelope, after ascertaining that the seals had not been broken.

At first sight, Richard and Moncharmin thought that the notes were still there; but soon they perceived that they were not the same. The twenty real notes were gone and had been replaced by twenty notes of the "Bank of St. Farce"!*

The managers' rage and fright were unmistakable. Moncharmin wanted to send for the commissary of police, but Richard objected. He no doubt had a plan, for he said:

"Don't let us make ourselves ridiculous! All Paris would laugh at us. O. G. has won the first game: we will win the second."

He was thinking of the next month's allowance.

Nevertheless, they had been so absolutely tricked that they were bound to suffer a certain dejection. And, upon my word, it was not difficult to understand. We must not forget that the managers had an idea at the back of their minds, all the time, that this strange incident might be an unpleasant practical joke on the part of their predecessors and that it would not do to divulge it prematurely. On the other hand, Moncharmin was sometimes troubled with a suspicion of Richard himself, who occasionally took fanciful whims into his head. And so they were content to await events, while keeping an eye on Mother Giry. Richard would not have her spoken to.

"If she is a confederate," he said, "the notes are gone long ago. But, in my opinion, she is merely an idiot."

"She's not the only idiot in this business," said Moncharmin pensively.

"Well, who could have thought it?" moaned Richard. "But don't be afraid . . . next time, I shall have taken my precautions."

The next time fell on the same day that beheld the disappearance of Christine Daaé. In the morning, a note from the ghost reminded them that the money was due. It read:

> Do just as you did last time. It went very well. Put the twenty thousand in the envelope and hand it to our excellent Mme. Giry.

And the note was accompanied by the usual envelope. They had only to insert the notes.

* Flash notes drawn on the "Bank of St. Farce" in France correspond with those drawn on the "Bank of Engraving" in England. —*Translator's Note.*

This was done about half an hour before the curtain rose on the first act of *Faust*. Richard showed the envelope to Moncharmin. Then he counted the twenty thousand-franc notes in front of him and put the notes into the envelope, but without closing it.

"And now," he said, "let's have Mother Giry in."

The old woman was sent for. She entered with a sweeping courtesy. She still wore her black taffeta dress, the color of which was rapidly turning to rust and lilac, to say nothing of the dingy bonnet. She seemed in a good temper. She at once said:

"Good evening, gentlemen! It's for the envelope, I suppose?"

"Yes, Mme. Giry," said Richard, most amiably. "For the envelope . . . and something else besides."

"At your service, M. Richard, at your service. And what is the something else, please?"

"First of all, Mme. Giry, I have a little question to put to you."

"By all means, M. Richard: Mme. Giry is here to answer you."

"Are you still on good terms with the ghost?"

"Couldn't be better, sir; couldn't be better."

"Ah, we are delighted. . . . Look here, Mme. Giry," said Richard, in the tone of making an Important confidence. "We may just as well tell you, among ourselves . . . you're no fool!"

"Why, sir," exclaimed the box-keeper, stopping the pleasant nodding of the black feathers in her dingy bonnet, "I assure you no one has ever doubted that!"

"We are quite agreed and we shall soon understand one another. The story of the ghost is all humbug, isn't it? . . . Well, still between ourselves,. . .it has lasted long enough."

Mme. Giry looked at the managers as though they were talking Chinese. She walked up to Richard's table and asked, rather anxiously:

"What do you mean? I don't understand."

"Oh, you understand quite well. In any case, you've got to understand . . . . And, first of all, tell us his name."

"Whose name?"

"The name of the man whose accomplice you are, Mme. Giry!"

"I am the ghost's accomplice? I? . . . His accomplice in what, pray?"

"You do all he wants."

"Oh! He's not very troublesome, you know."

"And does he still tip you?"

"I mustn't complain."

"How much does he give you for bringing him that envelope?"

"Ten francs."

"You poor thing! That's not much, is it?

"Why?"

"I'll tell you that presently, Mme. Giry. Just now we should like to know for what extraordinary reason you have given yourself body and soul, to this ghost . . . Mme. Giry's friendship and devotion are not to be bought for five francs or ten francs."

"That's true enough. . . . And I can tell you the reason, sir. There's no disgrace about it . . . on the contrary."

"We're quite sure of that, Mme. Giry!"

"Well, it's like this . . . only the ghost doesn't like me to talk about his business."

"Indeed?" sneered Richard.

"But this is a matter that concerns myself alone. . . . Well, it was in Box Five one evening, I found a letter addressed to myself, a sort of note written in red ink. I needn't read the letter to you, sir; I know it by heart, and I shall never forget it if I live to be a hundred!"

And Mme. Giry, drawing herself up, recited the letter with touching eloquence:

"MADAM:

1825. Mlle. Ménétrier, leader of the ballet, became Marquise de Cussy.

1832. Mlle. Marie Taglioni, a dancer, became Comtesse Gilbert des Voisins.

1846. La Sota, a dancer, married a brother of the King of Spain.

1847. Lola Monies, a dancer, became the morganatic wife of King Louis of Bavaria and was created Countess of Landsfeld.

1848. Mlle. Maria, a dancer, became Baronne d'Herneville.

1870. Theresa Hessler, a dancer, married Dom Fernando, brother to the King of Portugal."

Richard and Moncharmin listened to the old woman, who, as she proceeded with the enumeration of these glorious nuptials, swelled out, took courage and, at last, in a voice bursting with pride, flung out the last sentence of the prophetic letter:

"1885. Meg Giry, Empress!"

Exhausted by this supreme effort, the box-keeper fell into a chair, saying:

"Gentlemen, the letter was signed, 'Opera Ghost.' I had heard much of the ghost, but only half believed in him. From the day when he declared that my little Meg, the flesh of my flesh, the fruit of my womb, would be empress, I believed in him altogether."

And really it was not necessary to make a long study of Mme. Giry's excited features to understand what could be got out of that fine intellect with the two words "ghost" and "empress."

But who pulled the strings of that extraordinary puppet? That was the question.

"You have never seen him; he speaks to you and you believe all he says?" asked Moncharmin.

"Yes. To begin with, I owe it to him that my little Meg was promoted to be the leader of a row. I said to the ghost, 'If she is to be empress in 1885, there is no time to lose; she must become a leader at once.' He said, 'Look upon it as done.' And he had only a word to say to M. Poligny and the thing was done."

"So you see that M. Poligny saw him!"

"No, not any more than I did; but he heard him. The ghost said a word in his ear, you know, on the evening when he left Box Five, looking so dreadfully pale."

Moncharmin heaved a sigh. "What a business!" he groaned.

"Ah!" said Mme. Giry. "I always thought there were secrets between the ghost and M. Poligny. Anything that the ghost asked M. Poligny to do M. Poligny did. M. Poligny could refuse the ghost nothing."

"You hear, Richard: Poligny could refuse the ghost nothing."

"Yes, yes, I hear!" said Richard. "M. Poligny is a friend of the ghost; and, as Mme. Giry is a friend of M. Poligny, there we are! . . . But I don't care a hang about M. Poligny," he added roughly. "The only person whose fate really interests me is Mme. Giry. . . . Mme. Giry, do you know what is in this envelope?"

"Why, of course not," she said.

"Well, look."

Mme. Giry looked into the envelope with a lackluster eye, which soon recovered its brilliancy.

"Thousand-franc notes!" she cried.

"Yes, Mme. Giry, thousand-franc notes! And you knew it!"

"I, sir? I? . . . I swear . . ."

"Don't swear, Mme. Giry! . . . And now I will tell you the second reason why I sent for you. Mme. Giry, I am going to have you arrested."

The two black feathers on the dingy bonnet, which usually affected the attitude of two notes of interrogation, changed into two notes of exclamation; as for the bonnet itself, it swayed in menace on the old lady's tempestuous chignon. Surprise, indignation, protest and dismay were furthermore displayed by little Meg's mother in a sort of extravagant movement of offended virtue, half bound, half slide, that brought her right under the nose of M. Richard, who could not help pushing back his chair.

"*Have me arrested*!"

The mouth that spoke those words seemed to spit the three teeth that were left to it into Richard's face.

M. Richard behaved like a hero. He retreated no farther. His threatening forefinger seemed already to be pointing out the keeper of Box Five to the absent magistrates.

"I am going to have you arrested, Mme. Giry, as a thief!"

"Say that again!"

And Mme. Giry caught Mr. Manager Richard a mighty box on the ear, before Mr. Manager Moncharmin had time to intervene. But it was not the withered hand of the angry old beldame that fell on the managerial ear, but the envelope itself, the cause of all the trouble, the magic envelope that opened with the blow, scattering the bank-notes, which escaped in a fantastic whirl of giant butterflies.

The two managers gave a shout, and the same thought made them both go on their knees, feverishly picking up and hurriedly examining the precious scraps of paper.

"Are they still genuine, Moncharmin?"

"Are they still genuine, Richard?"

"Yes, they are still genuine!"

Above their heads, Mame Giry's three teeth were clashing in a noisy contest, full of hideous interjections. But all that could be clearly distinguished was this *Leit-motif*:

"I, a thief! . . . I, a thief, I?"

She choked with rage. She shouted:

"I never heard of such a thing!"

And, suddenly, she darted up to Richard again.

"In any case," she yelped, "you, M. Richard, ought to know better than I where the twenty thousand francs went to!"

"I?" asked Richard, astounded. "And how should I know?"

Moncharmin, looking severe and dissatisfied, at once insisted that the good lady should explain herself.

"What does this mean, Mme. Giry?" he asked. "And why do you say that M. Richard ought to know better than you where the twenty-thousand francs went to?"

As for Richard, who felt himself turning red under Moncharmin's eyes, he took Mme. Giry by the wrist and shook it violently. In a voice growling and rolling like thunder, he roared:

"Why should I know better than you where the twenty-thousand francs went to? Why? Answer me!"

"Because they went into your pocket!" gasped the old woman, looking at him as if he were the devil incarnate.

Richard would have rushed upon Mme. Giry, if Moncharmin had not stayed his avenging hand and hastened to ask her, more gently:

"How can you suspect my partner, M. Richard, of putting twenty-thousand francs in his pocket?"

"I never said that," declared Mame Giry, "seeing that it was myself who put the twenty-thousand francs into M. Richard's pocket." And she added, under her voice, "There! It's out! . . . And may the ghost forgive me!"

Richard began bellowing anew, but Moncharmin authoritatively ordered him to be silent.

"Allow me! Allow me! Let the woman explain herself. Let me question her." And he added: "It is really astonishing that you should take up such a tone! . . . We are on the verge of clearing up the whole mystery. And you're in a rage! . . . You're wrong to behave like that . . . I'm enjoying myself immensely."

Mame Giry, like the martyr that she was, raised her head, her face beaming with faith in her own innocence.

"You tell me there were twenty-thousand francs in the envelope which I put into M. Richard's pocket; but I tell you again that I knew nothing about it. . . . Nor M. Richard either, for that matter!"

"Aha!" said Richard, suddenly assuming a swaggering air which Moncharmin did not like. "I knew nothing either! You put twenty-thousand francs in my pocket and I knew nothing either! I am very glad to hear it, Mme. Giry!"

"Yes," the terrible dame agreed, "yes, it's true. We neither of us knew anything. But you, you must have ended by finding out!"

Richard would certainly have swallowed Mame Giry alive, if Moncharmin had not been there! But Moncharmin protected her. He resumed his questions:

"What sort of envelope did you put in M. Richard's pocket? It was not the one which we gave you, the one which you took to Box Five before our eyes; and yet that was the one which contained the twenty-thousand francs."

"I beg your pardon. The envelope which *M. le directeur* gave me was the one which I slipped into *M. le directeur's* pocket," explained Mame Giry. "The one which I took to the ghost's box was another envelope, just like it, which the ghost gave me beforehand and which I hid up my sleeve."

So saying, Mame Giry took from her sleeve an envelope ready prepared and similarly addressed to that containing the twenty-thousand francs. The managers took it from her. They examined it and saw that it was fastened with seals stamped with their own managerial seal. They opened it. It contained twenty Bank of St. Farce notes like those which had so much astounded them the month before.

"How simple!" said Richard.

"How simple!" repeated Moncharmin. And he continued with his eyes fixed upon Mame Giry, as though trying to hypnotize her.

"So it was the ghost who gave you this envelope and told you to substitute it for the one which we gave you? And it was the ghost who told you to put the other into M. Richard's pocket?"

"Yes, it was the ghost."

"Then would you mind giving us a specimen of your little talents? Here is the envelope. Act as though we knew nothing."

"As you please, gentlemen."

Mame Giry took the envelope with the twenty notes inside it and made for the door. She was on the point of going out when the two managers rushed at her:

"Oh, no! Oh, no! We're not going to be 'done' a second time! Once bitten, twice shy!"

"I beg your pardon, gentlemen," said the old woman, in self-excuse, "you told me to act as though you knew nothing. . . . Well, if you knew nothing, I should go away with your envelope!"

"And then how would you slip it into my pocket?" argued Richard, whom Moncharmin fixed with his left eye, while keeping his right on Mame Giry: a proceeding likely to strain his sight, but Moncharmin was prepared to go to any length to discover the truth.

"I am to slip it into your pocket when you least expect it, sir. You know that I always take a little turn behind the scenes, in the course of the evening, and I often go with my daughter to the ballet-foyer, which I am entitled to do, as her mother;

I bring her her shoes, when the ballet is about to begin...in fact, I come and go as I please. . . . The subscribers come and go too. . . . So do you, sir. . . . There are lots of people about . . . I go behind you and slip the envelope into the tail-pocket of your dress-coat. . . . There's no witchcraft about that!"

"No witchcraft!" growled Richard, rolling his eyes like Jupiter Tonans. "No witchcraft! Why, I've just caught you in a lie, you old witch!"

Mame Giry bristled, with her three teeth sticking out of her mouth.

"And why, may I ask?"

"Because I spent that evening watching Box Five and the sham envelope which you put there. I did not go to the ballet-foyer for a second."

"No, sir, and I did not give you the envelope that evening, but at the next performance . . . on the evening when the under-secretary of state for fine arts . . ."

At these words, M. Richard suddenly interrupted Mame Giry:

"Yes, that's true, I remember now! The under-secretary went behind the scenes. He asked for me.

"I went down to the ballet-foyer for a moment. I was on the foyer steps. . . . The under-secretary and his chief clerk were in the foyer itself. . . . I suddenly turned around...you had passed behind me, Mme. Giry...You seemed to push against me...Oh, I can see you still, I can see you still!"

"Yes, that's it, sir, that's it. I had just finished my little business. That pocket of yours, sir, is very handy!"

And Mame Giry once more suited the action to the word. She passed behind M. Richard and, so nimbly that Moncharmin himself was impressed by it, slipped the envelope into the pocket of one of the tails of M. Richard's dress-coat.

"Of course!" exclaimed Richard, looking a little pale. "It's very clever of O. G. The problem which he had to solve was this: how to do away with any dangerous intermediary between the man who gives the twenty-thousand francs and the man who receives it. And by far the best thing he could hit upon was to come and take the money from my pocket without my noticing it, as I myself did not know that it was there. It's wonderful!"

"Oh, wonderful, no doubt!" Moncharmin agreed. "Only, you forget, Richard, that I provided ten-thousand francs of the twenty and that nobody put anything in my pocket!"

XVII

THE SAFETY-PIN AGAIN

MONCHARMIN'S LAST PHRASE SO CLEARLY EXPRESSED THE SUSPICION IN which he now held his partner that it was bound to cause a stormy explanation, at the end of which it was agreed that Richard should yield to all Moncharmin's wishes, with the object of helping him to discover the miscreant who was victimizing them.

This brings us to the interval after the Garden Act, with the strange conduct observed by M. Rémy and those curious lapses from the dignity that might be expected of the managers. It was arranged between Richard and Moncharmin, first, that Richard should repeat the exact movements which he had made on the night of the disappearance of the first twenty-thousand francs; and, second, that Moncharmin should not for an instant lose sight of Richard's coattail pocket, into which Mame Giry was to slip the twenty-thousand francs.

M. Richard went and placed himself at the identical spot where he had stood when he bowed to the under-secretary for fine arts. M. Moncharmin took up his position a few steps behind him.

Mame Giry passed, rubbed up against M. Richard, got rid of her twenty-thousand francs in the manager's coat-tail pocket and disappeared.... Or rather she was conjured away. In accordance with the instructions received from Moncharmin a few minutes earlier, Mercier took the good lady to the acting-manager's office and turned the key on her, thus making it impossible for her to communicate with her ghost.

Meanwhile, M. Richard was bending and bowing and scraping and walking backward, just as if he had that high and mighty minister, the under-secretary for fine arts, before him. Only, though these marks of politeness would have created no astonishment if the under-secretary of state had really been in front of M. Richard, they caused an easily comprehensible amazement to the spectators of this very natural but quite inexplicable scene when M. Richard had nobody in front of him.

M. Richard bowed ... to nobody; bent his back ... before nobody; and walked backward . . . before nobody. . . . And, a few steps behind him, M. Moncharmin did the same thing that he was doing, in addition to pushing away M. Rémy and begging M. de La Borderie, the ambassador, and the manager of the Crédit Central "not to touch *M. le directeur*."

Moncharmin, who had his own ideas, did not want Richard to come to him presently, when the twenty-thousand francs were gone, and say:

"Perhaps it was the ambassador . . . or the manager of the Crédit Central . . . or Rémy."

The more so as, at the time of the first scene, as Richard himself admitted, Richard had met nobody in that part of the theater after Mame Giry had brushed up against him. . . .

Having begun by walking backward in order to bow, Richard continued to do so from prudence, until he reached the passage leading to the offices of the management. In this way, he was constantly watched by Moncharmin from behind and himself kept an eye on any one approaching from the front. Once more, this novel method of walking behind the scenes, adopted by the managers of our National Academy of Music, attracted attention; but the managers themselves thought of nothing but their twenty-thousand francs.

On reaching the half-dark passage, Richard said to Moncharmin, in a low voice:

"I am sure that nobody has touched me. . . . You had now better keep at some distance from me and watch me till I come to door of the office: it is better not to arouse suspicion and we can see anything that happens."

But Moncharmin replied. "No, Richard, no! You walk ahead and I'll walk immediately behind you! I won't leave you by a step!"

"But, in that case," exclaimed Richard, "they will never steal our twenty-thousand francs!"

"I should hope not, indeed!" declared Moncharmin.

"Then what we are doing is absurd!"

"We are doing exactly what we did last time...Last time, I joined you as you were leaving the stage and followed close behind you down this passage."

"That's true!" sighed Richard, shaking his head and passively obeying Moncharmin.

Two minutes later, the joint managers locked themselves into their office. Moncharmin himself put the key in his pocket:

"We remained locked up like this, last time," he said, "until you left the Opera to go home."

"That's so. No one came and disturbed us, I suppose?"

"No one."

"Then," said Richard, who was trying to collect his memory, "then I must certainly have been robbed on my way home from the Opera."

"No," said Moncharmin in a drier tone than ever, "no, that's impossible. For I dropped you in my cab. The twenty-thousand francs disappeared at your place: there's not a shadow of a doubt about that."

"It's incredible!" protested Richard. "I am sure of my servants . . . and if one of them had done it, he would have disappeared since."

Moncharmin shrugged his shoulders, as though to say that he did not wish to enter into details, and Richard began to think that Moncharmin was treating him in a very insupportable fashion.

"Moncharmin, I've had enough of this!"

"Richard, I've had too much of it!"

"Do you dare to suspect me?"

"Yes, of a silly joke."

"One doesn't joke with twenty-thousand francs."

"That's what I think," declared Moncharmin, unfolding a newspaper and ostentatiously studying its contents.

"What are you doing?" asked Richard. "Are you going to read the paper next?"

"Yes, Richard, until I take you home."

"Like last time?"

"Yes, like last time."

Richard snatched the paper from Moncharmin's hands. Moncharmin stood up, more irritated than ever, and found himself faced by an exasperated Richard, who, crossing his arms on his chest, said:

"Look here, I'm thinking of this, *I'm thinking of what I might think* if, like last time, after my spending the evening alone with you, you brought me home and if, at the moment of parting, I perceived that twenty-thousand francs had disappeared from my coat-pocket . . . like last time."

"And what might you think?" asked Moncharmin, crimson with rage.

"I might think that, as you hadn't left me by a foot's breadth and as, by your own wish, you were the only one to approach me, like last time, I might think that, if that twenty-thousand francs was no longer in my pocket. It stood a very good chance of being in yours!"

Moncharmin leaped up at the suggestion.

"Oh!" he shouted. "A safety-pin!"

"What do you want a safety-pin for?"

"To fasten you up with! . . . A safety-pin! . . . A safety-pin!"

"You want to fasten me with a safety-pin?"

"Yes, to fasten you to the twenty-thousand francs! Then, whether it's here, or on the drive from here to your place, or at your place, you will feel the hand that pulls at your pocket and you will see if it's mine! Oh, so you're suspecting me now, are you? A safety-pin!"

And that was the moment when Moncharmin opened the door on the passage and shouted:

"A safety-pin! . . . somebody give me a safety-pin!"

And we also know how, at the same moment, Rémy, who had no safety-pin, was received by Moncharmin, while a boy procured the pin so eagerly longed for. And what happened was this: Moncharmin first locked the door again. Then he knelt down behind Richard's back.

"I hope," he said, "that the notes are still there?"

"So do I," said Richard.

"The real ones?" asked Moncharmin, resolved not to be "had" this time.

"Look for yourself," said Richard. "I refuse to touch them."

Moncharmin took the envelope from Richard's pocket and drew out the bank-notes with a trembling hand, for, this time, in order frequently to make sure of the presence of the notes, he had not sealed the envelope nor even fastened it. He felt reassured on finding that they were all there and quite genuine. He put them back in the tail-pocket and pinned them with great care. Then he sat down behind Richard's coat-tails and kept his eyes fixed on them, while Richard, sitting at his writing-table, did not stir.

"A little patience, Richard," said Moncharmin. "We have only a few minutes to wait. . . . The clock will soon strike twelve. Last time, we left at the last stroke of twelve."

"Oh, I shall have all the patience necessary!"

The time passed, slow, heavy, mysterious, stifling. Richard tried to laugh.

"I shall end by believing in the omnipotence of the ghost," he said. "Just now, don't you find something uncomfortable, disquieting, alarming in the atmosphere of this room?"

"You're quite right," said Moncharmin, who was really impressed.

"The ghost!" continued Richard, in a low voice, as though fearing lest he should be overheard by invisible ears. "The ghost! Suppose, all the same, it were a ghost who puts the magic envelopes on the table . . . who talks in Box Five . . . who killed Joseph Buquet . . . who unhooked the chandelier . . . and who robs us! For, after all, after all, after all, there is no one here except you and me, and, if the notes disappear and neither you nor I have anything to do with it, well, we shall have to believe in the ghost . . . in the ghost."

At that moment, the clock on the mantlepiece gave its warning click and the first stroke of twelve struck.

The two managers shuddered. The perspiration streamed from their foreheads. The twelfth stroke sounded strangely in their ears.

When the clock stopped, they gave a sigh and rose from their chairs.

"I think we can go now," said Moncharmin.

"I think so," Richard agreed.

"Before we go, do you mind if I look in your pocket?"

"But, of course, Moncharmin, *you must*! . . . Well?" he asked, as Moncharmin was feeling at the pocket.

"Well, I can feel the pin."

"Of course, as you said, we can't be robbed without noticing it."

But Moncharmin, whose hands were still fumbling, bellowed:

"I can feel the pin, but I can't feel the notes!"

"Come, no joking, Moncharmin! . . . This isn't the time for it."

"Well, feel for yourself."

Richard tore off his coat. The two managers turned the pocket inside out. *The pocket was empty.* And the curious thing was that the pin remained, stuck in the same place.

Richard and Moncharmin turned pale. There was no longer any doubt about the witchcraft.

"The ghost!" muttered Moncharmin.

But Richard suddenly sprang upon his partner.

"No one but you has touched my pocket! Give me back my twenty-thousand francs! . . . Give me back my twenty-thousand francs! . . ."

"On my soul," sighed Moncharmin, who was ready to swoon, "on my soul, I swear that I haven't got it!"

Then somebody knocked at the door. Moncharmin opened it automatically, seemed hardly to recognize Mercier, his business-manager, exchanged a few words with him, without knowing what he was saying and, with an unconscious movement, put the safety-pin, for which he had no further use, into the hands of his bewildered subordinate. . . .

XVIII

THE COMMISSARY, THE VISCOUNT AND THE PERSIAN

THE FIRST WORDS OF THE COMMISSARY OF POLICE, ON ENTERING THE managers' office, were to ask after the missing prima donna.

"Is Christine Daaé here?"

"Christine Daaé here?" echoed Richard. "No. Why?"

As for Moncharmin, he had not the strength left to utter a word.

Richard repeated, for the commissary and the compact crowd which had followed him into the office observed an impressive silence.

"Why do you ask if Christine Daaé is here, *M. le commissaire*?"

"Because she has to be found," declared the commissary of police solemnly.

"What do you mean, she has to be found? Has she disappeared?"

"In the middle of the performance!"

"In the middle of the performance? This is extraordinary!"

"Isn't it? And what is quite as extraordinary is that you should first learn it from me!"

"Yes," said Richard, taking his head in his hands and muttering. "What is this new business? Oh, it's enough to make a man send in his resignation!"

And he pulled a few hairs out of his mustache without even knowing what he was doing.

"So she . . . so she disappeared in the middle of the performance?" he repeated.

"Yes, she was carried off in the Prison Act, at the moment when she was invoking the aid of the angels; but I doubt if she was carried off by an angel."

"And I am sure that she was!"

Everybody looked round. A young man, pale and trembling with excitement, repeated:

"I am sure of it!"

"Sure of what?" asked Mifroid.

"That Christine Daaé was carried off by an angel, *M. le commissaire*, and I can tell you his name."

"Aha, M. le Vicomte de Chagny! So you maintain that Christine Daaé was carried off by an angel: an angel of the Opera, no doubt?"

"Yes, monsieur, by an angel of the Opera; and I will tell you where he lives . . . when we are alone."

"You are right, monsieur."

And the commissary of police, inviting Raoul to take a chair, cleared the room of all the rest, excepting the managers.

Then Raoul spoke:

"*M. le commissaire*, the angel is called Erik, he lives in the Opera and he is the Angel of Music!"

"The Angel of Music! Really! That is very curious! . . . The Angel of Music!" And, turning to the managers, M. Mifroid asked, "Have you an Angel of Music on the premises, gentlemen?"

Richard and Moncharmin shook their heads, without even speaking.

"Oh," said the viscount, "those gentlemen have heard of the Opera ghost. Well, I am in a position to state that the Opera ghost and the Angel of Music are one and the same person; and his real name is Erik."

M. Mifroid rose and looked at Raoul attentively.

"I beg your pardon, monsieur, but is it your intention to make fun of the law? And, if not, what is all this about the Opera ghost?"

"I say that these gentlemen have heard of him."

"Gentlemen, it appears that you know the Opera ghost?"

Richard rose, with the remaining hairs of his mustache in his hand.

"No, M. Commissary, no, we do not know him, but we wish that we did, for this very evening he has robbed us of twenty-thousand francs!"

And Richard turned a terrible look on Moncharmin, which seemed to say: "Give me back the twenty-thousand francs, or I'll tell the whole story."

Moncharmin understood what he meant, for, with a distracted gesture, he said: "Oh, tell everything and have done with it!"

As for Mifroid, he looked at the managers and at Raoul by turns and wondered whether he had strayed into a lunatic asylum. He passed his hand through his hair.

"A ghost," he said, "who, on the same evening, carries off an opera-singer and steals twenty-thousand francs is a ghost who must have his hands very full! If you don't mind, we will take the questions in order. The singer first, the twenty-thousand francs after. Come, M. de Chagny, let us try to talk seriously. You believe that Mlle. Christine Daaé has been carried off by an individual called Erik. Do you know this person? Have you seen him?"

"Yes."

"Where?"

"In a churchyard."

M. Mifroid gave a start, began to scrutinize Raoul again and said:

"Of course! . . . That's where ghosts usually hang out! . . . And what were you doing in that churchyard?"

"Monsieur," said Raoul, "I can quite understand how absurd my replies must seem to you. But I beg you to believe that I am in full possession of my faculties. The safety of the person dearest to me in the world is at stake. I should like to convince you in a few words, for time is pressing and every minute is valuable. Unfortunately, if I do not tell you the strangest story that ever was from the beginning, you will not believe me. I will tell you all I know about the Opera ghost, M. Commissary. Alas, I do not know much! . . ."

"Never mind, go on, go on!" exclaimed Richard and Moncharmin, suddenly greatly interested.

Unfortunately for their hopes of learning some detail that could put them on the track of their hoaxer, they were soon compelled to accept the fact that M. Raoul de Chagny had completely lost his head. All that story about Perros-Guirec, death's heads and enchanted violins, could only have taken birth in the disordered brain of a youth mad with love. It was evident, also, that Mr. Commissary Mifroid shared their view; and the magistrate would certainly have cut short the incoherent narrative if circumstances had not taken it upon themselves to interrupt it.

The door opened and a man entered, curiously dressed in an enormous frock-coat and a tall hat, at once shabby and shiny, that came down to his ears. He went up to the commissary and spoke to him in a whisper. It was doubtless a detective come to deliver an important communication.

During this conversation, M. Mifroid did not take his eyes off Raoul. At last, addressing him, he said:

"Monsieur, we have talked enough about the ghost. We will now talk about yourself a little, if you have no objection: you were to carry off Mlle. Christine Daaé to-night?"

"Yes, *M. le commissaire.*"

"After the performance?"

"Yes, *M. le commissaire.*"

"All your arrangements were made?"

"Yes, *M. le commissaire.*"

"The carriage that brought you was to take you both away. . . . There were fresh horses in readiness at every stage. . . ."

"That is true, *M. le commissaire.*"

"And nevertheless your carriage is still outside the Rotunda awaiting your orders, is it not?"

"Yes, *M. le commissaire.*"

"Did you know that there were three other carriages there, in addition to yours?"

"I did not pay the least attention."

"They were the carriages of Mlle. Sorelli, which could not find room in the Cour de l'Administration; of Carlotta; and of your brother, M. le Comte de Chagny. . . ."

"Very likely. . . ."

"What is certain is that, though your carriage and Sorelli's and Carlotta's are still there, by the Rotunda pavement, M. le Comte de Chagny's carriage is gone."

"This has nothing to say to . . ."

"I beg your pardon. Was not M. le Comte opposed to your marriage with Mlle. Daaé?"

"That is a matter that only concerns the family."

"You have answered my question: he was opposed to it . . . and that was why you were carrying Christine Daaé out of your brother's reach. Well, M. de Chagny, allow me to inform you that your brother has been smarter than you! It is he who has carried off Christine Daaé!"

"Oh, impossible!" moaned Raoul, pressing his hand to his heart. "Are you sure?"

"Immediately after the artist's disappearance, which was procured by means which we have still to ascertain, he flung into his carriage, which drove right across Paris at a furious pace."

"Across Paris?" asked poor Raoul, in a hoarse voice. "What do you mean by across Paris?"

"Across Paris and out of Paris . . . by the Brussels road."

"Oh," cried the young man, "I shall catch them!"

And he rushed out of the office.

"And bring her back to us!" cried the commissary gaily. . . . "Ah, that's a trick worth two of the Angel of Music's!"

And, turning to his audience, M. Mifroid delivered a little lecture on police methods.

"I don't know for a moment whether M. le Comte de Chagny has really carried Christine Daaé off or not . . . but I want to know and I believe that, at this moment, no one is more anxious to inform us than his brother. . . . And now he is flying in pursuit of him! He is my chief auxiliary! This, gentlemen, is the art of the police, which is believed to be so complicated and which, nevertheless, appears so simple as soon as you see that it consists in getting your work done by people who have nothing to do with the police."

But M. le Commissaire de Police Mifroid would not have been quite so satisfied with himself if he had known that the rush of his rapid emissary was stopped at the entrance to the very first corridor. A tall figure blocked Raoul's way.

"Where are you going so fast, M. de Chagny?" asked a voice.

Raoul impatiently raised his eyes and recognized the astrakhan cap of an hour ago. He stopped:

"It's you!" he cried, in a feverish voice. "You, who know Erik's secrets and don't want me to speak of them. Who are you?"

"You know who I am! . . . I am the Persian!"

XIX

THE VISCOUNT AND THE PERSIAN

RAOUL NOW REMEMBERED THAT HIS BROTHER HAD ONCE SHOWN HIM that mysterious person, of whom nothing was known except that he was a Persian and that he lived in a little old-fashioned flat in the Rue de Rivoli.

The man with the ebony skin, the eyes of jade and the astrakhan cap bent over Raoul.

"I hope, M. de Chagny," he said, "that you have not betrayed Erik's secret?"

"And why should I hesitate to betray that monster, sir?" Raoul rejoined haughtily, trying to shake off the intruder. "Is he your friend, by any chance?"

"I hope that you said nothing about Erik, sir, because Erik's secret is also Christine Daaé's and to talk about one is to talk about the other!"

"Oh, sir," said Raoul, becoming more and more impatient, "you seem to know about many things that interest me; and yet I have no time to listen to you!"

"Once more, M. de Chagny, where are you going so fast?"

"Can not you guess? To Christine Daaé's assistance. . . ."

"Then, sir, stay here, for Christine Daaé is here!"

"With Erik?"

"With Erik."

"How do you know?"

"I was at the performance and no one in the world but Erik could contrive an abduction like that! . . . Oh," he said, with a deep sigh, "I recognized the monster's touch! . . ."

"You know him then?"

The Persian did not reply, but heaved a fresh sigh.

"Sir," said Raoul, "I do not know what your intentions are, but can you do anything to help me? I mean, to help Christine Daaé?"

"I think so, M. de Chagny, and that is why I spoke to you."

"What can you do?"

"Try to take you to her . . . and to him,"

"If you can do me that service, sir, my life is yours! . . . One word more: the commissary of police tells me that Christine Daaé has been carried off by my brother, Count Philippe."

"Oh, M. de Chagny, I don't believe a word of it."

"It's not possible, is it?"

"I don't know if it is possible or not; but there are ways and ways of carrying people off; and M. le Comte Philippe has never, as far as I know, had anything to do with witchcraft."

"Your arguments are convincing, sir, and I am a fool! . . . Oh, let us make haste! I place myself entirely in your hands! . . . How should I not believe you, when you are the only one to believe me . . . when you are the only one not to smile when Erik's name is mentioned?"

And the young man impetuously seized the Persian's hands. They were ice-cold.

"Silence!" said the Persian, stopping and listening to the distant sounds of the theater. "We must not mention that name here. Let us say 'he' and 'him'; then there will be less danger of attracting his attention."

"Do you think he is near us?"

"It is quite possible, sir, if he is not, at this moment, with his victim, in the house on the lake."

"Ah, so you know that house too?"

"If he is not there, he may be here, in this wall, in this floor, in this ceiling! . . . Come!"

And the Persian, asking Raoul to deaden the sound of his footsteps, led him down passages which Raoul had never seen before, even at the time when Christine used to take him for walks through that labyrinth.

"If only Darius has come!" said the Persian.

"Who is Darius?"

"Darius? My servant."

They were now in the center of a real deserted square, an immense apartment ill-lit by a small lamp. The Persian stopped Raoul and, in the softest of whispers, asked:

"What did you say to the commissary?"

"I said that Christine Daaé's abductor was the Angel of Music, *alias* the Opera ghost, and that the real name was . . ."

"Hush! . . . And did he believe you?"

"No."

"He attached no importance to what you said?"

"No."

"He took you for a bit of a madman?"

"Yes."

"So much the better!" sighed the Persian.

And they continued their road. After going up and down several staircases which Raoul had never seen before, the two men found themselves in front of a door which the Persian opened with a master-key. The Persian and Raoul were both, of course, in dress-clothes; but, whereas Raoul had a tall hat, the Persian wore the astrakhan cap which I have already mentioned. It was an infringement of the rule which insists upon the tall hat behind the scenes; but in France foreigners are allowed every license: the Englishman his traveling-cap, the Persian his cap of astrakhan.

"Sir," said the Persian, "your tall hat will be in your way: you would do well to leave it in the dressing-room."

"What dressing-room?" asked Raoul.

"Christine Daaé's."

And the Persian, letting Raoul through the door which he had just opened, showed him the actress-room opposite.

They were at the end of the passage the whole length of which Raoul had been accustomed to traverse before knocking at Christine's door.

"How well you know the Opera, sir!"

"Not so well as 'he' does!" said the Persian modestly.

And he pushed the young man into Christine's dressing-room, which was as Raoul had left it a few minutes earlier.

Closing the door, the Persian went to a very thin partition that separated the dressing-room from a big lumber-room next to it. He listened and then coughed loudly.

There was a sound of some one stirring in the lumber-room; and, a few seconds later, a finger tapped at the door.

"Come in," said the Persian.

A man entered, also wearing an astrakhan cap and dressed in a long overcoat. He bowed and took a richly carved case from under his coat, put it on the dressing-table, bowed once again and went to the door.

"Did no one see you come in, Darius?"

"No, master."

"Let no one see you go out."

The servant glanced down the passage and swiftly disappeared.

The Persian opened the case. It contained a pair of long pistols.

"When Christine Daaé was carried off, sir, I sent word to my servant to bring me these pistols. I have had them a long time and they can be relied upon."

"Do you mean to fight a duel?" asked the young man.

"It will certainly be a duel which we shall have to fight," said the other, examining the priming of his pistols. "And what a duel!" Handing one of the pistols to Raoul, he added, "In this duel, we shall be two to one; but you must be prepared for everything, for we shall be fighting the most terrible adversary that you can imagine. But you love Christine Daaé, do you not?"

"I worship the ground she stands on! But you, sir, who do not love her, tell me why I find you ready to risk your life for her! You must certainly hate Erik!"

"No, sir," said the Persian sadly, "I do not hate him. If I hated him, he would long ago have ceased doing harm."

"Has he done you harm?"

"I have forgiven him the harm which he has done me."

"I do not understand you. You treat him as a monster, you speak of his crime, he has done you harm and I find in you the same inexplicable pity that drove me to despair when I saw it in Christine!"

The Persian did not reply. He fetched a stool and set it against the wall facing the great mirror that filled the whole of the wall-space opposite. Then he climbed on the stool and, with his nose to the wallpaper, seemed to be looking for something.

"Ah," he said, after a long search, "I have it!"

And, raising his finger above his head, he pressed against a corner in the pattern of the paper. Then he turned round and jumped off the stool:

"In half a minute," he said, "we shall be *on his road*!" and crossing the whole length of the dressing-room he felt the great mirror.

"No, it is not yielding yet," he muttered.

"Oh, are we going out by the mirror?" asked Raoul. "Like Christine Daaé."

"So you knew that Christine Daaé went out by that mirror?"

"She did so before my eyes, sir! I was hidden behind the curtain of the inner room and I saw her vanish not by the glass, but in the glass!"

"And what did you do?"

"I thought it was an aberration of my senses, a mad dream. . . ."

"Or some new fancy of the ghost's!" chuckled the Persian. "Ah, M. de Chagny," he continued, still with his hand on the mirror, "would that we had to do with a ghost! We could then leave our pistols in their case. . . . Put down your hat, please . . . there . . . and now cover your shirtfront as much as you can with your coat . . . as I am doing. . . . Bring the lapels forward . . . turn up the collar. . . . We must make ourselves as invisible as possible. . . ."

Bearing against the mirror, after a short silence, he said:

"It takes some time to release the counterbalance, when you press on the spring from the inside of the room. It is different when you are behind the wall and can act directly on the counterbalance. Then the mirror turns at once and is moved with incredible rapidity."

"What counterbalance?" asked Raoul.

"Why, the counterbalance that lifts the whole of this wall on to its pivot. You surely don't expect it to move of itself, by enchantment! If you watch, you will see the mirror first rise an inch or two and then shift an inch or two from left to right. It will then be on a pivot and will swing round."

"It's not turning!" said Raoul impatiently.

"Oh, wait! You have time enough to be impatient, sir! The mechanism has obviously become rusty, or else the spring isn't working. . . . Unless it is something else," added the Persian anxiously.

"What?"

"He may simply have cut the cord of the counterbalance and blocked the whole apparatus."

"Why should he? He does not know that we are coming this way!"

"I dare say he suspects it, for he knows that I understand the system."

"It's not turning! . . . And Christine, sir, Christine?"

The Persian said coldly:

"We shall do all that it is humanly possible to do! But he may stop us at the first step! . . . He commands the walls, the doors and the trapdoors. In my country, he was known by a name which means the 'trap-door lover.'"

"But why do these walls obey him alone? He did not build them!"

"Yes, sir, that is just what he did!"

Raoul looked at him in amazement; but the Persian made a sign to him to be silent and pointed to the glass. . . . There was a sort of shivering reflection. Their image was troubled as in a rippling sheet of water and then all became stationary again.

"You see, sir, that it is not turning! Let us take another road!"

"To-night, there is no other!" declared the Persian, in a singularly mournful voice. "And now, look out! And be ready to fire."

He himself raised his pistol opposite the glass. Raoul imitated his movement. With his free arm, the Persian drew the young man to his chest and, suddenly, the mirror turned, in a blinding daze of cross-lights: It turned like one of those revolving doors which have lately been fixed to the entrances of most restaurants, it turned, carrying Raoul and the Persian with it and suddenly hurling them from the full light into the deepest darkness.

XX

IN THE CELLARS OF THE OPERA

"Your hand high, ready to fire!" repeated Raoul's companion quickly.

The wall, behind them, having completed the circle which it described upon itself, closed again; and the two men stood motionless for a moment, holding their breath.

At last, the Persian decided to make a movement; and Raoul heard him slip on his knees and feel for something in the dark with his groping hands. Suddenly, the darkness was made visible by a small dark lantern and Raoul instinctively stepped backward as though to escape the scrutiny of a secret enemy. But he soon perceived that the light belonged to the Persian, whose movements he was closely observing. The little red disk was turned in every direction and Raoul saw that the floor, the walls and the celling were all formed of planking. It must have been the ordinary road taken by Erik to reach Christine's dressing-room and impose upon her innocence. And Raoul, remembering the Persian's remark, thought that it had been mysteriously constructed by the ghost himself. Later, he learned that Erik had found, all prepared for him, a secret passage, long known to himself alone and contrived at the time of the Paris Commune to allow the jailers to convey their prisoners straight to the dungeons that had been constructed for them in the cellars; for the Federates had occupied the opera-house immediately after the eighteenth of March and had made a starting-place right at the top for their Mongolfier balloons, which carried their incendiary proclamations to the departments, and a state prison right at the bottom.

The Persian went on his knees and put his lantern on the ground. He seemed to be working at the floor; and suddenly he turned off his light. Then Raoul heard a faint click and saw a very pale luminous square in the floor of the passage. It was as though a window had opened on the Opera cellars, which were still lit. Raoul no longer saw the Persian, but he suddenly felt him by his side and heard him whisper:

"Follow me and do all that I do."

Raoul turned to the luminous aperture. Then he saw the Persian, who was still on his knees, hang by his hands from the rim of the opening, with his pistol between his teeth, and slide into the cellar below.

Curiously enough, the viscount had absolute confidence in the Persian, though he knew nothing about him. His emotion when speaking of the "monster" struck him as sincere; and, if the Persian had cherished any sinister designs against him, he would not have armed him with his own hands. Besides, Raoul must reach Christine at all costs. He therefore went on his knees also and hung from the trap with both hands.

"Let go!" said a voice.

And he dropped into the arms of the Persian, who told him to lie down flat, closed the trap-door above him and crouched down beside him. Raoul tried to ask a question, but the Persian's hand was on his mouth and he heard a voice which he recognized as that of the commissary of police.

Raoul and the Persian were completely hidden behind a wooden partition. Near them, a small staircase led to a little room in which the commissary appeared to be walking up and down, asking questions. The faint light was just enough to enable Raoul to distinguish the shape of things around him. And he could not restrain a dull cry: there were three corpses there.

The first lay on the narrow landing of the little staircase; the two others had rolled to the bottom of the staircase. Raoul could have touched one of the two poor wretches by passing his fingers through the partition.

"Silence!" whispered the Persian.

He too had seen the bodies and he gave one word in explanation:

"He!"

The commissary's voice was now heard more distinctly. He was asking for information about the system of lighting, which the stage-manager supplied. The commissary therefore must be in the "organ" or its immediate neighborhood.

Contrary to what one might think, especially in connection with an opera-house, the "organ" is not a musical instrument. At that time, electricity was employed only for a very few scenic effects and for the bells. The immense building and the stage itself were still lit by gas; hydrogen was used to regulate and modify the lighting of a scene; and this was done by means of a special apparatus which, because of the multiplicity of its pipes, was known as the "organ." A box beside the prompter's box was reserved for the chief gas-man, who from there gave his orders to his assistants and saw that they were executed. Mauclair stayed in this box during all the performances.

But now Mauclair was not in his box and his assistants not in their places.

"Mauclair! Mauclair!"

The stage-manager's voice echoed through the cellars. But Mauclair did not reply.

I have said that a door opened on a little staircase that led to the second cellar. The commissary pushed it, but it resisted.

"I say," he said to the stage-manager, "I can't open this door: is it always so difficult?"

The stage-manager forced it open with his shoulder. He saw that, at the same time, he was pushing a human body and he could not keep back an exclamation, for he recognized the body at once:

"Mauclair! Poor devil! He is dead!"

But Mr. Commissary Mifroid, whom nothing surprised, was stooping over that big body.

"No," he said, "he is dead-drunk, which is not quite the same thing."

"It's the first time, if so," said the stage-manager.

"Then some one has given him a narcotic. That is quite possible."

Mifroid went down a few steps and said:

"Look!"

By the light of a little red lantern, at the foot of the stairs, they saw two other bodies. The stage-manager recognized Mauclair's assistants. Mifroid went down and listened to their breathing.

"They are sound asleep," he said. "Very curious business! Some person unknown must have interfered with the gas-man and his staff . . . and that person unknown was obviously working on behalf of the kidnapper. . . . But what a funny idea to kidnap a performer on the stage! . . . Send for the doctor of the theater, please." And Mifroid repeated, "Curious, decidedly curious business!"

Then he turned to the little room, addressing the people whom Raoul and the Persian were unable to see from where they lay.

"What do you say to all this, gentlemen? You are the only ones who have not given your views. And yet you must have an opinion of some sort."

Thereupon, Raoul and the Persian saw the startled faces of the joint managers appear above the landing—and they heard Moncharmin's excited voice:

"There are things happening here, Mr. Commissary, which we are unable to explain."

And the two faces disappeared.

"Thank you for the information, gentlemen," said Mifroid, with a jeer.

But the stage-manager, holding his chin in the hollow of his right hand, which is the attitude of profound thought, said:

"It is not the first time that Mauclair has fallen asleep in the theater. I remember finding him, one evening, snoring in his little recess, with his snuff-box beside him."

"Is that long ago?" asked M. Mifroid, carefully wiping his eye-glasses.

"No, not so very long ago.... Wait a bit!... It was the night... of course, yes... It was the night when Carlotta—you know, Mr. Commissary—gave her famous 'co-ack'!"

"Really? The night when Carlotta gave her famous 'co-ack'?"

And M. Mifroid, replacing his gleaming glasses on his nose, fixed the stage-manager with a contemplative stare.

"So Mauclair takes snuff, does he?" he asked carelessly.

"Yes, Mr. Commissary.... Look, there is his snuff-box on that little shelf.... Oh, he's a great snuff-taker!"

"So am I," said Mifroid and put the snuff-box in his pocket.

Raoul and the Persian, themselves unobserved, watched the removal of the three bodies by a number of scene-shifters, who were followed by the commissary and all the people with him. Their steps were heard for a few minutes on the stage above. When they were alone the Persian made a sign to Raoul to stand up. Raoul did so; but, as he did not lift his hand in front of his eyes, ready to fire, the Persian told him to resume that attitude and to continue it, whatever happened.

"But it tires the hand unnecessarily," whispered Raoul. "If I do fire, I shan't be sure of my aim."

"Then shift your pistol to the other hand," said the Persian.

"I can't shoot with my left hand."

Thereupon, the Persian made this queer reply, which was certainly not calculated to throw light into the young man's flurried brain:

"It's not a question of shooting with the right hand or the left; it's a question of holding one of your hands as though you were going to pull the trigger of a pistol with your arm bent. As for the pistol itself, when all is said, you can put that in your pocket!" And he added, "Let this be clearly understood, or I will answer for nothing. It is a matter of life and death. And now, silence and follow me!"

The cellars of the Opera are enormous and they are five in number. Raoul followed the Persian and wondered what he would have done without his companion in that extraordinary labyrinth. They went down to the third cellar; and their progress was still lit by some distant lamp.

The lower they went, the more precautions the Persian seemed to take. He kept on turning to Raoul to see if he was holding his arm properly, showing him how he himself carried his hand as if always ready to fire, though the pistol was in his pocket.

Suddenly, a loud voice made them stop. Some one above them shouted:

"All the door-shutters on the stage! The commissary of police wants them!"

Steps were heard and shadows glided through the darkness. The Persian drew Raoul behind a set piece. They saw passing before and above them old men bent by age and the past burden of opera-scenery. Some could hardly drag themselves along; others, from habit, with stooping bodies and outstretched hands, looked for doors to shut.

They were the door-shutters, the old, worn-out scene-shifters, on whom a charitable management had taken pity, giving them the job of shutting doors above and below the stage. They went about incessantly, from top to bottom of the building, shutting the doors; and they were also called "The draft-expellers," at least at that time, for I have little doubt that by now they are all dead. Drafts are very bad for the voice, wherever they may come from.*

The Persian and Raoul welcomed this incident, which relieved them of inconvenient witnesses, for some of those door-shutters, having nothing else to do or nowhere to lay their heads, stayed at the Opera, from idleness or necessity, and spent the night there.

The two men might have stumbled over them, waking them up and provoking a request for explanations. For the moment, M. Mifroid's inquiry saved them from any such unpleasant encounters.

But they were not left to enjoy their solitude for long. Other shades now came down by the same way by which the door-shutters had gone up. Each of these shades carried a little lantern and moved it about, above, below and all around, as though looking for something or somebody.

"Hang it!" muttered the Persian. "I don't know what they are looking for, but they might easily find us. . . . Let us get away, quick! . . . Your hand up, sir, ready to fire! . . . Bend your arm . . . more . . . that's it! . . . Hand at the level of your eye, as though you were fighting a duel and waiting for the word to fire! Oh, leave

* M. Pedro Gailhard has himself told me that he created a few additional posts as door-shutters for old stage-carpenters whom he was unwilling to dismiss from the service of the Opera.

your pistol in your pocket. Quick, come along, down-stairs. Level of your eye! Question of life or death! . . . Here, this way, these stairs!" They reached the fifth cellar. "Oh, what a duel, sir, what a duel!"

Once in the fifth cellar, the Persian drew breath. He seemed to enjoy a rather greater sense of security than he had displayed when they both stopped in the third; but he never altered the attitude of his hand. And Raoul, remembering the Persian's observation—"I know these pistols can be relied upon"—was more and more astonished, wondering why any one should be so gratified at being able to rely upon a pistol which he did not intend to use!

But the Persian left him no time for reflection. Telling Raoul to stay where he was, he ran up a few steps of the staircase which they had just left and then returned.

"How stupid of us!" he whispered. "We shall soon have seen the end of those men with their lanterns. It is the firemen going their rounds." *

The two men waited five minutes longer. Then the Persian took Raoul up the stairs again; but suddenly he stopped him with a gesture. Something moved in the darkness before them.

"Flat on your stomach!" whispered the Persian.

The two men lay flat on the floor.

They were only just in time. A shade, this time carrying no light, just a shade in the shade, passed. It passed close to them, near enough to touch them.

They felt the warmth of its cloak upon them. For they could distinguish the shade sufficiently to see that it wore a cloak which shrouded it from head to foot. On its head it had a soft felt hat.

It moved away, drawing its feet against the walls and sometimes giving a kick into a corner.

"Whew!" said the Persian. "We've had a narrow escape; that shade knows me and has twice taken me to the managers' office."

"Is it some one belonging to the theater police?" asked Raoul.

"It's some one much worse than that!" replied the Persian, without giving any further explanation.†

* In those days, it was still part of the firemen's duty to watch over the safety of the Opera house outside the performances; but this service has since been suppressed. I asked M. Pedro Gailhard the reason, and he replied: "It was because the management was afraid that, in their utter inexperience of the cellars of the Opera, the firemen might set fire to the building!"

† Like the Persian, I can give no further explanation touching the apparition of this shade. Whereas, in this historic narrative, everything else will be normally explained, however abnormal the course of events may seem, I can not give the reader expressly to understand what the Persian meant by the words, "It is some one much worse than that!" The reader must try to guess for himself, for I promised M. Pedro Gailhard, the former manager of the Opera, to keep his secret regarding the extremely interesting and useful personality of the wandering, cloaked shade which, while condemning itself to live in the cellars of the Opera, rendered such immense services to those who, on gala evenings, for instance, venture to stray away from the stage. I am speaking of state services; and, upon my word of honor, I can say no more.

"It's not . . . *he*?"

"*He*? . . . If he does not come behind us, we shall always see his yellow eyes! . . . That is more or less our safeguard to-night. . . . But he may come from behind, stealing up; and we are dead men if we do not keep our hands as though about to fire, at the level of our eyes, in front!"

The Persian had hardly finished speaking, when a fantastic face came in sight . . . a whole fiery face, not only two yellow eyes!

Yes, a head of fire came toward them, at a man's height, but with no body attached to it. The face shed fire, looked in the darkness like a flame shaped as a man's face.

"Oh," said the Persian, between his teeth. "I have never seen this before! . . . Pampin was not mad, after all: he had seen it! . . . What can that flame be? It is not *he*, but he may have sent it! . . . Take care! . . . Take care! . . . Your hand at the level of your eyes, in Heaven's name, at the level of your eyes! . . . I know most of his tricks . . . but not this one. . . . Come, let us run. . . . it is safer. Hand at the level of your eyes!"

And they fled down the long passage that opened before them.

After a few seconds, that seemed to them like long minutes, they stopped.

"He doesn't often come this way," said the Persian. "This side has nothing to do with him. This side does not lead to the lake nor to the house on the lake. . . . But perhaps he knows that we are at his heels. . . although I promised him to leave him alone and never to meddle in his business again!"

So saying, he turned his head and Raoul also turned his head; and they again saw the head of fire behind their two heads. It had followed them. And it must have run also, and perhaps faster than they, for it seemed to be nearer to them.

At the same time, they began to perceive a certain noise of which they could not guess the nature. They simply noticed that the sound seemed to move and to approach with the fiery face. It was a noise as though thousands of nails had been scraped against a blackboard, the perfectly unendurable noise that is sometimes made by a little stone inside the chalk that grates on the blackboard.

They continued to retreat, but the fiery face came on, came on, gaining on them. They could see its features clearly now. The eyes were round and staring, the nose a little crooked and the mouth large, with a hanging lower lip, very like the eyes, nose and lip of the moon, when the moon is quite red, bright red.

How did that red moon manage to glide through the darkness, at a man's height, with nothing to support it, at least apparently? And how did it go so fast, so straight ahead, with such staring, staring eyes? And what was that scratching, scraping, grating sound which it brought with it?

The Persian and Raoul could retreat no farther and flattened themselves against the wall, not knowing what was going to happen because of that incomprehensible head of fire, and especially now, because of the more intense, swarming, living, "numerous" sound, for the sound was certainly made up of hundreds of little sounds that moved in the darkness, under the fiery face.

And the fiery face came on. . . with its noise. . . came level with them! . . .

And the two companions, flat against their wall, felt their hair stand on end with horror, for they now knew what the thousand noises meant. They came in a troop, hustled along in the shadow by innumerable little hurried waves, swifter than the waves that rush over the sands at high tide, little night-waves foaming under the moon, under the fiery head that was like a moon. And the little waves passed between their legs, climbing up their legs, irresistibly, and Raoul and the Persian could no longer restrain their cries of horror, dismay and pain. Nor could they continue to hold their hands at the level of their eyes: their hands went down to their legs to push back the waves, which were full of little legs and nails and claws and teeth.

Yes, Raoul and the Persian were ready to faint, like Pampin the fireman. But the head of fire turned round in answer to their cries, and spoke to them:

"Don't move! Don't move! . . . Whatever you do, don't come after me! . . . I am the rat-catcher! . . . Let me pass, with my rats! . . ."

And the head of fire disappeared, vanished in the darkness, while the passage in front of it lit up, as the result of the change which the rat-catcher had made in his dark lantern. Before, so as not to scare the rats in front of him, he had turned his dark lantern on himself, lighting up his own head; now, to hasten their flight, he lit the dark space in front of him. And he jumped along, dragging with him the waves of scratching rats, all the thousand sounds.

Raoul and the Persian breathed again, though still trembling.

"I ought to have remembered that Erik talked to me about the rat-catcher," said the Persian. "But he never told me that he looked like that. . . and it's funny that I should never have met him before. . . . Of course, Erik never comes to this part!"

"Are we very far from the lake, sir?" asked Raoul. "When shall we get there?. . . Take me to the lake, oh, take me to the lake! . . . When we are at the lake, we will call out! . . . Christine will hear us! . . . And he will hear us, too! . . . And, as you know him, we shall talk to him!"

"Baby!" said the Persian. "We shall never enter the house on the lake by the lake! . . . I myself have never landed on the other bank. . . the bank on which the house stands. . . . You have to cross the lake first . . . and it is well guarded! . . . I fear that more than one of those men—old scene-shifters, old door-shutters—who have never been seen again were simply tempted to cross the lake. . . . It is terrible. . . . I myself would have been nearly killed there. . . If the monster had not recognized me in time! . . . One piece of advice, sir; never go near the lake. . . . And, above all, shut your ears if you hear the voice singing under the water, the siren's voice!"

"But then, what are we here for?" asked Raoul, in a transport of fever, impatience and rage. "If you can do nothing for Christine, at least let me die for her!"

The Persian tried to calm the young man.

"We have only one means of saving Christine Daaé, believe me, which is to enter the house unperceived by the monster."

"And is there any hope of that, sir?"

"Ah, if I had not that hope, I would not have come to fetch you!"

"And how can one enter the house on the lake without crossing the lake?"

"From the third cellar, from which we were so unluckily driven away. We will go back there now. . . . I will tell you," said the Persian, with a sudden change in his voice, "I will tell you the exact place, sir: it is between a set piece and a discarded scene from *Roi de Lahore*, exactly at the spot where Joseph Buquet died. . . . Come, sir, take courage and follow me! And hold your hand at the level of your eyes! . . . But where are we?"

The Persian lit his lamp again and flung its rays down two enormous corridors that crossed each other at right angles.

"We must be," he said, "in the part used more particularly for the waterworks. I see no fire coming from the furnaces."

He went in front of Raoul, seeking his road, stopping abruptly when he was afraid of meeting some waterman. Then they had to protect themselves against the glow of a sort of underground forge, which the men were extinguishing, and at which Raoul recognized the demons whom Christine had seen at the time of her first captivity.

In this way, they gradually arrived beneath the huge cellars below the stage. They must at this time have been at the very bottom of the "tub" and at an extremely great depth, when we remember that the earth was dug out at fifty feet below the water that lay under the whole of that part of Paris.*

The Persian touched a partition-wall and said:

"If I am not mistaken, this is a wall that might easily belong to the house on the lake."

* All the water had to be exhausted, in the building of the Opera. To give an idea of the amount of water that was pumped up, I can tell the reader that it represented the area of the court-yard of the Louvre and a height half as deep again as the towers of Notre Dame. And nevertheless the engineers had to leave a lake.

He was striking a partition-wall of the "tub," and perhaps it would be as well for the reader to know how the bottom and the partition-walls of the tub were built. In order to prevent the water surrounding the building-operations from remaining in immediate contact with the walls supporting the whole of the theatrical machinery, the architect was obliged to build a double case in every direction. The work of constructing this double case took a whole year. It was the wall of the first inner case that the Persian struck when speaking to Raoul of the house on the lake. To any one understanding the architecture of the edifice, the Persian's action would seem to indicate that Erik's mysterious house had been built in the double case, formed of a thick wall constructed as an embankment or dam, then of a brick wall, a tremendous layer of cement and another wall several yards in thickness.

At the Persian's words, Raoul flung himself against the wall and listened eagerly. But he heard nothing, nothing. . . except distant steps sounding on the floor of the upper portions of the theater.

The Persian darkened his lantern again.

"Look out!" he said. "Keep your hand up! And silence! For we shall try another way of getting in."

And he led him to the little staircase by which they had come down lately.

They went up, stopping at each step, peering into the darkness and the silence, till they came to the third cellar. Here the Persian motioned to Raoul to go on his knees; and, in this way, crawling on both knees and one hand—for the other hand was held in the position indicated—they reached the end wall.

Against this wall stood a large discarded scene from the *Roi de Lahore*. Close to this scene was a set piece. Between the scene and the set piece there was just room for a body . . . for a body which one day was found hanging there. The body of Joseph Buquet.

The Persian, still kneeling, stopped and listened. For a moment, he seemed to hesitate and looked at Raoul; then he turned his eyes upward, toward the second cellar, which sent down the faint glimmer of a lantern, through a cranny between two boards. This glimmer seemed to trouble the Persian.

At last, he tossed his head and made up his mind to act. He slipped between the set piece and the scene from the *Roi de Lahore*, with Raoul close upon his heels. With his free hand, the Persian felt the wall. Raoul saw him bear heavily upon the wall, just as he had pressed against the wall in Christine's dressing-room. Then a stone gave way, leaving a hole in the wall.

This time, the Persian took his pistol from his pocket and made a sign to Raoul to do as he did. He cocked the pistol.

And, resolutely, still on his knees, he wiggled through the hole in the wall. Raoul, who had wished to pass first, had to be content to follow him.

The hole was very narrow. The Persian stopped almost at once. Raoul heard him feeling the stones around him. Then the Persian took out his dark lantern again, stooped forward, examined something beneath him and immediately extinguished his lantern. Raoul heard him say, in a whisper:

"We shall have to drop a few yards, without making a noise; take off your boots."

The Persian handed his own shoes to Raoul.

"Put them outside the wall," he said. "We shall find them there when we leave."*

He crawled a little farther on his knees, then turned right round and said:

"I am going to hang by my hands from the edge of the stone and let myself drop *into his house*. You must do exactly the same. Do not be afraid. I will catch you in my arms."

Raoul soon heard a dull sound, evidently produced by the fall of the Persian, and then dropped down.

He felt himself clasped in the Persian's arms.

"Hush!" said the Persian.

And they stood motionless, listening.

The darkness was thick around them, the silence heavy and terrible.

Then the Persian began to make play with the dark lantern again, turning the rays over their heads, looking for the hole through which they had come, and failing to find it:

"Oh!" he said. "The stone has closed of itself!"

And the light of the lantern swept down the wall and over the floor.

The Persian stooped and picked up something, a sort of cord, which he examined for a second and flung away with horror.

"The Punjab lasso!" he muttered.

"What is it?" asked Raoul.

The Persian shivered. "It might very well be the rope by which the man was hanged, and which was looked for so long."

And, suddenly seized with fresh anxiety, he moved the little red disk of his lantern over the walls. In this way, he lit up a curious thing: the trunk of a tree, which seemed still quite alive, with its leaves; and the branches of that tree ran right up the walls and disappeared in the ceiling.

* These two pairs of boots, which were placed, according to the Persian's papers, just between the set piece and the scene from the *Roi de Lahore*, on the spot where Joseph Buquet was found hanging, were never discovered. They must have been taken by some stage-carpenter or "door-shutter."

Because of the smallness of the luminous disk, it was difficult at first to make out the appearance of things: they saw a corner of a branch . . . and a leaf . . . and another leaf. . . and, next to it, nothing at all, nothing but the ray of light that seemed to reflect itself. . . . Raoul passed his hand over that nothing, over that reflection.

"Hullo!" he said. "The wall is a looking-glass!"

"Yes, a looking-glass!" said the Persian, in a tone of deep emotion. And, passing the hand that held the pistol over his moist forehead, he added, "We have dropped into the torture-chamber!"

What the Persian knew of this torture-chamber and what there befell him and his companion shall be told in his own words, as set down in a manuscript which he left behind him, and which I copy *verbatim*.

XXI

INTERESTING AND INSTRUCTIVE VICISSITUDES OF A PERSIAN IN THE CELLARS OF THE OPERA

THE PERSIAN'S NARRATIVE

IT WAS THE FIRST TIME THAT I ENTERED THE HOUSE ON THE LAKE. I had often begged the "trap-door lover," as we used to call Erik in my country, to open its mysterious doors to me. He always refused. I made very many attempts, but in vain, to obtain admittance. Watch him as I might, after I first learned that he had taken up his permanent abode at the Opera, the darkness was always too thick to enable me to see how he worked the door in the wall on the lake. One day, when I thought myself alone, I stepped into the boat and rowed toward that part of the wall through which I had seen Erik disappear. It was then that I came into contact with the siren who guarded the approach and whose charm was very nearly fatal to me.

I had no sooner put off from the bank than the silence amid which I floated on the water was disturbed by a sort of whispered singing that hovered all around me. It was half breath, half music; it rose softly from the waters of the lake; and I was surrounded by it through I knew not what artifice. It followed me, moved with me and was so soft that it did not alarm me. On the contrary, in my longing to approach the source of that sweet and enticing harmony, I leaned out of my little boat over the water, for there was no doubt in my mind that the singing came from the water itself. By this time, I was alone in the boat in the middle of the lake; the voice—for it was now distinctly a voice—was beside me, on the water. I leaned over, leaned still farther. The lake was perfectly calm, and a moonbeam that passed through the air hole in the Rue Scribe showed me absolutely nothing on its surface, which was smooth and black as ink. I shook my ears to get rid of a possible humming; but I soon had to accept the fact that there was no humming in the ears so harmonious as the singing whisper that followed and now attracted me.

Had I been inclined to superstition, I should have certainly thought that I had to do with some siren whose business it was to confound the traveler who should venture on the waters of the house on the lake. Fortunately, I come from a country where we are too fond of fantastic things not to know them through and through; and I had no doubt but that I was face to face with some new invention of Erik's. But this invention was so perfect that, as I leaned out of the boat, I was impelled less by a desire to discover its trick than to enjoy its charm; and I leaned out, leaned out until I almost overturned the boat.

Suddenly, two monstrous arms issued from the bosom of the waters and seized me by the neck, dragging me down to the depths with irresistible force.

I should certainly have been lost, if I had not had time to give a cry by which Erik knew me. For it was he; and, instead of drowning me, as was certainly his first intention, he swam with me and laid me gently on the bank:

"How imprudent you are!" he said, as he stood before me, dripping with water. "Why try to enter my house? I never invited you! I don't want you there, nor anybody! Did you save my life only to make it unbearable to me? However great the service you rendered him, Erik may end by forgetting it; and you know that nothing can restrain Erik, not even Erik himself."

He spoke, but I had now no other wish than to know what I already called the trick of the siren. He satisfied my curiosity, for Erik, who is a real monster—I have seen him at work in Persia, alas—is also, in certain respects, a regular child, vain and self-conceited, and there is nothing he loves so much, after astonishing people, as to prove all the really miraculous ingenuity of his mind.

He laughed and showed me a long reed.

"It's the silliest trick you ever saw," he said, "but it's very useful for breathing and singing in the water. I learned it from the Tonkin pirates, who are able to remain hidden for hours in the beds of the rivers."*

I spoke to him severely.

* An official report from Tonkin, received in Paris at the end of July, 1909, relates how the famous pirate chief De Tham was tracked, together with his men, by our soldiers; and how all of them succeeded in escaping, thanks to this trick of the reeds.

"It's a trick that nearly killed me!" I said. "And it may have been fatal to others! You know what you promised me, Erik? No more murders!"

"Have I really committed murders?" he asked, putting on his most amiable air.

"Wretched man!" I cried. "Have you forgotten the rosy hours of Mazenderan?"

"Yes," he replied, in a sadder tone, "I prefer to forget them. I used to make the little sultana laugh, though!"

"All that belongs to the past," I declared; "but there is the present. . .and you are responsible to me for the present, because, if I had wished, there would have been none at all for you. Remember that, Erik: I saved your life!"

And I took advantage of the turn of conversation to speak to him of something that had long been on my mind:

"Erik," I asked, "Erik, swear that. . ."

"What?" he retorted. "You know I never keep my oaths. Oaths are made to catch gulls with."

"Tell me. . .you can tell me, at any rate. . . ."

"Well?"

"Well, the chandelier…the chandelier, Erik?. . ."

"What about the chandelier?"

"You know what I mean."

"Oh," he sniggered, "I don't mind telling you about the chandelier! . . . *It wasn't I*! . . . The chandelier was very old and worn."

When Erik laughed, he was more terrible than ever. He jumped into the boat, chuckling so horribly that I could not help trembling.

"Very old and worn, my dear daroga!* Very old and worn, the chandelier! . . . It fell of itself! . . . It came down with a smash! . . .And now, daroga, take my advice and go and dry yourself, or you'll catch a cold in the head! . . . And never get into my boat again. . . . And, whatever you do, don't try to enter my house: I'm not always there. . . daroga! And I should be sorry to have to dedicate my Requiem Mass to you!"

So saying, swinging to and fro, like a monkey, and still chuckling, he pushed off and soon disappeared in the darkness of the lake.

From that day, I gave up all thought of penetrating into his house by the lake. That entrance was obviously too well guarded, especially since he had learned that I knew about it. But I felt that there must be another entrance, for I had often seen Erik disappear in the third cellar, when I was watching him, though I could not imagine how.

* Daroga is Persian for chief of police.

Ever since I had discovered Erik installed in the Opera, I lived in a perpetual terror of his horrible fancies, not in so far as I was concerned, but I dreaded everything for others.* And whenever some accident, some fatal event happened, I always thought to myself, "I should not be surprised if that were Erik," even as others used to say, "It's the ghost!" How often have I not heard people utter that phrase with a smile! Poor devils! If they had known that the ghost existed in the flesh, I swear they would not have laughed!

Although Erik announced to me very solemnly that he had changed and that he had become the most virtuous of men *since he was loved for himself*—a sentence that, at first, perplexed me most terribly—I could not help shuddering when I thought of the monster. His horrible, unparalleled and repulsive ugliness put him without the pale of humanity; and it often seemed to me that, for this reason, he no longer believed that he had any duty toward the human race. The way in which he spoke of his love-affairs only increased my alarm, for I foresaw the cause of fresh and more hideous tragedies in this event to which he alluded so boastfully.

On the other hand, I soon discovered the curious moral traffic established between the monster and Christine Daaé. Hiding in the lumber-room next to the young prima donna's dressing-room, I listened to wonderful musical displays that evidently flung Christine into marvelous ecstasy; but, all the same, I would never have thought that Erik's voice—which was loud as thunder or soft as angels' voices, at will—could have made her forget his ugliness. I understood all when I learned that Christine had not yet seen him! I had occasion to go to the dressing-room and, remembering the lessons he had once given me, I had no difficulty in discovering the trick that made the wall with the mirror swing round and I ascertained the means—of hollow bricks and so on—by which he made his voice carry to Christine as though she heard it close beside her. In this way also I discovered the road that led to the well and the dungeon—the Communists' dungeon—and also the trap-door that enabled Erik to go straight to the cellars below the stage.

A few days later, what was not my amazement to learn by my own eyes and ears that Erik and Christine Daaé saw each other and to catch the monster stooping over the little well, in the Communists' road and sprinkling the forehead of Christine Daaé, who had fainted. A white horse, the horse out of the *Profeta*, which had disappeared from the stables under the Opera, was standing quietly beside them.

* The Persian might easily have admitted that Erik's fate also interested himself, for he was well aware that, if the government of Teheran had learned that Erik was still alive, it would have been all up with the modest pension of the erstwhile daroga. It is only fair, however, to add that the Persian had a noble and generous heart; and I do not doubt for a moment that the catastrophes which he feared for others greatly occupied his mind. His conduct, throughout this business, proves it and is above all praise.

I showed myself. It was terrible. I saw sparks fly from those yellow eyes and, before I had time to say a word, I received a blow on the head that stunned me.

When I came to myself, Erik, Christine and the white horse had disappeared. I felt sure that the poor girl was a prisoner in the house on the lake. Without hesitation, I resolved to return to the bank, notwithstanding the attendant danger. For twenty-four hours, I lay in wait for the monster to appear; for I felt that he must go out, driven by the need of obtaining provisions. And, in this connection, I may say, that, when he went out in the streets or ventured to show himself in public, he wore a pasteboard nose, with a mustache attached to it, instead of his own horrible hole of a nose. This did not quite take away his corpse-like air, but it made him almost, I say almost, endurable to look at.

I therefore watched on the bank of the lake and, weary of long waiting, was beginning to think that he had gone through the other door, the door in the third cellar, when I heard a slight splashing in the dark, I saw the two yellow eyes shining like candles and soon the boat touched shore. Erik jumped out and walked up to me:

"You've been here for twenty-four hours," he said, "and you're annoying me. I tell you, all this will end very badly. And you will have brought it upon yourself; for I have been extraordinarily patient with you. You think you are following me, you great booby, whereas it's I who am following you; and I know all that you know about me, here. I spared you yesterday, in *my Communists' road*; but I warn you, seriously, don't let me catch you there again! Upon my word, you don't seem able to take a hint!"

He was so furious that I did not think, for the moment, of interrupting him. After puffing and blowing like a walrus, he put his horrible thought into words:

"Yes, you must learn, once and for all—once and for all, I say—to take a hint! I tell you that, with your recklessness—for you have already been twice arrested by the shade in the felt hat, who did not know what you were doing in the cellars and took you to the managers, who looked upon you as an eccentric Persian interested in stage mechanism and life behind the scenes: I know all about it, I was there, in the office; you know I am everywhere—well, I tell you that, with your recklessness, they will end by wondering what you are after here . . . and they will end by knowing that you are after Erik. . . and then they will be after Erik themselves and they will discover the house on the lake. . . . If they do, it will be a bad lookout for you, old chap, a bad lookout! . . . I won't answer for anything."

Again he puffed and blew like a walrus.

"I won't answer for anything! . . . If Erik's secrets cease to be Erik's secrets, *it will be a bad lookout for a goodly number of the human race*! That's all I have to tell you, and unless you are a great booby, it ought to be enough for you . . . except that you don't know how to take a hint."

He had sat down on the stern of his boat and was kicking his heels against the planks, waiting to hear what I had to answer. I simply said:

"It's not Erik that I'm after here!"

"Who then?"

"You know as well as I do: It's Christine Daaé," I answered.

He retorted: "I have every right to see her in my own house. I am loved for my own sake."

"That's not true," I said. "You have carried her off and are keeping her locked up."

"Listen," he said. "Will you promise never to meddle with my affairs again, if I prove to you that I am loved for my own sake?"

"Yes, I promise you," I replied, without hesitation, for I felt convinced that for such a monster the proof was impossible.

"Well, then, it's quite simple. . . . Christine Daaé shall leave this as she pleases and come back again! . . . Yes, come back again, because she wishes . . . come back of herself, because she loves me for myself! . . ."

"Oh, I doubt if she will come back! . . . But it is your duty to let her go."

"My duty, you great booby! . . . It is my wish. . . my wish to let her go; and she will come back again. . . for she loves me! . . . All this will end in a marriage . . . a marriage at the Madeleine, you great booby! Do you believe me now? When I tell you that my nuptial mass is written . . . wait till you hear the *Kyrie*. . . ."

He beat time with his heels on the planks of the boat and sang:

"*Kyrie!* . . . *Kyrie!* . . . *Kyrie eleison!* . . . Wait till you hear, wait till you hear that mass."

"Look here," I said. "I shall believe you if I see Christine Daaé come out of the house on the lake and go back to it of her own accord."

"And you won't meddle any more in my affairs?"

"No."

"Very well, you shall see that to-night. Come to the masked ball. Christine and I will go and have a look round. Then you can hide in the lumber-room and you shall see Christine, who will have gone to her dressing-room, delighted to come back by the Communists' road. . . . And, now, be off, for I must go and do some shopping!"

To my intense astonishment, things happened as he had announced. Christine Daaé left the house on the lake and returned to it several times, without, apparently, being forced to do so. It was very difficult for me to clear my mind of Erik. However, I resolved to be extremely prudent, and did not make the mistake of returning to the shore of the lake, or of going by the Communists' road. But the idea of the secret entrance in the third cellar haunted me, and I repeatedly went and waited for hours behind a scene from the *Roi de Lahore,* which had been left there for some reason or other. At last my patience was rewarded. One day, I saw the monster come toward me, on his knees. I was certain that he could not see me. He passed between the scene behind which I stood and a set piece, went to the wall and pressed on a spring that moved a stone and afforded him an ingress. He passed through this, and the stone closed behind him.

I waited for at least thirty minutes and then pressed the spring in my turn. Everything happened as with Erik. But I was careful not to go through the hole myself, for I knew that Erik was inside. On the other hand, the idea that I might be caught by Erik suddenly made me think of the death of Joseph Buquet. I did not wish to jeopardize the advantages of so great a discovery which might be useful to many people, "to a goodly number of the human race," in Erik's words; and I left the cellars of the Opera after carefully replacing the stone.

I continued to be greatly interested in the relations between Erik and Christine Daaé, not from any morbid curiosity, but because of the terrible thought which obsessed my mind that Erik was capable of anything, if he once discovered that he was not loved for his own sake, as he imagined. I continued to wander, very cautiously, about the Opera and soon learned the truth about the monster's dreary love-affair.

He filled Christine's mind, through the terror with which he inspired her, but the dear child's heart belonged wholly to the Vicomte Raoul de Chagny. While they played about, like an innocent engaged couple, on the upper floors of the Opera, to avoid the monster, they little suspected that some one was watching over them. I was prepared to do anything: to kill the monster, if necessary, and explain to the police afterward. But Erik did not show himself; and I felt none the more comfortable for that.

I must explain my whole plan. I thought that the monster, being driven from his house by jealousy, would thus enable me to enter it, without danger, through the passage in the third cellar. It was important, for everybody's sake, that I should know exactly what was inside. One day, tired of waiting for an opportunity, I moved the stone and at once heard an astounding music: the monster was working at his *Don Juan Triumphant*, with every door in his house wide open. I knew that this was the work of his life. I was careful not to stir and remained prudently in my dark hole.

He stopped playing, for a moment, and began walking about his place, like a madman. And he said aloud, at the top of his voice:

"It must be finished *first*! Quite finished!"

This speech was not calculated to reassure me and, when the music recommenced, I closed the stone very softly.

On the day of the abduction of Christine Daaé, I did not come to the theater until rather late in the evening, trembling lest I should hear bad news. I had spent a horrible day, for, after reading in a morning paper the announcement of a forthcoming marriage between Christine and the Vicomte de Chagny, I wondered whether, after all, I should not do better to denounce the monster. But reason returned to me, and I was persuaded that this action could only precipitate a possible catastrophe.

When my cab set me down before the Opera, I was really almost astonished to see it still standing! But I am something of a fatalist, like all good Orientals, and I entered ready for anything.

Christine Daaé's abduction in the Prison Act, which naturally surprised everybody, found me prepared. I was quite certain that she had been juggled away by Erik, that prince of conjurers. And I thought positively that this was the end of Christine and perhaps of everybody, so much so that I thought of advising all these people who were staying on at the theater to make good their escape. I felt, however, that they would be sure to look upon me as mad and I refrained.

On the other hand, I resolved to act without further delay, as far as I was concerned. The chances were in my favor that Erik, at that moment, was thinking only of his captive. This was the moment to enter his house through the third cellar; and I resolved to take with me that poor little desperate viscount, who, at the first suggestion, accepted, with an amount of confidence in myself that touched me profoundly. I had sent my servant for my pistols. I gave one to the viscount and advised him to hold himself ready to fire, for, after all, Erik might be waiting for us behind the wall. We were to go by the Communists' road and through the trap-door.

Seeing my pistols, the little viscount asked me if we were going to fight a duel. I said:

"Yes; and what a duel!"

But, of course, I had no time to explain anything to him. The little viscount is a brave fellow, but he knew hardly anything about his adversary; and it was so much the better. My great fear was that he was already somewhere near us, preparing the Punjab lasso. No one knows better than he how to throw the Punjab lasso, for he is the king of stranglers even as he is the prince of conjurors. When he had finished making the little sultana laugh, at the time of the "rosy hours of Mazenderan," she herself used to ask him to amuse her by giving her a thrill. It was then that he introduced the sport of the Punjab lasso.

He had lived in India and acquired an incredible skill in the art of strangulation. He would make them lock him into a courtyard to which they brought a warrior—usually, a man condemned to death—armed with a long pike and broadsword. Erik had only his lasso; and it was always just when the warrior thought that he was going to fell Erik with a tremendous blow that we heard the lasso whistle through the air. With a turn of the wrist, Erik tightened the noose round his adversary's neck and, in this fashion, dragged him before the little sultana and her women, who sat looking from a window and applauding. The little sultana herself learned to wield the Punjab lasso and killed several of her women and even of the friends who visited her. But I prefer to drop this terrible subject of the rosy hours of Mazenderan. I have mentioned it only to explain why, on arriving with the Vicomte de Chagny in the cellars of the Opera, I was bound to protect my companion against the ever-threatening danger of death by strangling. My pistols could serve no purpose, for Erik was not likely to show himself; but Erik could always strangle us. I had no time to explain all this to the viscount; besides, there was nothing to be gained by complicating the position. I simply told M. de Chagny to keep his hand at the level of his eyes, with the arm bent, as though waiting for the command to fire. With his victim in this attitude, it is impossible even for the most expert strangler to throw the lasso with advantage. It catches you not only round the neck, but also round the arm or hand. This enables you easily to unloose the lasso, which then becomes harmless.

After avoiding the commissary of police, a number of door-shutters and the firemen, after meeting the rat-catcher and passing the man in the felt hat unperceived, the viscount and I arrived without obstacle in the third cellar, between the set piece and the scene from the *Roi de Lahore*. I worked the stone, and we jumped into the house which Erik had built himself in the double case of the foundation-walls of the Opera. And this was the easiest thing in the world for him to do, because Erik was one of the chief contractors under Philippe Gamier, the architect of the Opera, and continued to work by himself when the works were officially suspended, during the war, the siege of Paris and the Commune.

I knew my Erik too well to feel at all comfortable on jumping into his house. I knew what he had made of a certain palace at Mazenderan. From being the most honest building conceivable, he soon turned it into a house of the very devil, where you could not utter a word but it was overheard or repeated by an echo. With his trap-doors the monster was responsible for endless tragedies of all kinds. He hit upon astonishing inventions. Of these, the most curious, horrible and dangerous was the so-called torture-chamber. Except in special cases, when the little sultana amused herself by inflicting suffering upon some unoffending citizen, no one was let into it but wretches condemned to death. And, even then, when these had "had enough," they were always at liberty to put an end to themselves with a Punjab lasso or bowstring, left for their use at the foot of an iron tree.

My alarm, therefore, was great when I saw that the room into which M. le Vicomte de Chagny and I had dropped was an exact copy of the torture-chamber of the rosy hours of Mazenderan. At our feet, I found the Punjab lasso which I had been dreading all the evening. I was convinced that this rope had already done duty for Joseph Buquet, who, like myself, must have caught Erik one evening working the stone in the third cellar. He probably tried it in his turn, fell into the torture-chamber and only left it hanged. I can well imagine Erik dragging the body, in order to get rid of it, to the scene from the *Roi de Lahore*, and hanging it there as an example, or to increase the superstitious terror that was to help him in guarding the approaches to his lair! Then, upon reflection, Erik went back to fetch the Punjab lasso, which is very curiously made out of catgut, and which might have set an examining magistrate thinking. This explains the disappearance of the rope.

And now I discovered the lasso, at our feet, in the torture-chamber! . . . I am no coward, but a cold sweat covered my forehead as I moved the little red disk of my lantern over the walls.

M. de Chagny noticed it and asked:

"What is the matter, sir?"

I made him a violent sign to be silent.

XXII

IN THE TORTURE CHAMBER
The Persian's Narrative Continued

We were in the middle of a little six-cornered room, the sides of which were covered with mirrors from top to bottom. In the corners, we could clearly see the "joins" in the glasses, the segments intended to turn on their gear; yes, I recognized them and I recognized the iron tree in the corner, at the bottom of one of those segments . . . the iron tree, with its iron branch, for the hanged men.

I seized my companion's arm: the Vicomte de Chagny was all a-quiver, eager to shout to his betrothed that he was bringing her help. I feared that he would not be able to contain himself.

Suddenly, we heard a noise on our left. It sounded at first like a door opening and shutting in the next room; and then there was a dull moan. I clutched M. de Chagny's arm more firmly still; and then we distinctly heard these words:

"You must make your choice! The wedding mass or the requiem mass!"

I recognized the voice of the monster.

There was another moan, followed by a long silence.

I was persuaded by now that the monster was unaware of our presence in his house, for otherwise he would certainly have managed not to let us hear him. He would only have had to close the little invisible window through which the torture-lovers look down into the torture-chamber. Besides, I was certain that, if he had known of our presence, the tortures would have begun at once.

The important thing was not to let him know; and I dreaded nothing so much as the impulsiveness of the Vicomte de Chagny, who wanted to rush through the walls to Christine Daaé, whose moans we continued to hear at intervals.

"The requiem mass is not at all gay," Erik's voice resumed, "whereas the wedding mass—you can take my word for it—is magnificent! You must take a resolution and know your own mind! I can't go on living like this, like a mole in a burrow! *Don Juan Triumphant* is finished; and now I want to live like everybody else. I want to have a wife like everybody else and to take her out on Sundays. I have invented a mask that makes me look like anybody. People will not even turn round in the streets. You will be the happiest of women. And we will sing, all by ourselves, till we swoon away with delight. You are crying! You are afraid of me! And yet I am not really wicked. Love me and you shall see! All I wanted was to be loved for myself. If you loved me I should be as gentle as a lamb; and you could do anything with me that you pleased."

Soon the moans that accompanied this sort of love's litany increased and increased. I have never heard anything more despairing; and M. de Chagny and I recognized that this terrible lamentation came from Erik himself. Christine seemed to be standing dumb with horror, without the strength to cry out, while the monster was on his knees before her.

Three times over, Erik fiercely bewailed his fate:

"You don't love me! You don't love me! You don't love me!"

And then, more gently:

"Why do you cry? You know it gives me pain to see you cry!"

A silence.

Each silence gave us fresh hope. We said to ourselves:

"Perhaps he has left Christine behind the wall."

And we thought only of the possibility of warning Christine Daaé of our presence, unknown to the monster. We were unable to leave the torture-chamber now, unless Christine opened the door to us; and it was only on this condition that we could hope to help her, for we did not even know where the door might be.

Suddenly, the silence in the next room was disturbed by the ringing of an electric bell. There was a bound on the other side of the wall and Erik's voice of thunder:

"Somebody ringing! Walk in, please!"

A sinister chuckle.

"Who has come bothering now? Wait for me here.... *I am going to tell the siren to open the door*."

Steps moved away, a door closed. I had no time to think of the fresh horror that was preparing; I forgot that the monster was only going out perhaps to perpetrate a fresh crime; I understood but one thing: Christine was alone behind the wall!

The Vicomte de Chagny was already calling to her:

"Christine! Christine!"

As we could hear what was said in the next room, there was no reason why my companion should not be heard in his turn. Nevertheless, the viscount had to repeat his cry time after time.

At last, a faint voice reached us.

"I am dreaming!" it said.

"Christine, Christine, it is I, Raoul!"

A silence.

"But answer me, Christine! . . .In Heaven's name, if you are alone, answer me!"

Then Christine's voice whispered Raoul's name.

"Yes! Yes! It is I! It is not a dream! . . .Christine, trust me! . . .We are here to save you. . .but be prudent! When you hear the monster, warn us!"

Then Christine gave way to fear. She trembled lest Erik should discover where Raoul was hidden; she told us in a few hurried words that Erik had gone quite mad with love and that he had decided *to kill everybody and himself with everybody* if she did not consent to become his wife. He had given her till eleven o'clock the next evening for reflection. It was the last respite. She must choose, as he said, between the wedding mass and the requiem.

And Erik had then uttered a phrase which Christine did not quite understand:

"Yes or no! If your answer is no, everybody will be dead *and buried*!"

But I understood the sentence perfectly, for it corresponded in a terrible manner with my own dreadful thought.

"Can you tell us where Erik is?" I asked.

She replied that he must have left the house.

"Could you make sure?"

"No. I am fastened. I can not stir a limb."

When we heard this, M. de Chagny and I gave a yell of fury. Our safety, the safety of all three of us, depended on the girl's liberty of movement.

"But where are you?" asked Christine. "There are only two doors in my room, the Louis-Philippe room of which I told you, Raoul; a door through which Erik comes and goes, and another which he has never opened before me and which he has forbidden me ever to go through, because he says it is the most dangerous of the doors, the door of the torture-chamber!"

"Christine, that is where we are!"

"You are in the torture-chamber?"

"Yes, but we can not see the door."

"Oh, if I could only drag myself so far! I would knock at the door and that would tell you where it is."

"Is it a door with a lock to it?" I asked.

"Yes, with a lock."

"Mademoiselle," I said, "it is absolutely necessary that you should open that door to us!"

"But how?" asked the poor girl tearfully.

We heard her straining, trying to free herself from the bonds that held her.

"I know where the key is," she said, in a voice that seemed exhausted by the effort she had made. "But I am fastened so tight. . . . Oh, the wretch!"

And she gave a sob.

"Where is the key?" I asked, signing to M. de Chagny not to speak and to leave the business to me, for we had not a moment to lose.

"In the next room, near the organ, with another little bronze key, which he also forbade me to touch. They are both in a little leather bag which he calls the bag of life and death. . . . Raoul! Raoul! Fly! Everything is mysterious and terrible here, and Erik will soon have gone quite mad, and you are in the torture-chamber! . . . Go back by the way you came. There must be a reason why the room is called by that name!"

"Christine," said the young man, "we will go from here together or die together!"

"We must keep cool," I whispered. "Why has he fastened you, mademoiselle? You can't escape from his house; and he knows it!"

"I tried to commit suicide! The monster went out last night, after carrying me here fainting and half chloroformed. He was going to his banker, so he said! . . . When he returned he found me with my face covered with blood. . . . I had tried to kill myself by striking my forehead against the walls."

"Christine!" groaned Raoul; and he began to sob.

"Then he bound me. . . . I am not allowed to die until eleven o'clock to-morrow evening."

"Mademoiselle," I declared, "the monster bound you. . .and he shall unbind you. You have only to play the necessary part! Remember that he loves you!"

"Alas!" we heard. "Am I likely to forget it!"

"Remember it and smile to him . . . entreat him . . . tell him that your bonds hurt you."

But Christine Daaé said:

"Hush! . . .I hear something in the wall on the lake! . . .It is he! . . .Go away! Go away! Go away!"

"We could not go away, even if we wanted to," I said, as impressively as I could. "We can not leave this! And we are in the torture-chamber!"

"Hush!" whispered Christine again.

Heavy steps sounded slowly behind the wall, then stopped and made the floor creak once more. Next came a tremendous sigh, followed by a cry of horror from Christine, and we heard Erik's voice:

"I beg your pardon for letting you see a face like this! What a state I am in, am I not? It's *the other one's fault*! Why did he ring? Do *I* ask people who pass to tell me the time? He will never ask anybody the time again! It is the siren's fault."

Another sigh, deeper, more tremendous still, came from the abysmal depths of a soul.

"Why did you cry out, Christine?"

"Because I am in pain, Erik."

"I thought I had frightened you."

"Erik, unloose my bonds. . . . Am I not your prisoner?"

"You will try to kill yourself again."

"You have given me till eleven o'clock to-morrow evening, Erik."

The footsteps dragged along the floor again.

"After all, as we are to die together . . . and I am just as eager as you . . . yes, I have had enough of this life, you know. . . . Wait, don't move, I will release you. . . . You have only one word to say: '*No*!' And it will at once be over *with everybody*! . . . You are right, you are right; why wait till eleven o'clock to-morrow evening? True, it would have been grander, finer. . . . But that is childish nonsense. . . We should only think of ourselves in this life, of our own death . . . the rest doesn't matter. . . . *You're looking at me because I am all wet*? . . . Oh, my dear, it's raining cats and dogs outside! . . . Apart from that, Christine, I think I am subject to hallucinations. . . . You know, the man who rang at the siren's door just now—go and look if he's ringing at the bottom of the lake-well, he was rather like. . . . There, turn round . . . are you glad? You're free now. . . . Oh, my poor Christine, look at your wrists: tell me, have I hurt them? . . . That alone deserves death. . . . Talking of death, *I* must sing his requiem!"

Hearing these terrible remarks, I received an awful presentiment. . . I too had once rung at the monster's door. . . and, without knowing it, must have set some warning current in motion. . . . And I remembered the two arms that had emerged from the inky waters. . . . What poor wretch had strayed to that shore this time? Who was "the other one," the one whose requiem we now heard sung?

Erik sang like the god of thunder, sang a *Dies Iræ* that enveloped us as in a storm. The elements seemed to rage around us. Suddenly, the organ and the voice ceased so suddenly that M. de Chagny sprang back, on the other side of the wall, with emotion. And the voice, changed and transformed, distinctly grated out these metallic syllables:

"*What have you done with my bag?*"

XXIII

THE TORTURES BEGIN

THE PERSIAN'S NARRATIVE CONTINUED

THE VOICE REPEATED ANGRILY: "WHAT HAVE YOU DONE WITH MY BAG? So it was to take my bag that you asked me to release you!"

We heard hurried steps, Christine running back to the Louis-Philippe room, as though to seek shelter on the other side of our wall.

"What are you running away for?" asked the furious voice, which had followed her. "Give me back my bag, will you? Don't you know that it is the bag of life and death?"

"Listen to me, Erik," sighed the girl. "As it is settled that we are to live together. . .what difference can it make to you?"

"You know there are only two keys in it," said the monster. "What do you want to do?"

"I want to look at this room which I have never seen and which you have always kept from me. . . It's woman's curiosity!" she said, in a tone which she tried to render playful.

But the trick was too childish for Erik to be taken in by it.

"I don't like curious women," he retorted, "and you had better remember the story of *Blue-Beard* and be careful. . . . Come, give me back my bag! . . . Give me back my bag! . . . Leave the key alone, will you, you inquisitive little thing?"

And he chuckled, while Christine gave a cry of pain. Erik had evidently recovered the bag from her.

At that moment, the viscount could not help uttering an exclamation of impotent rage.

"Why, what's that?" said the monster. "Did you hear, Christine?"

"No, no," replied the poor girl. "I heard nothing."

"I thought I heard a cry."

"A cry! Are you going mad, Erik? Whom do you expect to give a cry, in this house? . . . I cried out, because you hurt me! I heard nothing."

"I don't like the way you said that! . . . You're trembling. . . . You're quite excited. . . . You're lying! . . . That was a cry, there was a cry! . . . There is some one in the torture-chamber! . . . Ah, I understand now!"

"There is no one there, Erik!"

"I understand!"

"No one!"

"The man you want to marry, perhaps!"

"I don't want to marry anybody, you know I don't."

Another nasty chuckle.

"Well, it won't take long to find out. Christine, my love, we need not open the door to see what is happening in the torture-chamber. Would you like to see? Would you like to see? Look here! If there is some one, if there is really some one there, you will see the invisible window light up at the top, near the ceiling. We need only draw the black curtain and put out the light in here. There, that's it. . . . Let's put out the light! You're not afraid of the dark, when you're with your little husband!"

Then we heard Christine's voice of anguish:

"No! . . . I'm frightened! . . . I tell you, I'm afraid of the dark! . . . I don't care about that room now. . . . You're always frightening me, like a child, with your torture-chamber! . . . And so I became inquisitive. . . . But I don't care about it now . . . not a bit . . . not a bit!"

And that which I feared above all things began, *automatically*. We were suddenly flooded with light! Yes, on our side of the wall, everything seemed aglow. The Vicomte de Chagny was so much taken aback that he staggered. And the angry voice roared:

"I told you there was some one! Do you see the window now? The lighted window, right up there? The man behind the wall can't see it! But you shall go up the folding steps: that is what they are there for! . . . You have often asked me to tell you; and now you know! . . . They are there to give a peep into the torture-chamber . . . you inquisitive little thing!"

"What tortures? . . . Who is being tortured? . . . Erik, Erik, say you are only trying to frighten me! . . . Say it, if you love me, Erik! . . . There are no tortures, are there?"

"Go and look at the little window, dear!"

I do not know if the viscount heard the girl's swooning voice, for he was too much occupied by the astounding spectacle that now appeared before his distracted gaze. As for me, I had seen that sight too often, through the little window, at the time of the rosy hours of Mazenderan; and I cared only for what was being said next door, seeking for a hint how to act, what resolution to take.

"Go and peep through the little window! Tell me what he looks like!"

We heard the steps being dragged against the wall.

"Up with you! . . . No! . . . No, I will go up myself, dear!"

"Oh, very well, I will go up. Let me go!"

"Oh, my darling, my darling! . . . How sweet of you! . . . How nice of you to save me the exertion at my age! . . . Tell me what he looks like!"

At that moment, we distinctly heard these words above our heads:

"There is no one there, dear!"

"No one? . . . Are you sure there is no one?"

"Why, of course not . . . no one!"

"Well, that's all right! . . . What's the matter, Christine? You're not going to faint, are you. . .as there is no one there? . . . Here . . . come down . . . there! . . . Pull yourself together . . . as there is no one there! . . . *But how do you like the landscape?*"

"Oh, very much!"

"There, that's better! . . . You're better now, are you not? . . . That's all right, you're better! . . . No excitement! . . . And what a funny house, isn't it, with landscapes like that in it?"

"Yes, it's like the Musée Grévin. . . . But, I say, Erik . . . there are no tortures in there! . . . What a fright you gave me!"

"Why . . . as there is no one there?"

"Did you design that room? It's very handsome. You're a great artist, Erik."

"Yes, a great artist, in my own line."

"But tell me, Erik, why did you call that room the torture-chamber?"

"Oh, it's very simple. First of all, what did you see?"

"I saw a forest."

"And what is in a forest?"

"Trees."

"And what is in a tree?"

"Birds."

"Did you see any birds?"

"No, I did not see any birds."

"Well, what did you see? Think! You saw branches! And what are the branches?" asked the terrible voice. "*There's a gibbet*! That is why I call my wood the torture-chamber! . . . You see, it's all a joke. I never express myself like other people. But I am very tired of it! . . . I'm sick and tired of having a forest and a torture-chamber in my house and of living like a mountebank, in a house with a false bottom! . . . I'm tired of it! I want to have a nice, quiet flat, with ordinary doors and windows and a wife inside it, like anybody else! A wife whom I could love and take out on Sundays and keep amused on week-days . . . Here, shall I show you some card-tricks? That will help us to pass a few minutes, while waiting for eleven o'clock to-morrow evening. . . . My dear little Christine! . . . Are you listening to me? . . . Tell me you love me! . . .

No, you don't love me . . . but no matter, you will! . . . Once, you could not look at my mask because you knew what was behind. . . . And now you don't mind looking at it and you forget what is behind! . . . One can get used to everything . . . if one wishes . . . . Plenty of young people who did not care for each other before marriage have adored each other since! Oh, I don't know what I am talking about! But you would have lots of fun with me. For instance, I am the greatest ventriloquist that ever lived, I am the first ventriloquist in the world! . . . You're laughing. . . . Perhaps you don't believe me? Listen."

The wretch, who really was the first ventriloquist in the world, was only trying to divert the child's attention from the torture-chamber; but it was a stupid scheme, for Christine thought of nothing but us! She repeatedly besought him, in the gentlest tones which she could assume:

"Put out the light in the little window! . . . Erik, do put out the light in the little window!"

For she saw that this light, which appeared so suddenly and of which the monster had spoken in so threatening a voice, must mean something terrible. One thing must have pacified her for a moment; and that was seeing the two of us, behind the wall, in the midst of that resplendent light, alive and well. But she would certainly have felt much easier if the light had been put out.

Meantime, the other had already begun to play the ventriloquist. He said:

"Here, I raise my mask a little. . . . Oh, only a little! . . . You see my lips, such lips as I have? They're not moving! . . . My mouth is closed—such mouth as I have—and yet you hear my voice. . . . Where will you have it? In your left ear? In your right ear? In the table? In those little ebony boxes on the mantelpiece? . . . Listen, dear, it's in the little box on the right of the mantelpiece: what does it say? '*Shall I turn the scorpion?*'. . . And now, crack! What does it say in the little box on the left? '*Shall I turn the grasshopper?*'. . . And now, crack! Here it is in the little leather bag. . . . What does it say? '*I am the little hag of life and death!*'. . . And now, crack! It is in Carlotta's throat, in Carlotta's golden throat, in Carlotta's crystal throat, as I live! What does it say? It says, 'It's I, Mr. Toad, it's I singing! *I feel without alarm—co-ack—with its melody enwind me—co-ack!*' . . . And now, crack! It is on a chair in the ghost's box and it says, '*Madame Carlotta is singing to-night to bring the chandelier down!*' . . . And now, crack! Aha! Where is Erik's voice now? Listen, Christine, darling! Listen! It is behind the door of the torture-chamber! Listen! It's myself in the torture-chamber! And what do I say? I say, 'Woe to them that have a nose, a real nose, and come to look round the torture-chamber!' Aha, aha, aha!"

Oh, the ventriloquist's terrible voice! It was everywhere, everywhere. It passed through the little invisible window, through the walls. It ran around us, between us. Erik was there, speaking to us! We made a movement as though to fling ourselves upon him. But, already, swifter, more fleeting than the voice of the echo, Erik's voice had leaped back behind the wall!

Soon we heard nothing more at all, for this is what happened:

"Erik! Erik!" said Christine's voice. "You tire me with your voice. Don't go on, Erik! Isn't it very hot here?"

"Oh, yes," replied Erik's voice, "the heat is unendurable!"

"But what does this mean?. . .The wall is really getting quite hot! . . .The wall is burning! . . ."

"I'll tell you, Christine, dear: it is because of the forest next door."

"Well, what has that to do with it? The forest?"

"*Why, didn't you see that it was an African forest?*"

And the monster laughed so loudly and hideously that we could no longer distinguish Christine's supplicating cries! The Vicomte de Chagny shouted and banged against the walls like a madman, I could not restrain him. But we heard nothing except the monster's laughter, and the monster himself can have heard nothing else. And then there was the sound of a body falling on the floor and being dragged along and a door slammed and then nothing, nothing more around us save the scorching silence of the south in the heart of a tropical forest!

XXIV

"BARRELS! . . . BARRELS! . . . ANY BARRELS TO SELL?"

The Persian's Narrative Continued

I have said that the room in which M. le Vicomte de Chagny and I were imprisoned was a regular hexagon, lined entirely with mirrors. Plenty of these rooms have been seen since, mainly at exhibitions: they are called "palaces of illusion," or some such name. But the invention belongs entirely to Erik, who built the first room of this kind under my eyes, at the time of the rosy hours of Mazenderan. A decorative object, such as a column, for instance, was placed in one of the corners and immediately produced a hall of a thousand columns; for, thanks to the mirrors, the real room was multiplied by six hexagonal rooms, each of which, in its turn, was multiplied indefinitely. But the little sultana soon tired of this infantile illusion, whereupon Erik altered his invention into a "torture-chamber." For the architectural motive placed in one corner, he substituted an iron tree. This tree, with its painted leaves, was absolutely true to life and was made of iron so as to resist all the attacks of the "patient" who was locked into the torture-chamber. We shall see how the scene thus obtained was twice altered instantaneously into two successive other scenes, by means of the automatic rotation of the drums or rollers in the corners. These were divided into three sections, fitting into the angles of the mirrors and each supporting a decorative scheme that came into sight as the roller revolved upon its axis.

The walls of this strange room gave the patient nothing to lay hold of, because, apart from the solid decorative object, they were simply furnished with mirrors, thick enough to withstand any onslaught of the victim, who was flung into the chamber empty-handed and barefoot.

There was no furniture. The ceiling was capable of being lit up. An ingenious system of electric heating, which has since been imitated, allowed the temperature of the walls and room to be increased at will.

I am giving all these details of a perfectly natural invention, producing, with a few painted branches, the supernatural illusion of an equatorial forest blazing under the tropical sun, so that no one may doubt the present balance of my brain or feel entitled to say that I am mad or lying or that I take him for a fool.*

I now return to the facts where I left them. When the ceiling lit up and the forest became visible around us, the viscount's stupefaction was immense. That impenetrable forest, with its innumerable trunks and branches, threw him into a terrible state of consternation. He passed his hands over his forehead, as though to drive away a dream; his eyes blinked; and, for a moment, he forgot to listen.

I have already said that the sight of the forest did not surprise me at all; and therefore I listened for the two of us to what was happening next door. Lastly, my attention was especially attracted, not so much to the scene, as to the mirrors that produced it. These mirrors were broken in parts. Yes, they were marked and scratched; they had been "starred," in spite of their solidity; and this proved to me that the torture-chamber in which we now were *had already served a purpose.*

* It is very natural that, at the time when the Persian was writing, he should take so many precautions against any spirit of incredulity on the part of those who were likely to read his narrative. Nowadays, when we have all seen this sort of room, his precautions would be superfluous.

Yes, some wretch, whose feet were not bare like those of the victims of the rosy hours of Mazenderan, had certainly fallen into this "mortal illusion" and, mad with rage, had kicked against those mirrors which, nevertheless, continued to reflect his agony. And the branch of the tree on which he had put an end to his own sufferings was arranged in such a way that, before dying, he had seen, for his last consolation, a thousand men writhing in his company.

Yes, Joseph Buquet had undoubtedly been through all this! Were we to die as he had done? I did not think so, for I knew that we had a few hours before us and that I could employ them to better purpose than Joseph Buquet was able to do. After all, I was thoroughly acquainted with most of Erik's "tricks"; and now or never was the time to turn my knowledge to account.

To begin with, I gave up every idea of returning to the passage that had brought us to that accursed chamber. I did not trouble about the possibility of working the inside stone that closed the passage; and this for the simple reason that to do so was out of the question. We had dropped from too great a height into the torture-chamber; there was no furniture to help us reach that passage; not even the branch of the iron tree, not even each other's shoulders were of any avail.

There was only one possible outlet, that opening into the Louis-Philippe room in which Erik and Christine Daaé were. But, though this outlet looked like an ordinary door on Christine's side, it was absolutely invisible to us. We must therefore try to open it without even knowing where it was.

When I was quite sure that there was no hope for us from Christine Daaé's side, when I had heard the monster dragging the poor girl from the Louis-Philippe room *lest she should interfere with our tortures,* I resolved to set to work without delay.

But I had first to calm M. de Chagny, who was already walking about like a madman, uttering incoherent cries. The snatches of conversation which he had caught between Christine and the monster had contributed not a little to drive him beside himself: add to that the shock of the magic forest and the scorching heat which was beginning to make the perspiration stream down his temples and you will have no difficulty in understanding his state of mind. He shouted Christine's name, brandished his pistol, knocked his forehead against the glass in his endeavors to run down the glades of the illusive forest. In short, the torture was beginning to work its spell upon a brain unprepared for it.

I did my best to induce the poor viscount to listen to reason. I made him touch the mirrors and the iron tree and the branches and explained to him, by optical laws, all the luminous imagery by which we were surrounded and of which we need not allow ourselves to be the victims, like ordinary, ignorant people.

"We are in a room, a little room; that is what you must keep saying to yourself. And we shall leave the room as soon as we have found the door."

And I promised him that, if he let me act, without disturbing me by shouting and walking up and down, I would discover the trick of the door in less than an hour's time.

Then he lay flat on the floor, as one does in a wood, and declared that he would wait until I found the door of the forest, as there was nothing better to do! And he added that, from where he was, "the view was splendid!" The torture was working, in spite of all that I had said.

Myself, forgetting the forest, I tackled a glass panel and began to finger it in every direction, hunting for the weak point on which to press in order to turn the door in accordance with Erik's system of pivots. This weak point might be a mere speck on the glass, no larger than a pea, under which the spring lay hidden. I hunted and hunted. I felt as high as my hands could reach. Erik was about the same height as myself and I thought that he would not have placed the spring higher than suited his stature.

While groping over the successive panels with the greatest care, I endeavored not to lose a minute, for I was feeling more and more overcome with the heat and we were literally roasting in that blazing forest.

I had been working like this for half an hour and had finished three panels, when, as ill-luck would have it, I turned round on hearing a muttered exclamation from the viscount.

"I am stifling," he said. "All those mirrors are sending out an infernal heat! Do you think you will find that spring soon? If you are much longer about it, we shall be roasted alive!"

I was not sorry to hear him talk like this. He had not said a word of the forest and I hoped that my companion's reason would hold out some time longer against the torture. But he added:

"What consoles me is that the monster has given Christine until eleven to-morrow evening. If we can't get out of here and go to her assistance, at least we shall be dead before her! Then Erik's mass can serve for all of us!"

And he gulped down a breath of hot air that nearly made him faint.

As I had not the same desperate reasons as M. le Vicomte for accepting death, I returned, after giving him a word of encouragement, to my panel, but I had made the mistake of taking a few steps while speaking and, in the tangle of the illusive forest, I was no longer able to find my panel for certain! I had to begin all over again, at random, feeling, fumbling, groping.

Now the fever laid hold of me in my turn. . . for I found nothing, absolutely nothing. In the next room, all was silence. We were quite lost in the forest, without an outlet, a compass, a guide or anything. Oh, I knew what awaited us if nobody came to our aid. . . or if I did not find the spring! But, look as I might, I found nothing but branches, beautiful branches that stood straight up before me, or spread gracefully over my head. But they gave no shade. And this was natural enough, as we were in an equatorial forest, with the sun right above our heads, an African forest.

M. de Chagny and I had repeatedly taken off our coats and put them on again, finding at one time that they made us feel still hotter and at another that they protected us against the heat. I was still making a moral resistance, but M. de Chagny seemed to me quite "gone." He pretended that he had been walking in that forest for three days and nights, without stopping, looking for Christine Daaé! From time to time, he thought he saw her behind the trunk of a tree, or gliding between the branches; and he called to her with words of supplication that brought the tears to my eyes. And then, at last:

"Oh, how thirsty I am!" he cried, in delirious accents.

I too was thirsty. My throat was on fire. And, yet, squatting on the floor, I went on hunting, hunting, hunting for the spring of the invisible door . . . especially as it was dangerous to remain in the forest as evening drew nigh. Already the shades of night were beginning to surround us. It had happened very quickly: night falls quickly in tropical countries . . . suddenly, with hardly any twilight.

Now night, in the forests of the equator, is always dangerous, particularly when, like ourselves, one has not the materials for a fire to keep off the beasts of prey. I did indeed try for a moment to break off the branches, which I would have lit with my dark lantern, but I knocked myself also against the mirrors and remembered, in time, that we had only images of branches to do with.

The heat did not go with the daylight; on the contrary, it was now still hotter under the blue rays of the moon. I urged the viscount to hold our weapons ready to fire and not to stray from camp, while I went on looking for my spring.

Suddenly, we heard a lion roaring a few yards away.

"Oh," whispered the viscount, "he is quite close! . . . Don't you see him?. . . There . . . through the trees. . . in that thicket! . . . If he roars again, I will fire! . . ."

And the roaring began again, louder than before. And the viscount fired, but I do not think that he hit the lion; only, he smashed a mirror, as I perceived the next morning, at daybreak. We must have covered a good distance during the night, for we suddenly found ourselves on the edge of the desert, an immense desert of sand, stones and rocks. It was really not worth while leaving the forest to come upon the desert. Tired out, I flung myself down beside the viscount, for I had had enough of looking for springs which I could not find.

I was quite surprised—and I said so to the viscount—that we had encountered no other dangerous animals during the night. Usually, after the lion came the leopard and sometimes the buzz of the tsetse fly. These were easily obtained effects; and I explained to M. de Chagny that Erik imitated the roar of a lion on a long tabour or timbrel, with an ass's skin at one end. Over this skin he tied a string of catgut, which was fastened at the middle to another similar string passing through the whole length of the tabour. Erik had only to rub this string with a glove smeared with resin and, according to the manner in which he rubbed it, he imitated to perfection the voice of the lion or the leopard, or even the buzzing of the tsetse fly.

The idea that Erik was probably in the room beside us, working his trick, made me suddenly resolve to enter into a parley with him, for we must obviously give up all thought of taking him by surprise. And by this time he must be quite aware who were the occupants of his torture-chamber. I called him: "Erik! Erik!"

I shouted as loudly as I could across the desert, but there was no answer to my voice. All around us lay the silence and the bare immensity of that stony desert. What was to become of us in the midst of that awful solitude?

We were beginning literally to die of heat, hunger and thirst. . . of thirst especially. At last, I saw M. de Chagny raise himself on his elbow and point to a spot on the horizon. He had discovered an oasis!

Yes, far in the distance was an oasis. . . an oasis with limpid water, which reflected the iron trees! . . . Tush, it was the scene of the mirage. . . . I recognized it at once . . . the worst of the three! . . . No one had been able to fight against it . . . no one. . . . I did my utmost to keep my head *and not to hope for water*, because I knew that, if a man hoped for water, the water that reflected the iron tree, and if, after hoping for water, he struck against the mirror, then there was only one thing for him to do: to hang himself on the iron tree!

So I cried to M. de Chagny:

"It's the mirage! . . . It's the mirage! . . . Don't believe in the water! . . . It's another trick of the mirrors! . . ."

Then he flatly told me to shut up, with my tricks of the mirrors, my springs, my revolving doors and my palaces of illusions! He angrily declared that I must be either blind or mad to imagine that all that water flowing over there, among those splendid, numberless trees, was not real water! . . . And the desert was real! . . .

And so was the forest! . . . And it was no use trying to take him in . . . he was an old, experienced traveler . . . he had been all over the place!

And he dragged himself along, saying: "Water! Water!"

And his mouth was open, as though he were drinking.

And my mouth was open too, as though I were drinking.

For we not only saw the water, but *we heard it*! . . . We heard it flow, we heard it ripple! . . . Do you understand that word "ripple"? . . . *It is a sound which you hear with your tongue*! . . . You put your tongue out of your mouth to listen to it better!

Lastly—and this was the most pitiless torture of all—we heard the rain and it was not raining! This was an infernal invention. . . . Oh, I knew well enough how Erik obtained it! He filled with little stones a very long and narrow box, broken up inside with wooden and metal projections. The stones, in falling, struck against these projections and rebounded from one to another; and the result was a series of pattering sounds that exactly imitated a rainstorm.

Ah, you should have seen us putting out our tongues and dragging ourselves toward the rippling river-bank! Our eyes and ears were full of water, but our tongues were hard and dry as horn!

When we reached the mirror, M. de Chagny licked it . . . and I also licked the glass.

It was burning hot!

Then we rolled on the floor with a hoarse cry of despair. M. de Chagny put the one pistol that was still loaded to his temple; and I stared at the Punjab lasso at the foot of the iron tree. I knew why the iron tree had returned, in this third change of scene! . . . The iron tree was waiting for me! . . .

But, as I stared at the Punjab lasso, I saw a thing that made me start so violently that M. de Chagny delayed his attempt at suicide. I took his arm. And then I caught the pistol from him . . . and then I dragged myself on my knees toward what I had seen.

I had discovered, near the Punjab lasso, in a groove in the floor, a black-headed nail of which I knew the use. At last I had discovered the spring! I felt the nail. . . . I lifted a radiant face to M. de Chagny. . . . The black-headed nail yielded to my pressure. . . .

And then. . . .

And then we saw not a door opened in the wall, but a cellar-flap released in the floor. Cool air came up to us from the black hole below. We stooped over that square of darkness as though over a limpid well. With our chins in the cool shade, we drank it in.

And we bent lower and lower over the trap-door.

What could there be in that cellar which opened before us? Water? Water to drink?

I thrust my arm into the darkness and came upon a stone and another stone. . . a staircase. . . a dark staircase leading into the cellar. The viscount wanted to fling himself down the hole; but I, fearing a new trick of the monster's, stopped him, turned on my dark lantern and went down first.

The staircase was a winding one and led down into pitchy darkness. But oh, how deliciously cool were the darkness and the stairs? The lake could not be far away.

We soon reached the bottom. Our eyes were beginning to accustom themselves to the dark, to distinguish shapes around us. . . circular shapes. . . on which I turned the light of my lantern.

Barrels!

We were in Erik's cellar: it was here that he must keep his wine and perhaps his drinking-water. I knew that Erik was a great lover of good wine. Ah, there was plenty to drink here!

M. de Chagny patted the round shapes and kept on saying:

"Barrels! Barrels! . . . What a lot of barrels! . . ."

Indeed, there was quite a number of them, symmetrically arranged in two rows, one on either side of us. They were small barrels and I thought that Erik must have selected them of that size to facilitate their carriage to the house on the lake.

We examined them successively, to see if one of them had not a funnel, showing that it had been tapped at some time or another. But all the barrels were hermetically closed.

Then, after half lifting one to make sure it was full, we went on our knees and, with the blade of a small knife which I carried, I prepared to stave in the bung-hole.

At that moment, I seemed to hear, coming from very far, a sort of monotonous chant which I knew well, from often hearing it in the streets of Paris:

"Barrels! . . . Barrels! . . . Any barrels to sell? . . ."

My hand desisted from its work. M. de Chagny had also heard. He said:

"That's funny! It sounds as if the barrel were singing!"

The song was renewed, farther away:

"Barrels! . . . Barrels! . . . Any barrels to sell? . . ."

"Oh, I swear," said the viscount, "that the tune dies away in the barrel! . . ."

We stood up and went to look behind the barrel.

"It's inside," said M. de Chagny, "it's inside!"

But we heard nothing there and were driven to accuse the bad condition of our senses. And we returned to the bung-hole. M. de Chagny put his two hands together underneath it and, with a last effort, I burst the bung.

"What's this?" cried the viscount. "This isn't water!"

The viscount put his two full hands close to my lantern. . . . I stooped to look . . . and at once threw away the lantern with such violence that it broke and went out, leaving us in utter darkness.

What I had seen in M. de Chagny's hands . . . was gun-powder!

XXV

THE SCORPION OR THE GRASSHOPPER: WHICH?

The Persian's Narrative Concluded

The discovery flung us into a state of alarm that made us forget all our past and present sufferings. We now knew all that the monster meant to convey when he said to Christine Daaé:

"Yes or no! If your answer is no, everybody will be dead *and buried*!"

Yes, buried under the ruins of the Paris Grand Opera!

The monster had given her until eleven o'clock in the evening. He had chosen his time well. There would be many people, many "members of the human race," up there. In the resplendent theater. What finer retinue could be expected for his funeral? He would go down to the tomb escorted by the whitest shoulders in the world, decked with the richest jewels.

Eleven o'clock to-morrow evening!

We were all to be blown up in the middle of the performance . . . if Christine Daaé said no!

Eleven o'clock to-morrow evening! . . .

And what else could Christine say but no? Would she not prefer to espouse death itself rather than that living corpse? She did not know that on her acceptance or refusal depended the awful fate of many members of the human race!

Eleven o'clock to-morrow evening!

And we dragged ourselves through the darkness, feeling our way to the stone steps, for the light in the trap-door overhead that led to the room of mirrors was now extinguished; and we repeated to ourselves:

"Eleven o'clock to-morrow evening!"

At last, I found the staircase. But, suddenly I drew myself up on the first step, for a terrible thought had come to my mind:

"What is the time?"

Ah, what was the time?. . . For, after all, eleven o'clock to-morrow evening might be now, might be this very moment! Who could tell us the time? We seemed to have been imprisoned in that hell for days and days . . . for years . . . since the beginning of the world. Perhaps we should be blown up then and there! Ah, a sound! A crack!

"Did you hear that?. . . There, in the corner . . . good heavens! . . . Like a sound of machinery! . . . Again! . . . Oh, for a light! . . . Perhaps it's the machinery that is to blow everything up! . . . I tell you, a cracking sound: are you deaf?"

M. de Chagny and I began to yell like madmen. Fear spurred us on. We rushed up the treads of the staircase, stumbling as we went, anything to escape the dark, to return to the mortal light of the room of mirrors!

We found the trap-door still open, but it was now as dark in the room of mirrors as in the cellar which we had left. We dragged ourselves along the floor of the torture-chamber, the floor that separated us from the powder-magazine. What was the time? We shouted, we called: M. de Chagny to Christine, I to Erik. I reminded him that I had saved his life. But no answer, save that of our despair, of our madness: what was the time? We argued, we tried to calculate the time which we had spent there, but we were incapable of reasoning. If only we could see the face of a watch! . . . Mine had stopped, but M. de Chagny's was still going. . . . He told me that he had wound it up before dressing for the Opera. . . . We had not a match upon us. . . . And yet we must know. . . . M. de Chagny broke the glass of his watch and felt the two hands. . . . He questioned the hands of the watch with his finger-tips, going by the position of the ring of the watch. . . . Judging by the space between the hands, he thought it might be just eleven o'clock!

But perhaps it was not the eleven o'clock of which we stood in dread. Perhaps we had still twelve hours before us!

Suddenly, I exclaimed: "Hush!"

I seemed to hear footsteps in the next room. Some one tapped against the wall. Christine Daaé's voice said:

"Raoul! Raoul!"

We were now all talking at once, on either side of the wall. Christine sobbed; she was not sure that she would find M. de Chagny alive. The monster had been terrible, it seemed, had done nothing but rave, waiting for her to give him the "yes" which she refused. And yet she had promised him that "yes," if he would take her to the torture-chamber. But he had obstinately declined, and had uttered hideous threats against all the members of the human race! At last, after hours and hours of that hell, he had that moment gone out, leaving her alone to reflect for the last time.

"Hours and hours? What is the time now? What is the time, Christine?"

"It is eleven o'clock! Eleven o'clock, all but five minutes!"

"But which eleven o'clock?"

"The eleven o'clock that is to decide life or death! He told me so just before he went.... He is terrible.... He is quite mad: he tore off his mask and his yellow eyes shot flames! ... He did nothing but laugh! ... He said, 'I give you five minutes to spare your blushes! Here,' he said, taking a key from the little bag of life and death, 'here is the little bronze key that opens the two ebony caskets on the mantelpiece in the Louis-Philippe room . . . in one of the caskets, you will find a scorpion. In the other, a grasshopper, both very cleverly imitated in Japanese bronze: they will say yes or no for you. If you turn the scorpion round, that will mean to me, when I return, that you have said yes. The grasshopper will mean no.' And he laughed like a drunken demon. I did nothing but beg and entreat him to give me the key of the torture-chamber, promising to be his wife if he granted me that request.... But he told me that there was no future need for that key and that he was going to throw it into the lake! ... And he again laughed like a drunken demon and left me. Oh, his last words were, 'The grasshopper! Be careful of the grasshopper! A grasshopper does not only turn: it hops! It hops! And it hops jolly high!'"

The five minutes had nearly elapsed and the scorpion and the grasshopper were scratching at my brain. Nevertheless, I had sufficient lucidity left to understand that, if the grasshopper were turned, it would hop . . . and with it many members of the human race! There was no doubt but that the grasshopper controlled an electric current intended to blow up the powder-magazine!

M. de Chagny, who seemed to have recovered all his moral force from hearing Christine's voice, explained to her, in a few hurried words, the situation in which we and all the Opera were. He told her to turn the scorpion at once.

There was a pause.

"Christine," I cried, "where are you?"

"By the scorpion."

"Don't touch it!"

The idea had come to me—for I knew my Erik—that the monster had perhaps deceived the girl once more. Perhaps it was the scorpion that would blow everything up. After all, why wasn't he there? The five minutes were long past. . .

and he was not back. . . . Perhaps he had taken shelter and was waiting for the explosion! . . . Why had he not returned? . . . He could not really expect Christine ever to consent to become his voluntary prey! . . . Why had he not returned?

"Don't touch the scorpion!" I said.

"Here he comes!" cried Christine. "I hear him! Here he is!"

We heard his steps approaching the Louis-Philippe room. He came up to Christine, but did not speak. Then I raised my voice:

"Erik! It is I! Do you know me?"

With extraordinary calmness, he at once replied:

"So you are not dead in there? Well, then, see that you keep quiet."

I tried to speak, but he said coldly:

"Not a word, daroga, or I shall blow everything up." And he added, "The honor rests with mademoiselle. . . . Mademoiselle has not touched the scorpion"—how deliberately he spoke!—"mademoiselle has not touched the grasshopper"—with that composure!—"but it is not too late to do the right thing. There, I open the caskets without a key, for I am a trap-door lover and I open and shut what I please and as I please. I open the little ebony caskets: mademoiselle, look at the little dears inside. Aren't they pretty? If you turn the grasshopper, mademoiselle, we shall all be blown up. There is enough gun-powder under our feet to blow up a whole quarter of Paris. If you turn the scorpion, mademoiselle, all that powder will be soaked and drowned. Mademoiselle, to celebrate our wedding, you shall make a very handsome present to a few hundred Parisians who are at this moment applauding a poor masterpiece of Meyerbeer's . . . you shall make them a present of their lives. . . . For, with your own fair hands, you shall turn the scorpion. . . . And merrily, merrily, we will be married!"

A pause; and then:

"If, in two minutes, mademoiselle, you have not turned the scorpion, I shall turn the grasshopper. . . and the grasshopper, I tell you, *hops jolly high*!"

The terrible silence began anew. The Vicomte de Chagny, realizing that there was nothing left to do but pray, went down on his knees and prayed. As for me, my blood beat so fiercely that I had to take my heart in both hands, lest it should burst. At last, we heard Erik's voice:

"The two minutes are past. . . . Good-by, mademoiselle. . . . Hop, grasshopper! . . ."

"Erik," cried Christine, "do you swear to me, monster, do you swear to me that the scorpion is the one to turn? . . ."

"Yes, to hop at our wedding."

"Ah, you see! You said, to hop!"

"At our wedding, ingenuous child! . . . The scorpion opens the ball. . . . But that will do! . . . You won't have the scorpion? Then I turn the grasshopper!"

"Erik!"

"Enough!"

I was crying out in concert with Christine. M. de Chagny was still on his knees, praying.

"Erik! I have turned the scorpion!"

Oh, the second through which we passed!

Waiting! Waiting to find ourselves in fragments, amid the roar and the ruins!

Feeling something crack beneath our feet, hearing an appalling hiss through the open trap-door, a hiss like the first sound of a rocket!

It came softly, at first, then louder, then very loud. But it was not the hiss of fire. It was more like the hiss of water. And now it became a gurgling sound: "Guggle! Guggle!"

We rushed to the trap-door. All our thirst, which vanished when the terror came, now returned with the lapping of the water.

The water rose in the cellar, above the barrels, the powder-barrels—"Barrels! . . . Barrels! Any barrels to sell?"—and we went down to it with parched throats. It rose to our chins, to our mouths. And we drank. We stood on the floor of the cellar and drank. And we went up the stairs again in the dark, step by step, went up with the water.

The water came out of the cellar with us and spread over the floor of the room. If this went on, the whole house on the lake would be swamped. The floor of the torture-chamber had itself become a regular little lake, in which our feet splashed. Surely there was water enough now! Erik must turn off the tap! "Erik! Erik! That is water enough for the gun-powder! Turn off the tap! Turn off the scorpion!"

But Erik did not reply. We heard nothing but the water rising: it was half-way to our waists!

"Christine!" cried M. de Chagny. "Christine! The water is up to our knees!"

But Christine did not reply. . . . We heard nothing but the water rising.

No one, no one in the next room, no one to turn the tap, no one to turn the scorpion!

We were all alone, in the dark, with the dark water that seized us and clasped us and froze us!

"Erik! Erik!"

"Christine! Christine!"

By this time, we had lost our foothold and were spinning round in the water, carried away by an irresistible whirl, for the water turned with us and dashed us against the dark mirror, which thrust us back again; and our throats, raised above the whirlpool, roared aloud.

Were we to die here, drowned in the torture-chamber? I had never seen that. Erik, at the time of the rosy hours of Mazenderan, had never shown me that, through the little invisible window.

"Erik! Erik!" I cried. "I saved your life! Remember! . . . You were sentenced to death! But for me, you would be dead now! . . . Erik!"

We whirled around in the water like so much wreckage. But, suddenly, my straying hands seized the trunk of the iron tree! I called M. de Chagny, and we both hung to the branch of the iron tree.

And the water rose still higher.

"Oh! Oh! Can you remember? How much space is there between the branch of the tree and the dome-shaped ceiling? Do try to remember I . . . After all, the water may stop, it must find its level! . . . There, I think it is stopping! . . . No, no, oh, horrible! . . . Swim! Swim for your life!"

Our arms became entangled in the effort of swimming; we choked; we fought in the dark water; already we could hardly breathe the dark air above the dark water, the air which escaped, which we could hear escaping through some vent-hole or other.

"Oh, let us turn and turn and turn until we find the air hole and then glue our mouths to it!"

But I lost my strength; I tried to lay hold of the walls! Oh, how those glass walls slipped from under my groping fingers! . . . We whirled round again! . . . We began to sink! . . . One last effort! . . . A last cry:

"Erik! . . . Christine! . . ."

"Guggle, guggle, guggle!" In our ears. "Guggle! Guggle!" At the bottom of the dark water, our ears went, "Guggle! Guggle!"

And, before losing consciousness entirely, I seemed to hear, between two guggles:

"Barrels! Barrels! Any barrels to sell?"

XXVI

THE END OF THE GHOST'S LOVE STORY

THE PREVIOUS CHAPTER MARKS THE CONCLUSION OF THE WRITTEN narrative which the Persian left behind him.

Notwithstanding the horrors of a situation which seemed definitely to abandon them to their deaths, M. de Chagny and his companion were saved by the sublime devotion of Christine Daaé. And I had the rest of the story from the lips of the daroga himself.

When I went to see him, he was still living in his little flat in the Rue de Rivoli, opposite the Tuileries. He was very ill, and it required all my ardor as an historian pledged to the truth to persuade him to live the incredible tragedy over again for my benefit. His faithful old servant Darius showed me in to him. The daroga received me at a window overlooking the garden of the Tuileries. He still had his magnificent eyes, but his poor face looked very worn. He had shaved the whole of his head, which was usually covered with an astrakhan cap; he was dressed in a long, plain coat and amused himself by unconsciously twisting his thumbs inside the sleeves; but his mind was quite clear, and he told me his story with perfect lucidity.

It seems that, when he opened his eyes, the daroga found himself lying on a bed. M. de Chagny was on a sofa, beside the wardrobe. An angel and a devil were watching over them.

After the deceptions and illusions of the torture-chamber, the precision of the details of that quiet little middle-class room seemed to have been invented for the express purpose of puzzling the mind of the mortal rash enough to stray into that abode of living nightmare. The wooden bedstead, the waxed mahogany chairs, the chest of drawers, those brasses, the little square antimacassars carefully placed on the backs of the chairs, the clock on the mantelpiece and the harmless-looking ebony caskets at either end, lastly, the whatnot filled with shells, with red pincushions, with mother-of-pearl boats and an enormous ostrich-egg, the whole discreetly lighted by a shaded lamp standing on a small round table: this collection of ugly, peaceable, reasonable furniture, *at the bottom of the Opera cellars*, bewildered the imagination more than all the late fantastic happenings.

And the figure of the masked man seemed all the more formidable in this old-fashioned, neat and trim little frame. It bent down over the Persian and said, in his ear:

"Are you better, daroga?. . . You are looking at my furniture?. . . It is all that I have left of my poor unhappy mother."

Christine Daaé did not say a word: she moved about noiselessly, like a sister of charity, who had taken a vow of silence. She brought a cup of cordial, or of hot tea, he did not remember which. The man in the mask took it from her hands and gave it to the Persian. M. de Chagny was still sleeping.

Erik poured a drop of rum into the daroga's cup and, pointing to the viscount, said:

"He came to himself long before we knew if you were still alive, daroga. He is quite well. He is asleep. We must not wake him."

Erik left the room for a moment, and the Persian raised himself on his elbow, looked around him and saw Christine Daaé sitting by the fireside. He spoke to her, called her, but he was still very weak and fell back on his pillow. Christine came to him, laid her hand on his forehead and went away again. And the Persian remembered that, as she went, she did not give a glance at M. de Chagny, who, it is true, was sleeping peacefully; and she sat down again in her chair by the chimney-corner, silent as a sister of charity who had taken a vow of silence.

Erik returned with some little bottles which he placed on the mantelpiece. And, again in a whisper, so as not to wake M. de Chagny, he said to the Persian, after sitting down and feeling his pulse:

"You are now saved, both of you. And soon I shall take you up to the surface of the earth, *to please my wife.*"

Thereupon he rose, without any further explanation, and disappeared once more.

The Persian now looked at Christine's quiet profile under the lamp. She was reading a tiny book, with gilt edges, like a religious book. There are editions of *The Imitation* that look like that. The Persian still had in his ears the natural tone in which the other had said, "to please my wife." Very gently, he called her again; but Christine was wrapped up in her book and did not hear him.

Erik returned, mixed the daroga a draft and advised him not to speak to "his wife" again nor to any one, *because it might be very dangerous to everybody's health.*

Eventually, the Persian fell asleep, like M. de Chagny, and did not wake until he was in his own room, nursed by his faithful Darius, who told him that, on the night before, he was found propped against the door of his flat, where he had been brought by a stranger, who rang the bell before going away.

As soon as the daroga recovered his strength and his wits, he sent to Count Philippe's house to inquire after the viscount's health. The answer was that the young man had not been seen and that Count Philippe was dead. His body was found on the bank of the Opera lake, on the Rue-Scribe side. The Persian remembered the requiem mass which he had heard from behind the wall of the torture-chamber, and had no doubt concerning the crime and the criminal. Knowing Erik as he did, he easily reconstructed the tragedy. Thinking that his brother had run away with Christine Daaé, Philippe had dashed in pursuit of him along the Brussels Road, where he knew that everything was prepared for the elopement. Failing to find the pair, he hurried back to the Opera, remembered Raoul's strange confidence about his fantastic rival and learned that the viscount had made every effort to enter the cellars of the theater and that he had disappeared, leaving his hat in the prima donna's dressing-room beside an empty pistol-case. And the count, who no longer entertained any doubt of his brother's madness, in his turn darted into that infernal underground maze. This was enough, in the Persian's eyes, to explain the discovery of the Comte de Chagny's corpse on the shore of the lake, where the siren, Erik's siren, kept watch.

The Persian did not hesitate. He determined to inform the police. Now the case was in the hands of an examining-magistrate called Faure, an incredulous, commonplace, superficial sort of person, (I write as I think), with a mind utterly unprepared to receive a confidence of this kind. M. Faure took down the daroga's depositions and proceeded to treat him as a madman.

Despairing of ever obtaining a hearing, the Persian sat down to write. As the police did not want his evidence, perhaps the press would be glad of it; and he had just written the last line of the narrative I have quoted in the preceding chapters, when Darius announced the visit of a stranger who refused his name, who would not show his face and declared simply that he did not intend to leave the place until he had spoken to the daroga.

The Persian at once felt who his singular visitor was and ordered him to be shown in. The daroga was right. It was the ghost, it was Erik!

He looked extremely weak and leaned against the wall, as though he were afraid of falling. Taking off his hat, he revealed a forehead white as wax. The rest of the horrible face was hidden by the mask.

The Persian rose to his feet as Erik entered.

"Murderer of Count Philippe, what have you done with his brother and Christine Daaé?"

Erik staggered under this direct attack, kept silent for a moment, dragged himself to a chair and heaved a deep sigh. Then, speaking in short phrases and gasping for breath between the words:

"Daroga, don't talk to me. . . about Count Philippe. . . . He was dead . . . by the time . . . I left my house . . . he was dead . . . when . . . the siren sang, . . . it was an

. . . accident . . . a sad . . . a very sad . . . accident. He fell very awkwardly . . . but simply and naturally . . . into the lake! . . ."

"You lie!" shouted the Persian.

Erik bowed his head and said:

"I have not come here . . . to talk about Count Philippe . . . but to tell you that . . . I am going . . . to die. . . ."

"Where are Raoul de Chagny and Christine Daaé?"

"I am going to die. . . ."

"Raoul de Chagny and Christine Daaé?"

"Of love . . . daroga . . . I am dying . . . of love. . . . That is how it is. . . . I loved her so! . . . And I love her still . . . daroga . . . and I am dying of love for her, I . . . I tell you! . . . If you knew how beautiful she was . . . when she let me kiss her . . . alive. . . . it was the first . . . time, daroga, the first time I ever kissed a woman. . . .Yes, alive. . . . I kissed her alive . . . and she looked as beautiful as if she had been dead! . . ."

The Persian shook Erik by the arm: "Will you tell me if she is alive or dead."

"Why do you shake me like that?" asked Erik, making an effort to speak more connectedly. "I tell you that I am going to die. . . . Yes, I kissed her alive. . . ."

"And now she is dead?"

"I tell you I kissed her just like that, on her forehead . . . and she did not draw back her forehead from my lips! . . . Oh, she is a good girl! . . . As to her being dead, I don't think so; but it has nothing to do with me. . . . No, no, she is not dead! And no one shall touch a hair of her head! She is a good, honest girl, and she saved your life, daroga, at a moment when I would not have given twopence for your Persian skin. As a matter of fact, nobody bothered about you. Why were you there with that little chap? You would have died as well as he! My word, how she entreated me for her little chap! But I told her that, as she had turned the scorpion, she had, through that very fact, and of her own free will, become engaged to me and that she did not need to have two men engaged to her, which was true enough.

"As for you, you did not exist, you had ceased to exist, I tell you, and you were going to die with the other I . . . Only, mark me, daroga, when you were yelling like the devil, because of the water, Christine came to me with her beautiful blue eyes wide open, and swore to me, as she hoped to be saved, that she consented to be *my living wife*! . . . Until then, in the depths of her eyes, daroga, I had always seen my dead wife; it was the first time I saw my living wife there. She was sincere, as she hoped to be saved. She would not kill herself. It was a bargain. . . . Half a minute later, all the water was back in the lake; and I had a hard job with you, daroga, for, upon my honor, I thought you were done for! . . . However! . . . There you were! . . . It was understood that I was to take you both up to the surface of the earth. When, at last, I cleared the Louis-Philippe room of you, I came back alone. . . ."

"What have you done with the Vicomte de Chagny?" asked the Persian, interrupting him.

"Ah, you see, daroga, I couldn't carry *him* up like that, at once. . . . He was a hostage. . . . But I could not keep him in the house on the lake either, because of Christine; so I locked him up comfortably, I chained him up nicely—a whiff of the Mazenderan scent had left him as limp as a rag—in the Communists' dungeon, which is in the most deserted and remote part of the Opera, below the fifth cellar, where no one ever comes, and where no one ever hears you. Then I came back to Christine. She was waiting for me. . . ."

Erik here rose solemnly. Then he continued, but, as he spoke, he was overcome by all his former emotion and began to tremble like a leaf:

"Yes, she was waiting for me . . . waiting for me erect and alive, a real, living bride . . . as she hoped to be saved. . . . And, when I . . . came forward, more timid than . . . a little child, she did not run away . . . no, no . . . she stayed . . . she waited for me. . . . I even believe . . . daroga . . . that she put out her forehead . . . a little . . . oh, not much . . . just a little . . . like a living bride. . . . And, and . . . I . . . kissed her! . . . I! . . . I! . . . I! . . . And she did not die! . . . Oh, how good it is, daroga, to kiss somebody on the forehead! . . . You can't tell I . . . But I! I! . . . My mother, daroga, my poor, unhappy mother would never . . . let me kiss her. . . . She used to run away . . . and throw me my mask! . . . Nor any other woman . . . ever, ever! . . . Ah, you can understand, my happiness was so great, I cried. And I fell at her feet, crying . . . and I kissed her feet . . . her little feet . . . crying. You're crying, too, daroga . . . and she cried also . . . the angel cried! . . ."

Erik sobbed aloud and the Persian himself could not retain his tears in the presence of that masked man, who, with his shoulders shaking and his hands clutched at his chest, was moaning with pain and love by turns.

"Yes, daroga . . . I felt her tears flow on my forehead . . . on mine, mine! . . . They were soft . . . they were sweet! . . . They trickled under my mask . . . they mingled with my tears in my eyes . . . they flowed between my lips. . . . Listen, daroga, listen to what I did. . . . I tore off my mask so as not to lose one of her tears . . . and she did not run away! . . . And she did not die! . . . She remained alive, weeping over me, with me. We cried together! I have tasted all the happiness the world can offer!"

And Erik fell into a chair, choking for breath:

"Ah, I am not going to die yet . . . presently I shall . . . but let me cry! . . . Listen, daroga . . . listen to this. . . . While I was at her feet . . . I heard her say, 'Poor, unhappy Erik!' . . . And she took my hand! . . . I had become no more, you know, than a poor dog ready to die for her. . . . I mean it, daroga! . . . I held in my hand a ring, a plain gold ring which I had given her . . . which she had lost . . . and which I had found again . . . a wedding-ring, you know. . . . I slipped it into her little hand and said, 'There! . . . Take it! . . . Take it for you . . . and him! . . . It shall be my wedding-present . . . a present from your poor, unhappy Erik. . . . I know you love the boy . . . don't cry any more!' . . . She asked me, in a very soft voice, what I meant. . . . Then I made her understand that, where she was concerned, I was only a poor dog, ready to die for her . . . but that she could marry the young man when she pleased, because she had cried with me and mingled her tears with mine! . . ."

Erik's emotion was so great that he had to tell the Persian not to look at him, for he was choking and must take off his mask. The daroga went to the window and opened it. His heart was full of pity, but he took care to keep his eyes fixed on the trees in the Tuileries gardens, lest he should see the monster's face.

"I went and released the young man," Erik continued, "and told him to come with me to Christine. . . . They kissed before me in the Louis-Philippe room. . . . Christine had my ring. . . . I made Christine swear to come back, one night, when I was dead, crossing the lake from the Rue-Scribe side, and bury me in the greatest secrecy with the gold ring, which she was to wear until that moment. . . . I told her where she would find my body and what to do with it. . . . Then Christine kissed me, for the first time, herself, here, on the forehead—don't look, daroga!—here, on the forehead . . . on my forehead, mine—don't look, daroga!—and they went off together. Christine had stopped crying. . . . I alone cried. . . . Daroga, daroga, if Christine keeps her promise, she will come back soon! . . ."

The Persian asked him no questions. He was quite reassured as to the fate of Raoul Chagny and Christine Daaé; no one could have doubted the word of the weeping Erik that night.

The monster resumed his mask and collected his strength to leave the daroga. He told him that, when he felt his end to be very near at hand, he would send him, in gratitude for the kindness which the Persian had once shown him, that which he held dearest in the world: all Christine Daaé's papers, which she had written for Raoul's benefit and left with Erik, together with a few objects belonging to her, such as a pair of gloves, a shoe-buckle and two pocket-handkerchiefs. In reply to the Persian's questions, Erik told him that the two young people, as soon as they found themselves free, had resolved to go and look for a priest in some lonely spot where they could hide their happiness and that, with this object in view, they had started from "the northern railway station of the world." Lastly, Erik relied on the Persian, as soon as he received the promised relics and papers, to inform the young couple of his death and to advertise it in the *Epoque*.

That was all. The Persian saw Erik to the door of his flat, and Darius helped him down to the street. A cab was waiting for him. Erik stepped in; and the Persian, who had gone back to the window, heard him say to the driver:

"Go to the Opera."

And the cab drove off into the night.

The Persian had seen the poor, unfortunate Erik for the last time. Three weeks later, the *Epoque* published this advertisement:

"Erik is dead."

EPILOGUE

I have now told the singular, but veracious story of the Opera ghost. As I declared on the first page of this work, it is no longer possible to deny that Erik really lived. There are to-day so many proofs of his existence within the reach of everybody that we can follow Erik's actions logically through the whole tragedy of the Chagnys.

There is no need to repeat here how greatly the case excited the capital. The kidnapping of the artist, the death of the Comte de Chagny under such exceptional conditions, the disappearance of his brother, the drugging of the gas-man at the Opera and of his two assistants: what tragedies, what passions, what crimes had surrounded the idyll of Raoul and the sweet and charming Christine! . . . What had become of that wonderful, mysterious artist of whom the world was never, never to hear again? She was represented as the victim of a rivalry between the two brothers; and nobody suspected what had really happened, nobody understood that, as Raoul and Christine had both disappeared, both had withdrawn far from the world to enjoy a happiness which they would not have cared to make public after the inexplicable death of Count Philippe. . . . They took the train one day from "the northern railway station of the world." . . . Possibly, I too shall take the train at that station, one day, and go and seek around thy lakes, O Norway, O silent Scandinavia, for the perhaps still living traces of Raoul and Christine and also of Mamma Valérius, who disappeared at the same time! . . . Possibly, some day, I shall hear the lonely echoes of the North repeat the singing of her who knew the Angel of Music! . . .

Long after the case was pigeonholed by the unintelligent care of M. le Juge d'Instruction Faure, the newspapers made efforts, at intervals, to fathom the mystery. One evening paper alone, which knew all the gossip of the theaters, said:

"We recognize the touch of the Opera ghost."

And even that was written by way of irony.

The Persian alone knew the whole truth and held the main proofs, which came to him with the pious relics promised by the ghost. It fell to my lot to complete those proofs with the aid of the daroga himself. Day by day, I kept him informed of the progress of my inquiries; and he directed them. He had not been to the Opera for years and years, but he had preserved the most accurate recollection of the building, and there was no better guide than he possible to help me discover its most secret recesses. He also told me where to gather further information, whom to ask; and he sent me to call on M. Poligny, at a moment when the poor man was nearly drawing his last breath. I had no idea that he was so very ill, and I shall never forget the effect which my questions about the ghost produced upon him. He looked at me as If I were the devil and answered only in a few incoherent sentences, which showed, however—and that was the main thing—the extent of the perturbation which O. G., in his time, had brought into that already very restless life (for M. Poligny was what people call a man of pleasure).

When I came and told the Persian of the poor result of my visit to M. Poligny, the daroga gave a faint smile and said:

"Poligny never knew how far that extraordinary blackguard of an Erik humbugged him."—The Persian, by the way, spoke of Erik sometimes as a demigod and sometimes as the lowest of the low—"Poligny was superstitious and Erik knew it. Erik knew most things about the public and private affairs of the Opera. When M. Poligny heard a mysterious voice tell him, in Box Five, of the manner in which he used to spend his time and abuse his partner's confidence, he did not wait to hear any more. Thinking at first that it was a voice from Heaven, he believed himself damned; and then, when the voice began to ask for money, he saw that he was being victimized by a shrewd blackmailer to whom Debienne himself had fallen a prey. Both of them, already tired of management for various reasons, went away without trying to investigate further into the personality of that curious O. G., who had forced such a singular memorandum-book upon them. They bequeathed the whole mystery to their successors and heaved a sigh of relief when they were rid of a business that had puzzled them without amusing them in the least."

I then spoke of the two successors and expressed my surprise that, in his *Memoirs of a Manager,* M. Moncharmin should describe the Opera ghost's behavior at such length in the first part of the book and hardly mention it at all in the second. In reply to this, the Persian, who knew the *Memoirs* as thoroughly as if he had written them himself, observed that I should find the explanation of the whole business if I would just recollect the few lines which Moncharmin devotes to the ghost in the second part aforesaid. I quote these lines, which are particularly interesting because they describe the very simple manner in which the famous incident of the twenty-thousand francs was closed:

> As for O. G., some of whose curious tricks I have related in the first part of my Memoirs, I will only say that he redeemed by one spontaneous fine action all the worry which he had caused my dear friend and partner and, I am bound to say, myself. He felt, no doubt, that there are limits to a joke, especially when it is so expensive and when the commissary of police has been informed, for, at the moment when we had made an appointment in our office with M. Mifroid to tell him the whole story, a few days after the disappearance of Christine Daaé, we found, on Richard's table, a large envelope, inscribed, in red ink, "With O. G.'s compliments." It contained the large sum of money which he had succeeded in playfully extracting, for the time being, from the treasury. Richard was at once of the opinion that we must be content with that and drop the business. I agreed with Richard. All's well that ends well. What do you say, O. G.?

Of course, Moncharmin, especially after the money had been restored, continued to believe that he had, for a short while, been the butt of Richard's sense of humor, whereas Richard, on his side, was convinced that Moncharmin had amused himself by inventing the whole of the affair of the Opera ghost, in order to revenge himself for a few jokes.

I asked the Persian to tell me by what trick the ghost had taken twenty-thousand francs from Richard's pocket in spite of the safety-pin. He replied that he had not gone into this little detail, but that, if I myself cared to make an investigation on the spot, I should certainly find the solution to the riddle in the managers' office by remembering that Erik had not been nicknamed the trap-door lover for nothing. I promised the Persian to do so as soon as I had time, and I may as well tell the reader at once that the results of my investigation were perfectly satisfactory; and I hardly believed that I should ever discover so many undeniable proofs of the authenticity of the feats ascribed to the ghost.

The Persian's manuscript, Christine Daaé's papers, the statements made to me by the people who used to work under MM. Richard and Moncharmin, by little Meg herself (the worthy Madame Giry, I am sorry to say, is no more) and by Sorelli, who is now living in retirement at Louveciennes: all the documents relating to the existence of the ghost, which I propose to deposit in the archives of the Opera, have been checked and confirmed by a number of important discoveries of which I am justly proud. I have not been able to find the house on the lake, Erik having blocked up all the secret entrances.* On the other hand, I have discovered the secret passage of the Communists, the planking of which is falling to pieces in parts, and also the trapdoor through which Raoul and the Persian penetrated into the cellars of the opera-house. In the Communists' dungeon, I noticed numbers of initials traced on the walls by the unfortunate people confined in it; and among these were an "R" and a "C." R. C: Raoul de Chagny. The letters are there to this day.

If the reader will visit the Opera one morning and ask leave to stroll where he pleases, without being accompanied by a stupid guide, let him go to Box Five and knock with his fist or stick on the enormous column that separates this from the stage-box. He will find that the column sounds hollow. After that, do not be astonished by the suggestion that it was occupied by the voice of the ghost: there is room inside the column for two men. If you are surprised that, when the various incidents occurred, no one turned round to look at the column, you must remember that it presented the appearance of solid marble, and that the voice contained in it seemed rather to come from the opposite side, for, as we have seen, the ghost was an expert ventriloquist. The column was elaborately carved and decorated with the sculptor's chisel; and I do not despair of one day discovering the ornament that could be raised or lowered at will, so as to admit of the ghost's mysterious correspondence with Mame Giry and of his generosity.

However, all these discoveries are nothing, to my mind, compared with that which I was able to make, in the presence of the acting-manager, in the managers' office, within a couple of inches from the desk-chair, and which consisted of a

* Even so, I am convinced that it would be easy to reach it by draining the lake, as I have repeatedly requested the Ministry of Fine Arts to do. I was speaking about it to M. Dujardin-Beaumetz, the under-secretary for fine arts, only forty-eight hours before the publication of this book. Who knows but that the score of *Don Juan Triumphant* might yet be discovered in the house on the lake?

trap-door, the width of a board in the flooring and the length of a man's fore-arm and no longer; a trap-door that falls back like the lid of a box; a trap-door through which I can see a hand come and dexterously fumble at the pocket of a swallow-tail coat.

That is the way the forty-thousand francs went! . . . And that also is the way by which, through some trick or other, they were returned. Speaking about this to the Persian, I said: "So we may take it, as the forty-thousand francs were returned, that Erik was simply amusing himself with that memorandum-book of his?"

"Don't you believe it!" he replied. "Erik wanted money. Thinking himself without the pale of humanity, he was restrained by no scruples and he employed his extraordinary gifts of dexterity and imagination, which he had received by way of compensation for his extraordinary uglinesss, to prey upon his fellow-men. His reason for restoring the forty-thousand francs, of his own accord, was that he no longer wanted it. He had relinquished his marriage with Christine Daaé. He had relinquished everything above the surface of the earth."

According to the Persian's account, Erik was born in a small town not far from Rouen. He was the son of a master-mason. He ran away at an early age from his father's house, where his ugliness was a subject of horror and terror to his parents. For a time, he frequented the fairs, where a showman exhibited him as the "living corpse." He seems to have crossed the whole of Europe, from fair to fair, and to have completed his strange education as an artist and magician at the very fountain-head of art and magic, among the Gipsies. A period of Erik's life remained quite obscure. He was seen at the fair of Nijni-Novgorod, where he displayed himself in all his hideous glory. He already sang as nobody on this earth had ever sung before; he practised ventriloquism and gave displays of legerdemain so extraordinary that the caravans returning to Asia talked about it during the whole length of their journey. In this way, his reputation penetrated the walls of the palace at Mazenderan, where the little sultana, the favorite of the Shah-in-Shah, was boring herself to death. A dealer in furs, returning to Samarkand from Nijni-Novgorod, told of the marvels which he had seen performed in Erik's tent. The trader was summoned to the palace and the daroga of Mazenderan was told to question him. Next the daroga was instructed to go and find Erik. He brought him to Persia, where for some months Erik's will was law. He was guilty of not a few horrors, for he seemed not to know the difference between good and evil. He took part calmly in a number of political assassinations; and he turned his diabolical inventive powers against the Emir of Afghanistan, who was at war with the Persian empire. The Shah took a liking to him.

This was the time of the rosy hours of Mazenderan, of which the daroga's narrative has given us a glimpse. Erik had very original ideas on the subject of architecture and thought out a palace much as a conjuror contrives a trick-casket. The Shah ordered him to construct an edifice of this kind. Erik did so; and the building appears to have been so ingenious that His Majesty was able to move about in it unseen and to disappear without a possibility of the trick's being discovered. When the Shah-in-Shah found himself the possessor of this gem, he ordered Erik's yellow eyes to be put out. But he reflected that, even when blind, Erik would still be able to build so remarkable a house for another sovereign; and also that, as long as Erik was alive, some one would know the secret of the wonderful palace. Erik's death was decided upon, together with that of all the laborers who had worked under his orders. The execution of this abominable decree devolved upon the daroga of Mazenderan. Erik had shown him some slight services and procured him many a hearty laugh. He saved Erik by providing him with the means of escape, but nearly paid with his head for his generous indulgence.

Fortunately for the daroga, a corpse, half-eaten by the birds of prey, was found on the shore of the Caspian Sea, and was taken for Erik's body, because the daroga's friends had dressed the remains in clothing that belonged to Erik. The daroga was let off with the loss of the imperial favor, the confiscation of his property and an order of perpetual banishment. As a member of the Royal House, however, he continued to receive a monthly pension of a few hundred francs from the Persian treasury; and on this he came to live in Paris.

As for Erik, he went to Asia Minor and thence to Constantinople, where he entered the Sultan's employment. In explanation of the services which he was able to render a monarch haunted by perpetual terrors, I need only say that it was Erik who constructed all the famous trap-doors and secret chambers and mysterious strong-boxes which were found at Yildiz-Kiosk after the last Turkish revolution. He also invented those automata, dressed like the Sultan and resembling the Sultan in all respects,* which made people believe that the Commander of the Faithful was awake at one place, when, in reality, he was asleep elsewhere.

Of course, he had to leave the Sultan's service for the same reasons that made him fly from Persia: he knew too much. Then, tired of his adventurous, formidable and monstrous life, he longed to be some one "like everybody else." And he became a contractor, like any ordinary contractor, building ordinary houses with ordinary bricks. He tendered for part of the foundations in the

* See the interview of the special correspondent of the Matin, with Mohammed-Ali Bey, on the day after the entry of the Salonika troops into Constantinople.

Opera. His estimate was accepted. When he found himself in the cellars of the enormous playhouse, his artistic, fantastic, wizard nature resumed the upper hand. Besides, was he not as ugly as ever? He dreamed of creating for his own use a dwelling unknown to the rest of the earth, where he could hide from men's eyes for all time.

The reader knows and guesses the rest. It is all in keeping with this incredible and yet veracious story. Poor, unhappy Erik! Shall we pity him? Shall we curse him? He asked only to be "some one," like everybody else. But he was too ugly! And he had to hide his genius *or use it to play tricks with*, when, with an ordinary face, he would have been one of the most distinguished of mankind! He had a heart that could have held the empire of the world; and, in the end, he had to content himself with a cellar. Ah, yes, we must needs pity the Opera ghost.

I have prayed over his mortal remains, that God might show him mercy notwithstanding his crimes. Yes, I am sure, quite sure that I prayed beside his body, the other day, when they took it from the spot where they were burying the phonographic records. It was his skeleton. I did not recognize it by the ugliness of the head, for all men are ugly when they have been dead as long as that, but by the plain gold ring which he wore and which Christine Daaé had certainly slipped on his finger, when she came to bury him in accordance with her promise.

The skeleton was lying near the little well, in the place where the Angel of Music first held Christine Daaé fainting in his trembling arms, on the night when he carried her down to the cellars of the opera-house.

And, now, what do they mean to do with that skeleton? Surely they will not bury it in the common grave! . . . I say that the place of the skeleton of the Opera ghost is in the archives of the National Academy of Music. It is no ordinary skeleton.

« ORIGINAL SOURCES »

Alcott, Louisa May. "The Abbot's Ghost, or, Maurice Treherne's Temptation," *The Flag of Our Union*, January 1867.

Brown, Charles Brockden. "Somnambulism," *The Literary Magazine and American Register*, May 1805.

Chambers, Robert W. "In the Court of the Dragon," *The King in Yellow*. New York: F. Tennyson Neely, 1895.

Cram, Ralph Adams. "Sister Maddelena," *Black Spirits and White*. Chicago: Stone & Kimball, 1895.

Crawford, F. Marion. "The Dead Smile," *Wandering Ghosts*. New York: The Macmillan Company, 1911.

Ewers, Hanns Heinz. "The Spider," *The International*, December 1915.

Halidom, M. Y. "Execution," *Tales of the Wonder Club, Volume 2*. London: Harrison & Sons, 1899–1900.

Hardy, Thomas. "The Withered Arm," *Wessex Tales*. London: Macmillan and Co., 1888.

Hawthorne, Nathaniel. "Rappaccini's Daughter," *Mosses from an Old Manse*. New York: Wiley & Putnam, 1846.

Hoffmann, E. T. A. "The Sandman," *Tales from the German*. London: Chapman and Hall, 1844.

Lee, Vernon. "Marsyas in Flanders," *For Maurice: Five Unlikely Stories*. London: John Lane, 1927.

Le Fanu, J. Sheridan. "Carmilla," *In a Glass Darkly*. London: Richard Bentley & Son, 1872.

Leroux, Gaston. *The Phantom of the Opera*. New York: The Bobbs-Merrill Company, 1911.

Lovecraft, H. P. "The Rats in the Walls," *Weird Tales*, March 1924. Reprinted with the permission of Lovecraft Holdings, LLC.

Machen, Arthur. "The Great God Pan," *The Great God Pan and The Inmost Light*. London: John Lane, 1894.

Poe, Edgar Allan. "Metzengerstein," *The Works of the Late Edgar Allan Poe*. New York: J. S. Redfield, Clinton Hall, 1850.

Polidori, John. *The Vampyre*. London: Sherwood, Neely, and Jones, 1819.

Riddell, Mrs. J. H. "The De Grabrooke Monument," *Routledge's Every Girl's Annual*, 1879.

Shelley, Mary. "The Transformation," *Tales and Stories*. London: William Paterson & Co., 1891.

Shiel, M. P. "The House of Sounds," *The Pale Ape and Other Pulses*. London: T. Werner Laurie, 1911.

Smith, Clark Ashton. "The Ghost of Mohammed Din," *The Overland Monthly*, November 1910.

Stevenson, Robert Louis. "Olalla," *The Merry Men and Other Tales and Fables*. London: Chatto & Windus, 1887.

Stoker, Bram. "The Secret of the Growing Gold," *Dracula's Guest and Other Weird Stories*. London: George Routledge & Sons, 1914.

Tolstoy, Aleksey. "The Family of a Vourdalak," *The Russian Messenger*, January 1884.

Walpole, Horace. *The Castle of Otranto*. London: W. Clowes, 1817.